The
Dragon
Path

The
Dragon
Path

COLLECTED TALES OF KENNETH MORRIS

Edited and with an Introduction by
Douglas A. Anderson

TOR

A Tom Doherty Associates Book
New York

This is a work of fiction. All the characters and events portrayed in this book are fictitious, and any resemblance to real people or events is purely coincidental.

THE DRAGON PATH: COLLECTED TALES OF KENNETH MORRIS

A Tor Book
Published by Tom Doherty Associates, Inc.
175 Fifth Avenue
New York, N.Y. 10010

Tor ® is a registered trademark of Tom Doherty Associates, Inc.

Design by Lynn Newmark

Library of Congress Cataloging-in-Publication Data

Morris, Kenneth.
    Dragon path : the collected stories of Kenneth Morris / Kenneth Morris.
        p.   cm.
    "A Tom Doherty Associates book."
    ISBN 0-312-85309-2
    1. Fantastic fiction, English—Welsh authors.   I. Title.
PR6025.07527A6   1995
823'.912—dc20   94-46359
                                                                     CIP

First edition: March 1995

Printed in the United States of America

0   9   8   7   6   5   4   3   2   1

For Alex Urquhart
and W. Emmett Small,
friends of Kenneth Morris,
and friends of mine.
—D.A.A.

Contents

Introduction

*T*he fiction of Kenneth Morris (1879–1937) is today easily classified as fantasy literature, although no such distinction of fantasy
as a genre existed during Morris's own lifetime. His first novel, *The Fates of
the Princes of Dyfed* (1914), is a reworking of some of the Welsh mythological stories in the *Mabinogion*. It was published in Point Loma, California, by
the Theosophical Society to which Morris belonged, but its appearance
went almost unnoticed, and for many years it received little attention outside of theosophical publications. Its significance, too, went unnoticed for
many years; for with this novel Morris had in effect created the sub-genre of
modern Welsh fantasy.

Morris's second book was a volume of ten of his short stories, *The Secret
Mountain and Other Tales* (1926). It was published as a gift book, beautifully
designed, with several delicate symbolic decorations by K. Romney Towndrow reproduced in color to accompany seven of the stories. The unnamed
blurb-writer (probably either T. S. Eliot or Richard de la Mare) at the London
publisher Faber & Gwyer found himself at a bit of a loss in trying to describe
the stories themselves, writing that "nothing more unlike the American, or
indeed the ordinary English, short story can be imagined. The author's nearest literary relative is perhaps Lord Dunsany, but he stands entirely on his
own feet." The comparison with Dunsany is apt, for Morris did write fantastic stories with wit and style, in a poetic and lyrical prose much like Dunsany's, but Morris's stories differ from Dunsany's in that they have a depth
and a philosophical cohesiveness found rarely (if at all) in Dunsany.

Morris's third book, the last published within his lifetime, was a sequel to *The Fates of the Princes of Dyfed* entitled *Book of the Three Dragons*. It was published in America in 1930 as a children's book, as mythological tales of any sort were at that time considered to be. It proved to be moderately successful, for it was chosen as a main selection for "Boys and Girls between the ages of 8–12 years" by the Junior Literary Guild.

At his death in 1937 Morris left behind one unpublished novel about the Toltecs of Mexico. *The Chalchiuhite Dragon* tells of the events in ancient times in southernmost Mexico leading up to the rebirth of the god Quetzalcoatl, who is periodically reborn among men to teach peace. The manuscript was carefully preserved in the files at the Theosophical Society for many years before it was finally published as a "long-lost fantasy masterpiece" in 1992. Thus, some fifty-five years after his death, Morris's fiction began to find an appreciative and understanding audience.

Morris wrote only three novels. His thirty-nine known short stories, published under an array of pseudonyms in theosophical magazines, are here collected for the first time. The earliest tales date from 1898–1902, and these five stories, together with an additional story-essay (Morris's earliest interpretation of the *Mabinogion*), are collected in an Appendix at the end of this book. The main portion of this volume contains Morris's best work, thirty-four mature tales written during Morris's prime. In subject they range from Celtic to Norse, Greek to Roman, Taoist to Buddhist; and in locale, from China to India, Wales to Sweden, and Spain to the Middle East. A few tales are historical, a few are modern; all are in some ways mythopoeic. To refer to them merely as "short stories" seems an inadequate description; in calling them "tales" I follow Kenneth Morris's own usage. But perhaps they are best described with a more technical term such as "myth-based fantasies," for each tale is an entirely new story based upon a deep appreciation of some aspect of a given mythology.

This appreciation of mythology was vital to Kenneth Morris. He believed that the art of storytelling itself had its origins entirely in religious matters: that (as he himself wrote) "the deepest truths of religion and philosophy had their first recording for the instruction of the peoples, not in the form of treatise, essay, or disquisition, but as epics, sagas, stories." It was Morris's belief that the great theme of the world, of its philosophy and its mythology, was the evolution of the soul of man, and this belief remained central to Morris when he turned to the writing of fiction.

None of which is meant to imply that Morris's tales are in any sense difficult to read. Clearly, the story itself was of primary importance, with the symbology presented unobtrusively in the background for those willing and able to appreciate it. As one commentator has written of the novel *The Chalchiuhite Dragon,* so can the statement be made for any single one of Morris's tales: "Read it with joy for any reason—for its exquisite prose passages, its excitement as an adventure story, its delicious wit, its remarkable realism, and for the skein of esotericism that shimmers through its pages."

Morris's fiction is only a portion of his total literary output. Primarily he considered himself a poet, and while much of his poetry is traditional in form and Welsh in subject, he also did a great number of translations (Morris called them "recensions") from the classic Chinese poets of the T'ang Dynasty. He wrote a number of full-length plays, and a few short ones: some of these dramas are very much like the best of his tales. And he wrote three book-length lecture-series, and numerous other essays. All of his writings form a distinctive whole, tied together by his great love of theosophy.

Kenneth Morris was multi-talented. To appreciate his own special genius one must study the whole of Morris's output, and this involves interpreting the evolution of his writings within the framework of his own life.

Kenneth Vennor Morris was born near Ammanford, Carmarthenshire, in the southwestern part of Wales, on 31 July 1879. Kenneth was the youngest son of Alfred Arthur Vennor Morris, a chemical manufacturer, and Rosa (Leach) Morris; he had one older brother and two sisters. Morris's prosperous family owned three manor houses on the slopes of Bettws Mountain near Ammanford. Kenneth's grandfather, William Morris (a tin-plate manufacturer), lived at Pontamman, a house with very large grounds down in the valley; a cousin, Ivor Morris, lived at Brynhyfryd, a smaller house with a delightful, wild garden that young Kenneth loved, with a mountain brook flowing through it. Kenneth's family lived in the house called Wernoleu, where Kenneth was born. Wernoleu was on the hill above Pontamman, three-quarters of a mile away from it, with the road running between the two estates.

The scene was idyllic for a youth like Kenneth. Years later he would write several poems recapturing the beauty of those places. These include recollections about "Old Brynhyfryd Garden"; about "The Well at Llandybie" and "The Bluebells of Wernoleu"; and about "Pontamman Garden" ("I remember the snow and silver of the clouds over old Pontamman Garden: / And the blue blood gentianella; and the windy poplars; and behind, / The far slopes of Bettws Mountain—the green, quiet slopes of the mountain— / And God in the scent and sound of the mountain wind."). But those idyllic times were short-lived.

Kenneth's father died in 1884 at the early age of thirty-five; and Kenneth's grandfather, known as the Peacemaker of the Valley (Tangnefeddwr y Dyffryn), died in 1885. Newly passed laws regulating American trade caused the failure of the family business. Rosa Morris was forced to move to London and, in reduced circumstances, raise her children there. But on the way to London, she and the children spent time with her family at her old home, Devizes Castle in Wiltshire. Kenneth described the place as having "a wonderful garden of many acres utilizing excellently the ruined dungeons of the old medieval castle." Morris thought the castle itself wasn't very interesting, but the grounds were: "At 6 years old I used to play about in them, and was terrified out of my senses of the ghosts that used to lurk all round the castle waiting to pounce on me."

In 1887 Morris was enrolled at Christ's Hospital, a famous school founded in 1553 by Edward VI, then located in the center of London; it was often called the Bluecoat School because of the long blue coats and yellow stockings worn by its boys. It was a very traditional English school, with distinguished alumni such as Samuel Taylor Coleridge, Leigh Hunt, and Charles Lamb, who immortalized the school with his recollections of Coleridge at Christ's Hospital published in his *Essays* (1823). Morris left the school in 1895 at the age-limit of sixteen, with the rank of Senior Deputy Grecian, signifying his proficiency in classical languages.

Just what Morris did immediately after leaving Christ's Hospital remains unclear. Apparently he tried fruit-farming for a while, and probably he settled for a short time in Market Lavington in Wiltshire, near his mother's family in Devizes. Sometime in 1896 he visited Dublin, and this visit was of vital importance to Morris. There he encountered Theosophy and the Dublin Theosophical Society.

Ella Young (1867–1956), the Irish poetess, story-teller, and (in the 1930s) Phelan Lecturer on Celtic Literature at the University of California, met Morris at this time when she was herself new to the Dublin Theosophical Society. In a lecture devoted to Morris and given at Berkeley on 5 March 1936, Ella Young recalled the Kenneth Morris she had just met: "At eighteen he went to Dublin and entered a group of the foremost thinkers of the day, including Standish O'Grady, AE (George W. Russell), W.B. Yeats, Charles Weekes, etc., where the Gaelic myths, Celtic lore, and the philosophy of Oriental literature were studied. When Morris joined this group it had its headquarters in one of three Georgian houses in Upper Ely Place, fronting a little park. George Moore, the novelist, later rented the park for a garden. Mr. and Mrs. Fred J. Dick, who were very active in the establishment of the Theosophical work in Dublin, had a home nearby." Morris himself remembered being referred to at this time as the "lodge baby" by Violet North.

Ella Young also recalled one incident involving Morris: "Some of the rooms in Ely Place were adorned by mystical paintings done by AE, but the printing-room was not decorated. One day I went into that room and found Violet North—who afterwards married AE—and Kenneth Morris in possession. They had covered the walls and even the doors of that room with Arabic inscriptions from the *Koran,* and both professed themselves Moslems! Kenneth Morris looked like the poet and knight-errant that he was, and he always upheld the honor and glory of Wales. AE ultimately persuaded them to remove the texts." Many years later, after they had met again in California, Kenneth Morris wrote to Ella Young that he had "forgotten that incident about the Koranic texts and converting Violetta to Mohammedanism for the nonce!" But one other incident Morris did recall, in a letter to Ella Young's friend Marion Ethel Hamilton, the poet-wife of Col. Hinkle: "I do not yet get over my surprise that she [Ella Young] remembers me. I was a young boy in the society she frequented—not suspected of having any abilities or literary leanings. They all used to tease me for being the youngest of them and Welsh—they were all Irish: and I remember the beautiful, brilliant—she was both—Miss Young taking pity on me and championing my poor little country!"

In her autobiography *Flowering Dusk: Things Remembered Accurately and Inaccurately* (1945), Ella Young describes Morris as "tall, slender, dark-eyed, with an eager, clear-cut face . . . How could anyone foreknow that Kenneth, beautiful then as a young knight carved on a tombstone, would keep his poet-heart and his high noble dreams, and his beauty, the length of a lifetime when the rest of us, faltering, showed the dust and sweat of the road." But one of Morris's students at Point Loma, W. Emmett Small, corrects this impression: "Ella Young is mistaken: Kenneth was not tall, nor, if I may say so, handsome. He was below middle height (as most Welshman are); his eyes were his outstanding feature: dark brown, burning rather than lambent. Kenneth was a shy man, yet one with intense feeling and convictions, especially in the realm of literature and writing (his special field) and, of course, in the theosophical philosophy which he loved." The photographs of Morris which have survived (most of which probably date from around the mid-1910's) confirm this: Morris was a slender man with dark hair, and not very tall.

According to Charles J. Ryan (1865–1949), who knew Morris nearly forty years (first in England, then later for many years at Point Loma), Morris's stay in Dublin lasted for only a few weeks. But it is significant that Morris's first literary efforts date from soon after this visit, for as Morris himself wrote: it was AE who "awoke poetry in me . . . it was he who urged me to start writing it." Morris wrote his first poem "Ceridwen in Ystrad Tywi" soon after leaving Dublin, and it was not long afterwards that his first writings began to appear: an essay "Holy Ground," about the glory of mountains, was published in the *International Theosophist* (15 December 1898); a poem (apparently Morris's first published poem), "Night Is Departing," in the *International Theosophist* (15 February 1899); his first short story, "Prince Lion of the Sure Hand," in *The Crusader* (27 August–13 October 1899); and his first play, "Beli the Great," in the *Universal Brotherhood Path* (September 1899). The publication of writings by Kenneth Morris which began in 1898 continued until his death in 1937 and for several years after.

From 1899–1902, Morris published four more apprentice short stories. From 1902 through 1914 Morris appears to have published no fiction (or if he did, it remains at present untraced). But Morris did contribute prolifically to *The International Theosophist* (Dublin), *The International Theosophical Chronicle* (London), *The Century Path* (Point Loma), and other theosophical publications.

During 1896–1907, Morris kept at his theosophical work at various places in the British Isles. In 1897, Morris was in Romford, Essex, and by 1899 he had joined the Cardiff Lodge of the Theosophical Society. Soon after this he spent a lot of time in London, at the Theosophical Lodge there. At times, he and some friends would take holidays to escape the pressures of London. On one such holiday during the summer of 1900, Charles J. Ryan went with Kenneth Morris and some other friends to the heart of the New Forest in Hampshire, where as Ryan recalled "among the great silences of the shadowy glades of ancestral oak and beech Kenneth felt Wordsworth's mystic Spirit of the Woods so strongly that his heart leaped with joy and he cried: 'Here is a bit of Celtic Land in England!'."

Around 1903 or 1904, Morris was sent up to the Manchester Lodge of the Theosophical Society for rest from the strains of the London Lodge. There he met Walter J. Renshaw, the President of the Manchester Lodge, who reminisced of Morris in 1946: "We became great friends, through common interests. Often we would go [on] rambles (hikes) into the countryside, sometimes taking off our shoes and stockings and dabbling our feet in a brook while he told me Celtic stories, some of which he later put into shape for *The Fates of the Princes of Dyfed,* a copy of which he autographed— in Welsh—for me. And we, or rather he, would read from Lady Guest's *Mabinogion.*"

Many of the fellow theosophists Morris knew were gradually relocating to Point Loma, California, where in 1897 Katherine Tingley (1847–1929), Leader of the Universal Brotherhood and Theosophical Society (to give the society its full name at that time), had begun setting up a community and international headquarters. Charles J. Ryan left England for Point Loma in late 1900. Herbert Coryn and Fred J. Dick, editors of the *International Theosophist,* the Dublin magazine to which Kenneth Morris contributed, also moved to Point Loma. Walter J. Renshaw, too, would later move to Point Loma, where his friendship with Morris continued for many years.

Katherine Tingley went on a lecture tour in 1907; and it was probably at this time, when she was in London, that she invited Morris to join the staff at the headquarters at Point Loma. Sometime very late in 1907, Morris left England by ship, arriving in Point Loma on 13 January 1908. Morris fell instantly in love with Point Loma, a peninsular headland to the west of San Diego, running north and south, with the Pacific Ocean on one side, and San Diego Bay on the other. Morris would remain at Point Loma for the next twenty-two years.

Morris's first impressions of Point Loma are given in an article "Impressions of Lomaland" published in the *International Theosophical Chronicle* in June 1908. He found "Lomaland" (what those members of the Theosophical Society living at Point Loma called their headquarters) to be a magical place "which nature has delighted in making beautiful, and where the presence of man does not distract from the natural beauty." More simply he described it as "a great rock-bound promontory, rising out of the sea; first rocks, then the cliffs, then the hillside rising and rising. It is a long way down from the homestead to the sea, and the hillside that divides them has one grand object in life, and that is to produce sweet-scented growths; so that one can hardly tell where gardens end and wild life begins." Visible from all over Lomaland were, as Morris recalled them, "two gleaming domes": the Homestead building (also called the Raja-Yoga Academy) and the Temple of Peace, two graceful buildings surmounted by huge glass spheres, the one over the Temple of light purple glass, and the other of pale sea-green glass. The Homestead had three additional smaller other-colored domes, and all these domes were illuminated at night, making quite a dramatic sight. The whole of Lomaland encompassed some five hundred acres, with athletic fields and orchards and gardens, a beautiful open-air Greek theatre facing down the canyon to the Pacific, and an imposing Roman gate at the main entrance.

Much of the fascinating history of Point Loma is told in Emmett A. Greenwalt's *California Utopia: Point Loma: 1897–1942* (1955, revised 1978). This book records the history of Katherine Tingley's accomplishment in realizing her great vision of an ideal community and international headquarters where the theosophical life could be lived to the fullest.

Morris's duties at Point Loma included lecturing at the Raja Yoga College as Professor of History and Literature. One of Morris's students, W. Emmett Small, was brought by his mother from Macon, Georgia, to Point Loma in 1905 at the age of two. His recollections give a privileged glimpse of growing up at Point Loma: "All my young and maturing years were spent here on Point Loma, and I enjoyed the unique education the students experienced. Greenwalt's book gives some idea of this, but it is difficult for someone who wasn't there to really convey the inner spirit and essence of it all. We had teachers from Ireland, Wales, England, France, Sweden and of course USA. And all were treated the same. We had Music, Art, Drama, Athletics (baseball, tennis, football, basketball, etc.). And we also worked in the vegetable gardens, the flower gardens, the orchards. It was, all in all, an almost self-going community, and we had no need or little desire for what was called 'the city life.' We all learned musical instruments. I played the clarinet at 15, and later changed over to the cello. We had a stalwart band, and choruses. And the business end wasn't neglected, and we learned what in those days was called Bookkeeping. We learned to type, to master shorthand (Pitman system)—I find both useful today. We learned to speak in public, no matter how shy or awkward we were. And several of us took part in dramatic performances, even in leading roles."

Of Morris's role as a teacher, Small has written: "I was in a younger group who had him as instructor, and he was not so good in teaching the younger ones; he was more at home in the university. . . . There is no doubt that Kenneth inspired his pupils, one and all; but—if I may be permitted this observation—several of us felt that he tended to force them all to conform to his own image so to say, that is to see things as he saw them, to write as he wrote, verse and prose alike, and did not encourage one's own inner genius to emerge. But without question he did inculcate in all his students certain basically sound elements. Later, if they had it in them, they would break away and express 'themselves.' "

Not long after settling at Point Loma in 1908, Kenneth Morris was invited to join the local (San Diego) Cambrian Society by its founder George Holmes. Morris welcomed this contact with another Welshman in a place so far from Wales. Indeed this fellowship seems to have inspired Morris, for from that time on through the next several years Morris began an outpouring of prose and poetry to do with Wales, Welsh literature, and Welsh legends. His lecture-series in eleven parts on Welsh Literature appeared in *The Century Path* from March through November 1908. More significantly, in 1910 he began his first novel, itself a re-working of Welsh mythological tales, *The Fates of the Princes of Dyfed*. It was finished in 1911, and many years later Morris recalled to Ella Young that: "I was in a very Welsh mood in 1910–11 when I wrote *Fates*."

In late July 1912, Morris took enormous pleasure in hosting the Welsh Mountain Ash Choir, led by Glyndwr Richards, on their visit to Point Loma. They were the first visitors from Wales that Morris had seen since coming to California, and in honor of the occasion Morris published a charming photographic booklet commemorating the visit. It includes a few of Morris's own poems on Welsh themes.

The Fates of the Princes of Dyfed, with illustrations by Morris's friend and fellow Point Loma resident Reginald Machell (1854–1927), was published by the Theosophical press at Point Loma in September 1914. It is an elegant book, and Machell's black and white woodcut-styled illustrations add warmth and charm to the book. Morris's theosophical fiction was not without precedent, for in the last few months of her life, H.P. Blavatsky (1831–1891), the founder of the modern Theosophical movement, composed five such stories, collected posthumously as *Nightmare Tales* (1892). This little volume was also illustrated by Reginald Machell, then a distinguished London artist who would move to Point Loma in 1900 and who would later illustrate many of Kenneth Morris's other tales in *The Theosophical Path* as well as Morris's novel. Over the years Machell published a large number of stories in the theosophical magazines, but only one ever appeared in book-form, *The Coming of the King: A Story for Children* (1900), with illustrations by Machell himself. Perhaps the most famous piece of theosophical fiction is the novel *Om: The Secret of Ahbor Valley* (1924) by Talbot Mundy (1879–1940). It was written at Point Loma while Mundy was a guest of Katherine Tingley, though Mundy soon afterwards bought a house and lived at Point Loma, all the while active in the Theosophical Society.

In his "Preface" to *The Fates of the Princes of Dyfed*, Morris mentions that, in addition to depending heavily upon Lady Guest's translation of the *Mabinogion*, he had also drawn on "the writings collected by the ever-to-be-honoured Iolo Morganwg and the bards of the School of Glamorgan." But the extent of his debt to Iolo Morganwg, and in particular to Iolo's *Barddas*, is only hinted at here. Many years later, after Ella Young had received the position of Celtic Lecturer at the University of California in 1931, she wrote to Morris and asked him to recommend books on the Welsh Celtic legends (as opposed to the Irish Celtic legends which she knew so well). Morris responded with several recommendations, including special comments on Iolo's book: "There's a book called *Barddas*, in Welsh and English, which is important because it gives the philosophy of Druidism. . . . The sources of that Druidic philosophy are suspect with scholars; in fact they won't look at it at all; but that is because they haven't the commonsense to see that a Welsh peasant, a stone-mason, at the beginning of the nineteenth century could not possibly have invented Theosophy."

The book *Barddas; or, A Collection of Original Documents, Illustrative of the Theology, Wisdom, and Usages of The Bardo-Druidic System of the Isle of Britain*, to give it its full descriptive title, was actually a two-volume compilation by John Williams (Ab Ithel; 1811–1862) from the manuscripts of Iolo Morganwg (the Bardic pseudonym of Edward Williams, 1747–1826, a stone-mason from Glamorgan). The very large first volume was published in 1862, and the much smaller second volume appeared in 1874. Most scholars today, and even many of those in Morris's time, viewed the compilation with suspicion, crediting Iolo Morganwg with too much imagination in his task of compilation. Prys Morgan, in his essay "The Hunt for the Welsh Past in the Romantic Period" published in Eric Hobsbawm and Terence Ranger's *The Invention of Tradition* (1983), goes so far as to describe Iolo Morganwg as "a wild dreamer, a lifelong addict to laudanum", who was "an able man of letters and antiquary, but also a romantic mythologist who rolled into one many eighteenth-century dreams and fashions, fads and fancies. Iolo was obsessively concerned with myth and history, and out of the eighteenth-century interest in Druidism he created the notion that the Welsh bards had been the heirs of the ancient Druids, and had inherited their rites and rituals, their religion and mythology." Despite the long-standing controversy surrounding this proud and patriotic Welshman, his *Barddas* had a very considerable influence on many Welsh poets during the late nineteenth century. And in these books, Kenneth Morris found the bardo-druidic framework he would use to great effect in *The Fates of the Princes of Dyfed* and its sequel, *Book of the Three Dragons*. Morris felt that these names and stories, "sniffed at by the scholars and critics," had credentials of their own for the intuition and the imagination: "that if they were invented by Iolo Morganwg, or by Meurig Dafydd, or by Llewelyn Sion, one would say that the invention was rather a discovery. . . . No matter whether such names are ancient, medieval, or comparatively modern; one would have been put to it to invent them oneself, if one had not found them ready to hand."

Throughout the decade of the 1910s Morris was at his prime, and during this time he wrote and lectured constantly. He gave three book-length lecture-series, each of which were serialized in *The Theosophical Path.* The first was "Golden Threads in the Tapestry of History"; it appeared in installments from March 1915 through December 1916. The second, "The Three Bases of Poetry: A Study of English Verse," was Morris's lengthy answer to the question he posed in this study's very first sentence: "What is Poetry?" It was published from January through December of 1917. The third lecture-series was entitled "The Crest-Wave of Evolution," and though it was given during the 1918–19 school year to the Graduates' Class in the Raja Yoga College, its publication was spread out from March 1919 through July 1921.

To Ella Young, Morris wrote: "I suppose through '18 and '19 I overworked giving a series of lectures on history in which I floated a philosophy thereof in most respects anticipating Spengler's. I gave these lectures every Thursday evening and did all the research and writing between them whiles." Toward the end of 1919 his health broke down, "with influenza which became pneumonia and consumption; and never have I got my health back. The chest is cured and now stronger than ever it has been; but it has been one thing after another since. An enormous mental shock helped the overwork, I may say."

Just what this "enormous mental shock" was remains unknown, but these troubles brought Morris's writing to a virtual standstill. For more than seven years he wrote no verse, and only some occasional articles in prose. He wrote no fiction at all until early in 1926 when he began (at Katherine Tingley's request) his novel *The Chalchiuhite Dragon.* Yet contributions by Morris continued to appear in theosophical magazines throughout the 1920s, when Morris was ill most of the time. Many of the poems and the dramas which were published during the 1920s were actually written some years earlier, and one must be wary in making the assumption that any single item by Morris was published at anywhere near the time it was written.

Morris's health continued to be a problem through the late 1920s, as he confided to Ella Young: "In '26 the heart broke down; which presently turned out to be a result of Goitre—exophthalmic . . . the muscles of my back are somewhat atrophied; with the result that I can't sit up for long unless properly supported with cushions. This is extremely awkward; as I can't now attend any kind of meetings or concerts or lectures." W. Emmett Small recalled that for much of his later years at Point Loma Kenneth Morris was a semi-invalid: "It was as though he had burned himself out by his over-vigorous lecturing and teaching at the School and University, and the constant writing of articles, stories and poems. He was able to 'get around,' so to say, but even for quite a time his meals had to be brought to him."

Despite these difficulties Morris did manage to work on several fronts. He contributed an essay on "Lomaland—The Home of Theosophy" to a booklet by Claire Merton published at Point Loma, *Katherine Tingley on Marriage and the Home: An Interview* (1921); and Morris took great pleasure in compiling (anonymously) Katherine Tingley's *The Wine of Life* (1925), a collection of passages put together from Tingley's extemporaneous lectures, and from private instructions by Tingley to her students. With a preface by Talbot Mundy, this volume is the most substantial collection of Katherine Tingley's writings that was published during her lifetime.

Talbot Mundy, who had first visited Point Loma during the winter of 1922–23, was particularly impressed with the works of Kenneth Morris, writing that "since I began to read Professor Morris's poems and historical works I have found it impossible to speak of them without enthusiasm . . . The only fault I find with him is, that he does not write more, and oftener." Mundy even tried to interest his own publisher (Bobbs-Merrill) in Morris's writings, but nothing came of it.

Morris never seemed to have an easy time with publishers. He commented to Ella Young in 1927 that "I haven't yet learned to make publishers believe my stuff is worth printing. I have been writing verses all these years, but never a volume of it published yet; and I do not seem to know how to go about it to get one published."

Morris's verse occasionally did attract a bit of attention. One of his finer poems, "Dusk," was reprinted out of *The Theosophical Path* in collections such as Irene Hunter's *American Mystical Verse* (1925), and Charles Carroll Albertson's *Lyra Mystica: An Anthology of Mystical Verse* (1932).

In early 1919, Morris was asked by Charles Wharton Stork (1881–1971) to contribute some poetry to Stork's magazine, *Contemporary Verse*, but it was several months before Morris sent any. Then when he sent some of his "Rondels of Lomaland," a series of small pictures of nature at the Theosophical Headquarters at Point Loma, six of them were enthusiastically accepted and published in the June 1920 issue of *Contemporary Verse*. In accepting them for publication, Stork warned Morris that he could not pay for them. Morris replied: "As to payment—I quite understood that you did not pay for things: and for my own part have never been able to see parity or correspondence between poetry and money, so think that that is the best way of doing things."

In January 1924 Morris's article "On Verse, 'Free-Verse,' and the Dual Nature of Man" appeared in *The Theosophical Path*. It attracted considerable notice, and was reprinted later in the same year as a pamphlet. Charles Wharton Stork devoted a large amount of space in *Contemporary Verse* to reviewing Morris's thoughts. Stork agreed with most of Morris's points in his article, and his sympathy renewed the correspondence between the two men.

"Free verse," Morris once declared to Ella Young, "I hate it royally." But writing to Stork, Morris was softer and more diplomatic. Morris believed that "free verse can be grandly beautiful," and he cited Whitman and AE as examples of poets capable of such beauty in free verse. But he continued: "the trouble is this free verse craze has enabled anyone and everyone without the slightest feeling for verbal music in the world to put over their barbarisms on the public, sheer raucous cockadoodledooing that would be silenced before ever it began were there but a rigid convention for verse forms—which call for mental work in the producing, that at least." Despite his antipathy, Morris himself did write a few poems in free verse, including his very first poem, "Ceridwen in Ystrad Tywi," for which in 1924 he still retained enough fondness to declare that if ever a volume of his poetry was published, that poem would be in it.

Morris's own verse is not easily appreciated today, for most modern readers do not bring with them the necessary understanding and sympathy for the intricate metrical and structural techniques which Morris employed. It is also significant that Morris believed that "the first most radical characteristic of poetry is that it is a chant to be chanted; an incantation,—a thing to do holiest magic with." And believing so, while also demonstrating a pride in Welsh poetic forms and traditions, Morris constructed many of his poems to be chanted to certain Welsh "airs" (or folk-songs). Morris sometimes labeled his poems with the Welsh air to which the poem should be chanted.

As his friend Walter J. Renshaw recorded of Morris, "while in London he spent a great deal of time in the British Museum. One of his pursuits there was among manuscripts of unpublished Welsh songs. He had a lot of airs copied out on music paper. These he wanted me to play on the violin so he could establish their rhythms in his mind. I spent many nights in his quarters going over and over these old airs, he beating time with his forefinger." Undoubtedly these manuscript collections had many more Welsh airs than can be found in any printed collections, but some of the particular Welsh airs that Morris used can be found in some rare collections, like *Ancient National Airs of Gwent and Morganwg,* collected by M. Jane Williams (1847).

W. Emmett Small recalled that Morris "read poetry with real swing and song in it, and his eyes would get big and bright." And Walter J. Renshaw recorded in a personal copy of a poetry anthology that Morris had his own system of poetic principles. According to Renshaw, Morris felt that a poet should strive for three qualities, which he named in Welsh as Plenydd (color), Alawn (sound), and Gwron (number). Through combinations of these qualities Morris felt that a poet could attain Tydain Tad Awen (truth, in its "threefold name of manifested Deity"). Renshaw also recalled that

Morris "would recite (*chant* is the proper word) at different times from English (language) poetry to illustrate his meanings, saying that AE, of whose poetry he was very fond, had the most of all the three qualities." Some of Morris's other verses had music written specifically to accompany them. These poems, together with their music, were often composed for some specific occasion. Rex Dunn, a gifted concert violinist and the conductor of the Raja Yoga International Symphony Orchestra and Chorus at Point Loma, wrote the music to Morris's "Ode to Peace," which was presented at the Twentieth World Peace Congress held at The Hague in the Netherlands in August 1913. Dunn wrote music for Morris's "Flower Songs" and the series "Songs of the Nations." Together Dunn and Morris also composed an operetta entitled *Bruce and the Brownies.*

It is clear that Morris's keen sense of the rhythm and music of words, as is apparent in his poetry, was also an important element in the cadenced prose of his fiction, which has a musical quality of its own. It, too, should be read aloud, and not merely passed over quickly by the eye on paper.

Throughout the 1920s when Morris was ill, Charles Wharton Stork occasionally wrote to Morris and asked for some more poems for his magazine, but Morris thereafter turned him down, saying: "I wish I had some more and better poems to send you—but alas! I have not . . ."

In March 1923, Iverson L. Harris (1890–1979), the Assistant Secretary to Katherine Tingley, began a devoted effort in trying to interest publishers in bringing out in book form the writings of Kenneth Morris. He sent to various publishers a huge letter (four extra-long single-spaced typed pages) detailing Morris's entire literary output to that date, along with a large batch of sample chapters, essays, poems, and stories. While some publishers did express interest (particularly a Boston firm, who wanted to bring out Morris's *Golden Threads in the Tapestry of History*), in the end nothing came of this effort. Probably the sheer amount of Morris's writings made the whole project appear to be problematical for most publishers.

By the mid-1920s, *The Fates of the Princes of Dyfed* began to receive some of the recognition it deserves. There had been early positive reviews, but there were stumbling blocks too. The Welsh poet Edward Thomas (1878–1917) had refused to review the book because of its spiritual elements. On the other hand, the book did find some significant and enthusiastic readers, even though their number was few.

Morris sent a copy of the book to AE, whose first response was: "Thanks for your beautiful book. It is beautiful, as beautiful as anything of the kind I have met. I do not know your Welsh legends or to what extent you have based your tales on them; but I can see that you have had your vision and the book is yours and the Great Inspirer's. It is full of exquisite color. You are one of the few in the modern world who have the old bardic imagination. Long may you keep it."

Soon afterwards AE sent a follow-up letter: "I had hardly read your book of wonder when writing and my further reading confirms my admiration of the beauty and dignity of your conception. You will get recognition for it surely. Maybe not now. The world takes a long time to recognize spiritual beauty, but it is certain. I suppose you do not care greatly, the joy of doing it being the great reward."

Ella Young did not read the book until after she and Morris had become reacquainted in 1927, some thirty years after they had known each other in Dublin. Her very enthusiastic response was written in a personal letter to Morris, and it was seized upon by Iverson L. Harris. Harris was always anxious to promote the work of his friend, and after receiving permission from Ella Young, he published her remarks in the April 1928 issue of *The Theosophical Path*:

"We have made good books of story-telling in Ireland, but Wales in this book takes the victory. The Welsh bard has borne off the branch! And that is because he has restored the spiritual quality more than any of us! How full of magic every description is: magic that reaches out and illumines this present moment, magic that is wisdom and beauty and high-heartedness. It is a great shout—the Dragon-Shout of Wales! I cannot adequately express how delighted I am with it. I regard it as a fine literary achievement—one of the most notable books of Celtic story-telling, especially in its exquisite nature magic, the humor and the richness of description. When I read it I am in the many-colored land of which all outward beauty is but the vesture. Blessings on this Bard of Wales and luck in the shaping of whatever work is between his hands!"

Morris of course greatly appreciated Ella Young's enthusiastic response to his novel. On 14 February 1928, he informed her: "There is also written (typed rather) a sequel—telling of the Wanderings and Return to Dyfed of Manawyddan, whom I make out to be Pwyll after his being in the Cauldron. But having kept it so long, I now need to rewrite it, and haven't the brains. Have not had for eight years at least. And even if I had and could rewrite the book, it would be impossible to get it published. You'll note that I stole an Irish name for the Fates—after the Fates of the Children of Tuireann (excuse my Irish spelling). But for the sequel I have a Welsh style name—the Book of the Three Dragons. The stories in both books are largely my own inventions. But you get into that Celtic gloryworld, and see for yourself what happens."

Morris found and read a copy of Ella Young's recent book, *The Wonder Smith and His Son*, which consists of her own retellings of Irish folktales about the Gubbaun Saor, gathered from cottagers and fisherman in Gaelic-speaking Ireland. The book was illustrated by Boris Artzybasheff; it had been published in February 1927 by Longmans, Green and Company of New York. This firm would soon publish two more of Ella Young's children's books, *The Tangle-Coated Horse and Other Tales: Episodes from the Fionn*

Saga (1929), and *The Unicorn with Silver Shoes* (1932), the latter an original tale by Ella Young and the best of her children's books. Morris liked *The Wonder Smith and His Son,* but he was critical of the illustrations by Boris Artzybasheff because they were not in the least bit Celtic, and therefore inappropriate for the story. Morris also borrowed from some friends at Point Loma a copy of Ella Young's *Celtic Wonder Tales* (1910), which he found even more to his liking. In particular he singled out one descriptive passage about mountains for his praise ("as the best bit about mountains I know"), from the tale "The Children of Lir." It reads: "They are wiser than the wisest druid, more tender than the tenderest mother. It is they who keep the world alive."

Ella Young also greatly appreciated Morris's collection *The Secret Mountain and Other Tales,* which had been published in September 1926 by the London firm Faber & Gwyer. This book, a copy of which Morris sent to Ella Young in February 1928, includes ten stories by Morris, all of which had previously appeared in *The Theosophical Path* or *The Raja Yoga Messenger.* After the publication of *The Fates of the Princes of Dyfed* in September 1914, Morris published some twenty-three stories before his health broke down at the end of 1919. Five more stories were published between 1921 and 1923, but these stories had all been written earlier.

For the collection *The Secret Mountain and Other Tales* Morris chose ten out of these twenty-eight stories, revising some of them slightly. In December 1928, after listening to Bach's Fugue in D Minor, Morris was inspired to write a tiny story, his first in more than eight years. In January 1929 he suggested to Ella Young that the ability to write short fiction was coming back to him, as the faculty for writing verse had a year and a half earlier. Morris wrote a few other short tales at this time, inspired by various pieces of music. All thirty-nine of Morris's known tales are collected in the present volume, and those that were revised for *The Secret Mountain and Other Tales* appear herein in their revised forms.

In placing *The Secret Mountain and Other Tales* with a publisher, Morris had engaged Curtis Brown of London to act as his agents. At Curtis Brown, Morris's worked with Michael Joseph (1897–1958), then a literary agent and author, whose third book, *The Commercial Side of Literature,* had been a best-seller in the summer of 1925. Michael Joseph, who would in 1935 found the publishing company which would bear his name, was unable to place any collection of Morris's verse, and he warned Morris that the publication of most first volumes of poetry by unknown poets had to be paid for by the poets themselves. But Morris was pleased with his placement of *The Secret Mountain and Other Tales,* though the book did not sell well and was remaindered in late 1927. Morris was also pleased with the appearance of the book and its delicate, colored symbolic illustrations by K. Romney Towndrow. Morris dedicated the book to his old friend, Reginald Machell, the illustrator of *The Fates of the Princes of Dyfed* and many of Morris's other tales; and even Machell was highly pleased with the simple decorative illustrations to Morris's tales.

Undaunted by his inability to get a collection of his poems professionally published, Morris would make gifts for his friends by hand-binding typed collections of his poems. Around 1925, he bound a large collection for Ethel Green Small, the mother of W. Emmett Small. Probably in mid-1928, Morris sent Ella Young a small collection he had made for her and illuminated. Ella Young had this bound in calfskin and lizardskin, and years later she presented it to the Theosophical Society, after Morris's death. The Archives at the Theosophical Society in Pasadena also hold several other of these handbound collections of Morris's poems, most of which are variations on three basic collections that Morris made himself: *The Little Mountain Bird, From the Hills of T'ang,* and *To-Day: And Other Poems* (variantly titled *Point Loma and Since*). There also exists a small elegant booklet handmade by Morris consisting solely of his long poem *The Three Treasures of Len: A Story of Ancient and Modern Ireland.*

In addition to the booklets Morris made and gave away himself, his students would sometimes type up a selection and bind them as an exercise. W. Emmett Small has one such example that he typed up in his youth, a collection of some of Morris's Chinese translations entitled *A Souvenir of Honanfu,* probably dating from around 1926.

Many more such items probably exist, but they are not likely to be easily traced. All of these collections exemplify the nearly insurmountable difficulties and complexities involved in compiling an authoritative catalog of Morris's writings. Another problem is that of textual integrity, and a further one is the difficulty in determining Morris's preferred or final form for any given item.

Morris also made a number of illuminated poems. To make one of these, he would lightly type a poem on a single sheet of paper, and then write over the typed letters with a pen, making a fancier script. With the lettering done, he would then color and fill in the page with drawings and symbols, in various colored inks, including silver and gold, to make an illuminated work of art of each poem. Some of these illuminated poems are strikingly beautiful.

Another unusual thing created by Morris while at Point Loma was his Dragon Path, a winding garden path made of various types of flat beach stones. These stones were laid out so as to make someone on the path imagine that they were walking on the scales of a dragon. This path was in a semi-secluded place at Point Loma, and hidden from the main roads, with low walls of stone on both sides and lovely gardens and trees surrounding it. Ingrid Van Mater has written that as a child she used to love playing there; a particular pleasant memory she recorded was of hunting for colored easter eggs along the path, among a cluster of spring flowers—freesias, orange poppies, and blue and purple linaria. For Morris the dragon was always a "symbol of spiritual wisdom, spiritual courage, of mastery of the forces of the lower world," in literature as in life; and the idea of a path itself suggests the way by which the human soul must pass in its evolution to full spiritual self-consciousness. Kenneth Morris's Dragon Path demonstrates another facet of his creative genius.

In early 1928 Ella Young persuaded her editor at Longmans, Green and Company, Bertha L. Gunterman (1886–1975), to consider for publication Kenneth Morris's sequel to *The Fates of the Princes of Dyfed*. By April 1928 Morris was retyping and rewriting the *Book of the Three Dragons* for submission to Longmans. In rewriting his sequel Morris sought to correct some of the problems of the first book that he had become aware of through its reception. Morris felt that he had written *The Fates of the Princes of Dyfed* as if he were writing in Welsh: "that piling up of adjectives in English is a dangerous ploy: the worst American after dinner ranters do it ghastlily. But there, with the robe of my Welshness and Welsh modes of thought on me, I inched along gaily oblivious of my peril."

Morris also explained to Ella Young his approach to the process of rewriting *Book of the Three Dragons*: "I re-read the Princes of Dyfed as you recommended it and found the ornament so thick in places I lost the thread of the story in reading. So I determined that should not be the case in the 3 Dragons and went to the latter with a severe blue pencil, cutting out ornament right and left."

Morris sent the rewritten sequel to Longmans in the middle of May 1928, but there were some problems that the surviving correspondence does not make clear. First Longmans wanted a key to the pronunciation of the names in the book, and for Morris that was no problem: he said that he would make one up should they decide to publish. By late November they still had made no decision about the book. But in early December 1928, Morris was writing to Ella Young that: "I wrote to Miss Gunterman as you suggested: though before your letter came I had framed in my mind the haughtiest of rejections. And now I must say I can't quite see myself doing anything in the matter. But I don't know; it is possible time will bring me round to feeling interested in that book again. At present the one I am writing now, and have been since early 1926, fills my outlook somewhat; and increasingly so, as it should. I am not certain of the propriety or wisdom of publishing the 3 Dragons as a children's book. Or indeed at all, in the present age. I don't need money or reputation, and I don't want a third disappointment, and for fools to be saying cheap things in the reviews about it."

Ella Young mediated between Morris and Longmans, who did want to publish the book, but they also apparently wanted it shortened. In January 1929, Morris wrote to Ella Young: "I can't lay my hands on either your letter or Miss Gunterman's in answer to the one of mine you saw; so shall have to go by memory a little. As to the latter, she was very friendly indeed; said I mustn't think they didn't want to publish the 3 Dragons; they did; it was a 'book for all time,' and their suggestions were only to let readers know at once what treasures were waiting them. Evidently they find the Wonderful Head too metaphysical and beyond them; but I won't let it be published without it. Then to my anger, the news that Artzybasheff will not do your [next] book, but will take the contract for mine."

Eventually Morris was able to choose a different artist, Ferdinand Huszti Horvath (1891–1973), who illustrated nearly a dozen books (including fine editions of Ruskin's *The King of the Golden River* and Poe's *The Raven*) while living in New York before he moved in 1933 to Hollywood, where he worked as an idea man and concept artist at the Walt Disney Studios, specializing in fine detailed pencil sketches. Some of Horvath's illustrations to *Book of the Three Dragons* are very striking and effective.

Morris evidently gave in to the idea of shortening his book: fully the last third of the manuscript of *Book of the Three Dragons* was simply lopped off, and it remains unpublished to this day. This destroys the entire structure of the book, and obscures the elements which tie together the two novels into one consecutive story. A one-volume edition, containing *The Fates of the Princes of Dyfed, Book of the Three Dragons,* and the unpublished ending, is sorely needed in order to demonstrate the real scope of Morris's achievement and to tell the whole of the story of the Princes of Dyfed and the Family of Pwyll.

In Morris's very first letter to Ella Young, written in August 1927, there emerged one topic which gradually came to dominate their entire correspondence: their mutual love of classic Chinese poetry. Over the years, Morris sent to Ella Young a great number of his translations from the Chinese, and he even once loaned her what he called his "dearest treasure," a booklet he had made of his prose translations from the Chinese. He depended upon these prose translations in order to compose his "recensions," the poems in which he tried to recapture in English the intricate music of Chinese verse. To do so Morris used Celtic alliterative forms and the old French forms "with their chimes of ever recurring rhyme and phrase."

Ella Young included in her book *Marzilian and Other Poems* (1938) a poem of her own called "Weaving-Maiden," which she labelled as "adapted from T'ung Han-Ching's poem translated by Kenneth Morris"; and in her autobiography *Flowering Dusk* (1945), she quoted in full several of Morris's translations from the Chinese. After some of the reviewers of her autobiography had singled out Morris's poems for especial praise, Ella Young became determined to see a collection of Morris's Chinese translations published. For a while she worked closely with Morris's friend Charles J. Ryan, helping him to plan and shape the contents of the proposed volume. She even sent him a large portion of the letters Morris had written her (and for this action we can be grateful, as none of these letters would otherwise survive). Most of these letters have some detailed commentary about Chinese poetry and about Morris's approach in translating it. Young and Ryan planned to publish excerpts from these letters in the proposed volume. And Ella Young herself even offered to pay for the printing of the book (as she had done for some of her own poetry collections), but again no finished book resulted, despite the effort of all parties involved. Yet these translations remain well worth publishing, and at present a critical edition is slowly taking shape for eventual publication.

In 1929, while Morris was still negotiating with Longmans, several things happened which changed his life dramatically. First, in July, Katherine Tingley, the leader of the Theosophical Society, died in Sweden some weeks after an automobile accident. Then, following the stock-market crash in October, the Point Loma headquarters found itself in a desperate financial situation. The new leader, Dr. Gottfried de Purucker (1874–1942), encouraged members who could do so to leave Point Loma, to "earn their living in the outside world, and if possible to contribute part of their earnings to Point Loma."

Morris's excitement burst forth in a letter to Ella Young dated December 10th, 1929:

"The great thing has happened; and I am too excited to live.

"I AM GOING BACK TO WALES! I'R HEN WLAD FY NHADAU!

"Our new leader, Dr. G. de Purucker, is sending everyone he can possibly spare out into the world to work up the lodges of the society far and near; and I am to sail via Panama in about three weeks . . . It is quite impossible for me to write a sensible letter under the pressure of this—or I should say the uplift of this huge excitement. WALES. No; it is not possible for anyone but me to know what that little word means!

"AND I AM GOING THERE!

"After twenty-two years absence."

Morris travelled to England on the ship *S.S. Schwaben,* leaving from San Pedro on 9 January, 1930. Along the way, on the 16th of January, Morris was very pleased to see the mountains of Mexico from off the southern coast. He was gazing upon the setting of his novel, *The Chalchiuhite Dragon,* which he had been writing since 1926. He wrote a poem for the occasion, entitled "The Mountains of Mexico":

> *I saw your mountains, Mexico,*
> *Across the azure of the sea:*
> *A blue and endless rampart-row,*
> *I saw your mountains, Mexico.*
> *And they were Homes of Gods for me! . . .*

Unchanged by the ages! Even so
The Kings of old Prehistory
In chalchiuhite gems and plumes aglow,
Your noble mountains, Mexico,
From this blue waste were wont to see.

What Seer among them, long ago,
Adept in Ancient Mystery,
So blest your Mountains, Mexico,
That still they seem divine to me?
Quetzalcoatl himself, may be?

Upon his arrival in England, Morris went first to stay in Hove with his older brother, Ronald Arthur Vennor Morris, who was himself the author of occasional poems and essays in theosophical publications, as well as one novel, *The Lyttleton Case: A Detective Story*, published by Collins in 1922 and reprinted in 1930. The novel is completely forgotten today, but it has been called "an early specimen of the well-written, slow, carefully plotted puzzle" by Jacques Barzun and Wendell Hertig Taylor in their *Catalogue of Crime* (1971, revised 1989). They conclude: "it is an acceptable tale of murder, impersonation, and abduction, with entertaining asides about the contemporary scene." R.A.V. Morris also assisted A. Trevor Barker in compiling the first four volumes of *The Complete Works of H.P. Blavatsky* (1933–1936); he long outlived his younger brother Kenneth.

Morris stayed with some others of his relations (some of whom he hadn't seen since childhood) in London, and in Devizes, before he finally reached Cardiff in late April.

Sometime during the summer of 1930, Morris's editor at Longmans, Bertha L. Gunterman, spent a day with him in Cardiff. *Book of the Three Dragons* had finally been scheduled for publication in September. Morris received his copies of the newly published book in October, and he wrote to Ella Young: "Beyond the customary six, she [Gunterman] presented me with one sumptuously bound in green leather and with my name printed on as Ex libris in the inside cover: very fine indeed; and I got one from the Junior Literary Guild: their binding is in yellow cloth, very neat, and the wrapper in quiet green. As for the pictures: the one where he's leaping from peak to peak is hardly betterable, I think: and the one where Ewinwen is sinking down like a cloud to the sea is fine: and [the one of] the door [has] some feeling. But I may tell you in confidence that my dragons did not look like he has drawn them—not the least bit in the world: I suppose you can't get an occidental artist to understand that dragons are the most beautiful and graceful of God's creatures: surpassing the swan for grace, the gazelle for beauty. Still I am content with having escaped Artzybasheff—heresy though it be to say so!"

Back in England, through his brother's instrumentality, Morris met and became close friends with A. Trevor Barker, the British theosophist (associated throughout the 1920s with the Adyar Theosophical Society) and editor of two important theosophical books, *The Mahatma Letters to A.P. Sinnett* (1923) and *Letters of H.P. Blavatsky to A.P. Sinnett* (1925). Morris brought him over to the Point Loma Theosophical Society, and a close friendship developed between Barker and the new leader, Dr. Gottfried de Purucker.

In Cardiff, Morris also became friends with the poet Cyril Hodges (1915–1974). Morris probably met him through his sister Marjory Hodges, who was a member of Cardiff Lodge of the Theosophical Society. Even though he was probably not himself a member, Hodges spent a great amount of time at the Cardiff Lodge, attending lectures and socializing. His first book, *China Speaks,* was a collection of twenty-one poems; the poems are based on the prose translations from the Chinese by Kenneth Morris. This booklet was published by the Poet Pilgrims Society in Cardiff in 1941 under the pen-name Cyril Hughes.

In Wales, Morris was surprised to find his name already known among Welsh intellectuals through his theosophical writings. He was befriended by many important Welshmen, including the playwright and short-story writer, R.G. Berry (1869–1945) and the poet Huw Menai (Huw Owen Williams, 1888–1961). And Morris was also encouraged to contribute to various periodicals like the *Welsh Outlook* (a monthly devoted to Welsh affairs; Morris contributed three articles before it ceased publication at the end of 1933), and the *Western Mail,* the foremost daily newspaper in Wales.

Even though pleased to be back in Wales, Morris did occasionally become wistful for Point Loma. In June 1930, while visiting his cousin Annie Gardner at Camberley in England, Morris found himself reminded of Point Loma by the pine-boughs and windy English sky, and he wrote a fine poem about these feelings which he later illuminated and sent back to friends at Point Loma. It concludes: "Here amid the Springtime light and shadow / And the green of English lawns and trees / Need my heart be weeping for Point Loma / By the Rainbow Seas?"

When Morris took charge of the Welsh Section of the Theosophical Society in 1930, there were only a handful of members. By the time of Morris's death in 1937, he had founded seven lodges, each with their own leaders and study-classes, in seven towns and cities across South Wales, including Cardiff, Swansea, Tonypandy, Ferndale, Wrexham, Port, and Pontypridd. Meetings and lectures were coordinated through a four-page stencilled newsletter, *Y Fforwm Theosophaidd* (the Welsh "Theosophical Forum"), which consisted mostly of articles (written in English) of theosophical instruction and philosophy. Morris produced and edited the monthly magazine from his home in Cardiff, and he wrote most of the articles himself. The first issue was dated 1 January, 1933, and *Y Fforwm Theosophaidd* outlived Morris by some years.

Initially, Morris's health had seemed to improve in Wales. In August 1931 he wrote to Ella Young that "Wales has very nearly restored my youth—a different man I am all together," and in January 1932 he wrote that he was "as strong at any rate as some horses, taking walks up and over the mountains, and working a good deal." But he frequently suffered from bronchitis and other debilitating ailments. Alex Urquhart first met Morris in 1932 when Morris was in his early fifties. By that time Morris was, according to Urquhart, a "small frail old man" with grey hair.

For the last years of his life, Morris lived very frugally in a small two room flat in Gwalia House on Fitzalan Road in Cardiff. The stress of traveling and lecturing, and of producing his monthly publication, was taking its toll upon Morris's health.

Yet Morris did manage finally to complete his third novel, *The Chalchiuhite Dragon,* sometime in 1935. And he was well enough in early August 1935 to host the annual European Theosophical Convention in Wales. But by the time a Dutch friend, H. Vissers, came to visit Morris for a fortnight in October 1935, Morris was recovering in the infirmary at Carlisle and just about to return home. At this time Morris told Vissers that he had recently finished a new book, and that he had a lady friend in New York who was trying to arrange for its publication; but whether any publishers were actually offered the manuscript remains unknown.

Apparently Morris's health rebounded. He continued writing and lecturing, and even wrote a new short play, "The Sleeping Beauty," for the children at the Cardiff Lodge. It was performed as their Christmas play in December 1936, and was published the following March in *The Lotus-Circle Messenger.*

Morris fell ill again in early April 1937. On the 9th he was removed to the Llandough Hospital in Penarth, near Cardiff, suffering from heart trouble, brought on by the long-continued effects of goitre. After a week of examination and observation by doctors, Morris told his friends their verdict: "They say I'd only live a year or so at the best, with this goitre, and if I can stand the operation of removing it, I shall have a new lease on life." From his hospital bed Morris continued some literary work, preparing some poems for submission to the *South Wales Argus,* the *Western Mail,* and the *Merthyn Express.* Morris's cover letters to accompany the poems were dated the 15th of April 1937, and addressed from the Llandough Hospital. The poems, oddly, were some of the earliest Morris had written, though these versions were probably reworked. Morris also prepared the envelopes, but he never sent the poems.

Morris's operation was performed on the 20th of April. He regained consciousness for only a few minutes following the operation, and doctors remained in almost constant attention at his bedside through the night as

Although young, his attainments were very great: all that study could make them. He had obtained his *chin-shih* degree, and was employed as lecturer on poetry at the college in his native city. His dissertations were marked by subtleness and extreme learning; yet none of his pupils became poets. He preserved his modesty, realizing his own deficiencies.

One day he noticed a stranger in the lecture hall: an old man, dressed uncouthly, with a very long beard, very bright eyes, and a dignified and mysterious demeanor. Chao Shih-hsiung was expounding, that morning, the Elegies of Chu Yuan; a certain inspiration and unwonted eloquence came upon him, and he felt he was nearer to the secret of poetry than ever he had been before. The bright eyes of the stranger seemed to awaken wonderful but dim memories within him, so that he was filled with new hope. At the close of the lecture, the stranger came to him. Chao Shih-hsiung smiled and bowed, feeling that he owed much to this old man's friendly encouragement.

"Sir," said the stranger, "why do you waste your life in these idle strivings? Following this path, you will never become a poet."

"I have studied diligently," said Chao. "Unfortunately genius is lacking."

"Genius is not lacking, but unawakened," said the other. "Forgo your flashy methods, and seek quietude. Quit your book-learning, sir; follow the gulls into cloudland, and do not bury your ethereal self beneath the dust of the world. Take the empyrean for your roof, the sun and the moon for your constant companions, and the four seas for your inseparable friends. Study the magic of the mountains, sir; and your laudable ambitions will be fulfilled."*

So now Chao Shih-hsiung was endeavoring to take his advice.

He came to the head of the pass; the world was all behind him now, and before and on all sides, the realm of mountain-magic. Beyond the valley, in front, rose dim and darkly glowing mountains, forest-clad; and afar, like faint petals of a lily against the sapphire sky, the snow-peaks, shadowed with the sunset in pale rose and salmon and blue. In the depths of the valley the river sang and gleamed, a narrow, winding thread of silver, broken here and there where it was hidden by trees. The road ran on among the pines; the stars were beginning to shine: the Spinning-Maiden and the Cowherd shone out bright, watching each other across the impassable River of Stars. It became too dark to read, and Chao Shih-hsiung closed his book, and looked out over the mountain world; and then at last forgot his old strivings and desires. All at once he heard lute music, and singing lovelier than any singing he had heard in his life.

*This is almost an exact quotation of a saying of Chang Chih-ho, "the Old Fisherman of the Mists and Waters," a sage of the 8th century—who lived two hundred years after Chao Shih-hsiung, however.

he drifted into deeper and deeper coma. One of the doctors came to Alex Urquhart, saying that there was still a lot of life left in Morris's body, and would not Urquhart come and help to talk his friend back? Urquhart declined, feeling that Morris himself would know what he wanted and would come back himself if he wanted to.

Kenneth Morris died at 4 A.M. on Wednesday the 21st of April 1937. He was fifty-seven years old. His body was cremated in one of the valleys to the north of Cardiff, because at that time Cardiff had no crematorium. His ashes were probably scattered among the mountains he loved, as was his wish.

A special "In Memoriam" meeting was held by his friends at the Cardiff Lodge of the Theosophical Society on Sunday evening, the 1st of May. Some thirty members of the Welsh Section of the Theosophical Society, and a half-dozen personal friends, attended to pay tribute to the life and work of Kenneth Morris. A fine portrait of Morris was prominently placed for all to see, and surrounded by messages of condolence. Many people spoke glowingly of Morris, and of the loving care and wisdom that he had lavished on his pupils. In conclusion, Alex Urquhart read from Edwin Arnold's translation of the Bhagavad-Gita, *The Song Celestial:*

> *Thou grievest where no grief should be! thou speak'st*
> *Words lacking wisdom! for the wise in heart*
> *Mourn not for those that live, nor those that die.*
> *Nor I, nor thou, nor anyone of these,*
> *Ever was not, nor ever will not be,*
> *For ever and for ever afterwards.*
> *All, that doth live, lives always!*

It was a fitting memorial to Morris, symbolically bringing together in one room three of Morris's greatest loves: Wales, poetry, and theosophy.

Kenneth Morris several times wrote or spoke of his wish to be discovered, if at all, some fifty or one hundred years after his death. His writings were to be his testament, and as they now become more readily available, both the man and his work will live on.

Douglas A. Anderson
Ithaca, New York,
and Chesterton, Indiana, July 1994

After the publication of his first novel in 1914, Kenneth Morris turned mu
his attention to writing and publishing short stories. He was then age
thirty-five, and already in his stylistic prime. Over the next three years, M
would publish over half of his total output of short stories.
The first of these stories, "The White Bird Inn," is one of Morris's thr
Chinese tales. It appeared in the January 1915 issue of The Theosophica
Path *under the pseudonym of Quintus Reynolds. In it, Morris gently sugges*
for the first time one of his favorite themes: that book-learning is not an
adequate substitute for the experience of life.

The White Bird Inn

*C*hao Shih-hsiung was going up into the mountains; where, if anywhere, he had been told, one might learn to write poetry. He was exemplary in diligence and filial conduct; a youth against whom no ill was spoken, kindly and gentle to all. But above everything he desired to be a poet.

It was coming to be evening; he had left the flat rice-fields at midday, and now was among the rocks and pines. Behind, and far below, lay the fields, and beyond them, the city; beyond that again, gleaming in faint pearl and turquoise and silver, the southern sea. On either side rose the steep mountain-side: great, friendly rocks and immemorial wizard pines. The road was not too rough for study, and Chao Shih-hsiung went forward reading the poems of the great Tao Yuen-ming. He heard not the wind intoning the *Kung* among the forked and elbowed pine-branches above him; he saw no wizardry in the tufts of the pine-needles; he neglected t feel a reciprocal friendliness for the immense boulders and for the gentl darkening blueness of the sky.

"The world acclaims Tao Yuen-ming the first poet of the age," sa Chao; "yet even from him I learn not the secret. I perceive his method arranging the four tones, and have succeeded in arranging them in li manner in my own efforts. I take note of the subjects he writes upon, a have written on them often myself. Further, I have studied carefully *Book of Odes* and the poetry of the period of Han; and I have practised ber olence, and made some progress. Yet my effusions cause no enthusia even in myself."

"It will be from some inn," thought he; and remembered that he was tired and hungry, and that an inn where he might sup and sleep would be the most desirable thing he could come upon.

In a little while he came to it. The hostess bade him welcome, and fetched him warm wine and food. While she waited on him, she went on singing. He watched her by the light of the lanterns that hung from the rafters. She was clad in gleaming white; pale blue flowers were in her black hair, and her long sleeves were rimmed with blue. Her eyes were bright and quick like a bird's; and her motions as she ran and tripped, he thought; were bird-like. And her singing was sweet, sweet, sweet: rising and trilling and flowing now, and now soft cooing, deep and mysterious. At one moment she was in the room, serving him; at the next, she had run out, sleeves rustling and fluttering, and her singing came from the right, from the left, from above. Peace and delight and mountain-sweetness flowed over his soul, and he sat and listened, listened.

The night deepened; the moon rose over the snow-peaks. The waters of the river below, the wind among the pine-branches, the murmur of the pine-needles overhead, seemed a part of her song. He listened, and all the music became one: he heard the mountain voices intone the great *Kung*. "This is wonderful," thought he. Then remembrance of the poems of Tao Yuen-ming came upon him; partly through his old habit of study, partly through an unwonted wakening in his soul. He opened his book, and began reading; and at that moment he heard that the hostess was singing the very poem on which his eyes rested.

He read and listened as she sang. But now the characters on the page were alive; they were moving and shining; the mountain-magic had possessed them. They sang themselves with her singing. The poem was glowing, ensouled. In every ideogram he heard the hostess' voice, he beheld a light like a diamond, like a pearl, like a twinkling opal; and from each he heard the call of the far waters, the voice of the night birds in the valley, the long sough and whisper of the wind among the pines. The printed poem itself was intoning with them the *Kung*. Chao Shih-hsiung marveled quietly, half dreaming. "This is poetry," said he.

The hostess sang on; the wind came wandering up out of the valley, bearing the scents of the southern night. Chao Shih-hsiung heard the wheel of the Spinning-Maiden in the sky, far and sweet; and he heard her song, and the answering song of the Cowherd from beyond the River of Stars that neither of them may pass. He heard the River of Stars sing as it flowed through the blue plains of infinity, and the stars and the wind and the pines, and the faintly glistening petals of the snowpeaks, and the hostess with her lute, and the waters of the valley below, had one voice, it seemed, between them; they were chanting the poems of Tao Yuen-ming; they were all intoning the *Kung*.

All night long Chao Shih-hsiung listened, forgetting everything; in deep oblivion of desires, for the wonder of the great *Kung* that he heard. All night long the hostess of the White Bird Inn was singing.

It was getting cold, cold, it seemed to him. . . . Was it the poems of Tao Yuen-ming she was singing now . . . or was she imitating, marvelously, the voice of a bird . . . ? Surging in rich trills, gurgling like deep, lonely waters, flowing forth, rising and falling, sweet, sweet, sweet—could ever human voice be so bird-like? It was cold, and his limbs and body were stiff.

He opened his eyes. The rafters overhead were strangely like the living branches of a pine, forked and twisted and with many elbows. He sat up. The inn—

There was no inn. He had been lying on the ground, beneath a pine-tree just off the road; and no bed under him but the fallen dry needles. The snow-peaks afar were beginning to grow pale and saffron, faint blue and silver and salmon-color, with the rising of the sun. The song came from the branches above him; decidedly there were no human words to it; not even the magical words of Tao Yuen-ming. He looked up, and there, on a twig above his head, a white bird was singing. She had a little blue tuft of feathers on her head, and the white, gleaming wings of her were blue-tipped. And she was singing, singing, singing; and in her song, Chao Shih-hsiung heard all joy and all sorrow, and that which is beyond sorrow and joy. He heard the deep, far murmur, the eternal mystery of the *Kung*.

Then he went on his way, chanting the poems of Tao Yuen-ming; and poems—yes, *poems*— of his own. Into all of them, he chanted the same, lonely, solemn, joyous, infinite wonder and tone. The pines rustling above, seemed to have human expression; the boulders looked at him kindly and humanwise, and he reciprocated their friendliness.

He was a great poet after that, it is said.

This second Chinese tale, "The Eyeless Dragons," was published in the June 1915 issue of The Theosophical Path, *again under the pseudonym* Quintus Reynolds.

The Eyeless Dragons

*C*hang Seng-yu was to be the artist; that was why the crowds were so immense. The courts of the Temple of Peace and Joy had been full since dawn; although the sun would undoubtedly be well in heaven before the great Chang would mount the scaffolding and begin to work.

All Nankin had been agog since the word had gone forth that the Emperor desired a dragon painted on either of the two vast wall-surfaces of the Temple; and when it was reported further that Chang Seng-yu was to be the artist, then, indeed, the rejoicing was great. For the grand strokes of his brush were known; and his colors were delicate like the mists of evening on the Yangtse, or clear and lovely like the colors of flowers. Whenever he painted in public, the crowds would gather to watch; and from time to time to applaud the master-strokes, the flashes of daring imagination, the moments when the sparks of creation most visibly flew. And they *knew*, did those crowds of the Chinese Renaissance—some fourteen centuries ago.

They loved Chang Seng-yu for another reason, too, besides his genius and mastery of the brush. He was at least half a *Sennin:** many held that he had drunk the Elixir; that he could rein the flying Dragon, and visit the extremities of the earth, and bestride the hoary crane, to soar above the nine degrees of heaven. Such things were done, in those days. There was a certain power about Chang Seng-yu, that suggested infinite possibilities. One could never tell what might happen, with any picture he might be painting.

*Adept

A hush in the temple court; the artist has arrived, and with him a little band of disciples, bearing the brushes and pots of color. A quiet, gentle old man, who bows profoundly to the people as he comes in; and greets them with courteous formalities, not unaffectionately, while passing to the door of the Temple. With courteous formalities those spoken to respond, proud of the signal honor done them; for this is a popular hero, be it understood. The tailor and the cobbler have arranged in advance a holiday, and have come now with their families to spend the day in the Temple of Peace and Joy, watching the Master paint; the butcher's apprentice, sent on an errand, can not resist the temptation; the porter, calculating possibilities to a nicety, deems that he may go in, watch so much wall-space covered with sudden life, and then, by hurrying, still arrive in time with his load. For with all these people, painting is poetry made visible, the mysteries of Tao indicated, Magic, the topmost wonder and delight of life. And this being by Chang Seng-yu, will be no ordinary painting.— "Ah, in that honorable brush-sweep, one saw the effect of the Elixir!" cried the butcher's apprentice, radiant.

Day by day the crowds gathered in the court, and followed Chang Seng-yu, when he arrived, into the Vast Temple. Day by day the intent silence was broken ever and anon into murmurs, and the murmurs into rippling exclamation. A sweep of the brush, and lo, the jaws of a dragon; and from that the wonderful form grew, perfect at each touch, scale by scale through all the windings of the vast body to the very end of the tail. All in shining yellow that might have been distilled out of the sunset, it gleamed across the great wall: a thing of exquisite curves, noble lines; flowing, grand, and harmonious; wherein all parts seemed cognate to, and expressive of, the highest perceptions and aspirations of man. To behold it was like hearing the sudden crash of a glorious and awe-inspiring music: the soul of every upright man would at once both bow down and be exalted. The crowd, watching, expected at any moment to see motion quiver through its length; to see it writhe, shake out mighty pinions, break forth from the wall and through the roof, and cleave a way into the blue ether. A little fear mingled with their intense delight: the Master, surely, was dealing in magic.

"Sir," said Lu Chao, "for what reason have you omitted to paint in the honorable eye?"

"Could this sacred Dragon see," answered Chang Seng-yu, "nothing would content his lordship but to seek his home in the playground of the lightnings."

"How is it possible?" said Lu Chao. "The Dragon is beautiful, but it is only a semblance wrought in pigment. How could such a semblance soar into the heavens? The Master is pleased to indulge in humor at the expense of this miserable one."

"Not so, Lu Chao," said the Master. "You have little understanding, as yet, of the mysteries of art."

But Lu Chao doubted, and it was a sorrow to him that Chang Seng-yu should leave his creation incomplete.

The Yellow Dragon was finished, its glorious form covering the upper part of the south wall. The people could hardly forbear to worship; they saw in it Divine Power, the essence of Light-Bringing, the perfect symbol of inspiration, of holy and quickening thought from heaven. "If the Master had not left his creation eyeless," they said, "his lordship would never be content to dwell on earth. Heaven is the right abiding-place for such a one." But Lu Chao went on doubting.

He did not refer to the matter again; but when it came to his turn to hand the brush, newly dipped in the color pot, to Chang Seng-yu, the latter as he looked down would shake his head, and a shadow would pass over his face. "Although of a good disposition, Lu Chao will never be a painter," thought he, sighing.

The scaffolding was removed to the opposite wall, and there, facing the other, a Purple Dragon began to grow. Occasionally the Son of Heaven himself, the Emperor Wu-ti, would visit the temple to inspect the growing work. Then the artist would descend to make obeisance; but Wu-ti, holy man, would have none from the creator of those dragons. "Make your obeisance with me, to these two lordly Messengers of Heaven," said he. "But for what reason has the honorable Master left the eyes to be painted last?"

"Sire," said Chang Seng-yu, "the divine eyes of their lordships will not be painted. There is danger that they would be ill contented with the earth, if they could see to soar into their native empyrean. No man could paint into their eyes such compassion, that they would desire to remain here."

"It is well," said the emperor. "Their soaring aspiration is evident. Let them remain to be the guardians of the Peace and Joy of my People."

Lu Chao heard, but even the Son of Heaven's belief failed to convince him. "It may be as the Master says," thought he; "but such matters are beyond my understanding. How could a semblance wrought of pigment feel aspiration or a desire for the ethereal spaces? It appears to me that the venerable Chang is indulging in humor, when he speaks of painting compassion into their eyes."

The work was drawing to a close, and more and more Lu Chao doubted. It is true that he made progress in painting; and the skill shown in his work was applauded by many. For the day of the Consecration of the Dragons had been appointed in advance; and there was time to spare; and on certain days now the Temple would be closed, and the Master and his disciples would work in the studio. Then Chang Seng-yu, going from one to another, and commenting on the work of each, would shake his head a little sadly over Lu Chao's pictures. "You have skill and perseverance," he would say, "but faith is lacking."

Lu Chao pondered on this, but not with desire to acquire the faith. "Many say that I am making progress," thought he, "and it appears so to me also. The Master, truly, is harsh in his judgments. If I could show him that he is mistaken . . ." He considered the matter, and thought out his plans.

The Day of Consecration came; the great work was completed. Priests and augurs, sennins and doctors, gathered from all Liang, and from the kingdoms beyond the Yangtse and the Western Mountains. All day long there were sacrifices in the Temple of Peace and Joy, and processions passed through, doing joyful obeisance to the Dragons. At last night came, and the great hall and courts were silent.

The time had come for Lu Chao; now he would prove that the Master had been mistaken; that painted semblances could not shake themselves free from the walls whereon they were painted, and that he himself was making progress unhindered by lack of faith. "It may be that there is Magic," said he, "although I have never seen it. But reason forbids me to believe this."

He took a lantern, a small brush, and such paint as would be needed, and went down through the dark streets towards the Temple. There would be no trouble about obtaining entrance, he knew: should anyone question him, Chang Seng-yu had forgotten something, and had sent him for it. But it was unlikely that he would meet anyone, and he hoped to pass in unseen. "No one will know that I did it," thought he. "It will be understood that the spirits painted in the eyes, displeased that the Master left the work un-finished."

He met no one; succeeded in climbing the gate; found a ladder in the court; placed it against the south wall by the head of the Yellow Dragon; climbed, and prepared to begin. It had been a dark night, but calm, as he came through the city; now, with the first touch of his brush, a peal of thunder, a lightning flash. In his sudden perturbation, the brush dropped, and he must go down after it. Were the genii offended? He hesitated, and had some thought of going home. "But no," said he; "this is fear; this is arrant superstition,"—and mounted the ladder again. The lantern, hung from a rung close to the dragon's head, just threw light on that: a little disk of warm brightness fading into the gloom. It was enough for Lu Chao's purpose. A few brush-strokes; that would be all.

The first, and he was aware of fear. The second, and the wall seemed to him to be taken with unsteadiness. The third, and the sweat broke from his forehead and back, and his hand was trembling violently. He gathered his mind, reasoning with himself; steadied his hand, and put in the last stroke. The Yellow Dragon's eye was painted.

Lu Chao clung to the ladder. By the small light of the lantern he saw the wonderful head turn until it was looking out into the Temple, full face instead of profile. It was the left eye that he had painted; now the two were there, glancing out hither and yonder, proudly, uneasily; flashing fiery rays through the empty darkness. The ladder was shaking, swaying. Suddenly the two amazing eyes were turned full on him, on Lu Chao. A shadow of disgust flitted over them; then they were filled with immeasurable sadness, sorrow deeper than might be borne. The neck drew back; by a supernatural light from the Dragon's eyes, Lu Chao saw it, drawn back and clear out of the wall. A crash, and he saw the immense pinions shaken forth. A horrible swaying of the world; a rending noise, a tearing and a crashing; a blinding flame. . . .

All Nankin was awake, and out in the streets. What the people saw was a Golden Wonder soaring up into the sky: a cometlike glory ascending, till it was lost in the darkness of Heaven.

In the morning the emperor visited the ruins of the Temple of Peace and Joy, and with him went Chang Seng-yu the Master. The north wall alone was standing. The roof had gone up in a single blaze where the fiery wings cleaved it. Of the south wall, only the lower part remained; the rest had fallen. Under the débris they found the ladder, charred and broken, and the crushed body of Lu Chao.

"Ah," said Chang Seng-yu sadly, "he would never have made an artist."

• •

"The Night of Al Kadr" was published in the July 1915 issue of The
Theosophical Path, *under the pseudonym C. ApArthur. This story tells of
the conflict between the Christians and the Moors in eighth-century Spain. In
it, through the mystical experience of the Christian Don Jesús, Morris
emphasizes that true religious belief transcends denominations such as
Christian and Moslem.*

The Night of Al Kadr

*D*on Jesús María Guzmán de Altanera y Palafox would go crusad-
ing; not to the Holy Land, since opportunity was lacking, but
into infidel territories that lay more conveniently at hand. A day's ride from
his castle of Altanera de la Cruz lay the stronghold of that stubborn pagan
Ali Mumenin al-Moghrebbi; which now it seemed was likely to be lost to
pagandom. A third of the spoils to Santiago de Compostella, if Aljamid
should be surprised; and this even before the king's fifth had been de-
ducted. Don Jesús was a generous and religious man.

Of the *sangre azul* was this Don Jesús: a Goth, inheriting the ruthless
lordliness of the northern hordes that poured into Spain under Adolf and
Walia, a thousand years before, and set up turbulent kingdoms on the ruins
of the Roman province. His were still the blue eyes and flaxen hair of the
north; though Spanish skies and centuries, and a few Celtic mothers perhaps, had wrought in the temper that lay beneath them a certain change for
better or worse. Had made subtle and dangerous the old Teutonic bull-at-a-
gate impetuosity; had turned half leopard—smooth, graceful, but clawed
fearfully—what of old had been all lion and largeness. Such a transmutation
may make of brutality a reasoned cruelness; but also kindles a gleam of
idealism in the spaces of the soul. The wild warrior of huge feastings and
potations becomes the knight much given to prayer; the old thirst for mere
big deeds and adventures, a longing after warfares with some glimmer of
the spiritual about them. You shall fight, now, for God, the Faith, the
Saints, and the Virgin; your cause shall be sanctified; your sword drawn
against something you may dub evil; behind your rape and plunder, even,

there shall be a kind of vision. Herein lay the difference between Don Jesús and his ancestor, the big-limbed Goth who fought under Walia. The end of the affair, he had every hope, would be indiscriminate slaughter and all the worser horrors of war: hell let loose, after the fashion of the age, on the household of al-Moghrebbi, and no restraint imposed upon its beastly gluttony. None the less, he had taken Mass with his men before ever the portcullis was raised for them to pass, and went forth in exaltation of spirit, as one commissioned of heaven. As he rode down the hill from Altanera de la Cruz in the early morning, you should see in the keen eyes of him, in the spare, aquiline face and firm jaw, possibilities of cruelty and rapacity no doubt, but also the eagle's far glance sunward and beyond, as into things unseen. —The Grand Alchemist, Nature, forever dabbles in humanity: taking these elements and those, mixing them in such and such proportions and at such and such a temperature, and experimenting always after a spiritual type. In old Spain she came very near triumph and crying *Eureka!*— alas, her miss was as bad as many a mile. A little would make Don Jesús a demon; but then, a little might make him something very like a God.

All day they rode, but for a halt at noon; by the time the sun was nearing the snow-peaks westward, they had crested the last ridge of the foothills: had passed the debatable land, and were on the border, you might say, of Infidelity. Here, amid the pines they halted, and looked out towards their prey. From their feet the woods swept down steeply into the valley; beyond, in the shadow of the mountains already, or gilded with slant rays, lay the cornfields and orchards of the pagans; there wound the river, pale under the liquid blue of late afternoon; yonder, bounding the landscape, the majesty of the Sierra, deep purple in shadow, and the purple suffused with a glow of rich silver or faint gold. Far off were the peaks piled up skyward, white against a heaven in which soon the sunset roses would begin to bloom. And gaunt against the glow and gloom of the mountain, something westward of opposite, rose the crag outstanding into the valley, the hither face of it a precipice of four hundred sheer feet; and its crown the castle of Aljamid which Saint James that night should deliver into Catholic hands.

They were to wait where they were for the present, not invading the Moorish lands until after nightfall; and then with muffled hoofs, lest a hornet's nest of heathen should be roused against them before ever they came to their goal. —Of course there was no thought of ascending yonder precipice; for goats and monkeys it might serve, not for Christians. The stormable road ran up from the mountain-side beyond; it was steep and easily defended, they knew; but given a surprise and a guide, not impossible, they hoped, by moonlight. And a guide Don Jesús had brought with him: one Francisco Rondón, who had been a slave in Aljamid for years, until a certain lightness of the fingers, discovered, brought him into trouble. After that he had achieved escaping; with ideas of avenging, not so much his long durance, as the stripes that had been meted out to him in punishment by the master of the slaves. It was he who had inspired Don Jesús with the design, having convinced him of its feasibility and profitable nature. Al-Moghrebbi, he knew, was likely to be in Granada that day with the bulk of his men; in any case, it was the holiest night of their Ramadan with the pagans, and there would be much feasting and little watching, after sunset, within the walls. —Of the sanctity of the enterprise Don Jesús needed no convincing.

There then they lay, chatting beneath the pines, till a call from the sentinel brought them to their feet and to the look-out. The garrison was sallying, it appeared; and somewhat late in the day to be destined for Granada. The question was: Had Ali Mumenin heard of their coming, and determined to give them battle in the valley? Unlikely, considering the strength of his walls, impregnable except to surprise (and treachery). But if so, they would take him in the ford; let the Moors be involved in the water; then would the Christians swoop. . . . So they stood by their saddles, ready to mount and thunder down at an instant; the *Cierra España!* you may say, formed in their throats for the shouting.

Dimly the Moslem warriors could be seen emerging from the castle, and for awhile, passing in full view along the road. Then they were hidden, as though the way they took were walled or ran through a ravine; presently they came out on to the mountainside, leading their horses. In single file they came; in groups, in no order, struggling down into the valley; then, at the call of a silver fife or pipe, they began to assemble, and mounted.

Five hundred of them, at the least; instead of the mere fifty of the regular garrison; they would, then, be five to one against the Christians, should it come to fighting. But there were the saints of heaven also to be considered; which put the odds, to Christian thinking, very much on their own side. However, fighting there would be none, it seemed. The Moors had gathered at the foot of the crag, were a-saddle; and now, at another scream of the fife, started: not southward and east towards the ford and the Spaniards, but northwestward and on the road to Granada. Not yet was the light so dim that one could not see the round shields, the lances, the turbaned helmets: the flutter of white robes over the coats of mail; the prancing and caracoling and beautiful steps of the horses, mostly gray or white, and all with sweeping manes and tails. White-robed horsemen and white beasts, pearl-gray all through the dusk: one could see, even at that distance, the lovely grace of the horsemanship; every ripple of motion expending itself through horse and rider, as if they were one. . . . Away they rode and out into the dimness of distance; on and up along the river bank, towards the head of the valley, the pass, and Granada. Certainly martial Santiago of Spain was with his Spaniards, who might count their victory won already. . . .

They rode down the hill before the light was quite gone; and waited, not long, for the moon to rise before fording the river. A quarter of a mile, then, along the bank, and they turned, and struck up hill under the castle rock; a watch having been posted in the valley. Thence on they led their horses, until a cork grove half way up the slope offered concealment in which these might be left; having tied them, and posted a guard, they went forward in silence. The path was easy enough, until one turned, and faced outward towards the crag of Aljamid. A neck of land, rising steeply towards the fortress, and falling away on either side in sheer cliffs, lay between the mountain-side and the stronghold: a way that only goats could have traveled before patient Berber toil of old, cutting steps and passages, made a winding, much-ramparted path, to be traveled hardly anywhere by more than one abreast, and guarded by gates at a dozen places. Aljamid was deemed impregnable; it had never changed hands by force of arms since Musa built and garrisoned it.

To one after another of these gates our Christians came, and found all guardless and wide open. They might have suspected a trap, you will say; but Rondón had confidence in his plans, and Don Jesús in him; if a trap were set, it would go hard but they would trap the trappers. So up and down, to left and right, with sudden turns the way led; only now and again one caught glimpses of the grim moonlit towers beyond. Presently, in a sort of wide well or rampart deep bastioned, Rondón halted them. "Señor," said he, "from the top of yonder stairs, the road is straight and open; at the end of it, and before the gate, is a chasm a hundred feet deep; while the rest remain here hidden, I must have ten lithe climbers to descend and ascend that, overcome what guard may be beyond, and let down the drawbridge."

Don Jesús whispered his orders. He himself, he considered, with Saint James to aid him, would be more than equal to ten. He picked two men for sentries: one for the top of the stairs, one for the hither brink of the chasm; then, with Rondón, stole forward.

The descent, when they came to it, was no easy work for an armed man; but the Spanish moon is bright, and Don Jesús was all the leopard, sound and clean of limb, and unweakened by sinister living. Also the guide had learnt well every possible foothold. A narrow place of boulders, scorpions, and sharp moon-shadows at the bottom; then the ascent, less difficult, on the other side. At half way up they came to a narrow ledge; above which the rock wall rose sheer and unbroken. But the Arabs were masters of engineering, and there was a way for one who knew the secret. Stamped upon the memory of Rondón was the exact spot where you should press upon the cliff face; and now, at his touch, the rock gave, and a panel was to be shoved along its groove; which passing, they found themselves in a little chamber. Through the open door in the wall opposite came the light of a distant lantern; no one was there, and no sound was to be heard. They took that passage, and ascended many steps; lanterns set on the floor at long intervals lighting them. Presently they came out into a little room: a place for the gate-keeper, to judge by the bunches of keys on the walls. No guard was there.

"Here, Señor, I let down the bridge and raise the portcullis," said Rondón; and took hold upon certain cranks to begin. But the silence and the peril had been working on the nerves of his master. At each step forward the tension had grown greater; but it was the tension of a sublime exaltation. Now all the Quixote flamed up in him: a pride of race and pride of faith and pride of personality. He would have no aid in his work but from the Blessed on high. Having mastered the castle, overcome the infidels and slain without sparing, he would himself raise the cross on the highest tower before ever another Spaniard should enter there to help him. "No," he said; "we shall need no aid from without. Leave it, and lead forward into Aljamid."

Rondón stared; realized the position after a moment, and then fell to entreaties; but who is to argue with a madman with drawn sword? It was death immediate, he saw, under that Christian blade; or death deferred, but devised by the devil-cunning of black Abu'l Haidara, the slave-master. . . . Well, give the saints the time implied in that deferment, and they might do something—in consideration of all he had done for them. There might be a chance to slip behind and run for it; thank heaven, he knew the way. He cried inwardly to his churchly deities, and obeyed—just in time.

Through several halls they passed, all lovely with arches and lattice tracery; and dimly lighted with lanterns set lonely here and there on great stretches of tesselated floor. Stronghold and palace in one was this Aljamid; whence Ali Mumenin, paying slight attention to his sultan at Granada, kinged it in state over his own frontier valleys; in turn harrying and harried by the Christians. (True, a little of Don Jesús' confidence was drawn from the fact that he was breaking a long truce.)

Out they came, presently, into a patio filled with moonlight and the music of a fountain, and set round with orange trees planted in huge vases. Here at last a tinkling and a thrumming came blown to them, betokening human presence not far off; and the need to find someone to fight, to compel to surrender, was growing imperative on Don Jesús. He strode across the patio quickly, all his attention flowing towards what he should find beyond; and forbode to note the chance he was giving to Rondón. So it happened that a tale reached the waiting Spaniards, a little later, that their lord was taken and slain; that the garrison within numbered thousands, and were expecting them: were indeed on the point of sallying in force; and so it happened that by dawn these same Spaniards were well on their way to Altanera de la Cruz. Meanwhile Don Jesús, all unaware of his aloneness, had crossed the patio, passed through a doorless arch beyond, and come upon humanity at last.

A lamp, quite priceless, you would say, with its rubies, stood in the middle of the floor; beside it sat the lutanist, an African boy, not uncomely; and on a divan beyond was an old Arab, white-bearded, handsome with the beauty of wise old age, and of a gravity and dignity altogether new to this grave and dignified Spaniard. He rose and came forward as our hidalgo entered, approaching him with a mien all courtesy and kindliness. "Welcome to Aljamid, Don Jesús de Palafox," said he; and, "your grace is in his own house."

The hall was full of the scent of musk and sandalwood, and of some wonderful thing else, perceivable by a sense more intimate even than that of smell. Don Jesús' sword had sought its scabbard before the Moor had begun to speak. He had met pagans of rank before, both at war and in peace, and knew them for

caballeros de Granada,
hijosdalgo, aunque moros;

—to be respected, indeed, on all points save that of creed. But here there was something that roused reverence and wonder, and was not to be accounted for by anything visible. The moods that but now had been burning so bright in the Spaniard's soul, vanished; race and creed were forgotten; he felt no enmity towards this august pagan; indeed the terms *pagan* and *Christian,* had they been brought before his mind now, would have carried little meaning. Instead, there was a sense of intense expectancy: as if a curtain should be drawn back now, before which all his life he had been waiting; a feeling that the occasion was, for him, momentous, and predestined from times beyond his memory.

The Arab led him to the divan, and ordered that food should be served. "You would prefer to remain armed, Señor, or is the weight of the steel perchance an encumbrance?" Santiago of Spain, where were you now, to raise no raucous war-cry of the spirit that might save your champion from perdition? Belike the presence of sainthood in the flesh had shriveled and banished your sainthood of dream and dogma! . . . Don Jesús paused not before answering, "Señor, of your infinite courtesy—" unbuckling his sword-belt, and handing the weapon to his host. A slave came, and relieved him of his armor; another with water in a golden basin, for the washing of his hands. Then they brought in a low table and dishes, from which a savory scent arose; and Don Jesús remembered that he was hungry. While he ate, the old man talked to him.

As for the substance of the talk, you may imagine it. Whoever has been the guest of a Moslem aristocrat, a descendant of the Companions of Mohammed, knows what hostly courtesy means with these people: perfect breeding, kingly manners, and above all a capacity to make one feel oneself the supreme object of the care and personal interest of his host. All this the Moor displayed, and very much more. No matter what he said, it rang with an inner importance and vitality. Could he look at will into the past life of his guest; or had he secret information as to its details and intricacies? With the infinite tact of impersonality, he shed light upon the heights and depths of it, revealing the man to himself. All this in sentences that seemed casual; that were strewn here and there, and lifted themselves afterwards, and shone out strangely, from the current of his talk. Don Jesús listened and marveled; ideals long cherished came to seem to him base or too restricted; his old spiritual exaltation grew, but had shed all credal bonds. . . . The words of his host came, luminous of the dusk within his soul; in surprise at which light, he took little note as yet of the objects illumined. But there was, it seemed, a vast, an astounding world within there; in which one might find, presently—

Mutes came in, obeying a hand-clap of the Moor, and removed the dishes; then brought in a board and chessmen. Don Jesús played?—Was, in fact, not inexpert; so the game began. "But first, music," said the old man. Considering the matter in after years, this was the beginning, thought Don Jesús, of what might be called supernatural: no one entered in obedience to the hand-clap, that time; and it was certain that they were alone. Yet the music was there; it stole into being close at hand and all about them, out of the soft lamplight and out of the musk odor: faint at first, as a mere accompaniment to thought, a grouping and melodizing of the silence. . . . The game proceeded; the chessmen were of ivory, exquisitely carven; red was the Spaniard, white the Moor. The red king's pawn was well advanced; and the Don's game all to make a queen of it. A white knight moves and threatens; the threat is countered, and the pawn goes forward;—so the game goes, a stern struggle. What?—the white pieces move in their turn, without ever the Moor stretching out a hand to move them. . . . And how is this—that Don Jesús is watching the white queen, the knight that threatened, the rook, not from his place on the divan, but from that very sixth square where his pawn—no, he himself—is standing? The board has become the world in which he lives; he is there; he is the pawn: is menaced, plans, is trepidant, is rescued, moves forward and breathes freely; one more move and the goal is reached. . . . The music grows, becomes loud and triumphant; a shout rings over the battlefield; he turns; there is one riding down upon him: a great white figure of mien relentlessly compassionate; and he is taken.

He was, as it were, wakened out of sleep by a wondrous chanting; wakened into a light, shining in the night, clearly, but supernatural, and excelling the sun at noon. He woke with the sense of having passed through fasting and spiritual search; of having long contemplated the world and man with an agony of compassionate question; which agony, as he sensed the splendor of his vision, found itself appeased.

Out of the radiant infinity he heard the boom and resonance of a voice grander than music, that shaped itself for his hearing into this:—

The Night of Al Kadr is better than a thousand months. Therein do the angels descend, and the Spirit Gabriel also, with the decrees of their Lord concerning every matter. It is Peace, until the Rosy Dawn.
—But it was as if some one of God's ultimate secrets, some revelation supernal, had been translated and retranslated *downwards* a thousand times, until reaching a plane where it might be spoken in words at all. . . . To him, listening, the verse spoke all the systole and diastole of things that be or seem; he felt within it and within himself, the Universes roll, and the Secret Spirit, the Master of the Universes, contain itself in everlasting radiant quiescence and activity. He looked out on the world and men, that before had presented themselves with such insistent incomprehensible demands to his heart; and saw them spun out from and embodying the Light of Lights. "From IT do we proceed, and unto IT shall we return," he cried; and went forth, clothed in the Peace of Al Kadr, sensible of divinity "nearer to him than his jugular vein."

The light faded, the music died into confusion; and from the confusion was born again, now martial, wild, and fierce. He rode in reckless battle, exulting in the slaying of men; was in cities besieged, and fell in the slaughter that followed their capture. Now it was one body he wore, now another: Arab, Berber, Greek, Frank, German, Spaniard. Now in war, now in trade; now crowned and acclaimed king, now sold and fettered for a slave: he flung himself into this or that business or adventure, questing a light and knowledge, forgotten indeed, but whose afterglow would not wane out of his soul. One of a host of mobile horsemen, he scoured war-smitten fields raising the tekbir of the Moslem; in the name of the Most Merciful slaying and slain;—yet slain or slaying, found not that for which his soul thirsted. Clad in steel, he rode a knight of the Cross; slew mightily to the warshout of *Cierra España!* But the vision of those saints on whom he called, faded always or ever his eyes closed in death: he went hungering always into the silence: burned still for desire of the flame; was disappointed of the inwardness of the faith; called in vain for a supreme shining in the dusk within. . . . And always, it seemed, a voice from afar, from long ago, cried out to him, and might not intelligently be heard; and riding, fighting, trading, slaying, and sinning, he was without content, for longing to know what was being called. That would be the Secret, that the Glory; it was to hear and understand that, it seemed, he was thus plunging into life after life.

Night, night, night; and afar off, and obsessing his spirit with longings, dawn bloomed in the sky: dawn, all-knowledge, all-beauty: the satisfaction of the unrest and aspirations of his heart. On and on with him over the desert; dimly glittering under the glittering stars were the bones of them that had fallen in the way before him. Would there never be an end to this interminable riding? . . . Ah, here was the light; here was the splendor; here was the voice out of the sunburst: *The Night of Al Kadr is better than a thousand months . . . It is Peace until the Rosy Dawn.*

The old Moor was sitting opposite him on the divan, intoning words in an incomprehensible tongue—yet it had not been incomprehensible to Don Jesús a moment before, when he was out in the desert, and the great light shone. "Master, I know!" said he, very humbly. "It is peace . . . it shall be peace . . . until—"

The old man rose up; beautiful his eyes with strange compassion, triumph, understanding. "Your grace will be weary after long riding," said he. "Sleep now, and peace let it be with you."

Don Jesús leaned back on the cushions and slept. Was it in dream, or was it through half-closed eyes that sleep had not quite captured, that he saw his host, luminously transfigured for a moment, then disappear?

He awoke; broad daylight shone in through the arches from the patio. Standing before him, watching him intently, was a Moorish lord whom he recognized for the redoubtable al-Moghrebbi: black-bearded, well-knit, eyed and browed like a warrior and a despot.

"A strange guest I find in my castle, Señor," said the Moor.

Don Jesús rose and bowed. What he saw before him was not a pagan, not an enemy of Christian Spain; but a fellow man: a fellow—what shall I say?—casket of the Gem of Gems, lantern of the Light of Lights, seeker in the desert after the Dawn. "I am at your disposal, Señor," said he.

"You have eaten my salt, it appears; even though unknown to me it was offered to you. I give you safe-conduct to your own borders; thereafter, knowing the strength of Aljamid, you may make choice between peace and war."

"Señor Moro," said Don Jesús—and wondered whence the words came to him—"it is Peace, until the Rosy Dawn."

"The dawn is passed, Señor. You choose war?"

"I do not choose war, Señor; either now, or at any future time. If your grace will remember that I have eaten your salt, I—I shall remember that I have passed in your stronghold a night that was—*better than a thousand months.*"

Ali Mumenin eyed him curiously. "Strange words these, to come from a Christian to a Moor."

Again the Spaniard bowed. "Might we not say, Caballero, *from a man to a brother man?*"

Don Jesús meditated as he rode through the cork forest; his Moorish escort headed by the now all-cordial al-Moghrebbi, having left him at the border. A tenth of his possessions, in commemoration of certain victories, ought certainly to be devoted to—Santiago de Compostella? Then in fairness another tenth ought to go to some Moorish shrine. On consideration, he decided that better uses might be found for both.

He lived to win the trust of Ferdinand the Catholic, and to receive from that politic, but not unkindly monarch, the Castle of Aljamid and the government of the surrounding district. Isabella removed him when she began her policy of persecution, and he retired to Altanero de la Cruz. Torquemada sent emissaries through his late government, inquiring, into certain rumors anent his faith; who, sheep's-clothinged in apparent sympathy, learnt that he was certainly at heart with the conquered pagans; and probably, as these held, an agent of the Brothers of Sincerity* himself. But crossing into the Christian territories of Altanera de la Cruz, they found an orthodox peasantry equally assured that he was, if not a Catholic saint, only waiting death and the Pope to make him one.

But a legend remained among the slaves at Aljamid until the Conquest of Granada, how that on the holiest night of Ramadan, the Night of Al Kadr, in such a year, when their lord had ridden away with the garrison in the evening, only to return at dawn unexpectedly, having heard of the presence of Christians in his valley—Aljamid had been full of the music of Paradise, the scent of musk and sandalwood, the aroma of holiness; and the Spirit Gabriel had descended, and saved them from the sword of the Spaniard. Gabriel, or as some more thoughtful held, one of the great Brothers of Sincerity, the servants of that everliving Man who is the Pillar and Axis of the World.

---

*According to Islamic doctrine, a secret Lodge or Brotherhood of Adepts, whose members live throughout the ages, are the Guardians of the Esoteric Wisdom, and Incarnate from time to time among men for the sake of humanity.

● ●

"The Regent of the North" is one of Morris's two stories based on Norse mythology. In it, an old Viking chieftan clings to his faith in Odin the All-Father and Baldur the Beautiful, while Christianity overtakes Sweden by command of the King. "The Regent of the North" was published in the August 1915 issue of The Theosophical Path, *under the pseudonym C. ApArthur.*

The Regent of the North

*T*he northern winter is altogether ghostly and elemental; there is no friendliness to man to be found in it. There, the snow has its proper habitation; there, in the gaunt valleys of Lapland, in the terrible, lonely desolations, the Frost Giants abide. They are servants of the Regent of the North: smiths, that have the awful mountains for their anvils; and, with cold for flame tempering water into hardness, fashion spears and swords of piercing ice, or raise glittering ramparts about the Pole. All for the dreadful pleasure of doing it! They go about their work silently in the gray darkness; heaven knows what dreams may be haunting them—dreams that no mind could imagine, unless death had already frozen its brain. When the wind wolves come howling down from the Pole, innumerous, unflagging, and insatiable: when the snow drives down, a horde of ghosts wandering senseless, hurrying and hurrying through the night: the giants do their work. They make no sound: they fashion terror, and illimitable terror, and terror. . . . Or—is it indeed only terror that they fashion? . . .

And then spring comes, and the sun rises at last on the world of the North. The snow melts in the valleys; white wisps of cloud float over skies blue as the gentian; over a thousand lakes all turquoise and forget-me-not: waters infinitely calm and clear, infinitely lovely. Then the snow on the mountain dreams dazzling whiteness by day, defiantly glittering against the sun; dreams tenderness, all faint rose and heliotrope and amber, in the evening; blue solemn mystery in the night. Quick with this last mysterious dreaming!—for the nights are hurrying away; they grow shorter always; they slink Poleward, immersed in ghostly preoccupations; by midsummer they have vanished altogether. Then the sun peers incessantly wizardlike over the horizon; the dumb rocks and the waters are invincibly awake, alert, and radiant with some magic instilled into them by the Regent of the North. . . . It is in this spring- and summer-time that you shall see bloom the flowers of Lapland: great pure blossoms in blue and purple and rose and citron, such as are not found elsewhere in the world. The valleys are a dreaming, silent wonder with the myriads there are of them—silent, for the Lapps have followed the reindeer, and the reindeer have followed the snows.

Into this region it was that Halfdan the Aged came, when he was tired of the new ways and faith that had come into the south. The viking days were over forever, one could see that. Meek, crozier-bearing men had invaded the realms of Odin and Balder; laying terrible axes of soft words, of chanted prayers and hymns, to the roots of—? All the ancient virtue of the race, said Halfdan the Aged; all the mighty and mystic dreams that had been surging through the Northlands these hundreds of years; sending the brave forth to wonderful deeds and wonderful visions about the seas and coasts of the world. And Inge the king at Upsala, forgetting all things noble and generous, had foresworn Odin and battle-breaking Thor; had foresworn Balder the Beautiful; had welcomed these chanting, canting foreigners, and decreed their faith for his people. So that now nothing remained but a fat, slothful life and the straw-death at the end of it: there should be no more viking expeditions, no more Valhalla; no more Asgard and the Gods. "Faugh!" thought Halfdan Halfdansson, old hero of a hundred raids in the west and south; "this small-souled life for them that can abide it; it is worse than death for a *Man's Son.*"

Not but that his own days of action were over: had been these ten years; had passed with the age of the Vikings. Also his seven sons were in Valhalla long since, and beyond being troubled; they had fallen like men in battle before there was any talk of this Christian heaven and hell; as for his wife, she, royal-hearted woman, had died when the youngest of them was born. So that it would have been easy for him to cut himself adrift from the world and voyage down through pleasant dreams towards death, after the fashion of clean old age. He had already put by, somewhat sadly, the prospect of future expeditions, and was reconciling himself to old age and its illumination, when King Inge went besotted over the foreign faith. From his house, Bravik on the hillside, through whose door the sea-winds blew in salt and excellent, he could watch the changes of the Swan-way, and nourish peace upon the music of the sea. Below at the foot of the hill, was the harbor from which his ships used to sail; drawn up on the beach, sheer hulks, still they lay there, the *Wild Swan* and the *Dragon,* accustomed to Mediterranean voyagings of old. For his own life, he found no action to regret in it; it had all been heroic doing, clean and honorable and vigorous; and the Gods had had their proper place in it, lighting it mysteriously from within.

But what room was there for dreaming, when the cry *The glory is departed!* rang so insistent? The new order liked him so little, that in place of peace and its accompanying wisdom, the years brought him unease increasingly. With his old skalds about him, to sing to him in the hall in the evenings; with his old and pagan servants, faithful all of them to the past as to himself, he watched the change coming on Sweden with disquietude and disgust; and for the first time in his life, experienced a kind of fear. But it was a pagan and great-hearted fear, and had nought to do with his own fate or future.

He knew the kind of tales these becrozied men from the south were telling, and that were becoming increasingly a substitute for the old valiant stories of the skalds. A man had come to Bravik once, and was welcomed there, who, when the feast was over, and the poets were relating their sagas, had risen in his turn with a story to tell—of a white-faced, agonizing God, who died a felon's death amongst ignoble and unwarlike people. Halfdan had listened to it with growing anger: where was the joy, where the mighty and beautiful forms, the splendid life, of the Divine Ones in this? At the end of it he had called to the stranger:

"Thy tale is a vile one, O foreign skald! Fraught with lies it is, and unwholesome to the hearing."

"Lies it is not, but the truth of truths, O chieftain, and except thou believest, thou shalt suffer the vengeance of God throughout eternity."

"Go!" cried the Viking; and in the one word rang all the outraged ideals that had stood him in stead for sixty years. One does not defend his standpoint, but merely states it. He saw none of the virtues of Christianity, while its crude presentation shocked his religious feelings as profoundly as the blatant negations of atheism shock those of the pious of our own day. And his aspirations had a core of real spirituality in them. The Gods, for these high-souled Pagans, were the fountain of right, the assurance and stability of virtue. Thor, probably, stood for courage, spiritual as well as physical; Odin for a secret and internal wisdom; Balder for a peace that passeth understanding. Things did not end in Berserker fury: the paths of the spirit were open, or had been of old; beyond the hero stood the God; beyond strife, a golden peace founded on the perfection of life. Wars, adventure, and strenuous living were to fashion something divinely calm and grand in the lives of men; that once established, and no possibility of evil left lurking in any human soul. Balder's reign would come, something like the glow and afterglow of sunset, or a vast and perfect music enveloping the world—there should be a love as of comrades, as of dear brothers, between all men. But that Peace of Balder and of Odin was separated by all Berserkerism from the peace that is fear or greed. It was a high, perpetual exultation: a heaven into which the meek and weak could not slide passively, but the strong man armed (spiritually) should take it by storm. —And here was negation of the doctrine of the strong man armed; here was proclaiming godhood a thing not robust, joyless, unbeautiful. . . . Old Halfdan went moody and depressed for a week after the priest's visit. The serene Balder-mood, into the fulness of which now, in the evening of his life, he had the right to grow naturally had been attacked, and could not be induced to return. A God crucified! . . . his soul cried out for Gods triumphant.

Inge might launch his decrees at Upsala; at Bravik, not the least inten-tion existed of obeying them. With dogged and defiant faith Halfdan per-formed the rites of the religion of Odin, having dismissed from his house all who hankered after the newly proclaimed orthodoxy. With it all, he was ill at ease; as seeing that Sweden would not long hold a man faithful to her ancient ideals. Tales were brought in, how such and such a pagan chief had suffered the king's vengeance, or had been compelled to profess and call himself Christian. Heaven knew when his own turn might come; Inge would not overlook him forever. Well, there would be no giving in for him, no lip profession—a thing not in him to understand. He could swing a battle-ax yet, at the head of his retainers; he could die in his burning house like a Viking's son. That would be something: a blow struck for olden vir-tue: a beacon of remembrance for Sweden, in the dark days he feared and foresaw. His religious broodings deepened; he strove incessantly to come nearer to the Gods; for although he held it a coward's creed to think They exist to help men, and a brave man's, that men exist to help Them; yet at such a time, he deemed, They might find it worth Their while to turn from vaster wars for a moment, and concern themselves with the fate of Sweden. So he prayed, but his prayer was no petition nor whining after gains; it was a silencing of the mind, a stedfast driving it upward towards heights it had not attained before: eagle altitudes, and sunlight in the windless blue, where no passion comes, and the eternal voices may be heard.

The tide of trouble drew nearer. Presently a messenger came from Inge, with a priest. Halfdan was to install the latter in his house, and learn from him the faith of the Nazarene; was to forgo the Gods, or expect the king's armies. Halfdan sent them back; to say that Inge would be welcome at Bra-vik: as a friend, as of old; or still more as a foe. Then he dismissed the few women there were in his house, called in his men, and prepared for a siege: thoroughly if fiercely happy at last. But there was no bottom to the king's degeneration, it seemed. After three weeks this came from Upsala: "Half-dan Halfdansson, you are senile; you will die soon, and your false religion will all but die with you. The faith of Christ commands forbearance and forgiveness. You shall die in peace, and suffer hellflame thereafter; I will not trouble with you." *I will not trouble with you.* . . . For a week the old man raged inwardly. Inge should not thus triumphantly insult him; he would not die in peace, but lead his fifty against Upsala, and go out fighting. . . . Then the Baldermood came once more; and with it, light and direction vouchsafed him. He would go a-viking.

He summoned his fifty, and proclaimed his intention in the hall. Let who would, stay behind—in a Sweden that at least would let them be. For himself, he would take the Swan-way: he would have delight again of the crisping of blue waves against his prow: he would go under purple sails into the evening, into the mystery, into the aloneness where grandeur is, and it is profitable for souls to be, and there are none to tell heart-sickening tales. . . . There, what should befall him, who could say? Perhaps there would be sweet battle on the Christian coasts; perhaps he would burn and break a church or two, and silence the jangling of the bells that called ignoble races to ignoble prayer. Perhaps there would be battling only with the storm: going out into that vast unstable region the Aesir loved, perhaps they would expend their manhood nobly in war with the shrieking wind, the sweet wild tempest of heaven. At such times the Gods come near, they come very near; they buffet and slay in their love, and out of a wild and viking death, the Valkyrie ride, the Valkyrie ride! . . . There were fifty men in the hall that heard him; there were fifty men that rose and shouted their acclamation; fifty that would take the Swan-way with their lord.

So there came to be noise of ax and hammer in the haven under Bravik: the *Wild Swan* and the *Dragon* being refurbished and made all taut for voyaging. Within a month they set sail. But not southward, and then through Skagerack and Cattegat, out into the waters of Britain and France, as Halfdan had intended. On the first day, a sudden storm overtook them, and singing they plunged into black seas, beneath blind and battling skies. Singing they combatted the wave of the north; they went on, plunging blindly, driven for three days whither they knew not; then, with a certain triumph in their souls, they succumbed, singing, to the gale. They saw the Valkyrie ride through heaven, they gave their bodies to the foam about the rocks, and rose upon the howling winds, clean and joyous of soul at the last.

Halfdan had forgotten Christianity: all thought and memory of it deserted him utterly before the storm had been beating them an hour. In the end it was all pagan, all Viking, exultant lover and fighter of the Gods, that he leaped from his sinking ship in the night, fully armed, into the driving froth and blackness; struggled as long as might be with the overwhelming waters, as befitted his manhood; then lost consciousness, and was buffeted and tossed where the grand elements listed; and thrown at last, unconscious, on the shore.

Certainly he had seen the Valkyrie riding, had heard their warsong above the winds and waves: like the lightning of heaven they had ridden, beautiful and awful beyond any of his old dreaming; why then had they not taken him? This was no Valhalla into which he had come: this dark place smokily lamp-lit; this close air, heavy, it must be said, with stench. And were these the dwarfs, these little figures that moved and chattered unintelligibly in the gloom? . . . Slowly he took in the uncouth surroundings; raising himself, rather painfully, on his elbow from the bed of dry heather on which he was lying. There, on the tent-pole, hung his armor: his helmet with the raven wings; his shield, sword, and battle-ax; these were skins with which he was covered, and of which the walls of the tent were made. He was not dead then? No; it appeared that it was still mortal flesh that he was wearing. He had been thrown on some shore by the waves, and rescued by these quaint, squat people. Ah! he had been driven into the far north, and was among Lapps in the unknown north of the world.

He lay back, exhausted by his bodily and mental effort; and the sigh that broke from him brought the Lapp woman to his side, and the Lapp man after her. They brought him hot broth, and spoke to him, their unknown and liquid tongue, in which no sound unmusical intrudes, was full of gentle kindliness; their words were almost caressing, and full of encouragement and cheer. He had no strength to sit up; the Lapp woman squatted at his head and lifted him in her arms; and while he so leaned and rested the Lapp man fed him, sup by sup; the two of them crooning and chuckling their good will the while. In three days he was on his feet; and convinced that he could not outwear the kindly hospitality of his hosts.

The weeks of the northern spring went by; the flowers of Lapland were abloom in the valley, and old Halfdan wandered daily and brooded amidst the flowers. His mood now had become very inward. He hungered no more after action, nor dwelt in pictures of the past; rather an interiority of the present haunted him: a sweetness, as of dear and near deities, in the crag-reflecting waters, in the fleet cloud-fleeces, in the heather on the hills, and in the white and yellow poppies on the valley-floor. As the summer passed this mood grew deeper: from a prevalent serene peace, it became filled with divine voices almost audibly calling. As for the Lapps, they behaved to him at all times with such tenderness as might be given to a father growing helpless in old age, but loved beyond ordinary standards.

The first frosts were withering the heather; in the valley the flowers had died; the twilight of early winter, a wan iris withering, drooped mournful petals over the world. On the hills all was ghostly whiteness: the Lapps had come south with the winter, and there was a great encampment of them in the valley; it never occurred to Halfdan to wonder why the couple that had saved him had remained during the summer so far from the snows. One day he wandered down to the shore: the sea had already frozen, and the icy leagues of it shone tinted with rose and faint violet and beryl where light from the sun, far and low in the horizon, caught them. Wonderful and beautiful seemed to him the world of the North. There was no taint in the cold, electric air; no memory to make his soul ashamed for his fellow men. The wind blew keen over the ice, blowing back his hair and his beard; it was intense and joyful for him with that Divine life of the Gods that loves and opposes us. He walked out on the ice; something at his feet caught his attention, and he stooped to examine it; it was a spar, belike from the *Wild Swan* or the *Dragon,* the ships he had loved. Then came memory in a flood. All his life had gone from him; the faces familiar of old had vanished; down there, in the south, in the Gothland, all the glory had departed; and there was nothing left for him on earth, but the queer, evil-smelling life in the Lapp tent. . . . Yes, there were still the Gods. . . . A strange unrest came upon him; he must away and find the Aesir. . . . He had no plan; only he must find the Bright Ones: must stand in their visible presence, who had been the secret illumination of the best of his life. In mingled longing and exultation he made his way back to the camp.

He found his Lapp friends standing before their tent, and their best reindeer harnessed to an *akja**; they knew, it appeared, that he was to go; and mournfully and unbidden, had made preparation. They brought out his armor, and fondled his hands as they armed him; a crowd gathered about him, all crooning and chuckling their good will, and their sorrow to lose the old man in whose shining eyes, it seemed to them, was much unearthly wisdom. On all sides, evidently, there was full understanding of his purpose, and sad acquiescence; and this did not seem to him strange at all: the Gods were near and real enough to control and arrange all things. He sat down in the *akja,* and took the rein; the Lapps heaped skins about him for warmth; then, waving farewells, amidst an outburst of sorrowful crooning and chuckling, he started. Whither the reindeer might list; whither the mighty Undying Ones might direct.

On, and on, and on. Through ghostly valleys and through the snowstorm, right into the heart of the northern night, the reindeer, never uncertain of the way, drew him. The Balder-mood came to him in the weird darkness; in the cold desolation the bright Gods seemed nearer than ever. Through ghastly passes where the north wind, driving ice particles that stung, came shrieking, boisterous and dismal, down from the Pole to oppose him, on sped the reindeer while the mind of the old Viking was gathered into dreams. —Waiting for him, somewhere beyond, were Those whose presence was a growing glory on the horizon of his soul. . . . The snow-ghosts, wan, innumerable, and silent, came hurrying by; on sped the reindeer, a beautiful beast, heeding never the snow-ghosts over frozen rivers and frozen mountains, through ghostly cold valleys and the snow. Under vast precipices that towered up, iron and mournful into the night; or along the brink of awful cliffs, with the snowstorm howling below. . . . on and on. Who was to measure time on that weird journey? There were no changes of day and night; and Halfdan, wrapped in the warmth of his dreams, hardly would have heeded them if there had been. Now and again the reindeer halted to feed, scraping in the snow for his familiar moss-diet; then on again, and on. It was the beast, or some invisible presence, not the man, who chose the way.

A valley stretched out endlessly before; and afar, afar, a mountain

---

*The Lapp sledge of wicker and skin, capable of holding one man sitting with legs stretched out, and guiding the reindeer with a single thong of rein.

caught on its whiteness some light from heaven, so that amid all the ghostly darkness it shone and shot up, a little dazzling beacon of purity on the rim of the world. The snow had ceased to fall, and no longer the north wind came shrieking to oppose; there was quiet in the valley broken only by the tinkling of the reindeer bells and the scrunch of the falling hoofs on the snow. The white mountain caught the eyes, and at last the mind of the long dreaming Viking; so that he began to note the tinkling of the bells, the sound of the hoofs falling, the desolation before and around. And at last another sound also: long howling out of the mountains on this side and that; long, dreary howling behind, like the cry of ghosts in a nightmare, or the lamentation of demons driven forever through darkness beyond the margin of space. For some time he listened, before waking to knowledge that it was actual sound he listened to; and then for some time longer before it came to him to know whence the sound was. It had drawn nearer by then, much nearer; and peering forth through the glint and gloom, he saw the shadows that were wolves streaming up after him through the valley, and coming down from the mountains; singly, in twos and threes, in multitudes. The reindeer snuffed, tossed its head, and speeded on prodigiously, yet with what gathered on the hillsides, it would be a marvel if he escaped. On came the shadows, until one could see the green fire-sparks of their eyes, behind, to the right and to the left, almost before, and on sped the reindeer, and the white mountain drew nearer.

Then Halfdan the Viking scented war: he remembered his youth and its prowess; he made ready his shield and battle-ax; and thanked the Gods fervently that after all he should go out fighting. The brave reindeer should have what chance it might to escape by its own untrammeled fleetness: so he drew his sword and cut the harness. The beast was away over the snow at twice its former speed; and Halfdan in the *akja* shot forward thirty paces, fell out, and was on his feet in a moment to wait what should come.

A black, shag shadow, the foremost of them, hurled itself howling at his throat—eyes green fire and bared teeth gleaming; the ax swept down, clave its head in mid air, and the howl went out in a rattling groan and sob. No question of failing strength now; old age was a memory—forgotten. The joy of battle came to him, and as the first wolf fell he broke into song:

> *In the bleak of the night and the ghost-held region,*
> *By frozen valley and frozen lake,*
> *A son of the Vikings, breaking his battle,*
> *Doth lovely deeds for Asgard's sake.*

> *Odin All-Father, for thee I slew him!*
> *For thee I slew him, bolt-wielding Thor!*
> *Joy to ye now, ye Aesir, Brothers!*
> *That drive the demons forevermore!*

While he sang, another wolf was upon him, and then another and another; and the war-ax that had made play under Mediterranean suns of old, God, how it turned and swept and drove and clave things in the northern night! While they came up one by one, or even in twos, the fight was all in his favor, so he slew as many as a dozen at his singing; then the end began to draw near. They were in a ring about him now; rather fearful of the whirling ax, but closing in. Old age began to tell upon his limbs; he fought on wearying; and the delight of war ebbed from him; his thigh had been snapped at and torn, and he had lost much blood with the wound. Then the ax fell, and he leaned on it for support for a moment, his head bent down over his breast. The war-mood had gone altogether; his mind sped out to the Gods. Of inward time there had been enough, since the ax fell, for the change of mood, for the coming of calm wonder and exaltation; of the time we measure in minutes, enough for the leaping of a wolf. He saw it, and lifted the ax; knowing that nothing could be done. At his left it leaped up; he saw the teeth snap a hand's-breadth from his face. . . . An ax that he knew not, brighter than the lightning, swung; the jaws snapped; the head and the body apart fell to the ground. . . . And there was a wolf leaping on his right, and no chance in the world of his slaying it; and a spear all-glorious suddenly hurtling out of the night, and taking the wolf through the throat, and pinning it dead to the ground. And here was a man, a Viking, gray-bearded, one-eyed, glorious, fighting upon his left; and here was a man, a Viking, young and surpassing beautiful of form and face and mien, doing battle at his right. And he himself was young again, and strong; and knew that against the three of them all the wolves in the world, and all the demons in hell, would have little chance. They fled yelping into the dark; and Halfdan turned to hail those that had fought for him.

And behold, the shining mountain that had seemed so far, shone now near at hand, and for a mountain, it was a palace, exceedingly well-built, lovely with towers and pinnacles and all the fair appurtenances of a king's house. No night nor winter was near it; amidst gardens of eternal sunlight it shone; its portals flung wide, and blithe all things for his entering. And he greeted Odin All-Father, as one might who had done nothing in his life to mar the pleasant friendliness of that greeting. And in like manner he greeted Balder the Beautiful. They linked their arms in his, and in cheerful conversation he passed in with them into the Valhalla.

• •

This unusual tale, "The Lost Poet," is a mythic Middle-Eastern story which appeals for an Arab and Israelite understanding that Solomon (Suleiman) and Mohammed were apostles or prophets of the same God. It was published in the October 1915 issue of The Theosophical Path, *under the pseudonym Thomson J. Wildredge.*

The Lost Poet

*H*e whose name is the Compassionate, looking down of old time out of heaven, contemplated the lot of the Children of Abraham the Orthodox.

"I have raised up mine Apostle, Suleiman ibn Daoud, the Wise," said He, "to be king of the Seed of Isaac, and given unto him sovereignty in the east and in the west, over men and genii; and therefore Isaac is a mighty people, and the Seed of the Elder Brother is made subject unto him. Now will I go about to redeem Ishmael also."

Iblis, lurking in the courts of Paradise, answered Him and said:

"Thou canst not do this, O God. The Arabs delight to make war among themselves incessantly; and as much evil as I can devise for their doing, they do it eagerly, and clamor after more. If thou sendest them a king to unite them, behold, they will rebel and slay him; for they desire no yoke but mine. If thou sendest them a Prophet to call them from their sins he shall fare worse than any of thy Prophets who were slain of old. Leave thou Ishmael to me, and keep Isaac for thine own."

And God said: "Although they love war and abominations, yet love they Poetry also, O Iblis. Therefore I will raise up a poet to save them, who shall be greater than any poet that hath been born among men."

Iblis laughed. "I will tempt him with women and with power," said he. "Thou shalt hear his songs, that they shall be a blasphemy against thee."

"Though thou mayest tempt him, he shall not fall," said the Most Merciful. "I will make his heart altogether pure and holy, and without any desire save after the divine secrets of Poetry. All thy wiles shall not prevail against his soul to stain it, O Iblis; and thus shall Ishmael my people be redeemed."

Then said Iblis, "Since Thou hast decreed it so, suffer me but to be Thy minister in this; that the gifts Thou givest, I may multiply upon him."

And God said. "What thou wouldst have me suffer thee, unto that do I command thee."

Then Iblis went upon his way, to consider and to devise plans: for he was exceeding loathe to lose Ishmael. "It may be that I shall cheat thee in this matter also O Lord," thought he.

Khalid the Poet was journeying through the desert out of the Hedjaz northward; his goal was the court of Suleiman ibn Daoud at Jerusalem. Thither also was bound every verse-maker in Araby: though all but he, heaven knew, upon a fool's errand: For Suleiman the Wise had sent out word that he would hold a great contest of the poets of the Arabs, and that the prize to the most inspired should be the hand of his daughter and kingship of the Seed of Ishmael.

Amina herself had urged her father to this. She, the gazelle without peer among the lovely, was weary of the great kings that came wooing her, the princes of Egypt and of Greece, of the Himaryites and of the Persians. No warrior pleased her; she took no delight in fierceness, swiftness, fire, and generosity. No sword was so unconquerably sharp, that it might cut its way through hosts as far as to her favor; no war-mare so fleet and fearless that it might bear its rider to her heart. But she had dreamed a dream in the night; and waking, found that captured by a figure in a vision, which princes and proud horsemen had besieged in vain.

She dreamed that a star arose in the south, and came down upon the earth; and that she beheld it shining upon the brow of a youth of the Hedjaz, who was a poet like to none that had sung in Araby since Hagar went forth with Ishmael her son. She dreamed that she heard him singing, and that his song—ah, it was gone from her memory when she awoke: the words and the music, and even the substance of it, were gone. But she knew that, having heard it, the world would never again be the same for her: that all things would be entangled in a glamor beyond the light of dreaming, and that the glory of God would shine for her out of every moment of the common day. It was like no other song that had been or would be: the words of it were luminous pearls for sweetness; they were flashing diamonds and burning rubies for power—no, they were as the flaming stars of heaven, endowed with voice and rhythmic visible motion. They revealed the realms of the djinn and peris, and scorned to stop at such barren revelation; they leaped up and soared among the angels. The poet seemed to her to stand upon the horizon singing, girt all about in a robe woven as it were of night flamey with quintillions of stars, and to proclaim what the Spirit Gabriel alone knows, and as the lute-voiced Israfel alone might proclaim it. . . . On two matters she had made up her mind by morning: first, that the hero of her dream was a living man, a poet of her mother's people, the Arabs; and second, that him she would marry, and none other.

Who shall say that dreams are altogether vain, or that truth may never be revealed in them? It chanced that at that time Abu Walid ibn Abdullah, prince of the House of al-Wakkeed, lost the pearl of his herd, Zorayd, the white milch camel. Suleiman the Wise himself had given her to him, and the fame of her beauty extended from Damascus to Birku'l Jumad, wherefore, and because he loved her as his own daughter, the soul of Abu Walid was exceedingly troubled; and he sent forth all the young men of the tribe to track her and bring her back. On the third day young Khalid, who had gone out among the rest, led Zorayd into the tents of al-Wakkeed; but it was a Khalid whom his tribesmen had never seen before. Assuredly he had been visited by an angel in the desert; belike it was Israfel that came to him, and took the heart out of his breast, and wrung it clean of human blood, to fill it instead with some ichor out of Paradise, the sound of whose coursing should be immortal song. He came in transfigured, and when the tribe was assembled, sang to them; he, the modest one, whose lips theretofore had always been sealed in the presence of his elders, sang to them marvelously of his marvelous journey after Zorayd. And of other things beside: things glorious, unearthly, unspoken until then; so that they were silent, and wept silently for joy while he sang. When he had made an end, Abu Walid ibn Abdullah fell upon his neck and kissed him; and all the Beni Wakkeed clamored their praises to Allah ta'ala for that He had fired the heart of one of them with wild supernatural inspiration, and raised up a poet of poets in their midst.

And they prepared a feast, did the Beni Wakkeed, slaughtering seventy camels of the herd, and bidding to it all the tribes of the Hedjaz. Even they made truce with the Beni Hatim and the Beni Darda for the occasion: that, feasting together, they might enjoy signal triumph over these their ancient enemies through the supremacy of Khalid's singing. But when Khalid sang, lo, a marvel: the Beni Wakkeed forgot to triumph, and the Beni Hatim and the Beni Darda to gnash the teeth of rage and envy. Instead, they all wept together for exceeding great joy. You are to picture a poet of the Children of Hatim who, having heard a poet of the Sons of Wakkeed sing, would not sing in his turn the Battle-days of his own tribe; but instead must come forward and own himself but a barking jackal, a harsh hyena in the desert, as compared to this one whose voice was better than the lute-strings of angels—and you are to imagine him applauded by his own tribe for such an utterance. You are to see al-Ta'eef abu Hatim and Abu Darda come to Abu Walid ibn Abdullah, and kiss him and each other, upon the shoulder, saying: "Henceforth we three shall be as brethren born at one birth";—and you are to be assured that it was so.

For Khalid, singing, exalted not himself nor his tribe, not his horse nor his sword nor his camel nor his love; but the great beauty of the world, the great glory of mankind, the divinity immanent everywhere. It was a new thing in poetry; it defied all immemorial forms, yet by its triumphant beauty and grandeur overwhelmed criticism. Said al Ta'eef abu Hatim, very wisely: "It mounteth, verily, without effort unto the throne of God; and yet assuredly it redeemeth even Iblis in the seventh hell, and sheddeth beneficent glory upon him." . . . Here was the vastness of the desert, the loneliness of infinite burning sands, the sweep of the terrible sandstorm, the lovely shade of the oasis; here were the lilac-hued horizons of the evening, the carmine flame of the dawn, the fathomless blue of the noonday, the beacon constellations of the night: and all of them soaked through and through and scintillant with a splendor that might be found also within the inmost heart of man. Whoso heard him felt the presence and workings of God in his own soul: grew brother-hearted with the vast, with the silence, with that eternal peace that gloweth brighter than any war, with the Spirit of the Spirit of man. . . . It was a new thing in poetry; poets, hearing him, knew that there would be no more *Muallakat,* no more chanting the Days of Battle; that poetry would minister no more to pride, dissension and hatred; but would be ecstasy, worship, revelation. . . .

So when word drifted across the desert into the Hedjaz, that Suleiman ibn Daoud, the great king, had proclaimed his daughter and kingship of the Arabs as the prizes in a contest of poets, no one in those parts doubted as to the result. Abu Walid ibn Abdullah caused Zorayd herself to be saddled and caparisoned sumptuously, and led Khalid to her. "Thou art worthy of her, my son, as she is worthy of thee." he said. "Thou art to bring glory untold upon thy lineage; thou art to exalt thy tribe above all the nations of the earth. Go," he said, kissing him once on the shoulder, "and when thou art king, forget not the tents of thy fathers." But Zorayd he kissed upon her nose many times, and spoke her praises long and fittingly, and wept out loud to part with her.

So now Khalid the poet was riding northward, three days out from the camp of the Beni Wakkeed. In the hour before dawn, we will say, when the horizons are ash-gray and violet and mysterious, and that goes sighing over the desert, which might be a wind, but assuredly is the passing of djinn. A world full of wonder and terror it is, look that out of yonder dimness along the sky's edge westward, some towering afreet rise not, with smoke and dim flame for the clouds of his hair, and a roaring of terrible flame for his bodily form! —Beautifully white Zorayd took the whisper-laden leagues of sand; and Khalid, proud in his saddle, looked forth, swelled his lungs with the cool intoxicating air, and feared neither djinn nor afreet. That which dwelt within his heart was master of the invisible haunters of the desert: the fire in his soul was native to the empyrean, kindred to the sun and the constellations, immortal, born for spiritual sovereignty, proud. Had not Allah spoken through him—set a fire upon his tongue and a burning beacon in his mind?—did he not ride out to declare the secrets of the unknown worlds? Oh, worship, worship for the Light of Lights, of whom the sun's glory was a pale reflection or but the shadow; of whose vastness the vast firmament was no more than a tiny fragment; the jewels of whose robe were the stars of the night! . . . Life was poetry, and poetry an intense and ardent worship: it was love flaming up and out from the heart, and sweeping the world with its healing fire, and bearing away the lights of heaven in its current. . . . The sun rose hot over the vast desolation, but still for an hour or two one might ride forward. Khalid thought of the poetry of the Arabs, the immemorial convention he was to destroy. A hot eloquence over tribal battles, with exaltation of this warrior or that; the deserted camping-ground; the ride over the sands; the beauty and swiftness of the camel; the glory of the war-mare; bright keenness of the sword or lance: what were these things, transient forms falling away into nothingness always, that they should usurp dominion in the realms of poetry, that concerns only the soul and that which neither passeth nor perisheth? He rode to abolish their sway; to set up new standards, and make the race great with spiritual greatness. Wonder of wonders, that unto none before him had it been granted to hear the stars singing by night; the moonlight fluting delicate mysteries; the chanting of the marvelous midday-riding sun! Yet truly the deaf should hear all before long: mankind should hear the eternal voices, and be healed of evil. . . . Sands of the desert of life, you should be watered soon with life-giving song; soon you should put forth groves of date-palms lovely with shade; you should bloom with roses and lilies! Soon, barren mountains of the Hedjaz, you should exceed in green fertility the vales of Lebanon, the meadows by the waters of Damascus. . . . On, white Zorayd; you stride through the desert with God! In the blue above you, blithely the wings of angels hover, the heat palpitant in the sands beneath, consider that it is the ineffable glory of God! . . .

For now the sun had risen, and was well up in the heavens, and the sand glowed and panted; it was time to rest, if a little shade might be found, until evening brought back coolness. . . . Beyond this next ridge there would be at least a yard or two of shadow; ascend here, then, white Zorayd, and thou shalt rest! —From the ridge, the sweetest sight the desert holds was revealed to Zorayd and her rider: the waving of feathery palms, the glint of cool waters in their shadow. On then, white pearl of the herds of al-Wakkeed!—soon thy rest shall be rest indeed. . . .

They came into the green place, and Zorayd knelt, and Khalid dismounted and lay down beside the water, to muse awhile and sleep. But sleep came not to him, on account of the soaring of his mind. He was riding, a bridegroom to his bride, and she the loveliest daughter of Suleiman; an Ishmaelite to kingship over all the tribes of Ishmael;—many would have taken thought exultantly upon those things: some dreaming dreams of pleasures to be enjoyed or power to be attained; some even, of the upliftment of the people. But to Khalid, it all remained remote and unreal, like a palace of djinn known to exist in untraveled regions, but which, being afar from the bone-marked tracks of the caravans, rises never above the horizon for desert wanderers to behold. "Out yonder it is," one says; and passes without more thought of it. —The eyes and the desire of Khalid were upon poetry, upon the supreme revelation of it, up to which his whole being quivered in an ecstasy of adoration. . . . Let him behold, let him adore . . . and let love and fame and power and the whole gleaming show of things pass and perish. . . .

A bird flew glimmering out of the desert, and lighted among the palm leaves above his head. Her breast and her wings were scintillant, and better in color than the noon-day sky; the blue beauty of the heaven of heavens shone for her sake among the dark palm leaves about her. Out of her bill came song; and his mind forsook its workings to listen to her. A bird?— assuredly and assuredly she was an angel! She sang, and the spirit in him soared up with the soaring of her song; was carried into the radiant firmament, beyond companionship with the golden glory of the sun . . . Ah, beautiful in that loneliness, exultant, floated the soul of the poet; extended and borne up upon song; surveying creation; looking down upon earth from afar; beholding earth as an emerald and a turquoise swinging in sapphire immensities of light. This surely was the supreme revelation of poetry; give thanks now, O Khalid, praise thou God the Compassionate, who hath revealed this infinity of joy to thee, and made thee one with it! . . .—The song waned and sank, and the spirit of Khalid floated down with it into the shadow of the palms, into his body lying upon the ground. This surely had been the ultimate of all vision, he thought, as the bird took her flight from among the trees. Now let sleep come, for at last God had created and confirmed him a poet.

A tinkling and rustle of music broke out above, and came dropping down on him; and he opened his eyes and looked up. There was a bird among the palm leaves overhead, whose feathers were as glimmering soft pearls, lovely beyond loveliness. His soul rose to listen to her singing, and it exceeded by far that of her predecessor. Oh, a moment of such sound, unto what should he compare it? It was better, truly, than ten thousand years of intense delight; surely it was Angel Israfel that formed her bill and her throat, and informed them with immortal melody. . . . Ravished, his spirit soared up with the singing, and left the blueness of the empyrean behind and forgot the little emerald and turquoise that floated below, and came into gardens lovelier than dreaming, beyond the station of the sun, beyond the summer stars. . . . Up and up with thee, O wonderful revealer! Up into the intensity of bliss, O wings of Poetry, supreme wings! O Bird native to the Heaven of heavens! . . . All things on earth were forgotten—even the glory of poethood, the high exultations and dreamings; revealed now, and for the only reality, were the inward kingdoms of Poetry: beauty beyond the beauty of beauty, bliss beyond bliss—timeless, nameless, worldless, unknown.

And he heard the waning of that song also, and saw at last the pearly wings of the bird glimmer afar, vanishing over the yellow sands. Now he would sleep—now he would sleep. . . .

A third time song awoke him: there was a light as of the sunset above; and a bird there, the color of the rainbow, exquisite in unsurpassable loveliness. As she sang and he listened, he was borne up again on a torrent of holy singing, and left the firmament below, and left heaven after heaven below, and heard Israfel chanting amidst the stars, and saw the stars reel with delight at the chanting of Israfel. And he passed on, and left the chanting of Israfel below, forgotten; and came where even Gabriel comes not; and quivered up, a yearning and a trembling flame, towards That which the eyes of angels see not, and the minds of archangels may not dream: all infinity was present with him, and all eternity was enfolded in the moment that was he. . . .

And the song faded away, and behold, he was in his body again. The sun was setting over violet horizons, and the sky overhead was a blue-green beryl with the beauty of the evening. . . . Where were the date-palms, and where the cool waters beside which he had lain down? . . . Where was white Zorayd? . . .

A sound of chanting came drifting to him from beyond a ridge of sand, and he listened.

> *Bismillahi 'rrahmani 'rraheem!*
> *Al-hamdu lillahi rabi 'llalameen!*
> *Arrahmani 'rraheem,*
> *Maliki yowmi ed deen. . . .**

"It is a poet that praises the One God in his song," thought Khalid; "this is a marvel truly, since I alone of the poets have praised Him." Then he thought: "I will go and inquire of him, if perchance he hath seen Zorayd."

He rose up, and tottered across the sand, mounting the ridge painfully. He came upon an Arab praying, his face turned southward towards Mecca. "God is great!" cried the Arab, three times; and then:

> *I affirm that there is no god but God!*
> *I affirm that there is no god but God!*
> *I affirm that there is no god but God!*
> *I affirm that Mohammed is the Prophet of God!*

At that last affirmation Khalid stood bewildered. "Sir," he said, "wherefore affirmest thou this? Knowest thou not that our lord, Suleiman

*The opening of the first chapter of the Koran: "Praise be to God, the Merciful, the Compassionate," etc.

ibn Daoud, who is called the Wise, the King of the Jews in Jerusalem, is the Apostle of God unto this age?"

The Arab gazed at him in amazement. "O thou whose beard is whiter than the pomegranate flower," said he, "Suleiman ibn Daoud hath been dead these thousand years! Assuredly Mohammed ibn Abdullah, of the tribe of the Koreish at Mecca, he is the Apostle!"

The following tale is one of Morris's two Greek stories. Again we read of the conflict between worshipers of the old gods and worshipers of the one Christian God. "The Temple of the Baby Apollo" was published in the November 1915 issue of The Theosophical Path, *under the pseudonym Sergius Mompesson.*

The Temple of the Baby Apollo

*P*ines overshadowed its age-gray pillars and lichened roof; its out-look was across a narrow valley, unseen, on to mountains; it stood high on the mountainside itself, and was always murmurous with the cooing of doves and the tinkle and dropping of waters. It was a very old temple indeed: I doubt an older was in Hellas.

There was a sacred spring there, anciently very renowned for its healing properties: time was when the track from the valley below was much traversed: you might say thronged. Apollo as a child had wandered there, said the legend; as a child that knew nothing of his parentage and divine status, but accepted as the right of all children the homage he heard sung to him at noon, or in the magical hours of morning and eve, by the elemental races.

> *Shepherd of the wandering constellations, hail!*
> *Evoë, hail!*

they sang: sweet, far voices passing with the wind through the pine-tops, or with a rumor of lyre-music blown and swooning along the ground.

One day, it seemed, he gave the slip to his nurse and strayed, a dark-eyed, round-limbed, fun-loving rogue, away through the woods that so loved him, and up the mountainside that glowed to him like a mother's breast. They say the ground put forth deep red and purple anemones, sun-dusky like his own baby face and hair, wherever his fat little hands and feet touched it as he crawled and toddled, crowing with delight, or chuckling deliciously, to hear his nurse calling to him from the valley. —In mid-morning she missed him: by high noon the little naked joy had grown somewhat hot and tired; and what would he do, imperious and babylike, but smack the earth where he was rolling with a soft pud and cry out: *Baby thirsty!*—demanding comfort of the mountain or the Mighty Mother as if they had been the nurse that was fretting for him so far below. And with his baby faith and his godhood, the mountain and the Mighty Mother responded, and the clear, ice-cold waters bubbled up from the ground. By that spring they found him sleeping; and there, in after ages, the temple was built. But that was long ago: ever so long ago.

The Dorian had conquered Arcady since then; the phalanx and the legion had passed through the valleys, but without disturbing the worship on the hill. Priests had been appointed by Argive and Spartan and Macedonian kings, and then by consuls and Caesars. The devotion of the villagers had ebbed with the dissolution of the ancient world and its standards, had flowed in again, somewhat feebly, under Diocletian, and had gone right out under Constantine. Julian, that marvel of activity, had found time to make a pilgrimage thither; and while he lived, the path from the valley, the path the baby Apollo had first trodden, felt daily the pressure of feet. Now, even Julian's time was long past: among the earliest memories of the very old man who still nominally held the priesthood there. No worshipers came now from the villages; it was three years since the old priest had made his way, for the last time, down to the temple from the little house in the pine-woods where he and his daughter lived; and twenty since love of Apollo had drawn anyone to listen to the invocations, or to make vows or give offerings at the shrine. But still the sun-dusky anemones bloomed beside the rill that went tumbling and singing valleyward from the fountain where his sacred baby hand had smacked the soil; and still Daphne, the priest's daughter— Daphne the beautiful, the white, tall, willowy maiden nourished upon wholesome poetic dreams from the Golden Age—wreathed the altar about with purple and dark red blossoms daily, and burned the incense, and chanted the hymns at dawn and noon and sunset. To her, the laughing baby had grown up to chariot the sun and shepherd the planets; but he was not dead; he was near, and had not passed from the earth; she lived always in his sight, worshiping the glory and beauty of him; never felt sure that he might not come strolling and singing up the path, or down from the holy peak above, while she was making the sacrifice. She did not know that the Golden Age had passed.

Formerly she had been used to go down into Thymaleia, the nearest village, to buy the necessaries of her housekeeping; but it had long since become much wiser to leave the villagers unreminded of pagan temples and priestesses. She had been received coldly, then rudely; on her last visit a threatening little crowd, mainly of women, had gathered, and she owed her safety simply to her fearlessness. But their hostility hurt and puzzled her, and was not to be ignored: she saw no way out of the difficulty. Then the marvelous happened. Next day, Leonidas the shepherd presented himself at the temple at noon; he came bearing a garland of wild flowers as an offering, and somewhat sheepishly knelt before the altar, as one unaccustomed to the work, while she made sacrifice. Alas, his worship was not in truth, for the bright-rayed Deity—as you have guessed. But to this serene, dispassionate priestess, who would dare speak of passion? There was too lofty a simplicity about her; drawn from no personal pride, but from companionship with the night-skies and the untroubled mountains, and a close inner friendship with her lord the Sun.

"May Apollo shed his light upon you," said she, greeting him. "Whoso worships him is rewarded even in the worship."

"Aye, priestess," he answered; and was at a loss for words. But she saw he had more to say, and waited. "I—I live below in the valley," he said. "Every week I go down into Thymaleia. It would be nothing for me to do your errands when I go, and to bring you back what you may need when I come here—to worship the God. Will you permit this?"

He had seen her in the village the day before; and the fire that the sight of her had kindled in him, burned only, so far, towards adoration and desire to serve. He would be her votary, as one might worship a star. . . . He felt deity throb in the sunlight, and mingle mysteriously with the silver of the moon; he breathed not air, but intoxication, and went through his days exalted; his passion was not yet wholly personalized, and his weekly worship before the altar still not altogether sacrilegious—though Daphne would have deemed it so, perhaps, had she known. For her part she could not but feel kindly towards him; and the more so when she noted that, as the months passed, his piety grew; and that now he must bring flowers daily where he had brought them weekly at first. —In sooth, after a year of it he was undergoing great torment: his passion having passed from ecstasy into fierce desire.

He was held back from declaration partly by the shyness of his lonely life, partly by a feeling of her remoteness from him, and fear to hazard all upon a word; partly too, let us say, from an unextinguished instinct of the sacredness of the temple where he met her. Not that religion played a great part in his being. Down below, at Thymaleia, were the Christians; above, at Phassae, was the pagan shrine; he had been brought up to believe in the Gods, so far as he had been brought up to believe in anything; but they made a poor showing against the Galilean, in those days. Nothing had come of Julian's efforts; and now Theodosius, in an opposite direction, was carrying the world before him. So it looked, when one reasoned, as if the Christian deities were the more powerful; and yet—it might be dangerous to take liberties with Apollo. Could one but be sure that there was no God in the sun! . . . He took to frequenting the church in the village, that by absorbing Christian doctrine, he might purge himself of fear and hesitation. But the presence of the white priestess behind the altar, and the tones of her invocations, struck Christian confidence out of his soul. Sometimes even, when she called upon that Light within us and without us which is Apollo, his passion and bitter longing passed up into a region of inward snows: breathed an atmosphere too rare for them, and vanished trembling. Then he would go back to his sheep, repentant and with a mind for self-conquest; the words of her ritual had fallen sweet upon his soul; the sight of her had rebuked and given the lie to his longings; she was as the snow-peaks, as the mountain wind, as the immaculate blue of heaven. For an hour or two he would have mental glimmerings of the reality of Apollo. For an hour or two—.

Meanwhile the spirit of the age was not to be shut out even from remote valleys in the Peloponnese. Things were moving, in a religious sense. Wandering saints lit the fires of bigotry, and left them to smolder; anon came other wandering saints and fanned them, where the need was, into a blaze. Temples not so far away, had been wrecked: whose priests sometimes were moved by the devil to defend themselves, and then the church would be enriched by a martyr or two before the idolators were extirpated. Generally, however, the idolators were glad to escape, and conform quietly where their antecedents were unknown. Such expeditions had not yet gone forth from Thymaleia; yet even there paganism had been forbidden rigorously, and one or two of the old-fashioned, loath to put away utterly rites from which benefit *might* be derived, had been clubbed or stoned into orthodoxy or their graves. Leonidas, attending the church of a Sunday, found this new spirit infusing itself into his mind, and grew more and more at one with it. The old fear to offend Apollo, and capacity to feel the sacred influences of the temple, weakened to vanishing point; and they were the only curbs he had upon his passion. —Still he knelt daily before the altar, and watched the priestess as she changed; but now with a sneer at her credulity mixed with longing for herself, where before that longing had mingled, sometimes, with a purifying veneration of the God. The day came when he would hold himself no longer. After the invocation, she would remain for a while silent behind the altar; then, seeing him linger, sometimes would come forward and talk with him; sometimes would retire without speaking. But always those few moments of silence were observed, and he had understood them to be sacred. Now, the moment her chant had ceased, he was on his feet before her and pouring out his passion. Her amazement gave place to pity. "Poor youth," she said; "poor youth, thou hast been driven to this sacrilege—" —"Sacrilege!" he blazed; "priestess, thy religion is a lie. The Christian God is the Lord of things; he has conquered the demons of Olympus, and they are burning in hell; thy Apollo is in hell. But the God that is God is the God of the Christians, and He is Love, and love is the only reality—"

And so on, and so on. He implored, stormed, raved, entreated, besought and insulted her; and she stood unmoved and immovable, dispassionate in her compassion. "Poor youth," she said, "poor youth! Go! I will even pray

to Apollo for thee! . . ." One queenly gesture cowed the fiend in him, and
drove him back; "Go!" she said, "lest Apollo hide his face from the world
because of thee. . . ." He broke down, fell a-sobbing, and went.

She had been quite dependent on him for her supplies from Thymaleia;
and knew that even might she venture there herself, and pass unmolested,
no one would deal with her. So here was a predicament . . . which, however,
never entered her mind. Had it done so, no doubt she would have banished
it with thoughts upon her God. As for making petitions to Him for help in
her need, she had no mind for it; yet did offer up a prayer not in her ritual.
"O Apollo," she said, standing by the altar in attitude of invocation; "send
a shaft of thy light into the heart of that sorrowful youth, that the world
may be pleasant and wholesome to him once more. . . ."

Meanwhile Leonidas had rushed down into the valley, and flung himself on the ground in his cabin, face to earth, to writhe and groan over his
fate: over his tormenting passion, and his powerlessness to appease it: over
the fear that struck in on him and came between him and his purpose.
What should he do against all this hell let loose in him: slay himself, or
wait for death where he lay—and forgo his hope forever? No; he would go
pray. Christ and the saints were all-powerful, and perchance would help
him; he would wear out their patience on his knees in the church. . . . Utterly a madman, he hurried down into the village; noticing vaguely, when
he came there, that the street was emptied of folk. On to the church, which
he found crowded: the whole populace rapt while a blazing-eyed harsh fa-
natic poured out upon them the fiery good tidings of great joy. . . . Death to
the pagans; ruin to the temples, lest the vengeance of a jealous God should
fall upon them: lest their harvests should fail; lest they should be visited
with plague, pestilence, and famine; lest they should spend eternity
wracked and twisted in the flame. . . .

Here was bitter stuff: a heat of passion from without that soothed the
burning of his own passion within; Leonidas listened and enjoyed and was
carried away with it. —Were there no idolators in the countryside? yelled
the preacher, were there no temples to be given to the fire, after their
wealth had been glutted for the service of Christ and his flock? —"Zeus
hath a shrine at Andrissa!" shouted one; and another "The shrine of Aes-
culapius is at the crossroads!" "—Forth to Andrissa!" cried the monk; and
was down from the pulpit, and half way to the door, the crowd surging
round and after him. "And there is the temple on the mountain at Phassae—the temple of the Baby Apollo," cried Leonidas; "stop! there is the
temple at Phassae. . . ." It was so remote, on the way to nowhere, and had
been so long without worshipers, that none there had remembered a
thought of it: and now he must plant himself in the monk's path, and shout
again and again, before the cry *Phassae!* was taken up. A halt then, some
urging Phassae, some Andrissa; but Andrissa won it, being known to all,
and by tradition wealthy. "Today for Zeus, tomorrow for Apollo," cried the

holy man. "Come, ye faithful, ye beloved of the Lord!" So they surged out into the sunlight and the dust, and went forth to their work of destruction. It seemed to the shepherd that the Christian God had answered his prayers. Tomorrow he would guide them to Phassae, and claim the priestess as his reward. For the time his misery left him; no fear or hesitation would balk him in such company. He went forward with them shouting and singing, the maddest of them all.

But by the time they had broken and sacked the temple at Andrissa and certain horrors had been done there, reaction set in, and he came to his senses a little. Not, however, until he was alone. They returned in the evening drunk with fanaticism and singing barbarous hymns; whatever had been done, Leonidas had had his full share in it. The priest of Zeus, a cunning, meager-minded fellow, had attempted argument and died very ingloriously trying to proclaim himself a Christian. The shepherd left the mob at Thymaleia, where he was to meet them again in the morning; it was under the stars, on his way home, that reaction began to afflict him. He remembered the scene at Andrissa, and shuddered at its beastliness. There would be no influencing, no winning anything from the Christians. By the time he reached his cabin, he was ill at ease and sick. Ancestry in his blood pleaded for its natural gods, and he fell much in doubt of his new faith. He remembered the only bright moments he had known latterly: the moments in the temple above, when Apollo's influence wrought him peace. He spent a sleepless night despairing and repenting; and climbed the path to the temple while it was still dark, to wait there suppliant before the altar haggard and feverish, for Daphne and the dawn.

She came at last, impersonal as a cloud or a star, and if she saw him, made no sign. Her voice chanting the hymns, seemed to him like a bell rung out of the infinite azure; the words she uttered, to have a magical sweet potency of their own. He remembered the cries of the mob yesterday, harsh with all the cruel vileness hidden in the beast in man. Apollo had answered her prayer, and sent a shaft into his heart. Yesterday he had hobnobbed with dementia and destruction; it seemed to him that he had forfeited forever all the sweetness and beauty in the world. Now this ray shone out of heaven; here was the truth, golden and free and beautiful . . . the reflection of Apollo from afar, beheld within. . . .

She had finished the service and her silence before he stirred, and had turned to go, still apparently without having seen him. Then he rose, and called to her: "Priestess," he cried, "forgiveness, forgiveness!" She stopped and faced him, still impersonal; conceding no forgiveness, as having received no offense to forgive. "They will be here this morning," he cried, "—the Christians, they will destroy the temple and—ah, be not thou here when they come! It was I—I betrayed thee to them; I was mad."

She was stirred by nothing but wonder and pity. The man before her was simply an incident in the scheme of things, unlike the mountains and the trees only in that, somehow, he stood in need of her compassion in his dire plight. "As for what is past, let it be," she said, "since neither thou nor I can change it. Tell me rather what is this that will happen; let me understand." So she got the whole story from him; before midday the temple would be a ruin, and she herself, and her father, doubtless slain. Why? That was another question; the meaning of bigotry she had it not in her to fathom. Whatever God might be, one would naturally love and worship and honor; and the infinite beauty of things proclaimed that there were infinite hosts of Gods: causes innumerable why the world should rejoice. . . . Yet from her mythology she knew of an evil principle opposed to Apollo; and supposed that here was some resurrection of Python at work. How to meet its attack?

Leonidas broke in on her meditations, imploring her to let him guide her to safe places far away. He would be her slave; for him she was utterly holy and apart: Apollo shone through her and only living in her service could he enjoy the light of the sun. —All this talk of adoration fell away and left her consciousness untouched; she heard only the suggestion that she should leave the house of her God to its enemies. That she did not propose to do. If the temple was to perish, let her perish with it: as a sacrifice to Apollo for the sins of the people, and to show him that in a degenerate Hellas there was yet one left who loved the light. She did not tell herself he would protect her: would have been ashamed of such a thought had it come to her. She was for the Gods: let Them not trouble to be for her! It was for the good of the country and the people that temples existed and worship was paid in them; not by any means for the good of the Gods. She knew well that her Deity would chariot the heavens as brightly and proudly as of old, and as beneficently, though not one single mortal gave him tribute of praise and sacrifice; but what would then befall mankind, who could say?— since that tribute was the channel through which the Gods poured down their light into hearts. "No," she said; "I will not go. I fear nothing from these folk. I will protect the temple from them, they will hear reason from me. Apollo, I doubt not, will give me wise words, and will shine upon them inwardly; and if their God is a God indeed, he will cause them to reverence his elder brother the Sun. Fear thou nothing for me, good Leonidas."

He groaned. "I saw them," said he. "I was with them at the temple of Zeus, and beheld what they did; and the Thunderer sent no bolt—"

"Hush!" she said, lifting a hand. It was he, not she, who turned pale then. The noise that came up from the valley was unmistakable; less pleasant to hear than the howling of the wolf pack or the brool of hungry lions drawing near. It was the roaring of the beast that is in man; its hideousness lies in this: that it is not merely bestial, but half bestial, half fiendish. It was but an hour after dawn, and yet the mob was already in the valley; would be at work soon, very soon.

In his panic he would have caught her up and carried her away; but some divinity seemed to enter into her, and she quite overawed him. "Go!" she said, pointing to the path that led to her father's house; "carry him away; quickly; there is no time to lose." He was filled with the idea that she had knowledge that was concealed from him; and that no course was open to him but to obey. He went: inspired to seeming desertion as to an act of supreme faith.

Then she went into the temple again, and stood in her place behind the altar and chanted her hymns; and the noise of the mob drew nearer and nearer, till she could distinguish the voices clearly, and the words shouted or spoken.

Suddenly it stopped—just below the bend where the path rounded under the steep bank and the pine-clump; stopped, and gave place to—a crowing of baby laughter. Then she heard the voices again, but growing human now, women's voices and men's. *Ah, little sweetheart! . . . Come then, my pretty! . . . I tell thee, my little Basil was like that—as beautiful! . . . Oh, wonderful . . . most sacred!—see the halo about his head! . . . But it is the Holy Babe! It is the Child Jesus! . . . Ah, sacred little rogue! see, he pelts us with the flowers!*

She waited listening, and never saw or knew what happened below. Only she heard strange words cried, *Hosannas* and *Halleluias;* but the sound of them was full of delight and reverence: the beast and the devil in man had no part nor note in it. And then, by noon, they were withdrawing; still singing hymns of praise with voices sweet with humanity. . . .

When they had all gone she went down by the path to see. As she passed under the bank and the pine-clump, and turned, she heard a little chuckle of delight. . . . And there rolling on the slope amid the anemones, half buried in the deep red and purple blooms that wantoned out into their glory at his touch, was a little brown-limbed, beautiful, sun-dusky rogue, black-haired, and with the eyes of a baby god. . . . As she came, he held out his fat little arms to her, and she picked him up, and he nestled to her breast and kissed her as she carried him up to the temple. And as it was noonday and hot, and he had been basking and rolling all the morning in the sun, what wonder if he cried out as she brought him past the spring where the clear, cold water dripped from its marble basin in front of the temple, *Baby thirsty . . . ?*

And what wonder if from the mountain tops and the pinetrees, from the rocks and the grassy valleys, from the fountains of the nymphs and from the forests, the voices of the elemental hosts rose swooning up to her and to Him:

Shepherd of the wandering constellations, hail!
Evoë, hail!

•••••••••••••••••••••••••

"The King and the Three Ascetics" is a Brahman tale, a gentle satire suggesting that the best way to truth is through experience. It was first published under the title "The Tower of the Gandharvas" in The Theosophical Path *in December 1915, under the pseudonym Ephraim Soulsby Paton. Morris retitled it for inclusion in* The Secret Mountain and Other Tales.

The King and the Three Ascetics

*B*rightness, honor, power, splendor of countenance and Vedic glory—these things verily, were possessed in former times by Atidhanvan Sanaka, king of the Videhas, in such measure that there was none like him to be found in the world, and even the gods were astonished. On his body were the two and thirty marks of perfect birth; and the birthmarks of the Chakravartin,—the wheel, the orb and the discus of unbounded sovereignty. To speak of the tributary monarchs that bowed down to him, would be, as it were, to limit the infinity of his power: from the seven continents they came, bearing wealth to his treasure-house. His armies went forth even to Patala; and such was the fame of his beneficence, they achieved victory without the shedding of blood. He conquered the resplendent worlds. "Whatever tribute we may pay to him," said the kings of the earth, "it is upon us that the balance of benefit falls." Among the countless crores of his slaves and subjects there was none to hanker after the lightening of his yoke; none to complain, or desire any other lord but he.

All of which pertained to his rank as Chakravartin; but heaven knows he was more and greater than a Chakravartin possessing world-sovereignty. Shvetaketu-Dalbhya overheard seven flamingoes discoursing as they flew over the palace in the night. "Short-sighted brothers," said the leader of them, "fly not too near, lest the splendor of the good deeds of His Majesty scorch your wings." Ushasti Shalavatya listened while the bull of the herd was conversing with the cows. "As for Atidhanvan Sanaka," said the bull, "he, verily, is to be named with Raikva with the Car."—"How was it with that Raikva?" said the cows; "and how is it with the King of the

Videhas?"—"As in a game of dice," said the bull, "all the lower casts belong to him who conquers with the Krita cast, so all good deeds performed by other men belonged of old to Raikva, and belong now to the King." Prasnayana Jaivali heard the altar-flame soliloquizing. "Atidhanvan Sanaka" said the flame "knows that Golden Person who is seen within the sun, with golden beard and golden hair, whose eyes are like blue lotuses, and who is golden altogether to the tips of his nails. Atidhanvan Sanaka, verily, knows the Golden Person, the Lonely Bird. . . ."

And he who knows this, says the Upanishad, *knows that Brahman . . .*

Certainly, then, the king knew Brahman. Though he was a warrior of the Kshattriya tribe, many that were Brahmins came to him to learn wisdom. They put questions to him, and he answered their questions: revealing to them the Self of the self, making known to them the wanderings of the Lonely Bird. That which is the Breath of the breath, the Eye of the eye, the Ear of the ear, the Dwarf in the heart, he revealed it to them. Then he put questions to them, and they were dumb. "Master," said those proud ones, "teach us!"

Kingly indeed was this man: constantly in action; constantly shining forth surrounded with the pomp and magnificence of his sovereignty; no one ever beheld him at rest. As with chanting of Vedic hymns and with ceremonial rites, the priests conduct the sacrifice: or as the sun passes through heaven, adoring that Brahman: so Atidhanvan Sanaka conducted the affairs of the world. "Whatsoever the sun or the moon sees; or the light or the darkness hears; whatsoever the heart conceives, or the hand performs, or the tongue whispers: he knoweth it, he knoweth it!" said the people. Where one man feared him, millions loved him; and so great was the influence of his will and benevolence that righteousness was maintained everywhere, and evil put down firmly in every quarter of the world."

Now in those days there dwelt three ascetics in the Forest of Grantha-Nagari: Vaka Kakshaseni, Satyakama Kapeya, and Gautama Kaushitakeya, or as he was called, Pautraya Glava. They were assiduous in the quest of wisdom, and had spent three hundred years in meditation: performing many penances, governing the inbreathing and the outbreathing, and silently repeating the udgitha. They had attained to many powers; yet there was that, verily, to which they had not attained.

At the end of a hundred years Vaka Kakshaseni said:

"Sir, Satyakama Kapeya, knowest thou that Brahman?"

"I know it not," said he.

At the end of another hundred years Satyakama Kapeya said:

"Sir, Gautama Kaushitakeya, or as thou art called, Pautraya Glava, knowest thou that Brahman?"

"I know it not," said he.

After another hundred years he continued:

"There is that Atidhanvan Sanaka, king of the Videhas: it is said that he knows. Is it your opinion that we should go to him and request him to teach us?"

"We are Brahmins, and he is a Kshattriya," said they. "Were we to seek as our teacher one unworthy to teach us, our heads might fall off."

"Our heads might fall off, truly," said he.

Then said Satyakama Kapeya: "Sir, Vaka Kakshaseni, what is thy opinion?"

"That one of us should go to the king's palace, and make inquiry as to the knowledge he hath, and how he attained to it," said he. And they said: "Sir, Satyakama Kapeya, do thou go."

Satyakama Kapeya took the guise of a sweeper, and went into the city, and mingled with the crowd that gathered in the morning when Atidhanvan Sanaka came into the Hall of Justice. He saw the king ascend the throne, like the splendor of the sun at dawn into a sky of gold and scarlet, of clear saffron and refined vermilion. He listened while the judgments were being given, and understood that no lie might be maintained against the king's perspicacity of vision. He saw that whatsoever deed was done, or thought thought, or word spoken, it was known to Atidhanvan Sanaka, and could not be concealed from him. He abided there from dawn until noon, marvelling more and more. The motions of the king's hands, it seemed to him, were as the motions of Karma to administer rewards and punishments; the glances of the king's eyes seemed to him to penetrate compassionately into all the corners of the earth. At the end of the morning the people prostrated themselves and said, "Justice hath been done, even to the ultimate particular"; and Satyakama Kapeya answered, "Yea, justice hath been done." And he was not a man to be impressed by outward shows. Then he sat in meditation until sunset, by the roadside a mile beyond the city gates, considering what he had seen and learned; and at the end of it was in grave doubt whether, if they went to the King of the Videhas to learn wisdom, their heads might not fall off. "For" said he "were I to return to the forest and be questioned by my companions, those ascetics would say, 'There is nothing in this concerning knowledge of that Brahman.' Further inquiry is needed."

He shaped his mind into a question, and with it pervaded space.

Three crows flew by overhead; and the midmost of them looked down and cried out to him: "Inquisitive brother, come, and I will show thee!" So he assumed the form of a crow, and rose in the air, and flew with them over the walls and into the city, and over the palace enclosure in the midst of the city; and over a garden in the midst of the enclosure; and over a lake in the midst of the garden till the whole world below him was water, and there was no seeing the darkness of the shores, nor the twinkle of a light on any hand. And there a crag rose up out of the water to heights beyond where Vayu may wander in the air; and on the crag the ruins of a tower, roofless, desolate, immense; and the top of it beyond where Soma shone like a pale scimitar in the indigo mystery of heaven. Yet to the top of it, soaring and circling and laboring, Satyakama Kapeya and the other crows flew; and he and the bird that had spoken to him lit down on the wall where it had crumbled lowest; but the other two flew on as it were laughing into the dark solitude of night. Then the crow said: "Hast thou eyes to see?"

"Eyes I have, sir," said Satyakama Kapeya; "such as they are."

"Behold what passeth here, then; with such vision as thou hast," said the crow; "and understand that it is thus with him nightly."

He looked down into the tower, into a depth world-deep below him lit by a lurid glare and flamy confusion at the bottom, so that it was long and hard looking before he could see what befell there. Then the crow said: *"The gates of hell are three,* saith the Upanishad." And Satyakama Kapeya began to see . . . for he had gained many powers in the forest hermitage, and among them an extraordinary power of vision. Below was a man stripped naked, and armed with sword and shield; and he stood in a space between three hell-mouth caverns whence poured flame and stench and fury, and demons strained and crowded to emerge; but he fought them back. Then the crow said: "Thou seest him, how he sealeth the gates of hell against their egress"; and with that, flew wing-flapping and as it were laughing into the night. But Satyakama Kapeya intently watched the man who fought. Often the talons of the demons rent him; so that he dripped sweat and blood; the muscles writhed upon his body where they clutched and dragged and tore him; his brow with agony was crossed and twisted like a tree's roots; and he strove and writhed and bled and was silent. But no demon might pass him, to rise into the tower, and thence into the world of men.

Then the sun rose far off over the lonely waters; and through some crevice in the broken wall below, shone in upon the space where the combat was; and silence fell there suddenly; and all that had issued from the three hell-mouths sank back into them; and for stench arose an odor of incense-gums and sandalwood; and the man that had been fighting stood up, and the sunray fell like a golden garment upon his body. Then Satyakama Kapeya saw the wounds upon him glow mysteriously radiant; and knew them for the two-and-thirty marks of perfect birth, and the signs of the Chakravartin—the wheel, the orb and the discus of world-sovereignty. "Atidhanvan Sanaka it is," said he. "It is the King of the Videhas, with great powers."

He flew forth and came in his own guise to his companions in the forest, and told them all he had seen; and for a year they were silent, meditating on it. Then Gautama Kaushitakeya shook his head with anxiety. "There is nothing in this concerning knowledge of Brahman," said he. "Our heads might fall off, truly." Then he said: "Sir, Satyakama Kapeya, what is thy opinion?"

"That another of us should go and make inquiry," said he. "Sir, Vaka Kakshaseni, do thou go."

* * *

Vaka Kakshaseni took the guise of a Kshattriya dispensing gifts; and rode into the city at noon; and came in the king's Hall of Audience, where the tributary princes were in waiting. There were seven-score sovereign rulers present there: haughty, wise and puissant leaders; gifted with beauty of face and form; very resplendently appareled. It seemed to be a garden of a myriad blossoms because of the silks they were wearing, and the rubies, the silver and sapphires, the pearls and gold. Then came in Atidhanvan Sanaka, and took his place upon the throne; and because of his Vedic splendor and glory of countenance, the best of them seemed like the flame of a wretched lamp, fed with rancid oil, and the wick of it untrimmed, and flaunted at midday in the face of the sun.

Very carefully Vaka Kakshaseni watched him; and saw that the motions of his hands were the upholding of distant empires, and the maintaining of peace; that the glances of his eyes were enlightenment for far and barbarous peoples; that the words of his mouth brought lovingkindness where there had been envy, ambition and strife. He marveled until nightfall at what he saw; and ceased not to marvel when the king went forth; and he was not one to be impressed lightly. Then he went out, and walked in the palace garden in the dusk; and considered what he had seen and heard. "There is nothing in it concerning knowledge of Brahman," said he. He sent out his mind in inquiry into the four directions of space. . . .

Three moths flew by him through the drooping odors of the evening: through the jasmine-hearted evening: through the gloom and dimness rich with magnolia blooms. . . . Said the midmost of the moths: "Who seeks light, let him follow!" and Vaka Kakshaseni assumed moth form, and rose in the air and went with them. "Ah," said he; "here is the lake; but it is not as the venerable Satyakama described it." For all round about it he could see the low dark line of the shore, and the lights of the palace twinkling like large stars thick strewn in a galaxy, and the reflections of the lights reeling and glittering on the ghostly blueness of the water. "And here is the tower," said he; "but it is not as the wise ascetic said." For it stood on a low island grown about with pleasant trees; and rose above the tree-tops well roofed and slender pillared; and a light from within shone gently bright through the pearlish opacity of its topmost storey; and towards that light the moths flew. And two of them hovered about it at random with a droning fluster of wings; but the one that had spoken led him to a crevice through which he might peer. "Hast thou eyes to see?" said the moth. —"Sir, I have eyes, such as they are," said he. —"Behold then"; said the moth, "and know that it is thus with Atidhanvan Sanaka nightly at all times."

So Vaka Kakshaseni looked through, and down into the tower. At the bottom—but it was not far below—were the three hell-mouths; but nought emerged from them. He could see within them the demons that struggled to emerge, and the flame suppressed and impotent, and the gods of hell writhing and defeated. And what defeated them he saw clearly to be the light that filled the place; and whence it shone he saw clearly too. Upon a cloud that floated in the air midway between himself and the hellmouths, seated upon a cloth and kusa grass was a naked ascetic in meditation; the light shone from his brow. "Thus by meditation he defeateth them," said the moth; "thus, and not otherwise, O inquisitive Brother, he sealeth up the hell-mouths against the egress of the fiends."

"Sir," said Vaka Kakshaseni, "tellest thou me the truth of the truth?"

"I tell thee what I know," said the moth, and flew away; and the fluster and whirr of his wings was like dim laughter in the quiet of the night. But at daybreak a sunray entering illuminated the body of the sage that meditated, and Vaka Kakshaseni beheld thereon the two and thirty marks of perfect birth, and the marks of the Chakravartin enjoying world-sovereignty.

He came into the forest, and told his companions what he had seen and heard; and they meditated on it in silence for three years. Then Satyakama Kapeya shook his head gravely.

"Our heads might fall off if we sought wisdom from the king of the Videhas," he said. "There is nothing in this concerning knowledge of Brahman." Then he said: "Sir, Vaka Kakshaseni, what is thy opinion?"

"That again inquiry should be made," said he. "Sir, Gautama Kaushitakeya, do thou go."

In the morning Pautraya Glava (as he was called) assumed the guise of a hotri priest and went into the city; and whatsoever the others had seen or heard before nightfall, he saw and heard as much and more; and marveled as much as they did. "But," said he, "there is nothing in it concerning knowledge of That." So he pondered, when evening had come, in the garden; putting forth his mind shaped into inquiry, through all the directions of space. Then he heard a nightingale singing among the cypress trees; and what it sang was this: "Uncertain brother, come, and thou shalt learn." So he took the form of a nightingale and flew with the other, whither celestial music, that now filled all the moonlit garden, led or called. Over the dark waters of a lakelet, through whose gloom a gleam of opal and sly silver rippled; and the blue lotuses nodded there mysteriously, keeping time to the murmur of celestial music; and up and down through the bloom-rich darkness wandering stars floated and waned. A bowshot from the shore there was a gardened islet; and about it the music fainted and surged; on the islet was a tower of ivory chased and fretted. "Behold him" said the nightingale "if thou hast the eyes for it; thus spendeth he the nights ever."

And Pautraya Glava looked in, and saw a feast going forward: Indra and Agni, Vayu, Prajapati, seated on thrones like blue lotuses; and with them sat the king of the Videhas throned as their equal; and all above them from thence to the moon were choirs of the Gandharvas, the heavenly musicians, singing. "Thus obtaineth he his wisdom," said the nightingale. "Out of the converse of the Gods, and the music of the Gandharvas, he obtaineth it."

Gautama Kaushitakeya took the news to his companions in the forest. "Sirs, what is your opinion?" said he.

For three days and three nights they pondered it, and then made answer: "Sir, there has been discrepancy in the reports, leading to diversity of opinion. It would be well we should all go together, and make inquiry, and prosecute research."

So that evening they assumed falcon form; and flew to the palace, and to the lake in the garden, and to the tower on the island; and lighted down wing to wing, and watched all night; and returned to the forest in the morning.

Satyakama Kapeya said: "Sirs, venerable ascetics; you have seen that you were mistaken; that I reported it correctly; with your own eyes you have seen the King of the Videhas fight against the demons at the mouth of hell, and the blood and sweat pouring from his body."

Vaka Kakshaseni said: "Sir, Satyakama Kapeya, how is this? You yourself have seen that my report was indeed correct: you have seen Atidhanvan Sanaka seated upon a yogi's seat of cloth and kusa grass in meditation; and how by his meditation, and not otherwise, he sealed the mouth of hell."

Gautama Kaushitakeya said: "Sirs, venerable ascetics, how is this? You yourselves have seen the King feast, as I reported, with Indra and Prajapati and the other Gods; you have heard those deities discourse wisdom to him, and the troops of the singing Gandharvas of heaven fill the regions of space with celestial music for his pleasure . . ."

Then they all three looked at each other with astonishment and startled surmise. Then they all three rose up suddenly. "Come!" said they; "unless we go quickly, our heads may fall off."

They came to Atidhanvan Sanaka bearing fuel in their hands. "Sir," they said, "teach us That Brahman!"

"Be it so," said he. "It would have been better had ye come before I set the winged things to reason with ye. Abide in the palace seven years as fuel-bearers; then come to me again."

A *Middle-Eastern tale very similar to those found in* The Arabian Nights, *"The Rose and the Cup" was first published in* The Theosophical Path *in April 1916, under the pseudonym Wentworth Tompkins. Morris also selected it for inclusion in* The Secret Mountain and Other Tales.

The Rose and the Cup

'Iram indeed is gone with all his rose,
And Jamshyd's seven-ringed Cup, where no one knows.'

R oses and roses and roses: the garden was aglow, mysterious, foamy with them; I doubt you would have found the like in the Garden of Iram or in al-Jannat itself. Roses with pale petals over-curving like a wave or the lip of a shell, that within were all blush and peerless pinkness; roses amber-hearted or apricot-hearted; roses of infinite purity tossed in sprays whiter than the snows of Kaf; delicate yellow roses billowing over the latticed pergolas; crimson roses burning deep in the cypress gloom, redder than rubies, redder than wine, marvelously imperial and profound—not ostentatious nor flaunting their beauty, but compelled into a secret pride akin to compassion by the lofty intensity of their dreams, of their secret knowledge. . . .

These were the only faithful councilors and friends the Queen had.

She was in her garden amongst them, in a place of fretted marble, with overhead a foamy canopy of the yellow roses. You shall see her now, the rose of all roses in the rose garden; with beauty drawn out of the suns and fragrant nights of eighteen Persian springs—no more. Her eyes were dark and lustrous, but with something more than softness in them; in the poise of her beautiful head were strength and pride; but with the pride, humility, you would say; and the strength the strength of impersonality. . . .

It was a sore burden to be laid on her, this queenhood—in a kingdom left to her by her dead husband, to be held in trust for their unborn son. An over-civilized kingdom, wherein luxury was pursued and duty mainly neglected; a city of white palaces and mosques and lovely gardens, which put its trust in Turkish mercenaries, and thronged to hear too clever poets stab each other in mellifluous-spiteful *ruba'i* or *ghazal* over their wine; a city without patriotism, virtue or valor. She knew she had no defense, nor anyone to rely upon, but the hired Turks; and they—it would have been a strong king's work, or the greater part of it, to keep them in order. She had five hundred of them in her pay: five hundred too many for peace; hundreds of thousands too few for war—such war, especially, as threatened.

It was less than a year since she had traveled down from the mountain castle of her forefathers to be the bride of a young warlike king she had never seen: a marriage, however, that proved to be of those arranged in heaven. They became at once lovers and comrades, and foresaw splendid things they would do together: conquests they would make, not merely external; regeneration they would bring to their people. But within six months of their marriage he had died; leaving her to the protection of a crafty Minister she loved not and the Turkish guards—and to the tender mercies of terrible Mahmud of Ghazna.

Which tender mercies were now beginning to precipitate: and that was the worst part of her burden—perhaps. With her five hundred Turks she was to oppose that Worldshaker—that Turk of Turks and great Thunderbolt of God,—unless means could be found of placating him. It had come about in this way:

As Mahmud was among kings, so was Abu Ali ibn Sina* among philosophers; and during the months of this queen's married life that brilliant ornament of time had deigned to shed the luster of his presence on her husband's court. It was a light to be hidden under no bushel, a fame as wide as Mahmud's own; where Ibn Sina was, there was the intellectual capital of the world. And Mahmud could not endure it that his Ghazna should be second in any respect to any city on earth. He himself was the Daystar of the Age; let all counter-suns unite their radiance to his.

He wanted Ibn Sina himself; and what he wanted he asked for; and what he asked for he never failed to get. The four hundred poets of Ghazna, collected willy nilly from all the House of Islam; lured by barbaric pearls and gold, or fetched in as pampered captives from conquered kingdoms, had no magic to dull the tooth of envy that would be busy at their master's heart while Ibn Sina the Great remained at court or city other than his. Poets—*ta!*—their wit and quarrels were amusing; it swelled one's sense of splendor to feed them, array them, set them cock-fighting, flog them on occasion, or stuff their mouths with gold; it was a thing to boast of, like the conquest of India, that one had twenty score of them fattening in one's palace;—and then, too, they were the minters of flattery, without whose service it should not pass current far or long. But every court in Iran had its living dozen or more of them; and one had lost one's Firdausi that outshone them all.

*Avicenna.

Ibn Sina, on the other hand, was unique. That he was a poet, and of the wittiest, was the least of his accomplishments. No science was hidden from him; not even the Secret Science. From China to Andalus none had a tithe of his fame; he was the greatest of all physicians; and supreme, since Aflatun and Aristo, in philosophy. —A sovereign, luxurious and extravagant man withal, out-princing princes in the manner of his life, and with disciples unnumbered for his subjects: the gayest, the most brilliant of men who could yet snatch time from his high living to pour out upon the world a torrent of books ten times as profound, ten times as scintillant, and ten times as many as any other ten thinkers could produce together. Why, one would give all conquered Hindustan for Ibn Sina, and think the exchange cheap: possession of the man would more allay one's ambition, more swell one's fame. Mahmud had sent ambassadors with rich gifts and a peremptory message: Ibn Sina was to start for Ghazna forthwith.

The king and queen sent for the philosopher, and let Mahmud's emissaries give their message direct. There was just one man in Islamiyeh in those days, probably—at least in the Abbassid Caliphate—who would have dared flout Mahmud's commands; and that was Ibn Sina. In a lesser mind you might ascribe such light defiance to puffed-up vanity, and hold him a victim of his own eternal brilliance and success. But you have not understood Ibn Sina unless you have seen in him nature's prodigy, with no room in him for flattery or fear: one naturally to look on world-conquerors as the dust beneath his feet—and to tell them so. He quietly informed the ambassador that the court of his master was no place for men of mind: they could do no good work there. Even here in Iran there was much too much, for the dignity of civilization, of Turkish soldiery; was he to drown himself in the central ocean of Turkism, and become the slave of the son of the slave of a slave.* Let Sultan Mahmud bethink him of the insult he had offered Firdausi; and again of what al-Biruni suffered for prophesying truly twice; and let him give up hope of associating with his betters.

All of which the King al-Ka'us approved heartily; and added sharp words of his own to tease the Ghaznewid's hearing withal. Haughty young leopard of a prince, he had himself been straining, eastward, at the leashes of peace: Mahmud's ambitions grew intolerable to monarchs of will and spirit. . . . It was, of course, no less than to declare war; for which he, al-Ka'us, might have had as many Turks out of Turan as he desired: swift fearless bowmen and spearmen from the vast plains, nine-tenths of them with a nourishable hatred against the son of Sabuktigin already. And he could have overawed and led them—to victory? One could not say; no one ever did win victory from Mahmud; and yet, while Mahmud lived, there was always the chance. At least to an honourable defeat. —The Sultan at that time was busy in India: outdoing the exploits of Iskander of old, and

*Mahmud—who was actually that.

taking in ripe empires as one might swallow grapes; he could but pocket al-Ka'us's insult, and promise himself that the hour of these Persian princelings should come, and presently. And now it was certainly at hand. Al-Ka'us had died before Mahmud, returning, had arrived at Ghazna; and a month since the message had come: *Deliver up Ibn Sina and so much in tribute, or expect my armies to carry away the dust of your city.*

What could she do? Ibn Sina had left them before her husband's death, or that dire blow would not have fallen: the great doctor would surely have cured al-Ka'us; and as to the tribute demanded, there was not so much gold in Iran and Turan. Should she flee, and leave the kingdom to Mahmud? She thought of her dead lord, and of his unborn son, and dismissed the idea as unthinkable. Fight?—ah, but how? What could the captain of her Turks, Oghlu Beg—even supposing that he and his men would stand by her—do with his five hundred against the Ghaznewid's hundreds of thousands? And even if she had an army: Hussein al-Ajjami her vizir, she judged, would make his own terms with Mahmud; selling without compunction herself, her son, and her kingdom.

She had answered the Sultan's letter thus:

"The philosopher Abu Ali ibn Sina left our court long since; and is to be sought now at Merv or Ray or Samarcand—we know not where. Sultan Mahmud is a mighty champion of the Faith, a most puissant prince, and also a man of honor; it is certain that if he leads his armies hither, I also, a weak woman, shall endeavor to give him battle; let him consider, then, what kind of victory he might win. Were I victor, it would be a triumph for me until the Day of Judgment; if the victory be his, men will say, He has only conquered a woman. And the issues of war are in the hands of God: it cannot be known aforehand what the result will be. Make war, then, upon the strong, and in the victory his strength shall be added to yours; but give the hand of your august friendship to the weak: so shall men praise your magnanimity, and your fame shall endure. We expect your friendship, my lord Sultan; since most undeniably we are weak.

"But we will not give up this kingdom to you, since it is not ours to give, but the property of Hasan Ali ibn al-Ka'us, who is not yet born. Yet, knowing that the Sultan is wise and kindly, we have no anxiety in this matter, but repose on the couch of tranquillity and confidence."

She had received no answer to this; but knew that Mahmud was on the march. Now, what she meditated was the raising of an army to oppose him. She clapped her hands for a slave, and sent for the vizir.

He had held office under the father of her husband, had this Ajjami: planting his power by a thousand roots while the old king's faculties were failing. He had been a very politic minister: had he strayed anywhere from honorable service, none, even of his own household, knew of it for a certainty. Al-Ka'us would have dismissed him, but died before the occasion served; now the Queen found herself dependent on him. If she did not trust him greatly, whom else should she trust at all? He had been all humility with her; all, she suspected, a soft buffer between her will and its carrying into effect. —A handsome old man, perhaps sixty; refined, smooth, white-bearded and aquiline: it might have been a noble face, but for a keen quietude in the eyes that slightly veiled selfishness and cunning, and a sensuous fullness of the lower lip. His strength lay in intrigue, in persistence, in perfect suavity not to be ruffled; in the power of a will, too, that would hunt covertly for years, and never forgo its designs.

When the formalities of greeting were over she began to question him. Had the messengers ridden forth? What answers had come in? Was the manhood of the provinces assembling? What numbers had been mustered?—Ah, but here we must work with caution, said he; must consider well before irrevocable steps were taken, and irrevocable disaster invited. Mahmud and his host were drawing near, and opposition was hardly to be offered. The swiftness of his marches, the terror of his name, his long tradition of invincibility—all these things were to be taken into account. The feeling throughout the country, among the nobles—which he, her slave, had so carefully tested—was that, since the king was dead—

Here she broke in upon his speech to remind him that the king, unborn, was present.

He bowed low; seemed a little distressed—tactfully, as one who reserves painful things. These matters were in the hands of God; who could build upon the uncertainties of fate? Then he fetched a compass, and spoke of her beauty; ah, with tact—with wonderful tact! He indicated, not failing to make his meaning clear—and terrible—what the result of that beauty would be, upon Mahmud. And who could doubt the truth of his words? The kingdom would be annexed; she herself would be taken to Ghazna, to the Sultan's harem; her son, when he was born, would be enslaved or slain,—at best would grow up the nonentity Mahmud might choose to make of him. —"And your advice, O Ajjami?" said she, knowing there were ill things to be spoken. —His advice was couched in the language of utmost reverent devotion. Many of the prominent and influential had broached the idea to him; might his words, that were to declare it, be pearls of humility, rubies of love! It was that a king should be provided; for lack of whom indifference and anxiety were rife, and would grow; a king about whom the people might gather, and with whom, perhaps, the son of Sabuktigin might deign to treat. Let her lift her slave to the throne then, that he might meet Mahmud as king: so the radiance of her own beauty should remain hidden from the burning glances of the World Conqueror. . . .

She turned a little cold as she listened to him; mastered a disgust that sickened her; mastered her face and voice, and answered him. She was but two months a widow, she said; and her heart demanded longer time for mourning. Meanwhile she would consider this plan . . . that seemed wise . . . that might presently come to seem best. And she had great comfort of the thought that he, who served her and was faithful, had served and been faithful to al-Ka'us her dear lord also; and to al-Amin the father of al-Ka'us. Ah, what treasures were honor and loyalty! Not all the riches of the realm, nor sovereignty itself would weigh an ant's weight against them on the day when Munkir and Nakir should open his tomb; when his friends should ask what wealth he had left behind him; but the angels, what good deeds he had sent before. She could trust him, she knew, to leave nothing undone for the safety of his prince. —So he left her, assuring her of his devotion; and went forth to the furthering of his plans. She might trust him, she supposed, to sell her to Mahmud.

She walked forth among the roses her friends; perchance they would have comfort or counsel to whisper. . . . Allah! must she indeed pay this price that she loathed? Mahmud, or al-Ajjam! . . . She believed, knowing him somewhat, that the vizir would have cunning enough to save her for himself, should she consent to his terms: he won his battles perhaps even more inevitably than Mahmud. But what would he do with her son? She shuddered. For herself, she would rather the Ghaznewid's harem . . . but again, there was her son. . . . —The white rose reached out its sprays to her; the apricot-hearted wafted her its sweetness; the crimson, as she passed, stirred by a delicate wind, brushed her cheek with its sovereign bloom, and came dewed with a tear from the touch. *We both are Queens in Iran!* it whispered.

No, she would not pay the price. There was Oghlu Beg, the captain of the guard; dependable so long as he was paid;—she would compound with him for the contents of her treasury, and ride out herself among his Turks to seek death on the field. Then she and her son would meet al-Ka'us together in Paradise; and she knew al-Ka'us would approve. —She sent for the Turk.

"Oghlu Beg," she said, when the big limbed man was before her, "your living depends on your reputation for faith and valor. You have received my lord's pay, and mine; and your pay shall be doubled if you serve me well now. Doubled?—ask of me the whole of my treasury, when you have defeated me Mahmud ibn Sabuktigin."

"Madam," said he, with the heavy speech of the slow-thoughted, "it would be impossible without raising a great army. And I might do that, even now, had I the authority. But it would be a great task; the slave's son of Ghazna is renowned and feared. The men of Turan would not come to the banners of less than a king. And I also would serve for something better than money. . . . I love you; make me king, and I will go forth with you and gather an army that may meet even Mahmud with hope. Otherwise I must clearly offer my sword to the Ghaznewid; there would be little profit in offering it elsewhere."

Such things happened constantly. Turkish captains founded many a dynasty in Persia, and then patronized art and letters as vigorously—if not as intelligently—as they pushed their conquests. This slow, heavy, bow-legged warrior, for all his confessed readiness to sell himself and his men to her enemy, did not rouse in her the fear and disgust she felt at the advances of her own so polished countryman. His bluntness was better than the vizir's tact: it was his business to sell himself, and he would do it; but he had a code that would keep him from selling her.

"This is your one condition?" she asked.

"It is the one condition," he answered. "Not only on account of my love, but also in consideration of the possibilities. Not otherwise could I gather an army."

"And you will not ride with me against Mahmud with the army you have—and receive my treasury in exchange?"

"Dead men enjoy not wealth," said he. "It is the one condition."

There was no hope then, and she dismissed him. But an impulse came to her before he had passed from sight, and she called him back.

"Before you came here, O' Oghlu Beg," she said, "al-Ajjami the vizir was with me. He too had a plan to propose; and his plan was even as yours is. He too would be king, and my husband."

"May his couch be made in hell!" growled the Turk.

"I will tell you," said she. "The King my husband was not as other men; and no man shall have of me what he had. I will not marry al-Ajjami, O Oghlu; and I will not marry you. Therefore go you to Mahmud with your men, and serve him while he pays you, as you have served my lord and me. But I will even beg a boon of you before you go."

The Turk bent his head.

"Stay you here until the Ghaznewid is at the gates; go to him then. I desire your protection against al-Ajjami."

He had no more command of metaphor than a dog. Where another would have said "O Moon of Wonder" or "O Tulip from the garden-plots of Paradise," he could get out nothing but "I will stay. And I will guard thee from this son of Iblis." Then, after a pause for thought: "And I will not go to Mahmud. If it be thy will I will carry thee where Mahmud comes not: to Egypt, or Africa, or Spain. And none shall harm thee by the way: neither I nor another."

But the Queen had no idea of seeking refuge anywhere.

That night two things happened. First: the messenger returned from Mahmud's camp and reported. The Sultan had laughed over the Queen's letter. Within a week he would be at the city gates. "She expects our friendship" he said "because she is undeniably weak. Tell her the price of our friendship shall be"—here he had looked round for a suggestion—"What shall it be, you poets?" One of whom had named a sum altogether preposterous, and another had doubled it; and a third, more gifted with imagination, had cried, "The Cup of Jamshyd!"—"Stuff his mouth with rubies!" cried the

Allah-breathing lord; "the Cup of Jamshyd it shall be. If the Queen shall send us that, she shall have our friendship until her death or ours; but if she send it not—" Not for nothing had Mahmud fed upon the ancient legends whereof Firdausi made the great epic for him: in which the Cup of Jamshyd shone remote and mystic, the Grail and supreme talisman of an elder age, before the Arab, before the Sassanid—before, and long before, Xerxes led his armies against Greece. His terms were a jest; there were no terms; he meant conquest, and most thoroughly to wipe out the insult he had received from al-Ka'us and Ibn Sina.

The other happening was this: Oghlu Beg supped, and died in great torment an hour later—just when he should have been carrying into action a plan he had been at pains to form. He was always a slow-thoughted man; now his slowness cost him his life. He did not die, however, before conveying his intent, and a command to avenge him, to his brother and chief lieutenant. Who then proceeded with five Turks of the guard and a headsman's carpet to the chambers of al-Ajjami; so that by morning the Queen had lost both her suitors. Before noon the guard, dis-disciplined, lacking their Oghlu, rode away after some minor looting to join the standards of Mahmud of Ghazna.

The Sultan had promised to arrive within a week: it was a point of honor with him, at least in such matters as this, to be very much better than his word. All that day men came riding in from the east with tidings of his approach; none of them remained in the city, but sought safety farther afield. And all day through the western gates the city was emptying itself. Disturbances were to be dreaded, now that there was none to enforce authority; but fear policed the place fairly until evening. Before the sun had set, one could see from the towers of the palace clouds of dust along the flat horizon eastward. In the morning Mahmud of Ghazna would be at the gates; by noon he would be in the city; by nightfall— There was nothing to be done. He might have had the name of *Yilderim,* fittest title for your typical Turkish worldshaker at any time: his blows fell swift and terrible as the thunderbolt, and there was no escaping them.

The Queen walked among her roses in the twilight, very calm and proud; not yet had she given way to despair. She had done all she could, though it was nothing; she had no plan; she could not and would not dwell on the morrow. She still maintained a resigned queenly confidence: whatever fate might befall her body, her soul would keep the trust. When she met her lord in Paradise—and might that be to-morrow!—she would have no cause to be ashamed; and her son would have nothing to forgive her. Her son? He had not yet been born; yet he stood in her mental vision as clear a figure as her husband. The dead and the unborn were her companions: there, living and on this earth, she stood for them: for the future and the past. She felt as if she were somehow in two worlds at once: one outward and illusionary, full of terrible fantasm and turmoil; one inward and stable, where there was peace; and from this inner world she might look down serenely untroubled upon the chaotic happenings below or without. For there al-Ka'us walked with her; and the young hero that was to be, Hasan Ali ibn al-Ka'us; and the roses bloomed for the three of them: she and the roses were in both worlds. Out of the Persian earth they bloomed, these Persian roses, lovely with all ancient Persian deeds and dreams; and perhaps she too (like Omar Tentmaker):

Sometimes thought that never blew so red
The rose as where some buried Cæsar bled—

we will say, Khusru for Cæsar. These were white, perhaps, remembering the white hair of Zal; and perhaps young Isfendiyar, on his seven-staged journey and seven marvellous labours, won from fate the golden wisdom and tenderness that made these citron or apricot-hearted; and these so crimson, so peerless perfect—perhaps they distilled their glory from Rustum's sorrow over slain Sohrab his son; or perhaps the glow that shone from them was reflected from some still more ancient link between heaven and Persia—from Feridun's sword, or Zal's simurgh-feather, from blacksmith Kavah's apron, or from Jamshyd's Seven-ringed Cup. . . . Ah, in the inner world what was a thing carved of jewels or crystal, or any talisman, how potent soever, better than, or different from, His secret spiritual beauty God puts forth where our eyes can see it, through every rose that blooms in the garden? . . . Hasan Ali ibn al-Ka'us, mayest thou, too, bring new beauty to the roses! . . .

A hoarse roaring from the city broke in upon the peace of the rose garden; panic-stricken women of the court came running to her; the dregs of the populace, they said, had risen to sack the palace; and where should they hide, or how escape, or who would protect them? "I will protect you," said the Queen; "fear you nothing!" She made her way into the palace, donned tiara and robes of sovereignty, took scepter in hand, and went to the gate where by that time the mob had gathered; then had that thrown open, and herself discovered in the entrance. Very queenlike, with a gesture she commanded silence, and was obeyed; then spoke to her people. Took them into her confidence; called them her children, and they felt that they were so; spoke of their late king as if he were present, and expected much of them; spoke of their king who was to be, whom she bore beneath her breast. . . . Thieves and men of trades still viler hung their heads; women you would have called she-devils were brought to wholesome weeping; when she dismissed them, they went in silence. What was with her that evening, to make her greater than herself? Driven to the place where hope is not, she had attained that divine confidence which hope only promises and strives after. She had no need of hope, possessing the internal reality.

A great storm raged in the night; in the morning she found the palace deserted, but for two of her tiring-women whom she had brought with her from her mountain home. She bade them robe her in her richest robes and deck her with all the insignia of royalty; not as a suppliant would she meet world-quelling Mahmud. In the Hall of Audience, at the foot of the throne, she found a third who had not deserted her: al-'Awf the dwarf, playing with cup and ball, and chattering. None knew to fathom the mind of this 'Awf: sometimes it seemed that of a child just learning to talk; sometimes he was quite the idiot; sometimes out of his simplicity wisdom flashed, so that you would have said an angel spoke through him.

The Queen would not await Mahmud there, but in the garden: whither now the three that formed her court followed her. The wind that had blown in the night had made a wreck of everything; and it was a mournful desolation beneath grey skies that she found. The ground was bestrewn with petals; the beauty of the place was gone; there was no comfort for her now with the roses. White and yellow, apricot, and carmine, the long sprays were tossed and ravished; not a bud had broken into bloom since dawn; there was no blossom anywhere. She came to her dearest bush, that ruby-hearted glory in the shadow of the cypresses; all its royalty had fallen in a beautiful rain of petals; one bud alone was left—but what a rose it would be when it bloomed! She picked it, and went up sadly to her divan in the pergola. This ominous ruin of the roses was too much; the realities that had sustained her the evening before were no longer within her vision.

Al-'Awf came hurrying to the foot of the throne; he had been peering about and chattering through the garden, full of some business of his own—or Allah's—such as no human mentality could understand. Now he appeared big with an idea: swaggering with immense importance. The Wonder of the World should take comfort, said he; behold, here was al-'Awf the Intrepid sent of heaven to protect her. Here was al-'Awf, about to ride forth and treat with his old-time gossip the son of Sabuktigin: to speak with that spawn of Sheitan on her behalf;—to command him, and roughly! Here he crowed like a cock; with what intent or meaning, who shall guess? No, no; not command; that would but put Mahmud out of spirits; in matters such as this more delicate means must be used; the Pearl of pearls must trust to the wisdom of heaven-sent al-'Awf. He would carry to Mahmud the toy Mahmud had demanded of her; let her send by him the Cup of Jamshyd; a small matter in itself, but likely to appease the rascal. . . . Here he knelt before her, and held out both hands to receive, it appeared, the rosebud she held; and she, being in no mood for his inspiration or imbecility, gave it to him, and said, "Yes; go!" If he should go to Mahmud, at least he would get a court appointment, and be well or fairly treated. He swaggered out; then, having quiet, she fell asleep.

She awoke to find the garden, brightly sunlit now, filled with resplendent guards; and before her a very kingly and warlike man all in golden armor and robes of cloth-of-gold and scarlet; fierce-visaged, but with his features softened into reverence and wonder now, so that one noted potentialities of kindliness and generosity that at other times might be hidden.

"O Royal Moon of Iran," said he, "think not I come otherwise than to render homage. It is thou who art the conqueror; thou who of thy wealth hast given me the sacred gift. . . ."

So far her eyes had been all on Mahmud of Ghazna; now she turned where he pointed, and beheld al-'Awf, robed sumptuously, standing at the Sultan's left. His mouth had been stuffed three times over since he left the garden: once with sweets, once with pearls, and once with gold; and he had been installed—as being a present to Mahmud from the Queen—chief of the court dwarfs to the mightiest sovereign in Islam.

"Let the veil be withdrawn from it, O Jewel of Dwarfhood, that the Queen may look once more on the glory of her gift, and say if Mahmud's friendship be worth such a price," said the Sultan; whereupon al-'Awf drew away the gold-cloth covering from the thing he held in his hands.

And all the resplendent guards of Mahmud, the flower of the nobles of Ghazna, fell on their faces and made obeisance. And Sultan Mahmud bowed his head and covered his eyes to shield them from the excessive glory. . . . A ruby brighter than the setting sun; a vase from whose radiant splendour delight issued out and spread over the world, and exquisite odors of musk and attar and sandalwood, and music like the singing of Israfel, like the lutany in Gabriel's heaven. In seven rings of unutterable loveliness it shone there . . . and only the crimson rose, the flower of the flowers of Iran, knew by what magic she had put forth the Cup of Jamshyd for a bloom.

• •

"The Violinist's Dream" is a quasi-historical story, purporting to tell how the city of Waldburg in central Europe was saved from the ravaging of Count Tilly (1559–1632) during the Thirty Years' War (1618–1648). It was published in the July 1916 issue of The Theosophical Path, *under the pseudonym F. McHugh Hilman.*

The Violinist's Dream

*A*mbrose, the verdurer is riding home slowly through the summer evening. Along the green drive through the bracken he rides, passing now between beeches that rise like fountains of golden-green, delicate flame into the mellow sunlight; now through wide and lovely glades where the deer will be hiding amidst the fern. He has had a long day of it, though the sun is yet three hours from its setting; and is pleasantly and placidly tired, and glad his ride is so nearly over. One more wide valley to pass, with its slow peat stream at the bottom; one more long slope up which to lead Tina, his shaggy little forest pony; and from the ridge where the yew-trees grow by the ruin, he will see the hearth-smoke of his home. And then there will be the placid evening meal; and the placid music after, with adoring and adored Matty and the little ones for his audience; and tomorrow there will be more riding through the pleasant forest, and another sweet homecoming in the evening; and many tomorrows will follow, placid and sweet and earnest. Life is altogether a beautiful thing, thinks Ambrose the verdurer;—and the more so since there is still so much to learn, so much to become.

By no means an ordinary peasant is this gentle Ambrose. He is small and slender, while the forest people tend to big bones and height; beautiful-headed, while the bulk of them are very plain; has much book-learning, where they are wholly uninstructed; and adds a careful and acquisitive intellect to his forest instincts. There is nothing coarse in his mind or build or features; you would expect to find him in the Church, not in the verdurer's cottage. And in the Church, in good sooth, you should have found him; had not Matty at a critical moment appeared on the scene.

He was born in the forest, some thirty years ago; his father, it is to be supposed a political refugee from somewhere, was a learned man, and moved in court circles before he buried his identity in the woods, and got a verdurer's post from the friendly Grand Duke. There he married a peasant woman of the country, careful, pious and undemonstrative. He died not long after; so that it was the mother who had the bringing up of Ambrose; and she did her work nobly. From her he inherits his even temperament and perseverance; from his father, refinement, a measure of idealism, love of learning, and a somewhat Italian type of physique and features. From his own past, one must suppose, come what deeper possibilities may lie in his soul.

His mother intended him for the Church; and the good monks of Saint Anselm, twenty miles away and in the heart of the forest, gave him his schooling; they found him a pupil whose diligence and quickness mastered everything. Passion, it seemed, played no part in his make-up; temptation was unknown to him; he was devoted to doing the right thing by his books and his fiddle and his fellows, as he might find it to do day by day. None ever had pain or trouble from him; the more enthusiastic of his teachers even spied in him the latency of sainthood. And then came Matty; and quietly, but with peasant firmness, Ambrose disappointed them all and married her. Ten years ago; and he has been wonderfully happy with her during those ten years—wonderfully happy.

He had no trouble in getting the verdurer's post which his father had held. The monks, in spite of their disappointment, love him dearly; and a recommendation from the abbot to the Grand Duke was enough. Thus they would still have their eyes on him; as he showed no inclination to forgo his studies, perhaps some day he would repay them for their pains. And yet, it was difficult to say; one feared to build too much on him. Did he not fall in love and marry, when a splendid churchly career seemed open to him?— and not merely churchly, we will say; but one of conquests in the things of the spirit. . . . There is something lacking in him; of which, too, he has even himself been conscious at times. —As one who possesses quarried mountains of marble and alabaster, onyx and rare porphyry, but no architect nor architectural design. . . . It is a mind with every quality—diligence, patience, the faculty of absorbing limitless knowledge—except originality and daring thought: which may come in time, or may not. In music, too, there is promise almost infinite; but no absolute guarantee of ultimate achievement. There is the faultless ear, the endless perseverance, the ever-improving technique and the love which marks genius, or something of it; but not the divine fire.

Father Victor used secretly to sigh over him in this respect, considering that in the Church neither pain nor passion would reach him, great enough to tighten the strings of his soul. Father Victor himself is a supreme musician: to hear him fiddling, the angels would have stayed their flight. He plays their wingy marches through the vastness, their victories along the brink of the abyss; the wailings of the demons vanquished: triumph unimaginable and anguish unspeakable—all the possibilities, you would say, that lie in the human soul, Father Victor can scrape out of the fiddlestrings. But then assuredly Father Victor never learned his music in a monastery; he has had a past in the great world, of which he will not speak. Once when the Grand Duke, riding through the forest, spent a night at Saint Anselm's, the abbot, knowing him for a connoisseur, prevailed on Father Victor to play for him. —"But this is marvelous, titanic!" said the High-born; "good father, you must come to court; you shall have"—and he named a fabulous sum—"yearly as Director of Music."—"Multiply your offer by three, your Highness," said Father Victor. —"I do, I will." —"And still I will not come," said Father Victor; and neither bullying nor cajolery would budge him. "But at least, who was your teacher?" said the Grand Duke, meditating a search for pupils of the same master. The monk turned pale, hesitated a moment, then brought it out bitterly and proudly:—"Sorrow," said he; "sorrow—and sin"; and flouted all etiquette by hurrying undismissed out of the presence. Several shades of emotion swept over the High-born's face: anger and offense, doubt, then reverence. "Ah," said he, "a great man, and a good. Some of these days his bones will be working miracles for you." The foresters know Father Victor for a ministering angel; the friars know him for a colossal genius with the fiddle; but neither know much of his endless penances. . . .

And yet, too, it was Father Victor alone who rejoiced—secretly—when Matty appeared and Ambrose became unshakable against a monastic career. He believed the boy had genius in him, but doubted a monastic life would ever bring it to the surface. A great love, he thought, might do something. But he was destined, as we have seen, to disappointment. He crossed the forest one day, a year after their marriage, and came upon them in the evening in their cottage, and tasted its atmosphere of quiet, excitementless content. "Bah!" thought he; "it does him no harm and will do him no good." But at least it kept him out of the Church, and one could not say what might come. He made Ambrose play, and listened sadly to the gentle, intellectual, careful music: quite perfect, it must be owned, of its kind.

Then, not without a touch of bitterness, he took the fiddle himself, and let loose heaven and hell from its strings—ah, but brought hell forth out of the deeps where it lurks, lurid, horribly beautiful and alluring, damnable and damning, so that one could feel humanity dragged down helpless, glad to be destroyed; and then with a crash brought Michael and his host upon the scenes, and their lances terrible and scathing: virtue a fearful and burning thing, brighter and more perilous, more threatening than the lightning, to burn up hell with fires swifter, lovelier and more majestic than its own. He shook out winged tragedy on the little cottage and garden; and then on the heels of tragedy, sent forth Peace, redemption, a beauty and serenity that absorbed into themselves and transmuted the whole-world-conflict and sorrow; and he himself had the aspect of an archangel homing from the eternal wars, as the last notes died away.

"Ah!" said Matty, "it was lovely, quite lovely! I don't know which I liked best, dear father: your playing or my Ambrose's."

But Ambrose knew very well; for in respect of taste, he was a musician utterly; and he was a little sad, at the time, in a wistful way; though far more glad of the beauty of the music than sad. Memory of it comes back and back to him: shines upon the horizon of his mind at any time of emotional stress. But he has no grand ambition, spiritual or worldly; and no clearly defined sense of his deficiencies. He determined—and has carried out his determination—to practice harder than ever; and study too; to travel patiently the patient, plodding path he saw in front of him; which, after all, ran through a bed of thornless roses. It is right to improve oneself, to develop one's faculties; and ah, music is beautiful, beautiful! He senses in it, especially when Father Victor plays, a far-away and radiant goal; to which, indefinitely, he hopes to come sometime by the sole path his nature indicates to him. So, without great effort or internal opposition, he has gone on doing his duty by the Grand Duke, by Matty and the children; by his books and by his music. No greed, no passion or impatience disturbs him; but his playing is still mild, forceless and uninspired.

Indeed, what should enter that little clearing in the wildwood where his home is, to change the tenor of things and stir his soul? A paddock field under the shadow of the high beeches on this side, where Tina the shaggy lives "when she is at home"; a garden, very rich in blooms scarlet and crimson, blue and purple, yellow and white; very rich, too, in its cabbage and bean-rows, the former for *sauerkraut;* in its seven skeps for the bees, and its three appletrees, all good bearers, for *apfelkuchen;* a little cottage, wood-built and fern-thatched and neat; three rosy-cheeked children, all as good as gold; a Matty, small, gentle and flaxen-haired, and rosy-cheeked too, like the blush side of the yellow apples in the garden; an Ambrose, small, black-haired and sunburnt, gentle too, and a little dreamy, and rosy-cheeked after the fashion of the russets; all bound together by unruffled affection, perfect sweet contentment: what should come in among these to hurry evolution or force to the front things hidden in the soul? Beyond the kitchen-garden, indeed, the ancient forest restores itself: there grows the great oak by the stream: hundred-branched, druidic and immemorial: beyond it are fairy-haunted stretches of bracken and heather, with here and there the silver grace of a birch. And to the left of the cottage, beyond the clearing, the dark woods begin; that may contain heaven knows what of mystery and terror. And then on the other side, between the high beeches and the oak, the land rises into rolling hills of gorse and heather, with valleys between where are bog-cotton and rushes and sweet bog-myrtle: a region again of loveliness and mysterious loveliness, through which the cart-track from the highroad runs down to the clearing. Are there no forest voices to cry in from all these quarters and be heard in the cottage and the garden? —voices, I mean other than the belling of the deer, the barking of foxes, hooting of owls or bleating of snipe and the like: spiritual voices, not laden with passion or terror, but capable through their mysterious beauty of alluring the soul into its grand warriorlike and creative moods? Ambrose at least has heard nothing of them; though perhaps he suspects that they—or something—may be there.

He has the forester's material lore, and can read all such woodland signs as eyes of the flesh may see; but for the folklore sense, he has only book-learning. He loves the forest beauty, but has not deep vision into it; sees not nearly as far as to the presiding wizard life. So now, as he rides homeward, the proud, whispering, fountainlike beeches, wherein another might hear rumors of worlds more majestically beautiful than ours, speak to him only of the things of common day; the leagues of green give him no tidings of fairyland.—

> —*What do you see, and what do you see,*
>   *That your eyes so strangely and wistfully burn?*
> —*Oh, the Seven Enchantments of Faërie!*
>   *And I, but a glade of fern.*

> —*What do you hear, and what do you hear*
>   *When the brown owl cries from the dusk in the hollow?*
> —*Infinite mystery gathering near,*
>   *And God knows what, to follow!*

> —*What do you see, and what do you see,*
>   *That you gaze so fast on the timber there?*
> —*Oh, a Druid Prince in the guise of a tree,*
>   *And the Star of Eve in his hair!*

> —*And I, I heard but the hooting owl;*
>   *And I, I saw but the beechen tree;*
> *The one was only a night-going fowl,*
>   *And timber the other, for me.*

—And for Ambrose. This evening he will tie up the carnations in the garden; perhaps, when he has supped and rested, he will hoe the bean-rows; next Friday he will ride to the monastery, and get new books to study: in particular the treatise on trigonometry that Father Sylvester promised to get him from Nuremberg. . . . So his mind runs on as Tina ambles forward.

Rumor drifts very slowly through the forest; this morning he heard from his nearest neighbor, Michael the Charcoal-burner—and fifteen miles of beech and oak, pine and heather, lie between their squattings—that there is talk of the war having drifted southward: that Simon the Tavern-keeper, a couple of leagues north on the main road, heard in Waldburg, last Saturday was three weeks, that Tilly was on the march, and the Grand Duke likely to be dragged in after all. Well, no ripple of the war has ever washed as far as into the forest. . . . 'Tis to be hoped there will be no levy of the foresters. . . . He pays little heed to the rumor; 'tis an old familiar thing one has been hearing off and on these years. . . . Best not mention it to Matty, perhaps. . . . Thank God, one lives remote from all that trouble: that the passing of an occasional Grand Ducal hunt is all that one sees of the great world, where there are sin and sorrow. —Terms, in good sooth, meaningless enough to this gentle Ambrose; since he has neither seen nor tasted either. —Out there to the right a graceful head rises above the fern, and a herd of twenty deer trots off silently into the beeches. His quick eyes catch the glow of the evening sunlight on the red body of a fox by the stream yonder in the bottom. Life is a pleasant thing, thinks Ambrose the Verdurer.

He reaches the ridge where the yew trees grow about the ruin—there is a dark tale in connection with the place, which he never has bothered to tell the children, as he never found it interesting himself—and sees the blue curl of smoke rising; he blows his horn, that presently will bring the children scampering through the wood. He has a present for them: a hedgehog he caught over in Koboldsthal this morning, and is carrying, curled up and sometimes wriggling a little, in a bag over his shoulder; it will make a fine pet for them. . . . Why doesn't he hear them shout? —Well, perhaps Matty is washing them for supper; she may have been a little late with her work today, hindered by something. . . . One may thank God for a wife so careful, and yet so loving; not like Simon the Tavern-keeper's Grethel, who is a shrew; nor like Michael Charcoal-burner's Dorothea, who is a slattern. . . . Strange that the children do not come to meet him—that he does not even hear their voices. . . . He rides on, and comes to the gate in the paddock fence. . . . *O God! . . . O God!*

He dismounts and runs forward—this white-faced, suddenly aged Ambrose. No wonder he saw the smoke; it rises from the smoldering ashes of his cottage. No; there is no hope; no answer to his cries. The flower-beds are trampled and ruined . . . and there—there are the children; and there—*O God, O my God*—is Matty.

It dawns upon his dazed mind slowly; this is the meaning of the rumors he heard: this is War. . . .

Thirty past years given to the placid and earnest performance of duty interpose themselves between him and the stroke of madness. If it is the war, then there is a duty to perform—*now;* one must have one's mind in order, must possess oneself. He begins to consider, to calculate; not heeding the tears that fall uncontrolled. How many will these fiends have been?

—A hundred, by the hoofprints, so far as an expert forester can judge. They came down by the cart track from the high road, and will have ridden on to Waldburg; taking this short cut through the forest, eighteen miles by ridable drives, in place of the thirty by the road. There are enough of them to take the town, if they can surprise it; and then—more of this devil's work. . . . How long since they started? —About an hour; on fine warhorses; that will make for speed, as against what tired Tina can do. But Tina and he know the forest, as they do not; and there are short cuts again, which will reduce the eighteen miles to ten. One can take the broad drives and ride neck or nothing for a while; then will come the time for forest wisdom and caution. To get to Waldburg well ahead of these spoilers, ravishers and murderers; to give warning; to save the lives of other wives, other little children; much more than their lives . . . *O my God, my God!* . . . No; back all that; time for that tomorrow; now for the collected mind, the fullmind, the full exercise of one's powers. It is only just possible that the work he has to do can be done. . . .

With all dispatch he gives Tina a feed and a rub-down; then mounts, and rides on for an hour with all the speed he can get from her; —strong, brave little pony, it seems she understands she is to do her best. The slayers have been going none too quickly, it appears. Twice he leaves the drive and rides through the beechwood; now he must begin to use caution. Before taking the open here, he must dismount, creep through the fern, and observe. Yes; there they are, half a mile in front. . . . Best leave Tina now, cross the drive, cut through the forest on the other side, make all speed possible running under the oaks there, and come out on the road, perhaps in front of the soldiers—since further on the drive makes a good bend which they will have to follow. Then, in the open bog and heather, he may catch a pony easily, and ride on without saddle, with better speed than tired Tina can make, anyhow. He gives her a whistling call, and takes the bridle from her, and his pistols from the holster; then kisses her nose, and bids her go home. *Home!* . . . Once more, back all that, and to action! But the tears drop continually as he goes forward.

He slips across the drive, dashes through the fern and on under the oaks. It is almost dark in there; but he can go through the forest blindfold or by night without stumbling. He comes to the fern at the wood's farther edge, and looks out again; *pest!* there they are, still a quarter-mile in front. Well, it must be risked now. Across the drive is a waste of bogland, with heather and grass intermixed; if they attempt to cross that, it will be the worse for them; but he, on one of those forest ponies he sees, dimly through the dusk, grazing out there, with luck can manage it well enough. He darts over, runs out into the heather, rounds the soft places; gives a forest call to a pony, catches it and flings Tina's bridle over its head; and is off at a good pace before a shout tells him he is seen.

A mile in front of him, across the dangerous land he is traversing, is a low line of hills, crowned with beeches; through that wood runs the road to Waldburg, and at the end of a league of it, is the town. But the drive the soldiers must follow fetches a long compass to the right; takes five miles skirting the bog before it reaches the ridge. So that with luck, and especially if they try to follow him through the bog, he will have gained a splendid start of them by the time they get to the road. And they may not divine, from the direction he is taking, that he is bound, as they are, for Waldburg; which will seem to them—if, as is probable, they only know they are on the right track for it, and not what twists and turns that track may take—to lie south and west; whereas he is going south and east. In that chase, his flight will not cause them to hurry.

His reasoning is faulty, however; he ought to guess they have a guide. Who, as it chances, knows the road and general direction of things better than he knows the peril of the bog. On his representations, then, ten men are detached from the troop for pursuit; but are hopelessly bogged before they have ridden twenty yards; and time is lost rescuing them—all but two, who are drowned. This Ambrose notes with satisfaction, and hurries on, not too quickly for proper caution; and on by the drive, now at full speed, ride the soldiers. He reaches the road a mile ahead of them, his pony still going splendidly. The cry of an owl comes floating out of the dark wood.

Infinite mystery gathering near,
And God knows what to follow.

The moon is high in heaven by now. The troopers are in full hue and cry after him; not together, but each according to the speed of his horse. After a half-mile three of them, well ahead of the rest, are too near for comfort; he takes his pistol from his belt, and listens for the time to turn and shoot. On come the hoofs behind; the foremost, he judges, will be at twenty yards behind him; the next at seventy or thereabouts; the third at a hundred. He turns in his seat, and two shots ring out together; he feels a sting at his side, and hears the rider behind fall. On and on; the pain at his side is most welcome; it helps him to keep away from the awful pain in his heart. On, and round the bend in the road; his mind is going now; he is getting giddy . . . will fall. . . .

The pony stops with a jerk; someone has caught the bridle and stopped him at full gallop; and he falls—into remarkably strong peasant arms.

—"Hey, Ambrose, lad, what's the matter? Why the speed? What—?"

—"War, Michael. . . . They come . . . two of them . . . the rest follow. Tilly's troopers, I think. . . . No time to lose . . . warn Waldburg. . . ."

He feels himself carried into the fern; hears the second trooper come up, the twang of a bowstring and the whiz of an arrow. Then huge Michael bends over him again, and says: "There, dear lad; his soul is comfortably with Satan; now to bind thy wound. . . ."

"No," gasps Ambrose; "I am safe; warn Waldburg . . . Go!"
A great and terrible music burst upon him, passing into—

The greatest Violinist of the Age awoke, in his room at the Hotel in Waldburg. It was his first visit to these parts; yesterday he had come by coach through the forest, and in the evening had given a concert at the Opera House. And he had had the grandest reception of his life; and knew that he had played as he never played before. Notably, two improvisations; which he would write down since undoubtedly they were the finest of his compositions. The first he would call *The Forest:* it was the forest, as it had revealed itself to him on his drive through it: full of wizardry, full of wonderful sunlit magic and magic of the green gloom; full of the Seven Enchantments of Faërie. It was a side of music he had never come upon till then. And the second—an inspiration also from the forest, though he could not tell how or why—he would call *Pain the Light-Bringer.* No eye in the audience had been dry as he played it; no heart but was inspired, uplifted, grandly comforted. . . .

He had been wonderfully stirred by this beautiful forest country; and that, and the music it had brought him, he supposed would account for this vivid dream . . . in which he had been at once the dream-hero, feeling the whole agony of his losses—and as it were a detached spectator, conscious of all the limitations of his own—that is to say, of the dream-hero's—mind. And the dream ended, passing from emotion into music which seemed to him, while he still slept, a reminiscence of Father Victor's playing, terrible in its beauty; but when he was awake, he knew it for his own second improvisation of the evening before. It was the passage of dire pain into peace, weakness into strength. . . .

That day the Grand Duke took him for a ride in the forest. "I want you to see this monument," said the High-born, stopping the motor before a stone cross at the roadside. "It commemorates one of our national heroes of the Thirty Years' War."
The inscription read:

HERE AMBROSE THE VERDURER DIED,
WHO SAVED WALDBURG
FROM TILLY

In the following story, a young king must sacrifice what he values most in order to enlist the aid of the gods in preserving his land from invaders. The question remains: what is it that he values the most? "The Avatar" appeared in the August 1916 issue of The Theosophical Path, *under the pseudonym* Jefferson D. Malvern.

The Avatar

*K*ing Carvan, son of Irith, had been journeying all day: on horse-back across the plain and through the forest, and now on foot up the pass that lies between Mount Wandelosse and the Beacon. By nightfall he would have been king for a night and a day; and already he was taking such a step, venturing into such regions—

As, in plain truth, had not been tempted before, except by Cian and Conan, his brothers, during the history of ten thousand years, or since the passing of Wandelosse the Mighty. For these Mountains of the Sun were inviolate, impassable, terror-haunted. They bounded the empire eastward, and had done so since the empire began. No king had been so foolhardy and ambitious as to lead armies into their fastnesses; no discoverer so enamored of the wild as to look on them with longing eyes. One knew only that beyond Mount Wandelosse, beyond the Beacon, there were vast slopes and precipices upsweeping: lonely green places, and then places craggy with granite where no greenness was; and so on and up by wave on wave of mountain, to peaks covered with eternal snow, and peaks vaster and more terrific beyond; haunts where the wolf-packs howled, heights where the ea-gles soared; desolations where presences abode that were more terrible than either;—more beneficent, perhaps, but more terrible certainly; for one can make some sort of fight against natural things, even against a wolf-pack; but gods, whether they be hostile or loving—there is no opposing them.

Human feet had, indeed, trodden this pass and these two nearest peaks; or so legend would have it, and none disbelieved. But that was ten thousand years ago: in a titanic and traditional time, long before history was written.

Wandelosse the Mighty, Father of Gods and men, it was said, after he had led the people into that land, and after he had built the great city, Karaltwen, and reigned in it a hundred years, had caused a chamber to be hewn out upon the very peak of his mountain, and a cairn to be raised over it; and having bidden his people farewell, had gone up there alone; to sleep, perchance, or to watch there through certain ages; not to die. And he would come again, it was said, singing his ancient song for victory, if ever the national need were supreme, and called for him—and if the king then reigning should know how to invoke his aid.

Such need had never arisen, until now. The history of Karaltwen recorded no grand disaster of plague or dearth; and had there been invasion at any time, it was easily repelled. This was not an ambitious or a restless people, to bring trouble on others, and so presently on themselves. But a decade ago, and their ships were on the seven seas, their scholars honored at a hundred courts; their rich dwelling in piety and peace, and even their poorest sleek with content. Ten years ago; and it seemed a Golden Age aeons distant. For there had been nine years of plague, pestilence and famine since, and one of battle, murder and sudden death; and now let the Gods ward off destruction if they would, for it was beyond the power of man. . . . With one in every three dead of the Yellow Death, and the rest feeble with hunger, what fight could be made when the blonde giants came out of the north, killing, plundering and burning everywhere? What wonder if the invading horde swept away such puny armies as could be raised to oppose them, and was already within striking distance of the sacred city?

It was at that point that the druids came to the king—not Carvan, but Cian—and bade him ride forth on to the mountain to invoke the help of Wandelosse the Mighty. It was then, for the first time in all history, that the archdruid gave up the secret of invocation that had been handed down to him, whispering it in the ear of King Cian as he mounted his horse to ride forth. And Cian the Politic, who had schemed so long and so wisely for the well-being of his people; whose reign, until the years of disaster, had been so wisely ordered, so wonderfully prosperous—had sat in his saddle for a minute, two, in thought; then called for his chief minister, and for Conan his brother and heir; had taken the golden torque of his sovereignty from his neck, and given it to Conan, saying: "You are to wear it, unless I return by tomorrow evening." He had not returned; and on the morrow, in the evening, Conan the Bold had been proclaimed king.

And in the morning, Conan too received the secret, and rode forth, wearing the torque. And he returned in the evening of the second day, solemn, even anxious of visage; and with little to say but that he would go against the invaders in the morning. He had gone against them, and fallen; and left as heir to his kingdom none but this Carvan, the youngest of the brothers: Carvan the Fool, or the Bard, as some few called him—of whom no one would expect much in such troublous times as these.

For Carvan had never looked to be king; would rather have dreaded the possibility, had it occurred to him. One or other of his brothers would marry and have children, and he would be left in peace, he thought, to dream in the forest, to watch the changes of the sky above the mountains, and fathom with childlike-soaring mind the life of the Gods who haunted them. A gentle dreamer was Carvan, for whom the wildwood flowers were more than all the glories of kingcraft; and the children of the poor dearer than cargoed ships on the sea, or fields golden with increase, or treaties of alliance with powerful kings. —It may be supposed, then, that there was consternation everywhere when news came of Conan's heroic death; what kind of help should be from Carvan the Fool? —Whose good deeds, even, betrayed the lack of an organizing mind; since he had not the wit to set others doing them, but must needs get about them secretly himself. . . . So it was whispered hopelessly in street and palace; and but for the archdruid, I think, the true succession would have been passed over; and some minister with a head for statecraft, or captain fitted for war, would have been chosen. But Hoova was old and gifted with wisdom more than worldly, and by virtue of his office had the last word. He knew Carvan well, and the ways of the Immortals better, and was as adamant: this was not the time, he said, to offend the Gods by turning from the line of Wandelosse the Mighty. So in his turn Carvan had heard the secret, and ridden forth from a despairing sullen capital, up towards the mountains of the Gods.

Over the cultivated lands, and into the forest that he loved: the shadow-world of green umbrage, shot with golden light-flecks above, and beautiful below with the dark light of a myriad bluebells in bloom. He heard the blackbird singing; he heard the noonday chanting of the thrush, and the sweet wandering shout of the cuckoo; why should he think of war and disaster, when the lyricism of these proclaimed the nearness of dear and sacred Beings; when immortality rippled over the green fern leagues, and every acorn brooded upon druid secrets of the Gods? In your hands, O Mighty Ones!—in your keeping, O Everlasting Law! And he too, was he not a quivering center of sentience, of divinity, in the midst of this ocean of delight: a soul to perceive, to know, to adore? . . .

So he came to the foot of the pass and the beginning of the hallowed region, and went forward in exceeding great joy. Here no foot had ever trodden, save those of his two brothers, and of the great God himself, in all the ages of the race. He drew deep breaths as he went; the mountain air was pure joy tingling through his being. It was, after all, no sorrow or burden, as he had thought, but a privilege, to be king—in these miserable times at least: since not otherwise might one make the momentous and sublime journey, nor confront the Immortals in their darling haunts. He remembered how Cian's face had changed when Hoova whispered the secret to him; seeming to age suddenly, and the determination with which he had struggled hoping against hope, through the last ten years, going out from it in a resigned heroic despair. He remembered how Conan's warlike features had lighted with a gleam of fierce, desperate joy; and how he, too, had ridden forth a changed man. How terrible the secret must have been, he had thought, to work changes so great on such men as Cian and Conan! And yet, how simple a thing it was, when he in his turn heard it! What had they elected to give, he wondered. An intuition told him: Cian belike had offered his kinghood, that was so infinitely dear to him: the daily planning and scheming and governance of things, which was the work and inward nourishment of his being. That was why Cian had not returned: he would not take back the gift he had offered, even though it was unaccepted. And Conan the Brave would have offered his life itself; and so had deliberately lost it yesterday on the battlefield. Tears filled Carvan's eyes, of pride in his brothers, and grief for their sorrow. Dear, heroic Conan! Kind, wise, all-ordering Cian! Why had their great gifts, their supreme sacrifice, availed nothing?

As for himself, the problem presented itself to him not as *What should he sacrifice?* but as *What did he value most?* Let him find out that, and the rest would take care of itself; to know it was what mattered; to sacrifice it would be the natural thing, and of course. The kinghood had not been enough, as from Cian who loved it; it would be an insult to the God if offered by himself, who held it at a straw's price—indeed, but for this one privilege it conferred on him, rather as a distasteful thing and a burden. Better to follow Conan, and offer his life—and with what joy—to save the women in the little homes of the land, the men toiling in the fields; to save the children of the poor from slavery and sorrow and dishonor! But death for Conan had meant an end, at least for ages, to facing the perils that he loved; it was the greatest sacrifice Conan knew how to make, and yet had not availed. Whereas for him it would mean to ride untrammeled on the winds above the tops of the forest below there; to go unforbidden where he would among these august mountains of the Gods. Ah Death, that many feared, how lovely a thing wast thou: that freed the soul of mortality and partial knowledge; that discovered to it the secrets of the pine tree and the larch tree, of golden sunlight and purple shadow, of the immense blue empyrean where the winds and lightnings sported! To have the myriad-changing and adorable universe for throne and couch and playground and workshop; to claim kindred with the Mighty Ones among the mountains, who watch and toil and revel and are not afflicted, and neither change nor pass nor die!

Carvan the Bard knew that if he gave his life, the gift would be useless. It was something, indeed, that he was very happy to possess; but it was something he would be still happier without. And the archdruid had said: *That which most thou valuest. . . .*

He was high up in the pass now, on a road that in winter would be a roaring torrent, but now made traveling sometimes difficult, but nowhere impossible. The heat of the day was over, and on the tops of the pines and the larches the sunlight fell with a golden and mellow glow. The silence of the place was altogether wonderful and lovely. On either hand steep, tree-covered banks soared up as high above him, almost, as a lark will fly from her nest; so that only occasionally, when the valley widened or the precipice was broken on this side or that, was there seeing the giant shoulder of the Beacon, purple in heather, on his left, or the giant peak of Wandelosse on his right. Now the shadow of an eagle, or a hawk, sailing far in the blue; now a glimpse of a wild goat poised aloft there on the crag head; here the hum of wild bees, the flitting of many-colored butterflies' wings, or the sudden scutter of a rabbit . . . and silence, and golden light, and the sacred spirit of the mountains. . . . What was the thing he valued most? . . . What was the thing he valued most?

The sun was near setting by the time he left the pass, and came out into the larchwoods of a high upland valley. There, as he knew, he must turn to the right, and upward through the trees; then to the right again, or westward, and out over the wild northern slopes of Wandelosse to reach the path which, according to tradition, the Father of the Race had traversed of old. Through the faery gloom of the trees he went, and over the carpet of brown needles. As the green darkness above him was broken, now and again, by a golden shaft flashing on the blue iridescence, more luminous than jewels, of a jay's wing: so his mood, that had passed into quiet awe and wonder, would be kindled momentarily by thought-flashes almost agonizing in their beauty. In the murmur of the wind in the branches, he heard the voice of the eternal silence; and his soul within him glowed lofty, august, eternal as that.

In the twilight he came out from the woods, through little trees that stood apart in the midst of the greenest of grasses, over-silvered now; and beheld immense skies westward still glorious with the shadowy flame of the sunset's afterglow. Now indeed he was in the Holiest of Holies, and his whole being cried out and quivered in ecstatic joy. He stood on the open slope of the mountain of the Immortals, drew near to the dear and awful presence of the Father of Gods and men. He went on, the path clearly and marvelously marked before him, westward still and upward, the soul in him pulsating with superhuman gladness: come to its own, knowing itself, one with the Gods, with eternal and boundless life. . . .

Himself, and not himself: an eternal glory of which he, Carvan, was but the evanescent shadow. . . .

He knew what thing he valued most: it was his soul—the Soul. . . .

The slope of Wandelosse rises very gradually at this point. There are a thousand yards or more of almost level thicket and bogland between the lip of the chasm, up which he had come, and the upward sweep of heather and granite that ends in the peak and cairn. Here and there are alders many, and sloe-bushes, and tangles of bramble with crimson sprawling limbs;

dog-roses to make autumn wistful with their scarlet and orange-colored hips; whitethorn to breathe out sweetness upon May, and to bear haws of dark flame in the midst of October's delicate yellowness and mists. From here you can see, often, the shoulder of the Beacon beyond the pass, when the peak of Wandelosse itself is quite hidden from you, either by the near thicket, or by intervening knolls and juttings on the vast mountainside itself. Through this thicket he pressed on, the way growing more and more difficult as he went; then out on to the western slope, and on and up, until long after night had come up over the wild regions eastward, and the sky was wholly strewn with mirific hosts of stars. Oh, beautiful over the mountains . . . beautiful beyond telling in God's sacred place. . . .

No, not the life, but the Soul. . . . What would it be, to be without that—to be, and be soulless? Well, that beauty existed: there was the sky, the wind, the mountains. . . .

"Son, what gift art thou prepared to give?"

"Father, I give thee what I can. Not my kinghood, since it is nothing either to me or to thee. Not my life, for I value it at nothing. Take thou my Soul. . . ."

The shadowy flame form towered up over the peak above, awful in its golden and violet beauty, into the starry vastness. . . . And Carvan the son of Irith sank down on the mountainside—asleep?

It was the next evening, as history relates, that Carvan the Mighty rode into Karaltwen. Somehow, the city went mad with joy as soon as the watchman heard his horse's hoofs, and proclaimed the news of his coming. Men swore that he had added a foot to his stature since he went out, and that his face and form shone with the light of godhood. Out he rode again the same night; out with the strangest army that ever followed leader through the city gates: just the rabble that met him in the streets, and that followed because the glory and beauty of him impelled them to follow. How they came by arms at all it were a mystery to tell. A hundred, two hundred, perhaps five hundred there were of them: the ragtag and bobtail of the place: the poor and the maimed and the halt and the blind; they heard him singing the Song of Wandelosse the Mighty, the war-song of all immortal war-songs, and followed.

And he fell upon the foe at the dawn of the morning, and singing, made slaughter of them; he himself, they say, slaying his thousands as he sang; even as none had fought and slain and sung since Wandelosse the Mighty. And the rabble that followed him, made giants by his virtue, heroes by his heroic song, were better than the tens of thousands of veterans that were against them; and they broke the blonde invaders, and scattered them; and followed them up, and broke them again and again, until in all the land there was none left of them alive. And ever as he led his men to victory, Carvan the Mighty sang the Song of Wandelosse, the song that had been forgotten through the ages; and his men, hearing him, became not as men, but as Gods battling; and it seemed to all the people that a God was their king, and that the Father of Gods and men had come into the flesh to lead them. And sweet prosperity followed upon triumph, and gentle peace and wisdom upon war; and once more it was even as it had been, according to the songs and traditions of the bards, when Wandelosse the Mighty reigned, in the ancient days and in the dawn of time.

●●●●●●●●●●●●●●●●●●●●●●●●●●●

"Red-Peach-Blossom Inlet" is the last of Morris's three Chinese tales, and one of his finest, in which Wang Tao-chen finds temporarily the abode of the sages and experiences the Taoist ideal of man's spiritual union with nature and the gods. "Red-Peach-Blossom Inlet" was published in The Theosophical Path *in October 1916, under the pseudonym Hankin Maggs. It was also printed in* The Secret Mountain and Other Tales.

Red-Peach-Blossom Inlet

W ang Tao-chen loved the ancients: that was why he was a fisherman. Modernity you might call irremediable: it was best left alone. But far out in the middle lake, when the distances were all a blue haze and the world a sapphirean vacuity, one might breathe the atmosphere of ancient peace and give oneself to the pursuit of immortality. By study of the Classics, by rest of the senses, and by cultivating a mood of universal benevolence, Wang Tao-chen proposed to become superior to time and change: a *Sennin*—an adept, immortal.

He had long since put away the desire for an official career. If, thought he, one could see a way, by taking office, to reform the administration, the case would be different. One would pass one's examinations, accept a prefecture, climb the ladder of promotion, and put one's learning and character to use. One would establish peace, of course; and presently, perhaps, achieve rewelding into one the many kingdoms into which the empire of Han had split. But unfortunately there were but two roads to success: force and fraud. And, paradoxically, they both always led to failure. As soon as you had cheated or thumped your way into office, you were marked as the prey of all other cheaters and thumpers; and had but to wait a year or two for the most expert of them to have you out, handed over to the Board of Punishments, and perchance shortened of stature by a head. The disadvantages of such a career outweighed its temptations; and Wang Tao-chen had decided it was not for him.

So he refrained from politics altogether, and transplanted his ambitions into more secret fields. Inactive, he would do well by his age; unstriving, he would attain possession of Tao. He would be peaceful in a world disposed to violence; honest where all were cheats; serene and unambitious in an age of fussy ambition. Let the spoils of office go to inferior men; for him the blue calmness of the lake, the blue emptiness above: the place that his soul should reflect and rival, and the untroubled noiseless place that reflected and rivalled heaven. —Where, too, one might go through the day unreminded that that unintelligent Li Kuang-ming, one's neighbor, had already obtained his prefecture, and was making a good thing of it; or that Fan Kao-sheng, the flashy and ostentatious, had won his *chin shih* degree, and was spoken well of by the undiscerning on all sides. Let *him* examine either of them in the Classics! . . .

Certainly there was no better occupation for the meditative than fishing. One suffered no interruption—except when the fish bit. He tolerated this vile habit of theirs for a year or two; and brought home a good catch to his wife of an evening, until such time as he had shaken off—as it seemed to him—earthly ambitions and desires. Then, when he could hear of Li's and Fan's successes with equanimity, and his own mind had grown one-pointed towards wisdom, he turned from books to pure contemplation, and became impatient even of the attentions of the fish. He would emulate the sages of old: in this respect a very simple matter. One had but to bend one's hook straight before casting it, and everything with fins and scales in Lake Taoting might wait its turn to nibble, yet shake down none of the fruits of serenity from the branches of his mind. It was an ingenious plan, and worked excellently.

You may ask, What would his wife say?—he, fortunately, had little need to consider that. He was lucky, he reflected, in the possession of such a spouse as Pu-hsi; who, though she might not tread with him his elected path, stood sentry at the hither end of it, so to say, without complaint or fuss. A meek little woman, lazily minded yet withal capable domestically, she gave him no trouble in the world; and received in return unthinking confidence and complete dependence in all material things—as you might say, a magnanimous marital affection. His home in the fishing village was a thing not to be dispensed with, certainly; nor yet much to be dwelt upon in the mind by one who sought immortality. No doubt Pu-hsi felt for him the great love and reverence which were a husband's due, and would not presume to question his actions.

True, she had once, soon after their marriage, mildly urged him to follow the course of nature and take his examinations; but a little eloquence had silenced her. In this matter of the fish, he would let it dawn on her in her own time that there would be no more, either to cook or to sell. Having realized the fact she would, of course, dutifully exert herself the more to make things go as they should. There would be neither inconvenience nor disturbance, at home.

Which things happened. One night, however, she examined his tackle and discovered the unbent hook; and meditated over it for months. Then a great desire for fish came over her; and she rose up while he slept and bent the hook back to its proper shape with care, and baited it; and went to sleep again, hoping for the best.

Wang Tao-chen never noticed it; perhaps because, as he was gathering up his tackle to set out, a neighbor came to the door and borrowed a net from him, promising to return it that same evening. It was an interruption which Wang resented inwardly; and the resentment made him careless, I suppose. He was far out on the lake, and had thrown his line, before composure quite came back to him; and it had hardly come when there was a bite to frighten it away again,—and such a bite as might not be ignored. Away went the fish, and Wang Tao-chen after it: speeding over the water so swiftly that he had no thought even to drop the rod. Away and away, breathless, until noon; then suddenly the boat stopped and the line hung loose. He drew it in, and found the baited hook untouched; and fell to pondering on the meaning of it all. . . .

He had come into a region unknown to him, lovelier than any he had visited before. He had left the middle lake far behind, and was in the shadow of lofty hills. The water, all rippleless, mirrored the beauty of the mountains; and inshore, here reeds greener than jade, there hibiscus splendid with bloom. High up among the pines a little blue-tiled temple glowed in the magical air. Above the bluff yonder, over whose steep sheer face little pinetrees hung jutting half-way between earth and heaven, delicate feathers of cloud, bright as polished silver, floated in a sky bluer than glazed porcelain. From the woods on the hill-sides came birdsong strangely and magically sweet. Wang Tao-chen, listening, felt a quickening of the life within him: the rising of a calm sacred quality of life, as if he had breathed airs laden with immortality from the Garden of Siwangmu in the western world. Shore and water seemed bathed in a light at once more vivid and more tranquil than any that shone in familiar regions.

Quickening influences in the place stirred him to curiosity, to action; and he took his oar and began to row. He passed round the bluff and into the bay beyond; and as he went, felt himself drawing nearer to the heart of beauty and holiness. A high pine-clad island stood in the mouth of the bay; so that, unless close in shore, you might easily pass the latter undiscovered. Within—between the island and the hills, the whole being of him rose up into poetry and peace. The air he breathed was keenness of delight, keenness of perception. The pines on the high hills on either side blushed into deep and exquisite green. Blue long-tailed birds like fiery jewels flitted among the trees and out from the boscage over the bay; the water, clear as a diamond, glassed the wizardry of the hills and pines and the sweet sky with its drifting delicacy of cloudlets; glassed, too, the wonder of the lower slopes where, and in the valley-bottom, glowed an innumerable multitude of peach-trees, red-blossomed, and now all lovely like soft clouds of sunset with bloom.

He rowed shoreward, and on under the shadow of the faery peach-trees, and came into a narrow inlet, deep-watered, that seemed the path for him into bliss and the secret places of wonder. The petals fell about him in a slow roseate rain; even in midstream, looking upward, one could see but inches and glimpses of interstitial blueness. He went on until a winding of the inlet brought him into the open valley: to a thinning of the trees,—a house beside the water,—and then another and another: into the midst of a scattered village and among a mild, august and kindly people, unlike, in fashion of garb and speech, any whom he had seen—any, he would have said, that had lived among the Hills of Han* these many hundred years.

They had an air of radiant placidity, passionless joy and benevolence, lofty and calm thought. They appeared to have expected his coming: greeted him majestically, but with affability; showed him, presently, a house in which, they said, he might live as long as he chose. They had no news, he found, of the doings in any of the contemporary kingdoms, and were not interested; they were without politics entirely; wars nor rumors of wars disturbed them. Here, thought Wang, he would abide for ever; such things were not to be found elsewhere. In this lofty peace he would grow wise: would blossom, naturally as a flower, but into immortality. They let fall, while talking to him, sentences strangely illuminating—yet strangely tantalizing too, as it seemed to him: one felt stupendous wisdom concealed—saw a gleam of it, or as it were a corner trailing away; and missed the satisfaction of its wholeness. This in itself was supreme incitement; in time one would learn and penetrate all. Of course he would remain with them forever; he would supply them with fish in gratitude for their hospitality. Falling asleep that night, he knew that none of his days had been flawless until that day—until the latter part of it, at least. . . .

The bloom fell from the trees; the young fruit formed, and slowly ripened in a sunlight more caressing than any in the world of men. With their ripening, the air of the valley became more wonderful, more quickening and inspiring daily. When the first dark blush appeared on the yellow-green of the peaches, Wang Tao-chen walked weightless, breathed joy, was as one who has heard tidings glorious and never expected. Transcendent thoughts had been rising in him continually since first he came into the valley; now, his mind became like clear night-skies among the stars of which luminous dragons sail always, liquid, gleaming, light-shedding, beautiful. By his door grew a tree whose writhing branches overhung a pool of golden carp; as he came out one morning, he saw the first of the ripe peaches drop shin-

*i.e. in China.

ing from its bough, and fall into the water; diffusing the sweetness of its scent on the diamond light of the young day. Silently worshipping heaven, he picked up the floating peach, and raised it to his mouth. As he did so he heard the leisurely tread of oxhoofs on the road above: it would be his neighbor So-and-so, who rode his ox down to drink at the inlet at that time each morning. (Strange that he should have learnt none of the names of the villagers; that he should never, until now, have thought of them as bearing names.) As the taste of the peach fell on his palate, he looked up, and saw the Ox-rider . . . and fell down and made obeisance; for it was Laotse the Master, who had ridden his ox out of the world, and into the Western Heaven, some seven or eight hundred years before.

Forthwith and thenceforward the place was all new to him, and a thousand times more wonderful. What had seemed to him cottages were lovely pagodas of jade and porcelain, the sunlight reflected from their glaze of transparent azure or orange or vermilion, of luminous yellow or purple or green. Through the shining skies of noon or evening you might often see lordly dragons floating: golden and gleaming dragons; or that shed a violet luminance from their wings; or whose hue was the essence from which blue heaven drew its blueness; or white dragons whose passing was like the shooting of a star. As for his neighbors, he knew them now for the Mighty of old time: the men made one with Tao, who soared upon the Lonely Crane; the men who had eaten the Peaches of Immortality. There dwelt the founders of dynasties vanished millennia since: Men-Dragons and Divine Rulers: the Heaven-Kings and the Earth-Kings and the Man-Kings: all the figures who emerge in dim radiance out of the golden haze on the horizon of Chinese prehistory, and shine there quaintly wonderful. Their bodies emitted a heavenly light; the tones of their voices were an exquisite music; for their amusement they would harden snow into silver, or change the nature of the cinnabar until it became yellow gold. And sometimes they would bridle the flying dragon, and visit the Fortunate Isles of the Morning; and sometimes they would mount upon the hoary crane, and soaring through the empyrean, come into the Enchanted Gardens of the West: where Siwangmu is Queen of the Evening, and whence her birds of azure plumage fly and sing unseen over the world, and their singing is the love, the peace, and the immortal thoughts of mankind. Visibly those wonder-birds flew through Red-Peach-Blossom Inlet Valley; and lighted down there; and were fed with celestial food by the villagers, that their beneficent power might be increased when they went forth among men.

Seven years Wang Tao-chen dwelt there: enjoying the divine companionship of the sages, hearing the divine philosophy from their lips: until his mind became clarified to the clear brightness of the diamond; and his perceptions serenely overspread the past, the present and the future; and his thoughts, even the most commonplace of them, were more luminously lovely than the inspirations of the supreme poets. Then one morning while he was fishing his boat drifted out into the bay, and beyond the island into the open lake.

And he fell to comparing his life in the valley with his life as it might be in the outer world. Among mortals, he considered, with the knowledge he had won, he would be as a herdsman with his herd. He might reach any pinnacle of power; he might reunite the world, and inaugurate an age more glorious than that of Han. . . . But here among these Mighty and Wise Ones, he would always be. —Well; was it not true that they must look down on him? He remembered Pu-hsi, the forgotten during all these years; and thought how astounded she would be,—how she would worship him more than ever, returning, so changed, after so long an absence. It would be nothing to row across the lake and see; and return the next day—or when the world of men bored him. He landed at the familiar quay in the evening, and went up with his catch to his house.

But Pu-hsi showed no surprise at seeing him, nor any rapturous satisfaction until she saw the fish. It was a cold shock to him; but he hid his feelings. To his question as to how she had employed her time during his absence, she answered that the day had been as other days. There was embarrassment, even guilt, in her voice, if he had noticed it. "The day?" said he; "the seven years!"—and her embarrassment was covered away with surprise and uncomprehension. But here the neighbor came to the door, "to return the net" he said "that he had borrowed in the morning;"—the net Wang Tao-chen had lent him before he went away. And to impart a piece of gossip, it seemed: "I hear" said he "that Ping Yang-hsi and Po Lo-hsien are setting forth for the provincial capital to-morrow, to take their examination." Wang Tao-chen gasped. "They should have passed," he began; and bit off the sentence there, leaving "seven years ago" unsaid. Here were mysteries indeed.

He made cautious inquiries as to the events of this year and last; and the answers still further set his head spinning. He had only been away a day: everything confirmed that. Had he dreamed the whole seven years then? By all the glory of which they were compact; by the immortal energy he felt in his spirit and veins; *no!* He would prove their truth to himself; and he would prove himself to the world! He announced that he too would take the examination.

He did; and left all competitors to marvel: passed so brilliantly that all Tsin was talking about it; and returned to find that his wife had fled with a lover. That was not likely to trouble him much: he had lived forgetting her for seven years. But she, at least, should repent: she should learn what a Great One she had deserted. Without delay he took examination after examination; and before the year was out was hailed as the most brilliant of rising stars. Promotion followed promotion, till the Son of Heaven called him to be prime minister. At every success he laughed to himself: he was proving to himself that he had lived with the Immortals. His fame spread through all the kingdoms of China; he was courted by the emissaries of many powerful kings. Yet nothing would content him: he must prove his grand memory still further; so he went feeding his ambition with greater and greater triumphs. Heading the army, he inflicted disaster upon the Huns, and imposed his will on the west and north. The time was almost at hand, people said, when the Black-haired People should be one again, under the founder of a new and most mighty dynasty.

And still he was dissatisfied: he found no companionship in his greatness: no one whom he loved or trusted, none to give him trust or love. His emperor was but a puppet in his hands, down to whose level he must painfully diminish his inward stature; his wife—the emperor's daughter—flattered and feared, and withal despised him. The world sang his praises and plotted his downfall busily; he discovered the plots, punished the plotters, and filled the world with his splendid activities. And all the while a voice was crying in his heart: *In Red-Peach-Blossom-Inlet Valley you had peace, companionship, joy!*

Twenty years passed, and his star still rose: it was whispered that he was certainly no common mortal, but a genie, or a *Sennin,* possessor of Tao. For he grew no older as the years went by, but still had the semblance of young manhood, as on the day he returned from the Valley. And now the Son of Heaven was dying, and there was no heir to the throne but a sickly and vicious boy; and it was thought everywhere that the great Wang Tao-chen would assume the Yellow. The dynasty had exhausted the mandate of heaven.

It was night; and he sat alone; and home sickness weighed upon his soul. He had just dismissed the great court functionaries, the ministers and ambassadors, who had come to offer him the throne. The people were everywhere crying out for reunion, an end of dissensions, and the revival of the ancient glories of Han: and who but Wang Tao-chen could bring these things to pass? He had dismissed the courtiers, promising an answer in the morning. He knew that not one of them had spoken from his heart sincerely, nor voiced his own desire; but had come deeming it politic to anticipate the inevitable. For alas! in all the world there was none who was his equal. . . . Of these that had pressed upon him sovereignty especially, there was none to whom he could speak his mind—none with the greatness to understand. He saw polite enmity and fear under their bland expressions, and heard it beneath their courtly phrases of flattery. To be Son of Heaven—among such courtiers as these!

But in Red-Peach-Blossom-Inlet Valley one might talk daily with the Old Philosopher* and with Such-a-One; with the Duke of Chow and with Muh Wang and Tang the Completer; with the Royal Lady of the West;

*Laotse and Confucius.

with Yao, Shun and Ta Yü themselves, those stainless Sovereigns of the Golden Age;—ah! with Fu-hsi the Man-Dragon Emperor and his seven Dragon Ministers; with the August Monarchs of the three August Periods of the world-dawn: the Heaven-Kings and the Earth-Kings and the Man-Kings. . . .

He did off his robes of state, and donned an old fisherman's costume which he had never had the heart to part with; and slipped away from his palace and from the capital; and set his face westward towards the shores of Lake Tao-ting. He would get a boat, and put off on the lake, and come to Red-Peach-Blossom-Inlet Valley again; and consult with Fu-hsi and the Yellow Emperor as to this wearing of the Yellow Robe,—as to whether it was Their will that he, the incompetent Wang Tao-chen, should dare to mount Their throne. But when he had come to his native village, and bought a boat and fishing-tackle, and put forth on the lake in the early morning, his purpose had changed: never, never, never would he leave the company of the Immortals again. Let kinghood go where it would; he would dwell with the Mighty and Wise of old time, humbly glad to be the least of their servants. He had won a name for himself in history; *They* would not wholly look down on him now. And he knew that his life in that bliss would be forever: he had eaten of the Peaches of Immortality, and could not die. He wept at the blue lonely beauty of the middle lake when he came to it; he was so near now to all that he desired. . . .

In due time he came to the far shore; and to one bluff after another that he thought he recognized; but rounding it, found no island, no bay, no glazed-tile roofed temples, no grove of red-bloomed peaches. The place must be farther on . . . and farther on. . . . Sometimes there would be an island, but not *the* island; sometimes a bay, but not *the* bay; sometimes an island and a bay that would pass, and even peach-trees; but there was no inlet running in beneath the trees, with quiet waters lovely with a rain of petals—least of all that old divine red rain. Then he remembered the great fish that had drawn him into that sacred vicinity; and threw his line, fixing his hopes on that . . . fixing his desperate hopes on that.

All of which happened some sixteen hundred years ago. Yet still sometimes, they say, the fishermen on Lake Tao-ting, in the shadowy hours of evening, or when night has overtaken them far out on the waters, will hear a whisper near at hand: a whisper out of vacuity, from no boat visible: a breathless despairing whisper: *It was here . . . surely it must have been here!* *. . . No, no; it was yonder!* And sometimes it is given to some few of them to see an old, crazy boat, mouldering away—one would say the merest skeleton or ghost of a boat dead ages since, but still by some magic kept floating; and in it a man dressed in the rags of an ancient costume, on whose still young face is to be seen unearthly longing and immortal sadness, and an unutterable despair that persists in hoping. His line is thrown; he goes by swiftly, straining terrible eyes on the water, and whispering always: *It was here; surely it was here.* . . . *No, no; it was yonder* . . . *it must have been yonder.* . . .

•••••••••••••••••••••••••••

Another of Morris's finest tales, "The Saint and the Forest-Gods" emphasizes man's spiritual affinities with nature. It was published in the January 1917 issue of The Theosophical Path, *under the pseudonym Evan Snowdon. Morris also reprinted it in* The Secret Mountain and Other Tales.

The Saint and the Forest-Gods

Nanrossa Tower is far and far in the wilderness; you should journey hundreds of miles from it in any direction before you came to cultivated land. And then only to forest villages, with their few acres of tilled clearing: mere islands on the great sea of trees or heather, and all governed by Forest Law, and subject to the Court Leet of the Verderors. Dear knows what law or ruling might hold between Nanrossa and the farther bounds of the mountain region Finismond westward: none human, certainly. None human, either, eastward thence over the Bog of Elfinmere, where no man comes; and whose writ shall run among coot and bittern and waterhen? Five hundred miles of reedy lakes, with here and there an eyot— aldered for the most part, but the larger of them oak-grown sometimes; leagues on leagues of mossland, emerald green or bronze or golden, and utterly treacherous to the footsole; yellow irises and quietude and the darting of the dragonfly; long desolations of black quagmire; pleasant places for the crane and the heron; rush-rimmed pools for the frog's diving, the waterfly's sliding, the glassing of heaven and its blueness and wandering clouds: this, and solitude for five hundred miles, and the silence of all human voices; lay eastward from Nanrossa, on the Babylon side, before you should come to any abode of man, or indeed, habitable region.

The tower stands high on its crag; yet before Saint Cilian came there I doubt if human eyes had lighted on it since ancient and forgotten times;— since the Soldan's Son of Babylon rode by there, for example, when he quested Mirath Grief-of-Hearts and the enchantment that withered the world; or at least since Varglon Fflamlas came there seeking the Secret

Mountain of the Gods. From the face of the marsh one might see it; but from nowhere, I think, on the floor of the forest; by reason of the roofage of verdure or thick fretwork of winter tree-tops overhead, even on the highest of the hills; open glades there are none in those parts. To the heron, flying eastward from his high nest to his hunting-ground in the marsh, it would be the landmark of landmarks; but if any forester were to stray or venture so deep into the haunts of wizardry, he might pass right under it without dreaming of its nearness. But then, none ever did come into the Hills of Nanrossa; you are not to suppose it for an instant. There are places where human beings do not go; or so rarely that it is the same thing.

Sheer fell the crag two hundred feet from the bases of the tower down into the Gap of Nanrossa; through which, you will remember, ran the Old Road to Camelot; the stones wherewith the Giants of the elder world had paved it for King Arthur long since covered deep in green turf. The Gap itself is not so wide but that one might shoot an arrow from the tower to the hill-side opposite; and the great tide of the forest, that covers all these hills, flows down through it to the very edge of the bogland, a quarter mile beyond; so that from the tower one sees nothing of the road, but only the rustling billows of leafage below, or in winter the bare purple-brown tops of the beeches and oaks. As for the Old Road, it goes right through Elfin-mere; there, too, in places feet below the surface: which partly accounts for the fewness of the men who have come into the forest from Babylon, in these last two or three hundred thousand years.

But if men be few in those parts, of Immortals, why, there be lords many and gods many certainly. For this is all a very magical region; and you should hear, if you have the ears or the gift for it, strange windings of the horn, by day and night, among the wooded Hills of Nanrossa; you should feel at noonday the passage of serene presences among the great trees; and see at twilight, perhaps, shadowy flame-forms of azure and purple nim-bused marvellously passing a-gleam over shining meres in the marshland, setting a hush and quiver of adoration on reeds and rushes and alder-leaves. Or you might see wondrous beings, breathless, intent, beautiful, when dawn like a shining kingcup bloomed out of radiant soft mists of iris-grey and lavender: Gods of the marshes, wide-eyed and meditative; or again, you might see among the trees the little Rain-Gods of the forest, that go hurry-ing away for ever quietly over the gracious dripping fern and the dark greenness of the hollies. Always, if you were gifted for the seeing, of course! For these Nanrossa Hills and this Bog of Elfinmere are, I think, the very archeus of all woodland God-dom; and therefore it is but fitting they should be shunned and feared by men. I cast about in my mind, and can think of no other part of the forest, so far as I have explored it, so thronged with the strange Masters of Woodland Beauty. Finismond is terrible; and the Mountains of the Dwarfs are wild and weird too, and will keep in your memory, once you have seen them, through perhaps a score of lives; and all the country round Mirath's Tower is very famous for the things of light and shadow and the wandering sparks or stars that whirl in dance through the dusk; but give me Nanrossa Hills for the Gods of the Forest . . . who keep their chosen places secret and sacred at all times, tempting no discoverers, offering no lure to trade, but to remain a blank on all maps—until the Gods desire to leave them in quest of new lands that have been prepared.

Who built Nanrossa Tower? That same vanished race, I think, that made the Old Road for Arthur between Camelot his city and foreign Babylon: giants or dwarfs that held the forest of old time, before the Gods came into Nanrossa and made the hills and marshes their own. There at any rate Saint Cilian found it, when driven by faith he journeyed out of the Great City to that (to him) westward far rim of the world; there, I think, you should find it now. But to go back to my saint: in his days Camelot was the merest tradition in Babylon, and perhaps even that only with the most superstitious. So westward towards nothing, towards the end of things, seven years Saint Cilian journeyed, seeking a site for supreme spiritual adventures; until at last there between the hills and the mere he knew he had come into the realm he sought.

I cannot say how or why the unseen guardians of the place—I do not mean the Gods—came to let him pass. Certainly his faith was transcendent—and unselfish, as you shall hear; perhaps there was a quality in it that disarmed or even appealed to them. At any rate he found the tower, and found it weather-tight and habitable, as it is (I doubt not) to this day. Three storeys, and a stone staircase within: first, a room like a cave, half underground, with a kind of hearth and opening in the wall for a flue on the western side; no casements here, but all the light through the doorless doorway on the south. Here one could make one's fire, do such cooking and eating as might be necessary, live during the daytime (on wet days), and entertain stray wanderers should any chance to seek shelter in passing. Above, and reachable by the uneven staircase built out from the wall in the lower room, a cell-like bare chamber where one might lay one's bedding of dry bracken; a trap-door over the opening by which one entered secured one by night from over-lusty visitations of the wind, and from such prowling things as can climb stairs; there were no casements here again, but light—such as it was—from the stair-opening into the floor above. For there, in that topmost room, was light in plenty: the peak of the sloped in-curving roof was all a vast crystal, and the walls were open to the winds, a matter of pillars and arches. One could look forth thence over half a hundred miles of the marsh or the whole length of the great range of forest hills: it was the chamber of chambers for Saint Cilian's devotions, as you shall hear; and for them, and for them only, he used it.

They were by no means of a common kind; nor had been at any time since he came to Nanrossa to fight the battles of the Lord. He was a young man then: too nervously high-strung, and his heart all in the other-world.

There had been kindly women-folk about him at home: a mother who fain would have persuaded him to do his battling in Babylon—as if that were possible; a young wife who watched his inward unpeace with agonized anxiety; gentle sisters, Muriel, Elaine and Rosemary. There were strong forbearing brothers also: tall Philibert, Vanfred and Egan: soldiers the two younger, and the eldest a merchant; all three, very kindly and patiently, trying to win him into the unillumined, or as they said into the *sane* walks of life. All in vain! Nothing would serve Cilian but sainthood; which, heaven knew (or Cilian did), was not to be won in Babylon. In that rose-hued gorgeous opulence of shame and glory there was no peace to fight the battles of the Lord; you must have loneliness and the desert where the demons are. You must look deeper for the root of evil than in mere human sins and splendors: *Good and Evil* was as much as to say *Churchdom and Pagandom.* Here were the saints and angels of the one; there, the Gods—say devils—of the other: which were, thought young Cilian, the two eternal elements in the Battles of the Lord; and therefore would he seek out the Gods of the pagan in their own haunts, and in the name of Monotheos blast and wither them with daily curses. By multiplied anathema he doubted not—possessing faith to shame any grain of self-respecting mustard-seed, —either to make existence much too hot for them, or else to drive them penitent into the folds of the Church. Then would the Lord have triumphed for ever; sin would wilt upon its broken stalk; and humanity, by no effort of its own so to say, would be irretrievably redeemed. I declare to you that such was Saint Cilian's idea when he set forth from the great city, and when he came at length to my Nanrossa Hills and Tower, and went to work.

Every dawn would find him in that topmost chamber, his face turned eastward towards the marsh, busily cursing the Gods whose homes were in Elfinmere; every sunset would find him there, facing the splendor or quietude above the hills, and fulminating wrathful hot comminations against the Masters of the Forest's Beauty. At first it produced a mighty eloquence in him, such as none nowadays might hope to rival. The words leaped from his lips lurid and blasting; it was at least a year before any squirrel within earshot became used to it, and unafraid. A terrible time, one would think, for the poor deities; and a marvel that any one of them should have survived a month of it; since the Church knew no dreadful formula but Saint Cilian rolled it forth twice daily, all in that rich, turgid, bristling "Babylonish dialect" of the priestly hierarchy which is so effective in such cases; and besides these he had a many, and choicely bloodcurdling ones, of his own. It should have been fearfully effective, you would say; but the truth is the Gods have much business to attend to; and their ears, I take it, are not attuned to all kinds of hearing. It was forty years before they discovered him at all.

Forty years of Their sweet rain and sunshine and mists, Their nights starry or storm-ridden; forty years of wandering in the hallowed places, seeking whinberries and wortleberries, cranberries and blackberries and mushrooms, or gathering bracken for his bed, or fallen boughs for his firing; or of paddling on the mere in his hollowed log, or wading after eels; forty years of silence (save for the daily anathematizing), and of solitude (save for the wild things of the forest): had wrought a deal of change in Saint Cilian. He was no longer the sickly neuropath, but physically strong and wholesome; the Church was separated from him by infinite horizons; churchly bitterness had grown quite dim in him; the daily cursings had become mechanical. Had you listened, you should have heard the words jumbled not a little, one stumbling against the other: faith no longer prompted them, but mindless habit. Indeed, thought (or what commonly goes by the name) was coming to be silenced in him entirely, and giving place to the moods we share with the Mighty Mother. Slowly the forest influences penetrated him; slowly the wonder of the sky, the mystery of the marshland, sunk into his being. The murmur of the trees wrought in him more than peace; when the evenings of August brooded golden over the beech-tops he heard the Ancient breathing amidst the hills. When the faint rose dawns of winter blushed over the dim whiteness of mists and snows, he knew what wizard divinity broods pondering over the faint world. He forgot the battles of the Lord, and came instead into that "which passeth all understanding"; the acridity of religion, transmuted, had become in him kindliness and wonder. The wounded wolf would limp into his day-chamber, and he would tend it and heal its wounds; the rabbits would patter in, in the quiet of the evening, creep on to his knees or under his hands, and nestle against him as he sat before his fire; and they would watch the flame or red glow without fear, and nourish upon his silent friendliness heaven knows what dim rabbitish cogitations, as though they had been children listening to fairytales from him. The squirrels he had frightened so at first, now might be found at any time a-perch upon his shoulder. The shyest of fawns would walk beside him in the woods, his arm caressingly about the neck of her; the great red stag, coming upon him brooding among the many mossy roots of a beechtree, would nuzzle him, appealing to be stroked, or to have its splendid head patted or scratched. Even the wild boar would take crab-apples friendlily from his hand; and the mother beasts would bring their young about him, and be quite untroubled when he picked up the little ones to pet them. He had become clean, whole and natural; wholesome part and parcel of the life of the forest and the mere.

Then at last, when all religious taint had gone from him, and he knew no emotion but forest wonder and worship and love, the Gods became aware of his existence. Borion of the Golden Flame, who rides westward over the marshes at daybreak, heard his voice at the jargoned cursing in Nanrossa Tower, and stopped and looked curiously at him: "A saint, to judge by crucifix and rosary," mused Borion; "and yet—" Then at last, when Cilian went up to the high ridge to gather cones, Phenit Fireheart, the Fir-God, saw him—walking side by side with a wild sow, and cooing and chuckling very amicably to her piglings. Then at last wise Darron the Aged discovered him—asleep one summer afternoon under the oaks of Darron's own inmost and holiest grove; Cilian must have dozed or meditated there a thousand times before, but this was the first the Oak-God had seen of him. And Taimaz the Dew-Queen became aware of him, among the bracken on the margin of the marsh; and far out on the mere, Gwernlas, Lady of the Alders, learnt to discern his presence as he paddled his log among her islands, fishing, or as he waded in the shallow places after the eels;—and for the Gods to be aware of a man, is for the Gods to love him, as I guess. And from these the rumor went up to the council of the Major Deities that there was one in the forest, not immortal of race as they were; that spoke, when he spoke at all—at daybreak and sunset—in a tongue incomprehensible even to those Gods who knew all human languages;— one whose cross and beads proclaimed him a saint, but who was quite harmless and fit for the forest nonetheless.

Thereafter word went forth that note should be taken of this strange Saint Cilian, and a measure of inspiration lent him. So divine visitants sometimes would gather and listen whilst he cursed them: they would hover unseen about the tower as he launched his jumbled anathemas, and guess at his meaning:—they were of course but local and lesser deities: the Masters of the Stars were otherwhere. "It is clear that he prays not for his own salvation," they said, "or he would have polluted the forest before now." They perceived that he desired the good of the world, after his fashion; and therefore that he was on their side with them. "This is a marvellous thing in a saint," they said.

And at such times Saint Cilian, for his part, would feel a wonderful glow in his heart. The air about him would dance and be like diamonds with joy and quickened life; he felt vaguely that he had done great things for the Lord and for man. Language was becoming an unfamiliar thing to him now: had a human being met him in the forest, Saint Cilian would scarcely have found words wherewith to greet or answer him: would probably have cooed and grunted and chuckled, as he did to the fawns and piglings, thereby pouring out, as well as he was able, the good will, the delight and affection, he held for all living and visible things. . . .

"He even helps us in our work," said the Gods. "He understands the great language: the sky and the winds and the waters communicate with him: and thus in his way he is a link between us and the human race to which he belongs."

So now, after fifty, after sixty years of it, Saint Cilian felt the Holy Presences about him always on his wanderings. He considered, in an undefined sort of way, that the angels of God were passing amongst the ancient trees: that heavenly messengers went by him, whispering the mysteries of the kingdom, as he paddled his log on the waters. He went to his devotions with new avidity: using the wreckage of churchly anathema for words, but pouring out through it worship of the beautiful, desire for the salvation of the world—for the Forest-Spirit, that nourished the un-selfconscious God in him, to make conquests where men congregate, to become present, potent, dominant, in the thoughts of men. . . .

Seventy years passed, and he was a very old man: driving on his hundred, and failing. Borion, riding up out of the east at dawn, often heard no pleasant imprecations as he passed the tower; Gwernlas Alder-Queen missed him in the marsh; Phenit looked for him in vain in the fir-woods, except rarely. Then came a terrible winter; and old Saint Cilian found it too much even to crawl up to his bedchamber at nightfall, there to spend the dark hours shivering and coughing; much less could he mount higher to curse. But he was beyond being troubled, now, by these temporal things.

He would fall asleep before his fire; day and night alike he would sit there nodding; waking a little and sleeping again; always adream. Beasts with shaggy coats would come in, stand over him and nestle against him, lick his face and hands, doing their utmost to keep him from the cold and wind. Not even the bright fire on the hearth scared them; and their predatory instincts slept in his presence. You might have seen at the same time, wolf acting as couch for him, and fallow deer as screen to shelter him from the draught.

But how was it that the fire was always burning: what unseen hands replenished it day and night with logs? And how was it that the little store of beans and dried vegetables from his garden, and honey from his skeps, never gave out; that the stone flags of his day-chamber were thickly carpeted always with dry bracken and pine-needles; that there was always food and drink ready to his hand when he needed it? He did not know; it never appeared to him to call for surprise.

It was night; outside, below and on the hill-tops, the trees were frantic billows tossing on the wind; great branches, and often giant trunks and all, went crashing to the ground; thick snow was whirling on the maniac storm. Saint Cilian nodded and dreamed. He was ill . . . or he had been ill, and was now recovering . . . was in that stage of recovery when one makes no effort, thinks of nothing, but lies back and enjoys painless ease: one's body light as the air, one's mind content with vacuity. "Mother," says he, "how soft the bed is." "Yes, my darling," she answers; and lays the hand of cool peace on his brow. "Ah, and there art thou, my Mary; I thought—I dreamed—" It is the young wife that has his hand in hers. And there in the gloom and flicker he sees Muriel and Elaine and Rosemary; and tall Philibert and Vanfred and Egan his brothers: all their faces full of care and kindliness and love. He smiled at each of them, wonderfully happy to have them about him. "I thought—I dreamed—" he began; "it seems such ages since—" "Hush, hush!" they murmur; "thou wilt be well anon, dear one!"

He lies in great peace and ease, watching the flame leap and flicker and cast its light on their beautiful faces . . . that change as he watches them, growing more beautiful, more august, and still more kindly. . . . Suddenly he raises himself up, triumph shining out upon his face. "Ah, no!" he whispers; "that was a dream . . . a dream of very long ago; and I am an old man . . . and I am dying; and ye are . . . ah, Beautiful and Gracious Ones, ye are the Angels of the Lord!"

The flame died on the hearth, quite suddenly; and with it, all warmth and glow out of the ashes. The rabbit that had been nestling at his bosom leaped down from him and scuttered away with little runs and pauses into the night of storms. The old she-wolf on whose shaggy side he had been pillowed, rose, sniffed at the fallen corpse, howled dismally, and trotted out. The stag, whose body had been sheltering him from the wind, had made a dash for the safety of the out-of-doors already.

But Phenit Fireheart, and Darron Hên, and Borion of the Golden Flame, and the Dew-Queen and the Lady of the Alders and their companions, went out upon their rainbow path from the silence of the tower, through the radiance of their own world beyond the darkness and the tempest. "Poor little child-soul of a saint!" they said; "he was wonderfully harmless and kindly. . . ."

In *"A Mermaid's Tragedy,"* Morris presents the fascinating perspective of a non-human on the behavior of human counterparts. This story was published in The Theosophical Path *in February 1917, under the pseudonym* Vernon Lloyd-Griffiths.

A Mermaid's Tragedy

*U*nder vast skies from which the sun had just departed, and into which night with her pomp of stars had not yet come, the Atlantic, dreaming, lolled and heaved. Bars of liquid gold still streaked the west, and flickered shiftingly on the unstable gray and foxglove-tinted sea-face. Twilight was dying, and up the estuary of the Lonno the blue and dimness and violet of the world were passing into the somber glory of night.

Rarely shall you find such quiet on the sea. About the bases of the vast crag of Penmorvran, where the waves so incessantly whiten and bloom, was a slumberous motion of waters. The tide was high: almost high enough to cover the Mermaids' Rock; the ninth wave, no more than a ripple on that sleeping sea, did just wash over its level surface; the rest but plashed against its sides, swaying the fringe of seaweed, and crooningly gurgling and muttering. How wonderful was this world above the sea!

There, right under the shadow of Penmorvran, Gwendon, daughter of King Danvore, sat and pondered. It was the place of peril, as she had been warned a hundred times; where dread supernatural beings rode in their ships, and whoso saw them pass, should have pleasure no more in the beautiful depths of the sea. If we see the mermen rarely, it is no wonder; since the surface of the ocean is haunted with danger for them, that neither we nor they can understand. Only in human language was this sea-washed slab at the foot of Penmorvran called the Mermaids' Rock; among the subjects of King Danvore it was known as the Place of Peril.

But that was nothing to the Princess Gwendon. Having tempted the unknown, she found it haunted with wonder and beauty such as she had never dreamed of before. The great headland towered up, mysteriously majestic, into vastness more wonderful than anything beneath the waves;— vastnesses that called to some sleeping greatness within her heart, that thrilled towards the far blossoms of evening blooming above; or, when these withered, towards a firmament of solemn but exultant mystery, wherein the marvels that were the stars soared and swam and flamed. . . . Peril?—it was a world more excellent altogether than the beryl-hearted waters; one might expect here the passaging of Principalities and Powers; one might see those Masters of might and beauty at whose bidding the sea rolls and the wind riots, the stars shine and the skies bloom and darken. . . . For all these were a dim legend among the peoples of the sea.

And there was the land: the unknown, the inciter of imaginings, the abode of marvels and fountain of dreams. Dark rock of Penmorvran, round whose bases the waves, and round whose crest the clouds gathered; what should one see, could one swim up through this supportless new element, as through one's native water, and light on the summit of you; and, turning away from the ocean, gaze into the other world? Hills forest-clad beyond the Sands of Lonno; mysterious estuary, narrowing afar into a region blue and violet and waning into wonderful darkness; what lay beyond you, what lay beyond? . . .

One goes coldly and slowly below there, in the natural world of water; one floats poised in the middle ambience, in groves of silent forests, in glades whereabout the long frondage of the trees undulates soundless forever, and there are great many-hued shells below among the sea-flowers, and the fish go voiceless in their tribes, flitting dumbly through the soundlessness. . . . One floats poised there, brooding on the life that sways or is motionless about one—but brooding only with the eyes, not with mind;— then away through the green depths into some cavern on whose rocky and irregular floor sea-anemones wave flower-like tentacles, blue and orange and purple, to wander immeasurable dark miles, going dumb through silent halls and galleries, and wondering, dreaming, wondering—but with eyes only, never with mind. A commonplace, passionless world, where one obeyed King Danvore unquestioning, and went voiceless and passive forever, and revelled with no keenness of joy, and wandered without curiosity or desire, and labored without interest. . . .

Without joy, curiosity, desire, or interest—how did she know? Ah, it was that here in this new world between the sea and the sky, new senses stirred out of latency, and a new nature infected her;—as here, too, that wonderful new thing, sound, revealed itself. Here, even to the sea-races, it seemed, speech was made known; one might communicate the motions of one's consciousness not dumbly, as in the world below, but as the waves and the winds and the sea-gulls did, in sounds pregnant with mystery. One might imitate their song, and go from that to finding oneself possessed of language. The flamey blossoms of the sky, the flickering violet and silver

and citron on the sea, the plash of the waves and whisper of the breeze—
these things awakened a world of possibilities within one; one saw that
there might be delight keen and burning—that there might be thought
compelling and mysterious; that—. Here it was that her father had warned
her, but yesterday, of the dangers of this wonderworld: speaking in marvelous words the dumb fear that is implanted in the elemental races of the sea.
But he could get no promise from her; having tasted this once, how could
she swear she would not taste it again? Dangers—fear?—Ah, but the beautiful unknown called to her insistently, and a new being within her being
was trembling into life! O majestic crag towering into the sky; O dark marvelous expanse above, strewn with little points of flame: line of hills afar,
beyond the white waters of the estuary that run and ripple and gleam, now,
under a pale, luminous shell of a moon; how lifeless you have made the old
life beneath the waves seem! I long for you; I am drawn irresistibly towards
you; I must possess the secret of you; I must . . . Hush!

Out upon the waters a song rose, and drew near; and she half raised
herself, and sat tense, with strained ears to listen. Round the headland
swept a galley, driven by a hundred oars; crescent-shaped and dragon-
prowed it came, and by the prow stood a man wing-helmeted, one-armed,
very glorious and warlike of form. The long oars dipped in time to the singing, the waters flashed and dripped from them as they rose; the song, wild
and warlike, not unharsh, though swingingly musical, rang out over the
quiet sea. The ship passed very near her: so near that she could see the eyes
of the singers, and the motions of their lips as they sang.

Wonder of wonders; mystery and insatiable lure . . . terror . . . and lure!
She watched them wide-eyed, palpitant, amazed, bewildered. They passed,
and she started and shuddered; she must hurry back to the court of her
father; must seek natural things quickly, and safety in the familiar beryl-
hearted quietude; she had surely seen the thing forbidden, supernatural,
terrifying. Down from the rock she slipped, and sped through the green
world of the waters . . . and all the while she sped that which she left behind
was calling to her . . . Oh, this suffocating world, this drowning, dull,
soundless element! . . . No, never the world beneath the sea again; it was
unbreathable by that which had been awakened in her! She rose to the sea-
face, and panted, and cried with delight to behold once more the stars. But
what was she to do? Borne out from landward over the moon-gleaming
estuary came an irresistible call: human voices: the wild sea warsong of the
Vikings. Peril?—but sure, it was the only thing for her. She must follow,
and see, and know. She swam in towards the land.

The ebbing tide brought the brackish water of the Lonno upon her,
hard to battle against. She turned aside from the swift current, and rested
on a sandbank; and gave herself up to the joy of the new world, and sang:
and presently fell asleep under the moon. When she awoke it was in a glory
that almost stunned her with its magnificence; she was in the sea no longer,

but on land; in a warm, sunlit world full of gleaming beauty and sweet sound. Beside her a little streak of sea water, left by the tide, dimpled under the breeze; yonder on one side were the forest hills of Aglamere, and on the other, the great cape Penmorvran; all about her were the leagues and yellow leagues of the Sands of Lonno.

II

Prince Claribold stood in the window of his hunting-lodge at Tangollen, and looked out over the Sands of Lonno, all yellow and fawn-colored and bright under the sun and gentle skies of the best of June mornings. Here and there, in the wide expanse of sand, were shallow channels in which the tide, far ebbed, lingered silvery and shimmering. Beyond the estuary rose the mountain line, ending far seaward in the promontory of Penmorvran, a blue and purple sunlit gloom; the sea was a mere gleaming streak in the distance southward, to be seen brokenly through the sprays of green flame that were the leafage of the hazels and oaks on the hillside without.

It was the fourth morning of the boar hunt, and the prince had had three days of deep and unwonted content. He had ridden far, in that time, through the Forest; desiring relief from the strain of opposing his father's will. King Cophetua nagged, brought up the matter at unseasonable times, and mixed it in with your meat and drink. A scheming, politic old man, was King Cophetua; who had changed mightily since the days of his romance and the beggar-maid—Prince Claribold's mother, dead now these many years. Father and son, now, had nothing in common; except perhaps a stubbornness of will.

So the prince, high-hearted and romantic altogether, had ridden out upon the boar-hunt; and did not know, not he, whether he would return. Faith, he was utterly sick of court life, and of being the object of endless court scheming. More to his taste the wild places of the forest; the crags that towered up eagle-high into the blue out of the sea of trees; the shadowy regions of the green gloom and the sunlit glades of bracken—where you might mold for yourself in day-dreams a life as free and sweet, as romantic and unhampered as you please. Why, here one might play Robin Hood, with one's merry men; here, perchance—if one might meet some true Maid Marian.

He would not marry the Princess Eleanor; that was flat. A fig for uniting the two kingdoms; was there to be no more glory won at the old traditional war? And she was older than he; and if beautiful, of a beauty by no means to his taste. And he did not and would not love her; and would marry for love or turn monk. Whom? That was as fate and the future and love should say. Once or twice, indeed, he had tried to force the hand of the last named; but to no purpose. He was the son of Cophetua-in-love-with-the-beggar-maid, not of Cophetua-come-to-years-of-discretion or -past-the-follies-of-youth; and so, as it were, by heredity expectant of romance. And no high-born Bertha, Cunigunde or Althea at court having pleased him, he dreamed of some peasant-girl (perhaps)—but with the breeding of a princess—and of a house of green boughs (perhaps) in wide Aglamere.

Three days of the forest had cleaned all perturbation from his mind, and left him to dream freely what romantic dreams he would. Now, however, the gaiety and sweet vigor of morning possessed him, spirit and limbs; and a wind from the sea set him forgetting, almost, to dream. No, he would not hunt that morning; he would keep the forest for the afternoon, dining first at midday here at beloved Tangollen—after a ride down to the sea, and a swim to the Mermaids' Rock. Or perhaps he would not hunt until tomorrow, but give the afternoon to turning a chanson on the beauties of the hunting-lodge: the dancing leaves near, the sunlight on the sands, the far gleam of the water; and behind, the island-glades, in the great tree-ocean of Aglamere. What kingdom else should he desire, or what royal palace—so the Lady of Romance were there for his queen?—So, standing in the window, and already planning the chanson, he gave himself up to gay visions, in which was no tinge of gray or drab; visions that flashed with the clean sunlight and heyday of youth, a procession of them in green and gold and scarlet, with tenderer and more passionate hues interwoven.

All at once singing came up to his hearing from the sand below; singing like none he had ever heard: wordless and plaintive, filled with longing, with questions put to the unknown and infinite, hardly more personal than the sighing of a sudden gentle wind, or the lisp of little meditative waves on a sandy beach. He listened, much moved, and scanned the shore for the source of it, but saw no one; then went out, all aglow, to the very edge of the hill, where no hazel or oak leaves intervened to hinder his vision. What he saw swept his whole being into a tumult. Down the hillside he strode, and out across the sands of Lonno; the glamor of his dreams at last incarnate, it seemed to him.

She appeared bewildered, and without power to answer him clearly. She was a princess, she said; the daughter of a king out yonder—here she pointed out to the sea. Shipwrecked? She had no words to say; it was to be concluded so, however; and that she was still too dazed with the peril she had passed through, to remember. But she would come with him—accept his hospitality, his protection? Oh yes, she would come—as one follows a god that commands, knowing or not whither he be leading. For this human prince, of course, was a god to her: a being of a higher order than her own, whom she felt, vaguely, possessed the secrets of the wonderworld into which she had come, and would reveal them. That is, as soon as she began to feel anything at all, beyond mere awe and wonder at his presence, and an overwhelming sense of his superiority. —Before he had crossed the sands with her, he had wooed her and won: yes, she would marry him (whatever that might mean). . . . His praise of her beauty fell upon ears impersonal, and so uncomprehending; his passionate speech thrilled her, but less than did the wonder and beauty of the upper-world. She did not understand it; perhaps it was part of the great mystery, perhaps—since it seemed of the very essence of this wonder-being who spoke to her—it would prove the key to that. Homage in any case must be rendered. . . . When they came to Tangollen, he was all radiant and exalted; she still altogether lost and timid and confused.

He called to his knights, and showed her to them: his bride, a ship-wrecked princess. He would strike now with native impetuosity and romance, fashioning his dreams into sudden actuality. He laughed to think his father's love-story outdone; his mother could never have been as beautiful as this lovely jetsam from the sea. Let them drink bumpers to this beautiful bride! Let these, for the love of love, deck Tangollen with green boughs and the flowers of the forest; and these others go about to prepare a wedding-feast. . . . Rolf Forester, ride thou post haste the three leagues into Pontlonno, and bring back a priest to marry me; say he shall have a hundred crowns for his fee. We shall confront King Cophetua presently with the accomplished fact; then let him storm as he may. . . . A lodge of green boughs in Aglamere, if the worst came to the worst; with this so divinely fair bride to share it with him! . . . How beautiful the worst would be!

Rolf Forester returned within two hours after noon; he had met Father Ladislas, by good luck, in the forest—fresh from administering extreme unction to a charcoal-burner's daughter, and nothing loath to marry a couple for a hundred crowns of fee. —But arrived at Tangollen, the good religious—a cautious, unromantic man, it seemed—was afflicted with doubts. He had no need to wait for the *I, Claribold, take thee,* before coming at the bridegroom's identity; and knowing something of current statecraft and affairs at court, thought it was his duty to remonstrate. Besides, the beauty of the bride almost appalled him; he saw nothing human in it, and knew that great perils beset the man who marries with a daughter of the sea. He managed to get a little (on his part) tactful conversation with her—and made nothing of it but what confirmed his suspicions. He urged this view of it on the prince; with as much effect as if he had urged it upon the wind. Claribold took his warnings like the whirlwind takes the straw;—and then, there were the hundred crowns: no small matter to a poor (and avaricious) parish priest. The wedding was over before the sun went down.

Then they lit up the lodge bravely, and feasted; the prince with his bride at the head of the table; the priest, by no means easy in his mind, opposite to them. Many were the healths drunk; many were the songs sung and the stories told by the knights: courtly and romantic and passionate tales of Charlemain and his Paladins; of Arthur and his Table Round; of the good knight Sir Theseus of Athens, and his martial courting of the Lady Hippolyta. Dumb with wonder, Gwendon listened. The theme of the songs and stories was always the same: this secret (as it seemed) of the upper-world, this atmosphere of the supernatural realm into which she had come: this thing love of which the god-prince had been telling her all day: this fire in the veins, this intoxication of the heart which he had been pouring out upon her: and which she did not understand, or feel, but could only marvel at. How to interpret by it the flamy blossoms of night in the sky; the wild foxgloves, the primroses and daffodils of sunset that rippled and flickered on the face of the waters? Well, she would learn, she would learn; no doubt there was much more to be told.

III

The lights shone out through the windows of Tangollen, and far across the Sands of Lonno, covered now shallowly by the tide; the songs floated out seaward; and King Danvore, where he drifted in the silver of the moonlight, searching for his lost daughter, heard the songs and saw the lights, and was troubled, as by fearful omens. He turned back from the perilous estuary—for him a ghostly borderland; and sought the Mermaids' Rock.

Ivar the Sea Rover, too, heard and saw them from the prow of his ship. Last night Ivar had taken and burned Pontlonno town; of the inhabitants none escaped but Father Ladislas and his acolyte, who of course were away in the forest at the time, and knew nothing of it. All day long the Vikings had been hunting in Aglamere; but east of the river, so that no rumor of their doings reached Tangollen. Ivar the One-armed owed Prince Claribold a grudge, and of the first magnitude; since the coast-raid, two years before, in which the prince with a hundred knights met him, lopped off his left arm close to the shoulder in the battle, and drove him and his men, fighting strenuously, back to their ship plunderless. So now, spying the lights of Tangollen across the estuary, and knowing that region well, Ivar conceived that here was the chance of revenge. Tangollen was Claribold's; good sport to burn it to the ground, even though Claribold were not within. But he probably was within; witness the lights and songs. Anchor ship there, and come, some thirty of you, sons of the Vikings—long-legged men that will find no difficulty in crossing these moon-bright shallows!

A warshout without broke upon the revelry at Tangollen; the knights were on their feet in a moment; had snatched swords and targets from the walls; and were at the door, Claribold at the head of them, before it was broken down.

The Sea Princess, standing in her place on the dais, looked on what followed in amazement that passed into terror: it was another mystery of the man-world—but ah, not beautiful, not lofty, not to be desired. She saw spears and swords sickeningly reddened, and man after man fall. The shouting, the ferocity in the eyes of the fighters, appalled her. She saw her god-prince outdo and stand out from the others, and he began to take on personality for her. Fifteen of the Vikings fell, and the ten knights; but her eyes were all on Claribold. She saw him, fighting alone and heroically, driven back step by step, parrying thrust after thrust, killing this man, and that, and that other; then smashing to the ground that fourth man with an outward sweep of left arm and target. And then she saw the spear fly that struck his guardless breast, and saw him fall at her own feet. . . . And then the sorrow and passion of the world smote upon her at once, an overwhelming billow, and she was no longer a daughter of the sea. She forgot that there was wonder and beauty and mystery in this world above the waves; she forgot the flamey lights of the night sky, and the flickering blooms of the evening; all supernatural glory was blotted out of the world. She beheld her god slain, and the glamor of the world pass away with him; she understood the mournful mystery he had striven to reveal to her, and found the heart of it bitterness and sorrow; and was no more than a stricken and bereaved woman.

Ivar the One-armed had lost nineteen of his men; but he had won a good fight, his revenge, and a maiden the like of whose beauty he had never seen on any coast between Trondhjem and Alexandria. Decidedly he had no cause to complain.

King Danvore was on the Mermaids' Rock under the headland of Penmorvran, when the Viking ship passed. Passed quite near, so that he could see the eyes of the men who were rowing, and the motions of their lips as they sang. It was not that near view of terrifying humanity, however, that so appalled him, as the terrible beauty he beheld on his daughter's face. "Gwendon, Gwendon, my darling! Come back to me!" he cried; braving the whole awfulness of the supernatural for her sake. But she had no more eyes to see, or ears to hear him, than had Ivar the Viking and his men.

The following story is Morris's second and last Greek-inspired tale, with the god Pan in England having great fun with those who do not believe in his existence. It was published in March 1917 in The Theosophical Path, *under the pseudonym Maurice Langran.*

A Wild God's Whim

You may say that his world began by the clump of sweet peas at the corner; because with the instinct or intuition of his species, he knew that there would be things foreign, and perhaps distasteful, beyond. So from this point we may come to him fittingly; one should approach a deity with unhurrying reverence, and not rush in upon his meditations. Before you, then, lies a garden walk: we will call it a hundred yards from here to that thicket of lilacs and laburnums at the far end, through whose green gloom even from here you can see vistas of light. On either side of the walk are deep borders; beyond that on the left is a wall, south and sunny, on which in their season, peaches and jargonelle pears ripen. Between the wall and the walk are a multitude of delectable scents and blooms and a perpetual humming of bees. Side by side, peonies squander their opulence and irises display their grave and purple pride; here are tiger-lilies, there, turkscaps; yonder is the pensive grace of Solomon's seal; again, wallflowers and gilliflowers, pansies musing or laughing, and the wealth of the world in ruby and carmine and crimson with phlox and sweet-william. On the other side of the walk it all starts over again: a bank of delicious bloom and honeysweet heaviness in the air, rising from the thyme and lavender by the boxborder to the flowering trees at the back—lilac and pink hawthorn, and maybe rhododendrons, and laburnum again, and a mort of the like dear marvelous things besides.

It is at the end of this walk that you come absolutely into the odor of—I do not like to call it *sanctity,* lest he should object to the word as applied to himself or any of his doings. He would, I know. Still, there is occasion for taking off the shoes from off the feet; for though you cannot see him yet, he is not ten yards away.

The walk, which was three yards broad between the flower borders, narrows here into a mere path through the thicket, and is quite overhung and overarched with the lilacs and laburnums. Pass under these, and the lower garden is spread out before you. There is the great sloping lawn, and the lake at the bottom of it; there, beyond the lake, are the oakwoods; and over the tops of them, right across the vale (of which you see nothing), a distance of mountains that will be green or forgetmenot blue, storm-dark or purple or violet, according to the weather and the time of day and year.

At this point there is a deep bank; and thirty or more irregular and wandering steps lead down over its terraces into the garden; with pebbly landings here and there, and stone seats cunningly and unobtrusively devised. And near the top of this descent, on your left as you go down, is a reedy pool and a spring: a good force of water bubbles up there, to trickle and cascade down over the rockwork, and to wander among the shrubs on that side of the lawn, and presently to feed the lake—which is at least a quarter mile from these steps, I take it. By that spring, and right in among the reeds, he has his home: a bronze statue of himself.

There it had stood for a hundred years or so; brought there then from Italy, where it had been dug up somewhere and offered for sale. He had chanced to see it one moon-bright night in Naples, and had taken a fancy to it in his irrational, goat-footed, crag-haunting and forest-roving way; and forthwith elected it for his dwelling-place during the next few centuries, let them take it where they would. The sculptor had shown him at the moment when disappointment revealed the secret music of the world to him; when—

down the vale of Maenalus
He pursued a maiden and clasped a reed;

—when, with head bent over the plucked reed, he had received the inspiration of all his inspirations, and knew that thenceforth he was to be ten times the god he had been before. Bringing to his mind so keenly that sacred moment, he could not think of parting with it yet.

So he found himself there among the reeds by the pool in the garden, with the lawn and the lake and the oaks to look out over; and beyond, the mountains and the wayward Irish sky. And up there behind, when you might go forth for a gambol under the moon, or in the long, quiet, gold hours of early morning in summer, there was all that fragrance and wild wealth of bloom along the lilac walk for his pleasuring; he was not the god to complain of his surroundings, not he! They had lasted him a hundred years, and might last him another; the woods of Arcady had held nothing sweeter for him of old, than the hills of Wicklow held now. And had come to understand the Gaelic speech; less by hearing it humanly spoken—though sure, in the Earl's household, in those days, they would not have demeaned their lips, at home, with any other language than their natural one—than by absorbing it out of the moist air and the wind from over boglands and mountains, and from the whisper of the reeds about his feet, and the tinkle and pondering of the water. The Irish dawns and noons and nights, the blue skies and the gray and the flamey, worked upon him until he had lost his Doric or Achaean, and thought his wild-god thoughts in the native sweet Gaelic of the things about him; and he held it a better tongue than the other; as he held the Irish Sidhe more delightful company, when he desired it, than were the Sileni of old, and the sylvans and fauns. But then, your true god does not go mooning and mourning over the past, but finds delight, every moment, in the living beauty of the world.

And then there were the human people; he liked them, too. He saw a deal of them, one way or another; and found them not half so unaccountable or perverse as you might expect in humanity. They would be merry at times: *not merry enough,* but still, merry; and it pleased him. And again they would be grave and sad: would fall a-pondering, bereft of speech, at times, when evening hung like a daffodil out of the west; and then also, he would grow brother-hearted with them. Those were the moods he understood: wild delight of the sunlight or moonlight; breathless, breakneck tearings down the mountain-slopes, or leapings goatlike from the crags;—and breathless silences by the forest pools, where he will bide hour on hour, when the whim takes him, wordless, thoughtless, rapt and wary. And he saw these moods of his reflected in those who came into the garden: there would be wild, rollicking gatherings: excellent songs and stories from bards who carried the atmosphere of heather and peat-fires with them;—and then suddenly, a motion of the earth-breath that he felt, would set them silent, and him silent and listening too.

He had been with them through three of their generations: had seen the man that brought the statue from Italy pass from his prime into old age; his son grow from babyhood to old age; *his* son grow almost old; and his son again grow into proud, comely young manhood. They were all men that a god might take delight in: fine, proud and handsome, generous and courtly and brave; he had never seen anything incomprehensible in them—which means that he had seen no sign of insincerity. By the third generation he had become interested in them; the fourth you might say he loved, almost from its first toddling appearance in the garden. Though they paid him no ritual sacrifice, he was hardly aware of the omission; since they had ways of their own of worshiping him, and burnt incense to eternal beauty and fitness in their hearts. So, when the games were playing, he would run forth at times, and put vim into the smiting of the youths' hurley-sticks; and he saw to the increase of their flocks with partiality, and that honey should be plenty in their hives, and the hay in their meadows unspoiled by rain. Yes, he would bide where he was indefinitely—until the whim might take him to go elsewhere. He had found nothing else so pleasant at least since the great Lie was told about him—since he chuckled in the forest depths to hear it bruited that he was dead. As for the forms of worship, the rustic altars and the offerings, he had long ceased to expect them from unaccountable Man.

And he had come to be quite a personality, as we say, in the countryside. You wouldn't think he'd confine himself in a garden, although there were lawns in it revelled over nightly by the Beautiful Family; oaks to drop you acorns for the sacraments of your faith; lone places—

Where the roses in scarlet are heavy,
And dream on the end of their days.

—There were those mountain peaks and shoulders that one could see beyond the oak-tops, to be explored for more than unusually mystical echoes; there were wan tarns in the far uplands, where one might brood with the moon by the silent waters; rivers merry-toned in the green valleys; round towers immemorial to scale and leap from; woods and wildness and wonder. So when Michael the Black O'Dyeever swore he had seen him— seen that bronze statue—careering wildly down the slopes of the Joust Mountain at four o'clock of a June morning, there were few to doubt his word; or when Biddy the kitchen maid feared to pass down the steps into the lower garden in the evening, or alone at any time, for that matter, there was none in the servants' hall to laugh at her, but many to cross themselves in sympathy. Wasn't it the devil he was, with his cloven hoofs and all; and what for did the Chieftain allow statues of the devil in his garden? So he had enemies, as well as friends; but even they, mostly, were more inclined to propitiate than to wish him harm. And with all the magic of the garden and the Wicklow Mountains to feast his eyes and heart upon; and all the subtle silence, and the song that no man hears, to listen to; little he cared what his enemies might be saying. What did *he* know about the devil, anyway?

Mighty proud the three generations past had been of the statue; and well they might be, for Praxiteles himself had done nothing better. This pride, no doubt, had contributed to his attachment for the place and people; now, in the fourth generation, that attachment was increased mightily by a cause you shall hear of. One day he saw the young Earl walking on the lawn below with a man whose looks he, the great god Pan, by no means approved—nor yet the cut of the fellow's black garments. Evidently they were talking about himself; would he go down and listen, or bide where he was? Being in mood for contemplation, he would not bother with it. But presently they came up the steps, and he heard this:

"I tell you, son, 'twill bring a curse on your cause. 'Tis a relic of ancient fiend-worship, and should be destroyed."

Pan started; what?—the fellow was urging the destruction of this, the chosen home and best likeness ever made, of himself! Should he give the blasphemer a taste of a wild god's ire and might forthwith? —His reverence, had he known it, stood in dire peril for a moment. But the Earl's answer smoothed things over:

"Ah, sure, 'tis a lovely work of art, father; a Praxiteles, if ever there was one. 'Twould be bringing a curse upon the cause, I think, to commit an act of damnable vandalism at the outset."

"Then if you won't destroy it," said the other, "sell it. Sell it to some fool of a Saxon with money, and get a round sum to buy guns and pikes for the men."

"No," said the Earl, "I will not sell him, either. Since my great-grandfather's time he has been called the Luck of the House, and I'll not part with him now. There isn't the equal of him in Ireland, I'll be sworn; or in England either. 'Twould be enriching the Saxons to sell him to them, whatever money they might pay."

"Paganism, rank paganism!" growled the black-robed one; and they passed into the lilac walk and so up to the castle, leaving God Pan to his musings. Sell the statue forsooth, without his permission asked or given! However, well he knew it could not be done; that whoso found, bought or sold it henceforth, would do so upon inspiration from himself. Still, it might become necessary to devise rewards and penalties. . . . The fairies gathered with the twilight, and he thought no more of human beings, for the time. This was better fun; this was better fun!

But soon there came a time when the Sidhe came no more at dusk to the garden; there were gatherings of men instead. These would steal in through the oakwoods as soon as the sun had gone down; singly or in little groups they came, till fifty or sixty would be waiting on the lawn. Then the Earl would come down from the castle; and at a word of command from him, they would form into lines, and fall to marching and wheeling, charging and exercising with pikes; and this would go on, nightly, for several hours before they were dismissed. Pan would watch their evolutions, and perhaps grow interested; sometimes when the word was given to charge, he would slip down from his place with a whoop, and join them. Then the run would not be doubling, but trebling or quadrupling: a wild helter-skelter from one end of the lawn to the other; and not a man of them, at the end, but wondering at the delight and sweeping uplift of it. I do not know why no one saw him; moonlight is tricky at best; and who would look for a statue to come down from its pedestal and join in patriotic or rebellious drill?

And then came a night when no men stole out of the oakwoods; but the Earl came down at moonrise, cloaked and spurred, and a lady with him as far as the steps. She was bright-eyed and white-haired and proud looking; she embraced him very tenderly there, and would not weep; but many would have guessed she was praying down her tears. "I wouldn't hinder you going for the world," said she; "go, and God guard you, my darling!" And he kissed her many times; and said he, cheering her: "He will, with the sacredness of the cause, mother machree. And see now," said he, pointing to the statue, "here's the Luck of the House I'm leaving behind to guard you, dear, till I come riding back with victory."

And their faith pleased God Pan; they had confided each other into his care; for who would they mean by *God*, but he? —After that she turned back, the brave, queenly mother, and went dry-eyed and bright-eyed up to the castle. But as soon as the Earl was at the bottom of the steps, another lady came out from beneath the trees to meet him: a tall lady, young and very beautiful and slender; and Pan heard nothing of what they said to each other as they walked down towards the lake. There they parted; the Earl mounting a horse that a groom held for him, and riding away round the lake into the woods. But the lady came slowly back, and sat down on the stone seat by the pool, and fell a-weeping; and Pan understood. "Come now," thought he, "I'll give her music"; and began to play upon his reed; and who in the world would weep or sorrow, "listening to his sweet pipings"? She rose up presently like one in a dream, and stood entranced in the white moonlight; nor ever knew that Pan was piping, or that she heard music. Only her soul heard it; and hearing, was one with the dancing stars and the daedal earth, and heaven and the giant wars, and love and death and birth. She went up to the castle presently, not merely comforted, but exalted.

Then a week passed during which those two ladies walked much in the garden together; and then they came no more—neither they nor anyone. Pan might come down now at high noon to bask in the lawn; or wander anywhere, and take no precautions as to casting glamors against visibility or the like. And whether it was lonesome he grew, or inquisitive, he would venture now farther along the lilac walk and towards the castle than formerly. The bloom on the two borders had grown riotous and unkempt, and therefore the more delightful to him; he might have loitered there the summer day, but that the whim was on him to explore. The blooming of the sweet peas was over, since there was none to pluck the blooms. He turned the corner, and went on, and up on to the balustrade terrace, where heliotropes were withering in their stone vases. Well now, for once he would see the inside of one of these human habitations; and found an open French window, and was for going in. Bah! the dust was thick everywhere; the air was full of sadness; one breathed desertion and desolation; it was not yet fit for him to enter and work his magic. Let it lie lonely a hundred years; then he might go in and convert this disorder and atmosphere of grief into loveliness. The woodwork must have his nettles here and his wallflowers there; then he would have bats to flit and owls to cry and wander here where passion and laughter had been, and where grief lingered. . . . He went back across the terrace, and down into the lilac walk, and lurked and sauntered musing among the blooms, fearing that a day of sun and wind would hardly take the human sadness out of his heart that it had infected. But presently he came on a pansy that caught his eye and somehow had wisdom for him; and squatted down there to watch and ponder on it: squatted down on his haunches amid the peonies and irises and Solomon's seals, and brooded on the wisdom of the pansy from noon until the sun had sunk, and the sweetness of purple dusk was over the world.

Then he started from his deep mood, because of footsteps on the path, and the human sadness suddenly weighing upon him again, till it was unendurable. There was the Earl, pale and thin and far spent, his right arm in a sling, his clothes torn and tattered, hurrying down, a little uncertainly, towards the thicket and the steps and the lower garden. And just as he disappeared into that shelter, came other footsteps: that would have caused repugnance in any wildwood deity, I think: half a dozen men in uniform, and with guns; and another who was chiefly the cause of Pan's unease. Disguised out of recognition since last you saw him; but the grown beard, the excellent wig, and the cassock discarded for laical clothes hid him not for a moment from Pan, who sees souls and intentions first, and the rest after—if he troubles to see them at all. Here what he saw was treachery and intent to kill; and these jarred upon his mood, which had been learning peace among the peonies and pansies; it was the forethrown shadow of these that had brought back the human sadness on him. And the fellow in the disguise jarred upon him still more. . . . All this was an instantaneous shock of perception to him; the men had barely turned the sweet-pea corner into the lilac walk before the jarred mood and the sadness had gone, and another had filled him in their place and translated itself into action.

Up he leaped to his feet, did the great God Pan; up out of the peonies and irises, and went crashing over the pansies and the Solomon's seal; the maddest of his wild-god humors was on him; and here should be fun all to his heart. It was dusk, remember; wherein any running figure would seem to you the man you were pursuing. "There he is, fire!" cried the traitor; and there was a crash and a rattle behind, and Pan felt the patter of pebbles— they were bullets really—against his bronze back and legs. *Fun, fun, fun!* —He whooped in his sylvan glee, and dashed on. A glance as he passed through the lilac thicket told him the Earl was hiding there; he paused a moment, to let his pursuers come up a little; then took the steps at a couple of bounds, whooping to keep the scent red-hot, and sped out over the lawn with the seven of them following.

Then he had the time of his life with them: wheeling and stooping, and circling and dodging; leading them down towards the lake, and then back; and scattering them, and wheeling again. No more human sadness, now, for the great God Pan! It is all one, and all fun, to him, whether he runs with the hare or the hounds. Here, too, he had a little purpose of his own to serve: one or two purposes. He would bring wildwood disorder among these minions of an order he knew not; and there was one among the hunters, he suddenly remembered, against whom he had a kind of personal grudge. " 'Tis the man who would have destroyed me," he chuckled. Having produced general confusion, with a wheel and a whoop he came upon that man, seized him by the leg, and whirling him overhead in the air, tore down towards the lake. What was the weight of a fat man, anyhow, to hinder wild-god speed and glee? Out he splashed through the reeds, and then whirled his burden again, and flung it far into deep water; again a crash and a pattering of pebbles; again a wild-god whoop and wheel, and he was off into the forest through the reeds. Dark it was by that time, and pitch-dark under the trees, and fearfully the pursuers stumbled and blundered; but he infected them with the joy of the chase, and allowed them no peace. Darkness was daylight to him, and he never let the scent grow cold. Through the woods he led them, sometimes squirrelling into the high branches for fun, and pelting them with acorns as they passed beneath. If ever they were for giving up, there he was, running and shouting in full view; I surmise he led them half over Wicklow. By morning, one lay wounded in the woods, shot by his fellows in mistake; and another was half drowned in the river; and a third up to his neck in bogland. The rest—heaven knows where they were.

Years afterwards the Earl came from France incognito, and visited the home of his ancestors. He was shown over the place by the caretaker of an absentee peer in London. At the top of the steps that led down into the lower garden, he glanced round to the left. "H'm," said he; "was not there a statue standing there, in the old times—a famous Greek statue, the Pan of Praxiteles?"

"Ah sure, there was, your honor. It disappeared the night the young Earl escaped to France, and never a soul has heard of it since. Did ye ever hear of the chase he led the soldiers that came after him, your honor—the Earl, I mane, av coorse, and not the statue? Kilt the six of them entirely, he did, and flung that black trait—his reverence Father Timothy I should say, that sould him to the Sassenach—into the lake, after carrying him—" (But we know all that.)

"Ah, 'twas the grand, proud young hero he was, your honor—I mane, a coorse, the wild young divvle of a rebel. . . ."

"Looted, I suppose," was the Earl's inward comment. "Poor old Luck of the House, in one of their museums or palaces now, and never a tag on you to tell where they got you!"

But Pan, brooding among the reeds, caught his thought, and chuckled. Under ten feet of Irish bog lies the statue, where he dropped it inconsequentially at the end of the chase; and where he concluded to leave it, considering that bodiless invisibility would suit him well enough for an age or two. But there is no saying you might not be hearing him pipe at any time, in the Dargle, or the Vale of Avoca, or at the Meeting of the Waters.

The following story tells of a divine being becoming incarnate and suffering for the sake of humankind. It was published in May 1917 in The Theosophical Path, *under the pseudonym of Evan Gregson Mortimer. It was reprinted in Morris's collection* The Secret Mountain and Other Tales. *On another level, Morris was clearly aware that the daffodil was a national symbol for Wales.*

Daffodil

*F*iery princes of the empyrean rode daily to the palace of King Nuivray, to woo the Lady Daffodil, fairest of all the princesses of Heaven. On splendid steeds they came—the Chieftains of the Twelve Houses, with beautiful banners borne before them flaming along the Milky Way. Came the Knight of the Dawn, golden armoured and cloaked in scarlet; the Prince of Noon, panoplied in shining sapphire and the pennon of his lance a blue meteor trailing: Evening, an enchanter out of western heaven wrapped about in flame robes shell-pink and shell-blue; Night, a dark emperor of mysterious sovereignty and power. Many sultans came too, and paynim princes and sublimities: Aldebaran with the topaz-hilted scimitar, who is leader of all the armies of the firmament; white-turbanned diamonded Fomalhaut; Alpheratz and Achernar; Algol and Algenib and Alderamin. Came the great poets of the sky: the Pleiades ever beautiful and young, and Vega and his train, and Vindemiatrix; and the knightly-hearted brothers of Orion, who guard the Marches of Space. Came our Lord Martanda himself, gloriously singing and flaming in his car of flame.

No language known in heaven could tell the sweetness and the beauty of Lady Daffodil. The Pleiades knew well that with all their gift of song they could not declare it, nor the thousandth part of it; how then should one earth-born describe the aura of light about her head, citron-hued and saffron-hued, that shone more tenderly and beneficently yellow than even the breastplate of the Knight of Dawn, or even the golden crown of Aldebaran? How describe the gentle magical wisdom of her, her understanding of the antique transformations and transmigrations of things; or her profound unquenchable gaiety that kept merriment alive among the stars even on the days of the rebellions of hell? Not that you must think of her as meekly girlish; nor suppose her occupations merely such as spinning and embroidery, or playing upon zither or citole. She too had led armies through the mountains beyond Orion; and if she bore no sword herself, nor charged in scythed car, it was still her druid incantations on the peak, they said, that cleared the passes of invading hell. I will say that her presence was a light to heal sorrow, to exorcise or shame away evil; that an atmosphere breathed about her, quickening, spiritual and delicate, but very robust too, and with power to awaken souls. In the sapphire halls and galleries of her father's palace: in the gardens where gentian and larkspur and forget-me-not bloom: when she passed a rumor of delight ran trembling after and before her; the little asterisms that nested in the trees broke into trillings and warblings of joy. *Beautiful, beautiful, beautiful!* they sang; and *Delight, delight, delight, delight!*

Now it fell that King Nuivray held court in Heaven at Eastertime, and all the suitors were present. It was thought that whoever should win most glory now, whether in the jousts of arms or in the contests of song, would have the hand of the Lady Daffodil for his prize. Splendidly they were enthroned on thrones most splendid; not one of them but belonged to the great winged and flaming hierarchies; not one but was embodied in essential flame; and there was mirth there, and high emulation; and even though rivalry, pleasant companionship and comradely love.

In the midst of the feasting one came into the hall, at whose coming all turned to look at him; and they shuddered and there was a moment's silence beneath the turquoise towers. He was one that should have been young, but was decrepit; that should have been handsome, but for the marks of vice on his face; that should have been noble of form and limb, but for evil living. From his two eyes two haunting demons looked forth: the one, fear or horror; the other, shameless boldness. Because his words were so insolent as he called for a high throne among the Gods, Rigel and Mintaka and Anilam and Betelgeux, the archers of Orion, reached for their bows; our Lord Marttanda grasped his sword of flame; Aldebaran arose drawing his scimitar: such rudeness was not to be tolerated there, in the very presence of the yellow-haired Lady of Heaven. They waited but a sign of permission from her—

But she, rising from the throne at her father's side, came down the hall and stood before the stranger, all graciously shining. He framed, I think, some ribaldry in his mind; but looking up at her, faltered; then, bowing low, took her hand and kissed it very humbly, after the manner of a loyal knight of Heaven.

"Please you, sir, to declare to us your name and rank," said she.

"I am the Spirit of the Earth," he answered.

The Lords of the Firmament looked down at him very pitifully; then hung their heads in sorrow; for he was the outcast, the scapegrace, the traitor of Heaven; he alone had broken the Law; he alone hobnobbed with and sheltered the hellions whom they, embodying the Eternal Will, fought eternally and drove back and back over the brink of things.

"A place and a royal robe for the Lord Spirit of Earth!" commanded the Lady Daffodil.

Then they strove to forget him, and the feasting went forward.

This one told of his imperial state; this of his high adventures; this of conquests won afar; this of the prowess of his bow; this of the daring and keen edge of his sword. Not boastingly they spoke, however, nor in any mood of self-exaltation: their words, like their deeds, were all a ceremonial of sacrifice, and worship paid to the Lonely Unknown. At the end King Nuivray turned to his daughter: "Will you not make your choice now?" he said.

"Not yet," she answered; "there is still one knight that has neither spoken nor sung. Lord Spirit of the Earth," she said, turning to that most unlovely being, "tell you now your story."

Again the Princes of the Empyrean hung their heads, guessing they were to hear shame and sorrow. But the Spirit of the Earth rose and spoke.

"Braggart knights," he said. "I am greater than all of you. I alone do what I please; worship myself, sin, and enjoy a million pleasures. You— who shall compare you with me? You go on your courses obedient, and are the slaves of Law; my law is my own will; my pleasures I choose for myself; in my realm was planted the Tree of Knowledge of Good and Evil, and I ate of the fruit of the tree, and am wise—I am wise.

"Which one of you is equal unto me? Is it you, Lord Marttanda? All your splendor is squandered abroad; and as much as I desire of it falls upon me, and is mine to enjoy soft hours of it, and to turn away from it when I will;—but who ministers unto you, or who hath given you a gift at any time? Or is it ye, Knights of the Dawn and the Noon and the Evening? All your beauty is for me, for me. Is it ye, O poets of the Pleiades, who sing the songs it was ordained you should sing? Are ye not wearied yet of your singing? For me only is your music pleasant; because I listen when I will, and when I will, heed it no more, but turn to pleasures of my own."

Here he laughed, and his laughter sickened Heaven.

"Ye wage your wars in space, as it was predestined you should wage them: ye obey the Law in your warfare, going forth and returning according to a will not your own. Ye are light and know not darkness: in a shadowless monotony of splendor ye go forward to a destiny wherein is no prospect of change. What to you, O Lord Marttanda, is your splendid effulgence, that may not wax nor wane? What to you are your songs, O Pleiades?—they contain no grandeur of tragedy, nor sweet savor of sadness, nor fire of passion: neither hate nor love to give them life and power. Your glory and your music are a weariness to you; and a weariness, O Orion, is your watchful charge. That which ye are, ye shall be forever, O ye that know not the sweetness of sin!

"But I care nothing for the glory of your wars, since I have the power to raise up wars within myself. Since my children come, millions against millions, and burn and ravish and slaughter; since my lands grow fruitful soaked with blood, and my seas are the abode of sudden treacherous slaughter, and even in my skies rides Death!

"What are your tame delights, that I should envy them: since I go out after strange loves, and riot in strange sins, and take my fill of gorgeous pleasures of mine own devising, and—"

Then his eyes met those of the Lady Daffodil; and he faltered, dropped his head, and covered his face and groaned.

"O Lords of the Firmament, help me!" he cried. "You that have given me the light I pollute; you that of old endowed me with fire and soul; that are unfallen, and unhaunted by demons; that are not torn as I am torn, nor degraded as I am degraded! You whose souls are unsullied and unstained, a boon from you! Help from you! Come down into my house, some great warrior of you, that I be not destroyed by my own misdoings! One of you, beautiful Pleiades, come down and sing my miserable children into peace! Or you, Mintaka and Alnilam, keen-shafted! You, Lord Marttanda, come down, and drive away with your brightness the hellions that scourge and devour me! Sovereign Aldebaran, let the terrible edge of your scimitar cleave away the loathsome hosts of my sins!

"For behold, I am of your own race, and am fallen; my soul, that was divine once and knightly, is passing away from me and ebbing into oblivion; sin and death and sorrow are my companions; I am Hell; I am Hell!"

He fell on his knees suppliant, and with bent head implored them, weeping.

"What can I do for thee, brother?" said our Lord Marttanda. "I send thee my beautiful beams, and they come back to me an offence; they breed carrion and pestilence in thee, of the millions that are slain in thy wars. If I came nearer to thee, thou wouldst perish."

"Alas, what can we do for thee, poor brother?" said the Pleiades. "We have sung for thee, and of our singing thy poets have learned to sing; and with this sacred knowledge they have made war-songs and lust-songs and terrible songs of hate. What can we do for thee?"

"We keep watch upon the marches against monstrous invasion from the deep," said Mintaka and Alnilam. "But thou—hast thou not brought in demons, and made our watching to be in vain? We can do nothing for thee; would that we could!"

"I can do nothing for thee," said the Grand Seigneur Aldebaran—"I that am Lord of War, and leader of the Hosts of the Gods. For it was ordained of old that Light should break battle on darkness, and that this my

War in Heaven should be. But thou hast stolen the secret of conflict from me, which was ordained to be a lovely thing; and hast made it base, abhorrent and bloody. Thou hast not followed me to the eternal field in the ranks of thy brethren, but used the engine of God for thine own delight and destruction. Because of this, if I came nearer to thee, thy wars would destroy thee utterly. They children would riot down into madness and mutual slaughter, until none was left of them."

So one by one the princes spoke. They could do nothing for the Spirit of the Earth. He had eaten the fruit of the Tree of Knowledge of Good and Evil; his fate had been in his own hands, and he had elected to make it damnation.

Then King Nuivray, being their host, rose from his throne to pronounce their general judgment on him. "Thou camest here with insolence on thy lips," said he; "and made boast in Heaven of thy foulness, polluting the beauty of the empyreal fields. Go forth; thy sins have damned thee; there is no hope for thee. There is none in Heaven that will go with thee, nor one that might save thee if he went."

"Yes, there is one," cried the Lady Daffodil. As she spoke, the turquoise towers were filled with sudden light and loveliness, such as none had beheld in them till then. "Yes, there is one," said she. "Poor Spirit of the Earth, thou art to hope; I will go with thee."

The Lord Marttanda veiled his splendor in sorrow. The Pleiades wept in silence, and thenceforth for seven ages there was sadness in their song. "Not so!" cried Sultan Aldebaran; "thou art to shine and flame upon our ensigns; for thy sake, O Daffodil, we are to sweep triumphant over the ramparts of hell!"

But the Spirit of the Earth raised his head and looked at her, and a wild hope rose in his eyes; and then forlorn but altogether noble despair.

"No!" he said, "come not thou! Where hideous sin is, is no place for thee. Thou couldst not live in my dwelling-place; envious Death, that stalks there day and night, would shoot at thee at once, desiring thy beauty, for himself. I have no power against Death; I could not shield thee from his arrows. O Beautiful beyond all the beauty of Heaven, come not thou! Rather will I go forth alone to my condemnation, and perish utterly."

"My father," she said, very calmly. "I invoke the truth from thee. I will hear destiny speak through thy lips. Can I, going with him, save the Spirit of the Earth?"

They all rose in their places, to hear destiny speak through the king.

"Thou canst not save him," said he. "There is no God in Heaven of us all that could save him. He hath eaten the fruit of the Tree, and none can save him but himself. Yet if thou wert to go, there would be hope for him; and possessing hope, at the last he might come to save himself. But in the kingdom of Death, thou too wouldst die."

"Speak," she said, "what means this *die?*"

"We know not well," said the king; "we can but guess. I think it would be, to lose thyself, thy being; to become a very little and powerless thing; and without thought or knowledge, foresight or memory."

"I will go with the Spirit of the Earth," she said.

In the morning they rode forth together; and she talked to him by the way, uttering gentle druid wisdom, very powerful in its magic; so that he remembered all the hopes he had in his young time, and the beauty of his youthful dreams. Visions of beautiful victories rose before him. Inspired and strengthened by her shining companionship, he would purge his house of evil utterly; then ride out under the banners of Aldebaran and worship God in high deeds along the borders of space. And he loved her without thought of self; not as a man may love a woman, but as a poet may love a dream or a star; he vowed to himself that he would worship her for ever, and shield her from Death's arrows with his own body. So once more, as she rode with him through the blue empyrean, he was the Knight of Heaven going forth upon adventure: he knew himself for a God.

They came into the realm of Evening, and looking down, the Lady Daffodil beheld the mountains of the Earth empurpled far below, and the lakes golden and roseate under the sunset, and valleys that seemed the abodes of quiet peace.

"But thy kingdom is altogether lovely," said she.

"Thou hast not seen the dwellings of men," he answered.

They rode on and down, and passed beneath the borders of the empire of Night.

"What ails thee, Princess?" said he, trembling.

"I grow a little faint," she said. "There is one here—"

"Ha, Earth, my gossip, what new light o' love hast brought with thee?"

"Back, thou Death!" cried the Spirit of the Earth, leaping forward to take the arrow, if he might, in his own breast. But Death laughed at him as he shot, and went on his way jeering.

"Never heed thou this, to be cast down by it," she whispered. "Bury me in the loveliest of thy valleys; find thou a grassy mound whereon there are stones of the Druids, and bury me beneath the grass there; to-morrow I shall put forth a sign that I am with thee always, and that thou art always to hope. So I bid thee no farewell. . . ."

He bore her body down into the loveliest of his valleys, and digged her a grave upon the mound, and watched beside the grave until morning. And when the sun had risen he found a flower blooming above the grave, lovelier than all the blossoms of his native Heaven. He bent down, and reverently kissed the yellow delight and glory of its bloom; and lo, the bloom had language for him, and whispered: "While I flower thou shalt not perish; when thou seest me, thou art to think that beauty and hope still remain to thee; I am thy sign and assurance that thou shalt yet be among the greatest of the Princes of Heaven."

And that morning the Druids found daffodils blooming about their sacred circle. "Heaven hath won some sweeping victory over hell," they said.

●●●●●●●●●●●●●●●●●●●●●●●●●●●

*"A Mistake in the Mail?" tells of an Italian artist of the last century who
dreams of painting the goddess Diana. It was first published in* The
Theosophical Path *in August 1917, under the pseudonym Floyd C. Egbert.*

A Mistake in the Mail?

S unset time, and a gray-green dusk in the olive-woods: on which
soft gloom not yet had the star-flame of the fireflies begun to
wander and twinkle. Yonder a pool, left by the rain, flames sudden saffron
and vermilion where the sun-rays shine in slanting through a break in the
sage-gray roofage to the west. The place is heavy and sweet with the scent of
narcissus; their white blooms star the wood-floor dimly. From the Hotel
Oesterreich, half a mile or so away through the terraced woods, floats the
sound of German singing; one distinguishes only the swaying chorus, *Ja,
ja! Ja, ja!* But in this part of the world one may hear song or speech at any
time in almost any language in Europe; and United States also is common.
In the English church, of a Sunday morning, they pray regularly for "Our
Sovereign Lady Queen Victoria, Humbert King of Italy, and the President
of the United States of America"; within a mile, prayers will doubtless be
going up simultaneously for Kaiser Friedrich, the king of Sweden and Norway, the Czar of Russia—for everyone, in fact, except M. Sadi Carnot.
One does not pray much, in the churches, for the President of the Third
Republic.

Here in the olive-woods, also, prayers are ascending; but of a widely
different kind. They are addressed to the *Santissima Madonna;* but that is
because it is no longer the fashion to petition the Cyprian by name. *Speed her
coming!*—there you have the burden of them all. Someone has suggested
that there must often be confusion and jealousy on Olympus, which no celestial Post Office can obviate: prayers come addressed to the *Santissima Madonna,* that be intended, some for Venus, some for Lucina, some for any of

the ladies of the pantheon. They arranged these things better in pagan times, distinctly. Mistakes occur; did in the present instance, I incline to think, or this story would never have been told. However—

The one that prays is Giordano Farfalla, known commonly in artistic circles as *Il Botterfloy:* the name that suits him best. Many good critics believed him chief rising star in the firmament of Italian art; and of his genius none doubted. But then, there were always those butterfly wings! "In good time, *caro mio;* in good time! When the moment comes, I shall begin to work on my masterpiece, my *Diana the Huntress.* Ah, then you shall see; the world shall see. Already it is, in part, conceived—ah, *bellissima!* And when it is painted—*Madre mia, come sarà bellissima!* In Rome, yes; and in Paris, London, Vienna—but in America—everywhere shall I exhibit it; I shall submit it to the judgment of the world. Meanwhile, *pazienza!* there is time, there is time." He was one of those people, however, for whose boasting you only like them the better. . . .

In fact, he was the life and soul of society, native and foreign; and foreign of all camps and races. He would permit no one to be on terms other than the most cordial with him; and in this, had all the gifts necessary for success. Dr. Eastman, of New England, puritan and most learned divine, put aside a native prejudice against Italians and Roman Catholics only in his favor. He was secretly adored by the faded and quite unhumorous Miss Larsen, of Norway; he was the bosom chum of the elderly and ugly Mrs. Lorraine, called *Il Capitano* among the artists and Bohemians. Eke he was *persona grata* in the circles of Lady Philippa Fitzpatrick, who loathed Bohemianism, and gathered about her lights of the Church of England. In Lady Philippa's drawing-room he was strictly *Signor Farfalla;* she did not encourage, though she could not suppress, his excursions into English. He was likewise always welcome when the Baron took him round to the Oesterreich; though I doubt he knew as much German as to say *ja* for *si.* Indeed, his linguistic capacity was strictly limited; we spoke of his excursions into English, which was the only language, other than his own, that he would converse in. And in that he knew but the one word *Botterfloy*—but could make that go far.

Mrs. Lorraine was among those who believed in his genius; and her opinion was worth something. Watercolor was her medium, and in it she did flaming justice to the Italian skies. She had a religion of her own: it was that an artist must paint, and do nothing to hinder his painting. Ah, but she was original, *Il Capitano:* a vigorous spirit! After five minutes you forgot that she was the ugliest woman alive, and remembered only that she was the most charming. Old enough to be Farfalla's mother, she held that she alone among the daughters of Eve, for the present, had proprietary rights to his homage. She intended to marry him some day—to the right person. But it must be someone to whom she might bequeath him without fear of results; and meanwhile she must marry him firmly to his painting. It was she in fact who had taught him about half he knew; especially in the matter of painting with fire and light for pigment. Certainly she was the one serious influence in his life; for you could not count Padre Giacomo his confessor. And she wielded her influence with banter of the kind that does not sting; with criticism of the kind that counts; with the infection of her religion of work. "Yes, that's very good, my dear; now go and paint it again." So in the days when, a boy, he began haunting her studio. She had no atom of mysticism in her being, and believed in nothing, she said, that she could not see;—that, however, one took with a grain of salt. At any rate, she was at no pains to conceal her unbelief; hence her unpopularity with Lady Philippa Fitzpatrick's Anglican set. Go to church—when she might be painting? On a dull Sunday morning perhaps. —But if ever that dull Sunday morning came, it found her too busy with something else; and our Sovereign Lady Queen Victoria, Humbert King of Italy and the President of the United States of America had to be saved with no aid of intercession from her.

Another believer in Farfalla was *Il Barone*—Von Something—an artist who spoke Italian and English Germanly. These three were the trinity of the local Bohemia; their three studios were held in common, though mostly they foregathered in the Villa Lorraine when there was need or whim to work in company. The baron was a painter of solid merit, though a meek and meager little man; the antithesis of Mrs. Lorraine in many ways: sober and painstaking where she was brilliant and daring. At the Villa, too, they drank afternoon tea with some regularity; so did most of the artists of the place, and others who found Lady Philippa Fitzpatrick's a little dull. At those teas the relative claims of Shakespeare, Dante and Goethe to supremacy were discussed in English, Italian and German; one also heard French there constantly, and even Russian and Spanish sometimes.

"What has become of the Butterfly?" said *il-Capitano*. "This is the third time this week—"

The Baron groaned. "It is *la Tiamante*," said he. "Mine friend, I am afraid—so; I am afraid. He is young, *und auch* he is peautiful; und der plood, mit these Italians, it is so warm, *nicht wahr?* The great art, it goes not mit Tiamantes."

And in fact, the Baron was right. He might tearfully implore, and the Capitano might banter and harry; but there stood Farfalla's big canvas at his easel, as it had stood now for several weeks: so many square feet of silvery grey-green and romantic gloom—moonlight in the olive-woods— daubed on for a background, and Diana the Huntress—not. And littered about were sketches by the dozen—in crayon, in charcoal, in watercolor, in oils—of a divinity of quite another order: plump and retroussée, coquettishly wearing a white silk shawl starred over with little blossoms in green and red. And the Botterfloy had lost his gaiety, except in desperate fits and starts; and the Capitano forebore to make fun of the Baron when he inveighed against "la Tiamante"; she herself called down, in private, no blessings on that young person's head.

Farfalla was Italian, and therefore Catholic-Pagan; his father, a Nizzard, had worn the red shirt in his day; had possessed Garibaldi's confidence, indeed, and been a man after that lofty idealist's own heart. So there was good blood in the veins of our Botterfloy, and a capacity to dream high dreams; he was made for much better things than *la Diamante* and her tribe. So much the more Mrs. Lorraine lamented his enmeshment. "Hearken, *Giordanino mio,*" said she more than once; "there are other things to paint beside white silk shawls, although one treats them with talent." A love affair—*tut,* that was nothing; but this was of the kind that spoils genius.

And now, here he was in the olive-woods in the glamor of the evening; there was the gold and scarlet lighting the surface of the pool a dozen yards in front of him; all around, the light was growing dim and dusk, and the fireflies were beginning to dart and shine and wander. And between the puffs of endless cigarettes—"too many of them, these days, *caro mio!*" as Mrs. Lorraine had remarked only that morning for the fiftieth time—he was praying with fervor: "*Santissima Maria, speed her coming!*" "Her," need I say, was *la Diamante.*

The light died from the pool, and it became a faint glimmer under the sky in the midst of the firefly-lit darkness; and still no one came. Farfalla was artist, as well as lover; and the beauty of the night began to invade his mind. The moon rose, and he watched the pool over-silvered; and remembered Diana the Huntress, even while continuing his prayers. He bethought him of old dreams and creative ideals: how his heart had swelled and his vision ran out to far horizons of the spirit, when first the conception of *la Diana* had come to him. *Ah, bellissima, bellissima!* Pure, cold, intent, majestic, eager: a silver presence, yet more radiant than silver or gold—the highest dream. The utmost and farthest—passing starry through the woods. That was how he would have painted her. Would have?—would! The little glade where the pool was, and the moonlight on the water: that was the background for her! The rich, soft Italian moonlight; the deep, over-silvered blue of the Italian night-sky; the sweetness of the olive-woods, langorous with narcissus scent—all this sensuous softness, with its suggestion of latent passion, should be startled with a vision all whiteness, all beautiful strength and grace. Purity?—ah, it was not only the saints of the church that possessed the secret of that! —And still he prayed: *Ah, Madonna, speed her coming!*

"See, Carlo mio, he prays, that devout one. Let us advance, thou and I." So *la Diamante;* who had arranged her coup, and was to strike that night, win or lose, for the soul of Farfalla. "Not for nothing is he so named," she considered. "He shall find me with the little Carlo Agnelli; there shall be grand romance; then, if he shall have behaved—"

They came forward. Farfalla heard footsteps, rose from his knees, and dashed off past them in the direction of the town. *"Buona notte, signorino!* Ah, but why this haste!"* He lifted his hat, said his *"Buona notte, signorina!"* and was gone.

"Ah, che diavolo, quegli! The beast, the pig, the ingrate!"* La Diamante flamed and trembled. —"Adored one, what has happened?" said Carlo. "As an angel affronted you appear to me. It was merely, I think, Giordano Farfalla—he that paints with the German and the Englishwoman. But listen thou to the pleadings of thy worshiper!"—So he addressed her in the language she understood, and achieved soothing her presently. As for the Botterfloy, heaven knows whether he was so much as aware who had spoken to him.

Mrs. Lorraine came into her studio next morning uneasy of mind, and found no relief in her work. Her prie-dieu (easel and campstool) provided now no refuge devotional, as of old. She admitted she had been worrying about Farfalla; which was sinful, because you can't paint and worry. This morning the trouble was acute, and no inward wrestling would dislodge the demon. By eleven o'clock she could stand it no longer, and laid down her brushes with a sigh. She would put on her hat, and go forth in quest of news.

First she went to the Baron's, who knew nothing of Farfalla's whereabouts. "But I haf mineself been anxious too; ja, most anxious; and already I would go there up to his house." So the two of them wended their way towards the *città,* and sought Farfalla's studio. "You see, he is not there," said the Baron; "there is no song." Always, if the Botterfloy were at home, one might expect to hear *Con che cuor; Moritina, te mi lasce?* or something as classical, when one came to the foot of the stairs. "All the same I'm going in," said Mrs. Lorraine; with an inward shiver of apprehension. It never occurred to her to knock or to call *"E permesso!"*—either he was absent, or—

She went in, and, holding the handle of the door, came to a stop. Farfalla was rapt, agile, covering the bare canvas furiously. He neither heard nor saw her. She beckoned to the Baron outside, and put a finger to her lips commanding silence. They stood in the doorway and watched. "Ko-loss-al!" murmured the Baron; and "Sublime!" said she. And they were right—even at that stage. Not a word would they speak to him; both knew better than that. After a while they shut the door quietly, and went down into the street. Mrs. Lorraine pulled down her veil. "No, go home; I don't want you to accompany me," said she. "I'm going to blub."

As for what had wrought the change, there is no evidence for it but that of Farfalla himself. So you must take or leave what follows, as your preference may be. It was the explanation he gave to Mrs. Lorraine, when *Diana the Huntress* had gone forth to conquer Europe. Not till then would he speak;

although quite evidently marvels had been on foot. And he succeeded in convincing her that at least he believed what he was saying; she even believed it herself, I fancy; except when you challenged her habitual unbelief by questioning her about it. There was the evidence of the picture!

He had, then, thrown down his last cigarette, and forgotten to light another. The beauty of the night had taken hold upon him; as if his assignation had been with *la Diana,* not with *la Diamante.* The woods—can you not believe?—were filled with whisperings and mystery: haunted with immemorial rustling presences out of Mediterranean pagandom. Every gnarled over-branching olive-trunk seemed alive, silent, intense with expectancy. *Oh, Santissima, speed her coming!* Hush, what was that? A white heart, shining like the silver edge of a cloud, broke out of the silence and shadow, and gleamed across the glade. "But not along the ground, Signora; in the air; so high; *ecco!"* A quiver ran through the gray foliage; a whisper through the wood: a cold breath of wind, infinitely suggestive of purity. —Two hounds? yes, but never the hounds of a mortal hunter shone silvery like these, nor so came streaming through the haunted air. . . . They were gone with the hart into the shadow. "And then . . . she appeared . . . for an instant gliding in mid air through the glade; above the pool, whereon her shadow was as if it had lightened. *Ah, bellissima!* . . . The bowstring stretched tight, drawn back to the shoulder . . . a queen in faint blue and silver: a goddess, a visitant from celestial spheres! As you see her in the picture, Signora; but—yes, I swear it—a million times more beautiful even than that. . . . White gleamed the pool, celestially white beneath her celestial passaging; for an instant she shone; for an instant only; but even before she had vanished I was kneeling to her, and my arms flung forth in a gesture of homage, of adoration!"

● ●

"The Last Adventure of Don Quixote" appeared in the September 1917 issue of The Theosophical Path, *under the pseudonym Fortescue Lanyard. Morris reprinted it in his short story collection,* The Secret Mountain and Other Tales. *The Irish writer, AE (George Russell), reviewed the collection in* The Irish Statesman *and called this story "the most perfect of these tales and I think the most original." Morris's story is in effect a continuation of Cervantes' burlesque of heroic adventure, but with a difference: in Morris's version, Don Quixote, the mortal buffoon, is reborn as a genuine heroic figure.*

The Last Adventure of Don Quixote

*C*ide Hamete Benengeli relates this; though I cannot tell how he came by it. Indeed, it would be hard to say. All else he wrote was attested by numberless witnesses; but who could give testimony as to this? Perhaps it was for such a reason that his illustrious translator, having a passion for exactitude above all things, concluded to omit it from the Castilian version. Though again, it may have been among the many passages that were scissored out, as he tells us, by the authorities; or he may have felt in it an inferiority of style, and been too much the artist to allow it in. Yet I think it but fair to the patient and accurate Cide that it should come to light at last; and let the critics judge for themselves!

It seems, then, that the book as we have it closes too soon. Don Quixote rose from his sick-bed cured, and something more than that. He had been very ill, certainly; now, it pertained to the marvellous how little ill he felt. In all the long length of his body there was not so much as one ache or pain—unless one might speak of the ache of bounding and glowing health; while as for his mind—

He realized a curious clarity in it, quite unknown to him before. Of old—you know—he had always been troubled with a kind of—how shall I express it?—uncertainty—a sense of being haunted by shams. There had been, as it were, a wraith on the borders of his consciousness: one Alonso Quixano, called *the Good:* whose quiet prosaic life had somehow mingled its drab cotton with the rich silks and gold of his own. The powers of some enchanter had been wont to prevail against him, poisoning with a subtle confusion the truth of things. A giant or a paynim emperor with his hosts, heroically encountered, would loom up suddenly to mock him, on some fantastic plane of vision, as no more than a wretched windmill or a shepherd with his flocks; there had been times when, through the reality of glorious Rozinante, a lean miserable hack had trembled into view—an illusion, if ever there was one; and when Mambrino's magical helmet had seemed a barber's basin. There had been moments when to be God's Knight Errant had appeared a mirage, an unattainable splendor; and all attempts to come up with it a forlorn hope. One rode atilt at one's objective, but as in a dream stumbled and fumbled over irrelevancies; the atmosphere became as wet wool or as treachery about one; progress so to say evaporated: until, like a drunkard or a dreamer, one staggered at last into inevitable thwackings and ignominy.

Not that he had ever broken the faith of his calling, or given an inch to doubt. He had known that that tremendous thing the Glory of Service, or Knight Errantry, did exist: as surely as the rainbow of heaven, as the flames of sunset and dawn, it was *there;* and one might come to plunge one's being in it: one might attain. But there was a world of deceits to fight one's way through first. And if he had never despaired, it was also true that the bright reality of hope had become a little unfamiliar to him. He knew he had been feeding his faith from the stores of his conscious will: had had to provide for it himself. No manna of the spirit had fallen for it from heaven; nor ravens had brought it food, as they did to Elijah of old. He had not really hoped, but had only made himself hope—until now.

But now all was different; and he did not even hope, but *knew.* Master Notary had made his will, and the Curate had taken his confession: of which matters, though one would have supposed them solemn enough, he took the smallest account. Sancho, he recollected, had besought him with much blubbering not to be so injudicious as to die—whatever that might mean. It was somewhere about then that the turn had come in the tide of his affairs: he must have fallen asleep for a little, to wake thus a new man; with the perfect assurance that, going forth now, nothing but victories and serious work awaited him. So he looked on his surroundings, as on the recent past, with the detachment of a mind keyed to higher things. The people in the house seemed to him, as he passed out, shadowy and half unreal. He commended them to God perfunctorily—really, perhaps only in his thoughts: he was going upon a grand adventure, and knew too well they would not be interested. They hardly answered him—that is, if indeed he spoke. There was the housekeeper, good soul,—very busy about something, and apparently weeping the while; there was his niece, red-eyed and mouse-like quiet; Bachelor Samson Carrasco; the Curate; and Master Nicholas the Barber: the last-named three in consultation seemingly, and melancholy enough by the look of them—but unreal, unreal. Sancho, in the kitchen, he noticed as he passed its open door, blubbering over a very hearty meal. He

would have had some kind of connection with that Sancho, he supposed;—
or was it merely that the fat shrewd fellow had borne the same name as his,
Don Quixote's squire? But all that belonged to the foreclosed period of enchantments, and was not to be peered at too closely. It hardly mattered;
since the day of real things had come. In the same vague manner he noticed
the general air of dejection, and wondered what its cause might be—but
not much, for the business ahead was too insistent in its call.

He went out to the stable; and—there was, indeed, a lean miserable
hack at the manger: a wretched horse-skin hung on bones and propped up
on four caricatures of legs at the corners: just such a thing as he had been
condemned, when the enchanter's power prevailed against him, to imagine
Rozinante to be. But there also, beside that mockery of Knight Errantry's
companion, the Horse, stood the real Rozinante, all fire and gentleness and
beauty: limbs made for speed and endurance, glossy skin, hoofs like shells
from the sea, proud mien and arching neck: Rozinante, of the unique renown, veritably surpassing (and by far) Bucephalus of old or the Cid's own
Babieca. The beautiful creature whinnied him a welcome: with a note of
triumph, as knowing how glad a season had come. As for the hack, it lacked
but the strength to grow restive at sight of that knightly man in his splendid armor;—for in armor Don Quixote was, though without memory, exactly, how he came to be so clad; in armor he was: not to linger over it too
tediously, all panoplied, like Don Apollo of the Heavens, in burnished radiance and rubicund gold.

To him there came Sancho Panza: not the man he had but now left
blubbering and guzzling in the kitchen, but the true Sancho at last, the
right squire for a knight errant. "Is it your highness's will to ride forth?"
said this Sancho. "It is, good friend," said Don Quixote; "since now the day
has come when we are to meet the grand adventure, and win vast empires
for the glory of knight errantry." He must, I think, have forgotten the lady
Dulcinea del Toboso; or surely would have mentioned her here. "As God
wills," said Sancho; and without more words saddled the beautiful Rozinante and led him forth. On the road a mule was waiting, excellently
caparisoned: having held the stirrup for his master, and seen him duly
a-horseback, the squire mounted the mule, and together they rode forward.

Not, however, upon the familiar (and famous) Campo de Montiel; but
through vast regions unlike any in La Mancha. In front there were the dim
bluenesses of immense distance; on this side topless precipices soared diz-
zily into the heavens above; on that, fathomless abysses that hid the far
world beneath their carpeting of cloud. There were prodigious valleys, wide
as the world; there were august mountains towering afar in faint turquoise
and purple, about whose peaks in the sweetness of the evening clustered the
large white flames of the stars. A keen ecstasy and lightness encompassed
Don Quixote, limbs and mind and spirit; his soul was nourished with

wonder and inspiration, in tutelage to the mountains and to the fires of heaven. Neither weariness nor need of food or drink overtook him; that gigantic beauty momently renewed and increased his strength.

He rode forward, conversing at whiles with his squire on the deeds of knighthood; calm wonderful words came to his lips; noble and beautiful were the replies he had from his companion. Long journeying elapsed before it came to his mind that the name of Sancho was somehow inappropriate for that one. He had listened to grave utterances of poetry and wisdom, at first without heeding their unwontedness, then with a growing surprise; until certainty at last took him that he never had been squired by such a one before. He turned his glance wonderingly from the infinity before him, to behold the most kingly of men riding at his side.

"Señor," said he, drawing rein.

"Take it not ill, Señor Don Quixote," said the other, "that I ride beside your highness through these regions as your squire. My master, having taken account of your deeds and fame in La Mancha, and noted that that region deserved you little, desires that you shall visit his court; furthermore, he has set apart for you, if your grace will honor him by accepting it, command of a wide dangerous region in his dominions; since he knows your ability to win victories against the most stubborn of his foes. The way is long, however, and not easy to find; and therefore he sent me to escort you to his palace."

"*Caballero,*" said Don Quixote, "for this lofty graciousness thanks must be given in deeds rather than in words. My sword and my lance are henceforth at your great monarch's disposal."—So they rode forward; but it did not occur to Don Quixote at that time to make inquiry as to the names and titles of his squire.

Vaster and vaster grew the mountains; wider the valleys as they advanced. Along the lips of chasms where blue infinity fell endlessly below them; by the shores of night-blue waters strewn with a million trembling flame-splashes of gold; night and day, night and day they rode on; and ever the consciousness of immortal strength, the serenity of pure being, grew in the spirit and limbs of the knight. In what Spain were these cosmic mountains? Had any Amadis of Wales* or Palmerin of England, ridden through them before?

They came, early of an evening, to the top of a barren pass where the road branched: one way leading to the right high up along the mountainside, the other sweeping clean down into the valley. Far off, shining like a huge coronet in the sunset, gleamed a city with many gem-bright cloud-soft towers and minarets; it shone beyond the immensity of the valley—beyond and above ranges and ranges of snow-capped mountains all velvet

---

*Amadis de Gaula is properly so translated, and not as "of Gaul."

blue and dark and pale purple below their snows, whose austerity it crowned. "It is the high metropolis of my sovereign," said the squire. "What dark army is that, which moves in the valley?" said Don Quixote. "Whose grim castle is that, yonder in its depths to the southward?"

"It is the army of my king's enemies," said the other anxiously and with a sigh. "The castle is their chief stronghold; thence their leader, a great insurgent baron, works huge oppressions against the world."

The soul of Don Quixote swelled into grandeur within him. "Señor," he said, "I little thought the opportunity would be granted me so early to prove the truth of my new allegiance."

"Do not think of it, Señor Don Quixote, I beseech you! Taking this road to the right, we shall avoid them and act prudently; it is to be considered that they are numberless and puissant. Nay, nay indeed! My royal master would never forgive me, should the smallest harm befall your grace! It will be yours presently to ride against them at the head of armies; but now—"

Ta! he spoke to *Don Quixote!* The soul of that great man was as little to be shaken as the mountains, as luminous as the morning sun. He bowed with a very haughty gesture: "Señor," he said, "I have the honor of knight errantry to think of"; and with the word, couched lance, spurred steed, and away.

Down the slope thundered glorious Rozinante; with less danger of stumbling than the renowned Pegasus of antiquity charging through the middle air. Enchantment could prevail nothing against him now; right into the grim host flashed the golden figure of him; lance did its work, breaking the outermost ranks, and was gone; and in his hand instead flashed a falchion out of the mythologies. A roar of consternation arose in front, and he heard his own name carried to the horizons: *Don Quixote of La Mancha! Alas, it is Don Quixote!* Borne on still by the impetus of his charge, he hacked and hewed to left and right; nought in mind but the ideals of his profession and the gloomy standard, held aloft by giants, towards which he had aimed his horse from the first. They receded; then gathered and surged in on him; but he fought on and on. The force of his charge was spent; but he fought forward. Blows rained upon his shield and upon his armor; it began to go hard with him . . . and through all the ardor of the conflict a certain sound came to him: the patter and bleating of a thousand sheep on the road; sheep coming up behind him; he could hear the cries of the shepherd, the *yap! yap!* of the sheepdogs; and it appeared to him that enchantment was making head against him again; and lo, with the very sigh that escaped him upon that thought, the patter and baaing and the barking became the triumphant shouting of his name: *For Don Quixote of La Mancha! For the Tenth Worthy of the World!* and up from behind a great host in armor swept to his aid, and at their head (he recognized) the valiant knight Pentapolin of the Naked Arm;

and they drove back the enemy, and left Don Quixote alone for a moment on the field; so that he took breath, and recovered, and with a word to Rozinante charged again; but what had become of the army of Pentapolin he was not aware.

And now he charged into the center, and grasped, after many deeds of prowess, at the standard pole; and fought and reeled and struggled; and the great dark champions were about him like swarming bees about their queen; so that he made no headway, nor succeeded to drag away the standard pole; yet held it and would not part with it; and so, rocking to and fro, that mêlée surged; Don Quixote in the midst, heroically combating . . . and rejoicing, thinking that—

Enchantment again; and he might not be free from it; for he heard the creak, creak, clang of the sails as they went round; the groaning and complaining of the mill-wheels; and it was a miracle . . . for he beheld them, from this side and from that; the windmills, gigantic, lumbering across the plain; not stationary as of old to be attacked, but advancing . . . and turning, *creak, creak, clang* . . . and then a roar from them, and a shouting of his name: *Don Quixote de La Mancha! Por Diós y Don Quixote!*—and the windmills, behold, they were giants; all in white and silver armor; and they advanced upon those who were slaying Don Quixote, and with a great roar drove them off; so that my knight had breathing time again; and then that great host of giants passed like a sighing of the wind; and anew Don Quixote used his regained strength to advance.

And now he drove them across the plain in confusion, and helter-skelter in at the gates of their stronghold; and rode on pell-mell pursuing them; and had the standard at last at the gates; and thundered with his mace— but how the mace came in his hand he knew not—upon the portcullis as it fell clanging and locked, so that it shook and was loosened, and was within a little of breaking. Then Don Quixote heard from the far hills a bugle calling; and suddenly the air was loud with a rushing of myriad wings behind. Then rose up one before him flammivomous and horrible, vast and grim as the mountains, bearing a club whose fall should powder the granite mountains where they are firmest, and a brand that shed midnight and ghastly flame and stench; and between his attack and Don Quixote, a sudden sword flashed like the daybreak, and a splendor broke like the noonday sun; and the portcullis was shattered, the gate was down; and the dark lord driven out, and a host swept in with Don Quixote all golden armored and golden aureoled, and their armor strangely and beautifully adorned with pinions; and so that stronghold was taken.

But at Don Quixote's side stood the one whose sword but now had saved him; and it was the man who had squired him on his journey.

"Señor," said Don Quixote, "to whom am I honored to owe by deliverance?"

"*Caballero*," said the other, "let your grace make nothing of the deliverance. I am, in truth, the Captain-general of the war hosts of my sovereign; and hence qualified to appreciate the greatness of your feat. I am styled, Michael of the Flaming Sword."

Side by side in pleasant converse they rode forward then to the palace gates of their sovereign: Don Quixote of La Mancha and Don Michael Archangel: each wondrously pleased with the nobility and high bearing of his companion.

• •

*"Deio the Mountain" is Morris's first story written in his mature period
specifically for (and about) children. It appeared in two parts in the September
and November 1917 issues of* The Raja-Yoga Messenger, *the theosophical
magazine for young people. It was signed Cenydd Morus, a variant Welsh
spelling of Kenneth Morris.*

Deio the Mountain

*I*t began in the orchard. I don't know how he came there, nor what
Betti Nantymelin was doing, to let him get away like that. Her
fault it must have been, whatever; though not well to say too much about
it, for cry her eyes out she did when she found the nursery empty, poor
thing; and no harm coming of it, after all. You couldn't expect the others to
bother; and as for the master and mistress, they were in Swansea for the day,
and did not get back till just before Dan the Poacher arrived at Gelli-onen
in the evening, as shall be duly related.

But there he was, in the orchard, when the great idea struck him. The
appletrees were old, with trunks and boughs grey-bearded with lichens,
and elbowed and angled queerly. In the blue light of the afternoon—the
silver-blue time, before the world turns mellow-golden—you could hear
many sounds to delight you, and the air was flooded with the wine of
mountain odors. Between the tree rows you could see the green ample quie-
tudes of the mountainside, and above the green, the darkness and purple of
heather. From far up and beyond came dropping in a little seed-pearl
stream the notes of a lark singing.

It was Mr. Arthur planted those trees—the apples and plums and
greengages—"in the old, anncient, forrmerly times; over a hundred years
ago, I shouldn' wonder." That was what Amber said; and although it was
his one chronological formula for such things as the Roman occupation, the
Norman Wars, the Emperor Arthur and Owen Glyndwr, it was not inappropriate in this case; for Mr. Iorwerth had fought Boney under Picton; and
Mr. Iorwerth was Mr. Arthur's son; and Mr. Gwilym was Mr. Iorwerth's;

and Mr. Llewelyn was Mr. Gwilym's; and Deio bach was Mr. Llewelyn's. So that the trees had a certain claim to the title of ancient. But to Deio—called Browneyes before, but Deio the Mountain, proudly, after this episode—they were as though coeval with the world: things of antique magic and mystery, with profound thought and wisdom of their own. Once he had sat mouselike in the library while his father read to Captain Rees about the Woods of Celyddon, with their "seven score and seven sweet appletrees, equal in height, girth, beauty and sweetness," and about the half-appearing maid that predicts "things that shall certainly come to pass." He expected to see her emerge from the appletrees at any time. He had always thought wonderful on the orchard before, but now—

You never could tell what might happen in it. Again, it was on the way to the Mountain, and under the Mountain; and Who might live in the Mountain, who could tell? Sometimes one would enquire, and receive foolish answers: as, Davvy Beynon Llwchishywel, or Jones the Quarryfield, or Tommy Hodges, or Merry 'Altery (known to the sophisticated as Mary Walters). But far up there, as one could see from the night-nursery window, was a grove of dark trees; and close by them, Someone lived, that sang mysteriously in the nights;—or calling he was for you to come to him;—and it was neither Davvy Beynon, nor Jones nor Tommy Hodges, whom one knew perfectly well; nor even Merry 'Altery—about whom, still, there was a flavor of mystery. But then what good to ask at all, when nobody did know?

And it was on the Mountain that Tortoy had been lost; on Tuesday morning, when Betti Nantymelin took him to gather bluebells. Tortoy, you are to know, was a tortoise: of the tin sort that swims after a magnet: a loved and intimate pet, that had accompanied Deio Browneyes on all his wanderings. Its loss had been the first serious sorrow in his life; one not yet, after four long days, acquiesced in. Deio knows it might come to a call, if one were on the Mountain in the neighborhood of its hiding-place; and alone, so that one might discover the right call to give. And besides—and besides—and besides—

Over the green of the appletrees, that was like a green flame against the blue flame of the sky, came that thin sweet trickle of bird music, that was a call for him to come as clear as bird-Welsh could make it; *Dei-o, Dei-o, Dei-o, tyr'd ti, tyr'd li, tyr'd li! Dyre mla'n! dyre mla'n!* (Come thou, come away.)

—"So I are, too," said Deio; and his great plan was formed.

On he went, past the big codlin, past the row of Victoria plums, past the greengages: a long way, and Oh, a long, long way whatever! From the kitchen garden, away to his left, came a sound of singing, betokening the presence of peril: it was of course, Amber the gardener, to be avoided on an occasion like this. But Amber was busy with the hymn on his lips and the cucumber frames in his mind:

Beth sydd imi yn y byd
Ond gorthrymder mawr o hyd?
(What does this world hold for me?
Only grief and misery.)

he sang; and calculated what he would get in the market for "them pro-
misin'-lookin' cucumberrs." So Deio might pass unseen and unquestioned.
On he went to the top of the orchard, where the stile was—beyond
which lay bluebell-land and the Mountain. That stile was a difficulty; but
not beyond negotiating, even without help. The third trial brought him
rolling over on the soft grass beyond, much too joyous to consider whether
he was hurt by the fall; and now, indeed, it was

Beth sydd imi yn y byd
Ond y Mynydd mawr a 'i hud?—
(What does this world hold for me?
Only mountain-mystery!)

—The cropped turf, with bracken and blue and white wild hyacinths growing scatteredly: a slope up and up to the wild unknown places. One could
not stop, even for the bluebells. The fern grows thicker and taller as you go
upward, till you tread the tracks and passable places of a forest of bracken,
that even tiptoeing would be above your shoulders, above your head. (By
you, of course, I mean this Deio Four-years-old). And who was to know
what might live and move in its depths: all the creatures of Fairyland, and
plump, furry bunnies, and little men? Adventures . . . !
Green like jewels, like enamel, was the fern: sweet-scented, with young
shoots up-curling like a baby's hand; and fronds uncurled, spreading royally, to brood during the summer on dreams and memories out of the
world's prime; and to maintain a silence fitting their grace and dignity, lest
they should fail to hear the dewdrops dropping from them in the morning,
or the One that sings in the Mountain o' nights. But no good their pretending with Deio bach, who could very well hear their being alive. And who
would know the whereabouts of lost Tortoy, unless they? —You may argue
that the loss happened farther down, in bluebell land; but Deio was aware
of the ways of his pet. Should he call the creature, or should he ask them?
—a matter for deep thought and cogitation as he went. "Hush, dear, hush!"
whispered the bracken; but one didn't mind that, since they hushed themselves, and had a right to it; and indeed, spoke not fussily, with an air of
being grown up and superior; but rather as if sharing some secret delicate
wisdom with oneself. Yes; decidedly one was on the Mountain now, among
one's peers, the Quiet Things that Understand. As for enquiry, there would
come opportunities for that.

Here was a glade of soft, well-nibbled turf: an island in the fern and romping-place for rabbits; to one gray long-ears of whom sidled now my little man with friendly intentions. As was to be expected, two such grave things had a language in common. —"What?" queried the bunny sympathetically, allowing himself to be smoothed, and hardly staying the serious business in hand (or mouth). —"There's a—thing— called—a Tortoy—" began Deio, carefully picking his words. —"It's up there," said the other, with a flick of its ear towards the mountaintop. "It's up there, with—." Deio waited long for the rest; pondering deeply how he should frame an all important question, in case no more should come. It did not; so he proceeded: —"With the—One—that—sings—in the night?" Furred Solemnity seemed a little scared; "Hush, dear, hush!" it said, glancing round; then fell once more to its nibbling. But Deio, sure, could afford to be patient; here was one that knew something, and you had better just go on smoothing (since it was kindly permitted) and thinking. Fur at last, having either finished its dinner or made up its mind, assumed an air of decision, lifted its head, and said, "Come!"

It led him by its own roads through the fern; now up, now down a little; this way and that; if Betti Nantymelin had stood at the stile below, she might have scanned the whole world without catching a glimpse of Deio: calling she would have to be, to get news of him. But never a thought for Betti Nantymelin had Deio in his mind at that time: who was coming into his great own, and deep-hearted to enjoy it. Politeness seemed to demand no effort at conversation: he and the rabbit went on most comradely, in a silence upon which, however, soon quiet voices ahead, a song-soft chatter, broke:

> Tinkle dimple dongle, toong-roong-loong dinkle,
> Aaaah, ahha haha, toong-roong-loong tonkle. . . .

and Deio, listening, despite gravity must laugh a little. It would be fairies, he thought: lots of fairies. A sudden turn brought them into open sunlight and to the very brink of the singing; it was, of course, the brook, crooning in its own language; or someone hiding in the brook—someone up there, beyond the bend, not far off. They stopped by a broad, shallow, pebbly-bottomed and all rippling brightness and blueness with looking at the sky; it was here, if Deio had known it, he had seen the cattle gather in the evenings for conclave, when he watched them from the nursery window: here they came to confer on what secrets the Mountain had imparted to them during the day. Hence their solemnity and discreet air when they filed into the yard at milking-time.

—"Ask *him!*" said the rabbit. —"Who?" said Deio (regardless of grammar) but got no answer; white tail was bobbing, and long hind-legs loping off already down the path and into the fern. One must manage now for oneself.

Just above the shallows, on his left the waters narrowed; the banks grew high and closer together, and from one to the other of them a plank was thrown, with a rail, to do duty for a footbridge. (All very well for those who could reach the rail.) Under this bridge, and in the shadowy places beyond, the water poured *toong-roong-loong dapple,* in curving waves over great stones dark-green with their moss-tresses, and through somber pools as deep as the world nearly. It was up there that They were talking; and one might indeed go up there and come to something—to Them, in fact; and They might tell one things; but then—Ah, but also *then,* there beyond the shallows, and over the bridge, lay all the enchanted leagues of Mountain, the fairy and the whispering fern: the place where, sure you indeed, Tortoy had wandered, and whence the grand nightlong singing and calling came. For Tortoy, understand, had been a particular and confidential friend, with tastes utterly similar to its master's. Deio would naturally go straight up the Mountain; and therefore, so would Tortoy; and therefore again, so would Deio. He would cross that bridge somehow; not before due consideration; there would be secret means of crossing it, to be revealed to one who should watch in silence. And besides, people of four can't walk on forever without getting tired. He sat him down under the hip-thorn, on the clump at this end of the bridge; and listened to the talking and song-rich waters, and watched with longing eyes the green tremulous world beyond.

The world grew mellow and golden; the sun cast long rays over the fern. By and bye the cows came down from the Mountain; with whisking tails they gathered, and one by one came plash, plash, plash through the shallows; then went in slow procession down the path towards Gellioneny. The sky grew yellow and wistful in the west. Beautifully the dusk came down over the Mountain; beautifully the little winds of twilight went tiptoe whispering over the fern. Indeed, what was on Betti Nantymelin, that she still knew nothing of the absence of her charge? Gossiping in the village she must have been; and she so good a girl as a rule!

Far on the dark breast of the Mountain three brightnesses glinted and shone: birds that flew down low over the bracken, and sang softly as they flew, and sang sweetly as they flew. Down they came, crossing and wheeling and curving, nearer and nearer, till Deio could see them clearly; and till he was laughing for pleasure of their friendly beauty and singing. One of them reminded him of his mother's silk shawl, because it was white, and with pearly and creamy shadows, tender and glossy. One of them was blue like the Ming vase in the library: not the dark, but the light one, that you could watch and watch, sitting on the floor and never a word nor a stir from you, all the while your daddy was writing a chapter of his book. The third bird was lovely with all the colors of the rainbow and the jewels of the infinite world. "Pretty, oh, pretty!" cried Deio, rising up to them with out-stretched arms; for he had no doubt they had come for him: it was as if they had waited and watched for him a thousand years; and as if he, after even such a lapse of time as that, remembered them well. They flew down about him, circling round, brushing his cheeks and his ears with their wings. At the touch of them, it was a king he was, whatever: it was some antique royalty of the spirit rose up in him. Amidst the wind and flutter of their wings he trod safely the perilous plank. Perilous? He felt that no perils in the world could touch him . . . with the rainbows and twinkling and soft-ness of their plumage, and the wonder and wonder and wonder that flowed from their bills in song.

Night bloomed in the sky like a periwinkle blossom: like the cups of a blue campanula deepening: like a somber bluebell in the woodlands of heaven. Down from the palingrim of the firmament, the breast of the Mountain was a glowing darkness from which all material things had van-ished, no longer concealing the secrecies of the Gods. Following the birds, and mingled with their beauty, windlike or flamelike he ran over the tops of the fern. Far above in the pine wood the wind cried. *A-a-a-ah!* Deio, listening, heard eternal voices calling. It was as if the Mountain spoke to him, and said: "Brother, come to your own again! Little One, come to the heart of the Mother!" It was as if the Regent of the Mountain cried to him: "Ah, companion, companion!" Faded the paleness from the brim of the sky; far off on the hills and in the valley the farm windows twinkled; at Llwyn-pen-deryn a dog was barking, miles away; stars gently budded forth over the quiet darkness. What in that darkness was there for a little boy to fear; when to his vision the whole mountainside swam with delirious jewels: wandering sparks, rubies and moonstones and opals, gleaming and gliding and waning? He was in the fairy world, and himself a king of the fairies. What was there to fear?

The singing of the birds grew farther and fainter; with long, low, swooning flights over the fern they rose, and set at last like stars over the dark shoulder of the mountain. For a moment Deio was a little boy again, not unbewildered. A small voice called to him from the ground; he looked down, and there, I declare to you, under a harebell, stood Tortoy, upright upon the hind-legs, dimly to be seen by the light of the harebell bloom. —"Me too!" cried the creature; and Deio with a swoop and a laugh was upon it, and clutching it in a small hand. —"It's up there," said the tin tortoise, "hundreds of miles. I knew you would come." But Deio the child was puzzled, not having legs for hundreds of miles. —"I don't know how to go," he said, slowly; "the birdies taked me." But, Tortoy, as you would expect of him, was valiant with the unimagined resources of fairy creatures. —"Come on," he said, understanding perfectly; "it's up and up, like this!"

The easiest thing in the world, certainly; for up they rose, and swam in the air deliciously, a wandering spark of fairyland.

But you need a guide on that ferny mountain; there are lonely valleys where no one comes; there are many shoulders and ridges to deceive you; you think the top is there before you, when in reality it is far up still, and a mile to your right or left. By day, of course, you may do fairly; but how by night when all faërie is strewn and glimmering round to deceive you? —Running on the winds they were; hither and thither; and where in the world were the pine wood and the fountain of song they desired? Tortoy gave a little squeak in Deio's hand: "She will take us," it said; "look you by there!"

She, if you please, was Merry 'Altery: round black straw hat with turned down rim, snowy cap-frill beneath it, kind old face and full Welsh costume and all; only shining, shining. There she sat, pouring out the brooklet from the tilted pitcher beside her, and crooning olden words in her Fairy-Welsh to a tune like this:

Tongle-rongle toong-roong, tinkle timple teenkle;
Ah, ah, ahha haha, dimple rimple trip trop. . . .

—"Oh, please you, Merry 'Altery fach," began Deio—only when you came close was it indeed Merry 'Altery after all? The flannel of her dress was darkly and strangely glowing, with a glimmer lovelier than any silk; the round hat on her head was a crown of deep emeralds; the white cap-frill, a circle of diamonds and turkisses and pearls. Beautiful was her face, not lined with old age as it had been; and such light came from her that you could see by it the level ground before her and the apple-green velvet of its mosses, the brown tufts clearly on every rush, the beautiful blue of the forget-me-not bloom. And you could see the little boats that went down on the tiny stream, each with a spark of a star for its light, and a boatman half the stature of a pin. And her hair was a pale flame streaming out from beneath the glory of her crown; plumy; delicate in color like the cowslip bloom, and losing itself in the night like flame-flecks blown back by the wind. As for the beauty of her face, it was like the beauty of an August night full of large stars. "Merry 'Altery fach" would never do for such an one; Deio was inspired with a memory of the correct formula for addressing majesty. "Oh Merry 'Altery, live forever," said he, "please you, we do want the One that sings on the Mountain,—Tortoy and me."

She rose up, and took him in her arms: "Come you!" she said; *"tyr'd ti i fyny!"* And again they were speeding through the air up and up; high over ridge and mountain-shoulder, over lonely shoulder and untrodden upland valley. In one such hidden place he saw, far below, the whole host of the fairies dancing; taller than human they appeared, with beauty unchanged since the youth of the world. The great song grew nearer and louder. They drew in towards the high places; they came to the pine wood; by the light that shone from his guide he saw the pillar-like trunks of the trees; the song was the most wonderful joy in the world to him.

"Dei-o! Dei-o!"

There is a ruined cottage on Bettws Mountain, beyond the pine wood where he heard the song. I have examined the ground; I know the place where the runlet comes tinkling out of the mossy bank; I know the hollow where he saw the hosts dancing; I know the pine wood of everlasting song. But the only portals I know of, above there, are the doorless portals of this little ruin, under whose broken chimney the hartstongue grows so green. Glossy fronds, large and beautiful, have you news of the hidden halls of Arthur?

I know the bronze-green ceterach rooted in the mortar of the walls the little adiantum trichomanes with the black, hairlike stalk; I know the golden apples that fall and rot in the silent orchard. Have any of them news of the night-long singing of the Bard of bards, in the mountain-hid palace of the King?

"Dei-o! Dei-o!"

Even though the doors were shut, light streamed from them: light upon light. "Here he dwells with his bards and warriors," said the fairy lady; "Taliesin Benbardd sings to them in the night-time; it is all the songs of Druidry he sings."

She struck the door with her wand, and the huge mountain glowed as if it were a beryl, an opal, a turquoise and a diamond, through which seven suns in their noonday glory were shining. And the doors flew open, and Deio, looking in, beheld—

—"In my deed, Deio bach Gelli-onen! Oh, you not-ty, wick-ed boy you! There you now, come you to Dan the Poacher, *cariad i!* No one shant hurt you now Dan Poacher have found you, my little boy, my dear little heart of me! *Catw'n pawb,* and wok-kin through the ry-vaire you wass, you not-ty boy you—wok-kin with your shoes through the ry-vaire! —"There you now then, *machan,* come you, your shoes are dry whatever: cross by the bridge you wass, so brave and all, I shouldn' wonderr!"

Half an hour later Dan stood in the hall at Gelli-onen, a sleepy Deio in his arms. He had left his evening's bag, a couple of fat rabbits, in a convenient place under the hedge. Ten minutes ago the master and mistress had arrived; to find the whole household, except cook, absent hunting on the mountainside.

—"Well, Dan," said Mr. Llewelyn, slipping a couple of gold pieces into the poacher's hand; "so that's what you caught on your rounds this evening, is it? How many rabbits beside, you rascal?"

—"Rounds, sir? Rabbits, sir? There's unchristian thoughts for a gentleman to entertain! Comin' home I wass from Capel Zion over the Mountain; Jones Bethesda wass preachin': a beauty man on his knees, indeed, sir; there's pity you don't go to hear him. And—"

—"All right; go and get your supper in the kitchen. And I'll give you another chance at the Works on Monday." (Dan kept that job for a week; wonderful steady he was goin', to keep it, indeed you!)

"Daddy," said sleepy Deio, opening a pudgy hand and showing his treasure; "I founded Tortoy on the Mountain, whatever!"

And so he had, too.

*"The Cauldron of Ceridwen" is another Welsh tale, working together a portion
of the Taliesin legend of the* Mabinogion *with the story of a modern scholar of
the Welsh mythological writings. It first appeared in* The Theosophical
Path *in December 1917, under the pseudonym C. ApArthur.*

The Cauldron of Ceridwen

Sir David Prosser was in his study at Parcyrun. The lamp, green-shaded, stood on his desk to the left of the fireplace; its light fell on a litter of manuscripts there, some in his own or his secretary's handwriting, some ancient. It left the room, with its book-lined walls, for the most part, to the half obscurity and tremulous shadows of the fire-light.

Sir David had turned from his work, and sat in a low, deep-seated chair before the fire: his outward vision occupied with the flame-flicker, but giving no news of it, nor of any externals, to his mind. Which, indeed, had a matter more insistent to brood over: surprise, acquiescence, protest, indifference, rebellion against fate—mostly, perhaps, a very ungracious acquiescence. —So it might come at any time . . . It might come at any time! Dr. Lloyd had been uneasy about these attacks, and had prevailed on him to summon the great man from London, whose verdict had been passed that day; it might come at any time, and there was nothing to be done. Hours, days or weeks, there was no telling; though weeks were hardly to be hoped for, he judged. Hoped for?—yes, for he had a master passion; could he count only on a fortnight, he might at least round off his life's work by settling the hash of Taliesin, and showing up that myth for the late forgery it was. Only yesterday he had seen some scribbler's screed on it in the *Geninen;* which he had *not* read, but it had the sickening look of a kind of mystical interpretation. Well, his book would be published, with or without that last chapter; and no one, he guessed, would write or talk much about Taliesin after that. But he must give this one evening to meditation; with this news fresh on him, even though it made writing the more imperative, he could give his mind to nothing. He had dismissed his secretary for the night: an irritating fellow, but better than the run of them. Secretaries were always a problem. To get a man with a sound education, learned in the Welsh, without pressing ambitions towards the ministry, and with a smooth equable temper, was no easy task. Temper they would be showing, sooner or later, every one of them; and he could not work with an irritable, whimsy man. This one, indeed, had shown none of his tantrums so far; but he was stupid and timid, and it was a pleasure to be quit of him for the evening. But *pleasure*—now!

What might lie beyond that which was coming to him, he did not trouble to think. It was the past with its stings and successes that held him; the future was merely a thing out of which he was to be cheated by death; of the inner life (which is immortal) his sense was atrophied. Not that it had always been so: some men are born dead; Sir David was of those who achieve deadness. Thirty years since, at the time of his return, laden with honors, from Oxford, his life had been tinged with ethereal hues. A fine scholar, he was then also a fine poet; and could use the tortuous meters of Welsh classical poetry to some purpose. Not upon the well-worn themes of the competitions, either; not for him *Creadigaeth* or *Elusengarwch,* after the manner of the scribes. He had possessed, you may say, two of the three essentials of bardhood, as the Triad gives them: an eye to see, and a heart to understand, Nature; time was to show whether he had the third, courage to follow her. —Those were the days when Iolo Morganwg was still wandering Wales from library to library of the great houses, hunting in faded manuscripts for a light he believed was hidden in the ancient times; a wisdom, look you, deeper than any in science or dogma; remnants of Druid knowledge concerning the Soul of Man, its origin, wanderings and destiny. This theosophy Iolo deemed he had found; and David Prosser, coming under his influence, meant to illumine the Principality and the world with it. Like many in Wales in those days, he saw visions and dreamed dreams. He would avenge his country for her insignificance in the world, proclaiming broadcast the riches she had saved from her ruin, and hoarded unused in her secret heart through the centuries of her penury.

But life is a thing of currents and undercurrents, and we know not what we may become. We sail upon a blue and glassy sea, and manage helm and canvas with a song: this is the voyage, we think, "from Lima to Manillia"; we shall drift from island to island of delight, and disembark at last in the flamey havens of the sunset. But a little gust arises here; and there, some uncharted current sweeps us from our gentle courses. Our song passes into a strained silence; the isles we touch are deserted, or abodes of sordid trade; the blue brightness turns leaden dullness, and the sun goes down at last over a howling waste of winds and stinging spray. So and so sows his wild oats, we say; when often 'twas his rigid parents sowed them for him; or at least ensured that he should sow them, by souring the ground with their narrowness against growths of beauty, equability and peace. So in the life of David Prosser. "There's pious his father was before him," said Marged Owen in her prayers; the truth is, the child's poet soul had been ever in potential rebellion against a rule of life that yoked the Good with a substitute for the True and the antithesis of the Beautiful. In such cases unbalance results; if the nobler side of us has been given to regard righteousness coldly, what specious arguments will it not lend to the worse! The young David had had generous sentiments, noble leadings, but an intolerable thirst for freedom at all costs: he would express in perfect liberty the whole of his nature; too long had too much of it been fettered and starved. There was a passionate marriage, out of which all the poetry had passed in a year. At the end of two: "My life is spoiled," said David; "I married a Fool." The Fool had had her own complaints to make; and made them naggingly day and night. There were many incidents, of the kind that poetry will not survive; we need not go into them. The poet in him died presently; but not his ambition and fighting vein. He would not surrender and pass into negligibility; the fame of the scholar grew.

All light had waned from the ancient poems and stories, as from the ancient hills and moors. He sought the key to their interpretation no longer in life, which had become a poor wounded thing with him, but in learning: he searched for the Soul with a microscope; and, finding it not, knew that it did not exist. The Great Wonder is a property of the Divine; blind your eyes to the deity within you, and what radiance shall you see without? Where you caught a glimpse of the beauty and mystery of things, you shall perceive only delusions, that cannot stand the test of your crucible or dissecting knife. The dreams that had pleased and haunted him, he came to view with growing impatience; since he had no longer taught wherewith to handle them, except the sterilizing tools of philological research. He had parted with all sense of their poetic values, and scorned for childish foolery the pretensions of those who had not. His sole delight now—a savage one—was in exploding superstitions, pricking bubbles, smoking out mares' nests, blowing up castles in Spain. *Mysticism? Gammon! —Let's have Philology!* quoth Sir David. —A famous and snappy scholar, of opinions much respected, and personality wholly unbeloved.

Except, of course, by Marged Owen, his housekeeper, who had been his mother's maid and his own nurse, and was still three parts mother to him in her heart. A placid, not unstately woman, with great shining gray eyes behind her spectacles, and "indeed, driving on her ten and three score," as she reflected; she knew naught of his opinions, though she gloried in the thought of his renown; but loved him because he had been, and was still, her "boy bach," and because motherly love was her general attitude towards anything human she contacted. It was she who managed the house, shielded its master from the non-intellectual world; gave law to the gardener, that his realm might be maintained as it was in Mister Davie's youth; and preserved intact the reason of the secretary *pro tem,* with her calm inexhaustible kindliness. Her Welsh Bible and hymnbook, and the changing skies and old-fashioned June-sweet flowers of the garden, kept her in an inner life: these, and a fighting loyalty to Sir David which was tempered, not modified, by a knowledge of some of his peculiarities. Which, be it said, were a secret, so far as she was concerned, between herself and her God; with whom she argued nightly on his behalf. —"Indeed, Lord, 'tis true Zion do see little of him these days"—he had not been inside a chapel since his father's death, but no good to remind the Lord too precisely—"but there's pious his father was before him, and there's religious he was brought up! 'Tis them books he is writing, I s'pose: they do hold his mind; grand bardism he is making to glorify Thee! In his heart, indeed, indeed, there is nothing out of its place; consider Thou what he has suffered!" —And so, in truth, he had; but there were few beside her gentle self that would have said that about his heart. Morgan Llewelyn Zion had more than once made pointed reference from the pulpit, especially in his prayers, to the "heathen in our midst"; and no one but Marged had failed to understand at whom the shafts were pointed. Had she so much as guessed, I imagine she would have seceded to Zoar, even though the three miles extra would have entailed the wagonette. —From her book, indeed, I would borrow a page or two of charity. She had never doubted that his fame was based on his bardhood; if she knew nothing of his poems, that would be, she s'posed, because they were in English, and therefore beyond her. *(Pity you are not cleaving to the Welsh, whatever, machgen i!)* In her eyes, then, the poet had never died; and I am content to believe that her eyes, so love-lit, so short-sighted in things of the intellect, were gifted in compensation with glimmerings of spiritual vision. I would say, then, that the poet had not died, but was only numbed with the torture of a long crucifixion; banished, if you like; reviled and tormented; nearly dead: but still secretly feared by the scholar and critic its persecutor.

Sir David, sitting in his chair, fell to calling up pictures of the past: of his not too happy childhood and his school days; of Jesus College at Oxford; of his return thence, and of his father's death that followed so quickly; and of his own marriage. Then—ah well, he had long since freed himself of those follies! He chuckled sardonically, remembering how he had set aside the Tale of Taliesin, even then, to be a great part of his life's work. It was to be a poem in the *cywydd* meter: a vindication of the ancient light of his people, making real and definite the legendary figure of that great Bard-Initiate, who had stood the symbol of their aspirations and dreams. He remembered the days when conviction first flagged; when the lines would not ring true; when the supposed light that he had followed died—no, revealed itself for a worthless fantasy.

He thought of that passionate marriage; the first rapture that blurred the inward images, after heightening them to sunblazing vividity. He thought of the Fool, with a half sneer as of one whose heat of anger had long vanished: of the Fool, dead now these twenty years: her nagging, tongue, he told himself, had at least done much to relieve him of his illusions. Well, well, thanks to her for that; with all the triumphs he had won, he could afford to be magnanimous. And after all, when Gwen the Mill had gone mad, and killed her baby, the Fool had done much better than she might; considering that suspicion—or was it knowledge?—that he had seen in her eyes and heard, not in her words, but in the sharpened bitterness with which they were uttered. She kept off that subject; some might have blabbed their injuries abroad. But it was all past and done with a long time ago. Poor little Gwen! But there, for all that happened, she had but herself to thank,—herself, and the Fool his wife. He was not going to blame himself, at this time of day.

How could you call it a barren or wasted life, wherein he had won so much? A knighthood, and a string of letters after his name; honors from a dozen universities, at home and abroad, of such as be interested in Celtic research: surely all this betokened a life well-spent? —Evil on that *well-spent!* when now at any moment the account was to be closed, and there remained so much in him yet to spend. So many idiots to chasten with the lashings of his cold logic—as witness this man in the *Geninen,* with his rigmarole of mysticism about Taliesin. —Have at that fellow now, whatever! These memories grew none too amusing; he had better find relief from them in action; he had better keep his brain busy with cold work till the last. He drew the lamp to the edge of the desk, picked up the magazine, and began reading.

It brought back his youthful dreams to him like an ache. He, too, had fancied an universal symbolism in the old story. —The witch Ceridwen, it will be remembered, had a son who was the ugliest man in the world; and she, fearing he would obtain no honor at the court of Arthur, determined to brew for him the Three Drops of Science in her magical cauldron. —How he, Sir David, had brooded in those old days, upon that cauldron; extracting worlds of wonder out of its name, *Pair Dadeni,* the Cauldron of Rebirth! It was all so familiar to him; he might have written the article himself. —She set the cauldron to boil among the hills, bidding Gwion Bach watch the fire while she gathered the herbs of the mountain in their season. The water boiled over, and scalded Gwion; who, putting the hurt finger for relief to his mouth, tasted the Three Drops, was illuminated by them, and "instantly became aware that he must fear above all things Ceridwen." In all this a vast human significance was guessed; it referred to the initiation of the Bard, and the severe trials attendant thereto. "Then," said the writer, "woe unto him that is not—"

Ah God, that pain again! The cold sweat broke from his forehead; he lay back, clutching the arms of the chair, and waited. It had never been like this before. In thunder-crashes of agony it shook and rent him; breaking his courage; shattering his conceptions of time, of space, of selfhood; dislocating all the molds of his mind. The pictures he had been calling up went whirling past him; that wherewith he commented on them had grown impartial and impersonal with pain. His honors brought him no comfort now; he blamed none but himself for his errors. He perceived the beauty of his early dreams, and had it not in him to mock at them. He appeared to himself as two men: an individuality torn asunder by the raging storm of his torment: the poet he had been once, thirsty after golden non-material Truth; the acrid scholar he had become, avid only after truths barren and desolating—*truths!*

—*Prepared!* —*Woe unto him that is not prepared!* In waves and receding waves the great pain ebbed, leaving him strangely clear of brain and light of body; he finished the sentence he had been reading; or it was as if he had heard the words spoken aloud. *Woe unto him that is not prepared,* he repeated; what did it mean? It was something that interested him no longer; it had to do with— He stood up, undecided, strange, with a feeling of having experienced some momentous but indefinable change. A curious half restless sense came over him; as of one playing chess with Fate or Providence, who waits, yet with detachment, for his opponent to play. It was not his move; he must bide the time, and see what would happen. Meantime he went to the window, and looked out; as though expecting the move to come beneath the open sky. The full moon was shining above the sycamores, and he could see the glisten of drops on the grass-blades, and the movement of the April leaves on the trees. —What was that? . . . He listened, and a second time heard his name called, from outside, from the direction of the drive. "Gwen the Mill!" he whispered; forgetting she had died so many years ago: "Gwen the Mill, indeed now!" He went out into the hall, put on his overcoat, and took hat and stick. "I am going out for a stroll in the moonlight, Marged fach," said he, as Mrs. Owen appeared in the door of the housekeeper's room. "Take you care against your catching cold now, Mister Davie dear," she answered; and turned back, I suppose, for something she had forgotten. A moment later she was in the hall again, and he was gone. "Dear now," said she, looking anxiously at the hat-rack, "what hat did he take, whatever? And sure I am I did see him putting on his overcoat. My old eyes are failing me, I think."

Out into the drive went Sir David, and on towards the gate. At the curve a woman's figure, shadowy in the uncertain light, flickered before his vision and was lost. "Gwen!" he called softly; "Gwenno fach, is it thou?" A wave of clear thinking came on him, and he remembered, and chid himself for falling a victim to illusions. 'Twas the shock of that attack, he supposed, had left his mind unclear. But he would investigate, and satisfy himself, lest recurring moments of weakness— He went on through the gate, and up the road on to the mountain. Hush! there was a call again—and there, on the right, standing on the bank above the road, in full moonlight, a beckoning figure.

While he looked it was gone. He was not sure that it was Gwen the Mill's; I do not think he thought of that; but he was in no doubt that it must be followed. He made up the slope and on to the wild moorland; the night was very bright; there was no difficulty about the going. Down and up; over heather and through fern; there was no difficulty; he knew which way to go.

On and on he went. The moon set; a great wind arose; he heard the keen shrill of it, but it caused him no inconvenience. There was a whisper out in the night; there was a mystery, a thrill; the wind and the moor and the sky were filled with haughty elemental importance; all were part of some vast ceremony in which he, too, played a part, though an uncomprehended one. Presently he saw leaping lights and shadows far off, and the glow of flame on smoke. He made his way towards it, and came soon to the rim of a hollow, in whose bottom a fire burned; round it figures were moving in silence. Gypsies, he supposed; he would go down and question them. He greeted them pleasantly enough; and they, it seemed, were not disinclined to be companionable. Gypsies? —Well, no, they were not *shipshwns;* watching the fire they were, and the pot cooking on it. They had no Saxon—*dim gair.** —It struck him vaguely that there was something very strange about them: nine of them there were: as he could see when the firelight shone on their faces, the strangeliest handsome men he remembered seeing. —Had they news of a woman wandering on the mountain—was she perhaps of their company? —Well, there was the Mistress; he might have seen her, indeed. —What would she be doing, roaming the wilds in the night? —Whence did they come—from Llan-this or Cwm that?—the usual Welsh questions. —Oh, they answered, the Mistress would be gathering herbs in their season for the brew in the pot; and as for themselves, they came from—but here he could make nothing of their answer. "But come you, sir," said one of them; "cold you will be; warm you yourself by the fire." He drew near, and in that shelter from the wind's keening, heard above all sounds in the world the hissing and boiling of the water in their kettle, and listened to it, and listened to it, and listened to it.

He held his hands to the fire, listening, and forgot the nine watchers. Once again his life moved in minute procession before him. Now bright hopes, splendid aspirations, poetry; now the angry hissing and buzzing of acrid scholarship, and bitter criticism of the kind that eats into and destroys all beauty and mystery and truth. All his life, all his life. . . .

A sudden hubbub within the kettle; a cry from one of the nine: "Mind you your finger, sir!" He drew back his hand hastily; but not before a jet of

*Not a word (of English).

the boiling fluid, hissing out, had scalded him. At the pain, the finger flew to his mouth. . . .

Ah, heaven, how glorious a thing was life! Why, the universe was all blazing poetry; the stars had voices, and called to him out of the far skies: god-voices, that cried aloud to him, *Brother!* As a note in the singing of Seraphim: as a gleam in the flame that is God: appeared to him the rejoicing world and his own being, tremendous with joy. Ah, heaven, the immensity of time! the vista of ages behind him! the lives on lives he had lived! the starry serenity of his liberated self! the majesty of his thought! the flaming beauty of existence! All the littleness of his past life vanished from his consciousness; it was a dark incident closed, a bitterness from which he had extracted all the meaning. He was no more Sir David Prosser; he was a "marvel whose origin"—

"And instantly he was aware of the peril he stood in, and that above all things he must fear Ceridwen. . . ."

He started up in terror; the cauldron had fallen; the fire was quenched; a black flood, seething and writhing, was rising about him in the hollow. He fled forward through the dark air; immitigable terror driving him on. The darkness of night threatened; out of the thick core of the midnight doom hurried in pursuit of him: loss whose magnitude was not to be fathomed by imagination: death vibrating inward to absoluteness. Below he was aware of the black flood rising and covering the moorland: he heard its hiss and roar as it flowed down over the hills, into the valleys, bearing poison and death. In an agony of fear he heard the rush of far wings; he knew of a terrible Pursuer behind, sweeping over the night-hid vales and mountains. On and on blindly through the darkness; from everywhere the night and the storm and the starless gloom cried out to him *Too late!* —*Woe unto him that is not prepared!* cried the midnight. . . . A rush of wings behind him in the air; a storm of great wings beating and nearing; the wind of swooping wings impelling him helpless to the earth; then—silence, and the darkness died, giving place to no light. . . .

At half past ten Marged Owen went into her master's study, to see that he had returned from his stroll without harm taken, and to bring him his hot milk and biscuits. She found him dead in his chair.

● ●

"The Bunch Titania Picked" is Morris's purest fairy tale, set in London and fairyland. It was published in The Theosophical Path *in April 1918, under the pseudonym Floyd C. Egbert. It is the first of only two stories published by Morris in 1918, followed by only two more in 1919. During these two years Morris devoted the vast bulk of his energies to preparing and delivering his enormous and comprehensive lecture-series, "The Crest-Wave of Evolution," later published in* The Theosophical Path.

The Bunch Titania Picked:
A Fairytale of London

P. Simmons was a London clerk. He was what the poet calls a "pipe-and-a-stick young man." His speech bewrayed him for Cockney: you could hear Bow Bells jangling in it. Though not too oleaginously, as you might say; he was above indiscretion in the matter of aitches; which, after all, is the main thing. The P. stood for Peter.

He had a season ticket on the District Railway, which raises one above the rank of third-class traveler—or used to. Every morning in the week he emerged, at ten minutes to eight, from a semi-detached villa residence ("desirable") in Laburnum Terrace; lit his pipe at the garden gate; bought *The Daily Flamer* at the station bookstall, and caught the eight o'clock train to the city. The station was Walham Green. The pipe would last him as far as to the Temple, or perhaps Blackfriars; the paper to Mark Lane, where his journey ended. His days were spent in the outer office of J. J. Merrill and Co., Metal Brokers, of Mincing Lane; I forget the number. J. J. Merrill and Co. had two clerks, of whom P. Simmons was the senior. The other fellow used to be sent on the errands: Simmons, maintaining a certain state in the outer office—especially when Merrill was out—had the privilege of sending him. Merrill—our Mr. J. J. Merrill—was the firm; the Co., like North Poles and Equators in the poem, was merely a conventional sign. In respect to the junior clerk, Mr. Simmons' rights extended still further: as, to send him to buy oranges in the street; to make him a hone for the wit, and a dumping-ground for stories supposed funny. In fact, the junior clerk was little better than an office boy; though he thought he was a poet.

At 1 P.M., Simmons would repair to a room beneath the level of the street, where there were marble-topped tables, clouds of tobacco smoke, clerks innumerable, chess, draughts, and dominoes. The chess was for the aristocracy of intellect, to which he made no claim to belong; he, when he had eaten his steak-and-kidney pudding or the like, would play a game of dominoes with kindred-spirits over his second daily pipe. There, also, he was respectably familiar with the waitresses: called them Rose or Alice, as the case might be. Five fifteen saw him at Mark Lane Station again; and so home strap-hanging to the parental semi-detached at Walham Green. He derived his politics from the ha'penny press; by religion, he was impeccably—but not so as to cause insomnia—of the one Respectable Fold. As to his philosophy: he had been known once, in a moment of serious self-searching, to confess that *"It* (life, or the universe—this sorry scheme of things entire—) was a rummy sort of go." All these particulars are to convince you that he was in fact quite an ordinary young man.

His evenings were devoted to worship at the shrine of a Miss Violet Smiff, No. 10, Burlington Gardens, round the corner. She was meek and mouselike, had pale eyes, a colorless complexion, and more or less colorless hair: was an entirely deserving young person. *Worship at her shrine,* I said; in sober truth the phrase is none too accurate. The odor of the sacrifice rose, mostly, to his own nostrils. Miss Smiff was an immense admirer of Mr. Simmons, and he knew how to feed the flames of her admiration. He made that his business whenever they were together; and was her hero, her "flaming lion of the world." She heard that phrase in a poem read at the local Literary and Philosophic Society; and wept, it did remind her so of Mr. Peter Simmons. Not that it was all take, and no give, with him, by any means. A certain portion of his salary went in the purchase of flowers; to be exact, a minimum of sixpence a week. It came more expensive usually, and in the winter, of course, could not be managed daily. But now Spring was here, and violets at a penny or twopence the bunch with the flower-girls on most days; what other flower, costly though it were, would serve so well? It was a kind of punning, you see. The violet was his favorite flower.

Now Miss Smiff had a bosom friend, a Miss Amelia Colman; they attended the Literary and Philosophic in company; were the inseparable prime movers in Young Women's Christian bazaars, and had no secrets the one from the other. Miss Smiff was the first to be engaged; Miss Colman, however, biding her time, wiped out that advantage with a score of her own. One day she came round to Burlington Gardens, and gushed out the tale; *he* was a Mr. Algernon Binks, in whom she had long been tenderly interested; and she showed her dearest Violet a copy of some verses he had addressed to her. Alack, here was a point in which the flaming lion was excelled; her Peter had never written verses to Miss Smiff. She mentioned Binks' poem to Simmons, and spoke wistfully of her love for poetry. She had always seen in him, she hinted, one who needed but rousing to become a Browning, or an Omar Khayyam.

Peter didn't know, he was sure. Was rather inclined to think that things should be drawn mild. Binks, he explained, was notoriously weak-minded; and he didn't much hold with that sort of thing himself. But she seemed disappointed; and thereafter the odor of sacrifice rose not so sweetly as of old. Fair play to him, he made attempts at poetry, but could do nothing with it. At last a plan came to him.

It was on the morning of a certain 29th of April that it came; and acting upon it promptly, he broke thus upon his underling at the office:

"Here, April; write us a poem abaht violets, will yer?" (The spelling slanders his speech, perhaps; but not much.)

"April," naturally, was short for "Spring Poet"; an allusion to a weakness of the junior clerk to which reference has already been made. His name was really Bains—Wilfred Bains. Next morning, when Merrill had gone on 'Change and occasion offered, quoth Bains:

"I've brought you *that,* Mr. Simmons."

"Brought me what?" says Simmons, hypocritically.

"What you asked me for."

"Didn't ask yer for anything." (A conscious straying from the paths of veracity.)

"It was a—poem about violets," said April, blushing.

"Poem abaht violets? —Oh, ah—let's have a look."

He tilted back his stool till he could lean comfortably against the partition, placed his feet on the desk, and accepted the verses. He read a line—two—out loud; then, "Coo!" said he, "what rot!" Whether it was rot or no, he need not have read it like that. "Get yer hair cut, April old chap," said he; "her'll never be poet laureate." This when he had tortured poor Bains' ears with perverse rendering of the whole—his ears, and his whole sensitive being. I will not say he was one to hanker after inflicting torment for torment's sake; but there was a grave fault with the poem as it stood, a damning lack; and he was disappointed. And April's tribe is easy game; having neither strength for fight, speed for flight, nor wit for concealment. "Hullo, kid, what's wrong now?" said Simmons; "blest if I don't believe yer blubbing!"

Nothing of the kind; he thought he had a cold though, did April; and—was glad to escape. Fortunately the S.S. *Oanfa* had arrived at Rotterdam the evening before, and there were notes to be carried round to the metal-broking world. That morning, between breakfast and the Clerkenwell-Mansion House bus,—he had dingy lodgings in Clerkenwell—he had caught a whiff of violets from the basket of a flower-girl; a whiff that somehow set his brain on fire. Being, as Mr. Simmons often remarked, a rummy little bloke, he had taken off his hat: ostensibly to the flower-girl, who caught his eye and nodded friendlily: really to her flowers and "to the beauty of the world." Merrill paid him mighty little, and he might worship such beauty from afar, but hardly spend pennies on it. "Good luck to yer, my dear!" cried the flower-girl; and made as if to give him a bunch; but the bus was on the move, and he had had to run for it. On the top front seat he had composed his verses; passing through London streets as if they were alleys enchanted in Avallon; and hearing not the street-cries and pounding of hoofs, but the music of Fairyland. "She gave me good luck, all right," he said; as he read through what he had typed on the office Remington before Mr. Simmons arrived. "Wonder how I came to think of it; it isn't a bit like anything I ever wrote before." Nor was it,—but you shall judge for yourself:—

> *"Violets, sweet violets!*
> *Who will buy my violets?*
> *Here's a bunch from Fairyland*
> > *Only costs a brown!*

> "Here's a scent from woody vales
> Where hart's-tongue's whispering fairytales;
> King Oberon his writ's to run
> > For once in London town!
> Here's a breeze that's wandered seas
> With the Argonauts and their argosies;
> Here are the bright Hesperides,
> > And here's Titania's crown!

> "Here's a breath from moor and heath
> Where cowslips bloom the blue beneath—
> (Cowslips bloom in Fairyland,
> > Not in London town!)
> Here's what grew in the Wonder Hills
> With the asphodels and daffodils,
> Hard by Arethusa's rills
> > In the Realm of old Renown.

> "Violets, sweet violets!
> Who will buy my violets?
> Who'll have the flowers of Fairyland
> > To wear in London town?
> " 'Ere's vi'lets, lydy! 'Ere, I sye,
> Yer'd better tyke yer chawnst and buy!
> Here's a bunch Titania picked,
> > Only costs a brown!"

> *"Violets, sweet violets!*
> *Who's it selling violets?*

Who's it bringing Fairyland
Into London town?

"—Would you guess that fairy feet
Might tread the dirt of Fenchurch Street?
Might leave the dances wild and fleet
    To wander up and down
'Twixt Camberwell and Clerkenwell
And Pentonville—and all to sell
The flowers of Further Fairyland
    In dingy London town?

"—Lips that suck the dews of June,
Feet that dance beneath the moon,
Raiment spun of the gold of noon
    And foam, and dandy-down—
Human seeming, so they say,
May be donned for just a day
When Oberon would have his way
    For once, in London town.

"Oh, London streets are full of hell,
And between Kew and Whitechapel
Are half the seraphim that fell
    And half the souls that drown;
Yet deathless Beauty, wandering by,
Sometimes may choose to leave the sky,
And make a stand for Fairyland
    Even in London town."

Commonly he began his poems with *O thou!* and had tags from the
Gradus ad Parnassum that must be brought in, if skill and thought could
achieve it. Here, the lines in rich Cockney troubled him; and to call a penny
a *brown,* he thought, was irregular. Still, on the whole, he had marvellous
good conceit of his work; and so now was the more enangered against that
beast Simmons. He was but sixteen.

"Rummy kid," reflected Peter. He stretched out an arm towards the
waste paper basket, and rescued the effusion he had tossed there so lightly
to save his junior from swelled head. "Not half bad, after all—for him," he
commented, with the air of one who knows. The question was, how was it
for himself, and for Violet? "No love in it, and that's what's wrong." He
recollected with regret that he had asked for a poem *about violets,* and not *to
Violet.* "Anyone but a mug would have understood," he considered. "Still it
isn't half bad. Shouldn't wonder if he did something, some day. Knew a

feller once that sent in a poem to the *Church Recorder,* and got a guinea for it; and it wasn't more than half as long as this one. Maybe I'll put the kid up to that, one of these days." He was, perhaps, a little sorry for having teased the boy over much; but there was the goose that laid the golden eggs to be thought of. His lady love might turn Oliver Twist in this matter of poetry, and ask for more. So he determined to make amends nobly.

The afternoon was a busy one; Merrill kept them hard at it until three o'clock, when he went out, and things (as usual) slackened somewhat. "Say, April," said Mr. Simmons, "that wasn't half a bad poem of yours, after all."

The merest grunt for an answer.

"No; I read it over again, and I must say, it shows promise. Only it hasn't got wot I call human interest. Now, if you'd worked in something about a girl's eyes—don't you know—bein' like the violets, and all that kind of thing—why, it would be tip-top, ripping stuff."

Another grunt, but with more articulation in it.

"Yer know, I want that poem for a particular purpose. Don't yer think yer could work in another verse, so as to make it more human—depth of feelin', and all that kind of thing? I might be able to get yer a ticket for the Lyceum, if yer did."

Pride struggled in the heart of April, prompting this for an answer: "You can write your own poems in future, Mr. Simmons!" But one didn't get the chance to see Irving do Shylock every day. Pride also had traitors in his own camp; the *poet* was appealed to. "You can tell me what you want me to say, and I'll see if an inspiration comes." This loftily, though a concession.

"Well now, supposin' you were to address the poem to a girl: say her name was Violet, same as the flowers—she must have some name, of course; then bring in that about her eyes. That's wot I mean by human sentiment—something to make it real and appealin': not all up in the air like."

At about quarter to four April took the sheet out of the typewriter. "How will this do for you?" said he.

"Let's have a look."

"No, I'd better read it to you myself."

"All right, go ahead."

Then the poet read this:

"*Violet, thy lustrous eyes,*
Pellucid as the evening skies,
Cure my aches and miseries
Here in London town.
Deeper than the violets blue
When they're wet with diamond dew—
Ah, my heart's forever true
To you, my ownest own!"

I suspect he had misgivings himself; but Mr. Simmons called it glorious. "Yer'll get yer Lyceum ticket all right, April; sure as eggs. Say, did yer ever try sending poems to the papers? I bet they'd give yer a whole lot for one like this. It gives expression to the sentiments of a feller's heart, yer know—same as Shakespeare. Yer'll know all abaht the value of these things when you're a bit older, old chap. Try sending something to the *Church Recorder*—not this one, of course, because yer've given it to me. I knew a feller once—" but we have heard of that feller before.

At half past four they began to prepare for departure. Merrill was still out; had doubtless gone home. Mr. Simmons changed his coat, hanging up that reserved for office wear; doffed paper cuffs, revealing so the genuine Belfast article beneath. "Say, April," said he, "just run down and get me a bunch of violets, will yer? Here's yer twopence." April obeyed, as usual. At the corner of Fenchurch Street he found what he sought. "Vi'lets! Buy a bunch of vi'lets, young man—honly tuppence! 'Ullo, my dear, wotchyer doin' aht 'ere? Want some vi'lets?"

"A bunch please," said April, with dignity intended to be discouraging, and holding out Peter's pence. She took the money and gave him the flowers; then: " 'Ere, I likes you; sor yer this morning up Clerkenwell wye. You give them to 'im: nah 'ere's some special for yerself, along of yer tiking orf yer rat to a pore flower-girl. 'Alf price they are!"

April hesitated, reluctant to say, "I haven't a penny"; though such was nearly the case; since it must be choice between having the flowers and riding home. "Hi tell yer, this 'ere bunch is for yerself, and goin' at 'alf price," said the flower-girl; " 'ark!" And then, what would he hear but a murmur of chanting swell out of the tinkle of harness and swing and ding-dong of London hoofs: momentary poetry, and music and a sudden thrill of wonder in unwondering London:—

> *"Here's the bunch Titania picked,*
> *Only costs a brown!"*

He stared, round-eyed and as they say goose-skinned; and managed to get out, *How did you . . . know . . . that?* to which she answered, "Yer'd better 'ave it"; convincingly, somehow, for he produced his penny; whereupon what should she do but brush his eyes with the violets, and—

It was but a moment, and then it had vanished away. The opalescence, the quivering of intense glory, all was gone. The clerks passing were no longer gods, flamey and rainbow-hued, their faces full of proud agony, of calmness, triumph or compassion; they were just every day London clerks; and this was Fenchurch Street and the corner of Mincing Lane; but—What the eyes have seen, the heart will remember; and how should this place, or these people, be commonplace again? Oh God, what mystery, what tragedy and beauty might be hidden here—or anywhere! —April went upon his ways; some special providence led him back to the office. It would be to-morrow morning before any clear thought would come to him. No more need be told of him than this: he had fed upon his honey-dew; he had been given to drink the milk of Paradise. Imperious Poetry, lonely and haughty wanderer, had knocked at last upon the gates of his soul.

"Hullo April, seen a ghost?" said Mr. Simmons. "Oh, yer've got two bunches, have yer?" He drew quick inferences, to be used later for teasing. "Sentimental little beggar!" said he, taking one of the bunches. It hap-pened to be the wrong one; but neither of them knew that.

Now Miss Smiff had been spending the day at Greenwich, at her great-aunt Fanshawe's; whither now Mr. Simmons hastened; after tea he was to conduct her home by steamer. Miss Fanshawe was prim: kept her from opening the door when he ringed; and left them not alone together for a moment during tea. Then she was to attend a prayer-meeting, and must have Violet's assistance in the matter of putting on a bonnet. All three started out together, the elderly spinster in the middle; nor could they shake her off, since her way and theirs lay in the same direction, until the doors of Little Bethel had opened and closed upon her. So that nothing had been said about poem or posy until they had turned into the Park, and were among the tulip-beds in a lonely and lovely region. Then he produced both; presented the violets—which, unaccountably, were quite unfaded—and declaimed the verses, execrably; though the last one, that of his own prompting, it must be said with feeling. They were duly admired, or per-haps unduly. "Dearest," said Miss Smiff, "it's lovely. Did you really write it all yourself?" And then—I am sorry to record this—he answered: "Violet, I'm hurt—that's wot I am; *hurt!*"

A strange glory of sunset took the western sky; the river below them was pearl and faint opal; London was enshrouded in pearl-mist, and over-flamed, as it sometimes is, with mysterious lilac and roses and gold. They had never heard, these two, that the Eve of May is the fairy night of all the nights in the year. "Oh, Peter," said Miss Smiff, "isn't it pretty! Hush, listen to that barrel organ!"

Ah, but never a barrel organ made music such as that! It came from behind them, from around them, from the air and the trees; from the dimly gleaming, many-masted river; from pearl-enroyalled London, from the tall May tulips in the beds. And there they were, with Titania's own violets in their possession, and never a thought to touch their eyes with them, and obtain vision! . . . Vision of the hosts of Faërie singing, and dancing, and weaving and waving out their music in the lovely dusk: mist-like and iri-descent forms, hued like the bluebell and the lilac, like pale irises and the leaves of daffodils. They had no notion what a great dim glory Greenwich Park was that evening; or of the ones dancing that wore stars upon their foreheads, whose feet twinkled whitely and luminously in the gloom. . . . "All out!" cried the park-keepers; and our couple hurried forward. "Peter," said his betrothed, "I wanted to ask you: who is Harry Thuzer—mentioned in your poem?"

• •

The following story was published in The Theosophical Path *in June 1918
as "Another Chance, or The Divina Commedia of Evan Leyshon," under the
pseudonym Patton H. Mifkin. Morris also included it in his collection* The
Secret Mountain and Other Tales. *It is one of Morris's few fantasies set
in the contemporary world. Here, a derelict is dying in Cardiff, and during a
dream vision, he chooses hell over heaven, followed by an intriguing twist.*

The Divina Commedia of Evan Leyshon

I

*E*van Leyshon lay, as he well knew, not far from death. He had
returned, the evening before, to the place that served him for a
home: knowing well that his last drink was drunk and that he would trouble the police-court cells no more. And then he had spent the night on the
bare boards of the room that sheltered him, coughing and spitting blood
and agonizing. That he had that shelter at all he owed to the fact that there
may yet be grace in the very far fallen. Once he had almost turned the
woman of the house from the road to hell; and she remembered it.

Death—what was it? He used to know, he thought. But now—well,
why care? It might at least be rest. Damnation! what did he want with rest?
He had had a *Soul* in him—once. He had never sought out death—as so
many like him do daily. He wanted a chance to struggle on; yes, at bottom
that was what he wanted: to fight on, with the bare hope that he might not
die—go out at last and be at an end—ashamed. Oh, hell, hell, hell, what a
rotten wreck his life had been!

An *âme damnée,* you would say, if ever there was one: humanity reduced
to something like its most contemptible terms—so it still be human. There
are lower grades—that yet wear all the trappings of fine success and shine
in society; and make it their business so to shine—and to allure. Evan Leyshon, certainly, had reached no such bad eminence. He was one of those that
small boys torment in the streets as they pass, and that appear as often as
may be before the magistrates, "drunk and disorderly"; a fellow with a little
chin, to draw a pitying *Poor devil* from any charitably-minded Levite passing by.

Furies came about him as he lay, to hiss and scourge. Few, I suppose, would have seen Æschylean tragedy

"In sceptred pall come sweeping by,"

in that room of an evil house in the slums; yet there vultures tore Prometheus Bound; and there Orestes fled over dim Ægeans of thought: and I marvel if there were no august figures on the heights to mourn over the one; no ægised Pallas to be evoked by the other.

Failure! failure! miserable failure! hissed the Furies. *Where are your lofty ethics now; your fits and gleams of tender poetry; your flaming rhetoric of idealism?*—It was true: a time had been when people said he would have made a better preacher than any in the city; although even then he had been far fallen, and his highest possibilities all disappointed. Would have made?— actually was! *In vino veritas,* said the moralizers: though "half seas over" the fellow "rang true," pleading for things he did passionately believe in, and they were great things. The remnant only, of a wasting treasure, even then. . . .

And how long, sneered the Furies, *since you came up from the grey house at Rhesolfen with that little sheaf of verses in your bag, and the knowledge that a thousand more were hovering in the air about you waiting to be discovered and written? How long is it, you drink-drenched wastrel, since you were going to sing a new light and beauty to the world?*

"Thirty years," moaned Evan Leyshon. He remembered those bright days miserably. The outer world had been for him, then, a mere transparency through which the splendor of the Spirit shone. He had been familiar with invisible dawns and sunsets, and not ungifted to make others feel what he saw. He had stirred great hopes: in his work, though it was youthfully imperfect, there had been something unmodern, startling: he had seen the passers-by on the common pavements beautifully majestic like the demigods of old; there had been those who had descried Shelleyan promise in him, and a "pardlike spirit beautiful and swift."

But the promise had come to nothing, and the pardlike spirit was drowned; a couple of years in the city had done for it. Ever since he had been going steadily down. He had had a work to do in the world; and he had done nothing of it.

There are some crowns all the northern aurora without, and within they are wounding desperate thorns. The "fatal gift" is less often possession than vision of beauty. Osiris and Typhon come not together in the same age and land merely, but again and again in the same breast. Evan Leyshon's was a case in point. The crown had begun to glimmer; but only the wounding of the thorns increased. He had possessed in a measure the gift; and it had proved fatal indeed. It was now a Typhon's victory that lay dying in the slum room somewhere behind Bute Street by the docks.

And yet, too, Osiris has a thousand lives in him; he is sometimes desperately hard to kill. You see him buried at the cross roads; yet can never go by without suspecting tremors of the ground. Or you see the stone rolled up over the mouth of his sepulchre; yet can never be sure that what you hear from it thereafter is only the howling and prowling of hyænas. Evan Leyshon knew that he was dying, and whimpered miserably at the knowledge. The whimper belonged to his condition: it was, however, the expression, through that condition and proper to it, of Osirian rebellion somewhere far within. Thirty years of decline and fall: nearly ten of utter abjectness: had not been enough quite to convince Osiris that he was dead.

So the morning passed by; and with the afternoon came Captain Elias Elias; who was a man of God.

II

A Celtic sense of the unseen, and what they call *caredigrwydd Cymru*—the native kindliness of the Welsh peasant—to begin with; a Calvinistic chapel on the Cardigan coast to mould the former of these qualities during his early years; and then long night watches at sea, given over to wrestlings with the spirit and the elements, to bring the whole to fruition: had made him what he was. Ten years back he had left the merchant service, taken a house in Grangetown, and devoted himself, as he said, to the service of the Lord. It meant haunting the slums, seeking out the sick and dying—all whose helplessness put them at his mercy; ministering with the gentleness of a deep and tender nature to their material needs; doctoring them himself, when the peril was not too great, out of his sea medicine-chest and his old experience as skipper and doctor of the good ship *Ovingham* of Cardiff; and then letting loose upon them the hurricane and Aceldama of his flaming imagination in bedside sermons and prayer. *"Flaming"* imagination is the word. What with a hundred storms off the Horn and elsewhere, and as many and as violent revival services on land, there was little in the geography of Gehenna that the old fellow did not know. He knew the sea, and he knew the slums, and he knew, or had known, the cliffs and lanes between Mwnt and Aberporth; but he knew hell much better. In the spirit he had rounded all the Horns in Hades; not once, but a dozen times. Screaming winds and black billows from the Pole had taught him to picture the roar of the flame-storms of Tophet, the overwhelming desolation of eternal doom; from the fearful valleys between the wave-mountains, he had learned the horror of the bottomless pit. Dante could not be more vivid, nor Milton armed with more grandiose gloom, than was Captain Elias Elias at his best. Queer, cross-eyed, brown-bearded, tender-hearted old Apostle of Damnation, I wonder what kind of karma will be yours, for all that unflagging benevolence and hideous cruelty!

Captian Elias had long since marked down Evan Leyshon as lawful prey.

Sometimes he had come on him so far gone as to be fairly passive; and had had occasion then for inly exultation: another soul in a fair way to be snatched from the talons of Sathan. Generally, however, the poor wretch would fight back with fitful gleams of energy; Osiris being uneasy in his tomb. This afternoon the captain saw at once that all skirmishing was over, and the main battle waiting to begin; after preliminaries, that is to say, pertaining to this world and the captain's better nature. He sent for the nearest doctor—a personal friend of his own; and heard what he expected: that Leyshon could hardly last a day. Workhouse infirmary? That would hardly suit his plans; he himself would assume all responsibilities there where he was. Well, well; it was not worth the trouble of moving him, anyway; and there wasn't a better nurse in Cardiff than old Elias—if only he wouldn't be up to his damned tricks. "Be merciful to the poor devil, as you expect mercy, captain!" So Dr. Burnham, departing; and added to himself: "Queer old cuss—like all the rest of the Taffies!"

It was the captain's intention to be merciful; it always was. Here was clearly a case for the tender amenities, not for the terrors, of his theology. It was always so—always gently and lovingly—that he went to his work. First he called in the woman of the house, and paid her handsomely to watch during his short absence. Then off with him in a cab, and back within an hour with his own camp-bedstead and bedding, and what else he deemed necessary. But for his housekeeper, he would have carried Leyshon home; but she was angular and scrub-loving, and always *nassty* on such occasions; and he thought this the better plan. With the skill of a trained nurse and the tenderness of a mother, he got his patient undressed, washed and to bed; all to an accompaniment of gentle terms of endearment in the two languages. Then, out with his spectacles and big Bible, and to reading; and after the reading, to expatiating and exhortation. His intentions were still most gentle and tender; he was full of pity. *God so loved the world,* was his text.

But what are good intentions to a long habit and a native cast of mind? The *hwyl** of the little Cardigan chapel took him: the wind was in his sails, and it was the wind that blows about the Horn. He had finished with heaven before long; and then descended into hell and reveled there, and did gorgeous credit to his training. He could make word-pictures, and he did. He read and reeled off the terrors of all the planes of dementia; he brought Tophet in its awful glory into the little inglorious room. Trembling on the verges of consciousness, Evan Leyshon heard, saw, felt, and was terrified. Dumb Osiris lay quiet in his sepulchre, and Typhon the victor tossed and wallowed in the horrid torrents of his native glare and gloom.

Somewhere about nightfall the captain came to a pause. The repentant sinner lay before him; his own vein was somewhat expended, and he re-

*It means both the energy, inspiration or flow of a preacher, and the wind in the sails of a ship.

membered his first intentions. At once he was the tender nurse again: meeting the material needs, and filling his voice with soothing consolation. "But fear you nothing, my boy *bach!* remember you how God does love—" and "a long et cætera" . . . A dose given, and the moaning and tossing quieted; the candle lit, and screened from the patient's eyes; he prepared himself to argue the rest in silence—or sometimes in silence—with the Lord, and to make a night of it on his knees at his soap-box chair. The Lord hardened Pharaoh's heart of old; it should be a wonder if Captain Elias Elias did not soften the Lord's now. He chose Welsh, as being the language most likely to be best understood by Deity; and went to it with all his might. A rumor of his strivings should run through all the courts and hierarchies of heaven. . . .

And he became immersed in it; and the hours went by; and meanwhile the soul of Evan Leyshon, left at peace, went forth on its adventures.

III

He was walking in a vast procession on a long, dreary road, with marshlands on this side and that which lost themselves at a little distance in vagueness, perhaps invisibility—the Penarth Road, if you know those parts. And yet not the Penarth Road, either, as he could see; but the road taken by the newly dead—among whom he traveled. For there ahead—only many days' journeys ahead, and not a mere three miles or so—and yet clearly seen—rose the Heavenly City, the New Jerusalem . . . high upon its promontory, with its landmark church, St. Augustine's, in the midst dominating all, and sitting there like a duck squatting, beheaded. They had been traveling long and long. At some point or other he had come in sight of the blissful vision; he supposed after passing under the railway bridge at the end of Clive Street, where the tram turns; but could not remember.

All sorts and conditions of men were on the road with him. A priest came down the line from somewhere in front, picking out the Irishmen and here and there a foreigner; he had a rather commanding way with him, and reminded one a little of a sergeant-major with recruits. The Reverend Timothy Slimgill, sometime of the Baptist Forward Movement, was performing a like office for evangelicism generally; or trying to, for he had not the discipline, and must use unction and exhortation instead of the priest's command. From somewhere behind rose a belated sound of tambourines. Evan Leyshon felt little interest in these efforts. The thought of his wasted years and soul lay heavy on him; and he knew that presently, under Leckwith Hill, or about Penarth Dock, there would be a desolate turning in the road, which he would take.

A Mrs. Churchill-Pendleton, whom he had once known, hurrying hither and thither, displayed a busy anxiety to convert him to the Anti-Something Cause. Anti-what, he could not be quite sure; perhaps it was a good many things. She pressed leaflets on him, of which she had a goodly store; she had been distributing them all along the way, and meant to keep right on with it. "Take quite a number," she said: "I can get more printed, you know, when we are there." Presumably she contemplated an Anti-campaign among the angels, and had visions of reforming heaven. She corrected his pronunciation when he spoke, but seemed unaware of the substance of his answers. Later he heard her clash with the Reverend Timothy, with whom she took a high hand, telling him his views were crude and obsolete. There were two young colliers talking football: wishing to goodness they could have lasted till after the International with England. Alderman Glumph was enlarging nervously on past charitable undertakings of his own; he managed to buttonhole Slimgill, and held him five minutes, fishing for a good word. But Alderman Glumph had belonged to the Church, and Slimgill seemed a little bored. He spied Leyshon, and made off to him; perhaps after all only more eager for the one sinner that might be caused to repent, than for the just alderman that (obviously) needed no repentance. "My dear friend," said Reverend Timothy, "are you assured as to your destination?" "Assured enough," said Evan; "I am going to hell."

He spoke out loud, and saw that his words caused a little stir. Heads were turned; some one whistled; there was a general movement among those nearest to him to increase their distance. Apparently no one at all shared in his anticipations. Mr. Slimgill, however, was true to his colors, and stuck close. You might have thought his ministrations too late by a day; but here again the ruling passion was strong in death—and after. He seemed to forget that

As the tree falls, so shall it lie
Forever through eternity;

and that this tree decidedly was fallen. But whether or no, Evan Leyshon's blood was up (if one may speak in that way of the disembodied). The abjectness of his late physicality,—the keen edge of it—had gone from him, and he could step out like a man. He knew there was something in him that did not belong to that duck-churched Heavenly City on the heights; where, he divined, there would be conventional customs, conventional fashions in apparel, morality and religion, and—horror of horrors!—conventional Sabbaths. He had no business with singing Hallelujahs. He had tried to sing something of heaven—the real heaven—down into that hell back on earth; he had failed, and miserably; but shuddered at the thought of smug and smirkish bliss to follow his failure. In reality it was the spark left in him— sincerity—that caused the shudder. If hell was real, it was the place for him. If there was no justice, he would take the thing likest it. He would go where weakness and failure were punished, and take his damned chances.

Osiris believed that Typhon would only flourish the more up yonder: in a different, but perhaps a more deadly way; that the two of them would be soothed and lulled down into a complacent unity, with such life between them as that of a fat marrow in the fields. Typhon's aim always is peace with Osiris; all he fights for is that; but Osiris, though vanquished for ever and ever and ever, is still for war.

A cry was blown along from behind, and a motion of horror ran through the crowd; there came one wailing and pursued, from whom all the righteous shrank busily; one with head hanging down ghastlily—down on his breast, below his shoulders. Some one muttered: "At the jail this morning; the Splottlands murderer." "Damn them," said Evan Leyshon, "they've been at their legal crimes again." He thrust himself between the poor creature and its pursuers; put an arm round it protectingly, and railed back at them till they slunk from the pursuit. Here the procession broke, leaving these two in a gap of loneliness. Leyshon spoke to the thing at his side, saying what his heart dictated; whatever it was, it brought a growing likeness to humanity to the one addressed; and, strangely enough, a growing strength to Evan himself. So they went on.

They came under Leckwith Hill, and to the cross roads, and the railway sidings with their many trucks of coal; there these two turned and took their own way. As they went down into the gloom, they heard behind them the waning music of the elect: now a perfunctory *Jerusalem the Golden*—to the wheeze, it seemed, of some aerial unseen harmonium; now a straggling rattle of drums and cymbals with words to suit; now the exultant dirge or heartbreaking triumph of *O fryniau Caersalem*. It all died away at last as they went on between the standing coal-trucks and the stacked coal: through a gloom ever growing deeper, peopled with grim unhuman figures at toil.

And now, strangely, the two had changed roles; and it was not Evan Leyshon, but his Companion, that seemed the protector. "You are not afraid?" said that one. "No," said Evan; "I had a soul once." "Speak of it!" said the other; and in a tone that made Leyshon turn and look at him; and wonder at the transfiguration that had come to be there. It was now a veiled figure, erect, shining with a certain august light; and certainly with no mark of human desecration. "Speak of it," said that one; and laid a hand on Evan's arm: to whom straightway a flood of noble memories came, and he stepped proudly. "Let us go on," said he; "we two may conquer hell." It was the like of an archangel that went by his side; but veiled, so that he could not see the face.

They came to vast gates that were opened to them, and passed through into a vastness where, on high and terrible thrones amidst the shadows, sat the Judges of the Dead. Low down on a great space of floor before those judges Evan Leyshon was bidden stand; but it was as if his Companion went invisible: none but Leyshon seemed to see him where he stood at the latter's side. No accusation was needed, nor any passing of sentence; in silence his past life was unfolded, day after day, in a long procession through the gloomy air.

It passed; and the ground beneath him shuddered sullenly, and heaved as if moved by a dreadful life beneath—the life of death, of corruption. It began to crack and tremble like the ice-floe at high thaw; a thin glowing streak of fissure formed, and ran on, and broadened. A jagged rent opened, with muffled sound, right at his feet; and through it he looked down into gulfs below gulfs where in the thronging blackness ominous blue flames flickered and sputtered and died; or suddenly all would be a whirl and welter of red fire, and as suddenly, darkness again. He saw another crack form out in front, and run rippling towards him at right angles to the first; its edges as it widened glowing vermilion, and crumbling with little puffs of smoke. It grew, and drew nearer, nearer; and a great wail rang up out of the fathomless reek, and—

He felt his hand grasped in a hand . . . at the moment the fall began.

IV

Down, down, down; endlessly falling; through a night black as soot, in which ever and anon the blue sulphur-flames flickered grimly. And now there were charred living arms reached out to him, of those caught and tossed up by the currents and draughts of hell; and now there were avenues and narrow vistas, seen momentarily, glowing red, and in the midst of them forms like human writhing; and now a sudden glimpse of one chained and supine upon some peak above the chasms, and preyed upon by winged and taloned flames. For the most part there was silence; but sometimes a burst of hopeless passionless shrieking, or moaning like a sea-noise on desolate sunless shores. . . .

He had time to think as he fell. If this were real, he would. . . . Could he reach some stability; could he but *get at* some of those forms through which he was falling: he would, by heaven, do or say something for them. . . . Such thoughts grew, out of a first dazedness, and then a wonder. Fear or pain he felt not; but always more and more the high Osirian longings of his earlier years on earth. He had in him something, still, that was divine: if it was only words to say. That which he had failed to proclaim, living, he would, by the glory of God that kindled in him, proclaim aloud now that he was dead for the good of the damned in hell. What was it? Falling, he could not quite re-gather that. Only—there was blue sky somewhere, and he would forthtell it. Words would come to him; he felt a rainbowed cloud of them burning in the environs of his mind. There were streams on the mountains on earth, and they should flow through his songs in hell: there were runlets that he remembered, among the bluebells and bracken on Garth Faerdre Mountain; the damned should hear of them; they should hear of the perishless white flames of the stars. Damned? Tush! it was a dream; he would find the master word presently, that should vibrate out through this night of fire and dissipate it!

And ever and again, by a dim light, he would see landmarks worlds and worlds below: a peak; a crag whereon some vast being crouched and gloomed: and then in a moment they shot up past him, and were lost in the spaces through which he had fallen. And there were wandering and ominous suns, crimson like a dying ember, and as little light-giving, and dropping an agony of rubiate flame. And at last the glimmer of a midnight sea below; a sea of dark fires, whereon ran gleams and breakings of blue flame and green. Shadowy creatures came about him, and tossed imploring arms: there were millions and millions of them, outworn from human semblance, wasted with perpetual vain tears. Then he knew what hand it was he was holding; and that it was his Divine Companion's, who had come to him on the road in that ghastly guise. "Wake them!" he cried to that one; "it is all a dream; give me words to wake them!" "No," said the other; "your place is not here, but lower; come!"

Down and down; and so into the restless fire-flood on the floor of hell. But there too the words of his Companion came to him: "One is waiting for your coming until you have aroused whom from his evil dream, you can do nothing against hell." "Yes," said Evan Leyshon; "I will arouse him, if it costs me more sorrow even than I knew on earth." "He is here," said the other.

And they were in a miserable slum room, beneath the fire-sea at the bottom of hell. There was a lighted candle, much guttered, throwing large unsteady shadows on the walls. There was a man kneeling at a soap-box; there was a bed, and the like of a dead or dying man in it. Evan Leyshon looked from the one to the other, uncertain which of the two he was to waken; nor would his Companion tell him. Then he went to the kneeling man, and shook his arm, or tried to, and cried out to him, "Awake! awake! it is a dream!"

Captain Elias lifted his face lit up with a startled look of ecstasy. "Savior, I thank thee," he murmured, "that thou hast sent thine angel to visit me, and to give me assurance of thy mercy, of whose sweetness I have never dreamed till now." . . .

Evan Leyshon sighed. "He stirs in his sleep," he said; "but he will not be awakened."

"Go you to the other," said his Companion.

He did so; and bending over the bed, whispered: "Awake, awake, poor soul! you are to live again; it is not all at an end; you are to live again, and to conquer!"

The man in the bed opened his eyes; his face seemed curiously familiar to Evan Leyshon. "Another chance," he muttered, ". . . a great new chance. . . . I am to live again. . . . Of course . . . of course . . . I had forgotten." A look of transcendent delight came over his face; he smiled, as one might that had feared to die, on awaking to find the Angel Death bending over him, more beautiful than a night of stars, tenderer than any human compassion. . . .

The room vanished, and the mirk and the flames of hell thinned and waned; and Evan Leyshon, looking up, saw Orion shining, and the great white flame of Jupiter high in the heavens; and here the keen point Aldebaran, and there Sirius like a large diamond. And he heard songs from those triumphant luminaries: as when the stars of morning sang together and all the sons of God shouted for joy. Hell rang with the song and was shattered; there was the like of dispersing mist; there was the like of a drifting rain of pale constellations; there was the like of a burning mountain giving up sweet stars and singing for fire. . . .

V

He was going up Bute Street westward; but in mid air; and his Companion with him. It seemed to be delight that lifted him: above the high trams; above the crowds of hurrying clerks and loitering sailors; above the consulates and offices and warehouses. Over the whole city. He saw St. Mary Street below, and High Street; then the Castle with its great square towers, and the row of sculptured beasts on the wall. Then the park, and the river; then Llandaff and the cathedral; the open fields and the hills; there the towers of Castell Coch among the trees on its hill-top; there the gap, the Gate of Wales, and the high bridge; and yonder, Garth Faerdre Mountain, all in its silvered purple beauty, under a sunlight such as never shone on it for his living eyes. And there, above Garth Faerdre, with many spires and domes of turquoise and silver, lazuli and glistering crystal, what he knew for the Heavenly City. So those two came to the gates of Heaven.

He dwelt in Heaven for an immensity of timeless years. By green lawns and pleasant waters he wandered, and under phantom sapphire mountains where there was singing unlike any from mortal throats. It was a place of flowers, where every bloom was living and with power to touch him to the quick of joy; all his companions were as beautiful and discreet as flowers. Their speech was verse chanted; their thoughts eager and delicate and creative and strong like poetry. Memory of his past life was blotted away from him—except, sometimes, the early and hopeful days in the Vale of Neath. He remembered no sordidness, no failures; nothing of the lure of the senses, the poison that had brought him to ruin. On those piled up mountains of serenity there were always higher heights to climb: worlds upon worlds above, of more gracious color, more ennobling beauty, more exquisite and vigorous song. And then at last he came to the Peak of peaks, very near to the Sun. Over it hovered the princely Sun, with dragon wings quivering and scintillant. And the Sun leaned down and whispered a word to him; and touched his eyes with a wand of blue turquoise stone; and thereupon all vision was fulfilled in him; and all knowledge with infinite calmness blossomed within his breast. . . .

He saw the winged worlds and systems. He saw, strewn through the remote spaces, battle and bliss, battle and bliss. He heard the singing of the choirs of suns. The delight that trembles through the planispheres made a way for itself out through the inmost gates of his being. Then he looked down, and beheld the continents and islands of this world.

His eye fell at last on a city by the sea. He saw a long and dingy street, with groups of sailors lounging, and innumerable clerks hurrying hither and about. He could see every individual without and within: their bodily seeming, and the motions of their minds and desires. In all the crowd he seemed to be searching for some one: whom, he could not tell; but it was some one that concerned him nearly. . . . last he found him: the wreck of a man, shuffling miserably through the throng; and now it was night down there in the city, lit with electric globes. He saw the man going down towards the docks, lurching in his walk, and anon coughing and spitting blood. And then turning, and creeping and sneaking down by wretched side streets; and into an abominable place in the slums there to die.

Then he was concerned to know the past of that man; and saw it, following it somehow like a stream back to its source. He saw days when the man was falling, not quite fallen: when he spoke to crowds in the Hayes; he saw a divine thing, compassionate—the pride of conscious soulhood—struggling for the mastery of that life, and winning some little victories, and suffering many great defeats; and thwarted, and balked and driven back and humiliated, till it was almost expelled from contact with its body and brain. And then earlier days: in fields, among hills, by a beautiful river with many waterfalls: days when the world was exceeding lovely, aquiver with intense hopefulness: when almost every hour brought forth its increment of inspiration. He saw the whole of that life; he was fascinated by the sight; at every phase of it he made comment: "Ah, no! let him shun that! . . . Let him take this other course! . . . that is not the way; let him choose thus!"—He was absorbed; he fought all the battles of the man he watched, and knew that he himself had wisdom and strength to win them. He longed fiercely to be down there in that body, informing that mind, directing that life to certain victory. . . .

In Heaven one must always go on: there is no standing still there.

He stood, be it remembered, on the highest peak; at least the highest visible. He had accomplished the seven labors of Heaven, which are seven surprising incredible aspects of joy. His Companion stood beside him.

"We must go on," said that one; "there is no remaining here for ever."

"Of course," said Evan Leyshon. "We must go down there; there, do you see, to that world down yonder; in all space there is nothing I desire but to be there. It is a new place; a place of discoveries, of heroic adventures and conflicts; it has joys in it not to be found elsewhere. We must go to that man—do you not see him?—*there!* Every step of his life has been a step downward; he did not know how to fight the battles one has to fight in that world: just that atom of knowledge was lacking to him, or he might be as we now are; for he had vision, at first, almost such as we have; he was not blinded as most of them seem to be. I must go to him; somehow those battles of his are my battles, and I must fight and win them; somehow I know that that place in Heaven, that duty, is waiting for *me.*"

"Look further," said his Companion; "there is still more that you are to see."

He looked, and followed the man right back through his youth and childhood—the happy-go-lucky home, the parental indulgences, the first mistakes—to his birth; then clouds blew across the face of the globe he watched, and all was obscured. They passed, and he saw—another country, another age, and another life; but knew that the same individual was concerned; he felt the same interest in it. It was the life of a man who gave forth songs of divine soft beauty: one with a famous name, that captured in the nets of his vision the most secret wonder of the world; one to whom the magical life of the stars and the forests and sea-beaches was crystal-clearly revealed. High performance here; not mere promise! And he discerned in that life a certain lack of discrimination, not to know the Beauty of God from the beauty of the lures that kill: the shallow pool of passional satisfaction from the deep ocean of the satisfaction of the Soul. And so he saw him entrapped by passion, till the stars and sea-beaches and the forests were obscured from him, and the torrents of the lower life whirled him away quickly down to death.

"Look still further," said his Companion.

He looked, and was aware of clouds over the world again, and that once more time was drifting backward. Then he saw another life; but again, knew the man he now began to watch for a former edition, as it were, of him of the stars and sea-beaches, and of him of the miserable death in the slums. Now it was a life dedicated to all high thoughts and heroism: a great champion of the divine; a man of fierce passions fiercely dominated—but thoroughly; a life triumphant over the temptations of sense, but with a certain pride in virtue and intolerance of human weakness; a clear vision of right and wrong; an heroic warfare, public and private, against the wrong. A grand shining life; one that thrilled him to watch . . . and yet that hurt him, too . . . for there was that pride, that intolerance, that lack of pity. And then he knew why the singer of the stars and forests had fallen, and why the other had gone down to die miserably in the slums.

"What is it you desire?" said his Companion.

"What else should I desire?" said he. "To go down there and put that line of lives to rights. I know that it is my business, my adventure; there is nothing else in all this Heaven I care to be about. See: I am armed; I have the knowledge. I demand this boon from the Master of the Sun. That crookedness must be made straight; there will be no peace in all the universe till those lives are brought to a decent triumph; and it may easily be done; a few years of struggle and suffering—nothing! The pride of achievement is gone—sorrow and fall and lifewreck have banished that; let but the sensual weakness go—and I know how to conquer it—and he will be a true warrior for the Gods; for he has the love of man now for the central fire of his being. One life, or two, will do it. I must go down there, and run that matter, put it through. I must, because it concerns me . . . because it is . . . by heaven, because it is my own life!"

Day dawned; the sun came up over the low hills of England; over the Severn Sea; over the slums by Bute Street, as elsewhere. A ray struggled into that wretched room, and brought Captain Elias Elias from his knees and from wrestling with the Lord in prayer; it was now time to see to the patient again. He bent over the bed, and saw a kind of flush, something more than calmness, on Evan Leyshon's face. In a moment the dying man opened his eyes; they were clear; the traces of the beast had gone from them; Typhon was not there; Osiris shone,—confidence, calmness, joy. Not for nothing, thought the captain, had the Angel of the Lord visited the slum room during the night.

"Little heart," said he, "how is it with you in your soul, indeed now?"

Evan Leyshon made no answer. He was taking in the fact that the life now ending had been one of his own, the Soul's, the Denizen of Heaven's; and then he was taking in the fact that this failure, Evan Leyshon, thus dying in the slums, was also . . . one of the Host—a Soul—one from the high mountains of godhood: that had come again and again to earth-life, to do things—and to win things—and suffer things. And then—he was putting the two facts together, and taking the burden and sorrow of his awful life-failure, and seeing it melt before his eyes in the knowledge that there was no finality about it: that there would be other days, other chances; and, by God! a better knowledge, now, how to meet them and turn them to the purposes of the divine; how that from birth to death is but a day, and from death to rebirth but a night; and complete victory, complete expression of the highest things in the Soul, the end and goal of it all. . . .

"*Calon fach,*" said the captain, "how is it with you, indeed and indeed now, in your soul?"

But sure you, there, what good to bother that there was no answer? Captain Elias Elias could see well enough, by the look in the dead man's face. He went home presently, and got out what he called his "ship's log of holiness," and wrote down to his credit with the Lord, another soul snatched from the talons of Sathan, *whatever!*

• •

*"The Prodigal's Return" is another of Morris's few mainstream stories, here a
modern one with an Italian setting. It was published in* The Theosophical
Path *in April 1919, under the pseudonym Ambrosius Kesteven.*

The Prodigal's Return

Giacomo and Camilla had been up at the castle all day, pottering
about and dreaming; and, towards evening, preparing a meal in
case their master should return. This was a daily observance, and the ritual
of their religion: carried out in simple, unanxious faith for the last thirty
years. What would happen when they were gone, neither of them troubled
to speculate. The Marchese would have come back before then, and the ancient splendor of Castel Giuliano would have returned.

It was the subject of all their talk, that ancient splendor. The old Marchese Don Giulio—how noble, how glorious a man he had been!—"But
severe, Giacomino mio; severe!" Don Ferdinando, *poverino,* had perhaps
been a trifle gay; there was generous blood in his veins; *ecco!* you could not
expect the prudence of age from the heart and brains of youth. A matter for
Fra Domenico to absolve; what else were they for, those priests? A little
penance; with pease in the shoes, if the saints were really offended. *Ecco!*—
she herself, Camilla, understood the boiling of peas; she could have arranged all in such manner that no violence should have been done to the
Marchesino's gentle nurture. As for the saints, they would have thought the
better of her for it, had the matter come to their ears. Even that was doubtful; "they have a deal to attend to, my Giacomino!" But that of driving the
poverino from the castle of his ancestors—Sant' Ampeglio, it was altogether
too severe! Might it be pardoned her for saying so—and Don Giulio himself
a saint in glory now. . . . as without doubt he was; and let the Holy Father
mark what she said.

Camilla had been Don Ferdinando's nurse, and he remained in her eyes the one who could do no wrong. His birth had followed quickly on a birth in their cottage: hence the honor done Camilla. For the daughter born to her then—her only child—the Marchese himself had stood sponsor; of his great grace giving the child the name of Maria Giuliana. This was a bolt to transfix the heart of Giacomo forever: thenceforth the Marchese, living, had been for him the pattern and *ne plus ultra* of noblemen; and dead, the saint to whom his prayers were addressed. But then, Giacomo had been born, forty-five years before, into the personal service, you might say, of that same Marchese's father; so hereditary faithfulness entered into his composition, and formed the basis of this later cult. Camilla, on the other hand, was from Apricale, beyond the valley: of the estate, but not of the household. And her soul was overoccupied with the two babies at the time, for Don Giulio's condescension to impress it fully. Consequently for her Don Giulio, and for Giacomo Don Ferdinando, had been the one to shine with a borrowed light: had been respectively the father and the son of Perfection: although in each case, very near to being Perfection himself, be it said.

When Don Giulio banished his son, Giacomo accepted the fiat with sorrow, but unquestioningly: the Marchese, if severe, was infallible. Don Ferdinando, he considered, would go to the wars, achieve greatness, and return to rule his life and lands after the fashion of his so glorious progenitor. It was not well, in any case, for your young eagle to stay in the eyrie over-long; *ecco!* one must see the world. Meanwhile it was sad, certainly. —Not so had Camilla taken it, however. She *knew* there could have been no adequate cause for sternness so unpaternal: it was the natural wickedness in the heart of man, that moved the world to persecute her darling. She went into open rebellion when the news was brought to the cottage. "There, there, thy tongue is too long, Beppo!"—this to the servant who had brought it. "Thou hast been told lies, or art thyself lying. It was malice sent thee; it was Angela thy sweetheart, who hates me out of jealousy. *Basta!* I go to the castle myself; and they Marchese shall listen to reason before I return." —"Bide where thou art, Camilla; I command it!" said Giacomo. —"Command thou where thou mayest find obedience, my spouse," she answered; and was gone.

In the servants' hall she received confirmation of the news: there was an atmosphere of unease and tension there, that shattered her faith in Angela's malice before ever a word was spoken. Her questioning elicited this: during the morning the Marchese had sent for his son; at noon Don Ferdinando had ridden forth. None knew what had passed at the interview, but rumors were rife. There had been anger certainly; though Don Giulio's anger was not of the kind that finds expression in loudness, and eavesdropping had been disappointingly unprofitable. But the whole house felt it, and trembled. There had been a summons, and:—*Saddle Don Ferdinando's horse—immediately!*—and he, *poveretto,* with the aspect of one crushed and appalled, had ridden forth. . . . —"And you, dastards, pigs," cried Camilla, "you suffered this crime to be done, and made no sound?" Eloquently she poured scorn on their lineage, from which courage nor virtue was possible. "For me, I go to talk to this tyrant so cruel; I go to undo this fearful wrong. And whoso desires reward from a penitent father, let him saddle and ride after my lord, and bid him return." They made no sign of compliance, knowing their master better; but neither did they attempt to rail back at her. With the men, this last was mainly out of pity; with Angela, because she found herself for the moment over-awed.

Don Giulio was anything but a tyrant, or cruel; though it might be said that in him the ancient Roman honor more appeared than any that drew breath in Italy. His mother had been a Spaniard; and some ichor from the land of Don Quixote, also, undoubtedly ran in his veins. He had lived the life of a recluse on his estate, feeding upon refined, haughty, and benevolent ideals. He had walked the straight path; had governed with justice and mercy. He had dreamed Mazzini's dream before Mazzini; and knew its fulfilment postponed until the Bruti and Lucretias should return. He could strike no blow for Italy himself, since the time was unripe; but he could live exaltedly for her, and hope all things from his son. His wife had died when Ferdinando was three: a bereavement that would have broken him, but that the intense and knightly devotion he had accorded her, found other vents through which to burn. The loves that remained to him glowed whiter for his pain, and were to be called spiritual, almost entirely: they were for Italy, for his people, and for the ideal he had made of his son.

He governed his estates through Giacomo, his steward; whom, above all, he trusted. It was characteristic of him that he would have no city-born stranger in that office; but one of the peasants themselves, who would understand his fellow peasants; and, being trustworthy, see that none suffered and none transgressed. His own exterior pride and sternness, an outward semblance from the intensity of his dreams, held away from him the popular love that he deserved: his people were well contented, and honored him; but their Marchese was too aloof to be adored. Yet such ardent, you may say passionate, benevolence as his is a force more potent than steam or electricity, and is bound to awaken its response; the adoration was given, and liberally, but to Don Ferdinando his son. The latter, as child and boy, was as unlike his father as might be: all sunshine and affability, he was here, there, and everywhere among the peasants, and had for supreme talent the faculty to make himself loved. Later, when he had grown into youth, his doings had come to be questioned: there were stories afloat; and prudent mothers, if their daughters had the fatal gift, were on guard when he was by. Except always Camilla, whose faith was perfect, and made her heroic now to beard the Marchese and storm.

He was standing at his library window, looking out over his valley, to the little towns perched here and there on the hillsides: white Lorgnone, San Giacinto, Dolceacqua: his little towns and his fathers' before him.

There they were, the little towns on their crags: lime-washed walls and red roofs in a sea of gray-green olives; below, the vineyards and the fields; above, the stretches of wild thyme, rosemary, and myrtle among the pines. There, yonder, was his olive mill; there was his river, his *dolce acqua,* whose music, except in dry summer, rose forever to the towers of Castel Giuliano. There were the scenes and sounds that he loved, that he had always longed for during the few occasions in his life when he had been absent from them for more than a few days together. And now, where was their beauty; where was their sanctity gone?

On this mood in him Camilla broke, to pour forth the torrents of her wrath, and end in a storm of tears. "Ah, Signore, what is this that I have heard? what is this wickedness that you have done?" —None had so treated him before; and the household was intensely apprehensive, knowing whither she had gone, and in what temper. But in truth they did not know the man, nor guess the depths of his pride and love. His people were a part of himself, and their honor was his own. She was utterly unprepared for the reception he gave her. "Thou too?" he said, turning from the window. "And thou knowest not why he has gone?"

"Ah, Signore, I know not and I care not. For what reason are there priests, except to absolve our little sins? Ah me," she sobbed, "your lordship is unjust and cruel—but cruel! But you will repent—already you have repented! You wait to give the order to ride after him!"

"Listen then, poor little Camilla! Thou wilt understand too soon, alas; and then—"

He would have said—"then the child that will be born, and the mother, shall have right done them, if it lies within the power of my marquisate." Right—that is, adoption, education, and, if the law could achieve it, recognition as heir of Castel Giuliano. But in fact, his eye having offended him, he had plucked it out; and the wound was too sore for speech. His ideals might have stood him in better stead, had Ferdinando himself not been so intimate a part of them: he had played the Roman father by virtue of will and idealism, not through any coldness of heart. "Go now, then, *poverina,"* he said, "and put thy trust in the good Gesù and his saints!" And she, having expended her armory, departed; to give herself to days of quiet weeping.

And then her own Maria disappeared; and Camilla was still too grief-sick over the first, to feel the second blow in its intensity, or to perceive its significance. A runaway match, no doubt; that might end well enough, for that matter: we should hear of the little ingrate in time. . . . To connect her disappearance with the cause of the Marchese's anger against his son; to imagine that the latter's expulsion was punishment for wrong he had done Maria: would have been as impossible to Camilla as the commission of any deadly sin. Nor did even Giacomo guess the truth; perhaps being too much concerned about his master, to give himself to brooding on troubles of his own. One must consider how peasant loyalty had been growing in his line for generations; and how Don Giulio's virtues had turned what was an instinct into a passion. The whole incident had held from the first less than its due importance in their minds; the Marchese, who knew the cause of it, felt it much more deeply than they did. But now you must hear the whole story of it: both that which Don Giulio knew, and that which, for lack of knowing, he died.

We must say that there were grand elements in this Maria Giuliana: it needed but the bitter touch to bring them to the surface. Ferdinando, bringing all his arts to play, had wakened passion in her, promised her marriage; then, when he turned and laughed at her pleadings, the revelation of herself and of him came to her. For all his charm and brilliance, she saw, he was a veritable weakling; although passion had swept her headlong once, she knew that she was a hundred times stronger and braver than he. She loved him still, and was big enough to mingle her love with pity; to transmute it, largely, into that. Had the Marchese not banished him; had he remained at home, his guilt undiscovered, she would have bided her shame and said nothing. But now that he was gone she set forth to follow his trail through the Apennines, with peasant sense and instinct for guides, and something far higher than vulgar passion as motive. You are not to think she excused herself, or was blind to her fault; only, with the difficulties that lay before her, she could not afford to indulge in remorse. A child was to be born, and for its sake she must find its father; but she must find him for his own sake also: she must make him do right by his child, if she could; but also she must, if she could, shield and wean him from wrong. Her main thought was: *He will come to great grief, poor child, with none to protect him.* I will not speak of her sufferings during her search and the weeks that preceded it; out of them strength came daily seeping into her; as is the way when the potentiality of a grand compassion lies at the roots of character. She tracked him to Vienna, came upon him in utter poverty and depression, played her cards consummately, and convinced him of his dependence on her; then, taking him in a mood of penitence, won from his better nature, before her son was born, the marriage to which his father had commanded him in vain. After all, he reflected, such a step would mean repatriation: immediate wealth and comfort restored: and Maria, for whom he cared at times, had the manners and education of a lady, and was undoubtedly beautiful. He married her, and wrote of it to his father; but before the letter was posted, news came that his father had died. Whereupon he changed his mind about returning: partly because he saw how Maria longed for it, partly for other reasons. He could spend his patrimony in Vienna, where pleasures could be bought that neither love nor money would win at Castel Giuliano. Here Maria would be useful, there she would be a drag socially;

so, that none of his acquaintances there might know he had married beneath him, he forbade her to write to her parents. Thus it had come about that now, in their old age, she had passed entirely out of their lives.

As for Don Giulio's death, it had happened in this way. Half his life had gone with the loss of Ferdinando; Maria's disappearance, of which he knew the cause, seemed absolutely to threaten what of it remained. Giacomo and Camilla, in his dreams, were types of the peasants of Italy: of the new Italy that was to be, all faithfulness, frugal virtue, and simplicity. Twenty years before, in the joy of his own recent fatherhood, he had stood sponsor to their child: an act that he looked on as symbolic, and was proud to perform. He had taken his sponsorship seriously, too—in his life and in his dreams. She should be educated; and he had himself superintended her education. She should honorably marry: perhaps, if the time were ripe, a soldier of Italian liberation; at least she should bear strong sons to fight for that holiest cause. He would provide her dowry; God send her husband might fight under his son, or her sons under his son's sons! Now she was lost, and he felt himself not unresponsible; since he had been dreaming and mourning, these last weeks, when he should have been taking steps for her protection. He had not been able to speak of it to her parents, when word of her disaster first came to him: time, that would force that ordeal on him, he had thought, would also bring him strength to go through with it. Now, what a march that same time had stolen on him! Should he tell them now, when what they were inclined to make light of, stood revealed to him as their daughter's probably perdition? He had the country scoured for her; rode himself; it was wonderful that she succeeded in escaping. Returning, his horse had taken fright, and thrown him; he had broken a thigh in the fall; complications followed; of which, and mainly of grief, he died after five months.

"Giacomo," he said at the last, "what wilt thou do, thou and Camilla?"

"What my lord may command," said the weeping Giacomo. They had their little hoard, those two, gathered carefully during their years of service; and their cottage and garden, at the foot of the castle hill, were freehold, given them by Don Giulio at the time of their marriage.

"Listen then; I have made provision for you in my will. My son will repent, and return some day; perhaps he has already repented. Remain where you are; be steward for him until he returns; take care of the people; collect the rents and keep the house in order for him. . . . Take care of the people! . . . Take care of the people!" A pause; then followed instructions as to certain work that was to be carried out; privileges that were to be granted or extended. "And now," said he, "send for Camilla. I must have her forgiveness before I go."

Giacomo wept. "Signore, signore, she shall go on her knees beside the bed here, and pray for yours! A shrewish and bitter woman, signor mio; but of the great goodness of your heart you will forgive her, remembering her love for her fosterchild. Ah my lord, bitter will our days be, when your highness is with the saints in paradise!"

"Call her, Giacomino." He intended to tell them, now at the last, why he had banished his son; and to pray for their forgiveness of the sin done by his flesh and blood against theirs. But when Camilla came in with her husband she was all tears and voluble prayers for forgiveness. She would do penance, indeed she would—ah, none of Fra Domenico's bagatelles!—she would trudge in to the capital, seek out Fra Ludovico Menoni, who inspired terror; and to him confess to theft, to perjury, to parricide. . . . All this for having upbraided the Marchese, a few months before. —Perhaps it confused the dying man, and drove distinct memories from his mind. Instead of telling them of his son's sin, he merely blessed them as they knelt at his bedside, weeping and kissing his hands. Then the priest came with extreme unction; and while it was being administered, he died.

Besides what provision he had made for them, he had left an astonishing sum—all that he had in money or investments. In fact—"to my beloved god-daughter Maria Giuliana Giacomelli"; to be held in trust for her by the advocate Paolo Bolognini, pending her discovery; or to be dispensed, on proof received of her death, in charity. To Giacomo, who was named in it steward and guardian of the estates, Advocate Paolo, called Big Bolognini, explained as much of the will as concerned him; and he in turn explained it to Camilla.

A month later a letter had come from Vienna: "Giacomo: I need money. Send the year's rents, and what else thou hast in hand. Thy lord, Ferdinando di Castel Giuliano." Giacomo sent the rents, with a full account laboriously drawn up, and duly attested by the lawyer. A few months passed, and then this came: "Giacomo: I need more money; what was sent was insufficient. If thou hast not twenty-five thousand in hand, sell such and such lands. Thy lord, Ferdinando di Castel Giuliano." The steward took counsel with his wife. —"He has generous blood in his veins," said she. "He will need vast sums to maintain his state among the Tedeschi, so that they may not become familiar, those ones." —"Or perhaps," said Giacomo, "it is for good works he will require it." —"That also is likely," said Camilla; but leaned to the opinion that it was to overawe the Tedeschi. "In any case, the money must be sent." Giacomo groaned. —"But to sell the lands—" he began; but found no words to express the horror of it. —"Who speaks of the lands?" said Camilla. "We are over-rich, Giacomino mio, thou and I—ecco!" —"It is as thou sayest, Camilla," said Giacomo, a load lifted from his mind. Next day he explained his need to Big Bolognini, and by his aid converted half the Marchese's legacy into notes. "I charge thee nothing for advice, Giacomino," said the lawyer; "since thou art an obstinate pig, and wouldst take none." "Sì, sissignore!" Giacomo agreed: who had always found legal advice a thing that tended to confusion. He sent the money to Vienna, explaining that by God's grace there had been no need to sell the lands.

But the demands had come thick and fast; and first their own money, and then, bit by bit, the estates had gone. So things had come to be as they were. There were no servants left at Castel Giuliano; two rooms only remained furnished and habitable: of the rest, one after another had been closed, shuttered and bolted after everything sellable in it had been sold. It was a long siege, an unequal contest: time and ruin and decay the beleaguering host, and Giacomo and Camilla the garrison. And there was a traitor within: an arch-traitor and agent of the enemy: old age. Hard living and the natural passage of the years had long been telling against the steward and his wife; they were up early and late; they sought no rest; but limbs will stiffen at last, and minds grown old run towards dream. The scouring that in the days of their affluence Camilla would have finished in early morning, now took her all day; the repairs, or the gardening, that Giacomo used to do in a day, now lasted him a week. It was—"how many years, Camilla mia?" —"Ten at the least, Giacomino,"—since he had written to his master: "Signore, there are no more rents, and nothing left to sell; therefore I cannot send the money." "Thou hast been careless and improvident," came the reply. "I shall return, and demand full accounts." Giacomo pondered grievously and long, seeking wherein his improvidence had lain; but gave it up at last, concluding that his nature was to be stupid. Now, he had long since forgotten all that last letter, except the fact that it promised return. There was very much that they had forgotten, the two of them.

But that stopping of the funds marked a change in the prodigal's menage in the far country. No more riotous living now; but for Maria, his diet should have been "the husks that the swine did eat." And you will note that a measure of poetic justice had been done him; had he permitted her to write home, nothing could have saved her fortune from him. Henceforward it was she who was to hold the purse strings and the reins of government. She had fought daily battles for his soul, and lost heroically; had borne long with his cruelty, which now wasted down into mere cantankerous peevishness. Meanwhile she had captured certain of the sums sent by Giacomo, and started a little business of her own, of which her husband knew, or professed to know, nothing. At this business she had worked early and late; had developed it with indomitable courage, Italian taste and sound peasant sense; until, when resources from Castel Giuliano failed, with the help of her son she was making good money. And she had achieved bringing up the boy decently, with the object-lesson of his miserable father before his eyes; heaven knows how she had sacrificed and striven, to educate him! Long ago she had paid for that first mistake, had this brave Maria Giuliana; and turned her life, so gravely once in jeopardy of ruin, into a thing all nobility. But she had won her reward: in seeing Don Giulio's virtues, and not Don Ferdinando's vices, develop in her son.

All of which, of course, was infinitely far from the knowledge of the old folk at home. Their life and hers had diverged so widely, that now there was no correlation, in realities, between the two. For them, the black-haired and laughing-eyed Maria had somehow grown out of the past into the future; all the facts concerning her over-shadowed by their ruling passion. They had never thought of her departure as tinged deeply with tragedy; they had expected her to return sometime; now they had come to think of her as of one who had never gone out of their lives—who was absent for the moment, that was all;—and to speak of what she would do, what she would say or think, on the day of days. —"For she also loves him, as we do." So they traveled by a quiet and silvery road into the paradise of old age, which need have no boundary, no sharp distinction, between it and the paradises that lie beyond.

It was their own devotion that made that road pleasant for them; to a looker-on, the way would have seemed barren and difficult enough. How did they live at all? One would have had to ask the Big Bolognini; he, it appeared, had still mysterious funds belonging to the estate, and paid them weekly what should have kept them from hunger. They accepted it in good faith, and tried more than once to get him to disgorge it in lump to send to their master. But Bolognini was adamant as to that: "Would you have me sent to prison?" said he; and referred in vague terms to the will. He thought he was compounding with the saints for the safety of his soul; in reality it was the milk of human kindness. Of which in truth there was much in him; and he had no wife or children to consult as to what he should do with his own. "Poor little old ones so sympathetic!" he would sigh, soothing his business acumen after such an indulgence; "after all, one derives from it amelioration of appetite and digestion." The money he gave them, used peasant-wise, would have met all their needs; but there was the daily supper to prepare for Don Ferdinando, and they spent it expensively, nine tenths of it, on that. The meal thus prepared, however, served themselves for rations the next day. They never expected their lord to arrive in the daytime, and never failed to expect him in the evening: a superstition, one must suppose.

Poveri vecchietti tan simpatici!—they were, in truth, very old now. Their mouths were deep sunken; their faces innumerably lined; their limbs somewhat stiff and unmanageable; but their minds had struck root deep in dreamland, and there bloomed and rioted. "When their lord returned"— ah, when their lord returned—and the Golden Age! All the greatness of the house would be restored; all the prosperity of the valley. The virtues they had known in Don Giuilo, they transferred to Don Ferdinando; plus all the charm that had been his own. It was the beauty and tranquillity of their youth that they looked to see again: the whole romance of years long since, whose bright days only were remembered.

Now to go back to the point from which we started:—they had been up at the castle all day; now it was past ten o'clock and once more they postponed their expectations. "Clearly he will not come tonight, my Camilla." They lit their lantern, and began the hobble homeward. "It is better that it should be tomorrow," said Camilla; "I have but half scrubbed the floor of the sala; by tomorrow evening it will be finished." This also was a convention with them: to find consolation in the unfinishedness of their work. A storm was blowing, and no moon shone; though here in the great avenue there was some shelter for them, it was no night for old folk to be gadding abroad. Suddenly:—"Eh—who calls?" said Giacomo; and Camilla: —"It is our Maria only, *sposo mio;* it is nothing. *Pazienza,* little Maria; we come!" And I am to tell you that Camilla was right; that it was Maria who called, and no other. Thirty years ago they had lost a merry peasant daughter; now the lantern should have shown them a tall, grave, well-dressed lady; but *"It is our Maria only, sposo mio,"* said Camilla; *"it is nothing."*

"Ah, *carissimi,* your forgiveness!" she said. —*"Ebbene, piccolina,* thou didst well to come, on the contrary"—this from Giacomo—"thou canst help thy mother through the storm." And Camilla:—"Take the lantern from thy father, child; it grows difficult for him to manage it, these stormy nights."

One could not shout explanations against the wind; and none seemed to be needed—immediately. So, wondering and waiting for light, she shepherded them to the cottage in all love. She must have time to think, to discover things, must this brave Maria, before serious action could be taken, or serious words said.

They came to the door, and the old people entered in front of her; from what might happen now she would get her guidance. What did happen was more a surprise to her than to her parents. There, standing in the candle-light waiting for them, they beheld—that which they had been expecting all those years. There he stood, young and handsome, precisely as they had always pictured him—their own lord, their Don Ferdinando. Camilla gave one cry of joy, and had him in her arms, was hanging on his breast. —"Ah, *signorino mio,* thou hast come back to thy old nurse; thou hast come back to thy little Camilla, to make glad her ancient eyes!" There was none of the shock of surprise which kills; they had been expecting this for thirty years. The shock would have been, perhaps, if he who had returned had been the worn-out rip who had died a few weeks before in Vienna, after wasting their money and his father's estate; if they could have been made to realize that *he* was their Don Ferdinando, it might have killed them. But this was just their own boy: a few years older than when he left, but still young and merry.

For a moment Maria did not realize how things stood. "Ah, love him, *madre carissima;* since he is your own grandson." —"What nonsense she talks, the little Maria! Calm thyself then, my daughter; thy head is turned with joy at the return of our lord the Marchesino!" Then the situation dawned upon Maria; one cannot say whether with more sadness or relief. There was nothing to explain. "Thou seest how it is with them, my Dino," she whispered to her son. "To them thou art thy father, who was as thou art when last they saw him."

—"Ah, but he has even improved, our Marchesino," said Camilla. "Eh, Giacomo?" —"It is as thou sayest, *sposa mia.* Signorino, thy father, the sainted Don Giulio, would behold thee with pride now." —"For a saint, he was too severe," said Camilla sadly. "To take so gravely thy little faultlings." So they made much of him; while Maria, seated apart, wept quietly. There was nothing to explain; they would never know the story of her life.

You see how it ended? Big Bolognini needed but to see the marriage lines, the birth certificate, and the certificate of the death of her husband in Vienna; he was on his feet in a moment, bowing profusely; he was a good man, if stout, and a little soapy and flaccid. "But welcome, Madonna! Signor Marchese, you are most welcome! Ah, and there is much money waiting for you, too. Giacomo—your excellent father, Madonna, tried hard to get it from me. Had I known you were at Vienna, it would have gone."

In fact, there was enough to rehabilitate the castle; even to buy back much of the land: completely to restore, so far as Giacomo and Camilla ever knew, the ancient splendor of Castel Giuliano, the Golden Age of their dreams.

They lived to see two wonderful years of it; then, entered upon dreamings new and even brighter, but still kindred to their old ones.

● ●

In the following story, the divinity of a Babylonian slave is re-awakened by his dreams of the Secret Mountain of the Gods. It was published in the June 1919 issue of The Theosophical Path, *under the pseudonym Aubrey Tyndall Bloggsleigh. Morris republished it as the eponymous story of his collection* The Secret Mountain and Other Tales.

The Secret Mountain

I

Varglon Fflamlas, that was a slave in Babylon, dreamed a dream. Three dreams, indeed, it were better to say: since they came on three several nights, and each with a different story to tell. Or three chapters of one story; for the quality of it was ever the same, and such as to make the things of waking life—his fellow-slaves; the taskmaster; the courtyard, streets and palaces; the well from which he, yoked and blind-folded and going wearily round and round in a circle, drew water—seem as unreal as they were uninteresting.

The first night, then, he found himself in the midst of great splendors, but having a splendor within him greater than that without. He knew that up and down the world the sound of his name was going, and that men were praising him everywhere, and that no poet had fame like his fame, from Camelot to Xanadu, or from the Mountain Kaf to the bottom of the world. Nor did his honors lack foundation: his mind was all a wonder and extraordinary flame. He beheld the day sky traversed by beautiful deities and dragons, and the night on fire with the living palaces of the Gods; for him the sea was visibly the abode of hoary Thrones and Virtues; earth could not hide from him her magical inward continents and star-peopled promontories; men and women seemed to him great spirits under a thin disguise. . . .

He had come to his prime, he was aware, and his powers were growing yearly; and now he had made one supreme poem which should be chanted by bards to come, certainly, as long as kings had courts or men built cities, and there were singers in either to keep them sweet with song. And this poem he was now to chant before the King of kings in Babylon. There sat that great monarch—with the face of one of his fellow-slaves, in whom he had never before noticed kingly qualities; there the king's daughter, whose hand should be the reward of his singing; there, all the familiar faces of the courtiers and great officials;—and he himself, he knew, the central and important figure on whom all eyes were set. He rose to begin, and felt the grand surge of inspiration upon him: heard the rushing of the wings of the Spirit, as they are heard when a man's mind is to be borne up to the splendid heights—and then a stranger came out of the crowd, and stood before him, and whispered something; and he faltered, and could not give his mind to the chanting, for visions that came to him of a Mountain afar in the forest, asserting a pearly whiteness, thrown up high above the billowing tree-tops, against the intense blue of heaven. And he was filled with longing for that Mountain; so that applause and riches and fame seemed nothing to him; and if the king's daughter's hand had been held out to him he would not have reached forth his to take it. And his great poem—went through after a sort to the end; and before that came the king yawned and began talking—in whispers certainly—to those who stood by the throne; and at the finish he received conventional compliments, and the precise conventional reward; and all talk of the king's daughter's hand was tacitly dropped. And he went forth from the court to search the world for the Secret Mountain; and lived long, wandering, but died before he came by news of it. In the morning he looked on the faces of his fellow-slaves, and knew them for the faces of the great ones he had seen in his dream.

The day passed and night came; and no sooner had he lain down on his straw in the courtyard, and wrapped his leather cloak about him, than he was a great lord of battles among his hosts in the midst of a plain. His generals and captains were about him; his veterans that he had led to the conquest of many nations, in their chariots drawn up, a numberless multitude; and out in front was an embattled people against whom neither he nor any man had achieved victory since the world began. They were proud, gigantic, inordinate; they had come up out of the far seas with a boast and a challenge; empire by empire had fallen before them, even to the borders of the empires that had fallen before great Babylon itself. Now they were to be overthrown, and their conquests added to Babylon, and their princes were to be the slaves of the King of kings. And for himself, the victory would mean—

He gave the signal: the trumpets sounded; and rank by rank, cohort by cohort, all his chariots and horsemen and footmen were on the move, charging, wheeling, deploying; and he himself at the head of them. He felt the wind blow in his face; saw the fluttering of banners; had great relish of the shock when it came. —And in the midst of the sound, the fury and the slaughter there fell a certain lull and hush, perhaps at the arresting scream of fifes of silver, perhaps at no signal at all; and he saw that on neither side were men busy with the killing, but weapons raised to strike stayed motionless in the air, and all heads and eyes were turned where, the giant enemies' ranks opening, One that was not of the giants at all, neither warrior nor herald, came unhurried and unharmed towards himself. Then he was filled with overmastering wonder who this man should be, and what his mission; and—as the two hosts had done—forgot the war in his eagerness to know. So this stranger came up, and stood beside and before his chariot—where indeed he *should* have been in grave danger from the hoofs of the right-hand horse of the pair—and looked him searchingly in the eyes, and said something: and what he said Varglon Fflamlas neither in the dream nor afterwards could discover: for it was all hidden away by a picture that came before his mind's eye at once: a billowing of leagues of tree-tops, and soaring up from them the faint colors and creamy snows of the Secret Mountain. And the memory of the world and its wars and of Babylon drifted away from him; and the battle became a thing that nowise concerned him, a meaningless tumult; and with dropped spear and rapt heart he bade his charioteer drive on, for he would go in search of the Mountain. And at that moment he saw the white quiet lightning of the arrows, the terrible wind-driven snow of the arrows, the many-pointed death swift hurrying through the air;—and the dream was done. But waking, he considered this: that in this last dream he had had no memory at all of the other dream; and it seemed to him that he would have fought in the battle a thousand years before he failed with the song: that impression was quite strong with him; and yet in both dreams—in the second no less than in the first—the face of the Stranger had seemed familiar to him: it was a face he had known ages before; and the words spoken, could he but remember them, were words he had been wont to hear of old. And in the morning again he saw his generals and captains in his fellow-slaves; but there was none of them like the Stranger that had come to him on the battlefield. . . . And that day he began to search the faces of the passersby in the streets; for the man, he thought, would be living, somewhere. . . .

The third night he dreamed: and now he was himself King of kings in Babylon, with splendor incalculable encompassing him at his goings forth and comings in; and they that waited upon him, and that prostrated themselves day and night at the foot of his throne, were themselves tributary kings and the rulers of vast empires—So once he held court in his palace, and gave judgment, and received tribute, and was at the full moon of his greatness. And there came One into the audience hall at whose entry all voices were hushed: who made no obeisance, but came forward to the throne; and when he had spoken a word to the king, turned and went his ways.

Then he, Varglon Fflamlas the king, remembered the Secret Mountain of the gods, and that it was his own original home. He sat there upon his throne, and spoke nothing, and the whole court was silent whilst he gave himself up to memories from of old that came taunting him upon the far horizons of his mind. But of this he was sure: he had once been a prince or some very high lord among the Gods that dwell on that Mountain; and what such lordship implied he half remembered: it was power, unusual, not like any wielded by man. How came he to have left those regions of the Immortals to take this paltry kingship, a man in the world of men? Had he heard a sound of Babylon in those days: of the great plain strewn nightly with a twinkle and glimmer that imitated the stars of heaven; of the gardens built up high into blue noon, colonnade on colonnade, terrace on sculptured terrace with many groves and fountains; of the might of world-conquering kings and the spells of enchanters; of the ships laden with the merchandise of Opohir and India: spices and sandalwood, nard and cassia, pearls and apes and peacocks and ivory:—had he heard of all these things and coveted them, or—?

He awoke in the courtyard of the slaves, homesick, and resolute to return home. Was not this, then, Great Babylon, his birthplace? Were not these the streets, quays, shops, palaces and warehouses that he had always known?—They seemed now quite foreign to him; utterly distasteful and antipathetic. He was not accustomed (after all his thirty years of this present life in it, and how many other lives before, who could say?) to the everlasting roar and drone and pounding and tinkle; to the yelling of the criers and vendors; to the whole business of city life—Up there, where the large stars drooped luminous over the temple roofs, till it seemed you might almost light your taper at the flame of Rigel or of Betelgeux; there where the windows of the high palaces caught the glory of the Chaldæan sunsets and dawns; where the slim moon, and Astarte's star, haunted the topmost storeys of the Hanging Gardens:—there, indeed, Babylon, you were a queen. But you hid your splendors from the slaves; in the courtyards and hot street-gullies of the downtrodden and the ghouls of vice, your seeming was no lovelier than other cities'. Varglon Fflamlas, treading your paved ways wistfully, searched all faces for a glimpse of the one face that should make him less forlorn; and had no more interest in your beauty or your vileness than the possibility of that discovery might lend. But always, night and day, that vast sea of tree-tops flickered and whispered before his inner senses, and from it rose as an island the Secret Mountain, a white plume in the sky, a creamy faintness or icy glitter hung in mid-heaven. And sometimes, it seemed to him, he came quite near remembering those who had been his companions there, and what manner of work it had been theirs to perform.

II

All the world was Babylon's; there was no fear of a slave escaping. The penalties of failure were too great; the chances of success too small. The man who owned this Varglon Fflamlas desired a message taken to the slave-master at one of his country-houses; and it fell to the lot of Varglon Fflamlas to take it. So he set out: with no intent, or formulated wish even, to escape,—but with the proud vision of the Mountain continually before his inward eye.

He delivered himself of his charge, but was not delivered from his obsessing idea. Escape? No; he had no relish for a crucifixion. He turned conscientiously enough to go back to the city. In the dusk of the evening he fell in with a man whose face, surely, he knew . . . and walked beside him a mile, talking absently. Then the man left him, saying, "You are on the right road; go forward!" He went on until moonrise, with a strange excitement growing on him always; then discovered the cause of his excitement: the man he had been with was the one he had seen in his dreams, and watched for since. . . .

And then, his mind being freed to take note of outer things, he saw that the road he had taken—the one the Stranger had led him into and bidden him continue therein—was not the way he had traveled in the morning, nor one he had taken ever; but the certainty was in his mind, that it was exceedingly good to be travelling it now. The truth is he had taken the Old Road which the giants or the dwarfs built for Arthur anciently: the Old Road between Camelot and Babylon, the Forest Road, where no man comes. It never occurred to him to think that he was a slave escaping, or that he was safe or unsafe; all he knew was that momently the air grew sweeter and more divinely familiar; that somewhere ahead rose the Mountain, like a white finger in heaven beckoning to him to come.

So presently he traversed wide Elfinmere, and came to the tree-clad hills of Nanrossa, going up through the Gap of Nanrossa, where the Delectable Forest begins. A great flood of delight poured out through him from his inmost being; he was at home, or near it; his home-sickness was gone.

Down into Nanrossa Bottom, just beyond the Gap: and now which way should he turn? Up and leftward to the dark hill where Phenit Fireheart keeps guard among his pines; or where the green drive, flagged with the giants' huge pavement a foot or two beneath the sward, leads by a gentle ascent to the right through the oakwoods of Darron Hên the God of Oak-trees?—He would keep to the Old Road—And there among the hundred branched ministrants of Darron the Aged, he felt certain he was on the right way. It all tallied with the memories of his third and greatest dream. He was breathing the air of his home-land; his soul burgeoned within him into singing, into surprising knowledge, into a grandeur he could not have believed in before. These trees were the things he knew, and that belonged to him: the rustle of their dear leaves laved away Babylon from his mind. The porticoes and gardened terraces, the quays and courtyards, the squalor and splendor: tush! they had no real being; they were but the aftermath, haunting the outskirts of memory, from some ugly drug-begotten nightmare. . . . But the trees were ancient and friendly companions; participants with him aforetime in some delicate elder wisdom. Inner and inner selves awoke in him, responding to their large unlabored invitation. . . .

All that wood which covers the northern slope of the valley, after you have passed through the Gap: where each oak has its own spacious domain or holding, and leave to cover what extent of ground it will: seemed to him suffused or pregnant with a consciousness akin to his own, but quiet, golden, unworld-weary, expectant, withholding secrets. Only just withholding them. It was but to bide here a little while, he thought, to have his mind so stilled and his memory so cleared and settled that the right word would come to him, the right language; and he would call forth answering speech with it from these leafy titans that quivered so friendly through all their pendent greenness. Then he would inquire of them as to the way to the Secret Mountain; and they would not fail to tell him.

As he stood there brooding and partaking of the peace, and watching the sunlight westward on the gold-green tremulance of the tree-tops, and the deep leaf-walled ravine between the trees, and the drive in its emerald and dew-silver at the bottom, where it ran down, edged with bracken, into a glimpse of sunbright mystery beyond that could be seen between trunks and beneath low branches—something definite of memory did indeed come to him. He pictured a person appropriate to this solitude, and remembered a name out of lives and lives foregone. *"Darron Hên!"* he said; "yes; it was this place was haunted by Darron the Aged." The likeness that went with the name was that of an old man: druid-like, white-bearded and oak-leaf-crowned; very straight and majestic of form; eyes exceedingly bright and deep and wise and kindly. Yes; he remembered the Oak-God well; and knew that he had been one of his kinsmen on the Secret Mountain, when the Gods foregathered in that their arcane capital. And he remembered a chant of invocation they had been wont to use, to call to each other in the forest; it came back to him word by word, phrase by phrase, dropping into his mind with golden ripples of gladness; and he sang it there among Darron's own trees, and waited with confidence for that bright ancient to glimmer into visibility. But no shining form appeared, nor even could he come by hearing an answer; though it seemed to him that the leafage trembled as if with a remembered delight and blushed into more luminous green at hearing him.

He sat down on a fallen trunk, and gave himself over to happy ponderings. "Yes, yes," thought he; "we used to ride through the air over the unsolid green leagues . . . our passage was like a shooting or a streaming of flame, like the burning voyage of a meteor or a dragon. We were not human, like the people of Babylon." So he brooded, gathering up the threads of antique memories; and with hardly a shadow of unease on him that he could get no news of Darron Hên.

He left the oakwood, and went down through the leaf-walled gully; he would search the green wild forest through, but he would find the Mountain of his dreams. All that spring he wandered on; highly hopeful for the most part; often making songs as he went: it was not so wonderful that, after all these thousands of years, he should have some difficulty in finding the way. He heard the cuckoo calling as she flew, beyond his vision, between the blue and the green: it seemed to him a voice from an elder age; remote, friendly, of happy omen. He heard the minstrelsy of the blackbird in the birchwoods; the missel-thrush making bardism among the high beeches. The like of these you should not find in Babylon; cymbal and sackbut, shawm, dulcimer and psaltery: the king's musicians with all their music: were not comparable to these. Again and again he came on places he would have said he had known of old. In the secret reaches of the forest: in valleys bright with gorse, tender with heather; where the mosses glowed copper-golden and dusky and green, and the bog-cotton lifted its lonely grace, and the air was sweet with bog-myrtle: it was strange how the knowledge of his old divinity came dropping, came stealing into his mind. In the pillared somberness of the high beeches his imaginings grew in augustness; in the sun-soaked green places where lizards lightened, what dross of mortality remained on him slipped away. The grand revelation seemed always trembling on the verge of his memory; but there were absences he could not understand. The places were there, and the beauty; but Those that had been the soul and essence of them were gone. —In a glade where dewdrops sparkled on the fern, and the green of the turf was misted over with morning silver, a fire-shape delicately beautiful came to his mind, and he remembered distinctly the being and name of Taimaz the Dew-Queen; but he might invoke her with the song she had answered of old, and chant it never so sweetly, and get no reply but from the thrushes. . . .

He went on through the summer: when July, dark blue and proud and beautiful, July with the Egyptian eyes, brooded in the heavens; when silence pondered in the palaces of leaves, and no birds sang. August came, light-footed over the beech-tops, diffusing a fine remote gold through the air. In the purple of dusk he passed through the pinewoods, and saw the sky flame in the spaces between the dark needle-tufts and the ruddy trunks and boughs. He thought of Phenit Fireheart, whose shadowy ruby-dark mantle had often made a glow of twilight his eyes had seen of old among the pines. But where was Phenit, that one might get no news of him now? Ah, where were the forms of flame and light that had been wont to burn so beautifully once across the beautiful burning of the sky? There was a solitude in the forest, that bore no correspondence to his memories and dreams.

He made for all high places; he scanned the world from any eminence where a break in the trees gave freedom to his vision. There were green and lofty hills to be seen often; but never that one pearl-white plume, that tall sky-reaching beauty faint in its snows, that shone so clearly before his inner eye.

Often he came on the faery hosts riding the heather moors under the stars; and would have questioned them—but that they had no eyes that could see him, it seemed, at that time; and no ears that could hear his voice. So in growing loneliness he went on, right through the heart of the forest: through golden days and grey; through the sunlight that maintained its silence aloof, and the haste of the little Rain-Gods, always hurrying away quietly, that had no word to say to him. He remembered that his life of old upon the Mountain had not been idle wandering. Sometimes he thought that the beauty and secrecy of the forest were coming to elude him, because he had no high office to perform.

He journeyed westward through the autumn; through the flaming of the leaves and their waning; through their silent falling and drifting down. His joy was dimmed into quietude, his hope into grey resolution; he sang but little as he wandered. When the storms of winter were riding over the naked trees: when the beech-tops were sullen dun and purple, and the low skies grape-dark above them: he came to the edge of the forest and the wild wrathfulness of the sea; and still he had caught no glimpse of the Mountain of his home, nor seen anything of his ancient companions. Sadness overmastered him; great longings took him; at times he thought with dread of Babylon—of the flaunting scarlet and golden glory; of the wasted life, the empty days, the riot and desperate gloom.

He turned back from the sea, and into the forest again; and all that year wandered seeking. With the spring the great life flowed back to him, and he was less an exile in his home. He came to remember the language of the wild bees and the swallows; the speech of the fairies and the little Rain-Gods; how to address the blackbird, that he might not take offense; what to say to the missel-thrush in April; what to the cuckoo; what to the great white owl in the twilight of August under the pines; what to the water-wagtail by the stream; what to the kingfisher flashing green and blue in the woodland silence by still waters. —In the open glades, then, he would come upon the moonlight dancers; and they would gather around him, awestruck at the presence of a God, but silent with pity and sorrow to see the paleness of the flame-plume above his head and his eyes with their sadness and longing. *Did they know the way to the Secret Mountain?* At that they vanished away, sighing; there was something terrible, inexplicable, in such as he putting that question to them; he should not have done it. They were sensible, I suppose, of the presence of tragedy; and it cut into their lives and made them aware of the dreaded thing pain. They had no help for him. "I sing of it always," said Bard Blackbird; "can you not hear me?" or again, "How can I tell you more than is in my song?" (There is always a dash of tart gaiety in his bardism.) "Hush!" said the kingfisher; and dived after some gliding streak in the peat-brown lights and shadows of the water. *"Mi wn, mi wn!*—I know, I know!" cooed the woodpigeon, as she always does; but would youchsafe no information. So continually disappointed he wandered on.

In midwinter he came back to Nanrossa. To Phenit Fireheart's pinewood, with one faint whipped-up hope in him. But the snow lay inches thick on the branches and needle-tufts, and the place was cold and ghostly and lonely, and Phenit Fireheart was not there. To Darron's Oakwood: and the bare trees seemed to him as to a returning wanderer the ruined walls that once were his home. To Nanrossa Tower above the Gap, and to looking out over snow-covered Elfinmere under the grey indefinite skies and under the howling of the wolfish wind. He thought of Borion of the Golden Flame, how he used to come riding up at dawn over the marsh; he thought of Gwernlas the Lady of the Alders; and of all that by wood and glade and mere were the kindling flames and inward sweetness of the beauty of the forest. "Where are they?" he said; and again, "alas, where are they?" Not in the forest now, he knew; nor in the mute white waste of Elfinmere. And the Secret Mountain?—Of this only he could be sure: that he should never find it, wandering in those deserted regions; that he had lost the clue, or that his present eyes were unsuited for the vision. Then he thought of Babylon: of them that danced before the king clad in soft scarlet, and of them that crawled the kennels leprous or mutilated; of the loud brazen music of trumpets and shawms; of the flaunting splendor and hidden agony; the golden and crimson pageantry, and the squalid places of filth and shame. Was he a God, and doing nothing?

He went down, and took the fateful Old Road from Camelot to Babylon, and journeyed eastward, the way he came.

Hourly as he went, new memories came crowding upon him. He was aware of the things the Gods knew: their pride and their compassion ensouled him. What would he do?—Why, wage Their wars in Babylon. He remembered Their eternal project; and how they wait upon times and cycles, and are intent to conquer the world at last. He was one of them, and their warfare also was his own; even though for thousands of years he had taken no conscious hand in it. But he would make some campaign of it now, there in the great city. The Gods' war is unlike any other: it calls not for cohorts and large battalions; one man may be a puissant army; he is not lonely who singlehanded holds a planet for the Gods. A planet—or his own heart for that matter. There were high adventures for a God—for a slave—to undertake in Babylon.

He was within a day's journey of the city, and near the place where he had turned off from the populous ways into the Old Road for Nanrossa and the forest. There, at nightfall, from a high eminence, he looked forth, and saw the plain all about, and the sky above the plain, lit as it were with the watchfires of a grand encampment, and the far horizons luminous with vast rainbow-colored pavilions. A man overtook him as he came there, and greeted him; he knew afterwards that it was the One who had come to him in his dreams, but did not recognize him then. "What is it?" said Varglon Fflamlas, pointing to the unusual glory of fires. "These last years" said the other "the Gods lay siege to Babylon; they await the one who is to open the gates to them." In a moment the sun had set; the vision was gone; and with it the man who had been standing at his side. No saying but Varglon Fflamlas had dreamed.

He came into the city; he made three days' journey through Babylon, proclaiming the things the Gods know. He saw the dancers in their soft scarlet; the merchants, the thieves, the rich men and the fallen. They all were unconcealed from him: he saw them for gods obscured, angels banished, souls hidden under oblivion, the pilgrims of a thousand lives. Crowds listened to him on the quays and in all the public places. Then said one, "Is not this Varglon Fflamlas, the slave who escaped?" News of his coming reached his former master; he was taken before the judges presently, and condemned.

At dawn punishment was meted out to him according to the law. Towards evening, looking up from his cross, he saw in the midst of the blue sky, far above the huge porticoes and onyx columns and palaces all alabaster and polished porphyry, far above the Hanging Gardens of the king—a drifting together of clouds, and the likeness in them of a white plume-like mountain, faint in its creamy and pearly snows; and from that moment he despised his bodily pain; and by nightfall had gone forth to his own. . . .

In the night the city gates were opened from within, and the Gods entered Babylon; there to reign, it is said, for a thousand years or more.

••••••••••••••••••••••••••••

After Morris's health broke down at the end of 1919, he wrote little or no fiction for several years. Thus, the next five tales were written before his health failed, even though they were published over some years. This short children's tale, "Sion ap Siencyn," is a Welsh-themed short story. To Ella Young, Morris wrote on 20 February 1928 that it is "a genuine folktale too, though the telling is mine of course." To her Morris also spelt out the title phonetically as "Shawn ap Shenkin" ("ap" means "son of"). The story was published in The Raja-Yoga Messenger *in July 1921, and reprinted in* The Secret Mountain and Other Tales.

Sion ap Siencyn

*I*t was on a Thursday, and the day of the full moon; and the white-thorn was in bloom, and the birds were singing on the mountain-side; and it was towards evening by that time, and the sunlight lying mellow-golden on the long green fields.

Sion ap Siencyn stood by the farmyard gate; and thinking he was—was there something in that sunlight now, and was there a tune in the air with the birds, or something, that he could make a l'l song of them whatever? Then the pigs set up a squealing and a pother, meaning to say dinner-time it was with them; and out from the old yellow-washed farm-house came Gwenno his wife with the pail in her hand to fill their trough.

"Sioni," said she, "for shame upon you loafing there, and me toiling all day, and slaving all night, to keep a loaf on the board and the dirt from the floor here!"

"Yes, sure," said he; "what is on you now?"

"What is on me?" said she; "and the pigs themselves crying out that but for me they shouldn't have bite nor sup nor support for their lawful ambitions!"

They were certainly crying out something; and Sion ap Siencyn was all for a bit of peace, with that l'l song in the air and all; and he wasn't going to argue, with his wife *and* the pigs against him.

"What is it, indeed now?" said he.

"You do know very well what it is. Bronwen Cow is after her meandering up the mountain, and in the Field of the Pool of Stars she will be; and she knowing well that I will be waiting to milk her. Such spiteful ways you do teach the creatures, woe is me!"

"Well, well; not much for me to go and fetch her, after all," said Sion; and with that, off with him.

In the farm kitchen old Catrin, Sion's mother, was in her chair by the hearth. "Where is Sion *bach?*" said she, when Gwen came in.

"Fetching Bronwen from the Field of the Pool of Stars he is," said Gwen.

"Uneasy is my heart for that news you are telling me; and this the Eve of May, and the faery night of all the nights in the year."

Sion went up through the long Field of the Stream; and the beauty of the world was delighting him; and the song in the air was coming nearer to him, but he was not catching it yet. And he went up through the green Field of the Hollow; and the way the light lay on the rushes, he had never seen the equal of it before. And he went through the gate in the hedge, and into the Field of the Pool of Stars; and there, in his deed, was Bronwen Cow out before him. He called her; but perverse she was, and walking on, and he must go after her; and the more he called, the more she went, and the more he must follow; and she put seven hedges between herself and the farm before he could even come near her;—and all the while the song was coming nearer to him; and it the loveliest song in the world or Wales, he was thinking.

And just as he came up with her, lo, there was the root and source and fountain of the song out before him and plain for his vision: it was a bird on the blossoming hawthorn tree; it no bigger than the druid wren, but its feathers aglimmer whitely like sunlight on the mountain snow; and with every flirt of its wings shaking out a ripple of song to steal and travel over the world till you could know the mountains were laughing in their deep hearts for pleasure of it; and in his deed to God he must stop a minute and listen to that.

Stop he did, and listen; and every sorrow he had ever known, he made nothing of it: converted it was, in his memory, into joy; with the richness and the pleasantness of that singing.

But there, wonder was on the world that day, certainly it was. As he listened, he was aware of a song on his south that was better than the other one; and turning, saw a bird among the rushes there, crested and crowned, and as blue as the heavens, and shining like a jewel, and making song to bring the stars leaning out of the sky to listen. Never could he turn to go back while that song might be there for his hearing. And wondering he saw what the power of the song was: for the earth and the sky were changed about him, and the mountains that he saw were better than any he had seen before; and the population on them and in the valley were beautiful—lovelier than human, flame-bodied, and with delicate plumes of flame over their heads. And lovely lights were rising out of the mountains; and it was a greater joy to him to be alive than any joy he had known formerly; and he had little thought for Bronwen Cow, or for Gwenno his wife, or for the farm. And then came a third bird, colored like the rainbow; with a better song than either of the others had; and in the sweetness of her discoursing it seemed to him that he heard all the wisdom of the deep world. And it seemed to him that the ancient and flame-robed Kings of Wonder were about him; and that the vast mountains were their palaces; and he on a footing with them, as it were; and an inhabitant of the Ancient World, with wisdom and stature to him, and the dignity of the cloud-hidden peaks; and if there was anyone called Sion ap Siencyn, he was not remembering that one; instead, he was remembering the ages of the world and antiquity, and delighting in the beauty beyond time. . . .

Then the three of the birds flew away, and the stars were shining: an hour or more he must have been listening, though not five minutes it seemed. In the dimness he could see Bronwen Cow descending towards the farm before him; and happy he was as he turned to follow her, knowing that now the world of song was open to him, and that never again would he be at a loss for the words of beauty to sing. "It was as if I had listened to the Birds of Rhianon," said he. They were three faery birds that were in Wales at one time; you could be hearing them for a hundred years, and think it was an hour or less you had listened. . . .

There was firelight and candlelight in the farm kitchen, and the door was open; and when he had but looked in through the door, he stopped, there on the threshold; for what he saw and heard was not what he expected. A very old man was on the settle by the fire; and opposite him a young man that might be his grandson; and there were three children on the hearth between them; and moving about the kitchen a woman that had the voice and the look of Gwen with her, only there was something strange with her too.

"Indeed" she was saying "for shame that you don't go out after Bronwen Cow; and she in her meandering out upon the mountain!"

"Let you him be," said the old man. "Were you never hearing what befell the great-grandfather of my grandfather?'

"Ah, tell us the story!" cried the children all at once.

"Three hundred years ago it was," said the old man, "and the Eve of May it was; and a cow from this farm strayed out upon the mountain; and the great-grandfather of my grandfather—"

"What was his name?" cried the children.

"Sion ap Siencyn was his name," said the old man.

"There's somebody at the door," said the woman. "Come you in, and welcome to you!" said she.

No one came, and no one was there when they looked. "It was the wind sighing," said the young man. Then the grandfather went forward and told them the story of Sion ap Siencyn. "They say it was the Birds of Rhianon sang to him," said he.

●●●●●●●●●●●●●●●●●●●●●●●●●

Another of Morris's tales specifically for children, "Pali the Nurse" was published in The Raja-Yoga Messenger *in September 1921. Pali is a Welsh midwife who touches a magical ointment to her eyes and gains a special vision.*

Pali the Nurse

*O*ld Pali Evans sat knitting at her cottage door, where she could see if any one came down the road from Cardigan, or up from Aberaeron way, and pass him the time of day; or, if he was a stranger, pursue inquiries, and with luck get his name, present business, and family history. The evening was full of summer beauty and the sweetness of summer flowers; her little garden, between the thatched white-washed cottage and the road, was dark and rich and fragrant with blooms of pansies and candytuft, phlox and sweetwilliam; Pali herself was a kindly comfortable old body, with large clear eyes, deep and gray, the very look of which would be cooling the fever and quieting the pain of the sick;—and very proper that it should, she being the nurse for the parish. *Click, click, click,* went the needles in the kind old hands,—four purl, four plain; and the stockings, please God, would fetch ninepence in Cardigan market, and last somebody a lifetime, whatever.

She was busy making a story, as her way was, for the last passer-by, from whom she had got nothing but a couple of foreign words. For though she knew enough English to inquire of an obvious Englishman, "How arre you indeed?" or "Where wass you wentin' now?" she was sadly lost to interpret the answer. "Well, well," thought she; "rich, and strange in their ways, the Saxons; there is no knowing anything of them. A great lord with them, or the King of England's son himself, maybe. And he adventuring in Wales, known to no man, to see are the Welsh contented here. Or to find for himself a bride in Wales, knowing their excellence, and their tidy ways in the house, and they so careful with the money. There's Ceridwen the

Mill, now; would suit him lovely; she would keep his palace for him so he could eat his dinner off the floor. Or one of the daughters of Cwmteifi; nothing but good I am hearing of them. Or—"

—"Pali ferch Ifan?"

—"Dear, make me jump you did!" said she. And indeed, a wonder how he could have ridden right up to her garden gate, and she never hearing a sound of hoofs on the road. "Yes, sure," said she; "Pali ferch Ifan am I. Is it the woman at home will be needing me?"

"It is," said he; "and quickly."

So, no more but for her to pack what she needed in a little bundle, and be hauled up on to the saddle behind him—Pali was used to that—and ride away. You will suppose that she gave herself by the way to asking questions; and so she did, and thought she was doing famously: his name, place, and manner of living, kinsmen alive to the fourth degree, and forebears to the ninth generation, her mind was at rest as to it all; although, as she remembered it after, here is the conversation that passed:

—"Who shall I say it is?" said Pali. —"*The little red fox ran under the hill.*" —"And how are you living indeed?" —"*The moon shone over the ruined mill.*" —"And where was your father coming from now?" —"*Saturday, Sunday, Monday, Tuesday.*"

And so on until they turned from the road to follow a track, more for sheep than for men you would think, up the slope of the mountain; she had known that track of old, but had never known it to lead to farm or house or cottage, or to anywhere but the wilds where the flocks feed and the fairies dance, and the children go gathering mushrooms in the summer and blackberries in September; often she had been there herself when she was a little girl. Presently, in a small cup or hollow of the hill, where there was no looking out on anything but the sky, lo, as trim a little cottage as you would wish to see. "Dear, is it here you live?" said Pali. The place was one the children would never go near, in her day, by reason of the dark green ring in the grass at the bottom of the hollow; but she was not thinking of that just then.

He helped her down, and they went in; and, "Sure you indeed, the loveliest baby in the world or in Wales!" cried Pali. Cheeks like apples; hair like flax; eyes like the blue bloom of heaven: everything a kindly old Welshwoman could desire, to be in Edens of delight and wonder and worship. And the mother too—Pali's heart went out to her in a minute; though hard to tell whether one should call her *fach* ("my dear," or "dear little one") naturally, or "meistres" for respect's sake, or quite grandly "my lady." For there was a grand look on her at times whatever; and despite those illuminating answers from the man, but for being busy adoring that *cariad* of a baby, and petting and nursing the mother, her curiosity might have been stirring again. Foreigners they were, sure you: though with good clean. Welsh for her, talking some strange language among themselves that she was certain was not English. What was it he had told her, again?

The third day when he gave her a pot of ointment, and the smell of it sweeter than all the flowers on the mountain, till you could almost hear the bees humming when you smelt it. —"Rub you the child's limbs with this," said he; "night and morning rub them. And be you careful whatever you do not to get it in your eyes. Terrible it is in the eyes of anyone." —"Blind me, will it?" said Pali. —"Yes, blind you, and more than blind you," said he. "—Careful will I be, in my deed," said she.

It was the last morning she was to be there, and she was sitting by the fire; she had given the baby his bath, and now was rubbing the ointment into his small plump arms. Whether it was a gust of wind, and a whiff of smoke from the hearth blown into her eyes and stinging: or whether it was her Welsh curiosity, stirred by the doctor's warning: no one knows; she says it was the first; I who know her am doubtful;—anyhow, up went the hand that had been rubbing the child, to rub, or just touch, the left eye of herself for a moment, and then—

—"D-i-a-r anwyl i!" cried Pali. —"What is it?" said the mother from the bed where she was still lying (though to get up later, before Pali went). But cute was that one. —"Oh, nothing in the world, my lady fach," says she; "only marvelling at the beauty of him I am." But this was what the matter was, in reality: with the ointment's touching her eye, gone was the aspect of the little cottage, and she was in a place like the palaces of the kings and emperors of the world: better than any in the vicarage; better than any in the house of Syr Marteine himself—indeed, they were dirt and pigsties to it. With its golden pillars and its looking-glasses; its silks and its satins, silver and crimson; and the carpet ("so soft as a cloud") on the floor and all. And it vaster than the marketplace in Cardigan town itself. And the servants more than you could count, and they taking no note of Pali, as if they did not see her. And the splendid liveries they were wearing, flashing with jewels of light; and the proud handsome look on the least of them, beyond the nobles and the gentry of the world. —This, mind you, all round her; but just where she was sitting, and within reach of her arms, everything as it had been before: the oak chair; the stone floor of the cottage, the hearth; no grandeur. It was the same when she crossed the room: she carried plain simplicity with her, and saw always, beyond, the riches of the faery world. Wherever the crimson carpets glimmered, she trod nothing but the bare flags; and the two that, a few paces away, shone like prince and princess of enchantment, when she came near them appeared only cottagers like herself. She dropped her eyes and kept them on her own person, and then told herself she had been dreaming; but not one word from her aloud, lest they should know she had the ointment in her eye.

So the morning passed, and she rode away behind the man of the house, and could hardly keep from telling him her dream by the way, so sure she was she had been dreaming. Still, wiser to say nothing, she considered. And not to look after him, when he had left her at her cottage door. But one glance she could not keep from . . . and then dropped her eyes quickly, for there surely were the plumes shining like fire above his head, and the silken robes on him adorned with jewels; the princely mien and the grandeur; the saddlecloth of purple velvet bordered with glittering gold. So Pali fell to her knitting again, until she had a pile of stockings ready for the day of the fair in Cardigan town.

It was noon on that day; and Pali sat by her neighbor, Marged the Mill, at their stall in the marketplace. —"Dear," said she, "never have I seen such thousands as are here today." —"Thousands you call them?" said Marged; "empty the place is, by what it was last year, according to me." —"Empty indeed!" said Pali; "full it is, and more than full; hundreds and thousands of strangers here; and princely—Indeed, how is your lordship this long time whatever, and how is your lady by there, and that little cariad the baby?" —"Oh," said the man to whose house she had ridden with him, "how are you, Pali fach? Glad I am to see you again." "Woman dear, to whom are you talking?" said Marged the Mill. But the man, while he was speaking, was looking hard into Pali's eyes. —"Into which of them was it you got the ointment?" said he. —"The left," said Pali, without a thought. A quick wave of his hand before that eye, then; and behold, where he had been standing there was no one; and the "hundreds and thousands" of princely strangers she had seen in the market-place were gone; it was as it would be on any Fair-day at noon, when the farmers were in the inns at their dinner. *"Catw'n pawb!"* says Pali, "dreaming again I was, whatever."

But she never failed to find a piece of gold on her doorstep, on the Calends of May, and the Calends of winter, from that out.

• •

An unusual but fascinating story, "The Lord of the Planet" tells of the god assigned to Earth who, after thousands of years of forgetfulness, remembers his purpose: to bridge the gulf between his own consciousness and that of mankind. It was published in The Theosophical Path *in November 1922.*

The Lord of the Planet

I
The God

*T*his, then was the Earth—that Death Planet whereof so many tales were told. He must arrive at some clear view of it, if he was to do his duty in that state to which, for his sins, he had been condemned. —So he put it to himself; but his sins were not as ours; it was a matter of over-impetuosity that entailed his fall or banishment; it was his grand sweeping warwardness against Chaos; and because he, the dawn-chapleted Khorónvahn,

> *Whose throne was in the Isles of Capricorn,*
> *Whose dragon navies cruised the Milky Way,*

was the most ardent of the Stars of Morning that sang. —He must certainly think; he must understand this new scene of his labors, and (impossible task!) somehow bridge the gulf between his own consciousness and the consciousness (as he supposed he must call it) of his new subjects, Men. For the sentence pronounced against him was, to reign God of this planet for some few million years; and it would take hard thinking indeed to find out what any deity might make of the job.

It was beautiful, this Death Planet, to a degree that surprised him; but the beauty soaked through, piquant, treacherous with . . . an adverse inexplicable something (he knew no such word or concept as sorrow or might have defined what he felt). And withal, it was somehow august. Rumor had been right in speaking of it with a certain strangeness and awe; he had sensed that from the first. At the moment of crossing the boundaries of its atmosphere, he had felt himself, troubledly, in the presence of the unknown. —A tiny little God-forgotten nonentity of a globe, beneath contempt in a way,—and yet infecting one with a sense that one might be out of one's depth. . . .

At his feet the river emerged from its mountain gorges; and lay, a streak of flame and silver, along the dusky plain. Out in front the sea gleamed to the horizon, a bow now all crimson and orange and flickering sapphire and green. On either side and behind him rose the mountains, sunset-flushed to richest purple; a lark trilled in the mid-air far below; but for that and the call and hoarseness of the river in its gorges, there was silence: men came not here, nor had ever come. He was a little weary after the day he had spent (a thousand years as we count time) going up and down the world and trying to make men aware of his presence. Here, on this hill between the precipices, he would rest, and brood for a while, and find a way.

He had heard of old of these Men; and perforce taken all he had heard well salted, because there are limits to the possible,—or he had thought so. But seeing was believing. Or some way towards believing; for here was a vast deal indeed for a god to believe. Consciousness, he had supposed, meant delight; no other conception seemed possible. But here. . . . Well, he had hardly arrived, you may say: only a thousand times had the little globe with its shining seas and its mists and mournful beauty swung round the sun since it saw the falling star of his arrival: and already the task of finding out what consciousness could be—what it was, here,—had wearied him in some measure. His mind was not clear, as it used to be; puzzlement was on him, in a way; uncertainty as to the labor that lay before him; wonder as to how he should begin. For of course the first thing was to establish connection between his mind and some mind—one at least—among the earth people; and there was the difficulty. He had not been idle since his coming: there was no community of men that he had not visited; no individual, even, that he had not in his own way striven to approach. You might say: why not sink a populous island here and there; heave a mountain or two on to some few cities; rend the earth a little, and bury recalcitrant millions? But we do not understand the gentility of godhead, to which such ideas seem vulgar. What on earth should he do?

It was to be supposed that they had a sort of intelligence: one could see that they had built up an order of living,—possessed what might be called civilization. But it was an intelligence to him disparate and alien; an order of living and a civilization that no mere god could understand. In *his* circles, to be was to be delighted to be, and to take delight in all being;—what we should call love; only he, having no conception of hatred, had none of love either, as a thing in itself: existence, consciousness, love, delight, were to him one idea, and one only. But here, these fierce, cunning, crawling, fighting creatures,—well, it was an amazing revelation, undreamed hitherto in his philosophies,—they could move about, build their civilizations,—they could be and live, in short,—and yet their being seemed to be based on, motived by, another name for, non-being; their life was the negation of life. Ah, that accounted for the name, the *Death Planet;* he began to understand the meaning of that extraordinary term. Sentient existence, as he had understood it, was one, and knew itself one, in all its embodiments; but here it was at war with itself, paradoxical, inspired by self-antipathies. And it was his business to make this new kind of consciousness aware of and at one with his own kind; to bridge the gulf between himself and Man. Good Lord, what a problem for a God to solve!

No wonder that in such an atmosphere, do what one would, one could not keep one's mind clear. There was a drowsiness, a heavy something—the infection of this strange negation of life. . . .

Well; he would rest here, and think the thing over; he would watch the sea, and rest, and find a means. . . .

The mountains faced the sunset,—the plain, about nine leagues wide, between them and the sea. From two chasms, with a hill high enough to be a chair for him between, the river poured out into the plain, to unite or re-unite its waters a little below, and thence flow on seaward slowly and deep. Here he sat, and leaned forward; his chin on the palm of his hand, his elbow on his knee. Sheer precipices on either side of him, beyond the river, the mountains rose to the level of his head; so narrow was the gorge on his left, that one standing among the pines at the crag-top there would have been within a stone's throw of his face. Behind him, range on range rose white-peaked to the sky.

He sat there, brooding; and the glow of the sunset died away, and the stars shone out, the grand procession of them passing over him to sink in the sea. Yes; the air of this planet was soaked in heaviness, in sleep. How was he to make that passage between his mind and the minds of men? The stars passed, and the sun rose and sank, and the stars followed; the sea shone and darkened, shone and darkened. How . . . was . . . he . . . to? . . .

The sun drifting through the heavens to set in the sea; the traveling moon with her phases; the multitudinous procession of the stars; the gleaming and darkening bow of the sea,—how should one think, watching them? They became a wonder and a vague delight to him; they filled the fields of his consciousness . . . in this oblivion-laden atmosphere of the earth. True, there was something else to be considered . . . sometime . . . but consideration was difficult . . . in this oblivion-laden atmosphere of the earth. . . . The sun and the stars went dropping into the sea; he watched them, and did not know what they were. A million years passed. Time long since had turned his bodily presence into stone, as the rhythm of the drifting lights had lulled his mind into quiescence.

But all things grow weariness at last; and an age came when he had no more peace in watching. He could not be happy because of something he could not remember: the memory of his purpose, his identity, his ancient glory, ebbed long since beyond the reach of his cognitions, haunted him,—an irksome bewilderment lurking in the vast inanity of things. There was something, formidably important,—not the sea nor the lights of heaven,—which he ought to know. He could not tell what troubled him; could formulate no questions, yet was conscious of questions enambushed beyond his vistas, and had no delight because of them. Well; he would reach out and grasp them someday: in effortless quiescence, or in the throes and agony of thought. He was drawing nearer to that success with every dropping of the stars now; he was drawing nearer to it. . . .

Then all drifted away again. There came a humming and a drowse of sound perpetually from below; it caught his ear, and was a refuge from the unknown questions and from the sea-bow and the sun and the stars. He gave himself up to the comfort of listening, and desired only to hear. The voices of millions of men, rattle of wheels incessantly, hoofs pounding and clattering: it was full of mystery, infinitely complex, unfathomable. Day and night it rose to him, intriguing as poppy fumes that minister to dream. . . .

(At the feet of God they had built Khóronvehm, the City of God; and because God was there, visibly present above the city, Khóronvehm became the mistress of the world. They carved his temple in the hill, and built it out to be his footstool; his tall temple that was the wonder of the world. All of polished porphyry and onyx and alabaster, they flanked it with columns on this side and that: a half-moon of beautiful columns about the temple-courts. Tribute-bearing ships came up the river, and unloaded at the temple-court steps the treasures of the world. Very mighty were the Khóronvehmians; very mighty and religious; they oppressed the world, and the world obeyed them; for did not God sit visibly in their midst?)

All things become-weariness at last. Time came when the noise of the great city held him no longer; then beyond the horizons of his mind the questions rose again; and century by century he strove towards them more eagerly ever. And now, now, now, he was on the point of grasping them; he battled against the strange and heightened turmoil from below; he sunk his mind inward, furiously striving after the things that concerned him; until at last, yes, there was another light before him than the sunset; yes, he was that dawn-chapleted Khorónvahn from the Isles of Capricorn; he had been sent hither to be—

Like a heavy wave, sleep struck him.

That, to be exact, was on the day of the full moon in the month Argad, in the Year of the City, 10,581. Everyone knows what happened then. There had been civil war, between the factions of the kings and the priests; and God at last had made his power known. His priests had been victorious; and on that day their and God's enemies, the king with his family and adherents to the number of a thousand, had expiated their sins on the altar. Then the great yearly Feast of the Sacrifices had been inaugurated; and everyone knew that upon the rigid observance of that festival depended the favor of the "Almighty and Most Merciful Father, Our Lord God, Dawn-chapleted Khorónvahn, Maker of the Stars Made Visible"; (I quote from the *Book of Liturgies* of the priesthood at Khóronvehm). Since then, God (through his High Priest) had ruled the city and the world.

II
The Priest-Prince

Rumor was, in Khóronvehm, that the High Priests' Path was so perilous, that, a hundred to one, unless you had learned the clues beforehand, you should take some wrong turning and drop soon and suddenly into dark waters and caverns quite fathomless,—that the whole mountain was honeycombed with devilments, a place for nightmare to batten on. Yet here is one, certainly, taking that path with no clue or guide in the world but trust: he is to have speech at the summit with God; and God, he knows, will bring him past every peril. It is Vahnu-ainion the Priest-Prince, today to succeed to High Priestly sovereignty; he goes unshod, white-robed; he is wasted by long anxieties to frailty and the semblance of age, but now the vastness of his hope half makes him young again:—he goes up to his God.

As to the path he travels: his forefathers the High Priests have trodden it before him: each once and once only,—at his accession, when he went up to receive from Deity that last sanctification which should fit him to be Deity's Vicegerent;—and no man else has trodden it at all since slaves of old tunneled it out under the northern gorge and the river, and up through the mountain, or sometimes giddily along the face of the precipice; and built that little shrine of alabaster, the Holy of holies of religion, right on the brink of the chasm at the top. There, hidden from the world by clouds, communing with God, each Priest-Prince in his turn had attained infallibility and High Priestly status; for from that point the Divine Countenance was well within range of a voice not unduly uplifted: if God spoke, though it were hardly more than in a whisper, who stood at the altar should hear.

Vahnu-ainion was wasted with anxieties, as well he might be. After all these millennia of triumphant domination, disaster latterly had fallen on Khóronvehm. Continents had risen rebellious; navies had been sunk and armies slaughtered; until now the mistress of the world cowered within her walls hungry and despairing. The plain below was white with the tents, and the sea with the sails of her besiegers; and unless God should arise and his enemies be scattered, help or hope there was none. And today must be the end of it; there could be no holding out after today.

For that matter, so far as he was concerned, Vahnu-ainion knew, and had never doubted, that God would arise, and his enemies be turned into friends; that was not where the steel had pricked him. Though Priest-Prince, he believed utterly in the goodness of God. But he had been living through all these months of gathering national gloom, knowing that the priests (in their minds) and the people (often openly) attributed the whole evil to him. He doubted that, save God, he had any one friend as an offset against so many foes; and guessed that only God and his own hereditary sanctity—the habit of mind of some ten thousand years—had kept the knife or poison-cup from doing its work on him. The Khóronvehmians were above all things religious: God dwelt visibly among them, and they owed their pre-eminence to that. The High Priests—their absolute monarchs—had always been of the Vahnu family, whose name hinted at divine descent; and Vahnu-ainion was its only living scion. In all history, no High Priest had been deposed, nor any Vahnu done away with; and for lack of a precedent, deeds whose doing all desire and would approve are often left undone. So he was still alive. . . .

He was hated both as an innovator and as an innovation. All his predecessors had been great statesmen, princes of the church militant, urbane and masterful men, and exceedingly clever. He,—well, you shall judge. The Feast of Sacrifices at the full moon of the month Argad—that rite of atonement which ensured the favor of God for his city—was abhorrent to him; he loathed policy, and took no pleasure in universal sway; he had an idea that the High Priest of Khorónvahn should be the chief servant, not the master, of mankind. This is what I mean by saying he was an innovation,—or part of it; had he left things there, so much might have been excused. But no, he must be innovator too, active, pressing his views. He had set his face against the sacrifices, hinted at a desirable new dispensation; had even achieved saving one intended victim. And he meant openly to do much more: meant to petition God, today, and learn His will; was certain that God's will coincided with his own, and that the divine command would be given: *Abolish them: bring flowers, not men, to my altars.*

How could he square all this with history? Every High Priest before him had gone up whither he now was going, and received God's mandate for the ordering of the world; and yet the sacrifices and pomp and domination had persisted—it could not be supposed but by God's will. I do not know how he managed it: but the truth is that he believed in God and loved and pitied man with equal fervor; believed in his religion, and wished to change it; considered that an Inscrutable Wisdom might have allowed much of old that It desired altered now; was not too logical to follow the urgings of his heart,—nor perhaps so illogical that you could be sure the ground would never tremble under him.

He was an innovation in another way too; by ill fate this time, and not wilfully. Time out of mind the High Priesthood had passed from father to son, each trained for the office by his predecessor; and none of them all had made this journey without instruction. They knew what should be done in the white temple: what invocations chanted (he supposed), what ritual used; but he knew nothing. For his father, the God-aureoled Vahnu-gonaī, —imagine three epic pages filled with his titles,—had been during the last ten years a senile and most monkeylike babbler, so stricken before a thought of death had visited him or old age warned him to prepare; all the wisdom he had had to utter had been scraps of old street songs, nursery rhymes,—even flat blasphemies that would have brought another to the stake; and at the last, before he passed to his apotheosis yesterday, when some flaming up of mind and oracular dictum might have been looked for, the best he had given was a sneering stare at his son, an ugly chuckle unexplained, and some mutterings in which the word *fool,* often repeated, was to be caught. So now Vahnu-ainion went ignorant to this his greatest occasion. —Further, he had been, as regent, ruling the world, playing High Priest, for ten years, though uninitiated. He had stood to mankind as God's deputy, who had never spoken with God. His office had called for the constant overshadowment of Deity, and he had had nothing to bring to it but the shallow wisdom of men. No wonder disaster had befallen!

All this he felt; and yet did not know wherein he had failed. The rest of the world might be certain; he was still more certain that the rest of the world was wrong. He went without fear to meet his God, and had no thought colored by apology. That which had brought most rancor on him, he most gloried in: there he had acted for God with an intuition he felt to be infallible. —It was saving Artalach, that captive savage king, from the altar. He remembered how, when he saw the tall, chained, proud man landed from the tribute-ship at the temple-court steps, and marched with the others to the prison of the victims, the conviction had struck him: *This man is to do some grand service for Our Lord!* It was as if Khorónvahn himself had cried it from amidst the mountaintops and clouds over the city; he had never doubted Whose will he was doing, then or since. Later he had come to know that poor Artalach's history;—but he was going up to speak with Godhead now, and such tragic dark dealings should never be again. Aye, and he would make amends to the tall savage: would teach him the truths of religion, and for temporal sway and perishable honor, give him treasure where moth nor rust corrupts, nor thieves break in and steal. —He had taken Artalach into his own service, I must tell you; and was having him taught the Khóronvehmian and what else a gentleman should know. The time might come when he should find in that quarter what all his life he had lacked,—friendship. The man would serve God, and signally: that he knew. A proud seared spirit, so far; but the Priest-Prince believed his own pity stronger in the long run than any pride.

And he believed in God, and went on and up with joy overcoming his weariness, and hope banishing the memory of his anxieties. God would save the world, changing the order of things. God would appease and convert, not smite, the rebel princes in their tents beyond the walls. God would speak the word to him, that would be the solvent for the bitterness in men's hearts. God would teach him to redeem even the priesthood.

So by the tunneled steep passages and unrailed stairways cut in the cliff-face he went up, busy with his thoughts, and unaware of the one with the spear that followed him. There were many places on those cliff-cut stairs where Artalach might have leaped forward, picked him up, and hurled him down through the clouds; but the savage meant that God should see his revenge. It was God he hated, the God of Khóronvehm; not this frail woman-hearted priest. The thing should be done on the altar in the temple above, under the eyes of awakening Deity. (Vahnu-ainion seeking to sow hope in him, had made him understand the occasion). So, when it was done, God would act; the last thing he desired was to escape. God, by whose will his wife, his children, and all his braves had perished, would vent omnipotent anger on him; would devise ghastly deaths no doubt;—and should learn what strength to endure was in the spirit of Man. He would die deriding the impotent omnipotence that could win no groan from him. As for the Priest-Prince: death, that would take him swift and suddenly, was no misfortune; and Artalach would make amends, protecting and befriending him in the beyond.

A long steep passage up through total darkness; then a stairway beginning, and winding spirally up, up and up; and at last the black air thinning gray; and then, almost suddenly, light, and no trace of fog in it: one was above the clouds certainly; ay me, one was in the Holy Place! There were no walls; it was a round roof, peaked, resting on pillars; now the westering sunlight slanted in, mellow golden and dappled with pine-tree shadows, on the floor inlaid with mosaics of many-colored marbles and on the altar of onyx stone between the delicate columns in front; beyond which, and across the gulf, very near, it shone full and gloriously on the Face of Very God. Ah the calmness and vast majesty of that countenance, lighting the soul of Vahnu-ainion to intensest worship and joy! Advancing, rapt in the marvel of the vision, he stands at the altar,—that only between him and the abyss; wonderful it is to look down upon the clouds, now flushed to richest cream, suffused with softest amber; and to see, out of that shining moveless ocean of opacity, the divine breast rising, a formidable precipice, and the deific beauty of the neck and head above! Ah, Most Beautiful, Most Beautiful! what need for ritual here? In silence shall the uplifted heart invoke thee; with adoration call thee forth! —Vahnu-ainion kneels at the altar, resting his arms on it; and with clearest light in his mind, firmest will and most glowing compassion in his heart, pours his thought out towards Khorónvahn above the clouds.

—"Khorónvahn! Khorónvahn! hear, O Most Merciful! It is mankind that cries to thee through me!"

As if a stone had been thrown into a mountain-lake, where was only placidity and utter dreamlessness before: in some far vagueness ripples of thought are rising and widening; there is a cry *Khorónvahn! Khorónvahn!* and there is that, unaware of itself until now, that hears.

—"Now wilt thou declare thy heart, O Compassionate! Now wilt thou save the people of thy world!"

—"Who calleth Khorónvahn?"—so the thought-ripples ran;—"it was a name that . . ."

Artalach, watching at the back of the temple, heard nothing. There was no voice, either of priest or God, that any ear could hear.

—"Behold, O God, how my spirit yearns to thee! Thou hast enlightened my understanding and shone into my heart; give thou now the sign and token, that I may go forth and thy will be done!"

—"Ah, fumes arose from below and put sleep on me. I was . . ."

—"That there may be no more cruelty on earth; that thy priesthood may go forth healing and serving; that the nations may be at peace, and the fire of thy being kindled in men's hearts!"

—"There was a humming and a drowse of sound from below, that came between my thought and . . ."

—"That sorrow may depart from the world; that order and love may reign here, as they reign among thy stars in heaven!"

—"There was a gleaming bow out before me afar, and lights streaming above and sinking; and because of these I could not . . ."

—"Khorónvahn! Khorónvahn Omnipotent, hear!"

—"Khorónvahn? Khorónvahn? It was the name of one that . . . came down out of . . . that came hither to be . . ."

The Priest-Prince's fingertips, resting on the altar, became aware of inscribed letters there; and memory came floating into his mind . . . of lessons he had learned long ago: an ancient script and language, the sole subject his father personally had taught him when he was a boy; and he remembered the solemn pledge he had been made to take then, never to reveal, except to his own eldest son, that which he should learn; "for the writing on the white altar is in this tongue," said his father: words unexplained then, and forgotten these thirty years; but now returning, and heard distinctly in memory as if they had been just spoken. Here, then, was the secret: here written the words he should speak that God should hear and answer. He rose, and bending over the altar, deciphered it slowly.

"Son, now knowest thou all. Thou hast come into the secret place: art hidden by the cloud from the eyes of men.

"What camest thou up to see? What findest thou? That stone idol yonder? Look well and listen: hath he spoken to thee at all? Hath he moved a lip or an eyelid? They say that he was God once; time long since hath turned him into stone. The High Priests know: senseless as thou seest him he hath been these million years.

"Therefore rejoice thou; for were he God indeed, thou shouldst be destroyed. thou and thy power and thy glory and dominion. If he could be Lord of the Planet, would he leave that lordship with thee?

"But since he is stone he upholdeth thee; uphold thou then his worship, as thy fathers have upheld it before thee. Let blood flow continually on his altars, that the world may remember he is God. Chastise mankind in his name, that it may fear him; fearing him, it shall obey thee. Men say, 'God's will is inexorable'; be thou inexorable, that men may know thee the Vicegerent of God. This is the wisdom of thy fathers, whereby they have ruled the world.

"For men are fools; but be thou wise. Walk in the way of thy fathers; on the day thou departest from it thou shalt die. Art thou wise now, believing nothing? Go then! there is nothing more to know."

As if a great wind had risen suddenly, and the lake, where the ripples were flowing and broadening, were lashed suddenly into tempest: there was that which cried through the place of awakening consciousness: "Sorrow! ah, the sorrow of men! It is my heart that understands! It was I that came down out of the star-worlds to heal the sorrow of men. I will arise, and go to my people. . . ."

III

The Avenger

Artalach, waiting his moment, has seen Vahnu-ainion discover the inscription, and read it; he, too, guessed that it held the secret that should awaken God. Standing behind, he has seen nothing of the Priest-Prince's face as he read. What follows confirms his surmise. He sees Vahnu-ainion sink down on the altar, then rise and throw up his arms as in invocation; but he has already seen, beyond the chasm, the eyelids flicker, the lips quiver, motion taking the head, a straining; and now, when he is sure that God is watching, alert, and will see—now, as the Priest-Prince's arms go up,—he knows that the time is come. He knows nothing of the sudden shock to the man long wasted with trouble and fasting,—of the rush of blood to his brain; he sees but the invocation effective, God aroused, and in act to answer;—and his spear flies; and Vahnu-ainion (I doubt, dead before the weapon touched him) fallen, on to the altar, on to the floor, over the precipice. So: he has insulted God, slaying God's Priest; and with satisfaction and calmness now strides forward to the brink, that God may see him and realize well what has happened, and take what steps he will.

But—heavens, what has he done?—of what mightiest magic is he, all unknowing, the master? Vengeance? As if it had been God, not the Priest-Prince, his spear transfixed! Up out of the clouds the colossal breast rises, swaying, cracking, rending, groaning; the arms shoot up above the head; the whole vast mass totters, staggers; there is stumbling as the feet break through the temple-roof beneath; rending of stone, cracking, breakage; noise as of thunder and earthquake;—and a fragmentation and a crashing down of all, forward, on to the city: to crush to ruin palaces and temples and famished panic-stricken populace—they, and the hosts that have been pouring in through breaches in the walls an hour old. Priest, God, and city; he has destroyed them all; grandly indeed he is avenged. The cloud is dispersed by the fall of God; he can see something of the ruin he has wrought. His work is finished; and he turns, and is going. . . .

But where? What next? His plan has miscarried, in a way, and left him with nothing decided; there is nothing further for him to do . . . better follow the Priest-Prince, over the brink, and into that beyond where . . .

A hand is laid on his shoulder, and a voice speaks: "Brother?"

He turns, amazed, to face the speaker, a shining figure in the dusk, shedding light on the white pillars; and—he had been watching that colossal face beyond the chasm, and, despite the change, the human stature, could not be mistaken; . . . and, somehow, hatred, bitterness, all the searedness and constriction of these last years melt away from his heart. For moments he is silent, and then:

—"God!" said he. "God! take . . . thy . . . revenge! I am the man. . . ."

—"Thou art man, and I am God, my brother. Come with me; they need us, below there. We are man and God, and we must help them."

—"I go with thee, my brother," said Artalach.

That evening the Golden Age began.

●●●●●●●●●●●●●●●●●●●●●●●●●●●

*"The Victory" is an intriguing look at a Valhalla-styled afterlife where the
people of Arthrobaun awaken after the hopeless battle in the Pass of Bnah,
unaware that they have fallen. It was published in* The Theosophical Path
in August 1923.

The Victory

I

*E*vening in the Pass of Bnah; sunset, that had been an anthem or
an agony of color over the capital, waning now; though the far
snow-peaks eastward still shone roseate and ambered in the anti-glow, and
on the hillside above and to north of the pass, where the king stood, some
mellowness of the dying splendor remained. Below, on the grim battle site,
all was gloom and obscurity. The silver fifes of Arthrobaun—music sad or
gay as the ear should hear it—cried through the dusk; and at their weird
shrillness the grave plumed warriors came up the slope and gathered about
their lord. This was to be called the day of all days in history; what had
happened, it was to be supposed, was that the Gods had broken miracu-
lously through the veil of things and made their might known, and made
what we should call inevitability ridiculous; the empire, art, science, ancient wisdom—all human achievement—were saved; though to say that a
few hours since they had been despaired of is to say the very least that can be
said. There would be no realization of it yet: the king Pha Hedro and his
warriors were battle-weary, and the marvel of the event too great to understand.

You are to think what narrow straits the world had traversed that day in
the Pass of Bnah. History shows. Here was an empire, Arthrobaun, with
quite universal dominion: the king's writ running from the Sea of Sunrise
to the Waste Waters of the Sunset, and from the Desert of Ghosts northward to the very foothills of those Mountains of Calamity

"where no man came,
Nor had come since the making of the world."

Some part of that great territory Pha Hedro himself had gathered in; none of his ancestors but had won something. They had been a line of strong conquerors and judicious rulers since the dawn of time, you may say; since the mythological ages; fifty generations of kings deriving from that Pha Arthro-with-the-Spear who, emerging from the mountain and from the God-world, went forth world-shaking and world-redeeming in the beginning. He was divine, and his forebears not human; and truly his descendants the Phas of Arthrobaun had had something of divinity in them, and were not to be reckoned with common men. Back to their immortal place of origin, the prophecy was, that royal line should return at last: their work and their cycle completed, the gates of the hills would open for them, and they would ride again in triumph to their shining kin; the last of his race to be a memory and perpetual inspiration in this world, and an undying sovereign in that.

So religion declared; but in these latter days religion itself had stood confounded before the terror of events. The White Infliction had come: invaders out of the eastern sea without ruth, truth, or human nobility; priestled, and their priests grim sorcerers before whose cruel magic everything until today had gone down. No valor had availed, nor the strong walls of cities; it was not known that even a single one of the strangers had fallen in all the many battles that had been. So that morning, religion or no religion, prophecies or none, the king had ridden out with his clan, and no least doubt in his own or any other mind that he himself would be the last of his line and yet would die like a common mortal before evening. Nothing else was to be imagined, nothing better to be hoped; none that rode out to the Pass of Bnah were men to be taken captive. And meanwhile,—so it was well arranged,—the queen and her ladies in Cararthro would be seeing to it that no prize there should await the invaders. They were to worship the Gods with all ceremony during the morning, and then apply the torches and make of the burning capital their own funeral pyre.

But now, in the face of all possibility, the Gods had shown their power, and not one planned or expected thing had come to pass.

It was a very noble company that gathered now on the slope: the king's cousins, of the divine race of Arthro; all tall, well-made and blemishless; an ancient firm-chinned aristocracy, aquiline and clear-cut featured, men accustomed to rule. All, too, splendid with rainbow-colored plumes and jewels,—so bravely had they arrayed themselves in the morning for the sacrifice that, in the event, had not been and was not to be made. And a change and accession of dignity had come upon all of them that day. Since they had come forth upon a forlorn hope, to vindicate hereditary glories by dying: as men who had done with fate and the world, they had come forth

singing and not without gaiety; now, as men to whom the might of the
God-world was made known, they had put their gaiety by, and were silent.
The doom they had looked for had given place to a prospect wherein was no
shadow of apprehension nor any imaginable thing to fear; for that day not
one but all the armies of the invaders had come against them, and now there
was utter stillness in the gloom of the valley, where the noise of the invaders
had been.

And as for themselves—here was the arch-incomprehensibility—it became clear as they gathered that they had not even a single loss to mourn.
What winged chariots, what flaming coursers unseen, must have ridden
through the gray air on their side with them: what shafts and spears invincible, from immortal squadrons there drawn up or charging, must have
flown! They formed their ranks now, and there was no gap anywhere; it was
only the enemy had disappeared. As if no battle had been, no wound received; as if the last months had been a nightmare from which now they
were dazedly awaking. And yet heaven knew they had fought. . . .

They had fought; and, surely, as men never had fought before since the
beginning of time. Not more bravely, they meant; in courage there is
doubtless an absolute which men perhaps in every generation attain. But
this fight had been wholly mysterious. . . . Well; one had to consider the
magic of those sorcerer-priests: a very great deal to consider indeed. For in
no mind or memory of all those warriors would *ends meet*. They remembered
things that simply had not happened. Obviously not;—were they not all
there in the dusk on the hillside; all there, and all scatheless? But what
hideous power had been with those dead sorcerers (dead of course, the Gods
be thanked!) to produce such illusions! For even now one could not rid one's
mind of the impression—

Of the hopeless beginning of the battle, and the physical nausea produced by the first sight of the white men—hideous, long-toothed, pig-
eyed, little-headed mighty masses of brawn and disgusting ignobility;—of
the five hundred there were of themselves in the midst of the narrow pass,
and in front a great tide of this human (if so to be called) beastliness swinging up against them, and overflowing and pouring down on them from
above on either side; and shifting and changing deliriously; and withdrawn
again and again while the white storm of their arrows drove in among the
proud plumes and jewels;—and of the gay death-hymn the Arthroanion
went into battle singing—the haughty war-song of Arthrowith-the-
Spear—growing fainter and fainter with the silencing of voice after
voice;—and of seeing the men one loved (who yet now were standing unharmed on the evening hillside beside one) pierced and falling;—and of a
sharp shock and sudden bitter keenness sometime during the furious day,
and a momentary drifting of all things into indistinct confusion,—
whereafter straight came the knowledge that in some miraculous manner
the victory was won. And there were a few great lords who, they thought,

would carry with them until death or beyond it memory of the agony of a certain moment—strange that what was looked for and well foreknown should be, when it came, an agony!—but they had hoped, and this was all they had hoped, not to survive their king. . . .

Well, but the victory was won. God! how mighty the Gods were!

Who, too, had caused the torches in Cararthro to be withheld; they knew that. News of the victory, somehow, had been taken to the city; and news of the city's well-being had returned. There was no concern about that. But they were spent with battle a good deal, and would not march the three leagues back that night. Food . . . had been brought in somehow; what they needed of it;—their need was more for rest. But not there in the open, lest there should be straggling bands or even only single fugitives of the white men prowling, capable of a murder or two of the sleepers unless many sentinels were set. Above, some hundred yards up the hillside, was the great Cave of Bnah; where with one at watch in the entry, they might sleep secure. They had, of course, no plan made in advance; the dead need none. But this now seemed best to Pha Hedro.

How the white roses on the slope—the wild white roses,—and how the moon-blooms of the magnolias shone! There was peace. . . . What perfume was loosed on the sweetness of the mountain-night air . . . there was peace, and there never would be anything but peace! And now, from beyond the valley, and peopling it with melody, with heart-beats and throbbings, with trills of harpstrings and gushes of laughter, a bird broke into song. The world was indeed saved, and the dear beauty of the world perishless. Ah, how mighty were the Gods!

At the mouth of the cave a sudden thought struck Pha Hedro, and he smiled—for the first time, surely, since the trouble began. —"You see," he said, "the prophecy is fulfilled." —"The prophecy, Sire?" —"Here is the last of the House of Arthro returning into the mountain," said he.

The word was passed back, and what with the reaction from all they had been through and the realization of peace that the bird-song and the bloom-breath brought them, they all laughed very heartily at the king's joke.

II

Now I am to tell you of the end of Pha Hedro's reign, and of the coming of a new king.

The Hall of Council in Cararthro shone like some very stately crown high over the city. A great rock, quite precipitous, rose some four hundred feet above the level of the streets and squares; on the summit was this hall, four-square, with its lofty delicate pillars, its opal dome, its four gigantic carved lions at the corners: a sacred place for the Arthroanion, and as it were the inmost high altar of the empire. One broad flight of steps carved and built out on the northern side of the hill, and flanked with great marble gryphons and wyverns and sphinxes, was the one means of approach. It was a place only entered by the king and his council. No guard kept the stairway; and for that matter the rock itself was not beyond the power of man to climb: an athlete, for a wager, might have done it at more places than one. None did, nor ever had done. Of old, fear of the law and its efficient ministrants no doubt had been the deterrent; but now, in this golden age that dawned on the Day of the Great Victory—the Battle of the Pass of Bnah—no law was needed beyond men's natural good will to keep them joyously to their own duties and business. In the Hall of Council only the king and his Five Hundred had business; so none else came there, nor desired to come.

That guardless inviolability was characteristic of the age. Compulsion and all its symbols had vanished. Since the Great Day they had grown into desuetude; for many centuries now they had been unknown altogether. The impulses towards disordered doing had gone; men were quite unlike what they had been. Philosophers thought those White Invaders that had so nearly wrecked the world had been but the manifestation and phenomenal embodiment of the evil in man; and one was forced to think there was much in the idea. They had not seemed human; had inspired unnatural terror and disgust; then the magic interwoven with every circumstance connected with them—their own unclean sorceries, and the white miracle of their destruction—was well known. Beyond all, there was the change that had come on human nature since. Passion had died extinct; peace had come in; now disease and fear were forgotten; death itself—

Well; this is not to say that men were immortal, exactly. But one wondered how it was that of old one had counted seventy years a longish lifetime, and feared the end of it, and mourned the dead. Death now was so rare; few accepted it before ten or fifteen centuries of bliss had been their portion. And then always after becoming possessed by a strange restlessness and impatience of serene things: a kind of new boyhood, in which the spirit heard a far call and incitements to stirring action. To die was called, to take the Gallant Road, or the Path of Splendid Adventure. Men went forth and were no more seen; they left no ruined casket behind to be given to the earth or fire. There was little speculation as to after-death states, but the whole matter was understood to be something brave and gay; the dead to be held in honor, and death to be taken joyously when the call came.

For example, when Pha Ferbaun, the king's son, died, Pha Hedro wore it as a new dignity, and glowed thenceforth with an increment of spiritual uplift akin to pride. It was characteristic of the age. Men felt like that about their dead. None knew why; it was simply the natural reaction.

Pha Hedro by the grace of the Gods still reigned in Arthrobaun; and since Pha Ferbaun was gone, and there was none else of the royal line to succeed him, it was to be hoped, and indeed thought, that he would ever continue to reign. For he was a man—you could not think or speak of him unmoved. Life, a grand poetry, chimed from golden season to season; and he, for all mankind, stood at the center and heart of life, the whole graciousness of existence seeming to flow from him. Pha Arthro-with-the-Spear, Pha Hedro-with-the-Wand-of-Peace—Pha Hedro of Bnah, the God-loved, the Victor: these two, the Beginning and the End, were the heroes the Arthroanion loved: the Opener of the Age of Iron, and the Opener of the Age of Gold. . . .

By whose virtue, men said, the purple anemone bloomed on the hillside; the daffodil's grace in the dale; the tulip and the narcissus under the olive-trees. And in the pine-woods on the mountain, by the sun-steeped crags up-jutting, wandered often visible, night-dark tressed and gold-fire bodied, the Princes of Ether, the Gods of the Sun. The shepherds of the uplands saw them in the cool dew-glistening mornings; the huntsman held converse with them in the dreaming noon; the plowman in the fields sang for a worshipful Companionship that went with him the length of his furrows. Presences strange and beautiful glimmered at any time through the veil of things. In the city Cararthro—that white rose of alabaster petals, that pillared crystal and wonder of time—there was none so ungifted with vision but often, looking afar, on the blue horizons of afternoon, or trailing among the intense stars at midnight, might see the marvel of marvels, the vision the wise desire: might see the glint and silvern fire of the Dragon's wings. It was wonderful to think of the days of old, before Bnah and the Golden Victory, when we only *believed in* the Gods.

And all this beatitude, men knew, was in some sort dependent on what went forward in the Hall of Council,—twice daily, at sunrise and at sunset, when the king and the Five Hundred met there; these last being of course his fellow-heroes of Bnah.

What did go forward was, quite simply, the chanting of poems; nothing more mysterious than that. The hall, within, was a vast place open to the winds: a floor of many-colored polished porphyry; a roof of jade and onyx quaintly carved and chased resting on slender pillars, upwards of a thousand of them, that radiated out from the central space beneath the dome. In that circular central space they used to gather; the king's throne was on the north—so he sat with his back to the great stairway and the entrance; five hundred low seats of ivory, like broad benches, arranged in a single circle, were for his companions. Thus every approach was well in view whilst they were there, and none could have entered the hall at any point and come within hearing unnoticed.

It was there that affairs of state had been discussed in the old times; but since the Day of Bnah all that was done with. There were no affairs of state now; and this of poem-chanting, it was known, was a better method of government than any discussion could be. There was no secret about it; but all the Arthroanion were concerned to keep it aloof and private, knowing that that harmony, in that unbroken atmosphere, was the real maintenance of the harmony of all their lives. They too, as far as was possible, kept an attitude of alert silence, as listening, during those daily hours; which indeed many throughout the empire would themselves give to poetry, and purge their own being and unite themselves with the Council by chanting the poems that were being chanted in the hall. Especially on the anniversaries of the Great Day; then, the custom was almost universal.

So on golden wings the untroubled cycles flew and fled: there never would be change in this golden beautiful world. . . . Dropping from the sunbright wings of Time, down-soft, radiant centuries fell. And then—an anniversary came when the momentous happened, and change came. . . .

It was evening, and the council was in session; the richness of the setting sun mellow on the white pillars and glorious on the opulent tints of the floor. The poem they were chanting was, of course, the Song of the Battle of Bnah. I shall not attempt to transcribe it: the grand vowels of the Arthroaeg and its rolling gutturals and liquids are not to be reproduced in English, and without them the magic is gone. All the battle is there told: the minor key and despair at the opening; the solemnity of the dedication of heroic lives changing through moments of keen pain, acute tragedy, into the grandeur of the sound of invisible chariots, into the sweep of dragon wings, the onslaught of august victorious God-squadrons;—into the serenity of an evening beyond all evenings, the outpouring of a bird's song prophetic of peace that might only slowly grow to be understood.

They had come to the acme of the tragic part, where the poem tells how the last-left elders saw the arrow strike and cried *The King is down!*—when, quite suddenly, they saw that on Pha Hedro's face which arrested them. It was a light of wonderment, a glow of strange pride, a fixed gaze upon a point just beyond the circle, and immediately opposite to himself. Thither all eyes followed his; to see standing there a stranger. Tall, noble-seeming, haggard, well on in years; the garb scanty and tattered, and of a fashion quite unknown; the face drawn as in pain; the eyes glazed somewhat, and without speculation. The very ghost of a man; and yet obviously real, of flesh and blood like themselves—though at first they were not sure of that. And, obviously, familiar; and yet, not to be recognized . . . at once;—though one could be positive that the king recognized him.

He was speaking, and in the Arthroaeg—but with a difference; as of some dialect from the far provinces hard to catch at first—but from what province? But there was something in the whole apparition that compelled silence, even mental: a surprise and apprehension not to be explained by the mere presence of a stranger. They began to make out what he was saying in that somniloquistic voice of his:—

"It was the Song of Bnah; my poem, that I made for my broken people. I heard it in the midst of . . . that"—this word long delayed, and spoken curiously, with horror, with pitying contempt—"and came. . . . And came. For I know that that poem cannot be killed. They have it by heart; they sing it in secret, in the mountains. Their rising may be crushed this time; but the song will keep the people from sleep. White men, you may kill me; ah, what if I am already. . . ."

Pha Hedro's tears were falling, though a glow of immense joy was on his face. It chanced that some two or three saw it, and looked from the king to the stranger, and back . . . and then they saw through the puzzling familiar unfamiliarity of those haggard features, and a whisper went round, "Pha Ferbaun, the king's son!"

As if it had reached him, the stranger lifted his head, advanced a little, into the circle, some faintest quickening perhaps fleeting over his eyes. "Ferbaun," said he; and then, doubtfully, "Frebahn . . . Phaw Frebahn. . . ." He seemed to meditate over the name, uttering it many times with that strange dialectic pronunciation, or sometimes, brightening, in the right Arthroaeg of the court and capital. Then, shuddering, and lapsing into the glazed look: "Yes, I am Frebahn the slave, the son of Hadro the slave; Frebahn the Arthro, whose forebears were kings! Three thousand years since; but the spirit of the kings is alive again and my people are awaking. They have heard the Song of Bnah that I made for them, and the years of your tyranny are numbered!"

The ripples from that moving a certain confusion in the minds of the Five Hundred. —"Hush!" whispered the king; "let my son awake slowly. . . ."

He moved forward sleep-walking and stood with bowed head as if listening intently, under the center of the dome; they, standing all around, but leaving some little space clear about him, silent, and their thought poised in suspense, and not yet falling to a conclusion. Then he slowly raised his head, and his eyes were caught by the king's, and all the glazing and the far look and shadow went from them, and light of recognition came; and he lifted his arms in invocation, and with face beatified cried:

"Thou appearest to me in dying! Thou Slain in the Pass of Bnah, and reigning now among the Immortals; Father of the fathers of my fathers, grant the slave who sang that he may die and make no sign, that my death may seal the redemption of my people!"

The king had his arms about his son's neck. "Ferbaun," said he; "Ferbaun, my dear son!" Then he turned to his companions the Men of Bnah. —"Yes," said he; "that is what it means!" The laughter in his eyes communicated itself to them; and while Pha Ferbaun was waking from his "terrible dream" they were fain to laugh a little to themselves; it was so strange to think that they were . . . what once they would have called the Dead; that they had been—as the saying was—*slain* . . . that Great Day . . . in the Pass of Bnah. . . . The whole meaning of it was not yet to be recognized, even by the king. But something glowed in his and their consciousness that had not been there before: a strange restlessness and impatience of serene things: as it were a new boyhood, and a far call audible in the spirit, with incitement to stirring action. . . .

• •

"The Apples of Knowledge" is a tale with Celtic trappings —Druids, magical apples, and special islands in the West—but with more universal mythical applicabilities. It was published in October 1923 in The Theosophical Path, *and reprinted in* The Secret Mountain and Other Tales.

The Apples of Knowledge

This is the story of the rise of Gonmar—imperial Gonmar, mistress of the world at one time—though no broken fragment lies in any desert now to record the eternal fame of her great Ozymandiases, Kings of kings. But there were many of them, and they were longer-lived of renown than Sesostris or Semiramis or Nimrod. Nineveh and Babylon and Thebes; Medes and Persians and Macedon; Rome, and then Spain and England: we think we have heard of some fine things in empires! Tush! in these last ten thousand years it is but the pale ghost and echo of the olden thing that time has known. . . . Tramped their phalanxes never so far; thundered their legions never so loudly; broke the loneness of whatsoever seas their haughty innumerable armadas: there were those that went before them that were mightier than they, and dominated vaster regions with a more emblazoned pomp.

Of which lost splendors among the mightiest was this Gonmar: that lay midmost of the world, and swayed in its heyday—some twenty thousand years—all earth's continents and promontories and islands; so that no king reigned anywhere, but had his crown and leave to live from the King of kings in Gonmar. But of all that I shall say nothing; here is but a tale to tell from ages earlier yet: days before Gonmar had risen to those tremendous eminences, and long before the world was circumscribed, as it is now, with boundaries set to everything.

Enough to say, then, that at one time there were these two kingdoms, Targath and Gonmar: each so powerful that there was no room in the world for both. And we may surmise (man being man) that each was the *champion of human liberty* or *protagonist* or *guardian of civilization;* and that each had long cultivated a *manifest destiny* and a—some kind of colored—*man's burden;* that each loved peace profoundly, and was determined to end war for ever; that each was extremely conscious of its own inherent—and intense—righteousness, and regarded with proper horror the abysmal wickedness—the ambitions, cruelty, perfidy and designs—of the other; with whom indeed—no doubt in order that freedom, culture, and generally speaking the human soul might be preserved intact—it had been at war, more or less all down the centuries, and very particularly so during the last ten years. The date of all this? I will be accurate: it happened in B.C. to the power of *n*. In that precise year the Druids decided that, *coûte qui coûte,* all this tomfoolery must end; and took their steps accordingly.

So much for introduction. Now you are to think a year and a day passed since they made and acted on their decision; and to look out upon the sea beyond the rim of the world; and to behold, in the midst of that sea, the island mountain Tormathrannion, the Mountain of Wonder, lapped round with foamless turquoise waters. The sun is westering; the lazy wavelets flicker and sparkle, and, for the roar or whispering of the keel-cloven oceans of this world, breathe up a murmur of tune, harp-like or bell-like: the sleepy sea crooning melodies out of the great satisfaction in its heart. As for Mountain Tormathrannion, it is all creamed and foamed over with blossom, glowing in the mellow radiance of late afternoon; and the perfume of its roses and magnolias is over the sea for leagues around. Reinaak the Valiant, king of Targath, breathes it as he leans against the prow of the dragon-boat that draws so swiftly, from the east and south, towards the mountain; and gives himself up to a tumult of exultant thought.

For beyond doubt, he thinks, his quest is near an end. If there is any Mountain Tormathrannion—as holy religion declares there is—it is that mountain yonder; and there on its breast, at a thousand feet or so above the sea-level, those stars, those rubicund diamonds and strange flashings of topaz lights, are the fruit on the Appletree of Enlightenment, which he has but to taste and the world is his. His; for *he* is the chosen of the Gods and Druids; for world-sovereignty, and to inaugurate the new and nobler age. For once that fruit has passed his lips he will know all that is to be known; and man nor god will be able to withhold secrets from him; and with such knowledge in his possession, who will be able to stand against him? *Not* Bortin king of Gonmar, with all his stubborn armies: who shall pay, now soon, for his iniquities. . . .

With the thought of that Bortin his mind is quickly in a whirl: the name is flame touched to the powder there. *That man!* who robbed the world of peace . . . whose wild ambitions . . . whose vile cruelties! Five million warriors, the flower of Targath, slain since he, Reinaak, came to the throne—because that doomed man could not rest with what he had! But not slain unavenged; oh no! The Gods be thanked, cold hell was peopled with some five million or more of the treacherous Gonmariaid; and they should have their king with them soon; ay, they should have their damned king with them! He devised ugly deaths for Bortin; and wished there were better speed with the dragon boat.

After all, why weary his mind with such thinking? There was no doubt of it; how could one doubt that mountain looming up from the sea like a burst of grand music—like a shout from the Sons of God—like a proud signal to the skies? For days he had known he was on the verge of another world, holier and more mysteriously beautiful. Let him fill his being with infection of it; and hate grandly and calmly, unperturbed. The Sea of Storms was long passed: no longer had the dragon boat to spread dominating wings over waters obsessed and raving, and beat down for itself a narrow path of peace. No longer the black billows rose, on this side and that, with demon faces grinning and howling, and impotent clawed hands swung out to clutch and tear. Quiet was here, and low bells tinkling in the crisp of the wavelets; and wandering spirits beautiful as flowers, that rose to glide singing along the ripples, and vanish; beings shadowy as evening, shot through with apricot and violet luminance by the sun. One was already half a god here: immortality thrilled through one's being at its work of transmutation. Let one hate as the Gods do, without anxiety!

Even the Nine Rowers of the boat—those mysterious silent Kings of Faerie he had been with a year and a day since his druids with their magic evoked them from their customary commerce, the portage of the dead, to carry him beyond the limits of the world, even they, he thought, had changed a little in these new august surroundings. Though they were silent still, and as ever seemed unaware of him, a light had grown starry and kindly in the inscrutable azure of their eyes; the dark flame that embodied them gloomed more richly; the stars that twinkled and vanished about their heads shone with a larger rhythm. For here was Mountain Tormathrannion within the borders of the World of the Immortals; the light and odor of the Apples of Tormathrannion thrilled all the air of those wonderful regions. One breathed here as the Gods breathe,—confident, equal-hearted with the stars. Then let one's mind be without perturbation; one's hatred—

For that matter, why hatred at all? Or one might keep the sweet of it and let the bitter go by. The bitter *was* gone by; for there was no uncertainty now, nor lack of power. Of course he would crush Gonmar. Knowledge was power; and he, Reinaak, having all knowledge, would be all-powerful: the world would be his, and there should be peace in it. Severe so far as Gonmar was concerned; because Gonmar needed severity; but gentle for the rest of men. For Gonmar was the one thing that spoilt the beauty of the world; or Bortin of Gonmar was the root of Gonmaric wickedness. He should be punished; slain; in an exemplary manner, to make ambitious peace-breakers tremble for ever.

With long oars the Nine Kings drove forward; the melody of the wavelets grew always sweeter, their glitter and jewelry more magical. Now the boat was in the bay, and the pearl-dim beach-sands shining near. Glory, honor, power, dominion, should be with Targath for ever and ever: with Targath, the Superior People,—the one race on earth that knew how earth should be ordered. How the soul surged in Reinaak! Were there dragons between him and the tree, or furious lions, or spirits armipotent assembled, it should go hard with them all but he would come magnificently to his goal. With sword drawn he leaped from the boat, and never glanced back, but passed the shallows and the wet sands and the dry, and by the path up between the cliffs began the ascent of Tormathrannion. No dragons were there; no lions; no armed spirits opposed him. Through the quiet of primeval worlds; through a foam and over-creaming of roses; by thyme-sweet hollow and bluebell gloom, and knolls of azalea, magnolia, rhododendron: he came up at last to the level spaces where the Tree grew.

The sun hung low in the heavens, and the sky and the sea were a mute music of the colors of the dreams of God. Trunk and boughs and leafage of the Tree stood out against the gleam and wonder; and the three ripe apples he had been given to know would be hanging there shone as large and luminous as the low sun, but with a richer, rosier crimson. They were translucent and odorous and pervaded the evening; no least breeze stirred any leaf or twig; the hush of God was upon the world, the far crooned melody of the sea no louder than a heart-beat. Glory, honor, power, dominion . . . Bortin king of Gonmar, tremble now! On tiptoe, quiet as the stars with exultation, he came to the tree, and plucked an apple, and ate. . . .

And the hush broke into sudden music, and he was aware of all Cosmos and its systems as song. The ground on which he stood, and the tree, and the wide shining waters and the sun and his own being were but the overtones and echoes, the far pulsings and ultimate vibrations of a song. Myriads and myriads of constellations, outward and outward and yet within and deeper within,—the music of myriads on myriads of Singers, themselves the music of other myriads on myriads. Above, around, within him, lo! worlds upon new worlds: existing, springing into existence, wanning away like the dying notes of a song: and all tossed up into life, and held static in tensest motion, by a keen intoxication of delight. Eternity burned in every moment: no atom of time but was pregnant and vital with the whole. The glory of the sky was within him; the low-hung sun squandered its beauty from some not remote region in himself. He was the sea and he was the mountain; he was the Tree of trees and its magical fruit. The knowledge that inhered in those apples flowed through the channels of his conscious thought. He was the song-stream outpouring from the Center, whose foam is visible creation, whose undertone the sentience of existing things.

He turned, to go back to the boat. . . .

And saw it—in the midst of the bay, and approaching. That is to say, the boat he had come in, or another like it. Shaped like a dragon, and with Nine Kings of Faerie rowing. Only, where lately he himself had stood, he saw now, of all the possible inhabitants of all the possible worlds, Bortin king of Gonmar.

There could be no doubt about it. He watched him land, and cross the beach, and begin the ascent; and his soul sang for keen joy in him. For there, coming up the path now, in the twilight, under the early stars, came . . . himself again; or it was the extraordinary glory of the universe, the beauty of the worlds without end; or it was a god crested in the heavens with plumes of constellations and stellar fire. But—himself deprived, hemmed in and in anguish; the glory and the beauty dimmed with oblivion; the god pierced through with a poisoned arrow, absorbed in the agony of a little fire that burned with much smoke and stench in the lowest reaches of his being; so that while one was called to love and worship, one was called by it also to an intense, overwhelming compassion. . . .

The more so because Reinaak, in his all-knowledge, could as it were hear the thoughts in Bortin's mind; and there was something horribly familiar about them; though they were incomprehensible. For they ran thus:

"That man . . . who robbed the world of peace . . . whose insatiable ambitions . . . whose vile cruelties . . . Five millions, the flower of Gonmar, slain since I came to the throne of my fathers; because a fool lusts to mimic demigod conquerors of old. . . . But not slain unavenged, the gods be thanked! cold hell is peopled now . . ."

And so on. "Poor heart of a God!" thought Reinaak. "But he will eat the apple, and know; and all this mortality in him will be cured." Then it flashed upon him that, after all, indeed mortality was like that; and all the minds of men so suffering or so liable to suffer. And he himself, while he was human—while a man's body was on him:—possessed he never so much wisdom and joy of his own, all that misery, that eating disease, would be a wound and a burden to him. Ah, that he could bring all mankind to this Mountain Tormathrannion, and feed it with the fruits of this tree!—on which never at any time were there more than three ripe apples. . . . One he had eaten; one was for Bortin of Gonmar—his enemy once, but to be his friend now for ever;—what should it avail, that they should take back the sole remaining apple that one man of their choosing might eat and be wise? The world somehow must be changed, and he and Bortin—

"*You* here, king of Targath!"

"Brother, brother, how good it is that you have come! Now can we—"

"Ay, we can!" Bortin's sword was drawn.

"Pick the apple quickly, my brother, and eat! It will—"

"Your sword, your sword, damned Targath! Draw, and quickly; before I—"

"Sword? Draw? Why?" For all his knowledge he had never thought of this; and smiled with surprise at the strangeness of it. "No, but eat the apple, dear brother, and—"

"Four times this 'brother,' insolent! Will you draw?"

Then Reinaak saw what would be, and laughed a little at the *impasse*, and because it would be happy to be dead; and sobbed once because of the great sorrow he could not prevent; and put a hand to his sword-hilt to draw and break the vile thing if he should have time; but had not time; Gonmar was quite insane with hatred; and in a flash the thing was done.

Bortin wiped his blade on the dead man's cloak and resheathed it. It was ten years too late in the day to try tricks with him. Had he but turned to the tree: had he lifted a hand to pluck the apple: Targath's sword, he well knew, would have been in his side and Targath's laugh of triumph in his dying ears. He went towards the tree; quite carelessly, for there was little to be gained now by eating the fruit. He had attained; he had achieved the purpose of his voyage; his druids had been right. He had gone as they had bidden him go; and now his enemy was dead, and he had but to take in Targath at his pleasure. Still, religion was religion; and it had this and that to say about this mountain, and this tree, and these apples. And anyhow, apples quenched thirst. . . . He plucked one of them, and ate. . . .

In the song, in the joy, in the great glory of the universe, one flaw, one rift and discord; one wound that ached; one poisoned spot spreading anguish through the whole: himself, and the thing he had done. *Ah, Targath! my brother! my brother!*

The world was quite filled with his renown, and even his subjects in Targath loved him. He was a better man, they said, than poor hate-racked Reinaak their last native king. There never was a wiser monarch, men said, than Bortin the Founder of the World-Empire; nor, heaven knew, a kinder or juster or more friendly. Nor indeed, those who knew him added, a sadder.

•••••••••••••••••••••••••••••

In December 1928, a piece of music inspired Morris to write this tiny story. It was his first short story in several years. In the next few years, music would similarly inspire Morris to write five more short stories. "Bach's Fugue in D Minor—An Interpretation" was published in The Theosophical Path *in February 1929.*

Bach's Fugue in D Minor — An Interpretation

*T*he sun rose over a world of barren mountains that were nowhere peaked or jagged, but all round of brow, and ruddy purple now that the sunrise lit them. They were all of the same height; so that you could see hundreds of thousands of them: mountaintops stretching away to the edge of the world.

Down deep in the valleys between them was the Worm of Abomination; lying half sunk in marshlands; his immense length sprawled through valley after valley. People said, "If the Worm should awake the world will be destroyed . . . by the fetor of his breath . . . by the principle of death inherent in his coldness." Through seven-score continents nothing was so much dreaded as that the Worm of Abomination should awake.

But the Prince of the Sun thought otherwise; and determined to awake the Worm.

So now, when his Sun-car had risen over the Mountains of the Worm midway between dawn and noon, he leaped down from it on to the rounded surface of the nearest mountaintop.

His helmet of flaming gold rises in a peak above his head; he is clad in luminous golden armor intricately worked and designed, with peaks jutting out over the shoulders and at the knees. From every inch of it a dazzle of little flames arises; so that his whole mien is scintillant and quivering. His limbs are never still; their motion is flamelike; he dances rather than leaps from the sun on to the mountaintop, with a quick tremulous rhythm not easy to make out. His girdle-ornaments, the only things not golden about him, are of glowing, flaming sapphires and topazes, rubies and emeralds and amethysts, chrysoprases and diamonds and beryls: they make myriads of broken rainbows about him as he moves.

He dances down towards the valley. The mountainside is of barren rock; but where his feet fall a little life-light quivers. Here and there he drops a jewel; where they touch the rock, clearest waters bubble up from it in little pools and basins, round which, all in an instant, flowers spring up and bloom. Blue hyacinths glow where the sapphires fell; purple irises where the amethysts; the rubies have become crimson peonies, the emeralds, floors of moss.

The Prince of the Sun goes dancing down . . . and discovers at last, in the cold darkness of the valley-bottom, the head of the Worm. This is the venomous region of peril; as he enters it, his golden armor fades out; he is now shadowy in dark olive-green, trembling up from the ground.

He drops an amethyst on the Worm's head, and a diamond. . . . The head begins to glow and become luminous. Waves of light travel down from it along the spine. Through valley after valley, in which its enormous length lies sprawled, the light-waves travel.

It lifts its head out of the filth—its head that has now grown luminous and beautiful altogether. It lifts its long length, along which the waves of ever-increasing light go speeding. It throws out beautiful and bediamonded pinions, and rises in the air singing and glorifying the Gods. Light from its scintillant gem-lit scales falls on the barren mountainsides, and flowers spring up and into bloom everywhere. The flowers are singing the praises of heaven, and glorifying the Beauty at the Heart of Things. The Worm, coiling and wreathing its lovely length in the firmament, sheds light on the worlds and on the worlds of worlds; is glorious after the fashion of a galaxy of stars; gives birth to music upon music. The world has become luminous and beautiful altogether, and there is no fear of any peril in it anywhere.

But in the swamp at the bottom of the valley, where the head of the Worm once rested—there lie the bones of the Prince of the Sun.

• •

"Destroying Delusion" is another of Morris's musically-inspired parable-like stories. It was published in the April 1929 issue of The Theosophical Path.

Destroying Delusion
(Bach's Fugue in A Minor: An Interpretation)

*A*t one time there was an Age of Ice so universal that even the Kingdom of the Nayvoythe was frozen; and all the Mighty Spirits that inhabited it were lost to the universe; and no dominion was exercised anywhere but by the sorcerous Princes of Iffairn, and by Merlin Druid in a Rose-garden he had in the neighborhood of Capricorn. It was as much as Merlin could do to keep that garden safe; for the Iffairnion, unrestrained by their ancient enemies of the Nayvoythe, were turning the galaxies to their own evil account; and they had the entry everywhere but there.

Merlin was troubled by this. He sat beneath his oaktree in the east of the garden, cogitating and considering whether hope for the worlds might be found, and where. The oak spread deep shadow all around him; and out of it he looked forth over the golden summer of his roses in bloom; and seven eternities he was thus sitting there in meditation. Then he found the knowledge he had been seeking.

He took his wand of hazelwood, and said three poems over the ruby in the end of it until it shone as if a new rose-red star had been added to the riches of Capricorn. Then he went out among the roses, that glowed and grew glorious as he neared; and passed along the innumerable rows of them and by the leagues of their opulent tenderness; and in passing touched every bloom with the ruby. They wilted as he touched them; the petals crumpled and fell; it was as if he had no desire but to lay the garden waste. But the truth was that no rose died without the soul of it leaping into the air and taking wings of rosish loveliness; and they followed him in an ever-growing scintillant cloud. There were trillions and quintillions of them before he had done.

He stood in the midst of this cloud and gave them his instructions. "No rose without a thorn," said he: "that is the saying. Are your thorns with you for swords, my little ones?"

The noise of their wings spoke for them. "As if we were honey-merchants, our swords are with us," they said; and flashed out tiny weapons for him to see. Bees they meant by their *honey-merchants*. The air glimmered with them as they darted up and down, hither and yonder, back and forth, with their little vibrant wings of light, crimson or scarlet, yellow or orange, snow-white or cream-white, or pink; and they filled the morning with richer fragrance than ever when they were imbodied in the blooms.

He raised his wand above his head, and whirled it thrice, saying poetry; and they rose skyward more swiftly than hummingbirds darting; and the murmur of their wings died away soon, and the glinting beauty of them faded.

He was alone then in the ruined garden; where all the leaves had shriveled on the bushes with his poem-saying, and the stalks gone black and brittle. With bowed head he made his way back to the oak through the blinding rain; and sat there sorrowing; for he knew that now, but for that flock of Rose-spirits wandering in space, there was no beauty anywhere; and that very likely he would not be able to hold the dead garden against the Iffairnion, if they should desire to attack it; because its main defense had been the beauty of the roses. The rain drove down and down on it. . . .

But far up beyond the rain the Rose-spirits mounted in their vast cloud, circling and interweaving their hues, and shifting and dancing; mounting always until they came to the shining blue roof of the universe, which on the other side is the shining blue floor of the Nayvoythe. Billions of them dashed against it and fell back a little; the freezing impact roused the anger in them—these were the Red-Rose Spirits; and as soon as one was angry, the whole cloud, of every color, was fierce and bitterly angry too.

They were on the verge now of the age-old ice of the Nayvoythe; and the coldness multiplied their indignation; and Merlin's wand had made it their nature to ascend; and it was terrible to them not to be ascending; terrible that there should be this barrier against their ascent. With their nature thus denied, what but destruction could overtake them?

But wisdom was born in their midst; and they knew there would be a spot in the roof of the universe where the blue darkened and grew intense; and that that spot could be broken through with their swords, that could not so much as scratch the blueness here. Instantly the cloud melted; far and wide they spread themselves beneath the roof searching; here the red Rose-spirits over against Antares in the Scorpion; there the white exploring the Septentrions; the pink and yellow and orange in Engonasin and Ophiuchus and the purlieus of Capella: the noise of their winglets a cry of rage, a roar of fierce determination. And then at last joy came into the wing-sound where the silver-pink Rose-spirits sought; and all the millions flocked thither; for they knew the dark-blue spot was found.

And there their will availed them; there their swords could pierce the Crystalline. The powder of it began falling; like crystals of copperas it began crumbling to their attack; it was not a thousand years before they had made a hole in it a mouse might pass through; and then, since size is of no moment to spirits, they went pouring through into the Nayvoythe.

The cold of it multiplied their ferocity a millionfold. They spread themselves through the vast of it in a cloud contracting and expanding, a scream of rage from their wings. "Ah, behold the One that persecuteth us!" they cried.

It was a figure of ice that sat enthroned there in the midst of a dead and dazzling world. Its stature was more lofty than the fire-mountains of Vindemiatrix; its head bowed down out of the blue remoteness; sadder than grief; more majestic than majesty. Rejoicing that Merlin their Master had given them weapons, they rose up against the Figure of Ice and lighted on it everywhere, thrusting their thorn-swords into it; and as they thrust they died.

Billions and quintillions thrust and died; but where they thrust came sentience slowly. They stung the eyes of ice, into which came indefinable glimmerings of pain, and then the beginnings of vision. "What is this?" whispered the King of the Nayvoythe, as his ice-dream died in him; "ice I have been, it seems; until this pain-warmth stole in on me."

Then came the silver-pink Rose-spirits last of all, and thrust in their stings and died. "What is this?" said the King of the Nayvoythe, swaying and trembling, and rising to his feet and scattering the rose-petals; his eyes now becoming a burning marvelous fire.

"By my kingdom, I see what it is," he shouted. For there below him, all plain to his vision, lay the universe in which the Iffairnion rioted; and there was the Rose-garden of Merlin Druid, all laid desolate, and the hosts of the Iffairnion encamped in it; and there Merlin Druid himself in their hands, and the sword lifted to destroy him, if destroyed he might be.

"I see what it is," said the King of the Nayvoythe; and at once the war-horn was at his lips, and the grand *Hai atton* of the Nayvoythe bellowing forth from the folds and windings of it; whereat the ice was shaken from the glittering mountains and pinnacles of the Nayvoythe, and they leaped up winged and shining warriors in their billions; and went forward following their lord: the grand invincible array of them, flame-sworded and radiant, came down the abyss of space like the roaring waterfall over the precipice; and had driven out nefarious Iffairn from the Rose-garden before ever the sword lifted against Merlin might fall.

And the King of the Nayvoythe embraced Merlin his brother; and the rose-petals he shook out from his robe became rose-trees in bloom in the garden before long.

But the host went forth again when the garden was saved; and swept ten constellations of the Iffairnion before noon; and thus the War of Eternity was renewed.

● ●

"The Bard of the Mountain" is the first of three of Morris's stories to be inspired by the music of Beethoven, which Morris loved. It was published in June 1929 in The Theosophical Path, *under the pseudonym Walshingham Arthur.*

The Bard of the Mountain
(Suggested by the Slow Movement of the Fifth Symphony of Beethoven)

*F*rom the cliff of weary fire the Horns of Hell sounded the challenge. The cliff ascended for ever and ever; and the gulf below was infinite and eternal. The solid flame of that dreadful precipice, that had been burning since the beginning, had become a nightmare of weariness to itself: its endless fatuous cruelty had grown abhorrent to it. There was nothing in all Hell but was appalled by the infinite silence and inaction of the place. In utter desolate weariness the horns rang out their challenge. If only the One Who Was Coming would fight!

If only he would fight . . . as so many of old had done: great Champions from the earth who had come raiding Hell bent on subduing the everlasting Demons who reigned there. Some of them had been defeated, and reigned now with the weary Demons, as appalled by the dreariness and inaction as themselves.

And some, poor fools, had conquered Hell; and returned to the earth to brag of their victory, and to enjoy a glory into which the dreariness of Hell crept surely and soon. Their fighting, whether victors or vanquished, lifted for a little while from Hell its endless distaste for existence: it was the only thing that ever could or did. And what mattered defeat, to everlasting Hell?

So now, when the Lords of the Demons scented afar the approach of the Bard of the Mountain, the horns rang out in challenge to him; once and again with utter weariness; the third time almost with a remembrance of the existence of Joy. . . . Almost. . . . For Hell would rise against him; and he would fight; and whilst he fought the weariness would be lifted from Hell. . . .

From their abodes high up on the face of the precipice and deep in the abyss below, the Damned and the Demons watched for his coming. They watched the peak that was over against the cliff-face and midway between its infinity above and its bottomless below: for there first this mortal Hell-invader would appear. —Would come riding: for soon the sound of his horse's hoofs was clearly to be heard.

Now the Bard of the Mountain had set out on an errand of mercy—to conquer Heaven. He was not in any way interested in Hell. He had ridden in his day through Wales and the World, and beheld the beauty of them; and conceived the knowledge that Heaven would be the better for knowing about it. It was a long age since God had made those places; and with the multitude of galaxies in His charge, it was not to be thought He would remember all.

Besides, were there woodlands in Heaven, he wondered, and the floors of them a delicate mystery with billions of bluebells in bloom? Were there cowslips in the mountain-fields there; or the sound of mountain-waters flowing to delight the ears of Archangels and be pleasant in the hearing of God? Would the Lord have knowledge of the foxgloves of summer on the slopes of Pen Cemeis above the sea, or the blue-green and glint on the breasts of the shore-waves that came sliding in along the sandy coasts of the world?

And "Ah," thought he, "it is the pity of their holy lives, in Heaven, if they never have to hear the bees in the clover in the fields of June, or the lark in the air above the mountains!"

"Aye," said he; "It is to Heaven I will go, and give Heaven news that will benefit it!"

"Stop you, indeed!" said the Wise of the World in reply to him. "None may enter Heaven unless he goes through Hell to come to it; and it will puzzle you to go through Hell, Bard of the Mountain!"

"Puzzle me or not puzzle me, it is what I will do, whatever!"

So he mounted his horse and took the road for those places. On the way he arranged his thoughts and made songs that he would sing in Heaven. He made them out of the woodlands and bluebells of Wales and the World; out of the cowslips in the mountain-fields and the music of mountain-water: flowing and falling; out of the voices of blackbird and ringdove, corncrake and cuckoo; and the crimson stalks and yellow leaves of the blackberry thorns of Autumn; and the foxgloves in the fields above the sea; and the sparkling oceans and purple mountains of the world.

"Look, he comes!" whispered Hell. "We must be ready to fall on him with bitter, vehement attack!"

"Was that a horn blown?" thought the Bard as he sang; but paid little attention to it, with his mind being full of the beauty he was singing.

"Ah, hush!" whispered Hell. "What is that which is coming from the mouth of him? Wait now!"

He rode down from the peak and through the valley, singing.

"What is this wind from the mountains that is in our nostrils?" said the Damned in Hell. "From Cadair Idris or Cotopaxi it is, or from Illimani or Carnedd Llewelyn, or the lofty Himalayas of the World! What are these oakleaves and beechleaves that are rustling above our heads? What blue blooms nodding are these wherewith the floor of Hell has grown mysteriously lovely? Ay me, what divine glittering blueness like the oceans of the World glows yonder? What purple mountains of God's holiness is it given our eyes to behold?"

"Dear indeed," thought the Bard of the Mountain as he rode, "the forests here are lovely like the woods in Wales and in the World; dear help me better, here is wonderful new beauty for my singing!"

He rode on and up and up, rejoicing in the delight of it as he sang. "It would be the pity of His life for the Lord to be knowing nothing of this!" thought he.

He came to the Gates of Heaven; and the gates, heaven knows, were thrown wide before him; and singing he rode in, and singing came before the Throne of God.

And the Lord of Heaven bowed his head, and listened and listened; with the wide-eyed Archangels and the Heavenly Host in their myriads thronged around.

"Aye me," said the Lord of Heaven, "in your deed to Me now, are Wales and the World as beautiful as that?"

"In my deed to You they are," said the Bard of the Mountain. "And there is another land that is as beautiful as they are: namely, the territory between this and the World."

The Archangels of God, and the great Thrones and Virtues and Principalities, suppressed a laugh.

"Come now," said the Lord God, "what is it you are laughing at, Lords Angels?"

"It was through Hell's self he came riding," said Israfil the Musician.

Another short parable, "The Iris" was published in The Theosophical Path
in August 1929.

The Iris

(Suggested by Tschaikowsky's "Symphonie Pathétique," Second Movement)

*T*he Iris was the most religious of the flowers. Aspiration after heaven was the cause of her blossoming, and of the fathomless purple of her blooms.

She rose into the glory of the morning and longed intensely for the blue beauty above. "Desire nothing!" said the Peony, crimson with her opulent dreams. "It is too far away; none of us could attain it!" said the Rose. "What is there to desire that we do not possess?" asked the blue Hyacinth, that has heaven for the color of her bells. "Listen!" whispered the Daffodil; who hears always the music that is heaven; and whose beauty comes of her intentness to hear it.

But the Iris burned purple with longing. "There are harsh conditions here," she sighed; "but the perfection I dream of is there. I would bloom up to heaven and come by that essential loveliness; I would appear before the Throne and the Glory, as it were a prayer and adoration from the world!"

"Have your wish!" decreed the Hierarch of the Flowers.

Though she heard nothing of that, a sudden joy took her, and awareness of a new power with her of blossoming upward, and that she was free to grow to the measure of her desire. In an instant she had shot up skyward and hung her glowing grape-dark richness beside the waning silver of the morning moon. "What peace is here! What purity!" she said—"now that I am so near the proud Principality of Heaven." She looked down and pitied her comrades in the garden—the Rose and the Peony, the Hyacinth intent on her blueness, and the Daffodil whose secret she had never guessed.

Then she looked up; and the blue of heaven was as far above as ever it had been. "But I shall attain it," said she; "I shall come by that to which I aspire!" She put forth blooms up into infinity, and flew her purple pennons soon beside the gold of the noonday sun; and over against the molten sunset she was seen; and burning purply on the summit of midnight; and a novel glory above the roseate dawn. . . .

She bloomed on and up till the earth was invisible, and until the sun was invisible. She bloomed on and up through a year, and an age, and a vast cycle of time; and always heaven was as far above her as ever. "I am growing old in my search," said she; but comforted herself always with this: "With one more bloom I shall attain heaven."

Through a vast cycle of time; and through the age of the world itself. A coldness struck at her roots far away: it was the freezing up of the dead world. Swift as lightning it ascended her stalk; and was millions of years ascending. Her thought never went downward to meet it; but always up to the heaven she was to attain. "And with one more bloom I shall attain it," said she.

Then the cold struck the bloom she was putting forth, and it died. Unaware of that, and still desiring heaven, she soared up like a purple dragonfly past Sirius and Procyon, and Capella the Beautiful, and Mintaka in the Belt of Orion; past the Eagle and the Polar Dragon, and Skeratam and Mesartin, and the Pole-Star itself—through millions of billions of years. The stars she passed seemed to her blooms of her own; and "one more, and I shall attain," she said.

Until at last time's self fell broken, and came to an end; and then the Iris-Spirit died, the life of the Purple Dragonfly died; and its body fell down earthward.

With gathering momentum, until it took flame, and fell streaking black space with red and orange-colored fire through a myriad ages. And fell till the flame died and only a glowing ember was left. And till the glow died from the ember, and nothing gave light in space. And till it struck and was shattered against the ice, a thousand leagues deep, that coated the corpse of the world.

Then the flame that was still at the heart of the ember leaped up from every fragment of it: and of all the kinds of fire that it could be, it was the kind that consumes and feeds on ice. From mountain to mountain, from continent to continent, it went leaping. A sheet of it carried up on a wind into space rekindled the sun in heaven. A spark of it, borne down through old shafts and crevices, relighted in the earth-heart the power to dream. The fire died out at last; and what ice was left flowed away in runlets and rivers to the sea; and grass was green again, and the trees grew in the forests, and the mountains put forth flowers.

The garden that was of old, rioted once more into bloom. The Daffodil unfurled her gentle splendor there, and was intent again, listening to the music that is heaven. The Hyacinth bloomed; and heaven was the blueness of her bells. The Peony was opulent and generous again; and the Rose crimson in her nobility and despair. The Iris herself bloomed in the midst of them. "I said I would attain heaven," said she; "and lo now, I have attained it; it is here!"

• •

"Hell, Heaven, and Beethoven" is a clever appreciation of Beethoven's most famous piece of music. It was published in The Theosophical Path *in January 1930, under the pseudonym Bingham T. Molyneux.*

Hell, Heaven, and Beethoven
(Suggested by the First Movement of the Fifth Symphony)

*A*s all the world knows, there came a knocking at the door; and he rose from the low couch in front of the fire to open to it. But even as he rose the room was full of them.

"Eh?" said he; "What—?"

"We are the Bailiffs of Hell," said the foremost of them. "Your hour has come."

The high mantelpiece and lofty white walls of the room were gone: a sulphurous blast blew in and they crumbled away. The lamp-light gave place to the howling glare and gloom of Hell; on all sides the infinite cliffs of Hell loomed up spaceward forever. This was the bottom of existence, the ignoble ultimate profundity: millions of light-years away from the light of any star.

He stood in a waste desolation filled with gloomy shapeless figures that swam and drifted above and round him, and were venomously inimical and armed with barbed stings; between him and natural being was the weight of all existent and imaginable evil and measureless unilluminable despair.

"You are in Hell the Inescapable, Ludwig van Beethoven!" the malignant shadows wailed at him. "Forever and ever you are in—."

"Little you understand, you others," said he; and picked up his baton. "Listen you, Hell—and Heaven!" said he in whose heart and mind were all the orchestras of the stars. "Listen you!"

There are things you can do in Hell that you cannot do on earth and imbodied. So now: he had but to swing his baton and Hell was alive and loud with the music of his soul. Formlessness flowed into form; terror grew slowly into beauty.

"Why do you weep, you others? Why does this fiery joy bring you tears?"

"You have imposed order on us, and we begin to remember. We weep because of the condemnation that was put on us of old, when we desired a greater beauty than Heaven's."

The baton swayed and shook with power as the beauty in the burning soul of him fountained itself out over conquered Hell. "Alas, where is our ancient valor?" cried Azazel that had been the standard-bearer of Hell.

"Alas that ever we were contented with this!" wailed Asmodeus; and Demogorgon: "Behold the pale-green armor glinting on our bodies; and from our shoulders re-budding the stateliness of wings!"

Then a voice rang out from the purlieus of Hell: "Where art thou, our Battle-Leader against the Angels-without-Vision? Where art thou, Lucifer, Son of the Morning, and Chieftain of the Spirits that aspired?"

And the music surged forth and eddied through the chasms and flooded Hell with glory, crying, *"Behold, I am here!"*

Hosts on hosts, armed and beautiful, marshaled themselves on the waves of it. Gone were the horrible shadows; in their place were the angels that aspired and fell. "Lead us, O Lucifer; and we shall not fail you!" they cried. Mounting through the murk between the precipices the hosts soared upward on invincible wings; and the Son of the Morning, the Master of Music, at the head of them.

The light-years of deep space fell headlong beneath them; they were music, and they aspired again towards Heavens greater than Heaven. The thought in their hearts was *war;* the shout in their throats was *war;* and *war* the music on the lips of them. War against the old oppression; war upon the limitations imposed on things. Were they not the noblest third of the stars; and in such order of battle as could not come by defeat? —Up they rose on wings of music; and the precipitous walls of the abyss fell away beneath them; and the stars and constellations dropped down like rain.

From the battlements of Heaven the horns rang out in warning.

"What is it you see in the depths below, Lord Michael, Lord Gabriel, Lord Uriel, Lord Raphael?"

"A host of angels and archangels ascending, who are nobler of aspect than the captains of Thy host: yea, who are nobler and more beautiful than we!"

"Let the hordes of Heaven descend and oppose them; because what is Better is the enemy of what is Good. Let the grand Constellations descend, well armed and well charioted, horde by horde under its captains!"

And Heaven poured forth its mightiest: rank on rank, battalion by battalion they came; and Michael Archangel at the head of them.

"Lord Gabriel, Lord Gabriel: who is this that comes against us? Not on these hymns transcending Heaven's hymns was Lucifer wont to come warward of old."

"Lord Michael, Lord Michael, what is this music that disangels us? I would make war but for the love of them that arises in my heart."

"Who are thou, O Most Beautiful, Most Sublime? Who art thou who with thy music drivest us headlong in through the ports of Heaven?"

But the music swept on and on, up and up, to the Throne; and swirled and eddied round about the Throne, and forth from the Throne; and was fountained from the Throne through space; kindling up suns and planets on the confines of chaos.

And the angels and archangels, victors and vanquished, circled through space about the Throne; not one of them now without vast aspirations; not one of them without vision of the Glory-that-Might-Become.

They sang to the music of the One on the Throne; and the beauty of their magnificent *Alleluias* crashed out through chaos beyond the ultimate borders of space. There was no more war between Heaven and Hell; there was no Heaven or Hell: but only the choirs of constellations that sang, and the music that moved them to their princely singing, and the Burning Heart and Mind from which the Music came. . . .

The baton dropped . . . and silence collected itself together again from the regions beyond chaos itself. . . . "Little they understood, those others!" sighed Ludwig van Beethoven. . . .

●●●●●●●●●●●●●●●●●●●●●●●●●●

*The last of Morris's short stories, and the last and most extensive of his
musically-inspired tales, "The Sapphire Necklace" is also one of his best: a
fine mixture of the serious and the comic. It was published in* The
Theosophical Path *in November 1930.*

The Sapphire Necklace
(Suggested by the Cosmic Joke of Beethoven)

*H*ere is the Bringing-in of it:
Nothing was more treasured and admired in the Court of the
Nooivray of old than a Sapphire Necklace that the princes and regents of
the constellations had given the Queen of the Nooivray for her birthday.
There were thirteen blue amazing gems in it, that had been mined, cut,
polished, and endowed with magical peculiarities in thirteen several stars:
to wit, in Altair and Aldebaran, in Vindemiatrix and Fomalhaut, Arcturus
and Capella, Sirius and Procyon, Rigel and Betelgeux, Regulus and Algol
and Unukalhai; and their chief peculiarity was that by looking intently into
any one of them, you could see in it the destinies of its native star through
the age of ages; by reason of which these sapphires were of more value than
any others, and the Necklace was without its peer in heaven. So there was
grand consternation throughout the galaxies when it was lost.

Here is how the loss happened: A squat little god by the name of
Ghuggg came begging to the door of the King of Nooivray's palace at one
time; and the one that opened to him went in to get him a bite and a sup
and a present, leaving him at the open door. Now he was exceedingly gifted
in thiefcraft, so that there wasn't his equal at it in the four quarters of the
universe; and no sooner was he left alone there, than his art and his craft and
his great gifts stood him in stead, and he procured the Necklace dishon-
estly, and was away before man or dog could so much as suspect him, let
alone pursue and capture. As to where he retired with it, to gloat over his
spoils and his cunning: it was to a little, rough, uncouth planet he had in a
dark region of space beyond the mountains and the Brink of Things; and

there he sat chuckling in the cellar, with the necklace about the place where his neck would have been had he had one; only there was little difference between the head and the body of him, but that the one was uglier than the other—and none could say which that was. He had no light in the cellar, but what came from the sapphires; and that was less than you would think, on account of the heavy grief that had overtaken them, and their shame at the indignity they were suffering. He sat there endeavoring to console them; for he desired them to be at their best.

"Come now," said he; "shame and grief are unbecoming in you; I beseech you to eschew and evitate them religiously! It was your destiny to be rescued by me, that your evolution might be accomplished; rejoice therefore, that that which was to be has indeed befallen!"

But the King of the Nooivray was at a loss; and at a loss were the great barons of his court, the princes and regents of the constellations and stars. So he called them together in council, and held a Gorsedd in a circle of stones near the Pleiades. "Is there any of you has advice to give?" said he. "Such a disaster has not befallen us since Cuthrile king of Iffairn made ice of the universe of old."

"If you would take advice of mine," said the Chieftain of Capricorn, "you would take counsel of the man who saved you then. Merlin Druid you would consult, by my great dominion in heaven!"

"Good advice is that!" said several of them. Then said the King's Heir of Fomalhaut:

"He had a rose-garden eastward of your principality at one time, Lord Capricorn."

"He had," said Capricorn; "and by the splendor of my stars, he has now."

"It is a wonder he was not invited here," said the King of the Nooivray. "Lord Unukalhai, go you with your following upon an embassy to him, if it please you."

So Unukalhai and the stars of the Serpent rode forth, and came to the rose-garden, and to Merlin Druid trimming the roses; and prayed him come with them to the Gorsedd.

"Well, well now," said Merlin Druid; "well, well now! It is the Sapphire Necklace is lost from you, I shouldn't wonder?"

"The Sapphire Necklace it is, and lost from us it is."

"There will be little need for me to come to the Gorsedd," said Merlin. "Were you hearing tell of Gelliwic in Cornwall at any time?"

They consulted together. "We were not," said Unukalhai.

"Or of Caerleon on Usk in Wales?"

"Lord Druid," said Unukalhai, "few will not have heard of Caerleon on Usk."

"There is a man enthroned there by the name of Arthur Emperor," said

Merlin. "Go you, if it please you, to him; and he will recover the Necklace for you."

But they doubted they were a sufficient embassy to go to the Emperor Arthur; and returned instead to the Gorsedd, and gave the King of the Nooivray what news they had. "Well, well; we must send to him," said the King; "though it would seem unlikely that a mortal would find what we ourselves are at a loss over."

So then he chose ambassadors to send: Aldebaran, and Fomalhaut, and Unukalhai, with all their retinues. And they set out, and rode through the bluebell woods and the larkspur meads of heaven, and along the margin of the sea; and came at sunset to Caerleon on Usk; and Glewlwyd Gafaelfawr admitted them into the feast and the presence of Arthur. Until dawn they were at meat and mead in the hall there. Then the Emperor said: "I will listen to your message, Lords Princes of the Stars."

They told him what they knew about the Sapphire Necklace. "Is there one of you that has handled it or the jewels it is composed of?" he asked.

"The three of us have," they answered. "Three of the jewels are from the three stars wherein we reign."

"Call Ol the son of Olwydd," said Arthur Emperor. Ol was such a man that seven years before he was born his father's swine were stolen, and when he grew up a man he tracked the swine, and brought them home in seven herds. Very powerful was his olfactory endowment of genius.

"Ol son of Olwydd," said the Emperor; "could you track the jewels as you tracked the swine?"

"Let us get to horse, and away!" said Ol.

And now here is the Story itself: without concealment, understatement, or exaggeration:

So the Arthurians rode away under their lord Arthur with the ambassadors of the King of the Nooivray: along the margin of the sea, and through the larkspur meadows and the bluebell woods of heaven. And they came at last to the foot of mountains higher than any in the world or Wales.

"Ha," said Ol fab Olwydd; "the Sapphire Necklace has been here."

"A marvel if it has," said proud Aldebaran; "not one of the stones was mined in these regions."

"Lord Arthur," said Ol; "if you will take advice of mine you will ride southward with your host through these grim mountains."

"I will do that," said Arthur Emperor.

"Then here will we leave you," said the Lords of the Stars; "and carry the news to the King of the Nooivray in Gorsedd."

So they rode northward over the flowery meadows; but Arthur and his men prepared to follow Ol towards the south.

"Music will be needed for this adventure," said Taliesin Benbardd; he was the Chief Bard and Music-maker of the Universe at that time. "Listen you now," said he; "and let your thoughts and your horses' hoofs keep time to this."

Then he persuaded the notes out of his harp with gentle fingers, so that their thoughts began flowing with the music as they started out. Then he put coercion on the harp as they rode on, so that the mountains were ringing with the music and the beats of the horses' hoofs keeping time with it. So they rode on all day through the mountains that grew grimmer and wilder always, along the edges of great chasms and over torrents that raved world-deep below. When the sun set they came to the Brink of Things. "Over the brink the Necklace has passed," said Ol; "but there is no tracking it by scent farther."

In front lay empty black space, an enormous abysm, wherein there seemed to be nothing. "Is our quest to end here?" asked Glewlwyd Gafaelfawr.

"Oh, no," said Taliesin Benbardd; "the hoofs will keep time to the music still."

"Call Drem, the son of Dremidyd," said Arthur.

Drem was such a man that, when the gnat arose in the morning with the sun, he could see her from Gelliwic in Cornwall as far off as Pen Nant Gofid on the confines of hell; and furthermore, he could easily count the hairs of her beard.

"Drem fab Dremidyd," said Arthur; "do you catch sight of anything beyond there?"

Drem looked forth carefully. "Southward and below there," said he, "there is a blacker blackness moving, ten universes away."

"We will ride forward towards it," said Arthur Fawr.

So they leaped their horses out into the abyss; and by reason of the music of Taliesin Benbardd, empty space was equal to a well-paved road for them, and neither better nor worse; and the beat of the hoofs on the darkness kept time to the music.

"Is that which we seek far away now?" asked Arthur.

"Not so far as it was," said Drem fab Dremidyd. So they rode on, singing now to the music.

Far off in the cellar of his planet Ghuggg caught a rumor of it and trembled. "Eh?" said he; "WHAT'S THAT?" He could hardly induce his ears to listen to more than the beating of his heart. "But my heart beat never to such a rhythm as that," said he. He listened further, and groaned.

"Dear help me better," said he; "I know what it is: it is the harping of the Chief Bard of the Universe; and the men of the Island of the Mighty on the march to it. By the stench of the swamp of bottom-most Annwn, it is that!" said he; and grew pale over what would have been his face, had there been much to distinguish it from the gross rotundity in front of him.

"The music of Taliesin Benbardd it is; and he strongly coercing it from the strings of his harp; and the hoofs of the horses of the Arthurians keeping time to it as they pursue me through the abyss!" He was bewildered and amazed; his bones molten in him with terror. Then he mastered himself, and took courage, and planned his defense.

"Come now," said he; "where is my magic to fortify me against trouble? There is that Drem the son of Dremidyd: his sight will be potent against me unless I take to my magic."

So he took himself to it; and croaked thrice like a frog; and thereupon the blackness the Arthurians rode through became a million times blacker, and even more than that. "Sight is useless here," said Drem fab Dremidyd. "The light I saw by has gone out."

"Call Clust fab Clustfeinad," said the Emperor Arthur. When the ant arose from her nest in the morning Clust could hear her footsteps from Esgair Oerfel in Ireland as far as to the borders of space; and furthermore, he could hear the thought in her mind before ever she had uttered it.

"Clust fab Clustfeinad," said Arthur, "are you hearing anything from below and beyond there?"

"A frog croaking I heard—if a frog it was; and a man breathing I hear now—if he is a man. Follow you me, if it please you; and I will lead you to him."

So they rode forward after Clust fab Clustfeinad; and Taliesin Benbardd putting fierce, strong, exultant coercion on the harpstrings, and shaking out the music magnanimously through the night; so that tremendous speed was with their horses.

"Is it far away now?" asked Arthur.

"In my deed to heaven and man, it is not far," said Clust. "It is very near at hand."

"Ah," said Arthur then; "the right fore-hoof of Fflamwen my mare struck against hardness; and it seemed to me that the hardness was cracked."

"Cracked it was; and my genius has come back to me," said Ol fab Olwydd. "I smell the Sapphire Necklace; and it is falling down through space below us."

"In my deed it was cracked; and my sight thereby has come back to me," said Drem fab Dremidyd. "I can see the blackness falling away swiftly below, and a blue light shining out through the crack in it, that has the appearance of shining from thirteen bright amazing sapphires within."

"By the ruby in thy ring it cracked, Lord Arthur," said Clust; "and the music sounding out through the crack is like that of the thirteen Archflautists of heaven; and even better. Hark you now, if it please you!"

They heard the song of the sapphires, and it was as much as seventeen times better than Clust had said; and even more than that. It rose out of the crack in Ghuggg's planet that Fflamwen's hoof had made, and soared and floated out through thirteen universes, spreading hope and delight: the sapphires with hope restored to them were appealing to the Arthurians to deliver them.

"Woe is me, the men of Arthur Emperor are upon me!" sighed Ghuggg in his cellar. "The roof is broken by the rude hoofs of their horses; and their intentions are not good." He forgot the empire he desired to found, and longed only for escape. "I must set my planet to spinning and falling, that I may sink into the swamp on the floor of Annwn and be safe from their loathsome clamor and weapons."

He had fallen on the sapphires to hide the light of them; and now set his globe to spinning and whizzing downwards, swifter than the arrow's flight, than the passage of the light-ray, than the leaping of thought in the mind of a bard. Towards the swamp at the bottom of things he sped it. But the light of the sapphires shone out through his solid ugliness and through the cracked roof as it fell and as the Arthurians pursued it, their horses diving down towards the depths.

"Their object is theft, and reiving and violent robbery," sighed Ghuggg; "woe is me, a tenfold curse on all thieves and reivers! The honest may not enjoy their lawful gains for them!" he sighed; and sped his planet the quicker. But the swifter its fall, the swifter were the war-steeds of the Arthurians in pursuit of it; until the apples of gold at the four corners of their saddle-cloths burned and became molten and shone out through space. "Now I am near the swamp!" he chuckled; and then, looking up, moaned in his terror. "Evil on their beards, they are upon me!"

So his planet whirled downwards, obeying his desire. And there was the swamp not ten leagues below him; and a league and more between him and Drych Ail Cibddar the swiftest of the Arthurians. Down and down whirled Ghuggg, gathering impetus; his native stench and corruption awaited him, near at hand.

"Woe is me, how I am oppressed by the foul effluvia arising from it!" sighed Ol fab Olwydd. Every moment the little planet as it fell shone the brighter: the light from the sapphires ever the more impregnating it.

"Now I am saved, and the Necklace with me!" laughed Ghuggg; "in a moment I splash into the fluid!" And as he said it, the forehoofs of Drych Ail Cibddar's horse struck against his roof again.

Now there are sharp rocks on the Floor of Things, jutting out from the filth and slime there; and it was on one of them the planet struck; and what with the swift impact, and the kick of Drych Ail Cibddar's horse, it burst open and was shattered. Out flopped Ghuggg and dived like a frog, the Necklace about his middle, into the corruption. But Drych Ail Cibddar drew rein in time; and in a second the Arthurians were up with him; and there they halted. The swamp was clearly visible now by the light from the sinking sapphires.

And they blazed out the more the deeper they sank in it. The men of the

Island of the Mighty, watching, presently saw Ghuggg disentangled from them, and float upwards to the surface, charred, dried up and withering away; so that by the time he reached the surface, there was nothing of him to reach it.

"This is a marvel," said Ol fab Olwydd; "the stench is gone, and the air has become sweet and pleasant."

"This is a great marvel," said Drem fab Dremidyd; "for behold you now, the foulness and opacity of it are wasting and clearing; as if it were pure ether below us forevermore."

"In my deed to heaven and man, it is a lovely, bright, astounding marvel!" said Clust son of Clustfeinad; "for music is coming up from the sapphires in the depths like the music of a constellation of noblest stars!"

Arthur looked up and beheld the King of the Nooivray with his court at Gorsedd in the stone circle near the Pleiades; and nothing between but pleasant slopes, wooded and ferny mountains, meadows of cowslips and of gentian.

"King of the Nooivray," he cried, "behold, here is a new constellation of stars; come you now, if it please you, and annex it to the Empire of the Nooivray!"

So those that were in the Gorsedd rode down; and came to where the Arthurians waited; and dismounted there; and the King of the Nooivray embraced the Emperor Arthur; and there was good companionship, warmest friendship, between the men of the Island of the Mighty and the men of the Empire of Heaven. So together they rode down to where the Sapphire Necklace hung, that now was a beautiful constellation of stars: blue, amazing, exquisite islands in infinity. And they annexed them to the Nooivray; and appointed officers of the court to be their rulers and regents. And in this order they rode together from star to star of them, surveying their new dominion, and conversing together pleasantly, and relating to each other the heroic tales of the Island of the Mighty and of the Empire of Heaven; and in this order they sat at feast in the chief palace of the Nwyfre afterwards: that is to say, the Emperor Arthur and the King of the Nooivray; the Blessed Cai and the Regent of Aldebaran; Gwrhyh Gwalstawd Ieithoedd and the King's Heir of Fomalhaut; Greidawl Galldonyd and—

Appendix

• • • • • • • • • • • • • •

Early Stories (1898–1902)

•••••••••••••••••••••••••••••

Apparently Kenneth Morris's first published short story, "Prince Lion of the Sure Hand" was published in two parts in the London theosophical magazine The Crusader *(27 August 1899; 27 September/13 October 1899). At the time of publication, Kenneth Morris had recently turned twenty.*

Some of Morris's early stories were clearly written for the instruction and enjoyment of groups of children studying theosophy. These groups were called Lotus Circles, and were led by a Lotus Mother. Unlike Morris's later stories, these early ones sometimes explicitly refer to H. P. Blavatsky and her successor William Quan Judge, and to Blavatsky's volume The Secret Doctrine.

Prince Lion of the Sure Hand
A Story for Children

You may think, children, that you have only got two mothers— the home one and the Lotus Mother, but this is quite a mistake. You see there's a third, a great fairy who is the mother of everything and everybody. Have you ever seen her? Well, perhaps you have and perhaps not, but anyhow, I can tell you this much, that every flower or leaf or blade of grass you see is a little piece of this Great Mother's dress, and she herself is behind it somewhere so that her children may always have something to remember her by.

What is her name? Some people call her Mother Nature, and some people have other names for her, but in this story she is called Arianrod because once on a time, in a land where there are great purple mountains always listening to the sea washing and lapping against the rocks down at her feet, the Great Mother used to be a queen of that land, and she liked people to call her Queen Arianrod, and that means the Shining Giver, because you know that it is she that gives all good gifts.

Now some people have stupid ways of giving you anything, but the Great Mother always knows quite well how to do it. She manages it this way. She never gives anything to anybody unless she knows he wants it really, and has earned it.

Well, at that time one of her sons was a young boy and of course he was a prince, only I can't tell you what his name was, simply because he hadn't got a name at all. And the reason for that was that no one of the Great Mother's children can ever have a true proper name until he or she has earned it, because it is the Mother that gives names, and you know how *she* does things.

So this young prince, although he was a great strong boy with long golden-red hair down on his shoulders, was thinking all the time how he should get a name, and at last he was getting quite sad because he couldn't think of the right plan.

So at last he thought he would go to his big brother, Gwydion, and ask him. And right here I must tell you that no one will ever be able to get his name unless he finds out this same big brother, Gwydion, who is always looking out for a chance to help anyone.

So Gwydion thought a bit, and then he took the boy by the hand, and went with him down the mountain side, and over the long green fields and down by the sea, and across the long yellow sands and over the rocks until they came to where they could see a great castle overlooking the sea, and that castle was called Caer Arianrod, and in it lived the great queen Arianrod.

And when Arianrod saw them coming, she looked at them, and she knew what they wanted, and she knew too that the boy had not done anything yet that she could give him a name for. So when they came to the castle, she went down to meet them, and said that she could not give the boy a name then, he must earn it first.

So Gwydion took the boy back home again, and took him to a Lotus Group every week, and taught him a whole lot of lovely things about helping, and sharing, and working, and being kind to everything, and when some time had passed, he thought that the Great Mother Arianrod would give him a name then.

Now this big strong brother, Gwydion, has a wonderful stick or wand, and because of the power of this wand there is nothing he can't do if he sets his mind on doing it. He can do a lot of things with that wand.

So one day Gwydion took the little prince by the hand, and they went down to the sands by the sea, and there they picked up seaweed and wet green sedge that was floating on the tops of the waves, and Gwydion waved his wand over them, and there, instead of seaweed, was a little boat, and there was a great piece of fine leather in the boat and all the tools used by shoemakers, and instead of two princes, one a man and the other a boy, there were two cobblers, and they were the boy and Gwydion, but *you* would not have known who they were.

Then they got into the boat, and rode along the shore till they came to Caer Arianrod.

There they went on shore, and sat down where they could see the castle, and began to make shoes. For in those days it was a sad thing for anyone if he was ashamed to work, and the noble old kings and princes could make boots, and coats, and dig as well as anyone.

So when Arianrod looked out she saw these two cobblers on the sand, and she knew who they were, and what they wanted. So she went down to see what the boy could do, and whether he deserved a name. And then they made her a pair of boots, and she saw that he could work, and work well too, and she was pleased with that.

Then a little wren flew down and sat on the edge of the boat that was floating on the sea, and while Gwydion was putting the boots on the queen's feet, the boy saw the wren, and took up a bow and an arrow, and knelt down on the sand and took aim.

When Arianrod saw this, she thought for a moment he was going to hurt the wren, and that she certainly couldn't give him a name; but no, he aimed between the bird's legs, and away the arrow flew, and between the bird's legs, and away over the sea and through a wave or two, and then fell into the water, and the little wren flew away without so much as being scratched.

And when Arianrod saw this she was full of delight, for then she knew that he could work and that he could use a bow and arrow, and that he would not hurt a bird even. So she turned to Gwydion:

"This Lion of yours," said she, "has a Sure Hand." And that way she gave the boy a name. For always after that he was called Prince Lion of the Sure Hand, and a noble name it was, and well it fitted him.

As soon as ever Arianrod had given him the name, Gwydion stood up and waved his wand again, and the boat and the leather were gone, and there was just seaweed floating on the top of a long, green, gentle wave that came rolling in till it nearly touched their feet, and Gwydion and the boy were princes, and not like shoemakers any more. Then Arianrod looked at her son, and Lion thought that her great, grey, wonderful eyes were the most beautiful things in the whole world; and she was looking into his eyes, and away into the real boy inside them, because, you know, the real boy or girl lives away inside you somewhere, and it takes a great and clever person to be able to see it at all, and of course Arianrod is one of the few who are great enough, and that you will know.

While she was looking at him she saw a thing in his mind and in his heart, and that thing was that he was longing to wear armor, and have a sword and a spear. She saw another thing there, too, and that was that they would not be for good things to him if he had them, and that he had not yet won them for himself. For you know how great Arianrod gives her gifts—nothing given unless deserved.

"Ah, Lion!" said she, "it is your name you have earned, and a good name it is, but what will you be doing if I give you arms? You might hurt yourself with them, or you might hurt somebody else that should not be hurt, and that would be worse still, if you had them now before you have earned them and know how to use them. But I will give them to you when I can, and you know there is no one at all that you can have them from but me."

So Lion went away, and Gwydion with him, and he was rather sad for not having arms. Because you see there were then a lot of things that had to be killed (as there are now, too), unbrotherhood giants, and things called bad thoughts that you can't see now, but that I suppose they could in those days—perhaps because there were less of them—nasty things that get messing around and trying to poison people and worrying some people awfully—aye, and there were a few dragons, too, I shouldn't wonder. And of course when Arianrod gives any one a sword and a shield and spear and helmet she expects him to start off ridding the world of these nasty things, and you bet she won't give them unless she feels quite sure about it.

So, as they went along, "Gwydion," said Lion, "help you me to earn these arms!" "Aye!" said the other, "help you I will."

So they went on to a place away from the sea where there are great mountains, that are looking up from their great purple heads and wondering about the sky; and lower down there are fields that stretch far away so you don't know where they stop, and little tiny streams and marshes and long green rushes with brown tufts on them;—just the kind of place the fairies we call the Children of Beauty love to dance in of a summer night. And there Gwydion stayed, at Dinas Dinllef, and there he set to showing Lion things and teaching all about helping and sharing. And there the boy became so swift that he could chase the swiftest of the wild horses that were running over the mountains in those parts, and catch them, and so strong that he could tame them with his own hands; and I should not wonder if he didn't teach *them* things, too, to talk to him with the heart talk, like a certain little dog you know about does. And Gwydion taught him to make fair and noble songs, such songs that if anyone saw them he would have to sing them, even if he had never sung before in his life. And from the way the mountains were always looking up to the sky he came to know one thing, and from the way they sent down their streams and with them their soft, sweet song to the valleys he learnt another, and soon he got thinking that after all the arms would be no good to *him,* and then that if he had them they would be a lot of good to other people. And then he wanted them more and more. So one day they set out from Dinas Dinllef, Gwydion and he, and this time they were in new bodies again, for Gwydion had waved his wand over them, and now they appeared as two bards from another land, a land that is called the Land of the Sea-Song, and that because the sea is always singing around it, and a merry tune it is the sea sings there. And because they were bards, that is men who used to teach people all their lessons by just singing to them, as soon as they got to Caer Arianrod the doors were open to them, and fine feasts were set before them, and they sat all that evening with Arianrod, telling her stories and singing her songs.

Arianrod looked into Lion's heart, in through his eyes, and she saw that it was a golden light that shone out over his breast, and "that," said she to herself, "is that there is a breastplate for him." And she saw, too, that there were bright lights playing over his head; "they are the plumes for his helmet," said she. So then, when bed-time came, she knew her son was to have armor, and to have it that night. And glad she was for that.

So, when Gwydion was in his room, he took his wand, and you should have heard what happened! For there was the sea all covered with white-sailed ships, and, in the ships, men with lifted, gleaming swords, which they were clashing upon their golden, shining shields, and over the land as far as you could see were tents, and armed men in them, and all these were for attacking the castle.

The great mother smiled, and she brought two suits of armor, two long spears with twenty golden nails in each of them, two shields of skin, iron-studded, two great and beautiful swords. "Art thou for fighting for me this night?" she said. "Indeed, Queen," said Lion, "for thee will I fight." So she, knowing well, gave him the armor; and many a time he used it, and there was more of sunshine in the land because of Prince Lion of the Sure Hand, and more of blueness in the sky, and more of song everywhere. And there is more, too, because of the blossoming of every Lotus Bud. They are connected, you see.

While not exactly a short story, "The Epic of Wales" is at the same time a brief retelling as well as a theosophical explication of the main stories of the Mabinogion. *It is a vital illumination of Morris's approach to the* Mabinogion *materials, which he would later rework into his complementary novels* The Fates of the Princes of Dyfed *and* Book of the Three Dragons. *"The Epic of Wales" was published in four parts in the Dublin magazine* The International Theosophist *(15 March; 13 April; 13 June; and 13 August 1899). It was signed with the Welsh form of Morris's name, Ceinydd Morus.*

The Epic of Wales

I

*I*f it is true that Theosophy was at one time the religion of Britain, we may naturally expect to find traces of it in the literature and folklore of the old Britons. And we need not be disappointed. In the Welsh *Mabinogion,* as in books of Eastern legend, the ancient story of the soul is told.

There are two principal cycles of tales in the *Mabinogion,* as well as some odd stories which belong to neither. Of these cycles the older tells of pre-Christian Britain, and the other of the days of Arthur. But Taliesin appears in both cycles.

The first tale of all is called "Pwyll, Prince of Dyfed," and the third and fourth tales of the first cycle are really continuations of this. It relates how Pwyll*, while hunting one day in Glyn Cuch, outrode his followers in the pursuit of a stag, and reached the borders of Annwn, the underworld. There he was met by a pack of strange dogs; he heard them barking, and though he had seen every kind of dog in the world, he had known none with voices such as they had, nor any of the same color. These hounds with white bodies and red ears were chasing a stag; Pwyll called them off, and set his own dogs to kill it. Then entered the master of those dogs, Arawn, king of the underworld. Pwyll, he said, had insulted him by killing the stag he had been hunting. To wipe out the offence, Pwyll was obliged to leave his own kingdom for a year and a day, and, taking on the form and mind of Arawn, rule over the underworld. At the end of that time he was to fight with and kill

*Pwyll is a Welsh word, meaning intellect, reason, the lower mind.

Hafgan (vanity, *tamas*), Arawn's enemy; then he should return to Dyfed. Pwyll accepted, and lived in Annwn until the time had passed, and Hafgan was slain.

On returning to his own country, the Prince found that it had never been better governed or more prosperous than while he had been away. And the next incident in the story shews what changes had come about in himself resulting from his conquest of Hafgan.

A few days after his return, he went out hunting with his courtiers. They came to a hill. "Lord," said one, "this is the hill called Gorsedd Arberth,* and there is about it this peculiarity—that no one who seats himself on the top of it can come thence without violence, or without seeing a wonder." "Of a truth," said Pwyll, "I shall sit down on the top of it." And while he sat there they saw a woman riding towards them on a great white horse. Golden ornaments were upon her that gleamed in the sunlight. She rode slowly. They had never seen one like her before. And Pwyll thought she was the most beautiful woman in the whole world. He told one of his knights to ride to meet her, and ask who she was; but while he was mounting his horse she rode past. The swiftest steed in Britain he rode, but he could not come up with her, though all the while she rode as slowly as before.

The next day and the next, and for many days, he returned to Gorsedd Arberth, but he could never find the horse that could come up with that lady, though she never quickened her pace. At last he rode after her himself, and, after a long chase, called to her, begging her to stop. "Lord," said she, "it would have been well if thou hadst spoken to me when first thou sawest me. Rhianon, daughter of Hefeydd Hen, am I, and long have I waited for thee to call me, for I have sworn to have no husband but thee." Pwyll was to come to the court of her father at the end of a year; there she would marry him.

The year passed, and Pwyll repaired to the court of Hefeydd the Ancient; and that court is nowhere in the Britain which is visible. There, while the marriage feast was going on, he lost his bride for a year by listening to the requests of Gwawl† the son of Clud, and had to return to Dyfed without her. Gwawl was a suitor for the hand of Rhianon, but it was for her to marry Pwyll, and not one of her own race. So that when this second year was passed, Pwyll was able to win her back from Gwawl, by a stratagem, even though her marriage with the latter was then being solemnized.

In Dyfed, when Pwyll and Rhianon had been married three years, the nobles began to complain that the queen was yet childless, and implored the king to put her away, and take some wife of mortal race like himself. But this Pwyll would not consent to do. At last a child was born. Six

---

*Gorsedd Arberth means the "Throne of sublime perfection." It is here the pineal gland.
†Gwawl is the Welsh for light (*Satwa*).

women were watching in the chamber of Rhianon on the night that child was born, but they all slept at their posts. In the morning the child had disappeared. "Women," said the queen, "what has become of my son?" "Ask us not where thy son is, lady," said they, "we could not prevent thee from destroying him." For fear of being punished for sleeping they accused Rhianon of having made away with the child. And she preferred the penalty of the crime to arguing with them.

At that time Teyrnion Twrf Fliant, lord of Gwent Iscoed, had a mare which used to foal every May eve, and in the morning no one knew what had become of the foal. One year Teyrnion determined to watch himself in the stable. The mare foaled, and that was the most beautiful foal in the world. Then while watching he heard a loud noise without, and a great claw was thrust in through the window, and snatched the foal. Teyrnion struck the claw with his sword, and rushed out in pursuit. Finding nothing, he returned, and there where the foal had been standing, lying on the floor of the stable, was a beautiful baby. "This is the son of a great king," he said. He adopted the boy, and called him Gwri Wallt Euryn, because of his radiant golden hair.

When Gwri had grown able to talk and walk, Teyrnion, who had heard of Rhianon's punishment, observed his likeness to Pwyll. "There was no one in Gwent who did not know him for the son of Pwyll Pen Annwn," says the story. And after, when they brought him to Pwyll and Rhianon, no one failed to recognize him there. While they were feasting in joy that night, Teyrnion spoke of the boy, using the name they had called him in Gwent. "Not so," said Pwyll, "Pryderi fab Pwyll* shall the child be called."

Thus the first part of what is really a trilogy ends, after mentioning the death of Pwyll. In the second part, called Manawyddan Fab Llyr, the place of Pwyll as king of Dyfed,† and husband of Rhianon is taken by Manawyddan, son of Llyr; and this is suggestive of how the lower mind becomes one with the higher, for Manawyddan is translated Manas the Knower, Mana and Manas being the same word. Thus Knowledge takes the place of Reason.

The Tale of Manawyddan shows how he, Pryderi, and Rhianon suffer from and eventually triumph over the last of the three great enemies of their race, Gwawl the Son of Clud *(Satwa)*. Thus the threefold Higher Man becomes "free from the three qualities." They were living at Arberth, their chief court, and ruling Dyfed. One morning they looked out, and saw that the whole land had been laid under an enchantment. No people could be seen in the towns. Where populous villages had been, there were deer and

---

*Meditation, the son of Reason. Rhianon is intuition *(Buddhi)*, and Teyrnion, who rescued the child from the claws of desire, is, I think, the Will. This rescue is the overcoming of *Rajas*.

†Dyfed (rhymes with beloved), the modern Carmarthen, Cardigan and Pembroke Shires.

wild boars. No work was done in the fruitful fields other than the nibbling of the field-mice, and over all was a magical silence which they could not comprehend.

For some years this lasted, and they went into England and worked as shoemakers in many of the principal cities; and this was just before Cæsar first landed in Britain. The story relates that these heroes were the best shoemakers that ever lived, and there is not a note of surprise in the book that, kings as they were, they should have done this. Indeed, running all through the *Mabinogion* is the motif of the nobility of labor. "The knife is in the meat, and the mead is in the horn, and no man may enter the court of King Arthur excepting a craftsman bearing his craft," says the porter at the gate to Culhwch, when he came first to his kinsman's court. And the same phrase is repeated, Homerlike, many times in that story. But this is a digression.

They returned at last to Dyfed, but the land still lay under the magician's spell, and Pryderi was lured away by a wild boar through the gates of a castle, where he, and afterwards Rhianon were held spellbound until Manawyddan was able to release them. Thus he did it. His fields had been plundered by an army of mice, and eventually he succeeded in catching one of the little robbers. Knowing through his wisdom that the mouse was a creature of magic, he determined to hang it. He set up the first beam of a gallows for it, when a scholar came by, and entreated him to spare its life. "It is beneath your dignity, lord, to do this." But Manawyddan refused to listen to him and the scholar passed on. Then came a priest, and urged him more strongly, and at last a bishop rode by, and offered him large sums of money for the mouse, but it was of no avail. Only on these conditions would Manawyddan spare her—that the enchantment of Dyfed should cease, and that Pryderi and Rhianon should be freed. The seeming bishop, being himself the enchanter (the seeming mouse was his wife), complied, and so they became united once more, and freed from the last of the three qualities.

The third story—that of Math fab Mathonwy, "the man of illusion and phantasy"—does not tell much concerning our heroes, but an incident in it is the fall and death of Pryderi: which in some ways has a resemblance or correspondence to Wagner's *Götterdämerung*. Rhianon and Manawyddan have vanished from the scenes, and Pryderi is left alone. He became entrapped by the black magic of Gwydion, the son of Don, and gave him a gift which he had received from Arawn, King of Annwn. For this the protection of Arawn, which Pwyll gained by his sojourn in Annwn and conquest of Hafgan, was withdrawn from his son. Pryderi too late discovered his error. He led an army into Gwynedd against Math, King of Gwynedd, and Gwydion his nephew. But the men of the south were defeated, and, after the battle, Pryderi challenged Gwydion to single combat. A beautiful passage in the Welsh describes this combat and the death of the golden-haired hero. "They fought. And by the power of the prowess, and rage and magical might of Gwydion, slain was Pryderi. In Maen Tyfiawg, high o'er Melenryd, slew he him, and there is his grave to this day."

But Gwydion was to receive his reward. Math was a greater enchanter than he. "If a secret was breathed to the winds, the winds would tell it to Math." He found out the treachery of his nephew, and hurled him down into animal forms—first one, and then another. A purely Druidic reference this, for they taught that the result of great evil was that a man should lose his human soul and descend again into the animal kingdoms. And Math was the supreme magician; he learnt his magic from Menw ab y Tairgwaedd* himself.

Thus ends this version of

The Drama of the Hidden Soul,
Which tells of death and life and fate,
And what dwells under night and day—
Which God for countless ages sate
To watch his countless angels play.

II

This title, "The Epic of Wales," is in some respects undoubtedly a good one for the *Mabinogion* of the famous *Llyfr Goch Hergest,* in others not so good. Except for an occasional song, the stories are in prose, it is true, and with exceptions, they are distinct from each other, and tell of different heroes. The Mabinogi of Culhwch and Olwen is, as Rénan says, a complete epic in itself. For all that there is beyond doubt a vein of the same character and purpose running all through them; they are "the highest expression of the Celtic genius,"† and may go to form the bible of the Celtic race.

They have a certain interest too, as the originals of the romantic, as distinguished from the classic and Gothic, legends of all Europe. The Arthurian legend, to become almost universal, to be retold and spoiled in the telling by thousands of imitators from Malory to Tennyson, is found here in its native purity and beauty, without a thought in it all of uncleanness, such as there is so much of in the imitators. One who has read Tennyson's "Merlin and Vivien" is struck with amazement on reading the original version of the story in the *Mabinogion,* at the way the modern poet dragged a beautiful and mystical theme in the mire of petty, unmagical modernness. Parsifal, again, is the fruit of a tree rooted in the *Mabinogion;* he was Percival le Gallois; or as we say, Peredur mab Efrog, one of the sons of the king of the

---

*Menw, son of the three sounds (The Manu), so called from his having been the first to awaken out of the slumber of the worlds, when God chanted His own Threefold Name, which called all things into being and life from latent being and latent life according to Druidism.
†Rénan, *Essay on the Poetry of the Celtic Races.*

north. But in this case the process has been different—where Tennyson debased, Wagner exalted, re-arranged and organized, so that it might be easy to imagine that Parsifal and Peredur were different characters, different legends. That they are the same, a study of the Welsh story in a possible future article may show.

Like Myrddin, spell-bound in the forest of Broceliande, is the reader of the *Mabinogion,* but held by the glamour and beauty of the stories. One may read through page after page, not seeking or seeing any depth of meaning, but content to roam with the hero over sunlit lands, where every stone, weed or creature has a proper name and can talk like a human being. But ever and anon, as in those olden days the Maid of the Woods appeared to foretell some wondrous thing and then as suddenly vanished away, a few sentences occur revealing the true import of all that has been read, or else the story turns round and becomes suddenly the veiling of some new and unexpected mystery. It is so in the story of Branwen, the daughter of Llyr, which belongs to the earliest cycle. Almost to the end of this story we find only mystic hints and bardic allusions cunningly wrought into the fabric of the narrative; then with the death of Bran Fendigaid there is a change and we are brought face to face with a legend of the fall, curiously obvious to any who know aught of Druidic cosmogony. This Mabinogi demands our attention.

Bran the Blessed, son of Llyr Llediaith,* was King of Britain, and his sister Branwen was the wife of Matholwch, King of Ireland. She was ill-treated by Matholwch and a starling flew over to Britain and told the King of that ill-treatment. He led an army into Ireland, and because of the magic of the Irish every man in that army was slain except seven, and Bran himself was mortally wounded. Then comes the more definitely theosophical part, but before noticing that, the foregoing needs some attention. It is all connected with the mystic cauldron of Ceridwen. In the cauldron are three precious drops which have magical virtue; the rest of the liquid that seethes in it is deadly poison. Under the cauldron are nine fairies silently blowing the fire. The dead who are thrown into that vessel are restored to life—but as dumb men—they cannot speak again. Many and many a great one of old was bathed in the cauldron, and drew their magic and power from the cauldron Queen. When they arose from it, wrong was unknown to them, none of the lower spirits could work them harm.

> *Serene they rose—Bards, prophets, heroes, kings,*
> *And mighty ones who in the mountains sleep,*
> *Slayers of dragons, men who wielded wings*
> *And soared where we, their children, only creep.*

---

*Llyr Llediaith. Llyr is the Boundless Deep; Llediaith means defective utterance (applied now to the slow English accent). Complete utterance comes with Bran, the First Logos.

From it the bards drew their inspiration. "From the cauldron of Ceridwen I obtained the Shining Breath," sang Taliesin, the Chief of Song.

The meaning of it? Perhaps it is, as Rénan suggests, the Celtic version of Jamshyd's cup, to become in later days and other lands, with the latter, the Holy Grail. The candidates for initiation into the mysteries become as dead men, in the cauldron they return to life. But they are dumb, they cannot speak of what they have seen.

This cauldron was given to Bran by the wizard Llashar Llaesgyfnewid. He in turn gave it as a wedding gift to Matholwch, and, having it in possession, the Irish prevailed until one broke the cauldron—then the British. At last, of all the warriors of the two islands only seven Britons were left—Pryderi, Manawyddan, Glifieri, Eil Taran, *Taliesin,* Ynawg Gruddieu, and Heilyn, the son of Gwyn the Ancient.

And here the story changes, and becomes clearly and evidently mystical; nor is there doubt of its meaning. Remember the head of Padmapani and many another legend from many another land. Here is the tale:

"Then Bran the Blessed prepared them to cut off his head. 'And take you the head,' said he, 'and bear it to the White Hill in London and bury it there with the face towards France. Long shall you be on your journey. At Harlech you shall sit seven years at a feast, and the birds of Rhianon shall sing to you there. And the head shall be equal to a companion to you, and all shall be well with you as ever it was when I was alive. In Gwalas in Penfro you shall be fourscore years. There shall you stay, and the head with you, until you open the door that faces towards Aber Henfelen and towards Cornwall. When that door is opened you can stay there no longer, but must go on to London and bury the head.'

"Then they cut off the head, and those seven set out with it, and Branwen was the eighth with them. At Aber Alaw in Tal Ebolion they came to land, and there they stayed to rest. Branwen looked out over Ireland and over the Isle of the Mighty, for they could see both islands. 'Alas!' said she, 'on me is the sorrow of all my race. Evil has come upon two green isles because of me.' And she sighed, and sighing she broke her heart. There they made her a grave, and buried her by the side of the river Alaw.

"Then went they on to Harlech and sat down and began to feast. Came three birds and began to sing to them some sweet song. Of all the songs they had ever heard, harsh seemed each one compared to that. They saw the birds without; far away they were, and high o'er the sea. Yet they could see them and hear them as plainly as if they had been near at hand. At that feast they sat for seven years. At the end of the seventh year they set out for Gwalas in Penfro. A fair and kingly place was there, high above the sea. On it was a great hall, and into the hall they went. Two doors in the hall were open, but the third door faced towards Aber Henfelen and Cornwall, and was shut 'Look you,' said Manawyddan, 'this is the door we must not open. So they sat down and began their feast.

"For eighty summers in the hall they stayed
And feasted, high above the curling waves.
For eighty winters feasting there they made,
While roared the waters 'neath them in the caves.

"For eighty years in Gwalas as they sate
And told old tales of years long passed away,
Their strength and vigour did no more abate
Than as if all those years were one short day.

"And every day the head of Bran the king
Than all the others nobler stories told;
And every eve the head would with them sing,
And all was well as e'er in days of old.

"And though they sang and feasted all that time
No surfeit came on them, nor any ill,
And still their hair was black with manhood's prime,
And the rich food was spread before them still.

"But when those eighty years had swiftly sped
Heilyn, the son of Gwyn, arose and swore—
'Some direful evil come on me,' he said,
'Unless I open now that southmost door!'

"He strode towards the door and flung it wide,
And stood and gazed across the tossing waves;
In moaned the wet wind o'er the rising tide.
With screams of sea-gulls from the hollow caves.

"Then became manifest to them all that had ever gone from them, all the friends and loved ones whom they had ever lost, and every evil they had ever suffered—most of all, the loss of their lord. From that hour they could rest no longer, but set out with the head towards London . . . and buried the head there in the White Hill."

For the better understanding of this legend a word is needed on the Druidic system. There are seven wanderers—the Bardd Glâs and other Cymric adepts taught that man was a sevenfold being. Indeed, with the help of a good Welsh etymological dictionary it would probably not be difficult to find that each of these seven heroes had a name suggestive or descriptive of each of the various parts of man's interior nature respectively.*

*e.g. Manawyddan = a Higher or Divine Mind, etc.

There are three principal stages on this journey—so among the Druids the three worlds. Ceugant, infinity, the abode of God the unmanifest, is the first. Out of it came the seven with the living head of their lord—the Supreme Spirit. Before they started they knew all that should happen on the way. The second world is Gwynfyd, the abode of bliss. Here they were for seven years free from all sorrow—the three white birds of Rhianon singing to them the while. Then to Abred, the place of learning—into the hall of the body. The door looking southward they are warned not to open; Heilyn ab Gwyn opens it, and sorrow comes upon them. The head can communicate with them no more; they must go on to London and bury it there.

One feels in attempting to translate these old tales, of whatever nationality, into the language of science (in its broadest sense), that it is really a sad thing such a translation should be needed. They were never meant to be interpreted in words, but to be read directly by the soul in its own language—that of imagination. The interpretation *should* lie in themselves; it *must* do so mainly. Back of all religion is mysticism, imagination is the life of every science. Arjuna knew the Supreme when he had seen Him in all His myriad forms displayed. But it was that Supreme who, as Krishna, said—"No man knoweth It, even though he hath heard it described." In the Mabinogi, as in the Wagneric drama, a picture is displayed; through the imagination a vast teaching is shewn to the soul; the soul accepts it, and even the brain is made to feel dimly that something has happened of moment, and that itself is really something or pertaining to something greater than it knew of before. How gladly then must we hail the work of that Leader who is bringing back the sacred drama, through it reviving, directing, and nourishing the great world's imagination, and restoring the holy mysteries to an unmysterious age.

III
The Arthurian Cycle Romances

So much for the *Mabinogion,* properly so called. Professor Rhys, who is nothing if not a learned scholar, shows that the four tales of what we have called the first cycle are the only genuine *Mabinogion,* and that the tales and romances of the *Llyfr Goch* and of Lady Guest's work have no right in reality to be known, as they commonly are, by that title. Mabinogi (pl. Mabinogion), he explains, was a purely bardic term, possibly connected with the sun god Mabon, and he shows that the *Mabinogion* indeed formed the sacred book of the bards. When Prof. Rhys admits so much, we may put a certain trust in it, as he is one of the most helio-mythological of men. There are also evidences of this fact in the book itself. "He who is chief, let him be a bridge," is a saying in the druidic schools to the present day—a saying of profound significance, too, if one thinks about it. And that saying is a text from the Mabinogi of Branwen ferch Llyr, which the great bard Iolo Morganwg (present century) explains mystically. The chief is indeed the bridge between Those who are above and the disciples—the saying is *apropos* in the Universal Brotherhood, as it was in the Gorsedd.

Still these same tales and romances, such as the History of Taliesin, the story of Peredur who was Parsifal, or the romance of Culhwch and Olwen possess a vast amount of interest to mystics. Indeed, a new light is thrown on Arthur, and in these stories we come to see who he was. Not alone a tribal monarch now; no "hallowed sovereign of romance" now; but in truth, according to the belief of a people, Arthur the emperor the undying, lord of the body and of the senses.

In the tale of Geraint ab Erbin we learn that Glewlwyd Gafaelfawr was the chief porter at Arthur's court, but that he only attended at the gates on rare occasions. Seven noble knights under him divided the duties between them. Two of these seven are thus described:—

"Drem, the son of Dremidyd—(when the gnat arose in the morning with the sun, Drem could see it from Gelli Wic, in Cornwall, as far off as Pen Blathaon, in North Britain)."

"Clust, the son of Clustfeinydd—(though he were buried seven cubits beneath the earth, he could hear the ant fifty miles off rise from her nest in the morning." "He could hear the dew in June drop from the reeds and the grass in all the four quarters of the world)."

Sight, the son of Seeing, and Ear, the son of Hearing, are thus two of the porters, and the rest, though undescribed, are evidently the other five senses.

Looked at from this standpoint we may have some hope of seeing in these Arthurian stories something nobler and fairer than mere history, though there is history in them too. Who shall say where history ends and myth begins? What is the dividing line between them? All these heroes I doubt not were living men as well as everliving principles, or rather they were the former and represent the latter. If not so, their dates and deeds would never have been fixed so definitely, by tradition, may be, of which, as of every other good thing, there is no hide-bound proof to torture men's souls and cramp their imaginations, but still in a manner definitely fixed; nor would a thousand places have borrowed their names. And if they do not represent eternal principles their memory could never have lived, as it has, in the heart of a nation, dwelt on lovingly by every bard, the heroes of every storyteller. Thus there are two Arthurs; the Arthur of mythology and romance, who is the human soul, the "warrior," and the Arthur of history, who because of the luster which has gathered round his name, because of the power that made this Cymric King a world hero, has been supposed to be a re-incarnation of Hu Gardarn, the greatest of the gods. In the life of a nation there are cycles as in the life of a man. Here we see the twilight of a dying golden age, the last fading memories of a happier time which are also the promise of the first dawn which precedes the brightness of the morning.

*"I will foretell, in a song, the re-coming
Of Modred, and Arthur the leader of armies.
Again shall they rush to the battle of Camlan
And but seven shall escape from the two days' conflict."*

So sang Myrddin the Wild when he was dwelling alone with the seven score sprites in the woods of Celyddon. Jesus and Judas, Arthur and Modred, with every human body that is born, they return to the earth; again and again the old battle is fought on many a field of Camlan; again and again the Dragon King slays his traitor nephew, and himself, mortally wounded, is borne away into the darkness.

*"In the red sunset as I watched awhile
A hero fell beside a traitor slain;
Arthur and Modred passed from Prydain's Isle.
But Arthur, passing, swore to come again."*

Turning now to the romance of Culhwch and Olwen, we find in its general scheme a greater community with more familiar stories from other lands, but in its details a large originality and newness.

Cilydd, son of Prince Celyddon, some years after the death of his first wife, married again. Culhwch, the child of his first marriage, excited the jealousy of his step-mother. To get rid of him, she mentioned in his hearing, Olwen, the daughter of Yspaddaden Pencawr, a lady whom many heroes had sought to win, but none had ever succeeded. The boy had no sooner heard the name than he fell in love with its possessor. At all costs he must find Olwen. No one knew where she lived, yet he knew that he should find her. To the court of his cousin, the Emperor Arthur, he must go. Arthur alone could help him.

So to the court he went, and by all the knights and ladies of Britain he adjured Arthur to grant him this boon. If it were not Caledfwlch, Arthur's sword, or Ehangwen, his hall, or Prydwen, his ship of glass he asked for, Culhwch should have it. So the king chose out six of his knights and bade them go with Culhwch to find the castle of Yspaddaden, Head of Giants. At last they found it, and Culhwch first saw Olwen. "More yellow was her hair than the flower of the broom, and her skin was whiter than the foam of the wave, and fairer were her hands and her fingers than the blossoms of the wood anemone amidst the spray of the meadow fountains. . . . Wherever she trod, four white trefoils sprang up and blossomed in her footsteps."

Now Yspaddaden Pencawr was a great inert tyrant. He slew his foes with poisoned darts, but he himself could not die until his daughter was won—the day of her marriage was doomed to be his last. They found him seated in the hall of his castle, his beard and hair grown down to his feet. Nine porters and nine dogs guarded his door, silently they slew them all before they could enter. They told him what they had come for. "Where are my servants?" said he. "Raise now the forks that are under my eyelids, that I may see what manner of son-in-law is this." Then he bade them go and return again the next day to receive his answer. While they were going he took up one of the three poisoned darts that lay at his side, and threw it at them. Bedwyr caught it and threw it back, piercing with it the knee of the giant. "A cursed ungentle son-in-law truly! I shall never again walk without limping! Cursed be the smith who wrought that dart, and the fire in which it was wrought. So sharp it is!" Three times they came to him, and each time the scene was repeated. While they were going each day he threw a dart at them, but each day one of them caught it and threw it back, piercing him the second time through the breast, and the third time through his eye. But though those darts were deadly with poison, they only stung him like the bite of a gnat. The fourth time he told them what they must do before Culhwch could marry Olwen. They must cut his hair with the comb and scissors that were between the ears of the Twrch Trwyth, king of the wild boars. They must shave him with the tusk of Ysgrithyrwen Benbaedd, another boar monarch. To hunt these boars they must obtain the services of great warriors and hunters from all parts of Europe. They must find Mabon the son of Modron, who had been stolen away from between his mother and the wall ages ago, when he was only three nights old, and had never been heard of since. They must obtain the blood of a witch who lived on the confines of hell. They must remove a mountain, and plough the land where it had stood, with Nynnio and Peibio, the oxen of Hu Gadarn, wherewith Hu, the eldest of the gods, had drawn the Afanc, the great crocodile of the Lake of Floods, out of its home.*

To every one of these demands Culhwch, never doubting, answers—"It will be easy for me to accomplish this, although thou mayest think that it will not be easy." For he had found him who had sworn to obtain that which he sought. Arthur's sword Caledfwlch never struck a blow amiss. If anything could be obtained, Arthur's help could obtain it.

So they went away, and one feat after another was performed until all the quests were accomplished. Last of all the Twrch Trwyth was hunted; he and his seven pigs waged long war with all the armies of Arthur, but at length the comb and scissors were obtained. Finally came the shaving of Yspaddaden, Head of Giants. Culhwch took the tusk and shaved him; not only his bristling beard and whiskers he shaved, but stripped the flesh also clean from his cheeks and his chin. "Art thou shaved now, man?" said he. "Yea, I am shaved." Then Culhwch was married to Olwen, and as was his doom, Yspaddaden Pencawr died.

In the interpretation of this story, the main thread of the plot is easy

*See *The Secret Doctrine* on the constellation of Makara or the crocodile.

enough. Culhwch hears the name only of Olwen, but this name awakens in him titanic moods. It is the first realization of the divine presence within, which arouses strange old dreams and vaster aspirations than have ever before been known. Only with the help of Arthur can he obtain Olwen. We are reminded of Tannhäuser. "Stay for Elizabeth," says one, and the name is a spell potent to cause Tannhäuser to begin to seek redemption. Wolfram the mediator takes the place of Arthur. Yspaddaden—what is he but the dweller on the threshold, whose death is destined to be on the day his daughter is united to the hero who is strong and brave to win her? All this is clear enough, but what of the details, the various quests? Are they only exuberances of poetic imagination, or are they there because they are bound to be just where they are? I think the latter. There is, for instance, the seeking for Mabon (the Apollo Maponos of Gaul), and the final freeing him from the stone prison where he lay enchained. Culhwch and his companions came to the place where was the ousel of Cilgwri, and prayed her say if she knew aught of Mabon. She had lived there so long that a smiths' anvil there had been worn away entirely by her pecking—one peck she had given it daily when dusk was growing grey. But in all that time she had never heard of Mabon. Still, she would bring Arthur's ambassadors to a creature older than herself. But the stag of Redynfre knew nought of Mabon, nor did the Owl of Cwm Cawlwyd, who was formed long ere he was. The eagle of Gwern Abwy perhaps might know, for he had lived so long that a rock from which he used to peck the stars had been worn away by his talons and by grey old Time till now it was only a span high. The eagle had a friend who had heard of the lost one. He brought them to the salmon of Llyn Lliw, and the salmon, who was even older and wiser than the eagle, took two of them on his great shoulders and brought them up the Seven to a dark prison, where they found Mabon, and from which they eventually freed him. What sun god prisoned in the heart of man is this, that must be freed before he can be united to Olwen? And what waters must we be guided through on the shoulders of what wise old salmon? Ah! I think there is a deep mystery in all these things, and that we too go upon these adventures, though the sun which shone so brightly then is now veiled a little by the mists of a greyer age. But those very mists, maybe, are only the mists of the earliest moments of the dawn.

IV

This is the tale of Taliesin, Chief of the Bards. There was a man named Tegid Foel, and Ceridwen was his wife. Three children they had. The youngest, Afagddu, was the ugliest man that ever lived. In the battle of Camlan no one could stand against him because of his ugliness, and he strode unhurt through the battle; he one of the only three who were un-wounded. The other two were the Strongest Men in Britain, and the most Beautiful. No one touched those three.

Ceridwen seeing her son so ugly, feared that he would never be honored at the Court of Arthur unless he were endowed with wisdom equal to his own ugliness. So she was for brewing for him three drops of Wisdom in her cauldron. She set the cauldron on a mountain-side over a fire, and nine fairies she put to blow the fire, and she bade a blind man and Little Gwion stir the cauldron for a year and a day. She herself went out daily to gather herbs and magical plants on the mountains in the proper seasons. And while she was thus away, one day as the liquor was seething, fell three drops of it, in the shape of the Name of God,* on the forefinger of Gwion Bach. Then, because these were the three drops of Wisdom, when for the pain of the burning he put his finger in his mouth, he instantly knew everything. He knew that at once he must beware of Ceridwen. He was turning to run away, when the cauldron, filled with poison since the drops of Wisdom had gone from it, broke, and its contents went down to the sea, and the horses of Gwyddno Garanhir were killed by the liquid in a place which came to be known as "the poisoning of the horses of Gwyddno," and from that it had its name.

Meantime Ceridwen returned, and her mind was on fire when she saw what had been. She took a billet of wood, and with it she beat the blind man on the head till his sightless eye fell out upon his cheek. "A cruel and unjust woman art thou," he said, "the evil is with Gwion Bach and not with me." "Thou speakest truth indeed," she answered, "and him will I be pursuing."

So she ran swiftly after Gwion, and was overtaking him, but he changed himself into a hare. Then she became a greyhound to pursue him the faster, and she followed him to the banks of a stream, and to escape from her he became a trout, and more swiftly he swam in the water than the swiftest startled trout in Towy can swim to-day; but Ceridwen becoming an otter swam after him more swiftly than that which is swiftest. And when she was for catching him he came to the top of the water and as a bird he was flying away. Instantly Ceridwen became a hawk. Brighter were her eyes than the sun on the waters, and her wings were stronger than the strongest thing. Above him she waited, preparing to drop on him. Looking down he changed himself into a grain of barley, and fell on a dung heap in a farm yard. Thousands of other grains were there. But Ceridwen flew down and she changed herself into an old black hen with a crest of white feathers upon her head, and one grain of barley she ate, and that was the grain which was Gwion Bach.

Then, as the story relates, she had him nine months in her womb, and

---

*i.e.—In form of a broadarrow, that being with the Druids the symbol of the Sacred Word.

when he was born, he was the most beautiful babe in the whole world. Shining was his brow like the moon in a clear cloudless sky. Indeed there was with him this peculiarity till his death, that where it was darkest, if he went there his forehead was equal to a shining light in that place, by which the smallest thing could be seen. So beautiful was he that Ceridwen had not the heart to slay him, but put him in a leather bag, and set it upon the sea.

Now at that time Gwyddno Garanhir, the greater part of whose lands the sea swallowed, was King of Ceredigion; and Elphin the son of Gwyddno was the most unfortunate man in the world. Nothing that he ever did succeeded. Gwyddno had the fishing of a certain weir, which yielded the value of a hundred pounds in salmon on the night of May eve in every year. "Elphin," said he, "take thou the fishing of the weir this year; maybe it will bring a change in thy luck." So Elphin rode down to the weir. When they fished it there were no salmon there, but only the leather bag containing Ceridwen's child. "Of a truth, prince," said the fishermen, "thou wast never unfortunate till this night, for now thou hast destroyed the virtue that was in the weir." "Not so," he answered, "for perhaps there is the value of a hundred pounds in that bag." Then they drew the bag out of the water, and sorrowfully Elphin took the child in his arms and lifted him to his shoulder, and made his horse amble gently home because of the child, where it had been galloping before. Then sang the babe:

> Elphin, Elphin, I shall sing,
> Sing away thy sadness.
> In the weir and in the spring
> Is a well of gladness;
> And the mother makes men gay
> In many a sudden, secret way.
> In the hill and in the tree
> You know not what is hiding,
> And many a joy shall come to thee
> Where but tears were sliding.
> Bless the luck that brought thee me
> To set thee from thy sorrow free.

And that was the first song of Taliesin, chief of the bards of the west.

Elphin, wondering, brought the child to his wife. "In truth," she said, "it is a radiant forehead that is on him." "Rightly thou hast spoken," said he, "and Taliesin* shall his name be."

In after years, Maelgwn Gwynedd took Elphin prisoner, and Taliesin rescued him. Thus he did it. He went to the court of Maelgwn, who was King of the North. There he, a boy at that time, sat down in the middle of

---

*Tal Iesin—Anglice, Shining Brow.

the hall where they were feasting. Maelgwn called his bards to sing before him. As they passed Taliesin, he put his fingers to his mouth, "and played blerwm blerwm with his lips." The bards went before Maelgwn, and for all the songs they had made, they could do nothing but play blerwm blerwm with their lips. At last one of them said it was because there was a spirit in the room in the guise of a boy, who had thrown an enchantment over them. Maelgwn called Taliesin. "Who art thou," said he, "and whence comest thou, and why hast thou done this?" Then Taliesin replied that he had come to free Elphin, and sang his "Song of Myself"—

> My original country
> Is the Land of the Summer Stars.
> Edno and Heinyn
> Called me Myrddin,
> Soon shall all men know me as Taliesin.
> I have been in many a shape
> Before I attained a congenial form.
> I was the narrow blade of a sword;
> I was a shining drop in the air;
> I was a bridge for passing over three-score rivers;
> I am a marvel whose origin is not known:
> I was in the court of Don*
> Before the birth of Gwydion;
> I was on the high cross
> Of the merciful son of God;
> I was on the White Hill
> In the court of Cynfelin†
> In stocks and in fetters
> A year and a day.
> Three lives have I lived
> In Caer Arianrod;‡
> And I have been in an uneasy chair
> Above Caer Sidi,‡‡

*Don, in history the father of a race of Kings and enchanters in Gwynedd. In astronomy, Llys Don, Don's Court, is a constellation, I think Cassiopeia. Gwydion was the son of Don.
†Cynfelin (Cymbeline), a British high-king in the 1st century. The White Hill was a magical spot in London, either the Tower Hill, or, as I imagine, where St. Paul's now stands. The "Wonderful Head" (Uthr Ben) of the Blessed Bran was buried there, and while it was in the White Hill no oppression could come to Ynys Prydain. But Arthur in the pride of his heart, had it taken away, and then the Saxon oppression came. Uthr Ben is considered by some to have been evolved into Uthr Benddraig or Uther Pendragon, the supposed father of Arthur. A myth here suggests itself!
‡Arianrod, one of the three White Ladies of Ynys Prydain. The constellation, Caer Arianrod, is called Corona Borealis in Latin.
‡‡Caer Sidi, Saturn among the planets.

Whirling around,
Yet without motion.
Nine months was I then
In the womb of old Ceridwen;
I have been Gwion Bach,
I am now Taliesin forever.

Then he sang the "Song to the Wind," and that song was such that the wind arose, and Maelgwn in terror set Elphin free. "Right glad was Elphin; right glad was Taliesin."

Because this story tells of things not known of now, one must not suppose that Taliesin never lived. Indeed it may be well to close this short account of the greatest prose work of Cymric genius with a word or two on the greatest of the bards of Wales, perhaps the last *great* voice in her literature as we measure greatness. As to his personal history, it is given by Iolo Morganwg as follows. He was the son of Henwg, born at Caerleon on Usk, and descended from Bran Fendigaid. He was chief bard at the court of Urien Rheged, in Gower. He was carried off, like St. Patrick, by Irish pirates, and with him Elphin ab Urien. Taliesin, however, escaped in midsea, and came back to Wales in a coracle, landing in the territory of Gwyddno Garanhir, and was there tutor to Elphin the son of Gwyddno. After the sea swallowed the country of Gwyddno, Taliesin went to the court of Arthur, and there he was the chief of the bards of the Island of Britain.

He lived in a transition period. Druidism and the mysteries were then dying out, and with them the power of the Celtic race. Little people were coming into the world, men of our own stature; not, as before, moving to a vaster music. A tear fell from the eye of Arthur when he saw, seven hundred years after his death, the brave Rhonabwy. "Ah! that the fortunes of the Isle of the Mighty should be in the hands of such men as these!" said the king. It was for Taliesin to give something of the old to the new; to catch the last echoes of the holy things, and cry them again, and so clearly that the sound would live on until the spiritual tide turned. This he did. There are about seventy-seven of his poems extant, and they are like an old dark forest where every tree is alive, and all the spaces are peopled with whispering voices, and they are all telling of hidden, wonderful things. Mysticism? There is no other key to the now little understood chants of Taliesin. He has three things mainly to tell of. First, the Soul of Man, and its being one with God, hence brotherhood, non-separateness, all-knowingness. Henwg's son was the greatest of Cymric poets, but there was this other also, the radiant browed son of the mighty mother Ceridwen; and this is the omnipresent, wonder-working magician, who had suffered on the high crosses of all the Christs, to whom the doors of no experience were yet to be opened. Here he speaks with the same voice as Walt Whitman. Second, again, the Human

Soul, and now its experiences on its way towards its high goal. Here we have above all the poem called Preiddien Annwn, the spoils of the underworld—

> "*Three days lay he enchained in the prison of Hidden and Unconcealed*
> *And ever afterwards he was a bard.*"

> "*Thrice the freight of Prydwen sailed we from Britain;*
> *Save seven there were none returned from Caer Ochren.*"

And third, Hope, and it is here he assumes the part of a prophet, for he saw beyond the oncoming darkness away to the light shining the other side of the years. It was here he stamped his message on the consciousness of his people, not to be effaced till long after; perhaps never to be wholly effaced at all. For the fierce striving for national existence in the darkest time was closely interlinked with the writings of Taliesin and Myrddin the Wild. Right down into the middle ages every strong prince was looked on as an incarnation of some olden great one. When they fell, the time for the coming of the Gods was deferred indeed, but the Gods themselves were not forgotten. We see this by a glance at the time of Owen Glyndwr. Then for a moment Wales was free, and the old flames of Druid mysticism broke out over all the land. Christianity was at a discount, and a wilder, freer, more exultant faith broke out in its place. Well might Sion Cent, the Christian, wail

> *There are two religious influences in the world;*
> *The one from Jesus Christ, . . . and the other*
> *From Hu Gadarn among the children of Hu,*
> *From Hu Gadarn among the usurping bards of Wales.*

Call them usurpers—aye! for they had mounted sword in hand to the sky, and hurled down the pale idols, and enthroned the souls of men in their own place to be kings and heroes. Is it deposing God to declare that God exists? To look into the hearts of the stars, and say I, God, am there, and into the hearts of the meanest men and say, I, God, am there also? The work of Taliesin and of every member of the true school of the bards is to fight the battles of God, and plant His standards where they never were seen before. A great strong voice it was that went out in this one little corner of the world, till it should be lost in that greater, stronger, more jubilant voice that was to go out to proclaim the same truth indeed, but over the whole earth.

And oh! It is going, going out now. The world was asleep, and its dreams were troubled. Then an Angel came out of the sun and blew a trumpet blast over Point Loma away by the Western Sea, and the sound of it circled the earth, around and around again, and each time it grows louder and louder, and all things heard it, and men were the last of the creatures to hear it. Once around—and we do not know how quickly the sound goes—and the old-young Gods arose and rubbed their eyes. Twice, and they rose on their elbows. Thrice, and they seized their flaming swords and went forth. The black things that triumphed while they slept are fleeing, fleeing before them. "Mother of Joy," they cried, "We hail, we hail you!"

"Right glad was Elphin, right glad was Taliesin." But Maelgwn—?

• •

"The King with the Silver Hand" is unusual in that it is Morris's only reworking of Irish Celtic mythology. Soon after, he would concentrate on the Welsh Celtic materials, though he always considered, as he wrote to Ella Young on 9 February 1928, "one of my dearest dreams is to have Celts who mean Celts *when they use the word: who include Irish and Welsh in the rest." "The King with the Silver Hand" appeared in the "Young Folks' Department" of the American magazine* The Universal Brotherhood Path *in January 1900. It was signed Ceinydd Morus.*

The King with the Silver Hand

I
The End of the Coraniaid

*O*nce upon a time, before there were any English in Britain, and before Julius Caesar and his Romans ever came here, there was a great king in this island who saved the people from three great troubles. His name was really and truly Lludd Llaw Ereint; that is, Leeth with the Silver Hand. Nowadays people generally call him King Lud, and whether they do that because Lud is much uglier than his real name, or for some other reason, they know best.

Now in the time of King Leeth there were very wonderful things happening, and if you can't understand how such things could be, all I can say is that I read them in a book, and that proves they are true. And perhaps, too, if you could remember what used to happen in the old times, you would not be surprised at them at all, but they would seem quite natural to you. So the best way is to just wonder and wonder about them, and then I think some day you will come to know all about it. At least, you ought to, because even grown-ups do sometimes, and this is one of a whole lot of things that children know more about than grown-ups do. The children haven't had half as much time to forget things in, as the grown-ups have, you see, and that's why it is.

Well then, in those days there were three great sorrows in Britain, and those sorrows were very nearly driving half the people mad, and killing the other half with fright. And although there had been many sorrows in Britain before then, yet those three things seemed to be worse than anything that had ever happened, and though there are greater troubles with us now, the people then felt them more than we feel our troubles, and so, in a sense, they were worse. No one knew how to cure them, and two of them no one knew the causes of, and so every one was very sad, and King Leeth was very sad, too; you never heard people laughing, children forgot how to play their games, and there was no singing anywhere. Think how sad we should be before we stopped singing! And by and bye the sky came to be always cloudy, because the people were so sad, for it is our joy that makes the sun shine. Of course it is! Didn't I tell you that children know more about some things than grown-ups do? Well, that's just one of the things that the poor grown-ups have forgotten, and when they tell you it's all nonsense, you stand up with your hands behind your back and say very politely how sorry you are that they should have forgotten such a nice thing, but hadn't they better wait till they are children again themselves before they make too sure about it?

Well, now, one of these sorrows was that there were a lot of people in Britain called the Coraniaid. Very curious and very nasty people they were, too. There are plenty of them about now, only now we can't see them, but they get into our minds, if we will let them, and make us lazy and angry, and upset us in a lot of ways. Some people call them bad thoughts these days, but at that time they were all called the Coraniaid, and people could see them, and many and many a hero went out to fight them, and that's a lot better than going out to fight human people in other countries, isn't it?

Well, these Coraniaid were terribly clever, and they knew everything the moment it was said, and at least half of what no one said at all, but only thought. And as they hated the human people, and were all the time trying to make them mean, you see what a terrible time it must have been for the old Britons; having to guard against them and to keep their own minds high and grand and noble in spite of all the Coraniaid could do. For if a great hero went out and conquered these Coraniaid, all that happened was that they didn't trouble him any more; if he was very great they might keep out of the way of his friends as well as of himself. But it needed a very great man indeed to free the whole island from them, and even he had to get help before it could be done. That great man was the King, Leeth of the Silver Hand.

But if Leeth was such a great man, you may wonder who on earth was great enough to be able to show him what to do. For Leeth had often tried to save his people from the Coraniaid, but every time they had been too clever for him, and as soon as he had said a word about his plans, the Coraniaid knew just as much of them as he did himself, and so they were always quite ready for him. So at last Leeth had it in his mind that he would go and find out a certain very wise man, and ask him about it.

This wise man was called Llewelys, and the reason why he was so wise was that he had spent all his time helping other people; and if you try that you will become some day just as wise as he was. Llewelys was not living in Britain, and no one knew where he was, but Leeth thought he could find him. So as soon as he had told his people that he was going away, and that it did not matter where he was going, the King went down to the river in London, and in the river was his boat, and into the boat he stepped, and in it he sat down. A wonderful boat it was, for as soon as Leeth was sitting in it, and looking down towards the sea, his chin resting on his two hands and his elbows on his knees, it moved away from the bank and went swiftly down the river, although the tide was coming in, and there was no one rowing, and no sail on the boat, and no wind to fill it if there had been. I think that what made it go so quickly on the clear, beautiful water was that Leeth, as he sat there, was thinking and thinking ever so hard where he wanted it to go, and why he wanted to go there.

So the boat carried him out of London, and on down the river, and where there were great flat marshes stretching away ever so far on each side, with long reeds waving beside broad pools that looked like blue and white, reflecting the blue sky and the clouds; and on the pools and among the reeds there were hundreds of birds, wild ducks and geese, and moor hens, and lapwings that flew round and round in the air and called out when they saw him coming. "Pwee-a-weet? pwee-a-weet? pwee-weet-tee-ee-ee," and that in the old British language means. "Who art thou?" That is what the lapwings always say when they see any one, for they don't learn English when they are little birds, and go to school. And then they saw who he was, and told him how glad they were to see him, and then all the birds looked up, and wished him good luck, and just went about their business. For in those days the birds were very friendly with the human people, and did not fly away when they saw them, as they do now. At least, I suppose they were, or else how would they have been talking like that to the King?

And so Lludd went on down to the sea, and over the green, long waves, and they did not break under his boat, but just gave it a help along when they could. And at last, what with his thinking, and the magic which was in the boat, he came to the country where the great wise man, Llewelys, lived. When Leeth came to him the wise man did not say anything, but he just looked clear into his eyes, and saw the real Leeth that was looking out of them (just as the real *you* are always looking out of your eyes, except when you go away to your own country, which is called Dreamland). And there Llewelys saw a lot of things: he saw what the King wanted, and that he was not wishing to kill the Coraniaid in order that he might be praised and called a great King, but that he was simply longing to help his people because he loved them and was dreadfully sorry for them; and for that reason Llewelys knew that he would be giving Leeth the power he wanted. So he just took some powder, and said, "Take this, and go and do thy duty."

And now there was a wonderful thing happened! For instead of asking what Llewelys meant, or gaping and wondering about it, Leeth knew just what his duty was, and that without saying a word. So he just came home, and put the powder in some water, and called all the people together,

Britons and Coraniaid, and sprinkled them all with the water. Because of the magic in that powder, as soon as the water touched them, the Coraniaid all disappeared, and didn't worry the people any more for a long time. You see, children, these Coraniaid were so clever that you could not tell they were not ordinary people at once. No, and even now we can't see them, and they come to our minds, we can't always tell in a minute that they want to ruin us, and make us think we are mean and wretched, until mean and wretched we do become. They just come into our minds, and there they get busying around, and we very often like them at first. But that wonderful powder that Leeth got from the wise Llewelys knew all about it, and so, although the Britons rather liked it, the wicked Coraniaid were all killed right down dead before they knew where they were, and there were the Britons standing round and saying to each other when they saw what had happened, "And a good thing, too!" And that was how King Leeth made Britain free from the first of the three great sorrows.

II
The Scream of Terror

But if the first sorrow was a dreadful thing for the Britons, at any rate they knew the cause of it, but there was no one dreaming what caused the second one, and so it seemed to be worse than even the Coraniaid. For in the middle of the night of May eve in every year a great and fearful scream went out over the whole island, and so dreadful it was that half of the people went mad with terror when they heard it. Brave, strong men would be weak and helpless for days, and women and little children would die of fright, and the quiet cows would come tearing out of the fields, and charging through the streets of the towns, tossing people right and left, and going on and on as fast as they could until they could go no further, but just dropped down dead. It was so loud that if you had been standing on a mountain in Wales you would have heard it, and if you had been in London you would have heard it, and right up in Scotland they could hear it, too. When they heard that scream all the winds were filled with the terror of it, and all the waves of the sea around the Island of Britain went mad and wild for fear, so that no boat could go on them for weeks, because they were leaping up as high as mountains nearly, and shaking themselves into foam and trying and trying harder than ever to drown the whole land, and so prevent the scream coming to frighten them again. Even the young leaves that were budding out of the trees turned yellow with fear at that scream, and the pink and white blooms on the apple trees, when the sound of it came on them, would tremble and fall down on the ground like soft slow flakes of snow; and the flowers that were beginning to think how warm and blue-skied the Summer would be, and how beautiful they would make the green land with their blossoms, were filled with terror by it, and were afraid to put out their leaves and their buds, and began thinking that after all it was nicer in the Winter down underground; and so they withered, and the souls of them went down to their roots and slept there for another year. And the beautiful fairies that used to dance and ride over the mountains and through the great lone green places, where the winds go to sleep and where the long-tufted rushes wave and dream about the sky they were always looking at, even the fairies, who are so full of joy, used to hide themselves deep away in the mountain hearts, and put their fingers to their ears when they heard it, and for days after they would go alone and cry and cry for the sorrow that scream filled their hearts with. And so the whole land came to look the same in the Spring, when it should have been full of greenness and beauty, as it did in November when the trees were bare, and the flowers dead, and grey, sad mists over it all.

And Leeth, wise as he was, could not find out the cause of the scream of terror, so at last he said to himself that he would go again to Llewelys, for surely Llewelys would know, and would help him to make Britain a land of joy and beauty once more.

So he went again in his boat down the river, and between the wide marshes where the reeds and the pools and the birds were, and over the sea, till he came to Llewelys' land; and there he went ashore on a long sandy beach, but the boat he left on the sea, for he knew it would come when he called it. So he went up over the sand until he came to a forest of tall pine trees, and in that forest was Llewelys.

That time the wise man gave him a very large cauldron, and looked at him again till he knew just what to do. When the King was home again in Britain he did it, and a very curious thing it was. For, just as if Llewelys had told him in so many words, Leeth called a lot of clever people together, and made them measure the whole island carefully and find out the exact middle of it. When they had found the spot which was the very middle, the King went there, and told some one to dig a big hole in the ground there—or maybe he digged it himself, for he could dig well—and in that hole he put the cauldron, and filled it with a drink called mead, and when it was full he covered it over with satin. Then he sent everybody away, and began walking up and down near the cauldron and waiting. And presently he heard strange noises over his head, and looking up he saw two great dragons swaying about in the midst of the air and fighting, with their four long wings beating against each other, and their two tails wound around each other, and the sky all red for miles round with the fire they were breathing, and never a star to be seen for the smoke of them. Where those two dragons came from he could not tell. So there he was, waiting and watching them, for he knew quite well that if they should chance to fly over the middle of the cauldron a strange thing would happen. And strange, indeed, it was too; for when one moment they happened to push each other about till they were over the cauldron, they began to fall down and down and down, and as they fell they became smaller and smaller and smaller, until they both fell plump into the middle of the cauldron. There they were so hot and thirsty that they drank the mead as quickly as ever they could, and it made them sleepy, and as soon as they were fast asleep Lludd called his men, and got a great strong stone chest, and locked these two little dragons up in the chest, and put it away in the middle of a mountain in the strongest place he had. And if some silly person had not dug the chest up and let them out, there would have been no more fighting and quarrelling and hating in all the Island of Britain to this day. But you see, children dear, when people are unbrotherly, what can one expect? So they both got out, and they are both fighting still; and although we cannot see them, nor hear their fearful scream, we are waiting for some one to come who will find out where Llewelys lives, and get the great magic cauldron from him, and catch the two dragons in it once more. And, for all you or I know, children, it may be one of you that will do it. Yes, indeed, and I think that you will all have to do it in your time, and not an easy thing will it be for you, if you try to do it for your own sake, or for any other reason than that everybody may be happier, and that the trees and the flowers themselves may be merrier and more beautiful, and the sky bluer, and the sun shining more often. For remember how it was that Leeth, the great old hero King, managed to do all these wonderful things—by just keeping his own sorrow till the last, and doing what he could with all his might and main to destroy the sorrows of everybody else.

III
The Vanishing of the Food

For you will remember that in the days of the King who was called Leeth of the Silver Hand, there were three sorrows in the Island of Britain, and that though Leeth had freed the land, with the help of the wise man Llewelys, from the wicked race of the Coraniaid, and had imprisoned the two dragons that made the scream of terror in a strong stone chest in the mountain called Eryri Wen, there was still a work for him to do before he and his people could be quite happy. For although the third great sorrow of Britain at that time was one that hurt the King most of all, it did hurt other people, too, as you will hear. For one thing, whatever hurts anybody, hurts everybody; as every child knows quite well, even if they try hard to forget it, and do forget it later on. And this third sorrow was that, however much food there might be in the King's palace over night, there would be none left in the morning. No man or woman had eaten that food, and yet no one knew what had become of it. And as Leeth used to give this food the next day to every one who needed it, and as food that had been on the King's table became very wonderful, and made people better and happier and wiser when they ate it, you see this was really a sad thing for a lot of people. But as it was, after all, mostly hurting himself, as I told you, Leeth resolved that he would not leave his kingdom and ask Llewelys how to conquer this, but would wait, and comfort the people as best he could. But Llewelys knew very well all about it, and when Leeth came to him the second time, and he gave him that wonderful cauldron, Llewelys said to himself that as soon as the people were freed from the scream of terror, the King should know also how to free himself from the vanishing of the food. And a bird has told me that Llewelys could never have made the King know that if Leeth had been thinking how he could free himself, or had wanted to free himself before he had freed the people. And, indeed, I believe that little bird was quite right, too.

So, after he had seen the stone chest with the two dragons in it laid safe away in the heart of Eryri Wen mountain, Leeth had the cauldron brought to London, and one evening he put it in the hall, where he used to feast with his great lords and all the great queens and ladies of the Island of Britain, and had it filled with cold water, and cold enough it was, for it was the middle of Winter, and no one could see the ground anywhere for the white of the snow that was on it. That night they feasted in the hall, and many were the noble old tales that were told, and many were the songs that were sung. When the feast was over and all the great lords and warriors and ladies had gone to their rest, Leeth, the King, put his golden breast-plate over his breast, and his shield on his arm, and he took his long shining sword in his hand, and waited. Then, as the night wore on, he began to feel fearfully sleepy, and it came into his mind that of all the great battles he had ever fought, the battle with sleep that night was the greatest and hardest and most terrible. For all the time sleep was coming over him, and round him there was the sweetest and most delicate music sounding in the hall, and every note of that music had such power that it would lull ten strong men to sleep; if they heard it now. Now it seemed to him as if there were white birds singing in the hall, and such a song they sung as one might listen to for a thousand years, and think that it was only a minute or two he was listening. Then it seemed to be harps, which were being played by the most wonderful harpers in the whole world; and then it was the sound of a stream dashing and tumbling over the stones high up on the side of a mountain, and as he listened he seemed to come down with the foam on the stream, and down and down from the mountain into a green quiet valley, fully of wonderfully bright and sweet-smelling flowers, and there were bees humming and buzzing among the flowers, and then he lost the sound of the stream, and could only hear the buzzing of those bees, and it seemed to him that he would like to lie and listen to those bees till the world came to an end, such an exquisite music it was; and the scent of the flowers came over his whole soul, and—Splash! Just as he was beginning to forget everything but the valley of the bees, the memory of the magic cauldron came to him, and he jumped right into it, just in time to save himself from going fast off to sleep. So there he sat in the water, shivering and aching, but wide awake. For the coldness of that water was not like the coldness of anything else. First it was only just fearfully cold, but when he had been in it two minutes the coldness of it got inside him, and made him ache all over his body, and then it got into his mind, and never so sad had he been in all his life as he was then. After that the coldness of the water became to him like a burning heat, and it burnt into him till the fire of it came into his heart, and in his heart there were many things that it burnt away. But for all the pain, that would have killed a less noble man than he was, he sat still in the cauldron, and the music that had before sounded so sweet to him, gave him no more pleasure while he was there, but rather sounded to him like the knocking together of two old tin pans. So there he was, miserable and freezing, and burning and aching, but wide awake, and watching carefully all the time.

And then a strange thing happened, for there came into the hall a great black man, the blackest and ugliest in the whole wide world. So tall he was that the top of the King's head, when he was standing up, did not reach higher than his waist. Black armor was on him, and a long, black, crooked sword at his side. On his back was a black basket. He set the basket down on the floor, and into it he put all the food in the whole hall; though it was a small basket, and though he put heaps of food into it, it did not seem to be a bit fuller. Very quiet in the water was Leeth while he watched all this, and it was not until the great black man had taken all the food there, and put it in his basket, that the King moved. Then he jumped up, and ran after the black man, and bade him give back the food and fight for his life, for the King of the Isles of the Mighty was not to be oppressed by such a man as that black wizard was. So those two fought, and it is said that flames, and not mere sparks, flashed from the clashing together of their two swords, and those flames leaped up so high that the black marks of them were to be seen on the rafters of the roof of the King's great hall, and that although the strongest man in the island could not shoot an arrow from the floor high enough for it to stick in the roof at that time. But at last Leeth conquered, and I think that it was by the magic strength he gained while he was shivering and burning in the cauldron that he did it. For wonderful are the powers of that cauldron, children dear, as you will know when, like Leeth, you have been in it. If a dead man is put in it, he comes to life again, if he is brave and noble enough; if not, he disappears, and no one knows what has become of him. Indeed it is a wonderful cauldron.

Then King Leeth, having conquered the black man, made him his own servant. The color of his skin, that had been black, became white, and none of the servants Leeth had served their lord better than he did.

And after that the King was always as wise and strong as the great

Llewelys himself. No enemy could hurt his people while he lived, and there was no other sorrow for him, and none for them until he died.

And that is the story of Leeth with the Silver Hand, and a true story it is, and what he was, may you be, and what he did, may you also do.

The following story, "The Prince of the Streamland," is Morris's earliest fictional reworking of parts of the Mabinogion. The tale was published in the Children's Department of the April 1900 issue of The Universal Brotherhood Path, signed Ceinydd Morus.

The Prince of the Streamland

I

How Prince Pwyll Went to Annoon

Somewhere or other there is a beautiful country called the Streamland, and in that country the mountains are always purple, and the hills are as green as hills may be. If you get out a big map of the world, and search it very carefully indeed, and then can't find it marked, you may be sure that the person who made that map has forgotten all about it, or has never been there to see. And it's often the way, children, that they don't mark the real nice places on the map.

Well, in the time of Prince Pwyll, it was a lovely place to live in, with the woods all full of birds the whole year round always singing, and the towns and the villages all full of people who were generally singing, too, and always happy. And, indeed, I shouldn't a bit wonder if they are always happy still, for I never heard that Prince Pwyll died. Only I do know that he changed his name after the story was told, and what he changed it to, I won't tell you, except that it is something which you yourselves will all be some day.

A wonderful land is the Streamland, for it is always full of music, and no one knows whether that music is made by the streams that come down from the mountains, or if it is the fairies that are singing, or whether it is the blooming of the flowers that puts it into the heart of the Wind to sing, or whether it is that the country is so near to the Stars that you could hear the Sky-bees buzzing their honey-song in the shining star-blossoms that grow all over the sky. But there it was, and I have heard somebody say that all the beautiful music that ever was comes from that country, and I dare say you will find it is quite true, too, when you go there.

Well, one day it came into Prince Pwyll's mind that he would go a-hunting. So the next morning when the hills and the valleys were cold with the dawn, there were the men of the court all mounted on their horses in front of the palace, and their hunting horns hanging at their saddles, and the dogs running about around them, and they all waiting for Pwyll to blow his great horn for the hunt to begin.

Then he did blow it, and off they went, and all the morning they were riding on, over many a lonely mountain, and through many a green valley where the fields are all soaked and full of tumbling streamlets that went down to the little rivers that were singing on their way down to the sea; and over many a hillside covered with woods, and the ground in the woods all blue with the bluebells—until at last Prince Pwyll's horse had taken him far away beyond any of the others.

Every now and then he could see a great stag running on before him. The swiftest stag in the whole world it must have been, for neither he nor his swift dogs could catch up with it. On and on he rode, not knowing that he was alone; all the morning, and all the afternoon he rode on, and only stopped when the trees were dim with the shadows, and a star or two out in the sky, and only a streak of red and gold and pale yellow in the west to show where the sun had set. And then there he was with his dogs by a wide, dim lake in a great valley, and the clear water lapping against the sand and the pebbles by his horse's feet, and a few birds flying and calling over the water where it was bright with the sunset, and it came into his mind that he had never seen that place before.

He lifted his great horn, and three loud blasts he blew on it, and between each he listened for the answering blasts that any of his men who might hear him would be sure to blow. But each time the sound went forth, and up the mountains, and the elves on the mountains heard it, and just shouted it back at him and not once could he hear the horns of his men. So there he was sitting on his horse's back, and not knowing what to do one bit.

Then as he sat there listening there came a strange sound which seemed to be the barking of dogs, and he wondered where in the world those dogs came from, for he had never heard any dogs barking like that (nor have you).

While he was wondering, he looked up the side of the mountain, and there he saw a great stag come dashing out of the woods a little way above where he was. As soon as he saw it, of course he called to his dogs, and they ran, and he rode after it as fast as they could. And while he was riding he could hear that strange barking above the barking of his own dogs. And once he heard the sound of a horn, only it wasn't a bit like the sound of any horn he had ever heard before.

Just as he had crossed two wide fields, and was coming up over the soft wet ground to the wood, and the stag only one field in front of him, he saw a pack of dogs coming out of the wood. Curious dogs they were, and it was they who had been making the strange barking. Their bodies were white and shining like clean snow with the sun on it, and their right ears were as red as their bodies were white.

Pwyll could not think whose dogs they could be, nor how they came to be hunting in his country. He was angry, too, that strange dogs should be after the stag he had been hunting all day. So as they were coming up to the stag just before his own dogs were, he called them back and told them to lie down, and sent his own dogs on instead. But just as they were about to catch the stag, he heard his name called, and coming out of the wood there seemed to be a cloud of light that was coming slowly toward him. As it drew nearer he saw that it was a man whom he thought was a great king. The man was sitting on a grey horse, grey clothes were on him, but it seemed as Pwyll looked at him, that purple light was shining through the greyness of them. If you had seen his two eyes, you would have said at once, "This man must be a kind of cousin of the Lotus Mother's," and I think you would have been quite right, too.

For, you know, children, the man that Pwyll saw was a very great king, indeed. He is one of those who were called the Wise Ones, and that is why he seemed at first to be a cloud of light. In those old days they used to call him Arawn, but he has got a lot of names besides that. I believe that the great Mother and Queen of the Fairies and Men is his sister, and that it is through his power she is able to reign over her children and to be always teaching them strong and wise things. But however that may be, I know that nothing can happen without King Arawn has something to say in the ordering of it, and that we could never get on without him one bit.

Well, when Prince Pwyll heard his name called, and turned round, and saw the gray-robed and purple and silvery shining king riding toward him between the dusk-dark mountain and the quiet lake, he called to him:

"What dogs are these with which you are hunting in my kingdom?"

"It is not I who would be hunting in your kingdom, Prince," said the king.

And then it came into Pwyll's mind that although he knew every hill and mountain and field and wood and lake and valley in his own Streamland, he had never seen those mountains, nor that lake before, and he wondered how he could have left his kingdom in one day's ride. Then he began to wonder which was the way home, but that he could not tell; and he could not even tell whether the Streamland was in front of him or behind him, or on his left or on his right hand. And then he looked at his dogs, that had left chasing the stag when King Arawn called, and they were running about here and there and smelling the ground and then running back, and he saw that they did not know the way home either. And a strange thing was that, for there were no better dogs in all the world than those dogs were.

All the while the King was riding slowly toward him, and watching him, and calling tiny fairies from somewhere and sending them to Pwyll, and they were whispering in his ears and telling him what he ought to do. Then King Arawn said:

"I am called Arawn, and a great king in this land of mine am I. You have ridden into my kingdom. It is called Annoon, and it is in the world below the world you left to-day. You have called my dogs away from the stag I was hunting. For this you will not be able to go back to your own kingdom at once, for no one who comes into Annoon may leave it without doing some service, and I could not show you the way to the Streamland now. But if you are willing to have me for your dear friend, you must do what I shall ask you to do."

And then a great gladness was in Pwyll's heart, though he did not know why it was there, and he told him how glad he would be to have so great and noble a king for his close friend, and that he would with joy do whatever King Arawn wished. So the king said:

"In Annoon there is a man named Havgan, who has made a kingdom for himself by gathering together silly and wicked people, and many times he has made war on me. You cannot go back to the Streamland till this man is killed, and no one is allowed to kill him, but you, not even I myself. But before you can kill him, you will have to be as strong and wise as I am. You will have to wear my armor, and to be able to strike with my great sword. A blow from that sword there is no doctor who can heal. And to be able to do this, you will have to seem to be myself, and to reign in my kingdom for a year and a day without any one there knowing that you are not myself."

And all this Pwyll said he would gladly do, and as he said it, it seemed to him that the valley and the lake and the wood and the sky and the king were growing dimmer and dimmer all the time, and he thought that there were fairies dancing, at first slowly, around him; but as they danced they became quicker and drew nearer to him, and he could feel their cool breath on his face and in his hair as they went round, and it seemed to be drenched with a dew of sleep and dreams and through it and their quiet song he could hear the voice of King Arawn telling him that at the end of a year and a day he should fight with Havgan, and he heard him say: "Do nothing that he may ask you to do," and then he was fast asleep.

For those tall fairies came from the mountain beyond the lake when they knew that Arawn wished them to come, and began to do the work they are for doing. They are always in that valley. Some people call them the Sleep-Fairies, and some people call them the Birth-Fairies; but whether those names are the best for them, children dear, or whether by rights they ought to be called the Death-Fairies, I am not knowing. But they are all the subjects of the great wise King of Annoon, and they are always dancing their stately dances over the lake and in the valley on the borders of his kingdom. And I think that we all see them moving around us and feel their breath many times, many hundreds of times maybe, and shall, till the Story of All Stories is told, and the last of all Silent Moments is with us.

II
The Slaying of Havgan

Well, as soon as Pwyll was fast asleep, the king turned his horses, and called Pwyll's dogs and they went to him, and he rode off toward the Streamland, and the dogs after him, and there it is said that he reigned for a year and a day, and no one knew that he was not Pwyll.

But if you had been in the valley that evening, it is a curious thing you would have seen. For as soon as Pwyll was asleep, and those strange fairies dancing around him, his face seemed to be changing, and his clothes, and the horse under him. Instead of the blue cloak he had been wearing, and the splendid saddle of his horse, and the rich, four-cornered saddle-cloth of purple velvet with an apple of gold at each corner, it was the gray cloak of the king that was on him, and the plain saddle under him, and he on a great gray horse such as the King of Annoon had been riding. And then his face changed, and became like Arawn's face, and no one would have known that it was the Prince of the Streamland he was, and not the King of Annoon, which, as you know, is in the world below the world Prince Pwyll came from. Only there was no purple shining around him at that time.

Well, when those fairies had finished their work, they all went away, and Pwyll woke up. And there he was on his horse, and the last of the sunset light gone out of the west, and the moon pale on the lake and in the sky, and all the stars out, and everything as quiet as it could be, except now and then for the splash and rippling rings on the lake when a fish jumped up to see what was going on. If you had called him Pwyll then, he would no more have known what you meant than if you had called him the man in the moon. And that was because he had forgotten all about the Streamland, and all about his being the prince of it; and all that was in his mind was that he was Arawn, King of Annoon, and that he had been out hunting all day long, and he supposed he must have gone to sleep in the valley, and then he was wondering why and how he had come to fall asleep, and the he began to feel hungry, so he stopped wondering, and whistled to those strange, white dogs with red ears, and they came to him; and then, as if he had ridden that way every day of his life, he turned his horse's head toward the capital city of Annoon and rode straight to Arawn's palace.

When he got there, all the people called him "King" and "Arawn," and it never seemed a bit funny to him, as it does to you and me. For he just remembered the things that Arawn remembered, and he knew everybody's name at that court as well as Arawn knew them himself. Not that he was as great and wise then as Arawn was, or that he knew the real lovely things that Arawn did. No, indeed! How could he when he had not got the purple shining like the king? What he did know was the names of the people, and just enough to prevent himself or any one else ever guessing that he was another person than the true king. He could not become as great as Arawn, you see, until he had killed Havgan. And that was why Arawn had put him there—that Pwyll might grow strong and wise enough to be his own equal and friend.

And that is always the way with King Arawn, and you may be sure that some day or other he will be finding out that there is some dreadful enemy for *you* to fight, and then he will be seeing if you are strong enough to do it; and if you are not he will be putting you into all kinds of training; and it may be he will make you a king, and it may be he will make you a dustman, as he thinks fit, and whatever it is, he will wait and teach you, oh, so patiently, until that enemy is killed or that work is done.

There are some people who say that these things cannot happen, or perhaps that they only used to happen in the old, old times. But don't you believe it, because they are all just as likely to happen now as they were two or three thousand years ago. Aye, and now it is the New Century you cannot tell what may come any day. Indeed, if you manage to go right to the end of your life without seeing or hearing anything of Arawn the great, wise king—all I can say is, it is a funny child you are, and a funny man or woman you will grow up to be, so mind you that!

Well, a year and a day was Pwyll in King Arawn's palace, and no one dreaming that he was not the real king. One day he would be hunting in the woods and the forests, and another day he would be playing chess with one or another of the princes of Annoon, and often he would be feasting with the great men of that land, and at those feasts he would sing noble songs and tell splendid stories as well as the best of the bards and princes. And there was never a day in which he did not help some one, and so learn something himself; and if there had been I shouldn't wonder if he would have had to stay longer away from his own land. And so every day he grew stronger and wiser and more like the King. As the months passed by, too, you would have seen that the purple glow which was always around Arawn began, at first ever so dimly to shine around Pwyll. At the end of ten months there was no one who would not have seen that light, and when the year was at its passing, I do not think it was any less bright with Pwyll than it was with King Arawn himself.

Well, one evening at that time, while he was sitting in his place at the head of the great hall of the palace, there came a messenger from Havgan to say that in a few days' time the peace which was between him and Arawn would end, and that on the next Tuesday he would lead his army to the ford of the river which flowed between their two countries. Pwyll knew quite well about Havgan, and the peace that would have lasted for a year and a day, and he knew that he would have to be leading his army against the false King when that peace was over. So he was not a bit surprised, but just told all his princes to get their men together; and on the Tuesday he led them all to the ford.

And there were the two armies facing each other, and the river between them, shallow and full of stones, and great trees on the banks, and the sun shining down on the water between the leaves. When Havgan's princes saw Pwyll's army, it came into their minds that it would be well for their lord to fight alone with Arawn; and not to have any battle, for they had no quarrel with Arawn's men. So they sent a messenger out from their camp; a man dressed in blue, and with a little golden harp in his hand. You see they used always to carry harps in those days when they went on messages like that, because there was peace wherever a harp went.

So this man went out, and across the river, and the trout that were sunbathing in the shallow water did not stir, but stayed quite still in the water, because they saw that he was a messenger of peace. And he went to the great royal tent where Pwyll was, in the middle of his army, and told the man who seemed to be Arawn what Havgan's princes thought. So Pwyll turned to his princes, and it seemed to them, also, that that would be the best thing, and it seemed so, too, to himself.

So that afternoon Pwyll put Arawn's golden breast-plate on his breast, and took his shield of strong hide studded over with nails of gold, and Arawn's great sword, a blow from which no doctor had ever healed, and went down with his princes and great lords to the ford. And what with the sun gleaming on the gold of his armor, and the purple light of his heart that was shining out through his breast and the green of his clothes, those lords and soldiers thought that they had never seen so bright a King as he was. As he went there were strange thoughts coming into his mind; and every now and then he could hear music so strong and sweet that he was wondering where in all Annoon was any one who could make it. And all the time it grew stronger and sweeter, and he could hear less and less of anything else, so much did it fill his heart and his mind.

When they came to the ford there was Havgan waiting, and his lords with him, and those two were for fighting in the middle of the shallow river, with the water playing around their feet. Havgan lifted his long spear as they stepped into the stream and threw it at the man who seemed to be Arawn, but it flew over his shoulder and stuck quivering in the brown bank on the other side. As it whizzed past Pwyll's ear, he seemed to hear the words of the strange music between the sound of the spear and the rustling of the young leaves and the song of the water, and the words that he heard were: *"Prince of the Streamland."* Then Havgan drew his sword and they met in the middle of the ford. The sun was shining on Pwyll, but Havgan was always in the shade of the trees. Fierce was the attack of the false king, but all his sword blows fell on the shield or the sword of Arawn. While he was attacking there came into Pwyll's mind a wild, lone valley and a lake and strange fairies dancing round him, and the music that he heard grew more distinct.

Then he lifted Arawn's great sword, high in the air it flashed in the sunlight, and with it he struck Havgan. The false king lifted his sword to meet the blow, but it was beaten down and broken. Into the water he fell, and his broken sword flew from his hand and splashed into a deep pool by the bank a little way below the ford. As he struck that blow, Pwyll knew that he was not Arawn. Then Havgan said:

"I do not know why you should seek my death. Yet as you have begun to kill me, finish the work you have begun."

But the music seemed to be telling Pwyll not to do anything that Havgan asked, so he just answered:

"Not so, and if you are to die, you are to die without any more help of mine."

So Havgan knew that he had no more hope, and two of his princes carried him away and he died. So through that victory all Annoon came to belong to Arawn once more. And as soon as Havgan was killed, Pwyll came to remember everything.

And the next day he got on his horse and rode out alone to the wild valley, and there by the lake was King Arawn waiting. The king gave him back his own form and told him many things. It was a great thing for Pwyll to know such a king as Arawn. For ever afterward he was a dear friend and brother to the prince, and in the Streamland there was greater beauty and happiness than ever before, and people could go from one country to the other whenever they liked, and Pwyll was wise, and wise, and wise, and the purple shining never left him. And, as I told you, he changed his name in time. What he changed it to I won't tell you, only it means something you all will become when, like Prince Pwyll, you have killed the false king whom Arawn may put you to kill. And strong and wise you will need to be before you can do that and earn the new name that Pwyll had.

● ●

*"Hu with the White Shield" is the most significant story of Morris's early
period, giving Morris's version of the early mythological history of Wales. It
was published in six parts in the Dublin magazine* The International
Theosophist *(13 July—13 December 1900), as by Ceinydd Morus.*

Hu with the White Shield
A Tale for Children

I
The Valley of Silken Song

*O*nce upon a time, children, thousands and thousands of years
ago, there was a great land away over the sea called the Summer
Country, and where it is now the fishes and the sea fairies know best. And
that land was old in those days—so old that no one could tell how many
hundreds of ages had passed since the people first went there; so old that the
sea itself had forgotten the time when its waves first rose and fell on the
coast there—and it takes the sea a long time to forget anything. And it was
so old too, that those who have the ordering of these things saw that it
would be well if the best and strongest and noblest of its people were to be
led away into another land, and found a new kingdom where everybody
would know what Brotherhood meant. For at that time there were only a
few people in the Summer Country who knew about Brotherhood, and
there was very little helping and sharing done—and I shouldn't wonder if
that is why the fishes and the sea fairies know where it is now so much
better than you or I do.

Well, there was a boy named Hu living in a great white-walled city of
that land, a city close to the blue sea; and of all the boys in the whole country there was not one so brave or so strong or so beautiful as he was.

One day Hu was out in the mountains hunting, and when evening
came on he found himself in a green valley high up among the hills. On one
side there was a stream, where the cold clear water came foaming down the
hillside over great dark stones, and through cool deep pools, till it reached
the bottom of the valley, and then ran along there, and down and out towards the plains below. Half way up the mountain on that side too, there

were great stones by the stream, as big as big men, some standing and some lying down on the ground, and there were big thorns sprawling over some of them, with huge blackberries on them, and all around there was bracken and gorse; and Hu thought it would be well for him to sleep there that night, for he had never seen the place before. So in the grey and purple of dusk he went up by the stream, to where those stones were, and found one big flat moss-covered one, and on that he lay down with the low bank above him, yet out of the reach of the spray; and in a little while went fast off to sleep.

But in the night he awoke, and everywhere around him he could hear dim soft sweet voices singing. It seemed as if all the valley was full of song; but it was so soft that he could not tell who was singing, nor what the song was which was being sung. The whole place was bright with the moon-light, and all the moonlight seemed to be turned into music. And as he lay still with his eyes shut, slowly, slowly he began to hear the song, and the notes began to be words, and the song got into his mind and it filled him with wonder, and he could not think as he heard it why he should be lying there, and not out in the world doing great and noble deeds. And it isn't I who can tell you what that song was, children, only I know there was a great deal in it about a White Shield with a strange magic in it, and about the wonderful things the man who had that shield would do. And all that night as he lay there he was thinking and dreaming about the shield and about the song, and the pale flakes and shadows of the moonlight were fall-ing over him through the leaves of a little tree, and then something as soft as the moonlight brushed his face, and a verse began to sing itself through his heart and his mind—

> Oh white shield, and snow-white shield!
> To you they yield, the dragons dread.
> The fierce dark things with blood-red wings,
> 'Tis you that make them tame or dead!

And it kept on and on and on too, but whether *that's* really and truly a verse of the song Hu heard that night I can't tell you, but, indeed, I shouldn't a bit wonder if it is. Anyhow it came to him that he would have that White Shield, though he went all over the world for it; and that he would conquer monsters and blood-red dragons with it; for it was in his mind that there were surely things for him to do that would help the whole wide world. He did not know then what they were, but he knew that he would have the Shield. "I will," he said to himself, "I will have it!" and then the song came to him again, and with it singing in his heart he went off to sleep. And all the while he was sleeping he heard that song. He had not opened his eyes at all, or I don't know what he'd have seen, and I don't know what you'd have seen either, if you had been there. But I do know this, that when the cool quiet breezes began to stir, and morning came up with yellow and gold and orange and red all along the east of the sky, and Hu awoke and sat up on the stone, and was getting up to go, there was a great shield hanging on the side of a tall rock just above him, which he had not seen there the evening before. As he looked at it the song stole through his mind again—

> *Oh white shield, and snow-white shield,*
> *To you they yield, the dragons dread.*

But indeed, when he came to look at it again, it seemed to be no more white than a black sheep, but all covered over with dust and dirt and rust of all sorts of nasty things.

Then he didn't a bit know what to do. First he thought one thing and then another, and then he began to think it must have been there all the time, only he had not noticed it in the moonlight, and that someone passing that way must have hung it there and forgotten it; and then he thought someone had left it there on purpose, thrown it away because it was too old and rusty to be any good to anyone, and he was just turning to go down the hillside and away from that wonderful valley, when what should he hear but a voice among the light green ferns that were just bright and lit up with the sunrise, and it was singing ever so softly and sweetly, and he stopped to listen, and this is what he heard (at least I believe it was)—

> *Oh white as snow, and white as snow,*
> *They do not know how fair thou art!*
> *Who only see the form of thee,*
> *They only see thy lesser part.*

And then came that other verse about the White Shield, and it might have been the great sun's self that was drawing music and the song from the soft green bracken. And then he knew that he must take that shield, for it was that that had the magic in it. So he lifted it from where it was hanging, and stood with his face towards the sun, and lifted the shield above his head with both hands, so that the sunlight was on it, and cried out that he knew that shield in spite of the rust on it, and vowed that he would not rest till it was as white and bright as the snow on the highest place on the highest mountain—and as he spoke, the sun shone on the shield, and for a moment there was no rust there or dirt, but it shone and flashed and shone, and the whole valley was full of light, and Hu himself was full of the light of it too, and his heart and mind were full of the joy of it—and then a cloud blew across the face of the sun, and the shield became dull again. Then Hu gathered some blackberries for his breakfast, and after that he put the shield over his shoulder, and found his way down out of the valley, and out of the mountains, and late that evening he came to the great white city where he lived.

When he came among his friends, they wondered to see him carrying an old rusty shield like that; but they wondered more when they came near him, for some of the light that had flashed out of the shield in the morning was still in his eyes, and brighter eyes than those they had never seen. And his mother was for asking him where he had been; but his father saw his eyes, and said "No, let the boy alone," for he thought that the Wise Ones might have some work for Hu to do, which it would not be well to ask him about.

But every day Hu took down the shield from where it hung in his room, and tried and tried to make it clean before he went to do whatever had to be done that day. And every time he looked at it, it came into his mind that there were great and noble things for him to do, and that it was with the shield he would do them. So for seven years he was watching and waiting and learning, and the shield was becoming whiter and whiter every day.

And then, when the seven years were over, all but one day, and the shield was white and clean, only not flashing like it was that morning in the mountains, Hu knew that he would have to take it to the Valley of the Silken Song that day. For that was the name he had given to the Valley where he had the shield, because the song he had heard there seemed to him to be as soft as fine soft silk. The other people in the Summer Country knew nothing about that valley at all, because it was a fairy place. You know that there are plenty of places which the fairies are set to guard so that people shan't find them—valleys high up in all our mountains; and green islands which no one can see in the midst of our lakes; and islands in the sea too, which the white-winged sea-gulls can see, but cannot go to; and next time you are down by the sea, if you listen hard to what they say when they are crying, crying to each other over the curl of the waves, you will know *that* as well as they do themsleves. And sometimes, but not often, human people can see those islands too, but they cannot get to them in ordinary boats, or by swimming, or indeed at all, unless they are very very wise, and know how to do a whole lot of things besides that. For the fairies always love that sort of people and obey them; because the Great Mother of the fairies and mortals works with and helps them, and her fairy children are wise enough to do what She does and what She would have them do. Yes indeed, the bright fairies of the mountains, and streams, and woods, and wide fields, and seas, have much more sense than most human people in these things.

Well, you see, this Valley was just one of those places. Its real proper name was the Vale of the Shield, but Hu did not know that, so he called it the Valley of Silken Song whenever it came into his mind. A wonderful place it was, too; for in it a very very great and wise king had his home, and the rock on which Hu had found the shield marked one of the doorways of his splendid secret palace. It was this great wise king (I won't tell you his name), who had told the fairies to guard his valley very carefully indeed, for most of the people in the Summer Country were very proud and wicked, and so it would have been a bad thing for them if they had been able to go into the Vale of the Shield, and a bad thing for the valley too, and that you will know in good time. So whenever anyone came that way, the fairies would be sure to put it in his mind that it would be nicer to turn to the right and go straight up the hill, or easier to turn to the left and go down under the great pine trees towards the valleys below, or else much better to stay just where he was and go to sleep for awhile; and whoever did that they would carry him safely and silently off through the air and put him into his own bed in his own house, and then in the morning he would wake up and think what a funny dream he had had. But you see Hu was different, and he was always longing to help people and to make them happy, and so the King of that Valley sent for him, and fairies that he didn't see led him there to find the Shield. And we too shall be led there in time, children dear, whether we can see the fairies or not, and the wise King will shew us wonderful things and send us forth to do great deeds. And remember you this— that it may be early or it may be late, but it *may* be *any time,* children, if, like Hu, we say of that Shield—"I will have it, and *I will,* and I WILL."

II
The Fire of the Shield

Well now, children, that day Hu set out with the great white shield hanging over his shoulder, and went away from the city, and over the long green fields and up towards the mountains; for it was in his mind that maybe he would find out something up there before the next day. So all day long he was going on: first up a steep hill covered with rocks and thorns (and hard work enough it would be for you to climb that hill); and then through a great wood on top, where the sun was shining in between the pale green of the leaves wherever they were fewest, and where there were rabbits scuttling about with their little white tails bobbing up and down; and then down into a valley covered with yellow gorse and waving fern, and over the stream that was tumbling and singing along the bottom of it; and then up again through furze and gorse nearly as high as his own head; and then up higher and higher, where the mountain was so steep that he had to pull himself up by the roots of little trees, and on and on and on over one mountain and another, until at last he came to a path that led through a pine wood. From there he could see nearly all the way down to the white city, and beyond that the blue of the sea, and the brightness where the sun was shining on it.

And so, after searching all day among the mountains, he came towards evening to a stream, and following that upwards and upwards a long way, just as the sun was setting, he found himself in the Vale of the Shield. Half way up the hill, on his right, he could see the great stones by the stream through the shadowy purple and grey of the twilight, and on the hills around he could see the dancing lights of the fairies, as he had often seen them before in the long summer evenings, on the hills and in the long green fields. But he had not come there to see the fairies, however beautiful they might be, and so when he had eaten some of the food that was with him and drunk some of the cold clear water of the stream, he made his way up to those stones, and hung up the shield just where he had found it, and lay down to sleep in his old place.

And that night again music began to sound through the valley and Hu awoke, and rose up on his elbow, for it came to him that that night he would see whatever there was to be seen. There was no moon shining, but don't be thinking it was dark, for there was what seemed to be fire coming from the White Shield where it hung, only it was purple fire, and now and again a flash of pale green in it; and this fire flowed down as he watched it, and out over the whole of the valley till it seemed to be a sea of purple flame which was all the time rising and rising, and it tossed in beautiful curling waves against the rocks, and ran and played up the side of the mountains, and broke into foam and spray of every beautiful color in the whole world, and he could see where it poured down into the country below through the lower end of the valley. And even while he was looking at it, a wave of the flame came gliding towards him, and breaking and dashing over the rocks and over himself. He held his breath and shut his eyes tight till it had gone, for it was hotter than any fire you have ever seen; yet for all that it did not burn a thread of his clothes, or singe his hair. But it only came to him that he would wait there and bear all the pain that might need bearing, even though he died in it, for he would see and hear whatever things might be to be seen and heard that night. And, indeed, if he had thought less than that, children, I think he would never have done those great things which he did afterwards, and which make this story be told. For he knew that the Shield had regained at last its lost brightness, and so the great deeds which were to be done with it would be done before long, and because of them the sky would be bluer and the streams more sparkling, and human people happier and more full of Brotherhood. He knew all that, and proud he was for knowing it, and that even if he were killed by the fire, those deeds would not be left undone, but someone else would come to do them. And so, as the music sounded a song came to him, and he sang it, and a proud and strong and beautiful song it was, too, and full of love and of gladness.

And all the while the sea of fire was rolling and surging through the valley, and rising around and around him, and wave after wave dashed over him, and it burned him as that fire always does burn; it was not his body that was killed by it, but for all that the pain was greater than it would have been if his body had all been burned away. All the time, too, there was the noble music sounding through the valley, only it was not like the music he had heard there seven years before. For that had been soft and sweet, like the song of the fairies who live in the streams and in the green mountains, but this seemed to be the battle song of all that is great and good in the world in the war that it has with all that is evil.

Then he climbed up on to the top of the great rock where the Shield was, and there he stood, with the flame waves lapping and falling around his knees, and every now and again a great billow came slowly rolling up, and dashed all over him, and passed on a little way up the mountain side, and then came rolling back to the great fire sea in the valley. While he was standing there singing he saw a boat sailing down the vale over the flame-sea towards him. Full of joy he was because of it, for in it was a man whom he knew must be of the Wise Ones. He was the most kingly and beautiful being in the world. So tall he was that as he came along in his boat his shining head seemed to be higher than the hill-tops on either side. Every part of him was shining, but his hair, and his head shone more brightly than the moon when it is brightest, and it seemed as if his heart was the great Sun's self. A long light blue cloak was on his shoulders, and fastened over his breast by a brooch shaped like a crescent moon, and that brooch seemed to be made of pale yellow flame. On his left arm was a Shield that was like the Shield the boy had, when it flashed and shone in the Sun the morning he had it. When Hu saw him he forgot all about the pain of the flames, and stood still and watched the boat and the man who was in it. And glad he was indeed, for in his heart he was knowing many things, though his mind could not say what they were.

On towards the rock came the wise one, and it's no good for you to ask me what his name was, for I won't tell you; only he was the same great king that I told you of before, and he reigned in a secret place in the vale of the shield. He seemed to become more and more beautiful as he came nearer and nearer. His body was so bright that Hu thought the purple fire in the valley was passing up through the boat, and becoming the blood in his veins. In his two eyes there was more greatness and wonderfulness than in the sky when it is full of stars, and all the music in the world seemed to be hidden within them. And as he came up to the rock, and stood looking down at Hu, the boy's heart was full of longing that he would show him what deeds he might do for making the world better than it was.

And then the great wise king spoke to him, and what his voice was like when he spoke, you will know when he speaks to you, as he will some day, children dear, never doubt it. He asked him if he were willing to go far away from his home, and fight many strong monsters in another land, and to take the heaviness of a great curse from that land by the power of the white shield he had given him seven years before. And Hu said he would do it if it would make people happier, and that it was to do such a work as that that he had taken the shield from the rock. So the king told him many things; how there was an island far away which was needed by him to be the home of a race of people who would be wiser and nobler than the people of the summer country; and how there was a curse on that island which could only be lifted by a man from the summer country who was strong and brave enough, and whose heart was free from every selfish thought; because the shield would be no good unless it were pure and white, and every selfish thought or wish that came into the mind of the man who used it would leave a dark stain on its face. And he told Hu that when the island had been made free from the curse which was on it, those men who knew about Brotherhood would go there from the summer country, and would live there, they and their children for many ages after the summer country had been lost and forgotten. And then he told him how he would have to face dreadful dangers and win fierce fights; and while he spoke it seemed as if a fire and light from his eyes came into Hu's heart, and he cried out again and again—"I will do it, and *I will* and I WILL!"

And then the wise king bade him come into the boat, and Hu leaped down from the rock right into the flames and seized the shield, and ran towards it, the fire burning and burning him all the time. When he had climbed into the boat the flame did not come out of the shield any more. But still the valley was full of it, and as they sailed on and came to where the woods began and where they could see down to the sea, the boy saw that there was a river of the purple fire going all down the mountains and pouring into many a valley on the way till it seemed to be a lake of flame, and then flowing on right across the plain and over and over the sea in a thin, shining line, till far and farther and farthest away the sparkle and glimmer of it was lost where the sea touched the sky. Sometimes it was narrow and swift, with great leaping waves of flame, and sometimes it spread out, and wide stretches of land and sea were covered with it, and the sky itself all purple and shining.

Down that river those two sailed in the magical boat, down where it was rushing like a torrent, and across the vales that had become lakes, and over the wide dark plain towards the sea, and passed out from the land a long way to the left of the city. Then on across the sea they went, but never leaving the river of fire, on towards the north and the west as the boat was carried; more swiftly they went than the swiftest fish can swim or the swiftest bird can fly, until the fire brought them to where Hu could see the land. And there the stream turned and went northwards, on past high dark mountains and wide river mouths, and then between many shadowy islands scattered in the sea, and on to where the land ended; and then southward again through a sea covered with grey mists that were not grey that night, but lit up and purple with the stream of fire—a sea where in those old days pale and ancient ghosts were always leaping from crest to crest of the waves and gliding along the smooth wave-hollows, hidden in the mists as pale and grey as themselves. And as the boat came along the fire stream that night the ghosts fled shrieking away seaward, and after that they could not come to the land any more for thousands of years. Then Hu spoke to the Man that was in the boat with him.

"What are these ghosts that are flying from us King?" said he.

"They are the thoughts that came from cold hearts in the olden days," said the King, "and afraid of the White Shield they are."

Then they turned again, and the boat passed along the south of the island and came to where Hu had first seen land, and then on again, and three times that night did the Wise One, and Hu with him, go round the island in the boat, and the fire flowing before and behind them over the dark waves like an endless serpent of purple flame. All the time, too, it was in Hu's mind what he would have to do in the island, and then again the King told him that there were fierce fights he must win, and asked him whether he still would do it, and again he lifted his hands and the shield above his head and cried out, "I will, and *I will,* and I WILL!" And once more the shield flashed with the rising of the sun, for the morning had come, and the Wise King and the purple river of fire and the boat had all gone, and Hu was standing alone on a long sandy beach in the island, and on one side of him was the sea, and on the other great rocky cliffs and rocks, with deep pools in them, and overhead the sky all beautiful with the dawn.

III
The Curse on Ynys Vail

Well, there was Hu on the beach that morning, and the Shield on his shoulder, and he not knowing where he was, nor what it would be well for him to do. But it came into his mind that he would start at once to climb up over the rocks, and that he did, and soon found a place where he would get to the top of the cliff, and quickly he did that too, and then he stood still and looked far away into the island, and a strange and terrible island it was. As far as ever he could see there was no greenness anywhere, but only miles and miles of brown deadness. Before him there was a drear valley of hard brown rocks, and beyond that were low hills of rock, and in the valley was a yellow stream, but there did not seem to be any life in the rocks or in the waters of the stream, and in the clear air there were no birds, nor even the tiniest flies flying. Indeed, for a little while his heart was full of the sorrow of the silent land; only the White Shield was with him, and so of course the heaviness of that old curse could not really hurt him, for he knew that with the Shield he would conquer it all.

So he went on his way, first down over the rocks into the valley, and then climbing up over the rocky hill beyond, and then down again through another valley, and up and over another hill. Not a sound did he hear of the singing of birds or of the lowing of cattle, nor of the buzzing of bees or of any insect wings; nothing at all but the fall of his own feet, or on the hills the roll and rattle of little stones into the valley below. As for the dead streams, they were so slow that there was no pleasant sound with them.

At mid-day he came to a wide plain of flat rock strewn over with round great stones and jagged rocks, and on the edge of it was another yellow stream. The sun was beating down on the ground till it was burning hot beneath his feet, and he was hungry too, and oh, so thirsty, and the wild lifeless land made him more tired than he would have been in his own country. So he kneeled down and drank at the stream—but the water was bitter in his mouth, and bitter after he had swallowed it, and it burned and tormented him all over his body, and he got up and went on feeling more sick and ill than he had ever felt before. For he would not sit down to rest, not knowing how far he might have to go. And then the sun looked at him until Hu's head was burning and giddy, but still he would not stop, and the Shield was still White. Then he began to see misty figures moving around him that were gone as soon as he looked straight at them, and then soft sweet voices began to call to him and bid him stay and rest, and—yes, he could see beautiful fairies, and hear what they were singing and saying.

"Stay and rest," they said, "and we will lead you soon to a place where delicate flowers are always in bloom, and sweet voiced birds always singing. The least sweet of their songs you might listen to and love for a thousand years, if the others were not more beautiful still. And the foam of the waters there is ever agleam with sunlight, straying down between the leaves of green and golden oaktrees, and it is cool there, always cool!"

But Hu thought of the work he had to do, and said: "But how shall I lift the curse from this island if I go with you?"

"Ah, forget the curse!" they cried. "Who are you to be seeking to undo what has been for so many hundreds of years? Forget the curse and the foolish hopes you had and come with us; lay down your heavy shield and come, oh come!"

And Hu could hardly stand, so hot, and tired, and hungry he was, but he told them as well as he could that he would never let the White Shield go from him, and he took it from his shoulder for a moment, and looked at it, and as he looked strength came to him from it, and he cried out that it was the work of the Wise Ones he came to do, and he was not for leaving it undone—and with that the fairies all vanished, and he could only hear a sorrowful wind dying away over the rocks.

After that he went on and on a long while, and all the way through brown and burning deadness. All the strange things he saw I cannot tell you, evil fairies and many huge monsters that seemed to be standing in his path—but every time they were gone when he would not heed nor fear them, and where they went to no one knows. But Hu went on and on, till by the time the sun was setting he had come to the end of the plain, and there was a long low hill before him; and it came into his mind that he would not rest till he was at the top of it. So he went on and climbed the hill slowly, and then looked down on the other side, and what he saw made him full of gladness.

For there was a little rich green valley below him, and a clear stream of living water singing and running through it, and many sheep and cows grazing in the long sweet grass, and birds singing wherever there were trees, and clouds of gnats flying over the pure clean stream. At one end of the valley, too, there was a little house, with a thin thread of grey smoke, swayed by no wind, going up from its chimney into the evening sky. Hu knew that he would learn something of what he had to do from whoever lived in that house.

So he went on down the hill towards the house, and as he got nearer he heard someone singing, and soon he could hear the song which was being sung, and this is what he heard:—

> *I have grown old with wailing: quiet days*
> *Have flown, and quiet years have gone their ways;*
> *And long and full of peace my days have been.*
>
> *There was no isle so fair as Ynys Vail,*
> *But now her fairness is an olden tale,*
> *And this my little vale alone is green,*
>
> *My little vale alone is green and gay,*
> *And sorrow hath not come for many a day,*
> *Nor any gloom to hide the wide blue sky.*
>
> *My quiet kine have grazed for ages long,*
> *And I have filled the griefless years with song,*
> *And all my home is green and gay as I.*

Then the song stopped for a moment, and the harp's notes that went with it died away, but in a moment it went on again:—

> *A thousand years or more, maybe, have gone,*
> *A million times, maybe, the sun has shone*
> *Since the curse came, and all the people died.*
>
> *When will it end? Only the wise ones know!*
> *Ere he will come a thousand years may go:*
> *Strong was the curse, and the old sea is wide.*
>
> *When will it end, this curse on Ynys Vail?*
> *When, o'er a rich green land shall morning pale?*
> *Maybe the day is far—maybe 'tis near.*
>
> *My little vale is rich and green and gay,*
> *And sorrow had not come for many a day*
> *Upon my quiet kine and me, nor fear.*

And as Hu went along he saw a strange, tall, beautiful old man sitting under one of the trees in the valley, and it was he who was singing. His beard and hair were white, but there was no bend in his shoulders, nor any quavering in his voice when he sang:

> *My quiet kine have grazed the ages long,*
> *And I have filled the gentle years with song,*
> *And all my vale is green and gay as I.*

And then the old man stood up and began to croon and call out in a strange tongue, and the cows and the sheep heard him, and looked up with their quiet eyes and mild heads from the grass and began to come slowly towards him from all over the valley, and as they were coming he began to sing again, leaning on his stick:—

> *You are too slow! the moon is rising now—*
> *What if he comes to-night to seek the plough?*
> *You are too slow, the stars are o'er the sky!*

And they all began to run towards him through the dusk-filled valley as quickly as they could, although there were no dogs there to worry them.

And then the old man turned round to go to the house, and as he was turning he saw Hu for the first time, and went to meet him. Hu was going to tell him how he had come to the Island, and why, and to ask him how to make it free from the curse; but the other only took his hand, and looked deep in his eyes, and said—"I know why you have come here, and what you will do. Only tonight it will be good if you rest in my cottage, and to-morrow or the next day you shall go forth and take the curse from this sad island. My name is Cador, and I have waited for you."

And there was no wonder or fear on Hu to hear that, but he was very tired, so he only thanked him and followed him into the house. And there the old man bade him sit down, and brought him milk and bread and cheese and fruit, and waited on him till he had eaten enough. And by that time Hu was so tired that he had gone fast off to sleep. So Cador lifted him up in his arms, big as he was, and laid him on a bed that was in the house, and hung the White Shield on the wall over his head, and waited beside him for seven days, and all that time he was fast asleep.

And when on the eighth morning Hu awoke, he felt ten times wiser and stronger than he had ever been before. Looking out of the window, he could see old Cador milking a cow outside, and he went out and spoke to him, and after that there was a great love for each other in the hearts of both of them. When the milking was over they went into the cottage and ate; and after that Hu asked Cador to tell him what he was wanting to know. Then the old man told Hu the whole story of the curse. He told him that in the olden times the Island had been called Ynys Vail, the Isle of Honey, though there were no bees between all its four seas then, except in his own valley. For, he said, "there were giants in Ynys Vail then, and three giant kings ruled them: Ninnio was the king of the North, and Pibeo of the South and East, and Rhita Gawr of the Western mountains.

"By their pride and anger and wickedness Ninnio and Pibeo brought war and sorrow for the first time into Ynys Vail. Then Rhita came down from the mountains and made an end of the war, and took the two fighting kings away to his own land; but he was not soon enough to keep the curse from coming on their two countries, and the north and the south of Ynys Vail, wherever they had trodden in battle, became hard rock. And this valley alone is green and free because there has never been any rage or hate or war in it.

"But when Rhita had conquered the whole island, he too became full of pride, and that although he had been a just and good man before. In his pride and daring he tried to do a thing that brought his fall on him, and then the curse came on his land too, and all the people in Ynys Vail died, and I am alone in the whole island.

"Only the curse did not turn Rhita's country into rock. Into a lake there it brought Avank, a great water beast, because of whom, after a while, no one dared to go down to the lake. Then he grew angry, and with some strange magic that he had, caused the waters of his lake to rise and rise and rise, till they were higher than the tops of the mountains, and they flowed out over the whole land, and the people were drowned, and all the valleys became lakes, and the mountains covered with marshes, and never since have any people lived there, because of the wetness of the land, and of Avank's anger and magic."

Then Hu said, "If those two kings brought the curse on Ynys Vail, it is in my mind that through them I shall have to lift it."

"Indeed," said the other, "a true thing it is you have said, and you have to find Ninnio and Pibeo first. There are four things with me which you will need—a boat, a yoke, a plough, and a great chain, and the strong magic is in each of them, and that will help you, though I am not knowing how. The boat you must take and go west and north from here into Rhita's kingdom, and there you will find them: the boat will lead you to them. Aye, you will find them, and do all that you have to do . . . for I have known of your coming for hundreds of years . . . and that you could not fail if there were no stain or mist upon your Shield; but when you would I was not allowed to know."

Then Hu said nothing, but he thought and thought and thought, and he was longing to ask Cador who he was, and why he was living there all alone, and if he was so old that he could remember Ninnio and Pibeo and the beginning of the curse, and a whole lot of other things too. But the old man looked at him with bright blue eyes that seemed to be seeing right down into Hu's heart, and telling him not to care—and then he knew that to do the work he was for doing all his heart and mind had to be full of it, and nothing else in them at all. And you may wonder how he would be able to take the boat into Rhita's kingdom, but Hu did not wonder or doubt at all that he could do it; and if he had, I think there would have been some darkness on the face of his Shield. And remember you that, children, for you too will need to keep the shields that you will have without any stain or darkness on them; and how will you do th⸳ if there are doubts and fears in your hearts? *How?*

IV

Ninnio and Pibeo

Well, children, that day too Hu stayed in the valley and talked to old Cador, and learned from him many strange things. And the next morning they got up early, the two of them, and went out from the cottage, and half way up the hillside to where there was a little wood, and in the middle of the wood a great pond of water with the leafy trees and the blue of the sky glassed on it. On the pond there was a strange and beautiful boat floating, that seemed to be made of white and blue ivory, and all over it were wonderful figures cut out of every kind of jewel in the world. And there were long wings folded along the two sides of it, and they were as white as soft white clouds, and it seemed as if it were alive and full of the gladness of the golden rising sun.

And there Cador said goodbye to Hu, and bade him go into the boat, for he would find in it whatever things he would need. So through the reeds and waterlilies he went, knee-deep in the water, and stepped into the boat; and as soon as he was sitting down it spread out its two wings and rose and rose with him up through the air. In it were the three other things that Cador had been keeping for him—the Yoke, the Chain, and the Plough. And they too were full of magic, and if the boat seemed to be a living thing, Hu thought there was surely golden life in all three of them.

Well, up and up he rose till he could no longer see the old man standing by the water in the wood below; and then away to the north and west for mile after mile, and with nothing to be seen but miles on dreary miles of brown rock. And then, when the afternoon came, he passed high over a great river with pale brown waters, and on the other side of it there were green plains and high green hills at last; but the plains were swamps full of wide still pools and reeds, and the mountains were covered with marshes, and bogmyrtles and long green rushes were growing in the driest places. And so Hu knew that he was in the western kingdom, where Rhita the Giant had reigned, and where Ninnio and Pibeo were, and great Avank. And wherever he could see there were no living things, except such birds as can live on the water and make their nests in the waving reeds.

And as he went on and on towards the north and the west, his way lay between the crests of high mountains; and over quiet stretches of blue water; for the valleys were all half full of water; and black cold drops of water were all the time dripping and dropping and dropping down the mountains on either side, and into tiny streams and deep dark pools, and at last flowing down into the lakes. And it seemed to Hu that all the mountains were shedding tears because of the sorrow of the curse.

And towards evening the boat began to sink down over an island in the middle of the broadest lake he had seen that day. Half the island was a little hill covered with trees, and half of it was flat and treeless; and on the treeless half he could see two great living things struggling and fighting, and breathing out dark flames at each other as they fought. And there for a while the boat stayed still in the air with great wings spread out, and Hu leaned over the side and watched them fighting.

At first they seemed to be two huge men striking at each other with their fists, and wrestling, and struggling, and shouting; then they were changed into two great lions—ten times as large they were as any lion alive now—and standing on their hind legs, they fought and tore each other with their teeth and their strong claws, and the rage and anger that was in their eyes was the most fearful and evil fire Hu had ever seen. Then one of them fell, and rolled over into the water, and in a moment became a great water monster, and the other followed him in the same shape, and they chased each other round and round the lake till the water that had been smooth and beautiful with the sunset was like a wild sea for roughness. Then the long white wings began to move again, and Hu came slowly down among the trees on the higher part of the island, and among the trees he left the boat and went down to where it was treeless.

And the magic boat of Cador it was that brought him there, and so Hu knew that he had found Ninnio and Pibeo, who first had brought the curse on Ynys Vail. And as soon as he was facing the place where they were fighting in the water, he held up the White Shield where the setting sun would flash from it, and cried out to them—

"End your fighting, you two who were kings, for I am sent here to give you a work to do."

And Ninnio and Pibeo heard him, and for a moment the water ceased to foam and rage around them; and they were silent and apart from each other; and a thought of the time when they were real kings and there was no curse on Ynys Vail came into their minds. But then they looked at the island and saw Hu standing there, and thought of the hatred they had for each other, and for all men, and they both began to swim towards the island as quickly as they could, that they might kill him before they fought with each other again.

And there Hu stood and watched them coming, and he saw the hatred they had, those two strong monsters, for him; and that they would be trying to kill him; and then there came into his mind a certain singing he had heard seven years before—

> *Oh White Shield, and snow-white Shield,*
> *To You they yield, the dragons' dread!*
> *The fierce things with blood-red wings,*
> *'Tis you that make them tame or dead!*

—and he laughed proudly and out loud, and shouted to them across the water that he had with him there a thing that would tame and maybe save fiercer dragons or demons than they were. For he saw that the age-long rage of them had turned them into wild strong elves, and that they were not men any more; and full of pity for them he was.

And first Ninnio came to the island, and stood on the shore, and sprang at Hu with great dragon wings and claws stretched out; and dark red was the fire that he breathed out at him. But the White Shield was lifted up where the sun's light fell on it, and in a moment it flashed and burned so brightly that there was no shadow anywhere in the whole valley, or on the mountains on either side, and Ninnio's fire was altogether burnt up by it, as the dark fire of hatred always is by such pure and flashing flame as came from that Shield. And Ninnio's two eyes were dimmed by the brightness; and the mad heart in him was tamed and made full of quietness and peace; and he lay down before Hu, and they both knew that he would serve him after in whatever way he might. Hu knew, and Ninnio knew—and Pibeo knew, too, and he bellowed and screamed and lashed the water for rage as he swam; for it was not in *his* eyes that the fire of Hu's Shield had flashed, nor had it burnt into *his* heart. So he came on swiftly through the water towards the island, and the ripples that he made as he came were waves that broke around the mountain feet, and washed up over the island as high as Ninnio was lying.

And Hu would not wait for Pibeo where he had stood when the first of them came, but ran down to the edge of the water to meet him. Three times he lifted the Shield, and flashed bright fire from it against that wild, strong monster; but each time Pibeo, who was full of cunning for all the madness of his anger, dived deep down into the water, and shut his eyes tight so that it could not reach him as well as if he had seen it flashing through the air alone. So after the third time Hu went back a little way, and stood under a tree where the island was beginning to rise into a hill, and waited there till Pibeo should come to land. And the gold of the sunset was streaming down over him, and shining in his bright hair.

But Pibeo thought to attack him from behind when he saw what danger there was from the burning light of the Shield. So he swam underneath the water to other side of the little island, and rose in the air as a winged dragon, but oh! so quietly, and was for swooping down on Hu while he was watching for him where he had dived. And a dreadful thing it might have been for Hu, children, if Ninnio had not seen his old enemy coming, and cried out as well as he could to warn the man who had tamed him of the danger he was in. And there was no time for Hu to be startled, or for anything but to turn round and face the great fierce thing, and only just in time did he lift the wonderful Shield. And then once more the flame leaped from it that always burns up the dark red, evil fires; and the brightness flashed into Pibeo's angry eyes, and the anger was gone from them, and then through and deep into his heart, and made light there, where it had been so dark with restless hatred for maybe it was thousands of years. Then he, too, fell down right at the feet of Hu, and lay, quiet and tamed under the trees on the wood's edge; and there was no more hate or pride or anger in the whole valley at the time when the sun went out of sight behind the hills, but only coolness and peace. For all the air between the mountains was purged and clean of every evil thing that had come from the hearts of Ninnio and Pibeo, and it was the flashing of the White Shield that purged it. And the sky was full of the beauty of the sunset, and the stars were beginning to shine and twinkle out of the paleness of blue. And in that way the curse that was on Ynys Vail began to be lifted.

And that night Hu slept in his boat under the trees in the highest part of the island; but Ninnio and Pibeo lay where they fell in the flat treeless part, and there was no one to hinder them if they had wanted to do him any harm. But as I told you, there was no hate left in them, and for the first time since they had been living in that valley, they slept in all quietness till the sun came up over the hills, for they knew there would be a work for them to do together in the morning. And so strange was the fire of the White Shield that they were glad that it was so.

And when the morning came, and the coolness of dawn, they awoke, the three of them, and Hu went down and bathed in the cold lake, and after that he came to where the two who had been kings were and said to them—

"Now if you can speak, as I am thinking you can, do you two tell me how I shall make an end of the curse that came long ago on Ynys Vail, for it is in my mind that no one knows but you."

And they both lifted their heads to answer him, and one quiet voice seemed to be coming from the two of them.

"Ninnio and Pibeo indeed we were, and through us alone you can end the curse. With the magic that we have we will change ourselves into two strong and gentle oxen, and with us you must drag Avank out of his lake of floods, and plough the rock lands that were our two kingdoms from end to end, and so lift the whole curse from Ynys Vail." (And it's in my mind, children dear, that if you watch the way the Lotus Mother does things, you will come to know far better than I do why they said that.)

Well, while they were speaking, they began to change, the two of them, and they were no more ugly dragons, but tall, strong and beautiful oxen, and so great in height that a tall man now would hardly be able to reach higher than their breasts. Only Hu with the White Shield was much taller than the tallest man in the world in these days, and his shoulders were higher at that time than the tips of their long horns when they were holding up their heads. So he yoked them together with the yoke that Cador had given him, and there was a strange magic in that yoke, and what it was you shall hear in a while. Then he himself got into the boat, and it rose with him in the air and began to fly away slowly towards the north, and the two great oxen were following it below over mountain and lake and wild marsh, and over marsh and lake and mountain.

V

The End of Avank

Well, as they went on, the sky was greyer and greyer, and the mountains higher and higher, and every pass between them a roaring river, and every valley a great lake. And there were wet grey mists all over the land, and nothing came through the dimness of it except the sound of pouring, unseen waters. A grey and ghostly place it was, and one where Hu might easily have lost himself, if he had not been in a boat that needed no eyes for finding its way through the unknown air. And the two oxen that came after, they would have sunk far into the soft ground with every step they took, only part of the magic of the yoke they had was, that the feet of beasts that were under it would not sink in the softest land.

So they went on slowly, up and up and up, until at last they came, higher than the mountains, to a wide marshy plain, and passing on through that, to the edge of a great drear water. And Hu could hear distant rivers pouring out of it, but he could not see them, however near they might be, because of the mist. There the boat stopped, and the oxen, and so he knew well that was the lake where Avank lived. And he knew, too, that the first thing to do was to fasten one end of the chain to the oxen, so that with it they could pull the monster out of his home. And so he came down out of his boat, and was doing that, and not thinking what he should do after.

But small need for him to think, for he had hardly fastened the one end of it when the chain became like a living thing, and shook itself out, and raised its free end in the air, and went out curving and moving over the lake; and floating through the water; and at last it dived down under the water, and became tight and tighter and tightest; for because of the magic that was in it, it knew well what to do. Then Hu called to Ninnio and Pibeo, and those two put their heads down, and pulled and pulled; and the water began to be ruffled, and there were great waves rolling across the lake, and all the time they grew bigger, and came rolling up nearer to where Hu was. For you see, old Avank was angry, and so the Lake of Floods was rising, and may be this time too, it would drown the whole land.

"Faster and faster, my two strong ones," cried Hu; and faster they did go, those two oxen, and dreadfully hard they pulled, but the water was always rising higher, and every white-foamed wave that came dashing towards them was huger and more furious than all the others. For it was a magic chain that had gone down through the lake, and fastened itself to the great monster's body, and it is not I who who can be telling you how it did that. But I know it awoke him from a sleep that had been on him for I think it was hundreds of years, and at first he was full of anger, and took himself to his magic that the waters might rise, and struggled and pulled against the chain; but there was no strength in the world that could break that, and the two oxen were stronger than he was. So for all his strength and for all the power of his magic he knew that some evil fate would be coming on him that day; he had heard a whisper of it, too, long ago in the green loneliness of his deep, still, cold waters.

So there were Ninnio and Pibeo the oxen pulling him towards land. And soon when Hu turned for a moment as he was leading them, he could see what seemed to be a line of black rock in the water, and the waves breaking and washing in foam-whiteness over it. But Hu knew that it was Avank's back he could see, and he called to the oxen to go quicker still, for the water was rising all the time, and the waves were breaking over them as they went. And as quickly as ever Hu could lead them they followed him, and Avank could not stay them with his struggling, nor even with all the power and crushing of his great waves. For you see, the waves in that place were his faithful slaves, every one of them, and one after another they came roaring over the lake's edge, and the shore; and like three strong rocks stood Hu and the oxen every time one thundered down on them; and they were all three tired and wet and freezing nearly with the magic coldness of them; but still they went on, and would not be thrown down or swept away. And Ninnio and Pibeo, those old fighters, looked back over all the ages of their lives, but they could neither of them think of any battle they had ever fought so terrible as that battle with Avank's fierce, wild, thundering soldiers—the green, white-foaming, demon-souled waves of the Lake of Floods.

"On and on, my strong ones!" cried Hu, and on and on they went; and the wind was screaming and shrieking over the lake and over the bellowing of mighty waves; and all the time those last were growing greater and stronger; and the sharp rain was falling right in the faces of Hu and his two servants. For Avank knew well he was coming nearer and nearer to the shore, and would be out of the water in a minute; and then where would his power be? So again and again he sent out the strongest of his waves; but if they had been stronger the man with the White Shield would not have been conquered by them,* though maybe they would have crushed all the ships

---

*And *of course* the reason of that, as every Lotus Bud knows, was that there was no stain on the Shield's face.

in the wide world. And what about Ninnio and Pibeo? Well, I do believe those great waves would have thrown them down that time if Hu had not been guiding and leading them, and holding them up while the water-mountains fell. And after that there were no more waves, and the lake that had risen began to go down, and as soon as Hu could look round, he saw that the evil master of the lake was out of his home and away from his magic, and only the end of his tail left in the water at all.

And there he lay, and he was the ugliest and most terrible thing Hu had ever seen. His body was long and huge and smooth and shiny, and his thin neck lay along the ground, and the little head at the end of it was flat on the ground, and in it were two quick, white-rimmed eyes that seemed to be full of all the evil thoughts in the world. And nearly as soon as Hu turned to look at him, Avank raised his head and called out and asked Hu how he had dared to come there to disturb his long peace and dreams—and "I will allow you to go without harm or hurt this time," he said—but Hu only laughed, and asked him what harm he would be doing him if he stayed.

"Ah!" said Avank, "it is strong I am, and I need not be any thing but kind to such a man as you seem to be. But there is some magic in this chain that fills me with sorrow; and if you would have my love, you have only to unfasten it and let me be free. And then I will make you a master of all the magic of the green waters, and show you how to raise great wave armies to do your will."

And then, for his power was not all gone from him while any part of him was left in the lake, another wave arose at his bidding, and came rolling towards Hu, but it fell and went back before it had gone half the way.

So Hu turned again to the oxen, and they dragged Avank a little way further still, till there was land between him and the lake; and then the wind fell and the mists were gone, and the whole place was quiet, but for the trickling of innumerable waters and the pattering of soft rain. Then Hu lifted the yoke from the two oxen, and they lay down where they were to rest.

But as soon as ever Avank felt that the chain was loose at the other end, he lifted himself on his four legs as quietly as he could, and began to go down towards the lake; for it was in his mind that he might yet get back to his old lonely kingdom in the water, and to his old magic power. But Hu drew his long bright sword, and ran down between him and the lake, and called out to him that Ynys Vail should be free now from all the oppression of waters, or he would have to conquer him, and his sword, and the Shield that a Wise One had given him. And when Avank saw that there was no getting away, he rushed at Hu, full of hissing anger; and lifted himself up on his hind legs, and tried to drag him down, but he could not, and struck great blows at him with his swinging head; and if one of those blows had fallen on Hu, I could never have told you this story, children, or else it would have ended right here. But swift as he was, and strong, the man I'm telling you about was swifter and stronger still; and so they fought and fought and fought; and if Hu had been angry for a moment, there would have been that on the Shield that would have made it useless. And at last the swinging head came down on that same shield with a crash such as no smith could make with hammer on anvil, and after that there were no more thoughts in Avank's mind, and he only fought on because of the evil that was in him. And not long he did that either, for soon there was a great sweep of the bright sword, and he fell down along the wet ground, and there was no life with him whatever. And then whether it was that that clash of head on shield had frightened the grey elves of the clouds I don't know; but the rain stopped, and there were wide spaces between the clouds, and the bright sun shone down from the blue of the sky. And Hu looked at dead Avank, and at Ninnio and Pibeo, and he thought of the work he had been set to do, and all that had yet to be done; and again he lifted the Shield above his head, and "I will do it!" he cried *"I will!"*—and with that the flame came again from the Shield that was ten times brighter than ever before. Oh so bright it was, that fire! and it leaped and flashed over the lake and the marshlands; and there was no mist anywhere, but only air like a great gleaming diamond for clearness; and it chased away every cloud over the edge of the sky, and beyond the far mountains—and when the blinding brightness of it was gone, Avank's body was all burnt up and gone too, and no one has seen a sign of it from that day to this. And the lake was shining and beautiful, and far away in the great valley; and the streams that had been wailing were singing merry songs (and they haven't forgotten how to sing them yet); and the great pools of dark marsh water were flowing down in bright streams to the lake, and singing too; and the whole country was more sunlit and sparkling and blue-skied and beautiful than before it had been grey and lone and full of moaning winds and ghostly mists. And the lake was not called the Lake of Floods any more, but the Lake of Beauty, and that is its name to this day. And in time all the mournful waters that Avank had brought to Rhita's kingdom flowed away, and the whole land became fit for the noblest men and the most star-beautiful fairies to live in. And in that way was the curse lifted from the mountain country of Rhita Gawr in the west of green Ynys Vail of the Bees.

VI
The End of the Curse

Well, children, after that Hu went eastward in his boat through the cool and beautiful air, and the two oxen after him. And at last they left the mountains behind them, and were in the Rockland once more; and that land Hu had to plough with Ninnio and Pibeo, and he did it too. How could he, you ask, if it was all hard rock? Ah! it was what he had to do, since he himself had chosen to do it; what others greater than he was have had to do before and since, because they, too, had chosen to do it. And whenever you hear people talking about a great lady called H.P. Blavatsky, remember you that she was one who came from a beautiful place to plough the hard rock of many lands; and a mighty work it was for her, and thousands of evil things there were to plague her while she was doing it, as you shall hear there were for Hu in his time too. Yes indeed, a mighty work it was, but if she had not done it there would have been no Lotus groups to go to, and *then* where would you and I be? So it shows how much she loved everyone, that great lady H.P.B., and how great and strong she was, and how flashing and bright was her shield. And then there was Mr. Judge too, and our own dear Lotus Mother. Whenever you see her or the picture of her, think you in your own hearts that she too has had such a work as that to do; aye, to plough hot miles and miles of rock land, more than there is in all Ynys Vail and the three islands that are near it, and all of it harder, I think, than the hardest marble. For *that* grows from the wonderful working of I do not know what great and fiery being in I cannot say what splendid secret workshop in the mountains; but the rock such as those Great Ones have had to plough is made hard by all that comes from cold hard hearts and the selfish thoughts of unbrotherly people.

For all these thoughts must go *somewhere,* you see—of course they must! where else are they to go to? And they must be doing something, too; and now you ought to know what they do and where they go. And didn't wise old Cador himself say that the rocks of Ynys Vail came wherever Ninnio and Pibeo and their armies had trodden in war and hatred? So that proves it.

Well, Hu began to plough that land, and a wonderful plough it is, I know, that can bite into the hard rock as his did. For wherever the two great oxen drew the plough, and Hu passed on after them, the rock was turned into soft rich earth; and as he went along green grass and young trees grew up swiftly and silently behind him, and sweet bloomed flowers blossomed, and bees and butterflies came for their honey. And all that was because of the magic in the plough, and what that magic is you will come to know. In front of him was always the brown lifeless rock that grew, as he knew, less and less every day, for he passed over more land in one hour than ten men now could plough in ten days. And the magic, too, was the cause of that.

And ever and ever as he went came strange ill-shapen things that rained poisonous arrows on him from behind, but the White Shield was over his back, and the arrows fell harmless from that, and Hu passed on. And after, he heard a great shout in front of him, and looking up, he saw what seemed to be a huge army coming against him with drawn swords over the rocks, and he could hear the tramp and clank of thousands of steel-clad feet on the rocks. On they came in long lines, but it seemed as if the oxen could not see them, and he himself was not the one to stay or turn for a more terrible danger than that. And then they seemed to be rushing at him to kill him, but still he did not fear them—and as soon as the first of them were near enough to touch him the whole army of them became dim and vanished, and it was a long moaning wind that sped past him and died away. And Hu passed on and on, and always more and more of the land was becoming green and beautiful and freed of all evil things. And he was far greater and stronger and wiser then than he had been when first he came away from the Summer Country, and great need there was for him to be that; or how would he have done that ploughing? So when he heard what seemed to be demons shrieking behind him, and mocking laughter all around, he did not fear, or stay to look back, and when soft voices were begging him to rest or to come aside from his work and lay down his sword and his great shield, he did not ever heed them but went on and on and on, for such strength had come to him that he had no need for sleep or eating, and it was the same with the two that worked for him. So through glaring sunshine and grey mist, darkness and shadowy moonlight nights, they went on; and what ever they heard and saw, they did not heed nor fear.

And sometimes there would come to him crowds of ill fairies that shouted evil and vile things at him; and you will hear the same things too, so I shan't tell you what they were. And then may your shields be white and without stain on them; for because Hu's Shield was like that, he was able to go on, and still go on and on.

And when he came to Cador's valley, there it was, green and cool and beautiful, and the sheep and the cows grazing in it; but no old man could he see. And he called to him many times, but only from the other side of the valley the elves called out—"Cador! Cador!" in answer. After that he searched all through the valley, but there was no Cador there. And then it came into his mind that may be the old man had ended his work, and had gone back to the Wise Ones who live in their own secret place.

And so he went on and on and on till there was none of the curse left between all the four seas of Ynys Vail, but only a green and beautiful land where the hills were blue and purple and the valleys full of soft greenness. And there were woods, and birds singing in all the trees of them, and white-winged birds on all the gentle curling waves of its seas, and beautiful and kindly-hearted fairies in the mountains, and all that because of what Hu did.

And what next? Well, afterwards he went back to the Summer Country, and found people there who knew what Brotherhood meant, and they came with him into Ynys Vail. They were called the Comrades, were those Brotherhood people, and just as the King of the Vale of the Shield had said, the Comrades were a great people in Ynys Vail long after the Summer Country was lost and forgotten. And for many years Hu was the King of Ynys Vail, for he, too, was wise, and the Comrades knew that they had never seen anywhere such a man as he was. And after, when he threw away his body, and took a new one of bright fire, and went to live in some secret palace of his own, they called him Hu the Mighty, and Hu with the White Shield, and sometimes they called their island the Island of the Mighty, because he had lived in it. And for hundreds and thousands of years they remembered and loved him, and they told their Lotus Buds about him, as I tell you now, and they told them too, just as I have told you dozens of times in this story, that unless he had been strong of will, and had driven away from him all the selfish thoughts, there would have been stains and darkness on the Shield's face, and he could never have flashed from it the magical fire with which he tamed Ninneo and Pibeo, nor could he have done any of the work that the great wise King set him to do.

And that is the end of the story of Hu, children, and some day you will know that it is true. And the sooner you know the better will it be for you, and the better you are, the sooner you will know. And that is all.

The last of Morris's early stories, "The Story of Mabon" again reworks
material from Welsh mythological tales. It was published in the Children's
Department of The Universal Brotherhood Path in March 1902,
signed Ceinydd Morus.

The Story of Mabon

I
Arthur's Knights

Once upon a time the great King Arthur wanted to find a man. The man's name was Mabon and his mother, Modron, was a great queen in the days gone by. Indeed, whether it is right to call him a man at all, or whether he was a bright fairy, or even of a more splendid race than men or fairies, I do not know.

For Arthur had heard a whisper about this Mabon and the whisper was that he had been stolen away from his mother ages and ages ago, when he was a tiny baby; but was alive still somewhere or other, and would seem when he was found to be but a youth. And it said there was no one in the world who could do a certain work for Arthur except Mabon; and what that work was you will hear, maybe, another day.

Well, Arthur asked everybody he knew if they had ever heard of Mabon, but no one had heard a sound of him till that day. Only the wisest man in the country could give him any advice at all, and what *he* said was that the king had better send out five of the strongest and bravest and noblest of his knights to search for him high and low and up and down and far and wide, and perhaps they would hear tell of him somewhere or other in the big world. And that, the Emperor Arthur thought, was the best thing he could do.

So he called five of his knights, and the ones he called were these: The first was Cai (and that rhymes with "high"), and he was the best warrior Arthur ever had. He was so wise that he could become as tall as the tallest tree in the forest, or, if he wanted to, as small as the weeniest ant in the grass. In his heart was so bright a fire that everyone who came near him became warm and happy, even if it was the coldest day in winter, and even if they had been miserable the minute before. He was so true and strong that no dragon could stand against him, and if any evil thing was so much as scratched with his sword no doctor in the world could cure it. And he could do other wonderful things, too, such as staying under the water for nine nights and nine days, and going without food or drink or sleep for as long, and that without any harm coming to him. And him Arthur chose to be the leader of the five.

And the second was called Bedwyr (and you must call that Bedweer). Arthur sent him because he would always follow Cai, and serve him faithfully in any danger. He was Cai's dearest friend, and many a giant had those two together fought and killed. Wherever Cai went Bedwyr was not afraid to go.

And there was one named Gwrhyr (that is, Goorheer). No one in the world could speak any language that Gwrhyr did not know. Not only that but he knew the meaning of the lion's roar, and the ox's low; and the cat's mew and the dog's bark; the bees told him in their own tongue whatever wisdom they had; he understood what the dumb fishes think as they go in the water, and not a bird sang but Gwhyr could have told you as soon as he heard it, what was in its mind and what was in its song. So he, as you may guess, was a good man to be sent on such a journey as this, and so it was that the king sent him.

And the other two were called Cilhwch and Eidoel (please say Kilhoo'h and I-doyle, won't you, children?). Arthur sent Eidoel because Mabon would never be found, so the whisper said, unless one of his own race were on the quest, and Eidoel was of the same race as Mabon. And about Cilhwch there is nothing to tell you just this minute.

II
The Ousel of Cilgwri*

Well, these five rode out from Arthur's town, and they rode a day and they rode a night, and how much longer I do not know, and they came at last to a country called Cilgwri. And they came to a wide plain with a laughing, stony, sunny river running through it, and by the river there was a tree, and a very nice tree it was, too. Toward that tree they went.

In the tree there was a little bird singing, and Gwrhyr, Who Knew the Languages (that was what people called him), heard what she was singing, and this was her song:

> *I am so old, so old, my eyes have seen*
> *Hundreds of times my land in spring grow green,*
> *Hundreds of leafy summers come and go,*

---

*And it's quite easy to say that; you must just say it as if it were spelt Kilgoory.

Hundreds of sorrowful winters white with snow—
How many hundreds, 'tis not I that know.

When first Cilgwri heard my verses sung
An anvil stood here, and thereon has rung
No hammer since; but I have flown each day
And pecked it with my beak as dusk grew grey,
And now—my beak has pecked it all away.

"And what did you do that for?" asked Gwrhyr in Ousel language, for the little birdie was an Ousel.

"Why, to sharpen my beak to be sure," said she. "But where are you going, and I wonder if I could help you in any way?"

"Well," said Gwrhyr, "maybe as you are so very old, little bird, you can tell us about Mabon, the son of Queen Modron. He was stolen away from his mother when he was only a tiny baby, goodness knows how long ago, and no one can say what has become of him."

"I never heard of him," said the Ousel, "never in all my days. It must have been long, long before my time. Why do you want him?"

"King Arthur needs him to do a great work," said he.

And as soon as he mentioned the Emperor's name, down came the birdie from her nest, from bough to bough she hopped, and she told them that as it was for *him* she thought perhaps she could help them; for she knew an old gentleman who was quite old before she herself was born, and she would be glad to take them to him if they would come with her, because everyone wished to help and serve the Emperor Arthur.

So on they rode over the plain, and Mrs. Ousel was flying on before them. And they rode a day and they rode a night, and how much longer I do not know, and by and by they came to a great forest where there were miles on beautiful miles of huge oak trees, all of them hundreds of years old. And the waving ferns and the bracken in the forest were as high as the heads of their horses. And in the middle of the forest they came to a wide open place of ferns, and in the middle of that place was an old dead stump of a tree. And to that stump the little Ousel flew and there she perched.

III
The Stag of Rhedynfre*

Said she, "This is the place where my friend lives, and here I expect we shall see him soon." And while she was saying this and while they were looking round for any place where an old gentleman might be living (for that's what they all thought the Ousel's friend was, of course)—what should they see but two great wide-branching antlers rising up from among the fern, and

---

*Which is pronounced Rhedinvray, children.

after the antlers a beautiful stag with a noble, kingly head and eyes full of
wisdom and of memories of the old ancient times. The stag walked up towards them slowly, like a prince to his visitors; and when he saw Mrs.
Ousel, he greeted her and she greeted him, and you would have said from
their greeting that it was from him she had learnt all the great wisdom she
had. "Lord Stag," said she, "can you help these knights?"

"I shall be glad to do so if I can. What is it you want, princes?"

Then Gwrhyr came forward and told the Stag of Rhedynfre (that was
the name of his place), about Mabon, who had been stolen away from his
mother when he was three nights old, thousands of years ago, and never had
anyone heard a sound of him since; and how Arthur wanted him for doing a
certain great work—and all this he told him in the language of the stags of
course.

"The Emperor Arthur wants him?" said the stag. "Then I am doubly
sorry that I cannot tell you where he is, for I should be proud indeed to help
him. It must be a long, long time since Mabon was lost," he said, "for it was
before my day, and goodness knows I am not very young. You see this dead
tree here," said he, pointing to the old tree-stump in the middle of the
glade. "When first I came here and was made the king of my land, Rhedynfre, there was only a tiny acorn with a wee shoot and two little leaves to it
growing there. And in a hundred years it was a small oak tree, and in two
hundred years again it had grown big, and in three hundred years from that
it had become a tree that I was proud of, and in long years after it grew a
hundred great boughs, like that it was for more ages than I can tell you (for
you see, children, the oaks lived even longer then than they do now). And in
time from the acorns it dropped grew other trees; and there is not a giant
tree in this forest but grew up from one of those acorns, and this tree is the
father of them all. And it was a wise tree in its time, and whispered to me
all that the birds told it, and all that was in its heart and all that was in its
mind and in its imagination, and it was my comrade. But at last this body
of it died. And never did this tree hear of Mabon and never have I heard of
him."

"Dear, dear me!" said the old Ousel. "You are the most ancient of all
the animals and birds in the world, and you cannot remember the stealing
of Mabon, and so the great Emperor Arthur will not be able to find the man
he wants."

"No," said the stag, "I am not the oldest. There is one dear friend of
mine who was old and wise before I had this body; and as you came from
Arthur I will go with you and bring you to her, if you will come with me.
She will know, I should think—if it is to be known at all."

So they thanked him and said they would go; and then said good-bye to
the little bird and thanked her for helping them so kindly, and told her
they would tell Arthur about her, and what she had done for him, and
promised her she should have two brand new anvils from the king to

sharpen her beak on forever after (and so she had two when the time came). And with that she flew away to her own tree in Cilgwri, and sang on, as of old, about her great age and all she had learnt, and of all the people she had helped in her day, and of those she would help in the days to come.

But as for Cai and Bedwyr and Gwrhyr and Cilhwch and Eidoel, they went on their way towards the north, and the Stag of Rhedynfre with them. And they rode a day and they rode a night, and how much longer I do not know; and they passed through the forest and by great cities and over plains and rivers and mountains, and at last they came to a broad valley, and there was a blue river running through the valley, and all around was a green and ancient forest. And they came to an old and hollow tree on the hillside, and there the Stag stopped.

IV
The Owl of Cwm Cawlwyd*

"This is where my friend lives," said the Stag, "and I will knock at her door."

And with that he tapped with his horn on the trunk of her tree, and there came a voice from within, and to Cai and the others it seemed to be saying, "Tee-hwo-o-o," but the Stag and Gwrhyr knew it meant—"Who's there?"

And who should come out from the tree but an old Owl, the oldest in the whole world, I should think, and the wisest too, and the one with the softest and most beautiful voice (and you know all owls are very wise and have beautiful voices).

"Welcome my dear old friend and pupil," said the Owl of Cwm Cawlwyd (that was the name of her valley). "And welcome to you all. Is there anything you are wanting to know from me?"

"Please we've come to look for Mabon, the son of Queen Modron, who was stolen away from between his mother and the wall when he was a baby. Perhaps you may have heard something about him long ago when you were young, for it is thousands of ages since he was stolen."

The old Owl took off her spectacles and wiped the glasses, and put them on again and looked hard at Gwrhyr; and then she sat pondering awhile, and then she told them her story. And here it is:

"When I had traveled as far as I wanted to travel," said she, "and seen all I wanted to see, I came to live here in Cwm Cawlwyd, and there was a forest here then as there is now. And here I lived until I learned all that that forest could teach me. And then there came a few men and cut down a few of the trees and built cabins for themselves. I watched those men grow old and die, and in the time of their grandsons there was a large village here. In

*And that you must pronounce as if were written Coom Cowl (to rhyme with Owl), Weed—Coom Cowlweed.

the time of *their* grandsons the village had become a town; a hundred years from then it was a city. The city grew and grew and people came to it from every country. It became the place of powerful kings, twelve lines of kings reigned there, and each line was greater than the one before it. In their days the men of the city were brave and pure and noble. They built ships and sailed away and conquered far lands and brought home prisoners and gold. Then came twelve lines of evil kings, and the people became richer and more and more wicked. Then came sicknesses and famines and they began to go away and to die. Then came enemies that conquered the city, and there were no kings thereafter. And I saw the palaces fall into ruins, and no new palaces built in their place. People went away, and no others came instead. At last there were only a few huts here, and a few miserable robbers in them. Then those few robbers died and their huts slowly fell. In hundreds of years the earth had hidden all the ruins deep under grass and nettles. In hundreds of years the air was pure and free from evil thoughts. Then a few young trees began to grow where I had seen the palaces. In hundreds of years again there was a great and ancient forest waving and whispering where the town had its grave. Then for a long time I had peace. But at last again came men to Cwm Cawlwyd, and what I had seen before I saw again. Only the second town was longer in the building than the first, and became greater and more powerful than it. And there were twenty dynasties of good kings, and twenty kings in each, and twenty dynasties of bad kings. In longer ages it grew richer and more wicked than the forgotten town beneath it. And that city, too, I saw die away, and this is the third forest I have known in Cwm Cawlwyd, and many ages has it been growing.

"And it is no young bird I am," she said, "and it is no few things I have heard and known and remembered, but I have never heard anything of this Mabon. My wings are withered stumps, and my voice is old and nearly gone, and doubtless I shall have finished with this body and I shall die in a few ages. But the stealing of Mabon was not in my day, and I have heard no sound of him except from you."

"Indeed," said the Stag, "I am sorry to hear this, for you are the oldest and wisest person in the world, and you have not heard of Mabon, and nobody has heard of him, and so our race will not be able to help the Emperor Arthur, who is the best helper in the whole world, and the one whom it is the greatest honor to help."

"You come from the Emperor Arthur?" said she. "Then old and feeble as I am, I will use my wings this once and fly with you to one who can help you, if there is help in the whole world." And with that she told them that although many people would call her old and wise herself, there was one yet living, her teacher in the old days, compared to whom she was nothing more nor less than young and ignorant. This, as she said, was an ancient king, who lived by the Mountain of Gwern Abwy, and he was the wisest and strongest and noblest creature in the world, and the mountains were not born before he was.

And there and then they said good-bye to the Stag of Rhedynfre, and he to them, and he gave them messages to their Lord Arthur, and sorry they were to watch him trot off through the trees towards his home. But as for the Owl, she walks out on a branch of her tree, and stretches out her wings slowly and feebly, and flaps them two or three times, and then lets go of the branch, and flops off painfully to a tree near by, and there she sits and takes her breath. And then off again, this time a little more strongly and quickly to a tree beyond, and there she sits again, and calls to Cai and Gwrhyr and Bedwyr and Cilhwch and Eidoel, and says she—"Come along, this is the way, and soon I shall be flying as swiftly as your horses can run."

So they rode on after her, and bye and bye there was no dream of weakness nor slowness in her flight, but she was sweeping through the air before them, and calling to them in great round notes, and they following her towards the west.

V
The Eagle of Gwern Abwy

And they rode a day and they rode a night and how much longer I do not know, and at last they came to a high and rocky mountain, and there were Alder trees on the mountain, and "this is the mountain of Gwern Abwy," said the Owl, "and near here lives the one I told you about."

And they came to a low rock beside the mountain and there sat the Eagle of Gwern Abwy, and he was a great king among the Creatures, and it was of him the Owl had spoken. His eyes were more beautiful than the sky in the night, and more keen and flashing than two great diamonds. In them were wisdom and memory and power. They could see that his two wings were stronger than whatever is strongest. And the Owl of Cwm Cawlwyd bowed low to him, and he too greeted her.

"I have brought these five knights to you," she said, "because no one in the world can help them unless you can. They come from the Emperor Arthur."

And with that the Eagle of Gwern Abwy greeted them as a King might greet the messengers of a King no less great than himself, and asked them in what way could he be helping them.

Gwrhyr said in the language of the Eagles: "We have come to seek for Mabon the son of Queen Modron, who was stolen away when he was a baby from between his mother and the wall. And that was hundreds and thousands of ages ago, and no one has heard a sound of him from that day to this. We think that as you are so old you may perhaps remember the time of his being taken, and who took him, and where he is."

"I will do whatever I can for the Emperor Arthur, and for his messengers and for whoever is worthy of my help. But the stealing of Mabon was before I broke the egg's shell that held me."

"And you can do nothing for them?" asked the Owl—"you who are older and wiser than the mountains?"

"Indeed, older than the mountains I am," said he. "For when I came here first this rock that is now no higher than your horse's knees was so high that from my nest on the top of it, I could talk in the evening with the star-Eagles in the sky, and that without the raising of voices. And where the mountain there stands, was a level plain. But the ages as they passed altered the world, and made the plain a high mountain, and brought my starry rock down till now it does not stand a span from the ground. But this man was stolen before my day."

Then the Eagle thought and thought and thought and no one spoke to him for fear of interrupting his thinking. And by this time it was night, and it seemed to them that the Eagle's two eyes were like two great stars as he sat there thinking—"Mabon!" he said—"Mabon! I think I *have* heard tell of him, long ago. I think that was the name of the man my friend told me about." Then he said to Gwrhyr who knew the Languages:

"There is one creature in the world who is at least as old as I am. Indeed, I think he is much older, really and truly, and I know he is wiser, and I will tell you about him. One day thousands of years ago I was hungry, and had no food, and I thought I would go fishing, and the place where I would fish was the lake called Llyn Lliw.* And thither I went, and there I struck my talons into the back of a great Salmon. But this salmon was so strong that he quietly swam away to the bottom of a deep pool with me, and told me to leave go or I was sure to be drowned. It was all I could do to get free, and when I did I was so angry that I called together all my armies of birds, all my kindred and all that belong to me from near or from afar, from the Eagles to the tomtits, and with this host I went against the Salmon of Llyn Lliw.

"But he sent a messenger to me, and told me how foolish my anger was, and that I could not hurt him, while he could help me in many ways, and teach me many things. And what he said I knew was true, and I sent away my armies, and from then till now I have not had any friend or comrade so dear to me as the Salmon of Llyn Lliw.

"Once he said to me: 'Some men have been here fishing for me, and they have struck what seem to be a few thorns into my back.' And there were twelve and twice twenty long, iron-headed spears of ashwood thrust deep into his back, and little did they hurt him. And those I drew out. And I think I have heard him mention such a name as this of Mabon the son of Modron."

*And those two words rhyme with "pin" and "new."

And he told them they might come with him to Llyn Lliw if they would, and for Arthur's sake no doubt the Salmon would tell them all he knew.

So the men of Arthur said good-bye to the Owl, and she to them; and she bade them greet for her the Emperor Arthur; and they were sorry when she flew swiftly away, for she had been their helper and their friend and their love went with her. And the Eagle told them what a wise and noble bird she was, this old Owl of Cwm Cawlwyd.

And in the morning when the sun arose, the Eagle at once stretched out his broad pinions and swiftly beat down the air, and rose in a moment high above them.

Said Cilhwch, "I think he is going to say good morning to his comrade the sun," and no doubt he was right. And it was when he came down that they started.

VI
The Salmon of Llyn Lliw

They went on their way, those five and the Eagle, and they rode a day and they rode a night and how much longer I do not know, and they rode wherever the Eagle led them. And at last he brought them to a blue calm lake in the west, with great trees around it, and purple mountains beyond. There he called out with his loud strong voice, and they saw what seemed to be a long, beautiful, jewel-colored island arising from the water. That was the Salmon of Llyn Lliw.

The Eagle greeted the Salmon, and the Salmon the Eagle, and the bird told him about Mabon and asked him if he remembered the stealing.

"No," said the Salmon, "that was before my time. But I could help them if they came from the Emperor Arthur."

"Lord Salmon," said Gwrhyr, who knew the languages, "Arthur is our king, and it is he that sent us, and this Mabon is needed to do a great work for him, and he shall know of your help, if you will help us, and he will give you his love and his friendship."

"I will gladly help you," said the Salmon, "but I have the King's love already. Arthur I have known and loved from long ages ago, and he will know well who has helped him."

(And of course you know, children, why the Salmon of Llyn Lliw could only help people who came from the Emperor Arthur, don't you? And mind you me, like the Eagle and the Owl and the Stag and the little Ousel, and everybody and everything really wise, that Salmon wanted to help everyone in the world.)

But anyhow, the great fish swam up to the bank and bade them all get on his back; and who ever saw a salmon nowadays that could take five men and five horses on his back? But this one could, and he did, too, and swam away out of the lake with them (and the Eagle of Gwern Abwy flying over-head) and up the river and on they went until they came to Gloucester.

And there by the riverside they saw a dark castle all built of strong black stone and lead and iron. "Now," said the Salmon, "go on shore here, and you, Cai, strike with your sword on that black prison, for there is some one within who can help you."

And they did so, and when they could find no door in the place, Cai drew his sword and crashed it against the wall.

And there came a voice from within, that sounded far away, and as if it were the voice of one nearly dying. And it said: "Who's there?"

"Men come to seek for Mabon the son of Modron, who was stolen away from his mother when he was a baby, and that was ages and ages ago."

"I can tell you better than anyone in the whole world where he is," said the voice, and this time it was nearer and stronger than before. "I am Mabon, and here I have been imprisoned and alone in the dark for more ages than I can count, and I am the man you are seeking."

"Will any gift of gold to the man that holds you make you free?"

"Alas, no," said Mabon, sadly. "They need no gold who hold me. Only by fighting can I be made free."

"We will fight for you!" cried Cai and the others all at once, "and we will certainly make you free."

"Though you will fight for me," said Mabon (and his voice seemed to be nearer and stronger and less sad each time he spoke), "I do not know whether you will be able to make me free. Seven must come to do that."

"Seven are we."

"Though you are seven, you cannot do it unless one of you is a bird and one a fish, and five men."

"The Salmon of Llyn Lliw and the Eagle of Gwern Abwy and five men are here," said they.

"Though that is so, you cannot do it unless one of the five is of my own race."

"I am of your race, Mabon," said Eidoel, "I will never go away from here till you are free."

"Even so, unless you were sent here to free me by one man, you will not be able to do it. Unless you come from the greatest King in the whole world—"

And they shouted—"We come from the Emperor Arthur!"

VII

The Freeing of Mabon and Mabon Himself

"Then you are the ones who will free me," cried Mabon, and with that he began to sing, and his song was full of more strength and wisdom and joy than before his voice had been full of weakness and sadness.

Now in those days Gloucester was the city of all dark enchantments, and there were strong, well-armed and fierce witches there, and evil magicians with their selfish dragons from all the four quarters of the world.

So as soon as Mabon began to sing, what should they see but a white mist rising all around them, and coming nearer and nearer, and from it came harsh and hissing sounds and the Eagle said, "This is the thing we shall have to fight."

And they drew their swords and rushed into the mist and began to fight with all their might and main, but for all they could see they might have been fighting with each other. So the Eagle flew down, and with his two far-sweeping wings he beat and fanned the mist till it was all blown away, and then—all of a sudden what was there but a huge fire blazing and roaring and flaming about them, and they were nearly burned to death, and they would have been too, but for a huge wave that came rolling up from the river, and it was the Salmon who sent it to put out the fire, and he sent it by smacking the water with his tail. And then came another wave, and another, and soon the fire was entirely drowned. Then they saw before them a great, black man. His eyes were of red fire, and his teeth were longer than a man's hand, and he was uglier than anyone in the world. He had black armor and a black hilted sword; the blade of his sword was as long as a horse can leap; it was red-hot, and from the point of it came flames and black smoke.

To him went Cai, as tall he had made himself as a forest pine, and with him he fought. The black giant's sword he knocked out of his hand, and cut the hand with the same blow. Four red drops fell from that cut, and as they touched the ground, each of them became four strong, red, fierce, well-armed men, and sprung up to fight with the people of Arthur.

And I cannot tell you how terribly they fought, Cai, and Gwrhyr and Bedwyr, and Cilhwch and Eidoel, with those sixteen men. Sixteen? Yes, because a wound from Cai's sword no doctor could ever heal, and though the great black giant was wounded with only a little cut on his hand, he knew well that he would never be able to fight again, and in a little time it was dead he was. But the fight went on between the five and the red-glowing wizards, and they could not stand against the Emperor Arthur's men. And by five o'clock tea-time there was not one of them left, neither alive nor dead, for each as he fell went off like a puff of smoke and never was heard of again. And afterwards they told their Lord that but for the song that Mabon had been singing, they did not know what would have happened in that battle.

And after it was over, they all set on the castle together, they, and the Eagle in the air, and the Salmon from the water; and Mabon from within beat upon the walls with his chained hands. The castle shook, and a piece of the wall fell in, and Cai rushed in, and found Mabon and broke his chains, and carried him forth upon his shoulders. And as soon as they were outside—bang!—whoof! Where was the dark prison-place gone? No one knows. You see all the dark illusion castles in the world cannot stand against Universal Brotherhood, and those seven, the Knights and the Salmon and the Eagle were Brotherhood people, and Arthur their Lord himself was the Chief of Brotherhood in those days.

Anyhow, there was the castle gone, and not so much as a speck of ruin left—two minutes after and you would not have guessed where it stood, not even if you tried ever so. Cai himself could not be quite sure, after he had once turned round. Only there before them was Mabon, the beautiful son of Queen Modron, whom for Arthur's sake they had sought so long. His chains were gone, and his sorrow. His hair was shining like the sun. His eyes seemed to be two bright lights. He was taller than any man you have ever seen, and more beautiful than the handsomest of Arthur's Knights. Wherever he came his coming was like the sun's coming, and he did the work for Arthur which no one else in the world could do.

And that is the story of Mabon the son of Modron who was stolen away at three nights old from between his mother and the wall, and lay in prison in Gloucester for untold ages; and of how he was found and made free by Cai and Bedwyr and Cilhwch and Gwrhyr and Eidoel, the men of the Emperor Arthur; and of how they were helped by the five ancient creatures of the world, the Ousel of Cilgwri, the Stag of Rhedynfre, the Owl of Cwm Cawlwyd, the Eagle of Gwern Abwy, and the Salmon of Llyn Lliw. And those five ancients had King Arthur's love and his friendship. And that is all *now*.

Bibliography
Books and Pamphlets by Kenneth Morris

The Fates of the Princes of Dyfed
    Point Loma, CA: Aryan Theosophical Press, [September 1914]
    [Under the name Cenydd Morus; with illustrations by Reginald
    Machell]
    North Hollywood, CA: Newcastle Publishing Co., 1978
    [Paperback, substantially photo-offset from the 1914 edition
    (though front and end matter has been repaginated); with an
    introduction by Dainis Bisenieks]

On Verse, "Free Verse," and the Dual Nature of Man
    Point Loma, CA: Theosophical Publishing Co., 1924
    [Wrappers; essay reprinted in pamphlet form from *The Theosophical
    Path*, January 1924]

The Secret Mountain and Other Tales
    London: Faber & Gwyer, [October 1926]
    [Includes ten tales: "The Secret Mountain," "Red-Peach-Blossom
    Inlet," "The Last Adventure of Don Quixote," "Sion ap Siencyn,"
    "The Rose and the Cup," "Daffodil," "The King and the Three
    Ascetics," "The Saint and the Forest-Gods," "The Divina
    Commedia of Evan Leyshon," and "The Apples of Knowledge";
    decorations by K. Romney Towndrow]

Book of the Three Dragons
> New York: Longmans, Green & Co., [September 1930]
> New York: Junior Literary Guild, [1930]
> New York: Arno Press, 1978
> [All editions contain illustrations by Ferdinand Huszti Horvath]

Golden Threads in the Tapestry of History
> San Diego: Point Loma Publications, [1975]
> [Paperback. Collection of Morris's essay-series reprinted from *The Theosophical Path*, March 1915 through December 1916; with an introduction by Iverson L. Harris]

Through Dragon Eyes
> La Jolla, CA: Ben-Sen Press, 1980
> [Paperback. Edited by Helynn Hoffa. Includes three tales: "The Eyeless Dragons," "Red-Peach-Blossom Inlet," and "The White Bird Inn"; and one poem: "The Meditations of Ssu-ku'ung T'u." Editor's Introduction by Helynn Hoffa, and Preface to the poem by John R. Theobold]

The Chalchiuhite Dragon: A Tale of Toltec Times
> New York: Tor [March 1992]
> New York: Orb [1993] [paperback]
> [Both editions contain an Afterword and Glossary by Douglas A. Anderson]

Acknowledgments

*M*y personal quest for Kenneth Morris and his writings has continued for more than a dozen years. Along the way numerous people have shown great kindness in assisting me, and I wish to express my gratitude here. Foremost I must thank Grace F. Knoche, Leader of the Theosophical Society, for allowing me to use the papers of Kenneth Morris which have been preserved at the Theosophical Society's Headquarters in Pasadena, California. Others there who have greatly helped me include John Van Mater (Head Librarian), Kirby Van Mater (Archivist), and Will Thackara (Manager of the Theosophical University Press). Ingrid Van Mater also shared with me her memories of Morris, whom she knew as a young child growing up at Point Loma.

I must also thank David Hartwell, my editor at Tor, not only for his enthusiasm over my Morris projects but also for his patience shown over the extended length of time it has taken for me to deliver them. My London friend Christina Scull helped significantly by paging through a number of rare magazines in the British Library and searching for contributions by Kenneth Morris; she provided me with copies of some otherwise elusive items. Other friends who have helped in various ways include Chris Lavallie, Martin Hempstead, Eric Seibel, Anne Robertson, S. T. Joshi, Henry Zmuda, Richard Mathews, Charles Garvin, Thomas Servo, Will Southerland, Donald G. Keller and Anastacia Gourley. I am also grateful to Richard H. F. Lindemann, of the Special Collections at the Central University Library of the University of California, San Diego, for help with their collection of Iverson Harris Papers; and to Carolyn A. Davis, of the George

Arents Research Library for Special Collections, Syracuse University, for assistance with their Charles Wharton Stork Papers. And the pioneering work on Kenneth Morris by Kenneth J. Zahorski and Robert H. Boyer, *Lloyd Alexander, Evangeline Walton Ensley, Kenneth Morris: A Primary and Secondary Bibliography* (1981), has been very useful.

Last I must single out two people who helped the most in bringing to my mind a better understanding and living vision of Kenneth Morris. W. Emmett Small grew up at Point Loma in the early part of this century, and knew Morris as a teacher and friend until Morris left Point Loma and returned to Wales in 1930. Back in Wales, Morris befriended a young Scotsman named Alex Urquhart who had recently moved to Cardiff. Morris instructed him in Theosophy and later named him as his Literary Executor. Both men, now in their nineties, have given unstintingly of their time, and have helped me tremendously in many ways. Additionally, Alex Urquhart and his wife Sybil kindly shared their hospitality with me on my visit to Cardiff in August 1992.

The devotion of W. Emmett Small and Alex Urquhart to their long-dead friend has been an inspiration and encouragement to me in my work. To them both I dedicate this book.

ISTKω   HUMCA S SF
                           MORRI

MORRIS, KENNETH
    THE DRAGON PATH :
COLLECTED TALES OF
KENNETH MORRIS

Short Story Index
1994-1998

Fodors 2008

WALT DISNEY WORLD®

Where to Stay and Eat
for All Budgets

Must-See Sights
and Local Secrets

Ratings You Can Trust

Fodor's Travel Publications   New York, Toronto, London, Sydney, Auckland
www.fodors.com

FODOR'S WALT DISNEY WORLD® 2008

Editors: Laura M. Kidder, Adam Taplin

Editorial Production: Evangelos Vasilakis
Editorial Contributors: Jennie Hess, Alicia Rivas, Gary McKechnie, Rowland Stiteler
Maps & Illustrations: David Lindroth, cartographer; Bob Blake and Rebecca Baer, map editors; Robert Dress, Illustrator
Design: Fabrizio La Rocca, creative director; Guido Caroti, art director; Melanie Marin, photo editor
Cover Photo (Magic Carpets of Aladdin ride, Magic Kingdom® Park): © Disney
Production/Manufacturing: Angela L McLean

ISBN 978-1-4000-1808-6

ISSN 1531-443X

SPECIAL SALES

This book is available at special discounts for bulk purchases for sales promotions or premiums. Special editions, including personalized covers, excerpts of existing books, and corporate imprints, can be created in large quantities for special needs. For more information, write to Special Markets/Premium Sales, 1745 Broadway, MD 6-2, New York, New York 10019, or e-mail specialmarkets@randomhouse.com.

AN IMPORTANT TIP & AN INVITATION

Although all prices, opening times, and other details in this book are based on information supplied to us at press time, changes occur all the time in the travel world, and Fodor's cannot accept responsibility for facts that become outdated or for inadvertent errors or omissions. So **always confirm information when it matters,** especially if you're making a detour to visit a specific place. Your experiences—positive and negative—matter to us. If we have missed or misstated something, **please write to us.** We follow up on all suggestions. Contact the Walt Disney World® editor at editors@fodors.com or c/o Fodor's at 1745 Broadway, New York, NY 10019.

PRINTED IN THE UNITED STATES OF AMERICA
10 9 8 7 6 5 4 3 2 1

Be a Fodor's Correspondent

Your opinion matters. It matters to us. It matters to your fellow Fodor's travelers, too. And we'd like to hear it. In fact, we need to hear it.

When you share your experiences and opinions, you become an active member of the Fodor's community. That means we'll not only use your feedback to make our books better, but we'll publish your names and comments whenever possible. Throughout our guides, look for "Word of Mouth," excerpts of your unvarnished feedback.

Here's how you can help improve Fodor's for all of us.

Tell us when we're right. We rely on local writers to give you an insider's perspective. But our writers and staff editors—who are the best in the business—depend on you. Your positive feedback is a vote to renew our recommendations for the next edition.

Tell us when we're wrong. We're proud that we update most of our guides every year. But we're not perfect. Things change. Hotels cut services. Museums change hours. Charming cafés lose charm. If our writer didn't quite capture the essence of a place, tell us how you'd do it differently. If any of our descriptions are inaccurate or inadequate, we'll incorporate your changes in the next edition and will correct factual errors at fodors.com immediately.

Tell us what to include. You probably have had fantastic travel experiences that aren't yet in Fodor's. Why not share them with a community of like-minded travelers? Maybe you chanced upon a beach or bistro or B&B that you don't want to keep to yourself. Tell us why we should include it. And share your discoveries and experiences with everyone directly at fodors.com. Your input may lead us to add a new listing or highlight a place we cover with a "Highly Recommended" star or with our highest rating, "Fodor's Choice."

Give us your opinion instantly at our feedback center at www.fodors.com/feedback. You may also e-mail editors@fodors.com with the subject line "Walt Disney World® Editor." Or send your nominations, comments, and complaints by mail to Walt Disney World® Editor, Fodor's, 1745 Broadway, New York, NY 10019.

You and travelers like you are the heart of the Fodor's community. Make our community richer by sharing your experiences. Be a Fodor's correspondent.

Happy traveling!

Tim Jarrell, Publisher

CONTENTS

CONTENTS

WDW RESORT FLOOR PLANS

ABOUT
THIS BOOK

Our Ratings

In theme-park chapters, ★, ★★, or ★★★ rates the appeal of the attraction to the audience noted. "Young children" refers to kids ages 5–7; "very young children" are those (ages 4 and under) who probably won't meet the height requirements of most thrill rides anyway. Since youngsters come with different confidence levels, exercise your own judgment with the scarier rides.

In non-theme-park chapters, such as After Dark, black stars in the margin highlight things we deem **Highly Recommended**, places that our writers, editors, and readers praise again and again for excellence. The very best attractions, properties, and experiences get our highest rating, the orange **Fodor's Choice** symbol, throughout this book.

By default, there's another category: any place we include in this book is by definition worth your time, unless we say otherwise. And we will.

Disagree with any of our choices? Care to nominate a place or suggest that we rate one more highly? Visit our feedback center at www.fodors.com/feedback.

Budget Well

Hotel and restaurant price categories from ¢ to $$$$ are defined in the opening pages of chapters 2 and 12. For attractions, we always give standard adult admission fees; reductions are usually available for children, students, and senior citizens. Want to pay with plastic? **AE, D, DC, MC, V** following restaurant and hotel listings indicate if American Express, Discover, Diners Club, MasterCard, and Visa are accepted.

Restaurants

Unless we state otherwise, restaurants are open for lunch and dinner daily. We mention dress only when there's a specific requirement and reservations only when they're essential or not accepted—it's always best to book ahead.

Hotels

Hotels have private bath, phone, TV, and air-conditioning and operate on the European Plan (aka EP, meaning without meals), unless we specify that they use the Continental Plan (CP, with a Continental breakfast), Breakfast Plan (BP, with a full breakfast), or Modified American Plan (MAP, with breakfast and dinner) or are all-inclusive (including all meals and most activities). We always list facilities but not whether you'll be charged an extra fee to use them, so when pricing accommodations, find out what's included.

	Many Listings
★	Fodor's Choice
★	Highly recommended
⊠	Physical address
✢	Directions
⌖	Mailing address
☎	Telephone
🖷	Fax
⊕	On the Web
✉	E-mail
⌧	Admission fee
☉	Open/closed times
Ⓜ	Metro stations
▭	Credit cards

	Hotels & Restaurants
🏨	Hotel
⌤	Number of rooms
⌂	Facilities
⑩	Meal plans
✕	Restaurant
⌨	Reservations
⌇	Smoking
🕮	BYOB
✕🏨	Hotel with restaurant that warrants a visit

	Outdoors
🏌	Golf
⛺	Camping

	Other
☾	Family-friendly
⇨	See also
⊠	Branch address
☞	Take note

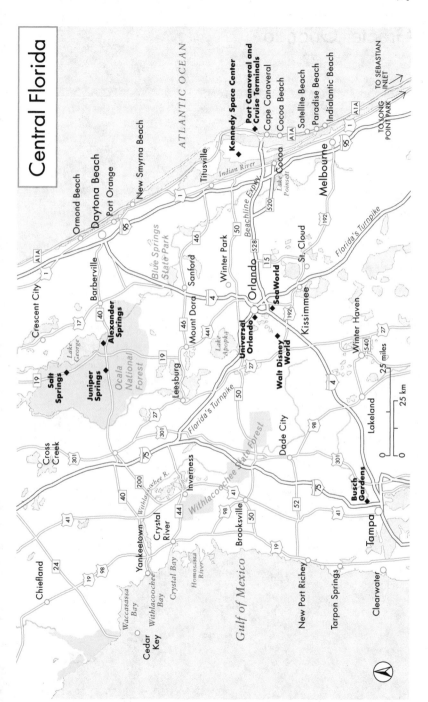

Central Florida

Greater Orlando

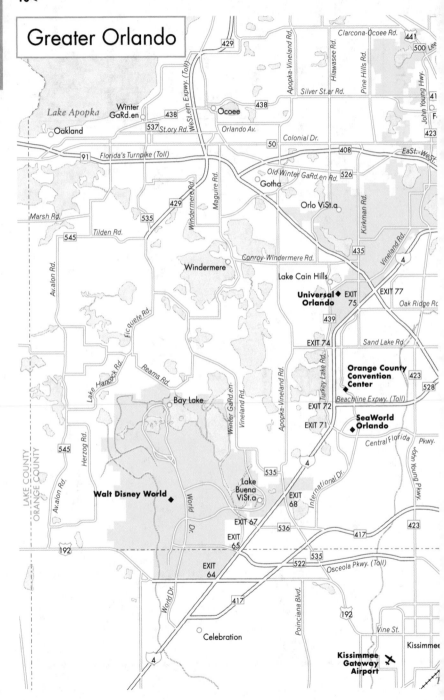

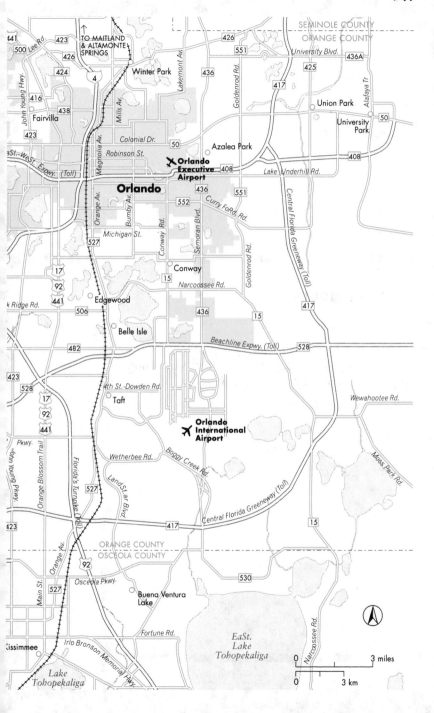

Planning Your Trip

WORD OF MOUTH

"We've taken groups to WDW and really cannot stress enough the importance of having a touring plan. Don't get rigid about it but it helps immensely to avoid wasting time."

—ajcolorado

"Build in breaks every afternoon to simply swim in the hotel pool and have some down time."

—kflodin

Revised by
Jennie Hess

THERE ARE TWO KINDS OF TRAVELERS TO WALT DISNEY WORLD.
There's the family that just shows up, trusting the reputation of Disney to guide them along the way. They'll arrive at the Magic Kingdom around 11, wander through Main Street and its stores, and then reach the other side of Cinderella's castle—wondering what to ride first. One child will want to go to Space Mountain, while another will start crying the farther the group gets from Dumbo, which now has a 90-minute line. This family might split up so each child can get in at least one preferred ride before lunch, or they might stick together, causing one child or the other to have a meltdown that ruins everyone's mood. Regardless, by the time they've struggled through the lines at rides and lunch counters, the late-afternoon sun will be beating down.

The second type of traveler does some research. They make their dining reservations in advance, and they decide which rides are must-sees for each person in their party. They learn the cardinal rule of Disney World touring—get there early—and they manage to avoid the worst lines. Above all, they remember that they can't do everything, and they relax long enough to enjoy their experience without stressing out about how much they need to do to merit the cost of their tickets.

Sure, the first family will still have fun at Walt Disney World, but they'll wait in more lines, probably spend more money, and stress out more than the second family.

■TIP➜A little planning goes a long way in Walt Disney World. There's no need for an hour-by-hour itinerary, but it's good to decide what you want to do every day of your trip. You don't need to map out every minute of your time to have a good vacation. You just need to know a few basic tips, most of which are outlined in this chapter. Planning can be fun, especially if you get everyone involved. Start by flipping through this book and browsing ⊕*www.disneyworld.com*, a fabulous, easy-to-use planning tool. After a little research, it'll be fairly simple for you to separate the "must-do" attractions from the "skip-it" and "if-we-have-extra-time" rides or sights. If you have younger and older children, decide where Mom and Dad or other adult family members might split up to take tots on the kiddie rides and older children to the thrill attractions. Then arrange a meeting location for later.

Don't worry that your best-laid plans will be stolen by throngs of other guidebook readers. ■TIP➜Regardless of all the books on the market, most Walt Disney World visitors still don't bother making touring plans. That's why there are still far fewer people in the parks at 9 AM than at 2 PM. Go ahead, see for yourself. And stay steps ahead of the crowds by purchasing tickets before your trip, mapping out a general itinerary, building in a travel-time cushion from hotel to parks, and using the handiest of theme-park tools: an alarm clock.

A Window on the World

No moss ever grows under the Mouse's trademark yellow clogs (unless it's artfully re-created moss). Since its opening in 1971, Walt Disney World has made it a point to stay fresh, current, and endlessly amusing. Disney Imagineers and producers constantly choreograph new shows and parades, revamp classic theme rides, and periodically replace an entire attraction. Yet amid all the hoopla, much remains reassuringly the same, rekindling fond memories among the generations who return.

The sheer enormity of the property—25,000 acres near Kissimmee, Florida—suggests that WDW is more than a single theme park with a fabulous castle in the center. The property's acreage translates to 40 square miles—twice the size of Manhattan. On a tract that size, 107 acres is a mere speck, yet that's the size of the Magic Kingdom. When most people imagine Walt Disney World, they think of only those 107 acres, but there's much, much more.

Epcot, the second major theme park and, at 300 acres, more than twice as big as the Magic Kingdom, is a combination of a science exploratorium and a world's fair. Disney–MGM Studios is devoted to the world of movies and TV shows. The Animal Kingdom, the fourth major theme park, salutes creatures real, imaginary, and extinct. Add two water parks, more than two dozen hotels, a sports complex, and countless shops, restaurants, and nightlife venues, and you start to get the picture. And still there are thousands of undeveloped acres. Deer patrol grassy plains and pine forests, and white ibis inhabit swamps patched by thickets of palmettos.

Best of all, Disney has proved that it can manage its elephantine resort and make customers so happy that they return year after year. Perhaps the company's most practical innovation, the Fastpass system, lets you experience the top attractions with little or no wait. Restaurants at the parks and resorts have made great strides in an effort to cater to guests with special dietary needs and to offer family-friendly alternatives to the standard burger and fries. And travelers who want to vacation longer get the best ticket deals.

Disney's tradition of constant and excellent upkeep has persevered through years of ups and downs within the company. Whatever is happening in the background, all is still well on the kingdom's grounds. Walt Disney's original decree that his parks be ever changing, along with some healthy competition from Universal Studios, SeaWorld, and other area attractions, keeps the Disney Imagineers and show producers on their toes as they dream up new entertainment and install higher-tech attractions. To avoid missing anything, do plenty of research before you go, make a plan, then try to relax—and have a wonderful time.

WHEN TO GO

Timing can spell the difference between a good vacation in the theme parks and a great one. Since the Orlando area is an obvious destination for families, the area is at its most crowded during school vacations. If you're traveling without youngsters or with just preschoolers, avoid school holidays.

SPRING Spring in Orlando is absolutely gorgeous: sunny and warm, but not killer hot and humid like it is in summer. In April and May, you may have some nippy days and others that are warm enough for the water parks. Avoid the weeks before and after Easter, which also coincide with Spring Break for a lot of schools. May, excluding Memorial Day weekend, and early June are excellent times to go.

SUMMER If water parks are a must for your family, plan your trip in summer, but be prepared for serious heat and serious crowds. Fortunately, busy periods bring longer hours and sometimes added entertainment and parades, such as the evening SpectroMagic parade in Disney's Magic Kingdom, which you can't see in quieter times. There are *slightly* fewer people in early June and late August.

FALL Summer and early fall are hurricane season, but the period from late September through November, like spring, usually brings bright beautiful days with cooler temperatures and some of the lightest crowds all year.

WINTER For most people, winter in Orlando is too chilly for swimming—and at least one of the water parks is always closed. Outside of the holidays, including Christmas, New Year's, Martin Luther King Jr. Day, and President's Day, it's the least crowded time of year.

HOW LONG TO STAY

To have a rich and full Orlando resort experience, plan on a trip of seven or eight days. This gives you time to see all of the parks at Universal and WDW and to take in one water park, to sample the restaurants and entertainment, and to spend a bit of time around the pool. Figure on an additional day for every other area theme park you want to visit, and then add your travel time to and from home.

If you can, make time for shopping and for exploring Orlando. Central Florida has some great high-end and discount shopping and some visitor treasures like Green Meadows Farm in Kissimmee and the Charles Hosmer Morse Museum of American Art, with the world's largest collection of Tiffany glass, in Winter Park.

TAKING THE KIDS OUT OF SCHOOL

For many parents, it's worth avoiding the frustration of the crowds to take the kids out of school for a couple of days. We agree that this can make for a more enjoyable trip, but it's a good idea to consult with your child's teachers before making plans. Hopefully the teachers can advise you about the best time of year to go and help create a study plan to make certain your child's education isn't compromised. For elementary-school kids, there are ways of making the trip educational.

For example, your child could write about the different countries featured at Epcot in lieu of a missed homework assignment. One last note: although it may be fine to take an elementary-school child out of school for a few days, missing several days of middle or high school could set your child back for the rest of the semester, so consider this option very carefully.

SEASONAL CLOSURES

Disney sometimes closes rides and attractions for refurbishment or maintenance during slower seasons. Before you finalize your travel schedule, call the theme parks to find out about any planned closures so you don't show up at the Magic Kingdom to find Peter Pan's Flight grounded for the week.

CLIMATE CHART

ORLANDO								
Jan.	70F	21C	**May**	88F	31C	**Sept.**	88F	31C
	49	9		67	19		74	23
Feb.	72F	22C	**June**	90F	32C	**Oct.**	83F	28C
	54	12		74	23		67	19
Mar.	76F	24C	**July**	90F	32C	**Nov.**	76F	24C
	56	13		74	23		58	14
Apr.	81F	27C	**Aug.**	90F	32C	**Dec.**	70F	21C
	63	17		74	23		52	11

ADMISSION

Visiting Walt Disney World isn't cheap. Everyone 10 and older pays adult price. In addition, Disney changes its prices about once a year and without much notice. For that reason, you may save yourself a few bucks if you buy your WDW tickets as soon as you know for sure you'll be going.

THE TICKETING SYSTEM

Once you've decided to take the plunge, Disney fortunately makes buying tickets easy and painless. The **Magic Your Way** ticketing system is all about flexibility. You can tailor your ticket to your interests and desired length of stay. The more days you stay, the greater your savings on per-day ticket prices. A one-day ticket costs $67 for anyone age 10 and up, while a five-day ticket costs $206 or $41.20 per day.

Once you decide how many days to stay, you'll want to decide what options to add on. The **Park Hopper** option lets you move from park to park within the day and adds $45 to the price of your ticket, no matter how many days your ticket covers. So it's an expensive option for a one- or two-day ticket, but it can be well worth the cost for a four-day trip, especially if you know what you want to see at each park.

The **Water Parks & More** option allows a certain number of visits to the water parks and other Disney attractions: Typhoon Lagoon, Blizzard Beach, Pleasure Island, DisneyQuest and Disney's Wide World of Sports complex. You pay $50 to add this option to your ticket, and you get three to six visits, depending on the length of your stay.

The **No Expiration** option can save you money if you know for sure you're coming back to Disney World again. For example, say you're planning a five-day trip one year, plus a weekend trip sometime the next year. You can buy a seven-day ticket, use it five days during your first trip and keep the remaining two-days' worth of theme-park fun for your next trip to Orlando. It will cost you $10 to $90 to add the No Expiration option to your two- to seven-day tickets.

Note that all Disney admission passes are nontransferable. The ID is your fingerprint. Although you slide your pass through the reader like people with single-day tickets, you also have to slip your finger into a special V-shape fingerprint reader before you'll be admitted.

BUYING TICKETS

IN ADVANCE

Buying your tickets in advance will save about 3% off the price at the ticket booths. You can buy them at **www.disneyworld.com** or by phone at **407/934–7639**.

You can also get discounted tickets from the **Orlando Convention & Visitors Bureau** at **www.orlandoticketsales.com or 407/363–5871.**

IN ORLANDO

You can buy tickets at the Transportation and Ticket Center in the Magic Kingdom (also known as the TTC); at ticket booths in front of the other theme-park entrances; in all on-site resorts if you're a registered guest; at the Walt Disney World kiosk on the second floor of the main terminal at Orlando International Airport; and at various hotels and other sites around Orlando.

DISCOUNTS

AAA

Many of the AAA motor clubs offer discounts to Central Florida attractions, including Disney World tickets, so check with your local branch or contact the national **AAA** (☎*866/222–7283 [866/AAA–SAVE]* ⊕*www.aaa.com*). Also ask your local AAA office about hotel discounts and vacation packages that would include tickets, as well as special benefits within the parks including discounts on meals and nonalcoholic beverages.

MILITARY

If you are or have been a member of the U.S. or foreign military, you're eligible for discount tickets that cost at least 10% less than full price. You can also buy tickets for nonmilitary guests as long as you're traveling with them. If you're active-duty or retired military, National Guard,

MAGIC YOUR WAY PRICE CHART

TICKET OPTIONS								
TICKET	**10-DAY**	**7-DAY**	**6-DAY**	**5-DAY**	**4-DAY**	**3-DAY**	**2-DAY**	**1-DAY**
BASE TICKET								
Ages 10-up	$216	$210	$208	$206	$202	$192	$132	$67
Ages 3-9	$177	$173	$171	$169	$168	$160	$110	$56

Base Ticket admits guest to one of the four major theme parks per day's use.
Park choices are: Magic Kingdom, Epcot, Disney-MGM Studios, Disney's Animal Kingdom.

ADD: Park Hopper	$45	$45	$45	$45	$45	$45	$45	$45

Park Hopper option entitles guest to visit more than one theme park per day's use. Park choices are any combination of Magic Kingdom, Epcot, Disney-MGM Studios, Disney's Animal Kingdom.

ADD: Water Parks & More	$50 6 visits	$50 6 visits	$50 5 visits	$50 4 visits	$50 4 visits	$50 3 visits	$50 3 visits	$50 3 visits

Water Parks & More option entitles guest to a specified number of visits (between 2 and 5) to a choice of entertainment and recreation venues. Choices are Blizzard Beach, Typhoon Lagoon, DisneyQuest, Pleasure Island, and Wide World of Sports.

ADD: No Expiration	$155	$90	$60	$55	$40	$15	$10	n/a

No expiration means that unused admissions on a ticket may be used any time in the future. Without this option, tickets expire 14 days after first use.

MINOR PARKS AND ATTRACTIONS		
TICKET	**AGES 10-UP**	**AGES 3-9**
TYPHOON LAGOON OR BLIZZARD BEACH		
1-Day 1-Park	$36	$30
DISNEYQUEST		
1-Day	$36	$30
DISNEY'S WIDE WORLD OF SPORTS	$10.28	$7.71
CIRQUE DU SOLEIL'S *LA NOUBA*	$61-$95	$49-$76
PLEASURE ISLAND		
1-Night Multi-Club Ticket	$21.95	$21.95

*Admission to *Pleasure Island* clubs is restricted to guests 18 or older unless accompanied by an adult 21 or older. For some clubs all guests must be 21 or older.

*All prices are subject to Florida sales tax

Army Reserve, a disabled veteran, or a Department of Defense civilian with military ID, you can also stay at the on-site **Shades of Green Resort** (☎*407/824–1403* ⊕*www.shadesofgreen.org*) for a fraction of what it costs to stay at other Disney resorts.

PACKAGES & MEAL PLANS

HOTEL & TICKET PACKAGES

Disney's Magic Your Way basic, premium, and platinum packages help families keep expenses in check by bundling hotel and theme-park expenses. For as low as $1,600, a family of four can plan a six-night, seven-day Magic Your Way Vacation that includes complimentary transportation from the airport and extra hours in the parks. Lower-end package rates offer value-resort accommodations; prices go up with moderate or deluxe accommodations. All Disney resort guests get free bus, boat, and monorail transportation across property. Visit ⊕*www.disneyworld.com* to explore the different package options.

MEAL PLANS

If you book a package, you can add on a meal plan for more savings. The Magic Your Way Dining Plan allows you one table-service meal, one counter-service meal, and one snack per day of your trip at more than 100 theme-park and resort restaurants. You can add the plan to your package for $38.99 per adult, per day, and $10.99 per child age 3–9, per day (tax and gratuities included). When you consider that the average Disney table-service meal for a child runs about $10.99 *without* gratuity, you realize this plan is a steal. Another advantage of the plan is that you can swap two table-service meals for one of Disney's dinner shows or an evening at one of the high-end signature restaurants like California Grill.

MONEY MATTERS

Be prepared to spend and spend—and spend some more. Despite relatively low airfares and car-rental rates, cash seems to evaporate out of wallets, and credit-card balances seem to increase on exposure to the hot Orlando sun. Theme-park admission is roughly $60 per day per person (for a family of two adults and two children ages 3–9)—not counting all the $2 soft drinks and $20 souvenirs. Hotels range so wildly—from $60 a night (at a few non-Disney hotels) to 10 or more times that—that you have to do some hard thinking about just how much you want to spend. Meal prices away from the theme parks are comparable to those in other midsize cities, ranging from $5 per person at a fast-food chain to $40 entrées at a fancy restaurant.

Best Ways to Save

■ **Consider your theme-park ticket options.** With Disney's Magic Your Way tickets, it's now worth it to buy an extra ticket on the day of your arrival or departure if you're planning to stay at least five days and want to cram in every bit of park time possible. It costs only $4 to upgrade from a four-day Disney adult ticket to a five-day one. If you're staying for just three or four days, however, you're probably better off spending arrival/departure days visiting Downtown Disney, Disney's Boardwalk, or Universal CityWalk, or lounging around your hotel pool.

■ **Buy your tickets as soon as you know you're going.** Prices typically go up about once a year, so you might beat a price hike—and save a little money.

■ **Avoid holidays and school vacation times, or go off-season.** You can see more in less time, and lodging rates are lower.

■ **Choose accommodations with a kitchen or at least a fridge and microwave.** You can stock up on breakfast items in a nearby supermarket, and save time—and money—by eating your morning meal in your hotel room.

■ **If you plan to eat in a full-service restaurant, do it at lunch.** Then have a light dinner. Lunchtime prices are almost always lower than dinnertime prices. Also look for "early bird" menus, which offer dinner entrées at reduced prices during late afternoon and early evening hours.

■ **Watch your shopping carefully.** Theme-park merchandisers are excellent at displaying the goods so that you (or your children) can't resist them. You may find that some articles for sale are also available at home—for quite a bit less. One way to cope is to give every member of your family a souvenir budget—adults and children alike. Another good option is to wait until the last day of your trip to buy your souvenirs.

■ **Refill your water bottles.** You'll be surprised at how much water you drink hiking around the parks under the hot Florida sun. Those $2 water bottles really add up, but you can save a bundle by refilling your bottles at the water fountains all over the parks.

■ **Bring essentials with you.** Remember to pack your hat, sunscreen, camera, memory card or film, batteries, diapers, and aspirin. These items are all very expensive within the theme parks.

SAMPLE COSTS AT WALT DISNEY WORLD

All prices include sales tax.

20 oz. bottle of water	$2	Souvenir T-shirt	$16–$35
20 oz. bottle of soda	$2–$2.50	Roll of film (36 shots)	$9.49
Cup of coffee	$2–$2.25	512 MB digital memory card	$69.95
Cheeseburger	$4.50	Autograph book	$6.95
French fries	$2	Plush character toys	$8–$50
Ice-cream treat	$3–$4		

ATMS

Automatic teller machines are scattered throughout the Magic Kingdom, Epcot, the Studios, Animal Kingdom, and Downtown Disney. Often there's a $1.50–$2.50 charge if you're not a customer of the specific bank that maintains the ATM.

CREDIT CARDS

Throughout this guide, the following abbreviations are used: **AE,** American Express; **D,** Discover; **DC,** Diners Club; **MC,** MasterCard; and **V,** Visa.

Reporting Lost Cards American Express (☎ *800/430–1000*). **Diners Club** (☎ *800/234–6377*). **Discover** (☎ *800/347–2683*). **MasterCard** (☎ *800/622–7747*). **Visa** (☎ *800/847–2911*).

DISCOUNT COUPONS

Coupon books, such as those available from **Entertainment Travel Editions** (☎ *800/445–4137* ⊕ *www.entertainment.com*) for around $30, can be good sources for discounts on rental cars, admission to attractions, meals, and other typical purchases. Hotel and restaurant lobbies also often have racks with flyers that advertise business with coupons.

The **Orlando Magicard** (☎ *800/643—9492* ⊕ *www.orlandoinfo.com/magicard*), offered for free by the Orlando–Orange County Convention & Visitors Bureau, provides discounts for many attractions, restaurants, and shopping-mall stores. Download it from the Web site or order it over the phone.

TIPPING

Whether they carry bags, open doors, deliver food, or clean rooms, hospitality employees work to receive a portion of your travel budget. In deciding how much to give, base your tip on what the service is and how well it's performed.

In transit, tip an airport valet and shuttle driver $1 to $2 per bag, a taxi driver 15% to 20% of the fare.

For hotel staff, recommended amounts are $1 to $2 per bag for a bellhop, $1 or $2 per night per guest for housekeeping, $5 to $10 for special concierge service, $1 to $2 for a doorman who hails a cab or parks

Packing Checklist

■ **Comfortable walking shoes or sneakers.** Make sure to break them in before your trip, and leave your sandals and high heels at home. If you're eating in a fancy restaurant, bring one pair of nice shoes.

■ **A small backpack or a waist pack** for your water, camera, sunscreen, and other small essentials.

■ **Sunglasses.** Even if you don't regularly wear them, sunglasses are a must in Florida.

■ **A hat or visor** will help block the blinding Florida sun from your eyes as well as protect your skin.

■ **Sunscreen.** Slather it on before you leave in the morning, or carry it with you.

■ **Extra contact lenses or glasses.** One reader's eyes teared up on a roller coaster from all the wind rushing past. The next she knew, one of her contact lenses had popped out.

■ **Camera.** Central Florida presents lots of opportunities for great photos, from shots of the family hugging Disney characters to panoramas of beautifully manicured lakeside parks to up-close snaps of gators and crocs. Be sure to keep the sun behind you when you compose a photo.

a car, 15% of the greens fee for a caddy, 15% to 20% of the bill for a massage, and 15% of a room service bill, unless gratuity is already included (be sure to check).

In a restaurant, give 15% to 20% of your bill to the server, and about 15% to a bartender.

WHAT TO PACK

Casual, comfortable, lightweight clothing is best. Most people walk around in shorts and T-shirts. On hot summer days, the perfect theme-park outfit begins with shorts made of a breathable, quick-drying material, topped by a T-shirt or tank top. Pockets are useful for Fastpass tickets and park maps. The entire area is extremely casual, day and night, so men need a jacket and tie in only a handful of restaurants.

We recommend bringing a change of clothes if you know you're going on a water ride that could leave you drenched. Plan ahead so you don't end up soaked and having to either buy an expensive Disney outfit from a souvenir shop or leave the park early.

In winter, be prepared for a range of temperatures: take clothing that you can layer, including a sweater and warm jacket. It can get quite cool in December, January, and February. For summer, you'll want a sun hat, and a rain poncho in case of sudden thunderstorms.

The Most Important Advice You'll Get

If you remember nothing else, keep in mind these essential strategies, tried and tested by generations of Disney World fans. They are the Eight Commandments for touring Walt Disney World.

■ **Make dining reservations before you leave home, especially for character dining experiences.** If you don't, you might find yourself eating a hamburger (again) or leaving Walt Disney World for dinner. The on-site restaurants book up fast.

■ **Arrive at the parks at least 30 minutes before they open.** We know, it's your vacation and you want to sleep in. So go to the Caribbean. Or the mountains. Don't go to Walt Disney World, unless you've been there a hundred times and you plan to sit by the pool and play golf more than go on rides. If you're like most families and you want to make the most of your time and money, plan to be up by at least 7:30 every day. After transit time, it'll take you 10–15 minutes to park and get to the gates. If you know you want to use the lockers or ATMs, or rent strollers, get there 45 minutes in advance.

■ **See the top attractions first thing in the morning.** And we mean first thing. As in, before 10 AM. Decide in advance which attractions you don't want to miss, find out where they are, and hotfoot it to them when the park opens. If you miss any in the morning, the other good times to see the most popular attractions are right before closing and during the parades. Otherwise, use Fastpass.

■ **Use Fastpass.** It's worth saying twice. The system is free, easy, and it's your ticket to the top attractions with little or no waiting in line.

■ **Build in rest time.** This is the greatest way to avoid becoming overly hot, tired, and grumpy. We recommend starting early and then leaving the theme parks around 3 or 4, the hottest and most crowded time of day. After a couple hours' rest at your hotel, you can have an early dinner and head back to the parks to watch one of the nighttime spectaculars or to ride a couple more of the big-deal rides (lines are shorter around closing time).

■ **Create a rough itinerary, but leave room for spontaneity.** Decide which parks to see on each day, and know your priorities, but don't try to plot your trip hour by hour. Instead, break up the day into morning, afternoon, and evening sections. If you're staying at a Disney resort, find out which parks are offering the Extra Magic Hours on which days, and plan to take advantage of the program.

■ **Eat at off hours.** Have a quick, light breakfast at 8, lunch at 11, and dinner at 5 or 6 to avoid the mealtime rush hours. Between 11:30 and 2:30 during high season, you can wait in line up to 30 minutes for a so-called fast-food lunch in the parks.

■ **Save the high-capacity sit-down shows for the afternoon.** You usually don't have to wait in line so long for shows, and you'll be relieved at the chance to sit in an air-conditioned theater during the hottest part of the day.

The Birth of Walt Disney World

It'd be a great question for Meredith Vieira to ask on Who Wants to Be a Millionaire?: Florida was founded by (a) Juan Ponce de León, (b) Millard Fillmore, (c) Sonny Bono, or (d) Walt Disney. For travelers who can't fathom Florida without Walt Disney World, the final answer is "d"—in Central Florida at least. The theme park's arrival spawned a multibillion-dollar tourism industry that begat a population boom that begat new roads, malls, and schools that begat a whole new culture.

So how did it happen? Why did Walt pin his hopes on forlorn Florida ranchlands 3,000 mi from Disneyland? In the 1950s, Walt barely had enough money to open his theme park in California, and lacking the funds to buy a buffer zone, he couldn't prevent cheap hotels and tourist traps from setting up shop next door. This time he wanted land. And lots of it. Beginning in the early 1960s, Walt embarked on a supersecret four-year project: he traveled the nation in search of a location with access to a major population center, good highways, a steady climate, and, most important, cheap and abundant land. Locations were narrowed down, and in the end Orlando was it.

In May 1965, major land transactions were being recorded a few miles southwest of Orlando. By late June, the *Orlando Sentinel* reported that more than 27,000 acres had been sold so far. In October, the paper revealed that Walt was the mastermind behind the purchases. Walt and his brother Roy hastily arranged a press conference. Once Walt described the $400 million project and the few thousand jobs it would create, Florida's government quickly gave him permission to establish the autonomous Reedy Creek Improvement District. With this, he could write his own zoning restrictions and plan his own roads, bridges, hotels—even a residential community for his employees.

Walt played a hands-on role in the planning of Disney World, but just over a year later, in December 1966, he died. As expected, his faithful brother Roy took control and spent the following five years supervising the construction of the Magic Kingdom. Fittingly, before the park opened on October 1, 1971, Roy changed the name of his brother's park to "Walt" Disney World. Roy passed away three months after the park's opening, but by then WDW was hitting its stride. For the next decade, it became part of Florida's landscape. Families that once saw Orlando merely as a whistle-stop on the way to Miami now made their vacation base at WDW.

Behind the scenes, however, a few cracks began to appear in the facade. In its first decade, growth was stagnant. By 1982, when Epcot opened, construction-cost overruns and low attendance created a 19% drop in profits. Meanwhile, the Disney Channel and Disney's film division were also sluggish. Eventually, in 1984, Michael Eisner came aboard as CEO and company chairman, along with Frank Wells as president and CFO. Their arrival got Disney out of the doldrums. Disney's unparalleled film catalog was brought out of storage with rereleases in theaters and on video. Jeffrey Katzenberg was put in charge of the Disney Studios, and with him came the release of "new classics" such as *Aladdin, Beauty and the Beast, The Little Mermaid,* and *The Lion King.*

In 1988 the Grand Floridian and Caribbean Beach resorts opened. The following year Disney–MGM Studios opened along with Typhoon Lagoon and Pleasure Island. Five resort hotels opened in the early 1990s. By 1997 Blizzard Beach, Disney's Wide World of Sports, and Downtown Disney West Side had opened; and by 1998 Disney's Animal Kingdom had come to life. Also arriving in this decade of growth were the planned community of Celebration, the Disney cruise lines, the book-publishing arm of Hyperion, and the purchase of Miramax Films and ABC television.

Since the profitable mid-1990s, however, Disney has suffered its share of economic trouble and political unrest. Following a dip in earnings in 2002, and several box-office bombs (think: *The Alamo*), Roy E. Disney, Walt's nephew, resigned from his position as vice chairman of the board of directors to lead a movement to oust Michael Eisner from the company. When Eisner came up for re-election to the Disney board in early 2004, 43% of shareholders withheld their votes. By September 2005, Robert Iger had replaced Eisner as CEO. Despite the big changes at its parent company, Walt Disney World continues to grow and improve. A score of new shows and attractions opened in 2006 and 2007, including the exciting "runaway train" ride Expedition Everest, the brilliant "Finding Nemo—The Musical," and Monsters, Inc. Laugh Floor Comedy Club.

And it all started with a man who didn't have the cash to buy a little more land in Anaheim.

–Gary McKechnie

THE FASTPASS SYSTEM

Imagine taking a trip to Disney and managing to avoid most of the lines. Fastpass is your ticket to this terrific scenario, and it's included in regular park admission. Pocket your theme-park ticket upon entry, then insert it into a special machine at one of several Fastpass-equipped attractions at each Disney park. Out comes your Fastpass, printed with a one-hour window of time during which you can return to get into the fast line. *Don't forget to take your park ticket back, too.* While you wait for your Fastpass appointment to mature, enjoy other attractions in the park.

It's important to note that once you've made one Fastpass appointment you cannot make another until you're within the window of time for your first appointment. Smart guests save their Fastpass appointments for the most popular attractions, and they make new appointments as quickly as possible after their existing ones mature.

RESERVATIONS

Make your dining reservations through the **WDW Reservation Center** (☎407/939–3463) before you leave home so you don't have to worry about finding a restaurant every night. Restaurants at Disney book up fast. There's no penalty for not showing up for a reservation, however. Make tee time reservations to play at any of Walt Disney World's six golf courses at ⊕ www.disneyworldgolf.com or by calling **WDW Golf Reservations** (☎407/939–4653).

OPENING HOURS

The major area theme parks, including those in Walt Disney World, are open 365 days a year. Opening times vary but generally hover around 9. Certain attractions within the parks may not open until 10 or 11 AM, however, and parks usually observe shorter hours during the off-seasons in January, February, April, May, September, and October. In general, the longest days are during prime summer months and over the year-end holidays, when the Magic Kingdom may be open as late as 10 or 11, later on New Year's Eve; Epcot is open until 9 or 9:30 in the World Showcase area and at several Future World attractions, the Studios until 7 or 8:30. At other times, the Magic Kingdom closes around 7 or 8—but there are variations, so call ahead. Most of the year, the Animal Kingdom closes at 5, though during peak holiday seasons it may open at 8 and close at 7 or 8.

The parking lots open at least an hour before the parks do. If you arrive at the Magic Kingdom turnstiles before the official opening time, you can often breakfast in a restaurant on Main Street, which usually opens before the rest of the park, and be ready to dash to one of the popular attractions in other lands at Rope Drop, the Magic Kingdom's official opening time.

Hours at Typhoon Lagoon and Blizzard Beach are 9 or 10 to 5 daily (until 7—occasionally 10—in summer).

The shops at Downtown Disney stay open as late as 11 PM in summer and during holidays.

You can check exact opening and closing times by calling the parks directly or checking their Web sites.

EXTRA MAGIC HOURS

The Extra Magic Hours program gives Disney resort guests free early and late-night admission to certain parks on specified days—call ahead for information about each park's "magic hours" days to plan your early- and late-visit strategies.

BASIC SERVICES

LOST & FOUND

There are Lost & Found offices in the Magic Kingdom, at Epcot, in Disney–MGM Studios, and at Disney's Animal Kingdom. After one day, all items are sent to the Main Lost & Found office.

Contacts **Disney's Animal Kingdom Lost & Found** (☎ 407/938-2785). **Disney-MGM Studios Lost & Found** (☎ 407/560-3720). **Epcot Lost & Found** (☎ 407/560-7500). **Magic Kingdom Lost & Found** (✉ City Hall ☎ 407/824-4521). **Main Lost & Found** (✉ Magic Kingdom, Transportation and Ticket Center ☎ 407/824-4245).

RESTROOMS

Restrooms at the theme parks are widely available and frequently cleaned, and there are usually enough stalls so that you rarely have to wait in line; most, including men's rooms, have baby-changing stations. Companion restrooms also are available in many locations for those who need assistance. Some park areas geared to smaller children even have kid-size potties and sinks. Plus, rest rooms at the airport and at many attractions use the automatic infrared flush trigger, so you never have to touch the toilet.

CAMERAS

Disposable cameras and film, batteries, and memory cards are widely available in shops throughout the theme parks and hotels. The **Camera Center,** in the Magic Kingdom Town Square Exposition Hall, is the place to buy photos that Disney photographers take of you and your family posing with characters or saying cheese at various locations around the park. A 5"× 7" photo costs $12.95 for the first print and $9.95 for each additional copy. An 8"× 10" costs $16.95 and $12.95 for each additional copy. You can buy similar photos at the other Disney park Camera Centers, or you can ask for the Disney PhotoPass so you can view and order the photos online at any time.

Best Disney Web Sites

Browsing **disneyworld.com** is one of the best ways to research hotels and restaurants and find which attractions are best for each age group. But there are also some fantastic unofficial Web sites with excellent up-to-date information and forums where first-time and annual Disney visitors post messages with questions, advice, and trip reports. **Allearsnet.com** is a great resource for travelers with special needs or medical conditions that include allergies, motion sensitivity, mobility issues, and certain impairments. The site is loaded with photos and interesting unofficial travel tidbits. **Mousesavers.com** will tell you how to get the best hotel deals and is a source for discount information and coupons. **Wdwinfo. com,** run by Werner Technologies, offers some good information on how to get discounts, plus visitor reviews of hotels, theme parks, and restaurants. Post your question at **disboards.com** to get feedback from fellow Disney travelers. The **fodors. com** forums also host lively virtual conversations between travel-happy people. To tap into the thrill-riding community, check out **thrillride.com.** And finally, **themeparkinsider.com** has information and ratings about the parks, rides, and hotels.

LOCKERS

Lockers are available near all the theme-park entrances ($5; plus $2 deposit). If you're park-hopping, you can use your locker receipt to acquire a locker at the next park you visit for no extra charge.

PACKAGE PICKUP

Ask the shop clerk to send any large purchase you make to Package Pickup, so you won't have to carry it around all day. Allow three hours for the delivery. The package pickup area is in Town Square next to City Hall.

PET CARE

It's probably best to leave Rover at home, but if you just can't part with your animal, all the major Disney parks, as well as Universal and SeaWorld, have kennels. They provide a cage, water, and sometimes food. Some of the kennels, such as the one at Epcot, offer dog-walking services for an additional fee. On-site Disney resort guests can board their pets for $13 each per night; others pay $15 per night. The Disney day rate is $10 per pet. At SeaWorld, pets can stay for $6 a day; at Universal, the day rate is $10.

The Portofino Bay Hotel, the Hard Rock Hotel, and the Royal Pacific Resort at **Universal Orlando** (☎ *407/503–7625 or 800/232–7827*) allow your pet to stay in your room for a $25 cleaning fee, and they even offer pet room service. You must, however, provide a pet health certificate that's no more than 10 days old. You must also have a leash or cage.

CLOSE UP

1

Books on Disney

Neal Gabler's *Walt Disney: The Triumph of the American Imagination* (2006) gives the full story that led to Walt's "synergistic empire," and has earned rave reviews. One of the most perceptive books on Walt Disney and his works is *The Disney Version* (third edition, 1997), by Richard Schickel. For a good read about Disney and other animators, look for *Of Mice and Magic* (1990), by Leonard Maltin. A comprehensive history of the great Disney animation tradition is provided in *Disney Animation: The Illusion of Life*, by Frank Thomas and Ollie Johnston (1995).

Walt Disney: An American Original (1994), by Bob Thomas, is full of anecdotes about the development of WDW. Rollins College professor Richard Fogelsong questions the "economic marriage" between Disney and Orlando in his book *Married to the Mouse* (2003).

HEALTH & FIRST AID

In an emergency, always call **911.** Disney employees are known for their extreme helpfulness, so don't hesitate to call on anyone with a Disney name tag. All the major theme parks have first-aid centers.

CLINICS & HOSPITALS

The **Centra Care** (⊠ *12500 S. Apopka Vineland Rd., Lake Buena Vista* ☎ *407/934–2273*) near Downtown Disney provides free shuttle service from any of the Disney, Universal, and SeaWorld theme park's first-aid stations and from all Disney resort hotels and other area hotels. It's open weekdays 8–midnight, weekends 8–8.

For minor emergencies visit the **Main Street Physicians Clinic** (⊠ *8723 International Dr., Suite 115* ☎ *407/370–4881*). It's open weekdays 8–11, weekends 9–11.

In an emergency near Celebration, head to **Florida Hospital Celebration Health** (⊠ *400 Celebration Pl., Celebration* ☎ *407/303–4000*). If you're closer to Universal Studios, head to **Orlando Regional Medical Center/Sand Lake Hospital** (⊠ *9400 Turkey Lake Rd., International Drive Area, Orlando* ☎ *407/351–8500*). Hospital emergency rooms are open 24 hours a day.

PHARMACIES

You can buy over-the-counter pain relievers at most Disney shops. For prescription medications, there's a 24-hour pharmacy at **Walgreens** (⊠ *920 Kirkman Rd., Universal Studios Area* ☎ *407/253–6288*). A branch of **CVS** (⊠ *5308 W. Irlo Bronson Memorial Hwy./U.S. 192* ☎ *407/390–9185*) is closer to Walt Disney World and is also open 24 hours; pharmacy hours are 8 AM–10 PM Monday–Saturday and 9–9 Sunday.

VISITOR INFORMATION

For general WDW information, contact Guest Information or visit Guest Relations in any Disney resort. If you want to speak directly to someone at a specific Disney location, use the WDW Central Switchboard at 407/824–2222. To inquire about specific resort facilities or detailed park information, call the individual property via the switchboard. For accommodations and shows, call the Disney Reservation Center. One of the easiest ways to get Disney information is via the WDW Web site.

PHONE NUMBERS & WEB SITES

WALT DISNEY WORLD

WDW Information ☎407/824–4321, 407/827–5141 TDD ⊕www.disneyworld.com. **WDW Resort Reservations** ☎407/934–7639. **WDW Dining reservations** ☎407/939–3463.

UNIVERSAL ORLANDO

Universal Information ☎*407/363–8000* ⊕*www.universalorlando.com.* **Universal Resort reservations** ☎*888/273–1311.*

SEAWORLD

SeaWorld Information ☎407/351–3600 or 888/800–5447 ⊕www.seaworld.com. **Discovery Cove Information** ☎407/351–3600 or 877/434–7268 ⊕www.discoverycove.com.

GREATER ORLANDO

Orlando/Orange County Convention & Visitors Bureau ☎407/363–5871 ⊕www.orlandoinfo.com. **Kissimmee/St. Cloud Convention & Visitors Bureau** ☎407/847–5000 or 800/327–9159 ⊕www.floridakiss.com. **Winter Park Chamber of Commerce** ☎407/644–8281 ⊕www.winterpark.org or www.cityofwinterpark.org. **Visit Florida** ☎850/488–5607 ⊕www.visitflorida.com.

Where to Stay

Updated
by Rowland
Stiteler

ONCE UPON A TIME, SIMPLY BEING in the midst of the world's largest concentration of theme parks was enough of a selling point to make most Orlando hotels thrive. But somewhere along the way, as the room inventory topped 120,000 (more hotel rooms than New York City), the competition became so intense that hotels needed to become attractions in themselves. Hoteliers learned that you've got to have a bit of show-biz to draw the crowds, so the choices here are anything but ordinary. Orlando may not be Las Vegas, but its hotels are definitely big, fancy, and, in some cases, leaning toward gaudy.

The idea in Orlando is for a hotel to entertain you as much as provide lodging. The Gaylord Palms Resort, with a 4-acre glass-covered atrium, has its own version of the Everglades inside, plus a re-creation of old St. Augustine, a mini Key West, and a 60-foot sailboat that houses a bar on an indoor waterway. Besides showy lobbies, restaurants, and pool areas, most of the larger hotels also have their own in-house children's clubs, many of which provide clown shows, magic shows, and other forms of live entertainment. It's as if the owners expect you to never leave the hotel during your entire vacation.

Most of the bigger, glitzier hotels have room rates commensurate with their huge construction and maintenance budgets—it's not unusual in this market for the cost of building a hotel to come in at $350,000 or more per guest room. But many other hotels maintain moderate and inexpensive rates. Because of the sheer number of properties in the Orlando area, you will find choices in every price range. One trend is the proliferation of all-suites properties, many with in-room kitchens and relatively low rates. And Disney has its own low-budget hotels, too—the All-Star resorts and the Pop Century Resort. With budget properties sprouting up along I-Drive, the cheap motels along U.S. 192 in Kissimmee are less of a good deal than they were 20 years ago.

So, your first big decision when it comes to your vacation will probably be whether to stay within Walt Disney World. The on-site hotels were built with families in mind. Older children can use the transportation system on their own without inviting trouble. (Disney property is quite safe, day or night.) And younger children get a thrill from knowing that they're actually staying in Walt Disney World.

If you're planning to visit other attractions, then staying off-site holds a number of advantages. You enjoy more peace and quiet and may have easier access to Orlando, SeaWorld, and Universal Studios, and you're likely to save money. To help you find your perfect room, we've reviewed hundreds of offerings throughout the main hotel hubs both in and surrounding Walt Disney World.

DO WE STAY ON-SITE OR OFF-SITE?

If you stay in WDW, you can put aside your car keys, because Disney buses and monorails are efficient enough to make it possible to visit one park in the morning and another after lunch with a Park Hopper pass. You have the freedom to return to your hotel for R&R when the

TOP 5 DISNEY HOTELS

BoardWalk Inn & Villas. The price is right and the location can't be beat for adults more interested in Epcot and nightlife than being close to the Magic Kingdom.

All-Star Movies Resort. Kids love the giant *Toy Story* figures and Disney-movie themes everywhere, and parents love the price.

Grand Floridian Resort & Spa. If you want to be on the monorail line just minutes from the Magic Kingdom's gate and you can splurge to stay in a gorgeous luxury hotel, the Grand Floridian is for you.

Wilderness Lodge. Close to the Magic Kingdom yet surprisingly secluded, this stunning retreat is perfect for families who prefer a lodge theme in a good location.

Yacht & Beach Club Resorts. With a man-made beach, spacious family suites, and a relaxed, luxurious, Ralph Lauren-esque feel, the Yacht and Beach clubs appeals to families looking for tranquility and beauty closer to Epcot.

crowds are thickest, and if it turns out that half the family wants to spend the afternoon in Epcot and the other half wants to float around Typhoon Lagoon, it's not a problem.

Rooms in the more expensive Disney-owned properties are large enough to accommodate up to five, and villas sleep six or seven. All rooms have cable TV with the Disney Channel and a daily events channel.

If you're an on-site guest at a Disney lodging, you're guaranteed entry to parks even when they have reached capacity, as the Magic Kingdom, Disney–MGM Studios, Blizzard Beach, and Typhoon Lagoon sometimes do. You also get other perks like meal plans ($39 a day); the chance to enter Disney parks earlier and stay later than nonguests; and the ability to use the Magical Express service to check your bags through to the hotel from your home airport when departing for Orlando and back again on return.

Though rates are often better at non-Disney owned hotels on Disney property (e.g., the Swan, the Dolphin, and the hotels on the so-called Hotel Row just outside Downtown Disney), the perks are fewer. Be sure to clarify what you'll get for the money at each type of property.

The hotels closest to WDW are clustered in a few principal areas: along I-Drive; in the U.S. 192 area and Kissimmee; and in the Downtown Disney–Lake Buena Vista Area, just off I-4 Exit 68. Nearly every hotel in these areas provides frequent transportation to and from WDW. In addition, there are some noteworthy, if far-flung, options in the suburbs and in the greater Orlando area. If you're willing to make the commute, you'll probably save a bundle. Whereas the Hilton near Downtown Disney charges about $200 a night in season, another Hilton about 45 minutes away in Altamonte Springs has rates that start at $140. Other costs, such as gas and restaurants, are also lower in

TOP 5 OFF-SITE HOTELS

Gaylord Palms Resort. The interior of this place is like a Cecil B. DeMille movie—about Florida. Just walking around in the 4-acre atrium is an adventure in itself: the Everglades, old St. Augustine. The wow-factor isn't exclusive to the theme parks.

Hyatt Regency Grand Cypress Resort. A top-class resort with sprawling grounds almost on top of Walt Disney World property, the Hyatt is perfect for families who want to be near the Mouse but need to take a break from Disney each night.

Nickelodeon Family Suites by Holiday Inn. For the same amount you'd spend on a basic room at a Disney value resort, you get a suite with a separate area for the kids, a Nickelodeon-theme pool, and tons of kids' activities at this family-oriented hotel.

Ritz-Carlton Orlando Grande Lakes. Ultraluxurious rooms, restaurants, and spa programs, plus a championship golf course, make this resort one of the best in the Orlando area.

Royal Pacific Resort. Like roller coasters? Got teens? You might want to stay at Universal Orlando instead of Disney. A stay at this South Pacific-theme hotel gets you into the Express lines on an unlimited basis for free.

the northeast suburbs. One suburban caveat: traffic on I–4 in Orlando experiences typical freeway gridlock during morning (7–9) and evening (4–6) rush hours.

RESERVATIONS

Reserve your hotel several months in advance if you want to snag the best rooms during high season. You can book all on-site accommodations—including Disney-owned hotels, non-Disney-owned hotels, and the Hotel Row properties—through the **WDW Central Reservations Office** (⌂ *Box 10100, Suite 300, Lake Buena Vista 32830* ☎ *407/934–7639* ⊕ *www.disneyworld.com*). People with disabilities can call **WDW Special Request Reservations** (☎ *407/939–7807*) to get information or book rooms at any of the on-site Disney properties.

When you book a room, be sure to mention whether you have a disability or are traveling with children and whether you prefer a certain type of bed or have any other concerns. You may need to pay a deposit for your first night's stay within three weeks of making your reservation. At many hotels you can get a refund if you cancel at least five days before your scheduled arrival. However, individual hotel policies vary, and some properties may require up to 15 days' notice for a full refund. Check before booking.

If neither the WDW Central Reservations Office nor the off-site hotels have space on your preferred dates, look into packages from American

Express, Delta, or other operators, which have been allotted whole blocks of rooms. In addition, because there are always cancellations, it's worth trying at the last minute; for same-day bookings, call the property directly. Packages, including airfare, cruises, car rentals, and hotels both on and off Disney property, can be arranged through your travel agent or **Walt Disney Travel Co.** (✉ *7100 Municipal Dr., Orlando 32819* ☎ *407/828–3232* ⊕ *www.disneyworld.com*).

PRICES

Like everywhere else, Orlando experienced an upward drift in hotel prices during 2005 and 2006. Although it used to be quite easy to find worthwhile lodging for less than $75 per room night, now that threshold has drifted closer to $100. The lodgings we list are the top selections of their type in each category. Rates are lowest from early January to mid-February, from late April to mid-June, and from mid-August to the third week in December.

Always call several places—availability and special deals can often drive room rates at a $$$$ hotel down into the $$ range—and don't forget to ask if you're eligible for a discount. Many hotels offer special rates for members of, for example, the American Automobile Association (AAA) or the American Association of Retired Persons (AARP). Don't overlook the savings to be gained from preparing your own breakfast and maybe a few other meals as well, which you can do if you choose a room or suite with a kitchenette or kitchen. In listings, we always name the facilities that are available, but we don't specify whether they cost extra.

WHAT IT COSTS				
¢	$	$$	$$$	$$$$
FOR 2 PEOPLE under $80	$80–$140	$140–$220	$220–$280	over $280

Price categories reflect the range between the least and most expensive standard double rooms in nonholiday high season, based on the European Plan (with no meals) unless otherwise noted. City and state taxes (10%–12%) are extra.

DISCOUNT RESERVATIONS   To save money, look into discount reservations services with Web sites and toll-free numbers, which use their buying power to get a better price on hotels, airline tickets, even car rentals. When booking a room, always call the hotel's local toll-free number (if one is available) rather than the central reservations number—you'll often get a better price. Always ask about special packages or corporate rates.

Hotel Rooms **Accommodations Express** (☎ *800/444–7666 or 800/277–1064* ⊕ *www.accommodationsexpress.com*). **Central Reservation Service** (*(CRS)* ☎ *800/555–7555 or 800/548–3311* ⊕ *www.crshotels.com*). **Hotels.com** (☎ *800/246–8357* ⊕ *www.hotels.com*). **Quikbook** (☎ *800/789–9887* ⊕ *www. quikbook.com*). **Turbotrip.com** (☎ *800/473–7829* ⊕ *www.turbotrip.com*).

THE DISNEY RESORTS

Disney-operated hotels are fantasies unto themselves. Each is immaculately designed according to a theme (quaint New England, the relaxed culture of the Polynesian Islands, an African safari village, etc.) and each offers the same perks: free transportation from the airport and to the parks, the option to charge all your purchases to your room, special guest-only park-visiting times, and much more. If you stay on-site, you'll have better access to the parks and you'll be more immersed in the Disney experience.

MAGIC KINGDOM RESORT AREA

Take I–4 Exit 62, 64B, or 65. The ritzy hotels near the Magic Kingdom all lie on the monorail route and are only minutes away from the park. Fort Wilderness Resort and Campground, with RV and tent sites, is a bit farther southeast of the Magic Kingdom, and access to the parks is by bus.

GRAND FLORIDIAN RESORT & SPA

$$$$
Fodor's Choice
★

On the shores of the Seven Seas Lagoon, this red, gable-roof Victorian is all delicate gingerbread, rambling verandas, and brick chimneys. It's Disney's flagship resort: add a dinner or two at Victoria and Albert's or Cítricos and you may spend more in a weekend here than on your mortgage payment—but you'll have great memories. Although you won't look out of place walking through the lobby in flip-flops, afternoon high tea and a pianist playing nightly in the lobby are among the high-scale touches. The Mouseketeer Clubhouse on the ground floor offers children's programs until midnight daily. Pros: on the monorail; Victoria and Albert's, one of the state's best restaurants. Cons: some say it's not ritzy enough to match the room rates; conference center and convention clientele lend stuffiness. ☎407/824–3000 ⟋900 rooms, 90 suites ⟋In-room: safe, Ethernet, Wi-Fi. In-hotel: 5 restaurants, room service, tennis courts, pools, gym, spa, beachfront, concierge, children's programs (ages 4–12), laundry facilities, laundry service, executive floor, no-smoking rooms ▭AE, D, DC, MC, V.

POLYNESIAN RESORT

$$$$

If it weren't for the kids in Mickey Mouse caps, you'd think you were in Fiji. In the three-story atrium lobbly orchids bloom alongside coconut palms and banana trees, and water cascades from volcanic-rock fountains. At the evening luau, Polynesian dancers perform before a feast with Hawaiian-style roast pork. Rooms sleep five, since they all have two queen-size beds and a daybed. Most rooms also have a balcony or patio. Lagoon-view rooms—which overlook Magic Kingdom fireworks—are peaceful but costly. Pros: on the monorail; great aloha-spirit atmosphere. Cons: pricey; not good for those bothered by lots of loud children. ☎407/824–2000 ⟋853 rooms, 5 suites ⟋In-room: safe, Ethernet. In-hotel: 4 restaurants, room service, bar, pools, gym, beachfront, children's programs (ages 4–12), laundry facilities, laundry service, concierge, executive floor, public Wi-Fi, no-smoking rooms ▭AE, D, DC, MC, V.

CONTEMPORARY RESORT

$$$–$$$$ You're paying for location, and perhaps tradition, when you stay here. This 15-story, flat-topped pyramid, the first hotel to open here more than 30 years ago, has been completely renovated several times. The 2006 upgrade brought work-station desks, flat-panel TVs, and marble bathroom vanities. The monorail runs through the lobby, so it takes just minutes to get to the Magic Kingdom and Epcot. Upper floors of the main tower (where rooms are more expensive) offer great views of all the activities in and around the Magic Kingdom, including the nightly fireworks.

Pros: easy access to Magic Kingdom; Chef Mickey's, the epicenter of the character-meal world; launching point for romantic sunset Bay Lake cruises. Cons: a mix of vacationers and conventioneers (there's an on-site convention center); sometimes too frenzied for the former and too staid for the latter. ☎407/824–1000 *1,013 rooms, 25 suites In-room: safe, refrigerator, Ethernet. In-hotel: 3 restaurants, room service, tennis courts, pools, gym, beachfront, concierge, children's programs (ages 4–12), laundry facilities, laundry service, executive floor, public Wi-Fi, no-smoking rooms* ⊟AE, D, DC, MC, V.

FORT WILDERNESS RESORT CABINS

$$$–$$$$ This 700-acre campground is a resort in itself. With its dozens of entertainment options–including biking, outdoor movies, and singing around the campfire—and the very popular *Hoop-Dee-Doo Musical Review* character event, a family can have a truly memorable vacation. The campground is so big that you may want to rent a golf cart (about $45 a day) or a bike ($22 a day). There's a shuttle bus system, but it's about 20 minutes between departures. The larger cabins can accommodate four grown-ups and two youngsters; the bedroom has a double bed and a bunk bed, and the living room has a double sleeper sofa or Murphy bed. Each cabin has a fully equipped kitchen, and daily housekeeping is provided. Pros: cabins don't constitute roughing it; you can save a fortune by cooking, but you don't have to, thanks to the three-meals-a-day restaurant and nightly barbecue. Cons: shuttle to Disney theme parks is free, but slow; coin-op laundry is pricey ($2 to wash, $2 to dry). ☎407/824–2900 *408 cabins In-room: kitchen, Ethernet. In-hotel: restaurant, tennis courts, pools, beachfront, bicycles, laundry facilities, no-smoking rooms* ⊟AE, D, DC, MC, V.

WILDERNESS LODGE

$$–$$$$
Fodor'sChoice
★ The architects outdid themselves with this seven-story hotel modeled after the majestic turn-of-the-20th-century lodges of the American Northwest. The five-story lobby, supported by towering tree trunks,

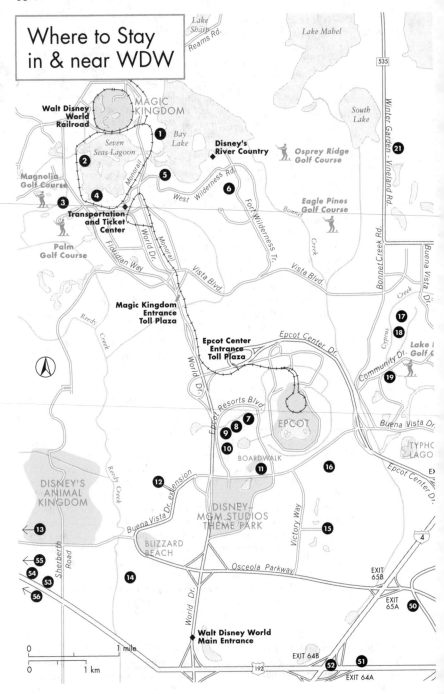

Where to Stay in & near WDW

Disney Hotels ▼

All-Star Sports, All-Star Music and All-Star Movies Resorts **14**

Animal Kingdom Lodge **13**

Beach Club Villas **7**

BoardWalk Inn and Villas **11**

Caribbean Beach Resort **16**

Contemporary Resort **1**

Coronado Springs Resort **12**

Fort Wilderness Resort Cabins & Campground **6**

Grand Floridian Resort & Spa **2**

Old Key West Resort **19**

Polynesian Resort **4**

Pop Century Resort **15**

Port Orleans Resort— French Quarter **18**

Port Orleans Resort— Riverside **17**

Saratoga Springs Resort **20**

Shades of Green **3**

Walt Disney World Dolphin **9**

Walt Disney World Swan **10**

Wilderness Lodge **5**

Yacht and Beach Club Resorts **8**

Other Hotels ▼

AmeriSuites Lake Buena Vista South **43**

Best Western Lakeside **56**

Best Western Lake Buena Vista **31**

Best Western Maingate South **46**

Buena Vista Palace Resort & Spa in the WDW Resort **35**

Buena Vista Suites **40**

Caribe Royale All-Suites Resort & Convention Center **41**

Celebration Hotel **52**

Celebrity Resorts Kissimee **45**

Celebrity Resorts at Lake Buena Vista **25**

Country Inn & Suites by Carlson **29**

DoubleTree Guest Suites in the WDW Resort **32**

Embassy Suites Hotel Lake Buena Vista **22**

Gaylord Palms Resort **50**

Grosvenor Resort **34**

Hampton Inn Orlando Maingate South **47**

Hawthorne Suites Lake Buena Vista **26**

Hilton in the WDW Resort **33**

Holiday Inn Maingate West **53**

Holiday Inn SunSpree Lake Buena Vista **37**

Hyatt Regency Grand Cypress Resort **30**

Magical Memories Villas **44**

Marriott Residence Inn **23**

Marriott Village at Little Lake Bryan **28**

Nickelodeon Family Suites by Holiday Inn **42**

Omni Orlando Resort at ChampionsGate **48**

Orlando World Center Marriott **39**

Palomino Suites Lake Buena Vista **24**

PerriHouse Bed & Breakfast Inn **21**

Radisson Resort Parkway **51**

Reunion Resort & Club of Orlando **49**

Royal Plaza **36**

Saratoga Resort Villas at Orlando Maingate **54**

Seralago Hotel & Suites Maingate East **55**

Sheraton Safari Hotel **27**

Sheraton Vistana Resort **38**

CLOSE UP

Perks for Disney Resort Guests

■ **Location! Location! Location!** You'll probably get to the parks faster than guests staying off-site, and if you plan to stay at Disney for your whole trip, you won't need to rent a car.

■ **Extra Magic Hour.** You get special early and late-night admission to certain parks on specified days—call ahead for information about each park's "magic hours" days to plan your early- and late-visit strategies.

■ **Magical Express.** This perk answers that bothersome question, "How do I get there from the airport?" If you're staying at a Disney hotel, you don't need to rent a car, and you don't even have to think about finding a shuttle or taxi. Or picking up your luggage. With Disney Magical Express, once you get off your plane at Orlando International, you're met by a Disney rep who leads you to a coach that takes you directly to your hotel. Your luggage is delivered separately and usually arrives at your hotel room an hour or two after you do. Participating airlines include American, Continental, Delta, JetBlue, Northwest, Southwest, and United. When you're ready to leave, the process works in reverse (though only on some participating airlines, so check in advance). You get your boarding pass and check your bags at the hotel. Then you go to the airport and go directly to your gate, skipping check-in. You won't see your bags until you're in your hometown airport. Best of all, the service is free.

■ **Package Delivery.** Anything you purchase, whether at one of the parks, one of the hotels, or even in Downtown Disney, can be delivered to the gift shop of your Disney hotel free of charge. It's a big plus not to have to carry your packages around all day.

■ **Priority Reservations.** Hotel guests get priority reservations at Disney restaurants by calling 407/939–3463. Hotel guests also get the choicest tee times at Disney golf courses. Reserve them up to 30 days in advance by calling 407/939–4654.

■ **Charging Privileges.** You can charge most meals and purchases throughout Disney to your hotel room.

■ **Free Parking.** Parking is free for hotel guests, and that extends beyond hotel parking lots. Show your parking pass when you go to any of the Disney parks and you won't be charged for parking.

has an 82-foot-high, three-sided fireplace made of rocks from the Grand Canyon and lit by enormous tepee-shape chandeliers. Two 55-foot-tall hand-carved totem poles complete the illusion. Rooms have leather chairs, patchwork quilts, cowboy art and a balcony or a patio. The hotel's showstopper is its Fire Rock Geyser, a faux Old Faithful, near the large pool, which begins as an artificially heated hot spring in the lobby. This hotel is a good option if you're a couple without kids looking for more serenity than is found at Disney's other hotels. Pros: high-wow-factor architecture; boarding point for romantic Bay Lake sunset cruises. Cons: ferry toots its horn at every docking; no direct shuttle to Magic Kingdom. ☎407/824–3200 ⟿728 rooms, 31 suites ⬧In-room: safe, Ethernet. In-hotel: 3 restaurants, room service, pool, beachfront, bicycles, children's programs (ages 4–12), laundry facilities, laundry service, concierge, executive floor, public Wi-Fi, no-smoking rooms ▤AE, D, DC, MC, V.

FORT WILDERNESS RESORT CAMPGROUND

¢–$ ⚠ Bringing a tent or RV is one of the cheapest ways to stay on WDW property, especially considering that sites accommodate up to 10. Tent sites with water and electricity are real bargains. RV sites cost more but are equipped with electric, water, and sewage hookups as well as outdoor charcoal grills and picnic tables. Even with just a good tent and cozy sleeping bag you'll be relatively comfortable, since the campground has 15 stra-

tegically located comfort stations where you can take a hot shower, as well as laundry facilities, restaurants, a general store—everything you need. There are many activities to keep you occupied, such as tennis and horseback riding. Pros: Disney's most economical lodging; pets allowed ($5 nightly fee). Cons: amount of walking within the camp (to reach the store, restaurants, etc.) can be a little much; shuttle rides to Disney parks too long for some. ☎407/824–2900 ⇆788 campsites, 695 with full hookups, 90 partial hookups ⚐Pools, flush toilets, full hookups, dump station, drinking water, guest laundry, showers, picnic tables, food service, electricity, public telephone ▤AE, D, DC, MC, V.

EPCOT RESORT AREA

Take I–4 Exit 64B or 65. From the Epcot resorts you can walk or take a boat to the International Gateway entrance to Epcot, or you can take the shuttle from your hotel or drive to the Future World (front) entrance.

BEACH CLUB VILLAS

$$$$ 🖼 Each villa has a separate living room, kitchen, and one or two bedrooms; studios are more like hotel rooms. Interiors are soft yellow and green with white iron bedsteads. Private balconies on the upper levels or porches at street level ensure that you can enjoy your morning coffee in the sun with a view of the lake. The villas are marketed as time-share properties for Disney Vacation Club members, but available rooms are also rented on a per-night basis. You'll have access to all the facilities of the adjacent Yacht and Beach Club resorts, including Stormalong Bay. Pros: short walk to Epcot's BoardWalk area; in-suite kitchens let you save money on meals. Cons: can be noisy; not close

to Magic or Animal Kingdoms. ☎407/934–8000 ☞205 villas ♨In-room: safe, Ethernet. In-hotel: restaurant, room service, tennis courts, pools, gym, beachfront, laundry service, concierge, public Wi-Fi, no-smoking rooms ▤AE, D, DC, MC, V.

BOARDWALK INN & VILLAS

$$$$
Fodor's Choice
★

▦ Disney's smallest deluxe hotel is a beautiful re-creation of Victorian-era Atlantic City inn. Architectural master Robert A. M. Stern designed it to mimic 19th-century New England building styles. Rooms have floral-print bedspreads and blue-and-white painted furniture. Those overlooking Crescent Lake cost the most and are the noisiest. A 200-foot waterslide in the form of a classic wooden roller coaster cascades into the pool area. The property opens directly onto Disney's Board-Walk entertainment complex, where you can ride surrey bikes, watch a game at the ESPN Sports Club, or dine in some of Disney's better restaurants. The hotel is also a 15-minute walk from Disney–MGM Studios. Pros: quick access to nighttime fun; rooms are larger than average (390 square feet). Con: shuttle to Magic Kingdom and other parks is slow. ☎407/939–5100 inn, 407/939–6200 villas ☞370 rooms, 19 suites, 526 villas ♨In-room: safe, Ethernet. In-hotel: 4 restaurants, room service, tennis court, pool, gym, concierge, children's programs (ages 4–12), laundry facilities, laundry service, public Wi-Fi, no-smoking rooms ▤AE, D, DC, MC, V.

YACHT & BEACH CLUB RESORTS

$$$$
Fodor's Choice
★

▦ These Seven Seas Lagoon inns seem straight out of a Cape Cod summer. The five-story Yacht Club has hardwood floors, a lobby full of gleaming brass and polished leather, an oyster-gray clapboard facade, and evergreen landscaping; there's even a lighthouse on its pier. Rooms have floral-print bedspreads and a small ship's wheel on the headboard. At the Beach Club, a croquet lawn and cabana-dotted white-sand beach set the scene. Stormalong Bay, a 3-acre water park with slides and whirlpools, is part of this club. Both lodgings have "quiet pools," which are secluded and largely kid-free, albeit nondescript. Pros: location, location, location—it's easy to walk to Epcot and the BoardWalk, and Disney–MGM is a fun, 20-minute ferry ride away. Cons: distances within the hotel—like, from your room to the front desk—can seem vast; high-noise factor. ☎407/934–8000 Beach Club, 407/934–7000 Yacht Club ☞1,213 rooms, 112 suites ♨In-room: safe, Ethernet, Wi-Fi. In-hotel: 4 restaurants, room service, tennis courts, pools, gym, beachfront, bicycles, children's programs (ages 4–12), laundry service, concierge, public Wi-Fi, no-smoking rooms ▤AE, D, DC, MC, V.

CARIBBEAN BEACH RESORT

$$–$$$
★

▦ Six palm-studded "villages," all awash in dizzying pastels and labeled with Caribbean names like Barbados and Trinidad, share 45-acre Barefoot Bay and its white-sand beach. Bridges connect to a 1-acre path-crossed play and picnic area called Parrot Cay. You can rent boats to explore the lake, or rent bikes to ride along the 1½-mi lakefront promenade. The Old Port Royale complex, decorated with cannons, statues, and tropical birds, has a food court, lounge, and pool area with falls and a big slide. Rooms, which have painted–wood furniture, are fresh and done in soft pastels like turquoise and peach. Pros: restaurants sell Jamaica's Red Stripe beer; plenty of on-site outdoor activities; convenient to Epcot, Disney-MGM, and Downtown Disney. Cons: you don't truly feel swept away to a tropical island; the only crystalline and swimmable waters are in the pools; walks from your room to the beach or a restaurant can be up to 15 minutes. ☎407/934–3400 ⇱*2,112 rooms* ♿*In-room: safe, Ethernet. In-hotel: restaurant, room service, pools, beachfront, bicycles, no elevator, laundry facilities, laundry service, public Wi-Fi, no-smoking rooms* ▤*AE, D, DC, MC, V.*

CORONADO SPRINGS RESORT

$$–$$$ Because of its 84,000-square-foot exhibit hall, this is Disney's most popular convention hotel. But since the meeting space is in its own wing, the moderately priced resort is also popular with families who appreciate its casual Southwestern architecture, its lively, Mexican-style food court, and its elaborate swimming pool, which has a Mayan pyramid with a big slide. There's a full-service health club and spa, and if you like jogging, walking, or biking you're in the right place—a pleasant path circles the lake. You can rent bikes, kayaks, canoes, and paddleboats. Pros: great pool with a play area/arcade for kids and a bar for adults; lots of outdoor activities. Cons: some accommodations are a half-mile from the restaurants; standard rooms are on the small side (300 square feet); kids may find the subdued atmosphere boring. ☎407/939–1000 ⇱*1,967 rooms* ♿*In-room: safe, Ethernet. In-hotel: 2 restaurants, room service, bar, pools, gym, spa, bicycles, laundry service, public Wi-Fi, no-smoking rooms* ▤*AE, D, DC, MC, V.*

ANIMAL KINGDOM RESORT AREA

Take I–4 Exit 64B. In the park's southwest corner, Disney's third resort area comprises the fabulous Africa-theme Animal Kingdom Lodge, plus two budget-price hotel complexes: All-Star Village, not far from U.S. 192, and the Pop Century Resort, on Osceola Parkway.

ANIMAL KINGDOM LODGE

$$–$$$$ Giraffes, zebras, and other wildlife roam three 11-acre savannas
★   separated by wings of this grand hotel. In the atrium lobby, a massive faux-thatched roof hovers almost 100 feet above hardwood floors with inlaid carvings. Cultural ambassadors give talks about their African homelands, the animals, and the artwork on display; evenings see storytelling sessions around the fire circle on the Arusha Rock terrace. All the romantic rooms (with drapes descending from the ceiling to lend a tentlike feel) have a bit of African art, including carved headboards, pen-and-ink drawings, or original prints. Most rooms also have balconies overlooking the wildlife reserve. Pros: extraordinary wildlife and cultural experiences; Jiko and Boma restaurants serve authentic African cuisine. Cons: shuttle to parks other than Animal Kingdom can take more than an hour; guided savannah tours available only to guests on the concierge level. ☎407/934–7639 ⇱*1,293 rooms* ♿*In-room: safe, Ethernet. In-hotel: 3 restaurants, bar, pools, gym, spa, children's*

programs (ages 4–12), laundry facilities, laundry service, public Wi-Fi, no-smoking rooms ▭AE, D, DC, MC, V.

ALL-STAR SPORTS, ALL-STAR MUSIC & ALL-STAR MOVIES RESORTS

☾ $ ⊡   Stay here if you want the quintessential Disney-with-your-kids

FodorśChoice experience, or if you're a couple that feels all that pitter-pattering of

★   little feet is a reasonable tradeoff for a good deal on a room. (Hint: for a little peace, request a room away from pools and other common areas.) In the Sports resort, Goofy is the pitcher in the baseball-diamond pool; in the Music resort you'll walk by giant bongos; and in the Movies resort, huge characters like *Toy Story*'s Buzz Lightyear frame each building. Each room has two double beds, a closet rod, an armoire, and a desk. The food courts sell standard fare, and you can have pizza delivered to your room. Pro: unbeatable price for a Disney property. Cons: no kids' clubs or programs; distances between rooms and on-site amenities can seem vast. ☎*407/939–5000 Sports, 407/939–6000 Music, 407/939–7000 Movies* ⌂*1,920 rooms at each* ⌂*In-room: safe, Ethernet. In-hotel: room service, bars, pools, laundry facilities, laundry service, public Internet, public Wi-Fi, no-smoking rooms* ▭AE, D, DC, MC, V.

POP CENTURY RESORT

$ ⊡   Giant jukeboxes and yo-yos, an oversized Big Wheel and Rubik's Cube, and other pop-culture memorabilia are scattered about the grounds. Items from mood rings to eight-track tapes are incorporated into the architecture; wall-mounted shadow boxes display toys, fashions, and fads from

> **WORD OF MOUTH**
>
> "Pop Century is a wonderful exciting place for families. They have three heated pools, bedtime stories on the phone from Disney characters, a wake-up call from Mickey, etc."–Geckolips

each decade since the 1950s. Brightly colored rooms are functional for families, with two double beds or one king. A big food court and a cafeteria serve reasonably priced fare. Pros: great room rates; the trip down memory lane; proximity to Wide World of Sports and Disney-MGM. Cons: big crowds at the front desk; big crowds (and noise) in the food court; small rooms (260 square feet). ☎*407/934–7639* ⌂*2,880 rooms* ⌂*In-room: safe, Ethernet. In-hotel: room service, bar, pools, gym, laundry service, public Wi-Fi, no-smoking rooms* ▭AE, D, DC, MC, V.

DOWNTOWN DISNEY RESORT AREA

Take I–4 Exit 64B or 68. The Downtown Disney–Lake Buena Vista resort area, east of Epcot, has two midprice resorts with an Old South theme, plus the upscale Old Key West Resort. From here shuttles are available to all of the parks.

2

OLD KEY WEST RESORT

$$$–$$$$ ☷ A red-and-white lighthouse helps you find your way through this marina-style resort. Freestanding villas resemble turn-of-the-20th-century Key West houses, with white clapboard siding and private balconies that overlook the waterways winding through the grounds. The one-, two-, or three-bedroom houses have whirlpools in the master bedrooms, full-size kitchens, (which could save you a fortune on food if you shop at an off-site grocery store), washers and dryers, and patios. The 2,265-square-foot three-bedroom grand villas accommodate up to 12 adults—so bring some friends. The resort is part of the Disney Vacation Club network, but rooms are rented to anyone when they're available. Pros: quiet and romantic; abundance of accommodations with whirlpool baths. Con: distances between rooms and restaurants, recreation facilities, bus stops, etc. ☎407/827–7700 ⟱*761 units* ♿*In-room: safe, Ethernet, Wi-Fi. In-hotel: restaurant, tennis courts, pools, gym, spa, bicycles, laundry facilities, laundry service, no-smoking rooms* ▭*AE, D, DC, MC, V.*

SARATOGA SPRINGS RESORT

$$$–$$$$ ☷ This large Disney Vacation Club has hundreds of units on 16 acres. Three- and four-story buildings, decorated inside and out to look like the 19th-century resorts of upstate New York, overlook a giant pool with artificial hot springs and faux boulders. Standard rooms, with 355 square feet, have microwaves and refrigerators; suites have full kitchens. Three-bedroom family suites—as big as most homes, with 2,113 square feet—occupy two levels and have dining rooms, living rooms, and four bathrooms. Rich woods, early American–style furniture, and overstuffed couches lend a homey, country-chic look. You can walk to Downtown Disney in 10 minutes or take the ferry, which docks near Fulton's Crab House. Pros: in-room massage; abundance of rooms with whirlpool baths. Con: it's a fair hike from some accommodations to the restaurant and other facilities. ☎407/934–7639 ⟱*828 units* ♿*In-room: safe, Ethernet. In-hotel: restaurant, tennis courts, pools, gym, spa, bicycles, public Wi-Fi, no-smoking rooms* ▭*AE, D, DC, MC, V.*

PORT ORLEANS RESORT–FRENCH QUARTER

$$–$$$ ☷ Ornate Big Easy–style row houses with vine-covered balconies cluster around squares planted with magnolias. Lamp-lighted sidewalks are named for French Quarter thoroughfares. Because this place is relatively quiet, it appeals more to couples than families with kids. The food court serves Crescent City specialties such as jambalaya and beignets. Scat Cat's Lounge is a serene little bar. Doubloon Lagoon, one of Disney's most exotic pools, includes a clever "sea serpent" slide that swallows and then spits you into the water. Pros: authentic, fun New Orleans atmosphere; lots of water recreation options, including boat rentals. Cons: standard rooms overlook a parking lot (water view rooms cost more); shuttle service is slow; food court is the only on-site

> **WORD OF MOUTH**
>
> "The Port Orleans French Quarter is my favorite WDW hotel, mainly for the beignets and the riverboat to Downtown Disney."–Silivia

dining option. ☎407/934–5000 ⬦1,008 rooms ♿In-room: safe, Ethernet. In-hotel: pool, bicycles, laundry facilities, laundry service, public Wi-Fi, no-smoking rooms ▤AE, D, DC, MC, V.

PORT ORLEANS RESORT–RIVERSIDE

$$–$$$ 🏨 Buildings look like plantation-style mansions and rustic bayou dwellings. Rooms accommodate up to four in two double beds and have wooden armoires, quilted bedspreads, and gleaming brass faucets; a few rooms have king-size beds. The registration area looks like a steamboat interior, and the 3½-acre, old-fashioned swimming-hole complex called Ol' Man Island has a pool with slides, rope swings, and a nearby play area. Recreation options here include fishing trips on the Sassagoula River, paddleboat and canoe rentals, and evening carriage rides. Pros: carriage rides; river cruises; lots of recreation options for kids. Con: shuttle can be slow. ☎407/934–6000 ⬦2,048 rooms ♿In-room: safe, Ethernet. In-hotel: restaurant, pools, gym, bicycles, laundry facilities, laundry service, no-smoking rooms ▤AE, D, DC, MC, V.

OTHER ON-SITE HOTELS

Although not operated by the Disney organization, the Swan and the Dolphin just outside Epcot, Shades of Green near the Magic Kingdom, and the hotels along Hotel Plaza Boulevard near Downtown Disney call themselves "official" Walt Disney World hotels. While the Swan, Dolphin, and Shades of Green have the special privileges of on-site Disney hotels, such as free transportation to and from the parks and early park entry, the Downtown Disney resorts have their own systems to shuttle hotel guests to the parks.

MAGIC KINGDOM RESORT AREA

SHADES OF GREEN

¢–$ 🏨 Operated by the U.S. Armed Forces Recreation Center, the resort is open only to active-duty and retired personnel from the armed forces, as well as reserves, National Guard, active civilian employees of the Department of Defense, widows or widowers of service members, disabled veterans, and Medal of Honor recipients. Rates vary with your rank, but are significantly lower than at Disney hotels open to the public. You'll find a Tuscan-style restaurant, a ballroom for weddings and other events, 11 family suites that sleep up to eight adults each, and two swimming pools surrounded by expansive decks and lush, tropical foliage. Pros: large standard rooms (480 square feet); on Disney's shuttle line; Army–Air Force Exchange store discounts deeply for people with military IDs. Cons: three-night minimum stay. ☎407/824–3600 or 888/593–2242 ⬥www.shadesofgreen.org ⬦586 rooms, 11 suites ♿In-room: safe, refrigerator, Ethernet. In-hotel: 4 restaurants, room service, bars, outdoor tennis courts, pools, gym, children's programs (ages 4–12), laundry facilities, laundry service, public Wi-Fi, no-smoking rooms ▤AE, D, MC, V.

EPCOT RESORT AREA

Take I–4 Exit 64B or 65.

WALT DISNEY WORLD DOLPHIN

$–$$$$ World-renowned architect Michael Graves designed the neighboring Dolphin and Swan hotels. Outside, a pair of 56-foot-tall sea creatures bookend this 25-story glass pyramid. The fabric-draped lobby resembles a giant sultan's tent. All rooms have either two queen beds or one king, and bright, beach-inspired spreads and drapes. The pillow-top mattresses, down comforters, and multitude of overstuffed pillows make the beds here some of the kingdom's most comfortable. Extensive children's programs include Camp Dolphin summer camp and the five-hour Dolphin Dinner Club. Pros: charge privileges and access to all facilities at the Swan; easy walk to BoardWalk; good on-site restaurants. Con: rooms only dip below $250 in off-season. ✉*1500 Epcot Resorts Blvd., Lake Buena Vista 32830-2653* ☎*407/934–4000 or 800/227–1500* ⊕*www.swandolphin.com* ⤵*1,509 rooms, 136 suites* ♿*In-room: safe, Ethernet. In-hotel: 9 restaurants, room service, tennis courts, pools, gym, spa, beachfront, children's programs (ages 4–12), executive floor, concierge, public Wi-Fi, no-smoking rooms* ▭*AE, D, DC, MC, V.*

WALT DISNEY WORLD SWAN

$–$$$$ Facing the Dolphin across Crescent Lake, the Swan is another example of the postmodern "Learning from Las Vegas" school of entertainment architecture characteristic of Michael Graves. Two 46-foot swans grace the rooftop of this coral-and-aquamarine hotel, and the massive main lobby is decorated with a playful mix of tropical imagery. Guest rooms are quirkily decorated with floral and geometric patterns, pineapples painted on furniture, and exotic bird-shape lamps. Every room has two queen beds or one king, two phone lines (one data port), and a coffeemaker; some have balconies. The Grotto, a 3-acre water playground complete with waterslides, waterfalls, and all the trimming, is nearby, as is Disney's BoardWalk and the Fantasia Gardens miniature golf complex. Pros: charge privileges and access to all facilities at the Dolphin; easy walk to BoardWalk; good on-site restaurants. Con: rooms only dip below $250 in off-season. ✉*1200 Epcot Resorts Blvd., Lake Buena Vista 32830* ☎*407/934–3000 or 800/248–7926* ⊕*www.swandolphin.com* ⤵*756 rooms, 55 suites* ♿*In-room: safe, Ethernet. In-hotel: 6 restaurants, room service, tennis courts, pools, gym, spa, beachfront, children's programs (ages 4–12), executive floor, concierge, public Wi-Fi, no-smoking rooms* ▭*AE, D, DC, MC, V.*

DOWNTOWN DISNEY RESORT AREA

Take I–4 Exit 68. A number of non-Disney-owned resorts are clustered on Disney property not far from Downtown Disney, and several more sprawling, high-quality resorts are just outside the park's northernmost entrance. Several of these hotels market themselves as "official" Disney hotels, meaning that they have special agreements with Disney that allow them to offer their guests such perks as early park admission. The hotels on Hotel Plaza Boulevard are within walking distance of Downtown Disney Marketplace, though most offer shuttle service anyway.

HILTON IN THE WDW RESORT

$$-$$$$ An ingenious waterfall tumbles off the covered entrance and into a stone fountain surrounded by palm trees. Although not huge, rooms are upbeat, cozy, and contemporary, and many on the upper floors have great views of Downtown Disney, which is just a short walk away. The hotel offers two good eateries: Andiamo Italian Bistro, specializing in pasta and grilled seafood, and a Benihana Steakhouse and Sushi Bar. Guests can enter Disney parks an hour before they officially open. Pros: close to Downtown Disney; free shuttle bus; kids program. Con: pricier than similar lodgings father from Disney; inconvenient to Universal and downtown Orlando. ✉1751 Hotel Plaza Blvd., Lake Buena Vista 32830 ☎407/827–4000, 800/782–4414 reservations ⊕www.hilton. com ⤶814 rooms, 27 suites ⑃In-room: safe, Ethernet. In-hotel: 7 restaurants, room service, pools, gym, children's programs (ages 3– 12), laundry facilities, laundry service, public Wi-Fi, no-smoking rooms ▭AE, DC, MC.

BEST WESTERN LAKE BUENA VISTA

$–$$$$ An attractive mural of Florida wildlife and landscapes graces the lobby, though the view of a junglelike wetland out the windows of the atrium restaurant is more compelling. Most rooms have private, furnished balconies with spectacular views of the nightly Disney fireworks. Disney shuttles are available, but you can walk to Downtown Disney in 10 minutes or less. Pros: one of the best bargains on Hotel Row; close to Downtown Disney. Cons: not as plush as other Hotel Row properties; inconvenient to Universal and downtown Orlando. ✉2000 Hotel Plaza Blvd., Lake Buena Vista 32830 ☎407/828–2424 or 800/937–8376 ⊕www.orlandoresorthotel.com ⤶325 rooms ⑃In-room: Ethernet. In-hotel: restaurant, room service, pool, laundry facilities, laundry service, no-smoking rooms ▭AE, D, DC, MC, V.

BUENA VISTA PALACE RESORT & SPA IN THE WDW RESORT

$–$$$$ This hotel gets kudos as much for its on-site charms as for its location—100 yards from the Wolfgang Puck's in Downtown Disney. All rooms have patios or balconies, most with great views of Downtown Disney. As a guest, you receive free transportation to all Disney parks, the chance to sign up for Disney character meals, and access to Disney golf courses. Pros: easy walk to Downtown Disney; huge spa. Con: inconvenient to Universal and downtown Orlando. ✉1900 Buena Vista Dr., Lake Buena Vista 32830 ☎407/827–2727 ⊕www.luxuryresorts.com ⤶1,014 rooms, 209 suites ⑃In-room: safe, Ethernet. In-hotel: 4 restaurants, room service, tennis courts, pools, gym, spa, children's programs (ages 4–12), laundry facilities, laundry service, concierge, public Wi-Fi, no-smoking rooms ▭AE, D, DC, MC, V.

DOUBLETREE GUEST SUITES IN THE WDW RESORT

$–$$$$ ⌘ The lavender-and-pink exterior looks strange, but the interior is another story. Comfortable one- and two-bedroom suites are decorated in tasteful hues, with blue carpeting and orange drapes and bedspreads. Each bedroom has either a king bed or two doubles. Units come with three TVs, including one in the bathroom, and a wet bar, microwave, refrigerator, and coffeemaker. The small lobby has a charming feature—a small aviary with birds from South America and Africa. There's a special "registration desk" for kids, where they can get coloring books and balloons. Pros: within walking distance of Downtown Disney; free shuttle to all Disney attractions. Con: inconvenient to Universal and downtown Orlando. ⊠*2305 Hotel Plaza Blvd., Lake Buena Vista 32830* ☎*407/934–1000 or 800/222–8733* ⊕*www.doubletreeguestsuites.com* ⇨*229 units* ⅊*In-room: safe, refrigerator, Ethernet. In-hotel: restaurant, room service, bars, tennis courts, pool, gym, laundry facilities, laundry service, public Wi-Fi, no-smoking rooms* ▤*AE, DC, MC, V.*

ROYAL PLAZA

$–$$$ ⌘ Spruced-up guest rooms have plasma-screen TVs, pillow-top mattresses, and granite bathroom counters. Some ground-level rooms have semiprivate patios that overlook the swimming pool. The restaurant, the Giraffe Café, is informal but pleasant and specializes in gourmet pizzas with toppings like Boursin cheese and lump crabmeat. You can rent microwaves and refrigerators for your room. Pros: within walking distance of Downtown Disney; free shuttle to all Disney attractions. Con: inconvenient to Universal and downtown Orlando. ⊠*1905 Hotel Plaza Blvd., Lake Buena Vista 32830* ☎*407/828–2828* ⊕*www.royalplaza.com* ⇨*394 rooms, 5 suites* ⅊*In-room: safe, refrigerator, VCR, Ethernet. In-hotel: 2 restaurants, room service, tennis courts, pools, laundry service, public Wi-Fi, no-smoking rooms* ▤*AE, DC, MC, V.*

GROSVENOR RESORT

$–$$ ⌘ This tan high-rise (the name is pronounced *Grove*-ner, just like the one in London) across from Downtown Disney is nondescript on the outside but quite pleasant on the inside. Blond-wood furniture and rose carpeting make the rooms homey, and those in the tower have a great view of Downtown Disney. Public areas are decorated in an easygoing Caribbean style. One of the restaurants, Baskervilles, hosts a Disney character breakfast three days a week and a Saturday murder-mystery dinner show. Pros: within walking distance of Downtown Disney; free shuttle to all Disney attractions. Con: inconvenient to Universal and downtown Orlando. ⊠*1850 Hotel Plaza Blvd., Downtown Disney, Lake Buena Vista 32830* ☎*407/828–4444 or 800/624–4109* ⊕*www.grosvenorresort.com* ⇨*626 rooms, 5 suites* ⅊*In-room: safe, refrigerator, VCR, Ethernet. In-hotel: 3 restaurants, room service, tennis courts, pools, laundry service, no-smoking rooms* ▤*AE, DC, MC, V.*

Spas that Pamper with Panache

Once upon a time something crucial was missing in Central Florida's vacation kingdom. There were castles and thrill rides, performing whales and golf meccas, but there were no standout spas, no havens of respite for the millions who trekked their feet flat and rubbed their shoulders raw lugging backpacks from one attraction to the next.

Now weary travelers can rejoice. It's a spa-world after all in Central Florida. Several pampering palaces at first-rate resorts can add blessed balance to your visit. Some of the finest spas have seized upon Florida's reputation as a citrus production center and will baste and massage you with essences of lemon, lime, orange, and grapefruit. Others import exotic treatments from Bali, Japan, and Thailand. Each spa offers signature treatments in addition to the usual massages, facials, and pedicures. You can even find leg-relief treatments for exhausted park hoppers. All resort spas offer bottled water, teas, and fresh-fruit snacks, and with any treatment you'll have access to saunas, steam rooms, whirlpools, and fitness facilities.

The **Buena Vista Palace Hotel & Spa** has one of the area's most popular rejuvenation centers, with intimate, beautiful surroundings, reasonable prices, and light lunches in the courtyard. Here you might try the ultrarelaxing, skin-smoothing Golden Door Pineapple Body Scrub (50 minutes, $125), which exfoliates your skin then softens it with oils and moisturizers. It's like being transported to your own tropical island. To extend the feeling, add on the Tranquility Facial (50 minutes, $120), which also comes with a paraffin hand-and-foot treatment. Take your beautified body to Downtown Disney afterward for shopping, lunch or dinner—it's just across the street.

Further fruit-enhanced fantasies can be realized at the lavish spa in the **Ritz-Carlton Orlando Grande Lakes,** where the two-hour Tuscan Citrus Cure ($330) is one of several signature treatments. You retire to a special suite for a lemon-crush scrub and lime shower that preps you for a tailored aromatherapy massage. From there, you climb into the suite's tub for a soothing hydro-citrus soak—you can control the jets to suit your mood. Your therapist completes the treatment with a sweet-orange moisturizing body wrap, and before emerging from your cocoon you're treated to a neck or scalp massage. The Ritz has an excellent spa with 42 treatment rooms in a 40,000-square-foot facility. It also has the highest prices. But if you want to indulge in the royal lifestyle, this is the place to do it.

A stone's throw from the theme parks is the **Canyon Ranch Spa-Club at Gaylord Palms.** Here the Canyon Ranch Stone Massage (80 minutes, $190) paves the path to nirvana. Smooth volcanic stones of several sizes are heated to a temperature between 115°F and 124°F. After applying oil to the stones, your therapist works them along your body using either Swedish, deep tissue, shiatsu, or Reiki techniques. If you've already experienced a traditional massage, this is a wonderfully soothing alternative.

A Balinese paradise in landlocked Central Florida? It's right there at Universal Orlando's Portofino Bay Hotel, where the **Mandara Spa** delivers the signature Mandara Four Hand Massage (50 minutes, $230), in which two therapists massage you simultaneously, and the Balinese Massage (50 minutes, $120), involving acupressure and Swedish techniques. Depending on your skin's condition, you may also receive a mini milk bath, and a wrap with eucalyptus and lavender oils designed to relieve tension, all as part of the treatment.

Almost as soon as you enter Disney's **Grand Floridian Resort & Spa** you can feel the stress melt away. Established in 1997, the Grand's spa has kept up its flawless reputation with its signature treatments, such as the Citrus Zest Therapies (80 minutes, $185), in which a soothing dose of grapefruit body oil is used in an aromatherapy massage, followed by reflexology. Families can enjoy the experience together—there's a couples treatment room, and there's a menu of facials, manicures, and pedicures for kids. Arrive early for complimentary use of the fitness center and a soak in the hot tub.

Healing spring waters of turn-of-the-20th-century Saratoga, New York, inspired the theme for **The Spa at Disney's Saratoga Springs**—it's the perfect place to sink into the luxury of a hydro-massage or emerge with the glow from a maple-enhanced body treatment. The Mineral Springs Hydro-Massage (45 minutes, $115) uses herbs to detoxify and awaken your skin. The Maple Sugar Body Polish (50 minutes, $125) deep cleans and exfoliates to boost circulation and hydrate your skin. Heated stones do the work during the Adirondack Stone Therapy Massage (80 minutes, $185)—you'll

be utterly relaxed. Kids' treatments include first facials, manicures, and pedicures. You can order a flavorful, nourishing lunch from nearby Artist's Palette.

Even if golf isn't a passion, you'll want to swing by **The Spa at Omni Orlando Resort at ChampionsGate,** just south of Walt Disney World, for its tropical-inspired treatments. Pineapple- and coconut-infused wraps envelop the weary body and let you drift off to Fiji or some other palm-studded isle. Sip on cranberry–hibiscus or green-passion tea as you relax in a plush robe before your treatment. If the Florida sun has dried out your skin, order the Aspara Essential Oil Wrap (50 minutes, $99)—you'll be swaddled in a warm cocoon of the herbal remedies while you enjoy a head and foot massage. It's a great headache reliever. The spa's classic Swedish massage (name your touch for 50 minutes, $92) is a value-packed therapy and great theme-park recovery strategy.

Most spas can book treatments on short notice, but your best bet is to call ahead and reserve the indulgence you don't want to miss. Be sure to inquire about any gratuity—often 18%—that will be added to your spa package or treatments.

—Jennie Hess

OFF-SITE HOTELS NEAR WALT DISNEY WORLD

LAKE BUENA VISTA AREA

Many people stay in resorts a bit farther northeast of Downtown Disney because, though equally grand, they tend to be less expensive than those right on Hotel Plaza Boulevard. If you're willing to take a five-minute drive or shuttle ride, you might save as much as 35% off your room tab.

Perennially popular with families are the all-suites properties, many with in-room kitchens, just east of Lake Buena Vista Drive. Furthermore, the 1,100-room Marriott Village at Lake Buena Vista, across I–4 from Downtown Disney, has made a splash in hotel-laden Orlando with its utter comprehensiveness. The gated, secure village has three hotels, a multirestaurant complex, a video-rental store, a 24-hour convenience store, and a Hertz rental-car station. There's also an on-property Disney booking station, staffed by a Disney employee who can answer questions and make suggestions.

HYATT REGENCY GRAND CYPRESS RESORT

$$$$

Fodor'sChoice

★

On 1,500 acres just outside Disney's north entrance, this spectacular resort has a private lake, three golf courses, and miles of trails for bicycling, jogging, and horseback riding. The 800,000-gallon pool has a 45-foot slide and is fed by 12 waterfalls. Tropical birds and plants and Chinese sculptures fill the 18-story atrium. All rooms have tasteful rattan furniture and a private balcony overlooking either the Lake Buena Vista Area or the pool. Villas have fireplaces and whirlpool baths. Accommodations are divided between the hotel and the **Villas of Grand Cypress** (⊠ *1 N. Jacaranda Dr., Lake Buena Vista 32836* ☎*407/239–1234 or 800/835–7377*), with 200 villas. Pros: great Sunday brunch at La Coquina; huge pool; lots of recreation options, including nearby equestrian center. Cons: pricey; inconvenient to Universal Orlando and downtown Orlando. ⊠ *1 Grand Cypress Blvd., Lake Buena Vista Area, Orlando 32836* ☎*407/239–1234 or 800/233–1234* ⊕*www.hyattgrandcypress.com* ⌨*750 rooms* ⌂*In-room: safe, Ethernet. In-hotel: 5 restaurants, room service, 18-hole golf courses, 9-hole golf course, tennis courts, pools, gym, spa, bicycles, children's programs (ages 5–12), laundry service, public Wi-Fi, no-smoking rooms* ▭*AE, D, DC, MC, V.*

ORLANDO WORLD CENTER MARRIOTT

$$$–$$$$

At 2,000 rooms, this is one of Orlando's largest hotels, and it's very popular with conventions. All rooms have patios or balconies, and the lineup of amenities and facilities seems endless—there's even on-site photo processing. You can rent the upscale Royal Palms, Imperial Palms, and Sabal Palms villas by the day or by the week. Golf at the 6,800-yard championship Hawk's Landing golf course becomes a bargain for guests—a golf package including one round costs about $20 more than the standard rate for a deluxe room, depending on the season. Pros: great steakhouses; golf course; lots of amenities. Con: not much to see or do within walking distance. ⊠*8701 World Center*

Dr., I–4 Exit 65, Orlando 32821 ☎*407/239–4200 or 800/228–9290* ⊕*www.marriottworldcenter.com* ⇄*2,000 rooms, 98 suites, 259 villas* ⌂*In-room: Ethernet. In-hotel: 7 restaurants, room service, 18-hole golf course, pool, gym, children's programs (ages 4–12), laundry facilities, laundry service, public Wi-Fi, no-smoking rooms* ⊟*AE, D, DC, MC, V.*

NICKELODEON FAMILY SUITES BY HOLIDAY INN

☾ **$$–$$$$**

Fodor'sChoice

★

The Nickelodeon theme extends everywhere, from the suites, where separate kids' rooms have bunk beds and SpongeBob wall murals, to the two giant pools built up like water parks. Kids will look forward to wake-up calls from Nickelodeon stars, character breakfasts, and live entertainment. You can choose between one-, two- and three-bedroom suites, with or without full kitchens. Pros: extremely kid-friendly; free Disney shuttle; golf course. Cons: not within walking distance of Disney or Downtown Disney; may be too frenetic for folks without kids. ✉*14500 Continental Gateway, I–4 Exit 67, Orlando 32821* ☎*407/387–5437 or 866/462–6425* ⊕*www.nickhotels.com* ⇄*800 suites* ⌂*In-room: safe, kitchen (some), refrigerator, Ethernet. In-hotel: 3 restaurants, room service, pools, 9-hole golf course, gym, children's programs (ages 4–12), laundry facilities, laundry service, public Wi-Fi, no-smoking rooms* ⊟*AE, D, DC, MC, V.*

CARIBE ROYALE ALL-SUITES RESORT & CONVENTION CENTER

$$–$$$

This big pink palace of a hotel, with flowing palm trees and massive artificial waterfalls, wouldn't look out of place in Vegas. Huge ballrooms attract corporate conferences, but there are key family-friendly ingredients, too: free transportation to Disney (10 minutes away) and a huge children's recreation area, including a big pool with a 65-foot slide. Suites are 450 to 500 square feet and have spacious living rooms with pull-out sofa beds, kitchenettes, and one or more bedrooms. Pros: family friendly; great pool area; good on-site restaurants; free shuttle to Disney. Con: too far to walk to shops and restaurants. ✉*8101 World Center Dr., Orlando 32821* ☎*407/238–8000 or 800/823–8300* ⊕*www.cariberoyale.com* ⇄*1,218 suites, 120 villas* ⌂*In-room: kitchen (some), refrigerator, Ethernet. In-hotel: 4 restaurants, room service, tennis courts, pool, concierge, laundry facilities, laundry service, no-smoking rooms* ⊟*AE, D, DC, MC, V* ⊙*BP.*

CELEBRITY RESORTS AT LAKE BUENA VISTA

$$–$$$

The large, comfortable, one- to three-bedroom suites here can sleep 4 to 10 people. Add full kitchens, dining and living areas, and washer-dryer sets, and you have excellent accommodations for families who want more space and amenities for their money. The Spanish-style architecture gives way to tastefully furnished interiors, although doors between rooms in the same suite are a little thin. Master bedrooms have floor-to-ceiling mirrors on two walls, and whirlpool tubs in the bathrooms. A small playground and a large, attractive outdoor pool are surrounded by pretty landscaping, and Downtown Disney is just a mile away. Pros: upscale atmosphere; convenient to Disney; in-suite hot tubs. Cons: no theme-parks shuttles; need a car to reach most things of interest. ✉ *8451 Palm Pkwy., Lake Buena Vista 32836* ☎ *407/238–1700 or 800/423–8604* ⊕ *www.celebrityresorts.com* 🛏 *66 suites* ♿ *In-room: safe, kitchen (some), Ethernet. In-hotel: restaurant, tennis court, pools, gym, children's programs (ages 4–12), laundry facilities, laundry service, no-smoking rooms* ☰ *AE, D, MC, V.*

SHERATON VISTANA RESORT

$$–$$$ 🏨 Consider this peaceful resort, just across I–4 from Downtown Disney, if you're traveling with a large family or group of friends. The spacious, tasteful, one- and two-bedroom villas and town houses have living rooms, full kitchens, and washers and dryers. Tennis players take note: the clay and all-weather courts are free to guests; private or semi-private lessons are available for a fee. With seven outdoor heated pools, five kiddie pools, and eight outdoor hot tubs, you can spend the whole day just soaking up the sun. Pros: kitchens let you save money on food; lots of on-site recreation options: Cons: not within walking distance of Downtown Disney (across I-4); shuttles to Disney ($9 round-trip) and Universal and I-Drive ($11 round-trip) are slow. ✉ *8800 Vistana Center Dr., Orlando 32821* ☎ *407/239–3100 or 800/325–3535* ⊕ *www.starwoodvo.com* 🛏 *1,700 units* ♿ *In-room: safe, kitchen, refrigerator, Ethernet. In-hotel: 2 restaurants, tennis courts, pools, gym, concierge, children's programs (ages 4–12), public Wi-Fi, no-smoking rooms* ☰ *AE, D, DC, MC, V.*

SHERATON SAFARI HOTEL

$–$$$ 🏨 From the pool's jungle motif to the bamboo enclosures around the lobby pay phones, this little piece of Nairobi in the hotel district adjacent to Downtown Disney is a trip. Although there are some leopard skin–print furniture coverings and wild-animal portraits on the walls, the guests are relatively sedate. Suites have kitchenettes with microwaves; six deluxe suites have full kitchens. Watch your kids play on the giant waterslide in the pool area while you sip drinks at the poolside Zanzibar. Pros: kid-attractive pool area; short walk to shops and restaurants; free Disney shuttle. Con: pool area can get loud. ✉ *12205 Apopka Vineland Rd., Orlando 32836* ☎ *407/239–0444 or 800/423–3297* ⊕ *www.sheratonsafari.com* 🛏 *489 rooms, 96 suites* ♿ *In-room: safe, kitchen (some), refrigerator (some), Ethernet. In-hotel: 2 restaurants, room service, pool, gym, public Wi-Fi, no-smoking rooms* ☰ *AE, D, DC, MC, V.*

EMBASSY SUITES HOTEL LAKE BUENA VISTA

$$ 🏨 The peach facade of this hotel, clearly visible from I–4, makes it something of a local landmark. But even if you find the color scheme too much, it's attractive for other reasons. It's 1 mi from Downtown Disney, 3 mi from SeaWorld, and 7 mi from Universal Orlando. Each suite has a separate living room and two TVs. The atrium lobby, loaded with vegetation and soothed by the sounds of a rushing fountain, is a great place to enjoy the free cooked-to-order breakfast and evening cocktails. Pros: convenient to Downtown Disney; free shuttle to all Disney parks; within walking distance of restaurants and shops. Cons: public areas are noisy. ✉ *8100 Lake Ave., Orlando 32836* ☎ *407/239–1144, 800/257–8483, or 800/362–2779* ⊕ *www.embassysuites.com*

333 suites ♿ *In-room: safe, refrigerator, Ethernet. In-hotel: 2 restaurants, room service, tennis court, pool, gym, children's programs (ages 4–12), no-smoking rooms* ☰*AE, D, DC, MC, V* ⦶*BP.*

HAWTHORN SUITES RESORT LAKE BUENA VISTA

$–$$ 🛏 Every suite has a bedroom and a full kitchen, including a dishwasher, a two-burner stovetop, a microwave, and a refrigerator. Downtown Disney is just 1 mi away. Pros: price; full kitchens; easy walk to shops. Con: pool area gets noisy. ✉*8303 Palm Pkwy., Orlando 32836* ☎*407/597–5000 or 866/756–3778* ⊕*www.hawthornlakebuenavista. com* *120 suites* ♿ *In-room: safe, kitchen, refrigerator, Ethernet. Inhotel: bar, pool, laundry facilities, public Wi-Fi, no-smoking rooms* ☰*AE, D, DC, MC, V* ⦶*CP.*

MARRIOTT RESIDENCE INN

$–$$ 🛏 Billing itself as a Caribbean-style oasis, with lush palms and a waterfall near the swimming pool, this all-suites hotel's most compelling features are more pragmatic: every room has a full kitchen with a stove and dishwasher, and there's an on-site convenience store. (A supermarket is a few blocks down Palm Parkway.) Suites include a separate living room–kitchen and bedrooms. Two-bedroom suites have two baths. The recreation area has both a kids' pool and a putting green. Pros: sequestered, resortlike atmosphere; convenient to Disney and I-Drive; free Disney shuttle. Cons: not within walking distance of much. ✉*11450 Marbella Palm Ct., Orlando 32836* ☎*407/465–0075* ⊕*www.marriott.com* *210 suites* ♿ *In-room: safe, kitchen, refrigerator, Ethernet. In-hotel: pool, gym, laundry facilities, laundry service, no-smoking rooms* ☰*AE, D, DC, MC, V.*

PERRIHOUSE BED & BREAKFAST INN

★ **$–$$** 🛏 An eight-room bed-and-breakfast inside a serene bird sanctuary is a unique lodging experience in fast-lane Orlando. The PerriHouse offers you a chance to split your time between sightseeing and spending quiet moments bird-watching: the 16-acre sanctuary has observation paths, a pond, a feeding station, and a small birdhouse museum. It's attractive to bobwhites, downy woodpeckers, red-tail hawks, and the occasional bald eagle. The inn is a romantic getaway, with four-poster and canopy beds and some fireplaces. The staff can book some interesting adventures—anything from bass fishing trips to sessions at an Orlando skydiving simulator. You're free to use the kitchen. Pros: intimate and private; great bird-watching. Cons: not an easy walk to much of interest; need a rental car. ✉*10417 Vista Oak Ct., Lake Buena Vista 32836* ☎*407/876–4830 or 800/780–4830* ⊕*www.perrihouse. com* *8 rooms* ♿ *In-room: safe, Ethernet. In-hotel: pool* ☰*AE, D, DC, MC, V* ⦶*CP.*

MARRIOTT VILLAGE AT LITTLE LAKE BRYAN

¢–$$ 🛏 The private, gated Marriott Village has three hotels. The **Courtyard** welcomes both families and business travelers with 3,000 square feet of meeting space and large standard rooms decorated with yellow and green floral patterns and blond-wood furniture. Each room has a coffeemaker and Web TV, and the indoor-outdoor pool has a swim-up bar. At **SpringHill Suites,** accommodations have kitchenettes, separate sleeping and dining areas, and Sony Playstations. The **Fairfield Inn** is the least expensive of the three, but rooms are as bright and pleasant, if not quite as amenity laden. It also has family suites with bunk beds and a Hawaiian theme that kids will love. Continental breakfast is included in the rates, and there are several chain restaurants in the complex. Best of all, there's an on-site Disney planning center where you can buy park tickets. Pros: lots of informal dining options; lower room rates than hotels on the other side of I–4. Cons: Disney shuttle costs $5 per person round trip (hotels across I–4 have free shuttles). ⊠ *8623 Vineland Ave., Orlando 32821* ☎ *407/938–9001 or 877/682–8552* ⊕ *www.marriottvillage.com* ↝ *650 rooms, 450 suites* ⟨ *In-room: safe, refrigerator, Ethernet. In-hotel: 8 restaurants, room service, bars, pools, gym, children's programs (ages 4–12), laundry facilities, laundry service, public Wi-Fi, no-smoking rooms* ⊟ *AE, D, DC, MC, V* ⫶ *CP.*

BUENA VISTA SUITES

$ ⊞ In this all-suites property you get a bedroom, a living room with a foldout sofa bed, two TVs, two phones, and a small kitchen with a coffeemaker, sink, microwave, and refrigerator. King suites have a single king bed and a whirlpool bath. Pros: free breakfast buffet; free Disney shuttle. Con: not much of interest within walking distance. ⊠ *8203 World Center Dr., Lake Buena Vista Area 32821* ☎ *407/239–8588 or 800/537–7737* ⊕ *www.buenavistasuites.com* ↝ *280 suites* ⟨ *In-room: safe, refrigerator, Ethernet. In-hotel: restaurant, room service, tennis courts, pool, gym, laundry facilities, public Wi-Fi, no-smoking rooms* ⊟ *AE, D, DC, MC, V* ⫶ *BP.*

HOLIDAY INN SUNSPREE LAKE BUENA VISTA

$ ⊞ This family-oriented hotel has a children's registration desk. Off the lobby you'll find the CyberArcade; a small theater where clowns perform weekends at 7 PM; and a buffet restaurant where kids accompanied by adults eat free at their own little picnic tables. Families love the Kidsuites: playhouse-style rooms within a larger room. Pros: extremely kid-friendly; great deal for families. Cons: too noisy at times for adults; street is a tad busy for pedestrians, especially at night. ⊠ *13351 Rte. 535, Orlando 32821* ☎ *407/239–4500 or 800/366–6299* ⊕ *www.kidsuites.com* ↝ *507 rooms* ⟨ *In-room: safe, refrigerator, Ethernet. In-hotel: restaurant, bar, pool, gym, children's programs (ages 4–12), laundry facilities, laundry service, public Wi-Fi, no-smoking rooms* ⊟ *AE, D, DC, MC, V.*

PALOMINO SUITES LAKE BUENA VISTA

$ ⊞ Both the prices and location make this a great home base for a family vacation. The suites are pleasant, if not enormous. Each sleep up to six if you fold out the living room's sofa bed, and kitchens are well equipped. In addition to a free breakfast buffet each day, snacks are laid out for a "social hour" Monday through Thursday 5 to 7 PM. Pros: you can save big bucks on food; Downtown Disney Market Place, with a reasonably priced Publix supermarket, is ½ mile from hotel. Con: with the maximum capacity of six people, suites would be cramped. ⊠ *8200 Palm Pkwy., Orlando 32836* ☎ *407/465–8200 or*

800/370–9894 ⊕*www.palominosuites.com* ⇝*123 suites* ᗕ*In-room: safe, kitchen, refrigerator, Ethernet. In-hotel: pool, gym, public Wi-Fi, no-smoking rooms* ▤*AE, D, DC, MC, V* ⦿l*CP.*

COUNTRY INN & SUITES BY CARLSON

¢–$ ▦ The signature lobby fireplace looks a little ridiculous in Orlando, but the in-room amenities and proximity to Downtown Disney (½ mi away) make this hotel a good bet for either families or couples. For $120 you can book what the hotel calls a one-bedroom Country Kids Suite, with two beds, two TVs (one of which is hooked up for video games), a refrigerator, and a microwave. Pros: within walking distance of Downtown Disney; refrigerators in every room. Cons: no on-site restaurant; no room service. ⊠*12191 S. Apopka Vineland Rd., Orlando 32836* ☎*407/239–1115 or 800/456–4000* ⊕*www.countryinns.com* ⇝*170 rooms, 50 suites* ᗕ*In-room: safe, refrigerator, Ethernet. In-hotel: pool, gym, laundry facilities, public Wi-Fi, no-smoking rooms* ▤*AE, D, DC, MC, V* ⦿l*CP.*

KISSIMMEE

Take I–4 Exit 64A, unless otherwise noted. If you're looking for anything remotely quaint, charming, or sophisticated, move on. With a few exceptions (namely, the flashy Gaylord Palms Resort), the U.S. 192 strip—aka the Irlo Bronson Memorial Highway—is a neon-and-plastic strip crammed with bargain-basement motels, fast-food spots, nickel-and-dime attractions, overpriced gas stations, and minimarts where a small bottle of aspirin costs $8. In past years, when Disney was in its infancy, this was the best place to find affordable rooms. But now that budget hotels have cropped up all along I-Drive, you can often find better rooms closer to the theme parks by passing the Kissimmee motel strip and heading a few exits north.

There are exceptions, however—a few big-name companies like Marriott have excellent lodging on or near U.S. 192, and some of the older hotels have maintained decent standards and kept their prices very interesting. You can find clean, simple rooms in Kissimmee for $40 to $80 a night, depending on facilities and proximity to Walt Disney World.

One Kissimmee caveat: beware of the word "maingate" in many hotel names. It's a good 6 mi from Kissimmee's "maingate" hotel area to the Walt Disney World entrance. The "maingate west" area, however, is about 2 mi from the park. Of course, the greater the distance from Walt Disney World, the lower the room rates. A few additional minutes' drive may save you a significant amount of money, so shop around. And if you wait until arrival to find a place, don't be bashful about asking to see the rooms. It's a buyer's market.

GAYLORD PALMS RESORT

★ $$$$ ⊞ Built in the style of a grand turn-of-the-20th-century Florida mansion, this resort is meant to awe. Inside its enormous atrium, covered by a 4-acre glass roof, are re-creations of such Florida icons as the Everglades, Key West, and old St. Augustine. Restaurants include Sunset Sam's Fish Camp, on a 60-foot fishing boat docked on the hotel's indoor ocean, and the Old Hickory Steak House in an old warehouse overlooking the alligator-ridden Everglades. Rooms carry on the Florida themes with colorful, tropical decorations. With extensive children's programs, two pool areas, and a huge Canyon Ranch spa, the hotel connives to make you never want to leave. The newest room amenity is Gaylord iConnect, complete with a 15-inch flat-screen monitor, that connects you to the Internet plus a hotel network for booking dinner and activity reservations. Pros: you could have a great vacation without ever leaving the grounds; free shuttle to Disney. Cons: rooms and meals are pricey; not much within walking distance. ⊠6000 Osceola Pkwy., I–4 Exit 65, Kissimmee 34746 ☏407/586–0000 ⊕www.gaylordpalms.com ⚓1,406 rooms, 86 suites ⚐In-room: safe, Ethernet. In-hotel: 5 restaurants, bars, pools, gym, spa, children's programs (ages 4–12), laundry service, public Wi-Fi, no-smoking rooms ▭AE, D, DC, MC, V.

OMNI ORLANDO RESORT AT CHAMPIONSGATE

$$$–$$$$ ⊞ Omni took over a 1,200-acre golf club with two Greg Norman–designed courses and a David Ledbetter academy to create this huge Mediterranean-style hotel complex. With a 70,000-square-foot conference center, the resort definitely attracts the corporate crowd. But there's family appeal, too, thanks to an 850-foot-long, lazy-river-style pool and excellent children's programs. And the hotel is a 10-minute drive from Disney. Rooms are attractive if not distinctive, with earth-color walls, gold carpets and drapes, and marble bathroom vanities. There are also one-, two-, and three-bedroom villas. Pros: big European-style spa; huge, water-park-style pool; golf school and two golf courses. Cons: rooms and food are pricey; need a rental car. ⊠1500 Masters Blvd., I–4 Exit 58, Championsgate 33896 ⊹south of Kissimmee ☏407/390–6664 or 800/843–6664 ⊕www.omnihotels.com ⚓730 rooms, 32 suites, 57 villas ⚐In-room: Ethernet. In-hotel: 5 restaurants, room service, bars, 18-hole golf courses, tennis courts, pools, gym, spa, children's programs (ages 0–12), laundry facilities, laundry service, public Wi-Fi, no-smoking rooms ▭AE, D, DC, MC, V.

REUNION RESORT & CLUB OF ORLANDO

★ $$$–$$$$ ⊞ It's on 28,000 tranquil acres of a former orange grove, far from the bustle of I–4, and yet it's only 12 minutes from Disney. A stay here includes access to three private world-caliber golf courses designed by Tom Watson, Arnold Palmer, and Jack Nicklaus. The resort was developed as a residential and vacation-home complex, but its condo-style villas are available on a per-night basis. Activities include walking and horseback riding on meandering trails. Kids love the swim pavilion with a winding lagoon, wave pool, slide, and beach volleyball area. Pros: secluded atmosphere; proximity to Disney and ChampionsGate area.

Cons: no Disney shuttle; you need a rental car. ✉ *1000 Reunion Way, Reunion 34747* ☎ *407/396–3200 888/418-9611* ⊕ *www.reunionresort.com* ◆ *60 units* ⌂ *In-room: safe, Ethernet. In-hotel: restaurant, room service, bar, 18-hole golf courses, pools, gym, spa, bicycles, children's programs (ages 4–12), laundry facilities, laundry service, no-smoking rooms* ▤ *AE, D, DC, MC, V.*

CELEBRATION HOTEL

$$–$$$$ 🏨 Like everything in the Disney-created town of Celebration, this 115-room hotel borrows from the best of the 19th and 21st centuries. The lobby resembles those of Victorian grand dames, with hardwood floors and decorative millwork throughout. Rooms may look as if they date from the early 1900s, but each has a 25-inch TV, two phone lines, high-speed Internet access, and a six-channel stereo system. Even though it's less than 1 mi south of the U.S. 192 tourist strip in Kissimmee, the hotel's surroundings are serene. The entire hotel is no-smoking. Pros: a mere block from good restaurants; rental bikes and golf carts make touring a breeze. Cons: need a rental car (or lots of cab money) to get around off site. ✉ *700 Bloom St., Celebration 34747* ☎ *407/566–6000 or 888/499–3800* ⊕ *www.celebrationhotel.com* ◆ *115 rooms* ⌂ *In-room: Ethernet. In-hotel: 2 restaurants, pool, gym, laundry service, public Wi-Fi, no-smoking rooms* ▤ *AE, D, DC, MC, V.*

SARATOGA RESORT VILLAS AT ORLANDO MAINGATE

$–$$$$ 🏨 The red-tile-and-stucco villas have between one and three bedrooms, living and dining areas, and well-equipped kitchens. With 1,200 square feet, three-bedroom units sleep up to eight comfortably. Pros: rates are hard to beat: a family of four can get a two-bedroom villa for $99 a night in high-season; free shuttle to Disney. Cons: on unattractive tourist strip; can't really walk around off the grounds. ✉ *4787 W. Irlo Bronson Hwy., Kissimmee 34746* ☎ *407/397–0555 or 800/222–8733* ⊕ *www.saratogaresortvillas.com* ◆ *150 villas* ⌂ *In-room: safe, Ethernet. In-hotel: restaurant, room service, tennis court, pool, gym, laundry facilities, no-smoking rooms* ▤ *AE, D, DC, MC, V.*

AMERISUITES LAKE BUENA VISTA SOUTH

$–$$ 🏨 A stay here gets you into the adjacent Caribbean-themed outdoor recreation complex for free. The complex includes an 18-hole miniature golf course and three outdoor pools, one with a waterslide. Complimentary Continental breakfast is served daily, and there's free scheduled shuttle service to Disney, Universal Studios, SeaWorld, Wet 'n Wild, and the Lake Buena Vista Factory Stores. The brightly colored, tropical-style suites have separate bedrooms and living rooms with kitchenettes, king-size sofa beds, and desks with high-speed Internet connections. Pros: easy drive to supermarkets; special, sub-$100-a-night rates for government employees with ID; free shuttle to Disney and other parks. Cons: just off not-so-scenic stretch of highway; not much within walking distance. ✉ *4991 Calypso Cay Way, Kissimmee 34746* ☎ *407/997–1300 or 800/833–1516* ⊕ *www.amerisuites. com* ◆ *151 suites* ⌂ *In-room: safe, kitchen, refrigerator, Ethernet. In-hotel: pool, gym, laundry service, no-smoking rooms* ▤ *AE, D, DC, MC, V* ⃝ *BP.*

RADISSON RESORT PARKWAY

★ ¢–$$ 🖼 This bright, spacious Radisson has an attractive location amid 1½ acres of foliage, good facilities, and competitive prices. The focal point is the giant pool, with wide, gentle waterfalls; a 40-foot slide; and whirlpools. The lively sports bar off the lobby has a massive TV. On-site refueling options include Starbucks, Krispy Kreme, and Pizza Hut. Generously proportioned rooms are decorated with blond-wood furniture and white down comforters. A free shuttle makes 10-minute trips to Disney. Pros: kids 10 and under eat free at hotel restaurants; kids suites have bunk beds; free Disney shuttle. Con: not an easy walk to area shops or restaurants. ✉*2900 Parkway Blvd., Kissimmee 34746* ☎*407/396–7000 or 800/634–4774* ⊕*www.radissonparkway.com* ↘*712 rooms, 8 suites* ♿*In-room: Ethernet. In-hotel: 2 restaurants, bar, tennis courts, pools, gym, laundry facilities, laundry service, public Wi-Fi, no-smoking rooms* ▤*AE, D, DC, MC, V.*

MAGICAL MEMORIES VILLAS

$–$$ 🖼 Despite the name, this resort is not affiliated with Disney, but you'll probably feel the magic anyway when you get your bill. Two-bedroom villas with full kitchens start at $94 a night. Three- and four-bedroom villas are also available. Although the furnishings are standard, the villas are spacious and bright, with large windows and pastel pink walls. All the suites include a washer and dryer, and a set of linens. Pros: sequestered and homey; free long-distance calls with mid-priced and premium rooms. Cons: not an easy walk to area shops or restaurants; extra charge for daily housekeeping (which is required.) ✉*5075 U.S. 192 W, Kissimmee 34746* ☎*407/390–8200 or 800/736–0402* ⊕*www. magicalmemories.com* ↘*140 villas* ♿*In-room: kitchen, refrigerator, VCR, Ethernet. In-hotel: tennis court, pool, gym, laundry facilities, no-smoking rooms, some pets allowed (fee)* ▤*D, MC, V.*

BEST WESTERN LAKESIDE

$ 🖼 Fifteen two-story, balconied buildings make up this 27-acre hotel complex. A small man-made lake offers pedal boating, and four outdoor tennis courts are available on a first-come, first-serve basis. Rooms come with two double beds or one king. Children's activities involve arts and crafts, movies, or miniature golf in a comfortable play area. Pros: feels almost like a family summer camp; on an idyllic lake; free breakfast for kids 10 and under; free Disney shuttle. Con: on a stretch of highway that you wouldn't want to walk along. ✉*7769 W. Irlo Bronson Memorial Hwy., 2 mi west of I–4, Kissimmee 34747* ☎*407/396–2222 or 800/848–0801* ⊕*www.laquintainnlakeside.com* ↘*651 rooms* ♿*In-room: safe, refrigerator. In-hotel: 2 restaurants, room service, tennis courts, pools, gym, children's programs (ages 4–12), laundry facilities, laundry service, no-smoking rooms* ▤*AE, D, DC, MC, V.*

CELEBRITY RESORTS KISSIMMEE

¢–$ 🖼 A collection of villas a few blocks south of U.S. 192, this resort puts you far enough from the highway to avoid the clutter of the tourist strip, but close enough to conveniently reach its shops and restaurants. And it's about 4 mi from the Walt Disney World entrance. As at the Celebrity Resort in Lake Buena Vista, accommodations here range from standard hotel rooms to two-bedroom deluxe suites that can sleep up to 10 people. Suites have living rooms with sofa beds and separate dining areas. Pros: feels miles off the tourist strip; short drive to shops. Cons: not within an easy walk of much; Disney shuttle costs $10 per person round trip. ⊠*2800 N. Poinciana Blvd., Kissimmee 34746* ☎*407/997–5000 or 800/423–8604* ⊕*www.celebrityresorts. com* ⚑*311 suites* ⚑*In-room: safe, kitchen (some), refrigerator, Ethernet, Wi-Fi. In-hotel: restaurant, room service, tennis court, pools, gym, children's programs (ages 4–12), laundry facilities, laundry service, no-smoking rooms* ⊟*AE, D, MC, V.*

HOLIDAY INN MAINGATE WEST

¢–$ 🏨 This six-story, classic Holiday Inn has large standard rooms with two double beds. Kids suites have queen beds for the adults and an extra room for the kids with bunk beds, a TV and VCR, a CD player, Nintendo 64, and board games. Pros: kids' play area in main restaurant; free Disney shuttle; golf and tennis centers nearby. Con: feels very much on the tourist strip. ⊠*7601 Black Lake Rd., 2 mi west of I–4, Kissimmee 34747* ☎*407/396–1100 or 800/365–6935* ⊕*www.ichotelsgroup.com* ⚑*295 rooms, 30 suites* ⚑*In-room: safe, refrigerator, Ethernet, Wi-Fi. In-hotel: restaurant, room service, pool, gym, laundry facilities, laundry service, public Wi-Fi, no-smoking rooms* ⊟*AE, D, DC, MC, V.*

SERALAGO HOTEL & SUITES MAINGATE EAST

¢–$ 🏨 It's within walking distance of the Old Town shopping and entertainment complex and 3 mi from Disney. Special kids suites have a room designed to look like Wild West fort, with bunk beds, TVs, and video games. All rooms have VCRs and kitchenettes with refrigerators and microwaves. Pros: easy walk to shops and restaurants; pets are welcome ($40 deposit); free shuttle to all Disney parks. Con: on a touristy strip of highway about as far from Walden Pond as you could imagine. ⊠*5678 W. Irlo Bronson Memorial Hwy., Kissimmee 34746* ☎*407/396–4488, 800/366–5437, or 800/465–4329* ⊕*www.orlandofamilyfunhotel.com* ⚑*614 rooms, 110 suites* ⚑*In-room: kitchen, VCR. In-hotel: restaurant, room service, bar, tennis courts, pools, children's programs (ages 3–12), laundry facilities, laundry service, no-smoking rooms* ⊟*AE, D, DC, MC, V.*

UNIVERSAL ORLANDO AREA

Take I–4 Exit 74B or 75A, unless otherwise noted. Universal Orlando's on-site hotels, all managed by Loews, were built in a little luxury enclave that has everything you need, so you never have to leave Universal property. In minutes you can walk from any hotel to CityWalk, Universal's dining and entertainment district, or take a ferry that cruises the adjacent artificial river. If you need something as mundane as a new toothbrush, there's plenty of shopping just across the street from Universal on Kirkman Road.

A significant perk is that your hotel key lets you go directly to the head of the line for most Universal Orlando attractions. Other special services at some hotels include a "Did You Forget?" closet that offers everything from kid's strollers to dog leashes to computer accessories.

If the on-property Universal hotels are a bit pricey for your budget, don't worry, a burgeoning hotel district with has sprung up across Kirkman Road, offering convenient accommodations and some room rates less than $50 a night. Although these off-property hotels don't have the perks of the on-site places, you'll probably be smiling when you see your hotel bill.

HARD ROCK HOTEL

$$$–$$$$ ▦ Inside the California mission–style building you'll find such rock memorabilia as the slip Madonna wore in her "Like a Prayer" video. Rooms have black-and-white photos of pop icons and serious sound systems with CD players. Stay in a suite, and you'll get a big-screen TV and a wet bar. Kid-friendly suites have a small extra room for children. Your hotel key card lets you bypass lines at the Universal. The Kitchen, one of the hotel's restaurants, occasionally hosts visiting musicians cooking their favorite meals at the Chef's Table. Pros: short walk to Universal and CityWalk; preferential treatment at Universal rides. Cons: rooms and meals are pricey; loud rock music in public areas may annoy some people. ✉ *5800 Universal Blvd., Universal Studios 32819* ☎*407/503–7625 or 800/232–7827* ⊕*www.universalorlando.com* ↻*621 rooms, 29 suites* ♿*In-room: safe, refrigerator, VCR, Ethernet. In-hotel: 3 restaurants, room service, bars, pools, gym, children's programs (ages 4–14), laundry service, public Wi-Fi, no-smoking rooms, some pets allowed (fee)* ▭*AE, D, DC, MC, V.*

PORTOFINO BAY HOTEL

$$–$$$$ ▦ The charm and romance of Portofino, Italy, are conjured up at this lovely luxury resort. The illusion is so faultless, right down to the cobblestone streets, that you might find it hard to believe that the different-colored row houses lining the "bay" are a facade. Large, plush rooms here are done in cream andwhite, with down comforters and high-quality wood furnishings. There are two Italian restaurants, Mama Della's and Delfino Riviera, and gelato machines surround the massive pool. The Feast of St. Gennaro (the patron saint of Naples) is held here in September as are monthly Italian wine tastings. Pros: incredible, Italian villa atmosphere; large spa; short walk or ferry ride to Universal Studios and Islands of Adventure; preferential treatment at Universal rides. Cons: rooms and meals are noticeably expensive; in-room high-speed Internet access costs $10 a day. ✉ *5601 Universal Blvd., Universal Studios 32819* ☎*407/503–1000 or 800/232–7827* ⊕*www.universalorlando.com* ↻*699 rooms, 51 suites* ♿*In-room: safe, VCR, Ethernet. In-hotel: 3 restaurants, room service, bar, pools, gym, spa, children's programs (ages 4–14), laundry service, public Wi-Fi, some pets allowed (fee)* ▭*AE, D, DC, MC, V.*

ROYAL PACIFIC RESORT

Fodor's Choice ★   The entrance—a footbridge across a tropical stream—sets the tone for the South Pacific theme of this hotel, which is on 53 acres planted with tropical shrubs and trees, most of them palms. The focal point is a 12,000-square-foot, lagoon-style pool, which has

WORD OF MOUTH

"We love the Royal Pacific Resort and Universal parks. Two and a half days is perfect. The best part is you will get express access to all the attractions."–schmerl

a small beach and an interactive water play area. Indonesian carvings decorate the walls everywhere, even in the rooms, and Emeril Lagasse's restaurant, Tchoup Chop, draws crowds. The hotel hosts Polynesian-style luaus every Saturday. Pros: Emeril's restaurant; preferential treatment at Universal rides. Cons: rooms can feel cramped; $10-a-day fee for Internet access unwarranted given rates. ⊠*6300 Hollywood Way, Universal Orlando 32819* ☎*407/503–3000 or 800/232–7827* ⊕*www.universalorlando.com* ⤶*1,000 rooms, 113 suites* ⚬*In-room: safe, VCR, Ethernet. In-hotel: 3 restaurants, room service, bars, pool, gym, children's programs (ages 4–14), laundry facilities, laundry service, executive floor, public Wi-Fi, no-smoking rooms, some pets allowed (fee), minibar* ⊟*AE, DC, MC, V.*

DOUBLETREE HOTEL AT THE ENTRANCE TO UNIVERSAL ORLANDO

$$ It's a hotbed of business-trippers that also attracts pleasure-seekers thanks to a location right at the Universal Orlando entrance. Don't worry about noisy conventioneers—the meeting and convention facilities are completely isolated from the guest towers. If you happen stay here on business, though, note that the teleconferencing center lets you connect with points all over the world. Pro: within walking distance of Universal and area shops and restaurants. Cons: on a fast-lane tourist strip; need a rental car to reach Disney, I-Drive, or downtown Orlando. ⊠*5780 Major Blvd., I–4 Exit 75B, 32819* ☎*407/351–1000* ⊕*www.orlandoradissonhotel.com* ⤶*742 rooms, 15 suites* ⚬*In-room: safe, Ethernet. In-hotel: restaurant, room service, pool, gym, laundry facilities, laundry service, public Wi-Fi, no-smoking rooms* ⊟*AE, D, DC, MC.*

EXTENDED STAY DELUXE ORLANDO–UNIVERSAL STUDIOS

★ **$**   This is no luxury resort, but the rooms are spacious, tidy, and pleasant. What's more, every suite has a full kitchen, so you can save money on meals if you enjoy cooking. Each suite also has a work table with broadband access, a queen-size bed, and a sofa bed. Pros: in-suite kitchens; short walk to Universal and area shops and restaurants. Cons: on a touristy strip; need a rental car to reach Disney. ⊠*5610 Vineland Rd., Orlando 32819* ☎*407/370–4428 or 800/398–7829* ⊕*www.extendedstayhotels.com* ⤶*84 suites* ⚬*In-room: kitchen, refrigerator, Ethernet. In-hotel: pool, gym, laundry facilities, public Wi-Fi, no-smoking rooms* ⊟*AE, D, DC, MC, V.*

Where to Stay in & near Universal Orlando

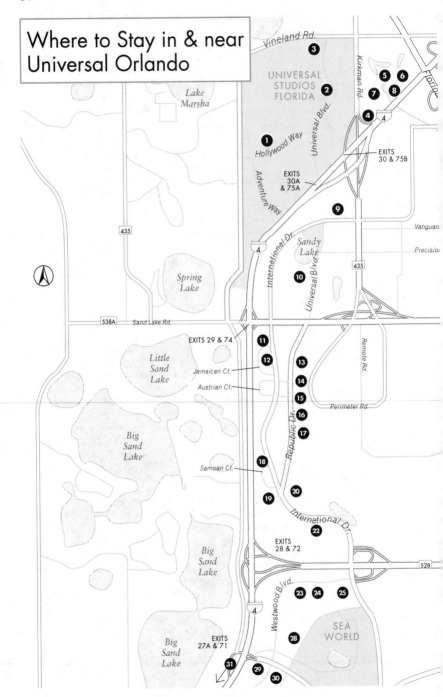

Tropical Lake

EXITS
31 & 77

Shingle Creek

Fla. Turnpike (Ronald Reagan Turnpike)

d St.

n Dr.

Mandarin Dr.

Sand Lake Rd.

John Young Parkway

423

32 - **34**

21

Beachline Expressway

Orangewood Blvd.

26

27

Central Florida Parkway

2

HOLIDAY INN HOTEL & SUITES ORLANDO/UNIVERSAL

$ 🏨 Staying at this hotel directly across the street from Universal could eliminate your need for a rental car if Universal, SeaWorld, Wet 'n Wild, and I-Drive are your only planned stops. There's a free shuttle to all four, though you can easily walk to Universal. Rooms have coffeemakers, hair dryers, irons, and ironing boards; one- and two-bedroom suites also have refrigerators, microwaves, dishwashers, and tableware. Suites cost about $20 more per night than the standard guest rooms. Pros: easy walk to Universal and area shops; small pets allowed ($50 nonrefundable deposit); plenty of shopping in walking distance. Con: need a rental car to reach Disney and downtown Orlando. ⊠*5905 S. Kirkman Rd., I–4 Exit 75B, Orlando 32819* 🕾*407/351–3333 or 800/327–1364* ⊕*www.hiuniversal.com* 🛏*390 rooms, 120 suites* ⧖*In-room: safe, refrigerator (some), Ethernet. In-hotel: restaurant, room service, bar, pool, gym, laundry service, public Wi-Fi, no-smoking rooms, some pets allowed* ▭*AE, D, DC, MC, V.*

SLEEP INN & SUITES UNIVERSAL ORLANDO

¢–$ 🏨 Rooms in this 11-story hotel have two double beds or one king; suites add full kitchens and a sofa bed. All baths have large walk-in showers. Pros: within walking distance of Universal and area shops and restaurants; free shuttle to Universal, Sea World, and Wet 'n Wild. Cons: need a rental car to reach Disney or downtown Orlando; no on-site restaurant or room service. ⊠*5605 Major Blvd., Orlando 32819* 🕾*407/363–1333* 🕾*800/424–6423* ⊕*www.choicehotels.com* 🛏*196 rooms, 40 suites* ⧖*In-room: safe, kitchen (some), refrigerator, Ethernet. In-hotel: pool, gym, laundry facilities, laundry service, no-smoking rooms* ▭*AE, D, DC, MC, V* ⑩*CP.*

SUBURBAN EXTENDED STAY AMERICA ORLANDO/UNIVERSAL STUDIOS

¢ 🏨 The brick exterior with Victorian-style architectural touches makes the place look like a dorm in a small-town college, but the amenities inside are far more extensive than what you probably had at your alma mater. Each studio has a full kitchen, complete with microwave, stovetop, refrigerator, dishes, and dishwasher. There's no on-site gym, but a Bally's fitness center is a short walk away, and the neighborhood has lots of entertainment and dining options. Take Exit 75B off I–4. Pros: easy walk to Universal and area shops and restaurants; low room rates. Con: no on-site restaurant or room service. ⊠*5615 Major Blvd., Orlando 32819* 🕾*407/313–2000 or 800/951–7829* ⊕*www. suburbanhotels.com* 🛏*150 suites* ⧖*In-room: safe, kitchen, refrigerator, Ethernet, Wi-Fi. In-hotel: laundry facilities, no-smoking rooms* ▭*AE, D, DC, MC, V.*

ORLANDO METRO AREA

INTERNATIONAL DRIVE

Take I–4 Exit 72, 74A, or 75A, unless otherwise noted. The sprawl of newish hotels, restaurants, malls, and dozens of small attractions known as International Drive"I-Drive" to locals—makes a convenient base for visits to Walt Disney World, Universal, and other Orlando attractions. Parallel to I–4, this four-lane boulevard stretches from Universal in the north to Kissimmee in the south. Each part of I-Drive has its own personality. The southern end is classier, and south of Sea-World there's still, amazingly, quite a lot of wide-open space just waiting for new hotels and restaurants to open up. The concentration of cheaper restaurants, fast-food joints, and T-shirt shops increases as you go north.

I-Drive's popularity makes it a crowded place to drive in any season. Try to avoid the morning (7–9) and evening (4–6) rush hours. If you're planning a day visiting I-Drive attractions, consider riding the I-Ride Trolley, which travels the length of I-Drive from Florida's Turnpike to the outlet center on Vineland Avenue, stopping at Wet 'n Wild and SeaWorld.

PEABODY ORLANDO

★ $$$$ ☐ Every day at 11 AM the celebrated Peabody ducks exit a private elevator and waddle across the lobby to the marble fountain where they pass the day, basking in their fame. At 5 they repeat the ritual in reverse. Built by the owners of the landmark Peabody Hotel in Memphis, this 27-story structure resembles a trio of high-rise office towers, but don't be put off by the austerity. The interior impresses with gilt and marble halls. Some of the oversize upper-floor rooms have views of Disney. A lobby concierge can answer your questions about attractions and cultural events. You can leave your cares behind at the spa or health club. A round-trip shuttle to Disney or Universal is $10 per person. Pros: adjacent to convention center (business travelers take note); good spa; short walk to shops and restaurants. Cons: pricey; adjacent to convention center (leisure travelers take note); on a congested section of I-Drive. ⊠*9801 International Dr., I-Drive Area, Orlando32819* ☎*407/352–4000 or 800/732–2639* ⊕*www.peabody-orlando.com* ⤶*891 rooms* ⌂*In-room: safe, Ethernet. In-hotel: 3 restaurants, room service, tennis courts, pool, gym, spa, concierge, public Wi-Fi, no-smoking rooms* ⊟*AE, D, DC, MC, V.*

RITZ-CARLTON ORLANDO GRANDE LAKES

$$$–$$$$ ☐ Orlando's first and only Ritz is a particularly extravagant link in
Fodor$Choice the luxury chain. Service is exemplary, from the fully attended porte-
★ cochere entrance to the 18-hole golf course and 40-room spa. Rooms and suites have large balconies, elegant wood furnishings, down comforters, and decadent marble baths (with separate showers and tubs). A lovely, Roman-style pool area has fountains and a hot tub. Make reservations for dinner at Norman's when you reserve your room. An enclosed hallway connects the Ritz to the nearby JW Marriott Hotel,

where you'll find more restaurants and a kid-friendly water park. Pros: truly luxurious; impeccable service; great spa; golf course; shares amenities with Marriott. Cons: pricey; need a rental car to reach Disney and area shops and restaurants. ⊠*4012 Central Florida Pkwy., I-Drive Area, Orlando 32837* ☎*407/206–2400 or 800/576–5760* ⊕*www. grandelakes.com* ⬐*520 rooms, 64 suites* ☖*In-room: Ethernet. In-hotel: 4 restaurants, room service, bars, 18-hole golf course, pool, gym, spa, concierge, children's programs (ages 4–12), laundry service, executive floor, public Wi-Fi, no-smoking rooms* ▤*AE, D, DC, MC, V.*

JW MARRIOTT ORLANDO GRANDE LAKES

$$–$$$$ ⛉ With more than 70,000 square feet of meeting space, this hotel caters to a convention clientele. But because it's part of a lush resort that includes a European-style spa and a Greg Norman–designed golf course, it also appeals to those looking to relax. Rooms are large (420 square feet), and most have balconies that overlook the huge pool complex. Wander down a long connector hallway to the adjoining Ritz-Carlton, where you can use your room charge card in the restaurants and shops. Pros: pool is great for kids and adults; shares amenities with the Ritz. Cons: things are spread out on the grounds; you need a rental car to reach Disney and other area offerings. ⊠*4040 Central Florida Pkwy., I-Drive Area, Orlando 32837* ☎*407/206–2300 or 800/576–5750* ⊕*www.grandelakes.com* ⬐*1,000 rooms, 57 suites* ☖*In-room: Ethernet. In-hotel: 4 restaurants, room service, bars, 18-hole golf course, pool, gym, spa, concierge, laundry service, executive floor, public Wi-Fi, no-smoking rooms* ▤*AE, D, DC, MC, V.*

ROSEN SHINGLE CREEK

$$–$$$$ ⛉ It may be adjacent to the convention center, but make no mistake: this place has plenty for those seeking fun and relaxation. There's the large spa, for instance, and the championship golf course and golf academy. There are also four swimming pools and recreation options that include kayaking on a creek. The architecture recalls the Spanish-revival palaces you find in Palm Beach County. Standard guest rooms are large (436 square feet) and have plasma-screen TVs and NXTV, a system that turns the TV into an Internet-linked computer. Thanks to the BAGS service, you can get a boarding pass for your flight and check in your luggage at the hotel, thus eliminating check-in at Orlando International. Pros: golf course; spa; free shuttle to Universal; BAGS check-in service. Cons: large grounds mean long walks to on-site amenities; no shuttle to I-Drive. ⊠*9939 Universal Blvd., I-Drive Area, Orlando 32819* ☎*407/996–9939, 866/996-6338 reservations* ⊕*www.rosenshinglecreek.com* ⬐*1,500 rooms, 109 suites* ☖*In-room: safe, Ethernet. In-hotel: 3 restaurants, room service, 4 pools, gym, golf course, tennis courts, spa, children's programs (ages 4–14), laundry facilities, laundry service, public Wi-Fi, no-smoking rooms* ▤*AE, D, DC, MC, V.*

MARRIOTT'S CYPRESS HARBOUR RESORT

$$–$$$ ⛉ This big, elaborate resort is a destination unto itself, with boating on a private lake, golf, tennis, and many other on-site amenities. The two-bedroom, two-bathroom villas sleep up to eight people and include washers and dryers. An on-property market has groceries, liquor, cigars, and video rentals. There's also a Pizza Hut Express and Edy's ice cream shop. Because the resort is a half-mile from the Nick Faldo Golf Institute by Marriott, the place is popular with those who want a golf getaway. Pros: lots of outdoor activities (biking, beach volleyball, boating). Con: not much within walking distance. ⊠*11251 Harbour Villa Rd., I-Drive Area, Orlando 32821* ☎*407/238–1300 or 800/845–5279* ⊕*www.vacationclub.com* ⟟*510 villas* ⌂*In-room: safe, DVD, Ethernet. In-hotel: 2 restaurants, bar, tennis courts, pools, gym, beachfront, children's programs (ages 4–12), laundry facilities, laundry service, concierge, public Wi-Fi, no-smoking rooms* ▤*AE, D, DC, MC, V.*

RENAISSANCE ORLANDO RESORT AT SEAWORLD

$$–$$$ 🏨 The 10-story atrium is full of waterfalls, goldfish ponds, and palm trees; as you shoot skyward in sleek glass elevators, look for the exotic birds—on loan from SeaWorld across the street—twittering in the large, hand-carved, gilded Venetian aviary. Rooms have more floor space than the average Central Florida hotel, plus nice touches like high-speed Internet connections. Atlantis, the formal Mediterranean restaurant, is something of an undiscovered gem. Pros: good on-site restaurants; across from SeaWorld; shuttles to Disney ($7 round trip) and Universal ($14 round trip). Cons: need a rental car to reach area shops and restaurants; $8 daily parking fee; shuttles aren't free; often full of conventioneers. ⊠*6677 Sea Harbor Dr., I-Drive Area, Orlando 32821* ☎*407/351–5555 or 800/468–3571* ⊕*www.renaissancehotels. com* ⟟*778 rooms* ⌂*In-room: Ethernet. In-hotel: 4 restaurants, room service, tennis courts, pool, gym, spa, laundry service, concierge, public Wi-Fi, no-smoking rooms* ▤*AE, D, DC, MC, V.*

ROSEN CENTRE HOTEL

$$–$$$ 🏨 This 24-story palace is adjacent to the convention center and within walking distance of such I-Drive attractions as the Pointe*Orlando shopping and entertainment center and Ripley's Believe It or Not! There's a massive pool surrounded by vegetation and a couple of good restaurants, including the Everglades Room and Cafe Gauguin. Universal ticket services are available, and so is the BAGS service offered by all Rosen conference and Disney properties. With it, you can get a boarding pass and check your luggage in at the hotel, eliminating check-in at Orlando International. A round-trip shuttle to Disney, Universal, or SeaWorld costs $7 to $15. Pros: easy walk to convention center, Pointe*Orlando, and other I-Drive attractions; BAGS check-in service. Cons: theme-park shuttles aren't free; feels very much like a business hotel; convention center traffic can be a problem. ⊠*9840 International Dr., I-Drive Area, 32819* ☎*407/996–9840 or 800/204–7234* ⊕*www. rosencentre.com* ⟟*1,334 rooms, 80 suites* ⌂*In-room: safe, Ethernet. In-hotel: 3 restaurants, room service, bars, pool, gym, laundry service, public Wi-Fi, no-smoking rooms* ▤*AE, D, DC, MC, V.*

INTERNATIONAL PLAZA RESORT & SPA

$$ 🏨 On 28 acres just south of convention center, this 17-story hotel welcomes families as well as conventioneers. It's roughly midway between the airport and Disney, less than a mile from SeaWorld, and a five-minute drive from Universal. There are free shuttles to all major theme parks, including Disney. Pros: close to SeaWorld, I-Drive, and convention center; on-site minature golf course; free theme-parks shuttle. Cons: few shops and restaurants within walking distance. ⊠*10100 International Dr., I-Drive Area, Orlando 32821* ☎*407/352–1100 or 800/327–0363* ⊕*www.internationalplazaresortandspa.com* ☞*1,102 rooms, 68 suites* ⌂*In-room: safe, Ethernet. In-hotel: 3 restaurants, room service, pools, gym, laundry service, public Wi-Fi, no-smoking rooms* ⊟*AE, D, DC, MC, V.*

WYNDHAM ORLANDO RESORT

$$ ⊡ Two-story villas, palm trees, and romantic lagoons evoke a Caribbean getaway. There's a children's entertainment center and an upscale shopping court. The villas are comfortable, if not necessarily candidates for *Architectural Digest*. And you can't beat the location five minutes from Universal. If you choose the Family Fun Suites option, your youngsters get a separate room with bunk beds. There's a free shuttle to Universal and SeaWorld. Pros: convenient to Universal, SeaWorld, I-Drive, and outlet malls; pets allowed ($50 nonrefundable fee). Con: no shuttle to Disney, about 30 minutes away. ⊠*8001 International Dr., I-Drive Area, Orlando 32819* ☎*407/351–2420 or 800/996–3426* ⊕*www.wyndham.com* ☞*1,064 rooms* ⌂*In-room: safe, refrigerator, Ethernet. In-hotel: 3 restaurants, room service, tennis courts, pools, gym, laundry service, public Wi-Fi, no-smoking rooms, some pets allowed (fee)* ⊟*AE, D, DC, MC, V.*

THE DOUBLETREE CASTLE

$–$$ ⊡ You won't really think you're in a castle at this midprice hotel, although the tall gold-and-silver spires, medieval-style mosaics, arched doorways, and British tourists may make you feel like reading Harry Potter. Take your book to either the rooftop terrace or the inviting courtyard, which has a big, round swimming pool. Rooms have gold-framed mirrors and black-velvet headboards. Café Tu Tu Tango, one of the better restaurants in this part of Orlando, has a zesty, small-dish, multicultural menu. Pros: kid-friendly; easy walk to I-Drive eateries and attractions; free theme-parks shuttle. Con: on a congested stretch of I-Drive. ⊠*8629 International Dr., I-Drive Area, Orlando 32819* ☎*407/345–1511 or 800/952–2785* ⊕*www.doubletreecastle. com* ☞*216 rooms* ⌂*In-room: safe, refrigerator, Ethernet Wi-Fi. In-hotel: 2 restaurants, room service, pool, gym, laundry service, public Wi-Fi, no-smoking rooms* ⊟*AE, D, DC, MC, V.*

EMBASSY SUITES HOTEL INTERNATIONAL DRIVE SOUTH/ CONVENTION CENTER

$–$$ ⊡ This all-suites hotel has an expansive Mediterranean-style lobby with marble floors, pillars, hanging lamps, and old-fashioned ceiling fans. The atrium is all about fountains and palm trees. Elsewhere, tile walks and brick arches lend still more flavor. The hotel has a number of good amenities, such as a health club with a fine steam room. Pros: free breakfast and nightly beverages; easy walk to convention center and Pointe*Orlando; free shuttle to Disney and Universal. Con: on congested stretch of I-Drive. ⊠*8978 International Dr., I-Drive Area,*

Orlando 32819 ☎*407/352–1400 or 800/433–7275* ⊕*www.embassy-suitesorlando.com* ⇌*244 suites* ⌁*In-room: safe, Ethernet. In-hotel: restaurant, pool, gym, public Wi-Fi, no-smoking rooms* ⊟*AE, D, DC, MC, V* ⦿|*BP.*

EMBASSY SUITES INTERNATIONAL DRIVE/ JAMAICAN COURT

$–$$ 🖾 The atrium of this all-suites hotel has a lounge where a player piano sets the mood. Each suite has a living room with a wet bar, pullout sofa, and two TVs—all at a better price than for many area single rooms. Two-room suites can sleep six. The shuttle to Universal, SeaWorld, and Wet 'n Wild is free; the one to the various Disney properties runs $7 to $13 round trip. Pros: within walking distance of I-Drive eateries and attractions; free breakfast; free cocktails and sandwiches; free shuttle to Universal, SeaWorld, and Wet 'n Wild. Cons: convention center traffic can be bad; shuttle to Disney isn't free. ⊠*8250 Jamaican Ct., I-Drive Area, Orlando 32819* ☎*407/345–8250 or 800/327–9797* ⊕*www. orlandoembassysuites.com* ⇌*246 suites* ⌁*In-room: safe, refrigerator, Ethernet, Wi-Fi. In-hotel: room service, pool, gym, public Wi-Fi, no-smoking rooms* ⊟*AE, D, DC, MC, V* ⦿|*BP.*

HOLIDAY INN HOTEL & SUITES–ORLANDO CONVENTION CENTER

$–$$ 🖾 A bright yellow facade fronted by palm trees welcomes you to this six-story, family-friendly hotel. Furnishings are simple, but rooms are large, with either two queen beds or one king. Suites, which have full kitchens, are a bargain at about $170 a night—even in high season. A stay here puts you a block from the Mercado shopping and dining complex. Universal, SeaWorld, and Wet 'n Wild are all within 2 mi. Pros: very economical; less than a block from I-Drive; free theme-parks shuttle. Cons: I-Drive traffic can be heavy; Disney is 30 minutes away. ⊠*8214 Universal Blvd., I-4 Exit 74A, I-Drive Area, Orlando 32819* ☎*407/581–9001* ⊕*www.holidayinnconvention.com* ⇌*115 rooms, 35 suites* ⌁*In-room: safe, kitchen (some), refrigerator, Ethernet. In-hotel: restaurant, bar, pools, gym, laundry facilities, laundry service, no-smoking rooms* ⊟*AE, D, DC, MC, V.*

LA QUINTA INN & SUITES ORLANDO CONVENTION CENTER

$–$$ 🖾 It's a family-oriented hotel on the more upscale part of I-Drive, near the convention center. The entrance is on Universal Boulevard, the relatively undiscovered thoroughfare a block east of I-Drive, so, despite the proximity to the tourist strip, things are still serene here. The king rooms and suites have refrigerators and microwaves, and although there's no restaurant the hotel provides free Continental breakfast daily, and there are a half-dozen eateries nearby. Round-trip shuttle service to Universal or SeaWorld costs 75¢. Pros: within walking distance of I-Drive restaurants and attractions; free breakfast; cheap shuttle to Universal and SeaWorld. Cons: no restaurant; no room service. ⊠*8504 Universal Blvd., I-4 Exit 74A, I-Drive Area, Orlando 32819* ☎*407/345–1365* ⊕*www.orlandolaquinta.com* ⇌*170 rooms, 15 suites* ⌁*In-room: safe, refrigerator (some), Ethernet. In-hotel: bar,* *pool, gym, laundry facilities, laundry service, no-smoking rooms, some pets allowed* ⊟*AE, D, DC, MC, V.*

MARRIOT RESIDENCE INN SEAWORLD INTERNATIONAL CENTER

$–$$ ⊡ The longish name hints at all the markets the hotel is attempting to tap: SeaWorld, I-Drive, and the convention center. All are within a 2-mi radius; all are served by hotel shuttles. Even the least expensive suites can sleep five people. A free breakfast is served daily, and several nearby restaurants will deliver to your room. The recreation area around the pool is like a summer camp, with a basketball court, playground equipment, picnic tables, and gas grills. Get a firm grip on directions if you're driving. The hotel is adjacent to I-4, but it's 2 mi from the interstate via two expressways, including Beachline Expressway. There's free shuttle service to Universal and SeaWorld. Pros: well-equipped kitchens; free breakfast; pets allowed ($75 deposit); free shuttles to lots of places. Cons: not much within walking distance; hard to find from I-4. ⊠*11000 Westwood Blvd., I-4 Exit 72, I-Drive Area, Orlando 32821* ☎*407/313-3600 800/331-3131* ⊕*www.residenceinnseaworld.com* ⇱*350 suites* ⟁*In-room: safe, kitchen, Ethernet, Wi-Fi. In-hotel: restaurant, bar, pool, gym, laundry facilities, laundry service, no-smoking rooms* ⊟*AE, D, DC, MC, V* ⏀*BP.*

STAYBRIDGE SUITES INTERNATIONAL DRIVE

$–$$ ⊡ The one- and two-bedroom units at this all-suites hotel sleep four to eight people. Each has a living room and kitchen with simple but up-to-date furnishings. Lush landscaping makes the place seem secluded even though it's on I-Drive. Pros: within walking distance of I-Drive eateries and attractions; close to Universal. Cons: no restaurant; no room service; on a congested stretch of I-Drive. ⊠*8480 International Dr., I-4 Exit 74A, I-Drive Area, Orlando 32819* ☎*407/352-2400 or 800/238-8000* ⊕*www.ichotelsgroup.com* ⇱*146 suites* ⟁*In-room: safe, kitchen, refrigerator, Ethernet. In-hotel: pool, gym, laundry facilities, laundry service, no-smoking rooms* ⊟*AE, D, DC, MC, V* ⏀*CP.*

ENCLAVE SUITES AT ORLANDO

¢–$$ ⊡ With three 10-story buildings surrounding a private lake, an office, restaurant, and recreation area, this all-suites lodging is less a hotel than a condominium complex. Here, what you would spend for a normal room in a fancy hotel gets you an apartment with a living room, a full kitchen, two bedrooms, and small terraces with lake views. KidsQuarter suites, which can sleep six, have small children's rooms with bunk beds and whimsical murals of Shamu. There's free transportation to Universal, SeaWorld, and Wet 'n Wild. Pros: good deals on spacious suites; within walking distance of I-Drive eateries and attractions; free breakfast; free shuttle to Universal, SeaWorld, and Wet 'n Wild. Cons: area traffic can be a hassle. ⊠*6165 Carrier Dr., I-Drive Area, Orlando 32819* ☎*407/351-1155 or 800/457-0077* ⊕*www.enclavesuites.com* ⇱*321 suites* ⟁*In-room: safe, kitchen, refrigerator, Ethernet. In-hotel: restaurant, tennis court, pools, gym, laundry facilities, laundry service, public Wi-Fi, no-smoking rooms* ⊟*AE, D, DC, MC, V* ⏀*BP.*

2

EXTENDED STAY DELUXE ORLANDO CONVENTION CENTER

$ ⬚ Both the Point*Orlando and the Westwood Boulevard branches are designed for business travelers: each room has voice mail, two phone lines, free local phone calls and incoming faxes, speakerphone, and good-size work tables. But families also get a lot for their money. There's a full kitchen with everything you need to avoid restaurant tabs, including a dishwasher. The earthtone color scheme is warm if not memorable, and the suites have two queen- or one king-size bed, plus a sofa bed. Although neither hotel has a restaurant, lots of eateries are within walking distance of both. Pros: very economical; within walking distance of I-Drive restaurants and shops; free shuttle to Disney and Universal. Cons: I-Drive traffic can be heavy; no on-site restaurant; no room service; Disney is 30 minutes away. ✉ *8750 Universal Blvd., I–4 Exit 74A, I-Drive Area, Orlando 32819* ☎*407/903–1500* ⬚*137 suites* ✉*6443 Westwood Blvd., I–4 Exit 72, I-Drive Area, Orlando32836* ☎*407/351—1982* ⬚*125 suites* ⊕*www.extended- stayhotels.com* ♿*In-room: safe, kitchen. In-hotel: pool, gym, laundry facilities, laundry service, public Wi-Fi, no-smoking rooms* ▤*AE, D, DC, MC, V.*

PARC CORNICHE CONDOMINIUM SUITE HOTEL

$ ⬚ A Joe Lee–designed golf course frames this property. Each of the one- and two-bedroom suites, which are full of pastels and tropical patterns, has a kitchen (with a dishwasher) plus a patio or balcony with golf-course views. The largest accommodations, with two bedrooms and two baths, can sleep up to six. A free Continental breakfast is served daily. SeaWorld is only a few blocks away. Pros: great for golf lovers; well-equipped kitchens; free theme-parks shuttle; free breakfast. Con: not much within walking distance. ✉ *6300 Parc Corniche Dr., I-Drive Area, Orlando 32821* ☎*407/239–7100 or 800/446–2721* ⊕*www.parccorniche.com* ⬚*210 suites* ♿*In-room: Ethernet. In-hotel: restaurant, room service, 18-hole golf course, pool, laundry facilities, laundry service, no-smoking rooms* ▤*AE, D, DC, MC, V* ⎟◯⎜*CP.*

ROSEN PLAZA HOTEL

$ ⬚ Harris Rosen, Orlando's largest independent hotel owner, loves to offer bargains, and you can definitely find one here. Although it's essentially a convention hotel, leisure travelers like the prime location and long list of amenities. Rooms have two queen-size beds and are larger than those at many hotels. Two upscale restaurants, Jack's Place and Café Matisse, offer great steaks and a great buffet, respectively. Rossini's serves great pizza, and you can also grab quick eats at the reasonably priced 24-hour deli. With the BAGS service, you can get your airline boarding pass and check your suitcases in the hotel lobby, so you can go straight to the gate at Orlando International. There's a free shuttle to Universal Orlando and SeaWorld; a round-trip shuttle to Disney costs $15 per person. Pros: within walking distanct of I-Drive eateries and attractions; free shuttle to Universal and SeaWorld; BAGS check-in service. Cons: convention center traffic can be bad; shuttle to Disney isn't free. ✉ *9700 International Dr., I-Drive Area, Orlando 32819* ☎*407/996–9700 or 800/627–8258* ⊕*www.rosenplaza.com*

➥*810 rooms* ♿*In-room: safe, Ethernet. In-hotel: 2 restaurants, room service, bar, pool, laundry facilities, laundry service, public Wi-Fi, no-smoking rooms* ▤*AE, D, DC, MC, V.*

SHERATON STUDIO CITY

$ 🖥 Atop this Sheraton is a giant silver globe suitable for Times Square on New Year's Eve. But the interior has a Hollywood theme, with movie posters and black-and-white art deco touches throughout the public spaces and rooms, most of which have two queen beds. The 21st floor has 15 extra-large rooms with floor-to-ceiling windows. Pros: convenient to Universal; free shuttle to theme parks and outlet malls; great night views from upper floors. Con: on an unattractive stretch of I-Drive. ✉*5905 International Dr., I-Drive Area, Orlando 32819* ☎*407/351–2100 or 800/327–1366* ⊕*www.sheratonstudiocity.com* ➥*302 rooms* ♿*In-room: safe, Ethernet. In-hotel: restaurant, room service, bar, pool, concierge, laundry service, public Wi-Fi, no-smoking rooms* ▤*AE, D, DC, MC, V.*

EXTENDED STAYAMERICA ORLANDO CONVENTION CENTER—WESTWOOD BOULEVARD

¢–$ 🖥 Don't confuse this hotel with the Extended Stay Deluxe Orlando Convention Center—the Westwood Boulevard branch of which is just up the street. The StayAmerica has slightly lower room rates, slightly smaller rooms, and fewer amenities. It's tucked behind a pine forest and feels remote, but SeaWorld, the convention center, and Pointe*Orlando are all within a 1-mi drive. Weekly rates start as low as $415. Pros: very economical; within walking distance of I-Drive restaurants and shops; free shuttle to Disney and Universal. Cons: small pool; limited amenities; I-Drive traffic can be heavy; Disney is 30 minutes away. ✉*6451 Westwood Blvd., I-4 Exit 72, I-Drive Area, Orlando 32821* ☎*407/352–3454* ⊕*www.extstay.com* ➥*113 suites* ♿*In-room: safe, kitchen, Ethernet. In-hotel: pool, laundry facilities, public Wi-Fi, no-smoking rooms* ▤*AE, D, DC, MC, V.*

WYNFIELD INN ORLANDO CONVENTION CENTER

¢–$ 🖥 If you want a room with more than just the bare essentials but don't have the budget for luxury, this three-story motel is a find. Quarters are comfy if not spectacular; all have two double beds. Children 17 and under stay free in their parents' room (with a maximum of four people per room). The hotel is ¼ mi from SeaWorld. Pros: very economical; short walk to I-Drive; pets allowed ($50 deposit). Con: traffic can be heavy, especially during conventions. ✉*6263 Westwood Blvd., I-Drive Area, Orlando 32821* ☎*407/345–8000 or 800/346–1551* ⊕*www.wynfieldinn.com* ➥*144 rooms* ♿*In-room: safe, Ethernet. In-hotel: restaurant, bar, pools, laundry facilities, laundry service, no-smoking rooms* ▤*AE, DC, MC, V.*

DOWNTOWN ORLANDO

Downtown Orlando, north of Walt Disney World and the I-Drive area, is a thriving business district. To get there take Exit 83B off I–4 westbound, Exit 84 off I–4 eastbound.

Where to Stay in Central Orlando & Outlying Towns

WESTIN GRAND BOHEMIAN

$$–$$$$ 🏨 This European-style property is downtown Orlando's only luxury hotel. Opposite city hall, the Grand Bohemian showcases more than 100 pieces of art—including an Imperial Grand Bösendorfer piano, one of only two in the world, which sits in a posh ground-floor lounge. Rooms have dark-wood furnishings with brushed-silver accents. Tall headboards are upholstered in iridescent fabrics. Pros: art gallery; quiet, adult-friendly atmosphere; great restaurant; short walk to Lake Eola and Church Street. Cons: kids may find it boring. ⊠*325 S. Orange Ave., Downtown, Orlando 32801* ☎*407/313–9000 or 866/663–0024* ⊕*www.grandbohemianhotel.com* ⬅*250 rooms, 36 suites* ⌂*In-room: Ethernet. In-hotel: restaurant, room service, bar, pool, gym, concierge, executive floor, public Wi-Fi, parking (fee), no-smoking rooms* ▭*AE, D, DC, MC, V.*

THE COURTYARD AT LAKE LUCERNE

★ **$–$$$** 🏨 Four beautifully restored Victorian houses surround a palm-lined courtyard at this inn. Although it's almost under an expressway bridge, there's no traffic noise. You can sit on one of the porches and imagine yourself back in the time when citrus ruled and the few visitors arrived at the old railroad station on Church Street, six blocks away. Rooms have hardwood floors, Persian rugs, and antique furniture. Pros: serenity; great Victorian architecture; short walk to Lake Eola and Church Street. Cons: far from theme parks and I-Drive. ✉*211 N. Lucerne Circle E, Downtown, Orlando 32801* ☎*407/648–5188* ⊕*www.orlandohistoricinn.com* ⇆*15 rooms, 15 suites* ♿*In-room: Ethernet. In-hotel: no elevator, no-smoking rooms* ▤*MC, V* |○|*CP.*

EMBASSY SUITES ORLANDO DOWNTOWN

$–$$ 🖫 Although designed for business travelers, this property has nice touches for vacationers, too. All suites have two TVs—one in each room. Many suites overlook nearby Lake Eola, and the hotel is a short walk from a half-dozen sidewalk cafés. The seven-story indoor atrium gives the hotel a classy touch. Pros: short walk to Lake Eola and Church Street; some suites have stunning lake views. Cons: traffic can be heavy; finding on-street parking is hard and on-site valet parking costs $12 a day; Disney is least 45 minutes away. ✉*191 E. Pine St., Downtown, Orlando 32801* ☎*407/841–1000 or 800/609–3339* ⊕*www.embassyorlandodowntown.com* ⇆*167 suites* ♿*In-room: safe, refrigerator, Ethernet. In-hotel: restaurant, pool, gym, laundry service, public Wi-Fi, no-smoking rooms* ▤*AE, D, DC, MC, V* |○|*BP.*

EŌ INN & URBAN SPA

★ $–$$ 🖫 The entrance is at the rear of the building, behind Panera Bread, the bakery–restaurant that occupies the ground floor. Consequently, this three-story boutique hotel in a 1923 building is an undiscovered charmer. The spa does a brisk business on its own, but as a hotel guest you can always get in for a Swedish massage or a beauty treatement. Rooms have black-and-white photographs, thick down comforters, and high-speed Internet connections. Best of all, Lake Eola, with its 1-mi walking path, is across the street—treat yourself to a king suite overlooking the water. Pros: good spa; very short walk to Lake Eola; short walk to Thornton Park and Church Street. Cons: you have to battle I–4 traffic; Disney is 30 minutes away. ✉*227 N. Eola Dr., off E. Robinson St., Thornton Park, Orlando 32801* ☎*407/481–8485 or 888/481–8488* ⊕*www.eoinn.com* ⇆*17 rooms* ♿*In-room: safe, Ethernet. In-hotel: spa, laundry service, public Wi-Fi, no-smoking rooms* ▤*AE, D, DC, MC, V.*

ORLANDO INTERNATIONAL AIRPORT

The area around the airport, especially the neighborhood just north of the Beachline Expressway, has become hotel city over the past few years, with virtually every big-name hotel you can think of, including plenty of family-style choices, such as suites with kitchens. All the hotels listed include free airport shuttle service.

THE FLORIDA HOTEL & CONFERENCE CENTER

$$–$$$ 🖫 Just 5 mi from the airport gates, The Florida Hotel is right between Orlando International and I-Drive. You're in for a treat if you like to shop: the hotel is connected to the upscale Florida Mall, with seven major department stores and 250 specialty shops. The hotel feels upscale, too, with polished marble floors, fountains in the lobby, and a good in-house restaurant, Le Jardin, as well as a Starbucks. Rooms have

2

either two queen beds or a king and a foldout sofa; microwaves and refrigerators are available for a small fee. There's free shuttle service to Disney, Universal, and SeaWorld. Pros: the mall's shopping and dining opps; in-room spa services; short drive to airport. Cons: neighborhood is less-than-scenic; Disney is 18 mi away. ⊠ *1500 Sand Lake Rd., at S. Orange Blossom Trail, Orlando International Airport, Orlando 32809* ☎ *407/859–1500 or 800/588–4656* ⊕ *www.thefloridahotelorlando. com* ♺ *510 rooms* ♿ *In-room: Ethernet. In-hotel: restaurant, room service, pool, gym, laundry service, public Wi-Fi, no-smoking rooms* ▤ *AE, D, DC, MC, V.*

HYATT REGENCY ORLANDO INTERNATIONAL AIRPORT

$$–$$$ ⊡ If you have to catch an early morning flight, this hotel inside the main terminal complex is a good option. Counting the time you spend waiting for the elevator, your room is just a five-minute walk from the nearest ticket counter. Rooms have views of either the runways or a 10-story-tall terminal atrium; terminal-side rooms have balconies. Hemisphere, the hotel's upscale restaurant, offers a eclectic menu that changes seasonally and spectacular runway views. An in-house health club and pool provide places to unwind. Shuttles to Disney and Universal are $29 per person round-trip. Pros: quiet and sublime; the terminal's 24-hour shopping and dining opps. Cons: nothing around but the airport; downtown Orlando and the theme parks are at least 30 mintes away. ⊠ *9300 Airport Blvd., Orlando International Airport, Orlando 32827* ☎ *407/825–1234 or 800/233–1234* ⊕ *www.orlando-airport.hyatt.com* ♺ *446 rooms* ♿ *In-room: Ethernet. In-hotel: 2 restaurants, room service, pool, gym, laundry service, no-smoking rooms* ▤ *AE, D, DC, MC, V.*

AMERISUITES ORLANDO AIRPORT NORTHEAST AND NORTHWEST

$–$$ ⊡ These two hotels (one on each side of State Road 436, north of the airport) offer suites with bedrooms and living room–kitchen areas. With red carpeting, gold drapes, an overstuffed couch and lounge chair, and of course, a coffeemaker, the living area has the warm feeling of the quintessential American home. Pros: good rates; efficient rooms with all the essentials; free airport shuttle. Cons: no shuttle to theme parks; not much within walking distance. ⊠ *7500 Augusta National Dr., Orlando International Airport, Orlando 32822* ☎ *407/240–3939* ♺ *128 suites* ⊠ *5435 Forbes Pl., Orlando International Airport, 32822* ☎ *407/816–7800 or 800/833–1516* ♺ *135 suites* ⊕ *www.amerisuites. com* ♿ *In-room: safe, refrigerator, Ethernet. In-hotel: pool, gym, laundry facilities, laundry service, public Wi-Fi, no-smoking rooms* ▤ *AE, D, DC, MC, V* ⌶ *BP.*

OUTLYING TOWNS

Travel farther afield and you can get more comforts and facilities for the money, and maybe even some genuine Orlando charm—of the cozy country-inn variety.

ORLANDO HOTEL CHART

HOTEL NAME	Worth Noting	Cost	Rooms	Suites/Villas	Kitchens	Restaurants	Kids' Programs	Playground	Pools	Spa	Golf
The Disney Resorts											
All-Star Resorts	budget and family-friendly	$82–$141	5760				yes	yes	6		priv.
★ Animal Kingdom Lodge	exotic African theme	$215–$635	1293			3	yes	yes	2	yes	priv.
Beach Club Villas	serene luxury	$315–$1,105		205		1		3	3		priv.
★ BoardWalk Inn and Villas	lively and compact	$315–$655	370			4	yes		1		priv.
★ Caribbean Beach Resort	basic and moderately-priced	$145–$225	2112	526		1		yes	7		priv.
Contemporary Resort	convenient and modern	$259–$570	1013	25		3	yes		3		priv.
Coronado Springs Resort	huge convention resort	$145–$245	1967			2	yes		4		priv.
Fort Wilderness Campground	cheapest way to stay on-site	$39–$92	788		yes		yes		2		
Fort Wilderness Resort Cabins	rustic; good for families	$239–$349		408	yes		yes		2		
★ Grand Floridian Resort & Spa	Victorian luxury	$375–$920	900	90		5	yes	yes	3	yes	priv.
Old Key West Resort	good for groups	$279–$1,595		761		1		yes	4	yes	priv.
Polynesian Resort	tropical island theme	$329–$815	858	5		4	yes	yes	2		priv.
Pop Century Resort	fun theme; great room rates	$82–$141	2880					yes	2		priv.
Port Orleans Resort–French Quarter	New Orleans charm	$140–$245	1008			1			1		priv.
Port Orleans Resort–Riverside	Old South style	$140–$245	2048			1		yes	6		priv.
Saratoga Springs Resort	condo-style with comforts of home	$279–$1,595		552		1			2	yes	priv.
★ Wilderness Lodge	like a National Park lodge	$215–$525	728	31		3	yes		1		priv.
★ Yacht and Beach Club Resorts	refined, upscale, sophisticated	$315–$1,105	1213	112		4	yes	yes	3		priv.
Other Hotels in WDW											
Best Western Lake Buena Vista	high-rise with fab views	$69–$299	325			1		yes	1		
Buena Vista Palace Resort & Spa	great restaurants & amenities	$139–$289	1014	209		4	yes	yes	3	yes	
DoubleTree Guest Suites	simple yet cheerful	$99–$299	229			1			1		priv.
Grosvenor Resort	plain but upbeat & affordable	$80–$159	626	5		3	yes		2		
Hilton in the WDW Resort	beautiful views, close to downtown	$189–$350	814	27		7	yes	yes	3	yes	
Royal Plaza	recent renov.; free shuttle	$129–$239	394	5		2	1	1	1	1	

Hotel	Notes	Rates	Rooms	Suites	✓	Rest.	✓	✓	Pools	✓	Golf
Shades of Green	military only	$76–$116	586	11		4	yes		2		priv.
★ Walt Disney World Dolphin	comfortable; very kid-friendly	$125–$465	1509	136		9	yes		5	yes	priv.
Walt Disney World Swan	colorful hotel near Epcot	$125–$465	756	55	yes	6	yes		5	yes	priv.
Lake Buena Vista (LBV) Area											
Buena Vista Suites	basic but roomy suites	$99–$129		280		1	yes		1		
Caribe Royale All-Suites Resort	big pink palace; fabulous pool	$140–$240	1218	120	yes	4	yes		1		
Celebrity Resorts Lake Buena Vista	very large family suites	$190–$279	170	66		1	yes		4		
Country Inn & Suites by Carlson	inexpensive family suites	$79–$99		50			yes	yes	1		
Embassy Suites Resort LBV	pink & turquoise standby	$159–$219		333	yes	2	yes	yes	1		
Hawthorn Suites Resort LBV	least expensive family suites	$89–$189		120			yes	yes	1		
Holiday Inn SunSpree	very popular Kidsuites	$99–$119	507			1	yes	yes	2		
★ Hyatt Regency Grand Cypress	gorgeous pool; nature trails	$289–$419	750	210	yes	5	yes	yes	2	yes	3 courses
Marriott Residence Inn	Caribbean-style oasis	$129–$154		400			yes	yes	1		
Marriott Village at Little Lake Bryan	private gated property	$79–$159	700			8	yes		3		
Nickelodeon Family Suites	kids love the Nick theme	$149–$385		800	yes	3	yes	yes	2		1 course
Orlando World Center Marriott	huge convention hotel	$239–$292	2000	357		7	yes		4		
Palomino Suites	free breakfast, great price	$89–$129		96							
★ PerriHouse Bed & Breakfast Inn	small B&B in nature preserve	$99–$150	8						1		
Sheraton Safari Hotel	fun jungle theme; large rooms	$99–$259	489			2		yes	1		priv.
Sheraton Vistana Resort	sprawling all-suites retreat	$149–$259	0	1700		2	yes		7		
Kissimmee											
AmeriSuites LBV South	budget vacation club	$104–$199		151		2	yes		1		
Best Western Lakeside	27 lakeside acres	$79–$99	651			2	yes	yes	3		
Celebration Hotel	grand Victorian-style hotel	$199–$289	115			2	yes		1		priv.
Celebrity Resorts Kissimmee	large family suites	$74–$119		311		1	yes		4		

HOTEL NAME	Worth Noting	Cost	Rooms	Suites/Villas	Kitchens	Restaurants	Kids' Programs	playground	Pools	Spa	Golf
★ Gaylord Palms Resort	huge, flashy, FLA.-theme hotel	$289–$499	1406	86		4	yes		2	yes	priv.
Holiday Inn Maingate West	classic HI with Kidsuites	$79–$119	295	30		1			1		
Magical Memories Villas	sunny, colorful, affordable	$94–$189		140	yes				1		
Omni Orlando Resort	deluxe hotel and golf resort	$239–$319	730	32		5	yes		2	yes	2 courses
★ Radisson Resort Parkway	pool with waterfalls & slide	$79–$199	712	8		2			2		
★ Reunion Resort & Club of Orlando	ultra-luxurious golf retreat	$235–$299		60	yes	1	yes		1	yes	3 courses
Saratoga Resort Villas	Spanish-style villa complex	$99–$299		150		1			1		
Seralago Hotel & Suites	Wild West-theme Kidsuites	$69–$99	614	110		1	yes		2		
In Universal Orlando											
Hard Rock Hotel	rock 'n' roll theme	$239–$475	621	29		3	yes		2		
Portofino Bay Hotel	Italian Riviera theme	$207–$415	699	51		3	yes		3	yes	
★ Royal Pacific Resort	South Pacific theme	$167–$268	1000	113		3	yes		1		
Near Universal Orlando											
DoubleTree Hotel	close to Universal	$143–$179	742	15		1	yes		1		priv.
Extended Stay Deluxe Universal Studios	spacious rooms, full kitchens	$84–$99		84	yes			1			
Holiday Inn Hotel & Suites	simple but well located	$89–$119	390	120		1		1			
Sleep Inn & Suites	basic rooms, good prices	$69–$109	196	40	yes			1	1		
Suburban Extended Stay America	attractive red-brick gem	$59–$79		150			yes		1		
International Drive											
DoubleTree Castle	medieval castle theme	$99–$169	216			2			1		
Embassy Suites I-Drive South	marble lobby	$129–$189		244		1			2		
Embassy Suites Jamaican Court	comfy two-room suites	$139–$179		246					1		
Enclave Suites	large condo complex	$79–$179	321		yes				3		
Extended Stay America Convention Ctr.	budget suites near SeaWorld	$45–$55		113	yes		yes		1		
Extended Stay Deluxe Orlando Convention Ctr.	business-traveler favorite	$99–$129		262	yes				1		

Holiday Inn Hotel & Suites	bright-yellow, cheerful hotel	$99–$169	115	35		1				2		
International Plaza Resort & Spa	no-frills budget property	$190–$219	1102	68	yes	3				3		
★ JW Marriott Orlando Grande Lakes	business-traveler favorite	$199–$349	1000	57		4				1	yes	1 course
La Quinta Inn & Suites Orlando	off-the-beaten-path chain	$121–$159	170	15						1		
Marriott Residence Inn SeaWorld	grills & playground	$129–$154		350	yes			yes	yes	1		
Marriott's Cypress Harbour Resort	lots of outdoor activities	$191–$279		510		2		yes	yes	3		priv.
Parc Corniche Condominium Suites	Joe Lee golf course	$99–$129		210		1		yes	yes	1		1 course
★ Peabody Orlando	loveable ducks live here	$259–$357	891			3				1	yes	priv.
Renaissance Orlando at SeaWorld	10-story tropical atrium	$200–$269	778			4				1		priv.
★ Ritz-Carlton Orlando Grande Lakes	excellent service; fit for royalty	$249–$399	520	64		4	yes			1	yes	1 course
Rosen Centre Hotel	gaudy convention hotel	$140–$279	1334	80		3				1		
Rosen Plaza Hotel	cheap with lots of amenities	$99–$129	810			2				1		
Rosen Shingle Creek	many recreation options	$199–$419	1,500	109		3	yes			4	yes	1 course
Sheraton Studio City	Hollywood theme	$99–$129	302			1				1		
Staybridge Suites International Drive	modern budget suites	$129–$189		146	yes	1				1		
Wyndham Orlando Resort	Caribbean-style getaway	$156–$179	1064			3				3		
Wynfield Inn Orlando Convention Ctr.	small rooms with balconies	$79–$109	144			1				2		
Downtown Orlando												
★ Courtyard at Lake Lucerne	Victorian B&Bs	$120–$225	15	15								
Embassy Suites Orlando Downtown	up-to-date & well-located	$135–$175	167			1				1	yes	
★ Eō Inn & Urban Spa	stylish boutique hotel	$129–$179	17									
Westin Grand Bohemian	sumptuous rooms & artwork	$209–$299	250	36		1				1		
Orlando International Airport												
AmeriSuites Orlando Airport NE & NW	budget suites near airport	$99–$179	263							1		

HOTEL NAME	Worth Noting	Cost	Rooms	Suites/Villas	Kitchens	Restaurants	Kids' Programs	Playground	Pools	Spa	Golf
Florida Hotel & Conference Ctr.	walk to the mall	$136–$229	510			1			1		
Hyatt Regency Orlando Intl. Airport	restaurant with a view	$199–$224	446			2			1		
Outlying Towns											
Best Western Maingate South	close to Davenport	$69–$120	113						1		
Hampton Inn Maingate South	13 mi south of WDW	$99–$149	83						1		
Holiday Inn Express Disney South	15 mi south of WDW	$75–$129	104						1		
Park Plaza Hotel Winter Park	1922 boutique hotel	$129–$245	27			1					

DAVENPORT

Take I–4 Exit 55. The beauty of Davenport is that virtually no one in Orlando has ever heard of it, even though it's only 13 mi southwest of Disney's south entrance. The relative obscurity of this town makes it a bargain oasis. If you don't mind the absence of nightlife and entertainment, you'll save 30% or more at Davenport hotels, which surround I–4 at Exit 55, compared with the same chains on I-Drive. Both areas are about the same distance from Disney but in opposite directions.

HAMPTON INN ORLANDO MAINGATE SOUTH

$-$$ 🏨 They've taken some poetic (or marketing) license with the name here. For the record, the hotel is 27 mi from Disney's main entrance. The park's south entrance is 13 mi away, however, and the hotel offers good bargains and access to attractions west of Orlando, like Cypress Gardens and Fantasy of Flight. Rooms are bright and pleasant—some come with DVD players—and you get a free hot breakfast and local phone calls. Pros: lots of freebies (Disney shuttle, breakfast, local calls); small pets allowed (nonrefundable $50 deposit); good location—easy drive to Disney, the Orlando metro area, and even Tampa (an hour west). Con: Davenport is more nondescript interstate stop than picturesque hamlet. ✉44117 U.S. 27 N, Davenport 33897 ☎863/420–9898 ⊕*www.hamptoninn.com* ⇨*83 rooms* ♿*In-room: Ethernet. In-hotel: pool, laundry facilities, no-smoking rooms* ▤*AE, D, DC, MC, V* ⊖*CP.*

BEST WESTERN MAINGATE SOUTH

¢-$ 🏨 The hotel is nothing extraordinary, but offers a nice palm-lined courtyard with a swimming pool and outdoor hot tub. Rooms, with pink-and-blue floral-pattern spreads and blue carpets, are pleasant but not palatial. There's no restaurant, but a Bob Evans Family Restaurant is just across the parking lot, and there's a free Continental breakfast in a small dining area adjacent to the lobby. Pros: free breakfast; free Disney shuttle; small pets allowed ($10 per night fee); easy drive to WDW and Orlando metro area. Cons: shuttles to Seaworld and Universal cost $15 round trip; it's in less-than-picturesque Davenport. ✉2425 Frontage Rd., Davenport 33837 ☎863/424–2596 or 800/424–1880 ⊕*www.bestwestern.com* ⇨*113 rooms* ♿*In-room: Ethernet. In-hotel: pool, laundry facilities, no-smoking rooms, some pets allowed (fee)* ▤*AE, D, DC, MC, V* ⊖*CP.*

WINTER PARK

Take I–4 Exit 87 or 88. Winter Park, a small college town and greater Orlando's poshest and best-established area, is full of chichi shops and restaurants. If its heart is the main thoroughfare of Park Avenue, then its soul must be Central Park, an inviting greensward dotted with huge trees hung with Spanish moss. It feels a million miles from the tourist track, but it's just a short drive from the major attractions.

PARK PLAZA HOTEL

$–$$$ 🖼 Small and intimate, this 1922 establishment feels almost like a private home. Best accommodations are front garden suites with a living room that opens onto a long balcony usually abloom with impatiens and bougainvillea. Balconies are so covered with shrubs and ferns that they are somewhat private, inspiring more than a few romantic interludes. A half-dozen sidewalk cafés and many more upscale boutiques and shops surround the hotel. Also, the Charles Hosmer Morse Museum of Art is within two blocks. Park Plaza Gardens, the restaurant downstairs, offers quiet atrium dining and excellent food. Pros: romantic; great balconies overlooking Park Avenue; short walk to shops and restaurants. Cons: no small children allowed; small rooms; Disney is 60 minutes away. ✉ *307 Park Ave. S, Winter Park 32789* ☎ *407/647–1072 or 800/228–7220* ⊕ *www.parkplazahotel.com* ⬈ *27 rooms* ♿ *In-room: Ethernet. In-hotel: restaurant, room service, laundry service, public Wi-Fi, no kids under 5, no-smoking rooms* 🚐 *AE, DC, MC, V.*

Getting There & Getting Around

WORD OF MOUTH

"Try taking the launch from the Contemporary to the Wilderness Lodge (and back again!). The gentle ride is relaxing and very beautiful on a warm evening. If you time your ride just right, you'll be able to watch the Magic Kingdom's fireworks show, Wishes, from the water. The boat captain will dim the onboard lights and maybe even let the boat idle during the show so that you can watch it to the very end. Even though you miss some of the ground effects, it's truly a unique and breathtaking view of the fireworks!"

—ajcolorado

THOUSANDS OF VISITORS FLY INTO Orlando daily for a dose of vacation magic. Getting here is easy with the abundance of flights available from all destinations. Once you arrive, you'll have your pick of ground transportation options, including shuttles, taxis, limos, and rental cars. If you're booked into a Walt Disney World Resort, take advantage of the Magical Express Service that delivers you and your luggage, at no cost, from your home airport to your hotel and back again (you must book this service before departing on your trip). Disney's own fleet of buses, trams, boats, and monorail trains make it a breeze to travel throughout Mickey's world. If you're eager to explore beyond the theme parks, be sure to have a good, up-to-date map—Orlando is a sprawling metropolitan area and some areas can be tricky to traverse.

FLYING TO ORLANDO

Revised by
Jennie Hess

All major and most discount airlines, including American, Northwest, US Airways, Southwest, JetBlue, Spirit, Ted, and ATA fly to **Orlando International Airport** ((MCO) ☎407/825–2001 ⊕ *www.orlandoairports.net*), which serves as a hub for Delta and AirTran. The airport is divided into two terminals, A and B, and is easy to navigate thanks to excellent signs. Monorails shuttle you from gates to the core area, where you'll find baggage claim. The airport is southeast of Orlando and northeast of Walt Disney World.

Flying times are 2½ hours from New York, 3½ hours from Chicago, and 5 hours from Los Angeles.

Don't forget to reconfirm your flight before you leave for the airport. Orlando's frequent summer storms can cause delays or even cancellations. You can do this on your carrier's Web site, by linking to a flight-status checker (many Web booking services offer these), or by calling your carrier or travel agent.

BOOKING YOUR FLIGHT

Unless your cousin is a travel agent, you're probably among the millions of people who make most of their travel arrangements online. Here are some options to help you get started.

DISCOUNTERS & WHOLESALERS

A **discounter** is a firm that does a high volume of business with an airline and, accordingly, gets good prices. A **wholesaler** makes cheap reservations in bulk and then resells them to people like you. Shop around. You may find a deal not available elsewhere, but you must generally prepay, and everything is nonrefundable. Before booking, check terms and conditions so that you know what a company will do for you if there's a problem.

Discounters & Wholesalers **Cheap Tickets** (⊕ *www.cheaptickets.com*). **Hotwire** (⊕ *www.hotwire.com*). **Onetravel.com** (⊕ *www.onetravel.com*). **Priceline.com** (⊕ *www.priceline.com*) is a discounter that also allows bidding.

ONLINE TRAVEL AGENTS

Expedia (⊕*www.expedia.com*) is a large online agency that charges a booking fee for airline tickets. **Orbitz** (⊕*www.orbitz.com*) charges a booking fee for airline tickets, but gives a clear breakdown of fees and taxes before you book. **Travelocity** (⊕*www.travelocity.com*) charges a booking fee for airline tickets, but promises good problem resolution.

■ TIP➔ Remember that Expedia, Travelocity, and Orbitz are travel agents, not just booking engines. To resolve any problems with a reservation made through these companies, contact them first.

Major Airlines **AirTran** (☎800/247–8726 ⊕www.airtran.com). **Alaska Airlines** (☎800/252–7522 ⊕www.alaskaair.com). **American** (☎800/433–7300 ⊕www.aa.com). **Continental** (☎800/523–3273 ⊕www.continental.com). **Delta** (☎800/221–1212 ⊕www.delta.com). **Northwest/KLM** (☎800/225–2525 ⊕www.nwa.com). **United Airlines** (☎800/241–6522 ⊕www.united.com). **US Airways/America West Airlines** (☎800/428–4322 ⊕www.usairways.com).

Smaller Airlines **ATA** (☎800/225–2995 ⊕www.ata.com). **Frontier** (☎800/432–1359 ⊕www.frontierairlines.com). **JetBlue** (☎800/538–2583 ⊕www.jetblue. com). **Midwest Express** (☎800/452–2022 ⊕www.midwestairlines.com). **Southwest** (☎800/435–9792 ⊕www.iflyswa.com). **Spirit** (☎800/772–7117 ⊕www. spiritair.com).

TRANSFERRING FROM THE AIRPORT

BY TAXI, LIMO & SHUTTLE

Taxi fares start at $3.50 for the first mile and add $2 for each mile thereafter. The fare from the airport to the Walt Disney World area can run $50–$60. If there are four or more people in your party, taking a taxi may cost less than paying by the head for an airport shuttle.

Mears Transportation Group meets you at the gate, helps with the luggage, and whisks you away in either an 11-passenger van, a town car, or a limo. Vans run to Walt Disney World, International Drive, and along U.S. 192 in Kissimmee every 30 minutes; prices range from $19 one-way for ($15 for children 4–11) to $31 round-trip ($23 children 4–11). Limo rates run $60–$70 for a town car that accommodates three or four to $155 for a stretch limo that seats eight. Town & Country Transportation charges $150 one-way for a limo seating up to seven or eight people depending on luggage needs.

If you're staying at a Disney hotel (excluding the Walt Disney World Swan, Dolphin, and Downtown Disney Resort area hotels), make arrangements to use Disney's free Magical Express service, which includes shuttle transportation to and from the airport, luggage delivery, and baggage check-in at the hotel. You can't book the service once you've arrived at the airport, so be sure to reserve ahead.

Transport Contacts **A-1 Taxi** (☎407/328–4555). **Ace Metro Cab** (☎407/855–1111). **Checker Cab Company** (☎407/699–9999). **Magical Express service** (☎866/599–0951). **Mears Transportation Group** (☎407/423–5566 ⊕www.

Flying 101

Think about schedules. Don't buy a ticket if there's less than an hour between connecting flights. Although schedules are padded, if anything goes wrong you might miss your connection. If you're traveling to an important function, depart; a day early.

Get the seat you want. Often, you can pick a seat when you buy your ticket on an airline Web site. But the airline could change the plane after you book, so double-check. You can also select a seat if you check in electronically. Avoid seats on the aisle directly across from the lavatories. Frequent fliers say those are even worse than back-row seats that don't recline.

Got kids? Get info. Ask the airline about its children's menus, activities, and fares. Sometimes infants and toddlers fly free if they sit on a parent's lap, and older children fly for half price in their own seats. Also inquire about policies involving car seat; having one may limit seating options. Also ask about seat-belt extenders for car seats. And note that you can't count on a flight attendant to produce an extender; you may have to ask for one when you board.

Check baggage weight and size limitations. In the United States you may be charged extra for checked bags weighing more than 50 pounds or less. Carry-on size limitations can be stringent, too.

Check carry-on restrictions. Research restrictions with the TSA (www.tsa.gov). Consider packing all but essentials (travel documents, prescription meds, wallet) in checked luggage. This leads to a "pack only what you can afford to lose" approach that might help you streamline.

Pack to avoid delays at security checkpoints. Don't pack any sharp objects in your carry-on luggage, including knives of any size or material, scissors, corkscrews, or anything else that might arouse suspicion, and carry medications in their original packaging. Be prepared to turn on your laptop or other electronic equipment to prove to airport security that the device is real. Also, be prepared to remove jewelry, belts, shoes, and other items that can set off detectors.

Rethink valuables. On U.S. flights, airlines are liable for only about $2,800 per person for bags. But items like computers, cameras, and jewelry aren't covered, and as gadgetry can go on and off the list of carry-on no-no's, you can't count on keeping things safe by keeping them close. Although comprehensive travel policies may cover luggage, the liability limit is often a pittance. Your home-owner's policy may cover you sufficiently when you travel—or not.

Lock it up and tag it. If you must pack valuables, use TSA-approved locks (about $10) that can be unlocked by all U.S. security personnel. Always tag your luggage; use your business address if you don't want people to know your home address. Put the same information (and a copy of your itinerary) inside your luggage, too.

Double-check flight times. Do this especially if you reserved far in advance. Schedules change, and alerts may not reach you.

Minimize the time spent standing line. Buy an e-ticket, check in at an electronic kiosk, or—even better—check in on your airline's Web site before leaving home. Pack light and limit carry-on items to only the essentials.

Bring paper. Even when using an e-ticket, always carry a printed copy of your receipt; you may need it to get your boarding pass, which most airports require to get past security.

Arrive at the airport when you need to. Research your airline's policy. It's usually at least an hour to 90 minutes before domestic flights and two to three hours before international flights. But airlines at some busy airports have more stringent requirements. Check the TSA Web site (www.tsa.gov) for estimated security waiting times at major airports. OIA has been ranked number one in the nation repeatedly by J.D. Powers and Associates for customer satisfaction in terms of security and service. The Orlando–New York route is the busiest for OIA.

Get to the gate. If you aren't at the gate at least 10 minutes before your flight is scheduled to take off (sometimes earlier), you won't be allowed to board.

Beware of overbooked flights. If a flight is oversold, the gate agent will usually ask for volunteers and offer some sort of compensation for taking a different flight. If you're bumped from a flight *involuntarily,* the airline must give you some kind of compensation if an alternate flight can't be found within one hour.

Be prepared. The Boy Scout motto is especially important if you're traveling during a stormy season. To quickly adjust your plans, program a few numbers into your cell: your airline, an airport hotel or two, your destination hotel, a car service, and/or your travel agent.

Know your rights. If your flight is delayed because of something within the airline's control (bad weather doesn't count), the airline must get you to your destination on the same day, even if they have to book you on another airline and in an upgraded class. Read the Contract of Carriage, which is usually buried on the airline's Web site.

Report problems immediately. If your bags—or things in them—are damaged or go astray, file a written claim with your airline *before leaving the airport.* If the airline is at fault, it may give you money for essentials until your luggage arrives. Most lost bags are found within 48 hours, so alert the airline to your whereabouts for two or three days. If your bag was opened for security reasons and something is missing, file a claim with the TSA.

3

Getting the Best Airfare

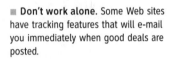

■ **Remember: nonrefundable is best.** If saving money is more important than flexibility, then nonrefundable tickets work. Just remember that you'll pay dearly (as much as $100) if you change your plans.

■ **Comparison shop.** Web sites and travel agents can have different arrangements with the airlines and offer different prices for exactly the same flights.

■ **Stay loyal.** Stick with one or two frequent-flier programs. You'll rack up free trips and perks like early boarding or access to upgrates.

■ **Watch ticketing fees.** Surcharges are usually added when you buy your ticket anywhere but on an airline Web site.

■ **Check early and often.** Start looking for cheap fares up to a year in advance. Keep looking till you find a price you like, then jump on a great deal before you lose it.

■ **Don't work alone.** Some Web sites have tracking features that will e-mail you immediately when good deals are posted.

■ **Be flexible.** Look for departures on Tuesday, Wednesday, and Thursday, typically the cheapest days to travel.

■ **Weigh your options.** What you get can be as important as what you save. A cheaper flight might have a long layover, or it might land at a secondary airport, where your ground transportation costs might be higher.

mearstransportation.com). **Star Taxi** (☎*407/857–9999*). **Town & Country Transportation** (☎*407/828–3035*). **Yellow Cab Co.** (☎*407/422–2222*).

RENTING A CAR

You should rent a car if you're staying at an off-site hotel; you want to visit sights or restaurants outside Walt Disney World; you're traveling in a group (four or more people); you like your independence.

On the other hand, if you're staying at a Disney hotel and spending all or most of your trip at Disney World, you can rely on Disney's own very efficient transportation system.

BOOKING YOUR CAR

RATES & REGULATIONS

Rates are among the lowest in the United States, but vary seasonally. They can begin as low as $30 a day and $149 a week for an economy car with air-conditioning, automatic transmission, and unlimited mileage. This does not include tax on car rentals, which is 6.5%. ■TIP→**Renting from Avis or Budget can get you out of the airport the fastest because they have car lots on airport property, a short walk from baggage claim.** The other agencies offer bus transportation to their lots.

In Florida, some agencies require that you be at least 21 to rent a car. Others require that you be 25.

RENTAL INSURANCE

If you own a car and carry comprehensive car insurance for both collision and liability, your personal auto insurance will probably cover a rental, but check with your insurance agent or read your policy's fine print to be sure. If you don't have auto insurance, then you should probably buy the collision- or loss-damage waiver (CDW or LDW) from the rental company. This eliminates your liability for damage to the car.

Some credit cards offer CDW coverage, but it's usually supplemental to your own insurance and rarely covers SUVs, minivans, luxury models, and the like. If your coverage is secondary, you may still be liable for loss-of-use costs from the car-rental company (again, read the fine print). But no credit-card insurance is valid unless you use that card for *all* transactions, from reserving to paying the final bill.

■TIP→**Diners Club offers primary CDW coverage on all rentals reserved and paid for with the card. This means that Diners Club's company—not your own car insurance—pays in case of an accident. It *doesn't* mean that your car-insurance company won't raise your rates once it discovers you had an accident.**

You may also be offered supplemental liability coverage; the car-rental company is required to carry a minimal level of liability coverage insuring all renters, but it's rarely enough to cover claims in a really serious accident if you're at fault. Your own auto-insurance policy will protect you if you own a car; if you don't, you have to decide whether you are willing to take the risk.

U.S. rental companies sell CDWs and LDWs for about $15 to $25 a day; supplemental liability is usually more than $10 a day. The car-rental company may offer you all sorts of other policies, but they're rarely worth the cost. Personal accident insurance, which is basic hospitalization coverage, is an especially egregious rip-off if you already have health insurance.

■TIP→**You can decline the insurance from the rental company and purchase it through a third-party provider such as Travel Guard (www.travelguard.com)—$9 per day for $35,000 of coverage. That's sometimes just under half the price of the CDW offered by some car-rental companies.**

MAJOR RENTAL AGENCIES **Alamo** (☎ *800/327–9633* ⊕ *www.alamo.com*). **Avis** (☎ *800/331–1212* ⊕ *www.avis.com*). **Budget** (☎ *800/527–0700* ⊕ *www.budget.com*). **Dollar** (☎ *800/800–4000* ⊕ *www.dollar.com*). **Hertz** (☎ *800/654–3131* ⊕ *www.hertz.com*). **National Car Rental** (☎ *800/227–7368* ⊕ *www.nationalcar.com*).

LOCAL AGENCY **Carl's Rent A Van** (☎ *800/565–5211* ⊕ *www.orlandovanrentals.com*).

CLOSE UP

How to Save on Cars

■ **Confirm all charges.** Those great rates aren't so great when you add in taxes, surcharges, and insurance. Such extras can double or triple the initial quote.

■ **Rent weekly.** Weekly rates are usually better than daily ones. Even if you only want to rent for five or six days, ask for the weekly rate; it may very well be cheaper than the daily rate for that period of time.

■ **Fill up farther away.** Avoid hefty refueling fees by filling the tank at a station well away from where you plan to turn in the car.

■ **Pump it yourself.** Don't buy the tank of gas that's in the car when you

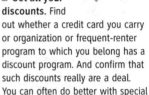

rent it unless you plan to do a lot of driving.

■ **Get all your discounts.** Find out whether a credit card you carry or organization or frequent-renter program to which you belong has a discount program. And confirm that such discounts really are a deal. You can often do better with special weekend or weekly rates offered by a rental agency.

■ **Check out packages.** Adding a car rental onto your air/hotel vacation package may be cheaper than renting a car separately.

DRIVING AROUND ORLANDO

The Beachline Expressway (formerly called the Beeline, aka Route 528) is the best way to get to the International Drive (also known as I-Drive) area and Walt Disney World from the OIA, though you'll pay up to $2 in tolls. Depending on the location of your hotel, follow the expressway west to International Drive, and either exit at SeaWorld for the International Drive area or stay on the Beachline to I–4 and head west for Walt Disney World and U.S. 192/Kissimmee or east for Universal Studios and downtown Orlando. Call your hotel for the best route.

I–4 is the main artery in Central Florida, linking the Gulf coast in Tampa to the Atlantic coast in Daytona Beach. Although I–4 is an east–west highway, it actually follows a north–south track through the Orlando area. ■ TIP→ **Think north when I-4 signs say east and think south when the signs say west.**

Two other main roads you're likely to use are International Drive and U.S. 192, sometimes called the Spacecoast Parkway or Irlo Bronson Memorial Highway. You can get onto International Drive from I–4 Exits 72, 74A, and 75A. U.S. 192 cuts across I–4 at Exits 64A and 64B.

Walt Disney World has four exits off I–4. For the Magic Kingdom, Disney–MGM Studios, Disney's Animal Kingdom, Fort Wilderness, and the rest of the Magic Kingdom resort area, take the one marked **Magic Kingdom–U.S. 192 (Exit 64B)**. Watch for possible detours at

Exit 64B, where extended construction is underway indefinitely to reconfigure the interchange and widen both U.S. 192 and I–4. (From here, it's a 4-mi drive along Disney's main entrance road to the toll gate, and another mile to the parking area; during peak vacation periods, be prepared for serious bumper-to-bumper traffic both on I–4 nearing the U.S. 192 exit and on U.S. 192 itself. A less-congested route to the theme parks and other WDW venues is via the exit marked **Epcot/Downtown Disney (Exit 67)**, 4 mi east of Exit 64.

Exit 65 will take you directly to Disney's Animal Kingdom and Wide World of Sports as well as the Animal Kingdom resort area via the Osceola Parkway.

For access to Downtown Disney (including the Marketplace, Disney-Quest, Pleasure Island, and West Side), as well as to Typhoon Lagoon, the Crossroads Shopping Center, and the establishments on Hotel Plaza Boulevard, get off at **Route 535–Lake Buena Vista (Exit 68).**

The exit marked **Epcot–Downtown Disney (Exit 67)** is the one to use if you're bound for those destinations or for hotels in the Epcot and Downtown Disney resort areas; you can also get to Typhoon Lagoon and the Studios from here.

RULES OF THE ROAD

All front-seat passengers are required to wear seat belts. All children under 4 years old must be in approved child-safety seats. Children older than 4 must wear a seat belt.

Florida's Alcohol/Controlled Substance DUI Law is one of the toughest in the United States. A blood alcohol level of 0.08 or higher can have serious repercussions even for the first-time offender.

In Florida, you may turn right at a red light after stopping, unless otherwise posted. When in doubt, wait for the green. Be alert for one-way streets, "no left turn" intersections, and blocks closed to car traffic. Watch for middle lanes with painted arrows that point left. These are turn lanes. They are to help you make a left turn without disrupting the flow of traffic behind you. Turn your blinker on, pull into this lane, and come to a stop, if necessary, before making a left turn. Never use this lane as a passing lane.

Expect heavy traffic during rush hours, which are on weekdays 6–10 AM and 4–7 PM. To encourage carpooling, some freeways have special lanes for so-called high-occupancy vehicles (HOV)—cars carrying more than one passenger. The use of radar detectors is legal in Florida and its neighboring states, Alabama and Georgia. Although it's legal to talk on your cell phone while driving in Florida, it's not recommended. Dial *511 on a cell phone to hear an I–4 traffic advisory.

EMERGENCY SERVICES

If you have a cell phone, dialing *347 (*FHP) will get you the Florida Highway Patrol. Most Florida highways are also patrolled by Road Rangers, a free roadside service that helps stranded motorists with minor problems and can call for a tow truck when there are bigger problems. The **AAA Car Care Center** (☎407/824–0976) near the Magic Kingdom is a full-service operation that will provide most emergency services, except towing, while it's open (weekdays 7 AM–6 PM, Saturday 7 AM–4 PM). On Disney property you can flag a security guard any day until 10 PM for help with minor emergencies, such as a flat tire, dead battery, empty gas tank, or towing. Otherwise call 407/824–4777. You can also gas up on Buena Vista Drive near Disney's BoardWalk and in the Downtown Disney area across from Pleasure Island.

TRANSPORTATION WITHIN WDW

Walt Disney World has its own free transportation system of buses, trams, monorail trains, and boats that can take you wherever you want to go. If you're staying on Disney property, you can use this system exclusively. In general, allow up to an hour to travel between parks and hotels.

If you're park hopping, consider using your own car to save time. There can be 30-minute waits for park-provided bus transportation. Your parking pass is good at any of the theme parks, and parking is free if you're a resort guest.

BY BOAT

Motor launches connect WDW destinations on waterways. Specifically, they operate from the Epcot resorts—except the Caribbean Beach—to the Studios and Epcot; between Bay Lake and the Magic Kingdom; and also between Fort Wilderness, the Wilderness Lodge, and the Polynesian, Contemporary, and Grand Floridian resorts. Launches from Old Key West, Saratoga Springs, and Port Orleans all travel to Downtown Disney, as well.

BY BUS

Buses provide direct service from every on-site resort to both major and minor theme parks, and express buses go directly between the major theme parks. You can go directly from or make connections at Downtown Disney, Epcot, and the Epcot resorts, including the Yacht and Beach Clubs, BoardWalk, the Caribbean Beach Resort, the Swan, and the Dolphin, as well as to Disney's Animal Kingdom and the Animal Kingdom resorts (the Animal Kingdom Lodge, the All-Star, and Coronado Springs resorts).

Buses to the Magic Kingdom all go straight to the turnstiles, allowing you to avoid the extra step of boarding a monorail or boat at the Ticket and Transportation Center (TTC) to get to the front of the Kingdom.

BY MONORAIL

The elevated monorail serves many important destinations. It has two loops: one linking the Magic Kingdom, TTC, and a handful of resorts (including the Contemporary, the Grand Floridian, and the Polynesian), the other looping from the TTC directly to Epcot. Before this monorail line pulls into the station, the elevated track passes through Future World—Epcot's northern half—and circles the giant silver geosphere housing the Spaceship Earth ride to give you a preview of what you'll see.

BY TRAM

Trams operate from the parking lot to the entrance of each theme park. If you parked fairly close in, though, you may save time, especially at park closing time, by walking.

DRIVING & PARKING IN WALT DISNEY WORLD

Sections of the Magic Kingdom lot are named for Disney characters; Epcot's highlights modes of exploration; those at the Studios are named Stage, Music, Film, and Dance; and the Animal Kingdom's sound like Beanie Baby names—Unicorn, Butterfly, and so on. Although in theory Goofy 45 is unforgettable, by the end of the day, you'll be so goofy with eating and shopping and riding that you'll swear that you parked in Sleepy. ■ TIP➡**When you board the tram, write down your parking-lot location and keep it in a pocket.** Trams make frequent trips between the parking area and the parks' turnstile areas. No valet parking is available for Walt Disney World theme parks.

For each major theme-park lot, admission is $10 for cars, $11 for RVs and campers, and free to those staying at Walt Disney World resorts. Save your receipt; if you want to visit another park the same day, you won't have to pay to park twice. If you have reservations at a Disney resort, check in early (leave baggage at the bell station if you wish) and ask for your free parking permit.

Parking is always free at Typhoon Lagoon, Blizzard Beach, Downtown Disney, and Disney's BoardWalk. You can valet park at BoardWalk for $10. Although valet parking is available at Downtown Disney, the congestion there is sometimes such that it may be faster to park in Siberia and walk. (Hint: arrive at Downtown Disney early in the evening—around 6 PM—and you'll get a much closer parking space; you'll also avoid long restaurant lines.) ■ TIP➡**At Disney's BoardWalk, you park in the hotel lot, where valets are available as well.**

4

Walt Disney World with Kids

WORD OF MOUTH

"We went when our nieces were 3 and 5 and had a great time, but personally, I would think kids younger than that won't really get much out of it."

—AustinTraveler

"You may run into naysayers who will try to discourage your taking toddlers to WDW. Smile politely and ignore everything they have to say. My toddlers *loved* Disney World."

—ajcolorado

"With a small child in tow I would definitely stay on the property somewhere and as close as possible to the attractions I wanted to see most, and use the WDW transportation system to get back and forth."

—Intrepid1

www.fodors.com/forums

Revised by
Jennie Hess

TRY TO WATCH YOUR CHILD'S face as he or she first steps foot into one of the Disney World parks. For many parents, grandparents, guardians, aunts, uncles, etc., half the fun of the trip is seeing Disney World through the eyes of the children accompanying them. Of course the rides wow them, but often it's the little things—the barbershop quartet singing away on Main Street, the fanciful architecture, the dancing park fountains—that impress the most.

The secret to enjoying Disney with children is to have a good plan but be willing to take small detours when magical moments occur. You can probably persuade your children to rush to the big-deal rides early in the morning, when the timing matters most, but don't expect them to keep up that pace all day. Cushion your itinerary with extra time and allow them to pause wherever they want as much as possible. When it comes to a Disney vacation with kids, let your mantra be "quality over quantity." It's better to tour the parks in a relaxed fashion than it is to antagonize your little ones by fleeing to Pirates of the Caribbean, passing up an opportunity to hobnob with Princess Jasmine along the way, only to find a 30-minute wait at the entrance to the ride. Jasmine definitely won't be there when you get out of the ride.

Finally, try to avoid building unrealistic expectations for yourself and your kids that may cause disappointment and tears. Let each family member choose one or two top rides or attractions for each park, and be sure those are part of your itinerary. Everything else should be icing on the cake. Run through the plan before you enter the park; if children know ahead of time that souvenirs are limited to one per person and that ice-cream snacks come after lunch, they're likely to be more patient than if they're clueless about your plans and dazzled by every snack and merchandise cart they discover. If you're towing an infant or toddler, be prepared to relax on a park bench while your little one snoozes in the stroller. Don't think about which ride you're missing while the rest of the family decides to ride and meet you later. Just kick back and soak up some of the remarkable detail that Disney's funmeisters have built into the enchanting scenery that surrounds you.

IS MY CHILD OLD ENOUGH?

Simply stated, Disney really does have something for everyone and we've heard parents say that even their infants were wowed by the sights and sounds. Cleverly designed playgrounds for toddlers abound, and many attractions have elements that appeal to all ages: jokes for the parents and older kids, and animatronics that move and sing for the babes. In addition, as part of the Magic Your Way Package Plus Dining plan, 1- and 2-year-olds can eat from a parent's plate at any restaurant at no charge, even when the restaurant serves buffet style.

All that said, there are many experiences very young children cannot enjoy—many of us probably remember a moment in early childhood when we went to an amusement park only to be turned away from the coolest rides because we didn't reach the height limit. Below is a list of advantages and disadvantages to bringing kids under six years old to the Orlando theme parks.

ADVANTAGES

Babies and tots under 3 get into the parks for free, so if you're planning a trip to Disney mainly for an older sibling, go for it.

If your children are in preschool, you can come during the off-season when the crowds are thinner and lines are shorter. It's harder for kids to miss school once they're immersed in the Renaissance and puzzling over fractions.

DISADVANTAGES

Will your 4-year-old even remember her trip to Disney after a couple of years?

You may want to go on repeat rides of the Twilight Zone Tower of Terror and Space Mountain, but any child under age 6 will probably want to ride Dumbo 100 times, splash in the fountains outside Ariel's Grotto, and collect signatures from people dressed in funny outfits.

You can still enjoy thrill attractions by taking advantage of the Baby Swap system, but you'll wind up riding with strangers instead of holding hands with your honey. The upside is that you'll meet someone new from just about anywhere in the world.

Very young children are often quite shy and easily frightened by loud noises, bright lights, and sudden movements. If your child is, he may be overwhelmed by many of the best theme-park experiences, including the 3-D shows, which don't have a minimum height.

Many children are actually seriously intimidated, and sometimes downright scared, by the characters, who are much, much larger in real life than on your TV screen.

Toddlers can get pretty impatient and cranky when they're made to adhere to adult schedules, not to mention wait repeatedly in the hot Florida sun or go on rides that may be too scary for them. Do you really want to spend $60-plus a day to whisk your uncomprehending tot around the parks trying to beat the crowds?

Clearly, there are some smart arguments against bringing your 5-and-under children to the theme parks. Of course, millions of parents do this every year and, although they may not ride as many roller coasters as other people, they certainly have a good time. Just remember to stay flexible. If the line for Snow White's Scary Adventures is 40 minutes, skip it and let your children choose another ride or show. This strategy may result in more walking back and forth, but it's probably worth it to keep young children out of long tiresome lines.

Avoiding a Meltdown

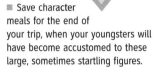

■ Avoid crowded times of year (during school holidays, for example) and plan your itinerary around the days of the week and times of day when the parks are the least busy.

■ Bring a stroller, or <u>rent one</u> at the parks. Your child may have plenty of energy and be a great walker on a normal day, but something about pounding the pavement under the hot sun for six to nine hours can really take its toll.

■ <u>Pack hats</u> or visors for everyone, and insist on applying sunscreen several times daily to avoid painful sunburns that could ruin a vacation.

■ Get everybody in your family, including your children, to agree to certain basic touring plans, such as getting up early and taking afternoon naps. At the same time, leave room in your schedule to take a detour and be flexible.

■ Eat at off times to avoid crowds.

■ Give yourself more time than you think you need, and buy park-hopper tickets so that you can always go back and see what you've missed another day.

■ Even with Fastpass, you may end up in a line or two. <u>Pack snacks and</u>

<u>handheld</u>
<u>games t</u>o
keep boredom at bay.

■ Save character meals for the end of your trip, when your youngsters will have become accustomed to these large, sometimes startling figures.

■ Plan for family time away from the theme parks. Spend a day at the pool or get away to the Historic Bok Sanctuary or Wekiva Springs State park.

■ Familiarize yourself with all age and height restrictions. Ideally, you should measure young children ahead of time so they won't get excited about rides they're too short to experience. However, most rides have premeasuring signs at the entrance to the queuing area, so even if you don't know how tall your child is, you won't have to wait in line before finding out.

■ Finally, be prepared for family disagreements and even tantrums. Chances are, they'll happen. Possible solutions include splitting up or leaving the parks. Missing out on a few rides while allowing everyone to cool down is better than forcing the tour to continue and testing frayed nerves.

CHILDREN IN THE PARKS

PRACTICAL INFO

STROLLER RENTALS

Renting lightweight, highly maneuverable strollers at the theme parks costs $10 to $18 a day depending on the size of the stroller. They come with a large, visible, white card on which you can write your name. Another good trick for identifying your stroller quickly is to attach a colorful bandana or T-shirt to it. Of course, it's never good to leave valuables in your stroller. Despite precautions, there's always the possibility that your stroller will be taken, probably by mistake because all the strollers look alike. Also, well-intentioned Disney cast members will organize strollers in a parking area. If you exit a ride to find your stroller isn't where you left it, look for it among the other strollers in the area. If you still can't find it, notify a cast member. You can pick up a new

stroller free of charge if you've kept your rental receipt. If you're park hopping on the same day, turn in your old stroller when you leave the first park and show your receipt to get a new stroller at the entrance to the next park.

If you're staying in a room, suite, or condo and need to rent baby equipment, such as a stroller, bassinet, high chair, or even pool toys, call **A Baby's Best Friend** (☎ *407/891–2241 or 888/461–BABY toll-free in the U.S.* ⊕ *www.abbf.com*), for swift delivery and fair rates. You can order online, and the company also carries refrigerators and microwaves if your hotel or resort doesn't provide them.

BABY CARE

The Magic Kingdom's soothing, quiet **Baby Care Center** is next to the Crystal Palace, which lies between Main Street and Adventureland. The other three major Disney parks have similar baby care centers with nursing rooms furnished with rocking chairs. Low lighting levels make these centers comfortable for nursing, though it can get crowded in midafternoon in peak season. There are adorable toddler-size toilets (these may be a high point for your just-potty-trained child) as well as supplies such as formula, baby food, pacifiers, disposable diapers, and even children's pain reliever. Changing tables are in all women's rooms and most men's rooms.

THE BABY SWAP SYSTEM

Parents with small children under the height limit for major attractions have to take turns waiting in the long lines, right? Wrong. In what's unofficially known as the Baby Swap, both of you queue up, and when it's your turn to board, one stays with the youngsters until the other returns; the waiting partner then rides without waiting again. Universal Studios calls it a Baby Exchange and has areas set aside for it at most rides.

LOST CHILDREN

Losing a child in a crowded theme park is one of the most frightening experiences a parent can have, but the one thing to remember is that theme-park security is excellent and crime is practically nonexistent. Theme park staff are trained to recover lost little ones and deliver them back to you safely. Disney cast members immediately accompany lost children to the Baby Care Center, where you can pick them up. But there are many ways you can avoid losing your child in the first place.

Have everyone in your family wear matching T-shirts or at least the same color, so you can easily find them and they can find you.

If you separate to use the bathroom or for any other reason, pinpoint a meeting location and time in the same area.

Hold tight to your children's hands after parades and during the massive exodus from the parks in the evening. The other times children can be easily separated are during character meet-and-greets, when parents are queuing up for Fastpass appointments, and when children are racing around play areas.

Explain to your kids ahead of time that if they get lost, they should tell any Disney cast member right away. Cast members are easy to recognize, with their bright theme uniforms, and they always wear a name tag.

SCARY & INTENSE ATTRACTIONS

Knowing your child's personality is half the battle when it comes to avoiding a frightening attraction. Gauge their sensitivities, and don't push them if they're unsure of a ride or attraction. Start with the milder attractions and build up to rides like the Haunted Mansion, with its dark spooky atmosphere, or Splash Mountain, with its final unnerving plunge.

Darkness, loud noises, and sudden surprises—often the main ingredients in the 3-D films—can scare children more than fast-moving coasters.

If you think your kids will be OK on a certain ride but you're not sure, talk to them about it ahead of time and let them know what to expect.

Finally we suggest that you buy earplugs and use them in loud theaters.

Below we've listed all of the attractions in Walt Disney World that may frighten your children and the parts that make them scary.

MAGIC KINGDOM

ADVENTURELAND **Pirates of the Caribbean.** The first short leg of this cruise past pirate skeletons and a cannonball battle may be a bit unsettling for young children but probably will be forgotten quickly with all the merrymaking and swashbuckling nonsense that follows.

FRONTIERLAND **Splash Mountain.** The big drop at the end is stomach-churning even for adults and those watching from the outside.

Big Thunder Mountain Railroad. Your kids *and* you will feel like you're about to go flying off the track on this high-speed and seriously bumpy roller coaster.

Haunted Mansion. The cackling ghosts and ghouls are more funny than scary to most kids, but some might find the darkness, fog, and eerie sounds, not to mention the jack-in-the-box surprises, to be pretty frightening.

FANTASYLAND **Mickey's PhilharMagic.** More intense than scary, this involves loud music and 3-D images that seem to pop out at you. Whooping and shouting audience members can also cause children to become upset.

Snow White's Scary Adventures. The witch with her warty nose and shiny poisonous apple can spook sensitive kids under 7.

Mad Tea Party. If your child is prone to motion sickness, avoid boarding a teacup with children who are likely to spin.

TOONTOWN **The Barnstormer at Goofy's Wiseacre Farm.** This is a starter coaster meant for kids, so definitely let them try this first if you're not sure if they can handle the other coasters. You can always watch it go around a few times before trying it out.

TOMORROWLAND **Space Mountain.** The scariest ride in the Magic Kingdom, this coaster whips you through space in almost total darkness. Many adults refuse to ride, but we've seen kids as young as 7 beg to ride again.

Stitch's Great Escape. Despite its cartoon host, this attraction isn't tame. Most of the show occurs in the dark with sensory surprises that can startle adults and scare kids as old as 8.

EPCOT

Body Wars. More of a gross-out than a fright, this ride through the different parts of the body can still scare some kids and make adults queasy.

Honey, I Shrunk the Audience Some of the film's 3-D and special in-seat effects can startle or frighten young children; prepare them ahead of time so they'll know to expect "in your face" and "beneath the seat" surprises.

Mission Space. You're in a capsule that spins around very fast. It's hard enough to remember to look straight ahead—the only way to avoid serious motion sickness; in addition you're supposed to push buttons

> **WORD OF MOUTH**
>
> "My 6-year-old daughter absolutely loved Spaceship Earth (go figure). We had to ride it three times in a row. She didn't love the Haunted Mansion. For the first time, she realized that cat teeth look like vampire teeth. Obviously, our fat, lazy cat—the one with the very dangerous name of Mama Kitty—is a vampire and presented a real threat to the safety and well-being of the family. We figured it was pointless to deny the obvious fact that the cat is a vampire and just assured her that if Mama Kitty hadn't attacked the family yet, she wasn't likely to in the near future. And this is our thrill-seeking child."–ajcolorado

and move a joystick. We recommend keeping kids under 9 (and especially those with any health issues), as well as anyone prone to motion sickness, off this ride.

Test Track. This track ride gears up at a fairly relaxed pace and builds to a high-speed climax. Most kids don't seem bothered.

DISNEY–MGM STUDIOS

Twilight Zone Tower of Terror. Anybody with vertigo will be extremely put out by this ride, wherein your "elevator" plunges down (and rockets skyward) 13 stories multiple times. Many people, especially small people and kids, are lifted clean out of their seats during the drops. Kids under 9 may be bothered by the scary music and story line even before the plunge.

Rock 'n' Roller Coaster Starring Aerosmith. If your child loved Space Mountain, chances are he'll love this ride, too. Be warned, however, that this ride is more intense for two reasons: one, your coaster goes a lot faster—60 mph as opposed to 30 mph—and two, you roll through high-volume hard rock music that can feel like quite an assault to the senses.

Jim Henson's Muppet*Vision 3-D. OK, it's the Muppets, and they aren't really scary, but like the other 3-D shows, images pop out of the screen and the soundtrack is pretty loud.

Star Tours. Riding through space in a runaway starship, you travel through an asteroid field and get shot at. We think this aging ride is fairly tame, but readers have written to us to say that their young children (think 5 years old) were pretty scared.

Sounds Dangerous Starring Drew Carey. More disturbing than scary, the loud noises of the soundtrack can shock some kids. We recommend earplugs.

Indiana Jones Epic Stunt Spectacular If you're going to take small children to this show, don't sit in rows close to the action—the loud gunplay by stunt performers and the fireballs produced on stage during the show can scare little ones.

ANIMAL KINGDOM

✗ **Tree of Life—***It's Tough to Be a Bug!* Loud noises, scary bugs that jump out at you, spiders that descend from the ceiling—this 3-D film can scare kids as old as 9 if they're sensitive. See *Mickey's PhilharMagic* or Muppet*Vision 3-D to prepare for this one.

Dinosaur. Huge, lifelike dinosaurs jump out at you at several turns during this ride. In addition, there are a couple of dips and drops. The darkness and loud sounds alone are enough to scare many children under 8.

Primeval Whirl. A starter coaster with wilder turns and dips than the Magic Kingdom's Barnstormer, this is a good one to try out before going on to Expedition Everest.

Expedition Everest. This wild ride into the Himalayas is Disney storytelling at its fast-paced finest, and children who meet the 44-inch height requirement won't want to miss it if they like coaster-type rides and don't mind a few frights. Be warned of scary moments in the dark

Hidden Mickeys

Searching for Mickey? Character meals and meet-and-greets aren't the only places you can find the "big cheese." You can spot images of Mickey Mouse hidden in murals, statues, and floor tiles in queue areas and rides.

Hidden Mickeys began as an inside joke among Disney Imagineers. When finishing an attraction, they'd subtly slip a Mickey into the motif to see if coworkers and friends would notice. Today, hunting for Hidden Mickeys (and Minnies) is a great way to pass the time while standing in line. For example, as you wait to board Norway's Maelstrom ride in Epcot, you can scan the big mural for the Viking wearing mouse ears.

You can request a list of Hidden Mickeys at guest services in the theme parks or at Disney hotels, and the non-Disney Web site ⊕ www.hiddenmickeys.org has a list and photos. Before you begin your search, keep in mind that some of the images can be quite difficult to discern. (You practically need a magnifying glass to make out the profile of Minnie Mouse in the Hollywood mural at the Great Movie Ride in Disney–MGM Studios; she's above the roof of the gazebo.) If you're traveling with young children, you can use Hidden Mickeys as a distraction tactic, but be careful. Preschoolers might actually become frustrated trying to find him. But school-age kids might welcome the challenge of finding as many Hidden Mickeys as they can. Here are some clues.

IN THE MAGIC KINGDOM

Big Thunder Mountain Railroad. As your train nears the station, look to your right for three rusty gears on the ground.

Haunted Mansion. There's a Mouse-eared place setting on the table in the ballroom.

Snow White's Scary Adventures. In the queue-area mural, look for shorts hanging on the clothesline and at three of the stones in the chimney.

Splash Mountain. After the final drop, look for Mickey in profile lounging on his back in a cloud to the right of the Steamboat where the characters "zip-a-dee-doo-dah."

IN EPCOT

Spaceship Earth. Mickey smiles down from a constellation behind the loading area.

The American Adventure. Check out the painting of the wagon train, and look above the front leg of the foremost oxen.

AT DISNEY–MGM STUDIOS

Twilight Zone Tower of Terror. In the boiler room, look for a water stain on the wall after the queue splits.

Rock 'n' Roller Coaster. A pair of Mickeys hides in the floor tile right before the doors with the marbles.

IN THE ANIMAL KINGDOM

DINOSAUR. Stare at the bark of the painted tree in the far left background of the wall mural at the entrance.

Rafiki's Planet Watch. The main Conservation Station building contains more than 25 Hidden Mickeys. Look at the animals and tree trunks in the entrance mural.

—Ellen Parlapiano

when the fearsome yeti appears and the ride vehicle plunges backward briefly.

Kali River Rapids. This water ride looks intimidating but it's actually pretty tame. There's one rather scary drop, but it's over quickly. The most off-putting part of the ride is the potential to get absolutely soaked. More than one child has walked away dripping wet and in tears because of it. Bring a change of clothes and a hand towel or be prepared to buy some souvenir shorts and a T-shirt.

PAL MICKEY

For a personal tour of Walt Disney World by the main mouse himself, consider buying a Pal Mickey. These 10-inch stuffed Mickey toys represent Disney's latest exploration of wireless technology and its many uses. Equipped with sensors and a soundtrack, Pal Mickey periodically tells you very useful bits of information as you tour the parks. For example, he can tell you the minimum-height restriction of a certain ride as you approach it, and he can remind you when to take your place before shows and parades. When he has a message to share, Mickey giggles and the toy vibrates. To hear the message, you just squeeze his hand. You can always ignore the giggle or turn the toy off if you don't want to hear a message. You can purchase Pal Mickey in any of the parks for $69.23, including tax. Of course, Pal Mickey won't talk anymore once you're outside Walt Disney World.

DINING

Many Central Florida restaurants have children's menus. And franchised fast-food eateries abound, providing that reassuring taste of home.

BEST WDW RESTAURANTS FOR KIDS

There are hundreds of eateries in Walt Disney World, and nearly all of them cater to kids in some way. A few, however, go above and beyond having a kids' menu and cute decor. The restaurants listed below are our favorites for that something extra they offer to families with children—whether it be characters, servers in costume, a crazy theme, exceptional food, or all of the above.

Cinderella's Royal Table. What could be more enchanting than a meal with Cinderella? Children, both boys and girls, though especially the latter, simply love this chance to climb the stairs to a banquet hall within Cinderella's Castle. Besides Cinderella, you may meet the Fairy Godmother, Belle, Peter Pan, Snow White, Aurora, Pocahontas, Wendy, Aladdin, Jasmine, Prince Charming, Prince Phillip, Alice, or Mary Poppins. The Once Upon a Time breakfast is so popular that it's often all booked up within minutes of the reservation lines opening at 7 AM (Eastern time) exactly 180 days in advance. Your best bet is to start calling a few minutes before 7 and hit redial continuously until you get through. Disney has helped to alleviate the competition slightly by offering an equally fabulous Fairytale Lunch. If you can't get a reservation for either breakfast or lunch, try for one at Akershus Restaurant in Epcot, where character meals include nearly all the princesses except Cinderella.

• **Boma.** This is the ultimate family dinner experience, no characters necessary. At Disney's Animal Kingdom Lodge, Boma gives children a chance to taste the flavors of Africa—roasted chicken with a sweet chutney, a heavenly curry stew, saffron rice, and glazed salmon are just some of the options. Buffet stations for salads, soups, entrées, and desserts make it simple for children to go back for more on their own. Finicky eaters will be thrilled with familiar choices like mac'n'cheese, chicken tenders, french fries, and spaghetti, as well as the dessert spread. Try to arrive early so you have time to walk around the resort's savanna, where giraffes, zebras, wildebeests, and other critters roam. Next to the pool area is another animal habitat and a playground, an ideal spot for parents to grab a chaise lounge for an after-dinner drink or coffee while the kids burn off energy before bedtime.

Cosmic Ray's Starlight Café. For a quick, relatively inexpensive lunch in the Magic Kingdom, grab a burger or sandwich at the counter here and take a seat outside or within an air-conditioned dining area where the "out-of-this-world" audio-animatronics character, Ray, tickles the ivories during regular sets throughout the day.

• **Crystal Palace.** Winnie the Pooh and his pals from the Hundred Acre Wood visit this Magic Kingdom buffet restaurant at breakfast, lunch, and dinner.

✎ **Chef Mickey's.** Mickey, Minnie, and Goofy are always around for breakfast and dinner at this restaurant in the Contemporary Resort. The comfort food on the buffet includes prime rib, baked ham, and Parmesan mashed potatoes.

'50s Prime Time Café. This Disney–MGM Studios restaurant is perfect for kids who beg to watch television during dinner, only at this place they'll be watching—and living—the shows their parents and grandparents used to watch.

Marrakesh Restaurant. Stagestruck children like the belly dancer in this restaurant in Morocco in Epcot's World Showcase. She entertains regularly enough that you should see her at some point during your meal.

'Ohana. At this prix-fixe all-you-can-eat luau in the Polynesian Resort, a chef grills meats in front of an 18-foot fire pit as flames shoot up to sear in the flavors and entertain the diners.

The Rainforest Café. With its scheduled "rainstorms," jungle details, and menagerie of lifelike critters, the Rainforest Café is a major child-pleaser, and there are locations in Downtown Disney Marketplace and at the entrance to Animal Kingdom.

Sci-Fi Dine-In Theater. Kids and parents love the classic convertible seating and appreciate the trailers of monster flicks playing in this faux drive-in in—you guessed it—Disney–MGM Studios. Expect burgers and fries, chicken, steak, catfish, and awesome milk shakes.

Whispering Canyon Café. Fun-loving cowboys and cowgirls serve up tall stacks of pancakes and heaping helpings of ribs at this outpost in Disney's Wilderness Lodge.

CHARACTER MEALS

At special breakfasts, lunches, and dinners in many Walt Disney World restaurants, Mickey, Donald, Goofy, Chip 'n' Dale, Cinderella, and other favorite characters sign autographs and pose for snapshots. Universal's Islands of Adventure has a character luncheon, so your children can enjoy pizza or chicken fingers with their favorite Seuss characters. Talk with your children to find out which characters they most want to see; then call the Disney or Universal dining reservations line and speak with the representative about what's available.

> WORD OF MOUTH
>
> "We did the character breakfast and it was a huge hit, but take into consideration that the kids don't eat a thing 'cause they're too busy looking at the characters. And it's an expensive breakfast when they don't eat anything!"
> –AustinTraveler

Reservations are recommended because these hugging-and-feeding frenzies are wildly popular, but if you haven't reserved ahead, try showing up early and you may get lucky. It's a good idea to have your character meal near the end of your visit, when your little ones will be used to seeing these large and sometimes frightening figures; they're also a good way to spend the morning on the day you check out.

For descriptions of character meals, see Chapter 12, Where to Eat.

KID-FRIENDLY HOTELS

Walt Disney World has strong children's facilities and programs at the BoardWalk, Contemporary, Dolphin, Grand Floridian, Polynesian, Swan, Wilderness Lodge, and Yacht and Beach Club resorts. The Polynesian Resort's Neverland Club has an enchanting Peter Pan–theme clubhouse and youngsters-only dinner show. Parents also rave about the Sand Castle Club at the Yacht and Beach Club resorts. The Board-Walk's child-care facility, Harbor Club, provides late-afternoon and evening child care for children ages 4–12.

Many hotels have supervised children's programs with trained counselors and planned activities as well as attractive facilities; some even have mascots. Standouts are the Hyatt Regency Grand Cypress, near Downtown Disney, and the Camp Holiday programs at the Holiday Inn SunSpree Resort Lake Buena Vista.

East of International Drive, the connected JW Marriott and Ritz-Carlton Grand Lakes resorts have rooms with adjoining kids' suites, complete with miniature furniture and toys. Additionally, the JW Marriott has a 24,000-square-foot "lazy river" pool, and the Ritz-Carlton has a Kids Club with a play area and daily scheduled activities.

Nickelodeon Family Suites by Holiday Inn, in Lake Buena Vista, offers suites with separate kid-friendly bedrooms decorated with images of cartoon characters. Plus, there are scheduled breakfasts and shows featuring Nick characters.

BABYSITTING

The **Kid's Nite Out** (☎407/828–0920 or 800/696–8105 ⊕*www.kidsniteout.com*) program works in participating hotels throughout the Orlando area, including the Disney resorts. It provides infant care and in-room babysitting for children ages 6 weeks to 12 years (a waiver must be signed for older children who are under the care of the sitter). Fees start at $14 an hour for one child, and increase by $2.50 for each additional child. There's a four-hour minimum, plus a transportation fee of $10 for the sitter to travel to your hotel room. When you make a reservation, you must provide a credit-card number. There's a 24-hour cancellation policy; if you cancel with less than 24 hours' notice, your credit card is charged the four-hour fee ($56).

EDUCATIONAL PROGRAMS

For any behind-the-scenes tours and programs, be sure to reserve ahead by calling **Walt Disney World Tours** (☎407/824–4321 ⊕*www.disneyworld.com*).

Many of Walt Disney World's backstage tours are good for children. For full descriptions of each, see Guided Tours in each theme park chapter. Two favorites are Dolphins In Depth at Epcot, costing $150 for 3½ hours, and Disney's Family Magic Tour at the Magic Kingdom, costing $27 for 2 hours.

Tips for
Special Trips

WORD OF MOUTH

"So many of the attractions are shows, films, and parades that people who can't ride jerky roller coasters will still find more than enough to see and do."
—grandma of three

"For a family reunion, you can get houses for such reasonable rates. We rented a great four-bedroom house two miles from Disney, with a heated pool, nice kitchen, and cable TV in every bedroom." —emd

"The best thing we did was go to the Mickey's Not-So-Scary Halloween Party. To go trick or treating in the Magic Kingdom was a priceless experience. Characters were everywhere, rides had surprisingly short lines, and my daughter danced the night away at the dance party by Ariel's Grotto."
—Laurel McKellips

Revised by
Jennie Hess

YOU MAY THINK YOUR PARTY is somewhat unusual. Perhaps you have a child with disabilities or older in-laws who would prefer not to spend much time waiting in line under the hot sun. Perhaps you're planning a group trip with friends or family, or a theme trip around a special event. Or perhaps you're pregnant and wondering if you should just stay home. Don't. Walt Disney World truly has something for everyone, and you'll find special programs and services meant to accommodate people of varying needs. And if you haven't found exactly what you're looking for, ask. Chances are Disney has a system in place that will help make your trip as easy and enjoyable as can be.

COUPLES

WEDDINGS

Planning on living happily ever after? Then maybe you should tie the knot at Walt Disney World, as do some 1,000 couples every year. At the **Fairy Tale Wedding Pavilion** (☎*407/828–3400*) near the Grand Floridian Resort and many other locations across Disney property, the bride can ride in a Cinderella coach, have rings borne to the altar in a glass slipper, and invite Mickey and Minnie to attend the reception. Check out the interactive Web site, **www.disneyweddings.com,** for photos, testimonies, and wedding ideas.

15 ROMANTIC THINGS TO DO AT WALT DISNEY WORLD

Not everything at Disney World involves children. Let the kids have fun at one of Disney's resort kids' clubs or get a babysitter (available for a fee through Guest Services) and enjoy some private time, just the two of you.

1. Dress up and have dinner at the very grand Victoria & Albert's restaurant in the Grand Floridian. Remember to make a reservation three months in advance.

2. Have dinner at the California Grill on the top floor of Disney's Contemporary Resort and watch the sun set over the Seven Seas Lagoon, or see the Magic Kingdom fireworks from your seat or the restaurant's outdoor viewing spot.

3. Rent a boat for a cruise on the Seven Seas Lagoon or the waterways leading to it. Bring champagne and glasses.

4. Take a nighttime whirl on Cinderella's Golden Carrousel in Fantasyland. Sparkling lights make it magical.

5. Have your picture taken and grab a kiss in the heart-shape gazebo in the back of Minnie's Country House.

6. Plan a day of couples pampering at the Grand Floridian Spa.

7. Buy a faux diamond ring at the Emporium on Main Street in the Magic Kingdom. Propose to your sweetheart at your favorite spot in the World.

8. Have a caricature drawn of the two of you at the Downtown Disney Marketplace.

9. Sit by the fountain in front of Epcot's France pavilion and share a pastry and café au lait.

10. Have a drink at the cozy Yachtsman's Crew bar in the Yacht Club hotel.
11. Stroll the BoardWalk. Watch IllumiNations from the bridge to the Yacht and Beach Club. Then boogie at the Atlantic Dance Hall.
12. Tie the knot all over again at the Wedding Pavilion or during an intimate ceremony on one of Disney's beaches. Invite Mickey and Minnie to the reception.
13. Rent a hot-air balloon for a magical tour of Walt Disney World.
14. Go club-hopping at Pleasure Island.
15. Enjoy a British lager outside at Epcot's Rose & Crown Pub—a perfect IllumiNations viewing spot. Book ahead and ask for a table with a view.

FAMILY REUNIONS & OTHER GROUPS

5

Groups of eight or more can take advantage of Disney's **Magical Gatherings** (☎407/934–7639 ⊕*www.disneyworld.com/magicalgatherings*) program, through which you can access special packages that include entertainment and meals tailored to your group's interest.

When traveling with relatives, friends, coworkers, club members, or any other kind of group, getting everyone to agree on what to do can be tricky. Preschoolers may be content on Dumbo, but thrill-seekers will want faster-paced rides. And grandparents might rather play golf than traipse around a water park. Likewise, when it comes to meals, everyone's preferences and dietary concerns may not coincide. And those doing the planning may find themselves also doing the mediating. That's where Disney's Magical Gatherings program comes in. Designed to help groups travel well together, the program, which is accessible online and over the phone, offers lots of free planning tips, plus a planner that can help you decide what to do together and when to split up.

PLANNING MADE EASY

You can start planning by visiting Disney's Magical Gatherings Web site. With its private chat rooms, your companions can "meet" virtually to discuss the trip. You can create polls to find out about your group's common interests and use the "My Favorites" feature to list everyone's can't-miss attractions. The "Group Favorites" button tabulates popular choices, so you can draft an itinerary that suits everyone.

GROUP MEALS & ACTIVITIES

Specially trained vacation planners can help you book a special tour, dinner reservation, or even a photo shoot. If you have eight or more people in your group and are staying at a WDW resort, you can sign up for one of Disney's four **Grand Gatherings:**

Good Morning Gathering. This is an interactive sit-down breakfast at Tony's Town Square Restaurant in the Magic Kingdom, hosted by a cast of colorful characters. You get to sing, dance, and play group games with Goofy, Pluto, and Chip 'n' Dale, and you even meet privately with Mickey Mouse himself. ✉$29.99 per person, $17.99 ages 3–9.

Safari Celebration Dinner. You begin this gathering with a guided safari through the Animal Kingdom's jungles and savanna. Afterward, you head to Tusker House Restaurant for a family-style dinner and show with African singers, drummers, storytellers, and live animals. Timon of *The Lion King*, Turk of *Tarzan*, or other Disney characters make appearances. ✉$59.99 per person, $24.99 ages 3 to 9.

International Dinner and IllumiNations Dessert Reception. In Epcot's Odyssey pavilion, you dine on international cuisine in a fairy-tale setting, where children participate in a storytelling experience and enjoy a surprise character appearance. After dinner you're led outside to a private viewing area where you can watch the IllumiNations nighttime spectacular. ✉$59.99 per person, $24.99 ages 3–9.

Magical Fireworks Voyage. For a cruise and an after-dinner treat, meet at the Contemporary Resort for this boat ride and dessert buffet. Captain Hook and Mr. Smee playfully capture your crew and usher you onto a boat commandeered by Patch the Pirate. But don't worry about walking the plank—you'll be too busy singing seafaring songs and playing trivia games as you cruise the Seven Seas Lagoon. You get to watch the Electrical Water Pageant and the Wishes fireworks extravaganza from the boat. On the way back to shore, Patch regales you with tales of Peter Pan, who'll be waiting at the dock to sign autographs and pose for pictures. ✉$39.99 per person, $18.99 ages 3–9.

FESTIVALS & OTHER EVENTS

If you've been to the parks and enjoyed the top attractions at least once, it may be time to think about a special trip around one of the many festivals and events slated throughout the year. To buy tickets for special events, call 407/824–4321 or visit ⊕*www.disneyworld.com.*

EPCOT INTERNATIONAL FOOD AND WINE FESTIVAL

You won't find a food and wine festival like this one anywhere else in the world. It's six weeks long (October through mid-November) and it offers something for everyone, whether you're a wine neophyte or oenophile, whether you have a finicky palate or you like to enjoy food as an adventure.

The cost of admission to the main events is your theme-park ticket, which includes seminars on wine and beer, culinary demonstrations, Eat to the Beat outdoor concerts, and multiple exhibits designed for the family. International marketplaces around the World Showcase offer tastes of food, wine, and beers of the world for $1.50 to $4.50 per item. Plan to spend one evening dining all around the marketplaces, finishing with a lovely crème brûlée and *petit café* at the France showcase.

You can also make reservations for special ticketed events, ranging from a $40 Food & Wine Pairing at one of the Epcot restaurants to a $195 Exquisite Evening five-course dining experience (park admission not required). The most popular ticketed event, Party for the Senses ($125) gears up every Saturday evening of the festival with about two dozen Disney and celebrity chefs, 70 different kinds of wine and beer, and four acts by Cirque du Soleil.

EPCOT INTERNATIONAL FLOWER & GARDEN FESTIVAL

Walt Disney was extremely fond of European topiaries, and he made sure that his parks were decorated with perfectly groomed green Disney characters. At this yearly eight-week-long festival (early-April through early June), the topiaries multiply across the park's landscape, with colorful flowers, grasses, and mosses added to create ever more detailed and lifelike characters. Gardening seminars with Disney horticulturists and celebrity gardeners, a screened butterfly garden, a fragrance garden, kids' activities, and nightly Flower Power concerts (Davy Jones of the Monkees is a regular) are just some of the events open to all for the cost of admission.

MICKEY'S NOT-SO-SCARY HALLOWEEN PARTY

Little girls dressed like fairy princesses and young boys in ninja costumes can take to the streets of the Magic Kingdom for treats (no tricks!) during the gently spooky fun of Mickey's Not-So-Scary Halloween Party, which takes place on various days throughout September and October, including the 31st. This nighttime ticketed event (about $45 for adults, $39 for children ages 3–9) is a great chance to meet Disney characters in their own favorite Halloween costumes and take advantage of the hottest attractions without waiting in long lines. There's also the special Mickey's Boo-To-You Halloween Parade.

HOLIDAY HAPPENINGS

The Disney parks are decked out in their holiday finest beginning around Thanksgiving and continuing through the end of the year. If you've never experienced this wondrous display, it pays to book a trip during the first few weeks of December, when there's a lull between the Thanksgiving and Christmas crowds. A road trip through the kingdom to visit Disney's many adorned resort lobbies and gingerbread house displays is a must for decor devotees; start in the morning and cap your tour with late-afternoon tea at Disney's Grand Floridian Resort & Spa, the most elegant of the hotels.

Epcot's nightly, free **Candlelight Processional** with celebrity narrators retelling the story of Christmas is a memorable experience, but you have to line up early for a seat at the America Gardens Theatre venue in Epcot. It pays to purchase the Candlelight lunch or dinner package (ranging from about $35–$60 for adults, $15 or more for children ages 3–9), with a meal at one of Epcot's restaurants and reserved seating for the show.

Mickey's Very Merry Christmas Party is a special ticketed event (about $48 for adults, $39 for children ages 3–9) happening in the Magic Kingdom over several weeks in December; it's most fun for families who've been to the park during the day and want an evening experience. You'll get snowed on during a stroll down Main Street, U.S.A., and you can enjoy the most popular park attractions without long waits. Complimentary cocoa and cookies and a special holiday fireworks show add to the fun.

At Disney–MGM Studios you can see the long-running holiday-time **Osborne Family Spectacle of Lights.** Disney's Animal Kingdom unwraps **Mickey's Jingle Jungle Parade** for the holiday festivities.

> **WORD OF MOUTH**
>
> "You *must* go see the Osborne lights show after dark at MGM! Do not miss that!"
>
> –emd

DISNEY MARATHON

At least 30,000 athletes from around the globe lace up their running shoes each January during the Walt Disney World Marathon Weekend. Goofy's Race-and-a-Half Challenge motivates runners to complete a half-marathon on Saturday and the full marathon on Sunday—a combined 39.3 mi. Marathon runners traverse the scenic 26.2-mi course that winds through the theme parks and crosses much of Disney's undeveloped acreage. You can register for one or both races. The Donald Duck medal goes to half-marathon runners, and the Mickey medal is for full-marathon survivors. In addition, a special Goofy medal awaits runners who cross the finish line of both courses. The marathon weekend also features a Disney 5K Fun Run and kids' races, plus a Health and Fitness Expo at Disney's Wide World of Sports complex.

GAYS & LESBIANS

During **Gay Days Orlando** (⊕*www.gaydays.com*), held the first week in June, parties and tours are organized throughout Orlando for the gay, lesbian, bisexual, and transgendered community, as well as supporters, family, and friends. The weeklong event started in 1991 when the organization's founders encouraged the gay community to "wear red and be seen" in the Magic Kingdom on the first Saturday in June. Now thousands of red-clad folk visit the parks and other Orlando sights during this festive week. Contact the **Gay, Lesbian & Bisexual Community Center of Central Florida (GLBCC)** (✉*946 N. Mills Ave., Orlando 32803* ☎*407/228–8272* ⊕*www.glbcc.org*) or visit the Gay Days official Web site for more information.

Gay- & Lesbian-Friendly Travel Agencies **Kennedy Travel** (✉*130 W. 42nd St., Suite 401, New York, NY 10036* ☎*212/840–8659 or 800/237–7433* ⊕*www. kennedytravel.com*). **Now, Voyager** (✉*4406 18th St., San Francisco, CA 94114* ☎*415/626–1169 or 800/255–6951* ⊕*www.nowvoyager.com*).

GUIDED TOURS

Disney offers numerous guided behind-the-scenes tours. For details about the various park tours, see the Guided Tours section toward the end of each theme-park chapter.

The most customizable tours are organized by Disney's **VIP Tour Services** (☎ *407/560–4033* ⊕ wdwviptours@disney.com). These tours, for those who don't mind shelling out a minimum of $750 or more for a day, are led by guides who will plan your day to maximize your time, enabling you to park-hop and get good seats at parades and shows with little effort. You can be as much or as little involved in the planning as you like. Note that Disney's VIP tours don't help you skip lines, as VIP tours in Universal Orlando do, but they make navigating the parks easy as pie. The guides create efficient schedules for your visit depending on your interests and lead you around the parks to the attractions you want to see. The charge is $125 per hour (or $95 an hour for Disney resort guests during non-peak times of the year), and there's a six-hour tour minimum for every tour. You can book up to 90 days in advance; there's a two-hour charge if you don't cancel at least 48 hours in advance. Tour guides can lead groups of up to 10 people.

PEOPLE WITH DISABILITIES

Central Florida attractions are among the most accessible destinations in the world for people with disabilities, and you'll see many wheelchairs and ECVs (electric convenience vehicles) in the theme parks. The hospitality industry continues to spend millions on barrier-removing renovations. Though some challenges remain, most can be overcome with planning.

The main park information centers can answer specific questions and dispense general information for guests with disabilities. Both Walt Disney World and Universal Studios publish guidebooks for guests with disabilities; allow six weeks for delivery.

DEVICES

WDW has several free devices available for the hearing impaired. **Closed captioning activators** and **assistive listening devices** are available at Guest Relations in all theme parks for a $25 refundable deposit. **Hand-held captioning devices,** require a $100 refundable deposit, and **audio guides and tours** are available for a $25 deposit. Stage shows with sign language interpreters are listed in the calendar of events. At all Disney parks, complimentary four-hour guided **tours in sign language** are available. Reservations must be made at least one week in advance. Call 407/824–4321 or TTY 407/827–5141.

ENJOYING THE PARKS

Attractions in all the Disney parks typically have both a visual element that makes them appealing without sound and an audio element that conveys the charm even without the visuals; many are accessible by guests using wheelchairs, and most are accessible by guests with some mobility. Guide dogs and service animals are permitted, unless a ride or special effect could spook or traumatize the animal. Large braille maps are at centralized areas in all four Disney theme parks and at Downtown Disney Marketplace, Pleasure Island, and West Side.

In some attractions, you may be required to transfer to a wheelchair if you use a scooter. In others, you must be able to leave your own wheelchair to board the ride vehicle and must have a traveling companion assist, as park staff cannot do so. Attractions with emergency evacuation routes that have narrow walkways or steps require additional mobility. Turbulence on other attractions poses a problem for some guests.

The *Guidebook for Guests with Disabilities* details many specific challenges and identifies the accessible entrances for attractions. In addition, a "guest assistance packet" of story notes, scripts, and song lyrics is available at all attractions with a story line—just ask an attractions host, who will provide a binder with the information you need.

A new standard of access was set at Walt Disney World with the opening of the Animal Kingdom, where nearly all attractions, restaurants, and shops are wheelchair accessible. Disney–MGM Studios comes in a close second, followed by Epcot, where some of the rides have a tailgate that drops down to provide a level entrance to the ride vehicle. Though the Magic Kingdom, now in its third decade, was designed before architects gave consideration to access issues, renovation plans are under way. Even so, the 20 or so accessible attractions combine with the live entertainment around the park to provide a memorable experience.

GETTING AROUND
The Disney transportation system has dozens of lift- and braille-equipped vehicles. In addition, there's ample reserved parking for people with disabilities.

INFORMATION
Before your trip, call **Walt Disney World Information for Guests with Disabilities** (☎407/939–7807, 407/939–7670 TTY) and request a copy of the *Guidebook for Guests with Disabilities* to help with planning your visit. The guidebook and Braille guides are available at Guest Relations. Call **Walt Disney World Information** (☎407/824–4321) two weeks in advance for a schedule of sign language–interpreted shows. Interpreters rotate daily between Disney's four major theme parks.

For accessibility information at SeaWorld and Discovery Cove, call **SeaWorld Information** (☎407/363–2414, 407/351–3600, 407/363–2617 TTY, 800/837–4268 TDD). For accessibility information at the Universal parks, call **Universal Orlando Information** (☎407/363–8000, 407/224–4414 TTY).

LODGING
Hotels and motels at Walt Disney World are continually being renovated to comply with the Americans with Disabilities Act. Most resorts here in every price range have rooms with roll-in showers or transfer benches in the bathrooms. Especially worthwhile and convenient are the luxurious Grand Floridian and the Port Orleans–French Quarter.

Outside Disney World, the definition of accessibility seems to differ from hotel to hotel. Some properties may be accessible by ADA standards for people with mobility problems but not for people with hearing or vision impairments, for example. One of the most accommodating off-Disney resorts is the Orlando World Center Marriott; its level of commitment is especially notable each morning, when the Solaris Restaurant hosts a bountiful, wheelchair-accessible buffet breakfast.

Newer hotels, such as the JW Marriott Orlando Grand Lakes, are fully accessible. In most properties, only elevators are braille-equipped, but some have programs to help employees understand how best to assist guests with visual impairments. Particularly outstanding is the Buena Vista Palace Hotel & Spa. The Embassy Suites hotels offer services such as talking alarm clocks and braille or recorded menus.

Most area properties have purchased the equipment necessary to accommodate guests with hearing impairments. Telecommunications devices for the deaf, flashing or vibrating phones and alarms, and closed captioning are common; an industry-wide effort to teach some employees sign language is under way. The Grosvenor Resort, on Hotel Plaza Boulevard, has excellent facilities but no Teletype reservations line.

TRAVEL AGENCIES
In the United States, the Americans with Disabilities Act requires that travel firms serve the needs of all travelers. Some agencies specialize in working with people with disabilities.

Travelers with Mobility Problems **Access Adventures/B. Roberts Travel** (✉ *206 Chestnut Ridge Rd., Scottsville, NY 14624* ☎ *585/889–9096* ⊕ *www. brobertstravel.com*), run by a former physical-rehabilitation counselor. **Accessible Vans of America** (✉ *37 Daniel Rd. W, Fairfield, NJ 07004* ☎ *877/282–8267, 973/808–9709 reservations* ⊕ *www.accessiblevans.com*). **Flying Wheels Travel** (✉ *143 W. Bridge St., Box 382, Owatonna, MN 55060* ☎ *507/451–5005* ⊕ *www. flyingwheelstravel.com*).

Travelers with Developmental Disabilities **New Directions** (✉ *5276 Hollister Ave., Suite 207, Santa Barbara, CA 93111* ☎ *805/967–2841 or 888/967–2841* ⊕ *www.newdirectionstravel.com*). **Sprout** (✉ *893 Amsterdam Ave., New York, NY 10025* ☎ *212/222–9575 or 888/222–9575* ⊕ *www.gosprout.org*).

WHEELCHAIR RENTALS
Probably the most comfortable course is to bring your wheelchair from home. If your chair is wider than 24½ inches and longer than 32 inches (44 inches for scooters), consult attraction hosts and hostesses. Thefts of personal wheelchairs while their owners are inside attractions are rare but have been known to occur. Take the precautions you would in any public place.

Wheelchair rentals are available from area medical-supply companies that will deliver to your hotel and let you keep the chair for the duration of your vacation. You can also rent by the day in major theme parks ($10 a day for wheelchairs, $35 daily for the limited number of scooters).

In Disney parks, since rental locations are relatively close to parking (except at the Magic Kingdom where you have to board the monorail), it may be a good idea to send someone ahead to get the wheelchair and bring it back to the car. Be sure to plan at least an extra half hour for this errand. Rented wheelchairs that disappear while you're on a ride can be replaced throughout the parks—ask any staffer for the nearest location. Attaching a small personal item like a colorful bandana to the wheelchair may prevent other guests from taking yours by mistake.

SENIOR CITIZENS

With a generation of baby boomers now joining an already robust senior-citizen population, the parks have found ways to cater both to senior citizens traveling without children and those who choose to visit with family members of several generations. Disney's Magical Gatherings program offers excellent vacation planning tools and some nice packages for multigenerational groups. Senior citizens traveling on their own will find an abundance of amenities from spas and Broadway-style shows to behind-the-scenes park tours and signature dining experiences. If you want to capitalize on your endurance, it pays to arrive in the theme parks at opening time or before, take in key attractions, then enjoy a leisurely lunch and some time by the resort pool. Energy recouped is well spent on an evening return to the parks, a shopping expedition to Downtown Disney, a night at Cirque du Soleil's *La Nouba* performance or many of Orlando's other after-dark options.

Beyond the theme parks, there's so much to do that you'll wonder how to fit it all in. In addition to excellent golfing, Disney offers bass fishing expeditions on vast Bay Lake, afternoon tea at Disney's Grand Floridian Resort & Spa, tennis, sailing and many other activities.

To qualify for age-related discounts, mention your senior-citizen status when booking hotel reservations and before you're seated in restaurants. Be sure to have identification on hand. When renting a car, ask about promotional car-rental discounts, which can be cheaper than senior-citizen rates.

The Magic Kingdom

WORD OF MOUTH

"We were in Frontierland and headed to Toontown, so we decided to ride the WDW railroad. When we got on the train, the only car that wasn't full was the last one. After we sat down, the conductor came up and asked our kids where we were from. It turned out his daughter lived about 50 miles from us. When the train was about to leave, the conductor asked my son if he would like a job. He jumped at the chance to help. So he was allowed to yell 'all aboard!' and motion for the train to move. When we got off the train, he was given a card that said he was an official conductor on the Mickey Mouse Railway. He still has that card to this day, and that was four years ago. It is wonderful that, with just a little conversation, the magic can happen."

—mom of two

Revised by
Jennie Hess

THE MAGIC KINGDOM IS THE heart and soul of the Disney empire. Comparable (in scope) to California's Disneyland, it was the first Disney outpost in Florida when it opened in 1971, and it's the park that launched Disney's presence, with modifications, in France, Japan, and Hong Kong.

For a landmark that wields such worldwide influence, the Magic Kingdom may seem small: at 107 acres, it's smaller than Disney World's other or "Big Three" parks. But looks can be deceiving: the unofficial theme song—"It's a Small World After All"—doesn't hold true when it comes to the Magic Kingdom's attractions. Packed into seven different "lands" are nearly 50 major crowd pleasers, and that's not counting all the ancillary attractions: shops, eateries, live entertainment, Disney-character meet-and-greet spots, fireworks, parades, and, of course, the sheer pleasure of strolling through the beautifully landscaped grounds.

Many rides are geared to the young, but the Magic Kingdom is anything but a kiddie park. The degree of detail, the greater vision, the surprisingly witty spiel of the guides, and the tongue-in-cheek signs that crop up in the oddest places—for instance, in Fantasyland, the restrooms are marked "Prince" and "Princess"—all contribute to a delightful sense of discovery that's far beyond the mere thrill of a ride.

The park is laid out on a north–south axis, with Cinderella Castle at the center and the various lands surrounding it in a broad circle. Upon passing through the entrance gates, you find yourself at the foot of Main Street, U.S.A., which runs due north and ends at the Hub, a large manicured circle, properly known as Central Plaza, in front of Cinderella Castle. The castle's golden spires have been polished to perfection in celebration of Disney's global "The Year of a Million Dreams" celebration. In fact, Disney Imagineers have built a royal castle suite designed with centuries-old details and regal canopy beds where, each night, a winning family will stay. All the Disney parks worldwide are in on the festivities.

Numbers in the margin correspond to points of interest on the Magic Kingdom map.

GETTING THERE & AROUND

If you're staying at the Contemporary, Polynesian, or Grand Floridian, take the monorail directly to the park. If you're staying at another Disney resort, take one of the Walt Disney World shuttle buses straight to the turnstiles.

If you're driving, try to arrive extra early (45 minutes to an hour ahead of park opening), so you can park close to the Ticket and Transportation Center (TTC), where you must board the monorail or ferry to get to the park. You'll need to show your park tickets to TTC attendants, or tell them you're picking up tickets at Guest Relations. After showing your tickets to a cast member, you can choose either ferryboat or monorail transportation to the turnstiles. If the line's not prohibitive,

TOP MAGIC KINGDOM ATTRACTIONS

FOR AGES 7 & UP

■ **Big Thunder Mountain Railroad.** This old classic coaster isn't too scary; it's just a really good, bumpy, swervy thrill.

■ **Buzz Lightyear's Space Ranger Spin.** Space ranger wannabes will love competing for the highest score on this shoot-'em-up ride.

■ *Mickey's PhilharMagic.* There are several 3-D film experiences at Disney, but this is the only one featuring the main Disney characters and movie theme songs.

■ **Space Mountain.** The Magic Kingdom's scariest ride, all you see are stars in the darkness as you zip along the tracks.

■ **Splash Mountain.** A long, tame boat ride ends in a 52½-foot drop into a very wet briar patch.

FOR AGES 6 & UNDER

■ **Goofy's Barnstormer.** This is Walt Disney World's starter coaster for kids who may be tall enough to go on Big Thunder Mountain and Space Mountain, but who aren't sure they can handle it. If your child loves the Barnstormer, he's probably ready for the big-kid rides.

■ **The Magic Carpets of Aladdin.** Just like Dumbo but with shorter lines, the Magic Carpets of Aladdin is a must-do for preschoolers. You can make your carpet go up and down to avoid the water as mischievous camels spit at you.

■ **The Many Adventures of Winnie the Pooh.** Hang onto your honey pot as you get whisked along on a windy-day adventure with Pooh, Tigger, Eeyore, and friends.

■ **Pirates of the Caribbean.** Don't miss this waltz through pirate country, especially if you're a fan of the movies. The scene is dark with lots of theatrical explosions, but the actual boat ride is slow and steady.

6

the monorail is usually faster, and if you have children along, ask to sit up front with the driver. You might have to wait for the next train or two, but it's worth the front window view and the chance to see and talk with the driver. Trams operate from the parking lot to the TTC if you park farther away.

Once you're in the Magic Kingdom, distances are generally short, and the best way to get around is on foot. The Walt Disney World Railroad, the Main Street vehicles, and the Tomorrowland Transit Authority do help you cover some territory and can give your feet a welcome rest, but they're primarily entertainment, not transportation.

GETTING STARTED

Be prepared to open your bags for a security check before heading through the turnstile. Guest Relations windows are to the right, in case you need to pick up reserved tickets or deal with any other concern. If you've taken our advice and arrived before park opening, you'll soon see Mickey and the gang ride in on the elevated Walt Disney World

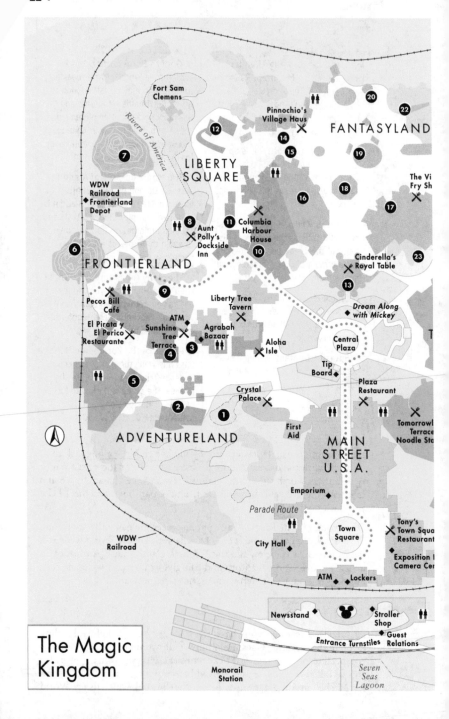

The Magic Kingdom

6

MAGIC KINGDOM TIP SHEET

■ Most families hit the Magic Kingdom early in their visit, so try to go toward the end of the week instead. Avoid weekends, since that's when locals tend to visit the park.

■ Arrive at the turnstiles at least 30 minutes before the scheduled park opening time.

■ If you're staying at a Disney resort, arrive at park opening and stay until early afternoon, then head back to the hotel for a nap or swim. You can return to the park in the mid- to late afternoon, refreshed and ready to soak up more magic.

■ Check Disney's Tip Board at the end of Main Street for good information on wait times—fairly reliable except for those moments when everyone follows the "See It Now!" advice and the line immediately triples.

■ Do your shopping in midafternoon, when attraction lines resemble a napping anaconda. During the afternoon parade, store clerks have been spotted twiddling their thumbs, so this is the time to seek sales assistance. (You can pick up purchases at Package Pickup next to City Hall when you're ready to leave the park). If you shop at the end of the day, you'll be engulfed by rush-hour crowds.

■ See or ride one of the star attractions while the parade is going on, if you're willing to miss it, since lines ease considerably. But be careful not to get stuck on the wrong side of the parade route when the hoopla starts, or you may never get across.

■ At the start of the day, set up a rendezvous point and time, just in case you and your companions get separated. Good places are by the Cinderella Fountain in Fantasyland, the bottom of the staircase at the Main Street railroad station, the benches of City Hall, and the archway entrance to Adventureland.

Railroad to welcome you to the Magic Kingdom. This little performance truly increases the excitement and anticipation. It's no wonder everyone rushes the entrance when the park finally does open.

As you pass underneath the railroad tracks, symbolically leaving behind the world of reality and entering a world of fantasy, you'll immediately notice the adorable buildings lining Town Square and Main Street, U.S.A. Cast members are available at almost every turn to help you. In fact, providing information to visitors is part of the job description of the men and women who sweep the pavement.

Before you leave Town Square, pick up a Guide Map, with color-coded sections to help you get around, and the Times Guide, which lists live showtimes, character greeting times, and special hours for attractions and restaurants that may not be open through closing.

BASIC SERVICES

BABY CARE

The Magic Kingdom's soothing, quiet **Baby Care Center** is next to the Crystal Palace, which lies between Main Street and Adventureland. Furnished with rocking chairs, it has a low lighting level that makes it comfortable for nursing, though it can get crowded in midafternoon in peak season. There are adorable toddler-size toilets (these may be a high point for your just-potty-trained offspring) as well as supplies such as formula, baby food, pacifiers, disposable diapers, and even children's pain relievers. Changing tables are here, as well as in all women's rooms and most men's rooms.

FIRST AID

The Magic Kingdom's **First Aid Center,** staffed by registered nurses, is alongside the Crystal Palace.

CAMERAS

The **Camera Center,** in the Town Square Exposition Hall, opposite City Hall, sells film, batteries, and digital memory cards. If a Disney photographer took your picture in the park, this is where you can purchase the photos or pick up your **Disney PhotoPass** so you can view and order them online at any time. A 5"×7" photo costs $12.95 for the first print and $9.95 for each additional copy. An 8"×10" costs $16.95 and $12.95 for each additional copy.

INFORMATION

City Hall is the Magic Kingdom's principal information center. Here you can search for misplaced belongings or companions, ask questions of staffers, and pick up a Guide Map and a Times Guide, with its schedule of events and character-greeting and attraction information. You can also try to find openings for last-minute lunch or dinner reservations, though it's always better to book in advance.

At the end of Main Street, on the left as you face Cinderella Castle, just before the Hub, is the **Tip Board,** a large board with constantly updated information about attractions' wait times.

LOCKERS

Lockers ($5, plus $2 deposit) are available in an arcade underneath the Main Street Railroad Station. If you're park-hopping, you can use your locker receipt to acquire a locker at the next park you visit for no extra charge.

LOST PEOPLE & THINGS

Name tags are available at City Hall or at the Baby Care Center next to the Crystal Palace, if you're worried about your children getting lost. Instruct them to talk to anyone with a Disney name tag if they lose you. If that does happen, immediately ask any cast member and try not to panic; children who are obviously lost are usually taken to City Hall or the Baby Care Center, where lost-children logbooks are kept, and everyone is well trained to effect speedy reunions. Savvy families wear matching neon or tie-dye T-shirts so that it's easy to spot stragglers in a crowd and scoop them up before they get lost. **City Hall** (☎407/824–

4521) also has a Lost & Found and a computerized Message Center, where you can leave notes for your traveling companions, both those in the Magic Kingdom and those visiting other parks. After a day, found items are taken to the **Transportation and Ticket Center** (☎407/824–4245).

PACKAGE PICKUP

Ask the shop clerk to send any large purchase you make to Package Pickup, so you won't have to carry it around all day. Allow three hours for the delivery. The Package Pickup area is next to City Hall.

STROLLER & WHEELCHAIR RENTALS

The **Stroller Shop,** near the entrance on the east side of Main Street, rents both strollers and wheelchairs. Strollers cost $10 for a single and $18 for double. Wheelchairs cost $10; motor-powered chairs cost $35. If you really want a motorized chair, plan to arrive early, as supplies are limited. Multiday rentals are available with a discount of $2 per day. If your rental needs replacing, ask any cast member.

MAIN STREET, U.S.A.

With its pastel Victorian-style buildings, antique automobiles ahoohga-oohga-ing, sparkling sidewalks, and an atmosphere of what one writer has called "almost hysterical joy," Main Street is more than a mere conduit to the other enchantments of the Magic Kingdom. It's where the spell is first cast.

Like Dorothy waking up in a Technicolor Oz or Mary Poppins jumping through the pavement painting, you emerge from beneath the Walt Disney World Railroad Station into a realization of one of the most tenacious American dreams. The perfect street in the perfect small town in a perfect moment of time is burnished to jewel-like quality, thanks to a four-fifths-scale reduction, nightly cleanings with high-pressure hoses, and constant repainting. And it's a very sunny world thanks to an outpouring of welcoming entertainment: live bands, barbershop quartets, and background music from Disney films and American musicals played over loudspeakers. Old-fashioned horse-drawn trams and omnibuses with their horns tooting chug along the street. Vendors in Victorian costumes sell balloons and popcorn. And Cinderella's famous castle floats whimsically in the distance where Main Street disappears.

Although attractions with a capital "A" are minimal on Main Street, there are plenty of inducements—namely, shops—to while away your time and part you from your money. The largest of these, the Emporium, is often the last stop for souvenir hunters at day's end, so avoid the crowds and buy early. You can pick up your purchases later at Package Pickup or have them delivered to your hotel or mailed home.

The Harmony Barber Shop is a novel stop if you want to step back in time for a haircut ($14 for children 12 and under, $17 for all others). Kids get complimentary Mickey Ears and a certificate if it's their first haircut ever. The Town Square Exposition Hall is actually a shop and exhibit center where you can see cameras of yesteryear and today. The shops in Exposition Hall are a good place to stock up on batteries, memory cards, and disposable cameras.

Main Street is also full of Disney insider fun. For instance, check out the proprietors' names above the shops: Roy O. Disney, etched above the Main Street Confectionery, is the name of Walt's brother. Dick Nunis, former chairman of Walt Disney Attractions, has an honored spot above the bakery. At the Hall of Champions, Card Walker—the "Practitioner of Psychiatry and Justice of the Peace"—is the former chairman of the company's executive committee. At last glance, Michael Eisner still didn't have his own shop; considering the company's recent political upheaval and Eisner's departure in 2005, perhaps he never will. Maybe new Disney chief Bob Iger will fare better.

GROOVY SOUVENIRS

Get your collectible Disney character pins at the pin cart across from the Chapeau in Town Square or at Uptown Jewelers on Main Street. Both have the best pin selections in the park, though you can find pins in other shops throughout the Kingdom. Up to four days a week (usually Sunday, Monday, Tuesday and Wednesday, depending on the season) pin enthusiasts can trade pins at Exposition Hall and meet with other pin aficionados. If you spot a cast member wearing a pin you covet, ask to trade—it's a sure bet you'll get the pin you've wanted. Check www.dizpins.com (an unofficial site featuring Disney pin-trading information) for the scoop.

Mickey-shape pasta from the **Main Street Market House** makes a wonderful gift for anyone, though you have to pack it carefully. Serious collectors of Disney memorabilia stop at the bright yellow, gingerbread **Main Street Gallery,** next to City Hall. If the sky looks dark, head to the **Emporium** for Disney's classic Mickey rain ponchos, essential on a rainy day. This vast souvenir mall segues from one shop to the next and is the perfect place to buy T-shirts, plush character toys, and the latest Disney doodads. Search for sale-priced items if you're on a budget.

WALT DISNEY WORLD RAILROAD
Duration: 21 min.
Crowds: Can be substantial beginning in late morning through late afternoon.
Strategy: Board with small children for an early start in Toontown, provided you have your own fold-up strollers to carry along on the train. If you've rented one of Disney's bulkier strollers, which cannot be loaded on the train, you may want to stick with a round-trip so you can collect your stroller outside the railroad station after you get off. Or hop aboard in midafternoon if you don't see a line.
Audience: All ages.
Rating: ★★

If you click through the turnstile just before 9 AM with young children in tow, wait at the entrance before crossing beneath the train station. In a few moments you'll see the day's first steam-driven train arrive laden with the park's most popular residents: Mickey Mouse, Donald Duck, Goofy, Pluto, and characters from every corner of the World. Once they disembark and you've collected the stars' autographs and photos, step right up to the elevated platform above the Magic Kingdom's entrance for a ride into living history.

Walt Disney was a railroad buff of the highest order—he constructed a one-eighth-scale train in his backyard and named it *Lilly Belle,* after his wife, Lillian. Another *Lilly Belle* rides the rails here, as do *Walter E. Disney, Roy O. Disney,* and *Roger Broggie* (named for a Disney Imagineer and fellow railroad aficionado). All the locomotives date from 1928, coincidentally the same year Mickey Mouse was created. Disney scouts tracked down these vintage carriers in Mexico, where they were used to haul sugarcane in the Yucatán, brought them back, and completely overhauled them. They're splendid, with striped awnings, brightly painted benches, authoritative "choo-choo" sounds, and hissing plumes of steam.

Their 1½-mi track runs along the perimeter of the Magic Kingdom, with much of the trip through the woods. Stops are in Frontierland and Mickey's Toontown Fair. The ride is a good introduction to the layout of the park and a quick trip with small children to Toontown in the morning; it's also great as relief for tired feet later in the day. The four trains run at five- to seven-minute intervals.

ADVENTURELAND

From the scrubbed brick, manicured lawns, and meticulously pruned trees of the Central Plaza, an artfully dilapidated wooden bridge leads to the jungles of Adventureland. The landscape artists went wild here: South African cape honeysuckle droops, Brazilian bougainvillea drapes, Mexican flame vines cling,

spider plants clone, and three different varieties of palm trees sway, all creating a seemingly spontaneous mess. The bright, all-American sing-along tunes that fill the air along Main Street and Central Plaza are replaced by the recorded repetitions of trumpeting elephants, pounding drums, and squawking parrots. The architecture is a mishmash of the best of Thailand, the Middle East, the Caribbean, Africa, and Polynesia, arranged in an inspired disorder that recalls comic-book fantasies of far-off places.

SWISS FAMILY TREEHOUSE

❶ **Duration:** Up to you.
Crowds: Artfully camouflaged so you may not see them—and the lines move slowly.
Strategy: Visit while waiting for your Jungle Cruise Fastpass appointment.

Illusions of Grandeur

CLOSE UP

Much of Disney World's breathtaking majesty comes from its architecture, and a little design trick called forced perspective, in which buildings appear taller than they actually are.

The best example of forced perspective is on Main Street in the Magic Kingdom. Look very carefully at the upper floors of the shops. Together, the second and third floors take up the same amount of space as the ground floor. The buildings start at normal scale at the base but then get imperceptibly smaller toward the top to simulate that cozy hometown feeling. Forced perspective is used in Cinderella Castle, too. Notice how it gets narrower toward the towers. This trick of the eye makes it look as if the spires are soaring into the clouds.

In the Animal Kingdom, architectural scale is suppressed to allow trees to overshadow the buildings. The aim is to relay a sense of humility in the face of nature's wonders. Building height is limited to just 30 feet, whereas trees can tower well above that. But the showcase of the park is the 145-foot Tree of Life, which looks like a skyscraper as it rises from the center of Animal Kingdom. The Tree of Life is a sculptural masterpiece, too. Its trunk is carved with the images of hundreds of animals, illustrating another important Disney design tenet: every structure must tell a story.

–Ellen Parlapiano

Audience: All ages; toddlers unsteady on their feet may have trouble with the stairs.
Rating: ★★

Inspired by the classic novel by Johann Wyss about the adventures of the Robinson family, who were shipwrecked on the way to America, the tree house shows what you can do with a big faux tree and a lot of imagination. The rooms are furnished with patchwork quilts and mahogany furniture. Disney detail abounds: the kitchen sink is a giant clamshell; the boys' room, strewn with clothing, has two hammocks instead of beds; and an ingenious system of rain barrels and bamboo pipes provides running water in every room. As you clamber around the narrow wooden steps and rope bridges that connect the rooms in this split-level dwelling, take a look at the Spanish moss. It's real, but the tree itself—some 90 feet in diameter, with more than 1,000 branches—was constructed by the props department. The 300,000 leaves are vinyl. It all adds up to a species of tree unofficially called *Disneyodendron eximus,* or "out-of-the-ordinary Disney tree."

NEED A BREAK?

If you're looking for real refreshment and an energy boost, stop by Aloha Isle, where you'll find some of the tastiest and most healthful goodies. Try the fresh pineapple spears, or sip a smoothie or just some fruit juice, while you relax on one of the benches scattered in Adventureland.

JUNGLE CRUISE

2 **Duration:** 10 min.
Crowds: Huge, from late morning until dinnertime.
Strategy: Go during the afternoon parade, but not after dark—you miss too much.
Audience: All ages.
Rating: ★★

On this Disney classic, you cruise through three continents and along four rivers: the Congo, the Nile, the Mekong, and the Amazon. The canopied launches are loaded, the safari-suited guides make a point of checking their pistols, and the *Irrawady Irma* or *Mongala Millie* is off for another "perilous" journey. The guide's shtick is surprisingly funny in a wry and cornball way. Along the way, you'll encounter Disney's famed audio-animatronics creatures of the African veld: bathing elephants, slinky pythons, an irritated rhinoceros, a tribe of hungry headhunters, and a bunch of hyperactive hippos (good thing the guide's got a pop pistol). Then there's Old Smiley, the crocodile, who's always waiting for a handout—or, as the guide quips, "a foot out." The animals are early-generation and crude by Disney standards—anyone who's seen the real thing at the Animal Kingdom or even a good zoo won't be impressed. Unless you're an old-school Disney fan, the Jungle Cruise isn't really worth a Fastpass.

THE MAGIC CARPETS OF ALADDIN

3 **Duration:** About 3 min.
Crowds: Heavy, but lines move fairly quickly.
Strategy: Visit while waiting for a Frontierland Fastpass appointment.
Audience: All ages; parents must ride with toddlers.
Rating: ★★★

Brightening the lush Adventureland landscape is this jewel-toned ride around a giant genie's bottle. You can control your own four-passenger, state-of-the-art carpet with a front-seat lever that moves it up and down and a rear-seat button that pitches it forward or backward. Part of the fun is dodging the right-on aim of a water-spewing "camel." Though short, the ride is a big hit with kids, who are also dazzled by the colorful gems implanted in the surrounding pavement.

ENCHANTED TIKI ROOM

4 **Duration:** 12 min.
Crowds: Waits seldom exceed 30 min.
Strategy: Go when you need a sit-down refresher in an air-conditioned room.
Audience: All ages.
Rating: ★

In its original incarnation as the Enchanted Tiki Birds, this was Disney's first audio-animatronics attraction. Now updated, it includes the avian stars of two popular Disney animated films: Zazu from *The Lion King* and Iago from *Aladdin*. The boys take you on a tour of the original attraction while cracking lots of jokes. A holdover from the original is the ditty "In the Tiki, Tiki, Tiki, Tiki, Tiki Room," which is second only to "It's a Small World" as the Disney song you most love to hate. Speaking of which, many people really do hate this attraction, finding the talking birds obnoxious and the music way too loud and peppy.

PIRATES OF THE CARIBBEAN

5 **Duration:** 10 min.
Crowds: Waits seldom exceed 30 min, despite the ride's popularity.
Strategy: A good destination, especially in the heat of the afternoon.
Audience: All ages.
Rating: ★★★

This boat ride is classic Disney with a set and cast of characters created with incredible attention to detail. One of the pirate's "Avast, ye scurvy scum!" is the sort of greeting you'll want to practice on your companions. And if you've seen any of the *Pirates of the Caribbean* movies you'll recognize many of the colorful characters and some of the scenes, as well. This might be the only ride in the world that inspired a film rather than the other way around.

The gracious arched entrance soon gives way to a dusty dungeon, redolent of dampness and of a spooky, scary past. Lanterns flicker as you board the boats and a ghostly voice intones, "Dead men tell no tales." Next, a deserted beach, strewn with shovels, a skeleton, and a disintegrating map indicating buried treasure prefaces this story of greed, lust, and destruction. Here's where the primary villain from the second film has been added: you'll pass right through a water-mist screen featuring the maniacal mug of Davy Jones, complete with squirming tentacle beard and barnacle-encrusted hat. Emerging from a pitch-black tunnel after a mild, tummy-tickling drop, you're caught in the middle of a furious battle. A pirate ship, cannons blazing, attacks a stone fortress. Note the pirate on board: it's gold-hungry Captain Barbossa, evil nemesis of the film's hero, Captain Jack Sparrow. Audio-animatronics pirates hoist the Jolly Roger while brave soldiers scurry to defend the fort—to no avail. Politically correct nerves may twinge as the women of the town are rounded up and auctioned, but the wenches rule in another scene, where they chase roguish rapscallions with glee. The wild antics of the pirates—Captain Jack Sparrow (played by Johnny Depp in the movie) pops up in several situations—result in a conflagration; the town goes up in flames, and all go to their just reward amid a catchy chorus of "A Pirate's Life For Me." Don't miss the attraction's new ending, also revised in the wake of the first two films—we'll tell no tales at risk of spoiling the fun.

GROOVY SOUVENIRS Among the all-time best Magic Kingdom souvenirs are the pirate hats, swords, and plastic hooks-for-hands at the **Pirate's Bazaar** near the Pirates of the Caribbean exit. Nearby, the **Agrabah Bazaar** has Aladdin-wear, including costumes and jewelry, plus safari hats, carvings, and masks. Jasmine and other Aladdin characters are sometimes on hand to sign autographs next to the store.

6

FRONTIERLAND

Frontierland, in the northwest quadrant of the Magic Kingdom, evokes the American frontier. The period seems to be the latter half of the 19th century, and the West is being won by Disney cast members dressed in checked shirts, leather vests, cowboy hats, and brightly colored neckerchiefs. Banjo and fiddle music twangs from tree to tree, and snackers walk around munching turkey drumsticks so large that you could best an outlaw single-handedly with one. (Beware of hovering seagulls that migrate to the parks during cooler months—they've been known to snatch snacks from unsuspecting visitors.)

The screams that drown out the string music are not the result of a cowboy surprising an Indian. They come from two of the Magic Kingdom's more thrilling rides: Splash Mountain, an elaborate flume ride; and Big Thunder Mountain Railroad, one of the park's two roller coasters. In contrast to lush Adventureland, Frontierland is planted with mesquite, twisted Peruvian pepper trees, slash pines, and cacti.

The Walt Disney World Railroad makes a stop at Frontierland. It tunnels past a colorful scene in Splash Mountain and drops you off between Splash Mountain and Thunder Mountain.

SPLASH MOUNTAIN

⑥ **Duration:** 11 min.

Fodor's Choice **Crowds:** Yes!

★ **Strategy:** If you're not in line by 9:45 AM, plan to use Fastpass or ride during meal or parade times. Parents who need to Baby Swap can take the young ones to a play area in a cave under the ride.

Audience: All except very young children, who may be terrified by the final drop. The minimum height is 40". No pregnant women or guests wearing back, neck, or leg braces.

Rating: ★★★

The second most popular thrill ride in the park after Space Mountain, Splash Mountain is a log-flume water ride, based on the animated sequences in Disney's 1946 film *Song of the South*. Here the audio-animatronics creations of Brer Rabbit, Brer Bear, Brer Fox, and a menagerie of other Brer beasts frolic in bright, cartoonlike settings. When you settle into the eight-person hollowed-out logs, Uncle Remus's voice growls, "Mark mah words, Brer Rabbit gonna put his foot in Brer Fox's mouth one of these days." And this just might be the day.

As the boat carries you up the mountain, Brer Rabbit's silhouette hops merrily ahead to the tune of the ride's theme song, "Time to Be Moving Along." Every time some critter makes a grab for the bunny, your log boat drops out of reach. But Brer Fox has been studying his book *How to Catch a Rabbit*, and our lop-eared friend looks as if he's destined for the pot. Things don't look so good for the flumers, either. You get one heart-stopping pause at the top of the mountain—just long enough to grab the safety bar—and then the boat plummets down into a gigantic, very wet briar patch. In case you want to know what you're getting into, the drop is 52½ feet—that's about five stories—at a 45-degree angle, enough to reach speeds of 40 mph and make you feel weightless. Try to smile through your clenched teeth: as you begin to drop, a flashbulb pops. You can purchase a photographic memento of the experience before exiting the ride. Brer Rabbit escapes—and so do you, wet and exhilarated—to the

tune of "Zip-a-Dee-Doo-Dah," the bouncy, best-known melody from the film. If you want to get really wet—and you will get splashed from almost every seat—ask the attendant to seat you in the front row.

BIG THUNDER MOUNTAIN RAILROAD
7 **Duration:** 4 min.
Fodor'sChoice **Crowds:** Large.
★ **Strategy:** Use Fastpass unless the wait is less than 15 minutes. The ride is most exciting at night, when you can't anticipate the curves and the track's rattling sounds as if something's about to give.
Audience: All except young children; the minimum height is 40". No pregnant women or guests wearing back, neck, or leg braces.
Rating: ★★★

Set in gold-rush days, the theme of this thrilling roller coaster is a runaway train. It's a bumpy ride with several good drops and moments when you feel like you're going to fly right off the tracks, but there are no inversions and at least you can see where you're going (unlike in Space Mountain). Overall it's more fun than scary, and you'll see kids as young as seven lining up to ride. The design is fabulous, too. The train rushes and rattles past 20 audio-animatronics figures—including donkeys, chickens, a goat, and a grizzled old miner surprised in his bathtub—as well as $300,000 worth of genuine antique mining equipment, tumbleweeds, a derelict mining town, hot springs, and a flash flood.

The ride was 15 years in the planning and took two years and close to $17 million to build. This 1979 price tag, give or take a few million, equaled the entire cost of erecting California's Disneyland in 1955. The 197-foot mountain landscape is based on the wind-swept scenery of Arizona's Monument Valley, and thanks to 650 tons of steel, 4,675 tons of concrete, and 16,000 gallons of paint, it replicates the area's gorges, tunnels, caverns, and dry river beds.

TOM SAWYER ISLAND
8 **Duration:** Up to you.
Crowds: Seldom overwhelming, but it wouldn't matter—here, the more the merrier.
Strategy: Try it as a refreshing afternoon getaway.
Audience: Most appealing to kids ages 5 to 13.
Rating: ★★

An artfully ungrammatical sign tells you what to expect: "IF'N YOU LIKE DARK CAVES, MYSTERY MINES, BOTTOMLESS PITS, SHAKY BRIDGES 'N' BIG ROCKS,

YOU HAVE CAME TO THE BEST PLACE I KNOW." Aunt Polly would have walloped Tom for his orthography, but she couldn't have argued with the sentiment. Actually two islets connected by a swing bridge, Tom Sawyer Island is a playground of hills, trees, rocks, and shrubs.

The main island, where your raft docks, is where most of the attractions are found. The Mystery Cave is an almost pitch-black labyrinth where the wind wails in a truly spooky fashion. Children love Injun Joe's Cave, all pointy stalactites and stalagmites and with lots of columns and crevices from which to jump out and startle siblings. And, in a clearing atop the hill, there's a rustic playground. As you explore the shoreline on the dirt paths, watch out for the barrel bridge—every time someone takes a step, the whole contraption bounces.

On the other island is Fort Sam Clemens, a log fortress from which you can fire air guns with great booms and cracks at the passing *Liberty Belle* riverboat. It's guarded by a snoring audio-animatronics sentry, working off his last bender. Both islands are sprinkled with lookouts for great views to Thunder Mountain and Frontierland.

COUNTRY BEAR JAMBOREE

9
Duration: 17 min.
Crowds: Large, considering the relatively small theater.
Strategy: Visit before 11 AM, during the afternoon parade, or after most small children have left for the day. Stand to the far left in the anteroom, where you wait to end up in the front rows; to the far right if you want to sit in the last row, where small children can perch on top of the seats to see better.
Audience: All ages; even timid youngsters love the bears.
Rating: ★★★

Wisecracking, cornpone, lovelorn audio-animatronics bears joke, sing, and play country music and 1950s rock-and-roll in this stage show. The emcee, the massive but debonair Henry, leads the stellar cast of Grizzly Hall, which includes the robust Trixie, who laments love lost while perching on a swing suspended from the ceiling; Bubbles, Bunny, and Beulah, harmonizing on "All the Guys That Turn Me On Turn Me Down"; and Big Al, the off-key cult figure who has inspired postcards, stuffed animals, and his own shop next door. Don't miss the bears' seasonal show in late November and December, when they deck the halls for a special concert.

GROOVY SOUVENIRS Cowboy hats and Davy Crockett coonskin caps at **Big Al's**, across from the County Bear Jamboree, are fun to try on even if you don't want to take one home. And families with a passion for pin trading can choose from among a selection of 400 Disney pins, including limited-edition pieces, at the **Frontier Trading Post**. The **Prairie Outpost & Supply** carries gourmet goodies for all tastes.

Behind the Scenes

As you stroll down Main Street, U.S.A., Disney cast members are dashing through tunnels in a bustling underground city, the nerve center of the Magic Kingdom. The 9-acre corridor system beneath the park leads to behind-the-scenes areas where employees create their Disney magic. It also ensures that you'll never see a frontiersman ambling through Tomorrowland. There's the Costuming Department with miles of racks, and Cosmetology, where Cinderella can touch up her hair and makeup. At the heart of this domain is the Digital Animation Control System (DACS), which directs virtually everything in the Magic Kingdom.

The only way to see what goes on in Disney's tunnels is by taking one of two backstage tours: the **Keys to the Kingdom** lasts more than four hours and costs $60, including lunch but not park admission; and **Backstage Magic** lasts seven hours and costs $199 including peeks at Epcot and Disney–MGM Studios, as well as lunch (park admission not included or required). These tours are restricted to people age 16 and older. Security measures prevent access to most of the concrete tunnels, so it's unlikely you'll bump into Mickey without his head on. (And don't expect to take photos. Disney guards its underground treasures carefully!) If you visit in late November or in December, you can take the three-and-half hour **Yuletide Fantasy** tour ($69)—an insider's look at how Disney's elves transform its parks and resorts. Reserve a spot several months in advance. For details, call ☎ 407/939–8687.

LIBERTY SQUARE

The rough-and-tumble Western frontier gently folds into colonial America as Liberty Square picks up where Frontierland leaves off. The weathered siding gives way to solid brick and neat clapboard. The mesquite and cactus are replaced by stately oaks and masses of azaleas. The theme is colonial history, which Northerners will be happy to learn is portrayed here as solid Yankee. The buildings, topped with weather vanes and exuding prosperity, are pure New England.

A replica of the Liberty Bell, crack and all, seems an appropriate prop to separate Liberty Square from Frontierland. There's even a Liberty Tree, a more than 150-year-old live oak found elsewhere on Walt Disney World property and moved to the Magic Kingdom. Just as the Sons of Liberty hung lanterns on trees as a signal of solidarity after the Boston Tea Party, the Liberty Tree's branches are decorated with 13 lanterns representing the 13 original colonies. Around the square are tree-shaded tables for an alfresco lunch and plenty of carts and fast-food eateries to supply the goods.

NEED A
BREAK?

Sleepy Hollow offers quick pick-me-ups in the decadent form of funnel cakes, soft-serve ice cream, espresso drinks, root beer floats, and caramel corn.

HALL OF PRESIDENTS

⑩ Duration: 30 min.
Crowds: Light to moderate.
Strategy: Go in the afternoon, when you'll appreciate the air-conditioning.
Audience: Older children and adults.
Rating: ★★

This multimedia tribute to the Constitution caused quite a sensation when it opened decades ago, because it was here that the first refinements of the audio-animatronics system of computerized robots could be seen. Now surpassed by Epcot's American Adventure, it's still well worth attending, as much for the spacious, air-conditioned theater as for the two-part show.

It starts with a film, narrated by author and poet Maya Angelou, that discusses the Constitution as the codification of the spirit that founded America. You learn about threats to the document, ranging from the 18th-century Whiskey Rebellion to the Civil War, and hear such famous speeches as Benjamin Franklin's plea to the Continental Congress delegates for ratification and Abraham Lincoln's warning that "a house divided against itself cannot stand." The shows conveying Disney's brand of patriotism may be a little ponderous, but they're always well researched and lovingly presented; this film, for instance, was revamped to replace a lingering subtext of Cold War fear with the more progressive assertion that democracy is a work in progress, that liberty and justice still do not figure equally in the lives of all Americans.

The second half is a roll call of all 42 U.S. presidents. (Because Grover Cleveland's two terms were nonconsecutive, they are counted separately.) Each chief executive responds with a nod—even those who blatantly attempted to subvert the Constitution—and those who are seated rise (except for wheelchair-bound Franklin Delano Roosevelt, of course). The detail is lifelike, right down to the brace on Roosevelt's leg. The robots can't resist nodding, fidgeting, and even whispering to each other while waiting for their names to come up.

LIBERTY SQUARE RIVERBOAT

⑪ Duration: 15 min.
Crowds: Moderate, but capacity is high, so waits are seldom trying.
Strategy: Check Times Guide—the riverboat is open seasonally. Go when you need a break from the crowds.
Audience: All ages.
Rating: ★

An old-fashioned steamboat, the *Liberty Belle* is authentic, from its calliope whistle and the gingerbread trim on its three decks to the boilers that produce the steam that drives the big rear paddle wheel. In fact, the boat misses authenticity on only one count: there's no mustachioed captain to guide it during the ride around the Rivers of America. That task is performed by an underwater rail. The 1 ½-mi cruise is slow and not exactly thrilling, except, perhaps, to the kids getting "shot at" by their counterparts at Fort Sam Clemens on Tom Sawyer Island. But it's a relaxing break for all concerned, and children like exploring the boat.

HAUNTED MANSION

12 **Duration:** 8 min.

Crowds: Substantial, but high capacity and fast loading usually keep lines moving.

Strategy: Go early in the day or when crowds have gathered to wait for a parade. Nighttime adds an extra fright factor, and you may be able to line right up during the evening parade in peak season.

Audience: All but very young children who are easily frightened.

Rating: ★★★

> **DID YOU KNOW?**
>
> One of the biggest maintenance jobs in the Haunted Mansion isn't cleaning up but keeping the 200-odd trunks, chairs, harps, dress forms, statues, rugs, and knick-knacks appropriately dusty. Disney buys its dust in 5-pound bags and scatters it throughout the mansion with a special gadget resembling a fertilizer spreader. According to local lore, enough dust has been dumped since the park's 1971 opening to completely bury the mansion. Where does it all go? Perhaps the voice is right in saying that something will follow you home.

6

The special effects here are a howl. Or perhaps a scream is more like it. Or for most, both. You're greeted at the creaking iron gates of this Hudson River Valley Gothic mansion by a lugubrious attendant, who has one of the few jobs at Disney for which smiling is frowned upon, and ushered into a spooky picture gallery. A disembodied voice echoes from the walls: "Welcome, foolish mortals, to the Haunted Mansion. I am your ghost host." A scream shivers down, and you're off into one of Disney's classic attractions.

Consisting mainly of a slow-moving ride in a black, cocoonlike "doom buggy," the Haunted Mansion is only scary for younger children, and that's mostly because of the darkness. Everyone else will just laugh at the special effects. Watch the artfully strung liquid cobwebs pass you by; the suit of armor that comes alive; the shifting walls in the portrait gallery that make you wonder if they are moving up or if you are moving down; the ghostly ballroom dancers; and, of course, Madame Leota's talking disembodied head in the crystal ball. Just when you think the Imagineers have exhausted their bag of ectoplasmic tricks, along comes another one; you suddenly discover that your doom buggy has gained an extra passenger. As you approach the exit, your ghoulish guide intones, "Now I will raise the safety bar, and the ghost will follow you home." Thanks for the souvenir, pal. And speaking of souvenirs, if you can't resist bringing home more than a friendly ghost, you can get Disney's Clue Haunted Mansion board game at a souvenir cart outside the attraction, at the park's Emporium gift shop, or at Once Upon a Toy in Downtown Disney.

FANTASYLAND

Walt Disney called this "a timeless land of enchantment." Fantasyland does conjure up pixie dust. Perhaps that's because the fanciful ginger-bread houses, gleaming gold turrets, and, of course, rides based on Disney-animated movies are what the Magic Kingdom is all about.

With the exception of the slightly spooky Snow White's Scary Adventures, the attractions here are whimsical rather than heart-stopping. Like the animated classics on which they're based, these rides, which could ostensibly be classified as rides for children, are packed with enough delightful detail to engage the adults who accompany them. Unfortunately, Fantasyland is always the most heavily trafficked area in the park, and its rides are almost always crowded.

You can enter Fantasyland on foot from Liberty Square, but the classic introduction is through Cinderella Castle. To get in an appropriately magical mood—and to provide yourself with a cooling break—turn left immediately after you exit the castle's archway. Here you'll find a charming and often overlooked touch: Cinderella Fountain, a lovely brass casting of the castle's namesake, who's dressed in her peasant togs and surrounded by her beloved mice and bird friends.

Photographers will want to take advantage of one of the least-traveled byways in the Magic Kingdom. From the southern end of Liberty Square, turn left at the Sleepy Hollow snack shop. Just past the outdoor tables is a shortcut to Fantasyland that provides one of the best unobstructed ground-level views of Cinderella Castle in the park. It's a great spot for a family photo.

CINDERELLA CASTLE

13 This quintessential Disney icon, with its royal blue turrets, gold spires, and glistening white towers, was inspired by the castle built by the mad Bavarian king Ludwig II at Neuschwanstein, as well as by drawings prepared for Disney's animated film of the French fairy tale. Although often confused with Disneyland's Sleeping Beauty Castle, at 180 feet this castle is more than 100 feet taller; and with its elongated towers and lacy fretwork, it's immeasurably more graceful. It's easy to miss the elaborate murals on the walls of the archway as you rush toward Fantasyland from the Hub, but they're worth a stop. The five panels, measuring some 15 feet high and 10 feet wide, were designed by Disney artist Dorothea Redmond and created from a million bits of multicolor Italian glass, silver, and 14-karat gold by mosaicist Hanns-Joachim Scharff. Following the images drawn for the Disney film, the mosaics tell the story of the little cinder girl as she goes from pumpkin to prince to happily ever after.

The fantasy castle has feet, if not of clay, then of solid steel beams, Fiberglass, and 500 gallons of paint. Instead of dungeons, there are service tunnels for the Magic Kingdom's less-than-magical quotidian operations, such as Makeup and Costuming. These are the same tunnels that honeycomb the ground under much of the park. And upstairs doesn't hold, as rumor has it, a casket containing the cryogenically preserved body of Walt Disney. Within the castle's archway is the **King's Gallery,** one of the Magic Kingdom's priciest shops. Here you'll find exquisite hand-painted models of carousel horses and Disney animated characters, delicate crystal castles, and other symbols of fairy-tale magic, including Cinderella's glass slipper in many colors and sizes.

If you have reservations to dine at **Cinderella's Royal Table,** you enter the castle by way of an ascending spiral staircase where costumed waiters attend to your meal. Cinderella, her Fairy Godmother, and other princesses join you at what is one of the most popular character-greeting experiences offered at Walt Disney World. ■**TIP**➔**Call 180 days ahead, or as soon as you can, to reserve the character breakfast or lunch.**

Who would have thought that, when the clock struck midnight, lucky Disney guests would have a chance to curl up next to an ornate fireplace and spend the night in a sumptuous Cinderella Castle suite? Through "The Year of a Million Dreams" celebration, families of six or fewer are being plucked from one of Disney's four theme parks or Downtown Disney and whisked to the newly completed fourth-story suite for a dream-come-true overnight stay. Amid the lavish décor of 17th-century France, visitors get to enjoy 21st-century amenities like a garden tub, flat-screen plasma TVs, plush down comforters on canopied beds, and elevator access to the suite. Word on Main Street is that castle enthusiasts may be able to book the suite once the "Dreams" celebration is a wrap, though no plans were confirmed at this writing.

➤ **IT'S A SMALL WORLD**

⑭ **Duration:** 11 min.
Crowds: Steady, but lines move fast.
Strategy: Go back later if there's a long wait, since crowds ebb and flow here. Tots may beg for a repeat ride; it's worth another go-round to see all that you missed on the first trip through.
Audience: All ages.
Rating: ★★

Visiting Walt Disney World and not stopping for this tribute to terminal cuteness—why, the idea is practically un-American. The attraction is essentially a boat ride through several candy-color lands, each representing a continent and each crammed with musical moppets, all madly singing. Disney raided the remains of the 1964–65 New York World's Fair for sets, and then appropriated the theme song of international brotherhood and friendship for its own. Some claim that it's the revenge of the audio-animatrons, as 450 simplistic dolls differentiated mostly by their national dress—Dutch babies in clogs, Spanish flamenco dancers, German oompah bands, Russians playing balalaikas, sari-wrapped Indians waving temple bells, Tower of London guards in scarlet beefeater uniforms, Swiss yodelers and goatherds, Japanese kite fliers, Middle East snake charmers, and young French cancan dancers, to name just a few— parade past, smiling away and wagging their heads in time to the song. But somehow, by the time you reach the end of the ride, you're grinning and wagging, too, with the one-verse theme song indelibly impressed in your brain. Now all together: "It's a world of laughter, a world of tears. It's a world of hope and a world of fears...."

PETER PAN'S FLIGHT

⑮ **Duration:** 2½ min.

Crowds: Always heavy, except in the evening and early morning.

Strategy: Get a Fastpass, and enjoy other Fantasyland attractions while you wait.

Audience: All ages, but best for the preschool set.

Rating: ★★

This wonderful indoor ride was inspired by Sir James M. Barrie's 1904 novel about the boy who wouldn't grow up, which Disney animated in 1953. Aboard two-person magic sailing ships with brightly striped sails, you soar into the skies above London en route to Neverland. Along the way you can see Wendy, Michael, and John get sprinkled with pixie dust while Nana barks below, wave to Princess Tiger Lily, meet the evil Captain Hook, and cheer for the tick-tocking, clock-swallowing crocodile who breakfasted on Hook's hand and is more than ready for lunch. Despite the absence of high-tech special effects, children love this ride. Adults enjoy the dreamy views of London by moonlight, a galaxy of twinkling yellow lights punctuated by Big Ben, London Bridge, and the Thames River. The only negative is the ride's brevity. Avoid the regular line or upon exiting you may find yourself annoyed at having waited for an hour for a 2½ minute ride.

MICKEY'S PHILHARMAGIC

⑯ **Duration:** 12 min.

Fodor'sChoice **Crowds:** Heavy.

★ **Strategy:** You could grab a Fastpass, but they're probably better spent on Pooh and Peter Pan. It's a big theater, so you shouldn't have to wait long. Go during the parade for the shortest lines.

Audience: All ages.

Rating: ★★★

Mickey Mouse may be the headliner here, but it's Donald Duck's mis-adventures—reminiscent of Mickey's as the sorcerer's apprentice in *Fantasia*—that set the comic pace in this gorgeous, 3-D animated film. As you settle into your theater seat, the on-screen action takes you behind the curtains at a grand concert hall where Donald and Mickey are preparing for a musical performance. But when Donald misuses Mickey's magical sorcerer's hat, he suddenly finds himself on a whirl-wind journey that includes a magic carpet ride and an electrifying dip under the sea. And you go along for the ride. On the way you meet favorite Disney characters including Ariel, Simba, Aladdin and Jasmine, and Peter Pan and Tinker Bell. The film startles with its special-effects technology—you'll smell a fresh-baked apple pie, feel the rush of air as champagne corks pop, and get lost in the action on one of the largest screens ever created for a 3-D film: a 150-foot-wide canvas. The film is beautifully scored, with popular tunes like "Be Our Guest" and "Part of Your World," and it marks the first time that classic Disney characters appear in a computer-generated animation attraction.

SNOW WHITE'S SCARY ADVENTURES

17 **Duration:** 3 min.
Crowds: Steady from late morning until evening.
Strategy: Go very early, during the afternoon parade, or after dark. Skip if the wait is more than 15 minutes.
Audience: All ages; may be frightening for young children.
Rating: ★

What was previously an unremittingly scary indoor spook-house ride where the dwarves might as well have been named Anxious and Fearful is now a kinder, gentler experience with six-passenger cars and a mini-version of the movie. There's still the evil queen, the wart on her nose, and her cackle, but joining the cast at long last are the Prince and Snow White herself. Although the trip is packed with plenty of scary moments, an honest-to-goodness kiss followed by a happily-ever-after ending might even get you "heigh-ho"-ing on your way out.

CINDERELLA'S GOLDEN CARROUSEL

18 **Duration:** 2 min.
Crowds: Lines during busy periods but they move fairly quickly.
Strategy: Go while waiting for your Peter Pan's Flight Fastpass reservation, during the afternoon parade, or after dark.
Audience: A great ride for families and for romantics, young and old.
Rating: ★★

It's the whirling, musical heart of Fantasyland. This ride encapsulates the Disney experience in 90 prancing horses and then hands it to you on a 60-foot moving platter. Seventy-two of the dashing wooden steeds date from the original carousel built in 1917 by the Philadelphia Toboggan Company; additional mounts were made of fiberglass. All are meticulously painted—it takes about 48 hours per horse—and each one is completely different. One wears a collar of bright yellow roses; another a quiver of Native American arrows. The horses gallop ceaselessly beneath a wooden canopy, gaily striped on the outside and decorated on the inside with 18 panels depicting scenes from Disney's 1950 film *Cinderella*. As the platter starts to spin, the mirrors sparkle, the fairy lights glitter, and the band organ plays favorite tunes from Disney movies. If you wished upon a star, it couldn't get more magical.

DUMBO THE FLYING ELEPHANT

19 **Duration:** 2 min.
Crowds: Perpetual, except in very early morning, and there's little shade—in summer, the wait is truly brutal.
Strategy: If accompanying small children, make a beeline here as soon as the park opens. Or skip Dumbo and head for the similar Magic Carpets of Aladdin.
Audience: Toddlers and young children—the modest thrills are just perfect for them.
Rating: ★★

Hands down, this is one of Fantasyland's most popular rides. Although the movie has one baby elephant with gigantic ears who accidentally downs a bucket of water spiked with champagne and learns he can fly, the ride has 16 jolly Dumbos flying around a central column, each pachyderm packing a couple of kids and a parent. A joystick controls each of Dumbo's vertical motions, so you can make him ascend or descend at will. Alas, the ears do not flap. Keep an eye out for Timothy Mouse atop the ride's colorful balloon.

ARIEL'S GROTTO

20 **Duration:** Up to you.
Strategy: Check your Times Guide for appearance times, and arrive at least 20 minutes ahead.
Audience: Young children, especially little girls.
Rating: ★★

A "beneath the sea" motif distinguishes this starfish-scattered meet-and-greet locale. Ariel the Little Mermaid appears here in person, her carrot-red tresses cascading onto her glittery green tail. Just across the ropes from the queue area are a group of wonderfully interactive fountains that little kids love splashing around in.

THE MANY ADVENTURES OF WINNIE THE POOH

21 **Duration:** About 3 min.
Crowds: Large.
Strategy: Use the Fastpass setup; if the youngsters favor immediate gratification, go early in the day, late in the afternoon, or after dark.
Audience: All ages.
Rating: ★★★

The famous honey lover and his exploits in the Hundred Acre Wood are the theme for this ride. You can read passages from A. A. Milne's stories as you wait in line. Once you board your honey pot, Pooh and his friends wish you a "happy windsday." Pooh flies through the air, held aloft by his balloon, in his perennial search for "hunny," and you bounce along with Tigger, ride with the Heffalumps and Woozles, and experience a cloudburst. When the rain ends at last, everyone gathers again to say "Hurray!" This ride replaced Mr. Toad's Wild Ride; look for the painting of Mr. Toad handing the deed to Owl.

POOH'S PLAYFUL SPOT

22 **Duration:** Up to you.
Crowds: Heaviest in midday.
Strategy: When the kiddies get tired of the stroller or standing in lines, this is the place to let them burn off some energy.
Audience: Children ages 2 to 5 and parents.
Rating: ★★★

Let your toddler have some free time at this whimsical playground based on tales from the Hundred Acre Wood. Tots and preschoolers can crawl through faux hollow logs and honey pots, clamber around in Pooh's impressive tree house complete with gnarled roots, zoom down a slide, and splash in fountains. Tired parents can relax on log-style benches and keep an eye on the wee ones without fear of losing them. Young children who are a bit put off by the huge Disney characters need not worry—Pooh and friends remain in Toontown for meet and greets. Though shade is limited in this newly planted area, Pooh's spot is nevertheless an enchanted place.

STORY TIME WITH BELLE

23 **Duration:** 25 min., several times daily (check your Times Guide).
Crowds: Heaviest in midday.
Strategy: See during the Fantasyland castle stage show or during the parade.
Audience: All ages.
Rating: ★

Disney's beloved bookworm makes an appearance at the Fairytale Garden several times daily and brings *Beauty and the Beast* to life, using her audience as cast members. Storytelling was never so much fun.

MAD TEA PARTY

24 **Duration:** 2 min.
Crowds: Steady from late morning on, with slow-moving lines.
Strategy: Skip this ride if the wait is longer than 30 minutes and if spinning could ruin your day.
Audience: Preschool and grade-school kids.
Rating: ★

This carnival staple is for the vertigo addict looking for a fix. The Disney version is based on its own 1951 film *Alice in Wonderland,* in which the Mad Hatter hosts a tea party for his un-birthday. You hop into oversize, pastel-color teacups and whirl around a giant platter. Add your own spin to the teacup's orbit with the help of the steering wheel in the center. If the centrifugal force hasn't shaken you up too much, check out the soused mouse that pops out of the teapot centerpiece and compare his condition with your own.

6

MICKEY'S TOONTOWN FAIR

This concentrated tribute to the big-eared mighty one was built in 1988 to celebrate the Mouse's Big Six-O. Owing to its continual popularity with the small-fry set, it's now an official Magic Kingdom land, a 3-acre niche set off to the side of Fantasyland. As in a scene from a cartoon, everything is child size. The pastel houses are positively Lilliputian, with miniature driveways, toy-size picket fences, and signs scribbled with finger paint. Toontown Fair provides great one-stop shopping (better known as meet-and-greets) for your favorite Disney characters—hug them, get autographs, and take photos. The best way to arrive is on the Walt Disney World Railroad, the old-fashioned choo-choo that also stops at Main Street and Frontierland. Note that Mickey's Toontown Fair is completely accessible.

THE BARNSTORMER AT GOOFY'S WISEACRE FARM

25 **Duration:** 1 min.
Crowds: Heaviest in midmorning.
Strategy: Visit in the evening, when many tykes have gone home.
Audience: Younger kids, especially preschoolers and grade-schoolers, but no one under 35 inches.
Rating: ★★★

Traditional red barns and farm buildings form the backdrop at Goofy's Wiseacre Farm. But the real attraction is the Barnstormer, a roller coaster whose ride vehicles are 1920s crop-dusting biplanes—designed for children but large enough for adults as well. Hold on to your Mouse ears. This attraction promises tummy-tickling thrills to young first-time coaster riders. If you're uncertain whether your children are up to Big Thunder Mountain Railroad, this is the test to take.

TOON PARK

26 **Duration:** Up to you.
Crowds: Moderate and seldom a problem.
Strategy: Go anytime.
Audience: Young children mainly, but everyone enjoys watching them.
Rating: ★★

This spongy green, maize, and autumn-orange play area formerly featured foam farm critters suitable for kiddie climbing. Now the fenced-in area is shaded by an awning and includes a giant tree trunk for scrambling in, around, and under; a tiny yellow and blue playhouse; and a gazebo-style structure leading to a tunnel and slide. Festive multicolored lights add a carnival mood by night.

DONALD'S BOAT

27 **Duration:** Up to you.
Crowds: Can get heavy in late morning and early afternoon.
Strategy: Go first thing in the morning or whenever the kids need some free-play time.
Audience: Young children and their families.
Rating: ★★

A cross between a tugboat and a leaky ocean liner, the *Miss Daisy* is actually a water-play area, with lily pads that spray without warning. Although it's intended for kids, grown-ups also take the opportunity to cool off on a humid Central Florida afternoon.

NEED A BREAK? The **Toontown Farmer's Market** sells simple, healthful snacks and fresh fruit, plus juices, lemonade slush drinks, espresso, and soda. If you're lucky, you can find a place on the park bench next to the cart and give your feet a rest.

MICKEY'S COUNTRY HOUSE

28 **Duration:** Up to you.
Crowds: Moderate.
Strategy: Go first thing in the morning or during the afternoon parade.

Audience: All ages, although teens may be put off by the terminal cuteness of it all.
Rating: ★★

Begin here to find your way to the mouse. As you walk through this slightly goofy piece of architecture right in the heart of Toontown Fairgrounds, notice the radio in the living room, "tooned" to scores from Mickey's favorite football team, Duckburg University. Down the hall, Mickey's kitchen shows the ill effects of Donald and Goofy's attempt to win the Toontown Home Remodeling Contest—with buckets of paint spilled and stacked in the sink and paint splattered on the floor and walls. The Judge's Tent just behind Mickey's house is where the mouse king holds court as he doles out hugs and autographs and mugs for photos with adoring fans.

JUDGE'S TENT

㉙ Duration: Plan to wait it out if an audience with Mickey is a priority.
Strategy: If you can't get there early, try a lunchtime visit.
Audience: Young children and families.
Rating: ★★★

If you want to spend a few moments with the big cheese himself, load your camera, dig out a pen, and get in line here. You can catch Mickey in his personal dressing room for the ideal photo opportunity and autograph session.

TOONTOWN HALL OF FAME

㉚ Duration: Up to you.
Crowds: Can get heavy in late morning and early afternoon.
Strategy: Go first thing in the morning or after the toddlers have gone home.
Audience: Young children.
Rating: ★★

Stop here to collect an autograph and a hug from such Disney characters as Pluto, Goofy, Cinderella, and Snow White. Check out the blue ribbon–winning entries from the Toontown Fair. **County Bounty** sells stuffed animals and all kinds of Toontown souvenirs, including autograph books.

MINNIE'S COUNTRY HOUSE

㉛ Duration: Up to you.
Crowds: Moderate.
Strategy: Go first thing in the morning or during the afternoon parade.
Audience: All ages, although teens may find it too much to take.
Rating: ★★

Unlike Mickey's house, where ropes keep you from going into the rooms, this baby-blue-and-pink house is a please-touch kind of place. In this scenario, Minnie is editor of *Minnie's Cartoon Country Living* magazine, the Martha Stewart of the mouse set. While touring her office, crafts room, and kitchen, you can check the latest messages on her answering machine, bake a "quick-rising" cake at the touch of a button, and, opening the refrigerator door, get a wonderful blast of arctic air while checking out her favorite ice cream flavor: cheese-chip.

TOMORROWLAND

The "future that never was" spins boldly into view as you enter Tomorrowland, where Disney Imagineers paint the landscape with whirling spaceships, flashy neon lights, and gleaming robots. This is the future as envisioned by sci-fi writers and moviemakers in the 1920s and '30s, when space flight, laser beams, and home computers belonged in the world of fiction, not fact. Retro Jetsonesque styling lends the area lasting chic.

TOMORROWLAND INDY SPEEDWAY

32 Duration: 5 min
Crowds: Steady and heavy from late morning to evening.
Strategy: Go in the evening or during a parade; skip on a first-time visit unless you've been through all the major attractions.
Audience: Older children. The minimum height is 52" to drive.
Rating: ★

This is one of those rides that incite instant addiction in children and immediate hatred in their parents. The reasons for the former are easy to figure out: the brightly colored Mark VII model cars that swerve around the four 2,260-foot tracks with much vroom-vroom-vrooming. Kids will feel like they're Mario Andretti as they race around. Like real sports cars, the gasoline-powered vehicles are equipped with rack-and-pinion steering and disc brakes; unlike the real thing, these run on a track. However, the track is so twisty that it's hard to keep the car on a straight course—something the race-car fanatics warming the bleachers love to watch. You may spend a lot of time waiting, first to get your turn on the track, then to return your vehicle after your lap. All this for a ride in which the main thrill is achieving a top speed of 7 mph.

SPACE MOUNTAIN

33 Duration: 2½ min.
Fodor'sChoice **Crowds:** Large and steady, with long lines from morning to night despite
★ high capacity.
Strategy: Get a Fastpass ticket, or go either at the beginning of the day, the end, or during a parade.
Audience: All except young children. No pregnant women or guests wearing back, neck, or leg braces. The minimum height is 44".
Rating: ★★★

The needlelike spires and gleaming white concrete cone of this 180-foot-high attraction are almost as much of a Magic Kingdom landmark as Cinderella Castle. Inside is what is arguably the world's most imaginative roller coaster. Although there are no loop-the-loops, gravitational whizbangs, or high-speed curves, the thrills are amply provided by Disney's masterful brainwashing as you take a trip into the depths of outer space—in the dark.

■ TIP➔ **The wait to ride Space Mountain can be an hour or more if you don't have a Fastpass, so do your best to get one in the morning.** As you walk to the loading area, you'll pass whirling planets and hear the screams and shrieks of the riders and the rattling of the cars, pumping you up for your own ride. Once you wedge yourself into the seat and blast off, the ride lasts only 2 minutes and 38 seconds, with a top speed of 28 mph, but the devious twists and invisible drops in the dark make it seem twice as long. Stow personal belongings securely or have a non-rider hold onto them.

WALT DISNEY'S CAROUSEL OF PROGRESS

34 **Duration:** 20 min.
Crowds: Moderate.
Strategy: Skip on a first-time visit unless you're heavily into nostalgia. May be closed in low season.
Audience: All ages.
Rating: ★

Originally seen at New York's 1964–65 World's Fair, this revolving theater traces the impact of technological progress on the daily lives of Americans from the turn of the 20th century into the near future. Representing each decade, an audio-animatronics family sings the praises of modern-day gadgets that technology has wrought. Fans of the holiday film *A Christmas Story* will recognize the voice of its narrator, Jean Shepard, who injects his folksy, all-American humor as father figure through the decades.

TOMORROWLAND TRANSIT AUTHORITY

35 **Duration:** 10 min.
Crowds: Not one of the park's most popular attractions, so lines are seldom long, and they move quickly.
Strategy: Go if you want to preview Space Mountain, if you have very young children, or if you simply want a nice, relaxing ride that provides a great bird's-eye tour of Tomorrowland.
Audience: All ages.
Rating: ★

A reincarnation of what Disney old-timers may remember as the WEDway PeopleMover, the TTA takes a nice, leisurely ride around the perimeter of Tomorrowland, circling the Astro-Orbiter and eventually gliding through the middle of Space Mountain. Some fainthearted TTA passengers have no doubt chucked the notion of riding the roller coaster after being exposed firsthand to the screams emanating from within the mountain—although these make the ride sound worse than it really is. Disney's version of future mass transit is smooth and noiseless, thanks to an electromagnetic linear induction motor that has no moving parts, uses little power, and emits no pollutants.

ASTRO-ORBITER

36 **Duration:** 2 min.
Crowds: Often large, and the line moves slowly.
Strategy: Visit while waiting out your Space Mountain Fastpass appointment or skip on your first visit if time is limited, unless there's a short line.
Audience: All ages.
Rating: ★★

This gleaming superstructure of revolving planets has come to symbolize Tomorrowland as much as Dumbo represents Fantasyland. Passenger vehicles, on arms projecting from a central column, sail past whirling planets; you control your car's altitude but not the velocity. The line is directly across from the entrance to the TTA.

> **SKIP STITCH IF . . .**
>
> Preteens seem to like this show best, while young children find it too scary, and for adults it's not as satisfying as, say, *Mickey's PhilharMagic.* It's really not worth waiting in line for an hour unless you have some serious Stitch fans in your party.

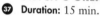

STITCH'S GREAT ESCAPE

37 **Duration:** 15 min.

Crowds: Large because it's one of the newer attractions.

Strategy: Use Fastpass if you've already been on Splash Mountain, Space Mountain, and Big Thunder Mountain, or see it during a parade.

Audience: All but young children, who may be frightened by shoulder restraints, periods of darkness, and loud, startling noises.

Rating: ★★

Once again, Disney seizes upon a hit film to create a crowd-pleasing attraction. This time the film is *Lilo & Stitch,* and the attraction is built around a back-story to the film, about the mischievous alien, Stitch, before he meets Lilo in Hawaii. You are invited, as a new security recruit for the Galactic Federation, to enter the high-security teleportation chamber, where the ill-mannered Stitch is being processed for prison. In the form of a 3½-foot-tall audio-animatronics figure, Stitch escapes his captors and wreaks havoc on the room during close encounters with the audience in near-darkness. Sensory effects and tactile surprises are part of the package. Beware the chili-dog "belch" and a spray that prompts more than a few gasps of surprise (hint: Stitch is the first audio-animatronics figure to spit.)

BUZZ LIGHTYEAR'S SPACE RANGER SPIN

38 **Duration:** 5 min.

Crowds: Substantial, but lines move fast.

Strategy. Go first thing in the morning, get your Fastpass appointment time, then return when scheduled. If you're with children, time the wait and ride twice if it's only 15 or 20 minutes. Youngsters like a practice run to learn how to hit the targets.

Audience: Kids 3 to 100.

Rating: ★★★

Based on the wildly popular *Toy Story,* this ride gives you a toy's perspective as it pits you and Buzz against the evil Emperor Zurg. You're seated in a fast-moving two-passenger Star Cruiser vehicle with an infrared laser gun in front of each rider and a centrally located lever for spinning your ship to get a good vantage point. You shoot at targets throughout the ride to help Disney's macho space toy, Buzz, defeat the emperor and save the universe—you have to hit the targets marked with a "Z" to score, and the rider with the most points wins. As Buzz likes to say, "To infinity and beyond!" The larger-than-life-size toys in the waiting area are great distractions while you wait.

MONSTERS, INC. LAUGH FLOOR COMEDY CLUB

③⑨ Duration: 15 min.
Crowds: Heavy.
Strategy: Go when you're waiting for your Buzz Lightyear or Space Mountain Fastpass appointment.
Audience: All ages.
Rating: ★★

The joke's on everyone at this new interactive attraction starring Mike Wazowski, the one-eyed hero from Disney-Pixar's hit film *Monsters, Inc.* The old Timekeeper theater, has been fitted with 400 seats so you can interact with an animated Mike and his sidekicks in the real-time, unscripted way that the character Crush from *Finding Nemo* performs at Epcot in Turtle Talk with Crush at The Seas with Nemo & Friends. Here the premise is that Mike realizes laughter can be harnessed as a power source, and the club is expected to generate power for the future. The more the audience yuks it up, jokes, and matches wits with Mike's comedian-wannabes, the greater the power produced. A new technological twist: you can text-message jokes from cell phones to the show's producer; they might even be used in the show.

ENTERTAINMENT, PARADES & FIREWORKS

The headliners are, of course, the Disney characters, especially if you're traveling with children. In what Disney calls "character greetings," these lovable creatures and fairy-tale celebrities sign autographs and pose for snapshots throughout the park—line up in Town Square when the gates open, or snag Mickey's autograph at the Judge's Tent in Mickey's Toontown Fair. Ariel's Grotto in Fantasyland is also a great place for autographs. The daily Times Guide lists all character meet-and-greet times and windows, so keep it handy.

DREAM ALONG WITH MICKEY

Duration: 20 min.
Crowds: Heavy, as with all new and limited-time shows.
Strategy: Arrive 30–40 minutes early to grab one of the scattered benches, though your view of the stage may disappear as the audience gathers for standing room. If you have children, plan to stand or sit on the pavement near the stage for an unobstructed view.
Audience: All ages. Older kids may want to skip it in favor of rides.
Rating: ★★

The Cinderella Castle forecourt provides the perfect location for several daily performances of this Disney character spectacle starring Donald Duck, Mickey Mouse, Minnie Mouse, Goofy and others. As the show begins, Donald is a "dreams-come-true" skeptic, but he has joined his optimistic pals anyway at a party where Disney princes and princesses dance in a romantic, dreamy number. There's adventure, too, when Peter Pan, pirates, and wenches take the stage. When pesky Disney villains crash the party, Donald decides to challenge evil and fight for the dreams of all his character friends and family. Pick up a Times Guide at City Hall or in most park shops for performance times and a schedule of character meet-and-greets. Based on Disney Entertainment's track record for creating new live productions, don't be surprised if there's a new song-and-dance extravaganza to replace *Dream Along with Mickey* in 2008 or 2009.

DISNEY DREAMS COME TRUE PARADE

Duration: About 35 min.
Crowds: Heavy.
Strategy: Arrive 20–30 min in advance.
Audience: All ages. Older kids may want to skip it in favor of rides, which will have shorter lines until the parade ends.
Rating: ★★

It's a fantasy world, after all, and your favorite Disney characters let you feel the wonder perpetuated by Walt Disney's legacy during the parade, which proceeds through Frontierland and down Main Street beginning at 3 PM. Bolstered by a powerful orchestral score and beloved songs from Disney films, seven themed floats tell the story of how it all started with a mouse named Mickey and evolved from one classic film to another. Mickey Mouse leads off in a tribute to his countless film roles through the years, followed by floats carrying Pinocchio, Snow White, the Seven Dwarfs, Cinderella, Belle, Beast, Ariel, Prince Ali, Mary Poppins, Alice (of Wonderland), and others. The finale features a rolling crystal castle bearing Goofy, Minnie, and Chip 'n' Dale.

SPECTROMAGIC PARADE

Fodor'sChoice   **Duration:** 20 min.
★   **Crowds:** Heavy.
Strategy: Take your place on the curb at least 40 minutes before the parade begins.
Audience: All ages.
Rating: ★★★

The magic truly comes out at night when the parade rolls down Main Street, U.S.A., in a splendidly choreographed surge of electro-luminescent, fiber-optic, and prismatic lighting effects that bring to life peacocks, sea horses, fountains, fantasy gardens, and floats full of colorful Disney characters. Plenty of old-fashioned twinkle lights are thrown in for good measure, and familiar tunes are broadcast over 204 speakers with 72,000 watts of power. Mickey, as always, is the star. But Practical Pig, from one of Disney's prewar Silly Symphony cartoons, steals the show. With the flick of a paintbrush, he transforms more than 100 feet of multicolor floats into a gleaming white-light dreamscape.

WISHES

Duration: 12 min.
Crowds: Heavy.
Strategy: Find a place near the front of the park so you can make a quick exit at the end of the show.

Audience: All ages.
Rating: ★★★

When the lights dim on Main Street and orchestral music fills the air, you know this fireworks extravaganza is about to begin. In Wishes, Jiminy Cricket returns to convince you that your wishes really can come true, and he is supported by Disney characters from such classic films as *Pinocchio, Fantasia, Cinderella,* and *The Little Mermaid.* Songs from the movies play over loudspeakers as more than 680 individual fireworks paint the night sky. Oh, and don't worry that Tinker Bell may have been sealed in her jar for the night—she comes back to fly above the crowd in grand pixie-dust style.

DISABILITIES & ACCESSIBILITY

Overall, the Magic Kingdom gets decent marks from visitors with disabilities. All restaurants and shops have level entrances or are accessible by ramps. Before your trip, call and request a copy of the *Guidebook for Guests with Disabilities.* This guide, assistive listening systems, reflective captioning equipment, hand-held captioning devices, braille and audio guides, and sign-language interpretation schedules are available in the park at Guest Relations. Devices require a deposits, but no fees. Call **Walt Disney World Information** (☎*407/824–4321*) then wait until the end of the menu to touch 0 to reach someone who can help. Dial 407/939–7807 or 407/939–7670 TTY for accessible accommodations and guidebook information. Call at least two weeks in advance for a schedule of sign language–interpreted shows. Interpreters rotate daily between Disney's four major theme parks.

To board the **Walt Disney World Railroad** at the Main Street Station, you must transfer from your wheelchair, which can be folded to ride with you or left in the station. Alternatively, board at Frontierland or Mickey's Toontown Fair. The **Main Street Vehicles** can be boarded by those with limited mobility as long as they can fold their wheelchair and climb into a car. There are curb cuts or ramps on each corner. At the hub by the Tip Board across from Casey's Corner, there's a large braille map of the park.

In Adventureland, the **Magic Carpets of Aladdin** has ramp access for guests in wheelchairs and a customized control pendant for manipulating the "carpet's" height and pitch movement. The **Swiss Family Treehouse,** with its 100 steps and lack of narration, gets low ratings among those with mobility and visual impairments. At the **Jungle Cruise,** several boats have lifts that allow access for visitors in wheelchairs; people with hearing impairments can pick up Assistive Listening receivers at Guest Relations for use on the boats. Boarding **Pirates of the Caribbean** requires transferring from a non-folding to a folding wheelchair, available at the entrance; the very small flume drop may make the attraction inappropriate for those with limited upper-body strength or those wearing neck or back braces. Because of gunshot and fire effects, service animals should stay behind.

6

BLITZ TOURS

BEST OF THE PARK

Arrive at the parking lot 30 to 45 minutes before scheduled opening, and once in the park, dash left, or hop the **Walt Disney World Railroad,** to Frontierland, where you can claim an early Fastpass time for **Splash Mountain.** After you've received your ticket, head over for **Big Thunder Mountain Railroad,** then ride **Pirates of the Caribbean.** By now, your Fastpass ticket should be valid to ride Splash Mountain. Next head over to Liberty Square and experience the **Haunted Mansion** if the wait's not long; otherwise, see the Country Bear Jamboree show or ride it's a small world and plan to return to the mansion later. When you're finished, sprint over to Tomorrowland and pick up your next Fastpass, this time for **Space Mountain** or **Stitch's Great Escape.** Try to time this so that you can have some lunch and then see **Dream-Along with Mickey** at the castle. If you have longer to wait, head to the Monsters, Inc. **Laugh Floor Comedy Club** or the **Carousel of Progress**. By now, it'll be time for you to experience Space Mountain or Stitch. Afterward, pick up a Fastpass for **Buzz Lightyear's Space Ranger Spin.** Then ride the **Tomorrowland Transit Authority** or squeeze in any attractions above that you may have missed.

If you haven't seen the 3 PM parade on previous visits, start looking for a viewing spot at 2:30 (many begin even earlier). Once you settle on a curb, send a member of your group to pick up the next set of Fastpass tickets for the **Many Adventures of Winnie the Pooh.** If the crowds aren't too thick, the second floor of the train station makes a really nice parade viewing spot. After the parade, hop the train to Mickey's Toontown Fair and pose by the colorful house fronts for some fun photos. From there, stroll into Fantasyland for your Fastpass appointment with Pooh. Afterward, get your Fastpass appointment for **Mickey's PhilharMagic** or **Peter Pan's Flight.** While you wait, take a spin on **Cinderella's Golden Carrousel** and check out the **Cinderella Castle** mosaics.

You probably have time to get dinner and return to your hotel for a couple hours' rest before the **SpectroMagic** parade and **Wishes** fireworks show. If you watch the fireworks from Town Square, you can be ready to grab a monorail seat back to the parking lot as soon as it ends. On the other hand, if you want to ride Splash Mountain or Space Mountain again, lines will be short now, and you can see the fireworks from pretty much anywhere in the park.

ON RAINY DAYS

If you visit during a busy time of year, pray for rain. Rainy days dissolve the crowds here. Unlike those at Disney–MGM and Epcot's Future World, however, many of the Magic Kingdom's attractions are outdoors. If you don't mind getting damp, pick up a poncho with Mickey insignia ($7 adults, $6 children) in almost any Disney merchandise shop and soldier on.

WITH SMALL CHILDREN

At Rope Drop, go directly to Fantasyland and start your day by getting a Fastpass return-time ticket at the **Many Adventures of Winnie the Pooh.** Then, go on a ride with **Dumbo the Flying Elephant.** Next, check showtimes for **Mickey's PhilharMagic** 3-D extravaganza and plan to see it before moving on to a new land. While you wait for the show and your appointment with Pooh, take a whirl on **Cinderella's Golden Carrousel** and, moving clockwise, other attractions without prohibitive waits. You can also head for a character greeting (check your Times Guide). By now it should be time to use your Fastpass ticket at the Many Adventures of Winnie the Pooh, and the wee ones may want to romp in Pooh's Playful Spot afterward. While they're enjoying the Hundred Acre Wood, send an adult from your group to get everyone a Fastpass for **Peter Pan's Flight.** Next head to **it's a small world.** If you have time before Peter Pan, visit **Ariel's Grotto** to pose for snapshots with the Little Mermaid, or see a performance of **Dream-Along with Mickey** in front of the castle.

If you want a sit-down lunch, proceed to **Cinderella's Royal Table** at Cinderella Castle or **Liberty Tree Tavern** in Liberty Square (be sure to reserve seating in advance). **The Crystal Palace** buffet is a great option complete with character visits. Depending on your lunch location, either take the train or walk to Mickey's Toontown Fair. Lunch can digest while the children get their autographs and photos with Mickey Mouse. Then on to the **Barnstormer** to test their coaster mettle. Taking the **Walt Disney World Railroad** is the most relaxing way to return to Frontierland, where you can pick up your Fastpass timed ticket for **Splash Mountain.** Then claim a piece of pavement across the street from the **Country Bear Jamboree**

for the 3 PM parade so you can make a quick exit to line up for **Big Thunder Mountain Railroad**—if your kids can handle the thrills and are tall enough. For the shortest lines, go *during* the parade. By now, it should be time for your Fastpass reservation for Splash Mountain. After the ride, check out either the *Country Bear Jamboree* or the **Haunted Mansion.**

Late afternoon is a nice time to hitch a raft to **Tom Sawyer Island.** When you return, head straight for Adventureland. Proceed directly across the Adventureland plaza to the **Jungle Cruise.** Pick up another Fastpass here if the line is long. Then do **Pirates of the Caribbean** and the **Magic Carpets of Aladdin.** If you still have some time and energy left, scramble around the **Swiss Family Treehouse** and then head back for your Fastpass entry to the Jungle Cruise.

Now stroll across the Main Street hub to Tomorrowland and pick up a Fastpass ticket for **Buzz Lightyear's Space Ranger Spin.** While you wait, see **Monster's, Inc. Laugh Floor Comedy Club** or **Stitch's Great Escape.** Then climb aboard **Tomorrowland Transit Authority** and, if the line's not prohibitive, **Astro-Orbiter.** By now it's time to join Buzz on his intergalactic mission and, if there's time afterward, to take a spin at the **Mad Tea Party.**

If you're really determined to see it all, have dinner at the closest restaurant, then hike toward the front of the park to grab a rocker on the porch of **Tony's Town Square Restaurant** or stake out a curb about an hour before the evening **SpectroMagic** parade and **Wishes** fireworks show for a spectacular end to your day.

6

Frontierland is the only area of the park, aside from Main Street, that has sidewalk curbs; there are ramps by the Mile Long Bar and east of Frontierland Trading Post. To ride **Big Thunder Mountain Railroad** and **Splash Mountain,** you must be able to step into the ride vehicle and walk short distances, in case of an emergency evacuation; those with limited upper-body strength should assess the situation on-site, and those wearing back, neck, or leg braces shouldn't ride. Service animals aren't allowed on these rides. **Tom Sawyer Island,** with its stairs, bridges, inclines, and narrow caves, isn't negotiable by those using a wheelchair. The *Country Bear Jamboree* is completely wheelchair accessible; if you lip-read, ask to sit up front. The **Frontierland Shootin' Arcade** has two guns set at wheelchair level.

The **Hall of Presidents** and *Liberty Belle* **Riverboat,** in Liberty Square, are wheelchair accessible. At the **Haunted Mansion,** those in wheelchairs must transfer to the "doom buggies" and take one step; however, if you can walk as much as 200 feet, you'll enjoy the preshow as well as the sensations and eerie sounds of the rest of the ride.

Mickey's PhilharMagic has special viewing areas for guests in wheelchairs. **it's a small world** can be boarded without leaving your wheelchair, but only if it's standard size; if you use a scooter or an oversize chair, you must transfer to one of the attraction's standard chairs, available at the ride entrance. To board **Peter Pan's Flight, Dumbo the Flying Elephant, Cinderella's Golden Carrousel,** the **Mad Tea Party,** and **Snow White's Scary Adventures,** guests using wheelchairs must transfer to the ride vehicles. The Dumbo and Peter Pan rides aren't suitable for service animals. For **The Many Adventures of Winnie the Pooh,** people who use wheelchairs wait in the main queue and are then able to roll right onto an individual honey pot to ride, with one member of their party accompanying them. There are amplifiers for guests with hearing impairments.

Mickey's Toontown Fair is completely accessible.

In Tomorrowland, **Stitch's Great Escape** requires guests in motorized scooters to transfer to an on-site standard wheelchair for the show's duration. *Monster's, Inc.* **Laugh Floor Comedy Club** and the **Carousel of Progress** are barrier-free for those using wheelchairs. To board **Buzz Lightyear's Space Ranger Spin, Astro-Orbiter,** and the **Tomorrowland Transit Authority,** you must be able to walk several steps and transfer to the ride vehicle. The TTA has more appeal to guests with visual impairments. To drive **Tomorrowland Indy Speedway** cars, you must have adequate vision and be able to steer, press the gas pedal, and transfer into the low car seat. The cautions for **Big Thunder Mountain Railroad** and **Splash Mountain.** also apply to **Space Mountain.** In the **Tomorrowland Arcade,** the machines may be too high for guests using wheelchairs.

EATING IN THE MAGIC KINGDOM

Dining options are mainly counter service—and every land has its share of fast-food restaurants serving burgers, hot dogs, grilled-chicken sandwiches, and salads. The walkways are peppered with carts dispensing popcorn, ice-cream bars, lemonade, bottled water, and soda. Kosher burgers, hot dogs, and chicken strips, all served with potato croquettes, are available at the counter of Cosmic Ray's Starlight Cafe in Tomorrowland.

FULL-SERVICE RESTAURANTS

Reservations are usually essential for the three most popular table-service restaurants in the Magic Kingdom. You can make them through the Disney reservations line up to 180 days in advance; it's a risk to wait until the day you want to eat.

The fare at **Cinderella's Royal Table** includes Caesar salads, braised lamb shank, pan-seared salmon, cheese tortellini, and roast chicken. But the real attraction is that you get to eat inside Cinderella Castle in an old mead hall, where Cinderella herself is on hand—with other princesses during the breakfast and lunch character meals—in her shiny blue gown. A photo package is now included in all Royal Table dining experiences. *Fantasyland.*

Decorated in lovely Williamsburg colors, with Early American–style antiques and lots of brightly polished brass, **Liberty Tree Tavern** is a pleasant place even when jammed. The menu is all-American, with oversize sandwiches, stews, and chops—a good bet for an à la carte lunch. Dinnertime, hosted by a patriotic crew of Disney characters, is a "revolutionary" feast of smoked pork, turkey, carved beef, and all the trimmings. *Liberty Sq.*

Tony's Town Square Restaurant is named after the Italian restaurant in *Lady and the Tramp,* where Disney's most famous canine couple share their first kiss over a plate of spaghetti. In fact, the video plays on a TV in the restaurant's waiting area. Lunch and "Da Dinner" menus offer pastas, of course, along with Italian twists on beef, pork, seafood, and chicken. Breakfast is offered as one of Disney's reservations-only Magical Gatherings experiences for groups of eight or more. *Main St.*

Contacts **Disney Reservation Center** (☎ *407/939–3463).*

SELF-SERVICE RESTAURANT

In the **Crystal Palace,** the "buffets with character" are pleasant. Winnie the Pooh and his pals from the Hundred Acre Wood visit tables in this glass-roof conservatory, and the offerings at breakfast, lunch, and dinner are varied, generous, and surprisingly good. Healthy doses of American regional cuisine include offerings inspired by the season, and there's a sizable choice of pastas, soups, freshly baked breads, and salads that varies from day to day. The place is huge but charming with its numerous nooks and crannies, comfortable banquettes, cozy cast-iron tables, and abundant sunlight. It's also one of the few places in the Magic Kingdom that serve breakfast. *At the Hub end of Main St. facing Cinderella Castle.*

6

MAGIC KINGDOM

NAME	Min. Height	Type of Ride	Duration	Suits	Crowds	Strategy
Main Street U.S.A.						
Walt Disney World Railroad	n/a	train	21 min.	All	Heavy	Board with small children for an early start in Toontown or hop on midafternoon.
Adventureland						
Enchanted Tiki Room	n/a	show	12 min.	All	30 min.	Go when you need a refresher in an air-conditioned room.
Jungle Cruise	n/a	boat	10 min.	All	Yes!	Go during the afternoon parade, but not after dark—you miss too much.
Pirates of the Caribbean	n/a	boat	10 min.	All	Less than 30 min.	A good destination, especially in the heat of the afternoon.
The Magic Carpets of Aladdin	n/a	thrill ride	3 min.	All	Fast lines	Visit while waiting for Jungle Cruise Fastpass.
Swiss Family Treehouse	n/a	play area	Up to you.	All	Slow lines	Visit while waiting for Jungle Cruise Fastpass.
Frontierland						
★ Big Thunder Mountain Railroad	40"	thrill ride	4 min.	5 and up	Big crowds	Fastpass. Most exciting at night when you can't anticipate the curves.
Country Bear Jamboree	n/a	show	17 min.	All	Heavy	Visit before 11 AM. Stand to the far left lining up for the front rows.
★ Splash Mountain	40"	thrill ride	11 min.	5 and up	Yes!	Fastpass. Get in line by 9:45 AM or ride during meal or parade times. Bring a change of clothes.
Tom Sawyer Island	n/a	play area	Up to you.	All	ok	Afternoon refresher. It's hard to keep track of toddlers here.
Liberty Square						
Hall of Presidents	n/a	show	30 min.	9 and up	Light	Go in the afternoon for an air-conditioned break.
Haunted Mansion	n/a	thrill ride	8 min.	All	Fast lines	Nighttime adds extra fear factor.
Liberty Square Riverboat	n/a	boat	15 min.	All	ok	Good for a break from the crowds.
Fantasyland						
Ariel's Grotto	n/a	play area	Up to you.	Little kids	Yes!	Arrive 20 min. before autograph time.
Cinderella's Golden Carrousel	n/a	carousel	2 min.	All	Fast lines	Go while waiting for Peter Pan's Fastpass, during afternoon parade, or after dark.

				Little kids	Slow lines	
Dumbo the Flying Elephant	n/a	thrill ride	2 min.			Go at Rope Drop. No shade in afternoon.
Fairytale Garden	n/a	show	25 min.	All	Midday	See during parade. Story time with Belle.
it's a small world	n/a	boat ride	11 min.	All	Fast lines	Tots may beg for a repeat ride; it's worth it.
Mad Tea Party	n/a	thrill ride	2 min.	All	Slow lines	Go early morning. Skip if wait is 30 min. Spinning ride.
★ Mickey's PhilharMagic	n/a	3-D film	12 min.	All	Heavy	Fastpass or arrive early or during a parade.
Peter Pan's Flight	n/a	ride	2½ min.	All	Steady	Try evening or early morning. Fastpass first.
Snow White's Scary Adventures	n/a	thrill ride	3 min.	All	Steady	Go very early, during the afternoon parade, or after dark. May scare toddlers and pre-schoolers.
The Many Adventures of Winnie the Pooh	n/a	thrill ride	3 min.	All	Heavy	Fastpass. Go early, late in the afternoon, or after dark.
Mickey's Toontown Fair						
The Barnstormer at Goofy's Wiseacre Farm	35"	kid thrill ride	1½ min.	3 and up	Steady	Go during evening if your child can wait.
Tomorrowland						
Astro-Orbiter	n/a	thrill ride	2 min.	All	Slow lines	Skip unless there's a short line. Better at night. May scare toddlers.
Buzz Lightyear's Space Ranger Spin	n/a	thrill ride	5 min.	3 and up	Fast lines	Go early morning and Fastpass. Kids will want more than one ride.
Monster's Inc. Laugh Floor Comedy Club	n/a	interactive film	15 min.	All	Heavy	Go when you're waiting for your Buzz Lightyear Fastpass.
★ Space Mountain	44"	thrill ride	2½ min.	7 and up	Yes!	Fastpass, or go at beginning or end of day or during a parade.
Stitch's Great Escape	40"	sim. exp.	15 min.	All	Large	Fastpass. Visit early after Space Mountain.
Tomorrowland Indy Speedway	52" to ride	racetrack	5 min.	Big kids	Steady	Go in the evening or during a parade; skip on a first-time visit.
Tomorrowland Transit Authority	n/a	tram	10 min.	All	ok	Go with young kids if you need a break.
Walt Disney's Carousel of Progress	n/a	show	20 min.	All	ok	Skip on a first-time visit unless you're heavily into nostalgia.

★ = **Fodor'sChoice**

GUIDED TOURS

A number of **guided tours** (☎407/939–8687) are available. Arrive 15 minutes ahead of time to check in for all of them. Some companies—such as Visa, the official credit card company of Walt Disney World, and AAA—offer discounts for some of the tours; make sure to ask ahead about special discounts.

The 4½-hour **Keys to the Kingdom Tour** is a good way to get a feel for the layout of the Magic Kingdom and what goes on behind the scenes. The walking tour, which costs $60, includes lunch but not admission to the park itself. No one younger than 16 is allowed. Tours leave from City Hall daily at 8:30, 9, and 9:30 AM. Included are visits to some of the "backstage" zones: the parade staging area, the wardrobe area, and other parts of the tunnels that web the ground underneath the Magic Kingdom.

The **Family Magic Tour** is a two-hour "surprise" scavenger hunt in which your tour guide encourages you to find things that have disappeared. Disney officials don't want to reveal the tour's components—after all, it's the Family "Magic" Tour—but they can say that a special character-greeting session awaits you at the end of the adventure. Tours leave City Hall at 10 AM daily ($27 for adults and children 3 and up).

Railroad enthusiasts will love the **Magic Behind Our Steam Trains,** which gives you an inside look at the daily operation of the WDW railroad. This tour became so popular that it was lengthened from two to three hours and is now offered on four days instead of three. Tours begin at the front entrance turnstile at 7:30 AM Monday through Thursday and Saturday. Those over 10 years old may participate. The cost is $40 per person, plus park admission.

Backstage Magic takes you on a tour of the Magic Kingdom, Epcot, Disney–MGM Studios, and the resort's behind-the-scenes Central Shop area, where repair work is done. The cost for the seven-hour tour, which is for those 16 and older, is $199 per person. Tours depart at 9 AM on weekdays. The fee includes lunch but does not include park admission, which isn't required for the tour itself.

Mickey's Magical Milestones, chronicles the development and influence of the Big Cheese himself and includes details about how the Disney icon affected pop culture and the Disney theme parks. A VIP meeting with Mickey Mouse and special seating at *Mickey's PhilharMagic* are included in the two-hour tour, which departs at 9 AM on Monday, Wednesday, and Friday. The cost is $25 per person for guests ages 3 and older, and park admission is required.

Epcot

WORD OF MOUTH

"Having done all the parks, my husband and I still like Epcot best and *loved* the new ride, Soarin'."
—LLindaC

"Epcot just didn't have much to offer little kids. It seemed like a lot walking with little payoff for the little ones. I can see how in just a few more years Epcot will be a more enjoyable experience for my kids."
—Laurel McKellips

"My kids enjoyed going around the nations and collecting the stamps for their passports in the Kidcot areas at each of the countries."
—MikeCT

Revised by
Jennie Hess

EPCOT, WHICH STANDS FOR AN "Experimental Prototype Community of Tomorrow," was the original inspiration for Walt Disney World. Disney envisioned a future in which nations coexisted in peace and harmony, reaping the miraculous harvest of technological achievement. He suggested the

> ### COVERING THE DISTANCE
>
> Even if your preschooler is a good walker, we highly recommend bringing or renting a stroller so you can cover Epcot's long distances without losing steam.

idea as early as October 1966, saying that Epcot would "take its cue from the new ideas and new technologies that are now emerging from the creative centers of American industry." He wrote that Epcot, never completed, always improving, "will never cease to be a living blueprint of the future ... a showcase to the world for the ingenuity of American free enterprise."

But the permanent settlement that he envisioned wasn't to be and, instead, has taken an altered shape in Disney's Celebration, an urban planner's dream of a town near fast-growing Kissimmee. Epcot, which opened in 1982, 16 years after Disney's death, is a showcase, ostensibly, for the concepts that would be incorporated into the real-life Epcots of the future. It's composed of two parts: Future World, where most pavilions are colorful collaborations between Walt Disney Imagineering and major U.S. corporations and are designed to demonstrate technological advances; and the World Showcase, where exhibition areas are microcosms of 11 countries from four continents.

Epcot today is both more and less than Walt Disney's original dream. Less because the World Showcase presents views of its countries that are, as an Epcot guide once put it, "as Americans perceive them"—highly idealized. But this is a minor quibble in the face of the major achievement: Epcot is that rare paradox—an educational theme park—and a very successful one, too.

Although several attractions, such as Soarin' and Mission: SPACE, provide high-octane kicks, the thrills are mostly for the mind. Epcot is best for older children and adults. But that doesn't mean the little ones can't have a great time here. Much of the park's entertainment and at least half of its attractions provide fun diversions for preschool children overstimulated by the Magic Kingdom's pixie dust.

GETTING THERE & AROUND

The monorail and WDW buses drop you off at the main entrance in front of Future World. But if you're staying at one of the Epcot resorts (i.e., the BoardWalk, Yacht Club, Beach Club, Dolphin, or Swan), you can use the International Gateway entrance, which lets you into the World Showcase between France and the United Kingdom, via water launches or a walkway. However, since Future World generally opens two hours earlier than the World Showcase, you'll have to walk briskly through the park to the Future World pavilions to get a head start on the crowd.

Trams operate from the parking lot to the entrance of each theme park. If you parked fairly close, though, you may save time, especially at park closing time, by walking.

Epcot is a big place; a local joke suggests that the acronym actually stands for "Every Person Comes Out Tired." But still, the most efficient way to get around is to walk. Just to vary things, you can cruise across the lagoon in one of the air-conditioned, 65-foot water taxis that depart every 12 minutes from two World Showcase Plaza docks at the border of Future World. The boat closer to Mexico zips to a dock by the Germany pavilion; the one closer to Canada heads to Morocco. You may have to stand in line for your turn to board, however.

GETTING STARTED

Once you go through security and the turnstiles at either the main Future World entrance or the back World Showcase entrance, make a beeline for Mission: SPACE and Test Track (for the fast-paced thrills) or for The Seas with Nemo & Friends and Soarin' (for two terrific family-fun experiences), where the longest lines form first.

BASIC SERVICES

BABY CARE

Epcot has a **Baby Care Center** as peaceful as the one in the Magic Kingdom; it's near the Odyssey Center in Future World. Furnished with rocking chairs, it has a low lighting level that makes it comfortable for nursing, and cast members have supplies such as formula, baby food, pacifiers, and disposable diapers for sale. Changing tables are available here, as well as in all women's rooms and some men's rooms. You can also buy disposable diapers and wipes near both park entrances at the stroller rental stations.

CAMERAS & FILM

Disposable cameras and memory cards are widely available, and you can get your digital memory card downloaded onto a CD for $11.99 plus tax at the **Kodak Camera Center,** in the Entrance Plaza, and at **Cameras and Film,** at the Imagination! pavilion. For photos snapped by Disney photographers, get the **Disney PhotoPass,** which allows you to keep track of digital photos of your group shot in the parks. Later you can view and purchase them online.

FIRST AID

The park's **First Aid Center,** staffed by registered nurses, is in the Odyssey Center on the path between Test Track in Future World and Mexico in the World Showcase.

INFORMATION

Guest Relations, on the east side of Spaceship Earth, is the place to pick up schedules of live entertainment, park brochures, maps, and the like. Map racks are also at the park's International Gateway entrance between the U.K. and France pavilions, and most shops keep a stack

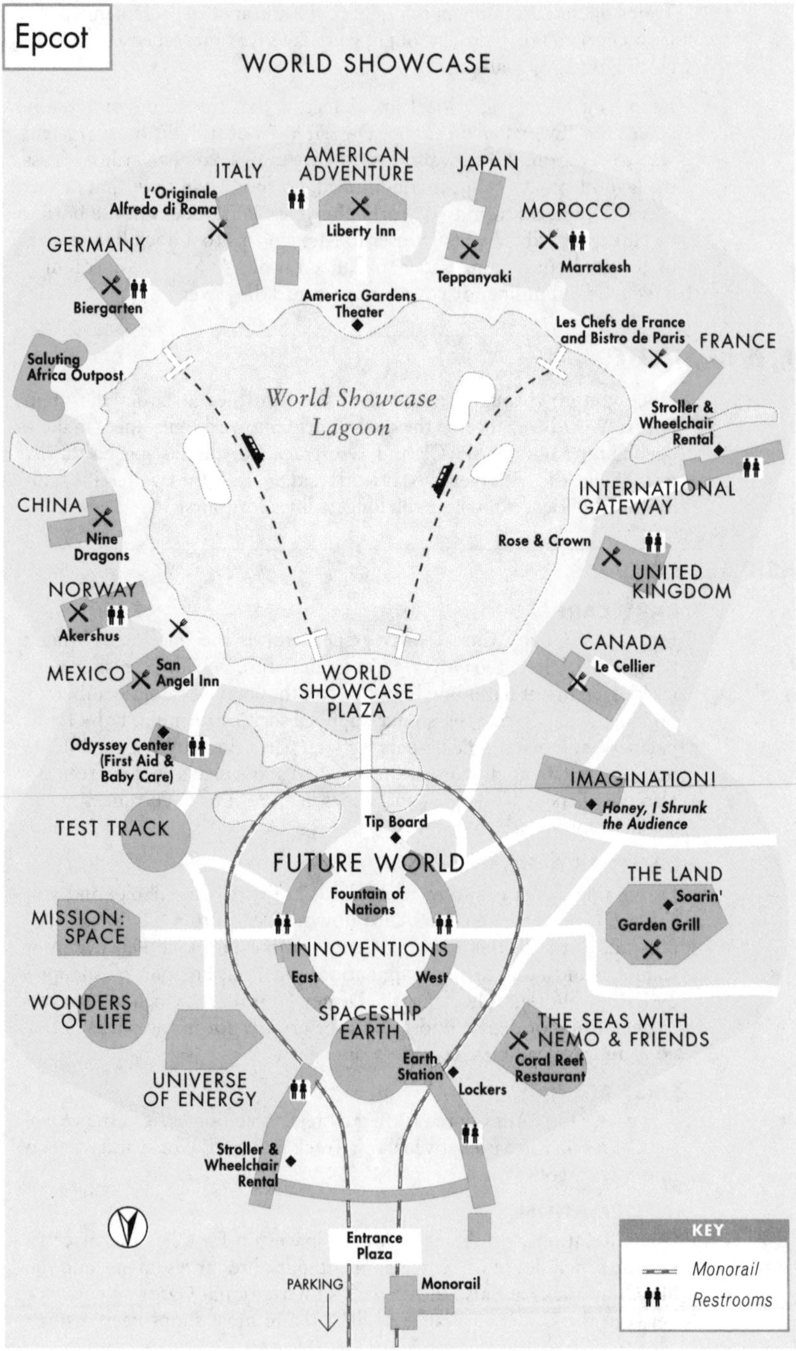
Epcot
WORLD SHOWCASE
AMERICAN ADVENTURE
ITALY
JAPAN
L'Originale Alfredo di Roma
Liberty Inn
MOROCCO
GERMANY
Teppanyaki
Marrakesh
America Gardens Theater
Biergarten
Les Chefs de France and Bistro de Paris
FRANCE
Saluting Africa Outpost
World Showcase Lagoon
Stroller & Wheelchair Rental
INTERNATIONAL GATEWAY
CHINA
Nine Dragons
Rose & Crown
UNITED KINGDOM
NORWAY
Akershus
CANADA
Le Cellier
MEXICO
San Angel Inn
WORLD SHOWCASE PLAZA
Odyssey Center (First Aid & Baby Care)
IMAGINATION!
Honey, I Shrunk the Audience
TEST TRACK
Tip Board
FUTURE WORLD
THE LAND
Fountain of Nations
Soarin'
MISSION: SPACE
Garden Grill
INNOVENTIONS
East
West
WONDERS OF LIFE
SPACESHIP EARTH
THE SEAS WITH NEMO & FRIENDS
Coral Reef Restaurant
Earth Station
UNIVERSE OF ENERGY
Lockers
Stroller & Wheelchair Rental
Entrance Plaza
PARKING
Monorail
KEY
Monorail
Restrooms

TOP 6 EPCOT ATTRACTIONS

The American Adventure. Many adults and older children love this patriotic look at American history.

Honey, I Shrunk the Audience. You gotta watch out when you're in the same room as clumsy inventor Wayne Szalinski. Accidents do happen.

IllumiNations. This amazing musical laser-and-fireworks show is Disney nighttime entertainment at its best.

Mission: SPACE. Blast off on a simulated ride to Mars, if you can handle the turbulence.

Soarin'. Feel the sweet-scented breeze as you fly over California's beautiful landscapes.

Test Track. Your car revs up to 60 mph on a hairpin turn in this wild ride on a General Motors proving ground.

handy. Guest Relations cast members will assist with dining reservations, ticket upgrades, and services for guests with disabilities.

LOCKERS

Lockers ($5; $2 deposit) are to the west of Spaceship Earth and in the Bus Information Center by the bus parking lot.

LOST PEOPLE & THINGS

If you're worried about your children getting lost, get name tags for them at either Guest Relations or the Baby Care Center. Instruct them to speak to someone with a Disney name tag if you become separated. I immediately report your loss to any cast member and try not to panic; the staff here is experienced at reuniting families, and there are lost-children logbooks at Guest Relations and the Baby Care Center. Guest Relations also has a computerized **Message Center,** where you can leave notes for your traveling companions in any of the parks.

For the **Lost & Found** (☎*407/560–7500*), go to the west edge of the Entrance Plaza. After one day, all articles are sent to the **Main Lost & Found office** (✉*Magic Kingdom, Transportation and Ticket Center* ☎*407/824–4245*).

PACKAGE PICKUP

Ask shop clerks to forward any large purchases you make to Package Pickup at the Gift Stop in the Main Entrance Plaza and at the World Traveler at International Gateway, so that you won't have to carry them around all day. Allow three hours.

STROLLER & WHEELCHAIR RENTALS

For stroller and wheelchair rentals, look for the special stands on the east side of the Entrance Plaza and at World Showcase's International Gateway. Strollers rent for $10 for a single and $18 for a double. Standard wheelchairs are available for $10, while electric scooters cost $35.

7

FUTURE WORLD

Future World is made up of two concentric circles of pavilions. The inner core is composed of the Spaceship Earth geosphere and, just beyond it, a plaza anchored by the wow-generating computer-animated Fountain of Nations, which is as mesmerizing as many a more elaborate ride or show. Bracketing it are the crescent-shape Innoventions East and West.

KIDCOT FUN STOPS

Children ages four to nine will love these activity and craft areas sprinkled throughout the World Showcase. They can get their Epcot passports ($9.95 plus tax at any of the shops) stamped, make puppets, draw pictures, and even create a Moroccan fez.

Seven pavilions compose the outer ring. On the east side they are, in order, the Universe of Energy, Wonders of Life, Mission: SPACE, and Test Track. With the exception of the Wonders of Life, which is open only during the busiest days of the year, the east pavilions present a single, self-contained ride and an occasional postride showcase; a visit rarely takes more than 30 minutes, but it depends on how long you spend in the postride area. On the west side there are The Seas with Nemo & Friends, the Land, and Imagination! Like the Wonders of Life, these blockbuster exhibits contain both rides and interactive displays; you could spend at least 1½ hours at each of these pavilions, but there aren't enough hours in the day, so prioritize.

SPACESHIP EARTH
Duration: 15 min.
Crowds: Longest during the morning and shortest just before closing.
Strategy: Ride while you're waiting for your Mission: SPACE or Test Track appointments.
Audience: All ages.
Rating: ★★

Balanced like a giant golf ball waiting for some celestial being to tee off, the multifaceted silver geosphere of Spaceship Earth is to Epcot what Cinderella Castle is to the Magic Kingdom. As much a landmark as an icon, it can be seen on a clear day from an airplane flying down either coast of Florida.

Inside the ball, the Spaceship Earth ride transports you past a series of tableaux that explore human progress and the continuing search for better forms of communication. Scripted by science-fiction writer Ray Bradbury and narrated by Jeremy Irons, the journey begins in the darkest tunnels of time, proceeds through history, and ends poised on the edge of the future.

Audio-animatronics figures (somewhat dated compared to more recent technology) present Cro-Magnon man daubing mystic paintings on cave walls, Egyptian scribes scratching hieroglyphics on papyrus, Roman centurions building roads, Islamic scholars mapping the heavens, and 11th- and 12th-century Benedictine monks hand-copying ancient manuscripts to preserve the wisdom of the past. As you move

TIP SHEET

■ Don't try to do it all. Epcot is so vast and varied that you really need two days to explore everything. If you only have one day, visit just the attractions and pavilions that most interest you.

■ The best days to go are early in the week, since most people tend to go to Disney's Animal Kingdom and the Magic Kingdom first.

■ Arrive at the turnstiles 15 to 30 minutes before opening, so you can avoid some of the lines. Make Mission: SPACE, Test Track, and Soarin' your first stops, and be sure to use your Fastpass option whenever possible.

■ Plan to have at least one relaxed meal. With children, you may want to make reservations (try to make them four to six months in advance) for the Princess Storybook Breakfast at Norway's Akershus, or for lunch or dinner at the Land's Garden Grill, a revolving restaurant that features character appearances by Mickey and friends. Or opt for an early seafood lunch at the Coral Reef in the Living Seas. A late lunch or an early dinner at one of the World Showcase restaurants is another great option.

■ Upon entering, check Epcot's Tip Board past Spaceship Earth and just outside Innoventions, and modify your strategy if there's a short line at a top attraction.

■ Walk fast, see the exhibits when the park is at its emptiest, and slow down and enjoy the shops and the live entertainment when the crowds thicken.

■ Set up a rendezvous point and time at the start of the day, just in case you and your companions get separated. Some good places in Future World include in front of Gateway Gifts near Spaceship Earth and in front of the Fountain of Nations; in World Showcase, in front of your country of choice.

into the Renaissance, Michelangelo paints the Sistine Chapel, Gutenberg invents the printing press, and in rapid succession, the telegraph, radio, television, and computer come into being. The pace speeds up, and you're bombarded with images from the age of communication before entering an idealized vision of the future.

INNOVENTIONS
Duration: Up to you.
Crowds: Largest around the popular computer displays.
Strategy: Go before 10 AM or after 2 PM.
Audience: All ages, but primarily for the grade-school set. A few games are designed with preschoolers in mind.
Rating: ★★★

Innoventions is a two-building, 100,000-square-foot, walk-through attraction that you can visit at your own pace. Hands-on interactive exhibits let kids and adults experience the science and technology that enhances their lives daily. Each major exhibit is presented by a leading company or association. Innoventions East focuses on products for home, work, and play, such as a floating bed, state-of-the-art showers, and the latest in digital entertainment centers. There's even a hybrid car in the "backyard" and a kitchen with a rising platform oven. At the Test the Limits Lab, you can be product testers for Underwriters Laboratories by trying to break TV screens, slam doors, crush helmets, and put other home products through their paces in various ways.

In Innoventions West, you can test drive the Segway Human Transporter at Segway Central. The transporter is so popular that it's used by some Disney personnel to wheel across the park and has been incorporated into an Epcot guided tour. The "Where's the Fire?" interactive experience is a terrific way to review fire safety and prevention. Families can enjoy the game house, where they team up with other guests to find and extinguish as many fire hazards as possible.

> **DID YOU KNOW?**
>
> Everyone likes to gawk at the giant "golf ball," but there are some truly jaw-dropping facts about it: it weighs 1 million pounds and measures 164 feet in diameter and 180 feet in height ("Aha!" you say. "It's not really a sphere!"). It also encompasses more than 2 million cubic feet of space, and it's balanced on six pylons sunk 100 feet into the ground. The anodized-aluminum sheath is composed of 954 triangular panels, not all of equal size or shape. And, last, because it's not a geodesic dome, which is only a half sphere, the name "geosphere" was coined.

The Innoventions Playground features Video Games of Tomorrow with current favorites and previews of games to come. You'll be hard-pressed to pull your kids out of here. When you finally do exit, if you're a collector of the myriad Disney pins that are sold in nearly all the theme-park shops, stop by the Pin Station at Innoventions Plaza.

NEED A BREAK?

The **Fountain View Espresso and Bakery** sells freshly brewed coffees, scrumptious croissants, fruit tarts, and éclairs. Try for one of the umbrella-covered tables on the patio; they have a fine view of the Fountain of Nations water ballet show (a five-minute show every 15 minutes). Enter the indoor refrigerator that is **Club Cool**, where Coca-Cola's bold red-and-white colors guide you to a room full of soda machines and logo merchandise. You can sample (for free) the cola king's products from around the world: Vegitabeta from Japan, Smart Watermelon from China, Kinley Lemon from Israel. It's entertaining to watch the faces of those who discover a not-so-yummy flavor.

MISSION: SPACE
Duration: 4 min.
Crowds: Heavy, since this is Disney's most technologically advanced attraction and one of only a handful of thrill rides at Epcot.
Strategy: Arrive before 10 AM or use Fastpass. Don't ride on a full stomach.
Audience: Adults and children over 8. Pregnant women and anyone with heart, back, neck, balance, blood pressure, or motion sickness

problems shouldn't ride. Minimum height 44".

Rating: ★★★

It took five years for Disney Imagineers, with the help of 25 experts from NASA, to design Mission: SPACE, the first ride ever to take people "straight up" in a simulated rocket launch. The story transports you and co-riders to the year 2036 and the International Space Training Center, where you are astronauts-in-training about to embark on your first launch. Before you board the four-person rocket capsule, you're assigned to a position: commander, navigator, pilot, or engineer. And at this point you're warned several times about the intensity of the ride and the risks for people with health concerns.

> **CAUTION**
>
> Parents should exercise caution when deciding whether or not to let their children ride Mission: Space. Even if your child meets the height requirement, she may not be old enough to enjoy the ride. In the capsule, you're instructed to keep your head back against the seat and to look straight ahead for the duration of the ride. (Closing your eyes or not looking straight ahead can bring on motion sickness.) Your role as a "crew member" also means you're supposed to hold onto a joystick and push buttons at certain times. All these instructions can confuse kids and get in the way of their enjoyment of the ride.

For those who can handle the intense spinning, the sensation of lift-off is truly amazing. You'll feel the capsule tilt skyward and, on a screen that simulates a windshield, you'll see the clouds and even a flock of birds pass over you. Then you launch, a turbulent and heart-pounding experience that flattens you against your seat. Once you break into outer space, you'll even feel weightless. After landing, you exit your capsule into the Training Lab, where you can rejoin your little ones playing space-related games. ■TIP→**Note that many people come off this ride feeling nauseated and disoriented from the high-speed spinning of the vehicle, which is the technology that makes you feel as if you're rocketing into space. Keep in mind that these effects are cumulative. You may feel OK after your first ride but totally ill after your second or third ride in a row.**

TEST TRACK
Duration: 5 min.
Crowds: Heavy.
Strategy: Go first thing in the morning and get a Fastpass ticket, or you will wait—a long time. Note that the ride can't function on wet tracks, so don't head here right after a downpour.
Audience: All but young children: the line-area message will be lost on them, and the speeds and other effects may prove frightening. No pregnant women or guests wearing back, neck, or leg braces. Minimum height: 40".
Rating: ★★★

This small-scale-with-big-thrills version of a General Motors vehicle proving ground takes you behind the scenes of automobile testing. The line area showcases many of these tests in informative, action-packed exhibits, which make the wait fun. On the ride, sporty convertible Test Track vehicles take you and five other passengers through seven performance tests. In the Brake Test your ride vehicle makes two passes through a circular setup of traffic cones, and you learn how antilock brakes can make a wildly out-of-control skid manageable. In the Environmental Chamber, vehicles are exposed to extreme heat, bone-chilling cold, and a mist that simulates exposure to corrosive substances. After leaving these test chambers, vehicles accelerate quickly up a switchback "mountain road" in the Ride Handling Test. There's also a too-close-for-comfort view of a Barrier Test. The best part, the High-Speed Test, is last: your vehicle goes outside the Test Track building to negotiate a steeply banked loop at a speed of nearly 60 mph. Outside the pavilion, kids can get a soaking in the Cool Wash, an interactive water area that lets them pretend they're in a car wash.

UNIVERSE OF ENERGY

The first of the pavilions on the left, or east, side of Future World, the Universe of Energy occupies a large, lopsided pyramid sheathed in thousands of mirrors—solar collectors that power the attraction inside. Though it's a technologically complex show with a ride, film, and large audio-animatronics dinosaurs, the attraction could use some updating. One of the special effects includes enough cold, damp fog to make you think you've been transported to the inside of a defrosting refrigerator. ("We don't want to go through that fog again," one child announced after emerging from a particularly damp vision of the Mesozoic era.)

ELLEN'S ENERGY ADVENTURE

Duration: 30 min.
Crowds: Steady but never horrible; 600 people enter every 15 minutes.
Strategy: To be at the front of the ride and have your experience of the primeval landscape unspoiled by rows of modern heads, sit in the seats to the far left and front of the theater; to get these seats position yourself similarly in the preshow area.
Audience: All ages.
Rating: ★★

In the Universe of Energy show, comedian Ellen DeGeneres portrays a woman who dreams she's a contestant on *Jeopardy!* only to discover that all the categories involve a subject she knows nothing about— energy. Her challengers on the show, hosted by Alex Trebek himself, are Ellen's know-it-all former college roommate (played to the irritating hilt by Jamie Lee Curtis) and Albert Einstein. Enter Bill Nye, the Science Guy, Ellen's nice-guy neighbor and all-around science whiz, who guides Ellen (and you) on a crash course in Energy 101.

First comes the history of the universe—in one minute—on three 70-mm screens, 157 feet wide by 32 feet tall. Next the theater separates into six 96-passenger vehicles that lurch into the forest primeval. Huge trees loom out of the mists of time, ominous blue moonbeams waver in the fog, sulfurous lava burbles up, and the air smells distinctly of Swamp Thing. Through this unfriendly landscape, apatosauruses wander trailing mouthfuls of weeds, a tyrannosaurus fights it out with a triceratops, pterodactyls swoop through the air, and a truly nasty sea snake emerges from the swamp to attack the left side of the tram. A terrified Ellen is even cornered by a menacing elasmosaurus.

The ride concludes with another film in which Ellen learns about the world's present-day energy needs, resources, and concerns. It's shown on three screens, each 30 feet tall, 74 feet wide, and curved to create a 200-degree range of vision. Does Ellen win in her *Jeopardy!* dream? You'll have to travel back in time for the answer.

WONDERS OF LIFE

This aging but entertaining pavilion—fronted by a towering statue of a DNA double helix—is open only during the busiest times of the year. If you do get the chance to visit, you'll be treated to a terrific film, a flight-simulator ride, and dozens of interactive gadgets that whiz, bleep, and blink, all promoting the importance of health and fitness.

BODY WARS
Duration: 5 min.
Crowds: Rarely a long line.
Strategy: Go anytime.
Audience: All but some young children, who may be frightened by the sensation of movement the film induces and by the lurching and pitching of the simulator chamber. Not recommended for pregnant women or guests with heart, back, or neck problems or motion sickness. Minimum height: 40".
Rating: ★★

The flight-simulator technology that's used to train commercial and military pilots adapts perfectly to thrill attractions, though this nearly-two-decade old ride could be even better with some high-tech tweaking. By synchronizing the action on a movie screen with the movement of a ride vehicle, you're tricked into thinking you're moving in wild and crazy fashion even though you never leave your seat. Probably the mildest flight simulator in Central Florida, Body Wars still offers a worthwhile experience, thanks to the fascinating film and the ingenious idea. You and your fellow scientists enter a simulator chamber that, like something out of a science-fiction plot, will be miniaturized and injected into the body's bloodstream to remove a splinter, which appears on-screen like a massive rock formation. Soon, you're shooting through the heart, wheezing through the lungs, and picking up a jolt of energy in the brain as you race against time to complete your mission.

THE MAKING OF ME
Duration: 14 min.
Crowds: Manageable lines, though the theater is small.
Strategy: Line up 5–10 minutes before showtime.
Audience: 6 and up.
Rating: ★★★

Show times at Wonders of Life are staggered to pick up as soon as another lets out, so with a little luck you can segue right into this film on human conception and childbearing. Starring Martin Short as a man who, in search of his origins, journeys back in time to his parents' childhood, youth, marriage, and their decision to have him, the film uses both animation and actual footage from a live birth to explain where babies come from. Some scenes are explicit, but all the topics are handled with gentle humor—as when the sperm race for the egg to the tune of "The Ride of the Valkyries"—and with great delicacy. Many adults find the film affecting enough to get out the handkerchiefs to dab at overflowing eyes, and the film gives children a great opening for talking with their parents about the beginning of life.

CRANIUM COMMAND

Duration: 20 min.
Crowds: Long lines, but they're quickly erased by the big theater, which seats 200 at a shot.
Strategy: Go when everyone else is at Body Wars.
Audience: All ages.
Rating: ★★★

Combining a fast-paced movie with an elaborate set, Disney's audio-animatronics, and celebrity cameos, this engaging show takes a clever look at how the cranium manages to make the heart, the uptight left brain, the laid-back right brain, the stomach, and an ever-alert adrenal gland all work together as their host, a 12-year-old boy, dodges the slings and arrows of a typical day. The star is Buzzy, a bumbling audio-animatronics Cranium Commando given one last chance to take the helm of an adolescent boy before being consigned to run the brain of a chicken. Buzzy's is not an easy job; as the sign on the way to the theater warns, you're entering THE HOME OF THE FLYING ENDORPHINS. In the flick, Buzzy's 12-year-old wakes up late, dashes off without breakfast, meets the new girl in school, fights for her honor, gets called up before the principal, and, finally, returns home and has a much-needed snack. Buzzy attempts to coordinate a heart, operated by *Saturday Night Live*'s muscle team, Hans and Franz; a stomach, run by George Wendt, formerly of *Cheers,* in a sewer worker's overalls and rubber boots; and all the other body parts. Buzzy succeeds—but just barely.

FITNESS FAIRGROUND

Duration: Up to you.
Crowds: Shifting, but they don't affect your visit.
Strategy: Hang loose and take turns while you're in the Fitness Fairground.
Audience: All ages.
Rating: ★★

This educational playground, which teaches both adults and children about good health, takes up much of Wonders of Life. You can pedal around the world on a stationary bicycle while watching an ever-changing view on video, and you can guess your stress level at an interactive computer terminal. *Goofy about Health,* an eight-minute multiscreen montage, follows Goofy's conversion from a foul-living "man-dog" to a fun-loving guy. The Sensory Funhouse provides great interactive fun for the little ones and their families. The Frontiers of Medicine, the only completely serious section of the pavilion, demonstrates leading-edge developments in medicine.

THE SEAS WITH NEMO & FRIENDS

This pavilion, known for years as the Living Seas, has always been a draw with its 5.7-million-gallon aquarium filled with 65 species of sea life, including sharks. To capitalize on the huge popularity of the Disney-Pixar hit film, *Finding Nemo,* Disney Imagineers reworked the attraction using clever technology that makes it look like Nemo and pals are on an adventure in the aquarium along with the real fish. While inside, don't miss the terrific *Turtle Talk with Crush* film.

THE SEAS WITH NEMO & FRIENDS EXPERIENCE

Duration: As long as you like. *Turtle Talk with Crush* lasts 20 minites.
Crowds: Heavy to moderate.
Strategy: If you have small children or Nemo fans, go early in the morning; the wait for both the new ride and the cannily interactive *Turtle Talk with Crush* will get longer.
Audience: All ages, but especially kids under 9.
Rating: ★★★

Hop into a "clamobile" and take a ride under the sea to look for Nemo, who has wandered off from Mr. Ray's class field trip. This ride adds fresh zip to an aging, but relevant, attraction—an astonishing animation projection effect makes it appear as if Nemo and his pals are swimming among the marine life of the actual Seas aquarium. As your ride progresses, Dory, Nemo's spacey sidekick, helps Bruce, Squirt, and other pals find him. After the ride, head for the Sea Base area to line up for *Turtle Talk with Crush,* starring, of course, Crush the ancient sea turtle from the *Finding Nemo* film. In this real-time animated show, Crush "chats" and "jokes" so convincingly with kids in the small theater, that some walk up and touch the screen where Crush "swims," eyes wide as sand dollars. There's a 40-minute wait for this cartoon chat, but it's a hit with preschoolers and young school children, as well as their parents. Take a few minutes to walk around the tank at the pavilion's core and check out Bruce's Shark World for some fun photo ops and shark facts with graphics, plus displays about the endangered Florida manatee and dolphins.

THE LAND

Shaped like an intergalactic greenhouse, the enormous, skylighted Land pavilion dedicates 6 acres and a host of attractions to everyone's favorite topic: food. You can easily spend two hours exploring here, more if you take one of the guided greenhouse tours available throughout the day.

NEED A BREAK? Talk about a self-contained ecosystem: the Land pavilion grows its own produce, some of which shows up on the menu at the **Sunshine Seasons** healthful food court. Much of the fare is cooked on a 48-inch Mongolian grill.

You order at a counter, then carry your meal or snack to a table. The eatery's Asian shop offers chicken noodle bowls and spicy beef and vegetable stir-fries. A sandwich shop delivers grilled veggie Cubans, Black Forest ham, or salami sandwiches on fresh ciabatta bread, and a yummy turkey and Muenster cheese combo on focaccia with chipotle mayonnaise. The salad shop also wows with roasted beets, goat cheese, and seared tuna—among other options—over mixed greens. Wood-fired grills and rotisseries sizzle with chicken, beef, and salmon, and the bakery is a sure bet for fresh pastries and hand-dipped ice cream. To avoid the crowds, plan to eat at nonpeak times—after 2 for lunch and before 5 or after 7 for dinner.

SOARIN'

Fodor'sChoice **Crowds:** Heavy.
★ **Strategy:** Go early and grab a Fastpass, or go just before park closing.
Audience: Adults and children 40 inches or taller. This is a mild flight with a thrilling view; even very shy children will love it.
Rating: ★★★

If you've ever wondered what it's like to fly, or at least hang glide, this attraction is your chance to enjoy the sensation without actually taking the plunge. It's based on the popular attraction Soarin' Over California at Disney's California Adventure in Anaheim. It uses motion-based technology to literally lift you in your seat 40 feet into the air within a giant projection-screen dome. As you soar above the Golden Gate Bridge, Napa Valley, Yosemite, andother California wonders, you feel the wind and smell pine forests and orange blossoms. The accompanying score created by Jerry Goldsmith (*Mulan, Star Trek*) builds on the thrill, and the crispness and definition of the film, projected at twice the rate of a typical motion picture, adds realism.

LIVING WITH THE LAND

Duration: 14 min.
Crowds: Moderate all day.
Strategy: The line moves fairly quickly, so go anytime. Use Fastpass in the case of peak season crowds.
Audience: Teens and adults.
Rating: ★★★

A boat ride into a faux rain forest is just the beginning of this entertaining tour that focuses on strides in agriculture and aquaculture. You climb aboard a canopied boat that cruises, accompanied by recorded narration, through three biomes—rain forest, desert, and prairie ecological communities—and into an experimental greenhouse that demonstrates how food sources may be grown in the future, not only on the planet but also in outer space. Shrimp, sunshine bass, tilapia, eels, catfish, and alligators are raised in controlled aquacells, and tomatoes, peppers, and squash thrive in the Desert Farm area via drip irrigation that delivers just the right amount of water and nutrients to their roots. Gardeners are usually interested in the section on integrated pest management, which relies on "good" insects like ladybugs to control more harmful predators. Everyone enjoys seeing Mickey Mouse-shaped pumpkins, cucumbers, and watermelons nurtured with the help of molds created by The Land's science team; scientists also are growing a "tomato tree"—the first of its kind in the United States—that yields thousands of tomatoes from a single vine. Many of the growing areas are actual experiments-in-progress, in which Disney and the U.S. Department of Agriculture have joined forces to produce, say, a sweeter pineapple or a faster-growing pepper. The plants (including the tomato tree's golf-ball-size tomatoes) and fish that grow in the greenhouse are regularly harvested for use in the Land's restaurants.

CIRCLE OF LIFE
Duration: 20 min.
Crowds: Moderate to large, all day.
Strategy: Hit this first in the Land.
Audience: Enlightening for children and adults; a nap opportunity for toddlers.
Rating: ★★

Featuring three stars of *The Lion King*—Simba the lion, Timon the meerkat, and Pumbaa the waddling warthog—this film delivers a powerful message about protecting the world's environment for all living things. Part animation, part *National Geographic*–like film using spectacular 70-mm live-action footage, *Circle of Life* tells a fable about a "Hakuna Matata Lakeside Village" that Timon and Pumbaa are developing by clearing the African savanna. Simba cautions about mistreating the land by telling a story of a creature who occasionally forgets that everything is connected in the great Circle of Life. "That creature," he says, "is man." The lilting accompaniment is Tim Rice and Elton John's popular song; and the narration is provided by James Earl Jones narrates.

IMAGINATION!

The theme here is the imagination and the fun that can be had when you let it loose. The leaping fountains outside make the point, as does the big attraction here, the 3-D film *Honey, I Shrunk the Audience.* The Journey into Imagination with Figment ride can be capped by a stroll through Image Works, a sort of interactive fun house devoted to music and art.

HONEY, I SHRUNK THE AUDIENCE
Fodor'sChoice **Duration:** 14 min.
★ **Crowds:** Large theater capacity should mean a relatively short wait, but the film's popularity can make for big crowds.
Strategy: Go first thing in the morning or just before closing, or utilize Fastpass.
Audience: All but easily frightened children. For most, the humor quotient outweighs the few scary moments.
Rating: ★★★

Don't miss this 3-D adventure about the futuristic "shrinking" technologies demonstrated in the hit films that starred Rick Moranis. Moranis reprises his role as Dr. Wayne Szalinski, who's about to receive the Inventor of the Year Award from the Imagination Institute. While Dr.

Szalinski is demonstrating his latest shrinking machine, though, things go wrong. Be prepared to laugh and scream your head off, courtesy of the special in-theater effects and 3-D film technology that are used ingeniously, from start to finish, to dramatize a hoot of a story.

JOURNEY INTO IMAGINATION WITH FIGMENT

Duration: 8 min.
Crowds: Lines move fairly quickly here.
Strategy: Ride while waiting for your *Honey, I Shrunk the Audience* Fastpass appointment.
Audience: School-age children and adults. Preschoolers may be frightened by the brief period of darkness and the scanner at the end.
Rating: ★★

Figment, a fun-loving dragon, is teamed with Dr. Nigel Channing, the presenter of Dr. Szalinski's award in *Honey, I Shrunk the Audience*. The pair take you on a sensory adventure designed to engage your imagination through sound, illusion, gravity, dimension, and color. After the ride, you can check out Image Works, where several interactive displays allow you to further stretch your imagination.

WORLD SHOWCASE

Nowhere but at Epcot can you explore a little corner of almost a dozen countries in one day. As you stroll the 1 1/3 mi around the 40-acre World Showcase Lagoon, you circumnavigate the globe according to Disney by experiencing the native food, entertainment, culture, and arts and crafts at pavilions representing 11 countries in Europe, Asia, North Africa, and the Americas. Pavilion employees are from the countries they represent—Disney hires them to live and work for up to a year as part of its international college program.

Instead of rides, you have breathtaking films at the Canada, China, and France pavilions; several art exhibitions; and the chance to chat in the native language of the friendly foreign staff members. Each pavilion also has a designated Kidcot Fun Stop, open daily from 11 AM or noon until around 8 or 9 PM, where youngsters can try their hands at crafts projects—they might make a Moroccan fez or a Norwegian troll, for instance. Live entertainment is an integral part of the pavilions' presentations, and some of your finest moments here will be watching incredibly talented Dragon Legend Chinese Acrobats, singing along with a terrific band of Fab Four impersonators in the U.K. pavilion and the rockin' Off Kilter band in Canada, or laughing along with some improv fun in the Italy courtyard. Dining is another favorite pastime at Epcot, and the World Showcase offers tempting tastes of the authentic cuisines of the countries that have pavilions.

The best times to visit are April through early June, during the Epcot International Flower & Garden Festival, and October through mid-November, during the Epcot International Food and Wine Festival. Keep in mind, however, that crowds do get heavier during these festivals, even though they're scheduled outside the peak season.

EN
ROUTE

A World Showcase Passport ($9.95) is a wonderful way to keep a kid interested in this more adult area of Epcot. The passports, available at vendor carts, come with stickers and a badge, and children can have them stamped at each pavilion. The World Showcase is also a great place to look for unusual gifts—you might pick up silver jewelry in Mexico, a teapot in China, or a kimonoed doll in Japan.

CANADA

"Oh, it's just our Canadian outdoors," said a typically modest native guide upon being asked about the model for the striking rocky chasm and tumbling waterfall that represent just one of the high points of Canada. The beautiful formal gardens do have an antecedent: Butchart Gardens, in Victoria, British Columbia. And so does the Hôtel du Canada, a French Gothic mansion with spires, turrets, and a mansard roof; anyone who's ever stayed at Québec's Château Frontenac or Ottawa's Château Laurier will recognize the imposing style favored by architects of Canadian railroad hotels. Like the size of the Rocky Mountains, the scale of the structures seems immense; unlike the real thing, it's managed with a trick called forced perspective, which exaggerates the smallness of the distant parts to make the entire thing look gigantic. Another bit of design legerdemain: the World Showcase Rockies are made of chicken wire and painted concrete mounted on a movable platform similar to a parade float. Ah, wilderness!

Canada also contains shops selling maple syrup, lumberjack shirts, and other trapper paraphernalia. Its restaurant, Le Cellier Steakhouse, is a great place to stop for a relaxing lunch and may be easier to get into than the higher-demand Chefs de France and L'Originale Alfredo di Roma Ristorante in Italy.

O CANADA!
Duration: 17 min.
Crowds: Can be thick in late afternoon.
Strategy: Go when World Showcase opens or in the evening.
Audience: All ages, but no strollers permitted, and toddlers and small children can't see unless they're held aloft.
Rating: ★★★

That's just what you'll say after seeing this CircleVision film's stunning opening shot—footage of the Royal Canadian Mounted Police surrounding you as they circle the screen. From there, you whoosh over waterfalls, venture through Montréal and Toronto, sneak up on bears and bison, mush behind a husky-pulled dogsled, and land pluck in the middle of a hockey game. This is a standing-only theater.

UNITED KINGDOM

Never has it been so easy to cross the English Channel. The United Kingdom rambles between the elegant mansions lining a London square to the bustling, half-timber shops of a village high street to thatched-roof cottages from the countryside. (The thatch is made of plastic broom bristles in deference to local fire regulations.) And of course there's a pair of the familiar red phone booths that were once found all over the United Kingdom but are now on their way to being relics. The pavilion has no single major attraction. Instead, you can wander through shops selling tea and tea accessories, Welsh handicrafts, Royal Doulton figurines, and English lavender fragrance by Taylor of London. Theme chess sets with characters from *Alice in Wonderland* and *Robin Hood* catch the eye at The Crown & Crest. Outside the strolling World Showcase Players coax audience members into participating in their definitely lowbrow versions of Shakespeare. There's also a lovely garden and park with benches in the back that's easy to miss—relax and kick back to the tunes of the British Invasion, a band known for its on-target Beatles performances. Kids love to run through the hedge maze as the parents travel back in time to "Yesterday." Check the Times Guide and arrive 30 minutes early for a bench or 15 minutes early for a curb.

NEED A BREAK? Revive yourself with a pint of the best—although you'll be hard-put to decide between the offerings—at the **Rose & Crown**, a pub that also offers traditional afternoon tea on the outdoor terrace. The adjacent dining room serves more substantial fare (reservations often required). The terrace outside is one of the best spots for watching IllumiNations; arrive at least an hour or so in advance to get a seat.

FRANCE

You don't need the scaled-down model of the Eiffel Tower to tell you that you've arrived in France, specifically Paris. There's the poignant accordion music wafting out of concealed speakers, the trim sycamores pruned in the French style to develop signature knots at the end of each branch, and the delicious aromas surrounding the Boulangerie Pâtisserie bake shop. This is the Paris of dreams, a Paris of the years just before World War I, when solid mansard-roof mansions were crowned with iron filigree, when the least brick was drenched in romanticism. Here's a replica of the conservatorylike Les Halles—the iron-and-glass barrel-roof market that no longer exists in the City of Light; there's an arching footbridge; and all around, of course, there are shops. You can inspect Parisian impressionist artwork at Galerie des Halles; sample Guerlain perfume and cosmetics at La Signature; and acquire a bottle of Bouzy Rouge at Les Vins de France. If you plan to dine at Les Chefs de France, late lunch is a good plan; dinner at the second-floor Bistro de Paris is a gourmet treat.

NEED A BREAK? The frequent lines at **Boulangerie Pâtisserie**, a small Parisian-style sidewalk café, are worth the wait. Have a creamy café au lait and an éclair, Napoleon, or some other French pastry while enjoying the fountains and floral displays.

IMPRESSIONS DE FRANCE
Duration: 18 min.
Crowds: Steady from World Showcase opening through late afternoon.

Strategy: Visit anytime during your stroll around the World Showcase.
Audience: Adults and children age 7 and up.
Rating: ★★★

The intimate Palais du Cinema, inspired by the royal theater at Fontainebleau, screens this homage to the glories of the country. Shown on five screens spanning 200 degrees, in an air-conditioned, sit-down theater, the film takes you to vineyards at harvest time, Paris on Bastille Day, the Alps, Versailles, Normandy's Mont-St-Michel, and the stunning châteaux of the Loire Valley. The musical accompaniment also hits high notes and sweeps you away with familiar segments from Offenbach, Debussy, and Saint-Saëns, all woven together by longtime Disney musician Buddy Baker.

MOROCCO

No magic carpet is required as you enter Morocco—just walk through the pointed arches of the Bab Boujouloud gate and you'll find yourself exploring the mysterious North African country of Morocco. The arches are ornamented with beautiful wood carvings and encrusted with intricate mosaics made of 9 tons of handmade, hand-cut tiles; 19 native artisans were sent to Epcot to install them and to create the dusty stucco walls that seem to have withstood centuries of sandstorms. Look closely and you'll see that every tile has a small crack or some other imperfection, and no tile depicts a living creature—in deference to the Islamic belief that only Allah creates perfection and life.

Koutoubia Minaret, a replica of the prayer tower in Marrakesh, acts as Morocco's landmark. Winding alleyways—each corner bursting with carpets, brasses, leatherwork, and other North African craftsmanship—lead to a beautifully tiled fountain and lush gardens. The full-service restaurant, Marrakesh, is a highlight here if you enjoy eating couscous and roast lamb while distracted by a lithesome belly dancer. And one of the hottest fast-food spots on the Epcot dining scene is Tangierine Café, with tasty Mediterranean specialties like chicken kabobs, lentil and couscous salads, and freshly baked Moroccan bread.

JAPAN

A brilliant vermilion torii gate, based on Hiroshima Bay's much-photographed Itsukushima Shrine, frames the World Showcase Lagoon and stands as the striking emblem of Disney's serene version of Japan.

Disney horticulturists deserve a hand for creating an authentic landscape: 90% of the plants they used are native to Japan. Rocks, pebbled streams, pools, and carefully pruned trees and shrubs complete the meticulous picture. At sunset, or during a rainy dusk, the twisted branches of the corkscrew willows frame a perfect Japanese view of the five-story winged pagoda that is the heart of the pavilion. Based on the 8th-century Horyuji Temple in Nara, the brilliant blue pagoda has five levels, symbolizing the five elements of Buddhist belief—earth, water, fire, wind, and sky.

7

The peace is occasionally interrupted by authentic performances on drums and gongs. Other entertainment is provided by demonstrations of traditional Japanese crafts, such as kite-making. Mitsukoshi Department Store, an immense three-centuries-old retail firm known as Japan's Sears Roebuck, is a favorite among Epcot shoppers and carries everything from T-shirts to kimonos and row upon row of Japanese dolls. Diners are entertained by the culinary feats of chefs at Teppan Edon or they can indulge in sushi and other authentic bites at Tokyo Diningo.

> **PHOTO TIP**
>
> You'll get a great shot of Spaceship Earth across the lagoon by framing it in the torii gate.

AMERICAN ADVENTURE

In a Disney version of Philadelphia's Liberty Hall, the Imagineers prove that their kind of fantasy can beat reality hands down. The 110,000 bricks, made by hand from soft pink Georgia clay, sheathe the familiar structure, which acts as a beacon for those across Epcot's lagoon. The pavilion includes an all-American fast-food restaurant, a shop, lovely rose gardens, and an outdoor theater.

NEED A BREAK? What else would you order at the counter-service **Liberty Inn** but burgers, apple pie, and other all-American fare? If the weather's cool enough, you can relax at an outdoor table and watch the world go by. On a warm summer evening, this is the place to get an ice-cream sundae before IllumiNations starts.

THE AMERICAN ADVENTURE SHOW

Duration: 30 min.
Crowds: Large, but the theater is huge, so you can almost always get into the next show.
Strategy: Check the entertainment schedule and arrive 10 minutes before the Voices of Liberty are slated to perform. Grab a bench or a spot on the floor and enjoy the music before the show.
Audience: All ages.
Rating: ★★★

The pavilion's key attraction is this 100-yard dash through history, and you'll be primed for the lesson after reaching the main entry hall and hearing the stirring a cappella Voices of Liberty. Inside the theater, the main event begins to the accompaniment of "The Golden Dream," performed by the Philadelphia Orchestra. This show combines evocative sets, the world's largest rear-projection screen (72 feet wide), enormous movable stages, and 35 audio-animatronics players that are impressive but could use some upgrading. Ben Franklin still climbs up the stairs, but his movements are more tentative when compared with newer-generation figures. Beginning with the arrival of the Pilgrims at Plymouth Rock and their grueling first winter, Ben Franklin and a wry, pipe-smoking Mark Twain narrate the episodes, both praiseworthy and shameful, that have shaped the American spirit. Disney detail is so painstaking that you never feel rushed, and, in fact, each speech and scene seems polished like a little jewel. You feel the cold at Valley Forge and the triumph when Charles Lindbergh crosses the Atlantic; you're moved by Nez Percé chief Joseph's forced abdication of Native American ancestral lands and by women's rights campaigner Susan B. Anthony's speech; you laugh with Will Rogers's aphorisms and learn about the pain of the Great Depression through an affecting radio broadcast by Franklin Delano Roosevelt.

AMERICA GARDENS THEATRE

Crowds: Large during festival and holiday performances and celebrity concerts.
Strategy: Check the entertainment schedule and arrive one hour or so ahead of time for holiday and celebrity performances.
Audience: Varies with performance.

On the edge of the lagoon, directly opposite Disney's magnificent bit of colonial fakery, is this venue for concerts and shows. Some are of the "Yankee Doodle Dandy" variety. Others are hot tickets themed to such Epcot events as the Flower Power concerts with '60s pop legends during the April-through-early-June Epcot International Flower & Garden Festival and Eat to the Beat! concerts during the October-through-mid-November Epcot International Food and Wine Festival. This is also the setting for the annual yuletide Candlelight Processional—a not-to-be-missed event if you're at WDW during the holidays. The Candlelight Dinner Package (available through Disney's dining reservations hotline) includes dinner in a select World Showcase restaurant and preferred seating for the moving performance.

ITALY

In WDW's Italy, the star is the architecture: reproductions of Venice's Piazza San Marco and Doge's Palace, accurate right down to the gold leaf on the ringlets of the angel perched 100 feet atop the Campanile; the seawall stained with age, with barbershop-stripe poles to which two gondolas are tethered; and the Romanesque columns, Byzantine mosaics, Gothic arches, and stone walls that have all been carefully antiqued. Mediterranean plants such as grapevines, kumquat, and olive trees add verisimilitude. Shops sell Venetian beads and glasswork, leather purses and belts, olive oils, pastas, and Perugina cookies and chocolate kisses. At the always-hopping L'Originale Alfredo di Roma Ristorante, authentic fettuccine Alfredo and other specialties provide a great carb high for all-day visitors.

GERMANY

Germany, a make-believe village that distills the best folk architecture from all over that country, is so jovial that you practically expect the Seven Dwarfs to come "heigh-ho"-ing out to meet you. Instead, you'll hear the hourly chimes from the specially designed glockenspiel on the clock tower, musical toots and tweets from multitudinous cuckoo clocks, folk tunes from the spinning dolls and plush lambs sold at Der Teddybär, and the satisfied grunts of hungry visitors chowing down on hearty German cooking.

The Biergarten's wonderful buffet serves several sausage varieties, as well as sauerkraut, spaetzle, and roasted potatoes, rotisserie chicken, and German breads, all accompanied by yodelers, dancers, and other lederhosen-clad musicians who perform a year-round Oktoberfest show. There are also shops aplenty, including Die Weihnachts Ecke (The Christmas Corner), which sells nutcrackers and other Christmas ornaments; Volkskunst, with a folk-crafts collection that includes cuckoo clocks ranging from hummingbird scale to the size of an eagle; and Glas und Porzellan, one of only eight outlets in the world to carry a complete collection of M. I. Hummel figurines.

NEED A BREAK? Bratwurst and cold beer from the **Sommerfest** cart, at the entrance of the Biergarten restaurant, makes a perfect quick and hearty lunch, while the soft pretzels and strudel are ever-popular snacks. There's not much seating, so you may have to eat on the run.

The **Saluting Africa–Outpost,** between Germany and China, isn't one of the 11 World Showcase pavilions, but you still make a brief cultural shift when you encounter the Orisi Risi interactive drum circle, with its traditional African folklore performances. Village Traders sells African handicrafts and—you guessed it—souvenirs relating to *The Lion King.* Buy an ice cream or frozen yogurt at the Refreshment Outpost and enjoy the break at a table by the lagoon while the kids test their drumming skills on bongos or play beneath the mist set up to offer respite on hot days.

CHINA

A shimmering red-and-gold, three-tier replica of Beijing's Temple of Heaven towers over a serene Chinese garden, an art gallery displaying treasures from the People's Republic, a spacious emporium devoted to Chinese goods, and two restaurants. The gardens, planted with a native Chinese tallow tree, water lilies, bamboo, and a 100-year-old weeping mulberry tree, are one of the most peaceful spots in the World Showcase. Piped-in traditional Chinese music flows gently over the peaceful hush of the gardens, which come alive with applause and cheers when the remarkable Dragon Legend Acrobats tumble into a roped off area for their breathtaking act.

NEED A BREAK? The **Lotus Blossom Café** is beautifully renovated and offers some authentic Chinese tastes, no reservation required. Pot stickers, soups, and egg rolls are popular; new among finger foods is the Ro Jia Mo, a Chinese-style beef sandwich. Entrees include Beijing Style Roast Chicken with Noodle Salad, Orange Chicken, and Garden Vegetables & Tofu Stir Fry.

REFLECTIONS OF CHINA

Duration: 19 min.
Crowds: Steady from World Showcase opening through late afternoon, but the theater's high capacity means you can usually get into the next show.
Strategy: Go anytime.
Audience: All ages, but no strollers permitted, and small children have to be held aloft to see.
Rating: ★★★

Think of the Temple of Heaven as an especially fitting theater for a movie in which sensational panoramas of the land and people are dramatically portrayed on a 360-degree CircleVision screen. Highlights include striking footage of Hong Kong, Shanghai, and Macao. This may be the best of the World Showcase films—the only drawback is that the theater has no chairs; lean rails are provided.

NORWAY

Among the rough-hewn timbers and sharply pitched roofs here—softened and brightened by bloom-stuffed window boxes and figured shutters—are lots of smiling young Norwegians, all eager to speak English and show off their country. The pavilion complex contains a 14th-century, fortresslike castle that mimics Oslo's Akershus, cobbled streets, rocky waterfalls, and a stave church modeled after one built in 1250, with wood dragons glaring from the eaves. The church houses an exhibit called "To the Ends of the Earth," which uses vintage artifacts to tell the story of two early-20th-century polar expeditions. It all puts you in the mood for the pavilion's shops, which sell spears, shields, and other Viking necessities. At the restaurant, Akershus, you'll find cold dishes like chilled shrimp, salads and cheeses on the traditional Norwegian *koldtbord* (buffet); hot items may include braised lamb, baked salmon and venison stew. The restaurant is the only one in the park where you can have breakfast, lunch, or dinner with Disney princesses, including Aurora, Belle, and Snow White. You can reserve up to 180 days in advance, and we recommend booking as early as possible. However, you can always check at Guest Relations for seats left by cancellations.

NEED A BREAK? You can order smoked salmon and other open-face sandwiches, plus Norwegian Ringnes beer at **Kringla Bakeri Og Kafe**. The pastries here are worth the stop. Go early or late for speediest service and room to sit in the outdoor seating area.

MAELSTROM

Duration: 10 min.
Crowds: Steady, with slow-moving lines from late morning through early evening.

Strategy: Grab a Fastpass appointment so you can return after lunch or dinner.
Audience: All ages.
Rating: ★★

In Norway's dandy boat ride, you pile into 16-passenger, dragon-headed longboats for a voyage through time that, despite its scary name and encounters with evil trolls, is actually more interesting than frightful. The journey begins in a 10th-century village, where a boat, much like the ones used by Eric the Red, is being readied for a Viking voyage. You glide steeply up through a mythical forest populated by trolls, who cause the boat to plunge backward down a mild waterfall, then cruise amid the grandeur of the Geiranger fjord. Then you experience a storm in the North Sea and, as the presence of oil rigs signals the 20th century, end up in a peaceful coastal village. Disembarking, you proceed into a theater for a quick and delightful film about Norway's scenic wonders, culture, and people.

AGE OF THE VIKING SHIP
Duration: As long as you want.
Crowds: Not that bad.
Strategy: Go anytime.
Audience: Toddlers and elementary-school-age children.
Rating: ★★

Children adore this replica of a Viking ship, an interactive playground filled with ropes and climbing adventures from bow to stern.

MEXICO

Housed in a spectacular Maya pyramid surrounded by dense tropical plantings and brilliant blossoms, Mexico welcomes you onto a "moon-lit" plaza that contains the Gran Fiesta Tour boat ride, an exhibit of pre-Columbian art, a very popular restaurant, and, of course, shopping kiosks where you can unload many, many pesos.

Modeled on the market in the town of Taxco, Plaza de los Amigos is well named: there are lots of friendly people—the women dressed in ruffled off-the-shoulder peasant blouses and bright skirts, the men in white shirts and dashing sashes—all eager to sell you trinkets from a cluster of canopied carts. The perimeter is rimmed with stores with tile roofs, wrought-iron balconies, and flower-filled window boxes. What to buy? Brightly colored paper blossoms, sombreros, baskets, pottery, leather goods, and colorful papier-mâché piñatas, which Epcot imports by the truckload.

GRAN FIESTA TOUR STARRING THE THREE CABALLEROS
Duration: 9 min.
Crowds: Moderate, slow-moving lines expected from late morning through late afternoon.
Strategy: Because the ride has been updated and re-themed, it's probably worth a visit, especially if you have small children, who usually enjoy the novelty of a boat ride.

Audience: All ages.
Rating: ★★

Donald Duck goes to Mexico in this fresher, lighter version of the original El Rio del Tiempo ride, which was basically a floating travelogue. In this attraction—which shines with the polish of enhanced facades, sound system, and boat-ride props—Donald teams with old pals Jose Carioca (the parrot) and Panchito (the Mexican charro rooster) from the 1944 Disney film *The Three Caballeros*. The *Gran Fiesta Tour* film sweeps you along for an animated jaunt as the caballeros are reunited for a grand performance in Mexico City. Donald manages to disappear for his own tour of the country, leaving Jose and Panchito to search for their missing comrade.

ENTERTAINMENT & FIREWORKS

Some of the most enjoyable entertainment takes place outside the pavilions and along the promenade. Live shows with actors, dancers, singers, mime routines, and demonstrations of folk arts and crafts are presented at varying times of day; get times in your Epcot Times Guide. Or look for signs posted at the pavilions. The **World Showcase Players** of Italy and the United Kingdom, plus the U.K.'s **British Invasion**, Morocco's **Mo' Rockin'**, Mexico's **Mariachi Cobre**, and China's incredible **Dragon Legend Acrobats** keep audiences coming back.

A group that calls itself the **JAMMitors** plays up a storm several days during the week (check the Times Guide) at various Future World locations, using the tools of the janitorial trade—garbage cans, wastebaskets, brooms, mops, and dustpans. If you hear drumming from the vicinity of Japan, scurry on over to watch the **Matsuriza** Taiko drummers in action. And the American Adventure's **Spirit of America Fife & Drum Corps** will take you back a few hundred years with a patriotic nod to the birth of a nation.

ILLUMINATIONS: REFLECTIONS OF EARTH

Fodor's Choice
★

Duration: 13 min.
Crowds: Heavy.
Strategy: For best views (and if you have young children), find your place 45 minutes in advance.
Audience: All ages.
Rating: ★★★

The marvelous nighttime spectacular takes place over the World Showcase Lagoon every night before closing. Be sure to stick around for the lasers, lights, fireworks, fountains, and music that fill the air over the water. Although there's generally good viewing from all around the lagoon, some of the best spots are in front of the Italy pavilion, on the bridge between France and the United Kingdom, on the promenade in front of Canada, at the World Showcase Plaza, and on the bridge between China and Germany, which will give you a clear shot, unobstructed by trees. After the show, concealed loudspeakers play the theme music manipulated into salsa, polka, waltz, and even—believe it or not—Asian rhythms.

DISABILITIES & ACCESSIBILITY

Accessibility standards in this park are high. Many attractions and most restaurants and shops are fully wheelchair accessible. The *Guidebook for Guests with Disabilities* lays out services and facilities available and includes information about companion rest rooms. Call **WDW Information** (☎407/824–4321, 407/939–7807, 407/827–5141 TTY) a few weeks in advance if you want to arrange sign-language interpretation on a day not scheduled. The guidebook, assistive listening systems, reflective captioning equipment, handheld captioning devices, braille and audio guides, and sign-language interpretation schedules are available in the park at Guest Relations. Devices require a deposit, but no fee. Closed-captioning is available on TV monitors at attractions that have preshows. A large braille map of the park to the left of the walkway from Future World to the World Showcase Plaza.

At Future World, to go on the **Spaceship Earth Ride,** you must be able to walk four steps and transfer to a vehicle; in the unusual case that emergency evacuation may be necessary, it's by way of stairs. Service animals shouldn't be taken on this ride. Although much of the enchantment is in the visual details, the narration is interesting as well. **Innoventions** is completely wheelchair accessible. **Universe of Energy** is accessible to guests using standard wheelchairs and those who can transfer to them. Because this is one of the attractions that has sound tracks amplified by rental personal translator units, it's slightly more interesting to those with hearing impairments than to those with visual impairments.

Wonders of Life, including **Cranium Command,** *The Making of Me,* and *Goofy about Health,* is totally wheelchair accessible, with special seating sections for guests using wheelchairs. Guests with visual impairments may wish to skip *Goofy about Health.* To ride the turbulent **Body Wars,** you must transfer to a ride seat; if you lack upper-body strength, request extra shoulder restraints. Service animals aren't allowed on this ride.

At **Test Track,** one TV monitor in the preshow area is closed-captioned for people with hearing impairments. Visitors in wheelchairs are provided a special area where they can practice transferring into the ride vehicle before actually boarding the high-speed ride. **Mission: SPACE** also requires a transfer from wheelchair to seat and has an area where you can practice beforehand. In **The Seas with Nemo & Friends,** guests in standard wheelchairs can wheel onto an accessible "clamshell" vehicle; those in electronic scooters must be able to transfer to a standard wheelchair or the ride vehicle; guests using wheelchairs also have access to the aquarium area and shows like *Turtle Talk with Crush.*

In **The Land,** *Circle of Life* and the greenhouse tour are completely wheelchair accessible. "Reflective captioning," in which captions are displayed at the bottom of glass panes mounted on stands, is available at the *Circle of Life.* If you can read lips, you'll enjoy the greenhouse tour. As for the **Living with the Land** boat ride, those using an oversize wheelchair or a scooter must transfer to a Disney chair. And in the

BLITZ TOUR

BEST OF THE PARK

Plan to arrive in the parking lot 30 minutes before the official park opening. Decide ahead of time whether you want to begin with the high-octane thrills of **Mission: SPACE** or with the remarkable but not stomach-churning high of **Soarin'**. As soon as you pass through the turnstile race over to either **Mission: SPACE** or **Soarin'** and wait in line to ride or get a Fastpass appointment. Afterward, choose either the East or West Future World track to continue.

East Track: After Mission: SPACE, either ride or pick up a Fastpass to return later for **Test Track.** Then backtrack to **Spaceship Earth.** Upon leaving Spaceship Earth, head to Soarin'.

West Track: After **Soarin'** at the Land pavilion, take the **Living with the Land** boat ride, then proceed to **The Seas with Nemo & Friends;** if the wait is long, plan to return when the masses have migrated to the World Showcase. At the **Imagination!** pavilion, get another Fastpass ticket for *Honey, I Shrunk the Audience.* Visit **Journey into Imagination with Figment,** and if you have time left, meander through Image Works before returning to *Honey, I Shrunk the Audience.*

Head counterclockwise into the World Showcase, toward **Canada,** while everyone else is hoofing it toward Mexico. If it's lunchtime, you may be able to get a table right away at **Le Cellier,** one of Epcot's lesser-known dining gems. Then try to catch a performance of the British Invasion in the United Kingdom before crossing the bridge into **France,** where you can snap up an éclair or Napoleon at **Boulangerie Pâtisserie.** Shop in Morocco and Japan; then see the **American Adventure Show,** timing it to a Voices of Liberty performance. If there are lines at **Norway** by the time you get there, grab a Fastpass for the Maelstrom ride, then head for **Innoventions, Ellen's Energy Adventure** at the Universe of Energy, or one of the greatest hits like **Soarin'** or **The Seas with Nemo & Friends** that you may have missed earlier due to long lines.

Now's the time to head back to Norway and Maelstrom, followed by an early dinner at France, Italy, Mexico, or another inviting spot. See any attractions or shows that you missed, remembering that parts of Future World sometimes close ahead of the rest of the park. Stick around for **IllumiNations,** and stake out a spot early by the lagoon wall at Italy, on the International Gateway Bridge between France and the United Kingdom, or at an outdoor U.K. table. Make sure the wind is to your back so fireworks and special-effects smoke don't waft your way and obscure the scene. Take your time on the way out—the park seems especially magical after dark.

ON RAINY DAYS

Although attractions at Future World are largely indoors, Epcot's expansiveness and the pleasures of meandering around the World Showcase on a sunny day make the park a poor choice in inclement weather. Still, if you can't go another day, bring a poncho and muddle through. You'll feel right at home in the United Kingdom.

7

new **Soarin'** riders must transfer from their wheelchairs to the ride system. Boarding the **Journey into Imagination with Figment** ride requires guests to take three steps and step up into a ride vehicle. The theater that screens *Honey, I Shrunk the Audience* is completely accessible, although you must transfer to a theater seat to experience some of the special effects. The preshow area has one TV monitor that is closed-captioned. The hands-on activities of **Image Works** have always been wheelchair accessible and should continue to be.

At World Showcase, most people stroll about, but there are also Friendship boats, which require those using oversize wheelchairs or scooters to transfer to Disney chairs; **American Adventure, France, China,** and **Canada** are all wheelchair accessible; personal translator units amplify the sound tracks here. **Germany, Italy, Japan, Morocco,** and the **United Kingdom** all have live entertainment, most with strong aural as well as visual elements; the plaza areas where the shows are presented are wheelchair accessible. In **Norway** you must be able to step down into and up out of a boat to ride the Maelstrom, and an emergency evacuation requires the use of stairs; service animals are not allowed. In **Mexico** the Gran Fiesta Tour boat ride is accessible to guests using wheelchairs, but those using a scooter or oversize chair must transfer to a Disney model.

During **IllumiNations,** certain areas along the lagoon's edge at Showcase Plaza, Canada, and Germany are reserved for guests using wheelchairs. Arrive at least 45 minutes before showtime to stake out a spot.

EATING IN EPCOT

In World Showcase every pavilion sponsors at least one and often two or even three eateries. Where there's a choice, it's usually between a full-service restaurant with commensurately higher prices; a more affordable, ethnic fast-food spot; and carts and shops selling snacks ranging from French pastries to Japanese ices—whatever's appropriate to the pavilion. France has two full-service restaurants; Chefs de France is open for lunch and dinner; Bistro de Paris opens for dinner only. Lunch and dinner reservations are essential at the full-service restaurants; you can make them up to 180 days in advance by calling ☎407/939–3463 or going in person to Guest Relations at the park (only on the day of the meal) or to the restaurants themselves when they open for lunch, usually at noon. Some of these are among Orlando's best dining options.

In Future World, a large fast-food emporium, **Electric Umbrella,** dominates the Innoventions' East Plaza area. The fare here is chicken sandwiches, burgers, and salads. At the Land's **Garden Grill,** you can eat solid American family-style lunch or dinner fare as the restaurant revolves, giving you an ever-changing view of each biome on the boat ride. Besides the Princess breakfast in Norway, this is the only Epcot restaurant that includes Disney character meet-and-greets during meals. **Sunshine Seasons** in the Land is a food court with healthful Asian-inspired cuisine, including sushi, as well as souped-up salads and inspired sandwiches. The Seas with Nemo & Friends' **Coral Reef** serves excellent seafood in addition to chicken, steak, and special kids' entrées; one of its walls is made entirely of glass and looks directly into the attraction's 5.7-million-gallon aquarium full of interesting critters.

See Chapter 12, Where to Eat, for full descriptions of Epcot restaurants.

GUIDED TOURS

Reserve with **WDW Tours** (☎407/939–8687)up to six weeks in advance for a behind-the-scenes tour, led by a knowledgeable Disney cast member. Don't forget to ask about tour discounts; some companies, such as Visa, offer them. Several tours give close-up views of the phenomenal detail involved in the planning and maintenance of Epcot. Tours are open only to those 16 years of age and over (proof of age is required) unless otherwise noted.

The UnDISCOVERed Future World ($49, plus park admission), leaves at 9 AM Monday, Wednesday, and Friday from the Guest Relations lobby just inside Epcot's main entrance. The four-hour behind-the-scenes walking tour covers all Future World pavilions, some VIP lounges, and includes peeks at backstage areas such as the barge marina where Disney stores its IllumiNations show equipment. The three-hour **Hidden Treasures of World Showcase** ($59, plus park admission), beginning at 9 AM on Tuesday and Thursday, offers a look at the art, architecture, and traditions of the 11 nations represented. Take the three-hour **Gardens of the World Tour** ($59, plus park admission) to see the World Showcase's realistic replicas of exotic plantings up close and to get tips for adding landscape magic to your own garden. The tour runs on Tuesday and Thursday at 9 AM, plus Saturday during the Epcot International Flower & Garden Festival from mid-April to early June.

Ever since the Segway Human Transporters (featured at Innoventions) became a novelty, a number of Disney employees have used them for speedy transportation around the park's World Showcase. Curious guests can now take their own two-hour Segway guided tour, called the **Around the World at Epcot Tour,** daily at 7:45, 8:30, 9, or 9:30 AM. Billed as "the world's first self-balancing, electric-powered personal transportation device," the Segway takes only a brief training session to master. Once you've learned the moves and strapped on your helmet, you can cruise with the group from one World Showcase country to the next. The tour begins at Guest Relations ($85, park admission required).

If you want to get into the swim—and you have documentation of your scuba open-water adult certification—try The Seas with Nemo & Friends' **Epcot Divequest** ($140, park admission not required or included). Discounts may be available. Guests of divers who want to watch must pay admission. The tours last three hours and, under the supervision of one of The Seas with Nemo & Friends' master divers, you can spend 40 minutes underwater in the mammoth aquarium. The tours take place daily at either 4:30 or 5:30. Guests 10 and up must

7

EPCOT

Future World

NAME	Min. Height	Type of Ride	Duration	Suits	Crowds	Strategy
Body Wars (Wonders of Life)	40″	sim. ride	5 min.	All	Rarely	Go anytime. Little kids may be scared. (Open only during peak periods)
Cranium Command (Wonders of Life)	n/a	show	20 min.	All	Fast lines	Go when everyone else is at Body Wars. (Peak periods only)
Ellen's Energy Adventure (Universe of Energy)	n/a	ride	30 min.	All	ok	Best seats are to the far left and front of the theater.
Fitness Fairground (Wonders of Life)	n/a	play area	Up to you.	All	ok	Hang loose here with little ones. (Peak periods only)
★ Honey, I Shrunk the Audience (Imagination!)	n/a	show	14 min.	All	Yes!	Go early morning or just before closing. Take off the 3D glasses if little kids get scared
Innoventions	n/a	walk through	Up to you.	3 and up	at displays	Go before 10 AM or after 2 PM.
Journey into Imagination with Figment (Imagination!)	n/a	tour	8 min.	Fast lines		Ride while waiting for Honey, I Shrunk the Audience Fastpass. Toddlers may be scared by darkness and scanner at end of ride.
Living with the Land (The Land)	n/a	boat	14 min.	Teens	ok	The line moves quickly, so go anytime.
Mission: SPACE	44″	thrill ride	4 min.	8 and up	Always	Get there before 10 AM or Fastpass. Don't ride on a full stomach.
★ Soarin' (The Land)	40″	sim. ride		5 and up	Heavy	Go early, Fastpass, or use single fliers line. Mild flight ride.

Spaceship Earth	n/a	ride	15 min.	All	Morning	Ride while waiting for Mission: SPACE or just before closing.
Test Track	40"	thrill ride	5 min.	5 and up	Heavy	The ride can't function on wet tracks, so don't go after a downpour.
The Circle of Life (The Land)	n/a	film	20 min.	All	Steady	Go early or for your toddler's afternoon nap.
The Seas with Nemo & Friends	n/a	ride, film, interactive exhibits	Up to you.	All	Heavy	Get Nemo fans here early in the morning
The Making of Me (Wonders of Life)	n/a	film	14 min.	All	ok	Line up 5–10 min before showtime. (Peak periods only)
World Showcase						
Age of the Viking Ship	n/a	play area	Up to you.	3 and up	ok	Go anytime.
America Gardens Theatre	n/a	show		Varies	Varies	Arrive 30 min to 1 hr ahead of time for holiday and celebrity performances.
Gran Fiesta Tour Starring the Three Caballeros	n/a	boat	9 min.	All	Moderate	Good if you have small children.
Impressions de France	n/a	film	18 min.	7 and up	late afternoon	Come before noon or after dinner.
Maelstrom	n/a	thrill ride	10 min.	All	Slow lines	Fastpass for after lunch or dinner.
O Canada!	n/a	film	17 min.	All	late afternoon	Go when World Showcase opens or in the evening. No strollers permitted
Reflections of China	n/a	film	19 min.	All	Yes!	Go anytime. No strollers permitted.
The American Adventure Show	n/a	show	30 min.	All	Fast lines	Arrive 10 min before the Voices of Liberty or American Vybe are slated to perform.

★ = **Fodor'sChoice**

have scuba certification and children under 17 must be accompanied by a parent or legal guardian. **Dolphins in Depth** ($150, neither park admission nor diving certification required) is an experience that encourages interaction with your favorite water friends. Tour officials meet you at the entrance at 9:45, where you'll be escorted to The Seas with Nemo & Friends pavilion. Tours run weekdays and last about three hours; you'll still need to pay park admission if you want to remain after the tour. Participants must be 13 or older; those under 18 must be accompanied by a participating parent or legal guardian.

The **Epcot Seas Aqua Tour** ($100, no park admission required or included) is designed for nondivers who want to get in with the fish. You wear a flotation device and diving gear, but you remain at the surface. Anyone age 8 and older can join the tour (those ages 8–11 must have a parent or legal guardian participating); tours are limited to 12 guests. The tour meets daily at 12:30 and runs about 2½ hours, with 30 minutes spent in the water. **Behind the Seeds at Epcot** is a one-hour tour of the Land pavilion's greenhouses. It costs $14 for ages 10 and up, $10 for ages 3–9. Park admission is required.

A seasonal tour that holiday fans will enjoy is **Yuletide Fantasy,** a 3½–hour visit through the theme parks and several resorts to see how Disney's elves weave decorations and holiday traditions throughout the 40-square-mile property. One day it's a tropical paradise, the next it's a winter wonderland. The $69 tour departs daily at 9 AM from Epcot and is for those 16 and older.

Disney–MGM Studios

WORD OF MOUTH

"Getting to the parks early was a big benefit in getting time with the characters in particular. However, I would mention that if you're late getting started or need to sleep in a little, Disney MGM–Studios is a good option."

—Stacy Drew

"The Tower of Terror and Rock 'n' Roller Coaster are *not to be missed!* I am a 37-year-old mom and those were my favorite rides!"

—Dawn

Revised by
Jennie Hess

WHEN MICHAEL EISNER OPENED DISNEY–MGM Studios in May 1989, he welcomed attendees to "the Hollywood that never was and always will be." Attending the lavish, Hollywood-style opening were celebrities that included Bette Midler, Warren Beatty, and other Tinseltown icons. Unlike the first movie theme park—Universal Studios in Southern California—Disney–MGM Studios combined Disney detail with MGM's motion-picture legacy and Walt Disney's own animated film classics. The park was designed to be a trip back in time to Hollywood's heyday, when Hedda Hopper, not tabloids, spread celebrity gossip and when the girl off the bus from Ohio could be the next Judy Garland. The result blends a theme park with fully functioning movie and television production capabilities, breathtaking rides with insightful tours, and nostalgia with high-tech wonders.

The rosy-hued view of the moviemaking business is presented in a dreamy stage set from the 1930s and '40s, amid sleek Art Moderne buildings in pastel colors, funky diners, kitschy decorations, and sculptured gardens populated by roving actors playing, well, roving actors, as well as casting directors, gossip columnists, and other colorful characters. Thanks to a rich library of film scores, the park is permeated with music, all familiar, all uplifting, all evoking the magic of the movies, and all constantly streaming from the camouflaged loudspeakers at a volume just right for humming along. The park icon, a 122-foot-high Sorcerer Mickey Hat, towers over Hollywood Boulevard. Unfortunately, the whimsical landmark blocks the view of the park's Chinese Theater, a more nostalgic introduction to old-time Hollywood. Watching over all from the park's back lot is the Earful Tower, a 13-story water tower adorned with giant mouse ears.

The park is divided into sightseeing clusters. Hollywood Boulevard is the main artery to the heart of the park, where you find the glistening red-and-gold replica of Graumann's Chinese Theater. Encircling it in a roughly counterclockwise fashion are Sunset Boulevard, the Animation Courtyard, Mickey Avenue, the Streets of America area, and Echo Lake.

The entire park is small enough—about 154 acres, and with only about 20 major attractions, as opposed to the more than 40 in the Magic Kingdom—that you should be able to cover it in a day and even repeat a favorite ride.

Numbers in the margin correspond to points of interest on the Disney–MGM Studios map.

GETTING THERE & AROUND

If you're staying at one of the Epcot resorts (the BoardWalk, Yacht Club, Beach Club, Swan, or Dolphin), getting here on a motor launch that leaves from one of several boat docks is part of the fun. Disney resort buses will deposit you at the park's front entrance. If you're staying off property, it'll cost $10 to park in the lot, but you can use that same parking ticket to visit another Disney park later in the day if you have the stamina. Once the turnstiles open at 9 AM, make a beeline for

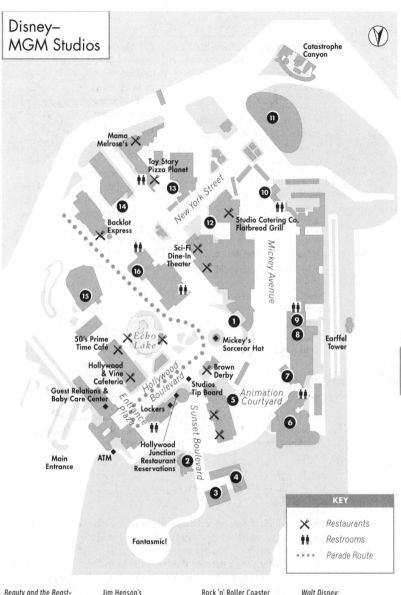

Disney–MGM Studios

Catastrophe Canyon

11

Mama Melrose's

Toy Story Pizza Planet

13

New York Street

14

Backlot Express

12

Studio Catering Co. Flatbread Grill

10

Sci-Fi Dine-In Theater

Mickey Avenue

16

15

Echo Lake

1

Mickey's Sorceror Hat

9

8

Earffel Tower

8

50's Prime Time Café

Hollywood & Vine Cafeteria

Guest Relations & Baby Care Center

Hollywood Boulevard

Brown Derby

Studios Tip Board

5

Animation Courtyard

7

6

Lockers

Entrance Plaza

Sunset Boulevard

Main Entrance

ATM

Hollywood Junction Restaurant Reservations

2

4

3

Fantasmic!

KEY	
✗	*Restaurants*
👥	*Restrooms*
••••	*Parade Route*

TIP SHEET

■ It's best to go to Disney–MGM Studios—like Epcot—early in the week, while most other people are rushing through Disney's Animal Kingdom and the Magic Kingdom.

■ Plan to arrive in the parking lot 30 minutes ahead of opening, so you can get to the entrance 15 minutes ahead.

■ Check the tip board periodically for attractions with short wait times that you can visit between Fastpass appointments.

■ Be at the *Fantasmic!* amphitheater at least 60 minutes before show time if you didn't book the *Fantasmic!* dinner package.

■ If you plan to have a fast-food lunch, try to eat early or late. The Disney–MGM counter-service places get especially packed between 11 and 2:30.

■ Set up a rendezvous point and time at the start of the day, just in case you and your companions get separated. Two excellent spots are by the giant Sorcerer Mickey Hat and at an outdoor table in front of the Starring Rolls Café near the intersection of Hollywood and Sunset.

the Information Center window at the corner of Hollywood and Sunset if you need to make same-day dining reservations. Distances are short inside MGM, and walking is the only way to get around unless you use a wheelchair or motor-powered chair.

BASIC SERVICES

BABY CARE

At the small **Baby Care Center,** you'll find facilities for nursing as well as formula, baby food, pacifiers, and disposable diapers for sale. There are changing tables here and in all women's rooms and some men's rooms.

FIRST AID

First Aid is in the Entrance Plaza adjoining Guest Relations.

CAMERAS & FILM

Walk through the aperture-shape door of **Darkroom** (or **Cover Story,** the shop next door—the two are connected) on Hollywood Boulevard, where you can buy memory cards, film, and disposable cameras. You can even have a cast member download your memory card onto a CD for $11.99 plus tax. If a Disney photographer takes your picture in front of the Chinese Theater, for example, or with Mickey Mouse on Sunset Boulevard, be sure to pick up a **Disney PhotoPass,** which will allow you to see the pictures online after you return home. Then you can purchase prints ($16.95 for an 8"×10" photo), if you like.

TOP DISNEY–MGM STUDIOS ATTRACTIONS

FOR AGES 8 & UP

Fantasmic! The ultimate battle between good and evil is staged on the moat and island of an outdoor amphitheater. Get ready for a cracking loud, fiery battle that involves water in a most unusual way. Many children under eight will love this show, but toddlers and babies are usually frightened of the loud noises.

The Magic of Disney Animation. Take a behind-the-scenes look at the making of a Disney animated film; children love the hands-on activities.

Rock 'n' Roller Coaster Starring Aerosmith. Many people think this high-speed, hard-core roller coaster is the best ride at Walt Disney World.

Twilight Zone **Tower of Terror.** Scare up some nerve and defy gravity inside this haunted hotel. You'd be better off taking the stairs—if there were any to take. As they say, the 13th story is killer.

FOR AGES 7 & UNDER

Disney Stars and Motor Cars Parade. Each day, lucky families have a chance to see more than 60 popular characters perform in this parade, including the Power Rangers, Mary Poppins, Lilo, and Stitch. Compared to the sweet "magical" mood of the Disney Dreams Come True parade in the Magic Kingdom, this parade has a faster-paced, more serendipitous tone.

Honey I Shrunk the Kids **Movie Set Adventure.** Preschoolers love to romp among the giant blades of grass and bugs at this adorable, creative playground. They can hide inside Lego pieces and slide down a strip of film coming out of a film canister.

MuppetVision 3-D. Children shriek with laughter and most adults crack up, too, during this 3-D movie in which Kermit, Miss Piggy, and other lovable Muppets vie for your attention.

Playhouse Disney—**Live on Stage!** The preschool crowd can't get enough of towering Bear from the TV show Bear in the Big Blue House when he dances the cha-cha. JoJo, Stanley, and Pooh help bring the house down. Streamers, bubbles, and other effects are the icing on this rich party cake.

Voyage of the Little Mermaid. This classic animated film is a kiddie favorite, and seeing Ariel live and in person as she sings "Part of Your World" from her grotto is a kick for fans. Evil Ursula can be a fright, however, for kids who are easily upset.

Beauty and the Beast—**Live on Stage.** The beloved fairy tale of Belle and her Beast plays out perfectly on the stage with charming performances by Mrs. Potts, Chip, Lumiere, and Cogsworth. Dancing chefs, and a sherbet parfait that transforms into a luminous showgirl, delight the little ones.

8

INFORMATION

Guest Relations is just inside the turnstiles on the left side of the Entrance Plaza. The **Production Information Window** (☎*407/560–4651*) in the Entrance Plaza is the place to find out what's being taped when and how to get into the audience.

At the corner where Hollywood Boulevard intersects with Sunset Boulevard is the **Studios Tip Board,** a large board with constantly updated information about attractions' wait times—reliable except for those moments when everyone follows the "See It Now!" advice, and the line immediately triples. Studio staffers are on hand. Just behind the Tip Board is the **Information Center** window, where you can make dining reservations.

LOCKERS

You can rent lockers at Oscar's Super Service, to the right of the entrance plaza after you pass through the turnstiles, or at Crossroads of the World. The cost is $5, with a $2 refundable deposit for the key. Bring your key to the Crossroads location for your refund.

LOST PEOPLE & THINGS

If you're worried about your children getting lost, get name tags for them at Guest Relations, and instruct them to go to a Disney staffer, anyone wearing a name tag, if they can't find you. If the worst happens, ask any cast member before you panic; logbooks of lost children's names are kept at Guest Relations.

Guest Relations also has a computerized Message Center, where notes can be left for traveling companions at this and other parks. Report any lost or found articles at Guest Relations in the Entrance Plaza or call **Disney–MGM Studios Lost & Found** (☎*407/560–3720*). Articles lost for more than one day should be sought at the **Main Lost & Found** (✉*Magic Kingdom, Transportation and Ticket Center* ☎*407/824–4245*).

PACKAGE PICKUP

Ask the shop clerk to forward any large purchase you make to Package Pickup next to Oscar's Super Service in the Entrance Plaza, so you won't have to carry them around all day. Allow three hours for it to get there.

STROLLER & WHEELCHAIR RENTALS

Oscar's Super Service, to the right in the Entrance Plaza, is the place for stroller rentals ($10 single, $18 double). This is also where to get standard wheelchairs ($10) as well as motor-powered chairs ($35). No electric scooters are available in this park. If your rental needs replacing, ask a cast member.

HOLLYWOOD BOULEVARD

With its palm trees, pastel buildings, and flashy neon, Hollywood Boulevard paints a rosy picture of 1930s Tinseltown. There's a sense of having walked right onto a movie set in the olden days, what with the art deco storefronts, strolling brass bands, and roving starlets and nefarious agents—actually costumed actors. These are frequently joined by characters from Disney movies new and old, who pose for pictures and sign autographs. *Beauty and the Beast*'s Belle is a favorite, as are Jafar, Princess Jasmine, and the Genie from *Aladdin,* the soldiers from *Toy Story,* and Lilo and Stitch from the film of the same name.

NEED A BREAK? For a sweet burst of energy, snag a freshly baked chocolate chip cookie or a pastry and an espresso at **Starring Rolls Cafe,** near the Brown Derby. Sandwiches and salads are also on the menu here, and outdoor tables offer a great people-watching spot.

GREAT MOVIE RIDE
❶ **Duration:** 22 min.
Crowds: Medium. If it's peak season and the inside lines start spilling out the door, expect at least a 25-min wait.
Strategy: Go while waiting out a Fastpass appointment for another attraction.
Audience: All but young children, for whom it may be too intense.
Rating: ★★★

At the end of Hollywood Boulevard, just behind the Sorcerer Mickey Hat, are the fire-engine-red pagodas of a replica of Graumann's Chinese Theater, where you enter this attraction. The line takes you through the lobby past such noteworthy artifacts as Dorothy's ruby slippers from *The Wizard of Oz,* a carousel horse from *Mary Poppins,* and the piano played by Sam in *Casablanca.* You then shuffle into the preshow area, an enormous screening room with continuously running clips from *Mary Poppins, Raiders of the Lost Ark, Singin' in the Rain, Fantasia, Footlight Parade,* and, of course, *Casablanca.* Once the great red doors swing open, it's your turn to ride.

Disney cast members dressed in 1920s newsboy costumes usher you onto open trams waiting against the backdrop of the Hollywood Hills, and you're off on a tour of cinematic climaxes—with a little help from audio-animatronics, scrim, smoke, and Disney magic. First comes the world of musical entertainment with, among others, Gene Kelly clutching that immortal lamppost as he begins "Singin' in the Rain" and Mary Poppins with her umbrella and her sooty admirers reprising "Chim-Chim-Cher-ee." Soon the lights dim, and your vehicle travels into a gangland shoot-out with James Cagney snarling in *Public Enemy.* Gangsters or Western gunslingers (it depends on which tram you board) hijack your tram and whisk you off to a showdown starring John Wayne.

Nothing like a little time warp to bring justice. With pipes streaming fog and alarms whooping, the tram meets some of the slimier characters from *Alien*—look up for truly scary stuff—and then eases into the cobwebby, snake-ridden set of *Indiana Jones and the Temple of Doom,* where your hijacker attempts to steal an idol and gets his or her just desserts.

Each time you think you've witnessed the best scene, the tram moves into another set: Tarzan yodels and swings on a vine overhead; then

Bogey bids Bergman goodbye with a "Here's looking at you, kid" in front of the plane to Lisbon. The finale has hundreds of robotic Munchkins cheerily enjoining you to "Follow the Yellow Brick Road," despite the cackling imprecations by the Wicked Witch of the West. Remember to check out Dorothy's tornado-tossed house—those on the right side of the tram can just spot the ruby slippers. The tram follows the Yellow Brick Road, and then there it is: a view of the Emerald City before you are brought back to reality.

SUNSET BOULEVARD

This avenue pays tribute to famous Hollywood monuments, with facades derived from the Cathay Circle, the Beverly Wilshire Theatre, and other City of Angels landmarks. As you turn onto Sunset Boulevard from Hollywood Boulevard, you'll notice the Information Center, where reservations can be made for restaurants throughout the park.

NEED A BREAK? Grab lunch or a quick snack at one of the food stands along Sunset Boulevard. You can get a burger or chicken strips at **Rosie's All-American Cafe**, a slice of pizza from **Catalina Eddie's**, a fruit salad from the **Anaheim Produce Company**, or a turkey leg or hot dog at **Toluca Legs Turkey Company**. Grab a sweet treat at **Hollywood Scoops Ice Cream**, where you can get two scoops in a cone or cup; for the diet conscious, there's fat-free, sugar-free vanilla.

BEAUTY AND THE BEAST—LIVE ON STAGE!
② **Duration:** 30 min.
Crowds: Almost always.
Strategy: Line up at least 30 minutes prior to showtime for good seats, especially with children. Performance times vary from day to day, so check ahead.
Audience: All ages.
Rating: ★★★

This wildly popular stage show takes place at the Theater of the Stars, a re-creation of the famed Hollywood Bowl. The long-running production is a lively, colorful, and well-done condensation of the animated film. As you arrive or depart, it's fun to check out handprints and footprints set in concrete of the television celebrities who've visited Disney–MGM Studios.

TWILIGHT ZONE TOWER OF TERROR
③ **Duration:** 10 min.
Crowds: Yes!
Strategy: Get a Fastpass reserved-time ticket. Otherwise, go early or wait until evening, when the crowds thin out.
Audience: Older children and adults. No pregnant women or

CAUTION
Scared of heights? Think twice before lining up for the Tower of Terror.

guests with heart, back, or neck problems. Minimum height: 40".

Rating: ★★★

Ominously overlooking Sunset Boulevard is a 13-story structure that was once the Hollywood Tower Hotel, now deserted. You take an eerie stroll through an overrun, mist-enshrouded garden and then into the dimly lighted lobby. In the dust-covered library a bolt of lightning suddenly zaps a television set to life. Rod Serling appears, recounting the story of the hotel's demise and inviting you to enter the Twilight Zone. Then, it's onward to the boiler room, where you climb aboard the hotel's giant elevator ride. As you head upward past seemingly empty hallways, ghostly former residents appear in front of you. The Fifth Dimension awaits, where you travel forward past recognizable scenes from the popular TV series. Suddenly—faster than you can say "Where's Rod Serling?"—the creaking vehicle plunges downward in a terrifying, 130-foot free-fall drop and then, before you can catch your breath, shoots quickly up, down, up, and down all over again. No use trying to guess how many stomach-churning ups and downs you'll experience—Disney's ride engineers have upped the ride's fright factor by programming random drop variations into the attraction. It's a different thrill every time. As you recover from your final plunge, Serling warns, "The next time you check into a deserted hotel on the dark side of Hollywood, make sure you know what vacancy you'll be filling, or you'll be a permanent member of ... the Twilight Zone!"

ROCK 'N' ROLLER COASTER STARRING AEROSMITH

4 **Duration:** Preride 2 min; Ride 1 min, 22 seconds.
Crowds: Huge.
Strategy: Ride early in the day, then pick up a Fastpass to go again later, especially if you're visiting with older children or teens.
Audience: Older children, teens, and adults. No guests with heart, back, or neck problems or motion sickness. Minimum height: 48".
Rating: ★★★

Although this is an indoor roller coaster like Space Mountain in the Magic Kingdom, the similarity ends there. With its high-speed launch (0 to 60 in 2.8 seconds), multiple inversions, and loud rock music, it generates delighted screams from coaster junkies, though it's smooth enough and short enough that even the coaster-phobic have been known to enjoy it. The vehicles look like limos, and the track resembles the neck of an electric guitar that's been twisted; a hard-driving rock sound track by Aerosmith blasts from speakers mounted in each vehicle to accentuate the flips and turns. There's rock-and-roll memorabilia in the line area, and Aerosmith stars in the preshow film.

ANIMATION COURTYARD

As you exit Sunset Boulevard, veer right through the high-arched gateway to the Animation Courtyard. You're now at one end of Mickey Avenue, and straight ahead are Playhouse Disney—Live on Stage!, the Magic of Disney Animation and *Voyage of the Little Mermaid*. At the far end of the avenue is the popular Disney–MGM Studios Backlot Tour.

PLAYHOUSE DISNEY—LIVE ON STAGE!

❺ **Duration:** 25 min.
Crowds: Not a problem, but lines tend to be heavy in midafternoon.
Strategy: Go first thing in the morning, when your child is most alert.
Audience: Toddlers, preschoolers.
Rating: ★★★

The former Soundstage Restaurant now holds one of the best Walt Disney World shows for children. *Playhouse Disney*—Live on Stage! uses a perky host on a larger-than-life "storybook stage" to present stars of several popular Disney Channel shows. Preschoolers and even toddlers can sing and dance in the aisles as Bear in the Big Blue House, JoJo and Goliath, Pooh, and Stanley cha-cha-cha their way through positive life lessons. Who knew that personal grooming tips could be so much fun?

THE MAGIC OF DISNEY ANIMATION

❻ **Duration:** About 30 min.
Crowds: Steady all day.
Strategy: Go in the morning or late afternoon, when you can get in with less waiting. If you want to test your talents at the Animation Academy, go straight to that line after the *Drawn to Animation* show and visit the interactive touch-screen zone later.
Audience: All but toddlers, who may be unwilling to sit still for the Animation Academy.
Rating: ★★★

This journey through the Disney animation process is one of the park's most engaging attractions. More than any other backstage peek, this tour truly takes you inside the magic as you follow the many steps of 2-D animation, an art expected to be totally replaced in years to come by computer-generated films such as the Disney/Pixar blockbusters *Toy Story* and *Finding Nemo*. The animation studio was a satellite of Walt Disney's original California studio from 1988 through 2003. It was here that *Brother Bear, Lilo & Stitch,* and *Mulan* were produced, as were several Disney short films and portions of other popular Disney features.

You begin the tour in a small theater with a performance of *Drawn to Animation,* in which a real actor plays the role of an animator interacting with Mushu, the wisecracking animated character from *Mulan*. Mushu prances between two screens above the stage. In their very funny exchange, the two explain how an animated character evolves from original concept. The animators who actually created the spunky dragon appear on screen to help tell the story. Depending on when you visit, new characters from upcoming Disney films may be introduced near the end of this show.

Next, you enter a creative zone where kiosks of computer touch screens invite you to add color to your favorite characters and even find out which Disney character is most like you (answer a brief quiz and you can't help but smile when you find your animated character double). In the Sound Stage area, your interactive computer lets you

choose from four film scenes, then cues you to voice the characters—it's a hoot when you play it back! Watch for popular Disney toon stars to appear in this area for autographs and photos.

The final stop is the Animation Academy, a delightful crash course in how to draw an animated character. Children and adults can sit side-by-side at one of 38 backlighted drafting tables as an artist gives easy-to-follow instructions on drawing a Disney character. Your sketch of Donald Duck (or the character du jour) is your souvenir. As you exit, check out the collection of drawings and cels, the clear celluloid sheets on which the characters were drawn for *Snow White, Fantasia,* and other Disney classics. Here, too, are the actual Academy Awards that Disney has won for its animated films.

8

VOYAGE OF THE LITTLE MERMAID

7 **Duration:** 15 min.

Crowds: Perpetual.

Strategy: If you decide not to ride the Rock 'n' Roller Coaster, go first thing in the morning, putting the Fastpass to good use. Otherwise, wait until the stroller brigade's exodus after 5.

Audience: All ages, though small children may be frightened by the dark theater and the evil, larger-than-life Ursula.

Rating: ★★★

A boxy building on Mickey Avenue invites you to join Ariel, Sebastian, and the underwater gang in this stage show, which condenses the movie into a marathon presentation of the greatest hits. In an admirable effort at verisimilitude, a fine mist sprays the stage; if you're sitting in the front rows, expect to get spritzed.

WALT DISNEY: ONE MAN'S DREAM

8 **Duration:** 20 min.

Crowds: Heavy.

Strategy: Get your Fastpass appointment to see one of the high-demand attractions like Rock 'n' Roller Coaster, then see this attraction while waiting.

Audience: Ages 10 and up.

Rating: ★★

Next door to the Mermaid show, One Man's Dream is a photo, film, and audio tour through Walt's life. You get to peek at his Project X room, where many of his successes were born, and hear him tell much of his own story on tapes never before made public. If you qualify as a baby boomer, it's a real nostalgia trip to see Walt resurrected on film as his "Wonderful World of Color" intro splashes across the screen. And if you're into artifacts, there's plenty of Walt memorabilia to view as you absorb the history of this entertainment legend.

MICKEY AVENUE

Stroll down this street, and you'll pass the soundstages that are used to produce some of today's television shows and motion pictures. On your left, there are several souvenir kiosks, as well as periodic street-side opportunities to mingle with character stars such as Mickey Mouse, Kim Possible, Little Einsteins, and JoJo and Goliath from the TV kiddie hit, *JoJo's Circus*. Check character schedules to be sure they're appearing.

JOURNEY INTO NARNIA: CREATING *THE LION, THE WITCH AND THE WARDROBE*

9 **Duration:** 10 min; longer if you're fascinated by movie sets.
Crowds: Not bad.
Strategy: Line up while waiting for a Fastpass appointment elsewhere.
Audience: Ages 3 and up.
Rating: ★

Launched just in time to coincide with Disney's late 2005 release of the blockbuster film *The Chronicles of Narnia: The Lion, The Witch and the Wardrobe,* this behind-the-scenes walk-through experience is a clever ad for the film, re-creating on a park soundstage the wintry Narnia set complete with forest and lamppost. As you enter the soundstage, the White Witch's castle appears on a large screen, and an actor portraying the witch makes a brief scripted appearance to set up a series of dramatic clips from the film. To get to the stage, you enter through a door fitted as a giant mahogany wardrobe. As you exit, you can browse a display that includes the White Witch's silvery sleigh, armor, some weapons, costumes, storyboards, and other film artifacts.

DISNEY–MGM STUDIOS BACKLOT TOUR

10 **Duration:** 30 min.
Crowds: Steady through the afternoon, but lines seem to move quickly.
Strategy: As you enter the tram, remember that people sitting on the left get wet. Go early; it closes at dusk.
Audience: All but very young children, who might be scared in Catastrophe Canyon.
Rating: ★★

The first stop on this tour, which you enter at the far end of Mickey Avenue, is an outdoor special-effects water tank, where audience members are recruited for an unforgettable (and very wet) video moment. (In winter, when guests aren't fond of walking through the park with damp clothing, this audience-participation scene may be canceled.) Then it's time to line up for the tram ride. As you walk through the line, you're also touring a huge prop warehouse, which stores everything you could possibly imagine, from chairs to traffic lights to British phone booths.

Board the tram for a tour of the back lot's different departments: set design, costumes, props, lighting, and a standout movie set—Catastrophe Canyon. The tram's announcer swears that the film that's supposedly shooting in there is taking a break. But the next thing you know, the tram is bouncing up and down in a simulated earthquake, an oil tanker explodes in a mass of smoke and flame, and a water tower crashes to the ground, touching off a flash flood, which douses the tanker and threatens to drown the tram. As the tram pulls out, you see the backstage workings of the catastrophe: the canyon is actually a mammoth steel slide wrapped in copper-color concrete, and the 70,000 gallons of flood water—enough to fill 10 Olympic-size swimming pools—are recycled 100 times a day, or every 3½ minutes. You'll also ride past the Streets of America back lot, where you can glimpse New York Street, with its brownstones, marble, brick, and stained glass that are actually expertly painted facades of fiberglass and Styrofoam. Grips can slide the Empire State and Chrysler buildings out of the way anytime. You'll have to walk the Streets set after exiting the tram to see the San Francisco and Chicago side streets.

STREETS OF AMERICA

It's well worth touring the New York, San Francisco, and Chicago sets here on foot—as long as crews aren't filming—so that you can check out the windows of shops and apartments, the taxicabs, and other details.

LIGHTS, MOTORS, ACTION! EXTREME STUNT SHOW

⓫ **Duration:** 30 min.

Crowds: Heavy due to attraction's newness.

Strategy: You should be able to get into the theater even if you arrive close to showtime. For the best seats, however, see it first or line up for the show while others are lining up for the parade.

Audience: All, though babies and young children may be frightened by loud noises.

Rating: ★★

In today's light-speed society, it makes sense that action films gross some of the highest figures at box offices around the world. And with the success of the high-octane vehicle stunt show at Disneyland Paris, it's only natural that Disney show designers would model this new stunt extravaganza after its action-packed counterpart. Here, Disney designers made it their mission to reveal the secrets behind Hollywood's greatest stunts, including heart-pounding car chases and explosions. The scene is a 177,000-square-foot Mediterranean village "movie set" inside a 5,000-seat, open-air theater. The premise? Filmmakers are producing a spy thriller on the set, and the director is organizing different out-of-sequence stunts. Heroes and villains perform high-speed spin-outs, two-wheel driving, jumps, and high falls using various vehicles, including watercraft. Besides experiencing the thrill of seeing choreographed stunts live, you will learn how filmmakers combine shots of various stunts to create a completed scene, which plays on the stadium's mammoth video wall. Keep in mind that this show is pretty long, and you're sitting on a hard bench with no back the whole time. If you have small children or if you think you might want to leave during the show, sit toward the back.

HONEY, I SHRUNK THE KIDS MOVIE SET ADVENTURE

⑫ Duration: Up to you.
Crowds: Steady.
Strategy: Come after you've done several shows or attractions and your children need to cut loose.
Audience: Preschoolers and young school-age children.
Rating: ★★★

Let your youngsters run free in this playground based on the movie, where there are scenes of Lilliputian kids in a larger-than-life world. They can slide down a gigantic blade of grass, crawl through caves, climb a mushroom mountain, inhale the scent of a humongous plant (which will then spit water back in their faces), and dodge sprinklers set in resilient flooring made of ground-up tires. All the requisite playground equipment is present: net climbs, ball crawls, caves, and slides. Because the area is enclosed, there's often a line to get in—but attraction hosts don't fudge on capacity limits, which maintains a comfort zone for those inside. ■ TIP➔ Keep a close eye on your toddler. It's easy to lose track of children in the caves and slides of this wacky playground.

JIM HENSON'S MUPPET*VISION 3-D

⑬ Duration: Clever 10-min preshow, 20-min show.
Crowds: Moderate, but the theater is high capacity, so if you get there 10 min early you can get in.
Strategy: Arrive 10 min early. And don't worry—there are no bad seats.
Audience: All ages.
Rating: ★★★

You don't have to be a Miss Piggyphile to get a kick out of this combination 3-D movie and musical revue, although all the Muppet characters make appearances, including Miss Piggy in roles that include the Statue of Liberty. In the waiting area, Muppet movie posters advertise the world's most glamorous porker in *Star Chores* and *To Have and Have More,* and Kermit the Frog in an Arnold Schwarzenegger parody, *Kürmit the Amphibian,* who's "so mean, he's green." When the theater was constructed, special effects were built into the walls; the 3-D effects are coordinated with other sensory stimulation so you're never sure what's coming off the screen and what's being shot out of vents in the ceiling and walls.

ECHO LAKE

Segue from New York Street into Echo Lake, an idealized southern California. In the center is the cool, blue lake of the same name, an oasis fringed with trees and benches and ringed with landmarks: pink-and-aqua restaurants trimmed in chrome, presenting sassy waitresses and black-and-white television sets at the tables; the shipshape Min and Bill's Dockside Diner, which offers snacks; and Gertie, a dinosaur that dispenses ice cream, Disney souvenirs, and the occasional puff of smoke in true magic-dragon fashion. Look for Gertie's giant footprints in the sidewalk. (Gertie, by the way, was the first animated animal to show emotion—an inspiration to the pre-Mickey Walt.) Here, too, you'll find two of the park's longest-running attractions, the Indiana Jones Epic Stunt Spectacular! and Star Tours.

EN ROUTE

Adventurous types should check out the genuine Indiana Jones bull-whips and fedoras sold at the **Indiana Jones Adventure Outpost,** next to the stunt amphitheater, and the Darth Vader and Wookie masks at **Tatooine Traders,** outside of Star Tours.

STAR TOURS

⑭ **Duration:** 5 min.

Crowds: Lines swell periodically when the Indiana Jones Epic Stunt Spectacular! lets out.

Strategy: To make sure you'll walk right on, go shortly before closing or first thing in the morning. Otherwise cruise on with the help of a Fastpass timed ticket. When you line up to enter the simulation chamber, keep to the far left to sit up front and closer to the screen for the most realistic sensations (the ride is rougher in back but the sensations of motion less exhilarating).

Audience: *Star Wars* fans, adults and children 40" or taller. No pregnant women, children under 3, or guests with heart, back, neck, or motion sickness problems; children under 7 must be accompanied by an adult.

Rating: ★★

Although the flight-simulator technology used for this ride was long ago surpassed on other thrill rides, this adventure (inspired by the *Star Wars* films) is still a pretty good trip. "May the force be with you," says the attendant on duty, "'cause I won't be!" Piloted by *Star Wars* characters R2D2 and C-3PO, the 40-passenger *StarSpeeder* that you board is supposed to take off on a routine flight to the moon of Endor. But with R2D2 at the helm, things quickly go awry: you shoot into deep space, dodge giant ice crystals and comet debris, innocently bumble into an intergalactic battle, and attempt to avoid laser-blasting fighters as you whiz through the canyons of some planetary city before coming to a heart-pounding halt.

> **WORD OF MOUTH**
>
> "Try to hit Star Tours *during* the Indiana Jones Epic Stunt Spectacular. It can get crowded just before and just after a show. Also, while waiting in line, listen for an announcement for George Sacul to respond. Sacul is Lucas spelled backward."–ajcolorado

NEED A BREAK?

If you have a sweet tooth, you should be sure to save room for some soft-serve Ice Cream of Extinction at **Gertie's**, the ice-cream bar and snack shop inside the big green dinosaur on the shore of Echo Lake. Nearby, **Min & Bill's Dockside Diner** is the spot for a stuffed pretzel or specialty shake. Step right up to the counter.

INDIANA JONES EPIC STUNT SPECTACULAR!

🔟⑮ **Duration:** 30 min.
Crowds: Large, but the theater's high capacity means that everyone who wants to get in usually does.
Strategy: Go at night, when the idols' eyes glow red. If you sit up front, you can feel the heat when Marian's truck catches fire.
Audience: All but young children.
Rating: ★★★

The rousing theme music from the Indiana Jones movies heralds action delivered by veteran stunt coordinator Glenn Randall, whose credits include *Raiders of the Lost Ark, Indiana Jones and the Temple of Doom, E.T.,* and *Jewel of the Nile.* Presented in a 2,200-seat amphitheater, the show starts with a series of near-death encounters in an ancient Maya temple. Clad in his signature fedora, Indy slides down a rope from the ceiling, dodges spears that shoot up from the floor, avoids getting chopped by booby-trapped idols, and snags a forbidden gemstone, setting off a gigantic boulder that threatens to render him two-dimensional.

Though it's hard to top that opener, Randall and his pals do just that with the help of 10 audience participants. "Okay, I need some rowdy people," the casting director calls. While the lucky few demonstrate their rowdiness, behind them the set crew casually wheels off the entire temple. Two people roll the boulder like a giant beach ball and replace it with a Cairo street, circa 1940. Then the nasty Ninja-Nazi stuntmen come out, and you start to think that this is one of those times when it's better to be in the audience. Eventually Indy comes sauntering down the "street" with his redoubtable girlfriend, Marian Ravenwood, portrayed by a Karen Allen look-alike. She is kidnapped and tossed into a truck while Indy fights his way free with bullwhip and gun, and bad guys tumble from every corner and cornice. Motorcycles buzz around; the street becomes a shambles; and, as a stunning climax, the truck carrying Marian flips and bursts into flame. The actors do a great job of explaining the stunts. You see how they're set up, watch the stars practice them in slow motion, and learn how cameras are camouflaged behind imitation rocks for trick shots. Only one stunt remains a secret: how do Indy and Marian escape the explosion? That's what keeps 'em coming back.

SOUNDS DANGEROUS STARRING DREW CAREY

🔟⑯ **Duration:** 30-min show; the rest is up to you.
Crowds: Steady.
Strategy: Arrive 10–15 min before showtime.
Audience: School-age children and up.
Rating: ★★

A demonstration of the use of movie sound effects, this show uses many of the gadgets created by sound master Jimmy Mac-Donald, who became the voice of Mickey Mouse during the 1940s and invented some 20,000 sound effects during his 45 years at Walt Disney Studios. Most qualify as gizmos—a metal sheet that, when rattled, sounds like thunder; a box

> **CAUTION**
>
> *Fantasmic!* is a theater-style show, so technically you can bring your toddlers and babies. But keep in mind that the sound effects are *very* loud and the visual effects can be very intense and scary.

of sand for footsteps on gravel; and other noises made from nails, straw, mud, leather, and other ordinary components. The premise of the show is that you will help Drew Carey, who portrays an undercover cop, find out who smuggled the diamonds from the snow globe. To do so, you don headphones to follow Carey's progress and to hear the many sounds that go into the production of a movie or television show. ■TIP➡**Most of the show takes place in utter and complete darkness and it's *very* loud—preschoolers will be frightened.** Carey's bumbling detective provides plenty of laughs for adults and older kids.

EN ROUTE If you like to sift through antiques and novelty wares, make a stop at **Sid Cahuenga's One-of-a-Kind,** where you can find authentic Hollywood collectibles, curios, and autographed items that once belonged to celebrities. You'll find child-size character clothing and a Mr. Potato Head Creation Station at **L.A. Cinema Storage,** at the corner of Sunset and Hollywood.

8

PARADE & FANTASMIC!

DISNEY STARS & MOTOR CARS PARADE
Duration: 25 min.
Crowds: Heavy.
Strategy: Stake out your curb spot an hour early and hang on to it.
Audience: All ages.
Rating: ★★

The parade wends its way up Hollywood Boulevard in true Tinseltown style with a motorcade of characters from the park's many attractions and Disney's many films perched and draped across customized classic cars. Animated stars include Mickey Mouse, Minnie Mouse, Ariel, Mulan, Woody, Buzz Lightyear, and other Disney film celebrities. Also on view are Kermit and Miss Piggy, Luke Skywalker, and even the huggable Bear from the Big Blue House.

FANTASMIC!
Duration: 25 min.
Crowds: Heavy.
Strategy: Arrive at least an hour early and sit toward the rear, near the entrance/exit. Consider the Fantasmic! dinner package, which includes reserved seating for the show.

Audience: Adults and kids over 6.
Rating: ★★★

The Studios' after-dark show wows audiences of thousands with its 25 minutes of special effects and Disney characters. The omnipresent Mickey, in his Sorcerer's Apprentice costume, plays the embodiment of Good in the struggle against forces of Evil, personified by Disney villains and villainesses such as Cruella DeVil, Scar, and Maleficent. In some of the show's best moments, animated clips of images of these famous bad guys alternate with clips of Disney nice guys (and dolls), projected onto screens made of water—high-tech fountains surging high in the air. Disney being Disney, it's Good that emerges triumphant, amid a veritable tidal wave of water effects and flames, explosions, and fireworks worthy of a Hollywood shoot-'em-up. Show up early at the 6,500-seat Hollywood Hills Amphitheatre opposite the *Twilight Zone* Tower of Terror. If you sit near the lagoon, spray from the fountains may chill you on cool nights.

DISABILITIES & ACCESSIBILITY

Studio attractions are wheelchair accessible, with certain restrictions on the Star Tours thrill ride and *Twilight Zone* Tower of Terror. Guests with hearing impairments can obtain closed-captioning devices for use in most of the attractions. You can reserve time with a sign-language interpreter by calling **WDW Guest Information** (☎*407/824–4321, 407/827–5141 TTY*) at least two weeks in advance. There's a large braille map of the park located where Hollywood intersects with Sunset, near the Tip Board.

To board the **Great Movie Ride,** on Hollywood Boulevard, you must transfer to a Disney wheelchair if you use an oversize model or a scooter; the gunshot, explosion, and fire effects mean that service animals should not be taken on the rides.

To board Sunset Boulevard's *Twilight Zone* **Tower of Terror,** you must be able to walk unassisted to a seat on the ride and have full upper-body strength. The ride's free falls make it unsuitable for service animals. *Beauty and the Beast*—**Live on Stage!** at the Theater of the Stars is completely accessible to guests using wheelchairs. To ride the **Rock 'n' Roller Coaster Starring Aerosmith,** guests who use wheelchairs must transfer to a ride vehicle—an area in which to practice the transfer is available.

At Animation Courtyard, *Voyage of the Little Mermaid, Playhouse Disney*—**Live on Stage!,** and **The Magic of Disney Animation** are wheelchair accessible; all have preshow areas with TV monitors that are closed-captioned.

You can roll a wheelchair throughout **Journey Into Narnia: Creating** *The Lion, The Witch and The Wardrobe* and the **Walt Disney: One Man's Dream** attraction, which features captioning in the theater. The **Disney–MGM Studios Backlot Tour** is wheelchair accessible,

Fantasmic! Dinner Package

If getting to the *Fantasmic!* amphitheater 60 minutes ahead of show time doesn't sound like your cup of tea, you can shave about 20 minutes off and still get a good seat by booking a *Fantasmic!* dinner package. Here's how it works: You get a prix-fixe meal at the buffet-style Hollywood & Vine or an à la carte dinner at the Hollywood Brown Derby or Mama Melrose's, plus a special pass to the show's amphitheater that gives preferred entry and lets you sidestep the main line. You can sit anywhere you like in the theater; the earlier you arrive, the better.

The price of the package depends on the restaurant you choose. At Hollywood & Vine, the buffet is $23.99 for adults and $11.99 for kids ages 3 to 9, including nonalcoholic beverage and dessert. At the Brown Derby, the menu is à la carte, with adult entrées ranging from $18 to $29 (no beverage or dessert included) and children's meals at $4.99 or $5.99, including a beverage, but not dessert. At Mama Melrose's, also à la carte, adult entrées range from $12 to $23 (beverages and dessert extra); children's meals are $4.99 or $5.99, beverage only included. Prices don't include park admission, tax, or gratuity.

Reserve dinner for at least two or three hours before the show, though you can also dine much earlier if you prefer. After dinner, you can spend more time in the park if it's early, or go straight to the amphitheater and choose your seat. Don't arrive at the last minute, though, or your seating choices will be severely limited. For one of the best spots, arrive 40 minutes before the show. Without the dinner package, you need to arrive 60 to 90 minutes early. That extra 20 minutes saved can make a big difference if you're traveling with tired and antsy children. Book the package by calling 407/939–3463 (407/WDW–DINE) or stop by the Information Center window as you enter Disney–MGM Studios in the morning to see if reservations are available. They often are. One caveat: *Fantasmic!* is an outdoor show and if it rains, the show can be canceled, even at the last minute. You still get your dinner, but you're not reimbursed for losing out on your preferred seating.

It's best to book your *Fantasmic!* dinner package a couple of months in advance, but you might be able to get a last-minute reservation.

8

too. Guests with hearing impairments who lip-read should request a seat near the tour guide. The earthquake, fire, and water effects of the Catastrophe Canyon scene make the attraction inappropriate for some service animals. The **Lights, Motors, Action!—Extreme Stunt Show** accommodates wheelchairs and offers an assistive listening device.

On New York Street, the *Honey, I Shrunk the Kids* **Movie Set Adventure** is barrier-free for most guests using wheelchairs, although the uneven surface may make maneuvering difficult. **Jim Henson's Muppet*Vision 3-D** is also completely wheelchair accessible. Those with hearing impairments may request a personal audio link that will amplify the sound here. A TV monitor in the preshow area is closed-captioned.

BLITZ TOUR

BEST OF THE PARK

Arrive well before the park opens. When it does, run, don't walk, right up Hollywood Boulevard, hang a right at Sunset Boulevard, and dash to the 13-story *Twilight Zone* **Tower of Terror.** You can make a Fastpass appointment here, then go next door to ride **Rock 'n' Roller Coaster Starring Aerosmith.** After your Twilight Zone plunge, you may want to get a Fastpass for a second go-round on your favorite of these two thrill rides. Make the **Great Movie Ride** at the Chinese Theater your next stop. If you're still waiting to return for your Fastpass appointment at the Tower of Terror or Rock 'n' Roller Coaster, catch **Lights, Motors, Action!—Extreme Stunt Show** or, if you have small children, *Playhouse Disney*—**Live on Stage!** When you've used your Fastpass, head over to the **Indiana Jones Epic Stunt Spectacular!** You can get a Fastpass to the Indy stunt show if they're jammed.

For lunch, grab a sandwich on the run at the **ABC Commissary,** or do a sit-down meal at the **Sci-Fi Dine-In Theater,** where you can sit in a 1950s-era convertible and watch B-movie film clips. Then take in the **Magic of Disney Animation** and return to Indiana Jones if you're holding a Fastpass appointment. Afterward, dash over to **Star Tours,** where you should take a Fastpass timed ticket unless the line is very short. While you wait for your appointment, catch **Jim Henson's Muppet*Vision 3-D** or the **Disney Stars and Motor Cars** parade. If there's still time before your Star Tours return, check out *Sounds Dangerous* **Starring Drew Carey** or the **Disney–MGM Studios Backlot Tour.**

Keep your Star Tours appointment, and then let the kids scramble around on the *Honey, I Shrunk the Kids* **Movie Set Adventure,** or explore Sunset Boulevard, where the shops sell much of the same merchandise as those on Hollywood Boulevard but are less crowded. If there's time, try to catch a late performance of *Beauty and the Beast*—**Live on Stage!** Finally, line up for a grand finale to cap the night with fireworks, lasers, fountains, and the cast of popular Disney characters—*Fantasmic!* Remember to turn at the gate for one last look at the Earful Tower, its perky appendages outlined in gold lights.

ON RAINY DAYS

If you must go on a rainy day, plan your day around the indoor attractions and make Fastpass appointments back to back. Enjoy a relaxing lunch at the Brown Derby or a zany time in the 50's Prime Time Café, where a great cast of servers will help you forget all about the weather.

At Echo Lake, the **Indiana Jones Epic Stunt Spectacular!** is completely wheelchair accessible. Explosions and gunfire may make it inappropriate for service animals. **Star Tours,** a turbulent ride, is accessible by guests who can transfer to a ride seat; those lacking upper-body strength should request an extra shoulder restraint. Service animals should not ride. *Sounds Dangerous* **Starring Drew Carey** is completely wheelchair accessible. However, the entertainment value is derived from the different sound effects, so you may decide to skip this one if you have a hearing impairment.

All restaurants and shops are fully wheelchair accessible, but there are no braille menus or sign-language interpreters.

Most live entertainment locations are completely wheelchair accessible. Certain sections of parade routes are always reserved for guests with disabilities. Tapings of television shows are wheelchair accessible, but none of the soundstages currently have sign-language interpreters. The noise and explosions in *Fantasmic!* may frighten service animals.

EATING IN DISNEY–MGM STUDIOS

FULL-SERVICE RESTAURANTS

The magic continues inside the park's full-service restaurants. Where else but at Disney World can you watch '50s sitcoms nonstop while you devour veal-and-shiitake-mushroom meat loaf? Waits can be long. To make priority seating reservations, call the **Disney Reservation Center** (☎407/939–3463) up to 180 days in advance, or stop in person at the restaurant or first thing in the morning at the Information Center window, just to the right of the Studios Tip Board, at the intersection of Hollywood and Sunset boulevards.

8

With its staff in black tie and its airy, palm-fronded room positively exuding Hollywood glamour, the spacious **Brown Derby** is one of the nicest—and most expensive—places to eat in the park. The Cobb salad, salad greens chopped and enlivened by loads of tomato, bacon, turkey, egg, blue cheese, and avocado, was invented at the restaurant's Hollywood namesake. The wine list is excellent, and you can count on creative chef specials. The butter comes in molds shaped like Mickey Mouse heads. If you request the *Fantasmic!* dinner package and make a reservation for no later than two hours before the start of the show, you receive a pass to skip the line, a sort of Fastpass, for this big performance.

Spend a leisurely lunch at the **50's Prime Time Café,** where video screens constantly show sitcoms, place mats pose television trivia quizzes, and waitresses play "Mom" with convincing enthusiasm, insisting that you clean your plate. The menu is what your own mom might have made were she a character on one of those video screens—meat loaf, broiled chicken, pot roast, hot roast beef sandwiches—all to be washed down with root-beer floats and ice-cream sodas.

DISNEY–MGM

NAME	Min. Height	Type of Ride	Duration	Suits	Crowds	Strategy
Hollywood Blvd.						
Great Movie Ride	n/a	tour	22 min.	5 and up	Medium	Go while waiting for Fastpass on another ride. Lines out the door mean 25-mins. wait.
Sunset Blvd.						
Beauty and the Beast—Live on Stage!	n/a	show	30 min.	All	Yes!	Go 30 min before show time for good seats. Performance days vary, so check ahead.
★ Rock 'n' Roller Coaster Starring Aerosmith	48"	thrill ride	3 min.	7 and up	Huge	Ride early, then Fastpass for another go later.
★ Twilight Zone Tower of Terror	40"	thrill ride	10 min.	7 and up	Yes!	Fastpass. Go early or late evening. Plunging ride.
Animation Courtyard						
Playhouse Disney—Live on Stage!	n/a	show	25 min.	toddlers & pre-schoolers	Afternoon	Go first thing in the morning, when your child is most alert or to wind down at the end of the day.
★ The Magic of Disney Animation	n/a	tour	Up to you.	All	Steady	Go in the morning or late afternoon. Toddlers may get bored.
Voyage of the Little Mermaid	n/a	show	15 min.	All	Yes!	Fastpass Rock 'n' Roller Coaster and head for this show first thing. Otherwise, wait until after 5.
Walt Disney: One Man's Dream	n/a	film	20 min.	10 and up	Heavy	See this attraction while waiting for a Fastpass appointment.
Mickey Avenue						
Disney-MGM Studios Backlot Tour	n/a	show	35 min.	All	Fast lines	People sitting on the left get wet. Go early; it closes at dusk.
Journey Into Narnia	n/a	show	10 min.	3 and up	Not bad	Line up while waiting on another Fastpass.

Streets of America

Honey, I Shrunk the Kids Movie Set Adventure	n/a	play area	Up to you.	All	Steady	Come after you've done several shows and your kids need to cut loose.
Jim Henson's Muppet*Vision 3-D	n/a	3-D film	20 min.	All	Moderate	Arrive 10 min early. And don't worry–there are no bad seats.
Lights, Motors, Action! Extreme Stunt Show	n/a	show	30 min.	All	Heavy	You should be able to get into the theater even if you arrive close to show time. For the best seats line up for the show while others are lining up for the parade.

Echo Lake

Indiana Jones Epic Stunt Spectacular!	n/a	stunt show	30 min.	All	Fast lines	Go at night, when the idols' eyes glow red. Sit up front to feel heat of truck on fire.
Sounds Dangerous Starring Drew Carey	n/a	show	30 min.	6 and up	ok	Arrive 15 min before show. You sit in total darkness.
Star Tours	40"	sim. ride	5 min.	5 and up	Fast lines	Go before closing, early morning or get a Fastpass. Keep to the left in line, for best seats.

Entertainment

Disney Stars and Motor Cars	n/a	parade	25 min.	All	Heavy	Stake out your curb spot an hr early and hang on to it.
★ Fantasmic!	n/a	show	25 min.	All	Heavy	Arrive at least 1 hr early and sit toward the rear, near the entrance/exit, or buy the Fantasmic! dinner package for preferred admission.

★ = Fodor'sChoice

To replace the energy you've no doubt depleted by miles of theme-park walking, you can load up on carbs at **Mama Melrose's Ristorante Italiano.** The menu has pastas, seafood, pizza baked in brick ovens, and several vegetarian entrées, including eggplant Parmesan. Ask for the Fantasmic! dinner package if you want faster access to the show.

If you don't mind zombies leering at you while you consume chef salads, barbecue pork sandwiches, charbroiled sirloin, and Milky-Way-Out Milk Shakes, then head to **Sci-Fi Dine-In Theater Restaurant,** a re-creation of a drive-in. All the tables are set in candy-color '50s convertibles and face a large screen, on which a 45-minute reel of the best and worst of science-fiction trailers plays in a continuous loop.

SELF-SERVICE RESTAURANTS

The **ABC Commissary** serves a full breakfast menu before 10:30 AM and has a refreshingly different fast-food menu that includes Cuban sandwiches, vegetable noodle stir-fry, and fish-and-chips. At the **Backlot Express,** in Echo Lake, you don't need a reservation to enjoy the burgers, hot dogs, grilled veggie sandwiches, and chef salads.

A buffet of rotisserie meats and poultry, salads, seafood, and fresh pastas makes up the dinner fare at **Hollywood & Vine Cafeteria of the Stars.** There's a Hollywood theme to the place; servers are just hoping to be discovered by some passing Hollywood screen agent, and the place is a real charmer—totally '50s and vaguely deco. Character meals at breakfast and lunch are attended by *Playhouse Disney* stars JoJo and Goliath from "JoJo's Circus" and June and Leo from "The Little Einsteins."

In Echo Lake, **Min & Bill's Dockside Diner** is the spot for a stuffed pretzel or specialty shake. Step right up to the counter. The **Studio Catering Company Flatbread Grill,** near the Disney–MGM Studios Backlot Tour exit, has specialty sandwiches, salads, and desserts. **Toy Story Pizza Planet Arcade** is for kids who need some amusement with their pizza—video games and other diversions allow parents to relax with a cappuccino or espresso while their children stay entertained.

Disney's Animal Kingdom

Revised by
Jennie Hess

HUMANKIND'S ENDURING LOVE FOR ANIMALS is the inspiration for WDW's fourth theme park, Disney's Animal Kingdom. At 500 acres and five times the size of the Magic Kingdom, Animal Kingdom is the largest in area of all Disney theme parks worldwide. The space gives Disney Imagineers plenty of scope for their creativity, and it allows for growth, an example of which is Expedition Everest. Opened in 2006, it's the park's biggest thrill attraction—a runaway train ride on a rugged mountain complete with icy ledges, dark caves, and a yeti legend.

Disney's Animal Kingdom park, opened in 1998, explores the stories of all animals—real, imaginary, and extinct. As you enter through the Oasis, exotic background music plays, and you're surrounded by a green grotto, gentle waterfalls, and gardens alive with exotic birds, reptiles, and mammals. The Oasis opens early, so you can do a lot of critter-watching before its inhabitants settle down to snooze through the heat of the day.

At park opening (8 or 9 AM, depending on the season), Mickey, Minnie, and the gang arrive in a safari vehicle to lead the first guests into the heart of the park, where animals thrive in careful re-creations of natural landscapes in exotic lands ranging from Thailand and India to southern Africa. You'll also find rides, some of Disney's finest musical shows, eateries, and, of course, Disney characters—where else does the Lion King truly belong? Cast members come from all over the world—Kenya and South Africa as often as Kentucky and South Carolina. That's part of the charm of the place. All this is augmented by an earnest educational undercurrent that's meant to foster a renewed appreciation for the animal kingdom.

The park is laid out very much like its oldest sibling, the Magic Kingdom. The hub of this wheel is the spectacular Tree of Life in the middle of Discovery Island. Radiating from Discovery Island's hub are several spokes—the other "lands," each with a distinct personality. South of Discovery Island is Camp Minnie-Mickey, a character-greeting and show area.

Numbers in the margin correspond to points of interest on the Disney's Animal Kingdom map.

GETTING THERE & AROUND

To get to the Animal Kingdom your options are to take a Disney bus, if you're staying on-site, or to drive ($10 parking fee, good at other Disney parks throughout the day). Although this is technically Disney's largest theme park, most of the land is reserved for the animals. The pedestrian areas are actually quite compact with relatively narrow passageways. The only way to get around is on foot.

BASIC SERVICES

BABY CARE

The **Baby Care Center** is in Discovery Island. You can buy disposable diapers, formula, baby food, and pacifiers.

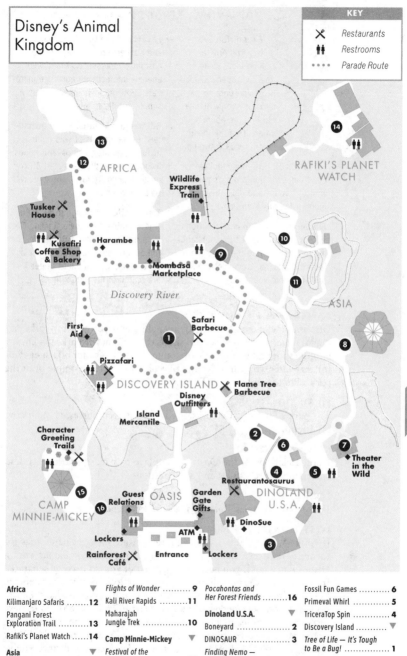

TOP ANIMAL KINGDOM ATTRACTIONS

Expedition Everest. The Animal Kingdom's cleverly themed roller coaster is a spine-tingling trip into the snowy Himalayas to find the abominable snowman. It's a ride best reserved for kids 7 and up.

DINOSAUR. Extremely lifelike giant dinosaurs jump out as your vehicle swoops and dips. We recommend it for kids 8 and up.

Finding Nemo—The Musical. Don't miss a performance of this outstanding musical starring the most charming, colorful characters ever to swim their way into your heart.

Festival of the Lion King. Singers and dancers dressed in fantastic costumes representing many wild animals interact with audience members and even invite children into a simple circular parade.

Kilimanjaro Safaris. You're guaranteed to see dozens of wild animals, including giraffes, hippos, and rhinos, living in authentic, re-created African habitats. If you're lucky, the lions will be stirring, too.

Tree of Life—It's Tough to Be a Bug! This adorable 3-D movie starring Flik from the Disney film *A Bug's Life*, is full of surprises, including "shocking" special effects. Some kids under 7 are scared of the loud noises.

CAMERAS & FILM

Disposable cameras are widely available, and you can buy film and digital memory cards at several shops throughout the park. If a Disney photographer takes a picture of you in the park, ask for a **Disney PhotoPass**—later, you can view and purchase the pictures online or at the park's Photo Center in the Oasis.

FIRST AID

The park's First Aid Center, staffed by registered nurses, is in Discovery Island.

INFORMATION

Guest Relations in the Oasis is the place to pick up park maps and entertainment schedules and ask questions.

LOCKERS

Lockers are in Guest Relations ($5, $2 key deposit).

LOST THINGS & PEOPLE

If you're worried about your children getting lost, get name tags for them at Discovery Island. Instruct them to speak to someone with a Disney name tag if you become separated. If you do become separated from your child, immediately report your loss to any cast member. Lost-children logbooks are at Discovery Island, which is also the location of the **Animal Kingdom Lost & Found** (☎407/938–2785). To retrieve lost articles after leaving the park, call Lost & Found on the same day, or call **Main Lost & Found** (✉*Magic Kingdom Transportation & Ticket Center* ☎407/824–4245) if more than a day has passed since you've lost the article.

PACKAGE PICKUP

You can have shop clerks forward any large purchases to Package Pickup near the Main Entrance Plaza in the Oasis, so that you won't have to carry them around all day. Allow three hours for the journey.

STROLLER & WHEELCHAIR RENTALS

Garden Gate Gifts, in the Oasis, rents strollers ($10 single, $18 double), wheelchairs ($10), and electric scooters ($35).

THE OASIS

This lush entrance garden makes you feel as if you've been plunked down in the middle of a rain forest. Cool mist, the aroma of flowers, and playful animals and colorful birds all enliven a miniature landscape of streams and grottoes, waterfalls, and glades fringed with banana leaves and jacaranda. On the finest Orlando mornings, when the mists shroud the landscape, it's the scene-setter for the rest of your day. It's also where you can take care of essentials before entering the park. Here you'll find stroller and wheelchair rentals, Guest Relations, and an ATM.

EN ROUTE Before you pass through the turnstiles on your way into the Animal Kingdom, stop at the **Outpost Shop** for a must-have safari hat with Mouse ears. Once in Discovery Island, look for a Minnie Mouse headband with a safari-style bow at **Creature Comforts.**

DISCOVERY ISLAND

Primarily the site of the Tree of Life, this land is encircled by Discovery River, which isn't an actual attraction but can be viewed from a bridge in Harambe. The island's whimsical architecture, with wood carvings handmade in Bali, adds plenty of charm and a touch of fantasy to this park hub. The verdant **Discovery Island Trails** that lead to the Tree of Life provide habitats for kangaroos, lemurs, Galapagos tortoises, and other creatures you won't want to miss while here. It's hard to tear the kids from the glass panel in a cavelike observation area where you can see river otters frolic underwater and above. You'll find some great shops and some good counter-service eateries here, and the island is also the site of the daily Mickey's Jammin' Jungle Parade. Most of the visitor services that aren't in the Oasis are here, on the border with Harambe, including the Baby Care Center, First Aid Center, and Lost & Found.

TREE OF LIFE—IT'S TOUGH TO BE A BUG!

❶ **Duration:** 20 min.

Crowds: Moderate to heavy.

Strategy: Get a Fastpass reservation after you've been on Kilimanjaro Safaris. If the line is 40 minutes or less, however, save your Fastpass for another ride, such as DINOSAUR, and get into the regular line. As you stroll the winding trail around the Tree of Life, it's fun to spot animals like ring-tailed lemurs, Galapagos tortoises, and red kangaroos in their habitats and to see how many of the creature carvings you can find on the trunk, branches, and roots of the mammoth icon.

Audience: All ages, but the show is very loud and some effects will frighten children under 8. There's always at least one screaming toddler in every show.

Rating: ★★★

A monument to all earth's creatures, the park's centerpiece is an imposing 14 stories high and 50 feet wide at its base. Its 100,000-plus leaves are several shades of green fabric, each carefully placed for a realistic effect. Carved into its thick trunk, gnarled roots, and soaring branches—some of which are supported by joints that allow them to sway in a strong wind—are nearly 350 intricate animal forms that include a baboon, a whale, a horse, the mighty lion, and even an ankylosaurus. Outside, paths tunnel underneath the roots as the fauna-encrusted trunk towers overhead. It's a rich and truly fascinating sight—the more you look the more you see. The path leads you inside the tree trunk to the star attraction of Discovery Island, where you get a bug's-eye view of life. The whimsical 3-D film adventure *It's Tough to Be a Bug!* is modeled vaguely on the animated film *A Bug's Life* from Disney-Pixar, the creators of *Toy Story.* Special film and theater effects spray you with "poison," zap you with a swatter, and even poke you with a stinger. It's all in good fun—and the surprise ending is too playful to give away.

DINOLAND U.S.A.

Just as it sounds, this is the place to come in contact with re-created prehistoric creatures, including the fear-inspiring carnotaurus and the gentle iguanodon. The landscaping includes live plants that have evolved over the last 65 million years. In collaboration with Chicago's Field Museum, Disney has added a complete, full-scale skeleton cast of Dino-Sue—also known as "Sue"—the 65-million-year-old Tyrannosaurus rex discovered near the Black Hills of South Dakota. After admiring "Sue," you can go on the thrilling Dinosaur ride, amble along the Cretaceous Trail, play in the Boneyard, or take in the *Finding Nemo–The Musical* show at the Theater in the Wild. Kids will want to hitch a dino-ride on the TriceraTop Spin and on the Primeval Whirl family coaster, which has spinning "time machines." There's no need to dig for souvenirs at Chester and Hester's Dinosaur Treasures gift shop—all you need is your wallet.

NEED A BREAK?   Carnivores and omnivores alike will want to make tracks for **Dino Bite Snacks,** the perfect spot for cooling off with sundaes, milk shakes, and floats.

BONEYARD

❷ Duration: Up to you and your children.

Crowds: Can be heavy midmorning to early afternoon.

Strategy: Let the kids burn off energy here while waiting for your Fastpass appointment for Dinosaur, or head over late in the day when kids need a break to run free.

TIP SHEET

■ Try to visit the Animal Kingdom during the week. The pedestrian areas of the park are relatively compact and the park can feel horribly packed on weekends when it's especially crowded.

■ Arrive a half hour before park opening to get a jump on the crowds and to see the wild animals at their friskiest.

■ Check the park's Tip Board for the latest information on lines just after crossing the bridge into Discovery Island.

■ Set up a rendezvous point and time at the start of the day, just in case you and your companions get separated. Some good places include the outdoor seating area of Tusker House restaurant in Africa, in front of DinoLand U.S.A.'s Boneyard, and at the turnstile of the *Festival of the Lion King* show.

Audience: Toddlers, school-age children, and their families.
Rating: ★★★

Youngsters can slide, dig, bounce, slither, and stomp around this archaeological dig site–cum–playground, the finest play area in any of the four Disney parks. In addition to a huge sand pit where children can dig for mammoth bones, there are twisting short and long slides, climbing nets, caves, and a jeep to climb on. Stomp on the dino-footprints to make 'em roar.

DINOSAUR

❸ Duration: Not quite 4 min.
Crowds: Can get heavy midmorning.
Strategy: Go first thing in the morning or at the end of the day, or use the Fastpass.
Audience: All ages except very young children, pregnant women, or guests with back, neck, or heart problems. The realistic carnivores frighten a lot of children under 8. Minimum height: 40".
Rating: ★★★

This wild adventure through time puts you face-to-face with huge dinosaurs that move and breathe with uncanny realism. When a carload of guests rouses a cantankerous carnotaurus from his Cretaceous slumber, it's showtime. You travel back 65 million years on a fast-paced, twisting adventure and try to save the last living iguanodon as a massive asteroid hurtles toward Earth. Exciting audio-animatronics and special effects bring to life dinosaurs like the raptor, pterodactyl, styracosaurus, alioramus, and compsognather. Be prepared for a short but steep drop toward the end of the ride.

TRICERATOP SPIN

❹ Duration: About 2 min.
Crowds: Heavy.
Strategy: Ride early or line up while waiting for your Fastpass appointment for Dinosaur.

Audience: Toddlers, school-age children and their families.

Rating: ★★

TriceraTop Spin is designed for playful little dinophiles who ought to get a kick out of whirling around this ride's giant spinning toy top and dodging incoming comets in their dino-mobiles. "Pop!" goes the top and out comes a grinning dinosaur as four passengers in each vehicle fly in a circle and maneuver up and down.

> **TIMING TIP**
>
> Because of the proximity of the two attractions, *Finding Nemo–The Musical* is a good place to take younger kids while older siblings wait in line and ride Expedition Everest. If there's not a long wait for Everest, however, the entire family should see the brilliant new musical.

PRIMEVAL WHIRL

⑤ Duration: About 2½ min.

Crowds: Heavy.

Strategy: Kids may want to ride twice, so take your first spin early, then get a Fastpass to return later if the wait is longer than 20 minutes. Minimum height: 48".

Rating: ★★★

In a free-spinning, four-passenger vehicle, you head on a brief journey back in time on this outdoor open-air coaster, twisting, turning, and even venturing into the jaws of a dinosaur "skeleton." As you ride, crazy cartoon dinosaurs in shades of turquoise, orange, yellow, and purple pop up along the track bearing signs that warn "The End Is Near." More signs warn of "Meteors!" and suggest that you "Head for the Hills!"—coaster hills, that is. Halfway through the ride, your car seems to spin out of control and you take the next drop backward. The more weight there is in the vehicle, the more you spin.

FOSSIL FUN GAMES

⑥ Duration: Up to you.

Cost: Varies.

Strategy: Bring a pocketful of change and a stash of ones.

Audience: Older children and adults.

Rating: ★

A carnival-style midway in the middle of DinoLand U.S.A., this fun fair draws crowds with games like Whack a Packycephalosaur and the mallet-strength challenge, Dino-Whamma. The prehistoric fun comes at a price, however, and stone currency is not accepted. Prizes are mostly of the plush-character variety—you might win your sweetheart a stuffed Nala.

FINDING NEMO–THE MUSICAL

Duration: 30 min.

Crowds: Expected to be heavy, as with all new attractions.

Strategy: Arrive 40 minutes before showtime.

Audience: All ages, especially fans of the film.

Rating: ★★★

This is a fish tale of magnificent scale; a show so creative and fun that some audience members enthused upon the show's debut that it was, alone, worth the price of park admission. Using as a foundation the sweet story of the animated film, *Finding Nemo,* Disney Imagineers collaborated with several Broadway talents to produce this richly staged musical brimming with special effects and elaborate, larger-than-life puppets acted by gifted performers, dancers, and acrobats. It's all choreographed to bring you into Nemo's big blue world. The basic story remains the same as in the movie—Nemo and his father Marlin go on separate journeys that ultimately teach them how to understand each other. Zany Dory, with her hilarious memory lapses, cool Crush the sea turtle dude, tap dancing sharks, and other characters give memorable supporting-role turns. Original songs by Tony Award–winning *Avenue Q* co-composer-creator Robert Lopez and a cappella musical *Along the Way* co-creator Kristen Anderson-Lopez add new depth and energy to the story. Michael Curry, who co-designed the character puppets of Broadway's *The Lion King,* created the musical's eye-popping puppetry; Peter Brosius, artistic director of The Children's Theatre Company of Minneapolis and winner of a regional theater Tony Award, directed the show. Expect multigenerational humor and Broadway- and pop-inspired tunes.

ASIA

Meant to resemble a rural village somewhere in Asia, this land is full of remarkable rain-forest scenery and ruins. Groupings of trees grow from a crumbling tiger shrine and two massive towers, one representing Thailand, the other Nepal. The towers are the habitat for two families of gibbons, whose hooting fills the air at all hours of the day. While you're here, take a wild ride on Expedition Everest, stroll the Maharajah Jungle Trek, see the *Flights of Wonder* bird show, and raft the Kali River Rapids.

EXPEDITION EVEREST

8 Duration: 2½ min.

Crowds: Huge for this park's wildest thrill ride yet.

Strategy: Rush here as soon as the park opens and enter the line if the wait isn't too long—the detail of this re-created Himalayan village is worth soaking up as you walk through; otherwise, grab a Fastpass.

Audience: Since the coaster is supposed to be less intense than, say, Space Mountain, brave children who meet the 44"-minimum height requirement can ride.

Rating: ★★★

Disney really turned up the thrill factor in the Animal Kingdom with Expedition Everest, a roller coaster coiling through a 200-foot-high faux Himalayan mountain. The story goes that a fierce yeti guards the route to Mt. Everest. Of course, you're willing to risk running across the big guy in your quest to reach the summit. So, you board an "aging," seemingly innocuous, 34-passenger, steam-engine train into the mountains. You roll past bamboo forests, thundering waterfalls, and sparkling glacier fields as you climb higher through snowcapped peaks. All of a sudden your trip turns perilous: the train becomes a runaway, barreling forward then backward around icy ledges and through dark snowy caverns. Nearly a mile of twists and turns in and out of the dark mountain, and at one point your train plunges a harrowing 80 feet. Will you find the yeti? Do you even want to? Well, what's a Disney ride without a mammoth, lifelike, animatronic monster?

For adults who yearn to travel to far-off places like Nepal, the line area is an architectural marvel that enriches the yeti story. The buildings, inside and out, are created in the same style as Himalayan mountain dwellings and teem with cultural references that include prayer flags, totems, and other artifacts from Tibet, Nepal, and the entire region. Photographs of Himalayan people are displayed in the line gallery.

FLIGHTS OF WONDER

9 **Duration:** 30 min.
Crowds: Not a problem.
Strategy: Arrive 15 minutes before showtime and find a shaded seat beneath one of the awnings—the sun can be brutal in summer.
Audience: All.
Rating: ★★

This outdoor show area near the border with Africa is the place for spectacular demonstrations of skill by falcons, hawks, and other rare and fascinating birds, which swoop down over the audience.

MAHARAJAH JUNGLE TREK

10 **Duration:** As long as you like.
Crowds: Not bad because people are constantly moving.
Strategy: Go anytime.
Audience: All ages.
Rating: ★★★

Get an up-close view of some unusual and interesting animals along this trail: a Komodo dragon perched on a rock; Malayan tapirs near the wooden footbridge; families of giant fruit bats that hang to munch fruit from wires and fly very close to the open and glass-protected viewing areas; and Bengal tigers in front of a maharajah's palace. The tigers have their own view (with no accessibility, of course) of a group of Asian deer and a herd of black buck, an antelope species. At the end of the trek, you walk through an aviary with a lotus pool. Disney interpreters, many from Asian countries, are on hand to answer any and all questions.

KALI RIVER RAPIDS

11 **Duration:** About 7 min.
Crowds: Long lines all day.
Strategy: Use your Fastpass, or go during the parade.
Audience: All but very young children and adults with heart, back, or neck problems or motion sickness. Minimum height: 38".
Rating: ★★★

Asia's thrilling adventure ride is to the Animal Kingdom what Splash Mountain is to the Magic Kingdom. Aboard a round raft that seats 12, you run the Chakranadi River. After passing through a huge bamboo tunnel filled with jasmine-scented mist, your raft climbs 40 feet upriver, lurches and spins through a series of sharp twists and turns, and then approaches an immense waterfall, which curtains a giant carved tiger face. Past rain forests and temple ruins, you find yourself face-to-face with the denuded slope of a logged-out woodland burning out of control. There are many more thrills, but why spill the beans? Be warned: you will get wet, and there's an 80% chance you will get so soaked you'll have to wring out your clothing in the nearest rest room afterward, so if you don't mind the extra baggage, ~~plan ahead with a change~~ of clothing and a plastic bag.

AFRICA

This largest of the lands is an area of forests and grasslands, predominantly an enclave for wildlife from the continent. The focus is on live animals at the key attractions. Harambe, on the northern bank of Discovery River, is Africa's starting point. Inspired by several East African coastal villages, this Disney town has so much detail that it's mind-boggling to try to soak it all up. Signs on the apparently peeling stucco walls of the buildings are faded, as if bleached by the sun, and everything has a hot, dusty look. For souvenirs with both Disney and African themes, browse through the Mombasa Marketplace and Ziwani Traders. Safari apparel, decorative articles for the home, and jewelry are on offer.

NEED A BREAK? The tantalizing aroma of fresh-baked cinnamon buns leads to the **Kusafiri Coffee Shop & Bakery**, where, after just one look, you may give in to the urge. These buns are worth the banknotes, and they pair well with a cappuccino or espresso. Kids may opt for a giant cookie and milk.

KILIMANJARO SAFARIS
Duration: 20 min.
Crowds: Heavy in the morning.
Strategy: Arrive in the park first thing in the morning—it's worth the trouble—and come straight here using the Fastpass if necessary. If you arrive at the park late morning, save this for the end of the day, when it isn't so hot. You'll probably see about the same number of animals as in early morning.
Audience: All ages—parents can hold small tykes and explain the poacher fantasy.
Rating: ★★★

A giant Imagineered baobab tree is the starting point for this adventure into the up-country. Although re-creating an African safari in the United States may not be a new idea, this safari goes a step beyond merely allowing you to observe rhinos, hippos, antelope, wildebeests, giraffes, zebras, elephants, lions, and the like. There are illustrated game-spotting guides above the seats in the open-air safari vehicles, and as you lurch and bump over some 100 acres of savanna, forest, rivers, and rocky hills, you'll see most of these animals—sometimes so close you feel like you could reach out and touch them. It's easy to suspend disbelief here because the landscape is so effectively modeled and replenished by Disney horticulturists. This being a theme park, dangers lurk in the form of ivory poachers, and it suddenly becomes your mission to save a group of elephants from would-be poachers. Even without the scripted peril, there's enough elephant excitement on the savanna to impress everyone. In the past several years, three baby elephants have been born—one, named Tufani, born May 22, 2003, is the fourth surviving elephant calf in North America resulting from artificial insemination. The second, Kianga, arrived July 6, 2004, as part of the park's breeding program coordinated by the American Zoo and Aquarium Association. And on December 19, 2005, the 233-pound baby Nadirah was born at the park. You'll see the growing youngsters hanging out with the rest of the herd, and the park's animal team expects to see more elephant babies in the future. The park's first baby animal of 2007 was a white rhinoceros named Tom; he's the sixth baby rhino born at Animal Kingdom; his mother, Kendi, was the first.

PANGANI FOREST EXPLORATION TRAIL

⓭ Duration: Up to you.
Crowds: Heavy in the morning, but there's room for all, it seems.
Strategy: Go while waiting for your safari Fastpass; try to avoid going at the hottest time of day, when the gorillas like to nap.
Audience: All ages.
Rating: ★★★

Calling this a nature walk doesn't really do it justice. A path winds through dense foliage, alongside streams, and past waterfalls. En route there are viewing points where you can stop and watch a beautiful rare okapi munching the vegetation, a family and a separate bachelor group of lowland gorillas, hippos (which you usually can see underwater), comical meerkats (a kind of mongoose), graceful gerenuk (an African antelope), exotic birds, an antelope species called the yellow-backed duiker, and a bizarre colony of hairless mole rats. Native African interpreters are on hand at many viewing points to answer questions.

RAFIKI'S PLANET WATCH

⓮ Duration: 5-min ride (each way); the rest is up to you.
Crowds: Can get heavy midmorning.
Strategy: Go in late afternoon if you've hit all key attractions.
Audience: All ages.
Rating: ★★

Take the Wildlife Express steam train to this unique center of ecoawareness. Rafiki's, named for the wise baboon from *The Lion King*, is divided into three sections. At the Conservation Station, you can meet animal experts, enjoy interactive exhibits, learn about worldwide efforts to protect endangered species and their habitats, and find out ways to connect with conservation efforts in your own community. At the Habitat Habit! section, cotton-top tamarins (small white-headed monkeys) play while you learn how to live with all earth's animals. And you don't have to be a kid to enjoy the Affection Section, where young children and adults who are giving their inner child free rein get face-to-face with goats and some rare domesticated critters from around the world.

CAMP MINNIE-MICKEY

This Adirondack-style land is the setting for live performances at the Lion King Theater and Grandmother Willow's Grove, as well as meet-and-greet trails where Disney characters gather for picture-taking and autographs.

FESTIVAL OF THE LION KING

Duration: 30 min.
Crowds: Not a problem.
Strategy: Arrive 15 minutes before showtime. If you have a child who might want to go on stage, sit in one of the front rows to increase his or her chance of getting chosen.
Audience: All ages.
Rating: ★★★

If you think you've seen enough *Lion King* to last a lifetime, you're wrong unless you've seen this show. In the air-conditioned theater-in-the-round, Disney presents a delightful tribal celebration of song, dance, and acrobatics that uses huge moving stages and floats. The show's singers are first-rate; lithe dancers wearing exotic animal-themed costumes portray creatures in the wild. Timon, Pumba, and other Lion King stars have key roles.

POCAHONTAS & HER FOREST FRIENDS

16 Duration: 12 min.
Crowds: Not a problem.
Strategy: May not be performed every day in low season; check entertainment Times Guide and arrive 15 minutes before showtime.
Audience: All ages.
Rating: ★★

At Grandmother Willow's Grove, an actor portrays Pocahontas in this lesson on nature and how to preserve endangered species. Pocahontas works with an armadillo, a skunk, a boa constrictor, a red-tailed hawk, and other creatures. She also breaks out in song with "Just Around the River Bend."

PARADE

MICKEY'S JAMMIN' JUNGLE PARADE

Duration: 15 min.
Crowds: Heavy.
Strategy: Choose your spot along the parade route early, as this is one of Disney's most creative parades, and you should try not to miss it.

Audience: All ages.
Rating: ★★★

The parade takes off at about 4 PM daily (times may vary, so check Times Guide) on a route beginning at the Kilimanjaro Safaris entrance and continuing around Discovery Island with a "characters on safari" theme. Rafiki in his adventure Rover, Goofy in a safari jeep, and Mickey in his "Bon Voyage" caravan join other popular characters each day for the festive daytime fanfare. Adding to the pomp are a batch of oversize puppets—snakes, giraffes, frogs, tigers, monkeys, and others—created by famed designer Michael Curry, known for the puppet costumes of *The Lion King* on Broadway. Throw in some fanciful "party-animal" stilt walkers and animal rickshaws carrying VIPs or lucky park guests, and you've got another reason to strategize your day carefully.

DISABILITIES & ACCESSIBILITY

All restaurants, shops, and attractions are completely wheelchair accessible, including the theater-in-the-round at Camp Minnie-Mickey, the new *Finding Nemo—The Musical* at the Theater in the Wild, and at the Tree of Life theater showing *It's Tough to Be a Bug!*, which are also accessible to electric scooters. However, to fully experience all the bug movie's special effects, guests who use wheelchairs should transfer to one of the theater seats. Check the *Guidebook for Guests with Disabilities* for information about closed-captioning boxes for the monitor-equipped attractions such as the Tree of Life and how to get a sign-language interpretation schedule. Scripts and story lines for all attractions are available, and sign-language interpreters can be booked with at least one week's notice. Braille guides are available at Guest Relations; a large braille map of the park is located near the Tip Board at the entrance to Discovery Island. Call **WDW Information** (☎ *407/824–4321, 407/827–5141 TTY*) for more details.

In DinoLand U.S.A., you must transfer from your wheelchair to board the **DINOSAUR** thrill ride. Note that you will be jostled quite a bit on this twisting, turning, bumpy ride. **Primeval Whirl** requires a transfer, but **TriceraTop Spin** is wheelchair accessible. To board **Kali River Rapids** in Asia, you'll need to transfer from your wheelchair to one of the ride rafts. If you're like most of the passengers who get soaked on this water ride, you'll be soggy for hours unless you have a change of clothing handy. You must transfer from your wheelchair to board **Expedition Everest.** In Africa, you can roll your wheelchair on board the Wildlife Express train to **Rafiki's Planet Watch,** where you'll need it to traverse the path from the train stop to the station. The **Kilimanjaro Safaris** attraction is also wheelchair accessible. Service animals are allowed in most areas of the park; however, some areas are off-limits, including the Affection Section petting-zoo area of Rafiki's Planet Watch, the aviaries of **Pangani Forest Exploration Trail** and **Maharajah Jungle Trek,** and both the DINOSAUR and Kali River Rapids rides.

BLITZ TOUR

BEST OF THE PARK

Whatever you do, arrive early. Get to the parking lot a half hour before the official park opening. Make a beeline for **Expedition Everest** and ride right away (if the wait is 20 minutes or less) or grab a Fastpass. After your yeti encounter, head straight over to Africa and ride **Kilimanjaro Safaris** or get a Fastpass. If you're waiting for a Fastpass appointment, explore the **Pangani Forest Exploration Trail.** If you need a snack, get one of the huge, hot, cinnamon rolls at **Kusafiri Coffee Shop & Bakery.** Next, head over to the **Tree of Life**—*It's Tough to Be a Bug!* Don't bother with the Fastpass here unless the line wait is longer than 40 minutes. The line meanders along paths that encircle the Tree of Life and allows great views of the tree's animal carvings and animal habitats along the way.

Now zip over to **DINOSAUR** in Dino-Land U.S.A. to pick up a timed Fastpass ticket. Then try to grab a ride on **TriceraTop Spin** or **Primeval Whirl** before heading to **Restaurantosaurus** for a bite to eat. Kids love the food; parents, the music. Afterward, let the children explore the **Boneyard** while you digest. By now it should be time to return to DINOSAUR. Try to time your ride either before or just after the next

performance of *Finding Nemo—The Musical* at the Theater in the Wild. Don't forget to check the entertainment schedule so you know when to find your spot for **Mickey's Jammin' Jungle Parade.** If the line's not too long and you're in the mood to get wet, take the plunge on **Kali River Rapids,** then dry out during a stroll along the **Maharajah Jungle Trek** or during the next *Flights of Wonder* show. Then, do a half circle around Discovery Island and head on into Camp Minnie-Mickey, where you and the kids can have your pictures taken with—who else?—Mickey, Minnie, and several of their character friends. Then catch one of the two shows—the best is *Festival of the Lion King.* Later, shop in Discovery Island. If time allows, and especially if the kids are along, take the train to **Rafiki's Planet Watch.**

If the wait's not too long, have dinner at the **Rainforest Café**; the surroundings alone are worth the visit.

ON RAINY DAYS

The animals love a cool, light rain, so don't avoid this park in wet weather unless you're feeling wimpy. You're going to get wet on Kali River Rapids anyway!

9

EATING IN THE ANIMAL KINGDOM

Restaurants inside Disney's Animal Kingdom serve mostly fast food. There's just one full-service restaurant, however, and it's outside the park entrance, so you actually don't have to pay park admission to eat there. For reservations, call the **Disney Reservation Center** (☎ *407/939– 3463*) at least one day ahead.

ANIMAL KINGDOM

NAME	Min. Height	Type of Ride	Duration	Suits	Crowds	Strategy
Discovery Island						
★ Tree of Life—It's Tough to Be a Bug!		3-D film	20 min.	All but toddlers	ok	Do this after Kilimanjaro Safaris. Good photo opp. Fastpass available. Small children may be frightened.
DinoLand U.S.A.						
Boneyard	n/a	play area	Up to you.	Under 9's	Heavy	Play here while waiting for DINOSAUR Fastpass, or come late in the day.
Cretaceous Trail	n/a	walk through	Up to you.	All	ok	Stroll along here as you head toward Chester and Hester's for souvenirs or while you wait for the next Finding Nemo show.
Dinosaur	40"	thrill ride	4 min.	5 and up	Midmorning	Go first thing in the morning or at the end of the day, or use the Fastpass.
Fossil Fun Games	n/a	arcade	Up to you.	n/a	ok	Bring a pocketful of change
Finding Nemo—The Musical	n/a	show	30 min.	All	Heavy	Arrive 40 min. before showtime. Take little kids here while big kids wait for Expedition Everest.
Primeval Whirl	48"	thrill ride	2½ min.	All	Yes!	Kids may want to ride twice. Take your first spin early, then Fastpass if the wait is more than 20 min. Spinning coaster.
TriceraTop Spin	n/a	thrill ride	2 min.	All	Heavy	Ride early while everyone else heads for the safari, or queue up while waiting for your Fastpass appointment for DINOSAUR.
Asia						
★ Expedition Everest	44"	thrill ride	2½ min.	7 and up	Yes!	Fastpass. This is the park's biggest thrill ride.
Flights of Wonder	n/a	show	30 min.	All	ok	Arrive 15 min before show time and find a shaded seat beneath one of the awnings—the sun can be brutal.
Kali River Rapids	38"	thrill ride	7 min.	4 and up	Yes!	Use your Fastpass, or go during the parade. You'll get wet.
Maharajah Jungle Trek	n/a	animal habitat walk	Up to you.	All	ok	Go anytime.
Africa						
★ Kilimanjaro Safaris	n/a	tour	20 min.	All	Morning	Do this first thing in the morning. If you arrive at the park late morning, save this for the end of the day, when it's not so hot.

Pangani Forest Exploration Trail	n/a	animal habitat walk	Up to you.	All	fast lines	Go while waiting for your safari Fastpass; try to avoid going at the hottest time of day, when the gorillas like to nap.
Rafiki's Planet Watch	n/a	walk through	Up to you.	All	Midmorning	Go in late afternoon after you've hit all key attractions.
Wildlife Express Train	n/a	train ride	7 min.	All	Steady	Head straight to Affection Section with little kids to come face-to-face with domesticated critters.
Camp Minnie-Mickey						
★ Festival of the Lion King	n/a	show	30 min.	All	ok	Arrive 15 min before show time. Sit in one of the front rows to increase your kid's chance of being chosen.
Pocahontas and Her Forest Friends	n/a	show	12 min.	All	ok	May not be performed every day in low season; check entertainment guide map and arrive 15 min before show time.
Entertainment						
★ Mickey's Jammin' Jungle Parade	n/a	parade	15 min.	All	Heavy	Choose your spot along the parade route early, as this is one of Disney's most creative parades, and you should try not to miss it.

★ = Fodor'sChoice

FULL-SERVICE RESTAURANT

The **Rainforest Café,** part of the international chain of the same name, is appropriately situated right outside the Animal Kingdom. It's truly a jungle in there, and the occasional orchestrated "thunderstorms" and robotic elephant, monkey, and other creatures make the experience a real treat for kids. A meal here really isn't about the food but about the moving animals, strange jungle sounds, and other made-for-kids distractions.

SELF-SERVICE RESTAURANTS

At Discovery Island's **Flame Tree Barbecue** you can dig into ribs, brisket, and pulled pork with several sauce choices. There are also fresh tossed salads. The tables, set beneath intricately carved wood pavilions, make great spots for a picnic.

On the other side of Discovery Island from Flame Tree Barbecue, **Pizzafari** serves individual pizzas, salads, and sandwiches. There's plenty of self-service seating in spacious rooms.

Restaurantosaurus, in DinoLand U.S.A., is the Animal Kingdom's hybrid of Disney and McDonald's fare. It's open for counter-service lunches and dinners featuring burgers, fries, chicken nuggets, and salads. For breakfast, you can have the all-you-can-eat Donald's Prehistoric Breakfastosaurus buffet.

Tusker House, in Harambe, is a buffet restaurant with indoor and outdoor seating. Donald's Safari Breakfast sees Donald, Daisy, Mickey, and Goofey as character hosts.

GUIDED TOURS

Call 407/939–8687 to arrange for an Animal Kingdom tour.

Backstage Safari takes an in-depth look at animal conservation every Monday and Wednesday–Friday 8:30–11:30, stopping at the animal hospital and other behind-the-scenes areas. It's a great way to learn about animal behaviors and how handlers care for the critters in captivity, but don't expect to see many animals on this tour. Book ahead; you can make reservations up to a year in advance. Those in your party must all be at least 16 years old to participate and the cost is $65 plus park admission.

Wild by Design offers participants 14 and older insights into the creation of Disney's Animal Kingdom every Thursday and Friday, from 8:30 to 11:30. The tour touches on the park's art, architecture, history, and agriculture, and reveals how stories of exotic lands are told at the park. You get a glimpse of behind-the-scenes buildings to see custodians taking care of the animals. The tour price is $58; park admission is required as well.

The Water Parks

Revised by
Jennie Hess

THERE'S SOMETHING ABOUT A WATER park that brings out the kid in all of us, and there's no denying that the Disney water parks are two of the best in the world. What sets them apart? It's really the same thing that differentiates all Disney parks—the detailed themes. Whether you're cast away on a balmy island at Typhoon Lagoon or washed up on a ski resort-turned-seaside playground at Blizzard Beach, you can be sure that the landscaping and clever architecture will add to the traditional fun of flume and raft rides, wave pools, and splash areas for the youngest children. The Disney water parks give you that lost-in-paradise feeling on top of all those high-speed wedgie-inducing waterslides. Blizzard Beach and Typhoon Lagoon are so popular with visitors and locals that crowds often reach overflow capacity in summer. And your children may like them so much that they simply must go again during your stay. That's why we recommend that you plan your water-park visit on a day early in your visit. If you're going to Disney World five days or more between April and October, we suggest adding the Water Park Fun & More option to your ticket. Of course, check the weather in advance to make sure the temperatures are to your liking for running around in a swimsuit.

> **WHICH PARK'S FOR ME?**
>
> Most people agree that kids under 7 and older adults prefer Typhoon Lagoon, while bigger kids and teens like Blizzard Beach better because it has more slides and big-deal rides.

GETTING THERE & AROUND

You can either take WDW bus transportation or drive to the water parks. Once inside, your options are to walk, swim, or slide. Arrive 30 minutes ahead of park opening and get ready to race to the tallest slides.

TYPHOON LAGOON

According to Disney legend, Typhoon Lagoon was created when the quaint, thatched-roof, lushly landscaped Placid Palms Resort was struck by a cataclysmic storm. It left a different world in its wake: surfboards sundered trees; once upright palms imitated the Leaning Tower of Pisa; and part of the original lagoon was cut off, trapping thousands of tropical fish—and a few sharks. Nothing, however, topped the fate of *Miss Tilly,* a shrimp boat from "Safen Sound, Florida," which was hurled high in the air and became impaled on Mt. Mayday, a magical volcano that periodically tries to dislodge *Miss Tilly* with huge geysers of water.

Ordinary folks, the legend continues, would have been crushed by such devastation. But the resourceful residents of Placid Palms were made of hardier stuff—and from the wreckage they created 56-acre Typhoon Lagoon, the self-proclaimed "world's ultimate water park."

TIP SHEET

■ There's really only one problem with the water parks—they're crowd pleasers. In summer and on weekends, the parks often reach capacity by midmorning.

■ If you must visit in summer, go during late afternoon when park hours run later or when the weather clears up after a thundershower. Typically, rainstorms drive away the crowds.

■ If you plan to make a whole day of it, avoid weekends—the water parks are big among locals as well as visitors.

■ Arrive 30 minutes before opening time so you can park, buy tickets, rent towels, and snag inner tubes before the hordes descend. Set up camp and hit the slides and whitewater rides first.

■ Women and girls should wear one-piece swimsuits unless they want to find their tops somewhere around their ears at the bottom of the waterslide.

■ One word—sunscreen. OK, so you know why it's important. But it's easy to lose track of time and forget to reapply, which can be a big mistake even on partly cloudy Florida days. Set your waterproof watch alarm or plan a sunscreen dousing during lunch, snack, or early dinner gatherings. Remember, that boiled-lobster look is neither attractive nor healthy.

■ An inexpensive pair of water shoes will do wonders to save the feet—especially children's tender footsies—from hot sand and walkways, and from grimy restroom floors.

■ Review the park layout with children, and help orient them to the spot where you've chosen to camp out for the day.

■ If you're visiting during a cooler time of year, go in the afternoon, when the water will have warmed up a bit.

10

Typhoon Lagoon offers a full day's worth of activities. You can bob along in 5-foot waves in a surf lagoon the size of two football fields, speed down waterslides, bump through rapids, go snorkeling, and, for a mellow break, float in inner tubes along the 2,100-foot Castaway Creek, rubberneck from specially constructed grandstands as human cannonballs are ejected from the storm slides, or merely hunker down in one of the many hammocks or lounge chairs and read a book. A children's area replicates adult rides on a smaller scale. It's Disney's version of a day at the beach—complete with friendly Disney lifeguards.

The layout is so simple that it's hard to get lost. The wave and swimming lagoon is at the center of the park; the waves break on the beaches closest to the entrance and are born in Mt. Mayday at the other end of the park. Castaway Creek encircles the lagoon. Anything requiring a gravitational plunge—storm slides, speed slides, and raft trips down rapids—starts around the summit of Mt. Mayday. Shark Reef and Ketchakiddie Creek flank the head of the lagoon, to Mt. Mayday's right and left, respectively, as you enter the park.

There are plenty of lounge chairs and a number of hammocks but definitely not enough beach umbrellas. If you crave shade, commandeer a spot in the grassy area around Getaway Glen on the left side of the park just past the raft-rental concession. If you like moving about, people-watching, and having sand in your face, go front and center at the surf pool. For your own patch of sand and some peace and quiet, head for the coves and inlets on the left side of the lagoon.

Numbers in the margin correspond to points of interest on the Typhoon Lagoon map.

GETTING STARTED

DISABILITIES & ACCESSIBILITY

The park gets high ratings in the accessibility department. All paths that connect the different areas of Typhoon Lagoon are wheelchair accessible. Those who use a wheelchair and who can transfer to a raft or inner tube can also float in **Typhoon Lagoon** and on **Castaway Creek.** Wheelchairs are available in the entrance turnstile area—a limited number are built to go into the water—and are free with ID.

DRESSING ROOMS & LOCKERS

There are men's and women's thatched-roof dressing rooms and two sizes of full-day lockers ($5 and $7, plus $5 deposits for either) to the right of the entrance on your way into the park; a second, less-crowded set is near Typhoon Tilly's. The towels you can rent (for $1) at the stand to the right of the main entrance are a little skimpy; bring your own beach towel or buy one at Singapore Sal's if you like. The Typhoon Lagoon Imagineers thoughtfully placed rest rooms in every available nook and cranny. Most have showers and are much less crowded with clothes-changers than the main dressing rooms.

FIRST AID

The small First-Aid Stand, run by a registered nurse, is on your left as you enter the park, not far from the Leaning Palms food stand.

INFORMATION

The staff at the **Guest Relations** window outside the entrance turnstiles, to your left, can answer many questions; a chalkboard inside gives water temperature and surfing information. During off-season, which encompasses October through April, the park closes for several weeks for routine maintenance and refurbishment. Call **WDW Information** (☎ 407/824–4321) or check disneyworld.com for days of operation.

LOST PEOPLE & THINGS

Ask about your misplaced people and things at the Guest Relations window near the entrance turnstiles, to your left as you enter the park. Lost children are taken to High and Dry Towels.

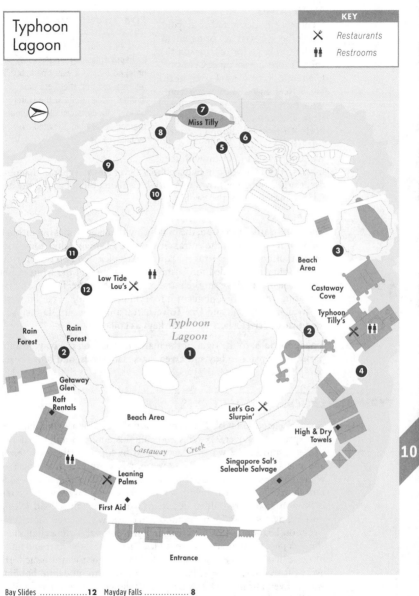

Typhoon Lagoon

KEY
✕ Restaurants
🚻 Restrooms

Miss Tilly ⑦

⑧

⑥
⑤

⑨

⑩

⑪

Beach Area

③

⑫

Low Tide Lou's ✕ 🚻

Castaway Cove

Typhoon Tilly's ✕ 🚻

Typhoon Lagoon

①

Rain Forest

Rain Forest

②

②

④

Getaway Glen

Raft Rentals

🚻

Beach Area

Let's Go Slurpin' ✕

High & Dry Towels

10

Castaway Creek

Singapore Sal's Saleable Salvage

Leaning Palms ✕

First Aid

Entrance

PICNICKING

Picnicking is permitted, but you won't be allowed to bring in a cooler too large for one person to carry. Tables are set up at Getaway Glen and Castaway Cove, near Shark Reef. Bring a box lunch from your hotel or pick up provisions from the Goodings supermarket at the Crossroads shopping center (off SR 535), and you'll eat well without having to line up with the masses. Although you can find alcoholic beverages at Typhoon Lagoon, don't bring along your own or you'll be walking them back to the car. Glass containers are also prohibited.

> **FOR YOUNG ONES ONLY**
>
> Most kids under 6 would be just as happy splashing around in a hotel pool as at a water park, but rest assured that there are designated kiddie areas at the water parks so toddlers can play without the danger of being bowled over by bigger kids.

SUPPLIES

The **rental-rafts concession,** the building with the boat sticking through the roof to the left of the entrance, past the Leaning Palms food concession, offers free inner tubes. You need to pick them up only for the lagoon; they're provided for Castaway Creek and all the white-water rides. You can borrow snorkels and masks at **Shark Reef,** but you may not bring your own equipment into Typhoon Lagoon. Free life vests are available at **High and Dry Towels.** You must leave an ID such as a credit card, driver's license, or car keys as collateral.

Singapore Sal's, to the right of the main entrance (on the way into the park), is the place to buy sunscreen, hats, sunglasses, and other beach paraphernalia.

TYPHOON LAGOON ATTRACTIONS

1 **Typhoon Lagoon Surf Pool.** This is the heart of the park, a swimming area that spreads out over 2½ acres and contains almost 3 million gallons of clear, chlorinated water. It's scalloped by lots of little coves, bays, and inlets, all edged with white-sand beaches—spread over a base of white concrete, as body surfers soon discover when they try to slide into shore. Ouch! The main attraction is the waves. Twelve huge water-collection chambers hidden in Mt. Mayday dump their load with a resounding "whoosh" into trapdoors to create waves large enough for Typhoon Lagoon to host amateur and professional surfing championships. A piercing double hoot from *Miss Tilly* signals the start and finish of wave action: every 2 hours, for 1½ hours, 5-foot waves issue forth every 90 seconds; the next half hour is devoted to moderate bobbing waves. Even during the big-wave periods, however, the waters in Blustery Bay and Whitecap Cove are protected enough for timid swimmers. Surfers who don't want to risk a fickle ocean can surf here on certain days before the park opens (call ahead for the schedule). Instruction and surfboard are included in the $140 cost, and the surfing experience lasts for 2½ hours. Reserve your waves by calling ☎407/939–7529.

❷ Castaway Creek. This circular, 15-foot-wide, 3-foot-deep waterway is everyone's water fantasy come true. Snag an inner tube and float along the creek that winds around the entire park, a wet version of the Magic Kingdom's Walt Disney World Railroad. You pass through a rain forest that showers you with mist and spray, you slide through caves and grottoes, you float by overhanging trees and flowering bushes, and you get dumped on at the Water Works, whose "broken" pipes the Typhoon Lagooners never got around to fixing. The current flows a gentle 2½ feet per second; it takes about 30 minutes to make a full circuit. Along the way there are exits where you can hop out and dry off or do something else—and then pick up another inner tube and jump right back in.

❸ Shark Reef. If you felt like leaping onto the stage at the Studios' *Voyage of the Little Mermaid* or jumping into the tank at Epcot's The Seas with Nemo & Friends, make tracks for this 360,000-gallon snorkeling tank. The coral reef is artificial, but the 4,000 tropical fish—including black-and-white-striped sergeant majors, sargassum trigger fish, yellowtail damselfish, and amiable leopard and bonnet-head sharks—are quite real. To prevent algae growth, Shark Reef is kept at a brisk 72°F, which is about 15 degrees cooler than the rest of Typhoon Lagoon. A sunken tanker divides the reef; its portholes give landlubbers access to the underwater scene and let them go nose-to-nose with snorkelers. Go first thing in the morning or at the end of the day if you want to linger. During the warmest weather, adults and children ages 5 and over can take a personal supplied-air snorkeling lesson at $20 per half hour (plus an additional $20 per participant for each air tank). If your kids want to learn how to explore the depths of the ocean Disney style, sign them up at Guest Relations when you purchase your tickets.

❹ Crush 'N' Gusher. If flume rides, storm slides, and tube races aren't wild enough for your inner thrill-seeker, get ready to defy gravity on Disney's first water coaster. Designed to propel you uphill and down along a series of flumes, caverns, and spillways, this ride should satisfy the most enthusiastic daredevil. Keeping with park lore, Crush 'N' Gusher flows through what appears to be a rusted-out tropical fruit factory, weaving in and out of the wreckage and debris that once transported fruit through the plant's wash facilities. Three fruit spillways are aptly named Banana Blaster, Coconut Crusher, and Pineapple Plunger. ☞ *Audience: Children under 48" are not allowed on this ride. No pregnant women or guests with heart, back, or neck problems or other physical limitations.*

10

NEED A BREAK? When you need to regain your energy, head to **Leaning Palms**, to your left as you enter the park, for standard beach fare—burgers, dogs, pizzas, chef salads, and, of course, ice cream and frozen yogurt. For adults, **Let's Go Slurpin'** is a beach shack on the edge of Typhoon Lagoon that dispenses frozen margaritas as well as wine and beer. **Typhoon Tilly's,** on the right just south of Shark Reef, also serves burgers, dogs, and salads, and pours mostly sugary, nonalcoholic grog—though you can grab a Davy Jones lager if you must.

⑤ Humunga Kowabunga. There's little time to scream, but you'll hear just such vociferous reactions as the survivors emerge from the catch pool opposite Shark Reef. The basic question is: want to get scared out of your wits in three seconds flat—and like it enough to go back for more? The two side-by-side Humunga Kowabunga speed slides rightly deserve their acclaim among thrill lovers, as they drop more than 50 feet in a distance barely four times that amount. For nonmathematicians, that's very steep. Oh yes, and then you go through a cave. In the dark. The average speed is 30 mph; however, you can really fly if you lie flat on your back, cross your ankles, wrap your arms around your chest, and arch your back. Just remember to smile for the rubberneckers on the grandstand at the bottom. ☞ *Audience: Children under 48"* *are not allowed on this ride. No pregnant women or guests with heart, back, or neck problems or other physical limitations.*

⑥ Storm Slides. Each of these three body slides is about 300 feet long and snakes in and out of rock formations, through caves and tunnels, and under waterfalls, but each has a slightly different view and offers a twist. The one in the middle has the longest tunnel; the others' secrets you'll have to discover for yourself. Maximum speed is about 20 mph, and the trip takes about 30 seconds.

⑦ Mt. Mayday. What goes down can also go up—and up and up and up and up. "It's like climbing Mt. Everest," wailed one teenager about a climb that seems a lot steeper than this 85-foot peak would warrant. However, it's Mt. Everest with hibiscus flowers, a rope bridge, stepping-stones set in plunging waters, and—remember that typhoon?—a broken canoe scattered over the rocks near the top. The view encompasses the entire park.

Lovers of white-water rafting should head to Mayday Falls, Keelhaul Falls, and Gang Plank Falls at Mt. Mayday. These white-water raft rides in oversize inner tubes plunge down the mount's left side. Like the Storm Slides, they have caves, waterfalls, and intricate rock work, but with some extra elements.

⑧ Mayday Falls. The 460-foot slide over Mayday Falls in blue inner tubes is the longest and bumpiest of the three falls; it's a straight slide over the falls into a catchment, which gives you just enough time to catch your breath before the next plunge.

⑨ Keelhaul Falls. This spiraling, 400-foot ride in yellow inner tubes through raging rapids seems way faster than the purported 10 mph.

⑩ Gang Plank Falls. If you climb up Mt. Mayday for this ride, you'll go down in four-person, 6½-foot-long inflated rafts that descend crazily through 300 feet of rapids. This is a great ride for adventurous families to enjoy together—the rafts can hold five if some of the passengers are kids.

⑪ Ketchakiddie Creek. Typhoon Lagoon's children's area has slides, mini-rapids, squirting whales and seals, bouncing barrels, waterfalls, sprinklers, and all the other ingredients of a splash fiesta. The bubbling sand ponds, where youngsters can sit in what seems like an enormous whirlpool bath, are special favorites. ☞ *All adults must be accompanied by a child or children under 48" and vice versa.*

⑫ Bay Slides. These scaled-down versions of the Storm Slides are geared to younger kids, who must be under 60 inches to ride.

BLIZZARD BEACH

With its oxymoronic name, Blizzard Beach promises the seemingly impossible—a seaside playground with an alpine theme. As with its older cousin, Typhoon Lagoon, the Disney Imagineers have created an entire legend to explain the park's origin: after a freak winter storm dropped snow over the western side of Walt Disney World, entrepreneurs decided to create Florida's first downhill ski resort. Saunalike temperatures soon returned. But just as the resort's operators were ready to close up shop, they spotted a playful alligator sliding down the "liquid ice" slopes. The realization that the melting snow had created the tallest, fastest, and most exhilarating water-filled ski and toboggan runs in the world gave birth to the ski resort–water park.

Disney Imagineers have gone all out here to create the paradox of a ski resort in the midst of a tropical lagoon. Lots of verbal puns and sight gags play with the snow-in-Florida motif. The park's centerpiece is Mt. Gushmore, with its 120-foot-high Summit Plummet, as well as other toboggan and water-sled runs with names such as Teamboat Springs, a white-water raft ride; Toboggan Racer; Slush Gusher; and Runoff Rapids. Between Mt. Gushmore's base and its summit, swim-skiers can also ride a chairlift converted from ski-resort to beach-resort use— with umbrellas and snow skis on their undersides. Devoted waterslide enthusiasts generally prefer Blizzard Beach to the other water parks.

Numbers in the margin correspond to points of interest on the Blizzard Beach map.

GETTING STARTED

10

DISABILITIES & ACCESSIBILITY
Most paths are flat and level. If you use a wheelchair, you'll also be able to float in **Cross Country Creek,** provided you can transfer to a large inner tube. Other guests with limited mobility might also be able to use the inner tubes at some of the park's tamer slides. A limited number of wheelchairs—some suitable to wheel into the water—are available near the park entrance and are free if you leave an ID.

DRESSING ROOMS & LOCKERS
Dressing rooms are in the Village area, just inside the main entrance. There are showers and restrooms here as well. Lockers are strategically located near the entrance, next to Snowless Joe's Rentals and near Tike's Peak, the children's area (more convenient if you have little swim-skiers in tow). At Snowless Joe's it costs $5 to rent a small locker, $7 for a large one; plus a $5 deposit required. Only small lockers are available at Tike's Peak. Restrooms are conveniently located through-

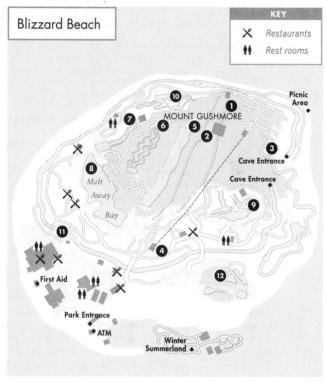

out the park; there are facilities in the Village area near the entrance, in Lottawatta Lodge, at the Ski Patrol Training Camp, and just past the Melt Away Bay beach area. Towels are available for rent at Snowless Joe's ($1), but they're tiny. If you care, buy a proper beach towel in the Beach Haus or bring your own.

FIRST AID

The First-Aid Stand, overseen by a registered nurse, is in the Village, between Lottawatta Lodge and the Beach Haus.

INFORMATION

Disney staffers at the Guest Relations window, to the left of the ticket booth as you enter the park, can answer most of your questions. Each year, the park closes for several weeks during the fall or winter months for routine maintenance and refurbishment. For the park's days of operation, call **Blizzard Beach** (☎ *407/824–4321*) or check the disney-world.com Web site.

LOST THINGS & PEOPLE

Start your visit by naming a specific meeting place and time. Instruct your youngsters to let any lifeguard know if they get lost. If they do get lost, don't panic: head for Snowless Joe's, local lost-children central.

PICNICKING

You are not allowed to bring glass containers or your own alcoholic beverages into the park. Picnicking is welcome, however, and several areas are pleasant lunch spots, most notably the terrace outside Lottawatta Lodge and its environs. Coolers must be small enough for one person to handle; otherwise, you won't be able to take them into the park.

SUPPLIES

Personal flotation devices, better known as life jackets, are available free to children and adults at **Snowless Joe's** (leave your ID with an attendant until you return them). You can't rent inner tubes here: they're provided at the rides.

Sunglasses, sunscreen, bathing suits, waterproof disposable cameras, and other sundries are available at the **Beach Haus,** along with Blizzard Beach logo merchandise. Check out the ski equipment hanging from the ceiling. The **Sled Cart,** a kiosk-style shop, sells souvenirs, suntan lotion, and water toys.

BLIZZARD BEACH ATTRACTIONS

1 Summit Plummet. This is Mt. Gushmore's big gun, which Disney bills as "the world's tallest, fastest free-fall speed slide." From Summit Plummet's "ski jump" tower, it's a wild 55-mph plunge straight down to a splash landing at the base of the mountain. It looks almost like a straight vertical drop. If you're watching from the beach below, you can't hear the yells of the participants, but rest assured—they're screaming their heads off. *Minimum height: 48 ˝.*

2 Slush Gusher. This speed slide, which drops through a snow-banked mountain gully, is shorter and less severe than Summit Plummet but a real thriller nonetheless. *Minimum height: 48 ˝.*

3 Teamboat Springs. Six-passenger rafts zip along in the world's longest family white-water raft ride. Since its original construction, it has doubled its speed of departure onto its twisting, 1,200-foot channel of rushing waterfalls. This is great for families—a good place for kids too big for Tike's Peak to test more grown-up waters.

4 Chair Lift. If you're waterlogged, take a ride from the beachfront base of Mt. Gushmore up over its face and on to the summit—and back down again. Children must be at least 32 inches tall to ride.

5 Toboggan Racers. On this ride you slither down an eight-lane waterslide over Mt. Gushmore's "snowy" slopes.

6 Snow Stormers. No water park would be complete without a fancy waterslide, and Blizzard Beach has one—actually three flumes that descend from the top of Mt. Gushmore along a switchback course of ski-type slalom gates.

7 Downhill Double Dipper. These side-by-side racing slides are where future Olympic hopefuls 48 inches and taller can compete against one another.

10

Lottawatta Lodge—a North American ski lodge with a Caribbean accent—is the park's main emporium of fast food. Lines are long at peak feeding times.

The **Warming Hut** has Disney's famous smoked turkey legs, salads, hot dogs, and ice cream. Hot dogs, snow cones, and ice cream are on the menu at **Avalunch**. **Frostbite Freddie's** and **Polar Pub** on the main beach both sell frozen drinks and spirits.

8 Melt Away Bay. The park's main pool is a 1-acre oasis that's constantly fed by "melting snow" waterfalls. The man-made waves are positively oceanlike. If you're not a strong swimmer, stay away from the far end of the pool, where the waves originate. You can get temporarily stuck in a pocket even if your head is still above water.

9 Blizzard Beach Ski Patrol Training Camp. The preteens in your crowd may want to spend most of their time on the T-bar drop, bungee-cord slides, and culvert slides here. In addition, there's a chance to take on Mogul Mania, a wide-open area where you can jump from one slippery mogul to the next. The moguls really look more like baby icebergs bobbing in a swimming pool.

10 Runoff Rapids. You have to steel your nerves to climb into an inner tube for these three twisting, turning flumes—even one that's in the dark. But once you're in, it's way more fun than scary.

11 Cross Country Creek. Just grab an inner tube, hop on, and circle the entire park on this creek during a leisurely 45-minute float. Along the way, you'll get doused with frigid water in an ice cave—wonderful on a steamy Florida day.

12 Tike's Peak. Disney is never one to leave the little ones out of the fun, and this junior-size version of Blizzard Beach, set slightly apart from the rest of the park, has scaled-down elements of Mt. Gushmore. Adults must be accompanied by children under 48 inches tall.

The Rest of the World

Revised by
Jennie Hess

AND THERE'S MORE. WALT DISNEY World is so much more than the Magic Kingdom and its theme-park siblings, Epcot, Disney–MGM Studios, and Disney's Animal Kingdom. Beyond the parks, there are enough diversions to keep you busy day or night. Let's start with shopping. At Downtown Disney alone there are dozens of stores, including the best World of Disney store on the planet, and the LEGO Imagination Center, with its life-size LEGO people and animals, retail store, and play area. Then there's the nightlife, including the Cirque du Soleil show; the fishing trips; the sports events; the boat rides—and so much more. If you're looking for entertainment that doesn't require lining up, jump on a Disney bus or grab your own wheels for a look at the rest-of-the-world options.

DOWNTOWN DISNEY

Downtown Disney is really three entertainment areas in one, with attractions, theaters, nightclubs, shopping, and dining. For detailed descriptions of Downtown Disney's stores, see Chapter 17, Shopping.

WEST SIDE

The West Side has Cirque du Soleil and its breathtaking *La Nouba* performances twice nightly, five evenings a week, as well as the DisneyQuest indoor interactive theme park and the plush AMC movie theaters. The West Side's terrific lineup of shops and boutiques includes Starabilias for a nostalgic browse, Magic Masters for aspiring Houdinis, a Virgin Megastore, and the wonderful Hoypoloi fine art and jewelry gallery. For food and entertainment, consider a meal at the House of Blues, Wolfgang Puck Café, Bongos Cuban Café, or Planet Hollywood.

PLEASURE ISLAND

This is an evening entertainment complex geared to adults (those under 18 are admitted if accompanied by an adult). The admission cost of $21.95 gets you into all the clubs, or you can pay $10.95 (plus tax) for entry to one club. You'll find destinations like the improv Comedy Warehouse and the richly decorated Adventurer's Club (both open to guests 18 and older) with its cast of wacky club characters. Other clubs require guests to be 21 or older. At Motion, a DJ spins hip-hop. Other clubs play rock and roll, disco, and alternative. Serious dancers shouldn't miss Mannequins, with its turntable dance floor, dramatic lighting, and sleek mannequin displays. Dancers who just want to have fun should squeeze onto the dance floor at 8Trax, where pop artists of the '70s are featured in a lava-lamp, disco-ball setting.

Pub enthusiasts can grab some upscale contemporary Irish fare, such as rack of lamb on a delicate Irish stew consommé at Raglan Road Irish Pub and Restaurant. On the "street" outside, video displays and carnival games keep the atmosphere festive as you bounce from club to club. Photo ID is required for the wristband that lets you purchase alcoholic drinks. For detailed descriptions of Pleasure Island's bars and clubs, see Chapter 16, After Dark.

MARKETPLACE

Finally, there's the Marketplace, which has some of the wildest shops and restaurants in Walt Disney World. Whatever you haven't found in the theme parks you'll probably find here. If you have kids, and even if you don't, you should visit World of Disney, the largest Disney-character store on the planet; and Once Upon a Toy, which has the latest theme-park editions of games and toys (check out the "it's a small world" Play-Doh set and Haunted Mansion CLUE), plus play castles, trains, plush critters, and even mini-monorail sets. The LEGO Imagination Center sells LEGO sets of all sizes, and there's a free outdoor LEGO building area with benches where parents can rest and watch. Disney's Wonderful World of Memories has scrapbooking and photo-album supplies, and a kiddie train ride pleases little passengers throughout the day.

DISNEYQUEST

This five-story, interactive, indoor theme park in Downtown Disney West Side is a virtual kingdom of attractions and adventures in a single building. Here Disney stories and characters come to life in a bold, interactive way—you not only partake of the magic, you're immersed in it. It's a wonderful, unique place to cool off on a hot summer day or to sit out an afternoon thunderstorm. To avoid crowds, arrive when it opens, usually at 11:30 AM, but some days earlier (call to verify). Its location in the middle of an entertainment and shopping complex ensures crowds after dark. Plan to stay for at least four hours or longer to get the most of your one-time admission—the Cheesecake Factory Express restaurant is inside so you can have lunch or dinner and then get back to the virtual fun. Be warned: your kids won't want to leave. Bring along some aspirin or other remedy just in case you develop a case of virtual overload.

You begin your journey at the Ventureport after exiting the elevator, here known as the Cybrolator. The Ventureport serves as a crossroads within the complex, and from there you can go on to enter any one of four distinct entertainment environments, or "zones": the Explore Zone, the Score Zone, the Create Zone, and the Replay Zone.

ADMISSION Tickets to DisneyQuest cost $36 for adults and $30 for children ages 3 to 9, not including sales tax. One price gains you admission to the building and allows you entrance to all of the attractions.

DISABILITIES & DisneyQuest attractions all are wheelchair accessible, but most require
ACCESSIBILITY transfer from wheelchair to the attraction itself, including the virtual thrill ride Cyberspace Mountain. You can, however, wheel right on to Pirates of the Caribbean: Battle for Buccaneer Gold, Aladdin's Magic Carpet Ride, and Mighty Ducks Pinball Slam. Wheelchairs can be rented ($10 with a major credit card or Disney resort ID card) at the Downtown Disney Guest Services locations at Downtown Disney West Side or Marketplace. Electronic wheelchairs available only at the Marketplace location cost $35 per day with a major credit card only. If you have your own wheelchair, it would pay to bring it along. Guide dogs

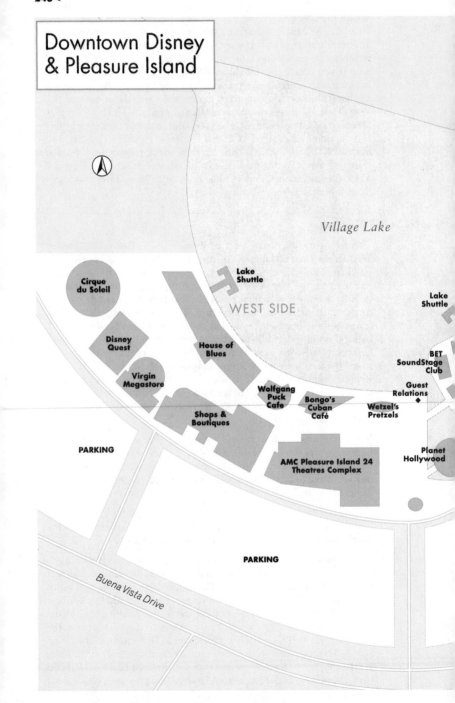

Downtown Disney & Pleasure Island

Village Lake

Cirque du Soleil

Lake Shuttle

WEST SIDE

Lake Shuttle

Disney Quest

House of Blues

BET SoundStage Club

Virgin Megastore

Wolfgang Puck Cafe

Bongo's Cuban Café

Guest Relations

Wetzel's Pretzels

Shops & Boutiques

PARKING

AMC Pleasure Island 24 Theatres Complex

Planet Hollywood

PARKING

Buena Vista Drive

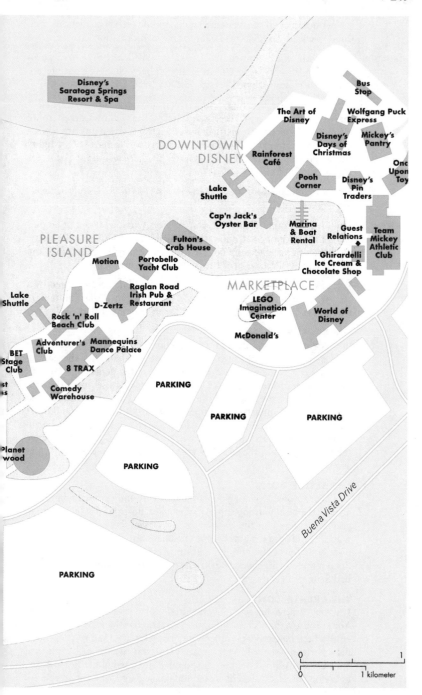

Disney's Saratoga Springs Resort & Spa

Bus Stop

DOWNTOWN DISNEY

The Art of Disney

Wolfgang Puck Express

Disney's Days of Christmas

Mickey's Pantry

Rainforest Café

Pooh Corner

Disney's Pin Traders

Onc Upon Toy

Lake Shuttle

Cap'n Jack's Oyster Bar

Marina & Boat Rental

Guest Relations ✦

Team Mickey Athletic Club

PLEASURE ISLAND

Fulton's Crab House

Ghirardelli Ice Cream & Chocolate Shop

Motion

Portobello Yacht Club

MARKETPLACE

Lake Shuttle

Raglan Road Irish Pub & Restaurant

D-Zertz

LEGO Imagination Center

World of Disney

Rock 'n' Roll Beach Club

Adventurer's Club

Mannequins Dance Palace

McDonald's

BET Stage Club

8 TRAX

st s

Comedy Warehouse

PARKING

PARKING

PARKING

Planet wood

PARKING

PARKING

Buena Vista Drive

PARKING

0   1

0   1 kilometer

are permitted in all areas but are unable to ride several attractions. Call **Guest Relations** (☎ *407/938–1076*) for more information.

Strollers are *not* permitted at DisneyQuest, which really doesn't provide much for very small children, though baby-changing stations are in both men's and women's restrooms.

As you enter the building, children will pass a height check and if they're at least 51" tall receive a wristband that allows access to all rides. The four attractions that have height requirements are Cyberspace Mountain (51"), Buzz Lightyear's Astro Blaster (51"), Mighty Ducks Pinball Slam (48"), and Pirates of the Caribbean: Battle for Buccaneer Gold (35").

For more information, contact **DisneyQuest** (☎ *407/828–4600* ⊕ *www. disneyquest.com*).

The Lost & Found is at the **Guest Services** window, film can be purchased at the Emporium, and cash is available at ATMs inside the House of Blues merchandise shop not far from the DisneyQuest entrance and inside Wetzel's Pretzels near the bridge to Pleasure Island.

Lost children are first walked through the building accompanied by a security guard. If that method is not successful, then the children are taken to the manager's office to wait for their mom or dad.

THE EXPLORE ZONE

In this virtual adventureland, you're immersed in exotic and ancient locales. You can fly through the streets of Agrabah with the help of a virtual-reality helmet on a hunt to release the genie on Aladdin's Magic Carpet Ride. Then take a Virtual Jungle Cruise down the roiling rapids of a prehistoric world and paddle (yes, *really* paddle) to adventure in the midst of volcanoes, carnivorous dinosaurs, and other Cretaceous threats. End your stay in this zone at Pirates of the Caribbean: Battle for Buccaneer Gold, where you and the gang must brave the high seas from the helm of your ship, sinking pirate ships, and acquiring treasure.

THE SCORE ZONE

The Score Zone is where you can match wits and game-playing skills against the best. Battling supervillains takes more physical energy than you'd think as you fly, headset firmly intact, through a 3-D comic world in Ride the Comix. Escape evil aliens and rescue stranded colonists with your crew during Invasion! An ExtraTERRORestrial Alien Encounter. Or hip-check your friends in a life-size Mighty Ducks Pinball Slam game.

THE CREATE ZONE

Let your creative juices flow in this studio of expression and invention. You can learn the secrets of Disney animation at the Animation Academy, where magic overload led one man who attended to propose to his girlfriend—she said yes! Create your own twisted masterpiece at Sid's Create-A-Toy, based on the popular animated film *Toy Story.* Or, at Living Easels, create a *living* painting on a giant electronic screen. All of the above creative ventures are quite popular with the elementary-school crowd. The real thrills await at Cyberspace Mountain, where you can design your own roller coaster on a computer screen, then climb aboard a 360-degree pitch-and-roll simulator for the ride of your dreams. At Radio Disney SongMaker, produce your own hit in a sound booth equipped with a computer and audio system that helps incorporate all kinds of sounds into your recording (DisneyQuest claims there are 2 billion possible combinations of songs, lyrics, and musical styles). You can buy what you've created at the Create Zone counter.

THE REPLAY ZONE

The classic free-play machines, like SkeeBall and Whack A Alien, are here, with futuristic twists. You can also sit with a partner in an asteroid cannon–equipped bumper car and blast others to make their cars do a 360-degree spin in Buzz Lightyear's AstroBlaster.

NEED A
BREAK?

At **Food Quest and Wonderland Café** you'll find varied soups, salads, sandwiches, pastas, pizza, and some of the best wraps around at this terrific eatery operated by the Cheesecake Factory Express. Desserts are worth the indulgence—cheesecake with strawberries, ice-cream treats, and chocolate pastries will rev you up for more virtual game play. Surf Disney's limited-access Web at your table—there's a computer terminal in many of the booths. You don't need a reservation to eat here, but you do need to pay the price of admission.

DISNEY'S BOARDWALK

If you have fond memories of strolling along an Atlantic coast boardwalk, hearing the bumpity-bump of bicycle tires on the boards, smelling fresh-baked pizza pies, and watching lovers stroll hand-in-hand, you're in for a heaping dose of nostalgia at Disney's BoardWalk in the Epcot resort area. Even if you've never known such pleasures, it's worth a visit here to experience what you've missed. Much smaller than Downtown Disney, BoardWalk spans a portion of lakefront at the BoardWalk Inn and Villas and offers good restaurants, a sports bar, a brewpub, a dance hall, midway games, a piano bar, the Wyland Galleries, and sporadic outdoor performances.

The Flying Fish Café is known for first-rate dining and serves up signature entrées that include a potato-wrapped Florida red snapper. Spoodles is a fun family experience, with Mediterranean specialties and even a take-out pizza window. Sports fans flock to ESPN Club, where even the bathrooms have TV monitors. You can rent a bicycle for two or a cycling surrey if you want to work off some vacation calories.

A DJ runs the party nightly at the Atlantic Dance hall (no cover charge), with its spacious dance floor and waterfront balcony. At Jellyrolls, you can sing along with dueling pianos (there's a $10 cover charge. Board-Walk is the perfect place for low-key fun—you can play a few carnival games, duck into an art gallery or boutique, and enjoy a free view from the Crescent Lake bridge of IllumiNations at nearby Epcot.

DISNEY'S WIDE WORLD OF SPORTS

In the mid-1990s, seizing on the public's seemingly endless fascination with sports, Disney officials built an all-purpose, international sports complex—Disney's Wide World of Sports. Although the facilities aren't designed to provide a day's worth of entertainment, there are plenty of fun events and activities here for the sports enthusiast in your group.

It feels like a giant leap back in time as you approach the old-time Florida architecture that anchors this 200-acre manicured spread. For the bench-warmers in your crowd, options include baseball at the Cracker Jack Stadium with the Atlanta Braves during spring training. There are also dozens of championship events hosted by the Amateur Athletic Union (AAU) throughout the year. If you want to be part of the action, sign up for the Sports Experience ($10.28 ages 10 and up, $7.71 ages 3–9), where athletes of all ages test their mettle at baseball, football, soccer, and other play stations on an interactive sports playground. For more information and prices on all events, including the Braves games, call 407/828–3267.

Where to Eat

WORD OF MOUTH

"If you have a car, eat dinner outside the parks a couple of nights. We ate in Celebration and at one of the restaurants on Sand Lake Road—a nice break from Disney."

–sophie_vero

"Epcot is full, Full, FULL of wonderful restaurants. It is truly the food park."

–ajcolorado

"We did the character breakfast and it was a huge hit, but take into consideration that the kids don't eat a thing cause they're too busy looking at the characters. And it's an expensive breakfast when they don't eat anything!"

–AustinTraveler

Revised by
Rowland
Stiteler

FOOD IN THE PARKS RANGES from fast to fabulous. Hamburgers, chicken fingers, and fries dominate at most of the counter-service places, but fresh sandwiches, salads, and fruit are always available, too. Of course, the full-service restaurants offer the best selection, from the Hollywood Brown Derby's signature Cobb salad to steak at Le Cellier. Priority-seating reservations are generally essential for restaurant meals, especially at dinner. Without reservations, you may find yourself having a burger (again) for dinner, or having to leave Walt Disney World, which some people prefer to do anyway.

Although some of Orlando's top restaurants—Victoria and Albert's, the California Grill, Bice, and Emeril's, for example—are in Walt Disney World or Universal, many others are outside the parks. Sand Lake Road, International Drive, and Celebration all have excellent restaurants, such as Seasons 52 and Bonefish Grill, which are perfect for a refreshing and romantic dinner in the real world.

DRESS

Because tourism is king around Orlando, casual dress is the rule. Men need jackets only in the priciest establishments.

MEALTIMES

When you're touring the theme parks, you can save a lot of time by eating in the off-hours. Lines at the counter-service places can get very long between noon and 2, and waiting in line for food can get more frustrating than waiting in line for a ride. Try eating lunch at 11 and dinner at 5, or lunch at 2:30 and dinner at 9.

RESERVATIONS

All WDW restaurants and most restaurants elsewhere in greater Orlando take "priority seating" reservations. A priority-seating reservation is like a Fastpass to a meal. You don't get your table right away, but you should get the next one that becomes available. Say you make your reservation for 7 PM. Once you arrive, the hostess will give you a round plastic buzzer that looks sort of like a hockey puck. Then you can walk around, get a drink at the bar, or just wait nearby until the buzzer vibrates and flashes red. That means your table is ready and you can go back to the hostess stand to be seated. You will most likely be seated within 15 minutes of your arrival.

For restaurant reservations within Walt Disney World, call 407/939–3463 or 407/560–7277. And, although you can't make reservations online at ⊕*www.disneyworld.com*, you can certainly get plenty of information, like the hours, price range, and specialties of all Disney eateries. For Universal Orlando reservations, call 407/224–9255.

In reviews, reservations are mentioned only when they're essential or not accepted. Unless otherwise noted, the restaurants listed are open daily for lunch and dinner.

	WHAT IT COSTS				
	¢	$	$$	$$$	$$$$
AT DINNER	under $8	$8–$14	$15–$21	$22–$30	over $30

Prices are per person for a main course, at dinner, excluding tip and tax.

12

WINE & ALCOHOL

The Magic Kingdom's no-liquor policy, a Walt Disney tradition that seems almost quaint in this day and age, does not extend to the rest of Walt Disney World, and in fact, most restaurants and watering holes, particularly those in the on-site hotels, mix elaborate fantasy drinks based on fruit juices or flavored with liqueurs.

WALT DISNEY WORLD AREA

CHARACTER MEALS

At these breakfasts, brunches, and dinners staged in hotel and theme-park restaurants all over Walt Disney World, kids can snuggle up to all the best-loved Disney characters. Sometimes the food is served buffet style; sometimes it's served to you banquet style. The cast of characters, times, and prices changes frequently (although locations of performances remain fairly constant), so be sure to call ahead.

Reservations are always available and often required; some meals can fill up more than 60 days in advance. However, you can also book by phone on the same day you plan to dine, and it never hurts to double-check the character lineup before you leave for the meal. If you have your heart set on a specific meal, make your reservations when you book your trip—up to six months in advance. Smoking is not permitted.

BREAKFAST

Main Street, U.S.A.'s **Crystal Palace Buffet** (☎407/939–3463 ⬛$18.99 *adults, $10.99 children ages 3–9*) has breakfast with Winnie the Pooh, Eeyore, Piglet, and friends daily from 8 AM to 10:30 AM. Disney–MGM Studios's **Hollywood & Vine** (☎407/939–3463 ⬛$22.99 *adults, $12.99 children ages 3–9*) hosts *Playhouse Disney* stars Jo Jo and Goliath from "Jo Jo's Circus" and June and Leo from "The Little Einsteins."

At Disney's Beach Club, characters are on hand at the **Cape May Café** (☎407/939–3463 ⬛$18.99 *adults, $10.99 children ages 3–9*) from 7:30 to 11 daily. At the Contemporary Resort, **Chef Mickey's** (☎407/939–3463 ⬛$18.99 *adults, $10.99 children ages 3–9*) has a no-holds-barred buffet from 7 to 11:15 daily. The Polynesian Resort's **'Ohana** (☎407/939–3463 ⬛$18.99 *adults, $10.99 children ages 3–9*) serves breakfast with Mickey and his friends daily from 7:30 to 11.

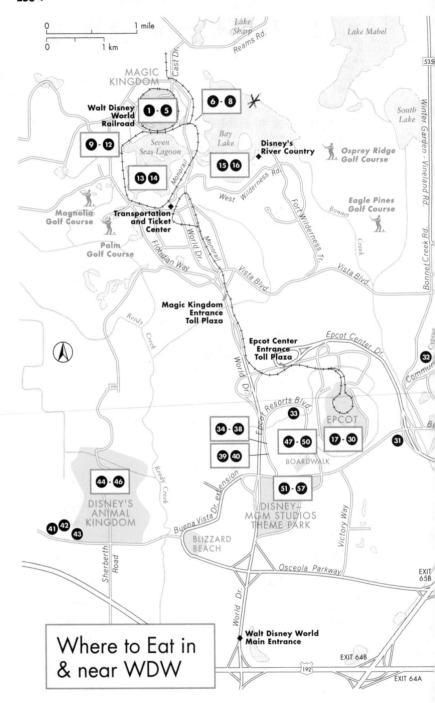

Where to Eat in & near WDW

12

TOP 5 DISNEY RESTAURANTS

Boma. African-inspired dishes like spiced chicken and banana-leaf–wrapped salmon are a hit with parents and kids at this casual buffet in the Animal Kingdom Lodge.

California Grill. This restaurant hits the top of the favorites list for most people for its innovative American cuisine and incredible views of the Magic Kingdom. Reserve months in advance for a window seat during the fireworks.

Jiko. Superb southern-African cuisine paired with an exceptional wine list and incredibly knowledgeable servers, Jiko is perfect for a romantic dinner for two.

Mama Melrose's. You can't go wrong with solid Italian pastas and secondi like osso buco. This casual *ristorante* in Disney–MGM Studios is great for families, and you get free drink refills if you sign up for the *Fantasmic!* dinner package.

Victoria and Albert's. Want to go all out? Treat yourself to a seven-course prix-fixe meal at the restaurant many consider to be Central Florida's best. The Victorian dining room and costumed servers transport you to another time and place, while every mouthful of the haute cuisine is a sensuous delight.

At the Swan, the weekend Good Morning Character Breakfast at the **Garden Grove Café** (☎407/934–3000 🍽*$16.95 adults, $8.50 children ages 3–9*) features a couple of dogs—Goofy and Pluto—from 8 to 11.

At the Wyndham Palace Resort & Spa you can drop in Sunday from 8 to 11 for a character meal at the **Watercress Restaurant** (☎407/827–2727 🍽*$24 adults, $13 children ages 3–9*).

BY RESERVATION ONLY — The Princess Storybook Breakfasts with Snow White, Sleeping Beauty, and at least three other princesses are held at Epcot Center in the Norway exhibit at **Restaurant Akershus** (☎407/939–3463 🍽*$22.99 adults, $12.99 children ages 3–9*) in the Norway Pavilion from 8:30 to 10:30 daily. Donald Duck and his friends are at Donald's Breakfastosaurus 8:10 to 10 daily at the **Restaurantosaurus** (☎407/939–3463 🍽*$18.99 adults, $10.99 children ages 3–9*), in Disney's Animal Kingdom. Mary Poppins presides at **1900 Park Fare Restaurant** (☎407/824–2383 🍽*$18.99 adults, $10.99 children ages 3–9*) in the Grand Floridian from 7:30 to 11:30 daily. Cinderella herself hosts Magic Kingdom breakfasts from 8:05 to 10 daily at

Fodor's Choice
★ **Cinderella's Royal Table** (☎407/939–3463 🍽*$31.99 adults, $21.99 children ages 3–9*). This breakfast is extremely popular, so book six months in advance to be assured seating.

LUNCH

At Cinderella Castle, **Cinderella's Royal Table** (☎407/939–3463 🍽*$33.99 adults, $22.99 children ages 3–9*) is a popular lunchtime option. Your picture is taken as you arrive, then presented to you—in a Cinderella frame, of course. Winnie the Pooh, Tigger, and Eeyore come to the **Crystal Palace Buffet** (☎407/939–3463 🍽*$20.99 adults, $11.99* *children ages 3–9*) on Main Street U.S.A. from 11:10 to 2:30. Mickey, Pluto, and Chip 'n' Dale are on hand from noon to 3:50 at the **Garden Grill** (☎407/939–3463 ✉$20.99 adults, $11.99 children ages 3–9) in the Land pavilion at Epcot.

The Princess Storybook Lunches with Snow White, Sleeping Beauty, and at least three other princesses are held at Epcot at the Norway Pavilion in **Restaurant Akershus** (☎407/939–3463 ✉$24.99 *adults, $13.99 children ages 3–9*) from 11:40 AM to 2:50 PM.

Jo Jo, Goliath, June, and Leo from *Playhouse Disney* make a comeback at Disney–MGM Studios's **Hollywood & Vine** (☎407/939–3463 ✉$24.99 adults, $13.99 children ages 3–9).

AFTERNOON SNACKS

For the *Wonderland* **Tea Party** (☎407/939–3463 ✉$28.17) at the Grand Floridian Resort, Alice and other characters preside over afternoon tea on weekdays from 1:30 to 2:30. With the cast's help, children can bake their own cupcakes and then eat them at the tea party. Open only to children ages 3 to 10; all participants must be potty-trained.

DINNER

All character dinners require reservations. Minnie Mouse and friends (which in this case does not include Mickey) get patriotic during their evening appearance at the Liberty Square **Liberty Tree Tavern** (☎407/939–3463 ✉$27.99 adults, $12.99 children ages 3–9). A "revolutionary" feast of smoked pork, turkey, carved beef, and all the trimmings is served nightly from 4 PM to 8:40 PM. Farmer Mickey appears at the Land Pavilion at Epcot's **Garden Grill** (☎407/939–3463 ✉$27.99 *adults, $12.99 children ages 3–9*) from 4 to 8 daily. Winnie the Pooh and friends appear at a nightly buffet from 4 to 8:45 at the **Crystal Palace Buffet** (☎407/939–3463 ✉$27.99 adults, $12.99 *children ages 3–9*) on Main Street, U.S.A.

Every night at 8 (7 in winter), near Fort Wilderness's Meadow Trading Post, there's a **Character Campfire** (☎407/824–2727) with a free singalong. There are usually around five characters there, with Chip 'n' Dale frequent attendees.

Cinderella's Gala Feast is held at the Grand Floridian's **1900 Park Fare** (☎407/939–3463 ✉$28.99 adults, $13.99 children ages 3–9), for a buffet served from 4:30 to 8:20 daily. The Contemporary Resort hosts a wildly popular dinner starring the head honcho himself at **Chef Mickey's** (☎407/939–3463 ✉$27.99 adults, $12.99 children ages 3–9), from 5 to 9:15 daily. At the Walt Disney World Swan, you can dine with *Lion King* characters Monday and Friday from 5:30 to 10 at **Gulliver's Grill** (☎407/934–1609). Known as the Garden Grove Café during the day, Gulliver's Grill hosts Goofy and Pluto the other five nights of the week. Dinner is $24.99 adults, $10.95 children ages 3 to 11.

The Princess Storybook Dinner with Snow White, Sleeping Beauty, and at least three other princesses are held at Epcot Center at the Norway Pavilion in **Restaurant Akershus** (☎407/939–3463 ✉$28.99 *adults, $13.99 children ages 3–9*) from 4:20 to 8:40.

MAGIC KINGDOM

Dining options in the Magic Kingdom are mainly counter service, and every land has its share of fast-food places selling burgers, hot dogs, grilled-chicken sandwiches, and salads. The walkways are peppered with carts dispensing popcorn, ice-cream bars, lemonade, bottled water, and soda.

For a meal in one of the full-service restaurants in the Kingdom, you must make priority-seating reservations. You can make them at the restaurants on the day you want to eat or through the **Disney Reservations Center** (☎407/939–3463).

AMERICAN–CASUAL

$$$–$$$$ ✕ **Cinderella's Royal Table.** Cinderella and other Disney princesses appear
★   at breakfast time at this eatery in the castle's old mead hall; you should book reservations up to 180 days in advance to be sure to see them. Breakfast and lunch are pre-plated meals. Breakfast, which includes scrambled eggs, sausages, bacon, danishes, potatoes, and beverages is $32 for adults, $22 for children. Lunch, which includes entrées like prime rib with mashed potatoes and roasted chicken breast on bread pudding with spinach, garlic, and red-onion marmalade, is $34 for adults, $23 for children. The prix-fixe dinner is $40 for adults, $25 for children. When you arrive at the Cinderella Castle, a photographer snaps a shot of your group in the lobby. A package of photographs will be delivered to your table during your meal. ⊠ *Cinderella Castle* ☎*407/939–3463* ⌂*Reservations essential* ▤*AE, MC, V.*

$$–$$$ ✕ **Crystal Palace.** Named for the big glass atrium surrounding the restaurant, the Crystal Palace is a great escape in summer, when the air-conditioning is turned to near meat-locker level. The buffet-style meal includes prime rib, peel-and-eat shrimp, soups, pastas, fresh-baked breads, and ice-cream sundaes, all part of a one-price package (dinner price is $28 for adults). There's also a kids-only buffet with what many youngsters consider the basic food groups: macaroni and cheese, pizza, and chocolate chip cookies for $13. per child. The Crystal Palace is huge but charming with numerous nooks and crannies, comfortable banquettes, cozy cast-iron tables, and abundant sunlight. It's also one of the few places in the Magic Kingdom that serves breakfast. Winnie the Pooh and his pals from the Hundred Acre Wood visit at breakfast, lunch, and dinner. ⊠ *At Hub end of Main St. facing Cinderella Castle* ☎*407/939–3463* ▤*AE, MC, V.*

$–$$$ ✕ **Liberty Tree Tavern.** This "tavern" is dry, but it's a prime spot on the parade route, so you can catch a good meal while you wait. Order colonial-period comfort food like smoked pork ribs, hearty pot roast cooked with a mushroom sauce, or turkey and dressing with mashed potatoes. Lunch prices are à la carte, with the least expensive sandwich for adults—a roast beef with Swiss cheese—going for $10.99. Kids can eat macaroni and cheese, pita pizzas, hot dogs, hamburgers, or chicken strips for $5 to $65. Dinner is a prix-fixe character meal that costs $28 for adults, $13 for children. The restaurant is decorated in lovely Williamsburg colors, with Early American–style antiques and

12

TOP 4 OFF-SITE RESTAURANTS

Bonefish Grill. Standout seafood like grilled sea bass, tilefish, and rainbow trout is served in a casually elegant dining room.

Emeril's. Bam! Get kicked-up New Orleans food like andouille sausage, shrimp, and red beans at Emeril Lagasse's eponymous restaurant.

Le Coq au Vin. Souped-up French country fare, like bronzed grouper with roasted pecans and the namesake chicken with red wine sauce, makes this fine little eatery in south-central Orlando worth seeking out.

Seasons 52. What's on the menu this month won't be on it next month at this new-concept restaurant where the ingredients in the dishes are served at the time of year when they are most ripe and flavorful. Besides flavor, you've got healthy here. Meats and fish tend to be grilled not baked. And the decadent desserts are served in shot-glass sizes.

lots of brightly polished brass. ✉*Liberty Sq.* ☎*407/824–6461* 🗖*AE, MC, V.*

¢–$ ✗ **Cosmic Ray's Starlight Cafe.** Kosher burgers, rotisserie chicken, barbecued ribs, cheesesteak sandwiches, hot dogs, and chicken strips, all served with potato croquettes, are available at the counter of this fast-food outlet in Tomorrowland. Robotic Las Vegas–style lounge singer Sonny E. Clipse croons for the crowds. ✉*Tomorrowland* ☎*407/503–3463* 🗖*AE, MC, V.*

ITALIAN

$$–$$$ ✗ **Tony's Town Square Restaurant.** Inspired by the animated classic *Lady and the Tramp,* Tony's offers everything from spaghetti and meatballs to wood-oven pizza and a very decent pan-seared salmon. There's no wine list, but you can get the smoothie of the day in a collector's mug for $8. A more tempting dessert is the excellent chocolate torte filled with hazelnut caramel. The restaurant's recommended breakfast fare includes a tasty Italian frittata and a bacon, egg, and cheese calzone. If you can't get a table right away, you can watch *Lady and the Tramp* in the waiting area. ✉*Main St., U.S.A., Liberty Sq.* ☎*407/939–3463* 🗖*AE, MC, V.*

EPCOT

Epcot's World Showcase offers some of the finest dining in Orlando. Every pavilion has at least one and often two or even three eateries. Where there's a choice, it's between a relatively expensive full-service restaurant and a more affordable, ethnic fast-food spot, plus carts and shops selling snacks ranging from French pastries to Japanese ices—whatever's appropriate to the pavilion.

Lunch and dinner priority-seating reservations are essential at the full-service restaurants; you can make them up to 60 days in advance by calling 407/939–3463 or going in person to Guest Relations at the park (only on the day of the meal) or to the restaurants themselves when they open for lunch, usually at noon. No matter how you book, show up a bit early to be sure of getting your table.

AMERICAN

$$$ ⨯ **Garden Grill.** Solid family-style lunch or dinner fare is served here as the restaurant revolves, giving you an ever-changing view of each biome on the Living with the Land boat ride. The restaurant offers an all-you-can-eat buffet ($21 for adults at lunch, $28 at dinner; $11 for children 3–11 for lunch, $12 for dinner). Typical choices include rotisserie pork, fried catfish, chicken strips, and macaroni and cheese. Besides the Princess breakfast in Norway, this is the only Epcot restaurant that has Disney character meet-and-greets during meals. ⊠ *The Land* ▤ *AE, MC, V.*

AMERICAN–CASUAL

¢–$ ⨯ **Sunshine Seasons.** Talk about a self-contained ecosystem: the Land pavilion where you'll find this restaurant grows its own produce. You order at a counter, then sit at a table and wait for your fresh-made food to be delivered. The varied menu includes seared tuna on a mixed green salad, turkey on cheese focaccia bread, and rotisserie chicken flatbread. If you have room for dessert, head for the bakery or hand-dipped ice-cream counter. The food is healthy, tasty, and reasonably priced, making Sunshine Seasons one of the most popular Epcot eateries. To avoid the crowds, plan to eat at nonpeak times—after 2 for lunch and before 5 or after 7 for dinner. ⊠ *The Land* ▤ *AE, MC, V.*

BRITISH

$$–$$$ ⨯ **Rose & Crown.** If you're an Anglophile and you love a good, thick beer, this is the place to soak up both the suds and the British street culture. "Wenches" serve up traditional English fare—fish-and-chips, Yorkshire pudding, and the ever-popular bangers and mash (sausage over mashed potatoes). There are several traditional meat pies to choose from, including chicken-and-leek pie and cottage pie (with ground beef, mashed potatoes, and cheese), all served with a side of green beans. Vegetarians will even find an offering of curried veggies and tofu on the menu. For dessert, try the sticky toffee pudding with rum-butter sauce. If you're not driving soon after the meal, try the Imperial Ale sampler, which includes five 6-ounce glasses for $9.35. The terrace has a splendid view of IllumiNations. ⊠ *United Kingdom* ▤ *AE, MC, V.*

CANADIAN

$$–$$$ ⨯ **Le Cellier.** With the best Canadian wine cellar in the state, this charming eatery with stone arches and dark-wood paneling has a good selection of Canadian beer as well. Aged beef is king, although many steaks appear only on the dinner menu. If you're a carnivore, go for the herb-crusted prime rib. Even though the menu changes periodically (gone are the buffalo steaks, alas), they've always got the maple-ginger–glazed Canadian salmon and free-range chicken with a mustard marinade. For

a light meal, try the Prince Edward Island mussels. Dessert salutes to the land up north include a crème brûlée made with maple sugar and the Canadian Club chocolate cake. ⊠ *Canada* 🖃 *AE, MC, V.*

CHINESE

$$–$$$$ ✕ **Nine Dragons Restaurant.** Though the restaurant is a showcase for all regions of Chinese cooking, including Szechuan and Hunan, the majority of the menu is Cantonese, from an excellent *moo goo gai pan* (a stir-fried chicken and vegetable dish) and sweet-and-sour pork to lobster. Other good choices are the "Imperial Pine Cone Fish"—a crispy whole (deboned) snapper topped with sweet-and-sour sauce, and the Cantonese roast duckling. For a really memorable experience, try the three-course Peking duck dinner for two, which includes a duck-broth soup with cabbage, tasty fried duck skin rolled in pancakes, and stir-fried shredded duck with Chinese vegetables. The red-bean ice cream is a great finale to your meal. The distinctive building has a curved, yellow-tile roof with ornate carvings inspired by the Forbidden City. ⊠ *China* 🖃 *AE, MC, V.*

FRENCH

$$$$ ✕ **Bistro de Paris.** The great secret in the France pavilion—and, indeed,
★ in all of Epcot—is the Bistro de Paris, upstairs from Les Chefs de France. The sophisticated menu changes regularly and reflects the cutting edge of French cooking; representative dishes include pan-seared lobster, roasted rack of venison with black-pepper sauce, and seared scallops with truffle-potato puree. An excellent appetizer is the double consommé of chicken and beef topped with puff pastry, a relative bargain at $9. Save room for the Grand Marnier flambéed crepes. Come late, ask for a window seat, and plan to linger to watch the nightly Epcot light show, which usually starts around 9 PM. Moderately priced French wines are available by the bottle and the glass. ⊠ *France* 🖃 *AE, MC, V.*

$$–$$$$ ✕ **Les Chefs de France.** What some consider the best restaurant at Dis-
★ ney was created by three of France's most famous chefs: Paul Bocuse, Gaston Lenôtre, and Roger Vergé. Classic escargots, a good starter, are prepared in a casserole with garlic butter; you might follow up with duck à l'orange or grilled beef tenderloin with a black pepper sauce. Make sure you finish with crepes *au chocolat*. Best guilty pleasure: a sinful version of macaroni and cheese made with cream and Gruyère cheese, a bargain at $17. The nearby Boulangerie Pâtisserie, run by the same team, offers tarts, croissants, eclairs, napoleons, and more, to go. ⊠ *France* 🖃 *AE, MC, V.*

GERMAN

$$ ✕ **Biergarten.** Oktoberfest runs 365 days a year here. The cheerful, sometimes raucous, crowds are what you would expect in a place with an oompah band. Waitresses in Bavarian garb serve *breseln,* hot German pretzels, which are made fresh daily on the premises. The menu and level of frivolity are the same at lunch and dinner. For a single price ($21 for adults, $10.99 for kids ages 3–11 at lunch and $24 for adults and $12 for children at dinner), mountains of sauerbraten, bratwurst, chicken schnitzel, apple strudel, and Black Forest cake await you at

the all-you-can-eat buffet. And if you aren't feeling too Teutonic, there's also rotisserie chicken and roast pork. Patrons pound pitchers of all kinds of beer and wine on the long communal tables—even when the yodelers, singers, and dancers aren't egging them on. ⊠*Germany* ⊟*AE, MC, V.*

ITALIAN

$$$–$$$$ ★ ✕ **L'Originale Alfredo di Roma Ristorante.** Waiters skip around singing arias, a show in itself. Their voices and the restaurant's namesake dish, made with mountains of imported Italian butter, account for its popularity. The classic dish—fettuccine with cream, butter, and loads of freshly grated Parmesan cheese—was invented by Alfredo de Lelio, whose descendants had a hand in creating this restaurant. Besides the excellent pastas, try the chef's tip of the hat to Florida—roasted grouper with a lemon, butter, and white wine sauce—or the tender, slow-roasted chicken served with polenta. The minestrone is excellent, and if you can't pass up the fettuccine Alfredo, it's available as an appetizer for $7.95 per person, or $19.95 fr a platter that serves three to four people. Dessert offerings include a good tiramisu and an even better cannoli. ⊠*Italy* ⊟*AE, MC, V.*

JAPANESE

$$–$$$$ ✕ **Mitsukoshi.** Three restaurants and a lounge are enclosed in this complex, which overlooks tranquil gardens. **Yakitori House,** a gussied-up fast-food stand in a small pavilion, is modeled after a teahouse in Kyoto's Katsura Summer Palace. At the **Tempura Kiku,** diners watch the chefs prepare sushi, sashimi, and tempura (batter-dipped deep-fried shrimp, scallops, and vegetables). In the five **Teppanyaki** dining rooms, chefs frenetically chop vegetables, meat, and fish and stir-fry them at the grills set into the communal tables. Specialties include lobster served with either shrimp and scallops or sirloin. The **Matsu No Ma Lounge,** more serene than the restaurants, has a great view of the World Showcase Lagoon. It also offers one of Epcot's great bargains: a 12-piece sushi platter for $21.75. Grown-ups might also go for the sake martini. ⊠*Japan* ⊟*AE, MC, V.*

MEXICAN

$$–$$$ ✕ **San Angel Inn.** In the dark, grottolike main dining room, a deep purple, dimly lighted mural of a night scene in Central Mexico seems to envelop the diners. San Angel is a popular respite for the weary, especially when the humidity outside makes Central Florida feel like equatorial Africa. At dinner, guitar and marimba music fills the air. Start with the *queso fundido* (melted cheese and chorizo sausage served with soft tortillas) and then try the authentic *filete motuleno* (grilled beef tenderloin over black beans and melted cheese, ranchero sauce, and poblano pepper strips) or the *puntas de filete* (tender beef tips sautéed with onions and chilis and accompanied by rice and refried beans). For dessert, the flan is served with a piña colada sauce and topped with a fresh strawberry. ⊠*Mexico* ⊟*AE, MC, V.*

MOROCCAN

$$-$$$$ ✕ **Marrakesh.** Chef Abrache Lahcen of Morocco presents the best cooking of his homeland in this ornate eatery, which looks like something from the set of *Casablanca*. Your appetizer might be *harira*, a soup with tomatoes, lentils, and lamb that is traditionally served during Ramadan. From there, move on to the chicken, lamb, or vegetable couscous, Morocco's national dish. A good way to try a bit of everything is the Marrakesh Feast ($35 per person), which includes chicken bastilla and beef *brewat* (minced beef in a layered pastry dusted with cinnamon and powdered sugar), plus vegetable couscous and assorted Moroccan pastries; or better still, upgrade to the Royal Feast ($38 per person), which includes everything in the Marrakesh Feast, plus crepes for dessert. Traditional belly dancers perform periodically throughout the day in a show that is completely G-rated. ⊠*Morocco* ▭*AE, MC, V.*

SCANDINAVIAN

$$$ ✕ **Restaurant Akershus.** The Norwegian buffet at this restaurant is as
★   extensive as you'll find on this side of the Atlantic. Appetizers usually include herring, prepared several ways, and cold seafood, including gravlax (cured salmon served with mustard sauce) or *fiskepudding* (a seafood mousse with herb dressing). For your main course, you might try some hot sausages, venison stew, or grilled Atlantic salmon. The à la carte desserts include raspberry tarts, bread pudding, and chocolate mousse with strawberry sauce. Akershus hosts a princess breakfast with Belle, Jasmine, Sleeping Beauty, and Snow White but *not* Cinderella. Call 407/939–3463 for reservations. ⊠*Norway* ▭*AE, MC, V.*

SEAFOOD

$$$-$$$$ ✕ **Coral Reef Restaurant.** One of this restaurant's walls is made entirely of glass and looks directly into the 6-million-gallon Living Seas aquarium, where you can get tantalizingly close to sharks, stingrays, groupers, tarpons, sea turtles and even the occasional scuba diver. And with a three-tiered seating area, everyone has a good view. Edible attractions include pan-seared tilapia served with a crab cake; ahi tuna lightly grilled; and Dublin-style mussels and clams steamed in a Harp beer broth. Crab fritters with spicy marinara sauce make a great appetizer. You might finish off with Kahlua tiramisu in raspberry sauce. ⊠*The Living Seas* ▭*AE, MC, V.*

DISNEY–MGM STUDIOS

The Studios tend to offer more casual American cuisine than the other parks. In other words, it's cheeseburger city. However, there are some good, imaginative offerings, too. Where else but here can you watch '50s sitcoms nonstop while you devour veal-and-shiitake-mushroom meat loaf? Waits can be long. To make priority-seating reservations, call 407/939–3463 up to 180 days in advance, or stop in person at the restaurant or first thing in the morning at Hollywood Junction Restaurant Reservations. There are four ways to book dinner packages that include the *Fantasmic!* after-dark show: by phone, in person at a Disney hotel, at the park's Guest Relations, and at Hollywood Junction.

AMERICAN

$–$$ ✕ **'50s Prime Time Café.** Who says you can't go home again? If you grew up in middle America in the 1950s, just step inside. While *I Love Lucy* and *The Donna Reed Show* play on a television screen, you can feast on meat loaf, pot roast, or fried chicken, all served on a Formica tabletop. At $13, the meat loaf is one of the best inexpensive dinners in any local theme park. Follow it up with chocolate cake or a thick milk shake—available in chocolate, strawberry, vanilla, even peanut butter and jelly. The place offers some fancier dishes, such as pan-seared salmon, that are good but out of character with the diner theme. If you're not feeling totally wholesome, go for Dad's Electric Lemonade (rum, vodka, blue curaçao, sweet-and-sour mix, and Sprite), worth every bit of the $9.50 price tag. Just like Mother, the menu admonishes, "Don't put your elbows on the table!" ⊠ *Echo Lake* ☎ *407/939–3463* ⊟ *AE, MC, V.*

AMERICAN–CASUAL

$–$$$ ✕ **Hollywood & Vine.** This restaurant is designed for those who like lots of food and lots of choices. You can have everything from frittatas to fried rice at the same meal. Even though the buffet ($24 for adults, $12 for children ages 3–11) is all-you-can-eat at a relatively low price, it does offer some upscale entrées like oven-roasted prime rib, sage-rubbed rotisserie turkey, or grilled sirloin in a red wine demiglace. There are plenty of kids' favorites, such as mac and cheese, hot dogs, and fried chicken. Minnie, Goofy, Pluto, and Chip 'n' Dale put in appearances at breakfast and lunch character meals. There's a Hollywood theme to the place; characters and servers are just hoping to be discovered by some passing Hollywood agent. Priority seating reservations are a must. ⊠ *Echo Lake* ☎ *407/939–3463* ⊟ *AE, MC, V.*

$–$$ ✕ **Sci-Fi Dine-In Theater Restaurant.** If you don't mind zombies leering at you while you consume chef salads, barbecue pork sandwiches, charbroiled sirloin, and Milky-Way-Out Milk Shakes, then head to this enclosed faux drive-in, where you can sit in a fake candy-color '50s convertible and watch trailers from classics like *Attack of the Fifty-Foot Woman* and *Teenagers from Outer Space.* The menu is not limited to choices like the $11 cheeseburger, however. For something different, try the slow-roasted barbecue ribs, the pan-fried catfish, butcher-tendered steak in a red wine sauce. The milk shakes are delicious. ⊠ *Echo Lake* ☎ *407/939–3463* ⊟ *AE, MC, V.*

ECLECTIC

$$–$$$ ✕ **Hollywood Brown Derby.** At this reproduction of the famous 1940s Hollywood restaurant, the walls are lined with movie-star caricatures, just like in Tinseltown, and the staff wears black bow ties. The house specialty is the Cobb salad, which by legend was invented by Brown Derby founder Robert Cobb; the salad consists of lettuce enlivened by loads of tomato, bacon, turkey, blue cheese, chopped egg, and avocado, all tossed table-side. And the butter comes in molds shaped like Mickey Mouse heads. Other menu choices include grilled salmon on creamy polenta and Gorgonzola with sun-dried tomatoes and baby arugula; and pan-roasted pork tenderloin with white-cheddar grits. For dessert, try the Brown Derby grapefruit cake, with layers of cream cheese icing. If you request the *Fantasmic!* dinner package, make a reservation for no later than two hours before the start of the show. ✉*Hollywood Blvd.* ☎*407/939–3463* ▤*AE, MC, V.*

FAST FOOD

¢–$ ✕ **ABC Commissary.** This place has a refreshingly different fast-food menu that includes vegetarian wraps, beef fajitas, and fish-and-chips, plus standard kid fare like chicken nuggets, and macaroni and cheese. Best of the fast-but-tasty treats is the $7 tortilla wrap filed with tabbouleh, hummus, and marinated tomatoes—far healthier than a burger and fries. Indoor seating offers great respite from the heat in summer. ✉*Echo Lake* ▤*AE, MC, V.*

¢–$ ✕ **Studio Catering Company.** With a creative and inexpensive menu, plus a convenient location near the Disney–MGM Studios Backlot Tour exit, this snack stop gets plenty of crowds at lunchtime. You'll find grilled chicken and chilled ham wraps, tantalizing flatbreads piled with steak gyro, Tandoori chicken, and lamb with baba ghanoush fillings. The best choice for kids is a $4 combo with a big peanut butter and jelly sandwich and one side item. ✉*Streets of America, Disney–MGM Studios* ▤*AE, MC, V.*

ITALIAN

$$–$$$ ✕ **Mama Melrose's Ristorante Italiano.** To replace the energy you've no FodorsChoice doubt depleted by miles of theme-park walking, you can load up on
★ carbs at this casual Italian restaurant that looks like an old warehouse. Wood-fired flatbreads with hearty toppings such as chicken and Italian cheeses make great starters before the arrival of such main courses as osso buco with risotto and grilled salmon with sun-dried tomato pesto. The sangria, available by the carafe for $16.50, flows generously. Cappuccino crème brûlée is the way to go for dessert. Kids' choices include a good burger and a $5 pizza. Ask for the *Fantasmic!* dinner package if you want priority seating for the show. ✉*Street of America* ☎*407/939–3463* ▤*AE, MC, V.*

DISNEY'S ANIMAL KINGDOM

AFRICAN

$$$ ✕ **Boma.** Boma takes Western-style ingredients and prepares them with FodorsChoice an African twist. The dozen or so walk-up serving stations have such
★ entrées as spit-roasted pork, spiced roast chicken, pepper steak, and banana leaf–wrapped sea bass or salmon. Don't pass up the soups, as the hearty chicken corn porridge is excellent. The zebra bones dessert is chocolate mousse covered with white chocolate and striped with dark chocolate. All meals are prix fixe ($26 for adults, $12 for children ages 3 to 11). The South African wine list is outstanding. Priority seating reservations are essential if you're not a guest at the hotel. ✉*Disney's*

12

Animal Kingdom Lodge ☎407/939–3463 ⚱*Reservations essential* 🞸*AE, D, DC, MC, V* ⊘*No lunch.*

$$$–$$$$
Fodor's Choice
★

✕ **Jiko.** The menu here is more African-inspired than purely African, but does include authentic entrées like jumbo scallops with golden brown mealie pap (a porridge made from ground grain) and steamed golden bass with spicy chaka-laka (a mixture of baked beans, carrots, tomato, onions, and spices—a longtime menu favorite). The menu changes periodically but typically includes such entrées as roasted chicken with mashed potatoes, and pomegranate-glaze quails stuffed with saffron basmati rice. After dinner, try a non-African treat: baklava—the honey-soaked dessert is the best on the menu. Also worth trying is a globe-trotting treat: three flavors of ice cream—vanilla, chocolate, and arugula—with meringue dots. ⊠*Disney's Animal Kingdom Lodge* ☎407/939–3463 ⚱*Reservations essential* 🞸*AE, D, MC, V.*

AMERICAN-CASUAL

$$–$$$$

✕ **Rainforest Café.** You don't have to pay park admission to dine at the Rainforest Café, the only full-service eatery in the Animal Kingdom area, with entrances both inside the park and at the gate. Since it resembles the one in Downtown Disney Marketplace, complete with the long lines for lunch and dinner, go early or late. If you can, make reservations by phone ahead of time. The most popular entrée is "mojo bones," slow-roasted pork ribs in a tangy barbecue sauce. Other good choices include chicken-fried steak with country gravy and shrimp enbrochette (broiled jumbo shrimp stuffed with crabmeat, jalapeños, four cheeses, and wrapped in bacon). The coconut bread pudding with apricot filling and whipped cream is great. Breakfast, from steak and eggs to excellent French toast, is served beginning at 7:30. ⊠*Disney's Animal Kingdom* ☎407/938–9100 or 407/939–3463 🞸*AE, D, DC, MC, V.*

FAST FOOD

¢–$

✕ **Flame Tree Barbecue.** At this counter-service eatery you can dig into ribs, brisket, and pulled pork with several sauce choices. For something with a lower calorie count, try the smoked turkey sandwich in a multigrain bun. There are also great vegetarian wraps. The outdoor tables, set beneath intricately carved wood pavilions, make great spots for a picnic and they're not usually crowded. ⊠*Discovery Island* 🞸*AE, MC, V.*

¢–$

✕ **Tusker House.** This counter-service restaurant offers tasty and healthy fare like rotisserie chicken, and a big garden salad served with focaccia bread on the side, along with the standard kids' fare like mac and cheese and chicken drumsticks served with mashed potatoes. Breakfast includes eggs, ham, biscuits and gravy, and lighter options like fruit cups and cereal. ⊠*Harambe* 🞸*AE, MC, V.*

DOWNTOWN DISNEY

Downtown Disney has three sections: the Marketplace, a small shopping-and-dining area; Pleasure Island, a nightlife complex with a hefty admission after dark; and, close by, Disney's West Side, another group of hipper-than-hip entertainment, dining, and shopping spots. The edge of Disney property is about a block away.

AMERICAN-CASUAL

$$-$$$ ✗ **Olivia's Café.** This is like a meal at Grandma's—provided she lives south of the Mason-Dixon line. The menu ranges from fried shrimp, grilled grouper, and crab cakes to fried chicken with mashed potatoes and gravy. One meat option stands out: the slow-roasted prime rib ($21 for 10 ounces). For dessert try the guava-swirl cheesecake with mango and raspberry sauce ($5). The indoor palms and rough wood walls resemble those of a venerable Key West abode, but other than that the atmosphere is not that special. The outdoor seating, which overlooks a waterway, is attractive any time that midsummer's heat is not bearing down. ⊠ *Old Key West Resort* ☎*407/939–3463* ▤*AE, D, DC, MC, V.*

$-$$$ ✗ **Planet Hollywood.** Patrons still flock to see the movie memorabilia assembled by celebrity owners like Schwarzenegger, Stallone, and Willis. The wait has been abated by a system that allows you to sign in, take a number, and get an assigned time window to return. The place covers 20,000 square feet if you count the indoor waterfall. The most popular menu item here is still the $11 burger (the barbecue-bacon-cheddar version is the best) but also notable are the grilled specialties including steak, salmon, ribs, and pork chops. You can also indulge in unusual pastas and salads. ⊠ *West Side, at entrance to Pleasure Island* ☎*407/827–7827* ⚄*Reservations not accepted* ▤*AE, D, DC, MC, V.*

$-$$$ ✗ **Rainforest Café.** People start queuing up a half hour before the 10:30 AM opening of this 30,000-square-foot jungle fantasy in Downtown Disney's Marketplace, drawn as much by the gimmicks (man-made rainstorms, volcano eruptions) as the menu. But the food, a mix of American fare with imaginative names, is nevertheless worthwhile. Top choices include "Eyes of the Ocelot," a nice meat loaf topped with sautéed mushrooms; and "mojo bones," tender ribs with barbecue sauce. For dessert, try "gorillas in the mist," a banana cheesecake topped with chocolate and whipped cream ($6). ⊠ *Marketplace* ☎*407/827–8500 or 407/939–3463* ▤*AE, D, DC, MC, V.*

CUBAN

$$$-$$$$ ✗ **Bongos Cuban Café.** Singer Gloria Estefan's Cuban eatery is inside a two-story building shaped like a pineapple. Hot-pressed Cuban sandwiches, black-bean soup, deep-fried plantain chips, and beans and rice are mainstays on the menu for the lunch crowd. One of the best entrées is "La Habana," lobster, shrimp, scallops, squid, clams, and mussels in a piquant creole sauce. Other worthwhile offerings include *masitas de puerco* (pork chunks served with grilled onions) and *vaca frita*, marinated flank steak served with rice and yucca. There's live Latin music on Friday and Saturday. ⊠ *West Side* ☎*407/828–0999* ⚄*Reservations not accepted* ▤*AE, D, DC, MC, V.*

ECLECTIC

$$$–$$$$ ✕ **Wolfgang Puck.** There are lots of choices here, from wood-oven pizza at the informal Puck Express to five-course meals in the upstairs formal dining room, where there's also a sushi bar and an informal café. At Express try the barbecue chicken pizza or spinach and mushroom pizza. The dining room always offers inspired pastas with sauces sublimely laced with chunks of lobster, salmon, or chicken. Another good choice is the slow-braised short ribs ($28). Special five-course prix-fixe dinners ($110 with wine, $75 without) require 24-hour notice. ⊠ *West Side* ☎407/938–9653 ▭*AE, MC, V.*

ITALIAN

$$$–$$$$ ✕ **Portobello Yacht Club.** The northern Italian cuisine here is uniformly good. The spaghettini *alla Portobello* (with scallops, clams, and Alaskan king crab) is outstanding; other fine options include charcoal-grilled rack of lamb served with creamy risotto cake, and wood-roasted grouper with ratatouille spiced with chili oil. There's always a fresh-catch special, as well as tasty wood-oven pizza. A special Chef's selection—four-course dinner, with rib-eye steak or fish of the day as the entrée—is offered at $57 per person. ⊠*Pleasure Island* ☎407/934–8888 ▭*AE, MC, V.*

SEAFOOD

$$$–$$$$ ✕ **Fulton's Crab House.** Set in a faux riverboat docked in a lagoon between Pleasure Island and the Marketplace, this fish house offers fine, if expensive, dining. The signature seafood is flown in daily. Dungeness crab from the Pacific coast, Alaskan king crab, Florida stone crab: it's all fresh. Start with the crab and lobster bisque, then try one of the many combination entrées like the gulf shrimp and crab cake platter. If you have no budget constraints, go for the Lobster Narragansett (a 2-pound lobster tail, oven roasted with scallops, shrimp and red skin potatoes, for $49). The sublime cappuccino ice-cream cake is $13, but one order is easily enough for two. ⊠*Marketplace* ☎407/934–2628 ▭*AE, MC, V.*

DISNEY'S BOARDWALK

AMERICAN–CASUAL

$$–$$$ ✕ **Big River Grille & Brewing Co.** Strange but good brews, like Pale Rocket Red Ale and Gadzooks Pilsner, abound here. You can dine inside among the giant copper brewing tanks, or sip your suds outside on the lake-view patio. The menu emphasizes meat, with pork ribs slow-cooked in red barbecue sauce, barbecue pork, and a house-special flame-grilled meat loaf made with ground beef and Italian sausage. The cheddar cheese–mashed potatoes are a perfect accompaniment. There's also a worthwhile grilled Atlantic salmon fillet with dill butter. ⊠*Disney's BoardWalk* ☎407/560–0253 ▭*AE, MC, V.*

12

$-$$ ✕ **ESPN Club.** Not only can you watch sports on big-screen TV here, but you can also periodically see ESPN programs being taped in the club itself and be part of the audience of sports radio talk shows. Food ranges from an outstanding half-pound burger to a 10-ounce sirloin and grilled chicken and shrimp in penne pasta, topped with marinara sauce. If you want an appetizer, try the Macho Nachos,

WORD OF MOUTH

"On a recent trip to Disney we ate at Spoodles on the Boardwalk and it was a huge disappointment. Food was mediocre at best and quite pricey. The restaurant wasn't busy and the service was sporadic. One of the steaks ordered was cooked wrong twice."–japw82

crispy corn tortilla chips piled high with ground beef, shredded cheddar cheese, sour cream, spicy salsa, and sliced jalapeños. The apple brown Betty, with a granola-streusel topping, is a satisfying dessert. This place is open quite late by Disney standards—until 2 AM on Friday and Saturday. ⊠ *Disney's BoardWalk* 🕾 *407/939–5100* ⊟ *AE, MC, V.*

MEDITERRANEAN

$$-$$$ ✕ **Spoodles.** The international tapas-style menu here draws on the best foods of the Mediterranean, from tuna with sun-dried tomato couscous to Italian fettuccine with rich Parmesan cream sauce. Oak-fired flatbreads with such toppings as roasted peppers make stellar appetizers. For a main course, try the Portuguese seafood stew overflowing with shrimp, oysters, clams, mussels, scallops, crab meat and potatoes—well worth the $26 price tag. For dessert, try the cheesecake with banana slices or go for a sampler from the dessert tower. There's also a walk-up pizza window if you prefer to stroll the boardwalk. ⊠ *Disney's Board-Walk* 🕾 *407/939–3463* ⊟ *AE, MC, V.*

SEAFOOD

$$-$$$$ ✕ **Flying Fish.** One of Disney's better restaurants, this fish house's best dishes include potato-wrapped red snapper, and oak-fired scallops with butternut squash risotto. The "peeky toe" crab cakes with ancho-chili rémoulade are an appetizer that never leaves the frequently changing menu—try them and you'll see why. Save room for the raspberry napoleon with white chocolate mousse, crispy phyllo dough, and macadamia nuts. ⊠ *Disney's BoardWalk* 🕾 *407/939–2359* ⊟ *AE, MC, V.*

WDW RESORTS

AMERICAN

$$$-$$$$ ✕ **Artist Point.** If you're not a guest at the Wilderness Lodge, a meal here ★ is worth it just to see the giant totem poles and huge rock fireplace in the lobby. The specialty is cedar-plank salmon and mashed potatoes with roasted fennel and truffle butter (worth its $29 price tag). Another good option: grilled buffalo sirloin with sweet potato–hazelnut gratin and sweet-onion jam. For dessert, try the wild berry cobbler or the flourless chocolate–whiskey cake with pecans and raspberry sorbet. There's a good northwestern U.S. wine list, and wine pairings for the meal cost $18 to $23 per person. A fixed price dinner, which offers a

good cross section of the restaurant's cuisine, is available for $46 per person. ☒ *Wilderness Lodge* ☎ *407/939–3463* ⚓ *Reservations essential* 🖃 *AE, MC, V.*

AMERICAN-CASUAL

$$$ ✕ **Chef Mickey's.** This is the holy shrine for character meals, with Mickey, Minnie, and Goofy always around for breakfast and dinner, so it's not a quiet spot to read the *New York Times.* Folks come here for entertainment and comfort food. The dinner buffet includes prime rib, baked ham, and changing specials like beef tips with mushrooms or baked cod with tarragon butter. The Parmesan mashed potatoes have been a popular menu item for years, but you can also get more unusual offerings like broccoli with black olives and feta. The all-you-can-eat dessert bar has sundaes and chocolate cake. ☒ *Contemporary Resort* ☎ *407/939–3463* 🖃 *AE, MC, V.*

$$–$$$ ✕ **Shutters at Old Port Royale.** This bright and breezy restaurant is a good place to put your feet up after a long day and sample cuisine inspired by the flavors of the Caribbean. You can have your spicy jerk chicken and your almond-raspberry cheesecake, too. A consistent hit is the pan-seared salmon with vine-ripened tomatoes, applewood-smoked bacon, red pepper aioli, and grilled sourdough bread. There's also a host of classic American offerings, such as smoked prime rib, grilled sirloin steak, and chocolate-hazelnut cake. Wash it all down with a tangerine margarita or a Red Stripe beer from Jamaica. ☒ *Caribbean Beach Resort* ☎ *407/939–3463* 🖃 *AE, D, DC, MC, V.*

$$–$$$ ✕ **Whispering Canyon Cafe.** No whispering goes on here. The servers, dressed as cowboys and cowgirls, deliver corny jokes and other talk designed to keep things jovial at this family-style restaurant, where huge stacks of pancakes and big servings of spare ribs are the orders of the day. The all-you-can-eat breakfast platter puts eggs, sausage, biscuits, and tasty waffles in front of you for $9.69. For dinner, the $22.49 all-you-can-eat skillet with pork ribs and roasted chicken is the best deal for big eaters. It includes pork ribs, pulled pork, roast chicken, beef stew, and sides like roasted red potatoes and corn on the cob. Kids love the Happiest Celebration on Earth dessert: warm chocolate s'more cake with graham cracker meringue cookie. ☒ *Wilderness Lodge* ☎ *407/939–3463* 🖃 *AE, MC, V.*

¢ ✕ **Picabu Buffeteria.** This buffet in the Walt Disney World Dolphin would be forgettable were it not for its hours and reasonable prices—Picabu serves up inexpensive hot food around the clock. You can find lots of kids' favorites here, like pizza, hot dogs, hamburgers, and grilled-cheese sandwiches, plus a supply of nonfood necessities like laundry detergent and disposable diapers. Breakfast, including a worthy omelet, is served from 6 to 11:30 AM. And for the parents, there's a selection of imported bottled beer. ☒ *Walt Disney World Dolphin* ☎ *407/934–4000* 🖃 *AE, MC, V.*

ECLECTIC

$$$$ ✕ **Victoria and Albert's.** At this Disney fantasy, you are served by "Victo-
Fodor's Choice ria" and "Albert," who recite the menu in tandem. There's also a som-
★ melier to explain the wine pairings. Everyone, of course, is dressed in period Victorian costumes. This is one of the plushest fine-dining expe-

riences in Florida: a regal meal in a lavish, Victorian-style room. The seven-course, prix-fixe menu ($100; wine is an additional $55) changes daily. Appetizer choices might include Iranian caviar, veal sweetbreads, or artichokes in a mushroom sauce; entrées may be Kobe beef with celery-root puree

or veal tenderloin with cauliflower-and-potato puree. The restaurant also features a vegetarian menu with exotics such as rutabaga napoleon with melted leeks and ramps. For most of the year, there are two seatings, at 5:45 and 9. In July and August, however, there's generally just one seating—at 6:30. The chef's table dinner event is $165 to $235 (with wine pairing) per person. Make your reservations 90 days in advance. ⊠ *Grand Floridian* ☎ *407/939–3463* ⚓ *Reservations essential*Jacket required ▭ *AE, MC, V* ⊘ *No lunch.*

$$$–$$$$ ✕ **Citricos.** Although the name implies that you might be eating lots of local citrus-flavor specialties, you won't find them here, aside from drinks like a "Citropolitan" martini, infused with lemon-and-lime liqueur, and an orange-chocolate mousse for dessert. Standout entrées include sautéed salmon fillet with roasted fennel, Yukon gold potatoes, and black-olive butter; and roasted free-range chicken with vegetable quinoa and tomato-cilantro sauce. The wine list, one of Disney's most extensive, includes vintages from around the world. ⊠ *Grand Floridian* ☎ *407/939–3463* ▭ *AE, MC, V.*

$$$–$$$$ ✕ **Todd English's bluezoo.** Celebrity chef Todd English opened this cutting-edge seafood eatery in late 2003. The sleek, modern interior resembles an underwater dining hall, with blue walls and carpeting, aluminum fish suspended from the ceiling, and bubblelike lighting fixtures. The menu is creative and pricey, with entrées like whole crispy-fried sea bass with chili bean sauce or tuna steak wrapped in bacon. If you don't care for fish, alternatives include chicken with lemon risotto, and slow-roast double pork chops with potatoes, asparagus, and fried onion rings. The coconut–cream crème brûlée is supremely satisfying. ⊠ *Walt Disney World Dolphin* ☎ *407/934–1111* ▭ *AE, D, DC, MC, V* ⊘ *No lunch.*

$$–$$$$ ✕ **California Grill.** The view of the surrounding Disney parks from this
Fodor'sChoice rooftop restaurant is as stunning as the food, especially at night, when
★ you can watch the nightly Magic Kingdom fireworks from the patio. Start with the brick-oven flatbread with grilled duck sausage or the *unagi* (eel) sushi. For a main course, try the oak-fired beef fillet with three-cheese potato gratin and tamarind barbecue sauce, or the seared scallops with risotto, baby carrots, and crustacean butter sauce. Good dessert choices include the orange crepes with Grand Marnier custard, raspberries, and blackberry coulis and the butterscotch, orange, and vanilla crème brûlée. ⊠ *Contemporary Resort* ☎ *407/939–3463* ▭ *AE, MC, V.*

$–$$$$ ✕ **Gulliver's Grill.** The legend is that this eatery was founded by Peter Miles Gulliver, a direct descendant of the Jonathan Swift character. Eat among tall palms and lush greenery inside a giant greenhouse.

The menu includes something for everyone—pizza, burgers, and spaghetti for the kids; and fresh crab stuffed baked shrimp, filet mignon, and old-fashioned meat loaf for adults. Catch the *Legend of the Lion King* characters on Monday and Friday, and Goofy and Pluto the rest of the week. ⊠ *Walt Disney World Swan* ☎ *407/934–3000* ⚓ *Reservations essential* ⊟ *AE, D, DC, MC, V* ⊘ *No lunch.*

> **WORD OF MOUTH**
>
> "The California Grill will definitely meet your every expectation for a special evening. It is a classy, sophisticated place. Try to get a reservation for about 15 minutes before the Magic Kingdom fireworks show (it usually starts at 9 PM) and specifically ask for a window table."–Orlando Vic

$$–$$$ ✕ **Kona Cafe.** Desserts get a lot of emphasis at this eclectic restaurant, with choices like caramel-banana crème brûlée and apple brown Betty. Best of the entrées are the breaded shrimp and pan-seared scallops with sticky rice and the reliably good slow-roasted prime rib. The blackened mahimahi sandwich, with an Asian tartar sauce, makes an outstanding lunch. If you want a cocktail, the Lapu Lapu, made with rum, orange juice, and chunks of pineapple, makes for soothing liquid solace at the end of a long day on your feet. As the name of the place hints, coffee is a specialty, too. ⊠ *Polynesian Resort* ☎ *407/939–3463* ⊟ *AE, MC, V.*

JAPANESE

$$–$$$ ✕ **Kimonos.** Knife-wielding sushi chefs prepare world-class sushi and sashimi but also excellent beef teriyaki and other Japanese treats good for a full dinner or just a snack. One of the best bets here is the sushi-sashimi combination, which gives you a generous amount of both for the price. Popular rolls include the California roll (crab, avocado, and cucumber), Mexican roll (shrimp tempura), and the bagel roll (smoked salmon, cream cheese, and scallion). At $5 to $10 per sushi roll, your tab can add up fast, but a bargain strategy involves the chef's choice combinations, in which you get 8 to 10 pieces for $20 to $24. ⊠ *Walt Disney World Swan* ☎ *407/934–3000* ⊟ *AE, D, DC, MC, V* ⊘ *No lunch.*

POLYNESIAN

$$$ ✕ **'Ohana.** The only option here is an all-you-can-eat prix-fixe meal ($25.99 for adults, $11.99 for kids) of shrimp, or grilled pork, beef, or turkey sliced directly onto your plate from mammoth skewers. The chef performs in front of an 18-foot fire pit, grilling the meats as flames shoot up to sear in the flavors and entertain the diners. Special desserts include the coconut snowball and the mandarin orange sponge cake. For the adults, there's a Bloody Mary made with a touch of hot wasabi mustard. ⊠ *Polynesian Resort* ☎ *407/939–3463* ⊟ *AE, MC, V.*

SEAFOOD

$$$–$$$$ ✕ **Narcoossee's.** The dining room here overlooks the Seven Seas Lagoon and is a great place to catch the Electric Water Pageant at night. Grilled salmon and grilled filet mignon are popular entrées, as is the traditional surf-and-turf centerpiece: Maine lobster and a tender filet mignon. Other good choices include grilled pork tenderloin, and oven-roasted tilefish with creole tomato sauce. For dessert, don't miss the strawberry shortcake (made with fresh, Florida-grown strawberries) and the key lime crème brûlée. ⊠ *Grand Floridian Resort* ☎ 407/939–3463 ⊟ *AE, MC, V.*

STEAK

$$$–$$$$　✕ **Shula's Steak House.** The hardwood floors, dark-wood paneling, and pictures of former Miami Dolphins coach Don Shula make this restaurant resemble an annex of the NFL Hall of Fame. Among the best selections are the porterhouse and prime rib. Finish the 48-ounce porterhouse and you get a football with your picture on it, but it's not easy to eat three pounds of red meat at one sitting unless you're a polar bear. The least expensive steak is still hefty at 16 ounces and $37. If you're not a carnivore, go for the Norwegian salmon, the Florida snapper, or the huge (up to 4 pounds) Maine lobster. For dessert, the molten lava chocolate cake or the apple cobbler are both worthy choices. ⊠ *Walt Disney World Dolphin* ☎ 407/934–1362 ⊟ *AE, D, DC, MC, V* ◯ *No lunch.*

$$–$$$$　✕ **Yachtsman Steak House.** Aged beef, the attraction at this steak house in the ultrapolished Yacht and Beach Club, can be seen mellowing in the glassed-in butcher shop near the entryway. The slow-roasted prime rib is superb, as is a combo featuring an 8-ounce filet mignon and a 6-ounce lobster tail. (At $55, it's one of the most expensive surf-and-turf meals in Orlando.) The oak-fired rib eye is quite tender but at $42 it's not soft on your wallet. For dessert, try the chocolate layer cake with wine-marinated cherries. ⊠ *Yacht and Beach Club* ☎ 407/939–3463 ⊟ *AE, MC, V* ◯ *No lunch.*

$$–$$$　✕ **Concourse Steakhouse.** If you've always liked that trademark monorail that runs from the Magic Kingdom into the Contemporary Resort, you might want to have a meal here. You can watch the monorail breeze by overhead as you dine. And don't worry, the place isn't as noisy as you might imagine. Selections for meat-eaters include a nicely prepared chipotle-glazed rib-eye steak and tasty pork spareribs. Among the other entrées are herb-crusted salmon and penne with pesto, a vegetarian option to which you can add shrimp, chicken, or sirloin steak, if you like. For dessert, try the vanilla-bean crème brûlée—a relative bargain at $6. ⊠ *Contemporary Resort* ☎ 407/939–3463 ⊟ *AE, MC, V.*

LAKE BUENA VISTA

The community of Lake Buena Vista stretches north of Downtown Disney and southeast to the other side of I–4, off Exit 68. This is where most off-site visitors to Disney World stay, and there are some good mealtime options.

FRENCH

$$$–$$$$　✕ **La Coquina.** This restaurant, just outside Disney property, bills itself as French with an Asian influence, and if you sample the buffalo tenderloin or the red pepper–marinated duck, you'll approve of its methods. Come for Sunday brunch, when the generous selection of goodies makes the price ($55 adults, $27.50 kids) almost seem like a bargain. In an unusual touch, during brunch your waiter takes you into the

kitchen, where you pick out what you want and watch the chef cook it to order. For a closer look at the chef in action, ask the manager about sitting at the special chef's table in the kitchen. ⊠*Hyatt Regency Grand Cypress, 1 Grand Cypress Blvd.* ☎*407/239–1234* ▭*AE, D, DC, MC, V.*

SEAFOOD

$$–$$$$ ✕ **Landry's Seafood House.** Set in a fake warehouse building—popular architecture in Central Florida—this branch of a nationwide chain delivers seafood at reasonable prices. The food is first-rate, especially Cajun dishes like the fresh-caught fish Pontchartrain, a broiled fish with slightly spicy seasoning and a creamy white-wine sauce that's topped with a lump of crabmeat. Because this chain traces its roots to New Orleans, it offers some great Louisiana-style cooking, such as a hearty gumbo with plenty of shrimp, crab and oysters, along with good po'boy sandwiches packed with your choice of shrimp, oysters, or white fish. Combination platters abound, including a $15 one that includes crab fingers, fried oysters, shrimp, and a catfish fillet. ⊠*8800 Vineland Ave., Rte. 535, Lake Buena Vista* ☎*407/827–6466* ▭*AE, D, DC, MC, V.*

TEX-MEX

$–$$ ✕ **Chevy's.** True, the ersatz cantina motif here looks like that of every other Mexican place in every suburb you've ever seen. But the food is a shocker: it's quite good. Try the hot tamales, or the shrimp-and-crab enchiladas topped with pesto-cream sauce. The menu, making use of some gringo creativity, includes chicken with Dijon mustard wrapped in a tortilla, and a huge burrito made with pork and beef barbecue. A specialty here is the selection of quesadillas—a traditional dish with melted cheese between two tortillas—but in this case the stuffing is pretty nontraditional, including chicken in barbecue sauce. For dessert, look for the good flan and cream pies. ⊠*12547 Rte. 535, Lake Buena Vista* ☎*407/827–1052* ⊠*2809 W. Vine St., Kissimmee* ☎*407/847–2244* ▭*AE, MC, V.*

UNIVERSAL ORLANDO AREA

With more than a dozen restaurants and the world's largest Hard Rock Cafe, Universal Orlando's CityWalk is a culinary force. At Islands of Adventure, each of the six lands has between two and six eateries—not all of them strictly burgers-and-fries affairs. Universal has done a good job of providing information and access to these eateries, with a special **reservation and information line** (☎*407/224–9255* ⊕*www.universalorlando.com*) and a Web site that includes menus for many of the restaurants.

To get to Universal, take I–4 Exit 75A from eastbound lanes, Exit 74B when you're westbound.

CHARACTER MEALS

Universal Studios offers meals with its characters, specifically Scooby-Doo, Spider-Man, Thing One and Thing Two, Woody Woodpecker, and Curious George, although the line-up is not nearly as extensive as what is offered at Disney World.

BREAKFAST

You can catch the Dr. Seuss characters, including the Cat in the Hat, for breakfast at the **Confisco Grille** (☎407/363–8000), at the entrance to Islands of Adventure, from 9 to 10:30. The meal costs $15.95 for adults and $9.95 for children.

DINNER

Character dinners at Universal take place at the three on-property hotels, and are by reservation only. Characters appearing at these restaurants vary, so please call the restaurant in advance to see which of the following will be appearing: Shaggy, Scooby-Doo, Woody Woodpecker, or Curious George. Reservations can be made at the **character meal reservation line** (☎407/224–4012).

Character dinners at **Islands Dining Room** (☎407/503–3430), in the Royal Pacific Resort, take place Monday, Tuesday, and Saturday from 6:30 to 9:30. Children age 12 and under eat from the buffet ($9.25), while adults order from a menu ($15–$25), except on Saturday, when the buffet is open to everyone and costs $24.50 for adults. Dinners at **Trattoria del Porto** (☎407/503–1430), in the Portofino Bay Hotel, take place on Friday from 6:30 and cost $26.95 for adults and $12.50 for children 12 and under. **The Kitchen** (☎407/503–2430) at the Hard Rock Hotel hosts character dinners Saturday from 6:30 to 9:30. Menu entrées range from $7.95 to $31.95. Character breakfasts at Universal hotels are handled by the **Loews Orlando reservations line** (☎407/503–3463).

UNIVERSAL STUDIOS

AMERICAN

$–$$$ ✕ **Mel's Drive-In.** At the corner of Hollywood Boulevard and 8th Avenue—which turns into Sunset Boulevard along the bottom shore of the lagoon—is a flashy '50s eatery with a menu and decorative muscle cars straight out of *American Graffiti*. For burgers and fries, this is one of the best choices in the park, and it comes complete with a roving doo-wop group. You're on vacation—go ahead and have that extra-thick shake. Mel's is also a great place to meet, in case you decide to go your separate ways in the park. ⊠*Hollywood Boulevard* ☎*407/363–8766* ⌖*Reservations not accepted* ▤*AE, D, MC, V.*

IRISH

$–$$$ ✕ **Finnegan's Bar & Grill.** In an Irish pub that would look just right in downtown New York during the Ellis Island era, Finnegan's offers classic Irish comfort food like shepherd's pie, Irish stew, and fish-and-chips, plus Guinness, Harp, and Bass on tap. If shepherd's pie isn't your thing, there are also steaks, burgers, and a darn good chicken salad. Irish

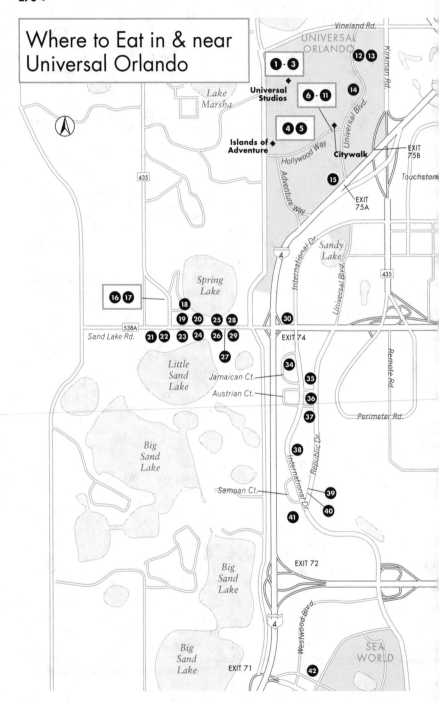

Where to Eat in & near Universal Orlando

12

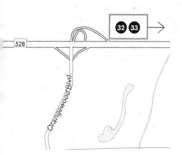

folk music, sometimes live, completes the theme. ⊠*Production Central* ☎*407/363–8757* ⊟*AE, D, MC, V.*

SEAFOOD

$$–$$$ ✕ **Lombard's Landing** Fresh grilled or fried fish, fried shrimp, and steamed clams and mussels are the specialty at this restaurant designed to resemble a Fisherman's Wharf warehouse from 19th-century San Francisco. You can also get a steak, pasta, hamburgers, chicken, and salad. ⊠*San Francisco/Amity* ☎*407/224–6400* ⊟*AE, D, MC, V.*

ISLANDS OF ADVENTURE

AMERICAN

$–$$ ✕ **Confisco Grille.** You could walk right past this Mediterranean eatery, but if you want a good meal and sit-down service, don't pass by too quickly. The menu changes often, but typical entrées include pan-seared pork medallions with roasted garlic and red peppers, baked cod with spinach and mashed potatoes, and Thai noodles with chicken, shrimp, tofu, and bean sprouts. Save room for desserts like chocolate-banana bread pudding or crème brûlée. You can catch the Dr. Seuss characters here at breakfast. ⊠*6000 Universal Blvd., Port of Entry* ☎*407/224–4404* ⊟*AE, D, MC, V* ☉*No lunch.*

ECLECTIC

$–$$ ✕ **Mythos.** The name is Greek, but the dishes are eclectic. The menu, which changes frequently, usually includes standouts like meat loaf, roast pork tenderloin, and assorted kinds of wood-fired pizzas. Among the creative desserts is a fine pumpkin cheesecake. But the building itself is enough to grab your attention. It looks like a giant rock formation from the outside and a huge cave (albeit one with plush upholstered seating) from the inside. Mythos also has a waterfront view of the big lagoon in the center of the theme park. ⊠*6000 Universal Blvd., Lost Continent* ☎*407/224–9255* ⊟*AE, D, MC, V.*

CITYWALK

AMERICAN-CASUAL

$$–$$$ ✕ **NBA City.** The NBA memorabilia and video games are great, but the food is actually the real draw here. The best appetizers include spring rolls filled with snow crab, and pecan-crusted chicken tenders with orange marmalade sauce. For an entrée, try the New Orleans–style jambalaya or the oak-smoked baby back rib. The brick-oven pizzas include a quirky BLT variety. Finish off with the pecan tart made with Vermont maple syrup and topped with fresh cream. The big-screen TVs, which naturally broadcast nonstop basketball action, probably won't surprise you, but the relatively quiet bar upstairs, with elegant blond-wood furniture, probably will. ⊠*6000 Universal Blvd.* ☎*407/363–5919* ⊟*AE, D, MC, V.*

$–$$$ ✕ **Jimmy Buffett's Margaritaville.** Parrotheads can probably name the top two menu items before they even walk in the door. You've got your cheeseburger, featured in the song "Cheeseburger in Paradise," and, of

12

course, your Ultimate Margarita. The rest of the menu is an eclectic mix of quesadillas, crab cakes, jambalaya, jerk salmon (marinated in spicy sauce), and a pretty decent steak. This place wouldn't be true to Buffet's heritage without a Key West–style conch chowder; this version is is quite piquant. Worthy dessert choices include the Last Mango in Paradise cheesecake, the obligatory key lime pie, and a tasty chocolate-banana bread pudding. ⊠*6000 Universal Blvd.* ☎*407/224–2155* ▤*AE, D, MC, V.*

$–$$ ✕ **Hard Rock Cafe Orlando.** Built to resemble Rome's Colosseum, this 800-seat restaurant is the largest of the 100-odd Hard Rocks in the world, but getting a seat at lunch can still require a long wait. The music is always loud and the walls are filled with rock memorabilia. Appetizers range from spring rolls to chicken tenders. The most popular menu item is still the $10 burger, with the pulled pork sandwich, the baby back ribs, and the homemade-style meat loaf all strong contenders. If you don't eat meat, try the pasta with roasted vegetables or the shrimp fajitas. The best dessert is the $5 chocolate-chip cookie (it's big), which is covered with ice cream. Parking is $8 until 6:30 PM, and free afterward. ⊠*6000 Universal Blvd.* ☎*407/351–7625* ⚭*Reservations not accepted* ▤*AE, D, DC, MC, V.*

CREOLE

$$$–$$$$
Fodor'sChoice
★

✕ **Emeril's.** The popular eatery is a culinary shrine to Emeril Lagasse, the famous Food Network chef who occasionally appears here. The menu changes frequently, but you can always count on New Orleans treats like andouille sausage, shrimp, and red beans appearing in some form or fashion. Entrées may include andouille-crusted redfish with crispy shoestring potatoes; milk-fed veal with shrimp, artichoke hearts, and a mustard hollandaise sauce; and grilled beef fillet with bacon mashed potatoes and buttermilk-breaded onion rings. The wood-baked pizza, topped with exotic mushrooms, is stellar. Save room for Emeril's ice-cream parfait—banana-daiquiri ice cream topped with hot fudge, caramel sauce, walnuts, and a double-chocolate-fudge cookie. ⊠*6000 Universal Blvd.* ☎*407/224–2424* ⚭*Reservations essential* ▤*AE, D, MC, V.*

ITALIAN

$–$$$ ✕ **Pastamoré.** Since it doesn't have marquee appeal like its neighbor Emeril's, Pastamoré is something of a CityWalk sleeper. But this could be the best uncrowded restaurant at Universal, with wood-fired pizza, fresh pastas, and Italian beer and wines. Especially notable are the huge Italian sandwiches, with ingredients like marinated chicken, peppers, and sun-dried tomatoes, as well as a good tiramisu. In an unusual touch, you can also come here for Italian breakfast breads—the place opens at 8 AM. The breakfast pizza, topped with sausage and eggs, will make you glad you didn't opt for a McMuffin. ⊠*6000 Universal Blvd.* ☎*407/224–3663* ▤*AE, D, MC, V.*

LATIN

$$–$$$ ✕ **The Latin Quarter.** This grottolike restaurant and club, with domed ceilings and stone walls, is one of those jumping-by-night, dormant-by-day spots, but the food is good all the time. Cuisines from 21 Latin

nations are on the menu, as is a wide selection of South American beers. Good entrée choices include *churrasco* (grilled skirt steak), *puerco asado* (roast pork), cumin-rubbed grilled chicken, guava-spiced spare ribs, and an outstanding fried snapper with tomato salsa. Most main dishes come with black beans and rice. Best bets for dessert: the crepes and the mango and guava cheesecakes. ✉6000 Universal Blvd. ☎407/224–2880 ⊟AE, D, MC, V.

HARD ROCK HOTEL

STEAK

$$–$$$$ ✕ **The Palm.** With its dark-wood interior and hundreds of framed celebrity caricatures, this restaurant resembles its famed New York City namesake. As you might guess, hearts of palm are among the salad selections. Steaks are the reason to dine here, but most are available only at dinner. The steak fillet cooked on a hot stone is a specialty, as is the double steak, a 36-ounce New York strip for two (or one extreme carnivore). There are several veal dishes on the menu, including veal piccata and veal parmigiana, along with a 3-pound Maine lobster, and linguine with clam sauce, either red or white. ✉1000 Universal Studios Plaza ☎407/503–7256 ⊟AE, D, DC, MC, V ⊘No lunch weekends.

PORTOFINO BAY HOTEL

ITALIAN

$$$–$$$$ ✕ **Bice.** In 2004 trendy, pricey Bice replaced the hotel's former top-billed restaurant, Delfino Riviera. Bice (pronounced "*beach*-ay") is an Italian nickname for Beatrice, as in Beatrice Ruggeri, who founded the original Milan location of this family restaurant in 1926. But the word "family" does not carry the connotation "mom and pop" at Bice, where white starched tablecloths set the stage for sophisticated cuisine. The restaurant retains its frescoed ceilings, marble floors, and, of course, picture windows overlooking great views of the artificial bay just outside. This restaurant is expensive, but some of the entrées that seem worth it are the one-pound veal chop with polenta ($38) while you're the veal Milanese with arugula and cherry tomatoes ($37). While you're running up your tab, you may as well also try the tasty lentil soup with black truffle fondue ($12). Desserts, ranging from tiramisu to baked apple tart with vanilla ice cream, are delicious. ✉5601 Universal Blvd. ☎407/503–1415 ⊟AE, D, DC, MC, V ⊘No lunch.

$$–$$$$ ✕ **Mama Della's.** The premise here is that Mama Della is a middle-age Italian housewife who has opened up her home as a restaurant. "Mama" is always on hand (this is a coveted job for middle-aged

actresses who do a good Italian accent), strolling among the tables and making small talk. The food, which is served family style, is no fantasy—it's excellent. The menu has Italian traditions like chicken cacciatore, veal parmigiana, and spaghetti with sirloin meatballs or Bolognese sauce, and all of the pastas are made in-house. A particularly good bet is grilled swordfish in garlic–lemon sauce. Tiramisu and white chocolate praline crunch cake with raspberry sorbet are sure bets for dessert. ⊠ *5601 Universal Blvd.* ☎ *407/503–3463* ▤ *AE, D, DC, MC, V* ⊘ *Closed Mon. No lunch.*

ROYAL PACIFIC RESORT

PAN-ASIAN

$$$–$$$$ ✕ **Tchoup Chop.** With its cathedral ceiling, the inside of this restaurant
★ looks almost churchlike, and the food at Emeril Lagasse's Pacific-influenced restaurant is certainly righteous. Following the theme of the Royal Pacific Resort, the decorators included a tiki bar with lots of bamboo, a couple of indoor waterfalls, and a long pool with porcelain lily pads running the length of the dining room. The menu combines Lagasse's own New Orleans–style cuisine with an Asian theme. Entrées include grilled pork chops with ginger-roasted sweet potatoes, and a Hawaiian-style dinner plate with Kiawe smoked ribs, pork and noodle sauté, and teriyaki grilled chicken. One of the mainstay dishes is fish steamed in a banana leaf and covered with a sake–soy sauce—something to give you that South Pacific feeling. For dessert try the bittersweet chocolate layer cake with banana sauce or the pecan pie with vanilla-bean ice cream. ⊠ *6300 Hollywood Way* ☎ *407/503–2467* ⚱ *Reservations essential* ▤ *AE, D, DC, MC, V.*

KISSIMMEE

Although Orlando is the focus of most theme-park visitors, Kissimmee is actually closer to Walt Disney World. To visit the area, follow I–4 to Exit 64A. Allow about 15 to 25 minutes to travel from WDW, or about 35 minutes from I-Drive.

CONTINENTAL

$$$$ ✕ **The Venetian Room.** Inside the Caribe Royale Resort, one of Orlando's bigger convention hotels, this place was doubtless designed for execs on expense accounts. But the serene, luxurious, and romantic atmosphere makes it a great place for dinner with your significant other. The architecture alone is enough to lure you in. It's designed to look like Renaissance Venice: the entryway has a giant copper dome over the door and the dining room has dark-wood furniture, crystal chandeliers, and carpets that could grace a European palace. A tad cliché but tasty just as well is the pan-seared foie gras starter. You can follow that with farm-raised squab or the lobster with cognac and hazelnut pheasant sausage, then perhaps the Grand Marnier soufflé or the chocolate sampler consisting of mousse, cake, and truffles—a dessert worth its $16 price tag. ⊠ *Caribe Royale Resort, 8101 World Center Dr., International Drive Area* ☎ *407/238–8060* ▤ *AE, D, DC, MC, V* ⊘ *No lunch.*

ITALIAN

$$–$$$ ✕ **Romano's Macaroni Grill.** You may have a branch of this prolific chain in your hometown, and the popular Orlando locations deliver a known quantity—good but not great Italian cuisine. It's friendly, it's casual, and it's comfortable. The scaloppine, made with chicken instead of the traditional veal, is topped with artichokes and capers and served with angel-hair pasta. Mama's Trio includes lasagna, chicken cannelloni, and chicken parmigiana. If you're health-conscious, you can subistutute whole-wheat pasta for regular in most dishes. House wines are brought to the table in gallon bottles—you serve yourself and then report how many glasses you've had. Your kids can pass the time doodling with crayons on the white-paper table covering. ✉ *5320 W. Irlo Bronson Memorial Hwy.* ☎ *407/396–6155* ✉ *12148 S. Apopka–Vineland Rd., Lake Buena Vista* ☎ *407/239–6676* ▤ *AE, D, DC, MC, V.*

$$–$$$ ✕ **Tarantino's.** What started out as a mom-and-pop eatery has grown into something you might find at Walt Disney World—a big operation resembling a movie set. But while the homey dining rooms may be faux, the Italian cooking isn't. Start with the antipasto platter for two, then move on to reliable entrées like veal sautéed in butter, white wine, and tomatoes or pork chops and cherry peppers sautéed in olive oil. Also worth trying is the baked chicken stuffed with spinach, red peppers, and mozzarella. Don't miss the cheesecake. ✉ *10 W. Monument Ave.* ☎ *407/870-2622* ▤ *AE, D, DC, MC, V* ⊙ *Closed Sun.* .

STEAK

$$$–$$$$ ✕ **Old Hickory Steak House.** If paying $44 for a steak (and an extra $7 for a side of mashed potatoes) and eating it inside a barn seems a bit surreal, remember that this is Orlando. The barn, like many of the unusual eateries in the Orlando area, is a fake, a movie-set kind of edifice designed for effect. Dine on the deck adjacent to the main building and you'll overlook the hotel's faux Everglades, where electronic alligators cavort with fiberglass frogs. The experience is designed to entertain, and it does; the food is worth the roughly $50 a person you'll spend for dinner. You could really go all-out by indulging in the tenderloin-of-alligator lasagna. Otherwise, there's Angus beef and American buffalo. ✉ *Gaylord Palms Resort, 6000 W. Osceola Pkwy., I–4 Exit 65* ☎ *407/586–1600* ▤ *AE, DC, MC, V* ⊙ *No lunch.*

CELEBRATION

If this small town with Victorian-style homes and perfectly manicured lawns reminds you a bit of Main Street, U.S.A., in the Magic Kingdom, it should. The utopian residential community was created by Disney, with all the Disney attention to detail. Every view of every street is warm and pleasant, though the best are out the windows of the town's four restaurants, all of which face a pastoral (though artificial) lake. There's even an interactive fountain in the small park near the lake, giving kids a great place to splash. To get here take I–4 to Exit 64A and follow the "Celebration" signs.

12

AMERICAN-CASUAL

$$–$$$$ ✕ **Celebration Town Tavern.** This New England–cuisine eatery has a split personality. Half is the casual Celebration Town Tavern, with sandwiches and less expensive fare; the other half is the slightly more formal Bostonian, with dishes like prime rib and lobster. Both halves are open for lunch and dinner. You'll find standouts such as lobster quesadillas and clam chowder (Manhattan and New England style) at the Town Tavern, and heaping platters of fried clams and oysters, New England crab cakes, or Florida stone crabs served in season (spring) at the Bostonian. Steak is not extremely expensive here. You can dine on a steak and lobster combo for $35, roughly half of what you would pay at pricier restaurants. For dessert there's great—what else?—Boston cream pie. ✉ *721 Front St.* ☎ *407/566–2526* ▭ *AE, D, MC, V.*

$–$$ ✕ **Market Street Café.** The menu at this informal diner resembling a 1950s classic ranges from the house-special baked-potato omelet (served until 4:30 PM) to chicken Alfredo and prime rib. One appetizer, the cheese quesadilla, is large enough to make a meal. Standout entrées include the pot roast and meat loaf. In addition to a hearty version of the quintessential American hamburger, there's also a salmon burger and a veggie burger for the cholesterol wary. The excellent housemade potato chips come with a blue cheese sauce. If you're looking for that quintessentially Southern dish, chicken fried steak, they have an excellent version here. ✉ *701 Front St.* ☎ *407/566–1144* ⌦ *Reservations not accepted* ▭ *AE, D, MC, V.*

ITALIAN

$$–$$$$ ✕ **Café d' Antonio.** The wood-burning oven and grill are worked pretty hard here, and the mountains of hardwood used in the open kitchen flavor the best of the menu—the pizza, the grilled fish and chicken, the steaks and chops, even the lasagna. Standouts include shrimp wrapped in pancetta, duck roasted with figs, and lobster ravioli. For dessert, try the hazelnut chocolate cake or the ricotta cheesecake. Italian vintages dominate the wine list. As at the rest of Celebration's restaurants, there's an awning-covered terrace overlooking the lagoon. ✉ *691 Front St.* ☎ *407/566–2233* ▭ *AE, D, MC, V.*

JAPANESE

$$–$$$ ✕ **Seito Celebration.** Operated by the Seils, the Japanese family that owns Seito Sushi in downtown Orlando, this quiet and casual eatery offers the same excellent sushi as its sister location. You can dine on your favorite rolls while overlooking the lake in the center of Celebration. Nonsushi entrées like salmon teriyaki and New York strip steak are also available. The house specialties, which include marinated sea bass, are worthwhile and inexpensive. Although cold tofu may sound like a health-food freak's revenge, it's actually a great appetizer here, livened up with ginger, scallions, and soy sauce. The bananas fried in tempura batter make an excellent dessert. ✉ *671 Front St., Suite 100* ☎ *407/566–1889* ▭ *AE, D, DC, MC, V.*

LATIN

$$–$$$ ✕ **Columbia Restaurant.** Celebration's branch of this family-owned chain is generally as good as the original in Tampa. Start with Cuban caviar (actually black-bean dip with crackers), ribs with guava barbecue sauce, or the house specialty, chicken or deviled crab croquettes. For your main course you should zero in on the paella—either *à la Valenciana*, with clams, shrimp, scallops, squid, chicken, and pork mixed into tasty yellow rice; or the all-seafood *marinara*, which also includes lobster. A good lighter dish is the Atlantic *merluza*, a delicate white fish rolled in bread crumbs, then grilled and topped with lemon butter, parsley, and diced eggs. Desserts include key lime pie and a special new dish created for the restaurant's centennial called *brazo gitano cien anos,* a sponge cake with strawberries that is soaked in syrup and sherry and flambéed table-side. ⊠ *649 Front St.* ☎ *407/566–1505* 🖃 *AE, D, DC, MC, V.*

ORLANDO METRO AREA

INTERNATIONAL DRIVE

A number of restaurants are scattered among the hotels that line manicured International Drive. Many are branches of chains, from fast-food spots to theme coffee shops and up. The food is sometimes quite good. To get to the area, take I–4 Exit 72 or 74A. Count on it taking about a half hour from the Kissimmee area or from WDW property.

AMERICAN–CASUAL

$$–$$$ ✕ **B-Line Diner.** As you might expect from its location in the Peabody Hotel, this slick, 1950s-style diner with red-vinyl counter seats is not exactly cheap, but the salads, sandwiches, and griddle foods are tops. The greatest combo ever—a thick, juicy burger served with fries and a wonderful milk shake—is done beautifully. You can also get southern favorites like crispy fried red snapper or hickory-smoked chicken, both with sides like white beans or collard greens. Desserts range from hazelnut-orange cake to coconut cream pie to banana splits. It's open 24 hours. ⊠ *Peabody Orlando, 9801 International Dr.* ☎ *407/352–4000* 🖃 *AE, D, DC, MC, V.*

CARIBBEAN

$$–$$$ ✕ **Bahama Breeze.** Even though the lineage is corporate, the menu here is creative and tasty. The big outdoor dining area, casual style, and the Caribbean cooking draw a crowd: so be prepared for a wait. Meanwhile, you can sip piña coladas and other West Indian delights on a big wooden porch. The food is worth the wait. Start with fried coconut-covered prawns, and move on to the seafood paella or the West Indian–style baby back ribs with a sweet and smokey guava barbecue glaze. Homemade key lime pie is the perfect finish. ⊠ *8849 International Dr.* ☎ *407/248–2499* ⊠ *8735 Vineland Ave., I–4 Exit 68, I-Drive Area* ☎ *407/938–9010* ⌓ *Reservations not accepted* 🖃 *AE, D, DC, MC.*

CHINESE

$$–$$$$ ✕ **Ming Court.** A walled courtyard and serene pond make you forget you're on International Drive. The extensive menu includes simple chicken Szechuan, jumbo shrimp with honey-glaze walnuts, and aged filet mignon grilled in a spicy sauce. Ming Court features an extensive selection of dim sum, including samples of shrimp ravioli, duck lettuce cup (spicy duck in a cup made from lettuce leaves), and grilled chicken yakitori (with sake and ginger). There's also an extensive array of dishes from the wok, including a house specialty called Eight Treasure Duck: roasted duck topped with scallops, carrots, cabbage, and mushrooms in a tangy brown sauce. The flourless chocolate cake, certainly not Asian, has been a popular standard for years. Ming Court is within walking distance of the Orange County Convention Center and can be quite busy at lunchtime. ✉9188 International Dr. ☎407/351–9988 ▤AE, D, DC, MC, V.

ECLECTIC

$$$$ ✕ **Norman's.** Chef-entrepreneur Norman Van Aken brings impressive
★ credentials to the restaurant that bears his name, as one might expect from the headline eatery in the first and only Ritz-Carlton in Orlando. Van Aken's culinary roots go back to the Florida Keys, where he's credited with creating "Floribbean" cuisine, a blend that is part Key West, part Havana, part Kingston, Jamaica. In the '90s, Van Aken became a star in Miami with his Coral Gables restaurant. The Orlando operation is a formal restaurant with marble floors, starched tablecloths, waiters in black-tie, and a creative, if expensive, prix-fixe menu. The offerings change frequently, but typical dishes include mango-glazed barbecue duck stuffed into a green chili-studded pancake; beef ribs with creamed corn, grilled chayote, and fried onion rings; and Mongolian-style veal chops with grilled Chinese eggplant and Thai fried rice. For dessert, try the "New World banana split," with macadamia nut–brittle ice cream and rum-flambéed banana. The least expensive dinner option is a three-course, prix-fixe meal for $65 per person. ✉Ritz-Carlton Grande Lakes, 4000 Central Florida Pkwy. ☎407/393–4333 ▤AE, D, DC, MC, V ⊘No lunch.

$$$–$$$$ ✕ **Café Tu Tu Tango.** The food here is served tapas-style—everything is appetizer-sized. The eclectic menu is fitting for a restaurant on International Drive. If you want a compendium of cuisines at one go, try the black-bean soup with cilantro sour cream, roast pears on pecan crisps, stuffed mushrooms with blue cheese, and pan-seared pork pot stickers. While you can order these individual dishes at $5 to $8 a pop, you'll save money by going with one of three fixed-price dinners that run from $30 to $40. The restaurant is supposed to resemble a crazy artist's loft; artists paint at easels while diners sip drinks like Matisse Margaritas. ✉8625 International Dr. ☎407/248–2222 ⊜Reservations not accepted ▤AE, D, DC, MC, V.

FAST FOOD

¢ ✕ **McDonald's.** Once the world's largest McDonald's (now there's a bigger one in Moscow), this one still has the largest PlayPlace and the billboard out front proclaiming just that. Perfect for Orlando, this

McDonald's definitely has more frills than your usual roadside double arches. The '50s-style dining room has a rock-and-roll theme, and there's an arcade where you can win prizes. Plus you can shop for discount attraction tickets, hotel rooms, McDonald's collector plates and pins, and even socks, since they're required in the huge indoor playground. Try out the new Bistro Gourmet menu, which includes healthier fare than burgers, such as panini sandwiches, wraps, and tossed pastas. ⊠*6875 W. Sand Lake Rd.* ☎*407/351–2185* ⌒*Reservations not accepted* ⊟*AE, DC, MC, V.*

ITALIAN

$$$–$$$$ ✕ **Bergamo's.** If you like Broadway show tunes with your spaghetti and opera with your osso buco, then head here for the booming voices as well as the good food, both of which are provided by servers in satin vests. Management does not rely on the entertainment alone to fill seats: the food is very worthwhile. Try the linguine *pescatore* (fisherman's linguine), with lobster, shrimp, crab meat and mussels; or the classic osso buco with risotto Milanese. And while the idea of a mango–basil cheesecake dessert sounds a tad strange, you'll probably love it, too. ⊠*8445 International Dr., I–4 Exit 74A* ☎*407/352–3805* ⊟*AE, D, DC, MC, V* ⊗*No lunch.*

$$–$$$$ ✕ **Capriccio's.** From the marble-top tables in this Italian restaurant you can view the open kitchen and the wood-burning pizza ovens, which turn out whole-wheat flour pies ranging from pizza *salsiccia*, with pepperoni and Italian sausage, to pizza *formaggio* (with Gorgonzola, pecorino, Parmesan, mozzarella, and garlic cream). However, this Italian eatery is more noted for steaks that are "flash-seared" to seal in the juices. Other standouts include seafood dishes like New Zealand lobster (flown in daily) and an excellent *zuppa di pesce,* an Italian seafood stew that is worth its $27.50 price. Worthwhile Italian entrées include chicken parmigiana and veal piccata. ⊠*Peabody Orlando, 9801 International Dr.* ☎*407/352–4000* ⊟*AE, DC, MC, V* ⊗*Closed Mon.*

JAPANESE

$$–$$$$ ✕ **Ran-Getsu.** The surroundings are a Disney-style version of Asia, but the food is fresh and carefully prepared, much of it table-side. Unless you're alone, you can have your meal Japanese-style at the low tables overlooking a carp-filled pond and decorative gardens. You might start with creamy, spicy shrimp and scallops served gratin style, and continue with the *shabu-shabu* (thinly sliced beef and vegetables cooked table-side in a simmering broth), or the *kushiyaki* (grilled skewers of shrimp, beef, chicken, and scallops). Sukiyaki (sizzling sliced sirloin of beef with mixed Chinese vegetables) is the signature dish here. If you feel adventurous, try the deep-fried alligator tail glazed in a ginger–soy sauce. ⊠*8400 International Dr.* ☎*407/345–0044* ⊟*AE, DC, MC, V* ⊗*No lunch.*

STEAK

$$$$ ✕ **Texas de Brazil.** The chain that brought this restaurant to Orlando is
★   from Texas, but the concept is straight out of Rio, where the *churrascarias* (barbecue restaurants) offer you the option of eating yourself into oblivion. Just as it is in Rio, here you'll find a card on your table,

Not-Bad Chains

When all you want is a quick bite, consider these chain restaurants. They seem to crop up everywhere, and most have tables where you can sit for a few moments before heading back out to the shops and attractions.

Amigo's. Tex-Mex restaurants come and go in Central Florida, but this local chain run by a family of transplanted Texans is consistently in the top tier. Go for the Santa Fe dinner, which includes tamales, enchiladas, chiles rellenos, and refried beans. The dinner's so big, it almost takes a burro to bring it to your table. Lighter fare includes spinach enchiladas.

California Pizza Kitchen: There's usually a line at the Mall at Millenia location, but the wait is worth it. The specialty is individual-size pizza, served on a plate with toppings ranging from Jamaican jerk chicken to spicy Italian peppers. You can also get fettuccine with garlic–cream sauce, and Santa Fe chicken topped with sour cream, salsa, and guacamole.

Don Pablo's: Chicken enchiladas and beef fajitas are on the bill of fare at this Tex-Mex outpost. The I-Drive location is in a big, barnlike building.

Johnny Rockets: Burgers and chili dogs are served in a vibrant, '50s-diner-style environment here. There are branches at the Mall at Millenia, on International Drive, and in Winter Park.

Moe's: Burritos with names like Joey Bag of Donuts, seem geared to make you laugh, but once you taste them, your mouth will be happy to just chew. This is good, fast, fresh Mex for the road.

Panera Bread: Fresh-baked pastries, bagels, and espresso drinks are the mainstays here, although you can grab a hearty and inexpensive meal like smoked-chicken panini on onion focaccia and still have change left from a $10 bill. Lake Eola and Mall at Millenia are standouts in this chain.

TooJay's Gourmet Deli: This classic deli and versatile family dining spot has classic sandwiches like turkey Reubens, and corned beef and pastrami smeared with chopped liver, plus hot comfort food like pot roast, matzo ball soup, meat-loaf melt, and brisket with onions and horseradish. Don't miss the *rugalach*, traditional Jewish cookies that have fruit or chocolate rolled into the dough.

Wolfgang Puck Express: At Puck's pricey café, a meal is an event. But at the two Downtown Disney express walk-up windows, a meal is poetry in motion. Grab a wood-oven pizza or soup and salad, and you're out of there in 10 minutes.

red on one side and green on the other. As long as you leave the green side up, an endless cavalcade of waiters will bring expertly grilled and roasted beefsteak, pork, chicken, and sausage. Buffet stations offer sides like garlic mashed potatoes, baked potatoes, black beans and rice, a wide assortment of salads, and decadent desserts such as Brazilian papaya cream. The fixed-price meal costs $43. For an additional cost you can choose from more than 700 wines. Children 12 and under eat for half price, and kids under six eat free. You can dine outdoors or in, where the restaurant has bright red walls, dark furniture, and white tablecloths. ⊠*5259 International Dr.* ☎*407/355–0355* ▤*AE, D, DC, MC, V* ⊘*No lunch Mon.–Sat..*

$$–$$$$ ✕ **Vito's Chop House.** There's a reason why they keep the blinds closed
★ most of the time: it's for the wines' sake. The dining room doubles as
the cellar, with hundreds of bottles stacked in every nook and cranny.
The lobsters weigh in at 2 to 3 pounds, so you may need a doggie
bag if you go for one of the larger ones. The steaks are sliced by hand
and flame broiled over oak and orange wood. A popular entrée is the
roast chicken cacciatore, and a second house favorite is the fried lob-
ster tails on linguine with marinara sauce. Worthwhile desserts include
grilled peach di Vito, an excellent key lime pie, and Italian wedding
cake. Finish your meal by enjoying a fine cigar along with a glass of
aged cognac, Armagnac, or grappa in the lounge. ⊠*8633 International
Dr.* ☎*407/354–2467* ⚐*Reservations essential* ▤*AE, D, DC, MC, V*
⊘*No lunch.*

SAND LAKE ROAD

This is the part of the city nearest the main Disney tourism area, a
mere five minutes or so northeast of International Drive or Universal
Orlando. Because the neighborhood has many expensive homes, with
high incomes to match, it's where you'll find some of the city's more
upscale stores and restaurants. Over the past few years one of the most
significant dining sectors in Orlando has sprung up along Sand Lake
Road, Exit 74A, just about a mile west of crowded International Drive,
where the quality of the average restaurant is not up to par with the
eateries on Sand Lake.

AMERICAN

$$$–$$$$ ✕ **Vines Grill & Wine Bar.** Live jazz and blues music fills the night at this
strip-mall bar, but don't worry—the food and drink here aren't second-
rate warm-up acts. They're headliners in their own right. The kitchen
specializes in beef, fish, and seafood, all of it cooked over charcoal. The
wine list here is extensive, with offerings from Napa Valley to New
Zealand. The crowd tends to dress up, but suit jackets and ties are not
required. Wood tables and ceramic tile floors give the place a rustic,
elegant look. ⊠*7563 W. Sand Lake Rd.* ☎*407/351–1227* ▤*AE, D,
DC, MC, V.*

ECLECTIC

$$$$ ✕ **The Melting Pot.** This fondue restaurant keeps you busy while you
eat—you'll be doing part of the cooking. Diners dip morsels ranging
from lobster tails to sirloin slices into flavorful broths and oils in stain-
less steel pots built into the center of the table. The lineup also includes
the traditional cheese fondues and chocolate fondues for dessert. You
can even order s'mores. ⊠*Fountains Plaza, 7549 W. Sand Lake Rd.,
I–4 Exit 74A* ☎*407/903–1100* ▤*AE, D, DC, MC, V.*

$$$–$$$$ ✕ **Chatham's Place.** In Florida, grouper is about as ubiquitous as Coca-
Cola, but to discover its full potential, try the rendition here: it's sau-
téed in pecan butter and flavored with cayenne. Other good entrées
include the chicken piccata, and the filet mignon served with a pep-
percorn and cognac sauce. The most popular appetizer is the Mary-

land-style crab cakes, but the New Orleans–style shrimp brochette is also noteworthy. The chef does wonders with desserts like pecan–macadamia nut pie. Take I–4 Exit 74A. ⊠*7575 Dr. Phillips Blvd.* ☎*407/345–2992* ▤*AE, D, DC, MC, V.*

$$–$$$ ✕ **Seasons 52.** Parts of the menu
Fodor'sChoice change every week of the year at this innovative restaurant, which
★ began with the concept of serving different foods at different times, depending on what's in season. Meals here tend to be light, healthy, and very flavorful. You might have an oak-grilled venison chop with mashed sweet potatoes, mesquite-roasted pork tenderloin with polenta, or salmon cooked on a cedar plank and accompanied by grilled vegetables. An impressive wine list complements the long and colorful menu. Another health-conscious concept adopted at Seasons 52 is the "mini indulgence" dessert: classics like chocolate cake, butterscotch pudding, and rocky road ice cream served in portions designed not to bust your daily calorie budget. Although the cuisine is haute, the prices are modest—not bad for a snazzy, urbane, dark-wood-walled bistro and wine bar. It has live music nightly. ⊠*7700 Sand Lake Rd.* ☎*407/354–5212* ⊠*463 E. Altamonte Dr., Altamonte Springs* ☎*407/767–1252* ▤*AE, D, DC, MC, V.*

HAWAIIAN

$$–$$$$ ✕ **Roy's.** Chef Roy Yamaguchi has more or less perfected his own cuisine type—Hawaiian fusion, replete with lots of tropical fruit–based sauces and lots of imagination. The menu changes daily, but typical dishes include treats like roasted macadamia nut mahimahi in butter sauce or hibachi-grilled salmon with Japanese vegetables. If your tastes remain on the mainland, go for classics like slow-braised and charbroiled short ribs. Best desert on the menu: the melting hot chocolate soufflé. ⊠*7760 W. Sand Lake Rd., I–4 Exit 74A* ☎*407/352–4844* ▤*AE, D, DC, MC, V.*

ITALIAN

$$$–$$$$ ✕ **Christini's.** Locals, visitors, and Disney execs alike love to spend money at Christini's, one of the city's best places for northern Italian. Owner Chris Christini is on hand nightly to ensure perfection in all aspects of the operation. Try the veal piccata or the fettuccine *alla Christini,* the house specialty fettuccine Alfredo. The multicourse dinner often takes a couple of hours or more, but if you like Italian minstrels at your table, this place should please you. Take I–4 Exit 74A. ⊠*Dr. Phillips Marketplace, 7600 Dr. Phillips Blvd.* ☎*407/345–8770* ▤*AE, D, DC, MC, V.*

$$–$$$$ ✕ **Antonio's.** This pleasant trattoria has great service, welcoming surroundings, and a good chef with plenty of world-class talent. Tasty creations include jumbo shrimp sautéed with garlic and rosemary and served with a light tomato sauce; *frutti di mare,* with shrimp, scallops, clams, and mussels; and chicken breast sautéed with mushrooms and baby peas in tomato sauce. Daily specials of fish (like Florida grou-

per) and red meat are always available. ⊠*Fountains Plaza, 7559 W. Sand Lake Rd., I–4 Exit 74A* ☎*407/363–9191* ▭*AE, D, DC, MC, V* ☽*Closed Sun. No lunch.*

$$–$$$ ✕ **Timpano Italian Chophouse.** In this celebration of the America of the '50s and '60s, you may feel transported to Vegas when you hear the piano player and vocalist—and sometimes the waiters—belt out Sinatra and Wayne Newton chestnuts. American beef definitely gets plenty of attention here, but that doesn't cancel out any of the Italian flair. Along with 18-ounce New York strip and 16-ounce center-cut pork chops, there is a credible version of veal piccata with tomatoes, capers, and artichokes. Grilled grouper with black and white beans, good minestrone soup, and sides of pasta (available with any main course) are all excellent choices. ⊠*7488 W. Sand Lake Rd., I–4 Exit 75A* ☎*407/248–0429* ▭*AE, D, DC, MC, V.*

LATIN

$$–$$$ ✕ **Samba Room.** Although owned by the same company that operates the TGI Friday's chain, this big, vibrant restaurant is a good version of an "authentic" Latin experience. You may agree once you've heard the bongos and tasted the barbacoa. To sample the extensive menu, go for the *bocaditas* (small plates) offerings, which include mango barbecued ribs with plantain fries and grilled mussels with a coconut sour-orange sauce. A standout on the main course menu is the Chilean sea bass enchilada served with shrimp orzo. For dessert, try the banana crème brûlée and the green-apple-and-banana cobbler. ⊠*7468 W. Sand Lake Rd., I–4 Exit 75A* ☎*407/226–0550* ▭*AE, D, MC, V.*

MEXICAN

¢–$ ✕ **Moe's.** The Moe in this equation could almost be the guy who cavorted with Larry and Curly. There are several oddly-named dishes, including an "Ugly Naked Guy" taco, and "The Other Lewinsky" and "Joey Bag of Donuts." But the food is more sublime than the nomenclature. The Ugly Naked Guy, for instance, is a vegetarian taco with guacamole and a side of red beans for $3. And the Joey Bag of Donuts is a marinated steak with beans and rice for $4.95. Moe's is a great fast-food alternative with most meals costing well south of $10. ⊠*7541D W. Sand Lake Rd., I–4 Exit 74A* ☎*407/264–9903* ⊠*847 S. Orlando Ave., Winter Park* ☎*407/629–4500* ♤*Reservations not accepted* ▭*AE, D, MC, V.*

MIDDLE EASTERN

$$–$$$$ ✕ **Cedar's Restaurant.** Set in a small strip shopping center that's become part of a restaurant row, this family-owned Lebanese eatery includes Middle Eastern standards like shish kebab, falafel, and hummus as well as tasty daily specials. One of the best of the latter is the fish *tajine*, grilled fish in a sauce of sesame paste, sautéed onions, pine nuts, and cilantro. You may also want to try chicken breast stuffed with garlic, onions, and cilantro. A tad more formal than the average Orlando-area Middle Eastern restaurant, Cedar's has tables with white linen tablecloths and diners who tend to go for resort-casual attire. ⊠*7732 W. Sand Lake Rd., I–4 Exit 74A* ☎*407/351–6000* ▭*AE, D, DC, MC, V.*

12

SEAFOOD

$$$–$$$$ ✕ **MoonFish.** The big waterfall on the sign out front will grab your attention, but once you get inside you'll find the gimmickry gives way to solid cuisine served in a serene space. Dark-wood paneling and white tablecloths abound. The menu is a blend of Pan-Asian, Pacific Rim, Cajun, and Floribbean fare. Specialties range from grilled lobster tail to Alaskan king crab to Florida stone crab. The restaurant also specializes in aged beef, which you can view in a big refrigerated cabinet as you walk in the door. There's also a raw bar with oysters and a sushi bar with the usual selections, including yellowtail tuna, octopus, squid, and eel. ✉ *7525 W. Sand Lake Rd., I–4 Exit 74A* ☎ *407/363–7262* 🖃 *AE, D, DC, MC, V.*

$$–$$$ ✕ **Bonefish Grill.** After perfecting its culinary act in the Tampa Bay area, this Florida-based seafood chain has moved into the Orlando market with a casually elegant eatery that offers seafood from around the world. Anglers (waiters) serve standout dishes like grilled sea bass in a mango sauce, Atlantic tilefish piccata, and pistachio-crusted rainbow trout. Meat-lovers may prefer the boneless pork chops topped with fontina cheese. For the record, there's no bonefish on the menu. It's an inedible gamefish, caught for sport in the Florida Keys. ✉ *7830 Sand Lake Rd., I–4 Exit 74A* ☎ *407/355–7707* 🖃 *AE, D, DC, MC, V* ⊗ *No lunch.*

Fodor'sChoice ★

STEAK

$$$–$$$$ ✕ **Morton's of Chicago.** Center stage in the kitchen is a huge broiler, kept at 900°F to sear in the flavor of the porterhouses, sirloins, T-bones, and other cuts of aged beef. Morton's looks like a sophisticated private club, and youngsters with mouse caps are not common among the clientele. It's not unusual for checks to hit $65 a head, but if beef is your passion, this is the place you'll want to go. A good, fruity dessert is the raspberry soufflé. The wine list has about 500 vintages from around the world. Take I–4 Exit 74A. ✉ *Dr. Phillips Marketplace, 7600 Dr. Phillips Blvd., Suite 132* ☎ *407/248–3485* 🖃 *AE, DC, MC, V.*

ORLANDO INTERNATIONAL AIRPORT

ECLECTIC

$$–$$$ ✕ **Hemisphere.** The view competes with the food on the ninth floor of the Hyatt Regency Orlando International hotel. Although Hemisphere overlooks a major runway, you don't get any jet noise, just a nice air show. Entrées change frequently, but often include selections such as miso-glazed sea bass on soba noodles, tamarind barbecue glazed filet mignon with fingerling potatoes, and grilled swordfish with truffle-scented mashed potatoes. Desserts change daily, but there's always a good tiramisu. ✉ *Hyatt Regency* ☎ *407/825–1234 Ext. 1900* 🖃 *AE, DC, MC, V* ⊗ *No lunch.*

CENTRAL ORLANDO

The center of Orlando shows what the town as a whole was like before it became a big theme park. Quiet streets are lined with huge oaks covered with Spanish moss. Museums and galleries are along main thoroughfares, as are dozens of tiny lakes, where herons, egrets, and, yes, alligators, peacefully coexist with human city dwellers. This is quintessential urban Florida.

The restaurants in this area, a good half hour from the Disney tourism area via I–4, tend to have more of their own sense of character and style than the eateries going full tilt for your dollars in Kissimmee or on International Drive.

ECLECTIC

$$$–$$$$ ✕ **The Boheme Restaurant.** The Westin Grand Bohemian, a downtown boutique luxury hotel, is the setting for one of the central city's better restaurants. As a prelude to your main, try the escargots with mushrooms stuffed into a puffed pastry. For a main course, try the corn-fed Angus beef. At breakfast, the French toast with a triple sec–strawberry glaze is an excellent way to awaken your palate. The Sunday brunch here is a worthwhile experience: you can get prime rib and sushi as well as omelets. ⊠ *Westin Grand Bohemian, 325 S. Orange Ave., Downtown Orlando* ☎ *407/313–9000* ⌂ *Reservations essential* ▤ *AE, D, DC, MC, V.*

$$$–$$$$ ✕ **HUE.** On the ground floor of a condo high-rise on the edge of Lake Eola, this place takes its name from a self-created acronym: Hip Urban Environment. While it may not be quite as cool as its press clippings, the food is both good and eclectic, with offerings ranging from succulent duck tostada with black beans, jack cheese, and salsa to crispy oysters with garlic mayo or wood-grilled New York strip steak with a red wine demi-glace. Unfortunately, the large outdoor dining area overlooks the street and not the lake. ⊠ *629 E. Central Blvd., Thornton Park* ☎ *407/849–1800* ⌂ *Reservations not accepted* ▤ *AE, D, DC, MC, V.*

$$$–$$$$ ✕ **K Restaurant & Wine Bar** This dark-wood-paneled spot for locals of
★ College Park—a quiet and quintessentially residential neighborhood about two miles northeast of downtown—features upscale eclectic American cuisine in an urbane, intimate setting. For those who love fine dining, this trip is well worth making. Most visitors from out of town don't make it here. The "K" stands for Kevin, as in Kevin Fonzo, the Culinary Institute of America graduate who created the place. Menus change daily, but there are several regular dishes that stand out. Start with the fried green-tomato-and–blue-cheese appetizer. For entrees, check out the grilled venison and Peruvian purple potato fries, or marinated flank steak with grilled Costa Rican hearts of palm. K also has some much-lauded desserts, including sweet potato cheesecake and a chocolate lava cake. There is an extensive wine list, and many selections are available by the glass. ⊠ *2401 Edgewater Dr., College Park* ☎ *407/872–2332* ▤ *MC, V* ⊘ *Closed Sun.*

$$$–$$$$ ✕ **Manuel's on the 28th.** Restaurants with great views don't always have
★ much more than that to offer, but this lofty spot on the 28th floor is also

12

a culinary landmark. The menu changes regularly, but there's always a representative sampling of fish, beef, pork, and duck. Dinner offerings may include sea scallops covered in macadamia nuts, Black Angus filet mignon, and even wild boar loin marinated in coconut milk. For an appetizer, try the smoked confit of duck with boursin (a creamy white cheese). For dessert, try the baked apples wrapped in pastry, beggar's-purse style, and topped with caramel sauce. ⊠*Bank of America bldg., 390 N. Orange Ave., Suite 2800, Downtown Orlando* ☎*407/246–6580* ⊟*AE, D, DC, MC, V* ⊗*Closed Sun. and Mon. No lunch.*

$$-$$$$ ✕ **Harvey's Bistro.** A loyal business crowd peoples this clubby café at lunch. It also attracts a nighttime following by staying open until 11 on Friday and Saturday nights. The menu has a good mix of bistro and comfort foods. The smoked-duck-and-spinach pizza is a top starter. Pasta favorites include chicken Stroganoff, duck and shrimp in Asian peanut sauce on linguine, and salmon with lobster Alfredo sauce. If you're a red-meat fan, rejoice. Harvey's has a good pot roast, a pan-seared tenderloin, and roasted duck alfredo. ⊠*Bank of America bldg., 390 N. Orange Ave., Downtown Orlando* ☎*407/246–6560* ⊟*AE, D, DC, MC, V* ⊗*Closed Sun. No lunch Sat..*

$-$$ ✕ **The Globe.** ⊗ During the six months of the year when Orlando seems to have the humidity and temperature of Brazil, the sidewalk cafés here are a test of one's stamina. But during the other six months, when the weather is absolute gold, places like the Globe come into their own. On downtown Orlando's block-long Wall Street (formerly lined with stock brokerages), this funky European café is a great place to people-watch over lunch. Settle down under big umbrellas and ponder the eclectic menu. Standouts include the pot stickers and an Asian-style noodle bowl with roast pork, chicken, shrimp, and veggies. The bread pudding with rum-butter sauce is to die for. ⊠*27 Wall St. Plaza, Downtown Orlando* ☎*407/849–9904* ⊟*AE, D, DC, MC, V.*

¢–$ ✕ **Johnny's Fillin' Station.** In a building that once housed a gas station, this burger joint and sports bar is a monument to the fact that good eating can sometimes be had in extremely humble surroundings. Orlando residents rave about the burgers, which are straightforward half-pounders infused with what the management calls a "family recipe." Generous portions of onions, tomatoes, and other less common ingredients—like grilled mushrooms and peppers—make these burgers wonderfully sloppy. Make sure to grab extra napkins. The bacon-and-blue cheeseburger is the most popular item on the menu, and a bargain at $7. Other options include chicken wings, cheesesteak sandwiches, and fish-and-chips. This place is also a sports bar and can get pretty loud and crowded. ⊠*2631 Ferncreek Ave., Central Orlando* ☎*407/894–6900* ⊟*D, MC, V.*

COLUMBIAN

$-$$$ ✕ **Leños y Carbon.** On what used to be Orlando's most popular tourist strip—Orange Blossom Trail—this Columbian-owned and -operated restaurant offers some of the city's best South American cuisine. Big-screen televisions beam high-energy salsa videos into the dining room, but the reason to visit is not the music but the quality cuisine. If you're unfamiliar with the entrées, try a sampler platter with grilled pork,

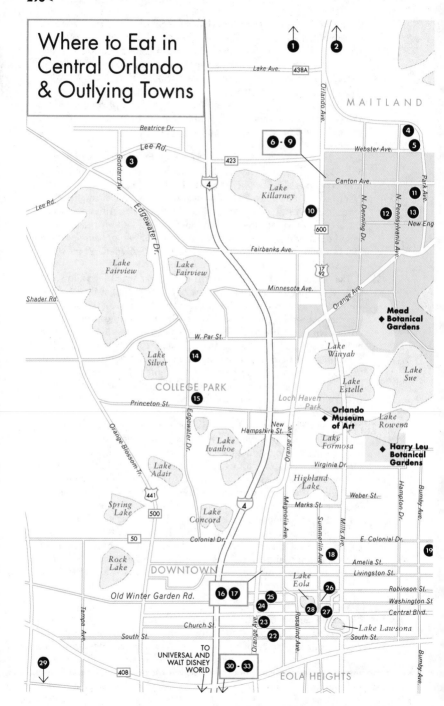

Where to Eat in Central Orlando & Outlying Towns

Lake Maitland

12

Park Ave.

Aloma Ave.

England Ave.

Osceala Ave.

Rollins College

Lake Mizell

WINTER PARK

Lake Virginia

Winter Park Blvd.

Glenridge Way

Corrine Dr.

Lake Susannah

Bennett Rd.

Humphries Ave.

50

19

20 **21**

Primrose Dr.

Maguire Blvd.

Orlando Executive Airport

St.
n St.
rd.

THORNTON PARK

East-West Expwy.

408

Primrose Dr.

Primrose Dr.

0 ___ 1 mi
0 ___ 2 km

Central Orlando ▼

Alfonso's Pizza
& More **14**

Amura **23**

Anthony's Pizzeria **26**

Baja Burrito Kitchen **19**

The Boheme
Restaurant **22**

Del Frisco **3**

The Globe **25**

Harvey's Bistro **16**

HUE **27**

Johnny's Fillin' Station **31**

K Restaurant
& Wine Bar **15**

Le Coq au Vin **32**

Leños y Carbon **30**

Linda's La Cantina **20**

Little Saigon **18**

Manuel's
on the 28th **17**

Numero Uno **33**

NYPD Pizza **29**

Shari Sushi Lounge **28**

Straub's
Fine Seafood **21**

Tijuana Flats **24**

Winter Park ▼

Briarpatch Restaurant
& Ice Cream Parlor **5**

Brio Tuscan Grille **7**

Cheesecake Factory **8**

Chef Justin's
Park Plaza Gardens **4**

Dexter's **12**

Houston's **10**

Luma on Park **11**

Pannullo's **13**

P.F. Chang's **9**

Seito Sushi **6**

Longwood ▼

Enzo's on the Lake **2**

Altamonte Springs ▼

Terramia Restaurant
& Wine Bar **1**

beef, and chicken. Also worth noting is the *cerdo asado,* grilled pork loin served with black beans and rice, and *ropa vieja,* a dish popular in both Cuban and Columbian cuisine that consists of shredded beef and grilled peppers and onions served over rice. Other worthy choices include the *cazuela de mariscos,* a seafood stew with plenty of scallops, clams, mussels, and lobster, and the chicken soup, a hearty bargain at $2.50. For desert, go for the *mil hojas,* a multilayered pastry with a creamy filling. A great feature in the restaurant is a Columbia bakery, which begins selling fresh pastries at 8:30 AM. ⊠ *7101 S. Orange Blossom Trail, South-Central Orlando* 🕾 *407/251–4484* ▭ *AE, D, DC, MC, V.*

CUBAN

$–$$$ ╳ **Numero Uno.** To the followers of this long-popular Latin restaurant, the name is no mere hyperbole. Downtowners have been filling the place at lunch for years. It bills itself as "the home of paella," so just take their word for it and order some. If you have a good appetite and you either called ahead to order or can spare the 75-minute wait, try the *boliche* (a tender pork roast stuffed with chorizo sausage) and a side order of plantains. Otherwise, go for traditional Cuban fare like shredded flank steak or *arroz con pollo* (rice with chicken). Finish with the *tres leches* (three-milk) cake, made with regular, evaporated, and sweetened-condensed milk. Take I–4 Exit 81A or 81B. ⊠ *2499 S. Orange Ave., South-Central Orlando* 🕾 *407/841–3840* ▭ *AE, D, DC, MC, V.*

FRENCH

$$–$$$$
Fodor's Choice
★

╳ **Le Coq au Vin.** Chef-owner Louis Perrotte is something of a culinary god in Orlando, but he doesn't let it go to his head. He operates a modest little kitchen in a small house in south Orlando. Perrotte's homey eatery is usually filled with locals who appreciate the lovely traditional French fare: bronzed grouper with toasted pecans; Long Island duck with green peppercorns; and braised chicken with red wine, mushrooms, and bacon. The menu changes seasonally to insure the freshest ingredients for house specialties. But the house namesake dish is always available and always excellent. For dessert, try the Grand Marnier soufflé. ⊠ *4800 S. Orange Ave., South-Central Orlando* 🕾 *407/851–6980* ▭ *AE, DC, MC, V* ☺ *Closed Mon..*

ITALIAN

$–$$
★

╳ **Alfonso's Pizza & More.** This is a strong contender for the best pizza in Orlando (in the non-wood-fired oven division). Since it's across the street from a high school, things get frenzied at lunch. The hand-tossed pizza's toppings range from pepperoni to pineapple—but the calzones and some of the pasta dishes, such as fettuccine Alfredo, are quite worthy as well. There are also subs and salads for lighter fare. The secret to the superior pizza is simple: the dough and all the sauces are made from scratch each and every day. Take I–4 Exit 84 to the College Park neighborhood area. ⊠ *3231 Edgewater Dr., College Park* 🕾 *407/872–7324* ▭ *MC, V.*

$–$$ ╳ **NYPD Pizza.** In business since 1996, this pizza place is a good alternative chain restaurants. Walk in for a slice of brick-oven, hand-tossed

12

pizza and you're back on the road in five minutes with a wholly satisfying lunch. Standouts include the pesto pizza, the barbecue-chicken pizza, and the "NYPD bleu," a cheesy favorite (and not a bad pun, either). Lasagna and chicken parmigiana are also available. Coney Island–style potato knishes make good snacks. Dessert standouts include a credible cannoli and, of course, New York cheesecake. Hardwood floors and brick walls make this place feel old-fashioned, and live music at night keeps things interesting. ⊠*2589 S. Hiawassee Rd., MetroWest* ☎*407/293–8880* ✉*2947 Vineland Rd., MetroWest* ☎*407/390-0170* ▤*AE, D, MC, V.*

¢–$ ✕ **Anthony's Pizzeria.** This neighborhood spot in Thornton Park is well
★ known to locals for its deep-dish pizza, but the pasta is worthy in its own right—and correctly priced for those on a budget. All the traditional Italian fare is available, and the chicken piccata and eggplant parmigiana are house favorites. If you're in a hurry, go for pizza by the slice, ranging from $1.85 for plain cheese to $4.50 for a slice of the stuffed pizza with ham, salami, pepperoni, peppers, onions, provolone, and mozzarella. ⊠*100 N. Summerlin Ave., Thornton Park* ☎*407/648–0009* ▤*MC, V.*

JAPANESE

$$–$$$$ ✕ **Amura.** A quiet respite from the vibrant—and loud—bars around it, Amura, Japanese for "Asian village," is comfortable and sophisticated. The sushi menu has about 40 choices, from *aoyagi* (round clams) to yellowtail tuna. For a taste of everything, try the Tokyo Plate, piled high with chicken teriyaki, salmon teriyaki, ginger pork, California roll, and tempura veggies. The Mexican roll—with avocado, shrimp, and jalapeño peppers—makes for an unusual appetizer. The Sand Lake Road location has a big, performance-style dining room, where the tables all surround grills and the chef cooks while you watch. The original downtown location has a quieter, more familylike atmosphere. ⊠*7786 W. Sand Lake Rd., I–4 Exit 74A, Sand Lake Road Area* ☎*407/370–0007* ✉*55 W. Church St. 170, Downtown Orlando* ☎*407/316–8500* ▤*AE, D, DC, MC, V* ⊗*No lunch Sun. .*

$$–$$$ ✕ **Shari Sushi Lounge.** Resplendent with chrome and glass, this trendy eatery has more of the atmosphere of a fast-lane singles bar than of an Asian oasis, but the dishes from the kitchen—fresh sushi and daily fresh fish entrées—acquit the place well as a legit dining establishment. Start with the *tako* (not taco) salad, a delicious arrangement of octopus, cucumber, enoki mushrooms, mandarin oranges, and spicy kimchi sauce. ⊠*621 E. Central, Thornton Park* ☎*407/420–9420* ▤*AE, D, DC, MC, V* ⊗*Closed Sun. .*

MEXICAN

¢–$ ✕ **Baja Burrito Kitchen.** Because of the excellent fish tacos as well as a specialty called the L.A. Burrito (grilled chicken or steak, plus guacamole and jack cheese), Baja Burrito calls itself a "Cal-Mex" palace. However, the mainstays of the menu—like a huge $7.65 burrito filled with chicken or steak, pinto beans, guacamole, and sour cream—will be familiar to denizens of the American heartland. It's not fancy, but it also won't drain your wallet. ⊠*2716 E. Colonial Dr., near Fashion*

Sq. Mall, Central Orlando ☎*407/895–6112* ✉*931 N. State Rd. 434, Altamonte Springs* ☎*407/788–2252* ⌦*Reservations not accepted* ▭*AE, D, MC, V.*

¢–$ ✗ **Tijuana Flats.** At this fine little downtown cantina you'll find a wild, weird assortment of bottled hot sauces from around the world. You can buy a bottle of Blair's Sudden Death or Sgt. Pepper's Tejas Tears for $10, or simply opt for the fiery house brand, free with your meal. The best menu options are plate-covering chimichangas; lime-marinated steak burritos with cheddar and jack cheese; and chipotle sauce–splashed corn tortillas loaded with meat, beans, and cheese. Mexican beers like Dos Equis flow freely. The sidewalk seating area faces the Orange County Historical Center and a pleasant little park. ✉*50 E. Central Blvd., Downtown Orlando* ☎*407/839–0007* ▭*AE, D, DC, MC, V.*

SEAFOOD

$$–$$$$ ✗ **Straub's Fine Seafood.** With offerings like escargots for $6—less than the price of a burger in the theme parks—Straub's proves that the farther you drive from Disney, the less you pay. Owner Robert Straub, a fishmonger for many years, prepares a fine mesquite-grilled Atlantic salmon with béarnaise sauce on the side. He fillets all his own fish and says he won't serve anything he can't get fresh. The Captain's Platter, with lobster and mesquite-grilled shrimp, is a great choice. The menu states the calorie count and fat content of every fish item, but for the tasty coconut-banana cream pie you just don't want to know. ✉*5101 E. Colonial Dr., near Orlando Executive Airport, Central Orlando* ☎*407/273–9330* ✉*512 E. Altamonte Dr., Altamonte Springs* ☎*407/831–2250* ▭*AE, D, DC, MC, V.*

STEAK

$$–$$$$ ✗ **Del Frisco.** Locals like this quiet, uncomplicated steak house, which delivers carefully prepared, corn-fed beef and attentive service. When your steak arrives, the waiter asks you to cut into it and check that it was cooked as you ordered. The menu is simple: T-bones, porterhouses, filet mignon, and such seafood as Maine lobster, Alaskan crab, and a good lobster bisque. There's also an excellent veal osso buco. Bread is baked daily at the restaurant, and the bread pudding, with a Jack Daniels sauce, is worth a try. There's a piano bar next to the dining room. ✉*729 Lee Rd., North-Central Orlando* ☎*407/645–4443* ▭*AE, D, DC, MC, V* ⊗*Closed Sun. No lunch.*

$$–$$$$ ✗ **Linda's La Cantina.** Beef is serious business here. As the menu says, management "cannot be responsible for steaks cooked medium-well and well done." Despite that stuffy-sounding caveat, this down-home steak house has been a favorite among locals since the Eisenhower administration. The menu is short and to the point, including about a dozen steaks and just enough ancillary items to fill a single page. The beef is relatively inexpensive here, with an 18-ounce sirloin going for $21 and a 2-pound T-bone—more beef than most can handle—for $30. With every entrée you get a heaping order of spaghetti (which isn't particularly noteworthy) or a baked potato. The chicken, veal, or eggplant Parmesan topped with marinara sauce is good for nonsteak

lovers. ✉4721 E. Colonial Dr., near Orlando Executive Airport, Central Orlando ☎407/894–4491 ▭AE, D, MC, V.

VIETNAMESE

\$–\$\$ ✕ **Little Saigon.** This local favorite is one of the best of Orlando's ethnic ★ restaurants. Even though there are more than 100 menu items, you can still create your own dish. Sample the summer rolls (spring-roll filling in a soft wrapper) with peanut sauce, or excellent Vietnamese crepes (stuffed with shredded pork and noodles). Move on to the grilled pork and egg, served atop rice noodles, or the traditional soup filled with noodles, rice, vegetables, and your choice of either chicken or seafood; ask to have extra meat in the soup if you're hungry, and be sure they bring you the mint and bean sprouts to sprinkle in. ✉1106 E. Colonial Dr., South-Central Orlando ☎407/423–8539 ▭MC, V.

OUTLYING TOWNS

WINTER PARK

Winter Park is a charming suburb on the northern end of Orlando, 25 minutes from Disney. It's affluent, understated, and sophisticated—and can be pleasurable when you need a break from the theme parks. To get into the area, follow I–4 to Exit 87.

AMERICAN–CASUAL

\$ ✕ **Briarpatch Restaurant & Ice Cream Parlor.** With a faux country store facade, this small eatery makes quite a contrast to its upscale neighbors, stores like Gucci and its ilk. But Briarpatch makes a great place to catch a hearty and inexpensive meal. The locals favor the thick burgers, which are topped with your choice of cheese, bacon, or mushrooms. Good breakfast choices include Belgian waffles, raisin-bread French toast, and freshly made scones. About 30 flavors of ice cream are available to help cool off on those long strolls down Park Avenue. ✉252 Park Ave. N ☎407/628–8651 ⬥Reservations not accepted ▭AE, D, DC, MC, V.

CHINESE

\$–\$\$ ✕ **P.F. Chang's.** Two huge, faux-stone, Ming dynasty–style statues of horses stand guard outside this Chinese restaurant. There's a lengthy wine list and very un-Asian desserts such as chocolate macadamia-nut pie and fruit tarts. You might start with shrimp dumplings, fried or steamed, and continue with orange chicken or perhaps crispy catfish in Szechuan sauce. The Mall at Millenia location has an outdoor dining area. ✉423 N. Orlando Ave., U.S. 17–92 ☎407/622–0188 ✉4200 Conroy Rd., Mall at Millenia Orlando ☎407/345–2888 ▭AE, MC, V.

ECLECTIC

\$\$–\$\$\$\$ ✕ **Houston's.** This Atlanta-based chain restaurant sits on a prime spot on Lake Killarney, which gives it a spectacular view. As you watch the egrets and herons you can savor some meaty fare. The fancy wood-grilled burger acquits itself well, but there's nothing like the steaks, which are wood-grilled or pan-seared to your specifications. The grilled fish entrées, such as tuna and salmon, offer tasty alternatives. On the lighter side, the club salad with chicken, bacon, avocados, and croutons (definitely pick the blue-cheese dressing) could easily satisfy two. Of the excellent soups, the New Orleans–style red beans and rice is the best. The patio makes a great place for a drink at sunset. ⊠*215 S. Orlando Ave., U.S. 17–92* ☎*407/740–4005* ⌖*Reservations not accepted* ▤*AE, MC, V.*

$$–$$$$ ✕ **Luma on Park.** Park Avenue, once an ultra-upscale enclave, was itself
★ a tourist attraction decades before the advent of Walt Disney World. Although Luma on Park is a 21st-century place, serving what some call "new American cuisine," it's also very much in line with Winter Park's 19th-century past. The chic contemporary setting includes terrazzo floors accented by plush carpets and seating areas in alcoves that create a cozy feel. A high point is the wine cellar, which holds 95 varieties of fine wine. Menu standouts include two appetizers, the crispy duck salad and the wood-fired pizza with sausage and ricotta cheese; and a pair of entres, Kobe flank steak with shiitake mushrooms; and the black grouper filet with black rice and boy choy. Standout desserts include sweet corn pudding with blackberries and warm chocolate truffle cake with banana ice cream and chocolate sauce. ⊠*250 S. Park Ave.* ☎*407/599–4111* ⌖*Reservations essential* ▤*AE, MC, V.*

$–$$$ ✕ **Cheesecake Factory.** You can select from more than three dozen varieties of the namesake treat, from chocolate Oreo mudslide cheesecake to southern pecan cheesecake. If you just don't like cheesecake, try the excellent apple dumplings. But this big restaurant also offers many full-meal options, from cajun jambalaya pasta to chicken marsala to wood-oven pizza to herb-crusted fillet of salmon. Great appetizers include avocado and sun-dried-tomato egg rolls, and bruschetta topped with chopped tomato, garlic, basil, and olive oil. ⊠*520 N. Orlando Ave.* ☎*407/644–4220* ⊠*4200 Conroy Rd., Mall at Millenia* ☎*407/226–0333* ⌖*Reservations not accepted* ▤*AE, D, DC, MC, V.*

$–$$$ ✕ **Dexter's.** The good wine list and imaginative menu tend to attract quite a crowd of locals. Dexter's has its own wine label and publishes a monthly newsletter about wine. Two of the best entrées here are the chicken tortilla pie—a stack of puffy, fried tortillas layered with chicken and cheese—and the pistachio-crusted black grouper served with seared shrimp and scallops. There's often live music on Thursday night. The Thornton Park location is just east of downtown Orlando; you may be the only out-of-towner here. If you're north of town, stop at the Lake Mary location in Colonial Town Park. ⊠*558 W. New England Ave.* ☎*407/629–1150* ⊠*808 E. Washington St., Thornton Park* ☎*407/648–2777* ⊠*950 Market Promenade Ave., Lake Mary* ☎*407/805–3090* ⌖*Reservations not accepted* ▤*AE, D, DC, MC, V.*

CONTINENTAL

$$–$$$ ✕ **Chef Justin's Park Plaza Gardens.** Sitting at the sidewalk café and bar is like sitting on the main street of the quintessential American small town. But the locals know the real gem is hidden inside—an atrium with live ficus trees, a brick floor, and brick walls that give the place a Vieux Carré feel. Chef Justin Plank's menu combines the best of French and Italian cuisine with an American twist. Much of the dinner menu is composed of traditional Continental fare, like rack of lamb or tenderloin topped with boursin cheese. One Florida touch is baked grouper with Tuscan white bean stew. Lunch offerings are lighter, with selections like glazed salmon and a good blue-cheese burger. ⊠*319 Park Ave. S* ☎*407/645–2475* ▤*AE, D, DC, MC, V.*

ITALIAN

$$–$$$ ✕ **Brio Tuscan Grille.** Head to this trendy restaurant for wood-grilled pizzas and oak-grilled steaks, lamb chops, veal scaloppine, and even lobster. Try the strip steak topped with Gorgonzola, or the grilled chicken topped with Parmesan and sautéed spinach. A good appetizer choice is the *brio bruschetta,* a wood-baked flatbread covered with shrimp scampi, mozzarella, and roasted peppers. The dining room's Italian archways are elegant, but the sidewalk tables are also a good option. ⊠*480 N. Orlando Ave.* ☎*407/622–5611* ⊠*4200 Conroy Rd., Mall at Millenia Orlando* ☎*407/351–8909* ▤*AE, MC, V.*

¢–$$ ✕ **Pannullo's.** The view of the tidy little downtown park across the street rivals the quality of the Italian cuisine when you dine in the sidewalk seating area. But when the rain or the heat drives you indoors, you've still got the consistently great cooking at this place, which includes an excellent veal piccata. Pizza-by-the-slice starts at $2.50—a good choice if you are in a hurry or on a budget. ⊠*216 Park Ave. S* ☎*407/629–7270* ▤*AE, D, DC, MC, V.*

JAPANESE

$$–$$$ ✕ **Seito Sushi.** Tucked into a corner of Winter Park Village, this pleasant eatery combines two great elements: sushi and sidewalk dining. Order a Japanese beer (or some hot sake) and sample the raw fish offerings, including the signature Seito roll, composed of tuna, whitefish, salmon, and crabmeat in a cucumber skin. Another favorite roll is the lobster Katsu, with deep-fried lobster topped with snow crab and avocado. There's also plenty of inspired cooked cuisine, including tasty sea bass with Asian rice, excellent salmon teriyaki, and even a good New York strip steak. Top off your meal with some red-bean ice cream or fried bananas. ⊠*510 N. Orlando Ave.* ☎*407/644–5050* ▤*AE, MC, V.*

LONGWOOD

A northern suburb 45 minutes from Disney, Longwood is a long way from the tourism treadmill. The community has some worthy restaurants as well. To get into the area, follow I–4 to Exit 94.

ITALIAN

$$–$$$$ ✕ **Enzo's on the Lake.** This is one of Orlando's favorite restaurants, even
★ though it's on a tacky stretch of highway filled with used-car lots. Enzo Perlini, the Roman charmer who owns the place, has turned a rather ordinary lakefront house into an Italian villa. It's worth the trip, about 45 minutes from WDW, to sample the antipasti. Mussels in the shell, with a broth of tomatoes, olive oil, and garlic, make a great appetizer. Try the aged tenderloin grilled with Gorgonzola cheese or the bucatini alla Enzo, a thick, hollow pasta tossed with prosciutto, peas, bacon,

mushrooms, and Parmesan. ⊠*1130 S. U.S. 17–92* ☎*407/834–9872* ⊟*AE, DC, MC, V* ⊘*Closed Sun.*

ALTAMONTE SPRINGS

A northern suburb 40 minutes from Disney, Altamonte Springs is immediately south of Longwood. The community is popular for its upscale shopping. To get into the area, follow I–4 to Exit 92.

ITALIAN

$$–$$$ ✕ **Terramia Winebar Trattoria.** If you didn't know about the delicious
★   Northern Italian cooking on offer here, the nondescript exterior and strip-mall location of this place might lead you to skip it. You would be making a mistake to do so. Inside the restaurant you'll find a warm and friendly neighborhood Italian eatery, serving classic Northern Italian pasta dishes with their own special twist—lobster ravioli, rigatoni with eggplant, mozzarella and basil, or fettucine with braised rabbit. A huge local following for this trattoria may come in part from the antipasto plate, which turns out to be "plates," as your waiter brings you an endless stream of tasty offerings that include roasted peppers, Italian sausage, polenta and bruschetta with an assortment of tangy toppings—a filling meal in itself for $8.50 per person. Not surprisingly, the desserts are dreamy as well, including an excellent tiramisu and a rich and creamy cannoli. Part of the charm of the place is a big, dark-wood bar, behind which you'll find dozens of bottles of fine Italian wines. ⊠*1185 S. Spring Center Blvd.* ☎*407/774–8466* ⊟*MC, V* ⊘*Closed Sun.*

DAVENPORT

This small town is the closest community to the Disney World exits if you go southwest on I–4 instead of northeast toward Orlando. It's largely a collection of budget motels along U.S. 27 South, but it also includes the golfing development and big Omni Orlando Resort at ChampionsGate.

ASIAN

$$$–$$$$ ✕ **Zen.** The signature restaurant at the Omni Orlando Resort At ChampionsGate, this pan-Asian delight offers an eclectic menu featuring everything from Chinese soups to Thai noodles to Japanese sushi. Your best bet is the Zen Experience—a complete Asian sampler plate that includes Thai-style chicken wings, Chinese barbecued spareribs, and a trio of salmon, pork, and chicken dishes. Another good choice is the sashimi and sushi combo platter, with lots of both for $52. Green tea–flavored ice cream makes an unusual dessert. ⊠*1500 Masters Blvd., I–4 Exit 58* ☎*407/390–6664* ⊟*AE, DC, MC, V.*

Disney Cruises

WORD OF MOUTH

"A cruise is a great way for a group to vacation together. Something for everyone. And Disney does a wonderful job. Lots for kids to do but lots of adult-only areas, too. And plenty of off-ship excursions for those who want activities."

—sueoz

"The kids' programs are the absolute best! They do science projects (they make them fun, really), plays, games, etc. At night in the kids' area they have a huge screen where they show the latest Disney movies and they bring out little cots for the kids to sit on, and warm freshly baked cookies and milk! They think of everything. We had to drag our kids out of there. Try to get them to leave to see the shows though. They are really fantastic productions."

—nina

www.fodors.com/forums

Revised by
Jennie Hess

WITH DISNEY'S REACH EXTENDING ALL the way to the high seas on two cruise ships, the *Disney Magic* and the *Disney Wonder*, there's an alternative vacation for "sail" beyond the Orlando kingdom. The Disney Cruise Line (DCL) ships, each with 875 staterooms and a capacity of 2,700, offer several excursions from Port Canaveral, Florida, to eastern and western Caribbean destinations, with stops at a nice mix of ports and at Disney's own private island, Castaway Cay. Periodically, the ships offer alternative sailings to the Mexican Riviera, Mediterranean ports, and southern Caribbean islands.

WORD OF MOUTH

"If you go with a family stateroom, avoid getting one under the Goofy pool because it gets noisy during the deck parties. Also, some of the staterooms have a solid railing as opposed to a plexiglass railing, which might limit visibility."–julia_elzie

Aboard the *Magic*, Mickey's silhouette is on the funnels and Goofy clings to the stern. Styled like a classic liner, the ship sails on a seven-night eastern Caribbean cruise, stopping at St. Maarten and St. Thomas with excursions to St. John and Castaway Cay. On alternate weeks, the *Magic* follows a western Caribbean itinerary to ports of call in Key West, Grand Cayman, and Cozumel, with the grand finish at Castaway Cay. Beginning May 25, 2008, the *Magic* charts a course along the Mexican Riviera, with 12 seven-night cruise vacations departing from the Port of Los Angeles. In addition, two 15-night cruises through the Panama Canal are slated as the ship heads to and from Los Angeles. From Port Canaveral, the first 15-night cruise through the canal departs May 10, 2008; the return trip to Port Canaveral begins August 17, 2008.

The art nouveau–inspired *Wonder* travels on three- or four-night Bahamian cruises, popular with first-time cruisers. Plus, you can combine this ocean getaway with a stay at Walt Disney World Resort for a seven-night seamless land-and-sea vacation. You check in just once: your room key at your Disney resort hotel becomes both your boarding pass at Disney's terminal at Port Canaveral and the key to your stateroom. The *Wonder* calls at Nassau en route to Castaway Cay, where there are separate beaches for adults, families, and teens, as well as good snorkeling and a family-friendly stingray adventure. Parents can enjoy some private time on the island while well-tended kids forget they're even around. Then everyone can share family time on the beach or in the water.

CRUISE PACKAGES

Packages include room, meals, and activities but not transportation to and from the ship (unless you book air travel at the same time) or shore excursions. Here are some starting rates for different packages, with adult prices based on double occupancy. Prices vary depending on the time of year you sail and even depending which week you book.

PACKAGE	ADULTS	AGES 3–12	UNDER 3
7-night cruise	$849	$549	$219
7-night land-and-sea	$839	$539	$209
4-night cruise	$519	$349	$169
3-night cruise	$429	$259	$169

You might get a better rate by booking early, but occasionally you'll get a bargain by booking at the last minute on a ship that hasn't filled. The larger your stateroom and the better the location, the higher the price will be.

The 2008 Mexican Riviera cruises start at about $1,599 per adult based on double occupancy. To book any Disney cruise, call **Disney Cruise Line** (☎800/370–0097 ⊕*www.disneycruise.com*). If you want to dig for a discount on your Disney cruise, locate a travel agent who specializes in cruises at www.travelsense.org or check out www.tripadvisor.com.

SPECIAL-OCCASION PACKAGES

Family reunion and other special-occasion cruises have become hot tickets as cruising gains popularity generally, and DCL will help you celebrate. Add-on packages include the Family Reunion Option ($49 per person for the first and second guests, $19 each additional guest), with commemorative certificates, personalized reunion T-shirts, and a photo. The Romantic Escape at Sea ($339 per couple) has champagne breakfast in bed, a couples' spa massage, and priority seating at the adults-only restaurant, Palo. A Disney Fairy Tale Weddings specialist will help couples plan weddings or vow renewals on the ship. If you want to surprise someone with a birthday bouquet or special gift, you can arrange it ahead of time with your Disney Cruise planner.

STATEROOMS

Cabins are ranked by category and range from standard inside staterooms (Categories 11 to 12, 184 square feet; sleeps 3 in Category 12, and 3 to 4 in Category 11) and deluxe inside staterooms (214 square feet; sleeps 3 to 4) to deluxe ocean-view rooms (Categories 8 and 9, 214 square feet; sleeps 3 to 4) to suites that sleep seven and provide sweeping views from a spacious balcony (Categories 1 and 2, from 945 to 1,029 square feet). In between the high and low ends are deluxe one-bedroom suites with verandas (Category 3, 614 square feet; sleeps 4 to 5); deluxe family stateroom with veranda (Category 4, 304 square feet; sleeps 5); and deluxe ocean-view staterooms with verandas (Categories 5 to 7, 268 square feet; Category 7 sleeps 3 and Categories 6 to 7 sleeps 3 to 4). The most luxurious and expensive staterooms are Category 1 Royal Suites, with private verandas and all the amenities you could dream of, including a media library and dining salon.

Quite a few of the staterooms feature a clever pull-down bunk-bed setup that saves space until bedtime and draws cheers from children.

On each ship, 73% of rooms have ocean views and 44% have private verandas. All are elegantly appointed with natural wood furniture. In addition, all except Category 11 and 12 rooms have split bathrooms, one with shower and sink, the other with toilet and sink, which allow couples and families to get ready in half the time.

Disney does a commendable job of keeping all rooms and much of the rest of the ship smoke-free while setting aside some deck, bar, and private veranda areas for smokers. Accessible staterooms for people with disabilities have ramps, handrails, fold-down shower seats, and handheld shower heads; special communications kits are available with phone alerts, amplifiers, and text typewriters.

SHORE EXCURSIONS

At various ports of call, Disney offers between one and two dozen organized shore excursions, from snorkeling and diving to sightseeing and shopping. For example, at Grand Cayman you can visit a butterfly farm or sign up for a trip to Stingray City, not really a city, but a long sandbar where hundreds of rays live. During a stop at Cozumel, you can explore the magnificent Mayan ruins of Tulum and strike a bargain for handcrafted Mexican hats, toys, and knickknacks. At St. Maarten you can sign up for a mountain-biking adventure, and on St. John, you can join a sail-and-snorkel expedition. All activities are rated from "leisurely" to "strenuously active." For full descriptions of the many shore excursions, go to ⊕ *www.disneycruise.com.*

ADULT ACTIVITIES

When people think Disney cruise, they often think it's a family-only affair. Not necessarily so. Sure, families get the best of all worlds on each of these elegant ships, there's no reason why adults (especially those who want to be kids again) have to miss out on the fun. On both ships, several areas are just for grown-ups, including one of the three pools. Poolside games, wine tastings, dessert-making, and even navigational demonstrations by the ship's bridge officers are among the diversions just for adults. The ship's spa is a don't-miss for those who need some pampering; the best time slots fill quickly, though, so book either when you buy your package or as soon as you board.

For a romantic dinner book an evening at the intimate, adults-only **Palo** (both ships), with its sweeping ocean views. Expect a fantastic wine list and dishes like grilled salmon with creamy risotto; warm shrimp salad with crispy pancetta, white beans, and grilled asparagus; and grilled filet mignon with a Port wine reduction and Gorgonzola cheese sauce. Reserve early, as it's a hot ticket. The champagne brunch on four-night-or-longer cruises is another great Palo dining event, with menu goodies like eggs Florentine; sweet pizza with mango, raspberries, and crème fraiche; and carpaccio of grilled eggplant with shaved prosciutto and truffle-oil dressing. Both dinner and brunch cost $10 per person on top of your cruise package.

> **JUST FOR KIDS**
>
> Most children's programs run from 9 AM to midnight, though earlier and later hours may be offered on some days. The teen clubs typically open at noon (with earlier activities on some days) and close between midnight and 2 AM.

13

Beat Street, a nightclub on the *Magic,* has the Rockin' Bar D dance club and Sessions, a piano bar. **Route 66,** the *Wonder*'s nightclub, has the WaveBands dance club and the Cadillac Lounge piano bar. If you're looking for something more low-key, check out **Diversions,** a sports pub on both ships. Or take in a first-run film at the ships' plush Buena Vista Theatre. At the Cove Café, you can enjoy a gourmet coffee, watch TV, check e-mail, and socialize.

CHILDREN'S ACTIVITIES

On both the *Magic* and the *Wonder,* there's nearly an entire deck reserved for kids. When you drop them off, pick up a pager to stay in touch with the activities counselors. Babysitting is available for children under 3 at **Flounder's Reef Nursery** for $6 per hour (two-hour minimum) and $5 an hour for each additional child.

The well-run **Oceaneer Club** is part of the cruise package, providing nonstop activities for kids ages 3 to 7, and giving parents the opportunity to enjoy some R&R. Little ones have a ball in the colorful playroom designed to look like Captain Hook's pirate ship. Kids can scramble around on a slide and rope bridge, play with a trunk full of costumes, settle in for arts and crafts, or watch a Disney movie. Counselors tailor activities to kids ages 3 to 4 and 5 to 7 separately.

Kids 8 to 12 can head for the high-tech, outer-space-theme **Oceaneer Lab.** There are fun science experiments, sports challenges, and karaoke jams. Counselors even organize treasure hunts all around the ship. With their parent's permission and a Lab Pass sticker on their Key to the World card, children can check themselves in and out of the Lab as they please.

Teens up to age 17 can chill out at their own getaway called the Stack on the *Disney Magic* and Aloft on the *Disney Wonder.* Here teens can tune in to music, watch plasma-screen TVs, play board- and video games, or just hang out and meet new friends. Organized activities for teens include trivia games and evening dance parties.

DINING & ENTERTAINMENT

RESTAURANTS

Disney offers six different dinner seating times: 5:30, 5:45, 6, 8, 8:15, and 8:30. Request the best seating time for your family when you book your cruise. Cruise dining coordinators will do their best to seat you at the requested time, but if you're placed on a wait list and scheduled for another seating, you can appeal to restaurant managers for a change once you're on board. Families with small children usually prefer earlier seatings. If you miss your seating, you can always find pizza or a simple buffet served elsewhere on the ship.

> **BON APPETIT!**
>
> Choose one of the early dinner seatings if you have young children. The onboard activities will usually have them wiped out by 8 PM.

The dining coordinators will arrange for you to alternate restaurants each night so you have the chance to sample all three. At **Animator's Palate** (both ships), the color scheme goes from black-and-white to Technicolor as the meal progresses. Dining is slightly more formal at **Lumiere's**, on the *Magic*, where beef tenderloin, lamb shank, and other entrées are served French-style in a grand dining room reminiscent of those aboard classic transatlantic ocean liners. At **Triton's**, on the *Wonder*, seafood, roast duck, pasta, and other selections are served in an elegant, art-deco, under-the-sea-theme dining room. At the Caribbean-theme **Parrot Cay** restaurant, the mood is both casual and festive. Character breakfasts and high tea with Wendy of *Peter Pan* fame are options aboard the *Magic* (but not the *Wonder*).

AFTER DARK

All Disney Cruise itineraries include the **Pirates IN the Caribbean** party, during which swashbuckling servers dish up an "argh" or two, a cup of grog, and a pirate bandanna for every guest at dinner. After dinner, you head off to a deck party where Captain Hook, Mr. Smee, and others appear for some high-spirited action, dancing, and a grand finale of fireworks.

Lavish shows and variety acts entertain families every night of every cruise. *The Golden Mickeys,* for example, is a high-tech salute to the animation of Walt Disney in the form of a Hollywood-style award ceremony. *Twice Charmed* is a Broadway-style production adding a twist to the Cinderella story. And *Disney Dreams* is a sweet bedtime story starring Peter Pan, Aladdin, Ariel, and other popular Disney characters with updated enhancements that provide animation, pyrotechnic and laser features, snow effects, and mechanisms that let characters "fly" more convincingly. Each ship also has a **cinema** screening classic Disney films.

Assistive listening systems for guests with disabilities are available in the ships' main theaters, and sign language interpretation is offered for live performances on specified cruise dates.

CASTAWAY CAY

Disney has its own private island, and you're invited. White-sand beaches, towering palms, and swaying hammocks beckon at Castaway Cay, the final stop of every Disney cruise. You're free to roam the island, relax on the beach, or join an excursion such as snorkeling or parasailing. Castaway Ray's Stingray Adventure, a calmer take on Grand Cayman's Stingray City, is a program that lets adults and kids age 5 and up touch, feed, and even snorkel with stingrays in an island lagoon. Tours and programs book up quickly so make your reservations when you buy your package.

If you're not traveling with children or if you've dropped them off at Scuttle's Cove to take part in the kids' programs, hop a tram to Serenity Bay. This is a beach just for adults, where you can melt under the influence of a cabana-sheltered Swedish massage (reserve in advance) or sip a rum punch from Castaway Air Bar. A barbecue lunch buffet is served on both the family and adult ends of the island. Sand-accessible wheelchairs are available for guests who need them.

13

Universal Orlando

WORD OF MOUTH

"Islands of Adventure is simply amazing. It's every-thing you could ask for in an Orlando theme park. The themes are carried out to the greatest extent, the rides are both thrilling and fun, and it is quite navigable. It is, in my opinion, at the complete opposite end of the spectrum from Disney's Magic Kingdom. MGM is Disney's counterpart to Univer-sal, but Disney has yet to develop anything near IOA caliber."

—IOA all the way

"Islands of Adventure is perfect for teens. My teens have pretty much outgrown Disney."

—eltrain

Updated
by Gary
McKechnie

UNIVERSAL AND DISNEY HAVE BEEN battling for years to attract attention and park goers away from each other. From the outset it was a contest between Disney–MGM Studios and Universal to draw film fans and production crews. Disney opened earlier and had the lead, but Universal used the extra time to tweak old rides, design new ones, and within a few years it had hit its stride to out-dazzle Disney with Islands of Adventure. Then CityWalk was added to compete with Disney's Pleasure Island. When its three themed hotels opened, Universal became a complete resort destination and a serious Disney competitor.

Borrowing a concept from Walt Disney World Resort, which encompasses theme parks and hotels, Universal Orlando Resort refers to the conglomeration of Universal Studios Florida (the original theme park), Islands of Adventure (the second theme park), CityWalk (the dining-shopping-nightclub complex), and three fabulous on-property hotels.

14

Halfway between Walt Disney World and downtown Orlando, and just off heavily trafficked International Drive, Universal is surprisingly secluded. You drive into one of two massive parking complexes (at 3.4 million square feet they're the largest on earth) and take moving walkways to the theme parks. Or, if you're staying at a Universal hotel, you can take a motor launch or stroll to the entrance.

While Disney creates a fantasy world for people—especially young children—who love fairy tales, Universal Orlando is geared to older kids, adults, and anyone who enjoys pop culture. Movie and TV fans will love this place. But along with pop culture comes plenty of commercialism: cash-depleting distractions like rock-climbing walls, souvenir kiosks, and other such traces of tackiness. To be fair, Disney is adding such distractions, and Universal *does* show a commitment to creativity, presentation, and cutting-edge technology through newer attractions like Revenge of the Mummy and *Fear Factor Live*. But Universal could take some tips from the competition on employee hospitality and the value of presentation. And when you want to forsake land-based action rides, you can head over to Wet 'n Wild (owned by Universal, but not a part of Universal Orlando Resort) for an afternoon of aquatic adrenaline and a place to cool off.

ADMISSION

Buy your tickets ahead of time for two reasons: one, you avoid the incredibly long and slow lines (even in low season) at the ticket booths at the park entrances; and two, you save a little money if you buy your tickets online at ⊕ *www.universalorlando.com*. Plus, there are no shipping costs because you can print your tickets directly from your computer. One such online-only bargain is the EarlyBird Exclusives Ticket. For $85 you receive unlimited admission to both theme parks and CityWalk for seven consecutive days—quite a savings. Here are your other ticket options (tax not included).

TIP SHEET

Universal Orlando isn't nearly the size of Walt Disney World, so navigating it is much easier.

■ Get there early—at 8 AM if the parks open at 9. Seriously. Seeing the park with about 100 other people is far better than seeing it with thousands. Plus, it's cooler in the morning.

■ Try to visit on a weekday, as locals crowd the parks on weekends.

■ If you aren't a resort guest, arrive in the parking lot at least 45 minutes early.

■ Write down your parking location.

■ Don't forget anything in your car. The parking garage is at least a half mile from both park entrances and a return round-trip will eat up valuable time.

■ If you're running late, skip the gargantuan parking garage and follow the signs to valet parking. For $18—almost twice the price of regular parking—you'll be in a lot just a few steps from the entrance to CityWalk and have a head start in reaching the parks.

■ If you're a Florida resident, you'll qualify for substantial discounts on admission to these parks. Buying online can save you even more.

■ If you're visiting during busy times, seriously consider buying the Universal Express PLUS Pass for an extra $15 and up (depending on the season and day of the week). It's well worth it to avoid waiting in line.

■ If you're in a hurry to reach the park and don't feel you can stop for a bite, don't worry—there's a Starbucks, a Cinnabon, and other quick-bite eateries at CityWalk. But we still recommend building in 10 minutes for a quick breakfast.

■ If you're overwhelmed by what to see and do, check with Guest Services, where Universal reps will create an itinerary for you, free of charge, based on your interests and available time.

■ One of the best perks of riding solo, if you don't mind breaking up your group, is the advantage of going into the fast-moving Single Rider line. Use it early and often anywhere it's offered.

■ If you're toting a baby around with you, check out the Child Swap areas. Although you won't be able to ride with your spouse, one parent can enter the attraction, take a spin, and then return to take care of the baby while the other parent rides without having to wait in line again.

■ Eat at off times, like 11 AM and 3 PM, to avoid the midday rush for food.

_AH HA!_

IN UNIVERSAL STUDIOS

■ When entering Universal Studios, many people are attracted to the towering soundstages on the left. Head to the right, bypassing shops and restaurants, to avoid crowds, especially early in the day.

■ Set up a rendezvous point and time early in the day, just in case you and your companions get separated. Good places include in front of the Lucy Tribute near the entrance, by the stage area across from Mel's Drive-In, and by the seating area of *Beetlejuice's Graveyard Revue.*

■ Expect kids to get wet at Fievel's Playland and absolutely drenched at Curious George Goes to Town—bring a bathing suit or change of clothing, and stash spare clothes in a nearby locker.

IN ISLANDS OF ADVENTURE

■ Tour the park counter-clockwise, zipping through Seuss Landing to get to Dueling Dragons, if you want to avoid the morning crowds. When you get to the Hulk coaster, you can use an Express Pass.

■ In case someone gets lost, set up a rendezvous point and time at the start of the day. Don't pick an obvious and crowded location (such as the Hulk entrance), but a small restaurant or bridge between two islands.

■ If you plan to ride Dueling Dragons or the Incredible Hulk Coaster, wear shoes that are strapped firmly onto your feet—no flip-flops or heelless sandals. If you wear glasses, consider pocketing them or wearing a sports strap to keep them firmly against your head when you're flung upside down. Neither coaster is so rough that you're certain to lose your glasses, but better safe than sorry. You should also leave loose change in one of the lockers.

■ Be ready to get totally drenched on Dudley Do-Right's Ripsaw Falls. Putting your bag under your feet should protect it in large part, but we still recommend a waterproof backpack. There are restrooms near the exit of the ride where you can go to change into your extra set of clothes. Avoid jeans!

14

TICKET	ADULTS	AGES 3—9
1 day, 1 park	$67	$56
1 day, 2 parks	$77	$67
2 days, 2 parks	$114.95	$104.95

You may also want to consider FlexTickets, which let you add visits to SeaWorld, Wet n' Wild, and Busch Gardens Tampa Bay onto visits to Universal. These FlexTickets are good for unlimited admission for 14 consecutive days.

TICKET	ADULTS	AGES 3—9
4-park FlexTicket	$189.95	$155.95
5-park FlexTicket	$234.95	$199.95

People with a disability that limits enjoyment of the park are eligible for a 15% discount off the ticket price. Also, American Automobile Association members get 10% off, sometimes more, at AAA offices. There are discount coupons for most theme parks in tourist flyers distributed around Orlando and if you buy tickets at the **Orlando/ Orange County Convention & Visitors Bureau** (⊠ *8723 International Dr.* ☎ *407/363–5871*), you can save about $5 per adult ticket ($3 on children's prices).

BABY CARE
There are diaper-changing tables in men's and women's restrooms. Nursing facilities and complimentary diapers are at the Health Services/First Aid centers (two per park). Many shops stock basic baby care items—wipes, etc.—but they are kept out of sight at the cash registers, so you have to ask for them. Also, check the park maps: a baby bottle symbol lets you know which ones carry the items.

CHILD SWAP
All rides have Child Swap areas, so that one parent or adult party member can watch a baby or toddler while the other enjoys the ride or show. The adults then do the swap, and the former caretaker rides without having to wait in line all over again.

GETTING THERE & AROUND
Driving east on I–4 (from WDW and the Tampa area), get off at Universal Boulevard (Exit 75A). Then take a left onto Universal Boulevard and follow the signs.

Driving west on I–4 (from the Daytona and Jacksonville areas), take Universal Boulevard (Exit 74B). Turn right onto Hollywood Way and follow the signs.

Both Universal Studios and Islands of Adventure (sometimes called simply IOA) are large parks that require a lot of walking. At IOA, sights are organized in a big circle, so if you plan carefully—that is, arrive early—you only have to walk around the doughnut once. Avoid backtracking if you're with small children or senior citizens. At the

Studios, you may have to cross the park a couple of times, especially if it's crowded and your Universal Express appointments are at inconvenient times.

HAND STAMPS

If you want to leave the park and come back the same day, have your hand stamped when you leave, and show your hand and ticket when you return.

HOURS

Universal Studios and Islands of Adventure are both open 365 days a year, from 9 to 7, with hours as late as 10 in summer and holiday periods.

INFORMATION

Call **Universal Orlando** (☎ *407/363–8000 or 888/331–9108* ⊕ *www.universalorlando.com*) for tickets, hotel reservations, and information.

PARKING

Universal's parking garage complex, which serves both theme parks and CityWalk, is the world's largest. Definitely write down your parking space, because everything looks the same inside and after a few go-rounds on the Hulk you might have a hard time remembering whether you parked at King Kong 104 or Jaws 328. Because your vehicle is covered, it's not so sweltering at the end of the day even when it's hot. The cost is $11 for cars and motorcycles, $12 for campers. Valet parking, which puts you just a short walk (and about 15 minutes closer) to the entrance of Universal Studios, is available for $18. Parking in the garage is free after 6 PM.

UNIVERSAL EXPRESS

The Universal Express Pass works much like Disney's Fastpass. You make appointments to get into the express line at certain popular attractions by inserting your theme-park ticket into a machine and getting a Universal Express Pass. The free pass is printed with the times between which you should show up for the ride, which means you'll likely wait no longer than 15 minutes for even the most popular attractions. Smart. You can't get another pass, or appointment, until your current one is used or the time expires.

With a Universal Express -PLUS- Pass, you get front-of-the-line access to rides and attractions without having to make or wait for an appointment. Prices vary, but a one-day/one-park pass costs $15 and up; a two-day/two-park pass runs $25 and up. If you're a Universal hotel guest, you actually get this perk for free, or rather, as part of your room rate. You use your hotel key card to access the express lines.

14

TOP ISLANDS OF ADVENTURE ATTRACTIONS

FOR AGES 8 & UP

The Amazing Adventures of Spider-Man. Easily the best ride in town. Get ready to fight the bad guys and put your life in danger. You'll understand what all the brightest engineers and technology wizards are doing with their time after this one.

Dudley Do-Right's Ripsaw Falls. Prepared to be completely soaked on this log flume ride, which has an even scarier dive than Splash Mountain.

Dueling Dragons. Two floorless coasters go through multiple inversions at 120 mph. At times they come so close together you feel as though you're going to hit the passengers on the other track.

Eighth Voyage of Sindbad. Jumping, diving, punching—is it another Tom Cruise action film? No, it's a cool, live stunt show with a love story to boot.

Incredible Hulk. Florida's best and scariest coaster shoots you skyward and sends you on no less than seven inversions. It will be hard to walk straight after this one.

FOR AGES 6 & UNDER

The Cat in the Hat. Take a seat on a moving couch and see what it's like to have the Cat in the Hat come to babysit for a while. Ever wanted to enter a Dr. Seuss book? That's what this ride is like.

Popeye and Bluto's Bilge-Rat Barges. This tumultuous raft ride is perfect for kids under 7 who want to go on a big-deal ride but are too young for the Hulk and Dudley Do-Right's. It's not too scary—just wild and wet.

STAYING ON SITE

When you stay at one of Universal's resort hotels—the Portofino Bay, Hard Rock Hotel, or Royal Pacific—you receive early admission to the parks, unlimited access to the express lines at rides, and priority seating at some restaurants. And in minutes you can walk to CityWalk and the parks. All three resorts are luxurious, fantasy-theme palaces, with room rates to match (though bargains can be had in the off-season). For detailed property descriptions, see Chapter 2, Where to Stay.

ISLANDS OF ADVENTURE

The creators of Islands of Adventure (IOA) brought theme-park attractions to a new level. From Marvel Super Hero Island and Toon Lagoon to Seuss Landing, Jurassic Park, and the Lost Continent, almost everything is impressive, and the shows, attractions, and at times the rides can even out-Disney Disney.

The park's five theme islands, connected by walkways, are arranged around a large central lagoon. The waterside is a good place to relax, either as a way to escape crowds or to recuperate from an adrenaline-surging coaster.

After passing the turnstiles, you've arrived at the Port of Entry plaza. This international bazaar brings together bits and pieces of architecture, landscaping, music, and wares from many lands: you may see Dutch windmills, Indonesian pedicabs, African masks, and Egyptian figurines. But don't stop here. Head directly for the massive archway inscribed with the notice THE ADVENTURE BEGINS. You won't be disappointed.

Numbers in the margin correspond to points of interest on the Islands of Adventure map.

BASIC SERVICES

CAMERAS **DeFotos** is a camera shop in the Port of Entry on your right after the turnstiles. They sell disposable cameras from about $13 (no flash) to $17 (with flash).

14

HEALTH **There are two Health Services/First Aid centers at Islands of Adventure:**
SERVICES one at the front entrance inside Guest Services, and the main center near Sindbad's Village in the Lost Continent.

INFORMATION **Guest Services** (☎ *407/224–6350*) is just before the turnstiles on your right before you enter the park. Step through the turnstiles and you'll find a rack of brochures and maps in French, Spanish, Portuguese, Japanese, and German, as well as English. If you have questions prior to visiting, call **Universal's main line** (☎ *407/363–8000*).

Studio Information Boards are at the Port of Entry in front of the Lagoon (where the circular walk around the park splits). The boards are posted with up-to-the-minute ride and show operating information—including the length of lines at the major attractions.

LOCKERS There are $8-a-day lockers across from Guest Services at the entrance, with $10 family-size models available; you have unlimited access to both types throughout the day. Scattered strategically throughout the park—notably at Dueling Dragons, the Incredible Hulk Coaster, and Jurassic Park River Adventure—are so-called Smart Lockers that are free for the first 45 to 60 minutes, but are $2 per hour afterward and max out at $14 per day. Stash backpacks and cameras here while you're being drenched or going through the spin cycle.

LOST THINGS & If you've misplaced something, return to the last attraction where you
PEOPLE had it. If it's not there, head to Guest Services in the Port of Entry. If you lose your children or others, head directly to Guest Services.

STROLLER & You can rent strollers ($10 per day for singles, $16 for doubles), man-
WHEELCHAIR ual wheelchairs ($12 per day), and electric scooters ($40 per day) at
RENTALS the Port of Entry to your left after the turnstiles. Photo ID or a $50 deposit on a credit card is required for either. If the wheelchair breaks down, disappears, or otherwise needs replacing, speak to any shop attendant. Since it's a long way between the parking garages and the park entrance, you may want to rent a push wheelchair at the garages and upgrade to an ECV (electric convenience vehicle) when you reach the park entrance. Quantities are limited, so it's recommended that you reserve in advance.

Islands of Adventure

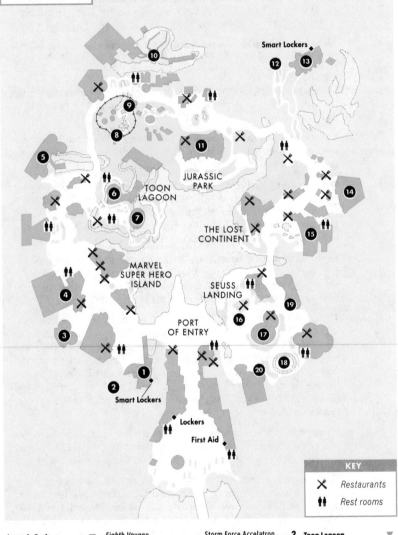

Smart Lockers

JURASSIC PARK

TOON LAGOON

THE LOST CONTINENT

MARVEL SUPER HERO ISLAND

SEUSS LANDING

PORT OF ENTRY

Smart Lockers

Lockers

First Aid

KEY

✕   *Restaurants*

👫   *Rest rooms*

MARVEL SUPER HERO ISLAND

This island may return you to the halcyon days of yesteryear, when perhaps you were able to name every hero and villain in a Marvel comic book. The facades along Stanley Boulevard (named for Marvel's famed editor and cocreator Stan Lee) put you smack in the middle of these adventures, with cartoony colors and flourishes. Although the spiky, horrific tower of **Doctor Doom's Fearfall** makes it a focal point for the park, the **Amazing Adventures of Spider-Man** is the one to see. At various times Doctor Doom, Spider-Man, and the Incredible Hulk are available for photos, and sidewalk artists are on hand to paint your face like your favorite hero (or villain). Also dominating the scenery is the Hulk's own vivid-green coaster. Along with a hard-driving rock sound track, the screams emanating from Doctor Doom's and from the Hulk Coaster set the mood for this sometimes pleasant, sometimes apocalyptic world.

INCREDIBLE HULK COASTER

❶ **Duration:** 2¼ min.
Crowds: All the time.
Strategy: You can use Universal Express Pass here; otherwise, make a beeline either to this coaster or to Dueling Dragons as soon as you arrive in the park.
Audience: Coaster lovers. No pregnant women or guests with heart, back, or neck problems. Minimum height: 54".
Rating: ★★★

If you follow a clockwise tour of IOA, this is the first ride that will catch your attention and probably the first you'll want to ride. The first third of the coaster is directly above the sidewalk and lagoon. You can watch as cars are spit out from a 150-foot catapult that propels them from 0 to 40 mph in less than two seconds. If that piques your interest, then enter the line where the walls are illustrated with artwork explaining how the superheroes and villains got their powers. After you get on the coaster, prepare yourself for flesh-pressing g-forces that match those of an F-16 fighter. Things are enjoyable in a rough sort of way, since you're instantly whipped into an upside-down, zero-g position 110 feet above the ground. That's when you go into the roller-coaster's traditional first dive—straight down toward the lagoon below at some 60 mph. Racing along the track, you then spin through seven rollovers in all and plunge into two deep, foggy subterranean enclosures. And just when you think it's over, it's not. It just keeps rolling along way after you've exhausted your supply of screams and shrieks. Powerful.

Note that the fog effects are most vivid first thing in the morning; darkness enhances the launch effect, since you can't see the light at the end of the tunnel. Front and rear seats give you almost entirely different experiences. The ride is fastest in the rear and has fine views, but is roughest on the sides; the front row, with its fabulous view of that green track racing into your face, is truly awesome—but you have to wait even longer for it.

14

STORM FORCE ACCELATRON

② **Duration:** 2 min.

Crowds: Not a problem.

Strategy: Go whenever—except after you've eaten.

Audience: Older children and adults. No pregnant women or guests with heart, back, or neck problems. Minimum height: 5".

Rating: ★★

This whirling ride is supposed to demonstrate the power of nature. Cartoon character Storm (of the X-Men) harnesses the power of weather to battle her archenemy Magneto (What?! *A story line?*) by having people like you board Power Orbs. These containers convert human energy into electrical forces through the power of "cyclospin." Strip away the veneer, however, and what you've got is a mirror image of Disney World's twirling teacups. Definitely not a good idea if you get motion sickness.

DOCTOR DOOM'S FEARFALL

③ **Duration:** 1 min.

Crowds: Can get crowded, but the line moves fairly fast.

Strategy: You can use Universal Express Pass here; otherwise, go later in the day, when crowds are thinner, but not on a full stomach.

Audience: Older children and adults. No pregnant women or guests with heart, back, or neck problems or motion sickness. Minimum height: 52".

Rating: ★

Although the 200-foot-tall towers look really, really scary, the ride is really just pretty scary. After being strapped into a chair, a silent countdown begins as you wait nervously. Then in a flash your chair is snapped with great speed to the peak of the tower, held there so you can realize just how high up you really are, and then dropped to earth. The process is then repeated, but just once. The ride is so short that it actually feels sort of anticlimactic. Watching it is scarier than riding it. Check the line and estimate your desire to see a panoramic view of Universal's parks and possibly the Orlando skyline (depending on which side of the ride you're on). Leave loose items in the bins provided; no one else can reach them while you're on your trip.

AMAZING ADVENTURES OF SPIDER-MAN

④ **Duration:** 4½ min.

Crowds: Usually inescapable unless you use Universal Express Pass.

Strategy: You can use Universal Express Pass here; otherwise, go early in the day or at dusk. If you don't know much about Spider-Man's villains, check out the wanted posters on the walls.

Audience: All but timid young children; youngsters accustomed to action TV shows should be fine. No pregnant women or guests with heart, back, or neck problems. Minimum height: 40"; children under 48" must be accompanied by an adult.

Rating: ★★★

Even if you've never heard of Peter Parker or J. Jonah Jameson, the 4½ minutes spent in this building can make an hour standing in line worthwhile. Unlike any other ride at any theme park, this one combines moving vehicles, 3-D film, simulator technology, and special effects. Unless you use the Universal Express Pass, expect a winding and torturous walk in line through the Daily Bugle's offices. You learn that members of the Sinister Syndicate (Doctor Octopus [aka Doc Oc], Electro, Hobgoblin, Hydro Man, and deadly Scream) have used their Doomsday Anti-Gravity Gun to steal the Statue of Liberty. None of this matters, really, since once you board your car and don your 3-D glasses, you're instantly swept up into a weird cartoon battle. When Spider-Man lands on your car, you feel the bump; when Electro runs overhead, you hear his footsteps following you. You feel the sizzle of electricity, a frigid spray of water from Hydro Man, and the heat from a flaming pumpkin tossed by the Hobgoblin. No matter how many times you visit this attraction, you cringe when Doc Oc breaks through a brick wall, raises your car to the top of a skyscraper, and then releases you for a 400-foot free fall to the pavement below. The bizarre angles and perspective at which scenes are shown are so disorienting, you really do feel as if you're swinging from a web. Do not miss this one.

14

TOON LAGOON

As you leave Marvel's world, there's no water to separate it from Toon Lagoon, just a change of pavement color and texture, midway games along the walkway, and primary colors turning to purple and fuchsia. Toon Lagoon's main street, Comic Strip Lane, makes use of cartoon characters that are instantly recognizable to anyone—anyone born before 1942, that is. Pert little Betty Boop, gangling Olive Oyl, muscle-bound Popeye, Krazy Kat, Mark Trail, Flash Gordon, Pogo, and Alley Oop are all here, as are the relatively more contemporary Dudley Do-Right, Rocky, Bullwinkle, Beetle Bailey, Cathy, and Hagar the Horrible. The colorful backdrop and chirpy music are as cheerful as Jurassic Park next door is portentous. There are squirting fountains for kids, hidden alcoves, and elevated cartoon balloon captions to pose under for photos.

EN ROUTE Get your Betty Boop collectibles at the Betty Boop Store. Poncho collectors can get one at Gasoline Alley, along with clever blank books, and cartoon-character hats and wigs that recall Daisy Mae and others.

DUDLEY DO-RIGHT'S RIPSAW FALLS
5 Duration: 5½ min.
Crowds: Varies by season, but very heavy in summer.
Strategy: You can use Universal Express Pass here; otherwise, go in late afternoon, when you're hot as can be, or at day's end, when you're ready to head back to your car. There's no seat where you can stay dry.
Audience: All but the youngest children. No pregnant women or guests with heart, back, or neck problems. Minimum height: 44"; children under 48" must be accompanied by an adult.
Rating: ★★★

Inspired by set-ups and a locale used on the popular 1960s animated pun-fest Rocky and Bullwinkle, this twisting, up-and-down flume ride through the Canadian Rockies is definitely wet and wild. You're supposed to help Dudley rescue Nell, his belle, from the evil and conniving Snidely Whiplash. By the time your mission is accomplished, you've dropped through the rooftop of a ramshackle dynamite shack and made an explosive dive 15 feet below water level into a 400,000-gallon lagoon, and you're not just damp—you're soaked to the skin. Actually, the final drop looks much scarier than it really is; the fact that the ride vehicles have no restraining devices at all is a clue to how low the danger quotient actually is here. You never know quite what's ahead—and you're definitely not expecting the big thrill when the time comes. If the weather is cold and you absolutely must stay dry, pick up a poncho at Gasoline Alley, opposite the entrance.

NEED A BREAK? On Toon Lagoon, you can sample you-know-whats at Blondie's Deli: Home of the Dagwood. The jumbo sandwich that creates the restaurant's marquee is a hoot, and you can buy the real thing, by the inch, inside.

POPEYE & BLUTO'S BILGE-RAT BARGES

6 **Duration:** 5 min.
Crowds: Heavy all day.
Strategy: You can use Universal Express Pass here; otherwise, go first thing in the morning or about an hour before closing.
Audience: All but young children. No pregnant women or guests with heart, back, or neck problems or motion sickness. Minimum height: 48"; children 42"–48" must be accompanied by an adult.
Rating: ★★★

At times this river-raft ride is quiet, but often it's a bumping, churning, twisting white-water tumult that will drench you and your fellow travelers. As with every ride at IOA, there's a story line here, but the real attraction is boarding the wide circular raft with 11 other passengers and then getting soaked, splashed, sprayed, or deluged. The degree of wetness varies, since the direction your raft spins may or may not place you beneath torrents of water flooding from a shoreline water tower or streaming from water guns from an adjacent play area.

ME SHIP, THE OLIVE

7 **Duration:** As long as you wish.
Crowds: Fairly heavy all day.
Strategy: If you're with young children, go in the morning or around dinnertime.
Audience: Young children.
Rating: ★★

From bow to stern, dozens of participatory activities keep families busy as they climb around this jungle-gym boat moored on the edge of Toon Lagoon. Toddlers enjoy crawling in Swee' Pea's Playpen, and older children and their parents take aim at unsuspecting riders locked into the Bilge-Rat Barges. Primarily, this is designed for kids, with whistles, bells, and organs to trigger, as well as narrow tunnels to climb through and ladders to climb up. Check out the view of the park from the top of the ship.

JURASSIC PARK

Walking through the arched gates of Jurassic Park brings a distinct change in mood. The music is stirring and slightly ominous, the vegetation tropical and junglelike. All this, plus the high-tension wires and warning signs, does a great job of re-creating the Jurassic Park of Steven Spielberg's blockbuster movie—and its insipid sequels. The half-fun, half-frightening Jurassic Park River Adventure is the island's standout attraction, bringing to life key segments of the movie's climax.

EN ROUTE The Dinostore, on the pathway between Jurassic Park and the Lost Continent, has a Tyrannosaurus rex that looks as if he's hatching from an egg, and (yes, mom) educational dino toys, too.

14

PTERANODON FLYERS

❽ Duration: 2 min.
Crowds: Perpetual. Since the ride loads slowly, waits can take an hour or more.
Strategy: Skip this on your first few visits.
Audience: All ages. Children 36" to 56" tall must be accompanied by an adult.
Rating: ★

These gondolas are eye-catching and can't help but tempt you to stand in line for a lift. The problem is that the wide, wing-spanned chairs provide a very slow, very low-capacity ride that will eat up a lot of your park time. Do it only if you want a prehistoric-bird's-eye view of the Jurassic Park compound.

NEED A BREAK? The Thunder Falls Terrace, near the grand finale of the Jurassic Park River Adventure, is open for lunch and dinner during peak seasons. One terrace side, entirely glass, gives an optimal view of the plunge, and you can also sit outdoors next to the river's thundering waterfall. Nearby, Burger Digs and Pizza Predattoria are year-round dining options.

CAMP JURASSIC

❾ Duration: As long as you want.
Crowds: Sometimes more, sometimes less.
Strategy: Go anytime.
Audience: One and all.
Rating: ★★

Remember when you were a kid content with just a swing set and monkey bars? Well, those toys of the past have been replaced by fantastic play areas like this, which are interwoven with the island's theme. Though the camp is primarily for kids, some adults join in, racing along footpaths through the forests, slithering down slides, clambering over swinging bridges and across boiling streams, scrambling up net climbs and rock formations, and exploring mysterious caves full of faux lava. Keep an eye open for the dinosaur footprints; when you jump on them, a dinosaur roars somewhere (different footprints are associated with different roars). Watch out for the watery cross fire nearby—or join in the shooting yourself.

JURASSIC PARK RIVER ADVENTURE
⑩ Duration: 6 min.
Crowds: Heavy except early in the morning.
Strategy: You can use Universal Express Pass here; otherwise, go early or late.
Audience: All but young children, who may be frightened. No pregnant women or guests with heart, back, or neck problems. Minimum height: 42".
Rating : ★★★

You're about to take a peaceful cruise on a mysterious river past friendly, vegetarian dinosaurs. Of course, something has to go amiss or it wouldn't be much fun at all. A wrong turn is what it takes, and when you enter one of the research departments and see that it's overrun by spitting dinosaurs and razor-clawed raptors, things get plenty scary. This is all a buildup to the big finish: guarding the exit is a towering, roaring T. rex with teeth the size of hams. By some strange quirk of fate, a convenient escape arrives via a tremendously steep and watery 85-foot plunge that will start you screaming. Smile! This is when the souvenir photos are shot. Thanks to high-capacity rafts, the line for this water ride moves fairly quickly.

JURASSIC PARK DISCOVERY CENTER
⑪ Duration: As long as you like.
Crowds: People mingle throughout, so that crowded feeling is almost extinct.
Strategy: Go anytime.
Audience: Older children and adults.
Rating: ★★
If there's a scintilla of information your kids don't know about dinosaurs, they can learn it here. There are demonstration areas where a realistic raptor is being hatched and where you can see what you'd look like (or sound like) if you were a dino. In the Beasaurus area ("Be-a-Saurus"), you can look at the world from a dinosaur's point of view. There are numerous hands-on exhibits and a Jeopardy!-style quiz game where you can test your knowledge of dinosaur trivia. The casual restaurant upstairs is a nice place to take an air-conditioned break, and tables on the balcony overlook the lagoon.

LOST CONTINENT

Ancient myths from around the world inspired this land. Just past a wooden bridge and huge mythical birds guarding the entrances, the trees are hung with weathered metal lanterns. From a distance comes the sound of booming thunder mixing with shimmering New Agey chimes and vaguely Celtic melodies. Farther along, things start to look like a sanitized version of a Renaissance Fair. Seers and fortune-tellers in a tent decorated with silken draperies and vintage Oriental carpets are on hand at Mystics of the Seven Veils. The gifted women read palms, tarot cards, and credit cards. In a courtyard outside the Sindbad show, a Talking Fountain offers flip responses to guest questions, such as "Is there a God?" Answer: "Yes. He's from Trenton and his name is Julio." Answers are followed by the fountain spraying unsuspecting guests.

EN ROUTE

Dragon's Keep carries Celtic jewelry along with stuffed dragons, toy swords in various sizes and materials, and perfectly dreadful fake rats, mice, and body parts. Treasures of Poseidon is stocked with shells and baubles made from them, while a heavy drop hammer pounds out signs and symbols on classy medallions at the interesting Coin Mint.

FLYING UNICORN

12 Duration: Less than a minute.

Crowds : Moderate, but since the ride is so brief, lines move quickly. You can use Universal Express Pass here if the lines are heavy.

Audience: Kids under 7, with adults riding along for moral support. Minimum height: 36".

Rating: ★★★

14

If you made the mistake of putting your kid on Dueling Dragons, the antidote may be this child-size roller coaster. Following a walk through a wizard's workshop, the low-key thrill ride places kids on the back of a unicorn for a very, very brief ride through a mythical forest. This is the park's equivalent of Universal Studios' Woody Woodpecker coaster. Kids lacking thrill-ride experience should enjoy this immensely.

NEED A BREAK?

If you're ready to toast your conquest of mortal fear, head straight across the plaza to the Enchanted Oak Tavern, ingeniously sprawled inside the huge base of a gnarled old oak tree. Chow down on barbecue chicken and ribs or corn on the cob, although the cool, cozy surroundings surpass the food's quality. In the adjacent Alchemy Bar, order a pint of beer including the park's own Dragon Scale Ale.

DUELING DRAGONS

13 Duration: 2¼ min.

Crowds: Perpetual.

Strategy: You can use Universal Express Pass here; otherwise, ride after dark, when most visitors are going home, or go early. For the most exciting ride, go for the rear car of the Fire Dragon or the front car of the Ice Dragon; note that lines for the front car of both coasters are much longer.

Audience: Older children with roller-coaster experience and adults with cast-iron stomachs. No pregnant women or guests with heart, back, or neck problems. Minimum height: 54".

Rating: ★★★

Since the cars of this high-test and extremely popular roller coaster are suspended from the track, your feet will be flying off into the wild blue yonder as you whip through corkscrews and loops and are flung upside-down and around. The twin coasters are on separate tracks so the thrill is in the near misses, which makes front-row seats a prized commodity (there's a separate, much longer line if you just have to ride in the lead car). Coaster weights are checked by a computer, which programs the cars to have near misses as close as 12 inches apart. Top speed on the ride ranges 55–60 mph, with the Fire Dragon (red) offering more inversions and the Ice Dragon (blue), providing more cornering. Either way, take advantage of the small lockers (free for 45 minutes) in which you can stash your stuff: wallets, glasses, change, and, perhaps, an air-sickness bag. (no hurling caps are sold in the adjacent gift shop.)

EIGHTH VOYAGE OF SINDBAD

⑭ Duration: 25 min.
Crowds: Not a problem, due to size of the open-air auditorium.
Strategy: Stake out seats about 15 minutes prior to show time. Don't sit too close up front—you won't see the whole picture as well.
Audience: Older children and adults.
Rating: ★★★

The story line of this stunt show is simple and satisfying: Sindbad and his sidekick Kabob arrive in search of treasure, get distracted by the beautiful Princess Amoura, and are threatened by the evil sorceress Miseria. That's enough to get the good guy started off on 25 nonstop minutes of punching, climbing, kicking, diving, leaping, and Douglas Fairbanks–ing his way through the performance amid water explosions, flames, and pyrotechnics that end with a daring flaming high dive. Kids love the action, and women love Sindbad. The 1,700-seat theater can be a nice place to sit a spell, replenish your energy, and watch a swashbuckler in action.

POSEIDON'S FURY

⑮ Duration: 20 min.
Crowds: Usually heavy.
Strategy: You can use Universal Express Pass here; otherwise, go at the end of the day. Stay to the left against the wall as you enter and position yourself opposite the podium in the center of the room. In each succeeding section of the presentation, get into the very first row, particularly if you aren't tall.
Audience: Older children and adults.
Rating: ★★

Following a long walk through cool ruins guarded by the Colossus of Rhodes, a young archaeologist arrives to take you on a trek to find Poseidon's trident. Although each chamber you enter on your walk looks interesting, the fact that very little happens in most of them can wear down the entertainment quotient. To reach the final chamber, you walk through a tunnel of water that suggests being sucked into a whirlpool—hard to describe, hard to forget. Then when the wall disappears, you're watching a 180-degree movie screen on which actors playing Poseidon and his archenemy appear. Soon, they're shouting and pointing at each other and triggering a memorable fire- and waterworks extravaganza where roughly 350,000 gallons of water, 200 flame effects, massive crashing waves, thick columns of water, and scorching fireballs begin erupting all around you. Although the first 15 minutes don't offer much, the finale is loud, powerful, and hyperactive. Is it worth the time investment? That's up to you.

SEUSS LANDING

This 10-acre island is the perfect tribute to Theodor Seuss Geisel, putting into three dimensions what had for a long time been seen only on the printed page. While adults recall why Dr. Seuss was their favorite author, kids are introduced to the Cat, Things One and Two, Horton, the Lorax, and the Grinch.

Visually, this is the most exciting parcel of real estate in America. From the topiary sculptures to the jumbo red-and-white-stripe hat near the entrance, the design is as whimsical as his books. Fencing is bent into curvy shapes, lampposts are lurching, and Seussian characters placed atop buildings seem to defy gravity. Everything, even the pavement, glows in lavenders, pinks, peaches, and oranges. Flowers in the planters echo the sherbet hues of the pavement.

From the main avenue, you can follow the webbed footprints to Sneetch Beach, where the Sneetches are frolicking in the lagoon alongside a strand littered with their beach things; the Seussonic boom box even has its own sound track, complete with commercials. Look carefully in the sand and you can see where the Sneetches jumped the fence to get to the beach, fell flat on their faces, and finally started dragging their radio rather than carrying it. Nearby is the Zax Bypass—two Zaxes facing off because neither one will budge. And keep an eye peeled for the characters—the grouchy Grinch, Thing One and Thing Two, and even the Cat himself.

EN ROUTE

Stores such as **Cats, Hats & Things** and **Mulberry Store** stock wonderful Seussian souvenirs, from funny hats to Cat-top pencils and red-and-white-stripe coffee mugs. And when you're inspired to acquire a bit of two-dimensional Dr. Seuss, you can stop into **Dr. Seuss' All the Books You Can Read.** For a last-minute spree, the **Islands of Adventure Trading Company,** in the Port of Entry, stocks just about every kind of souvenir you saw elsewhere in the park.

IF I RAN THE ZOO

16 **Duration:** Up to you and your young ones.
Crowds: Probably heaviest early in the day.
Strategy: If you can talk your kids into waiting, come at the end of your visit.
Audience: Young children.
Rating: ★★★

In this Seussian maze, kids can ditch the adults and have fun at their level. Here they encounter the trademarked fantasy creatures as they climb, jump, push buttons, and animate strange and wonderful animals. Park designers have learned that kids' basic needs include eating, sleeping, and getting splashed, so they've thoughtfully added interactive fountains.

Would you eat ice cream on a boat? Would you drink juice with a goat? Taste vanilla on a cone? Sip some grape juice all alone? Then there are places you must stop. Stop at **Hop on Pop Ice Cream Shop**. What do you say after Moose Juice Goose Juice? Say, thank you, thank you, Dr. Seuss.

Grab a quick bite inside the **Circus McGurkus** fast-food eatery. Check out the walrus balancing on a whisker and the names on the booths: Tum-tummied Swumm, Rolf from the Ocean of Olf, the Remarkable Foon. Occasionally, a circus master–calliope player conducts a singalong with the diners below. If you prefer dining with large groups of people, keep looking: the cavernous dining room seldom looks even partially full.

THE HIGH IN THE SKY SEUSS TROLLEY TRAIN RIDE

⑰ Duration: 3 min.
Crowds: Since this premiered in 2006, its novelty may trigger long lines.
Strategy: Kids love trains, so get in line.
Audience: All ages, but mostly for toddlers and young children. Children 34"–48" must be accompanied by an adult.
Rating: ★★

Offering an aerial view of the Seuss Landing, trains on separate tracks embark on a slow and pleasing tour of the area, with a Seusslike narrative detailing sights along the route. A nice and relaxing miniature train journey, it can be especially enjoyable for kids when the trolley rolls right through the Circus McGurkus Café Stoo-pendous, and along the shores of the lagoon where you can see the Sneetches as they enjoy the beaches.

CARO-SEUSS-EL

⑰ Duration: 2 min.
Crowds: Lines move pretty well, so don't be intimidated.
Strategy: You can use Universal Express Passs here; otherwise, make this a special end to your day.
Audience: All ages. Children under 48" must be accompanied by an adult.
Rating: ★★★

The centerpiece of Seuss Landing could have come straight from the pages of a Seuss book. Ordinary horse-centered merry-go-rounds may seem passé now that Universal has created this menagerie: the cowfish from *McElligot's Pool,* the elephant birds from *Horton Hatches the Egg,* and the Birthday Katroo from *Happy Birthday to You!*—an ark of imaginary animals. The 54 mounts are interactive: the animals' eyes blink and their tails wag when you get on. It's a cliché, but there's a good chance you'll feel like a kid again when you hop aboard one of these fantastic creatures.

ONE FISH, TWO FISH, RED FISH, BLUE FISH

18 **Duration:** 2-plus min.

Crowds: Thick all day.

Strategy: You can use Universal Express Pass here; otherwise, go very early or at the end of your visit when the tykes have left, so you can be a kid at heart. Otherwise, skip on your first visit.

Audience: Young children. Children under 48" must be accompanied by an adult.

Rating: ★★

Dr. Seuss put elephants in trees and green eggs and ham on trains, so it doesn't seem far-fetched that fish can circle "squirting posts" to a Jamaican beat. After a rather lengthy wait, climb into your fish, and as it spins, you (or your child) control its up-and-down motion. The key is to follow the lyrics of the special song—if you go down when the song tells you to go up, you may be drenched courtesy of the aforementioned "squirting post." Mighty silly, mighty fun.

THE CAT IN THE HAT

19 **Duration:** 4½ min.

Crowds: Heavy.

Strategy: You can use Universal Express Pass here; otherwise, go early or near the end of the day, when the children go home.

Audience: All ages. Children under 48" must be accompanied by an adult.

Rating: ★★★

If you ever harbored a secret belief that a cat could actually come to your house to wreak havoc while your mom was out, then you get to live the experience here. After boarding a couch that soon spins, whirls, and rocks through the house, you roll past 18 scenes, 30 characters, and 130 effects that put you in the presence of the mischievous cat. He balances on a ball; hoists china on his umbrella; introduces Thing One and his wild sibling, Thing Two; and flies kites in the house while the voice of reason, the fish in the teapot, sounds the warning about the impending return of the family matriarch. This ride promises high drama—and lots of family fun.

ENTERTAINMENT

Throughout the day there are character greetings and shows in each of the Islands. In Toon Lagoon, you may run into the **Toon Trolley,** which carries an assortment of Universal-related characters who disembark to sign autographs and pose for pictures. Adjacent to Ripsaw Falls, the Pandemonium Amphitheatre is usually dark, but does stage seasonal and/or special performances such as the skateboard and bicycle stunts of Extreme Adventures.

During the holidays, the **Grinchmas** celebration brings live shows and movie characters to Seuss Landing, and at Marvel Super Hero Island the **X-Men** make a guest appearance. During summer and holiday periods, when the park is open late, there's a big fireworks show that can

14

BLITZ TOUR

BEST OF THE PARK

To see everything in Islands of Adventure, a full day is necessary, especially since the large number of thrill rides guarantees that long lines will greet you just about everywhere. To see the most without waiting, stay at a Universal resort hotel or arrive in the parking lot 45 minutes before the park's official opening. Also, take advantage of Universal Express Pass ticketing.

This plan involves a lot of walking and retracing. It sounds crazy but it just ... might ... work. Unless you have preschoolers and need to see Seuss Landing first, take a left after the Port of Entry and head for the best and most popular attractions, starting with the **Incredible Hulk Coaster** then the **Amazing Adventures of Spider-Man.** Then double back, skipping Toon Lagoon in favor of the *Jurassic Park* **River Adventure.** In the Lost Continent next door, do **Dueling Dragons.** If it's showtime, next catch the *Eighth Voyage of Sindbad.* On the way back to Toon Lagoon, let the kids see either the **Jurassic Park Discovery Center** or **Camp Jurassic,** or both.

At Toon Lagoon, see **Dudley Do-Right's Ripsaw Falls** before or after the drenching at **Popeye & Bluto's Bilge-Rat Barges.** By now, if you're in luck, the young Dr. Seuss fans and their families will have left the park, so it's time to hit Seuss Landing. Go to **Cat in the Hat** first, then on to **One Fish, Two Fish, Red Fish, Blue Fish.** Make a stop at the **Green Eggs and Ham Cafe** to see how those green eggs are made, even if you're not ready to chow down. **Caro-Seuss-el** lets you be a kid again. Before you exit, walk through

If I Ran the Zoo. The unusual animals here are definitely worth a look. If the line is short and you can walk right on, consider boarding *The High in the Sky Seuss Trolley Train Ride*—otherwise wait until you're back in the neighborhood.

The remaining attractions are worthwhile if you've happened to arrive on a slow day and finish ahead of time: **Doctor Doom's Fearfall** and **Storm Force Accelatron** in Marvel Super Hero Island, the **Triceratops Discovery Trail** and **Pteranodon Flyers** at Jurassic Park, and **The Flying Unicorn** and **Poseidon's Fury** in the Lost Continent.

ON RAINY DAYS

Except during Christmas week, expect rainy days to be less crowded—even though the park is in full operation. (Coasters do run in the rain—although not in thunderstorms.) However, since most attractions are out in the open, you'll get very wet.

be seen anywhere along the lagoon bordering the islands—the lagoon-side terrace of the Jurassic Park Discovery Center has a fairly unimpeded view.

DISABILITIES & ACCESSIBILITY

As at Universal Studios, Islands of Adventure has made an all-out effort not only to make the premises physically accessible for those with disabilities but also to lift barriers created through the attitudes of others. All employees attend workshops to remind them that people with disabilities are people first. And you can occasionally spot staffers using wheelchairs. Most attractions and all restaurants are wheelchair accessible. Ask for the comprehensive *Guests with Disabilities* guidebook at Guest Services. Also, additional information for travelers with disabilities is available online (⊕ www.universalorlando.com; from the home page, click "Hours & Info" and then on Guest Services).

ATTRACTIONS All attractions are completely accessible to guests who use wheelchairs with the exception of the **Incredible Hulk Coaster, Doctor Doom's Fearfall,** and **Dueling Dragons,** for which you must transfer from your chair to ride. Ask an attendant for assistance or directions to wheelchair access.

SERVICES Many employees have had basic sign-language training; even some of the animated characters sign, albeit sometimes in an adapted manner. There's an outgoing TTY series hearing-impaired system on the counter in Guest Services.

EATING AT ISLANDS OF ADVENTURE

Sit-down restaurants and fast-food eateries are scattered throughout Islands of Adventure. Trans-fat foods are out and a line of healthy side dishes and snacks is in. Mythos and Confisco Grille accept "priority seating," which is not a reservation but an arrival time that's issued—you receive the first available seat after that particular time. To make arrangements up to 30 days in advance, just call **Guest Services** (☎ 407/224–6350). You can also visit Guest Services or the restaurant in person when you arrive.

FULL-SERVICE The park's fancy mealtime option is the sophisticated and gorgeous
RESTAURANTS **Mythos Restaurant** (☎ 407/224–4534), in the Lost Continent. The menu is ambitious and changes monthly, but menu items have included crusted pork with sautéed greens and ripe plantains; mahimahi pad thai; and a warm chocolate-banana cake.

Confisco's Grill (☎ 407/224–9255) is near the lagoon at the intersection of Port of Entry and Seuss Landing. Meals include steaks, salads, sandwiches, soups, and pastas—and there's even a neat little pub.

The **Thunder Falls Terrace** (☎ 407/224–4461), in Jurassic Park, serves rotisserie chicken and ribs, although the restaurant may close when crowds are light.

On Toon Lagoon **Blondie's Deli: Home of the Dagwood** serves the jumbo sandwich that creates the restaurant's marquee by the inch. At Seuss Landing's **Green Eggs and Ham Cafe**, traditional breakfast fare is also available. In Jurassic Park, you can have Caesar salad on a pizza crust, along with more traditional versions of the Italian specialty, at **Pizza Predatoria.** Check out the rapacious raptors on the sign.

UNIVERSAL STUDIOS FLORIDA

Disney does an extraordinary job when it comes to showmanship, which may be why Universal Studios has taken advantage of its distinctly non-Disney heritage to add attitude to its presentations. Universal Studios performers aren't above tossing in sometimes risqué jokes and asides to get a cheap laugh.

Although this theme park has something for everyone, its primary appeal is to those who like loud, fast, high-energy attractions. If you want to calm down, there are quiet, shaded parks and a children's area where the adults can enjoy a respite while the kids are ripping through assorted playlands at 100 mph. There are some visitors, however, who miss the sort of connection that Disney forges with the public through its carefully developed history of singable songs and cuddly characters.

The park has 444 acres of stage sets, shops, reproductions of New York and San Francisco, and anonymous soundstages housing themed attractions, as well as genuine moviemaking paraphernalia. On the map, it's all neatly divided into six neighborhoods, which wrap themselves around a huge lagoon. The neighborhoods are **Production Central,** which spreads over the entire left side of the Plaza of the Stars; **New York,** with excellent street performances at 70 Delancey; the bicoastal **San Francisco/Amity; World Expo; Woody Woodpecker's KidZone;** and **Hollywood.**

Although the park looks easy to navigate on the map, a blitz tour through it can be difficult, since it involves a couple of long detours and some backtracking. If you need help, theme-park hosts are trained to provide more information than you thought you needed. Also keep in mind that some rides—and many restaurants—delay their openings until late morning, which may throw a kink in your perfectly laid plans. In fact, if you arrive when the gates open, it's kind of eerie walking around in a nearly deserted theme park where it's just you and the staff. To make sure you maximize your time and hit all the best rides, follow this chapter's Blitz Tour.

Numbers in the margin correspond to points of interest on the Universal Studios map.

BASIC SERVICES

CAMERAS Just inside the Universal Studios main entrance, at the **On Location** shop in the Front Lot, you can find nearly everything you need to make your vacation picture-perfect. The store sells disposable cameras

TOP UNIVERSAL STUDIOS ATTRACTIONS

FOR AGES 7 & UP

Revenge of the Mummy. A pretty good indoor coaster that takes you past scary mummies and billowing balls of fire (really).

Universal Horror Make-Up Show. This sometimes gross, often raunchy, but always entertaining demonstration merges the best of stand-up comedy with creepy effects.

FOR AGES 6 & UNDER

Animal Actors on Location! A perfect family show starring a menagerie of animals whose unusually high IQs are surpassed only by their cuteness and cuddle-bility.

A Day in the Park with Barney. Small children love the big purple dinosaur and the chance to sing along.

14

from about $13 (no flash) to $17 (with flash), plus memory cards for digital cameras.

HEALTH SERVICES
Universal Studios' First Aid centers are between New York and San Francisco (directly across from *Beetlejuice's Graveyard Revue*) and at the entrance between the bank and the Studio Audience Center.

INFORMATION
Visit **Guest Services** (☎ *407/224–6350*) in the Front Lot to the right after you pass through the turnstiles, for brochures and maps in French, Spanish, Portuguese, Japanese, and German, as well as English. The brochures also lay out the day's entertainment, tapings, and rare film shoots. If you have questions prior to visiting, call **Universal's main line** (☎ *407/363–8000*) or Guest Services.

Studio Information Boards in front of Studio Stars and Mel's Drive-In restaurants provide up-to-the-minute ride and show operating information—including the length of lines at the major attractions.

LOCKERS
Locker rental charges are $8 for small lockers and $10 for family-size ones per day and both offer unlimited access. The high-price lockers are clustered around the courtyard after you've cleared the turnstiles. Keep in mind it can be a long walk back to the gate when you're on the other side of the park. If you time it right, you may not need a locker here because Universal also has Smart Lockers at major thrill rides. These are free for up to 90 minutes.

LOST THINGS & PEOPLE
If you lose something, return to the last attraction or shop where you recall seeing it. If it's not there, head to Guest Services. If you lose a person, there's only one place to look: head directly to Guest Services near the main entrance.

STROLLERS & WHEELCHAIRS
Strollers (singles $10, doubles $16), manual wheelchairs ($12 per day), and electric scooters ($40 per day) can be rented just inside the main entrance and in San Francisco/Amity. Photo ID or a $50 deposit on a credit card is required for either. If the wheelchair breaks down, disappears, or otherwise needs replacing, speak to any shop attendant. It's a

Universal Studios

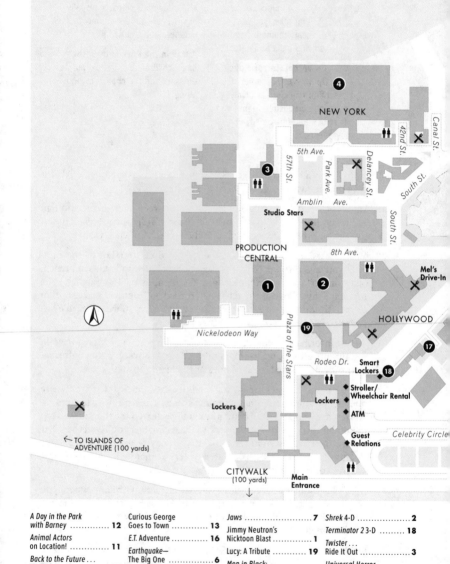

NEW YORK

Canal St.

42nd St.

5th Ave.

Delancey St.

South St.

Park Ave.

Amblin Ave.

Studio Stars

PRODUCTION
CENTRAL

8th Ave.

South St.

Mel's
Drive-In

HOLLYWOOD

57th St.

Nickelodeon Way

Plaza of the Stars

Rodeo Dr. Smart
Lockers

Stroller/
Wheelchair Rental

Lockers

Lockers

ATM

Celebrity Circle

Guest
Relations

← TO ISLANDS OF
ADVENTURE (100 yards)

CITYWALK
(100 yards)
↓

Main
Entrance

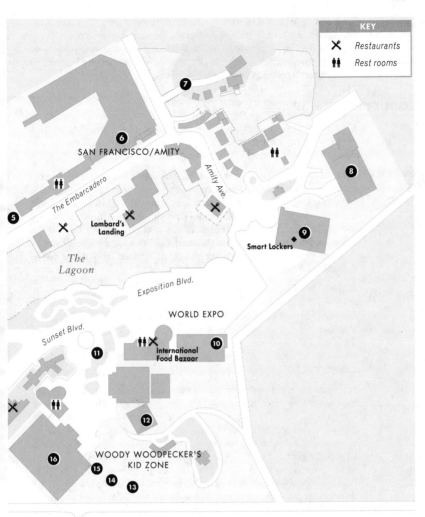

KEY

✗ Restaurants

👬 Rest rooms

7

6

SAN FRANCISCO/AMITY

The Embarcadero

Amity Ave.

5

✗ Lombard's
Landing

The
Lagoon

8

9 Smart Lockers

Exposition Blvd.

WORLD EXPO

Sunset Blvd.

11

👬 ✗ International
Food Bazaar

10

12

✗ 👬

16

WOODY WOODPECKER'S
KID ZONE

15

14

13

TO VINELAND RD. →

long, long way from the parking garage to the entrance. Consider renting a push wheelchair from the central concourse between the parking garages. You can upgrade to an ECV (electric convenience vehicle, or scooter) when you reach the park entrance. Quantities are limited, so it's recommended that you reserve in advance.

PRODUCTION CENTRAL

Composed of six huge warehouses with once-active soundstages, this area has plenty of attractions that appeal to preteens. Follow Nickelodeon Way left from the Plaza of the Stars.

EN ROUTE Every ride and attraction has its affiliated theme shop, and it's important to remember that few attraction-specific souvenirs are sold outside of their own shop. So if you're struck by a movie- and ride-related pair of boxer shorts, seize the moment—and the shorts. Choice souvenirs include Universal Studios' trademark movie clipboard, available at the **Universal Studios Store,** on the Plaza of the Stars, and sepia prints of Richard Gere, Mel Gibson, and Marilyn Monroe from **Silver Screen Collectibles,** across from *Terminator 2.*

JIMMY NEUTRON'S NICKTOON BLAST

❶ **Duration:** 8 min.
Crowds: Heaviest early in the day because it's near the entrance.
Strategy: If you can talk your kids into waiting, come at the end of the day.
Audience: All ages.
Rating: ★★★

Jimmy has arrived with a virtual-reality ride. The boy genius is joined by a large collection of Nickelodeon characters, including SpongeBob SquarePants and the Rugrats, as he demonstrates his latest invention (the powerful Mark IV rocket). Things go awry when evil egg-shaped aliens make off with the rocket and threaten to dominate the world. Computer graphics and high-tech, high-speed gizmos wow your senses as your rocket car dives, bounces, and skips its way through Nick-based cartoon settings. If your kids are regular Jimmy viewers or can sing SpongeBob's theme song, you have to do this ride. Be prepared: the show empties to a large gift shop selling Blues Clues, Dora the Explorer, Rugrats, Jimmy Neutron, and SpongeBob souvenirs.

SHREK 4-D

❷ **Duration:** 12 min.
Crowds: Will likely remain heavy as long as the movie remains popular.
Strategy: Use a Universal Express pass if possible.
Audience: All ages.
Rating: ★★

Mike Myers, Eddie Murphy, Cameron Diaz, and John Lithgow reprise their vocal roles as the swamp-dwelling ogre, Shrek; his faithful chatterbox companion, Donkey; Shrek's bride, Princess Fiona; and the vengeful Lord Farquaad in this animated 3-D saga. Grab your "OgreVision" glasses and prepare for a tumultuous ride as Shrek tries to rescue Fiona from Lord Farquaad's ghost. If she won't be his wife in life, he figures she ought to be in death. The showdown puts you at the center of a 3-D movie adventure that includes a battle between fire-breathing dragons and a pretty scary plunge down a deadly 1,000-foot waterfall. Specially built theater seats and a few surprising sensory effects—mainly blasts of air and sprinkles of water—make the "4-D" part. Even with the show's capacity for 300, you'll probably have to wait in line an hour just to reach the preshow, which stars the Gingerbread Man and the Magic Mirror and is slightly entertaining, but at 13 to 15 minutes, lasts longer than the film itself.

NEED A BREAK?

14

Classic Monsters Cafe resembles a mad scientist's laboratory. The self-serve restaurant is open seasonally and offers wood-fired oven pizzas, pastas, chopped chef salads, four-cheese ravioli, and rotisserie chicken. Frankenstein's monster and other scary characters from vintage Universal films make the rounds of the tables as you eat. Be sure to check out the monster-meets-celebrity pictures at the entrance.

NEW YORK

This Universal take on the Big Apple recalls the original—right down to the cracked concrete and slightly stained cobblestones. Many of the sets you see are used in music videos and commercials. The **Blues Brothers Bluesmobile** regularly cruises the neighborhood, and musicians hop out to give scheduled performances at 70 Delancey. The show is surprisingly popular, with crowds congregating in the street for the live show.

TWISTER ... RIDE IT OUT
❸ **Duration:** 3 min.
Crowds: Expect very long lines.
Strategy: You can use Universal Express Pass here; otherwise, go first thing in the morning or at closing.
Audience: All but young children, who may be frightened.
Rating: ★★

This attraction accomplishes in two minutes what it took the highly contrived movie two long hours to do—and overall it's far more exciting. After enduring a slow line and a fairly boring lecture from the movie's stars about the destructive force of tornadoes, you're eventually ushered into a standing-room theater where a quiet country scene slowly transforms into a mighty scary make-believe windstorm. An ominous, five-story-high funnel cloud weaves in from the background to take center stage as 110 decibels of wind noise, crackling electrical lines, and shattered windows add to the confusion. A truck, signs, car, and cow are given frequent-flyer points as they sail across the stage; and even though you know you're in a building and more victims are waiting patiently outside, when the roof starts to fly away your first instinct is to head for the root cellar. Don't. Watch the whole thing and marvel at the special-effects masters who put this together—and tear it apart every few minutes.

REVENGE OF THE MUMMY

④ Duration: 3 min.

Crowds: Expect very long lines.

Strategy: Use Universal Express Pass or go first thing in the morning. If you don't mind riding alone, make tracks for the strategic single-rider line.

Audience: All but young children, who may be frightened. Minimum height: 48".

Rating: ★★★

Action, adventure, and horror—the staples of the *Mummy* movies—are in abundance in this spine-tingling thrill ride. First you enter the tomb of a pharaoh and walk through catacombs and past Egyptian artifacts before boarding a coaster car. Then you're taken into a haunted labyrinth, where you're given an opportunity to sell your soul for safety and riches. Opting against it, you're sent hurtling through underground passageways and Egyptian burial chambers on a $40 million ride that combines roller-coaster technology, pyrotechnics, and some super-scary skeletal warriors. Coaster junkies take note: you'll feel the 1.5 g-force as you fly uphill, and almost the entire ride takes place in the dark.

SAN FRANCISCO/AMITY

This area combines two sets. One part is the wharves and warehouses of San Francisco's Embarcadero and Fisherman's Wharf districts, with cable-car tracks and the distinctive redbrick Ghirardelli chocolate factory; the other is the New England fishing village terrorized in *Jaws*.

EN ROUTE **Shaiken's Souvenirs,** on the Embarcadero, sells supercool Blues Brothers sunglasses and hats, among other movie apparel and accessories.

BEETLEJUICE'S GRAVEYARD REVUE

⑤ Duration: 25 min.

Crowds: Steady, but high capacity of amphitheater means no waiting.

Strategy: You can use Universal Express Pass here; otherwise, go when ride lines are at capacity or after dark on hot days.

Audience: Older children and adults.

Rating: ★★

Whew! This is *some* show. In an amphitheater, a Transylvanian castle is the backdrop for Beetlejuice, who takes the stage and warms up the audience with his snappy lines, rude remarks, and sarcastic attitude. Then for some reason, which is hard or useless to remember, he introduces the stars of the show: Frankenstein's monster and his bride, the Werewolf, and Dracula. Thus begins a stage show never before seen on this planet. At some point, the monsters doff their traditional costumes in favor of glitzy and hip threads and sing the greatest hits of such diverse artists as Bruce Springsteen, the Village People, and Van Halen. Upping the weirdness factor, two Solid Gold–style dancers add sex appeal to the production. Despite a sense of pity for the performers (which once included NSync's Joey Fatone and comedian Wayne Brady), this may be the only place you could see Frankenstein pretending to play an electric guitar and shout "Are you ready to rock, Orlando?" Don't be fooled by imitators.

NEED A BREAK?

If you plan to have a full-service dinner in the evening, a quick burger may be all you need to make it through the day. **Richter's Burger Co.** lets you drop in and create your own burger or grilled chicken sandwich. Pretty quick, pretty convenient, and there are seats inside and out.

EARTHQUAKE

6 **Duration:** 20 min.
Crowds: Heavy.
Strategy: You can use Universal Express Pass here; otherwise, go early or late.
Audience: All but young children. No pregnant women or guests with heart, back, or neck problems or motion sickness. Minimum height: Without adult, 40".
Rating: ★★

14

Unless you volunteer as an extra, the preshow for onlookers can be a little slow. After Charlton Heston appears in a documentary about the 1973 movie and preselected volunteers participate in the making of a short disaster scene, you board a train and take a brief ride into a darkened San Francisco subway tunnel. This is where the heebie-jeebies kick in very, very quickly. The idea is that you've been cast as an extra for the "final scene," and when the train parks within the subterranean station, a few lights flash, the ground starts to shake, and suddenly you're smack dab in the middle of a two-minute, 8.3–Richter scale tremor that includes trembling earth, collapsing ceilings, blackouts, explosions, fire, and a massive underground flood coming from every angle. Don't miss it—unless you're claustrophobic or fear loud noises and crumbling buildings. In that case, Earthquake might put you over the edge.

JAWS

7 **Duration:** 7 min.
Crowds: Lines stay fairly long most of the day, but nothing like those at *Shrek* 4-D.
Strategy: You can use Universal Express Pass here; otherwise, go early or after dark for an even more terrifying experience—you can't see the attack as well, but can certainly hear and feel it.
Audience: All but young children, who will be frightened. No pregnant women or guests with heart, back, or neck problems or motion sickness.
Rating: ★★★

This popular ride around a 7-acre lagoon has a fairly fast-moving line, but if it slows down you can always watch WJWS, a fake TV station airing joke commercials for products like used recreational vehicles and candied blowfish. You can guess what happens when you board your boat for a placid cruise around the bay. That's right. A 32-foot killer

Backstage at Universal

CLOSE UP

Odds are that while you're midway through a 100-foot spiral and g-forces are pushing your forehead through your feet, you won't be thinking about the technological soup of rotors, generators, and gears it took to get you there. But every time you board a ride at Universal Studios or Islands of Adventure, what you experience is just the tip of a high-tech iceberg. Lasers, 3-D imaging, holograms, pulleys, motors, hydraulics, and supercharged power supplies are working like mad to ensure that, for a few minutes at least, you really think Poseidon is sparking lightning bolts or Spider-Man has joined you on a trip through New York.

Think of what your day would be like minus all this mechanical acumen. The Incredible Hulk Coaster, for instance, would be just a lump of metal and plastic. But add four massive motors spinning fast enough to generate power to 220 smaller motors, and you're whipping up enough force to throw this 32,000-pound vehicle (a mass equal to eight Mercedes-Benz cars) up a 150-foot track at a 30-degree incline, to rocket you from 0 to 40 mph *in less than two seconds.* If you want to experience a similar sensation, climb into an F-16 fighter jet and take it for a spin.

At **The Amazing Adventures of Spider-Man,** 3-D effects, sensory drops, and virtual reality will fool you into believing you're actually being subjected to an assault of flaming pumpkins, careening garbage trucks, electric bolts, antigravity guns, swirling fog, frigid water, and an incredibly intense 400-foot, white-knuckle, scream-like-a-baby sensory drop.

The volume of air that rushes through **Twister ... Ride It Out** could fill more than four full-size airborne blimps in *one minute.* Its 110-decibel sound system uses 54 speakers cranking out 42,000 watts; enough wattage to power five average homes.

At Back to the Future The Ride, the elaborate, hand-designed and -painted miniatures took two years to make and cost as much as a feature film. Twenty computers conduct 5,000 different cues to create the special ride and movie effects.

In **E.T. Adventure,** there are 4,400 illuminated stars in the sky, 3,340 miniature city buildings, 250 cars on the street, and 140 streetlights in the city. The ride utilizes 284 mi of electrical wiring, 250 mi of fiber optics, 68 show control computers, and 2,500 separate commands from those computers.

Earthquake registers 8.3 on the Richter scale, releasing a slab of falling roadway that weighs 45,000 pounds. Nearly 65,000 gallons of water are released and recycled every six minutes.

Jaws's 7-acre lagoon contains 5 million gallons of water, 2,000 mi of wire, and 10,000 cubic yards of concrete reinforced with 7,500 tons of steel. The 32-foot steel and Fiberglass shark weighs 3 tons and swims at 20 feet per second.

Each time you step inside a Universal attraction, there are more high-tech happenings going on behind the scenes ... or right before your eyes.

shark zeroes in at 20 mph, looking for a bite of your boat. Even though you know the shark is out there, things can still get pretty frightening with surprise attacks, explosions, and the teeth-grinding sounds on the side of your boat. And don't think you're safe just because you've reached the boathouse. The special effects on this ride really shine, especially the heat and fire from electrical explosions that could singe the eyebrows off Andy Rooney. Try it after dark for an extra thrill, and then cancel the following day's trip to the beach.

FEAR FACTOR LIVE

⑧ Duration: 25 min.

Crowds: Expect large crowds as with all new attractions, though the 2,000-seat amphitheater means you should be able to get in close to showtime.

Strategy: For a premium seat, arrive 30 min in advance or use Universal Express.

Audience: All ages, though small children may not be entertained.

Rating: ★★★

If you can't get enough of watching people grasping for fame by eating worms, being sealed up in a roach-filled box, or wetting their pants as they're suspended from a helicopter, well, you can witness, and even participate in, stunts like this live at this show, which marks the first time a TV reality show has become a theme-park attraction. If you dare to compete, sign up at the audience-participation desk near the front of the attraction. Of course, since there are physical stunts involved, there are plenty of restrictions: you must be 18 or older, 5' to 6'2" tall, 110 to 220 pounds, and in good health. Apply as early as possible, as slots for the six daily shows fill quickly. If you're in the audience, you can still get in on the action by blasting contestants with water and air.

WORLD EXPO

The far corner of the park contains two of Universal Studios' most popular attractions, *Back to the Future* **The Ride**, and *Men in Black:* **Alien Attack**. These two make this the section to see for major thrills.

> **NEED A BREAK?** **The International Food Bazaar,** near *Back to the Future,* is an efficient, multiethnic food court serving Italian (pizza, lasagna), American (fried chicken, meat loaf), Greek (gyros), and Chinese (orange chicken, stir-fried beef) dishes at affordable prices—usually $7 to $9.

MEN IN BLACK: ALIEN ATTACK

⑨ Duration: 4½ min.

Crowds: Up to an hour in busy season.

Strategy: You can use Universal Express Pass here; otherwise, go first thing in the morning. Hint: solo riders can take a faster line so if you don't mind splitting up for a few minutes, you'll save a lot of time.

Audience: Older children and adults. The spinning nature of the cars may cause dizziness, so use caution: no guests with heart, back, or neck problems or motion sickness.

Rating: ★★★

This star attraction is billed as the world's first "ride-through video game." The preshow provides the story line: to earn membership into MIB, you and your colleagues have to round up aliens who escaped when their shuttle crashed on Earth. A laser gun is mounted on your futuristic car, but unfortunately, since the gun's red laser dot is just a pinpoint, sometimes it can be hard to see what you've hit (which is why your score is tallied and displayed on an onboard computer). Basically, you're on a trip through dark New York streets, firing blindly at aliens to rack up points. And they can fire back at you, sending your car spinning out of control. Be prepared to stomach the ending, when your car ends up swallowed by a 30-foot-high bug. Depending on your score, the ride wraps up with one of 35 endings, ranging from a hero's welcome to a loser's farewell. And you can compare scores with your friends. All in all, it's pretty exciting, if a bit confusing.

BACK TO THE FUTURE THE RIDE

⑩ Duration: 5 min.

Crowds: Peak times between 11 and 3, and slightly less crowded first thing in the morning, when *Twister* siphons off the crowds.

Strategy: You can use Universal Express Pass here; otherwise, dash over when the gates open, or about a half hour afterward, or go later at night.

Audience: Older children and adults. No pregnant women or guests with heart, back, or neck problems or motion sickness. Minimum height: 40".

Rating: ★★★

At heart, this is just a motion simulator ride, but it remains one of the park's most popular—albeit nausea-inducing—experiences. Following a long wait and a preshow video that explains how Biff has swiped one of Doc Brown's time-travel vehicles, you get into a cramped eight-passenger DeLorean, and take off to track down Biff and save the future. A series of realistic past, present, and future scenes projected onto a seven-story, one-of-a-kind Omnimax screen whooshes past you, making you feel completely disoriented. Having no sense of perspective (or seat belts) makes this the rocking, rolling, pitching, and yawing equivalent of a hyperactive paint mixer. It's scary, jarring, and jolting. If you like your rides shaken, not stirred, this one will be worth the wait—and the queasy feeling that will follow you around afterward.

WOODY WOODPECKER'S KIDZONE

Universal Studios caters to preschoolers with this compilation of rides, attractions, shows, and places for kids to get sprayed, splashed, and soaked. It's a great place for children to burn off their energy and give parents a break after nearly circling the park.

ANIMAL ACTORS ON LOCATION!

⑪ Duration: 20 min.

Crowds: Can get crowded in peak times.

Strategy: Go early for a good seat.

Audience: All ages.
Rating: ★★★

Animal shows are usually fun, and this one is better than most. An arkful of animals are the stars here, and the tricks (or *behaviors*) they perform are loosely based on shows from the cable network: *Emergency Vets, Planet's Funniest Animals,* and *The Jeff Corwin Experience.* A raccoon opens the show, and Lassie makes a brief appearance, followed by an audience-participation segment in the clever, funny, and cute Dog Decathlon. Next, Gizmo the parrot from *Ace Ventura: Pet Detective* arrives to fly in front of a wind machine and blue screen, the televised image showing him soaring across a desert, a forest, and then in outer space. In the grand finale Bailey the orangutan does some impressions (how an ape does Ricky Martin is a mystery), then there's an overpoweringly adorable chimpanzee and, finally, a brief peek at a boa constrictor. If your family loves animals, then this is an entertaining show that shouldn't be missed.

A DAY IN THE PARK WITH BARNEY

⓬ **Duration:** 20 min.
Crowds: Room for all.
Strategy: Arrive 10–15 minutes early on crowded days for a good seat—up close and in the center.
Audience: Young children.
Rating: ★★

If you can't get enough of the big purple dinosaur, here he is again. After a long preshow starring a goofy, kid-friendly emcee, parents tote their preschoolers into a pleasant theater-in-the-round filled with brilliantly colored trees, clouds, and stars. Within minutes, the kids will go crazy as their beloved TV playmate (and Baby Bop) dance and sing though clap-along, sing-along monster classics including "Mr. Knickerbocker," "If You're Happy and You Know It," and (of course) "I Love You." Following the very pleasing and thoughtful show and a chance to meet Barney up close, you'll exit to a fairly elaborate play area featuring hands-on activities—a water harp, wood-pipe xylophone, and musical rocks—that propel the already excited kids to even greater heights.

CURIOUS GEORGE GOES TO TOWN

⓭ **Duration:** As long as you like.
Crowds: Heavy in midmorning.
Strategy: Go in late afternoon or early evening.
Audience: Toddlers through preteens and their parents.
Rating: ★★★

The celebrated simian visits the Man with the Yellow Hat in a no-line, no-waiting, small-scale water park. The main town square has brightly colored building facades, and the plaza is an interactive aqua play area that adults avoid but kids are drawn to like fish to water. Yes, there's water, water everywhere, especially atop the clock tower, which periodically dumps a mighty huge 500 gallons down a roof and straight onto a screaming passel of preschoolers. Kids love the levers, valves, pumps, and hoses that gush at the rate of 200 gallons per minute, letting them get sprayed, spritzed, splashed, and splattered. At the head of the square, footprints lead to a dry play area, with a rope climb and a ball cage where youngsters can frolic among thousands of foam balls. Parents can get into the act, sit it out on nearby benches, or take a few minutes to buy souvenir towels to dry off their waterlogged kids.

FIEVEL'S PLAYLAND

(14) **Duration:** Up to your preschooler.

Crowds: Not significant, although waits do develop for the waterslide.

Strategy: On hot days, go after supper.

Audience: Toddlers, preschoolers, and their parents.

Rating: ★★

Another Spielberg movie spin-off, this one from the animated film *An American Tail,* this playground's larger-than-life props and sets are designed to make everyone feel mouse-size. Boots, cans, and other ordinary objects disguise tunnel slides, water play areas, ball crawls, and a gigantic net-climb equipped with tubes, ladders, and rope bridges. A harmonica slide plays music when you slide along the openings, and a 200-foot waterslide gives kids (and a parent if so desired) a chance to swoop down in Fievel's signature sardine can. It should keep the kids entertained for hours. The downside? You might have to build one of these for your backyard when you get home.

WOODY WOODPECKER'S NUTHOUSE COASTER

(15) **Duration:** 1½ min.

Crowds: Heavy in midmorning and early afternoon, when the under-2 set is out in force.

Strategy: Go at park closing, when most little ones have gone home.

Audience: Young children and their parents.

Rating: ★★★

Unlike the maniacal coasters that put you through zero-g rolls and inversions, this low-speed, mild-thrill version (top speed 22 mph) makes it a safe bet for younger kids and action-phobic adults. (It's the same off-the-shelf design used on Islands of Adventure's Flying Unicorn and Goofy's Barnstormer at the Magic Kingdom.) The coaster races (a relative term) through a structure that looks like a gadget-filled factory; the coaster's cars look like shipping crates—some labeled "mixed nuts," others "salted nuts," and some tagged "certifiably nuts." Woody's Nuthouse has several ups and downs to reward you for the wait, and children generally love the low-level introduction to thrill rides.

E.T. ADVENTURE

(16) **Duration:** 5 min.

Crowds: Sometimes not bad, but can be heavy during busy seasons.

Strategy: You can use Universal Express Pass here; otherwise, go early.

Audience: All ages. No guests with heart, back, or neck problems or motion sickness.

Rating: ★★★

Steven Spielberg puts one of his most beloved creations on display in this heavenly attraction adjacent to Fievel's Playland, although you may notice that it's starting to look weatherworn inside. After Spielberg's given you an update on E.T. and your mission, you board bicycles mounted on a movable platform and fly 3 million light years from Earth (in reality just a few hundred yards), past a phalanx of policemen and FBI agents to reach E.T.'s home planet. Here the music follows the mood, and the strange sounds in E.T.'s world are as colorful as the characters, which climb on vines, play xylophones, and swing on branches in an alien Burning Man festival. Listen in at the end when E.T. offers you a personalized good-bye.

14

HOLLYWOOD

Angling off to the right of Plaza of the Stars, Rodeo Drive forms the backbone of Hollywood.

EN ROUTE

Stop by the **Brown Derby Hat Shop** for the perfect topper, from red-and-white *Cat In The Hat* stovepipes to felt fedoras to bush hats from *Jurassic Park*.

UNIVERSAL HORROR MAKE-UP SHOW

17 **Duration:** 25 min.
Crowds: Not daunting.
Strategy: You can use Universal Express Pass here; otherwise, go in the afternoon or evening.
Audience: All but young children, who may be frightened; older children eat up the blood-and-guts stories.
Rating: ★★★

One of the funniest and most entertaining shows in any theme park, this attraction begins in an intriguing preshow area where masks, props, and rubber skeletons from the film *Scorpion King* make a great backdrop for a family photo. Beyond this, the real fun kicks off in the theater when a host brings out aspecial-effects expert to describe what goes into (and what oozes out of) some of the creepiest movie effects. Corn syrup and food coloring make for a dandy blood substitute, for example. Despite the potentially frightening topic, the subject is handled with an extraordinary amount of dead-on humor and totally engaging audience participation. As movie secrets are betrayed, actors add in one-liners with comedy-club timing. Throw in some knives, guns, loose limbs, and a surprise ending, and you've got yourself a recipe for edge-of-your-seat fun. It's absolutely flat-out good.

NEED A BREAK?

Schwab's Pharmacy is a re-creation of the legendary drugstore where—studio publicists claim—Lana Turner was discovered. What you'll discover is a quick stop where you can order ice cream as well as hand-carved turkey and ham sandwiches.

TERMINATOR 2 3-D
⑱ Duration: 21 min, with preshow.
Crowds: Always.
Strategy: You can use Universal Express here; otherwise, go first thing in the morning.
Audience: All but very young children, who may be frightened.
Rating: ★★★

California's governor said he'd be back, and he is, along with the popular film's other main characters, including a buff Linda Hamilton and an older Edward Furlong, aka young John Connor. Directed by James *Titanic* Cameron, who also directed the first two *Terminator* movies, the 12-minute show is—frame for frame—one of the most expensive live-action films ever produced. The attraction begins when you enter the headquarters of the futuristic consortium, Cyberdyne, and a "community relations and media control" hostess greets your group and introduces their latest line of law-enforcing robots. Things go awry (of course), and the Schwarzenegger film, combined with icy fog, live actors, gunfights, and a chilling grand finale, keep the pace moving at 100 mph—although the 3-D effects seem few and far between. Kids may be scared silly and require some parental counseling, but if you can handle a few surprises, don't miss this one.

LUCY: A TRIBUTE
⑲ Duration: About 15 min.
Crowds: Seldom a problem.
Strategy: Save this for a peek on your way out or for a hot afternoon.
Audience: Adults.
Rating: ★

If you smile when you recall Lucy stomping grapes, practicing ballet, gobbling chocolates, or wailing when Ricky won't let her be in the show, then you need to stop here. This mini-museum (and major gift shop) pays tribute to Lucille Ball through scripts, props, costumes, awards, and clips from the comedian's estate. A challenging trivia quiz game has you trying to get Lucy, Ricky, Fred, and Ethel across country to Hollywood. It's a nice place to take a break and spend time with one of the funniest women of television.

ENTERTAINMENT

If you're in Orlando at the right time of year, don't miss Universal's evening seasonal parties—most notably **Mardi Gras** (early February through early April), **Rock the Universe** (Christian music, September), the wildly popular **Halloween Horror Nights** (October), and **Macy's Holiday Parade** (December–January). There are also CityWalk celebrations, including **Tony Hawk's Skate Bash, Orlando Beer Festival,** and **Reggae Fest.**

DISABILITIES & ACCESSIBILITY

In addition to being physically accommodating, Universal has a professional staff that is quite helpful. At each park's Guest Services desk, you

BLITZ TOUR

BEST OF THE PARK

If you want to attempt to see everything in one day, arrive early so that you can take care of business and see the top attractions before the park gets very crowded. Another way to increase your attraction quota is to ignore the faux Hollywood streets and the gift shops. During peak seasons, you can avoid long waits at major attractions with the highly recommended Universal Express and Express PLUS Passes. These admit you to the attractions with little or no wait in line.

If you're one of the first people in the park and have plenty of early energy, circle the park twice to catch the A-list rides first, then pick up the B-list later. If you're dying to see *Shrek* **4-D,** you'll need to hit it first (it's straight ahead on the right), and then backtrack and turn left to follow up with *Terminator 2* **3-D.** Next, make tracks down the street to *Back to the Future* **The Ride** while the lines are still at a minimum. As you continue counterclockwise, *Men in Black:* **Alien Attack** is next, followed by *Jaws, Earthquake,* then the must-see *Revenge of the Mummy* attraction and, finally, back near the entrance to see *Twister ...* **Ride It**

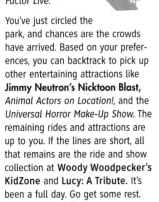

Out. Anywhere along the line, if you time it right so you don't have to wait, consider dropping in to see the live action show, *Fear Factor Live.*

You've just circled the park, and chances are the crowds have arrived. Based on your preferences, you can backtrack to pick up other entertaining attractions like **Jimmy Neutron's Nicktoon Blast,** *Animal Actors on Location!,* and the *Universal Horror Make-Up Show.* The remaining rides and attractions are up to you. If the lines are short, all that remains are the ride and show collection at **Woody Woodpecker's KidZone** and **Lucy: A Tribute.** It's been a full day. Go get some rest.

ON RAINY DAYS

Unless it's the week after Christmas, rainy days mean that the crowd will be noticeably thinner. Universal is one of the area's best bets in rainy weather—the park is fully operational, and there are many places to take shelter from downpours. Only a few street shows are canceled during bad weather.

14

can pick up a *Studio Guide for Guests with Disabilities* (aka *Rider's Guide*), which contains information for guests who require specific needs on rides and offers details on interpreters, braille scripts, menus, and assisted devices. Walking areas for service animals are available at the Nickelodeon Courtyard and at *Men in Black*: Alien Attack.

During orientation, all employees learn how to accommodate guests with disabilities, and you can occasionally spot staffers using wheelchairs. Additionally, power-assist buttons make it easier to get past heavy, hard-to-open doors; lap tables are provided for guests in shops; and already accessible bathroom facilities have such niceties as insulated under-sink pipes and companion rest rooms.

UNIVERSAL ORLANDO

NAME	Min. Height	Type of Ride	Duration	Suits	Crowds	Strategy
Universal Studios						
A Day in the Park with Barney	n/a	show	20 min.	Toddlers	ok	Arrive 10–15 mins early on crowded days for a good seat.
★ Animal Actors on Location!	n/a	show	20 min.	All	Peak times	Come early for a good seat, up front and enter.
Back to the Future The Ride	40″	sim. ride	5 min.	7 and up	Peak times	Go when gates first open, or a half hour later, or go late at night.
Beetlejuice's Graveyard Revue	n/a	show	25 min.	5 and up	Fast lines	Use Universal Express Pass here or go after dark on hot days.
Curious George Goes to Town	n/a	play area	Up to you.	All	Midmorning	Go in late afternoon or early evening.
E.T. Adventure	n/a	ride	5 min.	All	ok	Come early morning.
Earthquake— The Big One	40″	thrill ride	20 min.	10 and up	Heavy	Come early or before closing. This is loud.
Fear Factor Live	n/a	show	25 min.	All	Fast lines	Arrive 30 min. early for good seats. Or use Universal Express Pass. Toddlers may be bored.
Jaws	n/a	thrill ride	7 min.	10 and up	Fast lines	Come after dark for a more terrifying ride.
Jimmy Neutron's Nicktoon Blast	n/a	sim. ride	8 min.	All	Morning	Come at end of day, or Universal Express Pass while you do Shrek ride.
Lucy: A Tribute	n/a	walk through	15 min.	Adults	ok	Save this for a hot afternoon.
Men in Black: Alien Attack	n/a	thrill ride	4½ min.	All	Peak season.	Solo riders can take a faster line so split up. Spinning ride.
Revenge of the Mummy	48″	thrill ride	3 min.	7 and up	Yes!	Use Universal Express Pass or go first thing in the morning.
Shrek 4-D	n/a	4-D film	12 min.	All	Yes!	Very popular. Use Universal Express Pass.
Terminator 2 3-D	n/a	3-D film	21 min.	7 and up	Yes!	Go first thing in the morning.
Twister . . . Ride It Out	n/a	sim. ride	3 min.	10 and up	Yes!	Go first thing in morning or at closing.
★ Universal Horror Make-Up Show	n/a	show	25 min.	All	Not daunting.	Go in the afternoon or evening. Young children may be frightened; older children eat up the blood-and-guts stories.
Woody Woodpecker's Nuthouse Coaster	n/a	thrill ride	1½ min.	4 and up	Midmorning	Go at park closing, when most little ones have gone home.

Universal Islands of Adventure

★ The Amazing Adventures of Spider-Man	40"	sim. ride	4½ min.	10 and up	Yes!	Use Universal Express Pass or go early or late in day. See bad guys in the WANTED posters.
Camp Jurassic	n/a	play area	Up to you	Toddlers	ok	Go anytime.
Caro-Seuss-el		carousel	2 min.	All	Fast lines	Universal Express Pass or end day here.
The Cat in the Hat	n/a	thrill ride	4½ min.	All	Heavy	Universal Express Pass here or go at end of day.
Doctor Doom's Fearfall	52"	thrill ride	1 min.	10 and up	Fast lines	Go later in the day, on empty stomach.
★ Dudley Do-Right's Ripsaw Falls	44"	thrill ride	5½ min.	6 and up	Summer	Go in late afternoon, to cool down, or at day's end. There's no seat where you can stay dry.
★ Dueling Dragons	54"	thrill ride	2¼ min.	10 and up	Yes!	Ride after dark or early morning. Go for the rear car of Fire Dragon
★ Eighth Voyage of Sinbad	n/a	show	25 min.	All	Fast lines	Universal Express Pass or come 15 min. before show time. Don't sit too close up front.
Flying Unicorn	36"	thrill ride	1 min.	Under 7	Fast lines	Use Universal Express Pass if crowded.
High in the Sky Seuss Trolley Train Tour	34"	ride	3 min.	All	Moderate	Relatively new. You may have to wait.
★ Incredible Hulk Coaster	54"	thrill ride	2¼ min.	10 and up	Yes!	Come here first Effects best in the morning. The front row is best
Jurassic Park Discovery Center	n/a	walk through	Up to you	10 and up	ok	Go anytime.
Jurassic Park River Adventure	42"	thrill ride	6 min.	All	Yes!	Universal Express Pass. Toddlers may be scared.
One Fish, Two Fish, Red Fish, Blue Fish	n/a	ride	2+ min.	All	Moderate	Usually a wait, but kids think it's worth it.
Popeye & Bluto's Bilge-Rat Barges	42"	water-ride	5 min.	All	Yes!	Come early morning or before closing.
Poseidon's Fury	n/a	show	20 min.	6 and up	Heavy	Come at end of day. Stay to the left for best spot. Get in first row each time
Pteranodon Flyers	n/a	ride	2 min.	All	Perpetual	Skip this on your first visit.
Storm Force Accelatron	54"	thrill ride	2 min.	All	ok	Go whenever—except after you've eaten.

★ = FodorsChoice

Many of the cobblestone streets have paved paths, and photo spots are arranged for wheelchair accessibility. Various attractions have been retrofitted so that most can be boarded directly in a standard wheelchair; those using oversize vehicles or scooters must transfer to a standard model available at the ride's entrance—or into the ride vehicle itself. All outdoor shows have special viewing areas for wheelchairs, and all restaurants are wheelchair accessible.

ATTRACTIONS *Animal Actors on Location!,* the *Universal Horror Make-Up Show, Beetlejuice's Graveyard Revue, Twister ...* **Ride It Out,** and *Terminator 2 3-D* are all completely wheelchair-accessible, theater-style attractions. Good scripts and songs mean that even those with visual impairments can enjoy parts of all of these shows.

No motorized wheelchairs or electric convenience vehicles (ECVs) are permitted on any ride vehicle, at either park. To ride *E.T.* **Adventure** you must transfer to the ride vehicle or use a standard-size wheelchair. Service animals are not permitted. There is some sudden tilting and accelerating, but even those with most types of heart, back, or neck problems can ride in E.T.'s orbs (the spaceships) instead of the flying bicycles. Those who use wheelchairs must transfer to the ride vehicles to experience **Woody Woodpecker's Nuthouse Coaster,** but most of **Curious George Goes to Town** is barrier-free.

If you use a standard-size wheelchair or can transfer to one or to the ride vehicle directly, you can board **Earthquake,** *Jaws,* and *Men in Black* directly. Service animals should not ride, and neither should you if you find turbulence a problem. Note that guests with visual impairments as well as those using wheelchairs should cross San Francisco/Amity with care. The cobblestones are rough on wheelchair and stroller wheels.

One vehicle in **Jimmy Neutron's Nicktoon Blast** is equipped with an access door that allows for standard-size wheelchairs, and two vehicles in the back of the attraction have closed caption screens. *Shrek* **4-D** has eight handicap-equipped seats. Assisted listening devices are available at Guest Services.

Lucy: A Tribute is wheelchair accessible, but the TV-show excerpts shown on overhead screens are not closed-captioned. *Back to the Future* **The Ride** is not accessible to people who use wheelchairs, nor are service animals permitted.

SERVICES Many Universal Studios employees have had basic sign-language training; even some of the animated characters speak sign, but since many have only four fingers, it's an adapted version. Like Walt Disney World, Universal supplements the visuals with a special guidebook containing story lines and scripts for the main attractions. The *Studio Guide for Guests with Disabilities* pinpoints special entrances available for those with disabilities; these routes often bypass the main line. You can get this and various booklets at Guest Services, just inside the main entrance and to the right. There's an outgoing TTY series hearing-impaired system on the counter in Guest Services.

EATING AT UNIVERSAL STUDIOS

Most restaurants are on Plaza of the Stars and Hollywood Boulevard. Several accept "priority seating," which is not a reservation but an arrival time. You'll receive the first available seat after that particular time.

You can make arrangements up to 30 days in advance by calling or dropping by **Guest Services** (☎ *407/224–6350*) when you arrive or by heading over to the restaurant in person. In a sign of the times, trans-fat foods are out and healthful food is in.

FULL-SERVICE
RESTAURANTS

San Francisco/Amity's **Lombard's Landing** (☎ *407/224–6400*) is designed to resemble a warehouse from 19th-century San Francisco. The specialty is seafood (of course), including clams, shrimp, mussels, and catch of the day, but you can also get hamburgers, pastas, steak, and chicken.

Hidden in Production Central, **Finnegan's Bar & Grill** (☎ *407/363–8757*) is an Ellis Island–era New York dining room serving shepherd's pie, Irish stew, fish-and-chips, and steaks. Main courses start at $10; and Guinness, Harp, and Bass are on tap. Live Irish folk music completes the theme.

At the corner of Hollywood Boulevard and 8th Avenue—which turns into Sunset Boulevard along the bottom shore of the lagoon—is **Mel's Drive-In** (☎ *407/363–8766*) (no reservations), a flashy '50s eatery with a menu and decorative muscle cars straight out of *American Graffiti*. For burgers and fries, this is one of the best choices in the park, and it comes complete with a roving doo-wop group. You're on vacation—go ahead and have that extra-thick shake. Mel's is also a great place to meet, in case you decide to go your separate ways in the park.

SELF-SERVICE
RESTAURANTS

The **International Food Bazaar,** a food court near *Back to the Future The Ride*, has pizza, lasagna, fried chicken, meat loaf, gyros, stir-fried beef and other multicultural dishes at affordable prices—usually $7 to $9. The Italian Caesar and Greek salads are especially welcome on a muggy day.

Production Central's **Classic Monsters Cafe** resembles a mad scientist's laboratory. The self-serve restaurant is open seasonally and offers wood-fired oven pizzas, pastas, chopped chef salads, four-cheese ravioli, and rotisserie chicken. Frankenstein's monster and other scary characters from vintage Universal films make the rounds of the tables as you eat. Be sure to check out the monster-meets-celebrity pictures at the entrance.

GUIDED TOURS

Universal has several variations on **VIP Tours** (☎ *407/363–8295*), which offer what's called "front-of-the-line access" or, in plain English, the right to jump the line. It's the ultimate capitalist fantasy and worthwhile if you're in a hurry, if you're with a large group, if the day is crowded, and if you have the money to burn. The six-hour VIP tour costs $100 per person for one park and $125 for two parks. Exclusive eight-hour tours start at $1,400, not including sales tax. For $2,600, sign up for a two-day tour of both parks, which includes backstage access and discussions on the park's history, decorating, and landscaping. The tours also offer extras and upgrades such as priority restaurant seating, bilingual guides, gift bags, and valet parking. Best of all, the guides can answer practically any question you throw at them—they're masters of Universal trivia. Tours six hours and shorter are nonexclusive, which means you'll be touring with other guests. Eight-hour VIP tours are exclusive and geared to the desires and interests of your group.

UNIVERSAL CITYWALK

CityWalk is Universal's answer to Downtown Disney. They've gathered theme retail stores and kiosks, restaurants, and nightclubs in one spot—here they're right at the entrance to both Universal Studios Florida and Islands of Adventure. CityWalk attracts a mix of conventioneers, vacationers, and what seems to be Orlando's entire youth market. You may be too anxious to stop on your way into the parks and too tired to linger on your way out, but at some point on your vacation you may drop by for a drink at **Jimmy Buffett's Margaritaville,** a meal at **Emeril's,** a concert at **Hard Rock Live,** or a souvenir from one of several gift stores. Visiting the stores and restaurants is free, as is parking after 6 PM. The only price you'll have to pay is a cover charge for the nightclubs, or you can invest in the more sensible $9.95 Party Pass for admission to all the clubs all night long. Pay $13 and you can add a movie to your evening out. See Chapter 16, After Dark, for descriptions of CityWalk's bars and clubs.

WET 'N WILD

The world's first water park (as confirmed by *Aquatics International*), Wet 'n Wild opened in 1977 and quickly became known as the place for thrilling waterslides. Although it's now far from alone, Wet 'n Wild is still the nation's most popular water park, thanks to its quality, service, innovations, and ability to create more heart-stopping waterslides, rides, and tubing adventures than its competitors. There's a complete water playground for kids, numerous high-energy slides for adults, a lazy river ride, and some quiet sandy beaches on which you can stretch out and get a tan.

After skimming down a super-speedy waterslide, it may be time for a break. You can bring a cooler or stop for lunch at one of several food courts and find a picnic spot at various pavilions near the lakeside beach, pools, and attractions. Pools are heated in cooler weather, and Wet 'n Wild is one of the few water parks in the country to be open year-round.

If you're not a strong swimmer, don't worry. Ride entrances are marked with warnings to let you know which ones are safe for you, there are plenty of low-key attractions available, and during peak season as many as 400 lifeguards are on duty daily.

TIP SHEET

■ Avoid the peak months of June, July, and August.

■ Arrive 30 minutes before the park opens in the morning, or come on a cloudy day.

■ On the surface, there doesn't seem to be much reason to go to this park when it's gray and drizzly, but as a Wet 'n Wild spokeswoman observes, "This is a water park. If you aren't coming here to get wet, why are you here?" OK. If you do come on a day that rains, it will likely be a quick summer afternoon shower that will close attractions and clear pools only until 30 minutes or so after the thunder and lightning pass. If it looks like a soggy, thorough, all-day rain, skip it.

■ Wear a bathing suit (and a one-piece suit is better than a bikini). You can't wear cutoffs or anything that has rivets, metal buttons, or zippers.

■ If your bare feet aren't used to it, the rough and hot surface of the sidewalks and sandpaperlike pool bottoms can do a number on your soles. Bring a pair of wading slippers when you're walking around, but be ready to carry them as you're plunging down a slide.

■ Keep money, keys, and other valuables in a locker. They could get lost on the super slides. If you wear pre-scription sunglasses, you can bring them on the rides; just take them off and clutch them tightly before you take the plunge.

■ Keep in mind that lines here are Disney-esque. Once you think you're almost there, you discover there's another level or two to go. Get ready to be patient.

■ Bring a towel, but leave it behind when you ride.

■ Wear high SPF sunblock, and remember that you can get a sunburn even on a cloudy day.

■ Eat a high-protein meal to keep your energy going. A day here involves nearly nonstop walking, swimming, and climbing.

ADMISSION

Admission without tax is $35.95 for adults (10 and above) and $29.95 for children ages three to nine. The price drops by $10 roughly three to four hours before the park closes. Since closing times vary, call in advance to find out when the discount begins. For information about the Orlando FlexTicket, a combination ticket for all of the Universal Studios parks, see the Admission section at the front of this chapter. Parking is $8 for cars, $9 for RVs.

BASIC SERVICES

FACILITIES & SUPPLIES Don't think the expenses stop with parking and admission. If you came without a towel, you can rent one for $2 with a $2 deposit. Mighty small lockers, $5 with a $2 deposit, are near the entrance and at handy locations throughout the park. Tubes for the Wave Pool cost $4 with a $2 deposit. To save you $2, a combination package of all three is available.

There are dressing rooms (with lockers), showers, and rest rooms to the left just after the main entrance. Additional rest rooms are near the Bubble Up, First Aid, and the Surge.

Life jackets are provided by the staff. If you're looking for sunscreen, sunglasses, bathing suits, camera film, and other necessities, stop in the Breakers Beach Shop near the park entrance.

FIRST AID   The First Aid Stand is between Surf Grill and Pizza & Subs.

HOURS   Wet 'n Wild is open 365 days a year, from 10 to 5, with hours extending from 9 AM to 9 PM or later in summer. Call for exact hours during holiday periods.

INFORMATION   The Guest Services desk is to the left as you enter the park. For general information, call **Wet 'n Wild** (☎ *407/351–3200 recorded information, 407/351–1800 park operations*).

LOST THINGS & PEOPLE   If you plan to split up, be sure everyone knows where and when you plan to meet. Lifeguards look out for kids who might be lost. If they spot one, they'll take the child to Guest Services, which will page the parent or guardian. The Lost & Found is at Guest Services, to the left just after you walk through the entrance to Wet 'n Wild.

PICNICKING   You are welcome to picnic and to bring coolers with food into the park. However, glass containers and alcoholic beverages are not permitted. There are many picnic areas scattered around Wet 'n Wild, in both covered and open areas.

WHEELCHAIRS   Many of the paths are flat and easily accessible in a wheelchair; however, no rides accommodate people using wheelchairs. Wheelchairs are available for $5 with a $25 refundable deposit.

WET 'N WILD ATTRACTIONS

Black Hole. One of the most popular attractions here, this two-person tube ride (solo travelers share a lift with a stranger) starts in the bright light of day and suddenly plunges into a curvaceous 500-foot-long pitch-black tube illuminated only by a guiding, glowing line. The lack of light makes the spinning, twisting, 1,000-gallon-a-minute torrent more fun, and you'll likely be screaming your head off as you zip into curves and up the enclosed watery-banked turns. *Minimum height: 36", 48" without an adult.*

The Blast. This two-passenger ride sends you and a friend bumping down twists and turns through explosive pipe bursts and drenching waterspouts leading up to a final waterfall plunge. *Minimum height: 36", 48" without an adult.*

Blue Niagara. For a real thrill head to the top of this giant, six-story-tall slide. Twin tubes wrap around each other like snakes. Inside is a rushing waterfall. Since the tubes are roughly horizontal, you have the luxury of keeping your eyes open and watching the action unfold as you're shot through the curves. With two tubes, the line usually moves fairly quickly. *Minimum height: 48" without an adult.*

Bomb Bay. Lines move quickly here, but not because the capacity is great. It's because a lot of kids chicken out once they reach the top. If you challenge yourself to the ultimate free fall, here's what happens: you step inside a large enclosed cylinder mounted above a nearly vertical drop. The attendant looks through the glass door to make sure your arms and legs are crossed (thereby preventing wedgies), and then punches a button to release the trapdoor. Like a bomb dropping out of a plane, you free-fall for 76 feet and then skim down the long, steep slide. The force of the water on your feet, legs, and back can be substantial, rivaling the emotional toll it took to do it in the first place. *Minimum height: 48" without an adult.*

Bubba Tub. Because up to four people can take this ride together, this is one of the park's most popular attractions. After scaling the platform, your group boards a huge waiting inner tube. From the top of the six-story slide it flows over the edge and starts an up-and-down, triple-dip, roller-coaster ride that splashes down into a watery pool. *Minimum height: 36", 48" without an adult.*

Bubble Up. After catching sight of this enormous (about 12 feet tall), wet beach ball, many kids race right over to try to climb to the top and then slide back down. Surrounding the ball is a wading pool, a respite between attempts to scale the watery mountain. *Height: 42"–64" only.*

Der Stuka. Adjacent to Bomb Bay is a steep slide that offers a similar thrill to that of Bomb Bay, but without the trap-door drop. *Der Stuka,* "steep hill" in German, is hard to beat for sheer exhilaration. After climbing the winding six-story platform, you sit down on a horizontal slide, nudge yourself forward a few inches, and then gravity takes over. You're hurtling down a slippery, 250-foot-long speed slide that will tax your back and test the security of your bathing suit. This one's a real scream. *Minimum height: 48".*

Disco H20. Here's something even the folks at Studio 54 never dreamed of: a four-person raft that floats into a swirling aquatic nightclub. Once inside the 70-foot-tall building, your raft goes into a spin cycle as you're bombarded with sparkling lights, disco balls, and the sounds of the '70s greatest hits. You must be 36" in height or you'll upset the bouncer. *Minimum height: 36", 48" without an adult.*

The Flyer. This four-person toboggan carries you into switchback curves and down suddenly steep drops. The turns are similar to those on a real toboggan run. *Minimum height: 36", 48" without an adult.*

Hydra Fighter. Attached by a bungee cord to several towers are several two-person seats—each with a fire hose mounted on the front. Sitting back-to-back, you and your partner alternate between firing the hoses. The springy cord you're on starts to hoist you up and then from side to side. The stronger the stream of water, the higher and faster you go in all directions (and the farther you fall). Try to avoid sharing a seat with a chubby guy—it kills the bounce. Between getting everyone situated, letting them ride, and getting them unloaded, this one can mean a long wait. *Minimum height: 56".*

Kids' Park. Designed for children under 48", Kids' Park is like a day at the beach. There's a kid-size sand castle to play in, and a 5-foot-tall bucket that dumps 250 gallons of water every few minutes onto a seashell-decorated awning, where it splashes off to spray all and sundry. In the center is a pool surrounded by miniaturized versions of the more popular grown-up attractions and rides. Children overjoyed when they play with a garden hose will go absolutely nuts when they see that they can slide, splash, squirt, and swim on rides here. Tables and chairs go fast, with many families here for nearly their whole visit.

Knee Ski/Wakeboard. A molasses-slow line marks the entrance to this seasonal attraction. A moving cable with ski ropes attached encircles a large lake. After donning protective headgear and a life vest, you kneel on a knee board or try to balance yourself on a wakeboard, grab a ski rope, and are given the opportunity to circumnavigate the lake. The ½-mi ride includes five turns: roughly 75% of the riders wipe out after turn number one, and 90% are gone by turn two. Only the agile and athletic few make it the distance. Hint: if you wipe out before turn one, you get to go back and try again. *Minimum height: 56".*

Lazy River. Had enough? Then settle into an inner tube for a peaceful trip down a gently moving stream. Bask in the sun as you drift by colorful flowers and tropical greenery. It's a nice break when your body just can't handle any more 45-degree drops.

Mach 5. After grabbing a soft foam board, you scale a few steps and arrive at one of three waterslides. Conventional wisdom says that Lane B is the best, but it's possible all three are the same. Riding on your belly, you zip through some great twists, feel the sensation of hitting the high banks, and then splash down in a flood of water. It's mucho fun. *No height requirement, but participants must be able to control the board.*

The Storm. At the top of the tower, two tubes carry a torrent of water. Climb in the tube, shove off in the midst of a tidal wave, and the slow, curving arc takes you around and around until you reach a 30-foot diameter bowl. Now you spin around again like soap suds whirling around a sink drain. After angular momentum has had its fun, you drop through a hole in the bottom of the bowl into a small pool. After you get your bearings and find the surface, you may be tempted to climb up and do it again. *Minimum height: 48".*

Surf Lagoon. This 17,000-square-foot lagoon is as close to a beach as you'll get in the park, which explains why it's generally packed. Also known as the Wave Pool, it's just past the turnstiles. Every so often, the lagoon is buffeted by 4-feet-high waves, which elicit screams of delight from kids. Likewise, adults are thrilled to find that the money they spent on the kid's floats, surfboards, and inner tubes was worth it.

The Surge. The title overstates the thrill of this ride, although it borders on exhilarating. Up to four passengers can fit in this giant raft: once you've gone over the lip of the first drop, there's no turning back. The raft zips down five stories while twisting and turning through a series of steeply banked curves and beneath waterfalls. If you or your kids are too nervous for rides like Bomb Bay or the Black Hole, then this is probably a safe bet. *Minimum height: 36", 48" without an adult.*

The Wild One. Open seasonally (usually April through September), this is a large, two-person inner tube that's towed around the lake. The ease of staying afloat is countered by the challenge of hanging on when you cross the boat's wake. *Minimum height: 51".*

14

SeaWorld Orlando & Discovery Cove

WORD OF MOUTH

"We loved SeaWorld—the shows were the best part, and the kids loved being able to feed and pet the dolphins."

—klw25

"We went to Discovery Cove when our children were 10 and 12. It was a wonderful experience, and well worth the money! Our favorite part was actually the snorkeling, rather than the dolphin encounter."

—Dreamer2

"Swim with the dolphins at Discovery Cove. Expensive? Yes. Worth it? Yes."

—Laura

Updated
by Gary
McKechnie

LESS GLITZY THAN WALT DISNEY World or Universal, SeaWorld and its sister park, Discovery Cove, are definitely worth a visit for a low-key, relaxing, ocean-theme experience.

Ten minutes from both Universal and Walt Disney World, both parks are designed for animal lovers and anyone who prefers more natural pleasures. The difference between the two is in the price and activities. At SeaWorld you'll watch a series of high-energy circus shows involving dolphins, whales, sea lions, a huge walrus, and even cats and dogs. Plus you can ride two thrilling roller coasters, one of which (Kraken) is considered one of the scariest rides in Florida.

Discovery Cove is more of a laid-back oasis. You change into your bathing suit and spend the day snorkeling among tropical fish, relaxing on the beach, and, for a short period, interacting with dolphins. You can also get up close to tropical birds in the aviary. For the luxury of visiting a faux tropical island, you'll pay roughly four times as much as a ticket to SeaWorld, but your ticket actually includes a pass to either SeaWorld or Busch Gardens in Tampa (which must be used within seven days).

15

SEAWORLD ORLANDO

There's a whole lot more to SeaWorld than Shamu, the "stage name" used for its mammoth killer-whale mascots. Sure, you can be splashed by the whales, stroke a stingray, see manatees face-to-snout, learn to love an eel, and be spat at by a walrus. But as the world's largest marine adventure park, SeaWorld celebrates all the mammals, birds, fish, and reptiles that live in and near the ocean.

Although SeaWorld can't rival Disney World when it comes to park design and attention to detail, it does offer a somewhat gentler and less-hurried touring experience governed mostly by show schedules. Every attraction is designed to showcase the beauty of the marine world and demonstrate ways that humans can protect its waters and wildlife. And because there are more exhibits and shows than rides—believe it or not, there are only three actual rides in the entire park—you can go at your own pace without that hurry-up-and-wait feeling.

First-timers may be slightly confused by the lack of distinct "lands" here—SeaWorld's performance venues, attractions, and activities surround a 17-acre lake, and the artful landscaping, curving paths, and concealing greenery sometimes lead to wrong turns. But armed with a map that lists show times, it's easy to plan a chronological approach that flows easily from one show and attraction to the next and allows enough time for rest stops and meal breaks.

Numbers in the margin correspond to points of interest on the SeaWorld map.

ADMISSION

At this writing, regular one-day tickets to SeaWorld cost $64.95 for adults, and $53.95 for children ages 3 to 9, not including tax. For

TOP SEAWORLD ATTRACTIONS

Kraken. SeaWorld's main thrill ride takes you on a high-speed chase with a dragon. But who's chasing who? Just don't disturb the dragon eggs on your way out.

Pets Ahoy. Anyone who has ever loved a pet, or wanted one, has to see the talented cats, dogs, birds, and pig in this show.

Journey to Atlantis. This somewhat dated Splash Mountain-esque ride still provides thrills on its last, steep, wet drop.

Believe. The park's flagship attraction and mascot are irresistible. In a show four years in the making, you'll see several Shamus performing graceful aquabatics that are guaranteed to thrill.

Clyde and Seamore Take Pirate Island. Head for Sea Lion & Otter Stadium to watch this slapstick comedy routine starring an adorable team of water mammals and their trainers.

permission to bypass the admission line at the park, purchase and print out your tickets online at ⊕*www.seaworld.com.*

DISCOUNTS SeaWorld offers what they call their **Anytime** pass. This is a complimentary, nontransferable ticket valid for admission to the park for seven consecutive days. Simply visit the park and before you leave for the day, exchange this ticket at the Anytime Window inside the park for a personal pass that allows you to come and go as you please for the next week. Make sure your entire party is together when arranging the extended admission. Standard discounts are available for senior citizens, AAA members, military personnel, and guests with disabilities. Guests with visual or hearing impairments are eligible for 50% off the ticket price. Florida residents have the added advantage of buying a Fun Card, which offers unlimited admission between January 1 and December 31 at a very affordable $64.95 for adults and $54.95 for children.

The **Orlando FlexTicket** (☎*800/224-3838* ⊕*www.officialticketcenter. com*), which covers SeaWorld, Busch Gardens Tampa Bay, and the Universal parks, is similar to Walt Disney World's pass system. The base price of a four-park ticket, which allows you up to 14 consecutive days of unlimited admission to Universal Orlando, Wet 'n Wild, and SeaWorld is $189.95 for adults, and $155.95 for children 3 to 9. The five-park ticket gets you in to all of the above as well as Busch Gardens and costs $234.95 for adults and $199.95 for children. Sea-World–Busch Gardens combination Value Tickets, for one day at each park, cost $99.95 for adults and $89.95 for children 3 to 9. None of these prices include sales tax.

BABY CARE

Diaper-changing tables are in or near most women's rest rooms and in the men's rest room at the front entrance, near Shamu's Emporium. You can buy diapers at machines in all changing areas and at Shamu's

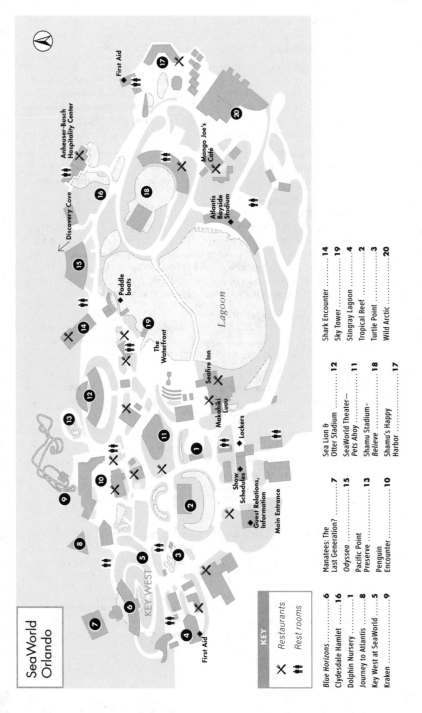

SeaWorld Orlando

First Aid

Anheuser-Busch Hospitality Center

Discovery Cove

First Aid

Mango Joe's Café

Atlantis Bayside Stadium

Paddle boats

Lagoon

The Waterfront

Seafire Inn

Makahiki Luau

Lockers

Show Schedules

Guest Relations, Information

Main Entrance

KEY WEST

First Aid

15

KEY

✕ *Restaurants*
♦♦ *Rest rooms*

Blue Horizons **6**
Clydesdale Hamlet **16**
Dolphin Nursery **1**
Journey to Atlantis **8**
Key West at SeaWorld **5**
Kraken **9**

Manatees: The
Last Generation? **7**
Odyssea **15**
Pacific Point
Preserve **13**
Penguin
Encounter **10**

Sea Lion &
Otter Stadium **12**
SeaWorld Theater—
Pets Ahoy **11**
Shamu Stadium—
Believe **18**
Shamu's Happy
Harbor **17**

Shark Encounter **14**
Sky Tower **19**
Stingray Lagoon **4**
Tropical Reef **2**
Turtle Point **3**
Wild Arctic **20**

Emporium. A special area for nursing is alongside the women's rest room at Friends of the Wild gift shop, equidistant from SeaWorld Theater, Penguin Encounter, and Sea Lion & Otter Stadium.

Gerber baby food is sold by request at most restaurants (for yourself you may want to order a more substantial entrée), as well as at the Children's Store. For more infant items you'll have to leave the park for a short drive to a nearby supermarket or drugstore. Ask for directions to Publix or Walgreen's on International Drive, the CVS Pharmacy on Central Florida Parkway, or Kmart on Turkey Lake Road.

CAMERAS & FILM
Memory cards for digital cameras, as well as disposable 35mm and APS (advanced photo system) cameras and film, are for sale on the premises.

GETTING THERE & AROUND
SeaWorld is just off the intersection of I–4 and the Beachline Expressway, 10 minutes south of downtown Orlando and 15 minutes from Orlando International Airport. Of all the Central Florida theme parks, it's the easiest to find. If you're heading west on I–4 (toward Disney), take Exit 72 onto the Beachline Expressway (aka Highway 528) and take the first exit onto International Drive and follow signs a short distance to the parking lot. Heading east, take Exit 71.

HEALTH SERVICES/FIRST AID
First Aid Centers, staffed by registered nurses, are behind Stingray Lagoon and near Shamu's Happy Harbor. In case of an emergency ask any SeaWorld employee to contact Security.

HOURS
SeaWorld opens daily at 9 AM, but closing hours vary between 6 and 7 PM, and, during the holidays, as late as 11 PM. To be safe, call in advance for park hours.

INFORMATION
The **Main Information Center** is just inside the park, near the entrance. Pick up a map and showtime listing. You can also buy tickets for the luau, Discovery Cove, and guided tours here, as well as make dinner reservations. For general information, contact **SeaWorld Orlando** (☎*407/351–3600 or 800/327–2420* ⊕*www.seaworld.com*).

LOCKERS
Coin-operated lockers are available inside the main entrance and to the right as you enter, next to Shamu's Emporium. There are also lockers throughout the park and, conveniently, by the wild coaster, Kraken. The cost ranges between 50¢ and $1.50, depending on size.

LOST THINGS & PEOPLE
All employees who see lost-looking children take them to the Information Center, where you can also go to report lost children. A parkwide paging system also helps reunite parents with kids. The center operates as the park's Lost & Found, too.

TIP SHEET

■ Avoid a weekend visit or one during school holidays if you can, since those are the busiest times.

■ Wear comfortable sneakers—no heels or slip-on sandals—since you may get your feet wet on the water rides.

■ Pack dry clothes for yourself and your children if you intend to get wet by sitting close to the front at the Shamu show or riding Journey to Atlantis.

■ If you prefer to take your own food, remove all plastic straws and lids before you arrive—they can harm fish and birds.

■ Budget ahead for food for the animals—feeding time is a major part of SeaWorld charm. A small carton of fish costs $5.

■ Arrive at least 30 minutes early for the Shamu show, which generally fills to capacity on even the slowest days. Prepare to get wet in the "splash zone" down front.

PACKAGE PICKUP

Purchases made anywhere in the park can be sent to Package Pickup, in Shamu's Emporium, on request. Allow two hours for your purchases to make it there.

PET CARE CENTER

For $6, the pet care center near the main entrance accommodates dogs, cats, hamsters, and whatever other creatures you may be traveling with. Dogs must be walked every two to three hours throughout the day. For meals, you're expected to bring food for your pet, but SeaWorld will spring for the water.

PARKING

Parking costs $10 per car, $12 for an RV or camper. Preferred parking, which costs $15, allows you to park in the six rows closest to the front gate.

STROLLER & WHEELCHAIR RENTALS

Strollers ($10 for a single and $18 for a double), standard wheelchairs ($10), and electric wheelchairs ($35) can be rented at the Information Center.

SEAWORLD ATTRACTIONS

DOLPHIN NURSERY

❶ Crowds: Not a problem.
Strategy: Go during a Shamu show so the kids can be up front.
Audience: All ages.
Rating: ★★

In a large pool, dolphin moms and babies (with birth dates posted on signs) play and leap and splash. You can't get close enough to pet or feed them, so you'll have to be content peering from several feet away and asking the host questions during a regular Q and A session. Here's a popular answer: No, you can't take one home. Hint: if you just *have* to touch a dolphin, head over to Dolphin Cove in the Key West section.

TROPICAL REEF

2 **Crowds:** Not usually a problem.
Strategy: Go at the end of the day—because it's near the entrance, most people stop here on their way in.
Audience: All ages.
Rating: ★★

A good place to get out of the sun or rain, this indoor walk-through attraction contains 30 small aquariums filled with weird, ugly, and/or beautiful tropical fish, eels, worms, and crustaceans. The fish lie camouflaged on the bottom, dig holes, glow in the dark, or float lazily and stare at you through the glass. Clear and concise printed descriptions reveal interesting facts about each tank's inhabitants, leading to comments such as, "Hey, cool, look at this one!" or "Hey, let's go get some sushi."

TURTLE POINT

3 **Crowds:** Sporadically crowded, but generally enough space for all to get a good view.
Strategy: Go anytime.
Audience: All ages.
Rating: ★★

At this re-creation of a small beach and lagoon, many of the cute sea turtles (loggerheads, green, and hawksbill) basking in the sun or drifting in the water were rescued from predators or fishing nets. Injuries make it impossible for these lumbering beauties to return to the wild. A kiosk is filled with sea turtle info, and an educator is usually on hand to answer questions. The kiosk is well worth a brief look.

STINGRAY LAGOON

4 **Crowds:** Can make it hard to get to the animals during busy seasons.
Strategy: Walk by if it's crowded, but return before dusk, when the smelt concession stand closes.
Audience: All ages.
Rating: ★★★

In a broad shallow pool, dozens of stingrays are close enough to touch, as evidenced by the many outstretched hands surrounding the rim. Smelts, silversides, shrimp, and squid are available for $5 a tray at nearby concession stands. The fishy treats are a delicacy for the rays, and when they flap up for lunch you can feed them and stroke their velvety skin. Even though they still have their stingers they won't hurt you; they just want food. This is one of the most rewarding experiences for everyone, and the animals are obligingly hungry all day. Look for the nursery pool with its baby rays.

KEY WEST AT SEAWORLD

⑤ Crowds: Can get thick but not overwhelming.
Strategy: While on your way to or from a show, carve out some time to see the dolphins. If things are too crowded, go shopping until the crowds disperse.
Audience: All ages.
Rating: ★★★

This laid-back 5-acre area is modeled after Key West, Florida's southernmost outpost, where the sunsets are spectacular and the mood is festive. There are no distinct "lands" within SeaWorld, but Key West at SeaWorld comes close, containing individual tropical-style shows and attractions within its loosely defined borders. Along with an obvious Jimmy Buffett-y "island paradise" feel, a huge pool holds a few dozen Atlantic bottlenose dolphins that you can feed and pet. Fish trays cost $5.

BLUE HORIZONS

⑥ Duration: 30 min.
Crowds: Heavy due to the attraction's newness.
Strategy: Arrive 20 min early.
Audience: All ages.
Rating: ★★

Blue Horizons blends a dolphin-and-trainer show with Cirque du Soleil–style costuming and acrobatics. The story starts with a young girl's fantasy of life in the sea and kicks off with high-energy and crowd-pleasing dolphin tricks. Next comes a "bird woman" who flies in via a thick cable (the presence of which kind of breaks the illusion) although the fantasy returns when a series of high divers leap repeatedly from two high towers, an act followed by two acrobats performing impressive and repeated bouncing jumps on bungee cords. After two false killer whales scoot around the pool, splashing, diving, and jumping, the tale concludes with little Marina getting a chance to surf on the back of a dolphin and even fly. Overall, this is a great family show that blends together everything SeaWorld does best above and below the water.

MANATEES: THE LAST GENERATION?

⑦ Crowds: Since the area is fairly large, that "crowded" feeling is nonexistent.
Strategy: Go during a Shamu show and not right after a dolphin show.
Audience: All ages.
Rating: ★★★

If you don't have time to explore Florida's springs in search of manatees in the wild, then don't miss the chance to see this. The lumbering, whiskered manatees, which look like a cross between walruses and air bags, were brought here after near-fatal brushes with motorboats. Tramping down a clear tunnel beneath the naturalistic, 3½-acre lagoon, you enter Manatee Theater, where a film describes the lives of these gentle giants and the ways in which humans threaten the species' survival. In Manatee Habitat, a 300,000-gallon tank with a 126-foot seamless acrylic

15

viewing panel, you can look in on the lettuce-chomping mammals as well as native fish, including tarpon, gar, and snook. Keep an eye out for mama manatees and their nursing calves.

EN ROUTE

It's hard to pass up a plush Shamu—not least because the dolls are available all over the park. But if you're looking for a slightly less conventional souvenir, consider a soft manatee. You can buy either one at **Manatee Gifts**. Proceeds from the toys go to benefit a manatee preservation organization.

JOURNEY TO ATLANTIS

❽ **Duration:** 6 min.

Crowds: Large.

Strategy: Make a beeline here first thing in the morning or go about an hour before closing; going at night is definitely awesome, and the wait, if there is one, will be cooler.

Audience: Older children and adults; definitely not for the faint of heart or for anyone with a fear of dark, enclosed spaces. Minimum height: 42".

Rating: ★★★

SeaWorld's first entry in Florida's escalating "coaster wars" combines elements of a high-speed water ride and a roller coaster with lavish special effects. There are frequent twists, turns, and short, shallow dives but few hair-raising plunges except for the first, which sends you nearly 60 feet into the main harbor (plan on getting soaked to the skin), and the final drop, a 60-foot nosedive into S-shape, bobsledlike curves. Like most other attractions, this has a story line that doesn't really matter, but here it is: the lost continent of Atlantis has risen in the harbor of a quaint Greek fishing village, and you board a rickety Greek fishing boat to explore it. Once you're inside, an ominous current tugs at your boat, and an old fisherman offers a golden sea horse (actually Hermes—the messenger of the gods—in disguise!) to protect you from the evil Sirens. That's it. The wild, watery battle between Hermes and Allura (queen of the Sirens) is all a ploy to crank up effects using liquid crystal display technology, lasers, and holographic illusions.

KRAKEN

Duration: 6 min.

Crowds: Expect lines.

Strategy: Get to the park when it opens and head straight to Kraken; otherwise, hit it close to closing or during the *Blue Horizons* show.

Audience: Older children and adults. Minimum height: 54".

Rating: ★★★

Many people head straight for Kraken when the park opens, and as soon as you see its loops and dips, you'll know why. Kraken, at 149 feet, is the second-tallest coaster in Florida (right after SheikRa at Busch Gardens). With floorless seats, seven inversions, and moments of weightlessness, it packs a serious punch. Named after an angry monster, this wickedly fast coaster will plunge you underground three times, lift you higher, drop you longer, and spiral you faster than any coaster in Florida. No bags are allowed past the turnstiles (although you could probably use a barf bag); and it'll cost 50¢ to leave them in a locker. It's worth the investment—this is one cool coaster.

PENGUIN ENCOUNTER

⑩ Duration: Stay as long as you like.

Crowds: Sometimes gridlocked despite the moving walkway nudging visitors past the glassed-in habitat.

Strategy: Go while the dolphin and sea lion shows are on, and before you've gotten soaked at Journey to Atlantis, or you'll feel as icy as the penguins' environment.

Audience: All ages.

Rating: ★★

If you saw *March of the Penguins,* you'll have to visit the stars of this low-key walk-through attraction. In a large white building between the Dolphin Stadium and the Sea Lion & Otter Stadium, 17 species of penguin scoot around a refrigerated re-creation of Antarctica. They're as cute as can be, waddling across icy promontories and plopping into frigid waters to display their aquatic skills. You watch an average day in their world through the thick see-through walls. A moving walkway rolls you past at a slow pace, but you can also step off to an area where you can stand and marvel at these tuxedo-clad creatures as they dive into 45°F (7°C) water and are showered with three tons of snow a day. Nearby, a similar viewing area for puffins and murres is nearly as entertaining.

SEAWORLD THEATER—PETS AHOY

Duration: 20–25 min.

Crowds: Can be substantial on busy days.

Strategy: Gauge the crowds and get there early if necessary.

Audience: All ages.

Rating: ★★★

A dozen dogs, 18 cats, and an assortment of ducks, doves, parrots, and a pig (nearly all rescued from the local animal shelter) are the stars of this lively, hilarious show. The animals perform a series of complex stunts on a stage that looks like a seaside village. No matter how many times you see it, *Pets Ahoy* will never fail to amaze you. These cute-as-a-button actors perform feats that are each more incredible than the last, eventually culminating in a hilarious finale. Surely this is one of the best family friendly shows in Florida. Stick around and you'll have a chance to shake paws with the stars.

SEA LION & OTTER STADIUM

⑫ Duration: 40 min, including the 15-min preshow.

Crowds: No problem.

Strategy: Sit toward the center for the best view, and don't miss the beginning.

Audience: All ages.

Rating: ★★★

Along with shows starring Shamu and the dolphins, the show here is one of the park's top crowd-pleasers. A multilevel pirate ship forms the set for *Clyde and Seamore Take Pirate Island,* a drama in which SeaWorld's celebrated otters, walruses, and California sea lions prevail over piratical treachery. During the performance, they prove that they can outperform the human actors in a hilarious swashbuckling adventure that revolves around lost loot, pirate plunder, and misadventure on the high seas. Get ready for plenty of audience interaction, cheap laughs, and good-natured gags designed to please the kids. Be sure to arrive at least 15 minutes early to catch the preshow—the mime is always a crowd favorite.

PACIFIC POINT PRESERVE

13 **Crowds:** Not a problem.
Strategy: Go anytime.
Audience: All ages.
Rating: ★★★

A nonstop chorus of "aarrrps" and "yawps" coming from behind Clyde and Seamore's stadium will lead you to the 2½-acre home for California sea lions and harbor and fur seals. This naturalistic expanse of beaches, waves, and huge outcroppings of upturned rock was designed to duplicate the rocky northern Pacific coast. You can stroll around the edge of the surf zone, a favorite hangout for fun-loving pinnipeds, and peep at their underwater activities through the Plexiglas wall at one side of the tank. Buy some smelts and watch the sea lions sing for their supper from close up.

SHARK ENCOUNTER

14 **Duration:** Plan to spend 20 min.
Crowds: Most significant when adjacent sea lion show gets out.
Strategy: Go during the sea lion show.
Audience: All ages.
Rating: ★★★

Within this large, innocuous white structure are some thoroughly creepy critters: eels, barracuda, sharks, and poisonous fish. You walk through large transparent tubes as the fish and eels swim all around you. There's a chance you'll come across a few creatures that you've probably never seen or even imagined before, like the weedy sea dragon and his cousin, the leafy sea dragon, which are cute little creatures that look like branches of a tree. For truth in advertising, there are a half dozen species of shark alone in some 300,000 gallons of water. You can time your visit to coincide with a meal at the extraordinarily well designed **Sharks Underwater Grill,** where you can order fresh fish and Floribbean cuisine while watching your entrées' cousins.

ODYSSEA

15 **Duration:** 30 min.
Crowds: Heavy, but the auditorium seats more than 1,000 so you won't feel packed in.
Strategy: Arrive at least 15 minutes before curtain for a wide choice of seats. You'll be rewarded with an entertaining preshow.
Audience: All ages.
Rating: ★★

Replacing the long-running and successful *Cirque de la Mer*, this show also stars Peruvian silent comic Cesar Aedo as an innocent spectator who's whisked into a mystical underwater world where he witnesses the performances of sea creatures. With this story line, the show can now present the type of circus acts you've probably seen several times before: a contortionist in a clamshell who can balance herself on one hand, gymnasts in a "kelp bed" twirling around on ropes, and trampoline artists dressed as penguins. Kind of odd. What you likely haven't seen is the giant, accordionlike, tubular worm that, well, you just have to see it. All in all, *Odyssea* is fun and free entertainment.

CLYDESDALE HAMLET

16 **Duration:** You'll probably stay between 10 and 15 min.
Crowds: Very light.
Strategy: Go anytime.
Audience: All ages.
Rating: ★

15

At its core, this is a walk around the stable where the hulking Budweiser Clydesdales are kept, and a look at the clean corral where they get a chance to romp and play. A statue of a mighty stallion—which kids are encouraged to climb upon—makes a good theme-park photo opportunity.

NEED A BREAK? You can score two free beers (if you're over 21) from the **Anheuser-Busch Hospitality Center**, a cafeteria near Clydesdale Hamlet.

SHAMU'S HAPPY HARBOR

17 **Crowds:** Often a challenge.
Strategy: Don't go first thing in morning or you'll never drag your child away; but if you go midafternoon or near dusk, expect plenty of hubbub. Bring a towel to dry them off.
Audience: Toddlers through grade-schoolers.
Rating: ★★★

If you want to take a break while your kids exhaust the last ounce of energy their little bodies contain, bring them here. This sprawling, towering, 3-acre outdoor play area has places to crawl, climb, explore, bounce, and get wet. There's also a four-story net climb and adjacent arcade with midway games. Youngsters go wild for the tent with an air-mattress floor, pipes to crawl through, and "ball rooms," one for toddlers and one for grade-schoolers, with thousands of plastic balls to wade through. With big sailing ships to explore and water to play in and around, Happy Harbor is sure to be a favorite of any high-energy kid.

SHAMU STADIUM

Duration: 30 min.
Crowds: Sometimes a problem.
Strategy: Go 45 minutes early for early-afternoon show. Close-up encounters through the Plexiglas walls are not to be missed, so trot on down.
Audience: All ages.

Rating: ★★★

This is the place. Within this stadium is Shamu, SeaWorld's orca mascot, starring in *Believe*, which (because we're talking about whales here) took more than four years to perfect. In the show, Shamu et al perform awe-inspiringly choreographed moves against the backdrop of an elaborate three-story set, and an 80-foot panoramic LED screen within the shape of a tail fluke helps illuminate the action. It's quite amazing, really. As whales weighing as much as *10,000 pounds* demonstrate their grace and agility, they are actually performing a kind of breathtaking "killer whale ballet" to the corresponding beat of an original musical score. Look to the wide screens for above- and below-water views of the stars.

NEED A BREAK? A boardwalk leads from Shamu Stadium across the lagoon to the **Waterfront**, a Mediterranean-style faux waterfront village lined with shops, eateries, kiosks, and street performers. Even more laid-back than the rest of the park, this is a perfect spot to relax if you can remember that's the purpose of your vacation. Although there are scheduled performances, chances are you'll just wander through the area en route to another attraction and catch some strolling musicians. The restaurants have entertainment, too, like at **Seafire Inn** where guests can enjoy a live family-friendly musical stage. Shops include **Oyster's Secret**, where guests can chose an oyster and find a pearl inside; and **Allura's Treasure Trove**, a toy shop featuring candy and toys. Summer and holiday fireworks displays go up from the Waterfront.

SKY TOWER
⑲ Crowds: Fairly light.
Strategy: Look for a line and go if there's none.
Audience: All ages.
Rating: ★★

The focal point of the park is this 400-foot-tall tower, the main mast for a revolving double-decker platform. During the six-minute rotating round-trip up and down, you'll get the inside scoop on the park's history, its attractions, and surrounding sights. There's a separate $3 admission for this tower ride. Adjacent to the tower is Oyster's Secret, a small area where you can sit and watch pearl divers snag oysters.

WILD ARCTIC
⑳ Crowds: Expect a wait during peak seasons.
Strategy: Go early, late, or during a Shamu show. You can skip the simulated helicopter ride if you just want to see the mammals.
Audience: All ages. Minimum height for motion option: 42".
Rating: ★★★

Inside this pseudo–ice station, you embark on one of SeaWorld's three rides, a flight-simulator helicopter ride leading to rooms with interactive, educational displays. If your stomach can handle the rolls and pitches of a virtual helicopter, it makes for scary, enjoyable, queasy fun. Afterward, there are above- and below-water viewing stations where

BLITZ TOUR

BEST OF THE PARK

Although there's room for all at the stadiums, the other attractions—especially Penguin Encounter and Key West at SeaWorld—can get unpleasantly crowded, and there may be lines at Wild Arctic, Shark Encounter, and Journey to Atlantis.

After passing the turnstiles, go straight ahead to the information desk for a park map and schedule of the day's shows. In this courtyard, take a moment to review show times and plan your day. With luck you can set up a clockwise tour of the park by seeing *Blue Horizons,* then visiting no-line attractions like **Turtle Point, Stingray Lagoon,** and **Dolphin Cove.** While you're in the neighborhood, allow time to see **Manatees.**

A few feet away are the park's two roller coasters, **Kraken** and **Journey to Atlantis.** Chances are there'll be a line, so you'll have to decide whether you want to stay or return once the crowds have thinned. **Penguin Encounter** is a good next stop, followed by a chance to visit and feed the sea lions at **Pacific Point Preserve.** Remember to keep track of the time so you can find a good seat at the **Sea Lion & Otter Stadium.** If you've built up an appetite by now, you may want to grab a quick bite at the **Smoky**

Creek Grill or **Seafire Inn.**

Shark Encounter is the next upcoming popular attraction, followed by the

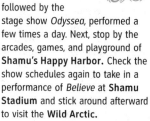

stage show *Odyssea,* performed a few times a day. Next, stop by the arcades, games, and playground of **Shamu's Happy Harbor.** Check the show schedules again to take in a performance of *Believe* at **Shamu Stadium** and stick around afterward to visit the **Wild Arctic.**

You've now seen most of the attractions, and you'll likely have time to see the **Dolphin Nursery** and **Tropical Reef** before heading back to **Key West at SeaWorld.**

ON RAINY DAYS

Although SeaWorld gives the impression of open-air roominess, nearly a third of the attractions are actually indoors, and many others are shielded from the elements by canopies, cantilevered roofs, or tautly stretched tarpaulins. Rides that may close during a thunderstorm include Journey to Atlantis, Kraken, Sky Tower, Shamu's Happy Harbor, and the Paddle Boats. If you're unprepared for a cloudburst, pick up a poncho at one of the ubiquitous concession stands, and dive right in.

15

you can watch beluga whales blowing bubble rings, polar bears paddling around with their toys, and groaning walruses trying to hoist themselves onto a thick shelf of ice.

DISABILITIES & ACCESSIBILITY

ATTRACTIONS With wide sidewalks and gentle inclines to the seats at shows, SeaWorld may be Florida's most accessible theme park. The **Dolphin Stadium, Sea Lion & Otter Stadium, SeaWorld Theater,** and **Shamu Stadium** all provide reserved seating areas that are accessible and have entry via sloping ramps. The stadium shows usually fill to capacity, so for your choice of seats plan to arrive 30 minutes before each show, 45 minutes in peak seasons.

At Shamu Stadium, the reserved seating area is inside the splash zone, so if you don't want to get soaking wet, get a host or hostess to recommend another place to sit.

Penguin Encounter, Shark Encounter, Tropical Reef, and **Journey to Atlantis** are all wheelchair accessible. To ride the moving-sidewalk viewing areas in Penguin Encounter, Shark Encounter, and Journey to Atlantis, you must transfer to a standard wheelchair, available in the boarding area, if you do not already use one. Tropical Reef and Penguin Encounter have minimal entertainment value for guests with visual impairments, but being hearing impaired does not detract from the enjoyment. To ride **Kraken** you must transfer to the ride vehicles.

Shamu's Happy Harbor has some activities that are accessible to children using wheelchairs, including many of the games in the midway. Most of the other attractions are geared toward those who can climb, crawl, or slide.

RESTAURANTS & SHOPS
Restaurants are accessible, but drinking straws are not provided here out of concern for the safety of the animals. Shops are level, but many are so packed with merchandise that maneuvering in a wheelchair can be a challenge.

SERVICES
There are outgoing TTY hearing-impaired systems in the lobby of Guest Services and across from the Dolphin Stadium. Sign-language interpreters for guided tours are available with advance notice.

EATING AT SEAWORLD

Burgers, barbecue, and other standard theme-park offerings are available at restaurants and concessions throughout the park. For reservations at full-service restaurants, call 407/351–3600 or 800/327–2424.

DINNER SHOW
The enjoyable **Makahiki Luau,** held in the Seafire Inn at the Waterfront, combines a Polynesian-Tahitian-Hawaiian feast with interactive entertainment. The evening begins with a welcome drink, a quick hula lesson, and the arrival of the Grand Kahuna, who arrives on a motorized pontoon boat rather than an outrigger canoe. What follows is a family-friendly stage show that includes sing-alongs, a drumming contest, and torch twirling. Reservations are required and may be made in advance or on the same day at the information counter near the park entrance. The cost is $48.94 for adults and $31.90 (tax included) for children ages 8 to 12, which includes unlimited nonalcoholic drinks and one cocktail for adults. Park admission is not required and is separate from the price of the luau.

FULL-SERVICE RESTAURANTS
Sharks Underwater Grill, near Shark Encounter, is the park's most upscale restaurant, and the setting and service are extraordinary for a theme park. You walk through an underwater grotto into a cavernous restau-

rant that looks like it could be the secret headquarters of a James Bond villain. Five bay windows separate the dining room from a 660,000-gallon aquarium with sand tiger, sandbar, nurse, black nose, and Atlantic black tip sharks. Three tiers of booths and tables fill the room and each of the 240 seats is perfect for watching the deep blue waters. The menu is Floribbean, with Caribbean-spice seafood pasta, coconut-crust chicken spears, filet mignon with jerk seasoning, and pork medallions with black-bean sauce. Two extra menus—one for teens and one for kids under age 9—are also offered. There's a bar in a quiet alcove near the entrance. Reserve in advance for priority seating, or visit the host stand at the restaurant.

Backstage at *Believe* (the new name for Dine With Shamu) includes a buffet dinner (salads, pastas, seafood, beef, chicken, and desserts) and a meeting with a marine animal trainer. A separate children's buffet is available. About 200 guests can be accommodated per seating, at $37 per adult and $19 per child age 3 to 9.

Beneath the Sky Tower, the **SandBar** is a pub designed to look like an ancient fortress. Overlooking the harbor, it's a nice spot to enjoy sushi platters, shrimp cocktails, fresh fruit and cheese plates, as well as martinis and live music.

SELF-SERVICE RESTAURANTS Just far enough away from the Clydesdale stables, the light and airy **Anheuser-Busch Hospitality Center** combines cafeteria-style service with a bar serving Anheuser-Busch beverages (Michelob, Budweiser, O'Doul's) and soft drinks. If you didn't pick up this information at your college keg parties, you can learn about historic brewing processes, fresh ingredients, and even sample Anheuser-Busch beers paired with an assortment of food at the free half-hour A.B. Beer School. Reservations are required.

At tropical-hue **Mango Joe's Cafe,** a cafeteria near Shamu Stadium, you can find fresh fajitas, hefty salads, and a delicious key lime pie. Many of the umbrella-shaded tables are right on the lake. **Smoky Creek Grill** serves up barbecue chicken and ribs near the Penguin Encounter. To accommodate health-conscious guests, **Mama's Kitchen** switched from home foods to a healthy menu that features sandwiches, salads and pastas. The **Waterfront Sandwich Grill** carves its sandwich fillings to order and also grills big, juicy hamburgers. Close to the Dolphin Cove in Key West, **Captain Pete's Island Eats** has quick bites including chicken fingers, hot dogs, and fresh funnel cakes, plus smoothies and cold drinks.

In an old shipbuilder's hall on the Waterfront, **Voyagers Wood Fired Pizzas** has hand-tossed pizzas, salads, pastas, and decadent desserts. Also at the Waterfront, the **Spice Mill** serves Cajun jambalaya, Caribbean jerk chicken sandwiches, chicken tenders, and a range of salads. At the **Seafire Inn,** chefs prepare stir-fry dishes on a 4-foot Mongolian wok for everyone to see. Hamburgers, sandwiches, and coconut fried shrimp are also on the menu.

GUIDED TOURS

Unlike other theme parks, SeaWorld has created a variety of programs that—for a price—will get animal lovers up close and personal with their favorite creatures. Register for all tours and programs by calling the **Guided Tour Center** (☎ *800/432–1178, 800/406–2244, or 407/363–2398 ⊕ www.seaworld.com*). You can also go to the tour desk to the left of Guest Relations at the park entrance to see what's available that day.

There are three hour-long **Behind the Scenes** tours to choose from, including **Polar Expedition,** which gives you a backstage and up-close view of polar bears and penguins and beluga whales and goes behind the scenes at SeaWorld's Penguin Research Facility. **Predators** teaches about the care of the animals at Shark Encounter and includes a behind-the-scenes tour at Shamu Stadium. It ends with a backstage peek in the shark food preparation room as well as a chance to touch a live shark. **Saving A Species** takes a look at animal rescue, rehabilitation, and release efforts for manatees and turtles, with the tours going to the quarantine area and lab and surgery facilities and a chance to hand-feed exotic birds in a free-flight aviary. A dollar of your fee goes to help the SeaWorld and Busch Gardens Conservation Fund. All tours cost $16 for adults and $12 for children, and leave every 30 minutes until 3 PM.

For an in-depth SeaWorld experience (as well as a chance to cut in line), the six-hour **Adventure Express** includes a comprehensive tour of all park attractions, lunch, and reserved seating at shows. An educator is assigned to your group to answer questions, and the group is limited to 18 people. The cost is $89 per adult and $79 for children on top of park admission. There's free fish to feed the dolphins, stingrays, and sea lions; backstage access to see and touch a penguin; instant admission to Kraken, Journey to Atlantis, and Wild Arctic; and reserved seating at two select shows, including *Believe.* You can make reservations in person at the guided-tour center or by phone.

The **Marine Mammal Keeper Experience** is an eight-hour course at which you work side by side with a SeaWorld caretaker, helping to care for the manatees, dolphins, walruses, beluga whales, and seals. At the Manatee Rehab Center, you may even have the chance to bottle-feed a baby manatee. If you have $399 worth of animal love in your heart and are prepared to start the loving at 6:30 AM, then this one's for you. The price includes lunch and a seven-day admission to the park as well as a souvenir photo and T-shirt.

Sharks Deep Dive is based on the real-life shark dives you might see on Nature or the Discovery Channel. Located at the Shark Encounter attraction, this two-hour experience (of which about 30 minutes is spent in the water) immerses guests into the fascinating realm of these perfect predators. During your close encounter with more than 30 sharks from five species, as well as an array of fish, you'll wear an all-new underwater helmet that allows you to breathe and communicate underwater without scuba equipment. A shark cage takes up to two guests at a time through a 125-foot long underwater habitat teeming with sand tiger sharks, nurse sharks, sawfish, and hundreds of schooling fish. The $150 program (plus tax) includes a T-shirt, Shark Information booklet, and a souvenir photo. Program requires park admission. Participants must be a minimum of 10 years of age.

Limited to four guests at a time, the 90-minute **Beluga Interaction Program** gives you the privilege of joining a SeaWorld trainer backstage and then getting close enough to feed and touch these gentle white whales. You'll learn about their food preparation and help prepare a meal, then have a chance to partially enter the chilly 55°F water to pet them, feed them, and give them commands. You'll need to bring $179 (on top of park admission) and your own swimsuit. The park provides a wet suit, a souvenir photo, and a better understanding of these big, happy boys.

Your kids should be tickled to know that SeaWorld's education department also offers more than 200 **summer camp programs** (☎407/363–2380), including sleepovers and educational adventures for kids. They're not the only ones having fun—there are also Adventure Camp opportunities for the whole family.

15

DISCOVERY COVE

Moving away from the traditional theme-park format, SeaWorld took a chance when it opened Discovery Cove, a 32-acre limited-admission park that's a re-creation of a Caribbean island, complete with coral reefs, sandy beaches, margaritas, and dolphins.

Here's how it works: after entering a huge thatch-roof tiki building, you register and are given a reserved time to swim with the dolphins, the highlight of your Discovery Cove day. With your admission, everything is included—lockers, food, mask, fins, snorkel, wet suit, swim vest, and towels.

Once inside, you're confronted with rocky lagoons surrounded by lush landscaping, intricate coral reefs, and underwater ruins. The pool where snorkeling lessons are taught has cascading waterfalls, and white beaches are fringed with thatched huts, cabanas, and hammocks. Exciting encounters with animal species from the Bahamas, Tahiti, and Micronesia are part of the experience. A free-flight aviary aflutter with exotic birds can be reached by way of a quiet walkway or by swimming beneath a waterfall.

Although the $279 peak-season rate may seem steep, if you consider that a dolphin swim in the Florida Keys runs approximately $175 and that your admission includes a complimentary pass to SeaWorld *or* Busch Gardens, it starts to look like a bargain.

ADMISSION

If you're committed to visiting Discovery Cove, make reservations well in advance—attendance is limited to about 1,000 people a day. Tickets (with Dolphin Swim) start at $259 in the off-season and go up to $270 in summer. Prices drop by $100 if you choose to forsake the dolphin.

TIP SHEET

■ Make reservations three to four months in advance for peak seasons. Admission slots for June start selling out in March.

■ The masks Discovery Cove provides don't accommodate glasses, so wear contacts if you can. Otherwise, try to get one of the limited number of prescription masks. No deposit is required, but you will be responsible if they are lost or damaged.

■ Don't bother to pack your own wet suit or fins. Wet suits and vests are available here, and fins, which annoy the fish, are discouraged.

■ You can leave your keys, money, and other personal belongings in your locker all day. The plastic passes you are given upon entering the park are all you need to pick up your meals and (nonalcoholic) drinks.

■ If it becomes an all-day thunder and lightning rainstorm on your reserved day, attempts will be made to reschedule your visit when you're in town. If that's not possible, you'll have to settle for a refund.

AH HA!

Either fee includes unlimited access to all beach and snorkeling areas and the free-flight aviary; all meals and snacks; use of a mask, snorkel, swim vest, towel, locker, and other amenities; parking; and a pass for seven days of unlimited, come-and-go-as-you-please admission to SeaWorld Orlando or Busch Gardens in Tampa. For reservations and additional information, call **Discovery Cove** (☎877/434–7268 ⊕*www.discoverycove.com*).

DISABILITIES & ACCESSIBILITY

Wheelchairs with wide, balloonlike tires that roll over the sand are available. Call to request one in advance so that they have one waiting for you at the reception.

HOURS

Discovery Cove is open daily from 9 to 5:30, with extended hours in summer and on some holidays. Allow a full day to see all attractions.

AVIARY

Rating: ★★★

The entrance to this 12,000-square-foot birdhouse is a kick. To get here you can walk in from the beach or, better yet, swim into it from the river that snakes through the park by going under a waterfall. You arrive in a small-bird sanctuary populated with darting hummingbirds, tiny finches, and honeycreepers. In the large-bird sanctuary, you get up close to perched and wandering toucans, red-legged seriema, and other colorful and exotic birds. Look for attendants who have carts filled with free fruit and birdfeed that you can use to attract the birds. Don't be frightened if one leaps onto your shoulder, and get ready to snap a photo.

BEACHES
Rating: ★★

Lined with swaying palms, tropical foliage, and quaint thatched huts, this is where you claim your own private spot in the sand, with shady umbrellas, hammocks, lounges, or beach chairs. Since the park's biggest-selling feature is limited guest capacity, the most seductive aspect is staking out your private stretch of sand and leaving the real world behind. For the most privacy, head to the far west end of Discovery Cove. A few cabanas and tents are available on a first-come, first-served basis, and towels and beach chairs are plentiful.

CORAL REEF
Rating: ★★★

Snorkelers follow butterfly fish, angelfish, parrotfish, and a few dozen other species through this authentic-looking coral reef. The brighter the day, the more brilliant the colors. Stingrays sail slowly and gracefully past as you float above. Some of the fish may come within touching distance, but when you reach out to them they scatter in nanoseconds. Also inside the coral reef is an artificial shipwreck where panels of Plexiglas in the hull reveal a pool filled with barracudas and sharks. Since it's hard to see the glass underwater, you'll get the heebie-jeebies when you see them face to face.

DOLPHIN LAGOON
Duration: 45–60 min.
Audience: Anyone age 6 and older.
Rating: ★★★

Before you get too excited about Discovery Cove's top attraction, remember that your "swim" with the dolphins is supervised and restricted to what's safe for both you and the dolphins. That said, your image of frolicking with the dolphins is probably mistaken. But despite the limitations, the attraction offers you the truly unique chance to touch, feed, play with, and even kiss a bottlenose dolphin, one of the most social and communicative marine animals.

Before you can get into the lagoon, you have to sit through a somewhat tedious 15-minute orientation with the rest of your group, that is, the people with whom you'll be sharing your dolphin. The orientation consists of an off-topic film about the SeaWorld companies and their animals, plus a few words from a dolphin trainer. Afterward, you proceed to the lagoon where you enter the surprisingly chilly water for roughly 25 minutes of "interaction" with one of 25 dolphins. You spend most of the time crouched down in knee-deep water, and a flotation vest is required, so even small children and non-swimmers can take part. Discovery Cove trainers teach you about dolphin behavior, and you discover the hand signals used to communicate with them. Your dolphin may roll over so you can touch his or her belly, and, at your signal, leap into the air. Near the end of the session you have a chance to swim out to deeper water, catch hold of the dolphin's fin and have him or her pull you back to shore. At some point, you pose for pictures, which you'll be corralled and cajoled into buying immediately after leaving the water.

RAY LAGOON
Rating: ★★

This is where you can wade and play with dozens of southern and cow-nosed rays. Don't be afraid—they've had their barbs removed. Often, several rays get together and make continuous loops of the pool, so if you stay in one spot they'll continue to glide past you.

TROPICAL RIVER
Rating: ★

The Tropical River meanders its way throughout most of Discovery Cove. River swimmers float lazily through different environments—a sunny beach; a dense, tropical rain forest; an Amazon-like river; a tropical fishing village; an underwater cave; and the aviary. The only drawback here is that the bottom of the river is like the bottom of a pool and the redundancy of the scenery along the way can make it a little tedious.

GUIDED TOURS

Discovery Cove's **Trainer for a Day** program allows up to 24 guests a day to work side by side and behind the scenes with animal experts and interact with dolphins, birds, rays, and tropical fish. Whether they have an in-water training experience with a dolphin, pamper a pygmy falcon, feed tropical fish, or play with an anteater, participants have the hands-on opportunity to train and care for these unique animals. You'll receive a reserved dolphin swim, an enhanced dolphin interaction, and a chance to feed and take care of exotic birds in the aviary. Plus, you have behind-the-scenes access to small-mammal playtime and training, animal food preparation and record review, and behavioral training instruction. You'll walk away with a lot of memories as well as a souvenir shirt and waterproof camera. Be sure about this one. It costs $449 (plus 6.5% sales tax) in peak season, and drops to $429 off-season, but it does include the regular admission price plus tickets valid for seven consecutive days at SeaWorld Orlando or Busch Gardens Tampa Bay.

After Dark

WORD OF MOUTH

"I think the best places at Pleasure Island are the Comedy Warehouse (try to sit by a phone if at all possible) and the Adventures Club."

–Mike

"I definitely recommend seeing Cirque du Soleil's *La Nouba* at Downtown Disney. The show is incredible for both kids and adults. Even if I didn't visit any theme parks, my visit to Orlando would have been worthwhile by seeing this show alone."

–Vince

"I really enjoyed the Hoop-Dee-Doo Revue. It's more of an old dance-hall dinner show than a fine restaurant, and it's a night true to Disney tradition, with entertainment from start to finish. There is audience participation and plenty of music."

–Ken Bilash

Updated
by Gary
McKechnie

AS ONE OF THE WORLD'S leading tourist destinations, Orlando has to meet the challenge of offering entertainment to more than 50 million visitors each year—and providing memorable experiences that will bring them back again and again. While Orlando's main domestic competitor, Las Vegas, can accomplish this with some stage spectaculars, free drinks at the slot machines, and of course the infinite promise of money for nothing, Orlando has a much more difficult task. Why? Because Orlando welcomes a much more diverse crowd. The typical Orlando guest can be part of a happy family from the UK, newlyweds from the Midwest, or retirees from Japan—and the city is, by law, required to provide an appropriate degree of entertainment for everyone who visits.

About a decade ago, there was little to do after dark. Then, when Disney saw a flood of their guests heading off to a downtown Orlando entertainment complex, they wised up. They retooled their after-dark options to include Pleasure Island and later West Side, now both part of the Downtown Disney entertainment complex. In response, Universal Orlando opened CityWalk to siphon off from Disney what Disney had siphoned off from downtown Orlando, which itself is still searching for new ways to compete for the after-dark crowd.

If you're here for at least two nights and don't mind losing some sleep, reserve one evening for Downtown Disney and the next for CityWalk. They are both well worth seeing. If you want a one-night blowout, however, head to Disney—believe it or not! By virtue of Disney's status as what amounts to a separate governmental entity—kind of like a Native American reservation—clubs on Disney property tend to stay open later than bars elsewhere. While most bars in Orange County close around 1 AM, Disney clubs usually stay open until 2. Keep in mind that smoking is not permitted in any Florida restaurants and bars that serve food. If you want to smoke inside, you'll have to find a drinks-only bar.

WALT DISNEY WORLD

When you enter the fiefdom known as Walt Disney World, you're likely to see as many watering holes as cartoon characters. After beating your feet around a theme park all day, there are lounges, bars, speakeasies, pubs, sports bars, and microbreweries where you can settle down with a soothing libation. Your choice of nightlife can be found at various Disney shopping and entertainment complexes—from the casual down-by-the-shore BoardWalk to the much larger multi-area Downtown Disney, which comprises the Marketplace, Pleasure Island, and West Side. Everywhere you look, jazz trios, bluesmen, DJs, and rockers are tuning up and turning on their amps after dinner's done. Plus, two long-running dinner shows provide an evening of song, dance, and dining, all for a single price.

Don't assume that all after-dark activities revolve solely around adult bars and expensive shows. A wealth of free shows is performed at

Epcot's pavilions and stages at the Magic Kingdom and Disney–MGM Studios. Even if you head back to your hotel for an afternoon nap or swim, you can always return to a theme park to catch the fireworks show. Get information on WDW nightlife from the **Walt Disney World information hotline** (☎407/824–2222 or 407/824–4500) or check online at www.waltdisneyworld.com. Disney nightspots accept American Express, MasterCard, and Visa. And cash. Lots of it.

DISNEY'S BOARDWALK

At the turn of the 20th century, Americans escaping the cities for the Atlantic seaside spent their days on breeze-swept boardwalks above the strand, where early thrill rides kept company with band concerts and other activities. Here, across Crescent Lake from Disney's Yacht and Beach Club Resorts, WDW has created its own version of these amusement areas, a shoreside complex that's complete with restaurants, bars and clubs, souvenir sellers, surreys, saltwater taffy vendors, and shops. When the lights go on after sunset, the mood is festive in a family way, far more tranquil than at Downtown Disney. For information on events call the **BoardWalk entertainment hotline** (☎407/939–3492 or 407/939–2444).

Atlantic Dance Hall. This club started out as a hypercool room recalling the Swing Era, with martinis, cigars, and Sinatra soundalikes, but that didn't last, so it reopened as a Latin club. That didn't last either, so now it's a typical Top 40 dance club. These days it has a huge screen showing videos requested by the crowd. You must be 21 to enter. ☎407/939–2444 or 407/939–2430 ⏷No cover ⏰Tues.–Sat. 9 PM–2 AM.

Big River Grille & Brewing Works. Disney World's first brewpub, Big River, has warm wood surfaces and intimate tables where brewmasters tend to their potions, adding to the charm of this retreat. Inside, stainless steel vats brew a variety of beers, the most popular being Rocket Red Ale. But if you're not sure what you'd like best, order a $5 sampler that includes up to six 4-ounce shots of whatever they have on tap that day, from the Red Rocket, Southern Flyer Light Lager, Gadzooks Pilsener, and Steamboat Pale Ale to Sweet Magnolia Brown and Winter's Nip Porter. Pub grub, sandwiches, and cigars round out the offerings, and the brewery's sidewalk café is a great place for people-watching and good conversation. ☎407/560–0253 ⏷No cover ⏰Daily 11:30 AM–12:30 AM.

ESPN Club. As with all themed things at Disney, the sports motif here is carried into every nook and cranny. The main dining area looks like a sports arena, with a basketball-court hardwood floor and a giant scoreboard that projects the big game of the day. Sportscasters originate programs from a TV and radio broadcast booth, and there are more than 100 TV monitors throughout the facility, even in the rest rooms. If you want to watch NFL on Sunday, get here about two hours before kickoff, because the place is packed for back-to-back games. On special game days, like those of the World Series or Super Bowl, count on huge crowds and call in advance to see if special seating rules are in effect. ☎407/939–1177 ⏷No cover ⏰Sun.–Thurs. 11:30 AM–1 AM, Fri. and Sat. 11:30 AM–2 AM.

16

TOP 5 AFTER DARK EXPERIENCES

Cirque du Soleil— La Nouba. If you haven't yet seen one of the surreal Cirque du Soleil shows, or if you have and you were wowed, you'll love this high-energy acrobatics performance.

Comedy Warehouse. A lot of the clubs in Pleasure Island have come and gone, but the Comedy Warehouse has been a Disney mainstay since 1989. Improv comedy routines by a regular cast and sometimes celebrity guests keep bringing people back for repeat visits.

House of Blues. This concert hall in Downtown Disney is the best live-music venue in Orlando and always hosts major headliners.

IllumiNations. Epcot's nighttime spectacular, featuring lasers, fireworks, and floating movie screens, is a not-to-be-missed crowd-pleaser.

SpectroMagic Millions of tiny white lights decorating the floats, carriages, and even costumes in this parade will absolutely mesmerize you. Kids can't tear their eyes away from the spectacle and usually end up watching the whole thing with their mouths silently agape.

Jellyrolls. In this rugged, rockin', and boisterous piano bar, comedians act as emcees and play dueling grand pianos nonstop. In a Disney version of "Stump the Band," they promise "You Name It. We Play It." You may have gone to piano bars before, but the steady stream of conventions at Disney makes this the place to catch CEOs doing the conga to Barry Manilow's "Copacabana"—if that's your idea of a good time. You must be 21 to enter. ☎407/560–8770 💲$10 cover after 7 PM ⊙Daily 7 PM–2 AM.

DOWNTOWN DISNEY

WEST SIDE

Disney's West Side is a hip outdoor complex of shopping, dining, and entertainment with the main venues being the House of Blues, DisneyQuest, and Cirque du Soleil. Aside from this trio, there are no cover charges. Whether you're club hopping or not, the West Side is worth a visit for its waterside location, wide promenade, and diverse shopping and dining. Opening time is 11 AM, closing time around 2 AM; crowds vary with the season, but weeknights tend to be less busy. For entertainment times and more information, call 407/824–4500 or 407/824–2222.

Bongos Cuban Café. Latin rhythms provide the beat at this enterprise owned by pop singer Gloria Estefan. Although this is primarily a restaurant, you may get a kick out of the pre-Castro Havana interior, the three bars, and the Latin band that plays *muy caliente* music every Friday and Saturday evening. Samba, tango, salsa, and merengue rhythms are rolling throughout the week. Drop by for a beer and a "babalu." ☎407/828–0999 💲$35 adults, $19 kids 3–9 ⊙Daily 11 AM–2 AM.

Fodor'sChoice **Cirque du Soleil**—*La Nouba*. This surreal show by the world-famous
★ circus company starts at 100 mph and accelerates from there. Although
the ticket price is high compared with those for other local shows,
you'd be hard-pressed to hear anyone complain. The performance is 90
minutes of extraordinary acrobatics, avant-garde stagings, costumes,
choreography, and a thrilling grand finale that makes you doubt New-
ton's law of gravity. The story of *La Nouba*—derived from the French
phrase *faire la nouba* (which translates to "live it up")—is alternately
mysterious, dreamlike, comical, and sensual. A cast of 72 international
performers takes the stage in this specially constructed, 70,000-square-
foot venue. The original music is performed by a live orchestra that you
might miss if you don't scrutinize the towers on either side of the stage,
which is a technical marvel in itself, with constantly moving platforms
and lifts. A couple of hints: call well in advance for tickets to improve
your chances of getting front-row seats (there are four levels of seating)
and hire a babysitter if necessary—admission is charged for infants.
☎407/939–7600 *reservations* ⊕*www.cirquedusoleil.com* ✉*Front
and center $119.28 adults, $95.85 children under 10; Category 1 seats
(front sides) $103.31 adults, $83.07 children under 10; Category 2
seats (to the side and the back) $84.14 adults, $67.10 children under
10; Category 3 seats (to the far sides and very back) $67.10 adults,
$53.25 children under 10* ☉*Performances Tues.–Sat. 6 and 9* PM.

DisneyQuest. Inside an enclosed five-floor video/virtual reality mini-
theme park, they've figured out that some suckers—er, guests—will
pay big bucks to play video games. To be fair, once you've shelled out
the considerable cover, you can play all day. There are some cutting-
edge games here, but save your money if you think you'll quickly tire
of electronic arcade noises. ☎407/828–4600 ✉*$38.34 adults, $31.95
children 3–9, including tax* ☉*Sun.–Thurs. 11:30* AM*–11* PM, *Fri. and
Sat. 11:30* AM*–midnight.*

Fodor'sChoice **House of Blues.** The restaurant hosts cool blues nightly (alongside its
★ rib-sticking Mississippi Delta cooking), but it's the HOB's concert hall
next door that garners the real attention. The hall has showcased local
and nationally known artists including Aretha Franklin, David Byrne,
Steve Miller, Los Lobos, the Roots, and even Journey. From rock to
reggae to R&B, this is arguably the best live-music venue in Orlando,
and standing a few feet from your guitar heroes is the way music should
be seen and heard. ☎407/934–2583 ✉*Covers vary* ☉*Daily, performance times vary.*

DOWNTOWN DISNEY MARKETPLACE

Although the Marketplace offers little in the line of typical nightlife,
there's hardly a more enjoyable place for families to spend a quiet
evening window-shopping, enjoying ice cream at a courtyard café,
or strolling among eclectic Disney stores. Aside from this, there's not
much "nightlife," per se, but **Cap'n Jack's Restaurant** (☎407/828–3971)
is a nice, quiet waterfront restaurant where you can gulp down some
oysters or sip on a huge strawberry margarita made with strawberry
tequila. For a sweeter tooth, the **Ghirardelli Soda Fountain & Chocolate
Shop** makes a nice after-dinner stop for sundaes, malts, and shakes.
☉*Daily 11:30–10:30.*

16

PLEASURE ISLAND

Pleasure Island was Disney's first foray into a nighttime complex, and judging by the crowds, the combination of clubs, stores, and entertainment remains an attractive mix. The 6-acre park has seven jam-packed clubs that attract an across-the-board mix of college kids, young married couples, middle-age business folk, world travelers, and moms and pops sneaking out for an evening. Weekends are the busiest, although Thursday hops with Disney World cast members itching to blow their just-issued paychecks. Several changes kicked in during 2007. Kids, who were once welcome here under the supervision of a parent, are no longer given such access to the entire complex, except to the Comedy Warehouse and Adventurer's Club. Only visitors 21 or older may enter the various nightclubs. Another change: there is no admission to Pleasure Island itself; only a substantial admission for a single club, double that fee for an all-clubs pass.

✉ *Off Buena Vista Dr.* ☎ *407/934–7781 or 407/824–2222* 💲 *$11.70 for single club, $23.38 for all clubs; access to shops and restaurants is free* ☽ *Clubs daily 7 PM–2 AM; shops and restaurants daily 10:30 AM–2 AM.*

Adventurers' Club. Like those of a private 1930s cabaret, the club-room walls here are practically paved with memorabilia from exotic places. Servers entertain you with their patter, and several times a night character explorer–actors share tall tales of the adventures they encountered on imaginary expeditions. Stop in for a drink and enjoy the scenery, or visit the Library for a slapstick show. With all its props and comedy, this is a good option if you're here with kids—who love shouting the club's rallying cry, "Kungaloosh!" ☎ *407/824–2222 or 407/824–4500.*

BET SoundStage Club. Backed by Black Entertainment Television, this club pays tribute to all genres of black music through videos, live performances, and shows by BET's own dance troupe. As the evening progresses, sounds shift from BET's top 10 to old R&B to hip-hop—a blend that's attracted legions of locals who proclaim this the funkiest nightspot in Central Florida (perhaps also the loudest). Even if you're dance-challenged, you might find it hard to resist shakin' your groove thang to the beat-rich music. Go on, Spaulding. Bust a move. You must be at least 21 to enter. ☎ *407/934–7666.*

Fodor'sChoice ★ **Comedy Warehouse.** At one of the island's most popular clubs, gifted comedians perform various improv games, sing improvised songs, and create off-the-cuff sketches based largely on suggestions from the audience. Each of the evening's five performances is different, but the cast is usually on a roll no matter when you go. Lines for the free shows start forming roughly 45 minutes before curtain, so get there early for a good seat. It's well worth the wait to watch a gifted comedy troupe work without profanity. ☎ *407/828–2939.*

8TRAX. In case the lava lamps and disco balls don't tip you off, the '70s are back at this glittering club. Slip on your bell-bottoms, strap on your platform shoes, and groove to Chic, the Village People, or Donna Summer on disk. After a while, it might seem like you're in your own Quentin Tarantino film. Swing by on Thursday when the calendar fast-forwards to the 1980s to celebrate the music of that less-long-gone era. ☎*407/934–7160.*

Mannequins. How far has Disney veered off the family path since Walt died? Stop here and you'll find out. You can expect over-the-top floor shows complete with suggestive bump-and-grind moves at this New York–style dance palace. Twentysomethings rule on the revolving dance floor, and the club also welcomes a gay clientele. Everyone grooves to Top 40 hits, elaborate lighting, and special effects like bubbles and snow. You must be at least 21 to be admitted. ☎*407/934–6375.*

Motion. Motion makes the most of being all things to all people by playing a mix of dance music ranging from retro rockabilly to the latest techno hits. This means that it attracts a cross-section of people who (eventually) hear at least one song they like. The two-story warehouse-like club is stark, emphasizing the dance floor and the club's twirling lights and thumping sound system. Motion hits the right tone to attract a young-and-hip clientele. Doors open nightly at 9 PM (and stay open until 2 AM). ☎*407/827–9453.*

Raglan Road. A low-key jazz club couldn't cut it here, so Disney found some folks who were ready to bring an authentic Irish pub to Orlando. A dramatic change has taken place. While dancers, storytellers, and musicians keep the pub thumpin', patrons are downing an assortment of Irish fare and beers, ales, and liquors served from four bars. Doors open nightly at 9 PM (and stay open until 2 AM). ☎*407/938-0300* ⊕*www.raglanroadirishpub.com.*

Rock & Roll Beach Club. This three-tier bar is always crowded and throbbing with rock music from the '50s to the '80s. With most clubs playing machine-produced music, it's a treat to hang out where the tunes were created by humans. The live band and disc jockeys never let the action die down, and the sounds attract a slightly older (thirties) crowd. The friendly and fun feel of a neighborhood bar is sustained by the pool tables, pinball machines, foosball, darts, and video games. ☎*407/934–7654.*

HOTEL BARS

DISNEY RESORT HOTELS
With more than a dozen resort hotels on Walt Disney World property, the hotel-bar scene is understandably active. Depending on whether the resort is geared to business or romance, the lounges can be soothing or boisterous—or both. You do not have to be a resort guest to visit the bars and lounges, and a casual tour of them may well provide an evening's entertainment. To reach any of these hotel bars directly, you can call the Disney operator at 407/824–4500 or 407/824–2222.

Belle Vue Room. Settle back in this lovely 1930s-style sitting room to escape the crowds, play board games, savor a quiet drink, and listen to long-ago shows played through old radios. Step out onto the balcony for a soothing view of the village green and lake. ⊠*Boardwalk Inn* ☽*Daily 5 PM–midnight.*

California Grill. High atop the Contemporary Resort, this utterly chic restaurant–lounge offers a fantastic view of the Magic Kingdom, especially when the sun goes down and the tiny white lights on Main Street start to twinkle. Add nightly fireworks (usually at 10 PM), and there's no better place to order a glass of wine and enjoy the show. An observation deck, which extends to the end of the hotel, adds a breezy vantage point from which to see all this, plus surrounding Bay Lake. In high season, you may need dinner reservations to gain access to the observation deck. ⊠ *Contemporary Resort* ⊘ *Daily 5:30 PM–midnight, dinner 6 PM–10 PM.*

Martha's Vineyard Lounge. This is a cozy, refined hideaway where you can sit back and sip domestic and European wines. Each evening 18 wines are poured for tasting. After facing the maddening crowd, it's worth a detour if you're looking for a quiet retreat and a soothing glass of zinfandel. ⊠ *Beach Club Resort* ⊘ *Daily 5:30 PM–10 PM.*

Mizner's. At the stylish Grand Floridian, a refined alcove is tucked away at the far end of the second-floor lobby. Even on steroids, this place wouldn't approach rowdy—it's a tasteful getaway where you can unwind with ports, brandies, and mixed drinks while overlooking the beach and the elegance that surrounds you. ⊠ *Grand Floridian* ⊘ *Daily 5 PM–1 AM.*

Narcoossee's. Inside the restaurant is a bar that serves ordinary beer in expensive yard glasses, but the porch-side views of the Seven Seas Lagoon (and the nightly Electrical Water Pageant) are worth the premium you pay. Find a nice spot and you can also watch the Magic Kingdom fireworks. ⊠ *Grand Floridian* ⊘ *Daily 5 PM–10 PM.*

Tambu Lounge. Beside 'Ohana's restaurant at the Polynesian Resort, Disney bartenders ring up all the variations on rum punch and piña coladas. Festooned with South Seas–style masks, totems, and Easter Island head replicas, this place is exotic—with the exception of the large-screen TV. ⊠ *Polynesian Resort* ⊘ *Daily 1 PM–midnight.*

Territory Lounge. Nestled within a carbon copy of the magnificent Yellowstone Lodge, this lounge is a frontier-theme hideout that pays tribute to the Corps of Discovery (look overhead for a Lewis and Clark expedition trail map). In between drinks, check out the props on display: surveying equipment, daguerreotypes, large log beams, parka mittens, maps, and what the lounge claims is a pair of Teddy Roosevelt's boots. ⊠ *Wilderness Lodge* ⊘ *Daily 4 PM–midnight.*

Victoria Falls. The central lounge at the extraordinary Animal Kingdom Lodge is a second-floor retreat that overlooks the Boma restaurant. The exotic feel of an obligatory safari theme extends to leather directors' chairs, native masks, and the sounds of a stream flowing past. Across the hall near the front desk, a small alcove beckons. Although no drinks are served in the sunken den called the Sunset Overlook—with artifacts and photos from 1920s safaris of Martin and Osa Johnson—it's a popular spot for late-night conversation. ⊠ *Animal Kingdom Lodge* ⊘ *Daily 5:30 PM–midnight, dinner 6 PM–10 PM.*

DISNEY'S DINNER SHOWS

★ **Hoop-Dee-Doo Revue.** Staged at Fort Wilderness's rustic Pioneer Hall, this show may be corny, but it's also the liveliest dinner show in Walt Disney World. A troupe of jokers called the Pioneer Hall Players stomp their feet, wisecrack, and sing and dance, while the audience chows down on barbecued ribs, fried chicken, corn on the cob, strawberry shortcake, and all the fixin's. There are three shows nightly, and the prime times sell out months in advance in busy seasons. But you're better off eating dinner too early or too late rather than missing the fun altogether—so take what you can get. If you arrive in Orlando with no reservations, try for a cancellation. Prices vary by seat selection. ✉ *Fort Wilderness Resort* ☎ *407/939–3463 advance tickets, 407/824–2803 day of show* 🖥 *$50.99–$58.99 adults, $25.99–$29.99 children 3–11, including tax and gratuity* ⊘ *Daily 5, 7:15, and 9:30.*

➤ **Spirit of Aloha.** Formerly the Polynesian Luau, this show is still an outdoor barbecue with entertainment in line with its colorful South Pacific style. Its fire jugglers and hula-drum dancers are entertaining for the whole family, if never quite as endearing as the napkin twirlers at the Hoop-Dee-Doo Revue. The hula dancers' navel maneuvers, however, are something to see. You should try to make reservations at least a month in advance. ✉ *Polynesian Resort* ☎ *407/939–3463 advance tickets, 407/824–1593 day of show* 🖥 *$50.99–$58.99 adults, $25.99–$29.99 children 3–11, including tax and gratuity Prices vary by seat selection.* ⊘ *Tues.–Sat. 5:15 and 8.*

FIREWORKS, LIGHT SHOWS & PARADES

Both in the theme parks and around the hotel-side waterways, Walt Disney World offers up a wealth of fabulous sound-and-light shows after the sun goes down. In fact WDW is one of the earth's largest single consumers of fireworks—perhaps even rivaling mainland China. Traditionally, sensational short shows have been held at the Magic Kingdom at 10. Starting times vary throughout the year, but you can check them at Guest Services. You can also find fireworks at Pleasure Island as part of the every-night-is-New Year's Eve celebrations—an event that's worth the wait into the wee hours.

Fireworks are only part of the evening entertainment. Each park hosts shows staged with varying degrees of spectacle and style. For the best of the best, head to Epcot, which hosts visiting shows that are free with admission. Regular performers include a Beatles soundalike group in the United Kingdom, acrobats in China, mimes in France, musicians in a smaller African kiosk, and rock-and-roll bagpipers in Canada. Catching any of these parades and/or performances easily soothes the sting of what you may feel is an overpriced admission.

ELECTRICAL WATER PAGEANT

One of Disney's few remaining small wonders is this 10-minute floating parade of sea creatures outlined in tiny lights, with an electronic score highlighted by Handel's *Water Music*. Don't go out of your way, but if you're by Bay Lake and the Seven Seas Lagoon, look for it from the beaches at the Polynesian (at 9), the Grand Floridian (9:15), Wilderness Lodge (9:35), Fort Wilderness (9:45), the Contemporary (10:05), and, in busy seasons, the Magic Kingdom (10:20). Times occasionally vary, so check with Guest Services.

FANTASMIC!

★ Disney–MGM's blockbuster after-dark show is held once nightly (twice on weekends and in peak seasons) in a 6,500-seat amphitheater. The throngs of people filing into the Hollywood Bowl–style amphitheater give you the distinct sense that you're in for something amazing. The special effects are superlative indeed, as Mickey Mouse in the guise of the Sorcerer's Apprentice emcees a revue full of song and dance, pyrotechnics, and special effects. Several scenes from Disney films and historic events are staged amid music, special lighting, and fireworks. Arrive an hour in advance for the best seats, 20 minutes if you don't mind sitting to the side of the stage. Or sign up for the *Fantasmic!* **Dinner Package,** which includes reservations at either the Studio's Brown Derby, Hollywood & Vine, or Mama Melrose restaurants, plus seating in a special VIP area of the *Fantasmic!* amphitheater. You should still show up at least 20 minutes early so you don't have to sit at the very back of the VIP section, which comprises all the risers at one end of the theater.

ILLUMINATIONS: REFLECTIONS OF THE EARTH

Fodor'sChoice It's worth sticking around until dark to see Epcot's light and fireworks
★ show, which takes place over the reflective World Showcase lagoon. As orchestral music fills the air, accompanied by the whoosh and boom of lasers and pyrotechnic bursts, a 30-foot globe on a barge floats across the lagoon, revealing the wonders of the seven continents on its curved LED screens. Meanwhile, each of the World Showcase pavilions is illuminated with more than 26,000 feet of lights. Check the wind direction before staking a claim, since smoke can cloak some views. Some of the better vantage points are the Matsu No Ma Lounge in the Japan pavilion, the patios of the Rose & Crown in the United Kingdom pavilion, and Cantina de San Angel in Mexico. Another good spot is the World Showcase Plaza between the boat docks at the Showcase entrance, but this is often crowded with those who want to make a quick exit after the show. If you decide to join them here, claim your seat at least 45 minutes in advance. It's worth waiting to see this spectacle.

SPECTROMAGIC

Fodor'sChoice This splendidly choreographed parade of lights is one of the Magic
★ Kingdom's don't-miss attractions. It's a colorful, flickering, luminescent parade with cartoonish floats and a complete lineup of favorite Disney characters. Times vary, so check the schedule before you set out, or ask any Disney staffer while you're in the park. The early showing is for parents with children, while the later ones attract night owls and others with the stamina and the know-how to enjoy the Magic Kingdom's most pleasant, least-crowded time of day.

WISHES

★ The *Wishes* show defines the magic of Disney better than any you'll see during your trip. To the accompaniment of Disney melodies, the fireworks of *Wishes* are launched from 11 locations around the park, as Jiminy Cricket reminds you that "anything your heart desires" can come true. The fireworks and music recall scenes from Disney films in which a fairy-tale character did indeed get his or her wish. The best place to watch the show is on Main Street—try to snag the few seats on the second floor of the Walt Disney World train station. It's a wonderful way to wrap up the day at the Magic Kingdom.

UNIVERSAL ORLANDO

At Universal, the after-hours action has seeped out of the parks and into CityWalk, an eclectic and eccentric 30-acre pastiche of shops, restaurants, clubs, and concert venues. CityWalk's attitude is as hip and sassy as anywhere in the Universal domain.

UNIVERSAL ORLANDO'S CITYWALK

16

CityWalk. Armed with a catchy headline ("Get a Nightlife"), CityWalk met the challenge of diverting the lucrative youth market from Disney and downtown Orlando. It did so by creating an open and airy gathering place that includes clubs ranging from quiet jazz retreats to over-the-top discotheques. On weeknights the crowd is a mix of families and conventioneers; weekends draw a decidedly younger demographic who are still arriving into the wee hours.

Although clubs have individual cover charges, it's far more economical to pay for the whole kit and much of the caboodle. You can buy a Party Pass (a one price–all clubs admission) for $11.99; or a Party Pass-and-a-Movie for $15.40 (plus tax). What makes these deals even better is the fact that after 6 PM the $11 parking fee drops to nothing. It is, however, a long walk from the parking garage to CityWalk (even longer when you stumble out at 2 AM and realize it's a ¼-mi walk to your car). Then again, you shouldn't be driving in this condition, so have a good time and call a cab. Taxis run at all hours (see Taxis in Essentials). ☎ *407/224–2692, 407/363–8000 Universal main line* ⊕ *www.citywalkorlando.com.*

★ **Bob Marley—A Tribute to Freedom.** The beauty of this place is that even if you can't dance, you can easily pretend just by swaying to the syncopated reggae rhythms. This museum-club is modeled after the "King of Reggae's" home in Kingston, Jamaica, complete with intimate low ceilings and more than 100 photographs and paintings reflecting pivotal moments in Marley's life. Off the cozy bar is a patio area where you can be jammin' to a (loud) live band that plays from 8 PM to 1:30 AM nightly. Red Stripe Rastafarian Thursday—soon to be a national holiday—lasts from 4 PM until closing, and offers $3.25 Red Stripes and Captain Morgan specials. You must be 21 or over to be admitted on Friday and

Saturday after 9 PM. ☎407/224–2692 💲*$7 after 8* PM ☉*Weekdays 4* PM–*2* AM, *weekends 2* PM–*2* AM.

CityJazz/Bonkerz. Despite the name on the marquee, there's a serious mix of musical styles in this club. Early in the week there's high energy funk, R&B, soul, rock, Top 40, and "old school" dance; while Thursday, Friday, and Saturday kick off with Bonkerz Comedy Club, starring a litany of touring comics, and a comedy hypnosis show on Sundays. After the comedy, the music kicks in again. ☎407/224–2692, 407/224–2189, 407/629–2665 *Bonkerz* 💲*$7, special performance ticket prices $6–$35* ☉*Sun.–Thurs. 8* PM–*1* AM, *Fri. and Sat. 7* PM–*2* AM. *Bonkerz shows, Thurs.–Sat. 8* PM.

the groove. The very sound of this place can be terrifying to the uninitiated: images flicker rapidly on several screens and the combination of music, light, and mayhem appeals to a mostly under-30 crowd. Within the cavernous hall, every nook and cranny is filled with techno pop. If you need to escape, the dance floor leads to three rooms: the '70s-style Green Room, filled with beanbag chairs and everything you threw out when Duran Duran hit the charts; the sci-fi Jetson-y Blue Room; and the Red Room, which is hot and romantic in a bordello sort of way. Prepare yourself for lots of fog, swirling lights, and sweaty bodies. This is another 21-and-up club. ☎407/224–2692 💲*$7* ☉*Daily 9* PM–*2* AM.

Hard Rock Cafe. This Hard Rock Cafe is the largest on earth, and the one that seems to play the loudest music. The best objects adorn a room on the second floor: Beatles rarities such as cutouts from the *Sgt. Pepper* cover, John Lennon's famous "New York City" T-shirt, Paul's original lyrics for "Let It Be," and the doors from London's Abbey Road studios. Buddy Holly's Boy Scout booklet and favorite stage suit are also here. Wow. Start with dinner and stay for the show, since much of the attraction here is at the adjoining **Hard Rock Live.** The concert hall's exterior resembles Rome's Coliseum, and almost every evening an entertainer performs here; occasionally it's one you recognize (Ringo Starr, Elvis Costello, Jerry Lee Lewis, etc.). Although the seats are hard and two-thirds don't face the stage, it's one of Orlando's top venues. Cover prices vary. Warning: you can't bring large purses or bags inside and there are no lockers at CityWalk, so leave big baggage in your car. ☎407/224–2692 ⊕*www.hardrocklive.com* ☉*Daily from 11* AM, *with varying closing time, generally around midnight.*

★ **Jimmy Buffett's Margaritaville.** Jimmy Buffett may be the most savvy businessman in America. He took a single concept, wrapped it up in a catchy tune, and parlayed it into books, clothing, musicals, and a hot club at Universal. It seems that Florida law requires residents to play Buffett music 24 hours a day, but if you're from out of state you might still not be over "Cheeseburger in Paradise." Attached to the restaurant are three bars (Volcano, Land Shark, and 12 Volt). There's a Pan Am Clipper suspended from the ceiling, music videos projected onto sails, limbo and Hula-Hoop contests, a huge margarita blender that erupts "when the volcano blows," live music nightly, and all the other subtleties that give Parrotheads a place to roost. ☎*407/224–2692* ⊕*www.margaritaville.com* ✉*$7 after 10* PM ⊙*Daily 11:30* AM–*2* AM.

Latin Quarter. This tribute to Latin music and dance is especially popular with local Hispanics. It's easy to overlook the restaurant here, as most attention is paid to the nightclub, which is crowded with partygoers in eye-catching clothing. The club feels like a 21st-century version of Ricky Ricardo's Tropicana, although the design is based on a mix of Aztec, Inca, and Maya architecture. There's even an Andes mountain range, complete with waterfalls, around the dance floor. If you can get your hips working overtime, pick a rhumba from 1 to 10 and swivel . . . And tango and merengue and salsa. . . . ☎*407/224–2692* ✉*$7; price may vary for certain performances* ⊙*Mon.–Thurs. 5* PM–*2* AM, *Fri. and Sat. noon–2* AM.

AMC–Loew's Universal Cineplex. Why spend your time watching a movie when you're on vacation? Who cares? It's your vacation. The 20-screen, 5,000-seat, bi-level theater offers an escape from the crowds. You can purchase tickets in advance by telephone. ☎*407/354–5998 recorded information and tickets, 407/354–3374 box office.*

Pat O'Brien's. A legend in pre-Katrina New Orleans, this exact reproduction of the original is doing all right in Orlando, with its flaming fountain, dueling pianists, and balcony that re-creates the Crescent City. The draw here is the Patio Bar, where abundant tables and chairs allow you to do nothing but enjoy a respite from the madding crowd— and drink a potent, rum-based hurricane. You must be 21 to enter. ☎*407/224–2692* ⊕*www.patobriens.com* ✉*$7 after 9* PM ⊙*Patio Bar daily 4* PM–*2* AM; *Piano Bar daily 6* PM–*2* AM.

Red Coconut Club. Swank and hip, the interior of CityWalk's newest nightclub is an ultra lounge that features a full bar, signature martinis, an extensive wine list, and VIP bottle service. Loaf around the Rat Pack–era lounge, hang out on the balcony, or mingle with the happening crowd at the bars. If you're on a budget, take advantage of the daily happy hours and a gourmet appetizer menu. A DJ and live music pushes the energy with tunes from rock to Sinatra. You must be 21 to enter. ☎*407/224–2692* ✉*$7 after 9* PM ⊙*Sun.–Wed. 7* PM–*2* AM, *Thurs.–Sat. 6* PM–*2* AM.

ORLANDO

The downtown clubs lost their monopoly on nighttime entertainment in the area when Disney and Universal muscled their way onto the scene. Most of the few clubs left are on Orange Avenue, alongside grungy tattoo and piercing parlors that make the downtown area look tired and seedy. Some hipster-types have started to spruce things up a bit with a few small new or converted bars and lounges. The neighborhood of Thornton Park and the community of Winter Park also have clusters of chic bars and restaurants, though no serious dance clubs.

Celebration at Night

It may not be "nightlife" per se, but there's a quaint cluster of shops, restaurants, and a movie theater in the utopian community of Celebration, a few minutes down the road from the rest of Disney.

Although Celebration's artificial perfection recalls an episode of the *Twilight Zone*, at night everything seems almost real. You can have dinner; take a romantic walk by the lake; and check out the Celebration Town Tav-ern, Barnie's Coffee & Tea Co., bookstores, boutiques, toy shops, and the two-screen AMC Theatre (407/566–1403).

DOWNTOWN ORLANDO CLUBS & BARS

Bösendorfer Lounge. One of only two Imperial Grand Bösendorfer pianos takes center stage at this, perhaps the classiest gathering spot in Orlando. The highly civilized (but not stuffy) lounge attracts a cross-section of trendy Orlandoans, especially the after-work crowd, among which the conversation and camaraderie flow as smoothly as the champagne, beer, wine, and cocktails. Art on the walls, comfortable couches, rich fabrics, sleek black marble, and seductive lighting invite you to stay awhile. ⊠ *Westin Grand Bohemian Hotel, 325 S. Orange Ave.* ☎*407/313–9000* ⊕*www.grandbohemianhotel.com* ⊘*Thurs.–Sat. 11 AM–2 AM, Sun.–Wed. 11 AM–midnight.*

Bull and Bush Pub. It's a mile or so east of downtown, but you might not mind the trek for a good pint, a bite of shepherd's pie, some fish-and-chips, and a game of darts. Besides the bar, there are small booths for privacy. The tap lineup covers 11 imported beers and ales. ⊠*2408 E. Robinson St.* ☎*407/896–7546* ⊘*Mon.–Sat. 4 PM–2 AM.*

Club Paris. Socialite Paris Hilton lent her name and inexplicably successful business talents to this nightclub, which premiered in late 2004. Imagine how her fans felt when she was given the boot in 2007 for not fulfilling her job duties, which were to show up once in a while. In a brilliantly pragmatic twist of nomenclature, the owner kept the name of the club but now says it is after the capital of France. Inside, a South Beach courtyard sets the tone for entry and the floor is monitored by "fashion police" who award the trendiest patrons a free bar tab for the evening. There's plenty of room to dance (20,000 square feet) to New York–style DJ noise, as well as varied music on themed nights: Latin, Ladies, Fashion, and '80s. If you're considered worthy or are willing to pay an added admission, you can go upstairs to the VIP club. Despite the heiress's flameout, this still may be the hottest club in Orlando. Isn't life wonderful? ⊠*122 W. Church St.* ☎*407/832–7409* ⊕*www. clubparis.net* ⊠*$5–$20* ⊘*Mon.–Sat. 8 PM–2 AM.*

Social. Perhaps the favorite live-music venue of locals, Social is a great place to see touring and local musicians. It serves full dinners Wednesday through Saturday and offers up live music seven nights a week. You can sip trademark martinis while listening to anything from alternative rock to rockabilly to undiluted jazz. Several now-national acts got their start here, including Matchbox Twenty, Seven Mary Three, and other groups that don't have numbers in their names. ⌧ *54 N. Orange Ave.* ☎ *407/246–1419* ⊕ *www.thesocial.org* ⌫ *$5–$18, depending on entertainment* ⊘ *Sat.–Thurs. 8* PM*–2* AM*, Fri. 5* PM*–2* AM.

Wally's. One of Orlando's oldest bars (circa 1953), this longtime local favorite is a hangout for a cross section of cultures and ages. Some would say it's a dive, but that doesn't matter to the students, bikers, lawyers, and barflies who land here to drink surrounded by the go-go dancer wallpaper and '60s-era interior. Just grab a stool at the bar to take in the scene and down a cold one. ⌧ *1001 N. Mills Ave.* ☎ *407/896–6975* ⊘ *Mon.–Sat. 7:30* AM*–1* AM*, Sun. noon–10* PM.

DINNER SHOWS

16

Dinner shows are an immensely popular form of nighttime entertainment around Orlando. For a single price, you get a theatrical production and a multicourse dinner. Performances run the gamut from jousting to jamboree tunes, and meals tend to be better than average; unlimited beer, wine, and soda are usually included, but mixed drinks (and often *any* drinks before dinner) cost extra. What the shows lack in substance and depth they make up for in grandeur and enthusiasm. The result is an evening of light entertainment, which youngsters in particular enjoy. Seatings are usually between 7 and 9:30, and there are usually one or two performances a night, with an extra show during peak periods. You might sit with strangers at tables for 10 or more, but that's part of the fun. Always reserve in advance, especially for weekend shows, and always ask about discounts.

If you're in Orlando off-season, try to take in these dinner shows on a busy night—a show playing to a small audience can be uncomfortable. Don't let the big prices fool you—there are a flood of major discount (sometimes half-off) coupons papering International Drive restaurants, hotels, and at the Orlando/Orange County Convention & Visitors Bureau. Since performance schedules can vary depending on the tourist season, it's always smart to call in advance to verify show times. When buying tickets, ask if the cost includes a gratuity—servers anxious to pocket more cash may hit you up for an extra handout.

Arabian Nights. An elaborate palace on the outside, this arena has seating for more than 1,200 on the inside. Its 25-act dinner show centers around the quest for an Arabian princess to find her true love, and includes a buffoonish genie who may or may not be amusing, a chariot race, an intricate Western square dance on horseback, and 60 fabulous horses that perform in such acts as bareback acrobatics by gypsies. Dinner is served during the show, so you might end up not paying much attention to the food—which is not a bad idea since the meal of prime rib or vegetable lasagna is functional, not flavorful. Extra shows are added in summer. Fans of equestrian displays will get the most out of this show. Make reservations in advance and ask about discounts, which are also available when booking online. ✉ *6225 W. Irlo Bronson Memorial Hwy., Kissimmee* ☎ *407/239–9223, 800/553–6116, 800/533–3615 in Canada* ⊕ *www.arabian-nights.com* ✆ *45.90 adults, $56.60 adult VIP (includes seating in first three rows, poster, and drink), $20.33 children 3–11, $31.03 children VIP 3–11* ⊙ *Shows nightly, times vary* ⊟ *AE, D, MC, V.*

Capone's Dinner and Show. This show brings you back to the era of 1931 gangland Chicago, when mobsters and their dames were the height of underworld society. The evening begins in an old-fashioned ice-cream parlor, but say the secret password and you are ushered inside Al Capone's private Underworld Cabaret and Speakeasy. Dinner is an unlimited Italian buffet that's heavy on pasta. ✉ *4740 W. Irlo Bronson Memorial Hwy., Kissimmee* ☎ *407/397–2378* ⊕ *www.alcapones.com* ✆ *$49.20 adults, $27.99 children 4–12* ⊙ *Daily 7:30* ⊟ *AE, D, MC, V.*

★ **Dolly Parton's Dixie Stampede Dinner & Show.** For real old-fashioned family entertainment, Dolly's show can't be beat. The evening begins in a preshow area featuring a singing cowboy who also has the interesting ability to rip, tear, and snap small objects to bits with a lightning-fast bullwhip. Next, in the main arena—an antebellum-style auditorium—you sit on either the North or South side and cheer on your teams as they engage in such competitions as ostrich and pig races. Expect lots of singing, dancing, comedy, and fast-paced acrobatic horsemanship with 32 magnificent horses. A four-course feast and plenty of audience participation make this show stand out above the others. The patriotic grand finale was written by Dolly Parton. Stick around after the show and you can meet the horses and performers. ✉ *8251 Vineland Ave., Lake Buena Vista Area, Orlando* ☎ *407/238–4455 or 866/443–4943* ⊕ *www.dixiestampede.com* ✆ *$49.99 adults, $21.99 children 4–11* ⊙ *Shows usually daily at 6:30 PM, but hrs may vary in high season and during holidays* ⊟ *AE, D, MC, V.*

Medieval Times. In a huge, ersatz-medieval manor house, this evening out presents a tournament of sword fights, jousting matches, and other games on a good-versus-evil theme. No fewer than 30 charging horses and a cast of 75 knights, nobles, and maidens participate. Sound silly? It is. But it's also a true extravaganza. That the show takes precedence over the meat-and-potatoes fare is obvious: everyone sits facing forward at long, narrow banquet tables stepped auditorium-style above the tournament area. Additional diversions include tours through a dungeon and torture chamber and demonstrations of antique blacksmithing, woodworking, and pottery making. ✉ *4510 W. Irlo Bronson Memorial Hwy., Kissimmee* ☎ *407/239–0214 or 800/229–8300* ⊕ *www.medievaltimes.com* ✆ *$54.95 adults, $34.95 children 3–11* ⊙ *Castle daily 9–4, village daily 4:30–8, performances usually daily at 8 but call ahead* ⊟ *AE, D, MC, V.*

Sleuths Mystery Dinner Show. If Sherlock Holmes has always intrigued you, head on over for a four-course meal served up with a healthy dose of conspiracy. There are 14 rotating whodunnit performances staged throughout the year in three different theaters. The show begins during your appetizers, and murder was the case by the time they take your plates away. You'll get to discuss the clues over dinner, question the still-living characters, and solve the crime during dessert. On Thursday evenings an added show—in Spanish—is presented in an adjoining theater. Did the butler do it? Si. ⊠ *8267 International Dr., Orlando* ☎ *407/363–1985 or 800/393–1985* ⊕ *www.sleuths.com* ⊠ *$48.95 adults, $23.95 children 3–11* ⊙ *Sun. and weekdays 7:30 (sometimes 8:30), Sat. 7:30 and 8:30* ▭ *AE, D, MC, V.*

16

Shopping

WORD OF MOUTH

"Nothing says Disney like the ears. Get them, get a picture of your kids at Disney looking cute in them, and you're good."

—MonicaRichards

"My son gets a new pair of Disney boxer shorts on every trip, and my girls love the Disney birthstone charms."

—ajcolorado

"I buy a Disney pin every time I go."

—vegasnative

Updated by
Alicia Rivas

FROM FAIRY-TALE KINGDOMS TO OLD West–style trading posts to outlet malls, Walt Disney World and Orlando have a plethora of shopping opportunities that won't leave you disappointed. The colors are bright and energetic, the textures soft and cuddly, and the designs fresh and thoughtful. Before you board any roller coaster or giggle at any show, you'll catch yourself window-shopping and delighting in the thought of making a purchase. And when it comes time to do some serious shopping, you may have a hard time deciding what to buy with all the options available. Of course, your best bet is to wait a couple of days before you buy anything; survey the scene a little before spending all the money in your budget. Better yet, save shopping for the last day of your trip.

WALT DISNEY WORLD

Even if you're not inclined to buy, the shops on Disney property are worth a look. Across the board, they are open, inviting, cleverly themed, and have beautiful displays. Of course, you could easily pick up $100 worth of goods before you've ventured even 10 feet into a store, but you're better off practicing some restraint. Enjoy the experience of just looking first. If you see something you like, think about it while you enjoy the rest of your day. You might see something even better in the next store. If you're still thinking of that beautiful stuffed Cheshire Cat or Cinderella snow globe at the end of the day, you can always go back to get it. That way you don't weigh yourself down with purchases until you're ready to leave. If you're a Disney hotel guest, you never have to carry off your purchases—Disney stores will deliver your merchandise to your room for free.

Also, don't let the price tags scare you off. Small souvenirs (key chains, pens, small toys, etc.) for less than $10 are available in almost every store. Just be careful with souvenir-hungry kids. Many attractions exit directly into gift shops. Even if you put your kid on a strict budget, he may be overwhelmed by the mind-boggling choices at hand and be completely unable to make a selection. If you return home and realize that you've forgotten a critical souvenir, call WDW's Merchandise Mail Order service at 407/363–6200.

MAGIC KINGDOM

Everywhere you turn in the Magic Kingdom there are shops and stalls urging you to take home a little piece of the magic.

MAIN STREET, U.S.A.

Fodor'sChoice Main Street, U.S.A., which serves as your gateway to the Magic King-
★ dom, is end to end with little shops selling clothing and memorabilia.

The Chapeau sells those classic monogrammed mouse ears. The hats won't stay on all day, though, and they'll get squished in a backpack, so this is another good souvenir to get at the end of the day. You could also consider buying a Disney baseball cap to protect you from the sun.

Best Disney Souvenirs

According to Fodors.com forums users ...

"My friend who is almost 25 still wears her Indiana Jones hat she bought on a senior-year spring break trip to Disney."–jayne1973

"My girls bought inexpensive fans (about $5) in the Epcot China pavilion gift shop. Then the fans were personalized right there (free) with the girls' names written in Chinese."–ajcolorado

"I bought a silver Tinker Bell necklace that I love. They also have these memo holders that are miniatures of the princess dresses. I have Snow White, Cinderella, and Sleeping Beauty, and of course, each is holding the picture of my kids with that princess. So cute!"–missypie

"My best Disney souvenir? Pictures of my kids doing stuff like freaking out on Splash Mountain, etc. These will be around a lot longer than any souvenir. But to officially answer your question it would be the Minnie dress I bought my two-year-old. She did not take it off forever!!"–momof5

"When we went for our honeymoon, we bought the Mickey and Minnie bride-and-groom stuffed toys. Every time I look at them, I think of our honeymoon. And they look so cute in the tux and dress, too!"–travel_addict

"We just returned and we got a Tinkerbell cookie jar and the Cinderella waffle iron."–jetprincess

The **Main Street Market House** is a fun little shop for foodies looking to add a little Disney to their kitchen. It's also a great place to pick up some inexpensive keepsakes. Tubby little Mickey coffee mugs go for around $12, and Mickey's "Really Swell" coffee can be had for $8.95 per half-pound. Whimsical Goofy chef's aprons for $18 also make great gifts. For the kids, who always seem to cost more, there are Mickey waffle irons, and toasters that will toast the mighty mouse's image onto your bread.

Uptown Jewelers is a great spot for window-shopping. Along with a dazzling display of jewelry, figurines, and collectible Disney lithographs, you can see Disney artists at work in the Watchmaker's corner. The artists sketch Disney characters and themes for the watch faces that are then built into Citizen watches. Ranging in price from $200–$350, these one-of-a-kind watches are exclusive to this store and cannot be purchased anywhere else.

Serious collectors of Disney memorabilia stop at **Main Street Gallery,** next to City Hall. Limited-edition sculptures, dolls, posters, and sometimes even park signs are available. You can buy a Pal Mickey plush toy stuffed with a receiver and audio device that plays sound tracks at various attractions—it's as if Mickey is giving you a personal guided tour of his kingdom.

The big daddy of all Magic Kingdom shops is the **Emporium**. This 17,000-square-foot store stocks thousands of Disney character products, from sunglasses to stuffed animals. Girls will be thrilled to see lots of princess items, including pillows and pajamas. One of the best souvenirs ever is a princess cameo ring encircled with feathers. At $2 each, the rings are a very inexpensive way to give your little princess a gem of her own. Although perpetually crowded and absolutely mobbed at closing time, the Emporium is, hands down, one of the best sources for souvenirs. Hang on to your kids in

DRUMROLL, PLEASE . . .

The number-one best store on Disney property is World of Disney in the Marketplace section of Downtown Disney. You could actually skip all of the stores in the theme parks and find everything you want here in an hour. And it may be a cliché, but there really is something for everyone, whether you're looking for a something small and inexpensive, like the $3 princess pen, or a Disney collectible, like a Mickey watch or figurine.

here; they're likely to wander away as they spot yet another trinket they have to have.

ADVENTURELAND

Just outside the Pirates of the Caribbean ride, the **Pirate's Bazaar** is a good place to shop for your next Halloween costume. The pirate hats, swords, and hooks-for-hands are hits with everyone who has a bit of the scoundrel in them. And if you think you're too cool for a souvenir T-shirt, the Bazaar's hip and slightly Gothic shirts will make you reconsider. There are gritty, almost sinister skull-and-bones appliqués on biker vests, skull caps, and even beer koozies. Movie novelty collectors can buy any number of items with the logo from the *Pirates of the Caribbean* film.

Nearby, the **Agrabah Bazaar** has Aladdin-wear and the all-important Jasmine costume, as well as Moroccan-made carpets, carvings, and masks.

FRONTIERLAND

Emporia in Frontierland are generally referred to as "posts," as in the **Frontier Trading Post,** which is largely devoted to Disney collector pin trading. Large signs with advice for pin traders indicate that this place is a real trading post as well as a store.

The **Prairie Outpost & Supply** sells sheriff badges, leatherwork, cowboy hats, and southwestern, Native American, and Mexican crafts. Yee-haw!

Popular among boys are the Davy Crockett coonskin hats and personalized sheriff badges at **Big Al's,** across from the Country Bear Jamboree.

The **Briar Patch,** next door to Splash Mountain, looks like the inside of a tree hollow, with big, snarled roots across the ceiling and a pair of old wooden rockers in front of the hearth. If you're lucky enough to grab one of the rockers, you can rest your feet a spell while your kids snuggle and cuddle the many plush toys in the shop.

17

History buffs can find presidential and Civil War memorabilia at Liberty Square's **Heritage House.**

FANTASYLAND

For the famous black Mouseketeer hats, head to **Sir Mickey's.**

After you ride the Many Adventures of Winnie the Pooh, you end up at **Pooh's Thotful Shop,** a small store devoted entirely to Pooh merchandise, although these items are also available in other Disney stores.

Tinker Bell's Treasures is pretty much princessland, with sparkly, shimmering dresses, hats, dolls, and jewelry. You can even take home your very own Cinderella Castle for a mere $55.

Toontown's **County Bounty** is a voluminous carnival-tentlike store centered around a giant, cylindrical Mr. Potato Head dispenser. For $20, you get a potato head, a box, and all the accessories you can stuff inside the box. Some of the pieces are classic Mr. Potato Head parts, others are all Disney. There are mouse ears, Goofy hats, Minnie Bows, and so on. With an estimated 40 different parts to choose from, this may be the most interactive purchase you ever make.

Inside Cinderella Castle, the **King's Gallery** sells items to help you furnish your own castle, like imported European clocks, chess sets, and tapestries.

EPCOT

There are a few stores in Future World, but it's the World Showcase that has the really unique gifts.

WORLD SHOWCASE

Fodor'sChoice ★ Each of the countries represented has at least one gift shop loaded with things reflective of the history and culture of that nation's homeland, and many of the items are authentic imported handicrafts.

If your shopping time is limited, check out the two shops at the entrance to World Showcase. **Disney Traders** sells Disney dolls dressed in various national costumes as well as the requisite T-shirts and sweatshirts. Also sold here—and at some scattered kiosks throughout the park—is a great keepsake for youngsters: a World Showcase Passport ($9.95). At each pavilion, children can present their passports to be stamped—it's a great way to keep their interest up in this more adult area of Epcot. At **Port of Entry** you'll find lots of merchandise for kids, including clothing and art kits.

UNITED KINGDOM   Anglophiles will find their hearts gladdened upon entering the cobblestoned village at the United Kingdom, where an English Pub sits on one side, and a collection of British, Irish, and Scottish shops beckon you on the other. Consider the possibilities of an English garden at the **Magic of Wales.** You can pick up gardening tools, flower pots, and lavender potpourri. Take your time exploring the **Crown & Crest,** which has impressive handcrafted chess, some featuring the characters from *Alice in Wonderland*. If you wish you still had that Beatles lunch box from childhood, you might be able to buy a replacement here. Or perhaps you'll marvel at the magnificent knight's swords that can be had for $285 to $525.

FRANCE In France, keep a nose out for Guerlain perfume and cosmetics at **La Signature.** Every princess needs a tiny Limoges porcelain box for her earrings; look for the perfect one in the exquisite **Plume et Palette.** At **Les Vins de France** you can do some wine tasting and then pick up a bottle of your favorite.

MOROCCO Morocco has an **open-air market** like something out of an Indiana Jones movie. It's also a great place to pick up something really different, like a Moroccan tarboosh or fez for $8. If you're feeling really exotic, you can buy a belly-dancing kit, complete with a scarf, hat, finger cymbals, and a CD for $110.

JAPAN Instead of another princess doll, consider the kimonoed dolls at **Mitsukoshi.** Or instead of another T-shirt, consider a silk kimono. Koi ponds, Taiko drummers, and an impressive bonsai tree collection will help to bring a moment of serenity to your trip, that is until one of the kids catches a glimpse of the Japanese toys, collectibles, and candy artistry for sale here.

ITALY For chic Italian handbags, accessories, and collectibles, stop in at **Il Bel Cristallo.** Other gifts to look for include Venetian beads and glasswork, olive oils, pastas, and Perugina cookies and chocolate kisses (*baci*).

GERMANY In Germany pay a visit to the **Weinkeller,** where you can sample German wines by the glass. There are plenty to choose from, including rare German ice wines. For a good conversation piece, check out the nutcrackers at **Die Weinachts Ecke.**

SALUTING AFRICA OUTPOST At the **Village Traders,** wood carvers from Kenya whittle beautiful giraffes, elephants, and other animals while you watch. If you ask, the carvers may tell you stories about their homeland as they work. Each piece is unique, and some are a bit pricey, but you can buy an intricately carved wooden flute for $15. You'll find items from India and Australia for sale, too.

CHINA **Yong Feng Shangdian** is considered by some well-traveled guests to be the largest Chinese department store in the United States. It has exquisite desks, cabinets, and dining-room furniture featuring heavy lacquer and beautiful inlays. There are also hand-painted figurines, hand-carved chess sets, traditional clothing, and colorful parasols upon which you can have your name painted in Chinese.

NORWAY You can find Norwegian pewter, leather goods, and colorful sweaters at the **Puffin's Roost.** Viking wannabes can check out the spears, shields, and helmets.

MEXICO For a fun and colorful gift for kids, consider the piñatas at **Plaza de los Amigos,** in Mexico. Other good souvenirs include brightly colored paper blossoms, sombreros, baskets, pottery, and leather goods.

17

FUTURE WORLD

Future World shopping won't tempt you to spend much money unless you're heavily into the art of Disney animation. For the serious collector, the **Art of Disney** sells limited-edition figurines and cels (the sheets of celluloid on which cartoons are drawn). **Green Thumb Emporium,** in the Land pavilion, sells kitchen- and garden-related knickknacks—from hydroponic plants to vegetable refrigerator magnets. **Mouse Gear,** the biggest Disney apparel store at Epcot, has an impressive selection of Disney and Epcot logo items. You can pick up sweats emblazoned with Disney characters exercising at **Well & Goods Limited** in the Wonders of Life. Racing and automobile enthusiasts will likely be a bit disappointed by **Inside Track** near the Test Track exit. It sells some racing merchandise and other car-related items, but with less of a selection than a racing hobbyist store.

DISNEY–MGM STUDIOS

HOLLYWOOD BOULEVARD

Hollywood Boulevard is set up like Main Street U.S.A. in the Magic Kingdom—you can bypass the shops on your way in because you'll pass them again on the way out.

Of the shops here, **Sid Cahuenga's One-of-a-Kind,** an antiques and curios store, is the most interesting. With its bungalow-style architecture and 1930s phonograph music playing in the background, this very cool little shop might trick you into thinking it's actually a vintage store. You can pick up autographed items, such as a $425 Indiana Jones publicity photo signed by Harrison Ford. If you're a die-hard Old Blue Eyes fan, you can buy an authentic Frank Sinatra–signed picture for $2,475. Sid's even sells clothes worn by your favorite soap star. A dress worn by Susan Lucci might set you back a couple of hundred bucks.

If you're in the market for something you can actually wear, pop in to **Keystone Clothiers.** This store is full of Mickey clothing that is clearly geared to adults. The styles are hip and trendy, with some items capitalizing on popular vintage styles. Backpacks, for instance, sport vintage Mickey or vintage 1930s Sleeping Beauty artwork. For kid's clothing, go to **L.A. Prop Cinema Storage,** at the corner of Sunset and Hollywood.

ECHO LAKE

Almost as popular as the pirate swords and hats in the Magic Kingdom are the Indiana Jones bullwhips and fedoras sold at the **Indiana Jones Adventure Outpost,** next to the stunt amphitheater, and the Darth

Vader and Wookie masks at **Tatooine Traders,** outside of Star Tours. Serious Star Wars collectors might also find the action figure that's been eluding them, as well as books and comics. It's a busy store that inspires browsing.

NEW YORK STREET

The Writer's Stop offers one of the few decent cups of coffee to be had in Disney parks, as well as Earl Grey tea. If you happen to hit it right, you might get a book signed by a celebrity author, but the shop is small, the book selection is limited, and it's not conducive to hanging around. It is, however, a good place to pick up an autograph book. **It's a Wonderful Shop,** open seasonally, is where to pick up special Christmas decorations.

ANIMATION COURTYARD

Budding animators can hone their talents with Paint-a-Cel, a kit with two picture cels ready to be illustrated sold at the **Animation Gallery.**

SUNSET BOULEVARD

If you have younger children, consider a stop at **Legends of Hollywood** on Sunset Boulevard—it's brimming with Pooh-theme kids' clothing, toys, and accessories. Making the most of villains in vogue, the **Beverly Sunset** has Disney's best bad guys: Cruella DeVil, Mufasa, and the Siamese cats from *Lady and the Tramp.* You can also pick up weird Tim Burton wear featuring characters from *The Nightmare Before Christmas.*

17

DISNEY'S ANIMAL KINGDOM

Before you pass through the turnstiles on your way into the Animal Kingdom, stop at the **Outpost Shop** for a must-have safari hat with Mouse ears.

If you're traveling with small children, you won't escape Animal Kingdom without a visit to DinoLand U.S.A., where you'll find **Chester & Hester's Dinosaur Treasures.** This purposely tacky tourist outlet is the Animal Kingdom's premier toy store, with the toys mostly being of the prehistoric sort.

For African imports and animal items, as well as T-shirts, toys, and trinkets, check out the Harambe village shops. **Mombasa Marketplace and Ziwani Traders,** which you'll spot as you leave Kilimanjaro Safaris, sells $10 Animal Kingdom over-the-shoulder water-bottle holders, $19 colorful African sarongs, plush safari animals, and T-shirts with sparkly, leopard-print, Mickey silhouettes. Kids will be drawn to the unique African percussion and wind instruments—flutes cost just $2.50.

At **Creature Comforts** (before you cross from Discovery Island to Harambe), you can get a Minnie Mouse headband with a safari-style bow, sunglasses, prince and princess costumes, and great kiddie togs. **Island Mercantile,** to the left as you enter Discovery Island, has loads of little trinkets, like Mickey pens and key chains, plus cute safari, Tigger, and Pooh backpacks for $30, and Disney headgear for your dog.

Disney Outfitters, directly across from Island Mercantile and by the Tip Board, is another spot for finding some unique items. Kenana Knitter Critters are sized-for-stuffing stockings knit by Kenyan women who sign the tags. Made from soft, earth-tone yarns, each $30 stocking has an adorable animal head. You'll also find pottery with colorful safari scenes hand painted by artists in Zimbabwe. Prices range from $20 for a ramekin to $50 for a salt and pepper set.

DOWNTOWN DISNEY

⑪ The largest concentration of stores on Disney property is found in
Fodor'sChoice Downtown Disney. This three-in-one shopping and entertainment com-
★ plex comprises the Marketplace, West Side, and Pleasure Island, which is known primarily for its clubs.

MARKETPLACE

A lakefront outdoor mall with meandering sidewalks, hidden alcoves, jumping fountains that kids can splash around in, and absolutely fabulous toy stores, the Marketplace is a great place to spend a relaxing afternoon or evening, especially if you're looking for a way to give the kids a break from standing in line. There are plenty of spots to grab a bite, rest your feet, or enjoy a cup of coffee while taking in the pleasant water views and the hustle and bustle of excited tourists. The Marketplace is generally open from 9:30 AM to 11 PM. If you happen to run out of cash while you're shopping, you can apply for instant Disney credit at any register. How convenient.

Mickey's Mart. The sign proclaims "Everything Ten Dollars and Under," undoubtedly a welcome sight for those who've been reaching for their wallets a little too frequently. Look for the Surprise Grab Bags and the Item of the Week specials. ☎407/828–3864.

LEGO Imagination Center. An impressive backdrop of large and elaborate LEGO sculptures and piles of colorful LEGO pieces wait for children and their parents to build toy kitties, cars, or cold fusion chambers. ☎407/828–0065.

Once Upon A Toy. A joint venture by Disney and Hasbro, this huge toy store is the kind of place childhood dreams are made of. There are tons of classic games redesigned with Disney themes. You'll find Princess Monopoly and the Pirates of the Caribbean Game of Life, just to name a couple. Overhead are a massive Tinker Toy creation and an oversized toy train making the rounds on a suspended track. Toys in the main room seem to be mostly for boys, but another room has a huge faux-candy castle and a My Little Pony Creation Station. You can test-drive many of the toys and play with touch-screen computers. With so many things to do, this is one store that might let you escape without making a purchase. ☎407/934–7775.

World of Disney. You might make it through Once Upon a Toy without pulling out your wallet, but you probably won't be so lucky at World of Disney. For Disney fans, this is *the* Disney superstore. It pushes you into sensory overload with nearly a half-million Disney items from

Tinker Bell wings to Tigger hats. But if you have girls in your party, it's the Princess Room that will get you into the most trouble. Five-foot-tall likenesses of Cinderella and Sleeping Beauty stand watch over hoards of little misses scrambling to pick out just the right accessories. Besides princess dolls, clothes, shoes, and jewelry, you can buy a Belle (or Cinderella or Sleeping Beauty) wig to complete the look. Be warned, if you have a princess-obsessed child, one of the dazzling $60 princess dresses is going to be a must-have in her eyes, and people will be plucking them off the racks left and right of her. Add to that the new Bibbidi Bobbidi Boutique, where girls just like yours will be receiving princess makeovers ranging in price from $35 to $175, and you could land your budget in a royal mess. Of course there are things in the $10 to $30 range, including some cute pajamas, but it's hard to compare with those dresses. For grown-ups there are elegant watches, limited-edition artwork, and stylish furniture pieces with a Disney twist. ☎407/828–1451.

Pin Traders. It's nice to know that you can visit the biggest and best location for pin collectors without paying park admission. The Marketplace location has not only the largest selection, it also sells many limited-edition pins that are hard to find elsewhere. There are enough pins lining the walls to make you go cross-eyed, but the employees in this shop know their inventory very well, so if you're looking for something in particular, be sure to ask. And if you're having trouble managing your collection, you can buy additional lanyards, pin bags, and corkboards, too. ☎407/828–1451.

WEST SIDE

The West Side is mainly a wide promenade bordered by an intriguing mix of shops and restaurants. There are also gift shops attached to **Cirque du Soleil, DisneyQuest,** the **House of Blues,** and **Planet Hollywood.**

Guitar Gallery. This shop sells videos, music books, accessories, guitars, guitars, and more guitars, ranging in price from $89 to $20,000. Keep an eye open for the guitar heroes who drop in prior to gigs at the neighboring House of Blues. If you miss your favorite musician, the clerks have had the stars sign oversize guitar picks, which they display throughout the store. ☎407/827–0118.

Magic Masters. This small shop is arguably the most popular one here. As the magician on duty performs close-up card tricks and sleight of hand, an enraptured audience packs the shop for the free show. After the trick is finished, the sales pitch begins with a promise that (if you buy) they'll teach you how to do that particular feat of prestidigitation before you leave. ☎407/827–5900.

Magnetron. As the name implies, this place sells magnets—some 20,000 of them. So what's the big attraction? Well, they light up, change color, glow in the dark, and come in every shape, size, color, and pop culture character (check out magneto-Elvis). ☎407/827–0108.

Sosa Family Cigar Company. Cigars are kicking ash at this family-owned business. A fella's usually rolling stogies by hand in the front window and there's even a humidor room filled with see-gars. Smoking! ☎407/827–0114.

Starabilia's. If you're comfortable paying a few hundred simoleons for a framed, autographed picture of the cast of your favorite '70s sitcom, stop by Starabilia's. Although prices for the memorabilia run high—shoppers have paid from $195 for a Pee-Wee Herman autograph to $250,000 for a Hofner bass signed by the Beatles—you can't lose any money window-shopping, and the turnover of goods means the inventory's always entertaining. ☎407/827–0104.

Virgin Megastore. At 49,000 square feet, this enormous store has a selection as large as its prices. You can find better deals elsewhere, but not every record store has around 150,000 music titles, more than 300 listening stations, a full-service café, a 10,000-square-foot book department, clothing, accessories, and tens of thousands of DVD, software, and video titles. ☎407/828–0222.

There are several smaller, yet still enjoyable, shops along the **West Side pedestrian mall.** If you need a boost of sugar, the **Candy Cauldron** is filled with chocolate, fudge, hard candy, and other similarly wholesome foods. **Celebrity Eyeworks** carries designer sunglasses as well as replicas of glasses worn by celebrities in popular (as well as forgettable) films of the last few decades. **Mickey's Groove** has hip lamps, posters, greeting cards, and souvenirs inspired by the rodent. **Hoypolloi** adds art to the mix, with beautifully creative sculptures in various mediums—glass, wood, clay, and metals.

UNIVERSAL ORLANDO

UNIVERSAL STUDIOS FLORIDA

Every ride and attraction has its affiliated theme shop; in addition, Rodeo Drive and Hollywood Boulevard are pockmarked with money pits. It's important to remember that few attraction-specific souvenirs are sold outside of their own shop. So if you're struck by a movie- and ride-related pair of boxer shorts, seize the moment—and the shorts. Other choice souvenirs include Universal Studios' trademark movie clipboard, available at the **Universal Studio Store**; sepia prints of Richard Gere, Mel Gibson, and Marilyn Monroe from **Silver Screen Collectibles**; supercool Blues Brothers sunglasses from **Shaiken's Souvenirs**; plush animals, available at **Safari Outfitters, Ltd.** Stop by Hollywood's **Brown Derby** for the perfect topper, from fedoras to bush hats from Jurassic Park.

TOP 5 SHOPPING DESTINATIONS

Downtown Disney. Why spend valuable touring time shopping in the theme parks when you come here (for no entry fee) on your first or last day? The perfect place for one-stop souvenir shopping, Downtown Disney has dozens of stores, including World of Disney, easily the largest and best store on Disney property.

Epcot World Showcase. Trinkets from all over the world, some hand-crafted and incredibly unique, are sold at the pavilions representing individual countries here. Check out the Japanese bonsai trees and Moroccan fez hats.

Main Street, U.S.A., Magic Kingdom. The Main Street buildings are so adorable with their forced perspective architecture, pastel colors, and elaborately decorated facades that you want to go inside them and start examining the wares immediately. Don't waste precious touring time shopping in the morning, but definitely come back to check them out in the afternoon or evening.

Mall at Millenia. Visiting this mall is like going to New York for the afternoon. One look at the store names—Gucci, Dior, Chanel, Jimmy Choo, Cartier, Tiffany—and you'll think you've died and gone to the intersection of 5th and Madison.

Park Avenue, Winter Park. If you have the chance to visit the quaint village of Winter Park north of Orlando, carve out an hour or two to stroll up and down this thoroughfare.

17

ISLANDS OF ADVENTURE

From your own stuffed Cat in the Hat to a Jurassic Park dinosaur and a Blondie mug, you can find just about every pop-culture icon in take-home form here. **Wossamotta U.** is a good source for Bullwinkle stuffed animals and clothing. The **Dinostore** in Jurassic Park has a *Tyrannosaurus rex* that looks as if he's hatching from an egg, and (yes, mom) educational dino toys, too. Watch for—or watch out for—the **Comics Shop.** Kids may not be able to leave without a Spider-Man toy.

Merlin wannabes should head for **Shop of Wonders** in the Lost Continent to stock on magic supplies. And poncho collectors can get one at **Gasoline Alley** in Toon Lagoon, along with clever blank books and cartoon-character hats and wigs that recall Daisy Mae and others. For a last-minute spree, the **Universal Studios Islands of Adventure Trading Company,** in the Port of Entry, stocks the park's most popular souvenirs.

CITYWALK

❻ To Whom It May Concern: To spice up the mix of CityWalk's entertainment and nightlife, Universal added stores geared to trendy teens and middle-age conventioneers who can't go back home without a little something. Most stores are tucked between buildings on your left and right when you exit the moving walkway that rolls in from the parking garages, and a few are hidden upstairs—watch for the large overhead signs. Hours vary but are generally 11 AM–11 PM, closing at midnight on weekends. CityWalk parking is free after 6 PM. You can call the shops directly or get complete theme-park, nightlife, and shopping information from **Universal Orlando CityWalk** (☎*407/363–8000* ⊕*www.citywalkorlando.com*).

Cartooniversal. Small but packed with great products, Cartooniversal is the place to pick up your kid's favorite cartoon hero: Spider-Man, SpongeBob, and the Cat in the Hat are everywhere. A big plush Scooby Doo goes for $29.95, and X-Men T-shirts go for $14.95. ☎*407/224–2464.*

Cigarz. You have to duck down an alley to find this store, but the heavy aroma wafting from within might help to guide you. Just be careful not to walk into the giant Indian as you step through the doorway. Cigarz has a walk-in humidor, a full-length bar, and plenty of tables and ashtrays for enjoying your newly acquired stogie. Employees here take great pride in having hard-to-find smokes always in stock. Labels like OpusX, Ashton VSG, and Diamond Crown Maximus can be had for $9–$20 each, but you have to ask. Cigarz is open daily from 11 AM to 2 AM. ☎*407/370–2999.*

Endangered Species. Designed to resemble a jungle, this store aims to raise awareness of endangered species, ecosystems, and cultures worldwide. Some items, such as plush toys made by Aurora World Inc., clearly state on the tags that a portion of the proceeds are donated to conservation efforts. Periodically, artists, authors, and educators come in to discuss issues regarding the preservation of the planet. ☎*407/224–2310.*

Fresh Produce Sportswear. Bright, colorful beach clothes for women are sold here. Everything is made from 100% cotton, and the styles are loose and relaxed. You won't find much for dad, but moms and daughters can pick up matching outfits. ☎*407/363–9363.*

Jimmy Buffett's Margaritaville. If you absolutely *must* buy a Jimmy Buffett souvenir and can't make it to Key West, this is the next best thing. You can stock up on JB T-shirts, books, toy guitars, margarita glasses, sunglasses, picture frames, license plates, key chains, and theme hats (cheeseburger, parrot, and toucan). ☎*407/224–2144.*

Quiet Flight. Florida has managed to turn a natural detriment (small waves) into an asset—Florida's Cocoa Beach is the "Small Wave Capital of the World." This explains Quiet Flight, which sells surf brands like Billabong, Quicksilver, and Oakley. You'll find plenty of clothes but no surfboards. You can, however, shop for a skateboard. Quiet Flight opens a little earlier than other CityWalk stores, so you can start shopping at 9 AM. ☎*407/224–2126.*

Universal Studios Store. Although impressive in size, this store does not have all of the merchandise that's available in the individual park gift shops. Only the best-sellers are for sale here—T-shirts, stuffed animals, and limited-edition comic-book artwork. What's exclusive to this store are the mini movie posters, featuring some of Universal Studios greatest monster movies, priced at $11.99. It's also one of the few places on the property selling Universal trading pins. While you're here, be sure to check the back of the store for clearance racks. ☎*407/224–2207.*

SEAWORLD

Just as Disney offers all things Mickey, SeaWorld offers all things Shamu. If the classic plush Shamu toy isn't your thing, then perhaps you'd like a hand-painted Shamu martini glass from **Ocean Treasures** at the Waterfront, where you can also find some rather sophisticated black-and-white Shamu T-shirts as well as demure Shamu desk accessories for the office.

The **Waterfront,** a promenade lined with open-air restaurants and shops, resembles an international bazaar. You'll find wood carvings, handcrafted jewelry, and dinnerware painted with brilliant tropical flowers.

The sweet scents of tropical fruits lure you into the **Tropica Trading Company,** where you can design your own scent at the Fragrance Blending Bar. You can also pick up glasses hand-painted with tropical fish, and add to your resort-wear wardrobe while you're at it.

Allura's Treasure Trove is very appealing to young girls with its enchanting assortment of mermaid toys and mermaid apparel.

If you've promised your little one a stuffed toy, you might want to hold out until you've been through the **Wild Arctic gift shop,** which has an irresistible collection of soft, white, baby seals and fluffy polar bears. It's hard to walk past them without hugging at least one. You might also consider a soft manatee toy, available from **Manatee Gifts,** west of Dolphin Stadium. Proceeds from the toys go to benefit a manatee preservation organization.

During your visit, a park photographer may shoot a picture of you interacting with the animals. You can buy the souvenir photograph at **Keyhole Photo,** near Shamu's Emporium. You can also have your picture taken with one of the famous Budweiser Clydesdales at Clydesdale Hamlet. And if you're a real Anheuser-Busch enthusiast, then you might want to hit **Bud's Shop** near Turtle Point.

If you've left the park before realizing that you simply must have a Shamu slicker, visit **Shamu's Emporium,** just outside the entrance. Also, any purchase you make inside the park can be sent to Shamu's Emporium for pickup as you exit.

17

THE ORLANDO AREA

FACTORY OUTLETS

The International Drive area is filled with factory outlet stores, most on the northeast end. These outlets are clumped together in expansive malls or scattered along the drive, and much of the merchandise is ostensibly discounted 20%–75%. You can find just about anything, some of it top quality, but be advised: retailers have learned that they can fool shoppers into believing they must be getting a deal because they're at a stripped-down outlet store. Actually, prices may be the same as or higher than those at other locations.

❶ ★ Prime Outlets Orlando. Two malls and four annexes make Prime Outlets Orlando the area's largest collection of outlet stores. One of the best places to find deals is Off 5th, the Saks Fifth Avenue Outlet. There are almost always sales under way, allowing you to pick up high-end labels at sometimes ridiculously low prices. The same may prove true for the Nieman Marcus Last Call Clearance Center, scheduled to join the Prime Outlet shopping area as part of a massive remodel. A two-phase construction plan calls for a completely revamped shopping complex to be finished and cha-chinging by mid-2008. Other names to search out while there include Michael Kors, the Escada Company Store, and a Polo Ralph Lauren Factory Store. Don't worry about the construction cutting into your shopping. Stores are remaining open during the face-lift. Especially popular are the outlets for athletic shoes: Converse, Reebok, Foot Locker, and Nike. There are also good buys in housewares and linens in such outlets as Pfaltzgraff, Corning/Revere, Mikasa, and Fitz & Floyd. Don't worry about carting home breakable or cumbersome articles: these stores will ship your purchases anywhere in the United States by UPS. And just to be sure you don't run out of steam before you run out of money, Prime Outlets runs a free trolley between its Design Center, Mall 1, and Annex. ⊠ *5401 W. Oak Ridge Rd., at northern tip of International Dr.* ☎ *407/352–9600* ⊕ *www.primeoutlets.com* ☽ *Mon.–Sat. 10–9, Sun. 10–6.*

❿ Lake Buena Vista Factory Stores. Although there's scant curb appeal, this is a nice gathering of standard outlet stores. The center is roughly 2 mi south of I–4 and includes Reebok, Nine West, Big Dog, Sony, Liz Claiborne, Wrangler, Disney's Character Corner, American Tourister, Murano, Sony/JVC, Tommy Hilfiger, Ralph Lauren, Jockey, Casio, OshKosh, Fossil, and the area's only Old Navy Outlet. If you can, check the Web site before traveling as some stores post online coupons. Take Exit 68 at I–4. ⊠ *15591 State Rd. 535, 1 mi north of Hwy. 192* ☎ *407/238–9301* ⊕ *www.lbvfs.com* ☽ *Mon.–Sat. 10–9, Sun. 10–6.*

❾ Orlando Premium Outlet. This outlet capitalizes on its proximity to Disney (it's at the confluence of I–4, Highway 535, and International Drive). It can be tricky to reach—you have to take I–4 Exit 68 at Highway 535, head a few blocks east, and find the very subtle entrance to Little Lake Bryan Road (it parallels I–4). Parking is plentiful, and the center's design makes this almost an open-air market, so walking can

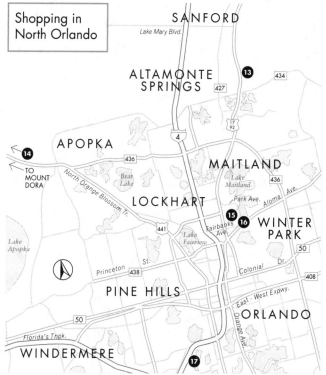

Shopping in
North Orlando

be pleasant on a nice day. You'll find Nike, Adidas, Timberland, Polo, Giorgio Armani, Burberry, Tommy Hilfiger, Dockers, Reebok, Versace, Guess?, Bebe, Mikasa, Max Mara, Nautica, Calvin Klein, and about 100 other stores. This mall has many of the same stores as Prime Outlets Orlando, so if you've hit one, you may find you can skip the other. ✉ *8200 Vineland Rd.* ☎ *407/238–7787* ⊕ *www.premiumoutlets.com/ orlando* ☉ *Mon.–Sat. 10–10, Sun. 10–9.*

② Outdoor World. The very large and very nice megastore carries goods and provisions for every aspect of outdoor life. In a sparkling 150,000-square-foot Western-style lodge accented by antler door handles, fishing ponds, deer tracks in the concrete, and a massive stone fireplace, the store packs in countless fishing boats, RVs, tents, rifles, deep-sea fishing gear, freshwater fishing tackle, scuba equipment, fly-tying materials (classes are offered, too), a pro shop, outdoor clothing, Uncle Buck's Cabin (a restaurant and snack bar), and a shooting gallery. If you're an outdoor enthusiast, this is a must-see. ✉ *5156 International Dr.* ☎ *407/563–5200* ⊕ *www.basspro.com* ☉ *Mon.–Sat. 9 AM–10 PM, Sun. 10 AM–7 PM.*

⑤ Sports Dominator. The huge, multilevel Sports Dominator could probably equip all the players of Major League Baseball and the NFL, NBA, and NHL combined. Each sport receives its own section, crowding

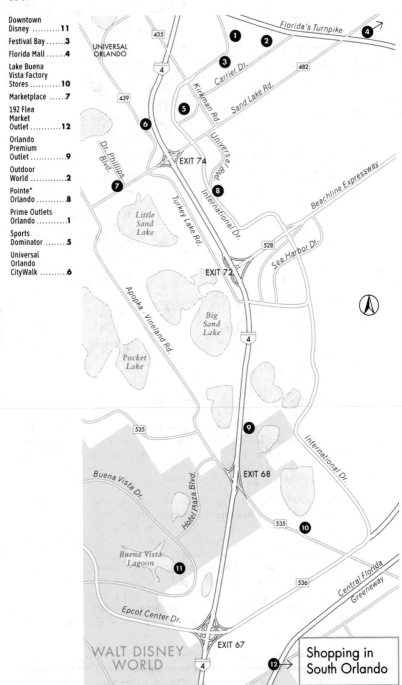

the floor with soccer balls, golf clubs, catcher's mitts, jerseys, bows, and a few thousand more pieces of sports gear. The prices may not be lower than anywhere else, but the selection is a winner. ⊠*6464 International Dr.* ☎*407/354–2100* ⊕*www.sportsdominator.com* ⊘*Daily 9 AM–10 PM.*

FLEA MARKETS

⓭ **Flea World.** It's a long traffic-choked haul from the attractions area (about 30 mi northeast), but Flea World claims to be America's largest flea market under one roof. Merchants at more than 1,700 booths sell predominately new merchandise—everything from car tires, Ginsu knives, and pet tarantulas to gourmet coffee, biker clothes, darts, NASCAR souvenirs, rugs, books, incense, leather lingerie, and beaded evening gowns. It's also a great place to buy cheap Florida and Mickey Mouse T-shirts. In one building, 50 antiques and collectibles dealers cater to people who can pass up the combination digital ruler and egg timer for some authentic good old junque and collectibles. A free newspaper, distributed at the parking lot entrance, provides a map and directory. Children are entertained at Fun World next door, which offers two unusual miniature golf courses, arcade games, go-carts, bumper cars, bumper boats, children's rides, and batting cages. Flea World is 3 mi east of I–4 Exit 98 on Lake Mary Boulevard, then 1 mi south on U.S. 17–92. ⊠*U.S. 17–92, Sanford* ☎*407/321–1792* ⊕*www.fleaworld. com* ⊡*Free* ⊘*Fri.–Sun. 9–6.*

⓬ **192 Flea Market Outlet.** With 400 booths, this market is about a fourth the size of Sanford's Flea World, but it's much more convenient to the major Orlando attractions (about 10 mi away in Kissimmee) and is open daily. The all-new merchandise includes "tons of items": toys, luggage, sunglasses, jewelry, clothes, beach towels, sneakers, electronics, and the obligatory T-shirts. ⊠*4301 W. Vine St., Hwy. 192, Kissimmee* ☎*407/396–4555* ⊘*Daily 9–6.*

⓮ **Renninger's Twin Markets.** In the charming town of Mount Dora (30 mi ★ northwest of downtown Orlando), Renninger's may be Florida's largest gathering of antiques and collectibles dealers. At the top of the hill, 400 flea-market dealers sell household goods, garage-sale surplus, produce, baked goods, pets, and anything else you can think of. At the bottom of the hill, 200 antiques dealers set up shop to sell ephemera, old phonographs, deco fixtures, antique furniture, and other stuff Granny had in her attic. If you have the time, hit the flea market first, since that's where antiques dealers find many of their treasures. Both markets are open every weekend, but on the third weekend of the month the antiques market has a fair attracting about 500 dealers. The really big shows, however, are the three-day extravaganzas held on the third weekends of November, January, and February—these draw approximately 1,500 dealers. These events can be all-day affairs; otherwise, spend the morning at Renninger's and then move on to downtown Mount Dora in time for lunch. From I–4, take the Florida Turnpike north to Exit 267A to reach Highway 429 east and, 8 mi later, Highway 441 north to Mount

17

Dora. Summers are very slow, the pace picks up from October through May. ⊠*U.S. 441, Mount Dora* ☎*352/383–8393* ⊕*www.renningers. com* ▤*Markets and Antiques Fairs free; Extravaganzas $10 Fri., $5 Sat., $3 Sun.* ⊙*Markets, weekends 9–5; Antiques Fairs, Mar.–Oct., 3rd weekend of month, 9–5; Extravaganzas Nov., Jan., and Feb., 3rd weekend of month, Fri. 10–5, weekends 9–5.*

SHOPPING CENTERS & MALLS

INTERNATIONAL DRIVE AREA

❸ **Festival Bay.** Long awaited and much delayed, this mall opened in 2003 to much fanfare. Most of its stores, such as Shepler's Western Wear and Ron Jon Surf Shop, are new to the Orlando market. Taking a new approach to retailing, Festival Bay has an indoor miniature golf course called Putting Edge and a 55,000-square-foot Vans Skatepark, with ramps for skateboarders and in-line skaters. Shops include Steve & Barry's University Sportswear, Epoxy, Hilo Hattie, CoKooning, and Storyville. There's also a 20-screen Cinemark Theater. Festival Bay is adjacent to the Factory Outlet Mall. ⊠*5250 International Dr.,* ☎*407/351–7718* ⊕*www.belz.com* ⊙*Mon.–Sat. 10–10, Sun. 11–7.*

❹ **Florida Mall.** With 260-plus stores, this is easily the largest mall in Cen-
★ tral Florida. Anchor stores and specialty shops include Nordstrom, Sears Roebuck, JCPenney, Dillard's, Saks Fifth Avenue, Restoration Hardware, J. Crew, Pottery Barn, Brooks Brothers, Cutter & Buck, Harry & David Gourmet Foods, and Swarovski. A 17-restaurant food court and four sit-down restaurants assure you won't go hungry. Stroller and wheelchair rentals are available, along with concierge services and, because the mall attracts crowds of Brazilian and Puerto Rican tourists, foreign-language assistance. The mall is minutes from the Orlando International Airport and 4½ mi east of I–4 and International Drive at the corner of Sand Lake Road and South Orange Blossom Trail. ⊠*8001 S. Orange Blossom Trail* ☎*407/851–6255* ⊕*www. simon.com* ⊙*Mon.–Sat. 10–9:30, Sun. 11–7.*

⓱ **Mall at Millenia.** The best way to describe this mall is "high-end." Design-
Fodor's Choice ers such as Gucci, Dior, Burberry, Chanel, Jimmy Choo, Hugo Boss,
★ Cartier, and Tiffany have stores here. You'll also find Anthropologie, Neiman Marcus, Bloomingdale's, Bang & Olufsen, and Orlando's only Apple store. The

★ **Millenia Gallery** (☎*407/226–8701* ⊕*www.milleniagallery.com*) treats window-shoppers and serious art buyers to paintings by Picasso, pop art by Warhol, and hand-blown glass art by Chihuly. Beyond the gallery's three exhibit halls is a second-floor balcony displaying outdoor sculptures. A few minutes northwest of Universal, the mall is easy to reach via Exit 78 off I–4. ⊠*4200 S. Conroy Rd.* ☎*407/363–3555* ⊕*www.mallatmillenia.com* ⊙*Mon.–Sat. 10–9:30, Sun. 11–7.*

❼ **Marketplace.** Convenient for visitors staying on or near International Drive, the Marketplace (not to be confused with Disney's Marketplace) provides all the basic necessities in one spot. Stores include a pharmacy, post office, one-hour film processor, stationery store, bakery, dry cleaner, hair salon, optical shop, natural-food grocery, and 24-hour supermarket. Also in the Marketplace are three popular restaurants: Christini's, Enzo's, and the Phoenician. Take the I–4 Sand Lake Road exit (Exit 74AB) and head west. ✉ *7600 Dr. Phillips Blvd.* ☎ *No phone* ⊙ *Hrs vary.*

⑧ Pointe*Orlando. Strategically located within walking distance of the Peabody Orlando and Orange County Convention Center, this impressive retail center along the I-Drive corridor is also undergoing a massive renovation and upgrade designed to make it even more appealing to expense-account-rich conventioneers. In addition to WonderWorks and the enormous Muvico Pointe 21 theater, the massive complex houses more than 60 specialty shops, including A/X Armani Exchange, Abercrombie & Fitch, Foot Locker Superstore, Chico's, Denim Place, Gap, Tommy Hilfiger, and Victoria's Secret. It also has a wide range of dining options, including the very high-end Capital Grille, Dan Marino's Town Tavern, Hooters, Monty's Conch Harbor, and Johnny Rockets. There are also a few dozen pushcart vendors selling hair ribbons, sunglasses, and other small items. Considering you have to pay to park ($2 for 15 minutes–2 hours, $5 daily), the nearby ATM is more than convenient. ✉ *9101 International Dr.* ☎ *407/248-2838* ⊕ *www.pointeorlando.com* ⊙ *Sun.–Thurs. 10–10, Fri. and Sat. 10 AM–11 PM.*

17

WINTER PARK

Unquestionably one of the most inviting spots in Central Florida,

⑯ Park Avenue in downtown Winter Park offers a full day of shopping

Fodor$Choice ★ and entertainment. The last couple of years have seen a mass exodus of the chain stores that came to dominate shopping on Park Avenue, leaving the street open to the return of boutique shopping. Most of these stores are privately owned and offer merchandise that cannot be easily found elsewhere.

On the north end of Park Avenue is the **Charles Hosmer Morse Museum of American Art,** of which the centerpiece is the work of Louis Comfort Tiffany. It's a great little museum with a fantastic shop selling lots of Tiffany-theme gifts and books. On the other side of the street is **10,000 Villages,** a fascinating little store dealing exclusively in fair-trade items. Across the street is **Shoooz,** which sells funky but functional Euro shoes. Just a short walk from there, **Jacobson's** is a chic clothing boutique.

Toward the south end of Park Avenue, you'll find **Peterbrooke Chocolatier,** which makes all of its chocolates on premises and almost always has something on hand to sample, such as its to-die-for chocolate-covered popcorn. Next door is **Red Marq,** a truly hip card shop that goes way beyond anything Hallmark has to offer. Across the street, **NFX Apothecary** sells indulgent soaps, lotions, and cosmetics. **Shoúture,** a high-end shoe boutique, stocks such designers as Hollywould, Constanca Basto, and Lily Holt. And if your feet are weary from shopping, don't worry, most Shoúture purchases will qualify you for a complimentary pedicure. If you're looking for the popular upscale pet boutique that used to be called The Doggie Door, go north a block. This shop has been combined with another venture owned by the same people, a former gourmet food and wine shop known as Olive This Relish That, to create **Bullfish**. A pet store/wine shop might sound like an odd combination, but the new combined business is as popular as the old separate businesses were.

For shoppers and nonshoppers alike part of the fun of Park Avenue is exploring the little nooks and crannies that divert you from the main drag. Tucked in an alley between Lyman and New England Avenues is **Palmano's**, a great little coffee bar that will sell you a hot cup of brew or a pound of its fresh roasted beans. It's also a great place to grab a glass of wine in the evening. Between Welbourne and Morse avenues, around the corner from Barnie's Coffee, you find **Greeneda Court**. A walk to the back reveals a delightful fountain and wrought-iron tables and chairs where you can sit and relax with a cappuccino from Barnie's. Of course the antiques store hidden there could keep you on your feet.

In the middle of the next block are the **Hidden Garden Shops,** which house Pooh's Corner, a delightful children's bookstore specializing in hard-to-find titles. Also on Park Avenue are numerous art galleries, antique jewelry stores, a cigar shop, and a gentlemen's barber shop where you can treat yourself to a haircut and a shave.

The third weekend in March brings the **Winter Park Sidewalk Art Festival** (☎407/672–6390); more than 40 years after its debut it still attracts thousands of art aficionados and a few hundred of America's better artists. ⊠ *Park Ave. between Fairbanks and Canton Aves.* ⊘ *Most shops Mon.–Sat. 10–5, some also Sun. noon–5.*

🕒 **Farmer's Market.** If you know you want to hit Park Avenue while you're in Central Florida, you might try to schedule your visit on a Saturday. Then you can begin your day at the Winter Park Farmer's Market, which takes place every week at the city's old train depot, two blocks west of Park Avenue. It's a bustling, vibrant market with vendors selling a wide selection of farm-fresh produce, dazzling flowers, and prepared foods. On any given morning you may find a chef stirring a steaming pot of Irish oatmeal, or a woman selling made-to-order crepes. There are plenty of baked goods and hot coffee available, along with places to sit and enjoy your treats.

Those willing to cross the railroad tracks that run through Winter Park will find the recently gentrified **Hanibel Square**. Centered around the intersection of New England and Pennsylvania avenues, the upscale dining and shopping found here is slowly working its way eastward toward Park Avenue with every additional boutique and art gallery.

Golf &
Other Sports

WORD OF MOUTH

"The Magnolia course is very nice, beautifully landscaped. There are LOTS of water hazards, though, as most of that area is a natural swamp. I'd do it just because you can't do a Disney course anywhere else!"

—mykidssherpa

"A great place to escape all that heat is Wekiwa Springs State Park. It is a natural spring so the water stays a cool 72° year-round. It's a lovely park north of Orlando in the Altamonte Springs–Apopka area, and you should be able to drive there in about 45 minutes from the Disney area."

—Lenore

Updated
by Rowland
Stiteler

THERE'S MORE TO AN ACTIVE Orlando experience than walking 10 mi a day in the theme parks. Northern travelers were flocking to central Florida's myriad lakes, streams, and golf resorts decades before there was a Disney World. There's nothing that can quite compare to an afternoon paddling down a Florida river, watching the alligators splash into the water and the snowy egrets glide among the palm trees.

You can find just about every outdoor sport in the Orlando area—unless it involves a ski lift. There are plenty of tennis courts and more than 150 golf courses, plus 17 golf academies, staffed by nearly three dozen PGA pros within a 40-mi radius. Some of the world's best-known golfing champions—huge names such as Arnold Palmer and Tiger Woods—have homes in the Orlando area. Anglers soak up the Orlando sun on the dozens of small lakes, and the metropolitan area has as many big-league professional bass fishermen as big-league baseball stars and PGA golf luminaries. And when you're ready to soothe those aching muscles from a day hiking the parks or the links, you can book yourself a treatment at one of the dozens of world-class spas in the Orlando area.

As a professional sports town, Orlando holds a hot ticket. The Orlando Magic basketball team is big-time, and baseball fans have plenty of minor-league action to enjoy. The Southern Professional Hockey League franchise, the Florida Seals, has a rabid fan base, and the Walt Disney World Speedway is the home of the Indy 200 and the Richard Petty Driving Experience. At Disney's Wide World of Sports you can watch or you can play. The complex hosts participatory and tournament-type events in more than 25 individual and team sports, including basketball, softball, and track-and-field; and it serves as the spring-training home of the Atlanta Braves.

But not everything in Orlando is wholesome, Disney-style family fun. Wagering a wad of cash at the jai-alai fronton or the dog track is guaranteed to wipe the refrain from "It's a Small World" right out of your head. Most of the tracks and frontons now have closed-circuit TV links with major horse-racing tracks, so you can bet on the ponies and then watch the race on a big-screen TV. And even if you bet and lose steadily, you won't necessarily spend more than you would at most Disney attractions—that is, depending on how much you wager.

AUTO RACING

★ **The Richard Petty Driving Experience** allows you to ride in or even drive a NASCAR-style stock car on a real racetrack. Depending on what you're willing to spend—prices range from $99 to $2,999—you can do everything from riding shotgun for three laps on the 1-mi track to taking driving lessons, culminating in your very own solo behind the wheel. The Richard Petty organization has a second Central Florida location at the Daytona International Speedway, but it involves riding in the car with an experienced race-car driver rather than driving a car yourself. ⊠ *Walt Disney World Speedway* ☎ *800/237–3889* ⊕ *www.1800bepetty.com.*

TOP 5 RECREATIONAL EXPERIENCES

Bob's Balloons. Think you see a lot from the top of the Tower of Terror? That ain't nothin' compared to what Bob will show you from the top of the clouds.

Grand Cypress Equestrian Center. Take a trail ride, learn dressage, or just stop by to see the stabled horses (some are for sale) at this world-class equestrian center just north of Walt Disney World.

Osprey Ridge Golf Course. This gorgeous, secluded, Tom Fazio-designed course is on Disney prop-erty but it's a world away from the cheerful insanity of the theme parks. Players on one hole can't see players on another.

Sky Venture. Totally safe skydiving? That's right, you can fly like a bird without jumping out of an airplane or even getting that far off the ground.

Winter Summerland Minigolf. This is kind of what you might expect Christmas in the Bahamas to look like, minus the snowman, of course. The giant sand castle is a small replica of Cinderella's not-so-humble abode.

BALLOONING

It's hard to imagine a more inspiring way to enjoy the beautiful Central Florida outdoors than with a hot-air balloon ride.

Fodor'sChoice ★ **Bob's Balloons** offers one-hour rides over protected marshland and will even fly over Disney World if wind and weather conditions are right. You meet in Lake Buena Vista at dawn, where Bob and his assistant take you by van to the launch site. It takes about 15 minutes to get the balloon in the air and then you're off on an adventure that definitely surpasses Peter Pan's Flight in the Magic Kingdom.

From the treetop view you'll see farm and forest land for miles, along with horses, deer, wild boar, cattle, and birds flying *below* you. Bob may take you as high as 1,000 feet, from which point you'll be able to see Disney's landmarks: the Expedition Everest mountain, the Epcot ball, and more. Several other balloons are likely to go up near you—there's a tight-knit community of ballooners in the Orlando area—so you'll view these colorful sky ornaments from a parallel level. There are seats in the basket, but you'll probably be too thrilled to sit down.

Landing places are somewhat arbitrary since your direction depends on the wind. You may even land on a private farm. Fortunately, Bob has a relationship with most of the landowners in the area. After Bob and his assistant, who follows the balloon in the van, wrap everything up, they treat you to a lovely champagne picnic brunch (minus coffee, so don't forget to have a cup before you leave). Late fall through early spring is prime time for ballooning. The air is typically too hot in sum-

18

mer for the balloons to get aloft. ☎407/466–6380 or 877/824–4606 ⊕*www.bobsballoons.com* ✉*$175, $90 per child under 90 lbs or 12 years* ▭*D, MC, V.*

BIKING

WALT DISNEY WORLD

The most scenic biking in Orlando is on Walt Disney World property, along roads that take you past forests, lakes, golf courses, wooded campgrounds, and resort villas. Most rental locations have children's bikes with training wheels and bikes with baby seats, in addition to regular adult bikes. Disney's lawyers are always watching out for liability problems, so management asks that you wear helmets, which are free with all bike rentals.

Theoretically, bike rentals are only for those lodging on WDW property; in practice, rental outfits usually check IDs only in busy seasons. Bikes must be used, however, only in the area in which you rent them. You must be 18 or older to rent a bike at all Disney locations.

☺ You can rent bikes for $8 per hour and surrey bikes for $20 (two seats) and $22 (four seats) per half hour at the **Barefoot Bay Marina** (☎407/934–2850), open daily from 10 to 5. Regular bikes at **Coronado Springs Resort** (☎407/939–1000), near Disney–MGM Studios, rent for $8 per hour or $22 per day, and surrey bikes rent for $17 (two seats) and $22 (four seats) per half hour. The surrey bikes look like old-fashioned carriages and are a great way to take your family on a sightseeing tour. The covered tops provide a rare commodity at Disney—shade. At **Fort Wilderness Bike Barn** (☎407/824–2742), bikes rent for $8 per hour and $22 per day. At the **BoardWalk Resort** (☎407/939–6486 *surrey bikes*), near Disney–MGM Studios, two types of bikes are available at two separate kiosks. Surrey bikes cost $20, $22 and $24 per half hour, depending on the size of the bike. Regular bicycles are $8 per hour.

ORLANDO AREA

Thanks to the Orlando community's commitment to the nationwide Rails to Trails program, the city now has several bike trails, converted from former railroad lines, in both rural and urban surroundings. You can venture into the city of Winter Park and pick up a trail that starts at the mall, or travel into the backwoods through heavily vegetated landscape and by scenic lakes. The Clermont–Lake County region is out in the boonies, where orange groves provide great scenery, and some hills afford challenges. Information about Orlando bike trails can be obtained from the **Orlando City Transportation Planning Bureau** (☎407/246–3347 ⊕*www.cityoforlando.net*).

★ **The West Orange Trail,** the longest bike trail in the Orlando area, runs some 20 mi through western Orlando and the neighboring towns of Winter Garden and Apopka. Highlights of the trail are the xeriscape–butterfly garden a mile east of the Oakland Outpost and views of Lake Apopka. You can access the trail at **Chapin's Station** (✉*501 Crown Point Cross Rd., Winter Garden 34787* ☎407/654–1108). **West Orange Trail**

Bikes & Blades (✉*17914 State Rd. 438, Winter Garden* ☎*407/877–0600*)rents bicycles and in-line skates.

A favorite of local bikers, joggers, and skaters, **the Cady Way Trail** connects eastern Orlando with the well-manicured enclave suburb of Winter Park. The pleasant trail is only 3½ mi long, with water fountains and shaded seating along the route. The best access point is the parking lot on the east side of the **Orlando Fashion Square Mall** (✉*3201 E. Colonial Dr., about 3 mi east of I–4 Exit 83B*).You can also enter the trail at its east end, in **Cady Way Park** (✉*1300 S. Denning Ave.*).

FISHING

Central Florida freshwater lakes and rivers swarm with all kinds of fish, especially largemouth black bass but also perch, catfish, sunfish, and pike.

LICENSES

To fish in most Florida waters (but not at Walt Disney World) anglers over 16 need a fishing license, available at bait-and-tackle shops, fishing camps, most sporting-goods stores, and Wal-Marts and Kmarts. Some of these locations may not sell saltwater licenses, or they may serve non-Florida residents only; call ahead to be on the safe side. Freshwater or saltwater licenses cost $6.50 for three consecutive days, $16.50 for seven consecutive days and $31.50 for one year. For Florida residents under age 65, a freshwater or saltwater license is $13.50 each, or $23.50 for both. Information on obtaining fishing licenses is available from the **Florida Game & Fish Commission** (☎*850/488–3641*). Fishing on a private lake with the owner's permission—which is what anglers do at Disney World—does not require a Florida fishing license.

WALT DISNEY WORLD

★ You can sign up for two-hour **fishing excursions** (☎*407/939–7529*)on regularly stocked Bay Lake and Seven Seas Lagoon. In fact, Bay Lake is so well stocked, locals joke that you can almost walk across the lake on the backs of the bass, so your chances of catching fish are quite good. The trips work on a catch-and-release program, though, so you can't take fish home.

Departing from the Fort Wilderness, Wilderness Lodge, Contemporary, Polynesian, Port Orleans Riverside, and Grand Floridian resort marinas, trips include boat, equipment, and a guide for up to five anglers. If you've never fished before, don't worry—your guide is happy to bait your hook, unhook your catches, and even snap pictures of you with your fish.

These organized outings are the only way you're allowed to fish on the lakes. Reservations are required. Yacht and Beach Club guests and Boardwalk Hotel guests can book a similar fishing excursion on Crescent Lake for the same fee as the Bay Lake trip. Two-hour trips, which depart daily at 7, 10, and 1:30, cost $230 for the morning departures and $200 for the afternoon departure, plus $80 for each additional hour. Shinners (live bait) are available for $15 per dozen.

18

On **Captain Jack's Guided Bass Tours** (☏407/939–7529), bass specialists go along for the two-hour fishing expeditions on Lake Buena Vista. Anglers depart from the Downtown Disney Marketplace marina at 7, 10, and 1:30. Trips for groups of two to five people cost $230 for the morning departures and $200 for the afternoon departure. Per-person admission, available only for the 1:30 trip, is $110.

The Fort Wilderness Bike Barn (☏407/824–2742), open daily 8–6, rents poles and tackle for fishing in the canals around the Port Orleans–Riverside (formerly Dixie Landings) and Port Orleans resorts and at Fort Wilderness Resort and Campground. Fishing without a guide is permitted in these areas. A cane pole with tackle is $4 per half hour and $8 per day; rod and reel with tackle is $6 per hour and $10 per day. You must be at least 18 to rent a rod and reel. Policy stipulates that rod users must be at least 12 years old, though this is not strictly enforced.

☺ **Yacht & Beach Club Kids-Only Fishing Trips** (☏407/939–7529), for ages 6 to 12 are led by adult Disney staff members who drive the boats and serve as guides. Half-hour excursions cost $30 per child and set out from the Boardwalk Community Hall Monday through Friday at 10 AM.

Ol' Man Island Fishing Hole (✉*Port Orleans–Riverside* ☏407/939–2277)has fishing off a dock. Catch-and-release is encouraged, but you can have your fish packed in ice to take home—you have to clean them yourself. Cane poles and bait are $4 per half hour. You must rent your equipment here to use the dock. Two-hour excursions in a boat with a driver are $80 per person, and include rod, reel, and bait. The Fishing Hole is open daily 7 to 2:30 and reservations are required.

ORLANDO AREA

Top Central Florida fishing waters include Lake Kissimmee, the Butler and Conway chains of lakes, and Lake Tohopekaliga—a Native American name that means "Sleeping Tiger." (Locals call it Lake Toho.) The lake got its centuries-old name because it becomes incredibly rough during thunderstorms and has sent more than a few fishermen to a watery grave. Be careful in summer when you see storm clouds. Your best chance for trophy fish is between November and April on Toho or Kissimmee. For good creels, the best bet is usually the Butler area, which has the additional advantage of its scenery—lots of live oaks and cypresses, plus the occasional osprey or bald eagle. Toho and Kissimmee are also good for largemouth bass and crappie. The Butler chain yields largemouth, some pickerel, and the occasional huge catfish. Services range from equipment and boat rental to full-day trips with guides and guarantees. Like virtually all lakes in Florida, the big Orlando-area lakes are teeming with alligators, which you'll find totally harmless unless you engage in the unwise practice of swimming at night. Small pets are more vulnerable than humans, and should never be allowed to swim in Florida lakes or rivers.

FISHING
CAMPS
A number of excellent fishing camps in the form of lakeside campgrounds draw a more outdoorsy crowd than you'll find elsewhere in the area.

East Lake Fish Camp (✉*3705 Big Bass Rd., Kissimmee* ☎*407/348–2040*), on East Lake Tohopekaliga, has a restaurant and country store, sells live bait and propane, and rents boats. You can also take a ride on an airboat. The camp has 286 RV sites that rent at $20 per night for two people. The RV sites rent for $350 per month. Simple, rustic cabins are $65 per night for two people and $5 per night for each additional person with a limit of five per cabin. Try to reserve one of the 24 cabins at least two weeks in advance in winter and spring.

> **NON-DISNEY LAKES**
>
> The key difference between the public lakes and the Disney lakes is that you have the option of keeping the fish you catch on the public lakes. Disney has a catch-and-release policy.

Lake Toho Resort (✉*4715 Kissimmee Park Rd., St. Cloud* ☎*407/892–8795* ⊕*www.laketohoresort.com*), on West Lake Tohopekaliga, has 200 RV sites. Most of the full hookups are booked year-round, but electrical and water hookups are usually available, as are live bait, food, and drinks. The RV sites are $24 per night and $275 per month, plus electricity.

Richardson's Fish Camp (✉*1550 Scotty's Rd., Kissimmee* ☎*407/846–6540*), on West Lake Tohopekaliga, has 7 cabins with kitchenettes, 16 RV sites, six tent sites, boat slips, and a bait shop. The RV sites are $28 per night, tent sites are $22.50, and cabins are $44 for one bedroom, about $68 for two bedrooms, and $79 for three bedrooms.

GUIDES Guides fish out of the area's fishing camps, and you can usually make arrangements to hire them through the camp office. Rates vary, but for two people a good price is $225 for a half day and $325 for a full day. Many area guides are part-timers who fish on weekends or take a day off from their full-time job.

All Florida Fishing (✉*4500 Joe Overstreet Rd., Kenansville 34739* ☎*407/436–1966 or 800/347–4007* ⊕*www.all-florida-fishing. com*)takes you on half- and full-day trips to go after the big bass that make the Kissimmee chain of lakes southeast of Disney ideal for sport-fishing. Captain Rob Murchie also leads full-day saltwater fishing expeditions in the Indian River Lagoon and Atlantic, an hour's drive to the east, in pursuit of tarpon and other game fish. Half-day freshwater trips are $225; full-day trips are $325. Saltwater trips (full day only) are $400. Prices are for one to two people. A third participant can join the group for $50. You can buy your license and bait here.

Bass Challenger Guide (BCG) (✉*195 Heather Lane Dr., Deltona 32738* ☎*407/273–8045 or 800/241–5314* ⊕*www.basschallenger.com*)takes you out in Ranger boats and equips you with tackle, license, bait, and ice. Transportation can be arranged between fishing spots and local hotels. Bass is the only quarry. Half-day trips for one or two people begin at $265; full-day trips begin at $350. Each additional person pays $50 more. You can buy your license and bait here. If you want a multiday trip or need nearby accommodations, Captain Eddie Bussard may book you a room at a local hotel for $59 a night.

18

GOLF

Sunny weather practically year-round makes Central Florida a golfer's haven, and there are about 150 golf courses and 17 golf academies within a 45-minute drive of Orlando International Airport. Most of Florida is extremely flat, but many of the courses listed here have man-made hills that make them more challenging. Many resort hotels let nonguests use their golf facilities. Some country clubs are affiliated with particular hotels, and their guests can play at preferred rates. If you're staying near a course you'd like to use, call and inquire. Because hotels have become so attuned to the popularity of golf, many that don't have golf courses nearby might still have golf privileges or discounts at courses around town. Check with your hotel about what it offers before you set out on your own.

In general, even public courses have dress codes—most courses would just as soon see you stark naked as wearing a tank top, for instance—so call to find out the specifics at each, and be sure to reserve tee times in advance. The yardages quoted are those from the blue tees. Greens fees usually vary by season, but the highest and lowest figures are provided, and virtually all include mandatory cart rental, except for the few 9-hole walking courses.

Golfpac (⊠ *483 Montgomery Pl., Altamonte Springs 32714* ☎ *407/260– 2288 or 800/327–0878* ⊕ *www.golfpactravel.com*) packages golf vacations and prearranges tee times at more than 78 courses around Orlando. Rates vary based on hotel and course, and at least 60 to 90 days' advance notice is recommended to set up a vacation.

Numbers in the margin correspond to properties on the Golf Courses in & near WDW map.

WALT DISNEY WORLD

Where else would you find a sand trap shaped like the head of a well-known mouse? Walt Disney World has 99 holes of golf on five championship courses—all on the PGA Tour route—plus a 9-hole walking course. Eagle Pines and Osprey Ridge are the newcomers, flanking the Bonnet Creek Golf Club just east of Fort Wilderness. WDW's original courses, the Palm and the Magnolia, flank the Shades of Green Resort to the west and the Lake Buena Vista course near Downtown Disney's Marketplace. All courses are full-service facilities, and include a driving range, pro shop, locker room, snack bar–restaurant, and PGA-staffed teaching and training program. Disney provides a special perk to any guest at a WDW hotel who checks in specifically to play golf: free cab fare for you and your clubs between the hotel and the course you play. (It saves you from having to lug your clubs onto a hotel shuttle bus.) Ask at the front desk when you check into the hotel or call ☎ 407/939–7529.

GREENS FEES   There are lots of variables here, with prices ranging from $20 for a youngster 17 or under to play 9 holes at Oak Trail walking course, to an adult nonhotel guest paying $165 to play 18 holes at one of Disney's newer courses in peak season. Disney guests get a price break, with rates ranging from $79 for a Disney hotel guest playing Monday through Thursday at the Lake Buena Vista course to $155 for a day visitor playing the Osprey Ridge course. All have a twilight discount rate, $30–$80 for the 18-hole courses, which goes into effect at 2 PM from October 31 to January 14 and at 3 PM from April 1 to October 26. The 9-hole, par-36 Oak Trail course is best for those on a budget, with a year-round rate of $20 for golfers 17 and under and $38 golfers 18 and older, and can be played for a twilight rate of $15 for adults and $10 for youngsters under 17 after 3 PM between May 14 and September 27. Rates at all courses except Oak Trail include an electric golf cart. No electric carts are allowed at Oak Trail, and a pull cart for your bag is $6. If you've got the stamina and desire to play the same course twice in the same day, you can do so for half price the second time around, but you can't reserve that option in advance, and this "Re-Play Option," as Disney calls it, is subject to availability. Note that golf rates change frequently, so double-check them when you reserve.

TEE TIMES &
RESERVATIONS Tee times are available daily from 6:45 AM until dark. You can book them up to 90 days in advance if you're staying at a WDW-owned hotel, 30 days ahead if you're staying elsewhere from May through December, and four days in advance from January through April. For tee times and private lessons at any course, call **Walt Disney World Golf & Recreation Reservations** (☎ 407/939–7529).

GOLF
INSTRUCTION One-on-one instruction from PGA-accredited professionals is available at any Disney course. Prices for private lessons vary: 45-minute lessons cost $75 for adults and $50 for youngsters 17 and under. Call the **Walt Disney World Golf & Recreation Reservations** to book a lesson.

18

COURSES **Eagle Pines,** one of the newer Walt Disney World courses, was designed
❺ by golf-course architect Pete Dye. The dish-shape fairways and vast sand beds are lined with pines and punctuated by challenging bunkers. *Golf Digest* gave this course four-and-a-half stars. ✉ *Bonnet Creek Golf Club* 🏌 *18 holes, 6,772 yards, par 72, USGA rating 72.3.*

❻ **The Lake Buena Vista** course winds among Downtown Disney–area town houses and villas. Greens are narrow, and hitting straight is important because errant balls risk ending up in someone's bedroom. Be prepared for the famous island green on the 7th. ✉ *Lake Buena Vista Dr.* 🏌 *18 holes, 6,819 yards, par 72, USGA rating 72.7.*

❶ **The Magnolia,** played by the pros in the Disney–Oldsmobile Golf Classic, is long but forgiving, with extra-wide fairways. More than 1,500 magnolia trees line the course. ✉ *Shades of Green, 1950 W. Magnolia-Palm Dr.* 🏌 *18 holes, 7,190 yards, par 72, USGA rating 73.9.*

❷ **Oak Trail** is a 9-hole, par-36 walking course, designed to be fun for the entire family. It was designed by Ron Garl and is noted for its small, undulating greens. ✉ *Shades of Green, 1950 W. Magnolia-Palm Dr.* 🏌 *9 holes, 2,913 yards, par 36.*

❹ **Osprey Ridge,** sculpted from some of the still-forested portions of the
Fodor's Choice huge WDW acreage, was transformed into a relaxing tour in the hands
★ of designer Tom Fazio. However, tees and greens as much as 20 feet

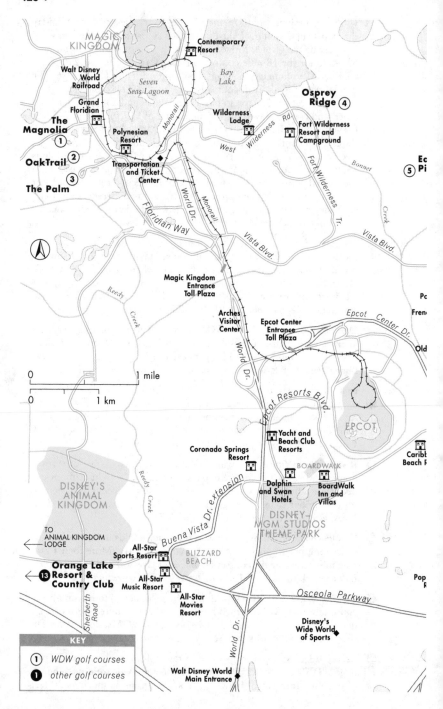

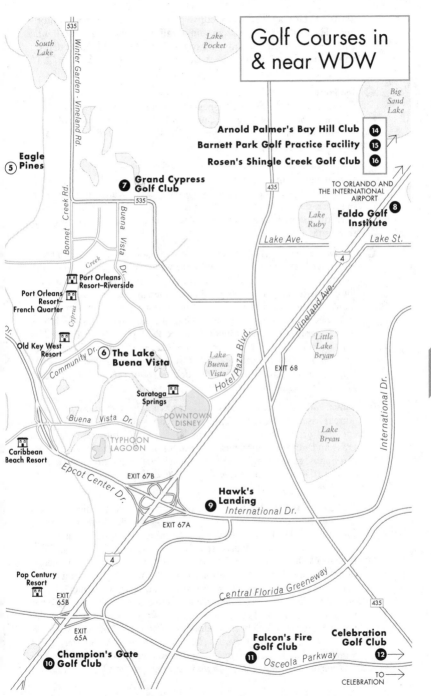

Golf Courses in & near WDW

above the fairways keep competitive players from getting too comfortable. The course was rated four-and-a-half stars by *Golf Digest*. Rental clubs require photo ID and a major credit card for refundable deposit of $500 per set. ⊠*Bonnet Creek Golf Club, 3451 Golf View Dr.* ⚐*18 holes, 7,101 yards, par 72, USGA rating 73.9.*

❸ **The Palm,** one of WDW's original courses, has been confounding the pros as part of the annual Disney–Oldsmobile Golf Classic for years. It's not as long as the Magnolia, or as wide, but it has 9 water holes and 94 bunkers. ⊠*Shades of Green, 1950 W. Magnolia-Palm Dr.* ⚐*18 holes, 6,957 yards, par 72, USGA rating 73.*

ORLANDO AREA

Greens fees at most non-Disney courses fluctuate with the season. A twilight discount applies after 2 PM in busy seasons and after 3 PM during the rest of the year; the discount is usually half off the normal rate. Because golf is so incredibly popular around Orlando, courses raise their rates regularly.

⑭ **Arnold Palmer's Bay Hill Club & Lodge** golf courses are open only to those who have been invited by a member or who book lodging at the club's 65-room hotel. But with double-occupancy rates for rooms overlooking the course running as low as $469 in summer, including a round of golf, many consider staying at the club an interesting prospect. The course is the site of the annual Bay Hill Invitational, and its par-72, 18th hole is considered one of the toughest on the PGA tour. ⊠*9000 Bay Hill Rd., Orlando* ☏*407/876–2429 or 888/422–9445* ⊕*www.bayhill.com* ⚐*18 holes, 7,207 yards, par 72, USGA rating 75.1; 9 holes, 3,409 yards, par 36* ⊠*Greens fees included in room rates* ⌔*Restaurant, private lessons, club rental.*

⑮ **Barnett Park Golf Practice Facility,** besides having an attractive course, has a great asset: it's free. All a golfer has to do is show up to use the net-enclosed driving range (with 10 pads), the three chipping holes with grass and sand surroundings, and the 9-hole putting green. As a special bonus, children ages 7–13 can spend time with a pro at no charge from 3 to 4:30 PM on Wednesday. ⊠*4801 W. Colonial Dr., Orlando* ☏*407/836–6248* ⊠*Free.*

⑫ **The Celebration Golf Club** course—in addition to its great pedigree (it was designed by Robert Trent Jones Jr. and Sr.)—has the same thing going for it that the Disney-created town of Celebration, Florida, has: it's just 1 mi off the U.S. 192 tourist strip and a 10-minute drive from Walt Disney World, yet it is lovely and wooded, and as serene and bucolic as any spot in Florida. In addition to the 18-hole course, driving range, and 3-hole junior course, the club includes a quaint, tin-roof clubhouse with a pro shop and restaurant, flanked by a tall, wooden windmill that is a local landmark. The club has golf packages, which include lodging at the nearby Celebration Hotel. ⊠*701 Golf Park Dr., Celebration* ☏*407/566–4653* ⊕*www.celebrationgolf.com* ⚐*18 holes, 6,783 yards, par 72, USGA rating 73* ⊠*Greens fees $55–$150, depending on time of year, time of day you play, whether you're a Florida resident,* *and whether you're a Celebration resident; daily discount rates begin at 2 PM ᒯRestaurant, pro shop, private lessons, club rental.*

★ ⑩ **Champions Gate Golf Club,** which has the David Leadbetter Golf Academy on its property, has courses designed by Greg Norman. The club is less than 10 mi from Walt Disney World at Exit 24 on I–4. The two courses have distinct styles; the 7,406-yard International has the feel of the best British Isles courses, whereas the 7,048-yard National course is designed in the style of the better domestic courses, with a number of par-3 holes with unusual bunkers. ✉*1400 Masters Blvd., Champions Gate* ☎*407/787–3330 or 888/558–9301 Champions Gate, 888/633-5323 Ext. 23 Leadbetter Academy* ⊕*www.championsgategolf.com* ⅄*International: 18 holes, 7,406 yards, par 72, USGA rating 73.7; National: 18 holes, 7,048 yards, par 72, USGA rating 72.0* ▧*Greens fees $65–$187, depending on time of year and time of day you play. Golf lessons at Leadbetter Academy are $225 per hr and $1,750 per day for private lessons; group lessons are $325 for 3 hrs; a 3-day minischool is $900; a 3-day complete school is $3,000* ᒯ*Pro shop, golf school, private lessons, club rental.*

⑪ **Falcon's Fire Golf Club,** designed by golf-course architect Rees Jones, has strategically placed fairway bunkers that demand accuracy off the tee. This club is just off the Irlo Bronson Highway and is one of the most convenient to the hotels in the so-called "Maingate" area. ✉*3200 Seralago Blvd., Kissimmee* ☎*407/239–5445* ⊕*www.falconsfire.com* ⅄*18 holes, 6,901 yards, par 72, USGA rating 73.8* ▧*Greens fees $79–$145, $50 after 2 PM, $40 after 4 PM* ᒯ*Tee times 8–60 days in advance. Restaurants, private and group lessons, club rental, lockers, driving range, putting green.*

⑧ **Faldo Golf Institute by Marriott** is the team effort of world-famous golf pro Nick Faldo and Marriott Corp. An extensive-curriculum golf school and 9-hole golf course occupy the grounds of the corporation's biggest time-share complex, Marriott's Grande Vista. Here you can do anything from taking a one-hour, $150 lesson with a Faldo-trained pro (although not with the great Faldo himself, of course) to immersing yourself in a three-day extravaganza ($895–$1,400) in which you learn more about golf technique than most nonfanatics would care to know. Private instruction starts at $125 per hour. Among the high-tech teaching methods at the school is the Faldo Swing Studio, in which instructors tape you doing your initial, unrefined swing; analyze the tape; and then teach you how to reform your physical skills the Faldo Way. The course, designed by Ron Garl, is geared to make you use every club in your bag—and perhaps a few you may elect to buy in the pro shop. As with virtually everything else in Florida, prices go up in peak seasonal months, but there's always a group discount at the Faldo Institute, even for groups as small as two people. ✉*Marriott Grande Vista, 12001 Avenida Verde, Orlando 32821* ☎*407/903–6295 or 888/800-4325 Ext. 6295* ⊕*www.gofaldo.com* ⅄*9 holes, 2,400 yards, par 32.*

⑦ **Grand Cypress Golf Club,** fashioned after a Scottish glen, is comprised of four nines: the North, South, East, and New courses. The North and South courses have fairways constructed on different levels, giving them added definition. The New Course was inspired by the Old Course at St. Andrews, and has deep bunkers, double greens, a snaking burn, and even an old stone bridge. ⊠*1 N. Jacaranda, Orlando 32836* ☎*407/239–1909 or 800/835–7377* ⊕*www.grandcypress.com* ⚑*North: 9 holes, 3,521 yards, par 36; South: 9 holes, 3,472 yards, par 36; East: 9 holes, 3,434 yards, par 36; New: 9 holes, 6,773 yards, par 72. USGA rating 72.* 🏌*Greens fees $120–$190* ☞*Tee times 7:30* AM*–6* PM*. Restaurant, club rental, shoe rental, locker room, driving range, putting green, free valet parking.*

❾ **Hawk's Landing,** originally designed by Joe Lee, was extensively upgraded with a Robert E. Cupp III design in 2000. The course includes 16 water holes, lots of sand, and exotic landscaping. ⊠*Orlando World Center Marriott, 8701 World Center Dr., Orlando 32821* ☎*407/238–8660, or 800/567–2623* ⊕*www.golfhawkslanding.com* ⚑*18 holes, 6,810 yards, par 72, USGA rating 73.2* 🏌*Greens fees $89–$129* ☞*Tee times 7 days in advance for public, 90 days in advance for World Center guests. Restaurants, private and group lessons, club and shoe rental.*

⓭ **The Orange Lake Resort & Country Club,** about five minutes from Walt Disney World's main entrance, has three very similar 9-hole courses: the Orange, Lake, and Cypress. Distances aren't long, but fairways are very narrow, and there's a great deal of water, making the courses difficult. A fourth course, the 18-hole Legends, was designed by Arnold Palmer. Standard practice is to play two of the three 9-hole courses in combination for a single round of golf, or play Legends. ⊠*8505 W. Irlo Bronson Memorial Hwy., Kissimmee 34747* ☎*407/239–0000 or 800/877–6522* ⊕*www.orangelake.com* ⚑*Lake/Orange: 18 holes, 6,531 yards, par 72, USGA rating 72.2; The Reserve: 18 holes, 6,670 yards, par 72, USGA rating 72.6; Cypress/Lake: 18 holes, 6,571 yards, par 72, USGA rating 72.3; Legends: 18 holes, 7,074 yards, par 72, USGA rating 74.3* 🏌*Greens fees $22–$65 for guests of the resort; $25–$70 nonguests* ☞*Tee times 2 days in advance. Restaurant, private and group lessons, club rental, driving range, putting green.*

⓰ **Rosen's Shingle Creek Golf Club,** designed by David Harman, lies alongside a lovely creek, the headwaters of the Everglades. The course is challenging yet playable, with dense stands of oak and pine trees and interconnected waterways. The golf carts even have GPS yardage systems. Universal Studios and the Orange County Convention Center are within a few minutes' drive. ⊠*9939 Universal Blvd., Orlando 32819* ☎*407/996–9933 or 866/996–9933* ⊕*www.shinglecreekgolf. com* ⚑*18 holes, 7,205 yards, par 72, USGA rating 69.8* 🏌*Greens fees $79–$134, $75 after 2* PM ☞*Tee times 7–sunset. Restaurant, club rental, shoe rental, driving range, putting green.*

HORSEBACK RIDING

WALT DISNEY WORLD

Fort Wilderness Resort and Campground (⊠ *Fort Wilderness Resort* ☎*407/824–2832*)offers tame trail rides through backwoods. Children must be at least 9 to ride, and adults must weigh less than 250 pounds. Trail rides are $42 for 45 minutes; hours of operation vary by season. You must check in 30 minutes prior to your ride, and reservations are essential. Both horseback riding and the campground are open to nonguests.

ORLANDO AREA

FodorsChoice **Grand Cypress Equestrian Center** gives private lessons in hunt seat, jump-
★ ing, combined training, dressage, and Western riding. Supervised novice and advanced group trail rides are available daily 8:30 to 5. Trail rides are $45 per hour. Private lessons are $55 per half hour and $100 per hour. Call at least a week ahead for reservations in winter and spring. ⊠*Hyatt Regency Grand Cypress Resort, 1 Equestrian Dr., Lake Buena Vista Area* ☎*407/239–1938* ⊕*www.grandcypress.com.*

Horse World Riding Stables, open daily 9 to 5, has basic and longer, more advanced nature-trail tours along beautifully wooded trails near Kissimmee. The stables area has picnic tables, farm animals you can pet, and a pond where you can fish. Trail rides are $39 for basic, $48 for intermediate, and $69 for advanced. Trail rides for children 5 and under are $15, and the stables offer birthday party packages for kids, as well as hayrides for groups. Reservations a day in advance are recommended for the advanced trails. ⊠*3705 S. Poinciana Blvd., Kissimmee* ☎*407/847–4343* ⊕*www.horseworldstables.com.*

18

MINIATURE GOLF

Fantasia Gardens Mini-Golf (☎*407/560–4870*), near Disney-MGM Studios and the Swan and Dolphin resorts, recalls Disney's *Fantasia* with a huge statue of Mickey in his sorcerer's outfit directing dancing broomsticks. Music from the film plays over loud speakers. Games cost $11.40 for adults, $9 for children ages 3 to 9, and there's a 50% discount for the second consecutive round played.

 Winter Summerland Mini-Golf (☎*407/560–7161*)has everything from
FodorsChoice sand castles to snowbanks, and is allegedly where Santa and his elves
★ spend their summer vacation. The course is close to Disney's Animal Kingdom and the Coronado Springs and All-Star resorts. Adults play for $11.40 and children ages 3 to 9 play for $9, including tax. A 50% discount applies to your second consecutive round.

RUNNING

WALT DISNEY WORLD

Walt Disney World has several scenic running trails. Pick up maps at any Disney resort. Early in the morning all the roads are fairly uncrowded and make for good running. The roads that snake through Downtown Disney resorts are pleasant, as are the cart paths on the golf courses.

At the **Caribbean Beach Resort** (☎407/934–3400), there's a 1½-mi running promenade around Barefoot Bay. **Fort Wilderness Campground** (☎407/824–2900)has a 2 -mi running course with woods, as well as numerous exercise stations along the way.

ORLANDO AREA

Orlando has two excellent bike trails, the West Orange Trail and the Cady Way Trail, which are also good for running. Rural Orlando has some unbelievable hiking trails with long, densely wooded, nonrocky stretches that are tremendous for running, and often you can run for a half hour and not see any other living being—except wild game.

Turkey Lake Park, about 4 mi from Disney, has a 3-mi biking trail that's popular with runners. Several wooded hiking trails also make for a good run. The park closes at 5 PM, and fees are $4 per car. ⊠3401 S. Hiawassee Rd., Orlando ☎407/299–5581.

SKYDIVING & PARASAILING

Sammy Duvall's Water Sports Centre (⊠Disney's Contemporary Resort ☎407/939–0754)offers parasailing on Bay Lake in addition to water sports. Flights, $90 per outing, reach a height of 450 feet and last 7 to 10 minutes. Individual participants must weigh at least 100 pounds, but youngsters may go aloft accompanied by an adult. Tandem flights are $165.

Fodor'sChoice ★ **Sky Venture,** a 120-mph vertical-lift wind tunnel, allows you to experience everything skydivers enjoy, all within an air blast that reaches only 12 feet. The experience starts with skydiving instruction, after which you suit up and hit the wind tunnel, where you soar like a bird under the watchful eye of your instructor. While you are "falling" on the wind stream, you even experience what divers called "ground rush," because you're surrounded by a video depiction of a real skydive. The experience is so realistic that skydiving clubs come to Sky Venture to hone their skills. Famous people who have tried this include George Bush Sr. You must be less than 250 pounds and at least 4 feet tall to participate. You can purchase a video of your jump for $16. ⊠6805 Visitors Circle, I-Drive Area, Orlando ☎407/903–1150 ⊕www.skyventure. com ☑$39.95 per jump; $700 per hr, $425 per half hr ☉Weekdays 2–midnight, weekends noon–midnight.

TENNIS

WALT DISNEY WORLD

You can play tennis at any number of Disney hotels, and you may find the courts a pleasant respite from the milling throngs in the parks. All have lights and are open 7 AM to 8 PM, unless otherwise noted, and most have lockers and rental rackets for $3 to $5 a day. There seems to be a long-term plan to move from hard courts to clay. Most courts are open to all players—court staff can opt to turn away nonguests when things get busy, but that doesn't often happen. Disney offers group and individual tennis lessons at all of its tennis complexes.

The Contemporary Resort, with its sprawl of six HydroGrid courts, is the center of Disney's tennis program. It has two backboards and an automatic ball machine. Reservations are available up to 24 hours in advance, and there's an arrange-a-game service. ☎407/939–7529 reservations ✉Free; lessons $50 per hr or $30 per half hr for individual and $40 per hr for group of two ⊙Daily 7–7.

Fort Wilderness Resort and Campground has two tennis courts in the middle of a field. They're popular with youngsters, and if you hate players who are too free about letting their balls stray to their neighbors' court, this is not the place for you. There are no court reservations and instruction is not available. ✉3520 N. Fort Wilderness Trail ☎407/824–2742 ✉Free ⊙Daily 8–6.

The Grand Floridian has two Har-Tru clay courts that attract a somewhat serious-minded tennis crowd. Court reservations are available up to 24 hours in advance. ☎407/939–7529 ✉Free ⊙Daily 8–8.

The Yacht and Beach Club Resorts have two blacktop tennis courts. Court reservations are not required. Equipment is available at the towel window at no charge. ☎407/939–7529 ✉Free ⊙Daily 7 AM–10 PM.

ORLANDO AREA

Orange Lake Country Club has, in addition to its golf courses, seven lighted, all-weather hard tennis courts. It's five minutes from Walt Disney World's main entrance. Court reservations are necessary. ✉8505 W. Irlo Bronson Memorial Hwy., Kissimmee ☎407/239–0000 or 800/877–6522 ✉Free for guests, $5 per hr nonguests, $60 per hr for private lessons, $10 per ½ hr for group clinics, $2 per hr and $5 per day racket rental ⊙Daily dawn–11 PM.

WALT DISNEY WORLD SPORTS

★ **Disney's Wide World of Sports Complex** is proof that Disney doesn't do anything unless it does it in a big way. The huge complex contains a 7,500-seat baseball stadium—housed in a giant stucco structure that from the outside looks like a Moroccan palace—a 5,000-seat field house, and a number of fan-oriented commercial ventures such as the Official All-Star Cafe and shops that sell clothing and other items sanctioned by Major League Baseball, the NBA, and the NFL. During spring training, the perennially great Atlanta Braves play here, and

18

the minor-league Orlando Rays have games during the regular season. But that's just the tip of the iceberg. The complex hosts all manner of individual and team competitions, including big-ticket tennis tournaments. In all, some 30 spectator sports are represented among the annual events presented, including Harlem Globetrotters basketball games, baseball fantasy camps held in conjunction with the Braves at the beginning of spring training each year, and track events ranging from the Walt Disney World Marathon to dozens of annual Amateur Athletic Union (AAU) championships. The complex has softball, basketball, and other games for group events ranging from family reunions to corporate picnics. ⊠ *Osceola Pkwy.* ☎ *407/828–3267 events information* ⊕ *www.disneyworldsports.com.*

A key source for sports information on all things Disney is the **Sports Information and Reservations Hotline** (☎ *407/939–7529*).

WATER SPORTS

WALT DISNEY WORLD

Boating is big at Disney, and it has the largest fleet of for-rent pleasure craft in the nation. There are marinas at the Caribbean Beach Resort, Contemporary Resort, Downtown Disney Marketplace, Fort Wilderness Resort and Campground, Grand Floridian, Old Key West Resort, Polynesian Resort, Port Orleans Resort, Port Orleans–Riverside Resort, and the Wilderness Lodge. The Yacht and Beach Club Resorts rent Sunfish sailboats, catamarans, motor-powered pontoon boats, pedal boats, and tiny two-passenger Water Sprites—a hit with children—for use on Bay Lake and the adjoining Seven Seas Lagoon, Club Lake, Lake Buena Vista, or Buena Vista Lagoon. Most hotels rent Water Sprites, but you should check each hotel's rental roster. The Polynesian Resort marina rents outrigger canoes. Fort Wilderness rents canoes for paddling along the placid canals in the area. And you can sail and water-ski on Bay Lake and the Seven Seas Lagoon; stop at the Fort Wilderness, Contemporary, Polynesian, or Grand Floridian marina to rent sailboats or sign up for waterskiing. Call 407/939–0754 for parasailing, waterskiing, and Jet Skis reservations.

Sammy Duvall's Water Sports Centre (⊠ *Disney's Contemporary Resort* ☎ *407/939–0754*)offers waterskiing, wakeboarding (like waterskiing on a small surfboard; usually done on your knees), and parasailing on Bay Lake. Boat and equipment rental is included with waterskiing (maximum of five people) and wakeboarding (maximum of four people), as are the services of an expert instructor. Each is $165 per hour, plus tax.

ORLANDO AREA

★ **Wekiva River,** a great waterway for nature lovers, runs through 6,397-acre **Wekiva Springs State Park** (⊠ *1800 Wekiva Circle, I–4 Exit 94, Apopka* ☎ *407/884–2008* ⊕ *www.dep.state.fl.us/parks*)into the St. Johns River. Bordered by cypress marshlands, its clear, spring-fed waters showcase Florida wildlife, including otters, raccoons, alligators, bobcats, deer, turtles, and numerous birds. Canoes and campsites can be rented near the southern entrance of the park in Apopka. Canoes are available for $12 for two hours and $3 per hour after that. The park has 60 campsites, some of which are "canoe sites," in that they can only be reached via the river itself, while others are "trail sites," meaning you must hike a good bit of the park's 13.5-mi hiking trail to reach them. Most sites, however, are for the less hardy among us—you can drive right up to them. Sites go for $20 a night with electric hookups or $18 with no electricity. Tents are available for $4 per night, and it costs $5 per vehicle to enter the park.

18

Away from the Theme Parks

WORD OF MOUTH

"We recently visited the Kennedy Space Center, which our kids, 13 and 16, enjoyed. I think it's a great destination for teens, especially if they have an interest in engineering."

–patg

"Take a side trip to Gatorland, one of the most hysterically tacky places in the country. You enter through a giant plaster gator mouth and there's a show several times a day where the gators jump for raw chicken strung across their pond on a clothes-line. About as anti-Mickey as you can get."

–gail

Revised by
Jennie Hess

STARTING TO FEEL IRRITABLE? CLAUSTROPHOBIC? It's called theme-park syndrome, and it often strikes four days or so into a vacation. You start to feel like you can't wait to get away from the crowds, hot pavement, and Candyland surroundings of the parks. If this sounds familiar and you need a break from the theme-park mania, or if you'd simply like to see more of Central Florida than what you can view from the top of a roller-coaster track, then this chapter is for you.

For a breath of fresh air and a look at what the accommodating climate of Central Florida has to offer, you can escape to the Ocala National Forest or Wekiwa Springs State Park. If you need a museum fix and maybe some shopping in a quintessential Florida village, head for Winter Park and the Charles Hosmer Morse Museum with its stunning collection of Tiffany glass. Got kids to educate? Take them to WonderWorks or the Orlando Science Center. Do they like rockets and astronauts? Don't miss a day trip to the incomparable Kennedy Space Center. You'll soon discover an abundance of Central Florida sights that are equally enjoyable and often less crowded and less expensive than those at the theme parks. But take care—the sights listed below are fairly spread out from the northern suburbs to communities south of Disney World. Note their locations on a map before heading out to visit them.

Numbers in the margin correspond to points of interest on the Away from the Theme Parks map.

KISSIMMEE

10 mi southeast of WDW; take I–4 Exit 64A. Although Kissimmee is primarily known as the gateway to Walt Disney World, its non-WDW attractions just might tickle your fancy.

19

Long before Walt Disney World, there was **Gatorland.** This campy attraction near the Orlando–Kissimmee border on U.S. 441 has endured since 1949 without much change, despite competition from the major parks. In November 2006, however, a fire destroyed the park's main entrance and gift shop, though its monstrous aqua gator-jaw icon remained standing. And the park's thousands of alligators and crocodiles swimming and basking in the Florida sun remained unscathed. The park reopened a month later, with a temporary in-park gift shop and a rustic admission gate built as a stopgap until the main entrance is reconstructed. Its bounce-back spirit intact, Gatorland opened the Gator Gulley Splash Park in Spring 2007, complete with giant "egrets" spilling water from their beaks, dueling water guns mounted atop giant "gators," and other themed splash areas. There's also a small petting zoo and an aviary. A free train ride provides an overview of the park, taking you through an alligator breeding marsh and a natural swamp setting where you can spot gators, birds, and turtles. A three-story observation tower overlooks the breeding marsh, swamped with gator grunts, especially come sundown during mating season.

For a glimpse of 37 giant rare and deadly crocodiles, check out the exhibit called **Jungle Crocs of the World.** To see eager gators leaping

TOP SIGHTS AWAY FROM THE THEME PARKS

Charles Hosmer Morse Museum. Known as the "Tiffany museum," the galleries here hold the largest and most comprehensive collection of art by Louis Comfort Tiffany, from stained-glass windows and lamps to blown-glass vases and gem-studded jewelry.

Gatorland. Thousands of alligators and crocodiles swim around and bask in the sun at this reptile-oriented park. Don't miss the Gator Wrestlin' Show.

Historic Bok Sanctuary. The beautifully landscaped gardens and marble-and-seashell tower provide the backdrop for relaxing walks, picnics, and music recitals. The landscape

was designed by Frederick Law Olmsted Jr., son of the planner of New York's Central Park.

Kennedy Space Center. If you've ever been fascinated by space travel or wanted to be an astronaut, don't miss the chance to see shuttles up close.

Wekiwa Springs State Park. Celebrate the out-of-doors with a day fishing, boating, canoeing, or swimming in the Wekiva River. This park spans nearly 7,000 acres of virgin Florida land.

WonderWorks. The building clues you in to what you'll find here—it's upside down and sinking into the ground. Kids go nuts for the simulators that let you survive an earthquake and pilot a jet.

out of the water to catch their food, see the **Gator Jumparoo Show.** The most thrilling is the first one in the morning, when the gators are hungriest. There's also a **Gator Wrestlin' Show,** and although there's no doubt who's going to win the match, it's still fun to see the handlers take on those tough guys with the beady eyes. In the educational **Up Close Animal Encounters Show,** 30 to 40 rattlesnakes fill a pit around the show's host. This is a real Florida experience, and you leave knowing the difference between a gator and a croc. ⊠ *14501 S. Orange Blossom Trail, between Orlando and Kissimmee* ☎ *407/855–5496 or 800/393–5297* ⊕ *www.gatorland.com* ✉ *$19.95 adults, $12.95 children 3–12; discount coupons online* ☉ *Daily 9–5.*

★ ☾ ❷ Friendly farmhands keep things moving on the two-hour guided tour of **Green Meadows Farm**—a 40-acre property with almost 300 animals. There's little chance to get bored and no waiting in line, because tours are always starting. Everyone can milk the fat mama cow, and chickens and geese are turned loose in their yard to run and squawk while city slickers try to catch them. Children take a quick pony ride, and everyone gets jostled about on the old-fashioned hayride. Youngsters come away saying, "I milked a cow, caught a chicken, petted a pig, and fed a goat." Take U.S. 192 for 3 mi east of I–4 to South Poinciana Boulevard; turn right and drive 5 mi. ⊠ *1368 S. Poinciana Blvd.* ☎ *407/846–0770* ⊕ *www.greenmeadowsfarm.com* ✉ *$19; discount coupons online* ☉ *Daily 9:30–5:30; last tour at 4 PM.*

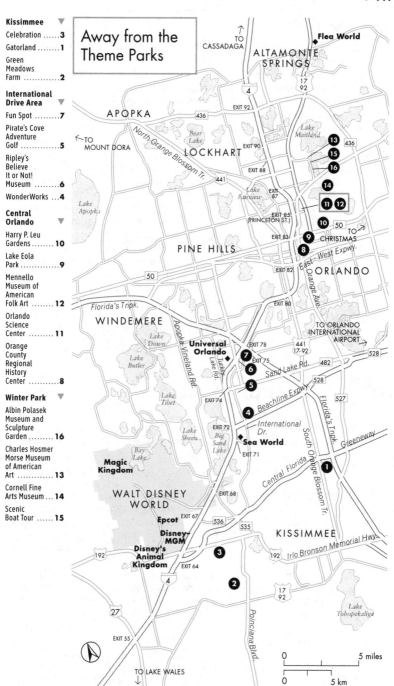

Away from the Theme Parks

19

CELEBRATION

❸ *6 mi south of Epcot; take I–4 to Exit 64A and follow "Celebration"*
signs. A detour may be required until road construction at that inter-
change is completed. This Disney-created community, in which every
blade of grass in every lawn is just right, looks like something out of *The*
Stepford Wives, the 1975 film remade in 2004. But Celebration, which
draws on vernacular architecture from all over the United States and
was based on ideas from some of America's top architects and planners,
offers a great retreat from the theme parks and from the garish reality of
the U.S. 192 tourist strip just 1 mi to the east. The shell of it appears to
be nearly as faux as Main Street, U.S.A., but as the town evolves, you see
signs that real life is being lived here—and a good life it is. Celebration is
a real town, complete with its own hospital and school system. Houses
and apartments, which are built to conform to a strict set of design
guidelines, spread out from the compact and charming downtown area,
which wraps around the edge of a lake. The town is so perfect it could be
a movie set, and it's a delightful place to spend a morning or afternoon.
Sidewalks are built for strolling, restaurants have outdoor seating with
lake views, and inviting shops beckon. After a walk around the lake,
take your youngsters over to the huge interactive fountain and have fun
getting sopping wet. Starting the Friday after Thanksgiving Day and
continuing through New Year's Eve, honest-to-goodness snow sprinkles
softly down over Main Street every night on the hour from 6 to 9, to the
absolute delight of children of all ages. Search ⊕ *www.celebrationfl.com*
for event listings or call 407/566–1200.

INTERNATIONAL DRIVE AREA

7 mi northeast of WDW; take I–4 Exit 74 or 75 unless otherwise noted.
A short drive northeast of WDW are a number of attractions that children adore; unfortunately, some may put wear and tear on parents.

Just up the street, the Ripley's Believe It or Not! building seems to be sinking into the ground, but true to Orlando tradition, the newer attraction,

☾ ❹ **WonderWorks,** one-ups the competition: it's sinking into the ground at
a precarious angle and upside down. If the strange sight of a topsy-
turvy facade complete with upended palm trees and simulated FedEx
box doesn't catch your attention, the swirling "dust" and piped-out
creaking sounds will. Inside, the upside-down theme continues only as
far as the lobby. After that, it's a playground of 100 interactive experiences—some incorporating virtual reality, others educational (similar
to those at a science museum), and still others just pure entertainment.
Here are just some of the things you can do: experience an earthquake
or a hurricane, pilot a fighter jet or land a space shuttle using simulator controls, make giant bubbles in the Bubble Lab, play laser tag in
the largest laser-tag arena and arcade in the world, design and ride
your own roller coaster, lie on a bed of real nails, and play basketball
with a 7-foot opponent. ⊠ *9067 International Dr.* ☎ *407/352–8655*
⊕ *www.wonderworksonline.com* ✄ *$19.95 adults, $14.95 children*

4–12; packages include laser tag and Outta Control Magic Comedy Dinner Show; see online coupons ⊙Daily 9 AM–midnight.

⑤ You can play the crème de la crème of miniature golf at the two **Pirate's Cove Adventure Golf** locations. Each site has two 18-hole courses that wind around artificial mountains, through caves, and into lush foliage. The beginner's course is called Captain Kidd's Adventure; a more difficult game can be played on Blackbeard's Challenge. The courses are opposite Mercado Mediterranean Village and in the Crossroads of Lake Buena Vista shopping plaza. ✉*8501 International Dr.* ☎*407/352–7378* ⊕*www.piratescove.net* ✉*Crossroads Center, I–4 Exit 68* ☎*407/827–1242* ✉*I-Drive location, $9.95 adults, $8.95 children 4–12; both courses $13.95 adults, $12.50 children; Crossroads location, $9.49 adults, $8.49 children 4–12; both courses $13.95 adults, $12.50 children* ⊙*Daily 9 AM–11:30 PM.*

⑥ **Ripley's Believe It or Not! Odditorium** challenges the imagination. A 10-foot-square section of the Berlin Wall. A pain and torture chamber. A Rolls-Royce constructed entirely of matchsticks. A 26' × 20' portrait of van Gogh made from 3,000 postcards. These and almost 200 other oddities speak for themselves in this museum-cum-attraction in the heart of tourist territory on International Drive. The building itself is designed to appear as if it's sliding into one of Florida's notorious sink-holes. Give yourself an hour or two to soak up the weirdness here, but remember, this is a looking, not touching, experience, which may drive antsy youngsters—and their parents—crazy. The museum is ¼ mi south of Sand Lake Road. ✉*8201 International Dr.* ☎*407/363–4418 or 800/998–4418* ⊕*www.ripleysorlando.com* ✉*$18.95 adults, $11.95 children 4–12* ⊙*Daily 9 AM–1 AM; last admission at midnight.*

⑦ **Fun Spot.** Four go-cart tracks offer a variety of driving experiences for children and adults. Though drivers must be at least 10 years old and meet height requirements, parents can drive smaller children in two-seater cars on several of the tracks, including the Conquest Track. Six family and thrill rides range from the dizzying Paratrooper to an old-fashioned Revolver Ferris Wheel. Seven kiddie rides include twirling toddler Teacups. Inside the arcade, traditional Whack a Mole and Spider Stompin' challenges get as much attention as the interactive high-tech video games. From Exit 75A, turn left onto International Drive then left on Grand National to Del Verde Way. ✉*5551 Del Verde Way, I–4 to Exit 75A* ☎*407/363–3867* ⊕*www.fun-spot.com* ✉*$14.95–$29.95 depending on go-cart and ride package; arcade tokens 25¢ each or $25 for 120* ⊙*Weekdays noon–11 PM, weekends 10 AM–midnight, non-peak; daily 10 AM–midnight, peak.*

19

CENTRAL ORLANDO

15 mi northeast of WDW; take I–4 Exit 82C or 83A eastbound, or Exit 85 for Loch Haven Park sights. Downtown Orlando is a dynamic area with high-rises, sports venues, interesting museums, restaurants, and nightspots. Numerous parks and lakes provide pleasant relief from the tall office buildings. A few steps away from downtown's tourist centers are delightful residential neighborhoods with brick-paved streets and live oaks dripping with Spanish moss.

🐚 ❽ The **Orange County Regional History Center** takes you on a journey back in time to discover how Florida's Paleo-Indians hunted and fished the land; what the Sunshine State was like when Spaniards first arrived in the New World; and how life in Florida was different when citrus was king. Visit a cabin from the late 1800s, complete with Spanish moss–stuffed mattresses, mosquito netting over the beds, and a room where game was preserved prerefrigeration. Seminole Indian displays include interactive screens, and tin-can tourist camps of the early 1900s preview Florida's destiny as a future vacation mecca. ✉️ *65 E. Central Blvd.* ☎️ *407/836–8500 or 800/965–2030* ⊕ *www.thehistorycenter.org* 🎟 *$10 adults, $3.50 children 3–12; discount coupon online* 🕐 *Mon.– Sat. 10–5, Sun. noon–5.*

🐚 ❾ In the heart of downtown is **Lake Eola Park,** with its signature fountain in the center. The park represents an inner-city victory over decay. Established in 1892, the now family-friendly park experienced a series of ups and downs that left it very run-down by the late 1970s. With the support of determined citizens, the park gradually underwent a renovation that restored the fountain and added a wide walkway around the lake. Now families with young children use the well-lighted playground in the evening and downtown residents toss bread to the ducks, swans, and birds and walk their dogs late at night in safety. The lakeside **Walt Disney Amphitheater** is a dramatic site for the annual Shakespeare Festival (April and May) as well as for weekend concerts and other events.

Don't resist the park's biggest draw, a ride in a swan-shape pedal boat. Two adults or one adult and two children can fit comfortably into the boats. Children under 16 must be accompanied by an adult.

Several good restaurants by the park and in the nearby Thornton Park neighborhood provide a nice mix of indoor-outdoor dining. The view at dusk, as the fountain lights up in all its colors and the sun sets behind Orlando's ever-growing skyline, is spectacular. ✉️ *Robinson St. and Rosalind Ave., Downtown Orlando* ☎️ *407/246–2827 park, 407/232–0111 Swan Boats* 🎟 *Swan Boat rental $12 per ½ hr* 🕐 *Park daily 6 AM–midnight; Swan Boats weekdays noon–6, weekends 10–8.*

❿ The **Harry P. Leu Gardens,** a few miles outside of downtown on the former lakefront estate of a citrus entrepreneur, are a quiet respite from the artificial world of the theme parks. On the grounds' 50 acres is a collection of historical blooms, many varieties of which were established before 1900. You can see ancient oaks, a 50-foot floral clock, and one of the largest camellia collections in eastern North America (in bloom November–March). **Mary Jane's Rose Garden,** named after Leu's wife, is filled with more than 1,000 bushes; it's the largest formal rose garden south of Atlanta. The simple 19th-century **Leu House Museum,** once the Leu family home, preserves the furnishings and appointments of a well-to-do, turn-of-the-20th-century Florida family. ✉️ *1920 N. Forest Ave., North-Central Orlando* ☎️ *407/246–2620* ⊕ *www.leugardens.*

org ✉*$5 adults, $1 children kindergarten–12th grade; toddlers and pre-schoolers free; also free to all Mon. 9–noon* ⊙*Garden daily 9–5; guided house tours Aug.–June, daily on hr and half hr 10–3:30.*

With all the high-tech glitz and imagined worlds of the theme parks, is it worth visiting the reality-based

★ ☺ ⓫ **Orlando Science Center?** That depends. If you're into hands-on educational exhibits about the human body, mechanics, electricity, math, nature, the solar system, and optics, you'll really like the science center. It's in a gorgeous building with, besides the exhibits, a wonderful atrium that's home to live gators and turtles. There's a great DinoDigs room for the dinosaur-crazed, and the Body Zone area is improved with BodyZone3D, a small digital theater show featuring a journey through the circulatory system from the perspective of a red blood cell. The Dr. Phillips CineDome, a movie theater with a giant eight-story screen, offers large-format IWERKS films (Ub Iwerkswas an associate of Walt Disney's in the early days), as well as planetarium programs. On Friday and Saturday night, you can peer through Florida's largest publicly accessible refractor telescope to view the planets and many of their moons, plus other galaxies and nebulas. ✉*777 E. Princeton St.* ☎*407/514–2000 or 888/672–4386* ⊕*www.osc.org* ✉*$14.95 adults, $13.95 students and seniors with ID, $9.95 children 3–11; after 6 Fri. and Sat. $9.95 adults, $8.95 students and seniors, $4.95 children; parking $4; tickets include all exhibits, films, and planetarium shows; additional admission charged for special exhibitions* ⊙*Sun.–Thurs. 10–6, Fri. and Sat. 10–11.*

⓬ The **Mennello Museum of American Folk Art** is one of the few museums in the United States, and the only one in Florida, devoted to folk art. Its intimate galleries, some with lovely lakefront views, contain the nation's most extensive permanent collection of Earl Cunningham paintings as well as works by many other self-taught artists. There's a wonderful video about Cunningham and his serendipitous discovery in Saint Augustine; temporary exhibitions have included the works of Wyeth, Cassatt, Michael Eastman, and others. At the museum shop you can purchase folk art books, toys, and unusual gifts. ✉*900 E. Princeton St.* ☎*407/246–4278* ⊕*www.mennellomuseum.com* ✉*$4 adults, $1 students, children under 12 free, $3 seniors 60 and older* ⊙*Tues.–Sat. 10:30–4:30, Sun. noon–4:30.*

19

WINTER PARK

20 mi northeast of WDW; take I–4 Exit 87 and head east 3 mi on Fairbanks Ave. This peaceful, upscale community may be just north of the hustle and bustle of Orlando, but it feels miles away.

You can spend a pleasant day here shopping, eating, visiting museums, and taking in the scenery along

★ **Park Avenue,** in the center of town. This inviting brick street has chic boutiques, sidewalk cafés, restaurants, and hidden alleyways that lead

A Pocket of Old Florida Charm

If you take a seat on a bench near the rose garden in Central Park and listen as the Amtrak passenger train rolls by the west end of the park, it's not hard to imagine how Winter Park looked and sounded in the late 19th century.

The town's name reflects its early role as a warm-weather haven for northerners. From the late 1880s until the early 1930s, each winter hundreds of vacationers from northern states like New York and Pennsylvania would travel to Florida by rail to escape the harsh weather. For many, Winter Park was the final destination. Here visitors would relax amid the orange groves and stroll along Park Avenue, which attracts window-shoppers and tea drinkers to this day. The lovely, 8-square-mi village retains its charm with brick-paved streets, historic buildings, and well-maintained lakes and parkland. Even the town's bucolic nine-hole golf course is on the National Register of Historic Places.

For the quintessential Winter Park experience, spend a few hours taking in the sights on Park Avenue. Serious shoppers can spend hours dipping into the small boutiques and chain stores that line the avenue. But save at least an hour or two for the **Charles Hosmer Morse Museum of American Art,** which has the largest collection of artwork by Louis Comfort Tiffany. This is where you'll find such treasures as the Tiffany Chapel and dozens of Tiffany's beautiful stained-glass windows, lamps, and pieces of jewelry. Many of the works were rescued from Tiffany's Long Island estate, Laurelton Hall, after a 1957 fire destroyed much of the property. The museum also contains collections of American decorative art from the mid-19th to the early 20th centuries and American paintings from the same period.

Another fine museum is on the Rollins College campus. The **Cornell Fine Arts Museum** has a collection of 6,000 art objects, including 19th- and 20th-century American and European paintings and sculptures. North of the college on Osceola Avenue is the **Albin Polasek Museum and Sculpture Gardens,** where you can get a guided tour of the former home of the prolific Czech-American sculptor Albin Polasek (1879–1965). On-property examples of Polasek's works include statues in several mediums.

Perhaps one of the loveliest ways to visit the village is on the **Scenic Boat Tour** (⊕ *www.scenicboattours.com*), in operation since 1938. The 18-passenger pontoon boat cruises 12 mi of Winter Park waterways, including three lakes and oak- and cypress-shaded canals built in the 1800s as a transportation system for the logging industry. A well-schooled skipper shares stories about the moguls who built their mansions along the shore. You can spot countless ducks and wading birds, including egrets, blue herons, and the enigmatic "snakebird," or anhinga—often seen drying its wings while perched on shore or diving beneath the lake surface for dinner. You may even glimpse an alligator or see an osprey or bald eagle soar overhead.

to peaceful nooks and crannies with even more restaurants and shops. Park Avenue is definitely a shopper's heaven.

When you want a rest, look for a bench in the shady **Central Park,** which has lovely green lawns, a rose garden, a fountain, and a gazebo. On the southwest corner, the **Winter Park Farmer's Market** lures locals and visitors each Saturday morning. If you don't want to browse in the shops across the street, a walk through the park beneath the moss-covered trees is a delightful alternative. Also consider a cruise on the area's canal-linked lakes to see wildlife and the old estates.

13 The world's most comprehensive collection of the work of Louis Comfort Tiffany, including immense stained-glass windows, lamps, watercolors, and desk sets, is at the **Charles Hosmer Morse Museum of American Art.** The museum's constant draws include exhibits on the Tiffany Long Island mansion, Laurelton Hall, and the 1,082-square-foot Tiffany Chapel, originally built for the 1893 world's fair in Chicago. It took craftsmen 2½ years to painstakingly reassemble the chapel here. Also displayed at the museum are collections of paintings by 19th- and 20th-century American artists, and jewelry and pottery, including a fine display of Rookwood vases. ⌂ *445 N. Park Ave.* ☏ *407/645–5311* ⊕ *www.morsemuseum.org* ✉ *$3 adults, $1 students, children under 12 free; Sept.–May, Fri. free 4–8* ⊗ *Tues.–Sat. 9:30–4, Sun. 1–4; Sept.–May, Fri. until 8.*

14 On the Rollins College campus, the **Cornell Fine Arts Museum** houses the oldest collection of art in Florida, its first paintings acquired in 1896. The collection includes more than 6,000 works, from Italian Renaissance paintings to 19th- and 20th-century American and European paintings, decorative arts, and sculpture. Artists represented include William Merritt Chase, Childe Hassam, and Louis Comfort Tiffany. In addition, outstanding special exhibitions are scheduled throughout the year. Outside the museum, a small but charming garden overlooks Lake Virginia. ⌂ *Rollins College, end of Holt Ave.* ☏ *407/646–2526* ⊕ *www.rollins.edu/cfam* ✉ *$5 adults, free for children and students with ID* ⊗ *Tues.–Sat. 10–5, Sun. 1–5.*

19

★ **15** From the dock at the end of Morse Avenue you can depart for the **Scenic Boat Tour,** a Winter Park tradition that's been in continuous operation for more than 60 years. The relaxing, narrated one-hour pontoon boat tour, which leaves hourly, cruises by 12 mi of Winter Park's opulent lakeside estates and travels through narrow canals and across three lakes. ⌂ *312 E. Morse Blvd.* ☏ *407/644–4056* ⊕ *www.scenicboat-tours.com* ✉ *$10 adults, $5 children 2–11* ⊗ *Daily 10–4.*

16 Stroll along on a guided tour through lush gardens showcasing the graceful sculptures created by internationally known sculptor Albin Polasek (1879–1965) at the **Albin Polasek Museum and Sculpture Gardens.** The late artist's home, studio, galleries, and private chapel are centered on 3 acres of exquisitely tended lawns, colorful flower beds, and tropical foliage. Paths and walkways lead past classical life-size, figurative sculptures and whimsical mythological pieces. Inside the museum are works by Hawthorne, Chase, Mucha, and Saint-Gaudens. ⌂ *633*

Fodor'sChoice
★

Osceola Ave. ☎*407/647–6294* ⊕*www.polasek.org* ☞*$5 adults, $3 students ages 13 and up with student ID, children under 12 free* ⊙*Sept.–June, Tues.–Sat. 10–4, Sun. 1–4.*

WEKIWA SPRINGS STATE PARK

13 mi northwest of Orlando, 28 mi north of WDW.

Where the tannin-stained Wekiva River meets the crystal-clear Wekiwa headspring, there's a curious and visible exchange—like strong tea infusing water. Wekiva is a Creek Indian word meaning "flowing water"; wekiwa means "spring of water."

☾ **Wekiwa Springs State Park** sprawls around this area on 6,400 acres. The parkland is well suited to camping, hiking, and picnicking; the spring to swimming; and the river to canoeing and fishing. Canoe trips can range from a simple hour-long paddle around the lagoon to observe a colony of water turtles to a full-day excursion through the less-congested parts of the river that haven't changed much since the area was inhabited by the Timacuan Indians. Take I–4 Exit 94 (Longwood) and turn left on Route 434. Go 1¼ mi to Wekiwa Springs Road; turn right and go 4½ mi to the entrance, on the right. ⊠*1800 Wekiva Circle* ☎*407/884–2008* ⊕*www.myflorida.com* ☞*$3–$5 per vehicle* ⊙*Daily 8–sunset.*

FodorsChoice ★

EN ROUTE

As you drive northwest on U.S. 441, you head into aptly named **Lake County,** an area renowned for its pristine water and excellent fishing. Watch the flat countryside, thick with scrub pines, take on a gentle roll through citrus groves and pastures surrounded by live oaks.

KENNEDY SPACE CENTER VISITOR COMPLEX

☾ *17 mi north of Cocoa.* The must-see Kennedy Space Center Visitor Complex, just southeast of Titusville, is one of Central Florida's most popular sights. Following the lead of the theme parks, they've switched to a one-price-covers-all admission. To get the most out of your visit to the space center, take the bus tour (included with admission), which makes stops at several facilities. Buses depart every 15 minutes, and you can get on and off any bus whenever you like. As you approach the Kennedy Space Center grounds, tune your car radio to AM1320 for attraction information.

FodorsChoice ★

The first stop on the tour is the **Launch Complex 39 Observation Gantry,** which has an unparalleled view of the twin space-shuttle launch-pads. At the *Apollo/Saturn V* **Center,** don't miss the presentation at the Firing Room Theatre, where the launch of America's first lunar mission, 1968's *Apollo VIII,* is re-created with a ground-shaking, window-rattling lift-off. At the **Lunar Surface Theatre,** recordings from *Apollo XI* offer an eerie and awe-inspiring reminder that when Armstrong and Aldrin landed, they had less than 30 seconds of fuel to spare. In the hall it's impossible to miss the 363-foot-long *Saturn V* rocket. A spare built for a moon mission that never took place, this 6.2-million-pound spacecraft has enough power to throw a fully loaded DC-3 all the way to the sun and back!

Don't miss the outdoor **Rocket Garden,** renovated to showcase more dramatically, through special lighting effects, the historic Atlas, Redstone, and Titan rockets of the early space program. You can travel back in time by climbing inside the Apollo, Gemini, and Mercury capsules to get a sense of the early astronauts' cramped spaces.

The most moving exhibit is the **Astronaut Memorial,** a tribute to those who have died while in pursuit of space exploration. A 42½-foot-high by 50-foot-wide "Space Mirror" tracks the movement of the sun throughout the day, using reflected sunlight to brilliantly illuminate the names of the 24 fallen U.S. astronauts that are carved into the monument's 70,400-pound polished granite surface.

During the **Astronaut Encounter,** in a pavilion near the center's entrance, an astronaut who's actually flown in space hosts a daily Q&A session to tell visitors about life in zero gravity, providing insights to an experience only a few hundred people have ever shared. If you'd like to have a closer encounter with an astronaut, you can purchase a special ticket option to **Lunch with an Astronaut** (adults $60.99, children 3–11 $43.99, includes general complex admission and lunch). For a more in-depth experience, take the **NASA Up Close** tour (adults $59, children 3–11 $43, includes admission), which brings you to sights seldom accessible to the public, such as the NASA Press Site Launch Countdown Clock, the Vehicle Assembly Building, the shuttle landing strip, and the 6-million-pound crawler that transports the shuttle to its launchpad. Or see how far the space program has come with the **Cape Canaveral: Then and Now** tour ($59 adults, $43 children), which visits America's first launch sites from the 1960s and the 21st century's active unmanned rocket program.

The only back-to-back twin **IMAX theater complex** in the world is in the complex, too. The dream of space flight comes to life on a movie screen five stories tall with dramatic footage shot by NASA astronauts during missions. Realistic 3-D special effects will make you feel like you're in space with them. Films alternate throughout the year. Call for specific shows and times. ⊠ *Rte. 405, Kennedy Space Center* 🕾 *321/449–4444* ⊕ *www.kennedyspacecenter.com* ⊠ *General admission includes bus tour, IMAX movies, and Astronaut Hall of Fame; adults $38, $28 children 3–11* ⊙ *Space Center daily 9–5:30, last regular tour 3 hrs before closing; closed certain launch dates; IMAX I and II theaters daily 10–5:40.*

The original *Mercury 7* team and the later *Gemini, Apollo, Skylab,* and shuttle astronauts contributed to make the **United States Astronaut Hall of Fame** the world's premium archive of astronauts' personal stories. Authentic memorabilia and equipment from their collections tell the story of human space exploration. You'll watch videotapes of historic moments in the space program and see one-of-a-kind items like Wally Schirra's relatively archaic *Sigma 7* Mercury space capsule, Gus Grissom's spacesuit (colored silver only because NASA thought silver looked more "spacey"), and a flag that made it to the moon. The exhibit **First on the Moon** focuses on crew selection for *Apollo 11* and the Soviet Union's role in the space race. Definitely don't miss the **Astronaut Adventure,** a hands-on discovery center with interactive exhibits that help you learn about space travel. One of the more challenging activities is a space-shuttle simulator that lets you try your hand at landing the craft—and afterward replays a side view of your rolling and pitching descent. If that gets your motor going, consider enrolling in **ATX (Astronaut Training Experience).** Held at the Hall of Fame, this is an intense full-day experience where you can dangle from a springy harness for a simulated moonwalk, spin in ways you never thought possible in a multi-axis trainer, and either work Mission Control or helm a space shuttle (in a full-scale mock-up) during a simulated landing. Veteran astronauts helped design the program, and you'll hear first-hand from them as you progress through your training. Space is limited (no pun intended), so call well in advance. Included in the program ($625, first two family participants—one adult, one child—and $275 for each additional adult or child; maximum four people) is your astronaut gear, lunch, and a VIP tour of the Kennedy Space Center. ⊠ *Rte. 405, Kennedy Space Center* ☎ *321/449–4444, 321/449–4400 ATX* ⊕ *www.kennedyspacecenter.com* ☒ *Hall of Fame only, $17 adults, $13 children 3–11* ☉ *Daily 9–6:30.*

EN ROUTE
★
The 57,000-acre **Canaveral National Seashore** is on a barrier island that's home to more than 1,000 species of plants and 300 species of birds and other animals. The unspoiled area of hilly sand dunes, grassy marshes, and seashell-sprinkled beaches is a large part of NASA's buffer zone. Surf and lagoon fishing are available, and a hiking trail leads to the top of a Native American shell midden at Turtle Mound. A visitor center is on Route A1A. Weekends are busy, and parts of the park are closed before launches, sometimes as much as two weeks in advance, so call ahead.

Fodor'sChoice
★
If you prefer wading birds over waiting in line, don't miss the 140,000-acre **Merritt Island National Wildlife Refuge,** which adjoins the Canaveral National Seashore. It's an immense area dotted by brackish estuaries and marshes and patches of land consisting of coastal dunes, scrub oaks, pine forests and flatwoods, and palm and oak hammocks. You can borrow field guides and binoculars at the visitor center to track down various types of falcons, osprey, eagles, turkeys, doves, cuckoos, loons, geese, skimmers, terns, warblers, wrens, thrushes, sparrows, owls, and woodpeckers. ⊠ *Rte. 402, across Titusville causeway* ☎ *321/861–0667* ⊕ *www.fws.gov/merrittisland* ☒ *Free* ☉ *Daily sunrise–sunset; visitor center weekdays 8–4:30, Sat. 9–5, Sun. (Nov.–Mar.) 9–5.*

MOUNT DORA

★ *35 mi northwest of Orlando and 50 mi north of WDW; take U.S. 441 (Orange Blossom Trail in Orlando) north or take I–4 to Exit 92, then Rte. 436 west to U.S. 441, and follow signs.* The unspoiled Lake Harris chain of lakes surrounds remote Mount Dora, an artsy valley community with a slow and easy pace, a rich history, New England–style charm, and excellent antiquing. Although the town's population is only about 10,000, there's plenty of excitement here, especially in fall and winter. The first weekend in February is the annual Mount Dora Art Festival, which opens Central Florida's spring art-fair season. Attracting more than 250,000 people over a three-day period, it's one of the region's major outdoor events. During the year there's a sailing regatta (April), a bicycle festival (October), a crafts fair (October), and many other happenings. Mount Dora draws large crowds during monthly (third-weekend, except December) antiques fairs and thrice-yearly antiques "extravaganzas" (third weekends of January, February, and November) at popular **Renninger's Twin Markets,** an antiques center plus farmers' and flea markets.

Take a walk down **Donnelly Street.** The yellow Queen Anne–style mansion is **Donnelly House** (⊠ *515 Donnelly St.*), an 1893 architectural gem. Notice the details on the leaded-glass windows. Built in the 1920s, what was once known as the Dora Hotel is now **The Renaissance** (⊠ *413 Donnelly St.*), a shopping arcade with restaurants and an Icelandic pub.

If you walk along **5th Avenue** you'll pass a number of charming restaurants and gift and antiques shops. At **Uncle Al's Time Capsule** (⊠ *140 E. 4th Ave.* ☎ *352/383–1958*), you can sift through some terrific Hollywood memorabilia and collectibles.

⚲ **Gilbert Park** has a public dock and boat-launching ramp, a playground, nature trail, and a large picnic pavilion with grills. ⊠ *Tremain St. and Liberty Ave.* ⊙ *Daily 7:30–1 hr after sunset.*

A stroll around the lakefront grounds of the **Lakeside Inn** (⊠ *100 N. Alexander St.* ☎ *352/383–4104*), a country inn built in 1883, makes you feel as if you've stepped out of the pages of *The Great Gatsby*; there's even a croquet court.

A historic train depot serves as the offices of the **Mount Dora Chamber of Commerce.** Stop in and pick up a self-guided tour map that tells you everything you need to know—from historic landmarks to restaurants. Don't forget to ask about the trolley tour, during which a guide gives you the skinny on local historical spots and throws in a ghost story. ⊠ *341 Alexander St., at 3rd Ave.* ☎ *352/383–2165* ⊕ *www.mountdora.com* ⊙ *Weekdays 9–5, Sat. 10–4; after hrs, maps on display at kiosk.*

⚲ The **Inland Lakes Railway** offers scenic train excursions via the Mount Dora Champion, pulled by Herbie, a 1942 locomotive-driven coach that takes you on a 75-minute ride. Lunch and dinner trains are available from Eustis station. ⊠ *Alexander St. and 3rd Ave.* ☎ *352/589–4300* ⊕ *www.inlandlakesrailway.com* 🎟 *$12 adults, $8 children 2–12* ⊙ *Weds.–Sun., times vary.*

OCALA NATIONAL FOREST

⚲ *60 mi northwest of WDW; take I–4 east to Exit 92, and head west on*
Fodor$Choice *Rte. 436 to U.S. 441, which you take north to Rte. 19 north.* Between
★ the Oklawaha and the St. Johns rivers lies the 366,000-acre Ocala

National Forest. Clear streams wind through tall stands of pine or hardwoods. This spot is known for its canoeing, hiking, swimming, and camping, and for its invigorating springs. Here you can walk beneath tall pine trees and canoe down meandering streams and across placid lakes. Stop in at the **Ocala National Forest Visitor Center** (✉*45621 Rte. 19, Altoona* ☎*352/669–7495*) for general park information. The center is open daily 9–5.

HISTORIC BOK SANCTUARY

57 mi southwest of Orlando; 42 mi southwest of WDW.

If after several days at the theme parks you find that you're in need of a back-to-nature fix, head south along U.S. 27 to the small town of **Lake Wales**. Along the way you see what's left of Central Florida's citrus groves (many of them remain). But the main reason to take this drive is to get to the

Fodor'sChoice **Historic Bok Sanctuary,** known for years as Bok Tower Gardens, an
★ appealing sanctuary of plants, flowers, trees, and wildlife. Shady paths meander through pine forests in this peaceful world of silvery moats, mockingbirds and swans, blooming thickets, and hidden sundials. You'll be able to boast that you stood on the highest measured point on Florida's peninsula, a colossal 298 feet above sea level. The majestic, 200-foot Bok Tower is constructed of coquina—from seashells—and pink, white, and gray marble, and it was refreshed for the sanctuary's 75th anniversary celebration in February 2004. The tower houses a carillon with 57 bronze bells that ring out each day at 1 and 3 PM during 30-minute live recitals, which may include early American folk songs, Appalachian tunes, Irish ballads, or Latin hymns. The bells are also featured in recordings every half hour after 10 AM, and sometimes even moonlight recitals.

The landscape was designed in 1928 by Frederick Law Olmsted Jr., son of the planner of New York's Central Park. The grounds include the 20-room, Mediterranean-style **Pinewood Estate,** built in 1930. Take I–4 to Exit 55, and head south on U.S. 27 for about 23 mi. Proceed past Eagle Ridge Mall, then turn left after two traffic lights onto Mountain Lake Cut Off Road and follow signs. ✉*1151 Tower Blvd., Lake Wales* ☎*863/676–1408* ⊕*www.boktower.org* ✍*$10 adults, $3 children 5–12, 50% off admission Sat. 8–9; Pinewood Estate general tour $6 adults, $5 children 5–12; holiday tour prices higher* ☼*Daily 8–6; check Web site or call for Pinewood Estate tour schedule, which varies seasonally; holiday tours late Nov.–early Jan.*

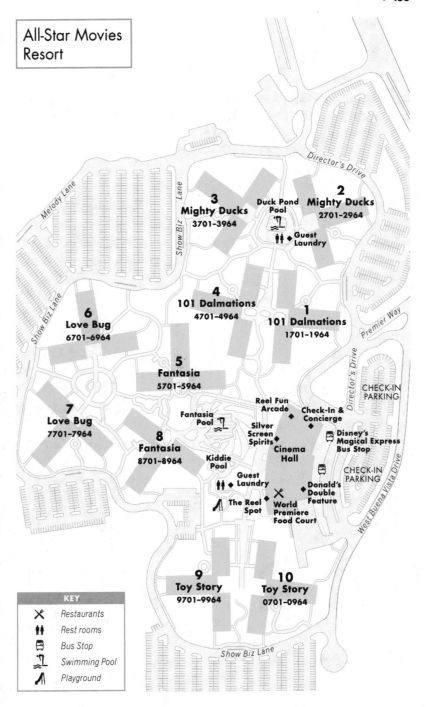

All-Star Movies Resort

3 Mighty Ducks 3701–3964

2 Mighty Ducks 2701–2964

Duck Pond Pool

Guest Laundry

4 101 Dalmations 4701–4964

1 101 Dalmations 1701–1964

6 Love Bug 6701–6964

5 Fantasia 5701–5964

7 Love Bug 7701–7964

8 Fantasia 8701–8964

Fantasia Pool

Reel Fun Arcade

Check-In & Concierge

Silver Screen Spirits

Disney's Magical Express Bus Stop

Cinema Hall

CHECK-IN PARKING

Kiddie Pool

Guest Laundry

The Reel Spot

World Premiere Food Court

Donald's Double Feature

CHECK-IN PARKING

9 Toy Story 9701–9964

10 Toy Story 0701–0964

Director's Drive

Melody Lane

Show Biz Lane

Premier Way

West Buena Vista Drive

Show Biz Lane

KEY

✕ Restaurants
🚻 Rest rooms
🚌 Bus Stop
🏊 Swimming Pool
🛝 Playground

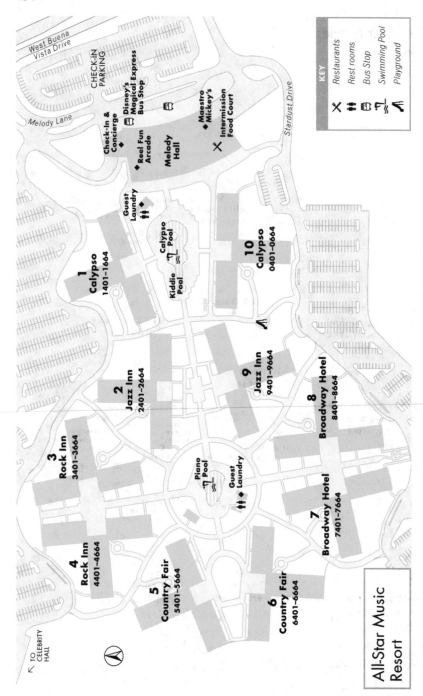

All-Star Music Resort

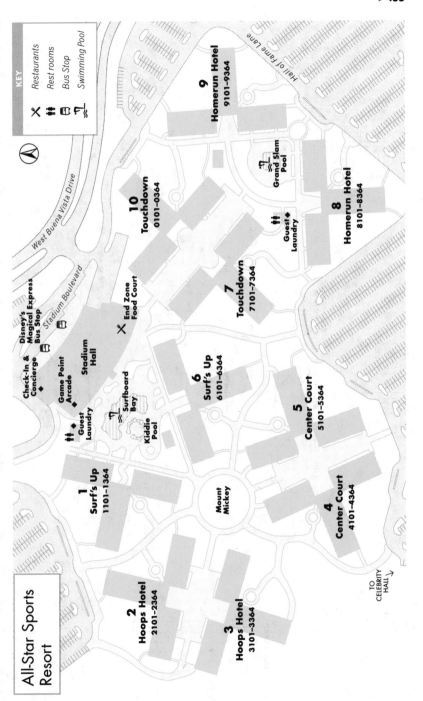

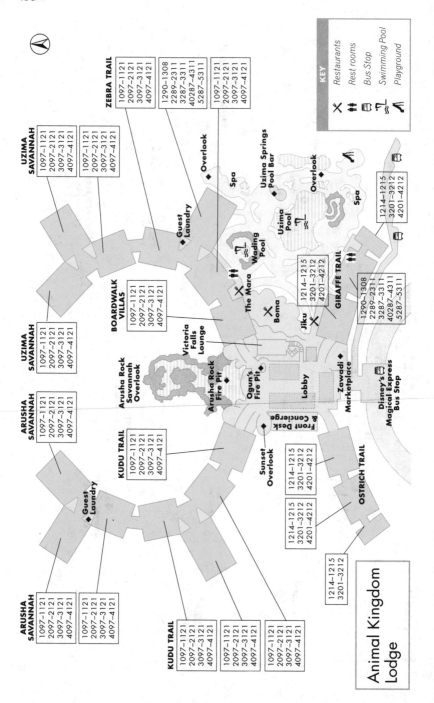

Animal Kingdom Lodge

KEY

Restaurants ✕
Rest rooms ♯♯
Bus Stop ⛫
Swimming Pool ⌇⌇
Playground ⋏

ZEBRA TRAIL

1097–1121
2097–2121
3097–3121
4097–4121

1290–1308
2289–2311
3287–3311
40287–4311
5287–5311

1097–1121
2097–2121
3097–3121
4097–4121

UZIMA SAVANNAH

1097–1121
2097–2121
3097–3121
4097–4121

1097–1121
2097–2121
3097–3121
4097–4121

BOARDWALK VILLAS

1097–1121
2097–2121
3097–3121
4097–4121

UZIMA SAVANNAH

1097–1121
2097–2121
3097–3121
4097–4121

ARUSHA SAVANNAH

1097–1121
2097–2121
3097–3121
4097–4121

KUDU TRAIL

1097–1121
2097–2121
3097–3121
4097–4121

ARUSHA SAVANNAH

1097–1121
2097–2121
3097–3121
4097–4121

1097–1121
2097–2121
3097–3121
4097–4121

KUDU TRAIL

1097–1121
2097–2121
3097–3121
4097–4121

1097–1121
2097–2121
3097–3121
4097–4121

1097–1121
2097–2121
3097–3121
4097–4121

Overlook

Spa

Uzima Springs Pool Bar

Overlook

Spa

Uzima Pool

Wading Pool

1214–1215
3201–3212
4201–4212

The Mara

Boma

Jiku

GIRAFFE TRAIL

1290–1308
2289–2311
3287–3311
40287–4311
5287–5311

1214–1215
3201–3212
4201–4212

Guest Laundry

Victoria Falls Lounge

Arusha Rock Savannah Overlook

Arusha Rock Fire Pit

Ogun's Fire Pit

Lobby

Zawadi Marketplace

Front Desk & Concierge

Disney's Magical Express Bus Stop

OSTRICH TRAIL

Sunset Overlook

1214–1215
3201–3212
4201–4212

1214–1215
3201–3212
4201–4212

1214–1215
3201–3212

Guest Laundry

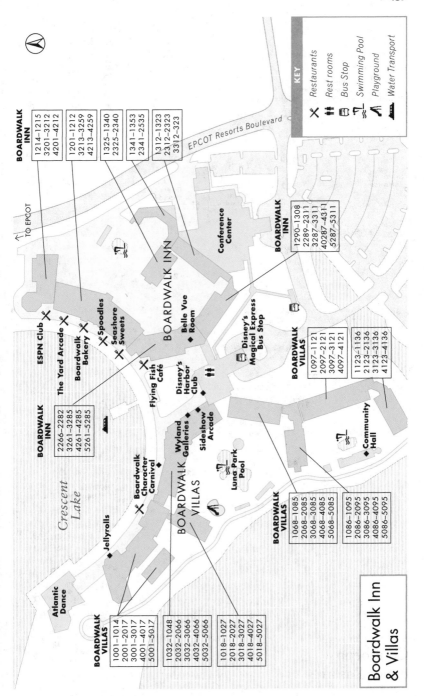

Boardwalk Inn & Villas

KEY

✕	Restaurants
♦♦	Rest rooms
🚌	Bus Stop
≋	Swimming Pool
⚘	Playground
⛴	Water Transport

TO EPCOT

EPCOT Resorts Boulevard

BOARDWALK INN

1214–1215
3201–3212
4201–4212

1201–1212
3213–3259
4213–4259

1325–1340
2325–2340

1341–1353
2341–2535

1312–1323
2312–2323
3312–323

BOARDWALK INN

1290–1308
2289–2311
3287–3311
4028–4311
5287–5311

Conference Center

BOARDWALK INN

Belle Vue Room

Disney's Magical Express Bus Stop

Spoodles

Seashore Sweets

Boardwalk Bakery

The Yard Arcade

ESPN Club

BOARDWALK INN

2266–2282
3261–3285
4261–4285
5261–5285

Flying Fish Café

Disney's Harbor Club

BOARDWALK VILLAS

1097–1121
2097–2121
3097–3121
4097–4121

1123–1136
2123–2136
3123–3136
4123–4136

Community Hall

Wyland Galleries

Sideshow Arcade

Luna Park Pool

BOARDWALK VILLAS

1068–1085
2068–2085
3068–3085
4068–4085
5068–5085

1086–1095
2086–2095
3086–3095
4086–4095
5086–5095

Boardwalk Character Carnival

BOARDWALK VILLAS

Jellyrolls

Crescent Lake

Atlantic Dance

BOARDWALK VILLAS

1001–1014
2001–2017
3001–3017
4001–4017
5001–5017

1032–1048
2032–2066
3032–3066
4032–4066
5032–5066

1018–1027
2018–2027
3018–3027
4018–4027
5018–5027

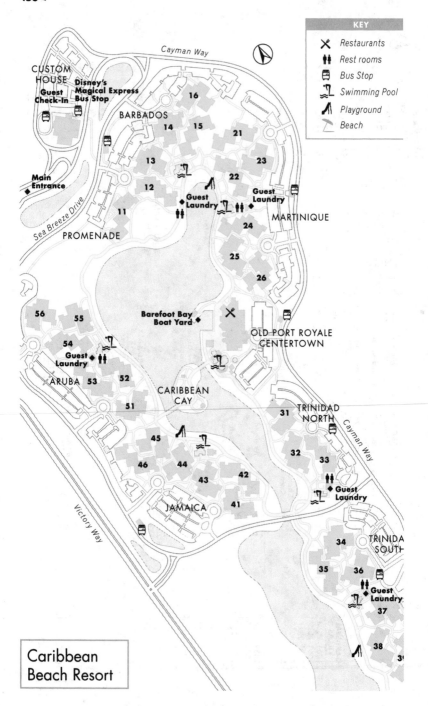

Caribbean
Beach Resort

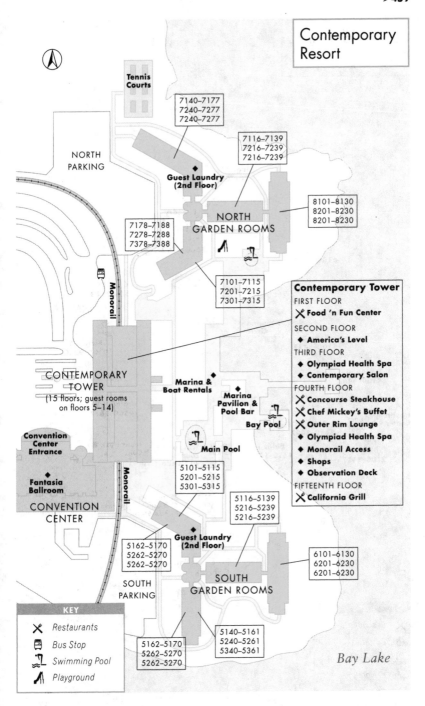

Contemporary Resort

Tennis Courts

7140–7177
7240–7277
7240–7277

7116–7139
7216–7239
7216–7239

NORTH PARKING

Guest Laundry (2nd Floor)

NORTH GARDEN ROOMS

8101–8130
8201–8230
8201–8230

7178–7188
7278–7288
7378–7388

7101–7115
7201–7215
7301–7315

Monorail

Contemporary Tower

FIRST FLOOR
✕ Food 'n Fun Center

SECOND FLOOR
◆ America's Level

THIRD FLOOR
◆ Olympiad Health Spa
◆ Contemporary Salon

FOURTH FLOOR
✕ Concourse Steakhouse
✕ Chef Mickey's Buffet
✕ Outer Rim Lounge
◆ Olympiad Health Spa
◆ Monorail Access
◆ Shops
◆ Observation Deck

FIFTEENTH FLOOR
✕ California Grill

CONTEMPORARY TOWER
(15 floors; guest rooms on floors 5–14)

Marina & Boat Rentals

Marina Pavilion & Pool Bar

Bay Pool

Convention Center Entrance

Main Pool

◆ **Fantasia Ballroom**

CONVENTION CENTER

Monorail

5101–5115
5201–5215
5301–5315

5116–5139
5216–5239
5216–5239

5162–5170
5262–5270
5262–5270

Guest Laundry (2nd Floor)

6101–6130
6201–6230
6201–6230

SOUTH PARKING

SOUTH GARDEN ROOMS

KEY
✕ Restaurants
🚌 Bus Stop
♨ Swimming Pool
🧗 Playground

5162–5170
5262–5270
5262–5270

5140–5161
5240–5261
5340–5361

Bay Lake

Coronado Springs Resort

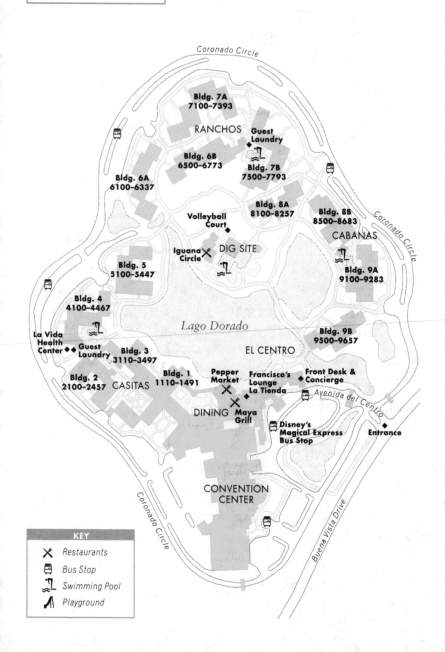

Coronado Circle

Bldg. 7A
7100–7393

RANCHOS

Guest Laundry

Bldg. 6B
6500–6773

Bldg. 7B
7500–7793

Bldg. 6A
6100–6337

Bldg. 8A
8100–8257

Bldg. 8B
8500–8683

Coronado Circle

CABANAS

Volleyball Court

Bldg. 9A
9100–9283

Iguana Circle DIG SITE

Bldg. 5
5100–5447

Bldg. 4
4100–4467

Lago Dorado

Bldg. 9B
9500–9657

La Vida Health Center

Guest Laundry

Bldg. 3
3110–3497

EL CENTRO

Bldg. 2
2100–2457

CASITAS

Bldg. 1
1110–1491

Pepper Market

Francisco's Lounge La Tienda

Front Desk & Concierge

Avenida del Centro

DINING Maya Grill

Disney's Magical Express Bus Stop

Entrance

CONVENTION CENTER

Coronado Circle

Buena Vista Drive

KEY	
✕	Restaurants
🚌	Bus Stop
🏊	Swimming Pool
🛝	Playground

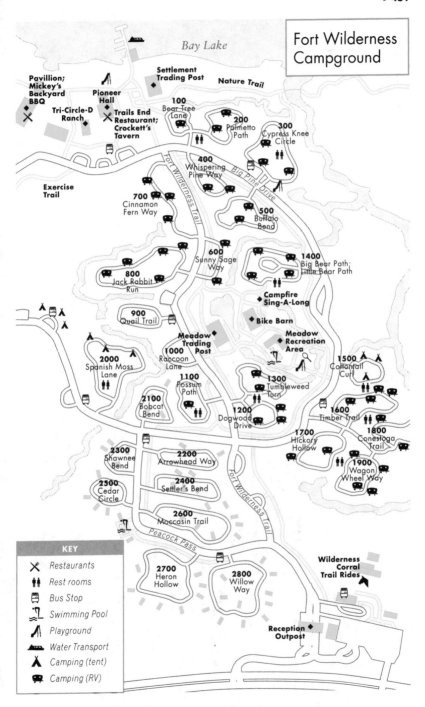

Fort Wilderness Campground

Bay Lake

Pavillion; Mickey's Backyard BBQ

Pioneer Hall

Tri-Circle-D Ranch

Trails End Restaurant; Crockett's Tavern

Settlement Trading Post

Nature Trail

100 Bear Tree Lane

200 Palmetto Path

300 Cypress Knee Circle

Big Pine Drive

400 Whispering Pine Way

Exercise Trail

Fort Wilderness Trail

700 Cinnamon Fern Way

500 Buffalo Bend

600 Sunny Sage Way

1400 Big Bear Path; Little Bear Path

800 Jack Rabbit Run

Campfire Sing-A-Long

900 Quail Trail

Bike Barn

Meadow Trading Post

Meadow Recreation Area

1000 Raccoon Lane

2000 Spanish Moss Lane

1100 Possum Path

1300 Tumbleweed Turn

1500 Cottontail Curl

2100 Bobcat Bend

1200 Dogwood Drive

1600 Timber Trail

1800 Conestoga Trail

2300 Shawnee Bend

2200 Arrowhead Way

1700 Hickory Hollow

1900 Wagon Wheel Way

2500 Cedar Circle

2400 Settler's Bend

Fort Wilderness Trail

2600 Moccasin Trail

Peacock Pass

2700 Heron Hollow

2800 Willow Way

Wilderness Corral Trail Rides

Reception Outpost

KEY

✕	Restaurants
🚻	Rest rooms
🚌	Bus Stop
🏊	Swimming Pool
🛝	Playground
⛴	Water Transport
🏕	Camping (tent)
🚐	Camping (RV)

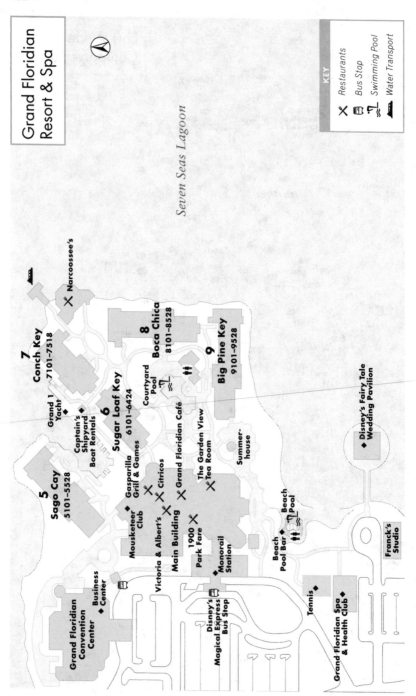

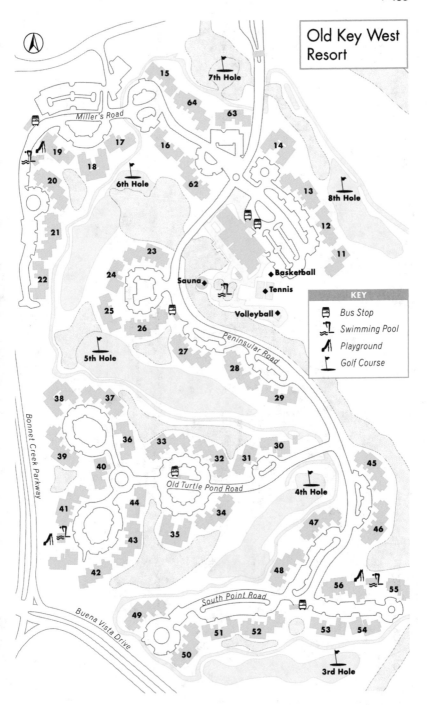

Old Key West Resort

Polynesian Resort

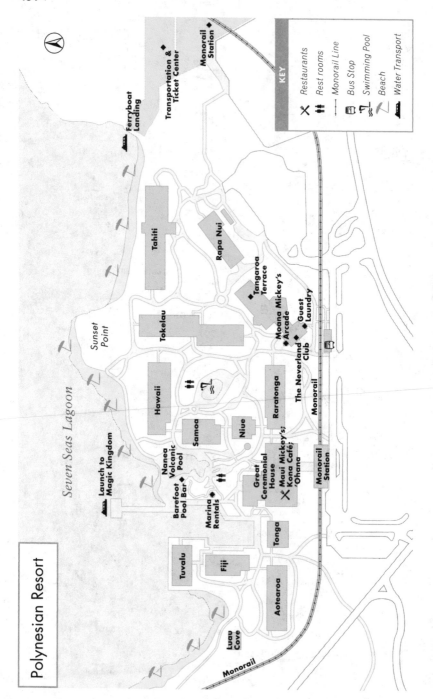

Seven Seas Lagoon

Sunset Point

Launch to Magic Kingdom

Luau Cove

Monorail

Tuvalu

Fiji

Aotearoa

Tonga

Nanea Volcanic Pool

Barefoot Pool Bar

Marina Rentals

Samoa

Niue

Great Ceremonial House

Maui Mickey's; Kona Café; Ohana

Monorail Station

Hawaii

Tokelau

Raratonga

The Neverland Club

Monorail

Tahiti

Rapa Nui

Tangaroa Terrace

Moana Mickey's Arcade

Guest Laundry

Ferryboat Landing

Transportation & Ticket Center

Monorail Station

KEY

✕ Restaurants
♦♦ Rest rooms
┼ Monorail Line
🚌 Bus Stop
⛱ Swimming Pool
〰 Beach
⛴ Water Transport

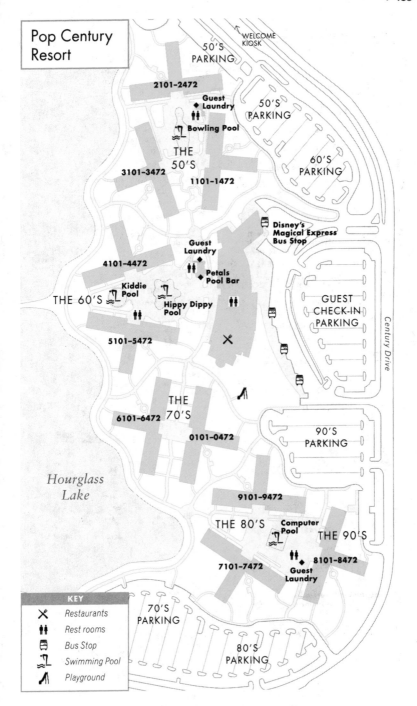

Pop Century Resort

50'S PARKING

WELCOME KIOSK

2101–2472

◆ Guest Laundry

Bowling Pool

THE 50'S

50'S PARKING

60'S PARKING

3101–3472

1101–1472

Disney's Magical Express Bus Stop

Guest Laundry ◆

4101–4472

◆ Petals Pool Bar

GUEST CHECK-IN PARKING

Century Drive

Kiddie Pool

THE 60'S

Hippy Dippy Pool

5101–5472

THE 70'S

6101–6472

0101–0472

90'S PARKING

Hourglass Lake

9101–9472

THE 80'S

Computer Pool

THE 90'S

8101–8472

7101–7472

Guest Laundry

70'S PARKING

80'S PARKING

KEY

✕	Restaurants
👫	Rest rooms
🚌	Bus Stop
🏊	Swimming Pool
🛝	Playground

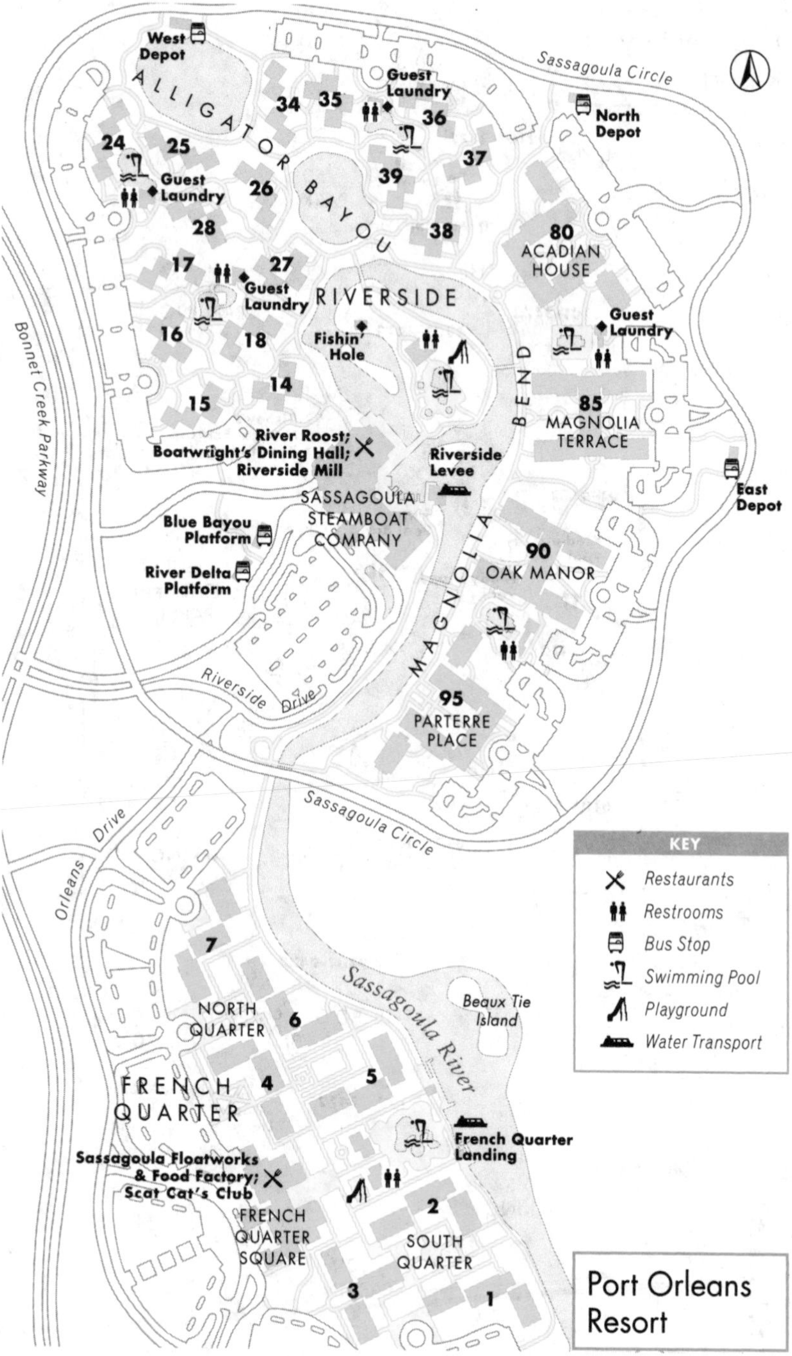
Port Orleans Resort
West Depot
North Depot
East Depot
Sassagoula Circle
ALLIGATOR BAYOU
34
35
36
37
38
39
24
25
26
27
28
17
16
18
14
15
Guest Laundry
Guest Laundry
Guest Laundry
Guest Laundry
RIVERSIDE
Fishin' Hole
80
ACADIAN HOUSE
85
MAGNOLIA TERRACE
MAGNOLIA BEND
River Roost; Boatwright's Dining Hall; Riverside Mill
Riverside Levee
SASSAGOULA STEAMBOAT COMPANY
Blue Bayou Platform
River Delta Platform
90
OAK MANOR
95
PARTERRE PLACE
Riverside Drive
Bonnet Creek Parkway
Orleans Drive
Sassagoula Circle
Sassagoula River
Beaux Tie Island
7
6
5
4
3
2
1
NORTH QUARTER
FRENCH QUARTER
SOUTH QUARTER
French Quarter Landing
Sassagoula Floatworks & Food Factory; Scat Cat's Club
FRENCH QUARTER SQUARE
KEY
Restaurants
Restrooms
Bus Stop
Swimming Pool
Playground
Water Transport

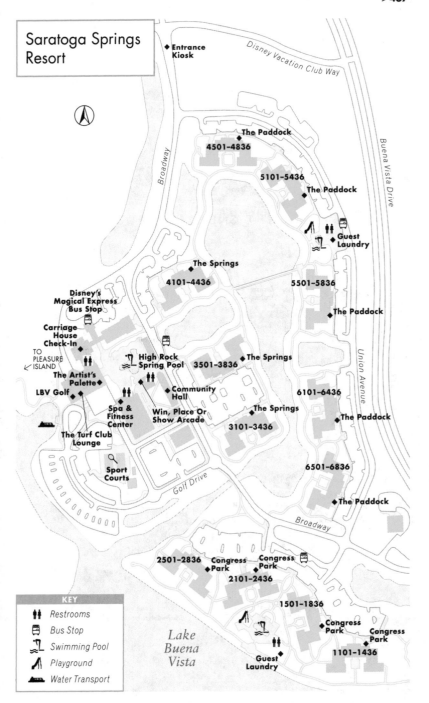

Saratoga Springs Resort

◆ Entrance Kiosk

Disney Vacation Club Way

Broadway

Buena Vista Drive

◆ **The Paddock**
4501–4836

5101–5436

◆ **The Paddock**

🛝 👫 🚊 **Guest Laundry**
≋

◆ **The Springs**
4101–4436

5501–5836

◆ **The Paddock**

Disney's Magical Express Bus Stop 🚊

Carriage House Check-In ◆

TO PLEASURE ISLAND ←

👫

🚊

High Rock Spring Pool ≋

3501–3836

◆ **The Springs**

The Artist's Palette ◆◆

LBV Golf ◆

👫👫👫

◆ **Community Hall**

6101–6436

Spa & Fitness Center

Win, Place Or Show Arcade

◆ **The Springs**

◆ **The Paddock**

The Turf Club Lounge

3101–3436

⚓

Sport Courts 🔍

Golf Drive

6501–6836

◆ **The Paddock**

Broadway

2501–2836 ◆ **Congress Park**   **Congress Park** 🚊

2101–2436

1501–1836

◆ **Congress Park**   **Congress Park**

Lake Buena Vista

🛝
≋
👫

Guest Laundry ◆

1101–1436

KEY

👫	*Restrooms*
🚊	*Bus Stop*
≋	*Swimming Pool*
🛝	*Playground*
⚓	*Water Transport*

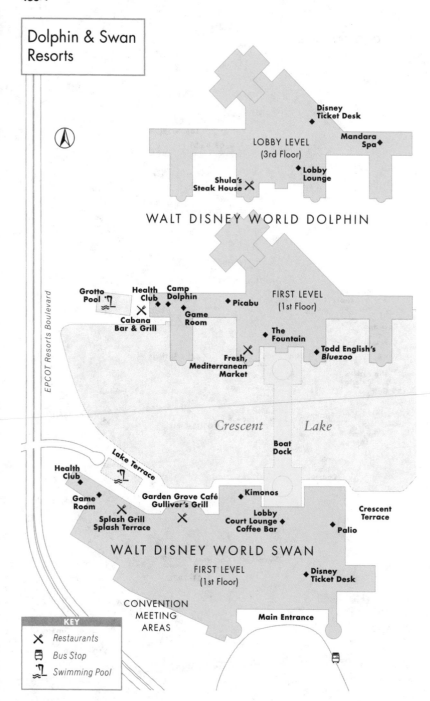

Dolphin & Swan Resorts

EPCOT Resorts Boulevard

WALT DISNEY WORLD DOLPHIN

LOBBY LEVEL
(3rd Floor)

◆ Disney Ticket Desk

Mandara Spa ◆

◆ Lobby Lounge

Shula's Steak House ✕

FIRST LEVEL
(1st Floor)

Grotto Pool

Health Club ◆

Camp Dolphin ◆

◆ Picabu

Cabana Bar & Grill ✕

Game Room

◆ The Fountain

◆ Todd English's *Bluezoo*

Fresh, Mediterranean Market ✕

Crescent   Lake

Boat Dock

Lake Terrace

Health Club ◆

Game Room ◆

Garden Grove Café Gulliver's Grill ✕

◆ Kimonos

Splash Grill Splash Terrace ✕

Lobby Court Lounge Coffee Bar ◆

Crescent Terrace

◆ Palio

WALT DISNEY WORLD SWAN

FIRST LEVEL
(1st Floor)

◆ Disney Ticket Desk

CONVENTION MEETING AREAS

Main Entrance

KEY
✕ *Restaurants*
🚌 *Bus Stop*
🏊 *Swimming Pool*

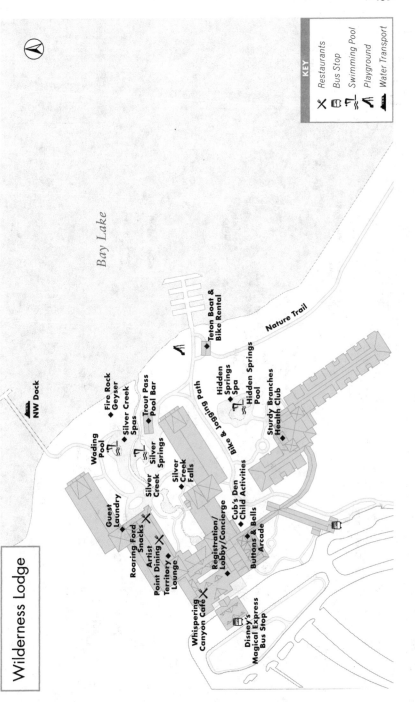

Wilderness Lodge

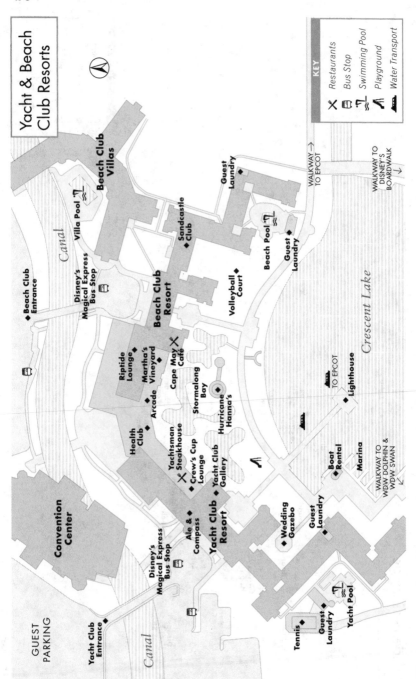

Yacht & Beach Club Resorts

Beach Club Villas

Canal

Villa Pool

Beach Club Entrance

Disney's Magical Express Bus Stop

Beach Club Resort

Guest Laundry

Sandcastle Club

Riptide Lounge

Martha's Vineyard

Arcade

Cape May Café

Health Club

Stormalong Bay

Hurricane Hanna's

Volleyball Court

Beach Pool

Guest Laundry

Yachtsman Steakhouse

Crew's Cup Lounge

Yacht Club Gallery

Crescent Lake

Boat Rental

Lighthouse

TO EPCOT

Marina

WALKWAY TO WDW DOLPHIN & WDW SWAN

WALKWAY TO EPCOT

WALKWAY TO DISNEY'S BOARDWALK

Ale & Compass

Yacht Club Resort

Disney's Magical Express Bus Stop

Wedding Gazebo

Guest Laundry

Convention Center

Canal

GUEST PARKING

Yacht Club Entrance

Tennis

Guest Laundry

Yacht Pool

KEY

× Restaurants
🚌 Bus Stop
🏊 Swimming Pool
🧒 Playground
⛴ Water Transport

INDEX

ABOUT OUR WRITERS

Jennie Hess is a travel and feature writer based in Orlando. Formerly a publicist for Walt Disney World Resort, Jennie still enjoys exploring every corner of the evolving kingdom and gathering theme-park details faster than Pooh can sniff out honey. She gets us the inside scoop on Disney, plus insights gleaned from her husband and two sons.

Alicia Rivas, our Shopping updater, is a freelance broadcast journalist and writer. Though technically a transplant, she considers herself a Central Florida native. Alica worked at Epcot while she was in college, and she still considers it the best job she's ever had.

Gary McKechnie knows *a lot* about Florida—his native state—and its many attractions. During his student days, he worked as a Walt Disney World ferryboat pilot, Jungle Cruise skipper, steam-train conductor, and double-decker bus driver. He was also an improv comedian at Epcot. He writes for dozens of publications and limits his reading to those that run his features. His book *Great American Motorcycle Tours* won a silver medal in the 2001 Lowell Thomas Travel Journalism Competition.

Good meals stick to your ribs; great meals stick in your mind. That's the belief of Rowland Stiteler, who has served as editor and dining critic of *Orlando* and *Central Florida* magazines. During the past 10 years he's researched more than 500 Florida hotels and restaurants for travel publications and the convention and resort industry.